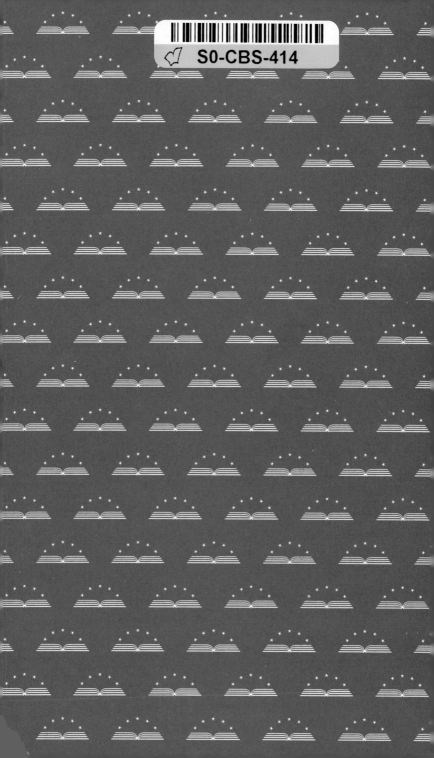

Library of America, a nonprofit organization,
champions our nation's cultural heritage
by publishing America's greatest writing in
authoritative new editions and providing resources
for readers to explore this rich, living legacy.

MARY McCARTHY

Mary McCarthy

NOVELS 1963–1979

The Group
Birds of America
Cannibals and Missionaries

Thomas Mallon, *editor*

THE LIBRARY OF AMERICA

Visit our website at www.loa.org.

The Group copyright © 1954 by Mary McCarthy, renewed 1982 by
Mary McCarthy. *Cannibals and Missionaries* copyright © 1979 by
Mary McCarthy. Published by arrangement with Houghton
Mifflin Harcourt Publishing Company.

Birds of America copyright © 1965, 1970, 1971 by Mary McCarthy.
Published by arrangement with Open Road Integrated Media.

"The Novels That Got Away," *The New York Times*, November 25, 1979,
copyright © 1979 by Mary McCarthy. Published by arrangement
with The Mary McCarthy Literary Trust.

This paper meets the requirements of
ANSI/NISO z39.48–1992 (Permanence of Paper).

Distributed to the trade in the United States
by Penguin Random House Inc.
and in Canada by Penguin Random House Canada Ltd.

Library of Congress Control Number: 2016946106
ISBN 978-1-59853-517-4

First Printing
The Library of America—291

Manufactured in the United States of America

Mary McCarthy: Novels 1963–1979
is published with support from
a friend of
Library of America

Contents

THE GROUP

1

I T was June, 1933, one week after Commencement, when
Kay Leiland Strong, Vassar '33, the first of her class to run
around the table at the Class Day dinner, was married to Harald Petersen, Reed '27, in the chapel of St. George's Church,
P.E., Karl F. Reiland, Rector. Outside, on Stuyvesant Square,
the trees were in full leaf, and the wedding guests arriving by
twos and threes in taxis heard the voices of children playing
round the statue of Peter Stuyvesant in the park. Paying the
driver, smoothing out their gloves, the pairs and trios of young
women, Kay's classmates, stared about them curiously, as
though they were in a foreign city. They were in the throes of
discovering New York, imagine it, when some of them had
actually lived here all their lives, in tiresome Georgian houses
full of waste space in the Eighties or Park Avenue apartment
buildings, and they delighted in such out-of-the-way corners as
this, with its greenery and Quaker meeting-house in red brick,
polished brass, and white trim next to the wine-purple Episcopal church—on Sundays, they walked with their beaux across
Brooklyn Bridge and poked into the sleepy Heights section of
Brooklyn; they explored residential Murray Hill and quaint
MacDougal Alley and Patchin Place and Washington Mews
with all the artists' studios; they loved the Plaza Hotel and the
fountain there and the green mansarding of the Savoy Plaza
and the row of horse-drawn hacks and elderly coachmen, waiting, as in a French *place*, to tempt them to a twilight ride
through Central Park.

The sense of an adventure was strong on them this morning,
as they seated themselves softly in the still, near-empty chapel;
they had never been to a wedding quite like this one before, to
which invitations had been issued orally by the bride herself,
without the intervention of a relation or any older person,
friend of the family. There was to be no honeymoon, they had
heard, because Harald (that was the way he spelled it—the old
Scandinavian way) was working as an assistant stage manager
for a theatrical production and had to be at the theatre as usual
this evening to call "half hour" for the actors. This seemed to

3

them very exciting and of course it justified the oddities of the wedding: Kay and Harald were too busy and dynamic to let convention cramp their style. In September, Kay was going to start at Macy's, to be trained, along with other picked college graduates, in merchandising techniques, but instead of sitting around all summer, waiting for the job to begin, she had already registered for a typing course in business school, which Harald said would give her a tool that the other trainees wouldn't have. And, according to Helena Davison, Kay's roommate junior year, the two of them had moved right into a summer sublet, in a nice block in the East Fifties, without a single piece of linen or silver of their own, and had spent the last week, ever since graduation (Helena had just been there and seen it), on the regular tenant's sublet sheets!

How like Kay, they concluded fondly, as the tale passed along the pews. She had been amazingly altered, they felt, by a course in Animal Behavior she had taken with old Miss Washburn (who had left her brain in her will to Science) during their junior year. This and her work with Hallie Flanagan in Dramatic Production had changed her from a shy, pretty, somewhat heavy Western girl with black lustrous curly hair and a wildrose complexion, active in hockey, in the choir, given to large tight brassières and copious menstruations, into a thin, harddriving, authoritative young woman, dressed in dungarees, sweat shirt, and sneakers, with smears of paint in her unwashed hair, tobacco stains on her fingers, talking airily of "Hallie" and "Lester," Hallie's assistant, of flats and stippling, of oestrum and nymphomania, calling her friends by their last names loudly —"Eastlake," "Renfrew," "MacAusland"—counseling premarital experiment and the scientific choice of a mate. Love, she said, was an illusion.

To her fellow group members, all seven of whom were now present in the chapel, this development in Kay, which they gently labeled a "phase," had been, nevertheless, disquieting. Her bark was worse than her bite, they used to reiterate to each other, late at night in their common sitting room in the South Tower of Main Hall, when Kay was still out, painting flats or working on the electricity with Lester in the theatre. But they were afraid that some man, who did not know the old dear as they did, would take her at her word. They had pondered about Harald; Kay had met him last summer when she was working as an apprentice at a summer theatre in Stamford and both sexes had lived in a dormitory together. She said he wanted to marry her, but that was not the way his letters sounded to the group. They were not love letters at all, so far as the group could see, but accounts of personal successes among theatrical celebrities, what Edna Ferber had said to George Kaufman in his hearing, how Gilbert Miller had sent for him and a woman star had begged him to read his play to her in bed. "Consider yourself kissed," they ended, curtly, or just "C.Y.K."—not another word. In a young man of their own background, as the girls vaguely phrased it, such letters would have been offensive, but their education had impressed on them the unwisdom of making large judgments from one's own narrow little segment of experience. Still, they could tell that Kay was not as sure of him as she pretended she was; sometimes he did not write for weeks, while poor Kay went on whistling in the dark. Polly Andrews, who shared a mailbox with her, knew this for a fact. Up to the Class Day dinner, ten days ago, the girls had had the feeling that Kay's touted "engagement" was pretty much of a myth. They had almost thought of turning to some wiser person for guidance, a member of the faculty or the college psychiatrist—somebody Kay could talk it out to, frankly. Then, that night, when Kay had run around the long table, which meant you were announcing your engagement to the whole class, and produced from her winded bosom a funny Mexican silver ring to prove it, their alarm had dissolved into a docile amusement; they clapped, dimpling and twinkling, with an air of prior knowledge. More gravely, in low posh tones, they assured their parents, up for the Commencement ceremonies, that the engagement was of long standing, that Harald was "terribly nice" and "terribly in love" with Kay. Now, in the chapel, they rearranged their fur pieces and smiled at each other, noddingly, like mature little martens and sables: they had been right, the hardness was only a phase; it was certainly a point for *their* side that the iconoclast and scoffer was the first of the little band to get married.

"Who would have thunk it?" irrepressibly remarked "Pokey" (Mary) Prothero, a fat cheerful New York society girl with big red cheeks and yellow hair, who talked like a jolly beau of the

McKinley period, in imitation of her yachtsman father. She was the problem child of the group, very rich and lazy, having to be coached in her subjects, cribbing in examinations, sneaking weekends, stealing library books, without morals or subtleties, interested only in animals and hunt dances; her ambition, recorded in the yearbook, was to become a vet; she had come to Kay's wedding good-naturedly because her friends had dragged her there, as they had dragged her to college assemblies, throwing stones up at her window to rouse her and then thrusting her into her cap and rumpled gown. Having now got her safely to the church, later in the day they would propel her into Tiffany's, to make sure that Kay got one good, thumping wedding present, a thing Pokey, by herself, would not understand the necessity of, since to her mind wedding presents were a part of the burden of privilege, associated with detectives, bridesmaids, fleets of limousines, reception at Sherry's or the Colony Club. If one was not in society, what was the point of the folderol? She herself, she proclaimed, hated being fitted for dresses, hated her coming-out party, would hate her wedding, when she had it, which, as she said, was bound to happen since, thanks to Daddy's money, she had her pick of beaux. All these objections she had raised in the taxicab on the way down, in her grating society caw, till the taxi driver turned round at a stop light to look at her, fat and fair, in a blue faille suit with sables and a *lorgnon* of diamonds, which she raised to her weak sapphire eyes to peer at him and at his picture, concluding, in a loud firm whisper, to her roommates, "It's *not* the same man."

"What perfect pets they look!" murmured Dottie Renfrew, of Boston, to quiet her, as Harald and Kay came in from the vestry and took their places before the surpliced curate, accompanied by little Helena Davison, Kay's ex-roommate from Cleveland, and by a sallow blond young man with a mustache. Pokey made use of her *lorgnon*, squinting up her pale-lashed eyes like an old woman; this was her first appraisal of Harald, for she had been away hunting for the weekend the one time he had come to college. "Not too bad," she pronounced. "Except for the shoes." The groom was a thin, tense young man with black straight hair and a very good, supple figure, like a fencer's; he was wearing a blue suit, white shirt, brown suède shoes, and dark-red tie. Her scrutiny veered to Kay, who was wearing a pale-brown thin silk dress with a big white *mousseline de soie* collar and a wide black taffeta hat wreathed with white daisies; around one tan wrist was a gold bracelet that had belonged to her grandmother; she carried a bouquet of field daisies mixed with lilies of the valley. With her glowing cheeks, vivid black curly hair, and tawny hazel eyes, she looked like a country lass on some old tinted post card; the seams of her stockings were crooked, and the backs of her black suède shoes had worn spots, where she had rubbed them against each other. Pokey scowled. "Doesn't she know," she lamented, "that black's bad luck for weddings?" "*Shut up*," came a furious growl from her other side. Pokey, hurt, peered around, to find Elinor Eastlake, of Lake Forest, the taciturn brunette beauty of the group, staring at her with murder in her long, green eyes. "But Lakey!" Pokey cried, protesting. The Chicago girl, intellectual, impeccable, disdainful, and nearly as rich as herself, was the only one of the group she stood in awe of. Behind her blinking good nature, Pokey was a logical snob. She assumed that it was taken for granted that of the other seven roommates, only Lakey could expect to be in *her* wedding, and vice versa, of course; the others would come to the reception. "*Fool*," spat out the Madonna from Lake Forest, between gritted pearly teeth. Pokey rolled her eyes. "Temperamental," she observed to Dottie Renfrew. Both girls stole amused glances at Elinor's haughty profile; the fine white Renaissance nostril was dinted with a mark of pain.

To Elinor, this wedding was torture. Everything was so jaggedly ill-at-ease: Kay's costume, Harald's shoes and necktie, the bare altar, the sparsity of guests on the groom's side (a couple and a solitary man), the absence of any family connection. Intelligent and morbidly sensitive, she was inwardly screaming with pity for the principals and vicarious mortification. Hypocrisy was the sole explanation she could find for the antiphonal bird twitter of "Terribly nice," and "Isn't this exciting?" that had risen to greet the couple in lieu of a wedding march. Elinor was always firmly convinced of other people's hypocrisy since she could not believe that they noticed less than she did. She supposed now that the girls all around her *must* see what she saw, *must* suffer for Kay and Harald a supreme humiliation.

Facing the congregation, the curate coughed. "Step forward!" he sharply admonished the young couple, sounding, as Lakey observed afterward, more like a bus conductor than a minister. The back of the groom's neck reddened; he had just had a haircut. All at once, the fact that Kay was a self-announced scientific atheist came home to her friends in the chapel; the same thought crossed every mind: what had happened in the interview in the rectory? Was Harald a communicant? It seemed very unlikely. How had they worked it, then, to get married in a rock-ribbed Episcopal church? Dottie Renfrew, a devout Episcopal communicant, drew her clasped furs closer around her susceptible throat; she shivered. It occurred to her that she might be compounding a sacrilege: to her certain knowledge, Kay, the proud daughter of an agnostic doctor and a Mormon mother, had not even been baptized. Kay, as the group knew too, was not a very truthful person; could she have lied to the minister? In that case, was the marriage invalid? A flush stole up from Dottie's collarbone, reddening the patch of skin at the V opening of her handmade crepe de Chine blouse; her perturbed brown eyes canvassed her friends; her eczematous complexion spotted. She knew by heart what was coming. "If any man can show just cause, why they may not be lawfully joined together, let him now speak, or else hereafter for ever hold his peace." The curate's voice halted, on a questioning note; he glanced up and down the pews. Dottie shut her eyes and prayed, conscious of a dead hush in the chapel. Would God or Dr. Leverett, her clergyman, really want her to speak up? She prayed that they would not. The opportunity passed, as she heard the curate's voice resume, loud and solemn, as if almost in reprobation of the couple, to which he now turned. "I require and charge you both, as ye will answer at the dreadful day of judgment, when the secrets of all hearts shall be disclosed, that if either of you know any impediment, why ye may not be lawfully joined together in Matrimony, ye do now confess it. For be ye well assured, that if any persons are joined together otherwise than as God's Word doth allow, their marriage is not lawful."

You could have heard a pin drop, as the girls agreed later. Every girl was holding her breath. Dottie's religious scruples had given way to a new anxiety, which was common to the whole group. The knowledge, shared by them all, of Kay's having "lived with" Harald filled them with a sudden sense of the unsanctioned. They glanced stealthily around the chapel and noted for the nth time the absence of parents or *any older person*; and this departure from convention, which had been "such fun" before the service began, struck them now as queer and ominous. Even Elinor Eastlake, who knew scornfully well that fornication was not the type of impediment alluded to in the service, half expected an unknown presence to rise and stop the ceremony. To her mind, there was a spiritual obstacle to the marriage; she considered Kay a *cruel, ruthless, stupid* person who was marrying Harald from ambition.

Everyone in the chapel had now noticed something a little odd, or so it seemed, in the curate's pauses and stresses; they had never heard "their marriage is not lawful" delivered with such emphasis. On the groom's side, a handsome, auburn-haired, dissipated-looking young man clenched his fist suddenly and muttered something under his breath. He smelled terribly of alcohol and appeared extremely nervous; all through the ceremony, he had been clasping and unclasping his well-shaped, strong-looking hands and biting his chiseled lips. "He's a painter; he's just been divorced," whispered fair-haired Polly Andrews, who was the quiet type but who knew everything, on Elinor Eastlake's right. Elinor, like a young queen, leaned forward and deliberately caught his eye; here was someone, she felt, who was as disgusted and uncomfortable as she was. He responded with a stare of bitter, encompassing irony, followed by a wink directed, unmistakably, at the altar. Having moved into the main part of the service, the curate had now picked up speed, as though he had suddenly discovered another appointment and were running off this couple as rapidly as possible: this was only a $10 wedding, his manner seemed to imply. Behind her large hat, Kay appeared to be oblivious of all slights, but Harald's ears and neck had turned a darker red, and, in his responses, he began, with a certain theatrical flourish, to slow down and correct the minister's intonations.

This made the couple on the groom's side smile, as if at a familiar weakness or fault, but the girls, in *their* pews, were scandalized by the curate's rudeness and applauded what they called Harald's victory over him, which they firmly intended to make the center of their congratulations after the ceremony. There were some who, then and there, resolved to speak to Mother and get her to speak to Dr. Reiland, the rector, about it; a capacity for outrage, their social birthright, had been redirected, as it were, by education. The fact that Kay and Harald were going to be poor as church mice was no excuse, they thought staunchly, for such conduct on the part of a priest, in these times especially, when everybody was having to retrench. Even among their own number, one girl had had to accept a scholarship to finish college, and nobody thought the worse of her for it: Polly Andrews remained one of their *very* dearest friends. They were a different breed, they could assure the curate, from the languid buds of the previous decade: there was not one of them who did not propose to work this coming fall, at a volunteer job if need be. Libby MacAusland had a promise from a publisher; Helena Davison, whose parents, out in Cincinnati, no, Cleveland, lived on the income of their income, was going into teaching—she already had a job sewed up at a private nursery school; Polly Andrews, more power to her, was to work as a technician in the new Medical Center; Dottie Renfrew was slated for social work in a Boston settlement house; Lakey was off to Paris to study art history, working toward an advanced degree; Pokey Prothero, who had been given a plane for graduation, was getting her pilot's license so as to be able to commute three days a week to Cornell Agricultural School, and, last but not least, yesterday little Priss Hartshorn, the group grind, had simultaneously announced her engagement to a young doctor and landed a job with the N.R.A. Not bad, they conceded, for a group that had gone through college with the stigma of being high-hat. And elsewhere in the class, in the wider circle of Kay's friends, they could point out girls of perfectly good background who were going into business, anthropology, medicine, not because they had to, but because they knew they had something to contribute to our emergent America. The group was not afraid of being radical either; they could see the good Roosevelt was doing, despite what Mother and Dad said; they were not taken in by party labels and thought the Democrats should be given a chance to show what they had up their sleeve. Experience was just a question of learning through trial and error; the most conservative of them, pushed to the wall, admitted that an honest socialist was entitled to a hearing.

The worst fate, they utterly agreed, would be to become like Mother and Dad, stuffy and frightened. Not one of them, if she could help it, was going to marry a broker or a banker or a cold-fish corporation lawyer, like so many of Mother's generation. They would rather be wildly poor and live on salmon wiggle than be forced to marry one of those dull purplish young men of their own set, with a seat on the Exchange and bloodshot eyes, interested only in squash and cockfighting and drinking at the Racquet Club with his cronies, Yale or Princeton '29. It would be better, yes, they were not afraid to say it, though Mother gently laughed, to marry a Jew if you loved him—some of them were awfully interesting and cultivated, though terribly ambitious and inclined to stick together, as you saw very well at Vassar: if you knew them you had to know their friends. There was one thing, though, truthfully, that made the group feel a little anxious for Kay. It was a pity in a way that a person as gifted as Harald and with a good education had had to pick the stage, rather than medicine or architecture or museum work, where the going was not so rough. To hear Kay talk, the theatre was pretty red in tooth and claw, though of course there were some nice people in it, like Katharine Cornell and Walter Hampden (he had a niece in the Class of '32) and John Mason Brown, the thingummy, who talked to Mother's club every year. Harald had done graduate work at the Yale Drama School, under Professor Baker, but then the depression had started, and he had had to come to New York to be a stage manager instead of just writing plays. That was like starting from the bottom in a factory, of course, which lots of nice boys were doing, and there was probably no difference between backstage in a theatre, where a lot of men in their undershirts sat in front of a mirror putting on make-up, and a blast furnace or a coal mine, where the men were in their undershirts too. Helena Davison said that when Harald's show came to Cleveland this spring, he spent all his time playing poker with the stagehands and the electricians, who were the nicest people in the show, and Helena's father said he agreed with him, especially after seeing the play—Mr. Davison was a bit of a card and more democratic than most fathers, being from the West and more or less self-made. Still, nobody could afford to be standoffish nowadays. Connie Storey's fiancé, who was going into journalism, was working as an office boy at *Fortune*, and her family, instead of having conniptions, was taking it very calmly and sending her to cooking school. And lots of graduate architects, instead of joining a firm and building rich men's houses, had gone right into the factories to study industrial design. Look at Russel Wright, whom everybody thought quite the thing now; he was using industrial materials, like the wonderful new spun aluminum, to make all sorts of useful objects like cheese trays and water carafes. Kay's first wedding present, which she had picked out herself, was a Russel Wright cocktail shaker in the shape of a skyscraper and made out of oak ply and aluminum with a tray and twelve little round cups to match—light as a feather and nontarnishable, of course. The main point was, Harald was a natural gentleman— though inclined to show off in his letters, which was probably to impress Kay, who was inclined to drop names herself and talk about people's butlers and Fly and A.D. and Porcellian and introduce poor Harald as a Yale man when he had only gone to graduate school at New Haven. . . . That was a side of Kay that the group did its best to deprecate and that drove Lakey wild. A lack of fastidiousness and consideration for the other person; she did not seem to realize the little social nuances. She was always coming into people's rooms, for instance, and making herself at home and fiddling with things on their bureaus and telling them about their inhibitions if they objected; it was she who insisted on playing Truth and on getting everybody in the group to make lists of their friends in the order of preference and then compare the lists. What she did not stop to think about was that somebody had to be on the bottom of every list, and when that somebody cried and refused to be consoled, Kay was always honestly surprised; *she* would not mind, she said, hearing the truth about herself. Actually, she never did hear it because the others were too tactful ever to put her at the bottom, even if they wanted to, because Kay was a little bit of an outsider and nobody wanted her to feel that. So instead they would put Libby MacAusland or Polly Andrews—someone they had known all their lives or gone to school with or something. Kay did get a bit of a shock, though, to find that she was not at the top of Lakey's list. She was crazy about Lakey, whom she always described as her best friend. Kay did not know it, but the group had had a pitched battle with Lakey over Easter vacation, when they had drawn straws to see who was to invite Kay home for the holidays and Lakey had got the shortest straw and then refused to play. The group had simply borne down on Lakey in a body and accused her of being a poor sport, which was true. After all, as they had swiftly pointed out to her, it was she who had invited Kay to group with them in the first place; when they saw that they could get the South Tower for themselves if they had eight in the group instead of six, it was Lakey's idea that they should invite Kay and Helena Davison to join forces with them and take the two small single rooms.

If you were going to use a person, then you had to make the best of them. And it was not "using," anyway; they all liked Kay and Helena, including Lakey herself, who had discovered Kay as a sophomore, when they were both on the Daisy Chain. She had taken Kay up for all she was worth, because Kay, as she said, was "malleable" and "capable of learning." Now she claimed to have detected that Kay had feet of clay, which was rather a contradiction, since wasn't clay malleable? But Lakey was very contradictory; that was her charm. Sometimes she was a frightful snob and sometimes just the opposite. She was looking so furious this morning, for instance, because Kay, according to her, should have got married quietly in City Hall instead of making Harald, who was not to the manor born, try to carry off a wedding in J. P. Morgan's church. Now was this snobbish of Lakey or wasn't it? Naturally, she had not said any of this to Kay; she had expected Kay to feel it for herself, which was just what Kay couldn't do and remain the blunt, natural, unconscious Kay they all loved, in spite of her faults. Lakey had the weirdest ideas about people. She had got the bee in her bonnet, last fall, that Kay had worked her way into the group out of a desire for social prestige; this was not at all the way it had happened, and it was a peculiar thing, really, to think about a girl who was so unconventional that she had not even bothered to have her own parents to her wedding, though her father was very prominent in Salt Lake City affairs.

It was true, Kay had rather angled to get Pokey Prothero's

town house for the reception, but she had taken it with good grace when Pokey had loudly lamented that the house was in dust covers for the summer, with only a caretaking couple to look after Father on the nights he spent in town. Poor Kay— some of the girls thought that Pokey might have been a little more generous and offered her a card to the Colony. In fact, on this score, nearly all the group felt a little bit conscience-stricken. Each one of them, as the others knew, had a house or a big apartment or a club membership, if it was only the Cosmopolitan, or a cousin's digs or a brother's that might possibly have been put at Kay's disposal. But that would have meant punch, champagne, a cake from Sherry's or Henri's, extra help—before one knew it one would have found oneself giving the wedding and supplying a father or a brother to take Kay down the aisle. In these times, in sheer self-protection, one had to think twice, as Mother said, fatigued; there were so many demands. Fortunately, Kay had decided that she and Harald should give the wedding breakfast themselves, at the old Hotel Brevoort down on Eighth Street: so much nicer, so much more appropriate.

Dottie Renfrew and Elinor Eastlake made their way out of the chapel together, onto the sunny pavement. The service had seemed awfully short. There had been no blessing of the ring and "Who giveth this Woman" had had to be left out, obviously. Dottie frowned and cleared her throat. "Wouldn't you have thought," she dared to suggest, in her deep military rumble, "that she would have had *someone*? Isn't there a cousin in Montclair?" Elinor Eastlake shrugged. "The plan miscarried," she said. Libby MacAusland, an English major from Pittsfield, thrust her head into the tête-à-tête. "What's this, what's this?" she said jovially. "Break it up, girls." She was a tall, pretty blonde with perpetually dilating brown eyes, a long, arching, inquisitive neck, and a manner of anxious conviviality; she had been president of the class sophomore year and had just missed being elected president of Students. Dottie laid a cautionary hand on Lakey's silken elbow; Libby, as everyone knew, was an unrestrained gossip and gabbler. Lakey lightly shook off Dottie's fingers; she detested being touched. "Dottie was asking," she said distinctly, "whether there wasn't a cousin in Montclair." There was a faint smile in the depths of her green eyes, which had a queer dark-blue rim around the iris, a sign of her Indian blood; she was searching the distance for a taxi. Libby became exaggeratedly thoughtful. She laid a finger to the center of her forehead. "I believe there is," she discovered, nodding three times. "Do you really think—?" she began eagerly. Lakey raised a hand for a taxi. "Kay kept the cousin in the background, hoping that one of us would supply her with something better." "Lakey!" murmured Dottie, shaking her head in reproach. "Really, Lakey," said Libby, giggling. "Nobody but you would ever think of such a thing." She hesitated. "If Kay wanted somebody to give her away, she had only to ask, after all. Father or Brother would have been glad, any of us would have been glad. . . ." Her voice broke off, and she precipitated her thin form into the taxi, where she took the jump seat, turning around, in half a minute, to survey her friends with cupped chin and brooding eyes: all her movements were quick and restive—she had an image of herself as a high-bred, tempestuous creature, a sort of Arab steed in an English sporting primitive. "Do you really think?" she repeated, covetously, biting her upper lip. But Lakey said no more; she never enlarged on a suggestion, and for this had been named the Mona Lisa of the Smoking Room. Dottie Renfrew was distressed; her gloved hand twisted the pearls that had been given her for her twenty-first birthday. Her conscience was troubling her, and she resorted, from habit, to the slow, soft cough, like a perpetual scruple, that caused her family such anxiety and made them send her to Florida twice a year, at Christmas and Easter. "Lakey," she said gravely, ignoring Libby, "one of us, don't you think, should have done it for her?" Libby MacAusland caracoled about on the jump seat, a hungry look in her eyes. Both girls stared into Elinor's impassive oval face. Elinor's eyes narrowed; she fingered the coil of Indian-black hair at the nape of her neck and readjusted a hairpin. "No," she said, with contempt. "It would have been a confession of weakness."

Libby's eyes protruded. "How hard you are," she said admiringly. "And yet Kay adores you," pondered Dottie. "You used to like her best, Lakey. I think you still do, in your heart of hearts." Lakey smiled at the cliché. "Perhaps," she said and lit a cigarette. She was fond, at present, of girls like Dottie who ran true to type, like paintings well within a style or a tradition. The girls she chose to collect were mystified, usually, by what she saw in them; they humbly perceived that they were very different from her. In private, they often discussed her, like toys discussing their owner, and concluded that she was awfully inhuman. But this increased their respect for her. She was also very changeable, which made them suspect great depths. Now, as the cab turned toward Fifth Avenue on Ninth Street, she made one of her abrupt decisions. "Let me out here," she commanded in her small, distinct, sweet voice. The driver instantly stopped and turned to watch her step out of the cab, rather stately, despite her fragility, in a high-necked black taffeta suit with a white silk muffler, small black hat, like a bowler, and black very high-heeled shoes. "Go *ahead*," she called back impatiently, as the cab lingered.

The two girls in the taxi interrogated each other. Libby MacAusland craned her gold head in a flowered hat out the window. "Aren't you coming?" she cried. There was no answer. They could see her straight little back proceeding south, in the sun, on University Place. "Follow her!" said Libby to the driver. "I'll have to go round the block, lady." The cab turned into Fifth Avenue and passed the Brevoort Hotel, where the rest of the wedding party was arriving; it went on into Eighth Street and back up University Place. But there was no sign of Lakey anywhere. She had disappeared. "Wouldn't that jar you?" said Libby. "Was it something I said, do you think?" "Go round the block again, driver," interposed Dottie quietly. In front of the Brevoort, Kay and Harald were climbing out of a taxi; they did not see the two frightened girls. "Did she just up and decide not to go to the reception?" continued Libby, as the cab made the second circuit, without any result. "She seemed terribly off Kay, I *must* say." The cab paused before the hotel. "What are we going to *do*?" demanded Libby. Dottie opened her pocketbook and gave a bill to the driver. "Lakey is her own law," she said firmly to Libby as they dismounted. "We must simply tell everyone that she felt faint in the church." A disappointed expression came into Libby's sharp-boned, pretty face; she had been looking forward to the scandal.

In a private dining room of the hotel, Kay and Harald stood on a faded flowered carpet, receiving their friends' congratulations. A punch was being served, over which the guests were exclaiming: "What *is* it?," "Perfectly *delicious*," "How did you ever think of it?" and so on. To each one, Kay gave the recipe. The base was one-third Jersey applejack, one-third maple syrup, and one-third lemon juice, to which White Rock had been added. Harald had got the applejack from an actor friend who got it from a farmer near Flemington; the punch was adapted from a cocktail called Applejack Rabbit. The recipe was an ice-breaker—just as Kay had hoped, she explained aside to Helena Davison: everyone tasted it and agreed that it was the maple syrup that made all the difference. A tall shaggy man who was in radio told several funny stories about Jersey Lightning; he warned the handsome young man in the knitted green necktie that this stuff packed an awful wallop. There was a discussion about applejack and how it made people quarrelsome, to which the girls listened with fascination; none of them had ever tasted applejack before. They were very much interested, just at this time, in receipts for drinks; they all adored brandy Alexanders and White Ladies and wanted to hear about a cocktail called the Clover Club that was one-third gin, one-third lemon juice, one-third grenadine, and the white of an egg. Harald told about a drugstore he and Kay knew on West Fifty-ninth Street, where you could get prescription whisky without a prescription, and Polly Andrews borrowed a pencil from the waiter and noted down the address: she was going to be on her own this summer, keeping house for herself in her Aunt Julia's apartment with a terrace, and she needed all the tips she could get. Then Harald told them about a liqueur called anisette that an Italian in the theatre orchestra had taught him to make, from straight alcohol, water, and oil of anis, which gave it a milky color, like Pernod. He explained the difference between Pernod, absinthe, arrack, and anisette; the girls spoke of green and yellow chartreuse, green and white crème de menthe, which Harald said varied only in the color that was added, artificially, to suit a fancy market. Then he told them about an Armenian restaurant in the twenties, where you got rose-petal jelly for dessert, and explained the difference between Turkish and Armenian and Syrian cooking. "Where did you get this *man*?" the girls cried, in unison.

In the pause that followed, the young man in the knitted tie drank a glass of punch and came over to Dottie Renfrew. "Where's the dark beauty?" he asked in a confidential voice. Dottie lowered her voice also and glanced uneasily toward the far corner of the dining room, where Libby MacAusland was whispering to two of the group. "She felt faint in the chapel," she murmured. "I've just explained to Kay and Harald. We've packed her off to her hotel to lie down." The young man raised an eyebrow. "How perfectly *frightful*," he said. Kay turned her head quickly to listen; the mockery in the young man's voice was evident. Dottie flushed. She cast about bravely for a new subject. "Are you in the theatre too?" The young man leaned back against the wall, tilting his head upward. "No," he said, "though your question is natural. In point of fact, I'm in welfare work." Dottie eyed him gravely; she remembered now that Polly had said he was a painter, and she saw she was being teased. He looked very much the artist—handsome as a piece of Roman statuary but somewhat battered and worn; the muscles of the cheeks were loosening, and there were somber creases on either side of the flawless, straight, strong nose. She waited. "I do posters for the Women's International League for Peace," he said. Dottie laughed. "That's not welfare work," she retorted. "In a manner of speaking," he said. He glanced down at her, carefully. "Vincent Club, Junior League, work with unwed mothers," he enumerated. "*My* name is Brown. I come from Marblehead. I'm a collateral descendant of Nathaniel Hawthorne. My father keeps a general store. I didn't go to college. I'm not in your class, young lady." Dottie remained silent, merely watching him sympathetically; she now thought him very attractive. "I am an ex-expatriate," he continued. "Since the fall of the dollar I occupy a furnished room on Perry Street, next to the bridegroom's, and do peace posters for the ladies, as well as a little commercial work. The john, as you girls call it, is down the hall, and in the closet there's an electric grill. Hence you must excuse me if I smell like a ham-and-egg sandwich." Dottie's beaver-brown eyes twinkled reproachfully; from the theatrical way he spoke she could see that he was proud and bitter, and she knew he was a gentleman from his well-cut features and his good, if old, tweed suit. "Harald is moving on to higher things," said Mr. Brown. "An apartment on the fashionable East Side—above a cordial shop

and a cut-rate cleaner's, I'm told. We met like two passing ele-
vators, to modernize the figure, one on the way up, one on the
way down. Yesterday," he went on, frowning, "I was divorced
downtown in Foley Square by a beautiful young creature
named Betty from Morristown, New Jersey." He leaned forward slightly. "We spent last night in my room to celebrate.
Are any of you people named Betty?" Dottie reflected. "There's
Libby," she said. "No Libbys, Beths, or Betsys," he cautioned.
"I don't like the names you girls have nowadays. But what of
the dark beauty? How is she called?"

At this moment, the door opened and Elinor Eastlake was
shown in by a waiter, to whom she handed two brown-paper
parcels she was carrying in her black kid-gloved hand; she appeared perfectly composed. "Her name is Elinor," whispered
Dottie. "We call her Lakey because her last name is Eastlake
and she comes from Lake Forest, outside of Chicago." "Thank
you," said Mr. Brown, but he made no move to leave Dottie's
side and continued to talk to her in an undertone, out of the
corner of his mouth, offering wry comments on the wedding
party. Harald had hold of Lakey's hand, which he swung back
and forth, as he stood back to admire her suit, a Patou model.
His quick, lithe movements went oddly with his solemn long
head and face, almost as if his head, a thinking machine, did
not belong to him and had been clapped on his body in a
masquerade. He was an intensely self-absorbed young man, as
the girls knew from his letters, and when he spoke of his career,
as he was doing now to Lakey, he had a detached impersonal
eagerness, as though he were discussing disarmament or deficit
spending. Yet he was attractive to women, as the girls knew
from his letters too; the group admitted that he had S.A., the
way some homely men teachers and clergymen had, and there
was something about him, a dynamic verve, that made Dottie
wonder, even now, as she and her companion watched him,
how Kay had brought him to the point. The idea that Kay
might be *enceinte* had stolen more than once into her quiet
thoughts, though Kay, according to herself, knew all about
taking precautions and kept a douche in Harald's closet.

"Have you known Kay long?" asked Dottie curiously, remembering in spite of herself the toilet he had mentioned in
the hall of Harald's rooming house. "Long enough," replied

Mr. Brown. This was so cruelly outright that Dottie flinched, just as though it had been said of *her*, at her own wedding reception. "I don't like girls with big legs," he said, with a reassuring smile—Dottie's legs and slim, well-shod feet were her best points. Disloyally, Dottie looked with him at Kay's legs, which were indeed rather beefy. "A sign of peasant forbears," he said, waving a finger. "The center of gravity's too low—a mark of obstinacy and obtuseness." He studied Kay's figure, which was outlined by the thin dress; as usual, she was not wearing a girdle. "A touch of steatopygy." "What?" whispered Dottie. "Excessive development of the rump. Let me get you a drink." Dottie was thrilled and horrified; she had never had such a risqué conversation. "You and your social friends," he continued, "have a finer functional adaptation. Full, low-slung breasts"—he stared about the room—"fashioned to carry pearls and *bouclé* sweaters and faggoting and tucked crepe de Chine blouses. Narrow waists. Tapering legs. As a man of the last decade, I prefer the boyish figure myself: a girl in a bathing cap poised to jackknife on a diving board. Marblehead summer memories; Betty is a marvelous swimmer. Thin women are more sensual; scientific fact—the nerve ends are closer to the surface." His grey eyes narrowed, heavy-lidded, as though he were drifting off to sleep. "I like the fat one, though," he said abruptly, singling out Pokey Prothero. "She has a thermal look. Nacreous skin, plumped with oysters. Yum, yum, yum; money, money, money. My sexual problems are economic. I loathe under-privileged women, but my own outlook is bohemian. Impossible combination."

To Dottie's relief, the waiters came in with the breakfast—eggs Benedict—and Kay shooed everyone to the table. She put the best man, a very silent person who worked on the *Wall Street Journal* (advertising department), on her own right, and Helena Davison on Harald's right, but after that all was confusion. Dottie was left stranded at the end of the table between Libby, her bête noire, and the radio man's wife, who was a stylist at Russeks (and who, of course, should have been seated on Harald's left). It was a hard table to seat, with so many girls; still, a more tactful hostess could have arranged it so that the duller ones were not all put together. But the radio man's wife, a vivacious beanpole of a woman, dressed in plumes and jet accessories like a film vamp, seemed perfectly content with her company; she was a graduate of the University of Idaho, Class of '28, who loved, she said, a good hen fest. She had known Harald from a boy, she announced, and his old folks too, though long time no see. Anders, Harald's father, had been the principal of the high school in Boise she and Harald had gone to, way back when. "Isn't Kay a honey?" she at once demanded of Dottie. "Awfully nice," said Dottie, warmly. Her neighbor was the sort that used to be called "peppy"; on the whole, Dottie agreed with the English teacher who said that it was wiser not to use slang because it dated you so quickly. "How come her parents didn't show?" the woman continued, lowering her voice. "'Show'?" repeated Dottie, at a loss—could she mean show dogs or cats? "Turn up for the wedding." "Oh," said Dottie, coughing. "I believe they sent Kay and Harald a check," she murmured. "Rather than make the trip, you know." The woman nodded. "That's what Dave said—my husband. He figured they must have sent a check." "So much more useful," said Dottie. "Don't you agree?" "Oh, sure," said the woman. "I'm kind of an old softy, myself. I was married in a veil. . . . You know, I told Harald I'd have liked to give the wedding at my place. We could have scrounged up a minister and Dave could have taken some pictures, to send to the folks back home. But Kay had made all the arrangements, it seemed, by the time I got my bid in." She stopped on a rising note and looked inquiringly at Dottie, who felt herself in deep waters. Kay's plans, she said tactfully, turning it into a joke, were "as the laws of the Medes and the Persians"; nobody could change her. "Who was it said," she added, twinkling, "that his wife had a whim of iron? My father always quotes that when he has to give in to Mother." "Cute," said her neighbor. "Harald's a swell gent," she went on, in a different voice, more thoughtful and serious. "Kind of a vulnerable gent, too. Though you might not think so." She looked hard at Dottie and her plumes nodded belligerently as she downed a glass of punch.

Across the table, farther down, on Kay's left, the auburn-haired descendant of Hawthorne, who was talking to Priss Hartshorn, caught Dottie's troubled eye and winked. Not knowing what else to do, Dottie gamely winked back. She had not imagined she was the type men winked at. The oldest of the group, nearly twenty-three now, thanks to the poor health that had kept her out of school as a child, she knew she was a bit of an old maid; the group teased her for her decorum and staid habits and mufflers and medicines and the long mink coat she wore on campus to keep off the cold, but she had a good sense of humor and quietly joined in the laugh. Her beaux had always treated her with respect; she was the sort of girl that people's brothers took out and she had a whole string of pale young men who were studying archaeology or musicology or architecture in the Harvard Graduate School; she read out bits of their letters to the group—descriptions of concerts or of digs in the Southwest—and, playing Truth, admitted to having had two proposals. She had fine eyes, everyone told her, and a nice flashing set of white teeth and a pretty, if thin, cap of hair; her nose was rather long, in the pointed New England way, and her brows were black and a little heavy; she resembled the Copley portrait of an ancestress that hung in the family hall. In a modest way, she was fun-loving and even, she suspected, rather sensuous; she loved dancing and harmonizing and was always crooning to herself snatches of popular songs. Yet nobody had ever tried to take a liberty with her; some of the girls found it hard to believe this, but it was true. And the strange thing was, she would not have been shocked. The girls found the fact funny, but D. H. Lawrence was one of her favorite authors: he had such a true feeling for animals and for the natural side of life.

She and Mother had talked it over and agreed that if you were in love and engaged to a nice young man you perhaps ought to have relations once to make sure of a happy adjustment. Mother, who was very youthful and modern, knew of some very sad cases within her own circle of friends where the man and the woman just didn't fit down there and ought never to have been married. Not believing in divorce, Dottie thought it very important to arrange that side of marriage properly; defloration, which the girls were always joking about in the smoking room, frightened her. Kay had had an awful time with Harald; five times, she insisted, before she was penetrated, and this in spite of basketball and a great deal of riding out West. Mother said you could have the hymen removed surgically, if you wanted, as royal families abroad were said to do; but perhaps a very gentle lover could manage to make it painless; hence it might be better to marry an older man, with experience.

The best man was proposing a toast; looking up, Dottie found Dick Brown's (that was his name) bright grey eyes on her again. He raised his glass and drank to her, ceremoniously. Dottie drank in return. "Isn't this fun?" cried Libby Mac-Ausland, arching her long neck and weaving her head about and laughing in her exhausted style. "*So* much nicer," purred the voices. "No receiving line, no formality, no older people." "It's just what I want for myself," announced Libby. "A young people's wedding!" She uttered a blissful scream as a Baked Alaska came in, the meringue faintly smoking. "Baked Alaska!" she cried and fell back, as if in a heap, on her chair. "Girls!" she said solemnly, pointing to the big ice-cream cake with slightly scorched peaks of meringue that was being lowered into position before Kay. "Look at it. Childhood dreams come true! It's every children's party in the whole blessed United States. It's patent-leather slippers and organdy and a shy little boy in an Eton collar asking you to dance. I don't know when I've been so excited. I haven't seen one since I was twelve years old. It's Mount Whitney; it's Fujiyama." The girls smiled forbearingly at each other; Libby "wrote." But in fact they had shared her delight until she began talking about it, and a sigh of anticipation went up as they watched the hot meringue slump under Kay's knife. Standing against the wall, the two waiters watched rather dourly. The dessert was not all that good. The meringue had browned unevenly; it was white in some places and burned black in others, which gave it a disagreeable taste. Underneath the slab of ice cream, the sponge cake was stale and damp. But fealty to Kay sent plates back for seconds. The Baked Alaska was the *kind* of thing that in Kay's place the group hoped *they* would have thought of—terribly original for a wedding and yet just right when you considered it. They were all tremendously interested in cooking and quite out of patience with the unimaginative roasts and chops followed by molds from the caterer that Mother served; they were going to try new combinations and foreign recipes and puffy omelets and soufflés and interesting aspics and just one hot dish in a Pyrex, no soup, and a fresh green salad.

"It's a hotel trick," explained the radio man's wife, speaking across the table to Priss Hartshorn, who was going to be married herself in September. "They have the ice cream frozen hard as a rock and then, whoosh, into the oven. That way they take no chances, but between you and me it's not what Mamma used to make." Priss nodded worriedly; she was a solemn, ashy-haired little girl who looked like a gopher and who felt it her duty to absorb every bit of word-of-mouth information that pertained to consumer problems. Economics had been her major, and she was going to work in the consumer division of N.R.A. "Working conditions," she declared, with her slight nervous stammer, "in some of our best hotel kitchens are way substandard, you know." She had begun to feel her liquor; the punch *was* rather treacherous, even though applejack, being a natural product, was one of the purest things you could drink these days. In her haze, she saw the radio man stand up. "To the Class of Thirty-three," he toasted. The others drank to the Vassar girls. "Bottoms up!" cried the man's wife. From the silent best man came a cackling laugh. Tiddly as she was, Priss could tell that she and her friends, through no fault of their own, had awakened economic antagonism. Vassar girls, in general, were not liked, she knew, by the world at large; they had come to be a sort of symbol of superiority. She would have to see a good deal less of some of them after she was married if she wanted Sloan to keep in with his colleagues on the staff of the hospital. She stared sadly at Pokey Prothero, her best friend, who was sitting sprawled out, across the table, putting ashes into her plate of melting ice cream and soggy cake with the very bad table manners that only the very rich could afford. There was a long spill down the front of her beautiful Lanvin suit. Mentally, Priss applied Energine; her neat little soul scrubbed away. She did not know how Pokey would ever get along in life without a personal maid to take care of her. Ever since Chapin, she herself had been picking up after Pokey, making her use an ashtray in the smoking room, collecting her laundry and mailing it home for her, creeping into the common bathroom to wash the ring off the tub so that the others would not complain again. Poor Pokey, when she was married, would be doomed to a conventional establishment and a retinue of servants and governesses; she would miss all the fun and the alarums, as Mother called them, of starting on your own from scratch, with just a tweeny to help with the dishwashing and the heavy work.

Great wealth was a frightful handicap; it insulated you from living. The depression, whatever else you could say about it, had been a truly wonderful thing for the propertied classes; it had waked a lot of them up to the things that really counted. There wasn't a family Priss knew that wasn't happier and saner for having to scale down its expenditures; sacrifices had drawn the members together. Look at Polly Andrews' family: Mr. Andrews had been in Riggs Clinic when the depression hit and all his investments went blotto; whereupon, instead of sinking deeper into melancholia and being put into a state hospital (grim thought!), he had come home and made himself useful as the family cook. He did every bit of the cooking and the marketing and served the most scrumptious meals, having learned about *haute cuisine* when they had their chateau in France; Mrs. Andrews did the scullery work and the vacuuming; everybody made his own bed; and the children, when they were home, washed up. They were the *gayest* family to visit, on the little farm they had managed to save near Stockbridge; Lakey went there last Thanksgiving and never had a better time—she only wished, she said, that *her* father would lose his money, like Mr. Andrews. She meant it quite seriously. Of course, it made a difference that the Andrews had always been rather highbrow; they had inner resources to fall back on.

Priss herself was a dyed-in-the-wool liberal; it ran in the blood. Her mother was a Vassar trustee, and her grandfather had been reform mayor of New York. Last year, when she had had to be a bridesmaid in a big social wedding at St. James', with the carpet and the awning and so on, she had not been able to get over the sight of the unemployed crowding round the church entrance, with the police holding them back. It was not that Priss felt she had to change the world singlehanded, as her brother, who went to Yale, was always jeering, and she did not blame the class she was born into for wanting to hold onto its privileges—that was part of their conditioning. She was not in the least bit a socialist or a rebel, though even Sloan liked to tease her about being one. To be a socialist, she thought, was a sort of luxury, when the world itself was changing so fast and there was so much that had to be done here and now. You could not sit down and wait for the millennium, any more than you could turn the clock back. The group used to play the game of when in history you would like to have lived if you could choose, and Priss was the only one who stuck up for the present; Kay picked the year 2000 (A.D., of course) and Lakey was for the *quattrocento*—which showed, incidentally, what a varied group they were. But seriously Priss could not imagine a more exciting time to come of age in than right now in America, and she felt awfully sorry for a person like Dick Brown, on her right, with his restless, bitter face and white unsteady hands; having talked with him quite a while (probably boring him stiff!), she could see that he was typical of that earlier generation of expatriates and bohemian rebels they had been studying about in Miss Lockwood's course who were coming back now to try to find their roots again.

The gabble of voices slowly died down. The girls, confused by alcohol, cast inquiring looks at each other. What was to happen now? At an ordinary wedding, Kay and Harald would slip off to change to traveling costume, and Kay would throw her bouquet. But there was to be no honeymoon, they recalled. Kay and Harald, evidently, had nowhere to go but back to the sublet apartment they had just left this morning. Probably, if the group knew Kay, the bed was not even made. The funny, uneasy feeling that had come over them all in the chapel affected them again. They looked at their watches; it was only one-fifteen. How many hours till it was time for Harald to go to work? Doubtless, lots of couples got married and just went home again, but somehow it did not seem right to let that happen. "Should I ask them to Aunt Julia's for coffee?" whispered Polly Andrews to Dottie, across the table. "It makes rather a lot," murmured Dottie. "I don't know what Ross would say." Ross was Aunt Julia's maid and quite a character. "Bother Ross!" said Polly. The two girls' eyes went up and down the table, counting, and then met, grave and startled. There were thirteen—eight of the group and five outsiders. How like Kay! Or was it an accident? Had someone dropped out at the last minute? Meanwhile, the radio man's wife had been exchanging signals with her husband; she turned to Dottie and spoke *sotto voce*. "How would some of you gals like to drop around to my place for some Java? I'll give Kay and

Harald the high sign." Dottie hesitated; perhaps this would really be more suitable, but she did not like to decide for Kay, who might prefer Aunt Julia's. A sense that everything was getting too involved, wheels within wheels, depressed her.

Pokey Prothero's voice, like a querulous grackle, intervened. "You two are supposed to go away," she suddenly complained, crushing out her cigarette and looking through her *lorgnon* with an air of surprised injury from the bride to the groom. Trust Pokey, thought the girls, with a joint sigh. "Where should we go, Pokey?" answered Kay, smiling. "Yes, Pokey, where should we go?" agreed the bridegroom. Pokey considered. "Go to Coney Island," she said. Her tone of irrefutable, self-evident logic, like that of an old man or a child, took everyone aback for a second. "What a splendid idea!" cried Kay. "On the subway?" "Brighton Express, via Flatbush Avenue," intoned Harald. "Change at Fulton Street." "Pokey, you're a genius," said everyone, in voices of immense relief. Harald paid the bill and launched into a discussion of roller coasters, comparing the relative merits of the Cyclone and the Thunderbolt. Compacts came out; fur pieces were clipped together; daily remembrancers of dark-blue English leather were consulted. The room was full of movement and laughter. "How did Pokey ever think of it?," "The perfect end to a perfect wedding," "Just right," the voices reiterated, as gloves were pulled on.

The party moved out to the street; the radio man, who had left his camera in the check room, took pictures on the sidewalk, in the bright June sunlight. Then they all walked along Eighth Street to the subway at Astor Place, while passers-by turned to stare at them, and right down to the turnstiles. "Kay must throw her bouquet!" shrieked Libby MacAusland, stretching on her long legs, like a basketball center, as a crowd of people massed to watch them. "My girl's from Vassar; none can surpass 'er," the radio man struck up. Harald produced two nickels and the newlyweds passed through the turnstile; Kay, who, all agreed, had never looked prettier, turned and threw her bouquet, high in the air, back over the turnstiles to the waiting girls. Libby jumped and caught it, though it had really been aimed at Priss just behind her. And at that moment Lakey gave them all a surprise; the brown-paper parcels she had checked in the hotel proved to contain rice. "*That* was what you stopped for!" exclaimed Dottie, full of wonder, as the wedding party seized handfuls and pelted them after the bride and the groom; the platform was showered with white grains when the local train finally came in. "That's banal! That's not like you, Eastlake!" Kay turned and shouted as the train doors were closing, and everyone, dispersing, agreed that it was not like Lakey at all, but that, banal or not, it was just the little touch that had been needed to round off an unforgettable occasion.

2

JUST at first, in the dark hallway, it had given Dottie rather a funny feeling to be tiptoeing up the stairs only two nights after Kay's wedding to a room right across from Harald's old room, where the same thing had happened to Kay. An awesome feeling, really, like when the group all got the curse at the same time; it filled you with strange ideas about being a woman, with the moon compelling you like the tides. All sorts of weird, irrelevant ideas floated through Dottie's head as the key turned in the lock and she found herself, for the first time, alone with a man in his flat. Tonight was midsummer's night, the summer solstice, when maids had given up their treasure to fructify the crops; she had that in background reading for *A Midsummer Night's Dream*. Her Shakespeare teacher had been awfully keen on anthropology and had had them study in Frazer about the ancient fertility rites and how the peasants in Europe, till quite recent times, had lit big bonfires in honor of the Corn Maiden and then lain together in the fields. College, reflected Dottie as the lamp clicked on, had been almost *too* rich an experience. She felt stuffed with interesting thoughts that she could only confide in Mother, not in a man, certainly, who would probably suppose you were barmy if you started telling him about the Corn Maiden when you were just about to lose your virginity. Even the group would laugh if Dottie confessed that she was exactly in the mood for a long, comfy discussion with Dick, who was so frightfully attractive and unhappy and had so much to give.

But the group would never believe, never in a million years, that Dottie Renfrew would come here, to this attic room that smelled of cooking fat, with a man she hardly knew, who made no secret of his intentions, who had been drinking heavily, and who was evidently not in love with her. When she put it that way, crudely, she could scarcely believe it herself, and the side of her that wanted to talk was still hoping, probably, to gain a little time, the way, she had noticed, she always started a discussion of current events with the dentist to keep him from turning on the drill. Dottie's dimple twinkled. What an odd comparison! If the group could hear that!

And yet when It happened, it was not at all what the group or even Mother would have imagined, not a bit sordid or messy, in spite of Dick's being tight. He had been most considerate, undressing her slowly, in a matter-of-fact way, as if he were helping her off with her outdoor things. He took her hat and furs and put them in the closet and then unfastened her dress, bending over the snaps with a funny, concentrated scowl, rather like Daddy's when he was hooking Mother up for a party. Lifting the dress carefully off her, he had glanced at the label and then back at Dottie, as though to match the two, before he carried it, walking very steadily, to the closet and arranged it on a wooden hanger. After that, he folded each garment as he removed it and set it ceremoniously on the armchair, looking each time at the label with a frown between his brows. When her dress was gone, she felt rather faint for a minute, but he left her in her slip, just as they did in the doctor's office, while he took off her shoes and stockings and undid her brassière and girdle and step-ins, so that finally, when he drew her slip over her head, with great pains so as not to muss her hairdo, she was hardly trembling when she stood there in front of him with nothing on but her pearls. Perhaps it was going to the doctor so much or perhaps it was Dick himself, so detached and impersonal, the way they were supposed to be in art class with the model, that made Dottie brave. He had not touched her once, all the time he was undressing her, except by accident, grazing her skin. Then he pinched each of her full breasts lightly and told her to relax, in just the tone Dr. Perry used when he was going to give her a treatment for her sciatica.

He handed her a book of drawings to look at, while he went into the closet, and Dottie sat there in the armchair, trying not to listen. With the book on her lap, she studied the room conscientiously, in order to know Dick better. Rooms told a lot about a person. It had a skylight and a big north window and was surprisingly neat for a man; there was a drawing board with some work on it which she longed to peek at, a long plain table, like an ironing table, monk's-cloth curtains, and a monk's-cloth spread on the single bed. On the chest of drawers was a framed photograph of a blonde woman, very striking, with a short, severe haircut; that must be "Betty," the wife. Tacked up on the wall, there was a snapshot that looked like her in a bathing suit and a number of sketches from the nude, and Dottie had the sinking feeling that they might be of Betty too. She had been doing her very best not to let herself think about love or let her emotions get entangled, for she knew that Dick would not like it. It was just a physical attraction, she had been telling herself over and over, while trying to remain cool and collected despite the pounding of her blood, but now, suddenly, when it was too late to retreat, she had lost her *sang-froid* and was jealous. Worse than that, even, the idea came to her that Dick was, well, *peculiar*. She opened the book of drawings on her lap and found more nudes, signed by some modern artist she had never heard of! She did not know, a second later, just what she had been expecting, but Dick's return was, by contrast, less bad.

He came in wearing a pair of white shorts and carrying a towel, with a hotel's name on it, which he stretched out on the bed, having turned back the covers. He took the book away from her and put it on a table. Then he made Dottie lie down on the towel, telling her to relax again, in a friendly, instructive voice; while he stood for a minute, looking down at her and smiling, with his hands on his hips, she tried to breathe naturally, reminding herself that she had a good figure, and forced a wan, answering smile to her lips. "*Nothing will happen unless you want it, baby.*" The words, lightly stressed, told her how scared and mistrustful she must be looking. "I know, Dick," she answered, in a small, weak, grateful voice, making herself use his name aloud for the first time. "Would you like a cigarette?" Dottie shook her head and let it drop back on the pillow. "All right, then?" "All right." As he moved to turn out the light, she felt a sudden harsh thump of excitement, right in *there*, like what had happened to her in the Italian restaurant when he said "Do you want to come home with me?" and fastened his deep, shadowed eyes on her. Now he turned and looked at her steadily again, his hand on the bridge lamp; her own eyes, widening with amazement at the funny feeling she noticed, as if she were on fire, in the place her thighs were shielding, stared at him, seeking confirmation; she swallowed.

In reply, he switched off the lamp and came toward her in the dark, unbuttoning his shorts.

This shift gave her an instant in which to be afraid. She had never seen *that* part of a man, except in statuary and once, at the age of six, when she had interrupted Daddy in his bath, but she had a suspicion that it would be something ugly and darkly inflamed, surrounded by coarse hair. Hence, she had been very grateful for being spared the sight of it, which she did not think she could have borne, and she held her breath as the strange body climbed on hers, shrinking. "Open your legs," he commanded, and her legs obediently fell apart. His hand squeezed her down there, rubbing and stroking; her legs fell farther apart, and she started to make weak, moaning noises, almost as if she wanted him to stop. He took his hand away, thank Heaven, and fumbled for a second; then she felt it, the thing she feared, being guided into her as she braced herself and stiffened. "Relax," he whispered. "You're ready." It was surprisingly warm and smooth, but it hurt terribly, pushing and stabbing. "Damn it," he said. "Relax. You're making it harder." Just then, Dottie screamed faintly; it had gone all the way in. He put his hand over her mouth and then settled her legs around him and commenced to move it back and forth inside her. At first, it hurt so that she flinched at each stroke and tried to pull back, but this only seemed to make him more determined. Then, while she was still praying for it to be over, surprise of surprises, she started to like it a little. She got the idea, and her body began to move too in answer, as he pressed *that* home in her slowly, over and over, and slowly drew it back, as if repeating a question. Her breath came quicker. Each lingering stroke, like a violin bow, made her palpitate for the next. Then, all of a sudden, she seemed to explode in a series of long, uncontrollable contractions that embarrassed her, like the hiccups, the moment they were over, for it was as if she had forgotten Dick as a person; and he, as if he sensed this, pulled quickly away from her and thrust that part of himself onto her stomach, where it pushed and pounded at her flesh. Then he too jerked and moaned, and Dottie felt something damp and sticky running down the hill of her belly.

Minutes passed; the room was absolutely still; through the skylight Dottie could see the moon. She lay there, with Dick's weight still on her, suspecting that something had gone wrong—probably her fault. His face was turned sideward so that she could not look into it, and his chest was squashing her breasts so that she could hardly breathe. Both their bodies were wet, and the cold perspiration from him ran down her face and matted her side hair and made a little rivulet between her breasts; on her lips it had a salty sting that reminded her forlornly of tears. She was ashamed of the happiness she had felt. Evidently, he had not found her satisfactory as a partner or else he would say something. Perhaps the woman was not supposed to move? "Damn it," he had said to her, when he was hurting her, in such a testy voice, like a man saying "Damn it, why can't we have dinner on time?" or something unromantic like that. Was it her screaming out that had spoiled everything? Or had she made a *faux pas* at the end, somehow? She wished that books were a little more explicit; Krafft-Ebing, which Kay and Helena had found at a secondhand bookstore and kept reading aloud from, as if it were very funny, mostly described nasty things like men making love to hens, and even then did not explain how it was done. The thought of the blonde on the bureau filled her with hopeless envy; probably Dick at this moment was making bitter comparisons. She could feel his breathing and smell the stale alcohol that came from him in gusts. In the bed, there was a peculiar pungent odor, and she feared that it might come from her.

The horrible idea occurred to her that he had fallen asleep, and she made a few gentle movements to try to extricate herself from under him. Their damp skins, stuck together, made a little sucking noise when she pulled away, but she could not roll his weight off her. Then she knew that he was asleep. Probably he was tired, she said to herself forgivingly; he had those dark rings under his eyes. But down in her heart she knew that he ought not to have gone to sleep like a ton of bricks on top of her; it was the final proof, if she still needed one, that she meant nothing to him. When he woke up tomorrow morning and found her gone, he would probably be glad. Or perhaps he would not even remember who had been there with him; she could not guess how much he had had to drink before he met her for dinner. What had happened, she feared, was that he had simply passed out. She saw that her only hope of saving her own dignity was to dress in the dark and steal away. But she would have to find the bathroom somewhere outside in that unlit hall. Dick began to snore. The sticky liquid had dried and was crusting on her stomach; she felt she could not go back to the Vassar Club without washing it off. Then the worst thought, almost, of all struck her. Supposing he had started to have an emission while he was still inside her? Or if he had used one of the rubber things and it had broken when she had jerked like that and that was why he had pulled so sharply away? She had heard of the rubber things breaking or leaking and how a woman could get pregnant from just a single drop. Full of determination, Dottie heaved and squirmed to free herself, until Dick raised his head in the moonlight and stared at her, without recognition. It was all true then, Dottie thought miserably; he had just gone to sleep and forgotten her. She tried to slide out of the bed.

Dick sat up and rubbed his eyes. "Oh, it's you, Boston," he muttered, putting an arm around her waist. "Forgive me for dropping off." He got up and turned on the bridge lamp. Dottie hurriedly covered herself with the sheet and averted her face; she was still timorous of seeing him in the altogether. "I must go home, Dick," she said soberly, stealing a sideward look at her clothes folded on the armchair. "*Must* you?" he inquired in a mocking tone; she could imagine his reddish eyebrows shooting up. "You needn't trouble to dress and see me downstairs," she went on quickly and firmly, her eyes fixed on the rug where his bare handsome feet were planted. He stooped and picked up his shorts; she watched his feet clamber into them. Then her eyes slowly rose and met his searching gaze. "What's the matter, Boston?" he said kindly. "Girls don't run home, you know, on their first night. Did it hurt you much?" Dottie shook her head. "Are you bleeding?" he demanded. "Come on, let me look." He lifted her up and moved her down on the bed, the sheet trailing along with her; there was a small bloodstain on the towel. "The very bluest," he said, "but only a minute quantity. Betty bled like a pig." Dottie said nothing. "Out with it, Boston," he said brusquely, jerking a thumb toward the framed photograph. "Does *she* put your nose out of joint?" Dottie made a brave negative sign. There was one thing she had to say. "Dick," and she shut her eyes in shame, "do you think I should take a douche?" "A douche?" he repeated in a mystified tone. "Why? What for?" "Well, in case . . . *you* know . . . birth control," murmured Dottie. Dick stared at her and suddenly burst out laughing; he dropped onto a straight chair and threw his handsome head back. "My dear girl," he said, "we just employed the most ancient form of birth control. *Coitus interruptus*, the old Romans called it, and a horrid nuisance it is." "I thought perhaps . . . ?" said Dottie. "Don't think. What did you think? I promise you, there isn't a single sperm swimming up to fertilize your irreproachable ovum. Like the man in the Bible, I spilled my seed on the ground, or, rather, on your very fine belly." With a swift motion, he pulled the sheet back before she could stop him. "Now," he said, "lay bare your thoughts." Dottie shook her head and blushed. Wild horses could not make her, for the words embarrassed her frightfully; she had nearly choked on "douche" and "birth control," as it was. "We must get you cleaned up," he decreed after a moment's silence. He put on a robe and slippers and disappeared to the bathroom. It seemed a long time before he came back, bringing a dampened towel, with which he swabbed off her stomach. Then he dried her, rubbing hard with the dry end of it, sitting down beside her on the bed. He himself appeared much fresher, as though he had washed, and he smelled of mouthwash and tooth powder. He lit two cigarettes and gave her one and settled an ashtray between them.

"You *came*, Boston," he remarked, with the air of a satisfied instructor. Dottie glanced uncertainly at him; could he mean that thing she had done that she did not like to think about? "I beg your pardon," she murmured. "I mean you had an orgasm." Dottie made a vague, still-inquiring noise in her throat; she was pretty sure, now, she understood, but the new word discombobulated her. "A climax," he added, more sharply. "Do they teach that word at Vassar?" "Oh," said Dottie, almost disappointed that that was all there was to it. "Was that . . . ?" She could not finish the question. "That was it," he nodded. "That is, if I am a judge." "It's normal then?" she wanted to know, beginning to feel better. Dick shrugged. "Not for girls of your upbringing. Not the first time, usually. Appearances to the contrary, you're probably highly sexed."

Dottie turned even redder. According to Kay, a climax was something very unusual, something the husband brought about by carefully studying his wife's desires and by patient manual stimulation. The terms made Dottie shudder, even in memory; there was a horrid bit, all in Latin, in Krafft-Ebing, about the Empress Maria Theresa and what the court doctor told her consort to do that Dottie had glanced at quickly and then tried to forget. Yet even Mother hinted that satisfaction was something that came after a good deal of time and experience and that love made a big difference. But when Mother talked about satisfaction, it was not clear exactly what she meant, and Kay was not clear either, except when she quoted from books. Polly Andrews once asked her whether it was the same as feeling passionate when you were necking (that was when Polly was engaged), and Kay said yes, pretty much, but Dottie now thought that Kay had been mistaken or else trying to hide the truth from Polly for some reason. Dottie had felt passionate, quite a few times, when she was dancing with someone terribly attractive, but that was quite different from the thing Dick meant. You would almost think that Kay did not know what she was talking about. Or else that Kay and Mother meant something else altogether and this thing with Dick *was* abnormal. And yet he seemed so pleased, sitting there, blowing out smoke rings; probably, having lived abroad, he knew more than Mother and Kay.

"What are you frowning over now, Boston?" Dottie gave a start. "To be highly sexed," he said gently, "is an excellent thing in a woman. You mustn't be ashamed." He took her cigarette and put it out and laid his hands on her shoulders. "Buck up," he said. "What you're feeling is natural. '*Post coitum, omne animal triste est,*' as the Roman poet said." He slipped his hand down the slope of her shoulder and lightly touched her nipple. "Your body surprised you tonight. You must learn to know it." Dottie nodded. "Soft," he murmured, pressing the nipple between his thumb and forefinger. "Detumescence, that's what you're experiencing." Dottie drew a quick breath, fascinated; her doubts slid away. As he continued to squeeze it, her nipple stood up. "Erectile tissue," he said informatively and touched the other breast. "See," he said, and they both looked downward. The two nipples were hard and full, with a pink aureole of goose pimples around them; on her breasts were a few dark hairs. Dottie waited tensely. A great relief had surged through her; these were the very terms Kay cited from the marriage handbooks. Down there, she felt a quick new tremor. Her lips parted. Dick smiled. "You feel something?" he said. Dottie nodded. "You'd like it again?" he said, assaying her with his hand. Dottie stiffened; she pressed her thighs together. She was ashamed of the violent sensation his exploring fingers had discovered. But he held his hand there, between her clasped thighs, and grasped her right hand in his other, guiding it downward to the opening of his robe and pressed it over that part of himself, which was soft and limp, rather sweet, really, all curled up on itself like a fat worm. Sitting beside her, he looked into her face as he stroked her down there and tightened her hand on him. "There's a little ridge there," he whispered. "Run your fingers up and down it." Dottie obeyed, wonderingly; she felt his organ stiffen a little, which gave her a strange sense of power. She struggled against the excitement his tickling thumb was producing in her own external part; but as she felt him watching her, her eyes closed and her thighs spread open. He disengaged her hand, and she fell back on the bed, gasping. His thumb continued its play and she let herself yield to what it was doing, her whole attention concentrated on a tense pinpoint of sensation, which suddenly discharged itself in a nervous, fluttering spasm; her body arched and heaved and then lay still. When his hand returned to touch her, she struck it feebly away. "Don't," she moaned, rolling over on her stomach. This second climax, which she now recognized from the first one, though it was different, left her jumpy and disconcerted; it was something less thrilling and more like being tickled relentlessly or having to go to the bathroom. "Didn't you like that?" he demanded, turning her head over on the pillow, so that she could not hide herself from him. She hated to think of his having watched her while he brought *that* about. Slowly, Dottie opened her eyes and resolved to tell the truth. "Not quite so much as the other, Dick." Dick laughed. "A nice normal girl. Some of your sex prefer that." Dottie shivered; she could not deny that it had been exciting but it seemed to her almost perverted. He appeared to read her thoughts. "Have you ever done it with a girl, Boston?" He tilted her face so that he could scan it. Dottie reddened. "Heavens, no." "You come like a house afire. How do you account for that?" Dottie said nothing. "Have you ever done it with yourself?" Dottie shook her head violently; the suggestion wounded her. "In your dreams?" Dottie reluctantly nodded. "A little. Not the whole thing." "Rich erotic fantasies of a Chestnut Street virgin," remarked Dick, stretching. He got up and went to the chest of drawers and took out two pairs of pajamas and tossed one of them to Dottie. "Put them on now and go to the bathroom. Tonight's lesson is concluded."

Having locked herself into the hall bathroom, Dottie began to take stock. "Who would have thunk it?" she quoted Pokey Prothero, as she stared, thunderstruck, into the mirror. Her ruddy, heavy-browed face, with its long straight nose and dark-brown eyes, was just as Bostonian as ever. Somebody in the group had said that she looked as if she had been born in a mortar-board. There was something magistral about her appearance, she could see it herself, in the white men's pajamas with her sharp New England jaw protruding over the collar, like an old judge or a blackbird sitting on a fence—Daddy sometimes joked that she ought to have been a lawyer. And yet there was that fun-loving dimple lurking in her cheek and the way she loved to dance and sing harmony—she feared she might be a dual personality, a regular Jekyll and Hyde. Thoughtfully, Dottie rinsed her mouth out with Dick's mouthwash and threw back her head to gargle. She wiped off her lipstick with a bit of toilet tissue and peered anxiously at the soap in Dick's soap dish, thinking of her sensitive skin. She had to be awfully careful, but the bathroom, she noted with gratitude, was *scrupulously* clean and placarded with notices from the landlady: "Please leave this room as you would expect to find it. Thank you for your cooperation"; "Please use mat when taking shower. Thank you." The landlady, Dottie reflected, must be very broad-minded, if she did not object to women's coming to visit. After all, Kay had spent whole weekends here with Harald.

She did not like to think of what women guests Dick had had, besides Betty, whom he had already mentioned. What if he had brought Lakey here the other night, after they took Dottie home? Breathing hard, she steadied herself on the washbasin and nervously scratched her jaw. Lakey, she argued,

would not have let him do what he had done with *her*; with
Lakey, he would not have dared. This line of thought, however, was too unsettling to be pursued. How had he known
that *she* would let him? There was one queer thing that her
mind had been running away from: he had not really kissed
her, not once. Of course, there could be explanations; perhaps
he did not want her to smell the liquor on his breath or perhaps she had hali herself . . . ? *No*, said Dottie firmly; she
would have to stop thinking this way. One thing was clear;
anyone could see it. Dick had been hurt, very much hurt, she
repeated, nodding, by a woman or women. That made him a
law unto himself, as far as she was concerned. If he did not feel
like kissing her, that was *his* business. Her lustrous contralto
rose humming as she combed out her hair with her pocket
comb: "He's the kind of a man needs the kind of a woman like
me-e." She did a gay dance step, stumbling a little in the long
pajamas, to the door. Her fingers snapped as she pulled out the
overhead light.

   Once she was settled in the narrow bed, with Dick sleeping
heavily beside her, Dottie's bird thoughts flew affectionately to
Mother, Class of 1908. Urge herself as she would to get her
beauty sleep after a *very* tiring day, she felt a craving to talk and
share the night's experiences with the person whom she designated as the nicest person in the world, who never condemned
or censured, and who was always so tremendously interested in
young people's doings. Tracing back the steps of her initiation,
she longed to set the scene for Mother: this bare room way
west in Greenwich Village, the moon's ray falling on the
monk's-cloth bedspread, the drawing table, the single wing
chair with the neat slip cover, some sort of awning material,
and Dick himself, of course, such an individual, with his restless chiseled face and incredible vocabulary. There were so
many details of the last three days that would appeal to Mother:
the wedding and going with him and Lakey that afternoon to
the Whitney Museum and the three of them having dinner afterward in a dinky Italian restaurant with a billiard table in
front and wine in white cups and listening to him and Lakey
argue about art and then going to the Modern Museum the
next day, again the three of them, and to an exhibition of
modernistic sculpture, and how Dottie had never suspected

that he was even thinking of *her* because she could see that he
was fascinated by Lakey (who wouldn't be?) and how she was
still sure of that when he turned up at the boat this morning to
see Lakey off, pretending that he wanted to give her some
names of painters in Paris for her to meet. Even when he had
asked *her*, at the dock, when the boat had sailed and there was
a sort of a letdown, to have dinner with him tonight at that
same restaurant (what a time she had finding it in a taxi, from
the New Weston!), she had told herself that it was because she
was Lakey's friend. She had been scared stiff at being alone
with him because she was afraid he would be bored. And he
had been rather silent and preoccupied until he looked straight
into her eyes and popped that question. "*Do you want to come
home with me?*" Would she ever, ever forget the casual tone of
his voice when he said it?

What *would* startle Mother, undoubtedly, was the fact that
there had been no thought of love on either side. She could
hear her own low voice explaining to her pretty, bright-eyed
parent that she and Dick had "lived together" on quite a different basis. Dick, poor chap, her voice announced coolly, was
still in love with his divorced wife, and, what was more (here
Dottie took a deep breath and braced herself), deeply attracted
to Lakey, her *very* best friend this year. In Dottie's imagination,
her mother's blue eyes widened and her gold curls trembled
with the little palsied shake of her head, as Dottie leaned forward, impressively, and reiterated, "Yes, Mother, I could still
swear it. Deeply attracted to Lakey. I faced the fact that night."
This scene, which her fancy was rehearsing, was taking place in
her mother's little morning room on Chestnut Street, though her
mother, in actuality, had already left for the cottage at Gloucester, where Dottie was expected tomorrow or the day after: tiny
Mrs. Renfrew was dressed in her tailored powder-blue Irish
linen dress, with bare, tanned arms, from golfing; Dottie herself was wearing her white sharkskin sports dress and brown-
and-white spectator pumps. She finished her piece, stared at
her toes, and fingered the box pleats of her dress, waiting
calmly for her mother to speak. "Yes, Dottie, I see. I *think* I
can understand." Both of them went on talking in low, even,
musical voices, her mother a little more staccato and Dottie
rumbling slightly. The atmosphere was grave and thoughtful.

"You are sure, dear, the hymen was punctured?" Dottie nodded, emphatically. Mrs. Renfrew, a medical missionary's daughter, had been an invalid too in her youth, which gave her a certain anxiety about the physical aspect of things.

Dottie turned restlessly in the bed. "You'll adore Mother," she said to Dick in imagination. "She's a terrifically vital person and much more attractive than I am: tiny, with a marvelous figure, and blue eyes and yellow hair that's just beginning to go grey. She cured herself of being an invalid, by sheer will power, when she met Daddy, her senior year at college, just when the doctors said she'd have to drop out of her class. She decided that it was wrong for a sick person to marry and so she got well. She's a great believer in love; we all are." Here Dottie flushed and inked out the last few words. She must *not* let Dick think she was going to spoil their affair by falling in love with him; a remark like that one would be fatal. To let him see that there was no danger, it would be best, she decided, to frame a statement of some sort, clarifying her position. "I'm very religious too, Dick," she essayed with an apologetic smile. "But I think I'm more pantheistic than most communicants of the Church. I love the Church for its ritual, but I believe God is everywhere. My generation is a little different from Mother's. *I* feel—all of us feel—that love and sex can be two separate things. They don't have to be, but they can be. You mustn't force sex to do the work of love or love to do the work of sex—that's quite a thought, isn't it?" she appended hurriedly, with a little nervous laugh, as her sources began to fail her. "One of the older teachers told Lakey that you have to live without love, learn not to need it, in order to live *with* it. Lakey was terrifically impressed. Do you agree?" Dottie's fancied voice had been growing more and more timid as she proffered her philosophy to the sleeping man by her side.

Her imagination had dared to mention Lakey's name to him in connection with love because she wanted to show that she was not jealous of the dark beauty, as he always called her; he did not like "Lakey" for a nickname. One thing Dottie had noticed was the way he absently straightened his tie whenever Lakey turned to look at him, like a man catching sight of himself in a subway mirror. And the way he was always serious with her, not mocking and saturnine, even when they disagreed about art. Yet when Dottie had murmured, several times, "Isn't she striking?" as they stood waving at her from the pier, in an effort to gain his confidence and share Lakey between them, he had merely shrugged his shoulders, as though Dottie were annoying him. "She has a mind," he retorted, the last time Dottie mentioned it.

Now that Lakey was on the high seas and *she* was in bed with Dick warm beside her, Dottie ventured to try out a new theory. Could it be, she asked herself, that Dick was attracted to Lakey platonically and that with herself it was more a physical thing? Lakey was awfully intelligent and knew a lot but she was cold, most people thought. Maybe Dick only admired her beauty as an artist and liked Dottie better the other way. The idea was not very convincing, in spite of what he had said about her body surprising her and all that. Kay said that sophisticated men cared more about the woman's pleasure than they did about their own, but Dick (Dottie coughed gently) had not seemed to be carried away by passion, even when he was exciting her terribly. A wanness crept over her as she thought of Kay. Kay would tell her bluntly that she did not have Lakey's "candle power," and that Dick obviously was using her as a substitute for Lakey, because Lakey was too much of a challenge, *too* beautiful and rich and fascinating for him to cope with in this bleak furnished room. "Dick wouldn't want a girl who would involve his feelings"—she could hear Kay saying it in her loud, opinionated, Western voice—"as Lakey would be bound to do, Renfrew. You're just an outlet for him, a one-night safety valve." The assured words crushed Dottie like a steam-roller, for she felt they were true. Kay would probably say also that Dottie had wanted to be "relieved" of her virginity and was using Dick simply as an instrument.

Was that true too—awful thought? Was that how Dick had seen her? Kay meant well, explaining things so clearly, and the terrible part was, she was usually right. Or at least she always *sounded* right, being so absolutely disinterested and unconscious of hurting your feelings. The moment Dottie let herself listen to Kay, even in imagination, she lost her own authority and became the person Kay decreed her to be: a Boston old maid with a "silver-cord" tie to her mother. It was the same

with all the weaker members of the group. Kay used to take
their love affairs, as Lakey once said, away from them and returned them shrunk and labeled, like the laundry. That was
what had happened to Polly Andrews' engagement. The boy
she was supposed to marry had insanity in his family, and Kay
had shown Polly so many charts about heredity that Polly had
broken off with him and collapsed and had to go to the infirmary. And of course Kay was right; anybody would agree that
Mr. Andrews was enough of a liability without marrying into
another family with melancholia in the background. Kay's advice was for Polly to live with him, since she loved him, and
marry someone else later, when she wanted to have children.
But Polly did not have the courage, although she wanted to
terribly. The whole group, except Lakey, had thought what
Kay did, at least about not marrying, but none of them had
had the heart to say it, straight out, to Polly. That was usually
the case: Kay came right out and said to the person what the
others whispered among themselves.

Dottie sighed. She wished that Kay would not have to find
out about her and Dick. But it was probably pretty inevitable,
Dick being Harald's friend. Not that Dick would tell, being a
gentleman and considerate; more likely, Dottie would tell
herself, for Kay was very good at getting things out of you. In
the end, you told Kay, wanting to hear her opinion more than
you did *not* want to hear it. You were afraid of being afraid of
the truth. Besides, Dottie saw, she could not really tell Mother
or not for a long time, for Mother, being a different generation, would never see it as Dottie did, no matter how hard she
tried, and the difference would just make her worried and unhappy. She would want to meet Dick, and then Daddy would
meet him too and start wondering about marriage, which was
utterly out of the question. Dottie sighed again. She knew she
would have to tell someone—not the most intimate details, of
course, but just the amazing fact that she had lost her virginity
—and that someone was bound to be Kay.

Then Kay would discuss her with Dick. This was the thing
Dottie shrank from most; she could not bear the idea of Kay
dissecting and analyzing her and explaining her medical history
and Mother's clubs and Daddy's business connections and
their exact social position in Boston, which Kay greatly

overestimated—they were not "Brahmins," horrid word, at all. A gleam of amusement appeared in Dottie's eye; Kay was such an innocent, for all her know-it-all airs about clubs and society. Someone ought to tell her that only tiresome people or, to be frank, outsiders were concerned about such things nowadays. Poor honest Kay: five times, Dottie recalled drowsily, before she was penetrated and so much blood and pain. Didn't Lakey say she had a hide like a buffalo? Sex, Dottie opined, was just a matter of following the man, as in dancing—Kay was a frightful dancer and always tried to lead. Mother was quite right, she said to herself comfily, as she drifted off to sleep: it was a *great* mistake to let girls dance together as they did in so many of the boarding schools of the second rank.

"Get yourself a pessary." Dick's muttered *envoi*, as he propelled her firmly to the door the next morning, fell on Dottie's ears with the effect of a stunning blow. Bewildered, she understood him to be saying "Get yourself a peccary," and a vision of a coarse piglike mammal they had studied in Zoology passed across her dazed consciousness, like a slide on a screen, followed by awful memories of Krafft-Ebing and the girl who had kept a goat at Vassar. Was this some variant she ought to know about, probably, of the old-maid joke? Tears dampened her eyes, though she tried to wink them back. Evidently, Dick hated her for what had taken place between them in the night; some men were like that, Kay said, after they had yielded to their passions: "an expense of spirit in a waste of shame." They had had the most dismal breakfast, which he had fixed, not letting her help him, on a grill in the clothes closet—scrambled eggs and coffee and the remains of a coffee ring from the bakery; no fruit or fruit juice. While they ate, he had hardly spoken; he had passed her the first section of the paper and then sat there, with his coffee, reading the sports news and the classified ads. When she had tried to give him the news section, he had impatiently pushed it back to her. Yet up to this very moment she had been telling herself that he might have just got up "on the wrong side of the bed," as Mother said; Daddy was cross too, sometimes, in the morning. Now she saw, though, that there was no use pretending any more; she had lost him. In his dressing gown, with his hair disordered and his cruel biting smile and bitter taunts, he reminded her of someone. Hamlet—of course—putting Ophelia away from him. "Get thee to a nunnery." "I loved you not." But she could not say, like Ophelia, "I was the more deceived" (which was the most pathetic moment in the whole play, the class had decided), because Dick had not deceived her; it was she who had been fooling herself. She stared at him, swallowing hard; a tear slid out of one eye. "A female contraceptive, a plug," Dick threw out impatiently. "You get it from a lady doctor. Ask your friend Kay."

Understanding dawned; her heart did a handspring. In a person like Dick, her feminine instinct caroled, this was surely the language of love. But it was a mistake to show a man that you had been unsure of him even for a second. "Yes, Dick," she whispered, her hand twisting the doorknob, while she let her eyes tell him softly what a deep, reverent moment this was, a sort of pledge between them. Luckily, he could never imagine the thing she had been thinking about the peccary! The happiness in her face caused him to raise an eyebrow and frown. "I don't love you, you know, Boston," he said warningly. "Yes, Dick," she replied. "And you must promise me you won't fall in love with me." "Yes, Dick," she repeated, more faintly. "My wife says I'm a bastard, but she still likes me in the hay. You'll have to accept that. If you want that, you can have it." "I want it, Dick," said Dottie in a feeble but staunch voice. Dick shrugged. "I don't believe you, Boston. But we can give it a try." A meditative smile appeared on his lips. "Most women don't take me seriously when I state my terms. Then they get hurt. In the back of their heads, they have a plan to make me fall in love with them. I don't fall in love." Dottie's warm eyes were teasing. "What about Betty?" He cocked his head at the photograph. "You think I love her?" Dottie nodded. He looked very serious. "I'll tell you," he said. "I like Betty better than I've liked any woman. I've still got hot pants for her, if you want to call that love." Dottie lowered her eyes and shook her head. "But I won't change my life for her, and so Betty lit out. I don't blame her; I'd have done the same if I were made like Betty. Betty is all woman. She likes money, change, excitement, things, clothes, possessions." He rubbed his strong jaw line with a thumb, as though he were studying a puzzle. "I hate possessions. It's a funny thing, because you'd think I hated them because they meant stability, wouldn't you?" Dottie nodded. "But I *like* stability; that's just the rub!" He had become quite tense and excited; his hands flexed nervously as he spoke. To Dottie's eyes, he suddenly appeared boyish, like the worried young lifeguards in their drifting boats at Cape Ann who sometimes dropped in at the cottage to discuss their futures with Mother. But of course that was what he must have been, once, growing up in Marblehead in the middle of the summer people; he was built like a swimmer, and she could picture him, brooding, in the lifesaving boat in one of those red jackets they wore—Mother said those boys were often marked for life by the experience of being betwixt and between, *with* the summer people but not *of* them.

"I like a man's life," he said. "A bar. The outdoors. Fishing and hunting. I like men's talk, that's never driving to get anywhere but just circles and circles. That's why I drink. Paris suited me—the crowd of painters and newspapermen and photographers. I'm a natural exile; if I have a few dollars or francs, I'm satisfied. I'll never pass third base as a painter, but I can draw and do nice clean work—an honest job. But I hate change, Boston, and I don't change myself. That's where I come a cropper with women. Women expect an affair to get better and better, and if it doesn't, they think it's getting worse. They think if I sleep with them longer I'm going to get fonder of them, and if I don't get fonder that I'm tiring of them. But for me it's all the same. If I like it the first time, I know I'm going to keep on liking it. I liked you last night and I'll keep on liking you as long as you want to come here. But don't harbor the idea that I'm going to like you more." A truculent, threatening note had come into his voice with the last words; he stood, staring down at her harshly and teetering a little on his slippered feet. Dottie fingered the frayed tassel of his dressing-gown sash. "All right, Dick," she whispered.

"When you get yourself fixed up, you can bring your things here and I'll keep them for you. Just give me a call after you've been to the doctor." A breath of last night's liquor wafted into her face; she fell back a step and averted her head. She had been hoping to know Dick better, but now, all at once, his strange philosophy of life gave her a sinking feeling. How would she fit him in this summer, for instance? He did not seem to realize that she would have to go up to Gloucester, the way she always did. If they were engaged, he could come up to visit, but of course they weren't and never could be; that was what he was telling her. To her horror, now that he had said he wanted her on *his* terms, Dottie found herself having second thoughts: what if she had lost her virginity with a man who scared her and who sounded, from his own description, like a pretty bad hat? For a moment, Dottie felt cornered, but her training had instilled the principle that it was a mark of low breeding to consider that you might have been wrong in a person. "I can't take you out," he said more gently, as if he read her thoughts. "I can only ask you to come here whenever you're in town. The welcome mat will be out. I've nothing but my bed to offer you. I don't go to theatres or night clubs and very seldom to restaurants." Dottie opened her mouth, but Dick shook his head. "I don't like ladies who want to pay my check. What I make with my posters and commissions takes care of my simple wants: my carfare, my bar bill, and a few frugal canned goods." Dottie's clasped hands made a gesture of pity and remorse; she had been forgetting he was poor, which was why, of course, he was so short and gruff about seeing her—it was his pride that made him talk that way. "Don't worry," he reassured her. "There's an aunt up in Marblehead who comes through with a check now and then. Some day, if I live long enough, I'll be her heir. But I hate possessions, Boston—forgive me if I think of you generically. I hate the itch to acquire. I don't care for this kinetic society." Dottie felt the time had come to interpose a gentle remonstrance; she thought Dick's aunt would not altogether approve of his point of view. "But Dick," she said quietly, "there are false possessions and true possessions. If everybody thought like you, the human race would never have got anywhere. We'd still be living in caves. Why, the wheel wouldn't even have been invented! People need an incentive, maybe not a money incentive . . ." Dick laughed. "You must be the fiftieth woman who has said that to me. It's a credit to universal education that whenever a girl meets Dick Brown she begins to talk about the wheel and the lever. I've even had a French prostitute tell me about the fulcrum." "Good-bye, Dick," Dottie said quickly. "I mustn't keep you from your work." "Aren't you going to take the phone number?" he demanded, shaking his head in mock reproach. She handed him her little blue leather address book, and he wrote down his name and his landlady's telephone number in heavy drawing pencil with a flourish; he had very striking handwriting. "Good-bye, Boston." He took her long chin between his thumb and forefinger and waggled it back and forth, absently. "Remember: no monkey business; no falling in love. Honor bright."

Notwithstanding this agreement, Dottie's heart was humming happily as she sat, three days later, beside Kay Petersen, in the woman doctor's office suite. Actions spoke louder than words, and whatever Dick might say, the fact remained that he had sent her here, to be wedded, as it were, by proxy, with the "ring" or diaphragm pessary that the woman doctor dispensed. With her hair freshly waved and her complexion glowing from a facial, she wore a look of quiet assurance, the look of a contented matron, almost like Mother and her friends. Knowledge was responsible for her composure. Kay would hardly believe it, but Dottie, all by herself, had visited a birth-control bureau and received a doctor's name and a sheaf of pamphlets that described a myriad of devices—tampons, sponges, collar-button, wishbone, and butterfly pessaries, thimbles, silk rings, and coils—and the virtues and drawbacks of each. The new device recommended to Dottie by the bureau had the backing of the whole U.S. medical profession; it had been found by Margaret Sanger in Holland and was now for the first time being imported in quantity into the U.S.A., where our own manufacturers could copy it. It combined the maximum of protection with the minimum of inconvenience and could be used by any woman of average or better intelligence, following the instructions of a qualified physician.

This article, a rubber cap mounted on a coiled spring, came in a range of sizes and would be tried out in Dottie's vagina, for fit, wearing comfort, and so on, in the same way that various lenses were tried out for the eyes. The woman doctor would insert it, and having made sure of the proper size, she would teach Dottie how to put it in, how to smear it with contraceptive jelly and put a dab in the middle, how to crouch in a squatting position, fold the pessary between thumb and forefinger of the right hand, while parting the *labia majora* with the left hand, and edge the pessary in, so that it would snap into place, shielding the cervix, and finally how to follow it with the right middle finger, locate the cervix or soft neck of the uterus and make certain it was covered by the rubber. When this process had been rehearsed several times, to the watching doctor's satisfaction, Dottie would be taught how and when to douche, how much water to use, the proper height for the douche bag, and how to hold the labia firmly around the lubricated nozzle in order to get the best results. As she was leaving the office, the nurse would present her with a Manila envelope containing a tube of vaginal jelly and a small flat box with Dottie's personalized contraceptive in it. The nurse would instruct her how to care for the pessary: to wash it after each use, dry it carefully, and dust it with talcum before returning it to its box.

Kay and Harald had just about fainted when they heard what Dottie had been up to, behind their back. She came to see them in their apartment, bringing a Georgian silver creamer for a wedding present, just the sort of thing an old aunt would have inflicted on you, and a bunch of white peonies; Kay could not have been more disappointed when she thought that for the same money they could have had something plain and modern from Jensen's Danish shop. Then, when Harald went to the kitchen to start their supper (minced sea clams, the new canned kind, on toast), Dottie had quietly told Kay, who wanted to know what she had been doing, that she had taken Dick Brown for her lover. Coming from Dottie, that imperial phrase was simply perfect; Kay immediately saved it to tell Harald. It had happened only the night before, it seemed, in that studio room of Dick's, and already, today, Dottie had scurried around to the birth-control bureau and got all this literature, which she had with her in her pocketbook. Kay did not know what to say, but her face must have shown how ap-palled she was. She thought Dottie must be insane. Under-neath that virile mask, which was what Harald called it, Dick Brown was a very warped personality, a dipsomaniac and a vio-lent misogynist, with a terrible inferiority complex because of what had happened with his socialite wife. *His* motives were plain enough; he was using Dottie to pay back society for the wound it had inflicted on his ego—Kay could hardly wait till she could hear how Harald would analyze it, when they were alone. But in spite of her impatience, she asked Dottie to stay for supper with them, greatly to Harald's surprise, when he came in with the tray of drinks: after Harald had gone to the theatre, Dottie would be bound to tell more. "I *had* to ask her," she apologized to Harald, in a quick exchange in the kitchen. She put her lips to his ear. "An awful thing has happened, and we're responsible! Dick Brown has seduced her."

Yet every time she looked at Dottie, sitting in their living room, so serene and conventional in her pearls and dressmaker suit, with white touches, and smart navy-blue sailor, sipping her Clover Club cocktail out of the Russel Wright cup and wiping a mustache of egg white from her long upper lip with a cocktail napkin, she just could not picture her in bed with a man. Afterward, Harald said that she seemed quite an appetizing piece, in her chipmunk style, with her brown friendly eyes gleaming with quiet fun and her lashes aflutter whenever she looked at him. What he did not see was that a lot of it was clothes, for, thanks to a clever mother, Dottie dressed to perfection: she was the only one of the Boston contingent at Vassar who knew better than to wear tweeds and plaid mufflers, which made the poor things look like gaunt, elderly governesses out for a Sunday hike. But, according to Harald, her deep-bosomed figure, as revealed by her bias-cut blouses, gave promise of sensuality. Probably it meant something, Kay could not deny it, that it was Dick himself, on his own initiative, it seemed, who had told her to go and get fitted with a pessary!

"He said to consult *me*?" Kay repeated, wondering and somewhat flattered, after Harald had gone and they were washing the dishes. She had always thought Dick did not like her. The fact was that, though she knew about pessaries, she herself did not possess one. She had always used suppositories with Harald, and it embarrassed her a little now to have to confess this to Dottie, who seemed to have forged ahead of her so surprisingly and after only one night. . . . She envied Dottie's enterprise in going to the birth-control bureau; until she was married, she herself would never have had the nerve. Dottie wanted to know whether Kay thought it was a good sign, Dick's saying that to her, and Kay had to admit that on the surface it was; it could only mean that Dick was expecting to sleep with her regularly, if you thought *that* was good. Examining her own emotions, Kay found she was piqued; it nettled her to guess that Dottie might have been better than *she* was in bed. Still, truth compelled her to tell Dottie that if it were only a halfhearted affair, Dick would just use condoms (the way Harald had at first) or practice *coitus interruptus.* "He must like you, Renfrew," she declared, shaking out the dish mop. "Or like you enough, anyway."

That was Harald's verdict too. Riding on the top of a Fifth Avenue bus, on the way to the doctor's office, Kay repeated to Dottie what Harald had said of the etiquette of contraception, which, as he explained it, was like any other etiquette—the code of manners rising out of social realities. You had to look at it in terms of economics. No man of honor (which Dick, in Harald's opinion, was) would expect a girl to put up the doctor's fee, plus the price of the pessary and the jelly and the douche bag unless he planned to sleep with her long enough for her to recover her investment. Of that, Dottie could rest assured. A man out for a casual affair found it simpler to buy Trojans by the dozen, even though it decreased his own pleasure; that way, he was not tied to the girl. The lower classes, for instance, almost never transferred the burden of contraception to the woman; this was a discovery of the middle class. A workingman was either indifferent to the danger of conception or he mistrusted the girl too much to leave the matter in her hands.

This mistrust, Harald said, which was deep in the male nature, made even middle-class and professional men wary of sending a girl for a pessary; too many shotgun weddings had resulted from a man's relying on a woman's assurance that the contraceptive was in. Then there was the problem of the apparatus. The unmarried girl who lived with her family required a place to keep her pessary and her douche bag where her mother was not likely to find them while doing out the bureau drawers. This meant that the man, unless *he* was married, had to keep them for her, in his bureau drawer or his bathroom. The custodianship of these articles (Harald was so entertaining in his slow-spoken, careful, dry way) assumed the character of a sacred trust. If their guardian was a man of any delicacy, they precluded the visits of other women to the apartment, who might open drawers or rummage in the medicine cabinet or even feel themselves entitled to use the douche bag hallowed to "Her."

With a married woman, if the affair were serious, the situation was the same: she bought a second pessary and a douche bag, which she kept in her lover's apartment, where they exercised a restraining influence if he felt tempted to betray her. A man entrusted with this important equipment was bonded, so to speak, Harald said, like a bank employee; when he did stray with another woman, he was likely to do it in her place or in a hotel room or even a taxi—some spot not consecrated by the sacral reminders. In the same way, a married woman pledged her devotion by committing her second pessary to her lover's care; only a married woman of very coarse fiber would use the same pessary for both husband and lover. So long as the lover had charge of the pessary, like a medieval knight with the key to his lady's chastity belt, he could feel that she was true to him. Though this could be a mistake. One adventurous wife Harald described was said to have pessaries all over town, like a sailor with a wife in every port, while her husband, a busy stage director, assured himself of her good behavior by a daily inspection of the little box in her medicine cabinet, where the conjugal pessary lay in its dusting of talcum powder.

"Harald has made quite a study of it, hasn't he?" commented Dottie with a demure twinkle. "I'm spoiling it," replied Kay seriously. "The way Harald tells it, you can see the whole thing in terms of property values. The fetishism of property. I told him he ought to write it up for *Esquire*; they publish some quite good things. Don't you think he should?" Dottie did not know what to answer; Harald's approach, she felt, was rather "unpleasant," so cold and cerebral, though perhaps he knew what he was talking about. It was certainly a different angle from what you got in the birth-control pamphlets.

Furthermore, Kay quoted, the disposal of the pessary and the douche bag presented a problem when a love affair was breaking up. What was the man to do with these "hygienic relics" after he or the woman tired? They could not be returned through the mail, like love letters or an engagement ring, though crude lads, Harald said, had been known to do this; on the other hand, they could not be put in the trash basket for the janitor or the landlady to find; they would not burn in the fireplace without giving off an awful smell, and to keep them for another woman, given our bourgeois prejudices, was unthinkable. A man could carry them, stuffed into a paper bag, to one of the city's wastebaskets late at night or dump them into the river, but friends of Harald's who had done this had actually been halted by the police. Probably because they acted so furtive. Trying to get rid of a woman's pessary and fountain syringe, the corpus delicti of a love affair, was exactly, as Harald put it, like trying to get rid of a body. "*I* said, you could do the way murderers do in detective stories: check them in the Grand Central parcel room and then throw away the check." Kay gave her rollicking laugh, but Dottie shivered. She saw that it would not be funny if the problem came up for her and Dick; every time she thought of the future, of the terrible complications a secret affair got you into, she almost wanted to give up and go home. And all Kay's conversation, though doubtless well meant, seemed calculated to dismay her with its offhand boldness and cynicism.

The upshot, continued Kay, was that no bachelor in his right mind would send a girl to the doctor to be fitted if he did not feel pretty serious about her. The difficulties only arose, of course, with respectable married women or nice girls who lived with their parents or with other girls. There were women of the looser sort, divorcées and unattached secretaries and office workers living in their own apartments, who equipped themselves independently and kept their douche bags hanging on the back of their bathroom door for anybody to see who wandered in to pee during a cocktail party. One friend of Harald's, a veteran stage manager, always made it a point to look over a girl's bathroom before starting anything; if the bag was on the door, it was nine to one he would make her on the first try.

They descended from the bus on lower Fifth Avenue; Dottie's complexion had come out in those blotches like hives or shingles—a sure sign that she was nervous. Kay was sympathetic. This was a big step for Dottie; she had been trying to give Dottie an inkling of just how big a step it was, much more than losing your virginity. For a married woman, naturally, it was different; Harald had agreed immediately that it would be a good idea for her to make an appointment and go along with Dottie to be fitted too. She and Harald both loathed children and had no intention of having any; Kay had seen in her own family how offspring could take the joy out of marriage. Her tribe of brothers and sisters had kept her Dads' nose to the grindstone; if he had not had so many children, he might have been a famous specialist, instead of a hard-worked G.P. with only a wing in the hospital to commemorate the work he had done in orthopedics and on serums for meningitis. Poor Dads had quite a kick out of sending her east to Vassar; she was the oldest and the brightest, and she had the feeling that he wanted her to have the life he might have had himself, out in the big world, where he would have got the homage he deserved. He still had invitations to come and do research in the big eastern laboratories, but now he was too old to learn, he said; the cerebral arteries were hardening. He had just crashed through nobly with a check; she and Harald had been moved almost to tears by the size of it—far more than he and Mums would have spent on trains and hotels if they had come on for the wedding. It was a declaration of faith, said Harald. And she and Harald did not intend to betray that faith by breeding children, when Harald had his name to make in the theatre. The theatre— strange coincidence!—was one of Dads' big passions; he and Mums went to see all the touring companies in Salt Lake City and had tickets every night, nearly, when they came to New York for medical meetings. Not leg shows, either; Dads' favorite playwright, after Shakespeare, was Bernard Shaw. Harald thought it would be a nice idea for Kay to keep the programs of the worthwhile plays he and she saw and send them on to Dads; that way, he would feel in touch.

Dads, like all modern doctors, believed in birth control and was for sterilizing criminals and the unfit. He would certainly approve of what Kay was doing. What he would think about Dottie was another question. Kay herself had been horrified to hear that Dottie had made the appointment in her real name: "Dorothy Renfrew," not even "Mrs." As though she were living in Russia or Sweden, instead of the old U.S.A. A lot of people who would not be shocked at her for sleeping with Dick (that could happen to anybody) would look at her askance if they could see what she was up to this minute. The things you did in private were your own business, but this was practically public! Kay ran an apprehensive eye up and down Fifth Avenue; you could never tell who might be watching them from a passing bus or a taxi. She had begun to be nervous herself, on Dottie's behalf, and to be crosser and crosser with Dick. Harald would never have exposed *her* to an ordeal like this. After the first few times, he had gone to the drugstore himself and bought her suppositories and a bulb type of douche and Zonite, so that she would not have to face the druggist herself. Kay gripped Dottie's arm, to steady her as they crossed the street with the traffic light; she rued the day she had invited Dick to her wedding, knowing what he was. Why, the office might be raided and the doctor's records impounded and published in the papers, which would *kill* Dottie's family, who would probably turn around and blame Kay, as the pathfinder of the college group. She felt she was making quite a sacrifice in coming with Dottie today, to lend moral support, though Dottie insisted that birth control was perfectly legal and aboveboard, thanks to a court decision that allowed doctors to prescribe contraceptives for the prevention or cure of disease. As they rang the doctor's bell, Kay had to laugh, suddenly, at Dottie's expression: you could almost see Mrs. Pankhurst in her resolute eye.

And indeed Dottie's zealotry was reflected in the furnishings of the woman doctor's office, which had a sort of militant plainness, like the headquarters of a missionary sect. There was a single upholstered couch, with two antimacassars aligned on its back; against the tan walls was a series of straight chairs. The magazine rack held copies of *Hygeia*, *Parents*, *Consumers' Research Bulletin*, a current issue of the *Nation*, and a back number of *Harper's*. On the walls were etchings showing overcrowded slums teeming with rickety children and a lithograph of an early hospital ward in which untended young women, with babies at their side, were dying—of puerperal fever, Dottie whispered. There was a pious hush in the atmosphere which was emphasized by the absence of any smoking equipment and by the solemn whirring of a fan. Kay and Dottie, who had automatically taken cigarettes out of their cases, replaced them after a survey of the room. There were two other patients waiting, reading *Hygeia* and *Consumers' Research Bulletin*. One, a sallow thin woman of about thirty, with a pair of cotton gloves on her lap, wore no wedding ring, a fact which Dottie silently called to Kay's attention. The second patient, in rimless glasses and worn Oxfords, was almost middle-aged. The sight of these two women, far from well-to-do, and of the prints on the walls had a sobering effect on the girls. Kay, made to reflect on "how much good the doctor was doing," a thing often said of her father by the elite of Salt Lake City, felt ashamed of the brittle, smart way she had talked about birth control on the bus, though she had only been quoting Harald. "Extend your antennae, girls," was a favorite apothegm of the teacher she had respected most, and Kay, reminded of her father's nonpaying patients, saw, to her discomfiture, that she and Dottie were just the frills on the doctor's practice.

What she could not remember, though Harald kept drilling it into her, was that she and her friends did not count any more, except as individuals, in the wider picture of American society, exemplified by these two women, right here in this office. Last night, after the theatre, when the three of them had gone to have a beer in a speak-easy, Harald had been explaining just that to Dottie. The transfer of financial power, he showed, from Threadneedle Street to Wall Street was an event in world history comparable to the defeat of the Spanish Armada, which had ushered in the era of capitalism. When Roosevelt, just now, had gone off the gold standard, it was a declaration of independence from Europe and an announcement of a new, flexible epoch. The N.R.A. and the eagle were symbols of the arrival of a new class to power. Their class, the upper middle, he told the two girls, was finished politically and economically; its best elements would merge with the rising class of workers and farmers and technicians, of which he, as a stage technician, was one. Take the theatre as an example. In the days of Belasco, the director used to be king; today, the director was dependent, first of all on his backers, who might be a combine, and second, and even more important, on his master electrician, who could make or break a play by the way he handled the lighting—behind every name director, like Jed Harris, for instance, there was a genius electrician, just as there was a genius camera-man behind every name movie director. The same in radio; it was the engineers, the men in the control room, who really counted. A doctor today was dependent on his technicians, on the men in the lab and the X-ray room. "They're the boys who can make or break a diagnosis."

Last night, it had thrilled Kay to imagine the future he predicted, of mass abundance through the machine. She had enjoyed watching him impress Dottie, who had not suspected he was such a social thinker since he did not put that side of himself in his letters. "As individuals," he said, "you girls have something to pass on to individuals in the rising class, just as old Europe still has something to pass on to America." It relieved her to hear him say this, with his arm clasping her waist and Dottie looking on, wide-eyed, for Kay did not want to be left behind by history and at the same time she was not really strong for the idea of equality; she liked, she had to confess, to be superior. Harald, when he was in a good mood, as he was last night, seemed to think this would still be possible, though with a difference, in the new age.

Last night, he had explained technocracy to Dottie, to show her there was nothing to fear from the future, if it was managed with scientific intelligence. In an economy of plenty and leisure, which the machine had already made feasible, everybody would only have to work a few hours a day. It was through such an economy that his class, the class of artists and technicians, would come naturally to the top; the homage people paid to money today would be paid in the future to the engineers and contrivers of leisure-time activities. More leisure meant more time for art and culture. Dottie wanted to know what would happen to the capitalists (her father was in the import business), and Kay looked inquiringly at Harald. "Capital will blend into government," said Harald. "After a brief struggle. That's what we're witnessing now. The administrator, who's just a big-scale technician, will replace the big capitalist in industry. Individual ownership is becoming obsolete; the administrators are running the show." "Take Robert Moses," put in Kay. "He's transforming the whole face of New York with his wonderful new parkways and playgrounds." And she urged Dottie to go to Jones Beach, which was an inspiring example, she really felt this herself, of planning on a large scale for leisure. "Everybody from Oyster Bay," she added, "drives over there now to swim. It's quite the thing to do, instead of swimming at a club." Private enterprise, suggested Harald, still had a part to play, if it had breadth of vision. Radio City, where he had worked for a while as a stage manager's assistant, was an

example of civic planning, undertaken by enlightened capitalists, the Rockefellers. Kay brought in the Modern Museum,
which had Rockefeller backing too. New York, she honestly
thought, was experiencing a new Renaissance, with the new
Medicis competing with public ownership to create a modern
Florence. You could see it even in Macy's, agreed Harald,
where enlightened merchant-Jews, the Strauses, were training
a corps of upper-middle-class technicians, like Kay, to make the
store into something more than a business, something closer
to a civic center or permanent fairgrounds, with educational
exhibits, like the old Crystal Palace. Then Kay talked about the
smart new renovated tenements in the Fifties and Eighties,
along the East River, black with white trim and white Venetian
blinds; they were still another example of intelligent planning
by capital! Vincent Astor had done them. Of course, the rents
were rather high, but look what you got: views of the river just
as good as from Sutton Place mansions, sometimes a garden,
the Venetian blinds, like the old jalousies but modernized, and
completely up-to-date kitchens. When you thought that they
had just been eyesores, probably full of vermin and unsanitary
hall toilets, till the Astor interests fixed them up! And other
landlords were following their example, turning old blocks of
barracky tenements into compact apartment buildings four
and five stories high, with central courts planted with grass and
shrubs and two- and three-room apartments for young people
—some with fireplaces and built-in bookcases and all with
brand-new plumbing and stove and refrigerator. A lot of waste
space was being eliminated in these buildings—no more foyers
or dining rooms, which were obsolete conventions. Harald,
Kay explained, was a perfect fanatic about waste space. A
house, he thought, should be a machine for living. When they
found a permanent apartment, they were going to have everything built in: bookcases, bureaus, chests. The beds were going
to be mattresses and springs, supported by four low pegs, and
they were thinking about having a table to eat on that would
fold up into the wall like a Murphy bed—a single leaf of wood
shaped like an ironing board but broader.

Kay had seldom been happier than she was just then, outlining these plans to Dottie, while Harald listened with one
quizzically raised eyebrow, correcting her whenever she made

a mistake. It was Dottie who slightly spoiled things by asking, in those gently rumbling tones, what happened to the poor people who had lived in those tenements before. Where did they go? This was a question Kay had never thought to ask herself, and Harald did not know the answer, which at once put him in a darker mood. "*Cui bono?*" he said. "'Who profits?' Eh?" And he signaled the waiter for another round of beer. This alarmed Kay, who knew he had an understudy rehearsal at ten in the morning. "Your question is at once simple and profound," he went on, to Dottie. "'What happens to the poor?'" He stared gloomily ahead of him, as if into empty space. "Do they go to Mr. Moses' big clean white antiseptic beach that Kay finds so inspiring and 'civic-minded'? No; they don't, my girls; they lack the price of admission and the car to transport them. Instead, it becomes the perquisite of the Oyster Bay set—damnable profiteers and grabbers, with their pretty powdered noses sniffing at the public trough." Kay saw that he was sinking into a Slough of Despond (they had coined this name for his sudden, Scandinavian fits of bitter depression), but she managed to steer the conversation into safer channels by getting him to talk to Dottie about recipes and cooking, one of his favorite themes, so that they were home and in bed by one-thirty. Harald was very paradoxical; he would whirl around and attack the very things he believed in most. As she sat in the doctor's waiting room and covertly examined the other patients, she could easily imagine him saying that she and Dottie were "profiteering" on the birth-control crusade, whose real aim was to limit the families of the poor. Mentally, she began to defend herself. Birth control, she argued, was for those who knew how to use it and value it—the educated classes. Just like those renovated tenements; if poor people were allowed to move into them, they would wreck them right away, through lack of education.

Dottie's thoughts too were running on the night before. She was fascinated by the way Kay and Harald had their whole life planned. When Kay started at Macy's in September, Harald would get their breakfast every morning and then sweep and clean and do the marketing, so that everything would be ready for Kay to get the dinner when she came home from work;

over the weekend, they would map out the meals for the week. Right now, Harald was teaching her to cook. His specialties were Italian spaghetti, which any beginner could learn, and those minced sea clams—terribly good—they had the other night, and meat balls cooked in salt in a hot skillet (no fat), and a quick-and-easy meat loaf his mother had taught him: one part beef, one part pork, one part veal; add sliced onions, pour over it a can of Campbell's tomato soup and bake in the oven. Then there was his chile con carne, made with canned kidney beans and tomato soup again and onions and half a pound of hamburger; you served it over rice, and it stretched for six people. That was his mother's too. Kay, not to be outdone —she said, laughing—had written *her* mother for some of the family recipes, the cheaper ones: veal kidneys done with cooking sherry and mushrooms, and a marvelous jellied salad called Green Goddess, made with lime gelatin, shrimps, mayonnaise, and alligator pear, which could be fixed the night before in ramekins and then unmolded on lettuce cups. Kay had found a new cookbook that had a whole section on casserole dishes and another on foreign recipes—so much more adventurous than Fannie Farmer and that old Boston Cooking School. On Sundays, they planned to entertain, either at a late breakfast of chipped beef or corned-beef hash or at a casserole supper. The trouble with American cooking, Harald said, was the dearth of imagination in it and the terrible fear of innards and garlic. He put garlic in everything and was accounted quite a cook. What made a dish, Kay said, was the seasonings. "Listen to how Harald fixes chipped beef. He puts in mustard and Worcestershire sauce and grated cheese—is that right?—and green pepper and an egg; you'd never think it bore any relation to that old milky chipped beef we got at college." Her happy laugh rang out in the speak-easy. If Dottie wanted to learn, she should study the recipes in the *Tribune*. "I *love* the *Tribune*," she said. "Harald converted me from the *Times*." "The *Tribune*'s typography has it all over the *Times*'s," observed Harald.

"How lucky you are, Kay," Dottie said warmly, "to have found a husband who's interested in cooking and who's not afraid of experiment. Most men, you know, have awfully set tastes. Like Daddy, who won't hear of 'made' dishes, except the good old beans on Saturday." There was a twinkle in her eye, but she really did mean it that Kay was awfully lucky. Kay leaned forward. "You ought to get your cook to try the new way of fixing canned beans. You just add catsup and mustard and Worcestershire sauce and sprinkle them with plenty of brown sugar, cover them with bacon, and put them in the oven in a Pyrex dish." "It sounds terribly good," said Dottie, "but Daddy would die." Harald nodded. He began to talk, very learnedly, about the prejudice that existed in conservative circles against canned goods; it went back, he said, to an old fear of poisoning that derived from home canning, where spoilage was common. Modern machinery and factory processes, of course, had eliminated all danger of bacteria, and yet the prejudice lingered, which was a pity since many canned products, like vegetables picked at their peak and some of the Campbell soups, were better than anything the home cook could achieve. "Have you tasted the new Corn Niblets?" asked Kay. Dottie shook her head. "You ought to tell your mother about them. It's the whole-kernel corn. Delicious. Almost like corn on the cob. Harald discovered them." She considered. "Does your mother know about iceberg lettuce? It's a new variety, very crisp, with wonderful keeping powers. After you've tried it, you'll never want to see the old Boston lettuce again. Simpson lettuce, they call it." Dottie sighed. Did Kay realize, she wondered, that she had just passed the death sentence on Boston lettuce, Boston baked beans, and the Boston School cookbook?

Nevertheless, Dottie did intend, when she got up to the cottage, to pass some of Kay's tips on to Mother. She had had Mother terribly on her conscience ever since she had got back to the Vassar Club that fatal morning (was it only two days ago?) and found a message that Gloucester had been calling the night before and again at 9:00 A.M. Telling her mother her first real lie—that she had spent the night with Polly in Polly's aunt's apartment—was one of the hardest things she had ever done. It still cut her heart to think that she could not tell Mother about her visit to the birth-control bureau and now to this doctor's office, all of which would have interested Mother so tremendously as a Vassar woman with Lucy Stoners and women's-rights fighters in her own college class. The cruel sense of withholding something had made Dottie more than usually alert to the small items of interest she could bring back to Gloucester in compensation—like Kay and Harald's menus and housekeeping arrangements, which would vastly amuse Mother. Perhaps she could even tell her that *Kay* had been to birth-control headquarters and been sent on here to get this new device?

"Miss Renfrew," called the nurse softly, and Dottie started and got up. Her eyes met Kay's in a last desperate look, like a boarding-school girl summoned to the headmistress' office, and she advanced slowly into the doctor's consulting room, her knees shaking and knocking so that they would hardly hold her. At the desk sat a white-coated, olive-skinned woman with a big bun of black hair. The doctor was very handsome, about forty years old; her large black brilliant eyes rested on Dottie briefly like electric rays, while one broad hand with tapering fingers motioned Dottie to a chair. She began to take the medical history, just as if it were an ordinary consultation; her pencil matter-of-factly wrote down Dottie's answers about measles and whooping cough, eczema and asthma. Yet Dottie became aware of a mesmeric, warm charm that emanated from her and that seemed to tell Dottie not to be afraid. It occurred to Dottie, almost with surprise, that they were both women. The doctor's femininity was a reassuring part of her professional aspect, like her white coat; on her hand shone a broad gold wedding ring, which seemed to Dottie serene and ample, like the doctor herself.

"Have you ever had intercourse, Dorothy?" The question appeared to flow so naturally from the sequence of operations and previous diseases that Dottie's answer was given before she had time to gulp. "Good!" exclaimed the doctor, and when Dottie glanced up, wonderingly, the doctor gave an encouraging smile. "That makes it easier for us to fit you," she said, commending, as though Dottie had been a good child. Her skill astonished Dottie, who sat with wondering eyes, anesthetized by the doctor's personality, while a series of questions, like a delicately maneuvering forceps, extracted information that ought to have hurt but didn't. This painless interrogation revealed no more curiosity about the why and the who of Dottie's defloration than if Dick had been a surgical instrument:

had Dottie been completely penetrated, had there been much bleeding, much pain? What method of contraception had been used, had the act been repeated? "Withdrawal," murmured the doctor, writing it down on a separate pad. "We like to know," she explained, with a quick, personal smile, "what methods our patients have used before coming to us. When was this intercourse had?" "Three nights ago," said Dottie, coloring and feeling that now, at last, they were going to touch the biographical. "And the date of your last period?" Dottie supplied it, and the doctor glanced at her desk calendar. "Very good," she said. "Go into the bathroom, empty your bladder, and take off your girdle and step-ins; you may leave your slip on, but unfasten your brassière, please."

Dottie did not mind the pelvic examination or the fitting. Her bad moment came when she was learning how to insert the pessary by herself. Though she was usually good with her hands and well co-ordinated, she felt suddenly unnerved by the scrutiny of the doctor and the nurse, so exploratory and impersonal, like the doctor's rubber glove. As she was trying to fold the pessary, the slippery thing, all covered with jelly, jumped out of her grasp and shot across the room and hit the sterilizer. Dottie could have died. But apparently this was nothing new to the doctor and the nurse. "Try again, Dorothy," said the doctor calmly, selecting another diaphragm of the correct size from the drawer. And, as though to provide a distraction, she went on to give a little lecture on the history of the pessary, while watching Dottie's struggles out of the corner of her eye: how a medicated plug had been known to the ancient Greeks and Jews and Egyptians, how Margaret Sanger had found the present diaphragm in Holland, how the long fight had been waged through the courts here. . . . Dottie had read all this, but she did not like to say so to this dark, stately woman, moving among her instruments like a priestess in the temple. As everybody knew from the newspapers, the doctor herself had been arrested only a few years before, in a raid on a birth-control clinic, and then been freed by the court. To hear her talk on the subject of her lifelong mission was an honor, like touching the mantle of a prophet, and Dottie felt awed.

"Private practice must be rather a letdown," she suggested,

sympathetically. To a dynamic person like the doctor, fitting girls like herself could not be much of a challenge. "There's still a great work to be done," sighed the doctor, removing the diaphragm with a short nod of approval. She motioned Dottie down from the table. "So many of our clinic patients won't use the pessary when we've fitted them or won't use it regularly." The nurse bobbed her white-capped head and made a clucking noise. "And those are the ones, aren't they, doctor, who need to limit their families most? With our private patients, Miss Renfrew, we can be surer that our instructions are being followed." She gave a little smirk. "I won't need you now, Miss Brimmer," said the doctor, washing her hands at the sink. The nurse went out, and Dottie started to follow her, feeling herself a rather foolish figure, with her stockings rolled down around her ankles and her brassière loose. "Just a minute, Dorothy," said the doctor, turning, and fixing her with her brilliant gaze. "Are there any questions?" Dottie hesitated; she wanted awfully, now that the ice was broken, to tell the doctor about Dick. But to Dottie's sympathetic eye, the doctor's lightly lined face looked tired. Moreover, she had other patients; there was still Kay waiting outside. And supposing the doctor, when she heard, should tell her to go back to the Vassar Club and pack and take the six o'clock train home and never see Dick again? Then the pessary would be wasted, and all would have been for nothing.

"Medical instruction," said the doctor kindly, with a thoughtful look at Dottie, "can often help the patient to the fullest sexual enjoyment. The young women who come to me, Dorothy, have the right to expect the deepest satisfaction from the sexual act." Dottie scratched her jaw; the skin on her upper chest mottled. What she especially wanted to ask was something a doctor might know, above all, a married doctor. She had of course not confided in Kay the thing that was still troubling her: what did it mean if a man made love to you and didn't kiss you once, not even at the most thrilling moment? This was something not mentioned in the sex books, so far as Dottie knew, and perhaps it was too ordinary an occurrence for scientists to catalogue or perhaps there was some natural explanation, as she had thought before, like hali or trench mouth. Or maybe he had taken a vow, like some people vowing never to shave or never to wash till a certain thing they wanted came about. But she could not get it out of her mind, and whenever she recalled it, not meaning to, she would flush all over, just as she was doing now. She was afraid, down in her heart, that Dick was probably what Daddy called a "wrong un." And here was her chance to find out. But she could not, in this gleaming surgery, choose the words to ask. How would you put it in technical language? "If the man fails to osculate?" Her dimple ruefully flashed; not even Kay could say such a thing. "Is there anything abnormal . . . ?" she began and then stared helplessly at the tall, impassible woman. "If prior to the sexual act . . ." "Yes?" encouraged the doctor. Dottie gave her throaty, scrupulous cough. "It's terribly simple," she apologized, "but I can't seem to say it." The doctor waited. "Perhaps I can help you, Dorothy. Any techniques," she began impressively, "that give both partners pleasure are perfectly allowable and natural. There are no practices, oral or manual, that are wrong in love-making, as long as both partners enjoy them." Goose flesh rose on Dottie; she knew, pretty well, what the doctor meant, and could not help wondering, with horror, if the doctor, as a married woman, practiced what she preached. Her whole nature recoiled. "Thank you, doctor," she said quietly, cutting the topic off.

In her gloved hand, when she was dressed and powdered, she took the Manila envelope the nurse in the anteroom handed her and paid out new bills from her billfold. She did not wait for Kay. Across the street was a drugstore, with hot-water bottles in the window. She went in and managed to choose a fountain syringe. Then she seated herself in the phone booth and rang Dick's number. After a long time, a voice answered. Dick was out. This possibility had never occurred to her. She had assumed without thinking that he would be there waiting for her, when she had carried out her mission. "Just give me a call." Now she walked slowly across Eighth Street and into Washington Square, where she sat down on a park bench, with her two parcels beside her. When she had sat there nearly an hour, watching the children play and listening to some young Jewish men argue, she went back to the drugstore and tried Dick's number again. He was still out. She returned to her park bench, but someone had taken her place. She

walked about a bit till she found another seat; this time, because the bench was crowded, she held the packages on her
lap. The syringe, in its box, was bulky and kept slipping off her
lap every time she moved or crossed her legs; then she would
have to bend down to pick it up. Her underwear felt sticky
from the lubricants the doctor had used, and this nasty soiled
sensation made her fear she had got the curse. Soon the children began leaving the park; she heard the church bells ringing
for Evensong. She would have liked to go in to pray, which she
often did at vesper time (and to take a hurried look, with no
one watching, at the back of her skirt), but she could not, because of the packages, which would not be decent in a church.
Nor could she face going back to the Vassar Club with them;
she was sharing a room with Helena Davison, who might ask
what she had been buying. It was getting late, long past six
o'clock, but the park was still light, and everyone, she thought,
now noticed her. The next time, she tried Dick from the phone
in the Brevoort Hotel lobby, after going first to the ladies'
room. She left a message: "Miss Renfrew is waiting in Washington Square, on a bench." She was afraid to wait in the hotel
lobby, where someone she knew might come in. Going back
to the square, she was sorry she had left the message, because,
after that, she did not dare annoy the landlady by calling back
again. It now seemed to her strange that Dick had not rung
her up at the Vassar Club, just to say hello, in the two and a
half days that had passed since she left him. She considered
calling there, to ask if there were any messages for her, but she
dreaded getting Helena. And anyway, she could not leave the
square, in case Dick should come. The park was getting dark,
and the benches were filling up with pairs of lovers. It was after
nine o'clock when she resolved to leave because men had
started to accost her and a policeman had stared at her curiously. She remembered Kay's remarks on the bus about the
"corpus delicti" of a love affair. How true!

It did not prove anything, she told herself, that Dick was not
at home. There could be a thousand reasons; perhaps he had
been called out of town. Yet it did prove something, and she
knew it. It was a sign. In the dark, she began quietly to cry and
decided to count to a hundred before going. She had reached
a hundred for the fifth time when she recognized that it was

no use; even if he got her message, he would never come to-night. There seemed to be only one thing left to do. Hoping that she was unobserved, she slipped the contraceptive equipment under the bench she was sitting on and began to walk as swiftly as she could, without attracting attention, to Fifth Avenue. A cruising taxi picked her up at the corner and drove her, quietly sobbing, to the Vassar Club. The next morning early, before the town was stirring, she took the train for Boston.

4

ONE afternoon in September, Harald lost his new job. When he told the director, softly, where to get off, the nance gave him notice. If Kay could only write, she could have sold the story of it to the *New Yorker*, she thought. She was just back from work that day and tying on her apron when she heard his step on the stairs and wondered—they did not usually break for dinner till six-thirty or seven. He had a pint of gin from the cordial shop with him, and there was a glitter in his hollow, dark eyes. The minute she saw him, she guessed what had happened. "I'm aware," he said to her stiffly, "of the bitter irony behind this. You seem to have picked a lemon." "Why do you say that?" protested Kay, starting to cry because that was not at all what she was thinking.

And yet it *was* ironical, you had to admit. October 1, their summer sublet was up, and they were due to move into an apartment of their own, in a new smart building made over from some old tenements, with a landscaped court and an inside doorman in a little booth, like a concierge. They had signed the lease and paid the first month's rent—$102.50, including gas and electricity. This was more than Harald had ever *dreamed* of paying, but Kay had argued that economists said you were supposed to count one-fourth of your income for rent; she made $25 a week at Macy's, and he would be making $75 when the show opened. This allowed them to pay $100 (or would have till this afternoon!), and they would really be paying less, when you subtracted the utilities. Manwise, Harald had pointed out that you weren't *obliged* to pay a quarter of your income—a mere factual observation, he insisted, when Kay wanted to quote it to their friends to show how witty he could be. She loved Harald's *risus sardonicus*, as Helena Davison's mother called it.

Yet now, strange to tell, as she followed him into the living room and watched him coolly fit a cigarette into his holder with that enigmatic half-smile he had, she felt her furies rising. She was certain, just looking at him, that he was going to want to renege on the lease because of losing his job, and the evil thought flashed through her mind that he had lost it as a *pre-text* for not moving into the apartment. "Slow there, Strong!" she warned herself (after three months, she still could not get used to "Petersen"). "Put on the brakes." Tonight, of all nights, Harald needed her sympathy, though his pride would not let him show it.

Poor Harald, he had been unemployed nearly all summer. The play he was with had folded when the hot weather came; the Saturday after their wedding, the closing notices went up. By that time, it was too late to get anything in one of the summer theatres, though in his place Kay thought she might have *tried*. Harald did not have her perseverance; that was a thing about him she had discovered. Getting married, instead of spurring him on, seemed, she sometimes feared, to have produced almost the contrary effect. But finally, out of the blue, he had been sent for about this new job, the best he had had yet, being in charge of the book of a satiric revue on the depression called "Hail Columbia" which was going to open in October; officially, he was only the stage manager, but the producer told him he could have a crack at directing the sketches, since the over-all director, an old Shubert whore, was only used to doing girl shows. The producer, it turned out, had had his eye on Harald for quite a while and was giving him this chance to prove himself.

"Isn't it almost too good to be true?" Kay had exulted; she could see Harald's name on the program with a credit as assistant director. But in the second week of rehearsals came the rift in the lute. The producer did not make clear the different spheres of authority; the way Harald analyzed it, it was because of an inner conflict: he was undecided himself as to just what kind of show he wanted, a literate revue with some bright songs and really topical sketches or the usual stupid omnium-gatherum held together by a couple of stars. So he was using Harald as a sort of guinea pig. Harald would rehearse a scene, and as soon as he had it set, the director would come and change it—introduce a line of show girls into an unemployment march or gag up a sketch about the milk strike with some farmerettes in straw hats. The authors were a hundred per cent on Harald's side, but the producer, when appealed to, would just vacillate, saying "Try it this way for a while" or "Wait!" Meanwhile, all through rehearsals, the director had been riding Harald every chance he got—if Harald was a few minutes late after the dinner break or missed a music cue—because Harald was loyal to the authors' conception, till finally, this afternoon, Harald, very quietly, in front of the whole company, had told him that he was incompetent to direct a book with a mind behind it. Kay would have given anything to have seen that. The director, unable, naturally, to match wits with Harald, had started screaming at him to get out of the theatre. So, before the show had even opened, there he was, out on the street. When he went upstairs to the office to protest (Kay could have told him that it was a mistake to delude himself that he still had the producer's ear), the producer, too ashamed to see him, sent word that at this stage he could not go over the director's head; the treasurer paid him two weeks' salary and offered him a drink, and that was that.

What Kay smelled was the prescription Scotch the treasurer had given him, to buck him up; for one awful moment, when she first opened the door for him and saw him standing there with the bottle of gin and alcohol on his breath, she was afraid that he might have been fired for drinking on the job. Once she had heard the story, she could see how unfair that was. Not only the treasurer, but the whole company had showed their sympathy for Harald. Most of the principals had made a point of stopping him, as he was leaving, to say they were sorry. The authors (one of them wrote regularly for *Vanity Fair*) had rushed up from their seats to argue with the director; one of the show girls had cried. . . .

Kay sat, nodding, in the cute red apron with white appliqués her mother had sent her, while Harald paced the living room, re-creating the scene in the theatre. Every now and then, she interrupted to ask a searching question, which she tried to make sound casual. Before she wrote her parents, she wanted to be sure that he was telling her the whole truth and not just his own partial view of it. That was the big thing they taught you at Vassar: keep your mind open and always ask for the evidence, even from your own side.

Though she believed Harald's version, because all the evidence she had supported it, she could see that an outside person, like her Dads, might think that Harald might have been wiser to tend to his knitting—see to the cues and the props and the prompt book and not give the director any excuse for picking on him. Like being late. But who was to blame for that? The producer or whoever was responsible for the awful hours they rehearsed. "Take an hour for dinner"! How did they expect Harald to get home, with those slow crosstown buses, eat, and go back again, all in sixty minutes? Most of the company, according to Harald, caught a bite in a drugstore or a speak-easy, next door to the theatre. But Harald was newly married, though nobody seemed to care or take that into consideration. Yet they knew he was married, because he had let her come once to a rehearsal and the star had caught sight of her in the house and made a rumpus, stopping right in the middle of a song and pointing to Kay and demanding to know what she was doing there; when she found it was Harald's bride, she said, "I'm so sorry, darling," and asked them both to her apartment for a drink. But the director had told Harald never to bring her again; it upset the principals, he said, to have strangers watching them rehearse, as Harald ought to know. It was the first time she had seen Harald eat humble pie, and it had given her the most dismal feeling, as if she were a sort of encumbrance; when they went to the star's apartment (a penthouse on Central Park South), she was conscious of her heavy legs and the hairs scattered on them and it was no consolation to remember that she had directed a Hall Play and been on the Daisy Chain at Vassar.

She thought that Actors Equity ought to *do* something about rehearsal hours, which Priss Hartshorn agreed were absolutely medieval and would not be tolerated in a substandard factory. She and Harald had hardly had intercourse since he got this job—how could they? The company did not break at night till one or two in the morning, and by that time *she* was asleep; when she left for work the next morning, *Harald* was still snoozing. One night, he did not get home till four, after a conference in the producer's office, yet he had to be back for rehearsal the next day at ten, even though it was a Sunday and the two of them might have had a leisurely breakfast together for once. And after rehearsals the show was going out of town to open, so that she would be alone for two weeks while Harald kept company with the dancers and the show girls—one of them was quite intelligent (Harald had found her backstage reading Katherine Mansfield) and had a house in Connecticut. So, naturally, Kay was glad when Harald tooled home (that was one of his favorite expressions) for dinner, instead of eating with the others in that speak-easy. Once he had brought one of the authors, and Kay had made salmon loaf with cream pickle sauce. That would have to be the night they broke for dinner early, and there was quite a wait ("Bake 1 hour," the recipe went, and Kay usually added fifteen minutes to what the cookbook said), which they had to gloss over with cocktails. Harald did not realize what a rush it was for her, every day now, coming home from work at Mr. Macy's and having to stop at Gristede's for the groceries; Harald never had time any more to do the marketing in the morning. And, strange to say, ever since *she* had started doing it, it had been a bone of contention between them. He liked the A & P because it was cheaper, and she liked Gristede's because they delivered and had fancy vegetables—the Sutton Place trade, Harald called it. Then Harald liked to cook the same old stand-bys (like his spaghetti with dried mushrooms and tomato paste), and she liked to read the cookbook and the food columns and always be trying something new. He said she had no imagination, following recipes with her glasses on and measuring the seasonings and timing everything: cooking was a lively art and she made it academic and lifeless. It was funny, the little differences that had developed between them, in the course of three months; at first, she had just been Harald's echo. But now if he said why not be sensible and open a can (this was another night when dinner was not ready), she would scream that she could not do that, it might be all right for him, but she could not live that way, week in, week out, eating like an animal, just to keep alive. Afterward, when he had left, she was sorry and made a resolution to be a better planner and budget her preparation time, the way the food columns said. But when she did manage to have dinner waiting in the oven, having fixed a casserole the night before, he would get irritated if she tried to hurry him to the table by reminding him what time it was. "Less wifely concern, please," he would say, waving his forefinger at her in the owly way he had, and deliberately shake up another cocktail before he would consent to eat.

This made her feel a bit guilty; he had never had the cocktail habit until he knew her. "Your class rite," he called it, and she was not sure whether he meant Class of '33 or social class; back in Salt Lake City, her parents never dreamed of having liquor even when they entertained, despite the fact that Dads could get prescription whisky. But in the East, it was the social thing to do, for older people too, as she knew from staying with Pokey Prothero and Priss and Polly. In Cleveland, as Harald had seen himself, Helena Davison's family had sherry. So, to please her, they had started having cocktails every night in the aluminum cocktail shaker. The difference between them was that what she liked was the little formality and what Harald liked was the liquor. One or two cocktails, of course, could never hurt anybody; still, during rehearsals, they should probably have done without, for Harald's sake. Yet it would have seemed such a comedown to just put the food on and sit down and eat, like her parents.

Harald had gone to the kitchen and fixed himself a gin and bitters; this was a bad sign—he knew Kay hated the taste of straight liquor and did not like to see him drink it. Now he put tobacco in his pipe, lit it, and poured a second. "What can I fix you?" he said. "A silver fizz?" Kay frowned; she was wounded by the mocking courtesy of his manner. "I don't think I'll have anything," she replied thoughtfully. Harald's dark, wiry eyebrows shot up. "Why this departure?" he said. Kay had suddenly determined to turn over a new leaf, but she felt this was not quite the right moment to announce it; you never knew how Harald would take things when he had been drinking. "I just don't feel like it," she said. "I'm going to start dinner." She rose from her chair. Harald stared at her, with his hands on his hips and pursed lips. "My God!" he said. "You are the most tactless, blundering fool that ever lived." "But what have I said?" cried Kay, too astonished, even, to be hurt. "'I don't think I'll have anything,'" he quoted, imitating her voice and adding a smug note that she could swear had not been there when she spoke. If he only knew, she was dying for a silver fizz and was doing without because she blamed herself, more than a little, for the trouble during rehearsals. What would happen if she went to work at Macy's after having had two cocktails before breakfast? It was the same thing, no? You could learn a lot, she always found, if you transferred your behavior to a different context and looked at it there, objectively. Had *she* just been fired, for instance, she would want to sit right down and trace the contributory causes, no matter how small. But maybe Harald was doing that and not letting on? "'I just don't feel like it,'" he went on. "Don't take that tone. It doesn't suit you. You're a terrible actress, you know." "Oh, can it!" Kay said abruptly and walked out to the kitchen. Then she listened to hear if Harald would go out, slamming the door, as he had the other night when she brought home from the store the Continental String Bean Slicer that did not work. But he was still there.

She opened a can of beans and dumped them into a baking dish; on top she put strips of bacon. On the way home on the El she had decided to make Welsh rabbit with beer, to surprise Harald, but now she was afraid to, in case it should curdle and give Harald a chance to lecture her. She pulled apart a head of lettuce and started her salad dressing. All at once, thinking of the Welsh rabbit that they were not going to have tonight just because Harald had lost his job, she gave a loud sob. Everything now was going to be changed, she knew it. By this, she really meant the Apartment; she was *living* for the moment they could move. Their present place belonged to the widow of an etcher who was now in Cornish, New Hampshire, and it was full of antiques and reproductions—Spanish chests and Oriental rugs and piecrust tables and Hepplewhite-style chairs and brass and copper that had to be polished. Kay could hardly wait to get out of this museum and move in with their own things. Harald knew this, yet so far he had not said a word about the Apartment, which he must have guessed was the thing uppermost in her mind from the moment she opened the door and saw him: what were they going to *do*? Hadn't this thought occurred to him too?

In her pocketbook on the lowboy in the living room were samples of upholstery material she had brought home to show him; she had spent her whole lunch hour in Macy's Forward House choosing a modern couch and two side chairs in muslin. And she had priced draperies just for fun, to show Harald how much they were saving thanks to the fact that the management gave you Venetian blinds free, the way they did in most of the smart new buildings. With the Venetian blinds you would not need draperies. To have had them made, she had found out today, even at Mr. Macy's with the discount, would have run to $100 or $120, so you could treat that amount as a reduction of the first year's rent. And that was unlined; lined would be even more.

She glanced at her beans in the oven—not yet brown. In the living room, she opened the drop-leaf table and set two places, meanwhile stealing a look at Harald, who was reading the *New Yorker*. He raised his eyes. "How would you like," he said, "to ask the Blakes in for bridge after dinner?" His negligent tone did not fool her; this, from Harald, was an apology. He was trying to make it up to her for nearly ruining their evening. "I'd love it!" Kay was delighted; it was a long time since they had had a foursome of bridge. "Shall I call them or will you?" "I will," he said, and, pulling Kay down to him, he kissed her hard. She released herself and hurried to the kitchen. "I've got three bottles of beer in the icebox!" she called out. "Tell them that!"

But in the kitchen her face fell. It struck her, all at once, that there was method in Harald's madness. Why the Blakes, of all people? Norine Blake, her classmate, was very left wing; at college she was always leading Socialist rallies and demonstrations, and her husband, Putnam, was a registered Socialist. And both of them had a complex about economy and living within a budget, though Putnam had a private income and came from a very good family. Kay could foresee what was coming. The Blakes, when they heard about Harald losing his job, would immediately start worrying the subject of the Apartment. Kay was already sick of hearing that Norine and Put had found a nice basement with a real garden for only $40 a month—why couldn't she and Harald? She wouldn't live in a basement; it was unhealthy. She glanced at her beans again and slammed the oven door. Put would argue (she could hear him!) that Harald was perfectly justified in going back on his legal obligation, which was what a lease was, because a lease was a form of exploitation and rent was unearned increment— something like that. And Norine would talk about carfares. She was hipped on the subject. The last time the four of them had played bridge, she had cross-questioned Kay about how she got to work. "You take the crosstown bus?" she asked, looking at her husband as if the crosstown bus were the most unheard-of luxury. "*And* the Sixth Avenue El?" Then she looked at her husband again, nodding. "That makes two fares," she relentlessly concluded. Norine's *idée fixe* was that all young couples should live near a subway stop. And she thought that Harald, because he worked in the Times Square area, should live on the West Side, not more than two blocks from an express stop. Kay and Harald had laughed at Norine's transportation obsession, but just the same it had put a bee in Harald's bonnet. And that very night, when Kay had served coffee and toasted cheese sandwiches after bridge, Norine had cried out, "What, real *cream*?" Apparently anybody but a millionaire was expected to live on evaporated. All these months Kay had been telling Harald that everybody bought cream as a matter of course (he wanted to use the top of the bottle), and she had turned red as a beet with confusion, as though Norine had exposed her in a lie. Yet Harald, strange to relate, instead of taking this amiss, had only teased Kay about it. "What, real *cream*!" he had murmured, afterward, squeezing her breasts.

Harald was always saying that she was transparent. Sometimes, like tonight, he meant it as a criticism, but sometimes he seemed to love her for being easy to see through, though what he saw or thought he saw she could not exactly make out. This reminded her of the funny letter she had found, night before last, when she was straightening up his papers to get ready for their move. It was a letter from Harald to his father and must have been written, she had figured out, the Saturday before she and Harald were married. She could not resist reading it when she saw her own name in the middle of the first page.

"Kay is not afraid of life, Anders"—that was what he called his father. "You and Mother and I are, all of us, a little. We know that life can hurt us. Kay has never found that out. That, I think, is why I've decided finally to marry her, though the cynics advise me to wait for a rich girl, who could buy me a piece of a show. Don't think I haven't thought of it. Between ourselves—this isn't for Mother's eyes—I've known a few such, in the Biblical sense. I've made love to them in their roadsters and raided their fathers' liquor cabinets and let them pay for me at the speak-easies where they have charge accounts. So I speak from experience. They're afraid of life too, have the death urge of their class in them; they want to annihilate experience in a wild moment of pleasure. They're like the Maenads who destroyed Orpheus—do you remember the old Greek myth? In the last analysis, they're afraid of the future, just like the Petersen family. You and Mother worry about your losing your job again or reaching retirement age; ever since the crash, the gilded girls worry that Papa might lose his money or have a revolution take it away from him. Kay is different; she comes from the secure class you never quite made, the upper professional class. Her father is a big orthopedist in Salt Lake City; look him up in *Who's Who* (if you haven't done so already!). That class still believes in its future and in its ability to survive and govern, and quite rightly too, as we see from the Soviet Union, where the services of doctors and scientists, no matter what their 'bourgeois' background, are at a premium, like the services of film directors and literary men. I see that belief, that pioneer confidence, in Kay, though she's unconscious of it herself; it's written all over her, the 'outward and visible sign of an inner and spiritual grace,' as the Episcopal prayer book says. Not that she is graceful, except in outdoor sports, riding and swimming and hockey too, she tells me. Speaking of the prayer book (read it some time for its style), Kay wants us to be married in J. P. Morgan's church; I'm agreeing, in a spirit of irony, and consoling myself with the thought that Senator Cutting (Bronson Cutting of New Mexico, one of my minor heroes— have I mentioned this?—a fighting gentleman progressive) worships there too when he's in town. (His sister has something to do with the Social Register.)

"I don't know how you feel out in Boise, but there's a big change here in the East since Roosevelt came in. Probably, as an old Townley man, you distrust him; frankly, I don't. You've read about the influx of professors into government; that is the key to the change, which may mean a bloodless revolution in our own time, with brain replacing finance capital in the management of our untapped resources. The Marxist boys here in New York make a mistake when they expect a final struggle between capital and labor; both capital and labor in their present morphology can be expected to dissolve. The fact that Roosevelt is a patrician is significant, and Kay tells me, by the way, proudly, that he was a trustee of Vassar. I'm wandering a little from the point, but I guess you see the bearing: I feel that my marriage to Kay is a pledge to the future. That sounds rather mystical, but I do have a mystical feeling about her, a sense of 'rightness' or destiny, call it what you will. Don't ask whether I love her; love, apart from chemical attraction, is still an unknown quantity to me. Which you may have divined. She's a very strong young woman with a radiant, still-undisciplined vitality. You and Mother may not like her at first, but that vitality of hers is necessary to me; it wants form and direction, which I think I can give her.

"By the way, would Mother mind asking Kay to call her Judith when she writes? Like all modern girls, she has a horror of calling a mother-in-law 'Mother,' and 'Mrs. Petersen' sounds so formal. Make Mother understand. Kay already thinks of you as Anders and is moved by the quality of our relationship—yours and mine, I mean. I've been trying to put the story of your life into a play, but Kay, who has studied theatre at Vassar under a funny, electric little woman, says I have no knack yet for dramatic construction; she may be right, I fear. Oh, Anders . . ."

Here the letter broke off; it had never been finished, and Kay wondered what he had said in the letter he finally wrote. There were other unfinished letters too in his rickety suitcase, some to her at Vassar, and several beginnings of a short story or novel, so old that the paper was turning yellow, and the first two acts of his play. The letter, Kay thought, was awfully well written, like everything Harald did, yet reading it had left her with the queerest, stricken feeling. There was nothing in it that she did not already know in a sense, but to know in a sense, apparently, was not the same as knowing. Harald, she had had to admit, had never concealed from her that he had had relations with other women and had even toyed with the idea of marrying them or being married by them. And she had heard all that about her social class (though, when he talked to her, he usually said it was finished) and Roosevelt and his not feeling sure that he loved her and "in a spirit of irony." Maybe it was just that that made reading the letter so disappointing. It was finding that Harald was just the same all through, which in a funny way made him different. Curiosity was a terrible thing; she had started reading the letter, knowing she shouldn't, with the thought that she might learn more about him and about herself too. But instead of telling her more about him, the letter was almost a revelation of the limitations of Harald. Or was it only that she did not like to see him "baring his soul" to his father?

Yet the letter *had* told her something, she reflected now as she listened to Harald on the telephone (the Blakes evidently were coming) and methodically tossed her salad. The letter explained, in so many words, what her attraction was—something she had never been clear about. When she had first met him in the summer theatre he had treated her like one of the *hoi polloi*, ordering her around, criticizing the way she hammered flats, sending her on errands to the hardware store. "You've got paint in your hair," he told her one night when the company was having a party and he had asked her to dance; he had just had a fight with the leading lady, a married woman, with whom he was sleeping—her husband was a lawyer in New York. Another time, when they were all having beer in a roadhouse, he had strolled over to her table, where she was sitting with some of the other apprentices, to say—guess what—that her shoulder straps showed. Kay could hardly believe it when he promised to write to her after she went back to Vassar, but he had—a short, casual note—and she had answered, and he had come up for a weekend to see the Hall Play she directed, and now here they were, married. Yet she had never felt sure of him; up to the last minute, she had feared he might be using her as a pawn in a game he was playing with some other woman. Even in bed, he kept his *sang-froid*; he did the multiplication tables to postpone ejaculating—an old Arab recipe he had learned from an Englishman. Kay dished up her beans. She was "not afraid of life," she repeated to herself; she had "a radiant vitality." Their marriage was "a pledge to the future." Instead of feeling chagrined by this and wishing he had said something more romantic, she should realize that this was her strong suit and play it; never mind those Blakes—a lease was a pledge to the future. No matter what people said, she would *not* give up the Apartment. She did not know why it meant so much to her—whether it was the Venetian blinds or the concierge or the darling little dressing room or what. She felt she would die if they lost it. And what would they do instead—go back to that sordid Village room across the hall from Dick Brown till Harald's plans were more "settled"? No! Kay set her jaw. "There are other apartments, dear," she could hear her mother say. She did not want another apartment; she wanted this one. It was the same as when she had wanted Harald and feared she was going to lose him every time she did not get a letter. She had not given up and said "There are other men," the way a lot of girls would; she had held on. And it was not only her; for Harald it would be an awful disaster psychologically to relinquish his Life plan and go backward after a single defeat— not to mention losing the deposit, a whole month's rent.

They sat down to the meal. The Blakes were coming at 8:30. Kay kept glancing at the lowboy, just behind Harald, where her pocketbook was lying stuffed with upholstery samples. She wondered whether she should not get it over with and show them to Harald before Norine and Putnam came. After bridge, it would be late, and Harald, she suspected, would be wanting to have intercourse; on a night like this she could hardly say no, even though it meant that after her douche, it would be one o'clock before she closed her eyes (thanks to those multiplication tables), and tomorrow morning before going to work would be no time to show him the samples; he would be snappish if she woke him up for that. Yet they would have to decide soon; two weeks on upholstery was the rule at Macy's. The beds and pots and pans and lamps and a table and all that would have to be ordered too, but at least they were there in the warehouse and you only needed two days for delivery. She thought they should have hair mattresses, which were more expensive but healthier; Consumers' Research admitted that. Her confidence fled as she passed the butter to Harald; only the other night, they had had quite a debate, ending in tears on her part, about margarine vs. butter—margarine, Harald maintained, was just as tasty and nourishing, but the butter interests had conspired to keep the margarine people from coloring their product; he was right, yet she could not bear to have that oily white stuff on her table, even if her reaction to the whiteness was a conditioned reflex based on class prejudice. Now he speared a piece of butter with a bitter smile, which Kay tried not to notice. Maybe she was not afraid of life, but she was certainly afraid of Harald.

She decided to edge in to the topic of the samples by a little light chatter about her day in the store; she was worried that if she did not talk Harald might sink into one of his Scandinavian glooms. "You know what?" she said gaily. "I think I was 'shopped' today." That was like having a sprung test in college: a professional Macy shopper, pretending to be a customer, was assigned to evaluate every trainee at one time during his or her six months' training. The bosses did not tell you this would happen, but of course the word leaked out. "I'm in 'Better Suits' this week, did I tell you?" Harald knew that Kay would be shifted around so that she would learn every aspect of merchandising, besides listening to lectures from the executives of the different departments. "Well, this afternoon I had this customer who insisted on trying on every suit on the floor and was dissatisfied with just about everything. It got to be almost closing time, and she couldn't make up her mind between a black wool with caracul trim and a blue severe tweed, fitted, with a dark-blue velvet collar. So she wanted me to send for the fitter, to get her opinion, and the fitter said she should take both and winked at me, to give me a tip, I guess. They grade you on politeness, good humor, general personality, but the main point is whether you can sell. You flunk if the shopper goes away without buying anything. And, what do you think, thanks to the fitter, this woman in the end bought both suits. Not really 'bought' of course; instead of going down to the workrooms, the suits are returned to stock if the customer is a Macy shopper. That way you can tell. But on the other hand if a real customer buys something and returns it, that counts as a mark against you; it means you oversold. . . ."

Harald sat chewing in silence; finally, he laid down his fork. In the face of this coldness, Kay could not continue. "Go on, my dear," he said, as her voice flagged and halted. "This is highly interesting. From what you say, I expect you'll be valedictorian of your Macy class. You may even find me a job in the rug department or selling refrigerators—isn't that considered a man's sphere?" "Yes," replied Kay, mechanically responding to a request for information. "Only they never start a man in those departments; you have to have other experience in selling first." Then she dropped her fork and buried her curly head in her hands. "Oh, Harald! Why do you hate me?"

"Because you ask tedious questions like that," he retorted. Kay's face flamed; she did not want to cry, because the Blakes were coming. Harald must have thought of the same thing, for when he spoke again it was in a different tone. "I don't blame you, dear Kay," he said gravely, "for comparing yourself to me as a breadwinner. God knows you have a right to." "But I *wasn't* comparing myself to you!" Kay raised her head in outrage. "I was just making conversation." Harald smiled sadly. "I was not blaming you," he repeated. "Harald! Please believe me!" She seized his hand. "The thought of a comparison never entered my mind! It couldn't. I know that you're a genius and that I'm just a B-average person. That's why I can coast along in life and you can't. And I haven't helped you enough; I know it. I shouldn't have let you come home to dinner while you were rehearsing; I shouldn't have made us have cocktails. I should have thought of the strain you were under. . . ." She felt his hand go flaccid in hers and realized she was blundering again; at least she had avoided naming his lateness at the theatre, which was the real thought that kept preying on her conscience.

He flung her hand aside. "Kay," he said. "How many times have I pointed out to you that you're an unconscionable egotist? Observe how you've shifted the center of the drama to yourself. It was I who was fired today, not you. You had nothing to do with it. Being late"—he smiled cruelly—"had nothing to do with it, despite what you've been insinuating in your clumsy way for the last two weeks. You've developed a time-clock mentality. Nobody takes that 'hour for dinner' seriously in the theatre—except you. You saw the night you were there; nothing started for half an hour after we pulled in. Everybody sits around playing pinochle. . . ." Kay nodded. "All right, Harald. Forgive me." But he was still angry. "I'll thank you," he said, "for keeping your petty-bourgeois conscience out of my affairs. It's your way of cutting me down to size. You pretend to accuse yourself, but it's me you're accusing." Kay shook her head. "No, no," she said. "Never." Harald raised a skeptical eyebrow. "You protest too much," he remarked, in a lighter tone; she could see that his mood was changing again. "In any case," he continued, "all that had nothing to do with it. You are on the wrong track, my girl. The nance hates me; that's all." "Because you're superior," murmured Kay.

"That, yes," said Harald. "Doubtless, there was that." "'Doubtless'?" cried Kay, affronted by the judicious, qualifying note in his voice. "Why, of course that was it." It would be just like Harald to start hairsplitting now, when they were both agreed that the basic motivations were as clear as noonday. "What do you mean, 'doubtless'?" He shook his head and smiled. "Oh, Harald, please tell me!" "Go and make us some coffee, like a good girl." "No. Harald, tell me!" Harald lit his pipe. "Do you know the story of Hippolytus?" he said finally. "Why, naturally," protested Kay. "Don't you remember, we did it at college in Greek, with Prexy playing Theseus? I wrote you, I built the scenery—the big statues of Artemis and Aphrodite. Golly, that was fun. And Prexy forgot his lines and ad-libbed 'To be or not to be' in Greek, and only old Miss MacCurdy, the head of the Greek department, knew the difference. She's deaf but she spotted it even with her ear trumpet." Harald waited, drumming his fingers. "Well?" said Kay. "Well," said Harald, "if you change the sex of Phaedra . . ." "I don't understand. What would happen if you changed the sex of Phaedra?" "You would have the inside story of my getting the ax. Now, make us the coffee." Kay stared, nonplused. She could not see the connection.

"Buggery," said Harald. "I, though not a virgin, am the chaste Hippolytus of the farce, which the play, incidentally, is. A male defending his virtue is always a farcical figure." Kay's jaw dropped. "You mean somebody wanted to bugger you? Who? The director?" she gasped. "The other way round, I believe. He assured me that he had a luscious ass." "When? This afternoon?" Kay was torn between horror and curiosity. "Flits have always been attracted to me"—he had told her that last summer (there had been two who were like that in the company), and then it had made her excited and sort of envious. "No, no. Some weeks ago," said Harald. "The first time, that is." "Why didn't you *tell* me?" The thought that he had kept such a thing from her cut her to the heart. "There was no reason for you to know." "But how did it happen? What did he say to you? Where were you?" "In Shubert Alley," he said. "I was a little liquored up that evening, and in my mood of geniality, I may have given him what he took for signs of encouragement. He suggested that we repair to his apartment later."

"Oh, God!" cried Kay. "Oh, Harald, you didn't—?" "No, no," he replied soothingly. "It was an uninviting prospect. The old fruit must be forty." For a second, Kay was relieved and, at the same time (wasn't that queer?), almost let down; then a fresh suspicion attacked her. "Harald! Do you mean you would have *done* it with someone younger? A chorus boy?" She felt sick thinking of the nights he had worked late, and yet there was this funny itch to know. "I can't answer hypothetical questions," Harald said, rather impatiently. "The problem hasn't come up." "Oh," said Kay, dissatisfied. "But the director—did *he* try again?" Harald admitted that he had. One night late, he had reached for Harald's crotch. "And what happened?" Harald shrugged. "Erection is fairly automatic in the normal male, you know." Kay turned pale. "Oh, Harald! You encouraged him!" All at once, she was frenzied with jealousy; it took Harald some time to calm her. In her heart was the horrible certainty that erection would not have been so automatic if she had not always been asleep when Harald tiptoed into their bedroom. And how did she know he tiptoed? Because (did he ever suspect this?) she was not always really asleep. Tonight, she decided, they would have intercourse no matter how tired she was when the Blakes left.

Kay yawned and slipped off Harald's lap, where he had taken her to comfort her ("I like your freckles," he had whispered. "And your wild black gipsy hair"). "I'll make the coffee," she said. As she turned to go, he reached out and patted her behind, which made her think, distrustfully, of the director. What had got into her, recently, that prompted her to distrust Harald and to always think there was something more than he was telling her behind every little incident he related? To tell the truth, she had wondered sometimes if there could not be some other explanation of the director's persecution, and now that she knew what it was ("Hell hath no fury like a woman scorned"), she still wondered whether there was not more to *that* than Harald said. How far had he let the "nance" go? She could not help remembering a story he had told her, while she was still in college, about undressing an older actress in her apartment and then just leaving her up in the air on her blue percale sheets with scalloped borders.

Kay believed in Harald completely; she had no doubt he was

bound to be famous, sooner or later, in whatever field he chose. But believing in him was different from believing him. In fact, the more impressed she was by him intellectually (his I.Q. must be in the genius percentile), the more she noticed his little lapses. And why was it that, with all his talent, he was still a stage manager when other people of his own age, people not nearly as bright, had forged ahead of him? Was there something wrong with him that was evident to producers and directors and not to her? She wished he would let her give him the Binet and some of the personality tests she had tried on the group at Vassar.

Once, during exam week (and nobody knew this but her), he had tried to commit suicide by driving somebody's car off a cliff. The car had rolled over without hurting him, and he had climbed out and walked back to the place where he was staying. The next day the couple he was visiting had sent for a tow truck to pull the car up and the only damage was that acid from the battery had dripped over the upholstery, making holes in it, and ruined Harald's English hat, which had fallen off his head when the car turned over. This suicide attempt had impressed her terrifically, and she treasured the letter in which he described it; she could not imagine having the coolness to do such a thing herself and certainly not in someone else's car. He had done it, he said, on a sudden impulse, because he saw his future laid out for him and he did not want to be a tame husband, not even hers. When the attempt failed so miraculously, he had taken it as a sign, he wrote her, that Heaven had decreed their union. Now, however, that she knew Harald better, she wondered whether he had not driven off the cliff by accident; admittedly, he had been drinking applejack at the time. She hated having these suspicions of Harald and she did not know which was worse: to be scared that your husband might kill himself if the slightest little thing went wrong or to be guessing that it was all a cover-up for something commonplace like driving-under-the-influence.

Harald was histrionic; Lakey had found the right word for him. Yet that was why, with his intellect and learning, he would make such a marvelous director. Kay had been giving a lot of thought to Harald's problems during her lonely evenings while he was at the theatre, and she had decided that the main thing that acted as a drag on him was his strong identification with his father. He was still fighting his father's battles; any psychologist could see that. No wonder, then, that Kay felt impatient with that relation. "Anders" and "Judith"!—she had come to loathe the very names of the old pair, if Harald only knew it. She would almost rather commit suicide herself than make Judith's "quick-and-easy meat loaf." The sight of her mother-in-law's labored pencil recipes, enclosed in letters from "Anders," made her cold and hard as nails. Ever since she had seen "Judith's" handwriting, she could not abide Harald's chile con carne, though it was still a big success with company, who did not know the source and thought it was something glamorous he had learned in the theatre. She had no doubt that "Judith" used oleomargarine; she could see a white slab of it on their humble oilcloth with a cheap plated-silver butter knife (the kind you sent in coupons for) lying by its moist side!

Turning off the coffee (Maxwell House), Kay made a face. She had a ruthless hatred of poor people, which not even Harald suspected and which sometimes scared her by its violence, as when she was waiting on some indigent in the store. Objectively, of course, she ought to pity old Anders, a poor Norwegian immigrant who had taught manual training in the Idaho public-school system and then had studied nights to become an algebra teacher and finally risen to be principal of a high school in Boise, where he made an enemy of the vice-principal, who brought about his dismissal. Harald's play told the story of that. In the play, he had made his father a college president and put him at odds with the state legislature. To her mind, that was very unconvincing and accounted for the weakness of the play. If Harald wanted to write about his father, why glorify him? Why not simply tell the truth?

According to Harald, his father, in real life, had been framed and railroaded out of his position because (shades of Ibsen!) he had discovered some funny business about the high-school book-keeping. But if he had really been as innocent as Harald claimed, it was peculiar that all through Harald's adolescence he could not get reinstated in the school system and had to support the family doing odd jobs of carpentry, non-union, while Harald went to work as a newsboy. Harald said it was all part of a conspiracy in which some crooked city officials had been involved too, and that they had to crucify his father to keep the real facts from being known. But then a reform party got elected (Harald's father was a sort of populist radical whose god was some man called Townley), and he was taken on again, as a substitute teacher; meanwhile, in high school Harald had made a big name for himself, being quarterback of the football team and star of the dramatic society and editor of the school paper. A group of Boise ladies had raised a scholarship fund to send him to Reed College, in Oregon, and then to Yale Drama School, and he could still have a job, any time he wanted, running their Little Theatre for them—you should see the silver water pitcher they had sent from Gump's in San Francisco for a wedding present. But Harald would not go back to Boise till his father's name had been vindicated. He meant till his play had been produced; he expected all of Boise to read about it in the papers and recognize poor old Anders, who was now a regular teacher again (half-time algebra and half-time manual training), in the wronged president of a big state university. The play was called *Sheepskin*, and Harald had merged in it the story of his father's life with some of the story of Alexander Meiklejohn at Wisconsin, not admitting to himself that his father and Meiklejohn were horses of a different color.

What worried Kay most, though, was that Harald was identifying with failure. One of her first thoughts, when she heard the news this afternoon, was that Harald might be repeating his father's pattern. She wondered how many people who knew Harald, besides herself, would think of this. This made it important to get the true facts into circulation, for it would hurt Harald's career if he got the name of a troublemaker, of a person who went around *wanting* to be fired, *needing* to fail. She did not think Harald should be soft about telling what the director had tried to do to him; knowing the director's proclivities, everyone would realize how he had been subtly provoking Harald to finally give him a piece of his mind; if it had not happened today, he would have goaded him till it did.

The doorbell rang just as they were finishing their coffee. Listening to the Blakes on the stairs (Norine had a heavy walk), Kay thought fast. Whatever was said about the Apartment, she was going to keep mum; let the others talk. And tomorrow morning, first thing, she would slip down to Forward House and order the upholstery job. She could always pretend that she had done it today, before she heard the news, and had not mentioned it on purpose, seeing how upset Harald was. She could even make up a story of trying desperately to cancel the order (that would be tomorrow morning) and being told it was too late—the material had already been cut. And it could have happened that way; it was just chance that she had decided to take the samples home to show Harald, instead of settling on the one she wanted—the Fireman Red—herself. If she had, it *would* be too late.

Kay opened the door. "Hi!" she said. "Greetings!" She spoke in a low, muffled voice, to prepare them, as though Harald, just behind her, lighting his pipe again, were sick or a specter or something—how were you supposed to act when your husband had joined the ranks of the unemployed right in the middle of the depression? For a moment, thinking of it that way, she felt a wild surge of fear, like what she had felt that first instant when she heard Harald's key scratching at the lock and *knew* what he was going to tell her. But something inside her hardened immediately and she had a new idea: now Harald would be able to work on his play and get that out of his system; the dinette would be perfect for a study for him, and he could build in shelves for his papers below the china cabinet. There was no reason, now, that he could not do all the carpentry and build in the bed too, the way they had once planned, and make a bookcase for the living room. Behind her, Harald spoke. "*Morituri te salutamus.* I've got the sack," he said. "Oh, Harald," said Kay eagerly. "Wait till they've got their things off. And tell it the way you told me. Start from the beginning and don't leave anything out."

HARALD and Kay were giving a party to celebrate Harald's having sold an option on his play to a producer. It was Washington's Birthday, and Kay had the day off from the store. The group had made a point of coming, in their nicest winter dresses and hats. Harald, poor fellow, had been out of work for months, it seemed, ever since September when, according to Polly Andrews, a director had molested him. They had not paid the rent for months either; the real-estate people were "carrying" them. When they got the check for the option ($500), the telephone was about to be shut off. It was a mystery what they had been living on, even with Kay's salary. On faith, hope, and charity, Kay said, laughing: Harald's *faith* in himself gave his creditors *hope*, which made them extend *charity*. And she told how Harald had proposed that they invite a select group of their creditors to the party: the man from the real-estate office, the man from the telephone company, Mr. Finn from the Internal Revenue, and their dentist, Dr. Mosenthal—wouldn't that have been a howl?

Kay had been showing the apartment to everyone who hadn't seen it. Two rooms, plus dinette and kitchen, plus a foyer, plus Kay's pride and joy, a darling little dressing room, so compact, with closets and cupboards and bureau drawers built in. Pure white walls and woodwork and casement windows, a whole row of them, looking out on a sunny court with young trees and shrubs. The latest models of stove, sink, and icebox; built-in cupboards for dishes, broom closet, linen closet. Every stick of furniture was the latest thing: blond Swedish chairs and folding table (made of birch with natural finish) in the dinette, which was separated from the kitchen by a slatted folding door; in the living room, a bright-red modern couch and armchairs to match, a love seat covered in striped gray-and-white mattress ticking, steel standing lamps, a coffee table that was just a sheet of glass that Harald had had cut at the glazier's and mounted on steel legs, built-in bookcases that Harald had painted canary yellow. There were no rugs yet and, instead of curtains, only white Venetian blinds at the windows.

Instead of flowers, they had ivy growing in white pots. In the bedroom, instead of a bed, they had a big innerspring mattress with another mattress on top of it; Harald had nailed red pegs to the bottom one to keep it off the floor.

Instead of a dress, Kay was wearing a cherry-red velvet sleeveless hostess gown (Harald's Christmas present) from Bendel's; they had an old colored maid from Harlem passing canapés in a modern sectioned hors d'oeuvre tray. Instead of cocktails, they had had Fish House Punch, made from One Dagger Rum, in a punch bowl with twenty-four matching glass cups they had borrowed from Priss Hartshorn Crockett, who had got it for a wedding present when she was married in Oyster Bay in September.

On *that* occasion, only four of the group had been able to make it. Today, *mirabile dictu*, the only one missing was Lakey, who was now in Spain. Pokey Prothero had flown down from Cornell Agricultural in a helmet and goggles; Helena Davison, who had spent the summer and fall in Europe, was in town from Cleveland. Dottie Renfrew had come back from Arizona, where her family had sent her for her health, with a marvelous tan and an engagement ring—a diamond almost as big as her eyes; she was going to marry a mining man who owned half the state.

This was quite a change from Dottie's modest plans for working in a settlement house and living at home in Boston. "You'll miss the concerts and the theatre," Helena had remarked dryly. But Dottie said that Arizona had a great deal to offer too. There were lots of interesting people who had gone there because of T.B. and fallen in love with the country— musicians and painters and architects, and there was the riding and the incredible wild flowers of the desert, not to mention the Indians and some fascinating archaeological digs that attracted scientists from Harvard.

The party was almost over; only one mink coat was left in the bedroom. At the high point, there had been five—Harald had counted them. Kay's supervisor's, Harald's producer's wife's, Connie Storey's, Dottie's, and a mink-lined greatcoat belonging to Connie's fiancé, that apple-cheeked boy who worked on *Fortune*. Now Dottie's lay in solitary state, next to Helena's ocelot and a peculiar garment made of old gray wolf

that belonged to Norine Schmittlapp Blake, another member
of the Vassar contingent. Harald's producer had left after half
an hour, with his wife (who had the money) and a star who
had replaced Judith Anderson in *As You Desire Me*, but the
Class of '33 had practically held a reunion, there was so much
news to keep up with: Libby MacAusland had sold a poem to
Harper's; Priss was pregnant; Helena had seen Lakey in Munich and met Miss Sandison in the British Museum; Norine
Schmittlapp, who was there with her husband (the one in the
black shirt), had been to the Scottsboro trial; Prexy (bless his
heart!) had had lunch on a tray with Roosevelt in the White
House. . . .

Helena, who was Class Correspondent, took a few terse
mental notes. "At Kay Strong Petersen's," she foresaw herself
inditing for the next issue of the *Alumnae Magazine*, "I saw
Dottie Renfrew, who is going to marry Brook Latham and live
in Arizona. 'The Woman Who Rode Away'—how about it,
Dottie? Brook is a widower—see the Class Prophecy. Kay's
husband, Harald, has sold his play, *Sheepskin*, to the producer,
Paul Bergler—watch out, Harald. The play is slated for fall
production; Walter Huston is reading the script. Norine
Schmittlapp's husband, Putnam Blake (Williams '30), has
started an independent fund-raising organization for labor and
left-wing causes. Volunteer workers take note. His partner is
Bill Nickum (Yale '29). Charles Dickens take note. Polly Andrews reports that Sis Farnsworth and Lely Baker have started
a business called 'Dog Walk.' It keeps them outdoors, Polly
says, and they're swamped with applications from people who
don't have butlers any more to take their canines walking in
the Park. . . ."

Helena puckered her little forehead. Had she mastered
(mistressed?) the idiom of the *Alumnae Magazine* Class
Notes? She and Dottie were in the living room, waiting tactfully to get their coats to leave. Harald and Kay were in the
bedroom with the door closed, having "words," she supposed.
The party, to quote the host, had laid an egg. The main body
of guests had decamped just as the old colored maid had appeared, all smiles, with a Washington's Birthday cake she had
brought for a present. Harald, reddening, had shooed her back
to the kitchen, so as not to let people see, presumably, that

they had been expected to stay longer. But Kay, who had always been a blurter, had let the cat out of the bag. "But Harald was going to read his play!" she cried sadly after the departing guests. The whole party had been planned around that, she confided. Now the maid had gone home with her satchel, and the only guests remaining, besides Helena herself and Dottie, were a radio actor, who was helping himself copiously at the punch bowl, the two Blakes, and a naval officer Harald had met in a bar, whose sister was married to a famous architect who used ramps instead of stairs. The actor, who had wavy hair in a pompadour, was arguing with Norine about Harald's play. "The trouble is, Norine, the line of the play is sheer toboggan. I told Harald that when he read it to me. 'It's very interesting, the way you've done it, but I wonder: is it a *play*?'" He gestured, and some punch from his cup fell on his suit. "If the audience identifies with a character, they want to feel he has a chance to win. But Harald's view of life is too blackly logical to give them that sop." Across the room, Putnam Blake, a thin, white-faced young man with a close collegiate haircut, an unsmiling expression, and a low, tense voice, was explaining what he called his "Principle of Accumulated Guilt" to the naval officer.

"Mr. Blake," said Dottie with a twinkle, "has a system for finding rich people to give money to Labor. He was telling about it earlier. It sounds terribly interesting," she added warmly. Glancing at their watches, at Norine and the actor, and at the closed bedroom door, the two girls drew near to listen. Putnam ignored them, dividing his attention between his pipe and the naval officer. Using Gustavus Myers' *Great American Fortunes*, Poor's *Register of Directors*, and Mendel's Law, he was able to predict, he said, when a wealthy family was "due." As a rule, this occurred in the third generation. "What I've done," he said, "is take the element of chance out of fund-raising and put it on a scientific basis. I'm simplifying, of course, but roughly speaking the money guilt has a tendency to skip a generation. Or if it crops out in the second generation, as with the Lamont family, you will find it in a younger son rather than in the first-born. And it may be transmitted to the females while remaining dormant in the males. This means that the guilt tends to separate from the chief property holdings, which are usually transmitted from first-born male to first-born male. Thus the guilt, being a recessive character, like blue eyes, may be bred out of a family without any profit to the Left." A ghostly quiver, the phantom of a smile, passed across his lips; he appeared eager to take the naval officer into his confidence, like some crazy inventor, thought Helena, with a patent, and it was as if some bashful ectoplasmic joke hovered in the neighborhood of his Principle. "I'm working now," he continued, "on the relation between mental deficiency and money guilt in rich families. Your ideal contributor (the Communists have found this), scion of a fortune, has a mental age of twelve." Without altering his expression, he gave a quick parenthetic little laugh.

Helena quirked her sandy eyebrows, thinking of the Rich Young Man in the Bible and idly imagining a series of camels with humps of accumulated guilt lining up to pass through the eye of a needle. The conversation at this party struck her as passing strange. "Read the *Communist Manifesto*—for its style," she had heard Harald telling Kay's supervisor (Wellesley '28). She grinned. "Take *her*," said Putnam suddenly to the naval officer, indicating Helena with a jab of his pipe. "Her people live on the income of their income. Father is first vice-president of Oneida Steel. Self-made man—first generation. Bright girl, the daughter—only child. Does not respond to fund-raising appeals for labor victims. Charities confined, probably, to Red Cross and tuberculosis stamps. But if she has four children, you can expect that at least one of them will evince guilt characteristics. . . ."

Impressed despite herself, Helena lit a cigarette. She had met Mr. Blake for the first time this afternoon and for a moment she felt he must have clairvoyance, like a mind reader in a movie house or, more accurately, a *fortune* teller. His confederate, of course, was Kay, drat her. She rued the day she had told her, as a curious fact, that her parents lived "on the income of their income"—*i.e.*, plainly. But Kay had had to turn it into a boast. Already this afternoon Helena had heard her telling Harald's producer that "Helena's parents have never *felt* the depression." "What was the name?" inquired the producer, turning to examine Helena, as they always did. Kay supplied the name of Helena's father. "Never heard of him," said the producer. "Neither have most people," said Kay. "But they know him down in Wall Street. And he's crazy about the theatre. Ask Harald. He saw a lot of the Davisons when his show was playing Cleveland last year. Her mother is president of one of the women's clubs there, quite a remarkable woman, always organizing classes and lectures for working-class girls; she scorns groups like the Junior League that don't mean business. . . ."

Helena blew smoke rings—an art she had perfected as an aid against self-consciousness; all her life, she had submitted to being talked *about*, first and foremost by her mother. She was a short, sandy-haired girl with an appealing snub nose and an air of being sturdy though she was really thin and slight. She very much resembled her father, a short, sandy Scot who had made a pile of money in steel through knowing about alloys; he had been born in a little town called Iron Mountain, Michigan. Helena was regarded as the droll member of the group, having a puckish sense of humor, a slow, drawling way of talking, and a habit of walking around nude that had startled the others at first. Her figure was almost undeveloped, and when you saw her from a distance, hiking down a corridor to the shower with a towel around her neck, you might have thought she was a freckled little boy on his way to a swimming hole in the woods somewhere; her legs were slightly bowed, and her little patch of hair down there was a bright pinky red. She and Kay, when they first knew each other freshman year, used to climb trees together on Sunset Hill, back of the lake, and perform strange experiments in the Chem Lab, nearly blowing each other up. Yet Helena was intelligent, the group discovered, and in some ways very mature for her age. She had read a tremendous lot, particularly in modern literature, and listened to modern music, which was way over most of the group's heads; she collected limited editions of verse and rare phonograph records of pre-polyphonic church music. The group considered her quite an asset, almost a little mascot, in her neat Shetland sweater and skirt, riding across the campus on her bicycle or chasing butterflies with a net in the Shakespeare Garden.

The worst, from Helena's point of view, was that she *knew* all this, knew, that is, about the mascot and the swimming hole and how she looked with the butterfly net; she had been watched and described too carefully by too many experts—all indulgent and smiling, like the group. She had been registered for Vassar at birth; her mother had had her tutored in every conceivable subject all through her childhood. Helena (as her mother said) could play the violin, the piano, the flute, and the trumpet; she had sung alto in the choir. She had been a camp counselor and had a senior lifesaving badge. She played a good game of tennis, golfed, skied, and figure skated; she rode, though she had never jumped or hunted. She had a real chemistry set, a little printing press, a set for tooling leather, a pottery wheel, a library of wild-flower, fern, and bird books, a butterfly collection mounted on pins in glass cases, collections of sea shells, agates, quartz, and carnelians; these educational souvenirs were still kept in cupboards in her little sitting room in Cleveland, which had formerly been the nursery—her doll's house and toys had been given away. She could write a severe little essay, imitate birdcalls, ring chimes, and play lacrosse as well as chess, checkers, mah-jongg, parcheesi, anagrams, dominoes, slapjack, pounce, rummy, whist, bridge, and cribbage. She knew most of the hymns in the Episcopal and Presbyterian hymnbooks by heart. She had had dancing lessons, ballroom, classical, and tap. She had done field walks in Geology and visited the State Asylum for the Insane, bunked in the Outing Cabin, and looked over the printing presses of the *Dutchess County Sentinel* in Poughkeepsie. She had swum in the waterfall near Washington's Crossing and attended the annual Greek play at the Bennett School in Millbrook. She and Kay, in Freshman Hygiene, were just about the only members of the class who actually inspected the dairies where the college cows were kept; one of the workmen had shown Helena how to milk. She knew china and had a small collection of snuffboxes at home that her mother had started for her; she knew Greek and Latin and could translate the worst passages of Krafft-Ebing without a shadow of embarrassment. She knew medieval French and the lays of the trouvères, though her accent was poor because her mother disapproved of French governesses, having heard of cases where these women drugged children or put their heads in the gas oven to make them go to sleep. At camp, Helena had learned to sail and sing old catches and sea chanties, some of them rather off-color; she improvised on the mouth organ and was studying the recorder. She had had art lessons since she was six and showed quite a gift for drawing. When Kay, senior year, had the group making those lists of who liked whom best, Helena cannily said she couldn't decide and instead drew a big colored cartoon which she called "The Judgment of Paris," showing them all in the nude, like goddesses, and herself very small in a jerkin with a dunce's cap on her head and a wormy apple in her hand. Tickled, they hung it in their common sitting room, and there was quite a controversy about whether they should take it down at Prom time when they had some of their beaux in to tea; the modest members of the group, like Dottie and Polly Andrews, were afraid of being considered fast because the likenesses were so realistic that somebody might have thought they had posed.

Having been Kay's roommate (before they all grouped together) and had her to stay in Cleveland, Helena accepted her mother's dictum, that Kay was her "best friend," though they were no longer as close as they had been before sex entered Kay's life. Helena had known about sex from a very early age but treated it as a joke, like what she called your plumbing. She was dry and distant toward the fond passion, as she called it, and was amused by Kay's ardors for Harald, whom she coolly dubbed "Harald Handfast"—an allusion to the Old English custom of bedding before wedding. To her, men in general were a curious species, like the unicorn; for Harald in particular her feelings were circumspect and consisted chiefly of a mental protest against the way he spelled his name. Her parents, however, liked him and approved of Kay's choice. When his play was in Cleveland last winter, Mr. Davison had offered him a card to his club, which he did not use much himself, he said, "being a plain fellow."

Kay herself was a favorite with Helena's mother, and, whenever she came to stay, Mrs. Davison, who was a great talker, liked to discuss Helena with her at breakfast, over her second cup of coffee in the handsome paneled breakfast room while Helena herself was still sleeping and only the toby jugs and Mr. Davison's collection of English china stirrup cups made in the form of foxes' heads were able (commented Helena) to listen. Knowing the two participants, Helena, in her sleep, could have told how the conversation would go. "She has had *every oppor-tunity*," emphasized Mrs. Davison, with an impressive look at Kay, who was respectfully drinking her orange juice, which was served in cracked ice. "*Every opportunity*." This way of stressing and repeating her words would lead Kay to think that Mrs. Davison was implying, for Kay's ears alone, that Helena had been a grave disappointment to her mother. But this was an error, as other chums of Helena's had found. Accustomed to public speaking, Mrs. Davison always paused and intensified to let her words slowly sink in, even with an audience of one. Her real belief was that Helena was turning out extremely well, though she greatly wondered, she said to Kay, that Helena had not "seen fit" to go on with her art at college. "Davy Davison and I," she explained, "would have had no objection at all to Helena's becoming a painter. *After* she had finished her college work. Her teacher here considered that she had unusual promise, a *decided bent*, and so did Mr. Smart at the museum. We had talked of giving her a year or two at the Art Students League in New York and of letting her have a studio in Greenwich Village. But her interests have widened at Vassar, dontcha know." Kay agreed. Mrs. Davison also wondered that Helena had failed to make Phi Beta Kappa. "I said" (Kay reported to Helena), "that only grinds made Phi Beta junior year." "Just as I told Davy Davison!" exclaimed Mrs. Davison. "Girls who have been coached and *crammed*." Mrs. Davison often spoke with detestation of "crammers."

"I am not a college woman myself," Mrs. Davison continued, "and it's a thing I've bitterly regretted. I shall blame Davy Davison for it till they put pennies on my eyes." This remark remained partly cryptic, like many of Mrs. Davison's utterances, in which learned allusions—like this one to Roman burial customs—mingled with obscure personal reminiscence. Kay took her to mean that Mr. Davison had married her (in Mrs. Davison's own parlance) "untimely," which she found hard to imagine because, much as she liked her, she could not imagine Mrs. Davison young. Helena's mother was a tall fat woman with piles of grey hair done in unfashionable puffs on either side of her ears and large, pensive, lustrous dark eyes that seemed misplaced in her big, doughy, plain countenance, which was white and shapeless, like bread punched down and set to rise again in a crock. She was a Canadian, from the province of Saskatchewan, and spoke in somewhat breathy tones.

In point of fact, she had been a country schoolteacher and well along in life, rising thirty, when Mr. Davison had met her, at the home of a metallurgist. If she could not write "B.A." after her name, it had been by her own choice: in the *annus mirabilis* (1901) when the university had opened at Saskatoon —a story she was fond of telling—she had gone to inspect the professors and found she knew more than they did. "Like the Child Jesus in the temple, *toute proportion gardée*," she avowed. Nevertheless, she harbored a mysterious grievance against Mr. Davison for not having been permitted to finish, as she put it, her education. "We'll have to buy Mother an honorary degree for her golden wedding anniversary," Helena's father sometimes remarked.

Both Mr. and Mrs. Davison had an emphatic distaste for show. Mrs. Davison wore no jewelry, except for her wedding and engagement rings and occasional Victorian brooches set with garnets, her birthstone, fastened to the bosom of her coin-print or polka-dot dresses. Helena had a set of moonstones, a cat's-eye brooch, an amethyst pin, and an Add-a-Pearl necklace that had been completed on her eighteenth birthday, when she was presented to society (that is, to the family's old friends) at a small tea given by her mother in their house, which was called "The Cottage" and had a walled garden and English wallflowers.

The Davison house—Kay had told the group—was almost magical, like a house you found in a fairy tale, though it was right in the heart of Cleveland, only two blocks from a streetcar stop but hidden by tall privet hedges and the garden wall. It was small, compact, and silent, with chintz-cushioned window seats and rocking chairs and cupboards and shelves and "dressers" full of fragile, precious things that were used for everyday, like instructive toys you could play with—milk glass, Sandwich glass, Wedgwood, Staffordshire, Lowestoft, Crown Derby. A table seemed almost always to be set, for breakfast, lunch, tea, or dinner, with toast racks, muffin warmers, a Lazy Susan (Kay had never heard the name before, even), muffineers full of powdered sugar, finger bowls in which flowers floated. Yet there were no butlers or footmen darting around to make you nervous for fear of using the wrong utensils. When Helena, who was always the last down, had finished her breakfast, the colored maid would bring in a big china basin with pretty pink roses on it and a pitcher full of hot water, and Mrs. Davison would wash the breakfast cups and saucers at the table (an old pioneer custom, she said) and dry them on an embroidered tea towel. At dinner, after the main course, the maid would bring in a salad bowl of Chinese porcelain, red and green, and an old cruet stand with olive oil, a mustard pot, and vials of different kinds of vinegar, and Mr. Davison, standing up, would make the salad dressing himself and mix the salad, which was always sprinkled with fresh herbs. They did not entertain very often; most of the family friends, Kay said, were rather old, bachelors or widows, and neither Mr. Davison (whose real name was Edward) nor Mrs. Davison was enthusiastic about what they humorously called "followers," though Helena, being an only child, had been given *every opportunity* at her progressive day school to meet boys and girls of her own age. Not to mention dancing school and Sunday school; neither Mr. Davison nor Mrs. Davison was a regular churchgoer (although Mrs. Davison was a sharp judge of a sermon), but they felt it only right that Helena should know the Bible and the beliefs of the principal Christian creeds, so that she could make up her own mind.

After day school, she had gone to a sound boarding school in New England with a well-rounded curriculum but no frills. In the summers, they had taken cottages at Watch Hill, Rhode Island, at Yarmouth in Nova Scotia, and at Biddeford Pool in Maine, and Helena had always had her friends come to visit her there and, after she was eighteen and had had driving lessons, the use of a small Ford runabout, as Mrs. Davison described it, which Mr. Davison had bought for a second car.

For the summer of 1930, after freshman year, they had planned a trip through the Lake District (Mrs. Davison was a great admirer of *Dorothy* Wordsworth), but with business conditions what they were, they had concluded that it was best to stay home, where Mr. Davison could keep an eye on developments. None of the other girls from Vassar was going, as Mrs. Davison had ascertained

This last June, it was Mr. Davison who had suddenly

declared that Helena needed a change. At Commencement, he had thought she looked peaked and had told her mother so. She had better go to Europe and look around for a few months by herself, before going to work at that nursery school, which was dang-fool nonsense anyway. With all Helena's education, she had elected to play the piano and teach Dalcroze and finger painting at an experimental school in Cleveland—to a darned lot of kikes' children, from what Mr. Davison had heard. Where was the sense in that, he had asked Kay angrily at lunch after Commencement, while Mrs. Davison said "Now, Daddy!" and Kay and Helena exchanged looks. "All right, Mother." Mr. Davison had subsided momentarily. Kay suspected that he was angry because Helena had failed to get *magna cum laude*, when a lot of the Jewish girls had. Mrs. Davison evidently had the same thought, because she now cleared her throat and re-marked that the simple *cum laude*, Helena's meed, was the sign of a real student as opposed to what, in *her* day, had been called "a greasy grind." "I *watched* those *magnas* go up for their diplomas," she announced, "and I didn't like the look of them at all; they smelled of the lamp, as I told Davy Davison. The midnight oil, dontcha know." "Oh, Mother!" said Helena and raised her eyebrows in distress. Mr. Davison would not be diverted. "Why should Helena take a job away from some girl who really needs it? Can you tell me that?" he demanded, pushing his fried chicken away. His small round cheeks had turned red. Kay started to answer, but Mrs. Davison inter-vened. "Now, Daddy," she said placidly, "do you mean to assert that a girl in Helena's position doesn't have the same rights as other girls?"

"I mean exactly that," Mr. Davison retorted. "You've hit the nail smack on the head. We pay a price for having money. People in my position"—he turned to Kay—"have 'privilege.' That's what I read in the *Nation* and the *New Republic*." Mrs. Davison nodded. "Good," said Mr. Davison. "Now listen. The fellow who's got privilege gives up some rights or ought to." "I'm not sure I understand," said Kay. "Sure you do," said Mr. Davison. "So do Mother and Helena." "Let's choose another example," said Mrs. Davison thoughtfully. "If Helena, say, were to paint a picture. Would she not have the right to sell it because other artists are impecunious?" "A painting isn't a service, Mother," said Mr. Davison. "Helena's offering a service that a hundred other girls in Cleveland could do as well." At this point, the discussion broke off; the waiter presented the check, which Mr. Davison paid. Helena herself had hardly said a word.

Afterward, Kay declared that Mr. Davison's ideas were surprisingly unfair and that the trip to Europe was a bribe that would corrupt Helena's integrity. She was amazed (and she repeated it today, right to Helena's face) that Helena had gone meekly off to Europe with her tail between her legs and stayed till just before Christmas. And now that she was back she was making no effort to get a job but talking of studying dry point in Cleveland and taking a course in acrobatic dancing at the Y.W.C.A., of all places. Nor was it a question of just marking time till she got married, like some other girls; Helena, Kay said, would never get married—she was a neuter, like a little mule. Therefore it was up to her to realize her potentialities. She and Kay were just the opposite of each other, Kay had been telling Mr. Bergler this afternoon.

"Really?" said Mr. Bergler. "How?" "In college I wanted to be a director," Kay replied. "Come here, Helena," she called loudly. "We're talking about you." Unwillingly, Helena approached; she was wearing a skullcap hat and a black velvet dress, with buttons straight down the front and a little old-lace collar with her cat's-eye brooch. "I was saying I always wanted to be a director," Kay continued. "Well!" said the producer, an unassuming grey-haired Jewish man with white soft skin and flat grey fish eyes. "So that's what you and Hal have in common." Kay nodded. "I directed one of the Hall Plays at college. That's different from DP—Dramatic Production, which Hallie teaches—Hallie Flanagan, have you heard of her? Anyway, the Hall Plays are part of Philaletheis, which is just a student thing. It sounds like stamp collecting. But it means something different—loving the theatre. In DP, Hallie would never let me direct. I worked on the lighting with Lester—Lester Lang, her assistant; you probably haven't heard of him. And I built scenery." "And now?" "I gave it up," said Kay with a sigh. "Now I work at Mr. Macy's, in the training squad. I have the drive but not the talent. That's what Harald said when he saw the Hall Play I directed. It was *The Winter's Tale*—in the Outdoor Theatre. Helena played Autolycus."

The producer turned his eyes to Helena. "That's what I started to say," Kay went on, remembering. "I lost the thread for a minute. I have the drive but not the talent, and Helena has the talents but not the drive." "You're interested in a stage career?" inquired the producer curiously, bending down to Helena. "Oh no," Kay answered for Helena. "Helena's a mime but not an actress. That's what Harald thinks. No. But Helena has so many other talents that she can't choose between them—canalize. She writes and sings and paints and dances and plays I don't know how many instruments. The compleat girl. I was telling Mr. Bergler about your parents, Helena. She has the most remarkable parents. How many magazines does your mother 'take in'? Her mother is a Canadian," she added while Helena stood pondering with a fresh cup of punch in her hand. She was being called upon, she recognized, to perform for Mr. Bergler, and she was going to do it, just as she used to recite or play under her mother's eye, feeling like a conscientious wind-up toy. She had a "searching" anxious little gaze, which she now directed upward at Mr. Bergler from under the reddish eaves of her brows.

"Well," she began, grimacing and drawling her words, "there's the *National Geographic*, *Christian Century*, the *Churchman*, *Theatre Arts Monthly*, the *Stage*, the *Nation*, the *New Republic*, *Scribner's*, *Harper's*, the *Bookman*, the *Forum*, the London *Times Literary Supplement*, the *Economist*, the *Spectator*, *Blackwood's*, *Life and Letters Today*, the *Nineteenth Century and After*, *Punch*, *L'Illustration*, *Connaissance des Arts*, *Antiques*, *Country Life*, *Isis*, the *PMLA*, the *Lancet*, the *American Scholar*, the annual report of the College Boards, *Vanity Fair*, the *American Mercury*, the *New Yorker*, and *Fortune* (those four are for Daddy, but Mother 'glances them over')."

"You're forgetting some," said Kay. Mr. Bergler smiled; he was supposed to be rather a Communist. "The *Atlantic Monthly*, surely," he suggested. Helena shook her head. "No. Mother is having a 'feud' with the *Atlantic Monthly*. She disapproved of something in the Jalna series and canceled her subscription. Mother dearly loves canceling her subscriptions—as a painful duty. Her feud with the *Saturday Review of Literature* has been very hard on her, because of the 'Double-Crostic.' She's thought of resubscribing in our maid's name, but she fears they might recognize the address." "She sounds a most awesome lady," said Mr. Bergler, responding to Helena's faint grin. "Tell me, what does she find objectionable in the *Saturday Review of Literature*? Has sex reared its head there?" "Oh," said Helena. "You misjudge my mother. She's impervious to sex." A publisher's reader who lived in the apartment downstairs had come up to listen; he gave Libby MacAusland's arm a little squeeze. "I love that, don't you?" he said. "Mother's shock area," continued Helena imperturbably, "is confined to the higher brain centers; the 'bump' of grammar and usage is highly developed. She's morally offended by impure English." "Like what?" encouraged Kay. "Dangling modifiers. Improper prepositions. 'Aggravating' to mean 'annoying,' 'demean' to mean 'lower,' 'sinister.'" "'Sinister'?" echoed the publisher's reader. "Mother says it only means left-handed or done with the left hand. If you tell her a person is sinister, all she will infer, she says, is that he's left-handed. A deed, she allows, may be sinister, if it's done sidewise or 'under the robe' or 'on the wrong side of the blanket.'" "I never heard *that*!" cried Pokey, as if indignant. The group around Helena had grown larger and was forming into a circle. "'Infer,' 'imply,'" prompted Libby, eager to be heard. "Ummhum," said Helena. "But that's too commonplace to be under Mother's special protection. 'Meticulous,' which is not a synonym for 'neat.' She sets great store by Latin roots, you notice, but she frowns on the ablative absolute as a construction in English." "Yow!" said Harald's friend, Mr. Sisson, the one who had taken pictures at the wedding. "Oh, and 'I cannot help but feel.'" "What's wrong with that?" asked several voices. "'I cannot help feeling' or 'I cannot but feel.'" "More!" said the publisher's reader. Helena demurred. "I cannot help feeling," she said, "that that is enough of Mother's 'pet peeves.'"

Her mother's habit of stressing and underlining her words had undergone an odd mutation in being transmitted to Helena. Where Mrs. Davison stressed and emphasized, Helena inserted *her* words carefully between inverted commas, so that clauses, phrases, and even proper names, inflected by her light voice, had the sound of being ironical quotations. While everything Mrs. Davison said seemed to carry with it a guarantee of authority, everything Helena said seemed subject to the profoundest doubt. "I saw 'Miss Sandison,'" she had been telling Kay and Dottie, "in the 'British Museum,'" signifying by the lifting of her brows and the rolling about of the names on her slow, dry tongue that "Miss Sandison" was an alias of some wondrous sort and the "British Museum" a front or imposture. This wry changing of pitch had become mechanical with her, like a slide inserted in a trombone. In fact, she had a great respect for her former Shakespeare teacher and for the British Museum. She had had a library card virtually from the time she could walk and was as much at home with the various systems of cataloguing as she was with the Furness *Variorum*. At college she had excelled at the "note topic"—a favorite with Miss Sandison too—and had many wooden boxes full of neatly classified cards on her desk beside the portable typewriter she had got for Christmas junior year—Mrs. Davison had not wished her to take up typing till her handwriting was formed; for a period in Cleveland she had had a calligraphy lesson every other day between her music lesson and her riding lesson and she had learned to cut her own quills from feathers. Nothing, moreover, was more natural than that she should find her teacher, an Elizabethan specialist, in the British Museum, yet Helena had gone on to explain methodically, as though it required accounting for, the circumstances that had brought this about: how Miss Sandison was doing a paper, in her sabbatical leave, on a little-known Elizabethan, "Arthur Gorges," and Helena was looking up an early publication of "Dorothy Richardson" and had stopped to see the "Elgin Marbles." In relating such "true particulars," Helena lowered her voice and gravely puckered her forehead, with a confidential air like her mother's, as though giving privileged news from a sickroom in which lay a common friend.

"A cute kid, that," the producer told Harald, when he was leaving. "Reminds me of the young Hepburn—before they glamorized her. Clubwoman mother there too." Helena found nothing to object to in the last part of this "tribute." "Mother *is* a clubwoman," she pointed out mildly to Kay, who felt that Mrs. Davison had been disparaged. "And I don't like Katharine Hepburn." She wished people would stop making this comparison. Mrs. Davison had been the first to notice a resemblance. "She was a Bryn Mawr girl, Helena. Class of '29. Davy Davison and I saw her with Jane Cowl. She wore her hair short like yours."

Wearily, Helena eyed the bedroom door. She wanted to go home or, rather, to go have dinner with Dottie at the Forty-ninth Street Longchamps, across from the Vassar Club. She knew that when she got back to Cleveland, she would be bound to report to her mother how she had "found" Kay and Harald, what their new apartment was like, and how Harald was making out in his career. "I have always been partial to Kay," Mrs. Davison would state, satisfied, when Helena had finished her narration. It was one of Mrs. Davison's peculiarities, well known to Helena, that, like royalty, she insisted that all news be favorable and reflect a steady advance of human affairs.

It was wonderful news, of course, that Harald's play was going to be produced, yet neither Kay nor Harald seemed very happy. Possibly, as Dottie suggested, success had been too slow in coming. Dottie had heard a painful story: that Harald had been helping a puppeteer who gave shows at vulgar rich people's parties; someone had seen him behind the scenes working the lights in the little portable puppet theatre—he was not allowed to mingle with the guests. Kay had never mentioned this to a soul. Today, she looked strained and tired, and Harald was drinking too much. He was right; the party had not "jelled." The producer and his wife had seemed mystified by so much Vassar; Helena feared Harald's stock had gone down. Kay craved the limelight for the group, but the limelight did not become them. As Harald said, they did not know how to "project." Of all the girls here this afternoon, only Kay, in his and Helena's opinion—they had agreed on this, by the punch bowl—was a genuine beauty. Yet she was losing her vivid coloring, which would distress Mrs. Davison, who admired the "roses" in Kay's cheeks.

The bedroom door opened. The love birds had made it up. Kay was smiling dewily, and Harald's cigarette holder was cocked at a jaunty angle. He had a big bowl of chile con carne, Kay announced, that he had fixed this morning, and everyone was to stay and eat. Afterward, if the guests were agreeable, he was going to read aloud an act from his play. There was no help for it, Helena and Dottie were bound to stay; Kay was counting on them. Harald went out to the kitchen, refilling his punch glass en route; he would not let Kay help him—she was tired, and this was her holiday. "Isn't that touching?" murmured Dottie. Helena was not touched. Harald, she presumed, knew Kay as well as she did, and if there was anything Kay hated, it was being left out; she was a glutton for making herself useful. They heard Harald moving about in the kitchen, the rattle of plates, the creak of drawers opening. Kay could not contain herself. "Can't I make the coffee?" she called out. "No!" Harald's voice retorted. "Entertain your guests." Kay looked around the circle with a defeated, anxious smile. "*I'll* help him," volunteered Dottie as the rattle of crockery continued. "No," said Norine. "I'll do it. I know the kitchen." With a purposeful stride, she went out; the shuttered door trembled as she pulled it shut. "She'll make the coffee too weak," Kay said sadly to Helena. "And she'll want to use paper napkins." "Forget about it," advised Helena.

The radio actor turned to Kay. He was more than a little drunk; the cigarette in his hand wavered. "Give me a light, will you?" Kay looked around; there were no matches; all the little booklets were empty. Putnam silently proffered his burning pipe. As the actor stabbed his cigarette into the bowl, some coals fell on the newly waxed floor. "Oh, dear!" cried Kay, stamping them out. "I'll get some matches from the kitchen." "I'll do it," said Helena.

In the small kitchen, behind the slatted door, she found Norine and Harald locked in an embrace. Her classmate's tall, rangy figure, like that of a big lynx or bobcat, was bent back as Harald kissed her, pressing forward in a sort of feral lunge. The scene reminded Helena, for some reason, of German silent films. Norine's tawny eyes were closed, and an Oriental turban she wore—her own millinery achievement—had come partly unwound. A dish towel was lying on the floor. Their wet mouths drew apart as Helena entered, and their heads turned to look at her. Then they heard Kay call. "Did you find them? Harald, give her the kitchen matches, will you?" Helena saw the box of matches on the stove. Norine and Harald backed away from each other, and she hurriedly dodged between them. "Gangway," she said. She picked up the towel and tossed it to Harald. Then she seized the matches and made for the living room. Her small hand shook with borrowed guilt as she struck the big sulphur match and held it for the actor to take a light from. It went out. She lit another. The room, she noted, was full of the smell of brimstone.

In a few minutes Norine strode in with a tray of plates and a box of paper napkins, and Harald followed with his chile. Everyone ate. The radio actor resumed his critique of *Sheepskin*. "The fall of a just man is precipitous," replied Harald, with a side glance at Helena. He set his plate down with a slight lurch. "Excuse me while I go to the toilet." "The fall of a just man," repeated the actor. "How well Harald puts it. The college president starts at the top, politicians put the skids under him, and he shoots right down to the bottom. It's a bold conception, no doubt, but not an *actor*'s conception." "Wasn't Shakespeare an actor?" suddenly spoke up the naval officer. "What's that got to do with my point?" said the actor. "Well, I mean, *King Lear*," said the officer. "Doesn't he start at the top?" "King Lear," remarked Helena, "was hardly a just man." They heard the closet flush. "And there's relief in *Lear*," said the actor. "Cordelia. Kent. The fool. In Harald's play there's no relief. Harald claims that would be fakery."

"Clara's cake!" cried Kay, as coffee was being served. "Harald! We've got to serve Clara's cake. I promised her. I'm afraid her feelings were hurt when we wouldn't let her pass it with the punch." "When *I* wouldn't let her pass it," corrected Harald with a melancholy air. "Why don't you say what you mean, Kay?" Kay turned to the others. "Wait till you see it. She made it for our party and brought it down from Harlem on a paper lace doily. Clara's a wonderful character. She runs a high-class funeral parlor. Tiger Flowers was buried from it. You ought to hear her description of him 'laying in state.' And I love it when she talks about her competitors. 'Those fly-by-night undertakers are takin' our business away.'" "Get the cake," said Harald. "Your darky imitation is terrible." "*You* imitate her, Harald!" "Get the cake," he repeated. They waited for Kay to come back. They could hear her washing up. The cat seemed to have got Norine's tongue, and "Putnam Blake" was no conversationalist. Dottie passed the coffee again. When it was his turn to be served, he nudged Helena. "Look, real cream!" he said, his peculiar eyes aglow. Helena could see that this excited him more than anything that had happened at the party.

Kay came in with fresh plates and a cake on a doily on a pink glass platter. The frosting was decorated with a maraschino cherry tree and a chocolate hatchet. "Oh, bless her heart!" said Dottie. "Her old black heart," said Harald, eying the cake askance. "Straight from a Harlem bakery," he pronounced. Kay put a hand to her cheek. "Oh, no!" she said. "Clara wouldn't tell me a lie." Harald smiled darkly. "A most villainous cake. 'Let them eat bread.' Don't you agree, my friend?" He turned to the naval officer. "Look at the frosting," said the actor. "It's pure Lavoris."

Tears appeared in Kay's eyes. Defiantly, she began to cut the cake. "Kay loves to be a gull," said Harald. "In the simplicity of her heart, she imagines that old coon happily baking for 'Miss Kay' and 'Mister Man.'" "*I* think it's touching," said Dottie quickly. "And I'll bet it tastes delicious." She accepted a piece and began to eat it. The others followed suit, except for Harald, who shook his head when the platter was passed to him. "Down the incinerator with it!" he declared with a flourish of his coffee spoon. There was a laugh and a silence. It appeared that Harald had been right. "It's like eating frosted absorbent cotton," murmured the actor to Helena. Helena set her plate aside. In Kay's place, she would not have served the cake—from a purely practical motive: so that the maid would not be encouraged to waste her money again. But she did not find Harald's "antic hay" very amusing, all things considered. He had put on the motley, she felt, for her special benefit to tell her that he was a Man of Sorrows. Was he afraid she would give him away, poor devil? Helena would have been glad to reassure him. "I shall listen to no tales, Helena," her mother had always admonished her if she came to report on a playmate. Helena did not "care for" what she had seen, but she assumed the bottle was responsible and felt a certain sympathy for Harald's present discomfort. He was being bad to Kay, she supposed, because if he were amiable, Helena would consider him a whited sepulcher.

Across the room Kay was talking—rather boisterously,

Helena felt—about wedding presents. Helena's pity for her had taken the form of acute embarrassment. Kay was on a stage without knowing it. Three ironic spectators, counting Helena, were watching her and listening. The *strangest* objects, she was saying, were still arriving by parcel post—right in a class with Clara's cake. "Look at these, for instance." She brought out an ugly red glass decanter and six little cordial glasses that had come (she could hardly believe it) from one of her childhood friends in Salt Lake City. "What can we do with them? Send them to the Salvation Army?" "Give them to Clara," said the actor. Nearly everyone laughed. "Down the incinerator with them!" said Harald suddenly.

They were examining the decanter, holding it up to the light, arguing about workmanship and mass production, when they heard the front door close. The pink glass platter with the remains of the cake on it was gone. Harald was gone too. "Where did he disappear to?" said the naval officer. "*I* thought he was in the kitchen," said Norine. Then the doorbell rang. Harald had locked himself out. "Where have you been?" they demanded. "Giving the cake a Viking's funeral. A *beau geste*, was it not?" He saluted the group. "Oh, Harald," said Kay sadly. "That was Clara's cake plate." The actor giggled. With an air of decision, Harald began to collect the little red cordial glasses. "You take the decanter, my friend," he said to the actor. The actor obeyed and followed him, humming the Dead March from *Saul*. "Are they spiffed?" whispered Dottie. Helena nodded. This time Harald left the door open, and the group in the living room could hear a distant crash of glass breaking as the set went down the incinerator in the hall. "Next?" said Harald, returning. "What next, my dear?" Kay tried to laugh. "I'd better stop him," she said to the others, "or he'll make a general holocaust of all our goods and chattels." "Yes, stop him," urged Putnam. "This is serious." "Don't be a wet blanket," said the actor. "Let's make a game of it. Everybody choose his candidate for the incinerator." Kay jumped up. "Harald," she said, coaxing. "Why don't you read us your play instead? You promised." "Ah yes," said Harald. "And it's getting late. And you have to work tomorrow. But you give me an idea." He went into the dinette and took a manuscript in a gray folder from a cupboard.

"Down the incinerator with it!" His tall, lean, sinewy figure paused a moment by the bookcase, then began to skirt the furniture: Norine's voice was heard ordering someone to stop him, and Putnam and the naval officer moved to block his way to the door. The actor leaped for the manuscript, and there was a sound of tearing paper as Harald wrenched it away. Holding it tight to his chest, with his free hand he pushed off his pursuers, like somebody racing for a touchdown. At the door, there was a scuffle, but Harald managed to open it, and it slammed behind him. He did not return. "Oh, well," said Kay. "Could he have thrown *himself* down the incinerator?" whispered Dottie. "No," said the actor. "I thought of that. It's too small for a man's body." For a moment no one spoke.

"But where has he gone, Kay?" said Norine. "He hasn't got an overcoat." "Downstairs probably," replied Kay matter-of-factly. "To have a drink with Russell." This was the publisher's reader. "I guess you'd better go home," Kay continued. "He won't come back till you're all gone. I always used to be scared when he disappeared like that. I thought he was going to throw himself in the river. Then I found out that he went to Russell's. Or over to Norine and Put's." Putnam nodded. "But he can't be there," he said simply. "Because we're here." They were all putting on their coats. "And his manuscript, Kay?" said Dottie, venturing a discreet reminder. "Oh," said Kay. "Don't worry. Bergler has a copy. And Walter Huston has one. And there're three on file with Harald's agent." Kay, reflected Helena for the second time, had always been a "blurter."

In the taxi, Helena and Dottie held a post-mortem. "Were you scared or did you guess?" asked Dottie. "I was scared," said Helena. "Everyone in that room was gulled good and proper." She grinned. "Except Kay," said Dottie. "That's funny," she added after a moment. "Harald must have known Kay knew. That he had other copies, I mean." Helena nodded. "Did he count on her silence?" Dottie wondered, in a voice that still sounded impressed. "And she betrayed him!" "She's not a gangster's moll," said Helena shortly. "Would you have exposed him like that, in her place?" persisted Dottie. "Yes," said Helena.

She was dourly composing a new version of the Class Notes. "Washington's Birthday Report. Yestreen I saw Kay Strong

Petersen's new husband in Norine Schmittlapp Blake's arms. Both were looking well, and Kay is expecting a promotion at Macy's. Later in the evening the guests were treated to a ceremonial manuscript-burning. Kay served Fish House Punch, from an old colonial recipe. Kay and Harald have an elegant apartment in the East Fifties, convenient to the river, where Harald will be able to throw himself when his marriage goes 'on the rocks.' Re this, Anthropology major Dottie Renfrew opines that the little things, like lying, become so important in marriage. If she married a man who was a born liar, she would conform to his tribal custom. How about this, '33? Write me your ideas and let's have a really stimulating discussion."

6

THE morning after Kay's party, Helena was planning to breakfast with her father, who had arrived on the sleeper from Cleveland; they were going to do the silversmiths together for her mother's anniversary present. She was to meet him at the Savoy Plaza, where he kept a bedroom and sitting room for the times when he was in New York on business; they gave him a special rate. Helena herself usually stayed at the Vassar Club in the Hotel New Weston, where her mother sometimes joined her, finding the atmosphere "suitable." Mrs. Davison had the heart of an alumna, and it was a cross to her not to be eligible for the Women's University Club in Cleveland, in which so many of her acquaintances were active and where she often figured as a guest. "I am not a university woman myself," she would begin when invited by the Chair to comment on a lecture that trenched on one of her fields of interest. "I am not a college woman myself," Helena would overhear her telling the Vassar Club secretary or some Class of '10 alumna in the lounge at teatime, laying aside the current issue of the *Vassar Alumnae Magazine* with the confidence of a born speaker. Simply by clearing her throat, her mother could command an audience, of which only Helena was an unwilling constituent. "We are taking out a five-year membership for Helena at the Vassar Club here," Mrs. Davison's measured tones continued, "so that she can always have a place to go, a *pied-à-terre*, like her father's in New York. 'A Room of One's Own,' dontcha know." Her mother's "decisions," especially those pertaining to Helena, were not simply announced, but promulgated. For this very reason, Helena was uncomfortable at the Vassar Club, which had come to seem to her like one of her mother's purlieus, yet she continued to stay there, whenever she was in New York, because, as Mrs. Davison said, it was central, convenient, economical, and she could meet her friends in the lounge.

This morning the phone rang while she was still in the shower. It was not her father; it was Norine, calling from a pay station in a drugstore and declaring that she had to see Helena right away, as soon as Putnam had gone out. He was in the bathroom now, shaving. All Norine wanted from her, plainly, was the assurance that she was not going to tell anybody, but since Norine did not say this on the telephone, Helena could not say, either, that Norine did not have to worry. Instead, she found herself agreeing philosophically to come to Norine's place and canceling her date with her father, who was quite put out; he could not see what was so urgent that it could not wait till afternoon. Helena did not specify; she never lied to her parents. She was unable to see, herself, to come down to brass tacks, why Norine couldn't have met her for tea or a cocktail or lunch tomorrow. But when Helena had proposed this in her driest tones, there had been a silence on the other end of the wire, and then Norine's clipped voice had said dully, "Never mind; forget it. I should have guessed you wouldn't want to see me," which had made Helena deny this and promise to come at once.

She did not look forward to the interview. Her light, mildly aseptic irony was wasted on Norine, who was unaware of irony and humorous vocal shadings; she listened only to the overt content of what was said and drew her own blunt inferences, as she had just now on the telephone. Under normal circumstances, Helena would have been interested to see Norine's apartment, which Kay had described as a "sketch," but right now she would have preferred to meet Norine in more impersonal surroundings—the Vassar Club lounge, for instance. She had no curiosity to hear whatever explanation or extenuation Norine, she supposed, was going to offer her, and it struck her as unjust that she should be haled to Norine's place just because, through no fault of her own, she had witnessed something that was plainly none of her business. It was like the time her father had been haled into court because he had innocently witnessed a traffic accident; when those darned lawyers got through with him, he declared he had no character left.

Norine, at any rate, did not live in some remote part of Greenwich Village, as might have been expected. Her apartment was quite near the New Weston Hotel, on a pretty street a block east of the Lexington Avenue subway stop that had trees and private houses with window boxes, a block just as good as Kay's block, if not somewhat better. This surprised

Helena. She found Norine, dressed in an old pair of ski pants, a sweat shirt, and a man's leather jacket, sitting on the front stoop of a yellow stucco house and anxiously scanning the street; her hand shaded her eyes. "Sister Ann, Sister Ann," Helena, who knew most of the fairy tales in Grimm and Perrault by heart, muttered to herself, "do you see anyone coming?" Putnam's bluish beard, a razored shadow on his white face, had caught her notice the night before. Sighting Helena, in her ocelot coat and bobbing Robin Hood cap with a feather, Norine waved and beckoned. "Put has just gone," she reported. "You can come in." She led Helena through an arched doorway into the ground floor of the house and past the open door of what appeared to be an office. The house, she explained, interrupting herself to call a greeting to someone unseen in the office, belonged to a firm of modern decorators, husband and wife, who had been hit by the depression; they lived on two floors upstairs and rented the garden apartment, which had formerly been a showroom, to Norine and Put; the top floor was rented to a secretary who worked for a law firm in Wall Street and doubled as a paid correspondent in divorce cases—"the Woman Taken in Adultery," Norine appended with a terse laugh.

Norine had a husky, throaty, cigarette voice and talked continuously, emitting a jerky flow of information, like an outboard motor. She had been regarded as "nervous" by the medical staff senior year at college, and her abrupt, elliptical way of speaking, as if through a permanent cloud of cigarette smoke, had been developed at that time. When not leading a parade or working on the college newspaper or the literary magazine, she could be found off campus drinking Coca-Cola or coffee and baying out college songs at a table at Cary's with her cronies, all of whom had deep hoarse voices too. "Here's to Nellie, she's true blue; she's a rounder through and through; she's a drunkard, so they say; wants to go to Heav'n, but she's going the other way." Helena's musically trained ear, unfortunately, could still hear those choruses and the thump of glasses that accompanied them after 3.2 beer was made legal; and she could remember seeing Kay, now and then, sitting with those gruff Huskies and adding her true voice, harmonizing, to their ensemble, putting ashes into her coffee, as they did, to see if it would give them a "lift" and playing a game they had invented of who could think of the worst thing to order: two cold fried eggs with chocolate sauce. Norine's chief interest at college had been journalism; her favorite course had been Miss Lockwood's Contemporary Press; her favorite book had been *The Autobiography of Lincoln Steffens*; her favorite art had been photography, and her favorite painter, Georgia O'Keeffe. Up until senior year, she had been one of the overweight girls, given to Vassar "Devils," a black fudgey mixture that Helena had never so much as tasted, and to trips to the Cider Mill, where doughnuts were served with cider; Helena and *her* friends bicycled to the Silver Swan, because the name reminded them of madrigals, or dined with a faculty member at the Vassar Inn, where they always ordered the same thing: artichokes and mushrooms under glass. But now Norine, like Kay, had grown thin and tense. Her eyes, which were a light golden brown, were habitually narrowed, and her handsome, blowzy face had a plethoric look, as though darkened by clots of thought. She rarely showed her emotions, which appeared to have been burned out by the continual short-circuiting of her attention. All her statements, cursory and abbreviated, had a topical resonance, even when she touched on the intimate; today she made Helena think of the old riddle of the newspaper—black and white and red all over. She spoke absently and with an air of preoccupation, as though conducting a briefing session from memorized notes.

"Your loyalties lie with her; I know it," she threw out over her shoulder as they came into the apartment. The barking of a dog in the garden rerouted the train of her ideas. "There's a bitch in heat upstairs," she said with a jerk of her head, "and we keep Nietzsche chained to prevent miscegenation." Her short, monosyllabic laugh came out like a bark. This laugh, of the type called "mirthless," was only a sort of punctuation mark, Helena decided—an asterisk indicating that Norine's attention had been flagged by one of her own remarks. Norine went on now, like some gruff veterinarian, to narrate the mating history of the dog upstairs, shunting off, via a parenthesis, to the mating history of its owners. Norine's language had roughened since she had been married; it was not clear to Helena whether the poodle or the wife of the landlord was the "bitch upstairs" who was going to have an operation on her

Fallopian tubes. "Both," said Norine shortly. "Margaret's tubes are obstructed. That's why she can't conceive. She's going to have them blown out. Insufflation. *Liza's* tubes are going to be tied up. They do it now instead of spaying. That way, she can still enjoy sex. Have some coffee."

Helena looked around the apartment. It was painted black, so as not to show the dirt, she would have presumed if Norine had been practical. But doubtless the color was a banner or slogan of some kind, as in Putnam's shirt, though a puzzling one to Helena, since black, she had always understood, was the color of reaction, of clerical parties and fascists. The kitchen was part of the living room, and the sink was full of unwashed dishes. Above it was a long shelf with cottage-cheese glasses, jelly glasses, plates, and cans of food, chiefly soups and evaporated milk. French doors tacked with orange theatrical gauze led to the garden. Along one wall, on either side of a white brick fireplace, were bookcases made of orange crates lined with folded black oilcloth and containing pamphlets, small magazines, and thin volumes of poetry. There were few full-size books, except for Marx's *Capital*, Pareto, Spengler, *Ten Days That Shook the World*, *Axel's Castle*, and Lincoln Steffens. Across the room, a big lumpy studio bed was covered with a black velveteen spread and piled with orange oilcloth cushions rudely stitched on a sewing machine and coming apart at the corners. On the black-and-white linoleum floor was a very dirty polar-bear rug. Below the sink stood a dog's dish with some half-eaten food. On the walls were framed reproductions of Georgia O'Keeffe's vulval flowers and of details from murals by Diego Rivera and Orozco and framed Stieglitz photographs of New York City slum scenes. There were two steel lamps with improvised shades made of typewriter paper, a card table, and four collapsible bridge chairs. On the card table were a toaster, a jar of peanut butter, an electric curling iron, and a hand mirror; Norine had evidently begun to curl her fine blond hair and stopped midway through, for the hair on one side of her head was frizzed in a sort of pompadour and on the other hung loose. This sense of an operation begun and suspended midway was the keynote, Helena decided, of the apartment. Someone, probably Norine's husband, had tried to introduce method and order into their housekeeping: beside the icebox, on a screen, was an old-fashioned store calendar with the days crossed off in red pencil; next to the calendar was a penciled chart or graph, with figures, which, Norine explained, was their weekly budget. On a spike driven into the wall by the stove were their grocery slips and other receipts; on the drain-board, a milk bottle was half full of pennies, which Norine said were for postage.

"Put makes us keep a record of every two-cent stamp we buy. He got me a little pocket notebook, like his, for my birth-day, to write down items like subway fares so I can transfer them at night to the budget. We do the accounts every night, before we go to bed. That way, we know where we are every day, and if we spend too much one day, we can economize on the next. All I have to do is look at the graph. Put's very visual. Tonight I'll be short a nickel—the one I used to call you. He'll take me back, step by step, over my day and say, 'Visualize what you did next,' till he can locate that nickel. He's nuts about accuracy." A brief sigh followed this eulogy, which had caused Helena's eyebrows to rise in disapproval; she had been given her own bank account at the age of ten and taught to keep her own check stubs. "Let me supply the nickel," she said, opening her pocketbook. "Why don't you make him give you an allowance?" Norine ignored the question. "Thanks. I'll take a dime if you don't mind. I forgot. I called Harald first to find out where you were staying." The click of the dime on the card table underscored the silence that fell. The two girls looked each other in the eyes. They listened to the dog bark.

"You never liked me at college," Norine said, pouring coffee and offering sugar and evaporated milk. "None of your crowd did." She sank into a bridge chair opposite Helena and inhaled deeply from her cigarette. Knowing Norine and feeling this to be a lead sentence, Helena did not contradict. In reality, she did not "mind" Norine, even now; ever since she had heard about the bookkeeping, she felt a kind of sympathy for the big frowsty girl, who reminded her of a tired lioness caged in this den of an apartment, with that other animal chained in the garden and the flattened polar bear on the linoleum. And at college she and Norine had worked together quite amicably on the literary magazine. "You people were the aesthetes. We were the politicals," Norine continued. "We eyed each other from across the barricades." This description appeared to Helena fantastic; the scholar in her could not allow it to pass. "Isn't that a rather 'sweeping statement,' Norine?" she suggested with a "considering" little frown shirring and ruching her forehead in the style of the Vassar faculty. "Would you call Pokey an aesthete? Or Dottie? Or Priss?" She would have added "Kay" but for an unwillingness to name her casually this morning or to seem to discuss her with Norine. "They didn't count," replied Norine. "The ones who counted were you and Lakey and Libby and Kay." Norine had always been an expert on who "counted" and who did not. "You were Sandison. We were Lockwood," pursued Norine somberly. "You were Morgan. We were Marx." "Oh, pooh!" cried Helena, almost angry. "Who was 'Morgan'?" In her cool character the only passion yet awakened was the passion for truth. "The whole group was for Roosevelt in the college poll! Except Pokey, who forgot to vote." "One less for Hoover, then," remarked Norine. "*Wrong!*" said Helena, grinning. "She was for Norman Thomas. Because he breeds dogs." Norine nodded. "Cocker spaniels," she said. "What a classy reason!" Helena agreed that this was so. "All right," Norine conceded after a thoughtful pause. "Kay was Flanagan, if you want. Priss was Newcomer. Lakey was Rindge. I may have been oversimplifying. Libby was M.A.P. Smith, would you say?" "I guess so," said Helena, yawning slightly and glancing at her watch; this kind of analysis, which had been popular at Vassar, bored her.

"Anyway," Norine said, "your crowd was sterile. Lockwood taught me that. But, God, I used to envy you!" This confession embarrassed Helena. "Dear me, why?" she inquired. "Poise. Social savvy. Looks. Success with men. Proms. Football games. Junior Assemblies. We called you the Ivory Tower group. Aloof from the battle." Helena opened her mouth and closed it; this view of the group was so far from the facts that she could not begin to correct it; she herself, for instance, had no particular looks and had never been to a college football game (Mrs. Davison despised "spectator" sports) or a prom, except at Vassar, where she had had to make do with Priss Hartshorn's brother for a "man." But she was not going to be drawn by Norine into a counter-confession; she supposed, moreover, that if you rolled the whole group into one girl, she would be what Norine said—a rich, assured, beautiful blue-stocking. "You mean Lakey," she said seriously. "She summed up the group. Or what Miss Lockwood would call its 'stereo-type.' But nobody was really like her. We were her satellites. Old Miss Fiske used to say that we 'shone in her reflected light.'" "Lakey had no warmth," asserted Norine. "She was inhuman, like the moon. Do you remember the apples?"

Helena felt herself color, remembering very well the quarrel with Norine over Cézanne's still lifes of apples in the new Museum of Modern Art. "The smoking room of Cushing," she admitted with a grimace. "When was that? Freshman year?" "Sophomore," said Norine. "You and Kay had come to dinner with somebody. And Lakey was there. You two were playing bridge. And Lakey was playing solitaire, as usual, and smoking ivory-tipped cigarettes. It was the first time she ever spoke to me." "Us too," said Helena. "And it was the first time I remember seeing *you*, Norine." "I was a mess," said Norine. "I weighed a hundred and sixty, stripped. All soft blubber. And you stuck your harpoons into me, the three of you." Helena raised her candid eyes from her coffee cup. "The 'spirit of the apples,'" she quoted, "versus 'significant form.'" She could not remember, exactly, what mushy thoughts Norine, sprawled on a sofa, had been expressing about the Cézannes to the smoking room at large, but she could see Lakey now, on whom she and Kay had had a distant crush, look up suddenly from her solitaire as she said coldly and distinctly that the point of the Cézannes was the formal arrangement of shapes. Norine had begun repeating that it was "the *spirit* of the apples" that counted; whereupon Kay, laying down her bridge hand and glancing toward Lakey for approval, had charged in with "sig-nificant form," which she had learned about in Freshman En-glish with Miss Kitchel, who had had them read Clive Bell and Croce and Tolstoy's *What is Art?* "You're denying the spirit of the apples," Norine had insisted, and Helena, laying down *her* bridge hand, had mildly cited T. S. Eliot: "The spirit killeth, and the letter giveth life." With everybody watching, Norine had started to cry, and Lakey, who had no pity for weakness, had called her a "bovine sentimentalist." Norine, yielding the field, had lumbered out of the smoking room, sobbing, and Lakey, uttering the single word "oaf," had gone back to her solitaire. The bridge game had broken up. On the way home to their own dormitory, Helena had said that she thought that three against one had been a bit hard on poor Miss Schmittlapp, but Kay said that Schmittlapp was usually in the majority. "Do you think she'll remember that we came to her rescue?" she demanded, meaning Lakey. "I doubt it," said Helena, having sat next to Miss Eastlake (Davison being just ahead of her in the alphabet) for a full half-term in an art-history course without evoking a sign of notice. But Lakey *had* remembered Kay, when they were on the Daisy Chain together that spring, and talked to her about Clive Bell and Roger Fry, so that you might say, Helena reflected, that the argument with Norine had pointed the way that had led, in the end, to their grouping with Lakey and the others in the South Tower. Helena, who was as immune to social snobbery as she was to the "fond passion," had not felt the charm of the South Tower group to the same extent as Kay, but she had raised no objections to the alliance, even though her teachers and her parents had worried a little, thinking, like Norine, that an "exclusive elite" was a dangerous set to play in, for a girl who had real stuff in her. Mrs. Davison's comment, on first meeting the group, was that she hoped Helena was not going to become a "clothes rack."

"I reacted against Lakey's empty formalism," Norine was saying. "I went up to my room that night and spewed out the window. That was Armageddon for me, though I didn't see it yet. I didn't discover socialism till junior year. All I knew that night was that I believed in something and couldn't express it, while your team believed in nothing but knew how to say it—in other men's words. Of course, I envied you that too. Let me show you something." She rose from her chair, motioning Helena to follow, and flung open a door, disclosing the bedroom. Over the bed, which was made, hung a reproduction of a Cézanne still life of apples. "Well, well, the apples of discord!" remarked Helena in the doorway, striving for a sprightly note; she had stumbled over a dog's bone in the matted fur of the polar bear; her ankle hurt; and she could not imagine what the apples were expected to prove. "Put had them in his college room," Norine said. "He'd made them the basis for his credo too. For him, they stood for a radical simplification." "Ummm," said Helena, glancing about the room, which was clearly Putnam's sphere. It contained steel filing cabinets, a Williams College pennant, an African mask, and a typewriter on a card table. It struck her that Norine's apartment was all too populous with "significant form." Every item in it seemed to be saying something, asserting something, pontificating; Norine and Put were surrounded by articles of belief, down to the last can of evaporated milk and the single, monastic pillow on the double bed. It was different from Kay's apartment, where the furniture was only asking to be admired or talked *about*. But here, in this dogmatic lair, nothing had been admitted that did not make a "relevant statement," though what the polar bear was saying Helena could not make out.

The two girls returned to their seats. Norine lit a fresh cigarette. She stared meditatively at Helena. "Put is impotent," she said. "Oh," said Helena, slowly. "Oh, Norine, I'm sorry." "It's not your fault," said Norine hoarsely. Helena did not know what to say next. She could still smell Put's tobacco and see his pipe in an unemptied ashtray. Despite the fact that she had had no sexual experience, she had a very clear idea of the male member, and she could not help forming a picture of Put's as pale and lifeless, in the coffin of his trousers, a veritable *nature morte*. She was sorry that Norine, to excuse herself for last night, had felt it necessary to make her this confidence; she did not want to be privy to the poor man's private parts. "We got married in June," Norine enlarged. "A couple of weeks after Commencement. I was a raw virgin. I never had a date till I knew Put. So when we went to this hotel, in the Pennsylvania coal fields, I didn't catch on right away. Especially since my mother, who hates sex like all her generation, told me that a gentleman never penetrated his bride on the first night. I thought that for once Mother must be right. We'd neck till we were both pretty excited, and then everything would stop, and he'd turn over and go to sleep." "What were you doing in the coal fields?" inquired Helena, in hopes of a change of subject. "Put had a case he was working on—an organizer who'd been beaten up and jailed. In the daytime, I interviewed the women, the miners' wives. Background stuff. Put said it was very useful. That way, he could write off our whole honeymoon on office expenses. And at night we were both pretty bushed. But when we came back to New York, it was the same thing. We'd neck in our pajamas and then go to sleep." "What possessed him to want to get married?" "He didn't know," said Norine.

"Finally," she continued hoarsely, "I faced the truth. I went to the Public Library. They've got a Viennese woman there in Information—very *gemütlich*. She drew me up a reading list on impotence, a lot of it in German; quite a bibliography. There are different types: organic and functional. Put's is functional. He's got a mother-tie; his mother's a widow. Some men are incapable of erection altogether, and some are incapable except in certain circumstances. Put's capable of full erection, but only with whores and fallen women." She gave her short laugh. "But you didn't find all that out in the library," objected Helena; she had heard her mother declare that it was possible to get a "university education in our great public-library system," but there was a limit to everything. "No," said Norine. "Only the over-all picture. After I'd read up on the subject, Put and I were able to talk. He'd had all his early sex experience with whores and factory girls in Pittsfield, it turned out. They'd pull up their skirts, in an alley or a doorway, and he'd ejaculate, sometimes at the first contact, before he got his penis all the way in. He'd never made love to a good woman and never seen a woman naked. I'm a good woman; that's why he can't make it with me. He feels he's fornicating with his mother. That's what the Freudians think; the Behaviorists would claim that it was a conditioned reflex. But of course he couldn't know any of that ahead of time. It's been an awful blow to him. I excite him but I can't satisfy him. His penis just wilts at the approach to intercourse. Lately, I've been bunking in the living room"—a jerk of her head indicated the couch—"because he has a horror of contact with a good woman's crotch in his sleep. Though we both wore pajamas, he had insomnia. Now at least I can sleep raw." She stretched.

"Have you tried a doctor?" Norine laughed darkly. "Two. Put wouldn't go, so I went. The first one asked me whether I wanted to have children. He was an old-fashioned neurologist that my mother knew about. When I said no, I didn't, he practically booted me out of the office. He told me I should consider myself lucky that my husband *didn't* want intercourse. Sex wasn't necessary for a woman, he said." "Good Heavens!" said Helena. "Yes!" nodded Norine. "The second one was a

G.P. with a few more modern ideas. Put's partner, Bill Nickum, sent me to him. He was pretty much of a Behaviorist. When I explained Put's sexual history, he advised me to buy some black chiffon underwear and long black silk stockings and some cheap perfume. So that Put would associate me with a whore. And to try to get him to take me that way, with all my clothes on, in the afternoon, when he got home from work." "Mercy!" said Helena. "What happened?" "It was almost a success. I went to Bloomingdale's and got the underwear and the stockings." She pulled up her sweat shirt, and Helena had a glimpse of a black chiffon "shimmy" with lace inserts. "Then I thought of that polar-bear rug. My mother had it in storage; it used to belong to my grandmother Schmittlapp, who was a rich old aristocrat. 'Venus in Furs'—Sacher-Masoch. I arranged so that Put would find me on the rug when he got home from the office." Helena smiled and made a noise like a whistle. "Put ejaculated prematurely," said Norine somberly. "Then we had a fight about how much I'd spent at Bloomingdale's. Put's an ascetic about money. That's why he won't consider psycho-analysis, though Bill Nickum thinks he should." Helena's eye-brows arched; she decided not to ask how "Bill Nickum" came to know of Put's "trouble." Instead, she put another question. "Are you *very* broke, Norine?" Norine shook her head. "Put has a trust fund, and my father gives me an allowance. But we put that into household expenses. Put and Bill sink most of their own dough in Common Causes." "'Common causes'?" repeated Helena, mystified. "That's the name of their outfit. Of course, they draw salaries, and the rest of the staff is volunteer. But their mailing and printing costs are pretty staggering. And then we have to entertain labor people and celebrities and rich do-gooders and some of the working press. We use this place as sort of a cross between a salon and a café." Helena looked around her and said nothing.

"Bill says it would take the strain off our marriage if Put could go to a brothel. Or find a taxi-dance girl. Though they're likely to be infected. But he could learn to use a prophylactic kit. Have you ever seen one? It's as simple as brushing your teeth. Put's offered me a divorce, but I don't want that. That's what the older generation would have done. The generation that ran away from everything. My mother and father are divorced. If Put were a drunkard or beat me up, that would be different. But sex isn't the only thing in marriage. Take the average couple. They have intercourse once a week, on Saturday night. Let's say that's five minutes a week, not counting the preliminaries. Five minutes out of 10,080. I figured it out in percentages—less than .05 per cent. Supposing Put were to spend five minutes a week with a whore—the time it takes him to shave? Why should I mind? Especially when I knew it didn't mean anything to him emotionally?" A dismayed expression had come over Helena's face as Norine jerked out these figures; she was fighting off the certainty that she had to go to the toilet. She had traveled all over Europe scoffing at a fear of germs, drinking the water, making use of a Spanish peasant's outhouse or of the simple drain in the floor provided as a urinal by an Italian *osteria*, but she shrank from the thought of Norine's bathroom. The need to relieve her bladder heightened the sense of unreality produced by Norine's statistical calculations and by the steady barking of the dog outside and the drip-drip of water in the sink; she felt she had slipped into eternity. Yet when she finally did ask for the john, it was a long time before she could urinate, though she put paper down on the toilet seat, which Put had left flipped up, like a morbid reminder of himself; in the end, she had to run the water in the basin to prime the pump.

When she returned to the living room, Norine suddenly came to the point. "I guess Harald had become a sort of male potency symbol for me," she said in her uninflected voice, blowing smoke with a careless air, but behind the smoke screen her narrowed topaz eyes were watching Helena as if to measure her reaction. As Norine went on talking, in her rapid-fire, memo-pad style, Helena lit a cigarette herself and settled down to listen critically, taking mental notes and arranging them under headings, just as though she were at a lecture or a meeting.

The reasons, she noted, for Harald's becoming "a male potency symbol" to the deprived Norine were as follows: (A) The Group. Norine had always envied them their "sexual superiority." (B) Kay's role as a neutral, "passing between both camps." *I.e.*, Norine had sat next to Kay senior year in Miss Washburn's Abnormal Psychology and found her "a good scout." (C) Envy of Kay for "having the best of both worlds." *I.e.*, she had lost her virginity and stayed at Harald's place weekends without becoming "*déclassée*." Norine's situation was the obverse. (D) Proximity. Norine had met Kay on the street the day she and Put came back from their honeymoon. They found they were neighbors and the two couples had started playing bridge together in the evenings. (E) Harald was a better bridge player than Put. *Ergo*, Harald had come to figure in Norine's mind as an "erect phallus" just out of her reach, like the Tower group. Which was why Helena had found the two of them kissing in the kitchen and why it did not "mean anything."

Helena wrinkled her forehead. It seemed to her on the contrary that, if you accepted Norine's chain of reasoning, it meant a great deal. If Harald was to be treated as a phallic symbol, instead of as Kay's husband, it made their kisses "meaningful" in just the sense that would appeal to Norine. She had been yielding to the Force of Logic, which poor Kay herself had set in motion.

"If it didn't mean anything, why dwell on it?" said Helena. "To make you understand," replied Norine. "We both know you're intelligent and we don't want you to feel you have to tell Kay." Something in Helena sat up at the sound of those "we"'s, but she puffed at her cigarette nonchalantly. What made them think she would tell Kay? That embrace, in her books, did not amount to a row of pins, so long as things stopped there; Harald, after all, had been drinking, as Norine ought to know for herself.

"I wouldn't want to wreck her marriage," mused Norine. "Then don't," said Helena, in a voice that sounded like her father's. "Forget about Harald. There're other fish in the sea. Don't feel you have to finish something just because you've started it." She grinned candidly at her hostess, believing she had read her psychology.

Norine hesitated. Idly, she picked up the curling iron. "It's not that simple," she threw out. "Harald and I have been lovers quite a while." Helena bit her lip; this was what, underneath, she had been afraid of hearing. She made a grimace. The simple word "lovers" had a terrible and unexpected effect on her.

Put was out all day, Norine went on to explain, and Kay was

out all day too. "It undercuts Harald that she works to support him. He has to assert his masculinity. You saw what happened last night—when he burned his play. That was a sort of immolation rite, to propitiate her; he was making a burnt offering of his seed, the offspring of his mind and balls. . . ." At these words Helena's normal droll self assumed command again. "Oh, Norine!" she protested. "Do come down to brass tacks." "'The Brass Tack,'" Norine said, frowning. "Wasn't that your name for a literary magazine at college?" Helena agreed that it was. Norine flicked on the curling iron. "What is it," she wondered, eying Helena, "that makes you want to puke at the imponderables? Do you mind if I curl my hair?" As the curling iron heated, she continued with her narrative. Harald, it seemed, left alone all day, had started dropping in, afternoons, for a cup of tea or a bottle of beer at Norine's place. Sometimes, he brought a book and read aloud to her; his favorite poet was Robinson Jeffers. "*Roan Stallion*," supplied Helena. Norine nodded. "How did you know?" "I guessed," said Helena. She well remembered the fatal weekend that Harald had read *Roan Stallion* to Kay. "One day," Norine said, "I told him about Put. . . ." "Enough said," dryly remarked Helena. Norine flushed. "My first *affaire*—before Harald—started the same way," she admitted. "It was a man I met in the Public Library, a progressive-school teacher with a wife and six children." She gave an unwilling laugh. "He was curious about the stuff I was reading. We used to sit in Bryant Park, and I told him about Put. He took me to a hotel and deflowered me. But he was afraid his wife would find out." "And Harald?" asked Helena. "Underneath his bravado, I guess he's afraid too. Married men are funny; they all draw a line between the wife and the concubine." She commenced to curl her hair. Soon the smell of singed hair was added to the smell of cigarette smoke, of dog, pipe tobacco, and of a soured dishcloth in the sink. Watching her, Helena granted Norine a certain animal vitality, and "earthiness" that was underscored, as if deliberately, by the dirt and squalor of the apartment. Bedding with her, Helena imagined, must be like rolling in a rich moldy compost of autumn leaves, crackling on the surface, like her voice, and underneath warm and sultry from the chemical processes of decay. It came back to her that Norine had written a famous rubbishy paper for Miss Beckwith's Folk Lore, on Ge, the Earth Mother, and the steamy chthonian cults, that had been turned down by the *Journal of Undergraduate Studies*, on the ground of "fuzzy thinking," a favorite faculty phrase. Helena chuckled inwardly. She felt she could write a fine paper herself this morning, in the manner of Miss Caroline Spurgeon, on the chthonic imagery of Norine's apartment, which, if not exactly a cellar, as Kay insisted on calling it, was black as a coalhole and heated by the furnace of the hostess' unslaked desires, burning like quicklime and giving off, Helena said to herself sharply, a good deal of hot air. Drolly, she considered the "bitch in heat upstairs," surely a totem or familiar, the Fallopian tubes of the landlady (a root system?), the Cerberus in the back yard. "Oh queen of hell," she said to herself, "where does your Corn Mother mourn?" On lower Park Avenue, she discovered, somewhat later in the conversation. Norine's mother lived on alimony from her father, who had remarried; Norine went to dinner with her at Schrafft's every other Wednesday.

"I'm not the first," Norine jerked out now, while the curling iron sizzled. "Harald tells me stuff he doesn't tell Kay. He had a long *affaire* with a show girl he met last fall; she wanted to marry him. She has a rich husband and a house in Connecticut, where he and Kay still go sometimes for weekends. But Harald won't sleep with her any more, though she begs him to. He has a horror of messy relationships. Before he and I went to bed, for instance, we both had to agree that we wouldn't let it affect our marriages."

"Isn't that easier said than done?" demanded Helena. "Not for Harald," said Norine. "He's a very disciplined person. And I'm fond of Put. Sometimes I get a bit jealous of Kay since I know Harald sleeps with her sometimes, though he doesn't talk about it. But I tell myself that every experience is unique; what he does with her can't alter what he does with me. And vice versa. I'm not taking anything away from her. Most married men perform better with their wives if they have a mistress. In other societies, that's taken for granted."

"Still," said Helena, "you'd rather Kay didn't find out. Or Put, I gather. And you must admit, you had a close call last night. What if Kay had marched in, instead of me?" Norine nodded somberly. "Check," she said. Then she laughed. "God!" she confided, "we had another close call the other day. . . ." Helena raised an eyebrow. "Do you want to hear?" said Norine. "All right," said Helena. "It happened right here," said Norine. "One afternoon. About ten days ago. We were fornicating there"—she indicated the couch—"when there was an awful banging on the door and a voice yelled, 'Open up there!'"

Helena shuddered. As she listened to her classmate, her imagination soberly reconstructed the scene, disrobing Norine and Harald and placing them, affrighted in the midst of their 'transports,' on the couch. What could the knocking mean? Harald, it seemed, did not wait to find out; he seized his trousers from the collapsible chair she was now sitting on and raced into the bedroom. Norine sat up and wrapped herself in the couch cover as the banging continued. She was sure it was the police—the Red Squad—after Putnam's files. It sounded as though they would break the door down any minute; they must have heard her and Harald whispering. "Answer it!" hissed Harald from the bedroom. Clutching the black couch cover around her, in her bare feet, Norine opened the door a crack. Two men in plain clothes and a woman burst into the room. "That's her!" cried the strange woman, a middle-aged type, in jewels and a fur coat, pointing to Norine. "Where's my husband?" Before Norine could stop them, the plain-clothes men pushed open the door into the bedroom, where they found Harald buttoning his fly. "Here he is, ma'am!" they yelled. "Partially disrobed. In his undershirt. Trousers unbuttoned." The woman went in to see too. "But that's not my husband," she exclaimed. "I never saw this man before. Who is he?" And she turned angrily to Norine.

At this point in Norine's narrative, Helena laughed. "The secretary upstairs?" she surmised. "How did you guess?" said Norine. Helena had grasped the situation. The plain-clothes men were private detectives, matrimonial specialists, and they had picked the wrong apartment. All the time, the woman's husband was upstairs with "Grace," the secretary, waiting to be caught by his wife and the detectives; it was an "arranged" divorce case. "And of course," Norine continued, "they weren't really supposed to be fornicating—just to have their clothes 'disarrayed.' And they were supposed to open the door right away and let the detectives in quietly; otherwise John makes a stink. He keeps telling Margaret they're running a 'disorderly house.'" "'John' is the landlord?" said Helena. Norine nodded. "Actually, he can't say much, because Margaret caught him with the previous tenant and threw her out. But he's pretty stuffy about Grace sometimes—the profit motive, as usual. He uses the house as a sort of showroom for his decorating clients and he's afraid the address will get in the paper in some divorce case. This time, it was all the stupidity of those detectives; they'd been clearly told to raid the top-floor apartment and instead they came to the ground floor. When we didn't open the door and they could hear us inside, they decided there was some funny business, that the husband was reneging on the deal. So, instead of calling up the lawyer, as they should have done, for instructions, they straight-armed their way in here. The wife didn't know what was up when she found me in the coverlet and her husband, she thought, hiding. She'd been told to expect a blonde (it has to be a blonde), so naturally she assumed I was Grace. Probably she figured her husband had decided to suit the action to the word." She laughed.

Harald had been "magnificent." Very quietly, he had elicited all the facts from the detectives and then given them a tongue-lashing. He had told them they were a pair of stupid goons who had got their training in violence on the New York police force and been "broken" for extortion or sheer witlessness. He dared them to deny it. They ought to have learned that they could not enter a private residence without a policeman and a search warrant, and in Norine's place, he said, he would bring suit against them for housebreaking, which was a felony, and send them and their lady-client to jail. "You were hardly in a position to carry out that threat," commented Helena. "The detectives must have seen that." Norine shook her head, which was now frizzed all around in a pompadour. "They were livid with fear," she declared.

Luckily, she went on, more prosaically, the house had been empty that afternoon, except for Grace and the man with her on the top floor; otherwise, the banging and shouting would have brought everyone running. "Where was Nietzsche, by the way?" inquired Helena. "I should have thought he would have added his voice." Nietzsche had gone to the country for the day with the landlord and his wife; it was Lincoln's Birthday, which was why Grace had the afternoon off; normally she was raided at night, unless John and Margaret had a dinner party. "And Kay?" said Helena. "Kay was working," said Norine. "The stores don't observe Lincoln's Birthday. They cash in on the fact that the other wage slaves get the day off. It's a big white-collar shopping spree. When do you think a forty-eight-hour-week stenographer gets a chance to buy herself a dress? Unless she goes without her lunch? Probably you've never thought." She stared at Helena and lit a cigarette, holding the burning match for a moment, as though to lighten the darkness of Helena's mind.

Helena got up; she was resolved to speak her piece. The careless, cursory tone of "Kay was working" had made her lips tighten. "I'm not a socialist, Norine," she said evenly. "But if I were one, I would try to be a good person. Norman Thomas is a good person, I think." "Norman used to be a minister," put in Norine. "That's his big handicap. He doesn't appeal to the modern worker. They smell the do-gooder in him. He's been helpful to Put, but Put thinks the time has come when he's got to break with him. There's a new group of Congressmen in Washington—Farmer-Laborites and Progressives—that Put feels he can work with more effectively. They're closer to the realities of power. A couple of them are coming this afternoon for drinks; probably we'll go to the Village with them afterward, to a night club—one of them likes to dance. Put and Bill—did he tell you?—want to start a newspaper syndicate and get out of fund-raising, where the Communists have a pretty formidable edge. Now these Congressmen have a lot of small-town newspapers behind them, in the farm states, that are hungry for real, uncensored labor news and the latest on co-operatives and profit sharing. I've asked Harald and Kay too this afternoon, because Harald has his roots in Veblen—" "Norine," interrupted Helena. "I said if I were a socialist, I would try to be a good person." Her voice, though she strove to maintain its careful drawl, began to tremble. Norine, staring, slowly put out her cigarette. "You say your husband can't sleep with you because you're a 'good woman.' I suggest you enlighten him. Tell him what you do with Harald. And about the progressive-school teacher with the wife and six children. That ought to get his pecker up. And have him take a look at this apartment. And at the ring around your neck. If a man slept with you, you'd leave a ring around him. Like your bathtub." Norine sat staring up at her, perfectly impassive. Helena gulped; she had not spoken so fiercely since she was a spunky child and angry with her mother. She hardly recognized some of the language she was using, and her voice was doing curious slides. In her dry constricted throat, a crowd of disconnected sentences seemed to be milling, like a mob she was trying to moderate. "Get some ammonia," she heard herself declare all of a sudden, "and wash out your brush and comb!" She stopped with a gasp, afraid that she might cry from sheer temper, as used to happen with her mother. Swiftly, she walked to the French windows and stood looking out into the garden, endeavoring to frame an apology. Behind her, Norine spoke. "You're right," she said. "Dead right." She picked up the hand mirror and examined her neck. "Thanks for telling me the truth. Nobody ever does."

At these gruff words, Helena jumped. She turned around slowly in her brown lizard pumps. Gratitude was the last thing she had expected from Norine. Helena was no reformer; she had "reacted," as Norine would say, against her mother's measured and stately meliorism and bridled at the very notion of changing people, as much as at the notion of being changed. She did not know, now, what had possessed her to fly off the handle—a defensive loyalty to Kay or to a canon of honesty or simply the desire to show Norine that she could not fool all of the people all of the time. But to find Norine receptive was quite a responsibility to shoulder. "Go on. Tell me more," she was urging. "Tell me what I need to do to change my life." Helena sighed inwardly and sat down opposite Norine at the table, thinking of her appointment with her father and of how much she would rather be looking at old silver than playing the new broom to Norine's life. But she supposed that at least the Congressmen and perhaps Putnam would thank her if she advised her to begin by cleaning up the apartment.

"Well," she said diffidently, "I'd start with a little 'elbow grease.'" Norine looked absently around her. "Scrub the floor, you mean? O.K. Then what?" Despite herself, Helena warmed to the opportunity. "Well then," she proceeded, "I'd get some toilet paper. There isn't any in the bathroom. And some Clorox for the garbage pail and the toilet bowl. And boil out that dishcloth or get a new one." She listened. "I'd unchain the dog and take him for a walk. And while I was at it, I'd change his name." "You don't like Nietzsche?" "No," said Helena, dryly. "I'd call him something like Rover." Norine gave her terse laugh. "I get it," she said appreciatively. "God, Helena, you're wonderful! Go on. Should I give him a bath to christen him?" Helena considered. "Not in this weather. He might catch cold. Take a bath yourself, instead, and wash your hair in the shower." "But I just curled it." "All right, wash it tomorrow. Then get some new clothes and charge them to Putnam. When he makes a fuss over the bill, tear up the budget. And buy some real food—not in cans. If it's only hamburger and fresh vegetables and oranges." Norine nodded. "Fine. But now tell me something more basic."

Helena's green eyes looked around thoughtfully. "I'd paint this room another color." Norine's face was dubious. "Is that what you'd call basic?" she demanded. "Certainly," said Helena. "You don't want people to think you're a fascist, do you?" she added, with guile. "God, you're dead right," said Norine. "I guess I'm too close to these things. I never thought of that. And you can't be too careful. The Communists are completely unscrupulous. One day they're your bedfellow and the next day they're calling you a fascist. They even call Norman a social fascist. O.K. Go ahead." "I'd get rid of that polar bear," said Helena mildly. "It's just a dustcatcher, and it seems to have outlived its usefulness." Norine agreed. "I think Put's allergic to it, anyway. Next?" "I'd take some real books out of the library." "What do you mean, 'real books'?" said Norine, with a wary glance at her shelves. "Literature," retorted Helena. "Jane Austen. George Eliot. Flaubert. Lady Murasaki. Dickens. Shakespeare. Sophocles. Aristophanes. Swift." "But those aren't seminal," said Norine, frowning. "So much the better," said Helena. There was a pause. "Is that all?" said Norine. Helena shook her head. Her eyes met Norine's. "I'd stop seeing Harald," she said.

"Oh," murmured Norine. "Fill up your time some other

way," Helena went on briskly. "Register for a course at Columbia. Or write up what you saw in the coal mines. Get a job,
even a volunteer one. But, Norine, don't see Harald. Not even
socially. Cut it clean." With this plea, her voice had grown
earnest; she resumed in a lighter key. "In your place, I'd get a
divorce or an annulment. But that's something you have to
determine—you and Putnam. It's nothing you should discuss
with anyone else. If you want to stay with him, then I think
you should decide to do without sex. Don't try to have it both
ways. Make up your mind which you want: sex or Putnam.
Lots of women can live without sex and thrive on it. Look at
our teachers at college; they weren't dried up or sour. And lots
of women," she added, "can live without Putnam."

"You're right," said Norine dully. "Yes, of course you're
right. It's a choice I have to make." But her tone was flaccid.
Helena had the feeling that some time back Norine had ceased
to listen to the program she had been outlining or was only
listening mechanically and making noises of assent. "The subject," she concluded, "is no longer fully co-operative." And
despite herself, she was vexed and disappointed. Why should
she care, she asked herself, whether Norine heeded her advice
or not? Except on Kay's account, but it was not only, she admitted, on Kay's account that she minded. She had got carried
away by a vision of a better life for Norine. And now, inflamed
by her own missionary zeal, she did not want to give that vision up. "Whatever choice you make, Norine," she said firmly,
"don't talk about it. That's my principal advice to you. Don't
talk about yourself or Putnam to anyone but a lawyer. Not
even another doctor. If anybody talks to a doctor, it ought to
be Putnam, not you. And as long as you're married to him,
resolve not to mention sex. In any form—animal, vegetable, or
mineral. No Fallopian tubes." "O.K.," said Norine, sighing, as
if this would be the most difficult part.

A weighty silence followed; the dog resumed its barking; the
Elevated rumbled on its trestle. In this Homeric contest, Zeus,
opined Helena, was taking out his golden scales. Norine
coughed and stretched. "You're a precocious kid," she said,
yawning. "But you're still in short pants, emotionally. *Si jeunesse savait . . . !*" She yawned again. "Seriously, I'm grateful
to you for trying to help me. You've told me the truth, accord-

ing to your lights. And you've given me a few damn good ideas. Like having to make a choice between sex and Put. Commit myself one way or the other. Instead of straddling the issue, the way I've been doing. What are you smiling at?" "Your choice of words." Norine gave a brief guffaw. Then she frowned. "That's an example," she said, "of what I'd call the limitations of your approach. You're hipped on forms, while I'm concerned with meanings. Do you mind if I tell you that most of your advice is superficial?" "Such as?" said Helena, nettled. "Cleaning up the apartment," replied Norine. "As if that were primary. Buying toilet paper, buying Clorox, buying a new dress. Notice your stress on bourgeois acquisition. On mere *things*. I ask for bread and you offer me a stone. I grant you we ought to have toilet paper in the bathroom; Put bawled me out for that this morning. But that won't solve the important questions. Poor people don't have toilet paper." "Still," suggested Helena, "I should have thought that one of your aims was to see that they did have toilet paper." Norine shook her head. "You're dodging my point," she said. "Your obsession with appearances. You don't touch on the basic things. The intangibles." "The 'spirit of the apples,'" remarked Helena. "Yes," said Norine. "It seems to me your 'central problem' is rather tangible," Helena drawled. She perceived that Norine did not intend to follow any of her prescriptions, unless perhaps she would change the dog's name to Rover—as a conversation-maker. "No," Norine replied thoughtfully. "There's an underlying spiritual malaise. Put's impotence is a sign of a Promethean loneliness."

Helena picked up her ocelot coat from the studio couch. After her last remark, Norine had sunk into meditation, her chin cupped in her hand, and seemed to have forgotten that Helena was there. "Do you have to go?" she said absently. "If you stick around, I'll give you some lunch." Helena refused. "I have to meet my father." She slipped her coat on. "Well, thanks," said Norine. "Thanks a lot. Drop in this afternoon if you're free." She put out her big hand with its bitten, dirty fingernails. "Harald and Kay will be here, if you want to see them again." Her memory appeared to jog her, and she reddened, meeting Helena's eye. "You don't understand," she said. "Put and I can't just drop them. I have to see Harald socially. He and Put have a lot in common—in their thinking. Probably they mean more to each other than I mean to either of them. And Harald depends on us for intellectual stimulation. I told you—we run sort of a salon. We're being written up this month in *Mademoiselle*. 'Put and Norine Blake, he Williams '31, she Vassar '33, keep open house for the conscience of young America.' With pictures." Her laugh jerked out. Then she frowned and ran a hand through her hair. "That's the element you miss in your analysis. The vital center of my marriage with Put. We've come to stand for something meaningful to other people, and when that happens you're no longer a free agent. From *your* perspective, you can't see that. And that leads you to overemphasize sex." Norine's tone had grown instructive and kindly as she stood looking down on her little visitor. "You won't repeat what I've told you?" she added, on a sudden note of anxiety. "No," said Helena, adjusting her jaunty hat. "But *you* will." Norine followed her to the door. "You're a peach," she declared.

A week later, in Cleveland, Mrs. Davison looked up from yesterday's New York *Times*. She was sitting in her morning room, in the corner she called the ingle, to which she always repaired with the mail after the postman's visit. The *Times* came a day late, but Mrs. Davison did not mind this, since she only read it for "background." The room was done in blue and violet and white chintzes and English furniture; it had a small-paned Tudor bow window of the kind that had made Helena, as a schoolgirl, imagine Sir Walter Raleigh writing on it with a diamond. There was a handsome Queen Anne secretary, with pigeonholes and a secret drawer, where Mrs. Davison tended to her correspondence; her collection of patch boxes held stamps of various denominations, like colored treasures; on a sturdy Jacobean table stood the month's periodicals, arranged in stacks, as in a school library. On the paneled wall above the secretary hung Mrs. Davison's "lares and penates"—faded late-Victorian photographs of the family seat in Somerset, "a plain gentleman's manor" which her ancestor, a clergyman, had left for Canada. The fireplace was tiled in a pretty blue-and-white heraldic pattern, and next to it sat Mrs. Davison in her easy chair, glancing over the newspaper, her porcelain-handled

letter opener in her large polka-dotted lap. "Helena!" she
called in her sonorous windy voice, like the foghorn of a majestic Cunarder. Helena appeared in the doorway. "Harald has
been arrested!" "My stars!" said Helena. "For fighting with
some private detectives, it appears," continued her mother,
rapping on the paper with the letter opener. "He and a man
named Putnam Blake. Do you know who that would be?"

Helena blanched. "Let me see it, Mother!" she implored,
bolting across the room as though to wrench the newspaper
and the awful information it contained from her mother's
custody. Harald and Norine must have been surprised again in
their illicit embraces, and the prospect of submitting to her
mother's cross-examination on the subject made her gold
freckles stand out dark on her cheekbones. Her mother, always
tantalizing, fended her off. "You'll muss it, Helena!" she
chided, slowly folding the paper. In the midst of her concern,
it struck Helena as peculiar that Mrs. Davison did not appear
to be as shocked as she should have been; rather, her attitude
was, if that were possible, one of comfortable and dignified
alarm. "I'll read it out to you," Mrs. Davison said. "Here it is,
on page five. And there's a picture too. These newspaper photographs are so *blurry*." Helena put her small sandy head next
to her mother's large grey one, her cheek grazing the hairnet
that restrained Mrs. Davison's "puffs." "I don't see where you
mean," she said, her eye running apprehensively down the
headlines, which all concerned labor disputes. "There!" said
her mother. "'Guests Walk Out in Waiters' Strike, Two Held.'"
Helena's teeth caught her lip; she gulped down her astonishment and sank onto a footstool, prepared to listen to her
mother's reading. "I don't know, Helena, whether you're
aware that a group of waiters has been striking in some of the
leading New York hotels. Daddy and I have been interested
because of the Savoy Plaza. Daddy's breakfast waiter told him,
only last week—" "Please, Mother," Helena interrupted.
"Let's hear about Harald." Thereupon Mrs. Davison commenced to read, with her customary stresses and pauses:

"The striking waiters at the Hotel Carlton Cavendish received
support last night from an unexpected quarter. A sympathy
strike of guests led by Putnam Blake, publicist, 24, was staged

in the candlelit Rose Room while the band played. The striking guests wore evening dress and included, besides Mr. Blake, who was taken to the East 51st Street station house, Dorothy Parker, Alexander Woollcott, Robert Benchley, and other literary celebrities. The signal for the walkout was a speech by Mr. Blake, urging the seated guests to demonstrate in sympathy with the waiters, whose union was picketing outside the hotel. Service was disrupted for three-quarters of an hour. Mr. Blake was charged with disorderly conduct on a complaint by Frank Hart, assistant manager of the Carlton Cavendish; also held on disorderly conduct charges was Harald Petersen, 27, a playwright. Both men, appearing in night court, were released in temporary bail of $25 each. Mr. Blake told reporters that he and Mr. Petersen intended to prefer charges against Mr. Hart and two house detectives employed by the Carlton Cavendish Corporation, who, he said, had 'roughed them up' and attempted to hold them prisoners in the hotel basement. Mr. Petersen charged that brass knuckles were used. He and his party, Mr. Blake said, were exercising their rights in leaving the Rose Room when they discovered that they were to be served by non-union waiters, and that Mr. Hart and the two detectives had acted to restrain them from leaving peaceably. Mr. Hart stated that the 'group of troublemakers' had ordered drinks and other refreshments and left without paying. Mr. Blake and Mr. Petersen denied this; all their party, they said, which consisted of about thirty persons, scattered at individual tables in the luxurious, newly decorated Rose Room, had left 'adequate compensation' for the beverages they had consumed before embarking on the walkout; they had, however, refrained from tipping. It was possible, Mr. Blake added, that other guests had quitted the dining room without paying, in the confusion that ensued when he and Mr. Petersen were allegedly attacked by a 'flying squad' of non-union waiters and detectives. In night court, Mr. Blake and Mr. Petersen were accompanied by their wives, smartly dressed in evening gowns, and by a group of friends in silk hats and tail coats. Their trial will be held March 23. The 'strikers,' it was said, included a number of Vassar girls. A similar walkout was staged a few weeks ago at the lunch hour in the Hotel Algonquin, led by Heywood Broun, newspaper columnist. On that occasion, no arrests were made."

"My word!" said Helena. "Do you suppose Kay's in the picture? Let's see!" The photograph showed a milling scene in the hotel dining room; a table and some chairs had been overturned. But unfortunately, as Mrs. Davison said, it was blurry. They could not find Kay, but they thought they spotted Harald, pale and shadowy in a dinner jacket, an arm raised aloft as a corps of waiters bore down on him. While her mother searched for Dorothy Parker ("She was convent-bred, Helena; did you know that?"), Helena identified Norine, in the center of the picture, facing the camera, wearing what appeared to be a low white satin evening dress and a jeweled tiara, as though she were in a box at the opera; she had on long white gloves, presumably *glacé* kid, with the hands rolled back over her wrists. A small inset showed Putnam as he was arraigned in night court; it was hard to tell whether the print was smudged or whether he had a black eye; he was dressed in a tail coat, apparently, but his white tie was missing.

Mrs. Davison laid down the paper. "That big photo shows you, Helena," she observed trenchantly, "that the whole affair was *staged*." "Of course it was staged, Mother," retorted Helena impatiently. "That was the point. To get publicity for the waiters' grievances." "It was *engineered*, Helena," said her mother. "They must have tipped off the newspaper to send a camera-man. Yet that Putnam Blake says in his statement that they left 'when they *discovered* that they were to be served by non-union waiters.' Notice the inconsistency." "That's only *pro forma*, Mother. Probably his lawyers advised him to say that. Otherwise, he might be charged with conspiracy or something. It's not meant, really, to fool anybody." "I'm going to call Daddy at the office," said Mrs. Davison. "He may have missed the story. It's just as his breakfast waiter at the Savoy Plaza told him; outside elements have got hold of the waiters and are *manipulating* them. I'm afraid Harald may be in for some very serious trouble. Letting himself be a party to a charade like that. Do you think you should put in a call for Kay?" Helena shook her head. She did not want to talk to Kay with her mother standing by. "Not now," she said. "She'll be at work, Mother." "Well, at least," returned Mrs. Davison, "they didn't put her in the paper. And Petersen is a common name. It's a wonder to me, by the bye, that the *Times* spelled it correctly. We can only hope that Macy's doesn't find out about this; I should hate to have Kay lose her position."

She rose to go to the telephone, which was on a table in the corner. "Run along now," she said, "while I talk to Daddy." Mrs. Davison's communications with Davy Davison, even on the most trivial matters, always took place *in camera*. In a little while, Helena was summoned back. "Daddy knows about it already. He's sent out for today's edition. If it's come yet. And for yesterday's *Tribune* and the yellow press. Daddy wonders whether the New York office could help Harald out of this scrape. Find him a reputable lawyer. Who is this Putnam Blake? I never heard Harald speak of him. Neither has Daddy." She spoke in tones of mild affront; Helena did not remind her that she had not seen Harald for many months. "He went to Williams," she said patiently. "He and another boy run an organization called Common Causes—to help raise money for the 'forgotten man' in labor cases. He's married to Norine Schmittlapp, in our class. She's the one in the tiara and long gloves. She was always leading demonstrations at college." "Exactly," said Mrs. Davison. "I knew it! '*Cherchez la femme*,' I said to Davy Davison. 'You mark my words; you'll find there's a woman behind this.'" Helena was taken aback by her mother's astuteness. "What do you mean, exactly, Mother?" she inquired cautiously.

Mrs. Davison patted her hairnet. "I said to your father that what this fracas reminded me of was the old suffragette demonstrations. Chaining themselves to lampposts, and that young woman, Inez Something Something, Vassar she was too, who rode a white horse down Fifth Avenue to demonstrate for the vote. Dressed to kill. It was all in the papers then, when you were a baby. They were very fond of getting themselves arrested. Your father would never let me take part in those shenanigans. Though there were many fine women— Mrs. McConnaughey and Mrs. Perkin, right here in Cleveland —who were active in the movement." These two friends of Mrs. Davison's, one a Smith woman, the other a Wellesley woman, figured frequently in her conversation and had loomed over Helena's childhood like secular patron saints. Mrs. Davison sighed. "But those suffragette shindigs were all staged too," she added in a more vigorous and cheerful voice, as though mastering her regrets. "With the press invited ahead of time. No, as soon as I saw that article"—she picked up the

Times and tapped it significantly—"I said to myself: 'No man ever planned this.'" "But why?" asked Helena. "No grown-up man," said her mother, "will ever put on a tuxedo unless a woman makes him. No man, whatever his politics, Helena, is going to put on a tuxedo to go out and sympathy-strike, or whatever they call it, unless some artful woman is egging him on. To get her picture in the paper. Don't tell me Harald did this for Putnam Blake's blue eyes. No; she's probably got Putnam Blake and Harald wound round her little finger. That tiara now—probably she wanted to wear that. And those gloves. It's a marvel to me she didn't have an ostrich-feather fan." Helena laughed and patted her mother's plump arm. "Why, you'd think, Helena," Mrs. Davison continued umbrageously but clearly feeling herself to be in "good vein," "she was in the receiving line at some charity ball. I'll wager she bought the whole outfit for the occasion. Or did she find it in her grandmother's trunk?" Helena laughed again; she could not help marveling at her mother's inductive powers. "A publicity hound," said Mrs. Davison, administering a final tap to the paper. "What was her field at college?" "English," said Helena. "She did her main work for Miss Lockwood. Contemporary Press." Mrs. Davison smote her forehead. "Oh, my prophetic soul!" she said, nodding.

IN New York two nights before (the story Mrs. Davison read had been reprinted from the previous day's late edition), Hatton, the Protheros' English butler, in his royal-purple wadded dressing gown of Chinese embroidered silk with *moiré* lapels, had been seated in a wing chair in his bedroom on the top floor of the Prothero town house, reading the *Herald Tribune*, his radio set turned on. He was smoking a pipe, and his feet, in silk socks and red leather slippers, were resting on a footstool. The dressing gown, the slippers, the wing chair, the radio set—all of Hatton's costume and stage properties, except the pipe he was smoking—had been passed on to him by Mr. Prothero, a mature sporty fashion plate of Hatton's age and build. Hatton was somewhat taller, more dignified, and less purple in the face; one of the footmen had overheard the Vassar young ladies, Miss Mary's classmates, declare that the butler looked like Henry James, an American novelist and London diner-out, it seemed, who had moved in the best circles—facts that Hatton himself had unearthed on his day out, in the reference room of the Society Library, not trusting the chauffeur, who exchanged Mrs. Prothero's crime story, picked for her every Friday by the head librarian, to do the job properly. (Mr. Prothero's library, as Hatton observed to the younger footman, was more what you might call a gentleman's library; it contained chiefly sporting books—histories of the thoroughbred, stud and yachting registers, memoirs of turf and field, bound in morocco and calfskin—and some volumes of pornography in dummy cases.)

The newspaper Hatton was conning had been glanced at by Mr. Prothero this morning and turned over to the butler in almost mint condition, like the dressing gown and the slippers, which scarcely showed signs of wear. Hatton, in fact, was a sort of double or slightly enlarged replica version of Mr. Prothero, and he was not displeased by this, feeling himself to be, on the whole, an improvement on his American master: Mr. Prothero's suits showed to better advantage on him because of his greater height; he enjoyed his evening read of the newspaper more than Mr. Prothero did the morning's brief, bloodshot stare at the stock-market pages. When valeting Mr. Prothero, he could not help seeing him sometimes, as he flicked the brush over his shoulders and adjusted the handkerchief in his pocket, as a sort of tailor's dummy in relation to himself—a mere padded form of wire and cloth on which clothes and other accoutrements were tried in rough stitching by a fitter for the "man" who was their real and final destination. Mr. Prothero, you might even say, broke in his shoes for him. He not only succeeded to Mr. Prothero's wardrobe, his chair, newspaper, and radio set, practically as good as new; he "stood in" for Mr. Prothero in household emergencies, such as fire alarms, for Mrs. Prothero, a huge, "delicate" lady, soft as a plump bolster or sofa cushion, had a great fear of fire, and Hatton, trained by her to "smell smoke," often led the family and the footmen and the maids downstairs to safety in the middle of the night, while Mr. Prothero slept. To meet Hatton, like a big wattled purple bird, in the corridors or on the stairways of the tall house late at night (Mrs. Prothero also had a fear of "prowlers") had often confused Miss Mary's house guests, coming back from a ball somewhat the worse for champagne; Hatton was aware of the fact that, seeing him without his livery, they took him for Mr. Prothero, whom they might have met during the evening in an identical dressing gown helping himself from the decanter of whisky in the library. Hatton himself was a total abstainer.

Hatton was not only the "man" but also the "man of the house" and a very responsible character. He had been with the family for years, ever since the girls were small, and though he had once had a secret plan of retiring to England on his savings and marrying a young woman, he had done the distinguished thing of losing all he had in the stock-market crash, four and a half years before. They had sold Hatton out, on the Street, and here too he had outshone Mr. Prothero, who, after a short setback in '29, had gone through the depression getting steadily richer without any effort on his part but because of a patent he had bought from a man someone had introduced to him at the Piping Rock Club after a polo game. This fellow, who had looked like a swindler, had killed himself shortly afterward by diving into an empty swimming pool. But the patent, which controlled one of the processes in making the new synthetics, turned out to be worth a mint. Making money, Mr. Prothero confessed, must be in the blood. He went downtown, now, to an office most weekdays, to provide what he called the window dressing for the firm that administered the patent; they made him a director, though he did not, as he said, understand what the hell they were manufacturing or leasing for manufacture, whichever it was. But he supposed it was his duty, in these times, to put his shoulder to the wheel.

The Prothero family, on both sides (Mrs. Prothero was a Schuyler), was dim-witted and vain of it, as a sign of good breeding; none of them, as far back as they could trace their genealogy, had received a higher education, until Pokey, or Mary, as she was called at home, came along; her younger sister, Phyllis, had been dropped from Chapin, to Mrs. Prothero's relief, in the sophomore year, and after a few months in Miss Hewitt's Classes, had been able to leave school, according to state law, as soon as she turned sixteen. By now, she had had her coming-out party and was ready for marriage at nineteen —just the right age, Mrs. Prothero thought, although she would be sorry to lose her, for she was a lonely woman and enjoyed having Phyllis' companionship on her trips to the hairdresser and the Colony Club, where she could sit in the lounge while Phyllis and her friends swam in the pool. Mrs. Prothero, poor soul, her staff agreed, was a woman of few resources: unlike most ladies, she did not care for shopping; fittings fatigued her, for she did not believe she could stand long, having suffered from milk leg after the births of the girls; matinees made her cry (there were so many sad plays nowadays), and she had never been able to learn the bidding for contract bridge. She took no interest in interior decoration, the way so many ladies were doing; the furniture, carpets, and pictures in the main rooms of the house had scarcely changed since Hatton had been there. The servants, except for the younger footman and Annette, the girls' maid, had not changed either. Mrs. Prothero had a pale, dusty tannish skin—the color of the upholstery and stair carpets; the paintings in the drawing room were of white and brown ruminants, cows and sheep, sitting in dark-brown fields. Hatton approved of the paintings, which he understood to be Dutch and valuable, and of the subdued brownish tone of the furnishings, but the women servants said that the place needed livening up. The trouble was that you could not get either Mrs. Prothero or the girls to take any notice. Recently, Forbes, the girls' nursery governess, who now looked after the linen and the heavy mending, had taught Mrs. Prothero to do petit point, which, as Forbes said, was like having a bit of company in the house, what with Miss Mary away at Cornell, studying to be a vet and never bringing her friends to stay any more, weekends, the way she had at Vassar, and Mr. Prothero at the office, and Miss Phyllis, who had been such a mainstay, off with girls of her own set to lunches and teas and fashion shows.

The Protheros entertained, but only at dinner; Mrs. Prothero was not equal to leading the talk at luncheon. Mr. Prothero always took his lunch at the Brook or the Racquet or the Knickerbocker, and the girls were told to have their friends to lunch at the Club, to save making extra work for Hatton. That was the Madam's way of putting it, but Hatton had never shirked work, as she ought to know. It was Hatton who planned Mrs. Prothero's dinners, bringing her the menus and a diagram of the seating arrangements, before writing out the place cards; the conundrum of seating eight or sixteen had never been unriddled by Mrs. Prothero, who always looked up at Hatton with faint surprised alarm when she found another lady opposite her, where she was used to seeing Mr. Prothero, at the other end of the long table. Mrs. Prothero's life was too inactive to warrant her having a social secretary, except during the two seasons when the girls were coming out. Hatton managed her invitations and her acceptances, told her who was coming to dinner and whom she was going to. He directed her contributions to charity and sometimes, on a night when they were entertaining, was able to suggest a topic for conversation.

Needless to say, he was also in the habit of giving the girls a hand. "Hatton, you're a genius!" Miss Mary and Miss Phyllis were always shrieking when they did a list or seated a table in consultation with him. "Infallible social sense," Mr. Prothero often muttered, of the butler, with a wink and a peculiar movement of the cheek muscle that gave him a paralyzed appearance. The girls had more confidence too in Hatton's judgment in matters of dress than they had in Annette's or Forbes's; they would come up to his room in their ball gowns, twirl around before him, and ask whether they should wear the pearls or the Madam's diamonds or carry a scarf or a fan. It had been Hatton, in alliance with Forbes, who had seen to it that Miss Phyllis was made to wear a patch over one eye, as well as keep the braces on her teeth; if Hatton had not backed up Forbes, poor Miss Phyllis would be, as Forbes said, a regular Ben Turpin today.

The whole family adored Hatton. "We all adore Hatton," Miss Mary would announce in a vigorous whisper, shielding her pursed mouth with one hand, to a young man who was seeing her home, for the first time, from a tea dance or a young lady who was coming, for the first time, to stay; the butler's trained features would remain impassive as he led the way up the stairs, though the pretense of not hearing would have tried an inferior servant, since both the young ladies were not only blind as moles but had loud, flat, unaware voices like the voices of deaf people, so that even when they whispered everyone turned around to look at them and listen to what they were saying. They had inherited this trait, another sign of blue blood, from their grandmother on their father's side.

Hatton, though he took no notice, partly from habit, was not displeased that the young ladies made it a point that nobody who stayed in the house or came to dinner should fail to appreciate him. The slow ceremoniousness of his manners, his strict austere bearing ought to have spoken for themselves, but it was a convention, he understood, among the better class of Americans, to pretend that the service was invisible, which was *their* little way of showing that they were used to being waited on. This offended Hatton's professional pride and had caused him to leave his last place. With the Prothero family, being more of the old school, his exceptional endowment and qualifications were brought into the limelight, and the more unobtrusive he made himself, the more all heads turned surreptitiously to watch his deportment as he entered or left a room. He had only to close a door, noiselessly, or retire into the pantry to know that the family and its guests were discussing him. To be aware of Hatton was a proof of intimacy with the family—a boast, you might say, particularly among the young people. "Hatton's a wonder," the tall young gentlemen who were going on to a

dance in white ties and tails would confide to each other, profoundly, over the coffee and the brandy when the young ladies
had left the dining room. "Hatton's a wonder, sir," they would
say to Mr. Prothero, at the head of the table. Hatton did not have
to be psychic (which Miss Mary liked to let on he was) to surmise, from a glance through the pantry door, the trend of the
conversation. The Vassar young ladies upstairs not all being
used to society, the footman who served the Benedictine and the
crème de menthe sometimes came down with a tale to tell, but
with the young gentlemen over the brandy it was always the same.

"Like one of the family," Mr. Prothero would reply. "Kind
of an institution, Hatton is. Famous." Hatton was not sure
that he cared to be described as "like one of the family"; he
had always maintained his distance, even when the young ladies were toddlers. But he did feel himself to be an institution
in the household and was used to being looked up to, like a
portrait statue raised on a tall shaft in a London square. With
this end in mind, he had perfected an absolute immobility of
expression, which was one of his chief points, he knew, as a
monument and invariably drawn to the attention of visitors.
The signals directing attention to his frozen, sculptured face
on the part of the young ladies and their friends Hatton was
perfectly familiar with and accepted as a form of compliment
while not, even inwardly, moving a muscle. When asked about
the family he had served so long and with such apparent sup-
pression of self ("Hatton is *devoted* to us," Mrs. Prothero declared, in one of her rare positive assertions of any kind), he
would answer, with reserve, that it was "a good place." Miss
Phyllis, when she was younger, used to pester him to say he
liked her, being the ugly duckling, not that the rest were swans,
but all Hatton would answer was simply, "It's a good place,
miss." The same with the master when he was half-seas over
and Hatton was guiding him to bed: "You like us, eh, eh,
Hatton? After all these years, eh?" Forbes, a stout party from
Glasgow who had been with the family ever since Miss Mary
was born, sometimes reminded Hatton that there were better
places: a first-class butler, she said, was not supposed to act as a
social secretary and valet, besides being a Holmes Protective
man and a human fire-alarm system (this was Forbes's joke).
"Beggars can't be choosers," Hatton, who was fond of a

proverb, coldly retorted, but he really meant the opposite: a
butler of his capacities could choose to take on extra duties
without prejudicing his legend. He was the bigger man for it.
Hatton, through doing crossword puzzles, was familiar with
the principal myths, and his mind sometimes vaguely dwelt on
the story of Apollo serving King Admetus, not that he would
place Mr. Prothero so high. Yet the comparison occasionally
flashed through his head when he was waiting on table, throwing a spacious aureole or nimbus around him as he moved
from one chair to the next, murmuring "Sherry, madam?" or
"Champagne, miss?" Miss Mary, he felt, was aware of the
nimbus, for he would find her nearsighted eyes frowningly focused on him, as if observing something unusual, and her
nostrils sniffing, a sign of aroused attention she had probably
picked from the Madam; the poor young lady herself had no
sense of smell. Miss Mary swore by telepathy; she had a sixth
sense, she insisted, to make up for the missing one. She had
decided that Hatton had too. "Are your ears burning, Hatton?" she often asked him when he came to answer the bell in
a room where she and her friends were playing one of those
mind-reading games, with cards, she had learned at Vassar. He
explained to her that it was the job of a good servant to read
his master's mind and anticipate his wishes; for him, he added
reprovingly, it was all in the day's work, no fun and games
about it. "How did you become a butler, Hatton?" she sometimes asked, seating herself on his bed. "Yes, how did you,
Hatton?" said Miss Phyllis, occupying his footstool. But Hatton declined to answer. "That is my private affair, miss." "*I*
think," said Miss Mary, "you decided to become a butler because you were psychic. Natural selection." This was over
Hatton's head, but he did not allow the fact to be seen. Miss
Mary turned to Miss Phyllis. "It proves my point, Phyl. Don't
you get it? Darwin. The survival of the fittest." Her loud peremptory voice resounded through the servants' quarters. "If
Hatton wasn't psychic he'd be a flop as a butler. *Ergo*, he is
psychic. Q.E.D." She scratched her head and beamed victori-
ously at Hatton. "Pretty smart, eh wot?" "Very smart, miss,"
Hatton agreed, wondering if this was the Darwin who had
discovered the missing link. "Girrls!" came Forbes's voice from
below. "Come down and get into your baths."

The fact was, Hatton had become a butler because his father had been in service. But he too had come to feel that there was something more to it than this; like Miss Mary said, he had had a vocation or a higher call that had bade him assume the office. This conviction had slowly overtaken him in America, where genuine English butlers did not grow on trees. "You're the real article, Hatton!" a gentleman who had come to stay in the Long Island house had said to him one morning with an air of surprise. He was like a stage butler or a butler you saw on the films, the gentleman doubtless meant to imply. Hatton had been pleased to hear it; being somewhat younger then and on his own, so to speak, in a foreign country, he had tried to conform to an ideal of the English butler as he found it in films and in crime stories and in the funny papers that Cook read, for the wise man knew how to turn the smallest occasion to profit. Yet he now felt that study alone could not have done it. When the young ladies told him he was a genius, he believed they had hit on the truth: "out of the mouths of babes." He had long accepted the fact that he was the brains of the family and the heavy obligation that went with it. The eternal model of the English butler, which he kept before his eyes, even in his moments of relaxation and on his day off, required that he have the attributes of omniscience and ubiquity, like they taught you in the catechism: "Where is God?" "God is everywhere." Hatton was Church of England, and did not mean to blaspheme, but he could not help noticing those little correspondences, as when he had observed, in his earlier situation, that he was expected to be invisible too.

Folding the newspaper, Hatton sighed. One of the duties or accomplishments of the classic English butler, of which he personally was the avatar, was to be well informed on matters that would not at first glance seem to be relevant to the job in hand and also to be a past master of proper names. That was why, at present, he was reading the *Herald Tribune*, on behalf of the family, having already had a hasty look at Cook's tabloid for the murders, and why he had started with the society columns and the sporting pages, to have a go at them while his mind was fresh. Hatton was not a sporting man, except for the races and, back home, the cricket, but duty obliged him to take cognizance of the proper names and lineage of dogs, cats, boats, horses, polo players, golfers, as they appeared in the news, together with all sorts of figures and ratings, since it was these names and figures that were most commonly wanted in the Prothero household. Then there were the society columns, for the Madam and the girls. When a young gentleman got married, it was Hatton who struck his name off Miss Mary's list, and when a young lady announced her engagement, it was Hatton who reminded Miss Mary or Miss Phyllis to buy a wedding present—a thing Miss Mary often neglected or sent Annette to do.

Selecting a green pencil, Hatton made a small check on the society page; this meant: present, Miss Phyllis; a red-pencil check meant: present, Miss Mary. With a new sigh, this time of content, he folded the paper to the obituary page—one of his favorite sections. Yet even here the voice of duty intruded, though not, he saw at a glance, this evening: he would not have to warn Yvonne, Mrs. Prothero's personal maid, to look over her mistress' blacks, nor get Mr. Prothero ready to be a pallbearer. He settled down to the obits. Next, he turned to the stock-market pages, which no longer interested him much personally; he had not had a flyer since the fall of '29; but he kept abreast of the market in order to follow the conversation at the dinner table when the senior Protheros were entertaining and the ladies had left the room. In the back of his mind, there was always the thought of picking up a tip from one of the older gentlemen, but he had not yet refound the courage to call his broker with an order.

Relighting his pipe, he studied the entertainment news, to make sure the film he planned to see on his day out was still playing. He read Percy Hammond's review of the play that had opened the night before. Hatton had never been to a proper theatre, only to music hall, but he took an interest in the stage partly because he understood that it was customary to begin a play with a scene between a butler and a parlormaid with a feather duster. He would have given something to see that. Miss Mary's friend, Miss Katherine from Vassar, had promised to get him tickets some time on his night out, but that was the last he had heard of it. She was the one who had married the actor or whatever he was, something connected with the stage; Miss Mary had gone to the wedding. Hatton had never been partial to Miss Katherine; he did not see eye to eye with Forbes, who called her "the bonny lass." Forbes would have changed her tune if she had seen what he had, coming downstairs one night, still tying his dressing-gown sash in his hurry and his bridgework not in, because the Madam had "heard a noise, Hatton. Please go and see." For once, the Madam was right: there the two of them were, in the front hall, on the landing, the "bonny lass" and her "fiancé," going right at it. Hatton had not liked the look of him at dinner. "Harald Petersen," he was called, like some blasted Viking; Hatton had taken special notice of the spelling as he made out the place card. When Miss Katherine was going to get married, Miss Mary, Hatton recalled, had consulted him as to whether it would be possible for the young lady to have the use of the town house for the wedding, since the rest of the family, except Mr. Prothero, would already have gone down to the country. Bearing in mind what he had seen ("Just a bit of kissing," Forbes said; did you do that on the floor with your skirts up and the "fiancé" planted on top of you for anybody from the street to see?), not to speak of the tickets, Hatton had said no, the furniture would be in dust covers, and it would upset the master, if he was staying in town that night, to find strangers in the house. "You're a treasure, Hatton!" Miss Mary had proclaimed. Hatton had not been surprised to read in the paper this last summer that the play Mr. Petersen was with had closed, despite Miss Katherine's telling them that it was going to run for years and years; since then, he had not seen the name in the theatrical columns, though he had observed in the real-estate notices that a Mr. and Mrs. Harold Peterson (sic) had taken an apartment in the East Fifties, near Sutton Place. That was them, said Miss Mary, who had been there only the other day. She had not had them to the house, though, since she had been up there at agricultural college; when she gave a dinner party nowadays, it was more for her own sort; she would just phone down to Hatton to have twelve covers and make up the list himself and to be sure and see to it that Miss Phyllis was not home for dinner that night. But if Miss Katherine and Mr. Petersen *were* ever asked again, Hatton had made a mental note to address her as "madam" when he opened the door. "Good evening, madam" (not "miss"), and a small, discreet smile; it was those little touches that counted. "He called me 'madam'; isn't that perfect?" Miss Katherine would whisper to her husband. "Hatton called me 'madam,' Pokey; what do you know?"

Hatton turned to the front page, which he had saved for the last; he liked the sense of exercising his intellect which the world and general news gave him. A labor dispute had been occupying a small part of the front page for over a week; the waiters of the principal hotels were on strike. Hatton made it a point to take no sides in American politics; he believed that it was against the law for an alien to interfere in the domestic affairs of a foreign country and consequently refrained from having any thoughts on the subject. "Who would *you* vote for, Hatton?" Miss Katherine had asked him at the time of the last election, when she was staying in the house. "I am not an American citizen, miss," Hatton had replied. Nevertheless, the waiters' strike had enlisted his sympathies, to a certain degree, for they were his fellow-creatures, even if there was a gulf, a very wide gulf, between private service and what you might call common service. For a brief time, while he was getting his training, he had worked at a hotel in London. Hence, he had been following the strike news, and he knew from Cook's *Daily Mirror* that something had happened last night at the Cavendish—another demonstration.

Now his grey eyes imperturbably widened; he shook the newspaper on his lap. When he had finished reading the item and turned to page five for the continuation, he refolded the paper back to page one, selected a blue pencil from his table and slowly drew a border around the story. His hands trembled slightly with suppressed excitement. Then he refolded the paper still again, into a shape that would fit onto a salver, which he would present to Mrs. Prothero at breakfast: "Beg pardon, madam; I thought this would interest Miss Mary." He then mentally withdrew to the sideboard or, better, to the serving pantry, within earshot.

"Hatton!" he heard the mistress' voice call in agitation the next morning, and he slowly re-entered the dining room. "What *is* this? Why have you brought me this?" Mrs. Prothero quivered through all her shapeless, cushiony form. "Excuse the liberty, madam, but I ventured to think that one of the gentlemen referred to was Miss Katherine's husband." He bent forward and indicated to his mistress with his pink, manicured forefinger the name of Harald Petersen (spelled "Harold Petersen"). "Miss Katherine?" demanded Mrs. Prothero. "Who is she? How do we know her, Hatton?" She turned her head away from the group photograph on page five he was attempting to show her. "The young lady who came to stay, madam, over the Christmas holidays and on one or two other occasions when Miss Mary was in school at Vassar." He paused, waiting for Mrs. Prothero's otiose memory to begin to work. But Mrs. Prothero shook her head, a mass of pale-brown, lusterless, trembling ringlets that, despite all Yvonne's and the hairdresser's labors, resembled a costumer's wig. "Who were her people?" "We never knew, madam," Hatton replied solemnly. "'Strong,' she was called. From one of the western states." "Not Eastlake?" queried Mrs. Prothero, with a momentary, uncertain brightening. "Oh no, madam. We *know* Miss Elinor. But this other young lady was dark too, and pretty, in a natural sort of way. Forbes, if you remember, took a fancy to her. 'A Highland rose,' she used to say." He imitated Forbes's burr. Mrs. Prothero gave a faint cry. "Oh, dear, yes," she said. "I remember. *Very* pretty, Hatton. But rather uncouth. Or was that the person she married? What was it she always called him?" "'My fiancé'?" supplied Hatton, with a smile in abeyance. "That's it exactly!" cried Mrs. Prothero. "Still, we oughtn't to laugh at her. Mr. Prothero used to recite a poem when she stayed here. 'Maud Muller, on a summer's day . . .' And then something about the hay. Oh dear, how did it go? Help me, Hatton." But Hatton for once was caught napping. "I've got it!" Mrs. Prothero exclaimed. "'Stood listening while a pleased surprise/Gleamed in her long-lashed hazel eyes.' Tennyson, I suppose." "I daresay, madam," replied Hatton austerely. "But we never knew who she was," Mrs. Prothero reminisced, sighing. "Mr. Prothero often used to ask me, 'Who's that girl who's always staying here? The Maud Muller girl.' And I was never able to tell him. Her people were early settlers out West, I believe she said." She put on her glasses and peered again at the folded rectangle of newspaper. "And now, Hatton, you tell me she's in jail. What has she done?

Shoplifting, I expect." "I believe," Hatton intervened, "that it's her husband who was in custody. Something to do with a labor dispute." Mrs. Prothero waved a pale plump hand. "Don't tell me any more, Hatton. And I beg you not to bring it to Mr. Prothero's attention. We had the man to dinner. I remember it distinctly." She reflected, her pale, dim eyes turning anxiously behind her gold-rimmed spectacles. "The best thing, I think, Hatton, would be for you to take that article out to the kitchen and burn it in the stove. Without saying anything to Cook, if you please. People in our position can't afford, Hatton—" She looked up at the butler expectantly, for him to finish her thought. "Quite, madam," he agreed, picking up the folded paper and replacing it on the salver. "'People who live in glass houses,' Hatton . . . How does it go? Oh, dear, no, I mean another one. 'Should be above reproach.' Shakespeare, isn't it? *Julius Caesar.*" She smiled. "We are being quite highbrow this morning," she went on. "Quite the intellectuals. We must blame Vassar for that, mustn't we, Hatton? Though you've always been quite a thinker." Hatton bowed in acknowledgment and retired a few steps. "Now mind you burn it, Hatton. With your own hands," his mistress cautioned.

When the butler had left the room, Mrs. Prothero gave way; she leaned on a podgy milk-blue elbow and let the tears rise to her eyes. Hatton watched her through the porthole in the pantry door. He knew what the Madam was thinking. She was thinking how brave she had been in the butler's presence, not letting him see how upset she was by that nasty story in the newspaper. Disgraceful. And of how she blamed everyone, starting with the Chapin School, for contriving to send Miss Mary to that college that was always getting in the paper—not that the others were any better, but you heard less about them. Everyone she trusted, starting with the Chapin School, had turned against her on the college issue: the schoolmistress, what was her name, who had helped Miss Mary fill out her own application forms; Forbes, who had lent her the price of the registration fee out of her savings; the Hartshorn girl, who had smuggled her out of the house three days running, it seemed, to take the college entrance exams; and Hatton, Hatton himself, who had got round her and her husband, when Miss Mary was accepted, by announcing that he did not believe a year or two of college would do the young lady any harm. It was like a case in Bar Harbor she had heard about only the other day at the Colony Club. She had told Hatton about it, just to show him that she had not forgotten. An elopement, *that* was, out a French window of one of the big houses and through a parting in the hedge. The staff, as usual, there too (Yes, she had said "as usual" straight out to Hatton) had gone against the family's wishes; the butler had actually crept out at night with a pair of garden shears and cut a hole through the hedge. What if the couple *were* married immediately, by a minister who was waiting in the rectory, so they said? He was only another accomplice. As for her own staff, she had always suspected that someone—Forbes or, more likely, Hatton—had signed her name to the Vassar application forms; Miss Mary swore she had done it herself and was brash as paint about it, but Mrs. Prothero still felt that Hatton had guided her hand.

Hatton turned away from the porthole; the Madam's sobs were becoming audible, and he went to ring for Yvonne. When she reached that point, the Madam was quite unreasonable. She was very much mistaken in thinking, as she still did, that he had forged her signature. They had kept their secret from him too; he had known nothing about the whole affair until it was over, and Miss Mary had been accepted. At the present time, he rather shared the Madam's views on higher education, though the Madam was not consistent: why give Miss Mary a plane if you did not want her to fly up every week now to learn to be a horse doctor? But Miss Mary always had her way, except with him.

He compressed his lips and went to take another peek at Mrs. Prothero. He was sorry now he had showed her the newspaper story, for what she did not know would not hurt her, poor lady. It had been an excess of zeal that had prompted it, he recognized—a certain over-perfectionism, if that was the term, in the performance of his role. "Hatton," he said to himself, "pride goeth before a fall." In the dining room, Mrs. Prothero would be reflecting that, thanks to higher education, she had had a jailbird in the house.

"A jailbird!" she repeated indignantly, with a wobble of her receding chin, so loud that Yvonne, coming down the stairs, could hear her. Clutching her wrapper around her and holding

Yvonne's arm, she retired upstairs to her bedroom and canceled the car, which was to take her to the hairdresser at eleven. Meanwhile Hatton, who had already told the chauffeur that he would not be needed, was cutting out the newspaper clipping and preparing to paste it in his scrapbook.

In Boston, the next morning, Mrs. Renfrew met Dottie for lunch at the Ritz. They were lunching early in order to go to Bird's for the wedding invitations and announcements; later in the afternoon, they had an appointment at Crawford Hollidge for a fitting. Dottie's wedding dress and going-away costume were being made in New York, but on most items, country suits and simple sport things above all, you could do just as well in Boston and at half the price. After Crawford Hollidge, if there was time, they were going to stop at Stearns' to look at linen and compare prices with Filene's. The Renfrews were not rich, only quite comfortably off, and Mrs. Renfrew economized wherever she could; she felt it was poor taste, in these times, to splurge when others were doing without. They had had the dressmaker in to see if Mrs. Renfrew's wedding gown, which *she* had got from *her* mother, could possibly be made over for Dottie, who was dying to wear it, but there was not enough material in the seams; Dottie, they discovered (and there was progress for you!), was nearly four inches wider in the waist, bust, and hips, though not at all "hippy" or "busty"; it was a question of larger bones. Mrs. Renfrew's mind this morning was full of measurements—sheet and glove and dress sizes; she was thinking too of the bridesmaids' presents. Silver compacts from Shreve Crump? Tiny sterling cigarette lighters? There would only be the three: Polly Andrews, of course, and Helena Davison, and Dottie's cousin, Vassar '31, from Dedham, who was going to be matron of honor. Since the groom was a widower, both Dottie and Mrs. Renfrew felt it was better for the wedding to be quiet, just the matron of honor and the two attendants behind her. Dottie had been pining to have Lakey, but Lakey had written, from lovely Avila, that she could not come back this year. In her letter she said that she was sending a little Spanish primitive of a Madonna (perfect for the Southwest) and that Dottie should have no trouble clearing it through the Customs House, as an antique. Mrs. Renfrew hoped that Sam, Dottie's father, whose firm had been clearing Customs since the days of sailing ships, would see to that for them; there was such a great deal to do.

On her way here to meet Dottie, who had gone to Dr. Perry for a check-up, Mrs. Renfrew had stopped at the Chilton Club to have a manicure and leafed through the day's New York papers in the library, in case she saw anything in the ads for Dottie that could be ordered by mail. Her eye was caught by a photo of some young people in evening dress on one of the inner pages, next to a Peck & Peck ad. She turned back to start the story, reprinted from yesterday's late edition, on the front page. When she saw Harald's name, she immediately made a note to tell Dottie at lunch; Dottie might want to call Kay to get all the gory details. Mrs. Renfrew was a cheerful, lively person who always looked on the gay side of things; she imagined it must have been quite an adventure for those radical young people to get dressed up and do battle with the hotel staff, rather like a *Lampoon* prank; Kay's husband, she was sure, when he came up for trial, would be let off after a lecture from the judge, the way the Harvard boys always were when they got in trouble with the Cambridge police force. Apropos of that, she meant to ask Sam to stop at City Hall and pay a parking ticket she and Dottie had got the other day.

It was only because she had so many other things on her mind, such as type faces, sheet sizes (would Brook and Dottie sleep in a double bed? It was so hard to know, with a widower, what to expect), and the bridesmaids' dresses (such a problem, unless Helena could come on from Cleveland early to be fitted), that she quite forgot to mention Harald's fracas till they had finished luncheon and were walking down Newbury Street, side by side, like two sisters, Mrs. Renfrew in her beaver and Dottie in her mink. "Dottie!" she exclaimed. "I nearly forgot! You'll never guess what I was reading this morning at the Club. One of your friends has run afoul of the law." She looked quizzically up at her daughter, her blue eyes dancing. "Try to guess." "Pokey," said Dottie. Mrs. Renfrew shook her head. "Not even warm." "Harald Petersen!" repeated Dottie, when her mother had told her. "That wasn't fair, Mother. He's not exactly a friend. What did he do?" Mrs. Renfrew related the story. In the middle of it, Dottie stopped dead, between

Arlington and Berkeley. "Who was the other man?" she asked. "I wonder who it could have been." "I don't know, Dottie. But his picture was in the paper. He had quite a 'shiner.'" "You don't remember the name, Mother?" Mrs. Renfrew ruefully shook her head. "Why? Do you think it's someone you know?" Dottie nodded. "It was a fairly common name," said Mrs. Renfrew, pondering. "It seems to me it began with B." "Not Brown?" cried Dottie. "It might have been," replied her mother. "Brown, Brown," she repeated. "I wonder if that was it." "Oh, Mother!" said Dottie. "Why didn't you clip it out?" "Darling," said her mother. "You can't clip newspapers in the Club. It's against the house rules. And yet you'd be surprised, the number of members that do it. Magazines too." "What did he look like?" said Dottie. "Rather artistic," said Mrs. Renfrew. "Dissipated-looking. But that may have been the black eye. A gentleman, I should think. Now, what did it say he did? Sad to say, Dottie, my memory's going. 'Harald Petersen, playwright,' and the other one was something like that. Not 'ditchdigger,' anyway," she added brightly. "'Painter'?" suggested Dottie. "I don't *think* so," said her mother.

All this time, they had been standing in the middle of the sidewalk, with people brushing past them. It was cold; Mrs. Renfrew pushed back her coat sleeve and glanced at her watch. "You go on, Mother," said Dottie abruptly. "I'll meet you. I'm going back to the Ritz to buy the paper." Mrs. Renfrew looked seriously up at Dottie; she was not alarmed, having guessed for a long time that some little love trouble had happened to Dottie early last summer in New York. That was why she had sent her out West, to get over it. "Do you want me to come with you?" she said. Dottie hesitated. Mrs. Renfrew took her arm. "Come along, dear," she said. "I'll wait in the ladies' lounge while you get it from the porter."

A few minutes later, Dottie appeared with the *Herald Tribune*; the *Times* had been sold out. "Putnam Blake," she said. "You were right about the B. I met him at Kay's party. He raises funds for labor. We got an appeal from him the other day for something. And he married Norine Schmittlapp, who was in our class. You can see her in the big picture. The four of them have got very inty this winter." From Dottie's flat tone, Mrs. Renfrew could tell that this was not "the one." The poor girl laid the paper aside quietly; then she sank her chin into the palm of her hand and sat thinking. Mrs. Renfrew took out her compact, so as not to seem to watch Dottie. As she powdered her pretty, bright features, she considered what to do. Dottie still "had it bad," as the girls said nowadays; that was all too clear. Her mother's sympathies, like delicate feelers, fluttered out to her; she knew how it felt to yearn for the sight of a certain name long after the man who owned it had passed out of one's life forever. The very prospect of seeing his name and his photograph had got Dottie all "hot and bothered" again. Yet Mrs. Renfrew could not decide whether it would be wiser to let Dottie bear her disappointment in silence or to help her talk it out. The danger of this was that Dottie's flame might only be fanned by talking; if she had the strength to stamp it out alone, she would come through, in the end, a finer person. And yet it made little Mrs. Renfrew wince and bite her lips to sit pretending to fix her hair when a few words from her might be balm to Dottie's soul.

Mrs. Renfrew had complete confidence in Dottie's judgment: if Dottie considered this man in New York, whoever he was, unsuitable for her, Dottie must be right. Some girls in Dottie's position might give up a fine young man because he was poor or had a dependent mother and sisters to support (Mrs. Renfrew had known such cases), but Dottie would not do that; through her religion, she would find the patience to wait. Whatever the reason, Dottie's heart had made its decision last summer and stuck to it splendidly; it was Mrs. Renfrew's guess that the man was married. There *were* cases (the wife hopelessly insane and shut up in an institution and no prospect of her death) in which Mrs. Renfrew might have counseled a liaison for Dottie, no matter what Sam Renfrew threatened, but if it had been something of *that* sort, Dottie would surely have told her. No; Mrs. Renfrew did not doubt that Dottie had done the wise and brave thing in cutting this man out of her life; it only troubled her that Dottie might be marrying too hastily, "on the rebound," before her former feelings had had a chance to die naturally. She had come back from Arizona quietly happy and looking fit as a fiddle, but with Brook still out West and the strain of the wedding preparations, she had begun to seem a little over-tired and nervous. It worried Mrs.

Renfrew, now, to realize that Dottie, with two fittings yet to come on her wedding dress, would be in New York and exposed, probably, at every turn, to memories of this man.

These thoughts, sharp as bird tracks, passed through Mrs. Renfrew's pretty little hatted head as she sat, tense with sympathy for her daughter, in the Ritz ladies' lounge. She wondered what Dr. Perry or Dr. Leverett, the dear old rector, would advise; perhaps Dottie would be able to talk to one of them, in case she had any real doubts about the state of her feelings. She snapped shut her handbag. "How was Dr. Perry today?" she asked smiling. "Did he give you a clean bill of health?" Dottie raised her head. "He wants to try some diathermy for my sciatica. But he says I'll be better when I get back into the sun—the great open spaces." She forced a twinkle into her brown eyes. Mrs. Renfrew hesitated; this was neither the time nor the place, but she was a believer in impulse. She looked around the lounge; they were alone. "Dottie," she said. "Did Dr. Perry say anything to you about birth control?" Dottie's face and neck reddened, giving her a rough, chapped look, like an ailing spinster. She nodded briefly. "He says you told him to, Mother. I wish you hadn't." Mrs. Renfrew guessed that Dr. Perry had been having one of his gruff days and had offended Dottie's maiden modesty; engaged girls often had the most unaccountable reactions to the prospect of the wedding night. Mrs. Renfrew moved her chair a little closer. "Dottie," she said. "Even if you and Brook are planning to have children, you mayn't want them just yet. There's a new device, I understand, that's ninety-per-cent effective. A kind of rubber cap that closes off the uterus. Did Dr. Perry tell you about it?" "I stopped him," said Dottie. Mrs. Renfrew bit her lip. "Darling," she urged, "you mustn't be frightened. Dr. Perry, you know, isn't a woman's doctor; he may have been a bit brusque. He'll arrange to send you to a specialist, who'll make it all seem easier. And who'll answer any questions you want to ask—you know, about the physical side of love. Would you rather see a woman doctor? I don't think this new device is legal yet here in Massachusetts. But Dr. Perry can fix it for you to have an appointment in New York, the next time we go down for your fittings."

It seemed to Mrs. Renfrew that Dottie shivered in reply.

"I'll go with you, dear," she added, brightly. "If you want moral support . . . Or you could ask one of your married friends—Kay or Priss." Mrs. Renfrew did not know what had done it—the mention of New York, perhaps—but Dottie began to cry. "I love him," she said, choking, as the tears ran in furrows down either side of her long, distinguished nose. "I love him, Mother."

At last it had come out. "I know, dear," said Mrs. Renfrew, fishing in Dottie's pocketbook for a clean handkerchief and gently wiping her face. "I don't mean Brook," said Dottie. "I know," said Mrs. Renfrew. "What am I going to do?" Dottie repeated. "What am I going to do?" "We'll see," promised her mother. Her principal object now was to get Dottie's tears dried and her face powdered and take her home, before any of their friends could see her here. "We'll give up the fitting," she said. The doorman brought the car around (he and Mrs. Renfrew were old friends); Mrs. Renfrew put her small foot on the accelerator and in a few minutes they were home and up in Dottie's bedroom, with the door closed, having let themselves in so softly that Margaret, the old parlormaid, had not heard them. They sat on Dottie's chaise longue, with their arms around each other.

"I thought I was over it. I thought I loved Brook." Mrs. Renfrew nodded, though she had not yet learned the circumstances or even the young man's name. "Do you want to marry him?" she asked, going straight to the heart of the matter. "There's no question, Mother, of that," Dottie answered, in a cold, almost rebuking tone. Mrs. Renfrew drew a deep breath. "Do you want to 'live' with him?" she heard herself bravely pronounce. Dottie buried her head in her mother's strong small shoulder. "No, I guess not," she acknowledged. "Then what do you want, darling?" said her mother, stroking her forehead. Dottie pondered. "I want to see him again," she decided. "That's all, Mother. I want to see him again." Mrs. Renfrew clasped Dottie tighter. "I thought he'd be at Kay's party. I was *sure* he'd be there. And you know, when I first came in, I only wanted him to be there so that he could hear about my engagement and see my engagement ring and watch how happy I was. I looked awfully well that day. But then, when he didn't come, I started wanting to see him just to see him—not to show him he didn't mean a thing to me any more. Was that first feeling just sort of an armor, do you think?" "I imagine so, Dottie," said her mother. "Oh, it was awful," said Dottie. "Every time the doorbell rang, I was convinced it was going to be Dick"—she pronounced the name shyly, looking sidewise at her mother—"and then when it wasn't I nearly fainted, each time, it hurt me so. And all those new friends of Kay's were terribly nice but I almost hated them because they weren't Dick. Why do you think he didn't come?" "Was he invited?" asked Mrs. Renfrew practically. "I don't know and I couldn't ask. And it was so peculiar; nobody mentioned him. Not a word. And all the time a drawing by him of Harald was hanging right there on the wall. Like Banquo's ghost or something. I felt sure he'd been invited and was staying away on purpose and that everybody there knew that and was watching me out of the corner of their eye." "Your grammar, Dottie!" chided her mother, absently; her sky-blue eyes had clouded over. "Does Kay know about this?" she asked, taking care to make the question sound casual, so that she would not seem to be reproaching Dottie. Dottie nodded mutely, not looking at her mother, who made a little grimace and then controlled herself. "If she knew, dear, and knew you were engaged," she said lightly, "she doubtless *didn't* invite him. For your sake." Mrs. Renfrew was "fishing," but Dottie did not bite. "How cruel," she answered, which told Mrs. Renfrew nothing. "You mustn't be unfair, dear," she said mechanically, "because you're unhappy. Your father would say," she added, smiling, "that Kay 'showed good judgment.'" And she looked questioningly into Dottie's eyes. How far had this thing gone? Mrs. Renfrew had to know, yet Dottie did not seem to be aware of the fact that she had left her parent in the dark.

"Then you think I shouldn't see him?" Dottie answered swiftly. "How can I say, Dottie?" protested her mother. "You haven't told me anything about him. But I think *you* think you shouldn't see him. Amn't I right?" Dottie stared pensively at her engagement ring. "I think I *must* see him," she decided. "I mean I feel I'm fated to see him. If I don't do anything about it myself. As if it would be arranged, somehow, before I was married, that I would meet him just once. But I think I mustn't *try* to see him. Do you understand that?" "I understand," said

Mrs. Renfrew, "that you want to have your cake and eat it too, Dottie. You'd like God to arrange for you to have something that you know would be wrong for you to have if you chose it of your own free will." A look of relief and wonder came into Dottie's face. "You're right, Mother!" she cried. "What a marvelous person you are! You've seen right through me." "We're all pretty much alike," consoled Mrs. Renfrew. "Judy O'Grady and the Colonel's lady, you know." She squeezed Dottie's hand. "And yet," said Dottie, "even if it's wrong, I can't stop hoping. Not hoping, even. Expecting. That somehow, somehow, I *will* see him. On the street. Or on a bus or a train. The day after Kay's party, I went to the Museum of Modern Art; I made believe I was going to see an exhibition. But he wasn't there. And the time's getting so short. Only a month left. Less than a month. Mother, in Arizona, I hardly thought about him at *all*. I'd almost forgotten him. It was Kay's party that brought it all back. And ever since then I've had the most *peculiar* feeling. That he was thinking about me too. Not just that, Mother. Watching me, sort of skeptically, wherever I went, like to Dr. Perry today or a fitting; he has the most thrilling grey eyes that he narrows. . . ." She hesitated and broke off. "Do you believe in thought transference, Mother? Do you remember *Peter Ibbetson*? Because I feel that Dick is listening to my thoughts. And waiting." Mrs. Renfrew sighed. "Your imagination has got over-active, dear. You're letting it run away with you." "Oh, Mother," said Dottie, "if you could only see him! You would like him too. He's terribly good-looking and he's suffered so much." All at once, she dimpled. "How could you ever have thought that I'd have fallen for someone that looked like that Putnam Blake? Why, he's white as a leper and needs to wash his hair! Dick isn't the unwashed type; he comes from a very good family—descended from Hawthorne. Brown is a very good name."

Mrs. Renfrew put her hands on her daughter's shoulders and shook her gently. "I want you to lie down now. And I'll bring you a cold compress for your eyes. Rest till dinner. Or till Daddy comes home." It was just as she had feared; talking about this man had revived all Dottie's feeling for him; having started by crying, she had finished in smiles and dimples. In the bathroom, wringing out two hand towels in cold water,

Mrs. Renfrew wondered whether it might not be a good thing, however, for Dottie to see this man again. In her own environment, among her own friends . . . Despite what Dottie said, he was evidently a bit of a rough diamond. If Dottie had not been engaged, she could have asked him to a little party in New York, perhaps at Polly Andrews' place. Or to dine quietly with herself and her mother some night, and to go to a play or a concert afterward, with some older man present to make a fourth? Six would be better still—less pointed. Dottie could simply telephone him and say that her mother had an extra ticket and could he dine first? But an engaged girl was not free to ask whomever she chose, even with all the chaperonage in the world. And what would Brook say to Dottie's mother if anything were to happen as the result?

Mrs. Renfrew sharply wrung out the compress, which had got tepid while she was thinking, and held it afresh under the cold-water tap. For Dottie's own sake, she *had* to know how far the thing had gone. If it had gone the whole way and the man had aroused her senses, the poor child was in a fix. Some women, they said, never got over the first man, especially if he were skillful; he left a permanent imprint. Why, they even said that a child conceived with the legal husband would have the features of the first lover! That was nonsense, of course, old wives' talk, yet the thought stirred Mrs. Renfrew's blood a little. She was forty-seven years old and had just had her twenty-fifth reunion (where she had been voted the youngest-looking member of the class) at the time of Dottie's Commencement, and yet at heart, she feared, she was still a romantic; it excited her foolish fancy to think that a man who took a girl's virginity had the power to make her his forever. She could not make out what Dottie's own heart was dictating. Dottie was independent; she had her own bank account in the State Street Trust. What then was holding her back from seeing this man if she wanted to?

She laid the compress on Dottie's forehead, briskly drew the shades, and sat down on the bed, meaning to stay only a minute, to feel Dottie's pulse. It appeared to be normal. "Dottie," she said impulsively, tucking the coverlet around her, "I think you have to be true to your own lights in this. If you love 'Dick'"—she brought out the name with difficulty—"perhaps you should take the initiative in trying to see him. Is it your pride that's holding you back? Did he hurt you in some way? Did you have a quarrel or a misunderstanding?" "He doesn't love me, Mother," said Dottie in a low voice. "I just excite him sexually. He told me so." Mrs. Renfrew closed her eyes for an instant, feeling something click inside her, rather unpleasantly, at hearing, with finality, what she had already guessed to be the case; then she picked up Dottie's hand and squeezed it warmly. "So he *was* your lover." There had only been one night, it seemed; the night she had tried to reach Dottie at the Vassar Club and Dottie did not come in. That was the time. "But you hardly knew him," said Mrs. Renfrew. "Dick's a fast worker," replied Dottie with a twinkle and a cough. "And what happened afterward?" said Mrs. Renfrew gravely. "You never heard from him again? Was that it, Dottie?" Compassion for her daughter moved her heart. "I can't explain," said Dottie. "I don't know myself what happened. I ran away, I suppose you could say." Mrs. Renfrew clicked her tongue against the roof of her mouth. "Was it a very painful experience? Did you bleed a great deal, dear?" "No," said Dottie. "It wasn't painful that way. Actually, it was terribly thrilling and passionate. But afterward . . . Oh, Mother, I simply can't tell you, I can never tell anyone, what happened afterward." Mrs. Renfrew's sensitive conjectures were wide of the mark. "He made me"— Dottie suddenly spoke up—"go to a doctor and get a contraceptive, one of those diaphragm things you were talking about." Mrs. Renfrew was stunned; her wide bright eyes canvassed her daughter's face, as if trying to reassemble her. "Perhaps that's the modern way," she finally ventured. "That's what Kay said," replied Dottie. She described her visit to the doctor. "But what were you supposed to do with it then?" asked Mrs. Renfrew. "That was the whole trouble," said Dottie, flushing. And she told how she had sat for nearly six hours in Washington Square with the contraceptive apparatus on her lap. "I knew then he couldn't care for me at all or he couldn't have put me through that." "Men are strange," said Mrs. Renfrew. "Your father—" She stopped. "I sometimes think that they don't want to know too much about that side of a woman's life. It destroys an illusion." "That was your generation, Mother. No. The truth is, Dick didn't give me a thought. I have to be unsentimental, like Kay, and face that. I left the whole caboodle under a bench in Washington Square. Imagine the junkman's surprise! What do you suppose he thought, Mother?" Mrs. Renfrew could not help smiling too. She understood now what had made Dottie shed tears in the Ritz. "So you thought," she said gaily, "Dr. Perry and I were going to make you go back to the same woman doctor. Like seeing the same movie over. Oh, poor Dottie!" Despite themselves, both mother and daughter began to laugh.

Mrs. Renfrew wiped her eyes. "Seriously, Dottie," she said, "it's queer that your 'Dick' wasn't home all that time. What do you suppose he could have been doing? I rather agree with Kay that he couldn't have sent you to the doctor just to make game of you." "He just forgot," said Dottie. "He stopped to have a drink in a bar, probably. That's another thing, Mother. He *drinks*." "Oh, dear," said Mrs. Renfrew.

He was a thoroughly bad hat, then, but that was the kind, of course, that nice women broke their hearts over. Mrs. Renfrew remembered the gay days of the war, when Dottie was still in short dresses with her hair in a big ribbon, and Sam, home on leave from camp, had christened a member of their set "the matrimonial submarine." How attractive he had been, too, to dance with, though all the men disliked him and in the end he had drunk himself into the sanatorium after torpedoing three happy marriages! She nodded. "You're right, Dottie," she said firmly. "If he were serious about you, he would have realized the shock he'd given your feelings and tracked you down through Kay. Or there may be *some* good in him. He may have decided to leave you alone, knowing that he'd ruin your life if you fell in love with him. Had he been drinking when he seduced you?" "He didn't seduce me, Mother. That's *vieux jeu*. And I *am* in love with him. Do you think if he knew *that* . . . ? He's very proud, Mother. 'I'm not in your class,' he said. That's one of the first things he told me. If I were to go to him and tell him . . . ?"

"I don't know, Dottie," Mrs. Renfrew sighed. It was not clear to her whether she herself was trying to dissuade Dottie from seeking this Dick out or the opposite. More than anything else, she wanted to guide Dottie to discover her own real feelings. There was one simple test. "Dear," she said. "I think we'd better postpone your wedding for a few weeks. That will give you time to know what your real feelings are. Meanwhile, you rest, and I'll get you a fresh compress." She got up and smoothed down the counterpane, feeling decidedly more cheerful as she began to see that it really would be practicable, and probably the best solution, to put off the wedding for the present. "Luckily, Dottie," she murmured, "we didn't order the invitations today. Just think, if I hadn't stopped at the Club for a manicure this morning, I should never have seen that newspaper, and you would never have told me what you did, and the invitations would be ordered. 'For want of a nail . . .'" "But what about the dresses?" said Dottie. "The dresses will still be good a month from now," replied Mrs. Renfrew. "We'll lay the blame on Dr. Perry." By this time, her active and sanguine mind had raced ahead another step; she was checking off the eventualities in case the wedding should be called off altogether in the end. She and Sam would have to compensate the bridesmaids for their dresses, but that would not amount to much: because of Polly Andrews, they had chosen an inexpensive model. And a few pieces of silver had already been marked, but fortunately in the old way, with the bride's initials, so that they would come in handy some time. No wedding presents would have to be returned, barring Lakey's Madonna, which could wait till Lakey came back. As for the wedding gown, it could either be kept or passed on to one of the younger cousins. At Mrs. Renfrew's age, she had learned to cope with disappointments; young people, she had noticed, found it a great deal harder to adjust to a change of plans.

When she came back with a fresh compress, she at first thought Dottie had fallen asleep, for her eyes were closed and she was breathing regularly. Mrs. Renfrew raised the window a crack and laid the cold towels gently on Dottie's forehead, noticing with tenderness the strong widow's peak. Then she tiptoed out of the room, thanking her stars that she had found the right remedy; as soon as the pressure of the oncoming wedding had been removed, Dottie had been able to relax. But just as she was closing the door, carefully, Dottie spoke.

"I don't want the wedding postponed. Brook would never understand." "Nonsense, Dottie. We'll just say that Dr. Perry—" "No," said Dottie. "No, Mother. I've made up my mind." Mrs.

Renfrew came into the room again and shut the door behind her; she had heard old Margaret, who was an eavesdropper, prowling about. "Darling," she said, "you thought you'd made up your mind before. You were very sure you loved Brook and could make him happy." "I'm sure again," said Dottie. Mrs. Renfrew advanced into the room with her precise, light step; she had limped as a young girl and overcome it with exercises and golf. "Dottie," she said firmly, "it's cruel and wicked to marry a man you only half love. Especially an older man. It's a kind of cheating. I've seen it happen among my own friends. You promise the man something that you can't give. As long as that other man remains in the back of your mind. Like a hidden card up your sleeve." She had grown quite agitated, and her golden head, with its silver glister, had begun to tremble a little, as if in memory of that old invalidism which they had called palsy in those days.

To her immense distress, they began to quarrel, in low-pitched, well-bred voices; Mrs. Renfrew would not have thought this could happen between her and Dottie. She was telling Dottie that she must see Dick again, if only to make sure. "If you order me to, I'll do it, Mother. But afterward I'll kill myself. I'll throw myself off the train." "Please don't be melodramatic, Dottie." "It's you who're being melodramatic, Mother. Just allow me to marry Brook in peace." Distractedly, Mrs. Renfrew was aware of the oddity of this situation, in which the roles were reversed, and the daughter was hurrying herself into a "suitable" marriage while the mother was pleading with her to seek out an unsuitable rake. This was, apparently, that "gulf between the generations" that had been discussed at her class reunion last June; one of the faculty members of Mrs. Renfrew's class had stated it as a generalization that this new crop of girls was far less idealistic, less disinterested, as a body of educated women, than their mothers had been. Mrs. Renfrew had not believed it, noting to herself that Dottie and her friends were all going out to work, mostly at volunteer jobs, and were not trammeled by any of the fears and social constraints that had beset her own generation. And yet here was Dottie virtually demonstrating what that faculty member had said. Was it a sign of the times? Had the depression done it? Were girls nowadays afraid of taking a risk? She suspected that Dottie, with her poor health and Boston heritage, was terrified of becoming an old maid. That (not the other) was the "fate worse than death" for Dottie's classmates. Yet marriage, as she had always impressed on Dottie, was a serious thing, a sacrament. Dottie did not love Brook; the certainty of this was beyond any doubt to Mrs. Renfrew's eyes, and she felt as though she would be condoning a very grave sin if, knowing what she knew, she let her go ahead unreflecting. Did Dottie even respect Brook? If so, she ought to hesitate.

"You're unwilling to make a sacrifice," Mrs. Renfrew said sorrowfully, her head commencing to tremble again. "Not even to wait a month to keep from hurting a man who isn't in his first youth. You're unwilling to sacrifice your pride to see 'Dick' again and live with him, if you love him, and try to re-form him. Women in my day, women of all sorts, were willing to make sacrifices for love, or for some ideal, like the vote or Lucy Stonerism. They got themselves put out of hotels for registering as 'Miss' and 'Mr.' when they were legally married. Look at your teachers, look what they gave up. Or at women doctors and social workers." "That was your day, Mother," Dottie said patiently. "Sacrifices aren't necessary any more. Nobody has to choose between getting married and being a teacher. If they ever did. It was the homeliest members of your class who became teachers—admit it. And everybody knows, Mother, that you can't reform a man; he'll just drag you down too. I've thought about this a lot, out West. Sacrifice is a dated idea. A superstition, really, Mother, like burning widows in India. What society is aiming at now is the full development of the individual."

"Oh, I agree; I quite agree," said Mrs. Renfrew. "And yet it's such a little thing I'm asking of you, Dottie. Bear with your Aged P." She put in this family joke in a nervous conciliatory manner. "It isn't necessary, Mother. I truly do know my mind. Because I slept with Dick doesn't mean I should change my whole life. He feels the same way himself. You can fit things into their compartments. He initiated me, and I'll always be grateful to him for making it so wonderful. But if I saw him again, it might not be so wonderful. I'd get involved. . . . It's better to keep it as a memory. Besides, he doesn't want my love. That's what I was thinking about when you were in the bathroom. I can't *throw* myself at him." "It often works," said Mrs. Renfrew, smiling. "Men—unhappy, lonely men, particularly—" she continued gravely, "respond to a faithful heart. An unswerving faith, Dottie, moves mountains; you should have learned that from your religion. 'Whither thou goest I will go. . . .'" Dottie shook her dark head. "*You* try sitting in the Common, Mother, with a douche bag and what-not on your lap. And anyway you don't really want me to live with him either. You're only talking, because you want me to 'pay the price.' Postpone my wedding and upset everybody's plans, just to allow a 'decent interval' to elapse. Of mourning for Dick. Isn't it true?" A faint teasing smile came into her brown eyes as she interrogated her mother.

Mrs. Renfrew considered the accusation. It was true, she had to confess, that *she* did not want Dottie to "live with" Dick. But she would want *Dottie* to want to do it. Yet how to express this? Perhaps Dottie was right, and she was only being conventional in wishing to postpone the marriage. It might be the conventional Bostonian in her that felt that Dottie ought to make *some* gesture toward the past. Yet was this enough to account for the deep sad sense of disappointment she had—disappointment in Dottie? It seemed to her, looking at it as charitably as she could, that Dottie was being tempted by Brook's wealth and by the glorious outdoor life he had to offer her, of which she had painted such a vivid unforgettable picture—the desert and the silver mines and the pack trips into the mountains. "You were 'just talking' yourself, Dottie," she chided, "when you said you loved Dick. I was only going by what you told me. I don't believe you do love him. But I think you like to say so. Because if you didn't you would be too shamed and degraded." "Please, Mother!" said Dottie haughtily.

Mrs. Renfrew turned away. "Try to get some rest," she said. "I'm going to lie down myself." There were tears in her bright-blue eyes as she lay on her chaise longue, which faced the window, hung with pretty Swiss-embroidered curtains, overlooking Chestnut Street. She had certainly not married Sam Renfrew for money or for what they called "security" nowadays, and yet she felt as if she had and as if some dreadful pattern were being repeated in Dottie. Had she and Sam given Dottie false values, despite all their efforts to the contrary? She and Sam had married for love, and there had never been

anyone before him, and yet she felt as if, long ago, she had had
a lover whom she had given up for this house and the State
Street Trust and the golf and the Chilton Club, and it was all
being visited on Dottie or on that poor man out in Arizona.
The sins of the fathers. This was all perfect *stuff*, she knew, and
Dottie, she supposed, might learn to love Brook, especially
since her senses seemed to have been awakened; that, at least,
was the positive side of all this sad affair—or could be, if Brook
were careful. The Arizona climate, too, was "just what the
doctor ordered" for Dottie. A few tears, nevertheless, rolled
out of one eye, and she stanched them with the handkerchief
of fine Irish linen and lace old Margaret had given her for
Christmas. An idea of a lost lover, of someone renounced,
tapped at her memory like a woodpecker. Whom could she be
thinking of, she asked herself demurely. The matrimonial
submarine?

LIBBY MacAusland had a spiffy apartment in the Village. Her family in Pittsfield was helping her pay the rent. The job she had been promised by a publisher, just before graduation, had not exactly materialized. The man she had interviewed, who was one of the partners in the firm, had shown her around the offices, given her some books they published, and introduced her to an editor, who was smoking a pipe in his sanctum. Mr. LeRoy, a portly young man with a dark mustache and bushy eyebrows, had been very forthcoming as long as the partner was there, but afterward, instead of settling her at a desk right away (Libby had spied an empty cubbyhole in the editorial department), he had told her to come back in a week or so. Then he said he was going to give her manuscripts to read at home to try her out. They paid $5 apiece for reading a manuscript and writing a summary and an opinion, and she ought to be able, he thought, to do three a week, which was the same as having a half-time job—better. "If we started you in the office," he said, "we could only give you $25 full time. And you'd have your carfare and your lunches to pay." When he asked her if she needed the work, Libby had let on that she did; she thought if he thought she was pretty desperate he would find her more manuscripts to read.

Anyway, that ought not to have been his business. Her background was perfect for a berth in publishing: fluent reading knowledge of French and Italian; copy editing, proofreading, and dummying as editor in chief of the Vassar literary magazine; short-story and verse-writing courses; good command of typing—all the tools of the trade. But mindful of the competition, Libby took special pains with her reports for Mr. LeRoy, typing them triple-spaced on a kind of sky-blue typing paper that was still manufactured in one of the mills in Pittsfield and stapling them in stiff blue covers. The "presentation" of her themes had been outstanding at Vassar. She always added a title page with a colophon—her device, the same she used for her bookplate—to her weekly papers and put them between covers; her handwriting was distinctive, with Greek e's and embellished capitals. Miss Kitchel had noticed her immediately in English 105 as "the artistic young lady with the fine Italian hand." Her "effusions," as Miss Kitchel, who was a hearty soul, used to call them, had been printed in the freshman *Sampler*, and she had been invited, while still a freshman, to serve on the board of the literary magazine. Libby's forte was descriptive writing. "This hopeful beauty did create" (Carew) was the motto beneath her picture in the yearbook.

Her mother's sister had a villa in Fiesole, and Libby had spent a year there as a child, going to the sweetest dame school in Florence, and countless summers afterward—to be exact, two; Libby was prone to exaggerate. She spoke a breathless Italian, with a nifty Tuscan accent, and had been dying to take her junior year abroad, at the University of Bologna, for she had read a fascinating novel called *The Lady of Laws*, about a learned lady in Renaissance times who had been a doctor of law at Bologna and got raped and carried off by one of the Malatestas (Libby had been an alternate in a debate on censorship with Wesleyan freshman year). But she had misdoubted that being a year away from college might cost her the "crown" she coveted; she counted on being elected President of Students.

Libby played basketball (center) and had a big following among the dimmer bulbs of the class; she was president of the Circolo Italiano and had been president of the class sophomore year. She was also active in the Community Church. But running for President of Students, she had been mowed down, as it turned out, by the big guns of the North Tower group, who were more the hockey-playing, ground-gripper, rah-rah Vassar sort and carried off all the class offices senior year. They had asked her to group with them at the end of freshman year, but she had thought Lakey's crowd was snazzier. Came the dawn when Lakey and the others would not even electioneer for her.

It seemed to be Libby's fate (so far) to start out strong with people and then have them lose interest for no reason she could see—"They flee from me that some time did me seek." That had happened with the group. Libby adored *Of Human Bondage* and Katherine Mansfield and Edna Millay and Elinor Wylie and quite a lot of Virginia Woolf, but she could never get anybody to talk with her about books any more, because Lakey said her taste was sentimental. The paradox was that she was the most popular member of the group *outside* and the least popular *inside*. For instance, she had put Helena, who was one to hide her light under a bushel, on the board of the literary magazine; then Helena had blandly turned around and sided with a minority that wanted to print "experimental literature." She and the arch-enemy, Norine Schmittlapp, had collaborated on an "Open Letter to the Editor," claiming that the college magazine no longer represented Vassar writing but had become the inheritance of a "pallid" literary clique. Libby, counseled by the faculty, had let herself run with the current and printed an "experimental number"; the tide turned *her* way when one of the poems in it proved to be a hoax, written by a cute freshman as a spoof on modern poetry. But in the very next issue a story she had battled for was discovered to be plagiarized, word for word, from a story in *Harper's*. It was hushed up, for the sake of the girl's future, after the Dean had had a talk with *Harper's* about it, but someone (probably Kay) whom Libby had told in strictest confidence betrayed her, and soon the rebel clique was busy spreading the news. It was one thing, they said, to be generously taken in by a hoax and another to print as original writing an unadventurous theft from a stale, second-rate magazine. Libby literally could not understand this last part; one of her highest ambitions was to have a story or a poem published by *Harper's*. And lo and behold, hold your hats, girls, it had happened to her finally a year ago this last winter.

She had been in New York nearly two years now, living first with two other girls from Pittsfield in Tudor City and now alone, in this spiffy apartment she had found. She was avid for success, and her parents were willing; Brother was settled, at long last, in a job in the mill, and Sister had married a Harkness. So Libby was free to try her pinions.

Mr. LeRoy had given her stacks of manuscripts to start out with. She had had to buy a ladies' briefcase at Mark Cross to lug them all back and forth—black calf, very snazzy. "You're *made*, Libby!" her roommates in Tudor City used to gasp when they saw her stagger in with her load. And to pile Pelion on Ossa, she had got herself some book-review assignments from the *Saturday Review of Literature* and the *Herald Tribune Books*—no less. Her roommates were green with envy because they were only going to Katharine Gibbs Secretarial School themselves. Her family was jubilant; that was why they had let her have the apartment. Libby was obviously dedicated to the idea of a literary career, as Brother reported to headquarters when he came home from a visit to New York. Father had had her first check photostated and framed for her, and it hung above her desk, with a little branch of laurel from the parental garden, to show that she was crowned with bays.

The idea of the book reviews was completely Mr. LeRoy's. "You might try for some reviewing," he said to her one day when she wanted to know how she could get ahead faster. So with that flea in her ear, she had gone to Miss Amy Loveman and Mrs. Van Doren (Irita, the wife of Carl), and they had both let her have a chance. She still had the New York *Times* to crack.

Most of the manuscripts Mr. LeRoy gave her were novels; biographies (which Libby doted on) he kept for specialists, and he had not yet tried her on a French or an Italian book—she was too much of a tyro, she supposed. Libby wrote exhaustive plot summaries, for she did not want the whole burden of decision to rest on her, and she labored far into the night on her critical exegeses, making constructive suggestions. She was eager to get into editing, which was the more glamorous part of publishing—not just copy editing, but creative rewriting. She tried to read creatively too, making believe she was a housewife in Darien or a homely secretary when she sat in the seat of judgment. It stood to reason, she argued, that publishers were in business to reach the public and not to please Libby Mac-Ausland. So she tried to look on every novel as a potential best seller. That was what the editor of the *Herald Tribune Books* thought too; she had told Libby, in the sweetest Southern accent: "We believe here, Miss MacAuslan', that there's something good in evvra book that should be brought to the attention of evvra reader."

Yet Mr. LeRoy had begun to eye her reflectively when she brought in her reports. It could not be her clothes; she made it a point to dress the way she imagined a publisher's reader should: neat but not gaudy, in a plain skirt and shirtwaist, with sometimes a pleated front or an old cameo brooch of Great Grandmother Ireton's at the throat—general effect a smitch

Victorian, like an "operative" in a Howells novel (Libby loved old words). If she ever got a regular job in an office, she was going to pin paper cuffs over her real ones. On cold days she wore a sweater and skirt with some gold beads or her pearls, which were not Oriental, only cultured, but as far as Mr. LeRoy could tell they might have come from the five-and-ten. It must be something about her reports, she was afraid. He dropped a hint once that she need not go to quite such length in describing a novel that she was turning thumbs down on. But she said she was only too happy to do the job right; the laborer must be worthy of his hire.

She often found him reading a magazine: the *New Masses*, she noticed, or another one called *Anvil* or still another with the peculiar name of *Partisan Review*, which she had tried to read in the Washington Square Bookshop. That was what gave her the idea of slipping words like "laborer" into her conversation, to remind him that she too was one of the downtrodden. Rumor had it that there were quite a few pinks in the publishing biz. Be that as it might, Mr. LeRoy was no Lord Chesterfield, sitting there in his shirt sleeves, phlegmatic and rather porky, tipping back in his desk chair, rubbing his mustache, and Libby sometimes got the feeling that he was not used to feminine women. She had a way of tilting her head to one side and thrusting her chin forward eagerly, with lips slightly parted, like one listening to music, that seemed to embarrass him, for whenever she did this he would stop in the middle of a sentence and frown and wring his eyebrows.

"You don't need to read them all through," he observed to her suddenly one day, balancing her blue folder on two fingers and puffing at his pipe. "Some publishers' readers just smell 'em." Libby shook her gold head in its navy beret emphatically. "I don't mind, dear sir," she cried. "And I'd like to scotch the legend that manuscripts aren't read by publishers. You can swear on the Book these have been. And you can't object if I'm doing it on my own time."

He got up from behind the desk and began to walk around with his pipe. "If you're seriously trying to make a living out of this, Miss MacAusland," he said, "you must treat it as piece work and rationalize your time like any sweated worker." "Don't call me 'sweated,'" she smiled. "Odo-Ro-No." He did not smile back. "Seriously," she went on, "I love doing it. I'm one of those unhappy few mortals that can't put down a novel till I know how it comes out. Words cast a spell on me. Even the worst words in the worst order. I write myself, you know." "Write us a novel," he proposed abruptly. "You write damned well." Libby lit herself a cigarette. She said to herself warily that she must not let him deflect her by flattery into a writing career. "I'm not ready for that yet. Construction is my fatal weakness. But I'm learning. Reading these manuscripts has taught me a lot. When my day comes and I open up the old Remington and type 'CHAPTER ONE,' I'll profit from their mistakes." He went back to his desk and knocked out his pipe. "You do it on your own time, as you say, Miss MacAusland. But the function of the first reader is to save the second reader's time. *And* his own. What you're doing is uneconomic." "But I have to make the work interesting to myself," Libby protested. "All work ought to be interesting. Even manual labor. Hear, hear!" she added jovially, in the manner she had learned at Vassar. "Sound of falling bricks," she muttered, when Mr. LeRoy remained silent.

Libby punched out her cigarette. She usually made it a policy to stay fifteen minutes, as if she were paying a call, but it was hard work, often, with Mr. LeRoy to stretch the visit that long. Now came the moment she dreaded. Some men in offices stood up to indicate that the interview was over, but Mr. LeRoy stayed seated at his desk or else he was pacing around restlessly anyway. He sometimes acted as if he had forgotten what she had come for, which was to get a fresh supply of manuscripts. He would let her put her coat and gloves on without seeming to notice that she was ready to make her adieux and without a single glance at the desk drawer where, she had discovered, the incoming manuscripts were kept. It was a big drawer, like a bin; lowering herself to pun, Libby called it the loony bin, because the suspense of waiting each time for him to open it drove her crazy. Sometimes she had to remind him, but generally she found that if she waited long enough he remembered. Each time, though, she felt her whole career hanging by a thread for what was probably only a minute by the clock but, measured by her heart's beat, eternity. Finally he would fish out a couple of manuscripts and toss them on the desk. "Here, have a look at these." Or, peering into the drawer, "There doesn't seem to be much here this week, Miss MacAusland," he would say, coughing. When Libby, arching her neck, could see that the drawer was practically full. Some day, she feared—and she used to tell it to herself as a story—the drawer would remain closed. She would put on her coat (simple navy blue with a velvet collar) and go out into the wintry streets with her empty briefcase; after that, she could never see Mr. LeRoy again—her pride would not let her.

In fact, Libby usually repaired to Schrafft's for a malted after a session with Mr. LeRoy. On this day of evil omen, she tottered out of the office in a shaken condition, with one measly manuscript to show for her trouble. Total blackness; ice and desolation. "The function of the first reader is to save the second reader's time." Fanning her brow with the tea menu, she called on herself to face the truth: he had been letting her down gradually for months, preparing her for the final blow, hint by hint, like an author preparing the reader! How much kinder if he had simply said to her, "I'm afraid you haven't worked out, Miss MacAusland. Sorry." Nothing would have been simpler than that. She would have understood. After all, publishers could not farm out manuscripts as a charity. "Thank you, Mr. LeRoy, for your frankness," she would have told him. "Do come and have tea with me some time. I shall always remember you as my friend."

After a while, sucking at her malted, Libby began to realize what a solipsist she was: all that was in her own mind. The trouble was, she had been looking at their interviews from *her* point of view, which was one of secret, mad apprehension concentrated on that drawer. But from Mr. LeRoy's point of view, it was all in the day's work. She was one of many readers he had to distribute manuscripts among. And he could not *make* manuscripts out of thin air, if authors did not send them in. Moreover, he had to be fair; he could not favor her over older readers who probably depended on it for their livelihood. You could see he was fair from his eyebrows, which always looked so perplexed. When he talked to her today like a Dutch uncle, it was because he was trying to teach her the trade, curb her "instinct of craftsmanship," which was too creative for the marts of commerce. He probably had not the faintest inkling of the tumults of hope and fear he stirred up in her girlish bosom. He took it for granted she was on the payroll. When he said there wasn't much this week, the emphasis in his mind was on "this week." And what she had said to herself just now was perfectly true: nothing would have been easier for him than just to tell her that she had been found wanting—*if* he thought so. He must have to tell some poor soul that every day. Each time he rejected a manuscript. Why had she never considered that?

It struck her that it would be a fascinating exercise in narrative point of view to tell the story of their relation first from her standpoint and then from Mr. LeRoy's. What would stand out, of course, would be the complete contrast. It would show how each of us is locked in his own private world. "The Fatal Drawer," you could call it. Or "The Secret Drawer," which would give the idea of secret, closed lives and would be an evocation of secret drawers in old desks, like Mother's desk at home. Tapping on her glass, Libby summoned the Irish waitress and borrowed a pencil; she began scribbling notes on the back of the menu. She had an inspiration that she wanted to catch on the wing. What if the heroine (never mind her name) had been enthralled, all through her childhood, by a secret drawer in her mother's (grandmother's?) desk, which she had never succeeded in opening? That would give a sort of poetic depth to the story and help explain the heroine's psychology: the granite Victorian house in the shadow of the mills, the tall hedges, the monkey tree in the garden, the summerhouse or pergola where the lonely child had tea, and the Queen Anne secretary in the dark hall at the top of the stairs, beyond the curving banisters. . . . Later, when the heroine met the publisher, you could have her imagine all sorts of grisly things, like making her suspect that his precious drawer was really bulging with manuscripts and that a not-so-bad-looking girl she had seen waiting outside with a cardboard briefcase was a rival for Mr. LeRoy's favors. When really it would turn out that the girl was an author whose manuscript was going to be given to Libby to pass on. That would be clear when you got the story from Mr. LeRoy's angle.

Libby was chock full of ideas for stories, which she generally wrote down in her diary. Every writer ought to keep a diary, Mrs. M. A. P. Smith said. Libby had been keeping hers faithfully for the last three years, noting her impressions and new words and her dreams. And titles for stories and poems. "'The Drawer'!" she exclaimed now. That was it, of course—the first rule for good writing was to strike out adjectives. Libby signaled for the hostess. "You don't mind if I take this?" she queried, showing her the menu and pointing to the briefcase. The hostess of course was delighted: all the world loves a writer, Libby had found. The old French waiters at the Lafayette Café had got so they gave her a regular table when she dropped in, *toute seule*, on Sunday afternoons, to read or take notes at the marble-topped table and watch the odd characters playing checkers or reading the newspapers, which were rolled up on wooden poles the way they were in France.

Libby was not all work and no play; she was managing to have a splendiferous time for herself without overspending her allowance. During the winter, she would go up to ski in the Berkshires on those weekend cut-rate excursions the New York Central ran; the trains were full of skiers, and she had made a lot of new friends that way. Most of them were flabbergasted when they heard she had broken into print. Last winter she had discovered a beauteous young man who taught English at one of the private schools and who knew, it turned out in the spring, a nifty picnic spot that could be reached for five cents on the subway: Pelham Bay Park; you took the Lexington Avenue Express to the end of the line and then got out and walked. Libby would pack a lunch of cucumber sandwiches, hard-boiled eggs, and big fat strawberries, and they would throw in a leather volume of poetry to read aloud after they had eaten and were lying on a steamer blanket in a sheltered spot overlooking the water. Libby was crazy about the Cavalier Poets, and he doted on the Elizabethans, especially Sidney and Drayton ("Since there's no help, come let us kiss and part.— Nay I have done, you get no more of me . . ."). He told Libby she looked just the way he imagined Penelope Rich (Penelope Devereux that *was*, the sister of the Earl of Essex), the "Stella" of Sidney's "Astrophel and Stella." "Stella" had blond hair and dark eyes, from which came killing darts, like Libby's. The combination of brown eyes and gold hair was the

Elizabethan *ne plus ultra* of womanly beauty. This spring, Libby could hardly wait for the first pussy willows for those picnics to start again. He was full of the most intriguing comparisons, which sometimes introduced her to complete new realms of reading. For instance, when he came last spring to pick her up one Saturday morning at the Tudor City apartment for their picnic, wearing heavy shoes and carrying a student's bookbag, she was in the kitchen buttering bread for their sandwiches. Whereupon he started reciting:

> "*Werther had a love for Charlotte*
> *Such as words could never utter.*
> *Would you know how first he met her?*
> *She was cutting bread and butter.*"

Her roommates nearly popped, they were so impressed, having only gone to Smith and Holyoke. That was a parody by Thackeray of Goethe's *Sorrows of Werther*, which Libby had promptly devoured in the library. She often demanded of herself, placing her index finger on her forehead dramatically to indicate deep thought, whether this delirious young man could be in love with her, though he didn't have a bean, except his teacher's salary. This Christmas he had taken her skating in Central Park twice, which was the only time he had put his arm around her, to hold her up on the ice, but unfortunately he had had a cold most of the winter and just taught his classes and afterward had a hot lemonade and went to bed.

Then she had other heavy beaux—a young actor she had met at Kay's who took her to the theatre in cheap seats they got at Gray's cut-rate ticket place in the bowels of the earth underneath the New York *Times* building; they always stopped outside to read the illuminated ribbon of news (the snappy comparison was Libby's) that ran around the *Times* building. And a young man from the Yale Music School who took her to Harlem to hear jazz. And there was this Jewish boy she had met on the ski train, with a lisp and curly eyelashes (from a very nice family who had changed their name legally), who took her dancing at the Plaza; he was studying politics and had been a poll watcher for the Democratic party at the Congressional elections last fall. She knew some young lawyers downtown, former flames of Sister's, who sometimes took her to the opera or a concert in Carnegie Hall. Or to the Little Carnegie Playhouse, where they showed foreign movies and you could get free demi-tasses and play ping-pong in the lounge. Libby was a whiz at ping-pong, as you might guess from her height and her long arms; Brother had taught her a wicked serve. On Sundays she sometimes went to church, with a Buchmanite boy she knew, to hear Sam Shoemaker, who was rector at Calvary; at college, she had been steamed up about the Oxford Group.

Right next to her apartment, practically, was the Fifth Avenue Cinema, where you could see foreign movies too and have a demi-tasse on the house; she went there mostly with other girls—Kay, when Harald was working, which he was again, Polly Andrews, Priss, when Sloan was at the hospital (so sad, she had lost her baby in the sixth month of pregnancy), and some of the old North Tower gang, whom she had rediscovered on the ski train. On her list too for manless evenings were two girls she had met in her career of crime as a book reviewer —the editorial secretary of the *Saturday Review of Literature*, Libby would have you know, and the editor's assistant on the *Herald Tribune Books*. One of them had gone to Smith, Class of '30, and the other had gone to Wellesley, ditto, and they both lived alone in the Village and had taken a big shine to Libby. The girl from the *Tribune* lived on Christopher Street, and she and Libby often forgathered for cocktails at Longchamps on Twelfth Street and then they might go on to Alice McCollister's on Eighth Street or to the Jumble Shop, where there were lots of artists and writers that this girl pointed out and Filipino waiters. Libby usually tried to stand treat to cocktails. "I asked *you*," she would gaily insist. She had both girls to a mulled-wine party she gave in January, to which she also invited their bosses, who unfortunately couldn't come. Kay said you should not invite the boss and her secretary to the same occasion; that cheapened your invitation. She also thought that Libby should have invited Mr. LeRoy, but Libby did not have the nerve. "He pictures me in a garret," said Libby. "I don't want to destroy his illusions. And besides, how do I know whether he's married?" "A flimsy excuse, MacAusland," replied Kay.

Libby was too much of a lady (she preferred the old word,

gentlewoman) to presume on a business acquaintance. Why, when she was making friends with the *Trib* and the *Saturday Review* girls, she would just poke her head in their door and wave till she was sure of her welcome. Now, of course, she would sally right in for a chat and a peek at the new books, so that she would know, when it was her turn, what to ask the editor for; it paid to ask for a specific book. Some reviewers followed the *Publishers' Weekly* religiously. There was a whole science to getting books for review; Libby honestly thought she could write an article on the subject. First, you had to know that the editors had "days," like hostesses, when they were at home to reviewers. Tuesday was the "day" at the *Tribune* and Wednesday at the *Saturday Review*. The *Times* was Tuesday too, though, so far, Libby had just sat there, ignored, in the waiting room, till the office boy came and said there was nothing this week. The book-review editors were like kings (or queens), she always fancied, holding levees, surrounded by their courtiers, while petitioners waited eagerly in the anteroom and footmen (that is, office boys) trotted back and forth. And, like kings, they had the power of life and death in their hands. She had got to know the other reviewers or "clients," as the Romans would have called them, quite well by sight—middle-aged bohemian women with glasses or too much rouge and dangly earrings and worn briefcases or satchels; pimply young men in suits that looked as if they were made of paper. And their shoes! Half-soled and with broken laces tied in frayed knots; it broke Libby's heart to study their shoes and the red, raw ankles emerging from cheap imitation-lisle socks. It reminded her of going to the eye doctor (she had to wear reading glasses), where you waited for hours too, and seeing all the poor people with cataracts patiently camping there. Among the book reviewers, there was a great deal of jealousy and spite; the young men with acne and eroded teeth always looked her up and down contemptuously and then positively hissed when she got ushered in ahead of them. Yet a lot of these would-be reviewers were dishonest; instead of reviewing the book, *their* object was to walk off with an armful and sell them to some little second-hand man without even looking at them. Which was unfair to the honest reviewer and even more so to the author and the publisher; any book that got published deserved the courtesy of a review. These "raiders," which was Libby's name for them, were supposed to be much more prevalent at magazines like the *New Republic* and the *Nation*, where no attempt was made to "notice" every book that came out. At the *Nation* and the *New Republic* they said too that you had to run a gauntlet of Communists before getting in to see the book editor—all sorts of strange characters, tattooed sailors right off the docks and longshoremen and tramps and bearded cranks from the Village cafeterias, none of them having had a bath for weeks. This was the effect of "proletarian literature," which was all the rage right now. Why, even up at Vassar, they were teaching it in courses; Miss Peebles gave it after "Multiplicity" in Contemporary Prose Fiction. Kay said that Libby ought to try the *Nation* and the *New Republic*, for they had a high standing among thinking people like her doctor father, but Libby said, "*Mon ange*, it's the *sitting* that interests me; I don't want to get fleas!"

Book reviewing, moreover, was only a means to an end: it got your name known in publishing circles, where they read every review, no matter how short. And it was there that Libby was going to make her way, come hell or high water, and despite her bouts of discouragement, when it seemed to her that she could not face another "Blue Monday" watching Mr. LeRoy scratch his mustache as he looked through her reports. Monday was her established "day" with Mr. LeRoy, a day she had fixed herself and never varied from, unless it was a holiday; men were creatures of habit.

After that grim session when he had given her such a scare, Libby decided that she must have another string to her bow. "You write damned well. . . ." This put the bee in her bonnet of talking to him about doing translations; the idea was really Kay's originally. Kay said Harald said that Libby's problem was to become a specialist in something. Otherwise, she was just competing with all the English majors who graduated every June and who had all been class poet or editor of their literary magazine. Libby should use her foreign languages—particularly her Italian, having lived there—to carve a field for herself. She should offer to do a sample chapter free, then, if they liked it, translate the book, setting aside an hour a day for the purpose. The literary exercise would be good for her style, and meanwhile she would be becoming an expert—a kind of technician. Other publishers would send her Italian books to read and editors would come to her to review Italian authors; she would meet scholars and professors and become an authority. In a technological society, Harald said, it was all a question of having the right tool.

Libby did not exactly feature herself as a translator; editing was much more exciting because you worked with people. Besides, Harald's project, like most of his ideas, was too long-term to stimulate her imagination. At the same time, she felt that she could not allow her relation with Mr. LeRoy to stand still. It dawned on her that this might be a way of moving into the foreign-book line. They paid more ($7.50) for reading foreign books, she had discovered. So the very next time she saw Mr. LeRoy, she did not even wait for him to riffle through the manuscript bin; she took the bull by the horns and said she wanted him to let her have a chance at reporting on a French or an Italian novel; she was going to try her hand at translating. "I'll do the report and then if we want to publish the book, I'll do you a sample chapter."

Mr. LeRoy, she thought, rather squirmed at that "we," which she had put in on purpose to sound professional. But by the strangest coincidence, that very day he had had an Italian novel back from his regular Italian specialist, a professor at Columbia, with a report that ended "Suggest you get another opinion." It was fate, plainly, that Libby had happened in at that moment, and Mr. LeRoy clearly felt that too. "O.K.," he said. "Take it home with you." He reflected. "Your Italian is pretty fluent?" "*Fluentissimo*." It would not pay her, he warned, to try to set up as a translator if she were not completely at home in the language; speed was of the essence. Libby left the office slightly daunted; something in Mr. LeRoy's attitude made her feel he was giving her her last chance.

Back in her apartment, she saw the trap he had laid for her. The conversation in the book was mostly in Sicilian dialect. Libby, who was used to the pure Tuscan, nearly passed away. In fact, she was not even sure it was Sicilian; the characters seemed to be peasants and small landowners, and the village they inhabited could be anywhere. She thought of dashing up to Vassar to consult Mr. Roselli, but, woe was her, he was on sabbatical leave, and the other members of the department, who were not her particular friends, would probably broadcast the fact that she had fled back to college for help. A small voice told her to return the book to Mr. LeRoy and admit that it was too hard for her, but she could not face the thought; this would give him an excuse to tell her that she was through.

Libby took a stance in the middle of her living room, one hand clapped to her brow, the other holding the book outstretched in a declamatory manner. "Lost, lost, all lost," she exclaimed. "Farewell, sweet maid." She then staggered to the couch and reopened the book—521 pages! It fell from her pale, limp hand, the leaves sadly fluttering. One of the big features of living alone was that you could talk to yourself all you wanted and address imaginary audiences, running the gamut of emotion. She rose from the sofa now, shaking her head, and went to contemplate herself in the mirror, scrutinizing her features as if for the last time. Then, shifting mood, she gave herself a nudge in the ribs and went to feed her lovebirds some lettuce, reminding herself that she still had a week in which to cope. "Be brave!" she clarioned, popping on her hat, and stamped out to Alice MacCollister's to dinner, where she saw a girl she knew, eating with a man. Stopping by their table on the way out, Libby instantly confided her problems with this Italian novel, which she showed them, having brought it along, with her pocket dictionary, to work on during dinner. "We *saw* you!" the girl said. "Gosh, it must make you feel important to have a job like that!" "I may not have it long," Libby prophesied. "Five hundred and *twenty*-one pages of the thickest Sicilian. And me nurtured on Dante."

She did not get her report done till late the following Sunday, though she stayed home nearly the whole weekend and did not even do the *Times* crossword puzzle. Her summary of the plot was short. Some features of the action had baffled her, despite some heavy work with the atlas and the dictionaries in the Public Library. She described the book as a "study of the agrarian problems of modern Italy, seen against the background of a feudal past. Don Alfonso, the protagonist, representative of the old order, is at odds with the mayor of the village, who stands for progress and innovation. The peasants, who are sharply characterized and who speak a rich, racy idiom redolent of the sty and the barnyard, are divided between the point of view of Don Alfonso and that of the mayor, Don Onofrio. Don Onofrio's daughter, Eufemia, is drawn into the political struggle and is stabbed by accident during a tumultuous meeting in the piazza. The peasants treat her as a saint and attempt to venerate her remains. The parish priest intervenes. The *carabinieri* appear, and order is finally restored, after a 'miracle' worked at the tomb of Donna Eufemia. This occurs just as the obsequies of Don Alfonso, the last of his race, are being performed and suggests an intended symbolism. There is much curious folklore, well presented, particularly the tapestry or, better, mosaic of pagan belief, Christian superstition, and primitive animism seen darkly glittering in the minds of the peasants, as in some ancient, dim-lit, bat-flittery church with its uneven pavement marked by the worn, sunken tombs of Norman Crusaders and the clerestory upheld by defaced pillars ravaged from Greek temples. The political 'slant' of the author is not sufficiently defined. Where does he stand in the struggle? With Don Alfonso or with the mayor? He does not say, but it is important that we, as readers, should know. The place assigned the 'miracle' tends to make us believe that he stands with the mayor; *ergo*, with present-day Italy and Il Duce. The *carabinieri* enter as virtual deliverers. If we attempt to peer into the cauldron of boiling *minestra* which this tale constitutes, we are driven back by the steam of pungent, scalding language. But this reader, at any rate, could not escape the suspicion that the author has written an apologia for the corporate state. For this reason, I would register a negative opinion on the book's chances here."

Libby had often heard her aunt in Fiesole say that Mussolini was doing the Italians a great deal of good; and she had been thrilled herself as a little girl by the Blackshirt rallies in the Piazza della Signoria. But she had tried to look at the novel from Mr. LeRoy's point of view, what with Ethiopia and Haile Selassie and the League, and she felt pleased, on the whole, with her "effort" when she brought it in to him on Monday, especially with the way she had managed to *suggest* that the book was laid in Sicily without actually naming it, in case she might be wrong.

She sat there lacing her fingers as he glanced through her

report. "Sounds like a damned opera," he remarked, raising his eyes from the first sentences. Libby just waited. He went on reading and suddenly shot her a quizzing look from under his bushy brows. He put her blue folder down, pulled the silk cord abstractedly, raised one pained eyebrow as if he had *tic douloureux*, and slowly lit his pipe. "Oh me oh my!" he commented. He was chuckling. "What book did you read?" he demanded and handed her the first reader's report. ". . . a too-little-known classic of militant Italian liberalism tempered with Chekhovian pity and ironic detachment . . . The author, whose place in Italian letters was made by this one novel, died in 1912. . . ."

Libby was speechless. "Sound of hollow laughter," she said finally, venturing a peal of same. "I can explain," she went on. "It's not important," he said. "I can see how you were misled. Probably customs and manners haven't changed much in Italy in the last fifty years." "The words out of my mouth!" ejaculated Libby, almost bounding out of her chair with relief. "Time has stood still in the *Mezzogiorno*. That's what I was going to say. I thought the author was trying to emphasize the backwardness. *You* know, that it was part of his thesis. Oh, did you ever hear anything so funny? But I'll have to redo my report. 'In the light of recent discoveries'—ha, ha. If you'll just give it back to me . . ." She turned her bright face anxiously to him, realizing that she had become horribly nervous, which was the effect his musing silences had on her.

He sighed. "Miss MacAusland," he said, "I'm going to have to give it to you straight. I think you'd better look for some other kind of work. Have you ever thought of trying for a job with a literary agent? Or on one of the women's magazines? You've got a real writing talent, believe me, and plenty of drive. But you're not cut out for straight publishing." "But why?" said Libby quite calmly; now that the blow had fallen, she felt an actual relief; she was only curious as to what he would say—not concerned. He puffed on his pipe. "I don't know that I can explain it to you. I've tried in my own mind to figure out exactly what's wrong. You just don't have the knack or maybe the common sense or the nose or whatever it is for picking out a publishable manuscript. Or let's say you're not hard-boiled enough. You're essentially a sympathizer. That's why I see you with a literary agent. You keep telling me you want to work with authors. Well, that's what agents do, work hand in glove with them, especially on magazine stuff. Encourage them; ride them; tell them what to cut; hold their hand; take them out to lunch." "But publishers do that too," put in Libby sharply. She had often pictured herself, in a snappy hat and suit, taking authors out to lunch on the expense account and discussing their work over coffee. "Those rumors are greatly exaggerated," said Mr. LeRoy. "You probably think I lunch every day with famous authors at the Ritz. As a matter of fact, I eat at least two lunches a week alone in the Automat. I'm dieting. Today, I lunched with an agent—a damned smart one, a woman. She makes three times what I do." Libby's well-arched brows manifested surprise and incredulity. "That's another thing, Miss Mac-Ausland." He leaned forward. "Publishing's a man's business. Book publishing, that is. Name me a woman, outside of Blanche Knopf, who married Alfred, who's come to the top in book publishing. You find them on the fringes, in publicity and advertising. Or you find them copy editing or reading proof. Old maids mostly, with a pencil behind their ear and dyspepsia. We've got a crackerjack here, Miss Chambers, who's been with us twenty years. I think she was Vassar too. Or maybe Bryn Mawr. Vinegary type, with a long thin nose that looks as if it ought to have a drop on the end of it, a buttoned-up sweater, metal-rimmed glasses; a very smart, decent, under-paid, fine woman. Our galley slave; pardon the pun. No. Pub-lishing's a man's business, unless you marry into it. Marry a publisher, Miss MacAusland, and be his hostess. Or make connections with an agent. Or work your way up in the slicks."

"What a picture you conjure up," said Libby thoughtfully, her chin cupped in her hand. "I wonder . . . Would you let me do an interview with you for the *Vassar Alumnae Maga-zine*?" Mr. LeRoy put up his hand. "I don't think that would be in keeping with the firm's policy," he said stuffily. "Oh, but I wouldn't have to name you, if you didn't want. I could just take a few notes now. Or, better, if you were free some day for a cocktail . . . ?" But he rudely brushed this aside. "We're having sales conference this week, Miss MacAusland. And next week, let's see—" he glanced at his desk calendar—"next week I have to be out of town." He cleared his throat. "You can write what you want, of course, but I'd rather not be involved in it." "I understand," said Libby.

She started to get up then, till it dawned on her that she was just tamely accepting her dismissal without having heard one adequate reason. He was only talking in generalities, not telling her frankly where she had failed, so that she could have a chance to correct it. And if she did not think of something fast, she would have no excuse, like the interview, for seeing him again. What did you do in a case like that?

She lit a cigarette. "Couldn't you try me at something else? Writing blurbs, for instance. I'm sure I could write blurbs." He cut her short. "I fully agree that you could write very passable jacket copy. But that's one of the mechanical trades in this business. No honor attaches to it. Everybody pitches in. I do it; all the editors do it; my secretary does it; the office boy does it. It comes down to this, Miss MacAusland; we really have no work that you're uniquely qualified to do. You're one of thousands of English majors who come pouring out of the colleges every June, stage-struck to go into publishing. Their families back them for a while; a year is about the limit. Till the girls finally find somebody to marry them and the boys go into something else."

"And your opinion," said Libby, "is that I'm just one of those. Those anonymous hordes." "You're more persevering," he said, with a glance at his watch and a sigh. "And you say your family isn't supporting you. Which makes your perseverance more redoubtable. And you do seem to have some eerie relation to literature. I wish you luck." And with that, he was standing up and vigorously shaking her hand across the desk. Her lighted cigarette dropped on the rug. "Oh, my cigarette! Oh, horrors!" she cried. "Where is it?" "Never mind," he said. "We'll find it. Miss Bisbee!" he called, to his secretary, who promptly poked her head in the open doorway. "There's a lighted cigarette in here somewhere. Find it, will you? And see that Miss MacAusland gets her check in the mail." He grabbed up Libby's coat and held it for her; the secretary was on her hands and knees scrabbling around the floor; Libby's head was reeling with the shock and confusion. She took a step backward and, girls, can you imagine it, she fainted kerplunk into Mr. LeRoy's arms!

It must have been the overheated office. Mr. LeRoy's secretary told her afterward that she had turned quite green and the cold sweat had been standing out on her forehead. Just like the summer day her aunt was with her when she passed out cold in the Uffizi in front of "The Birth of Venus." But Gus LeRoy (short for Augustus) was convinced it was because she was hungry—she confessed she had not eaten any lunch. He insisted on giving her $10 out of his own pocket and a dollar for a taxi besides. Then the next morning he rang her up and told her to go to see this literary agent who needed an assistant. So that now, lo and behold, she had this snazzy job at $25 a week, reading manuscripts and writing to authors and having lunch with editors. She and Gus LeRoy were the best of friends; he was married after all, she learned from her boss.

Gus LeRoy met Polly Andrews at a party given by Libby in May the following year. It was 1936, and half the group were married. Of the old crowd, Libby had invited only Priss, who couldn't come, and Polly and Kay; the others, she had rather lost sight of. She was serving a May *bowle*, made of Liebfraumilch and fresh strawberries and sweet woodruff. There was a special store where you could get the woodruff, dried and imported from Germany; it was over on Second Avenue, under the El, a dusty old German firm with apothecary jars and old apothecaries' scales and mortars and pestles in the window. Polly could not possibly miss it, Libby said on the phone; it was right around the corner from where she lived, and she could stop and get the woodruff for Libby any day on her way home from work. If she brought it the day before the party, that would be in plenty of time; it only had to steep overnight. Polly worked as a technician at Cornell Medical Center, giving basal metabolism tests chiefly, which meant that she had to be at the hospital the first thing in the morning, when the patients woke up. But she got off early in the afternoons, which Libby didn't, and took the Second Avenue El home quite often—she lived on Tenth Street, near St. Mark's Place, almost catercorner from St. Mark's-in-the-Bouwerie, where the rector, Dr. Guthrie, had such beautiful liturgy, though Polly never took advantage of it and slept Sunday mornings.

The herbal firm was nine blocks from Polly's place; trust Polly, who could be prickly in her mild, smiling, obstinate way, to let that transpire when she appeared with the woodruff at Libby's apartment. But they were nine short blocks, dear, Libby retorted, and Polly could use the fresh air and exercise. When she heard Polly's description of the shop's display of pharmacopoeia—all the old herbs and simples and materia medica in big stoppered glass jars with the Latin names written in crabbed Gothic lettering—she was sorry she had not gone herself, in a taxi. But to reward Polly for her pains, Libby had taken them both out to dinner at a new place in the Village, and afterward they had come back to the apartment and got the *bowle* started and everything organized for the party. Polly had a passion for flowers (she did wonders that evening with Libby's mountain dogwood), and she was efficient in the kitchen. Libby had persuaded her to make Mr. Andrews' famous chicken-liver *pâté*, a receipt he had brought back from France, and, having splurged on chicken livers at the market, she stood by watching Polly *sauter* them and laboriously push them through a sieve. "Aren't you doing them too rare?" she suggested. "Kay says *she* always cooks everything fifteen minutes longer than the recipe calls for." Libby was scandalized by the amount of fresh print butter Polly mixed in afterward, *plus* brandy and sherry—no wonder the Andrews family was insolvent. But Polly was sweet to do it and tenacious about having her own way, once she started on something. All the Andrews were like that. Mr. Andrews, Polly said, clung to making his own stock and boiling it down for the glaze, but Polly consented to use Campbell's consommé to line the mold, thank Heaven; otherwise, they would have been up till dawn. As it was, Libby was completely exhausted by the time Polly left. Just pushing those livers through a sieve had taken nearly an hour. She would not hear of Polly's washing up; a colored maid was coming the next afternoon to clean and serve at the party.

Fortunately, Polly could take the Eighth Street bus home; it was a long walk from Libby's place, just west of Fifth Avenue, and you had to pass some pretty sinister lofts and warehouses. Polly's apartment, though in a fairly decent block, was not as attractive as Libby's, which had high ceilings and a fireplace and windows almost down to the floor. In fact, it was flattery to call Polly's an apartment. It was really a furnished room and bath, with a studio bed, which Polly had covered with a pretty patchwork quilt from home, and some worn Victorian chairs and a funny old marble-topped table with lion's-claw feet, and a two-burner hot plate and some shelves covered with bright-blue oilcloth in one white-curtained-off corner, and an icebox that leaked. At least it was clean; the family were professional people (actually, the wife was Vassar, Class of '18), and Polly had made friends with the other lodgers—two refugees, one a White Russian and the other a German-Jewish socialist—and always had funny stories to tell about them and their violent discussions. Polly was a sympathetic soul; everybody she met told her their troubles and probably borrowed money from her. Yet, poor girl, her family could not afford to send her a cent. Her Aunt Julia, who lived on Park and Seventy-second, had given her some china and a chafing dish, but she did not realize how the other half lived; for one thing, she had heart trouble and could not climb Polly's stairs. In her day, St. Mark's Place had been a nice neighborhood, and she did not know that things had changed. Still, Polly's apartment would be perfectly suitable if she did not have this habit of letting herself be imposed on by strangers. The German-Jewish man, for instance, Mr. Schneider, was constantly bringing her little presents, colored marzipan in the shape of fruits (once he brought her a marzipan hot dog, which for some reason delighted Polly), chocolate-covered ginger, a tiny pot with a St. Patrick's Day shamrock, and in return Polly was helping him with his English, so that he could get a better job. This meant that almost every evening he was tapping at her door. Libby had met him one night—a dwarf, practically, with frizzy grey hair in a mop and a thick accent but old enough (Libby was glad to see) to be Polly's father, if Mr. Andrews had not been almost old enough himself to be her grandfather. You found the most curious visitors at Polly's, most of them ancient as the hills: Ross, her Aunt Julia's maid, who you had to admit was a sketch, sitting there doing her knitting, having brought Polly some lamb chops from her aunt's butcher on Park Avenue; the White Russian, poor devil, who liked to play chess with Polly; the iceman. Well, that was a bit exaggerated, but Polly did have an awfully funny story about the Italian iceman, a veritable troglodyte, coming in one day with the ice on his shoulder this last March and saying "Tacks" over and over and Polly offering him thumbtacks and him shaking his head and saying "No, no, lady; *tacks*!"; it turned out, believe it or not, that he was having trouble with his income-tax return, which he whipped out of his back pocket with his horny hand—only Polly would have an iceman who paid income tax. Naturally, she sat down and helped him with the arithmetic and his business deductions and dependents. Yet when one of her friends asked something of her, she might suddenly flush up and say, "Libby, you can perfectly well do that yourself."

To look at, she was one of those "gentle ray of sunshine"

girls—very fair, with almost flaxen hair, the color of pale straw or rough raw silk, big blue eyes, and milk-white skin, bluish, like skim milk; she had a soft, plump chin with a sort of dimple or cleft in it, plump white arms, and a wide, open brow. Some people thought she looked like Ann Harding in the movies, but she was not as tall as Ann Harding. She had taken to wearing her hair in braids around her broad head; she thought it was neater, for the hospital, all coiled around like that. The trouble was, it made her look older. When Priss was having her last miscarriage, in New York Hospital, in semi-private, Polly had stopped in to visit her every day, which was easy for *her* since she worked there; seeing her in her white coat and low-heeled shoes and those matronly braids, the other patient thought that Polly must be at least twenty-six. She had been on the Daisy Chain (that made four in the group—Libby herself, Lakey, Kay, and Polly—which was sort of a record), but Libby had never agreed that Polly was beautiful. She was too placid and colorless, unless she smiled. Kay had cast her as the Virgin in the Christmas pantomime senior year, which she directed, but this was to give her a pickup from having broken her engagement to the boy with the bad heredity. Actually, behind that placid exterior, Polly was rather emotional but very good fun, really a delightful companion, with an original point of view. All the Andrews were original. Polly had majored in Chemistry, thinking that she might be a doctor, but when Mr. Andrews lost his money, naturally she had to give that up; luckily, the college Vocational Bureau had got her placed at New York Hospital–Cornell Medical Center. All the group hoped she would meet some ravishing young doctor or pathologist who would want to marry her, but so far this had not happened or if so no one knew about it. About herself, Polly was very reserved. It sometimes sounded as if she saw nobody but her aunt and those strange inhabitants of her rooming house and other girls with jobs, some of them pretty dreary—the type, as Kay said, that had bulbs of paper narcissuses growing in their windows in a dish from the five-and-ten. This capacity for making lackluster friends, especially of her own sex, was Polly's *faiblesse*. The Chem majors at college were a case in point, worthy souls, no doubt, but the science majors as a group (credit Kay for this observation too) were about the lowest stratum at Vassar. They were the ones, as Kay said, you would not remember when you came back for your tenth reunion: pathetic cases with skin trouble and superfluous hair and thick glasses and overweight or underweight problems and names like Miss Hasenpfeffer. What would happen to them afterward? Would they all go home and become pillars of their community and send their daughters back to Vassar to perpetuate the type or would they go into teaching or medicine, where you might even hear of them some day? "Dr. Elfrida Katzenbach is with the Rockefeller Institute—Congratulations, Katzy," you would read in the alumnae news and "Who was she?" you would ask yourself. Astronomy and Zoology were a little different— Pokey had majored in Zoology and, would wonders never cease incidentally, last year she had up and married a poet, a sort of distant cousin who was in Graduate School at Princeton—her family had bought them a house down there, but Pokey still commuted by plane to Ithaca and was still planning to be a vet. Anyway, Astronomy and Zoology were different—not so dry, more descriptive; Botany too. Next to the Physics and Chem majors in dreariness came the language majors; Libby had narrowly escaped that fate. They were all going to be French or Spanish teachers in the high school back home and had names like Miss Peltier and Miss La Gasa. Polly had her followers among them too, who were even invited up to stay in Stockbridge, to talk French with Mr. Andrews. Polly was a democrat (all the Andrews voted for Roosevelt, being related to the Delanos), though Lakey used to say that the democracy was all on the surface and that underneath Polly was a feudal snob.

Be that as it might, Libby saw Polly as often as she could and almost always asked her to her parties. The trouble was, Polly, though wonderful company when you were alone with her, did not shine at big gatherings. Her voice was very low, like her father's, who virtually whispered his mild remarks. If you did not explain her family background (a nest of gentlefolk with a few bats in the belfry; Mr. Andrews' sisters had all been painted by Sargent), people were inclined to overlook her or ask after she had gone home who that quiet blonde girl was. That was another thing; she always left early unless you gave her something to do, like talking to a bore, to make her feel useful. All you had to do was tell her to go rescue some stick who was standing in a corner, and Polly would engage him in animated conversation and find out all sorts of wondrous things about him that nobody had ever suspected. But if you told her someone was a great catch, she would not make the slightest effort—"I'm afraid I must make my excuses, Libby" (all the Andrews talked like that).

But the minute you started a game, be it poker or "Pin the Tail on the Donkey," Polly was in her element, delighted to sort chips or cut out pieces of paper or make blindfolds; she was always the court of authority or the umpire—the person who decided the rules and kept everybody in order. That was the Andrews family again. Having lost their money and had so much trouble, they kept cheerful by doing charades and playing games. Anybody who stayed with them in that rambling old farmhouse, with its big fireplaces and attics and storerooms, was immediately drafted to be "It" after dinner and hastily told all the rules, and woe to him or her who was not quick to catch on. Some nights they did charades, very complicated ones, in costumes in the barn with kerosene stoves to keep warm. Some nights they played "Murder," though that made Mr. Andrews very nervous, they discovered, for it seemed he had had violent spells in the hospital and trembled if he had to do the carving at the table on one of his darker days. Some nights they played "*Cache-Cache*," which was just the French version of good old "Hide and Seek" with slightly different rules that they had learned in their chateau in France. Or "Ghosts," which the family had renamed "Punkin" because Mr. Andrews sometimes burst into quiet tears or laughed strangely when he missed a question and had to say "I'm one-third of a ghost"; so now instead they said "one-third of a punkin," after "pumpkin head." Then they played "Geography," which Mr. Andrews was a perfect fiend at, having traveled so much and knowing all the Y's and K's like Ypres, which he called "Wipers," and Yezd and Kyoto and Knossos. And a new version of "Ghosts" that they called the "Wily Austrian Diplomat" game ("Are you a wily Austrian diplomat?" "No, I am not Metternich"). Polly's family, being brainy, liked these guessing games almost best, next to charades, but they played silly ones too, like "I Packed My Grandmother's Trunk." And on rainy days there were chess and checkers and parcheesi; the family had had to give up Monopoly (some kind friend had sent them a set), again because of Mr. Andrews, poor lamb, who was always reminded of his investments. When they had to make a joint decision, like where to send young Billy to college or what to have for Christmas dinner, they would solemnly do the "*sortes Virgilianae*" in full concourse assembled with Mr. Andrews' old *Aeneid*; the idea was that the children became voting members of the family when they were able to construe Latin—think of that! Then the children got up treasure hunts, with homemade pincushions and calendars and a single amaryllis bulb for prizes, to take the place of paper chases, because they could not afford riding horses any more— only a few cows and chickens; one winter they had tried a pig. Polly used to hunt and ride sidesaddle, and she still had her riding habit and boots and bowler, which she took with her down to Princeton when Pokey remembered to ask her (Pokey had her own stables and hunted weekends); she had had to let out the coat, because she was a little fatter now than she was at eighteen, but they said she still looked very pretty, with her white skin and pale hair in the full-skirted black riding costume with a stock. Black was Polly's color.

Weekdays, she dressed very plainly, in an old sweater and plaid skirt and low-heeled shoes. But for parties, like today, she had one good black crepe dress, with a low scalloped neckline and a fringed sash, and she had two wide-brimmed black hats, one for winter and one for summer. The summer one, which she was wearing today, was a lacy straw trimmed with black lace. The crepe of her dress was getting a little rusty (black crepe did that, alas), but it set off her full white neck, fleshy chin, and bosom; she had done her hair low on her neck, in a big knot, which was much more becoming. Harald Petersen said she looked like a Renoir. But Libby thought a Mary Cassatt. Libby herself was in high-necked brown taffeta (brown was *her* color) with topaz earrings to bring out the gold lights in her hair and eyes. She thought Polly, who did not have any good jewelry left, might have worn a white rose in her corsage.

Libby had balanced her guests carefully: a little bit of Vassar, a little bit of publishing, Sister and her husband, who were just back from Europe, a little bit of Wall Street, a little bit of the stage, a lady author, a man from the *Herald Tribune*, a woman from the Metropolitan Museum. *E così via*; she had not asked anybody from the office, because it was not that kind of party. A rather mixed bag, Sister commented, narrowing her amethyst eyes, but Sister had always been critical of Libby's aspirations. "Noah's Ark, eh?" chuckled Sister's husband. "Bring on your menagerie, Lib!" He never failed to tease her about leading "the literary life." Libby usually played up to this, but today she had other fish to fry. She wanted Sister and her husband to impress her latest flame. His name was Nils Aslund; she had met him this winter on the ski train. He was the ski jumper at Altman's and a *genuine Norwegian baron*! Her brother-in-law, who was getting too fat, nearly choked on a gob of Mr. Andrews' *pâté*, when Nils came in, wearing the most beautiful Oxford-gray suit, and bent to kiss Sister's hand—you only did that with married women, Nils had explained to her. He had the most heavenly manners and a marvelous figure and danced divinely. Even Sister had to admit he was pretty snazzy, after talking to him for a while. His English was almost perfect, with just the trace of an accent; he had studied English literature at the University, and imagine, before he knew Libby, he had read her poem in *Harper's* and remembered it. They had the same interests; Libby was almost certain he was going to propose, which was partly why she had decided to have this party. She wanted him to see her in her setting; hence the dogwood, girls. She had never let him come up to the apartment before; you never knew, with Europeans, what they might assume. But at a party, with some of her family present, that was different. Afterward, he was going to take her to dinner, and that was where, she expected, if all went well, he was going to pop the question. Her brother-in-law must have smelled a rat too. "Well, Lib," he said, "is he gainfully employed?" Libby told him that he was in charge of the ski run at Altman's; he had come to America to study business. "Seems a funny place to start," said her brother-in-law, thoughtfully. "Why not the Street?" He chuckled. "You certainly can pick 'em. But seriously, Lib, that rates him socially about on a par with a golf pro." Libby bit her lip. She had been afraid of this reaction from her family. But she mastered her vexation and disappointment; if she accepted Nils, she decided, she could make it a condition that he find some other work. Perhaps they could open a ski lodge in the Berkshires; another Vassar girl and her husband had done that. And still another couple had a ranch out West. It was just a question of waiting till his father died, when he would go home and run the ancestral estate. . . .

With all this on her mind, it was no wonder that Libby, at the height of her party, forgot to keep an eye on Polly and see that she was circulating. When things calmed down a bit, what was her amazement to discover her deep in conversation with Gus LeRoy, who had said, when he arrived, that he could only stay a minute. Libby never did find out who had introduced them. They were standing by the window, looking at Libby's lovebirds. Polly was feeding them bits of strawberry from her glass (the poor birds would be tight as ticks on Liebfraumilch), and Gus LeRoy was talking to her a mile a minute. Libby nudged Kay. Polly's blue-white breasts were rather in evidence, which was probably the source of the attraction, and her strawy hair, which had a tendency to be untidy, it was so fine, was slipping a little from its pins in the back, at the nape of her neck.

Libby started to tell Kay Gus LeRoy's history. Her baron was hovering nearby, and she signaled to him to join them. "We're prophesying a romance," she explained. Gus came from Fall River, where his family had a printing business. He and his wife were separated, and there was one child, about two and a half years old, Augustus LeRoy IV. The wife taught at a progressive school and was a Communist party member; she was having an affair with somebody in her cell—that was why Gus had left her. Up to now, he had been pretty pink himself but never a party member, and he had brought several important authors who were Communist sympathizers to the firm, but now the Communists were turning a cold shoulder on him because he wanted to divorce his wife and name this other man, which they called a "splitting tactic" or something. "Nils is a Social Democrat," she added, smiling. "No, no," said the baron. "As a student, I was. Now I am neutral. Not neuter." He gave his jolly, boyish laugh and looked sidelong at Libby. The reason Libby had heard all this, she continued, flashing a reproachful look at Nils, was that there was an open Communist right in her office—a very homely girl, built like a truck, with nothing to do but drink by herself in the evenings or go to Party meetings. This girl or woman (she must be almost thirty) knew Gus LeRoy's wife. "Oh well, homely women!" said the baron, making a disdainful face. "For them it's like the church." Libby hesitated. The story that popped into her mind was a bit off color, but it would point a moral to Nils. "I beg to differ, dear sir. You should hear the horrible thing that happened to this girl the other night. Quite another pair of gloves from the Girls Friendly Society or the Altar Guild of St. Paul's. I had to take over this girl's work for her till they let her out of the hospital. Four teeth knocked out and a fractured jaw. That was what she got for being a Communist." "Picketing," cried Kay. "Did you hear that Harald led a picket march the other day?" Libby shook her head. "*Quite* another pair of gloves," she repeated. "This girl—I won't tell you her name— being a Communist, is very sympathetic to the workingman. Point two: she drinks. You should smell her breath some mornings. Well, one night—actually it was over a month ago; you remember that cold spell we had late in March?—well, she was coming home in a taxi, having had one too many in a bar somewhere, and she started talking to the taxi driver and commiserating with him about his lot, naturally, and they both mentioned how cold it was. She noticed—anyway, that's how she told the story—that he didn't have an overcoat or extra jacket on. So, as one comrade to another, she asked him up for a drink, to get warm." Kay caught her breath; Libby nodded. Several other guests drew near to listen; Libby had quite a reputation as a storyteller. "Maybe she thought being so homely was some protection," she pursued. "But he had other ideas. And he assumed she did too. So when he had had the drink, he made overtures. She was very startled and pushed him away. The next thing she knew, she came to on her floor, in a pool of blood, with her teeth all over the place and her jaw broken. He was gone, of course." "Did—?" "No," said Libby. "Apparently not. And nothing was stolen. Her purse was lying right beside her on the floor. My boss wanted her to go to the police. So did the hospital. They had to wire her jaw together, and it will take her *years* to pay for the dental work. But she wouldn't do a thing about it. It's against Communist principles, it seems, to call the police against a 'worker.' And she

said, between her clamped jaws, that it was her own fault."
"Quite right," said Nils firmly. "She was in the wrong." "Oh, I
don't agree at *all*," cried Kay. "If every time someone misunderstood you, they had a right to knock your teeth out . . . ?
Or if every time you tried to be nice, it was taken the wrong
way?" "Girls should not try to be nice to taxi drivers," said Nils.
"Old Europe speaking," retorted Kay. "I'm always nice to taxi
drivers. And nothing has ever happened." "Really? Never?" said
Sister, looking rather pityingly at Kay. "Well, actually," said Kay,
"once one did try to get into the back of the cab with me."
"Heavens!" said Libby. "What did you do?" "I talked him out
of it," said Kay. The baron laughed heartily; he had evidently
caught on to the fact that Kay was an inveterate arguer. "But,
Kay, my child, what had you done to encourage him?" said
Libby. "Absolutely nothing," said Kay. "We were talking, and all
of a sudden he said I was beautiful and that he liked the perfume
I was wearing. And he stopped the cab and got out." "He had
good taste. Don't you think so, Elizabeth?" Nils spoke of Kay,
but he looked deeply into Libby's eyes with his bright burning
blue ones till her knees nearly knocked together.

    After that, discussion was general. Kay wanted to tell about
Harald's picketing. "His picture was in the tabloids," she declared. Libby sighed, because of Sister and her husband. But
the story, it turned out, was fascinating—not the usual kind of
thing at all. It seemed that Harald had been directing a play for
a left-wing group downtown. It was one of those profit-sharing
things, co-operatives, but run really by Communists behind
the scenes, as Harald found out in due course. The play was
about labor, and the audiences were mostly theatre parties got
up by the trade unions. "So when Harald found out that these
Communists in the management were cooking the books, he
organized the actors and threw a picket line around the theatre." The man from the *Herald Tribune* scratched his jaw. "I
remember that," he said, looking curiously at Harald. "Your
paper played the story down," said Kay. "So did the *Times*."
"Because of advertising?" suggested the lady author. Harald
shook his head and shrugged. "Go on, if you must," he said to
Kay. "Well, the audience couldn't cross a picket line, obviously,
even if most of the actors hadn't been in it. So the management
had to agree right then and there to show its books every week

to a committee of the actors, which Harald is head of. Then they all marched into the theatre." "And the show went on!" concluded Harald, with an ironical flourish of his hand. "So you won," said Nils. "Very interesting." In practice, Kay said, the actors were still only getting the $40 Equity minimum, because the show was not doing too well. "But in principle," Harald said dryly, "''twas a famous victory.'" His skeletal face looked sad.

He was not drinking, Libby noted; perhaps he had promised Kay. His own play, poor man, had not been done after all, because the producer's wife had suddenly sued for divorce, just as they were casting, and withdrawn her money; a lawsuit was going on, which Harald's play was somehow tied up in. Harald had never been a special favorite of Libby's. They said that he was constantly sleeping with other women, and that Kay either did not know about it or did not mind, she was still so dominated by him intellectually. But he had thoroughly charmed Nils today, talking a little bit of Norwegian to him and reciting a few lines of *Peer Gynt* (you pronounced it "Per Gunt"), in which Nils had joined. "A delightful fellow, Petersen," Nils said to Libby. "You have such charming friends." And even Sister remarked that he was an ugly-attractive man.

All this time, Polly and Gus LeRoy had been standing by the window, paying no attention to the conversation. Their wine glasses were empty. Polly was very temperate because of the alcoholism in her family (one of her uncles had ridden a horse, while drinking, into the Copley Plaza in Boston), but usually she made an exception for wine and for odd liqueurs like Goldwasser and the one that had a tree growing in the bottle. Libby floated up to them and took their glasses to refill. "I think he's asking her to dinner," she reported to Kay. "And mark my words, she'll refuse. She'll find some bizarre reason for having to go home."

Sure enough, before long, Polly was "making her excuses" and wondering if she could have a little of the *bowle* to take home with her to that Mr. Schneider. Libby threw up her hands. "Why?" she wanted to know. "He can perfectly well go around the corner to Luchow's if he wants a glass of May wine. Why do you have to bring it to him?" Polly colored. "I'm afraid it was my idea. I told him about your *bowle* when I

brought the woodruff home. And he and Mr. Scherbatyeff had
a violent nationalistic argument about what to put in white-
wine punches. Mr. Scherbatyeff"—she gave her quick humorous smile—"favors cucumber rind. Anyway, I offered to bring
them home a sample of yours. If you can spare it, Libby."
Libby glanced at the punch bowl, calculating; it was still a
third full, and the guests were thinning out. "It won't be good
tomorrow," put in Kay, tactlessly. "The strawberries will go
bad. Unless you strain it. . . ." "If you have a cream bottle I
can take it in," persisted Polly, "or an old mayonnaise jar."
Libby bit her lips. Unlike Polly, she had no patience with the
kind of German refugee who was homesick for the old country
and the "good old German ways." She and Polly had argued
about this before, and Polly said it was their *country*, Libby,
but Libby said they would have to adapt to America. And,
frankly, she thought it was a bit unseemly for a German Jew to
be such a supporter of German products; why, there were
people who believed that even we Americans should boycott
Nazi goods. She would probably be criticized herself for having served Liebfraumilch at her party. Gus LeRoy, she noticed,
had got his hat and was standing there—waiting to say
good-bye to her, she supposed.

She was afraid her irritation showed. "Here," she felt like
saying, "Polly has a chance to go out to dinner with you at
some nice place, and instead she's going home to those lodgers,
because of a silly promise she made! Isn't that perverse?" Besides, no man, not even a parlor pink, liked a girl who carried
things around in old cream bottles stuffed into paper bags.
Libby turned to Polly. "You can't take it home on the bus. It'll
spill." Gus LeRoy stepped forward. "I'm taking her in a taxi,
Miss MacAusland."

Libby fanned herself. "Come into the kitchen," she said to
Polly. She had to talk to her alone. "Now, Polly," she said, "I
don't mind giving you the *bowle*. After all, you got the woodruff for *me*. But don't, please don't, take Gus into that place of
yours and introduce him to all those weird characters. For my
sake, if not for your own, don't." What Libby meant was that
the quaint life of Polly's rooming house was all very well to
dilate on to other girls, when you were having a bite alone, but
a man would think, to hear about it, still more to see it in the

flesh, that you were desperate for company if you had to fall
back on that. A man, any man, wanted to imagine that you
were courted by all sorts of glamorous rivals. . . . Libby
frowned. No, that was not exactly her thought. What was it
about those roomers, about the brownstone house itself, the
very carpet on the stairs, Polly's little tray of gold-speckled liqueur glasses with the worn gold rims, Mr. Scherbatyeff's
smoking jacket, that Libby's feminine instinct told her would
cook a girl's goose with any normal member of the opposite
sex? As though a visit to that house would betray something
horribly personal, like a smell, about Polly. The smell of poverty? But Gus LeRoy might like that. No; the smell of having
seen better days. That was it. That was what they all—the
house, the lodgers, and Polly herself, alas—had in common.
Having seen better days and not making those crucial distinctions any more, not having any real ambition. Hoarding a few
sepulchral joys, like the pomander balls Polly made for Christmas presents—oranges stuck with cloves and rolled in orrisroot
and tied with ribbons to hang in your closet or perfume your
drawers. Actually, those pomander balls were quite snazzy;
they were a very original present and cost practically nothing.
Libby had written down the receipt in her Florentine-leather
receipt book, and she was going to get Polly to help her make
some herself for next Christmas. But somehow it would be all
right for Libby to do it, whereas for Polly . . . ? It would
even be all right, strangely enough, for Libby to live in that
rooming house, not that she would; she could say she was
gathering material for a story. . . .

"I wasn't planning to, Libby," answered Polly, rather stiffly.
"Anyway, let's forget about the *bowle*. Please." "Now don't be
trying," said Libby. "Here, Ida," she called to the maid, "get
Miss Andrews that little glass cocktail shaker. Go and fill it
from the punch bowl, and make sure it's clean, please. Perhaps
Miss Andrews would like some of the *pâté* too. You're sure?"—
she turned swiftly to Polly. "Now what are you going to do?
He's going to drive you to your door. . . ." By dint of close
questioning, Libby established that Polly intended to leave the
bowle at her house and then she and Gus LeRoy were going to
have dinner at that famous Yiddish restaurant right around the
corner from Polly's—the Café Royal, where all the stars from

the Yiddish Theatre went and the journalists from the Jewish newspapers. "Whose idea was that? His?" "Mine, I'm afraid," said Polly. "It's not the *quietest* place." "Nonsense," said Libby. "It's just the thing. Pluperfect." She thought it clever of Polly, since Gus was so hard to talk to, to pick out a place where you could just look at the other patrons and not try to make yourself heard. She herself had been in transports when Polly took her there one night, frankly turning around and rubbernecking and getting Polly to tell her who the celebrities were (every *one* of them was a "name" to his co-religionists, which showed you the emptiness of fame) and uttering cries of delight when the food came, till Polly told her to stop, claiming that it would hurt their feelings to be looked at as curiosities, when anyone could see that that was why they came here—to show off. "No, it's perfect," she said thoughtfully, putting her index finger to her cheek. "Now what are you going to have to eat? That wonderful scarlet borscht *we* had, with the boiled potato popped into it . . . ?" "I haven't thought, Libby," said Polly, taking the cocktail shaker, filled, from the maid. "No, no," said Libby. "Ida will wrap it up for you. You just go to my dressing table and straighten your hair a bit." She lightly pushed some of Polly's silvery hairpins back into the knot at the nape of her full neck and then stood back so that she could examine her profile: Polly was going to have to watch her chin line. "Help yourself to some of the perfume in my atomizer." As Polly was leaving, with Gus LeRoy behind her awkwardly fingering his mustache and then leaping forward to settle Aunt Julia's old silver-fox tippet over her almost bare shoulders, Libby stepped in and extracted Polly's promise to bring back the cocktail shaker tomorrow evening, because Libby might be needing it; that way, Libby would be able to hear the post-mortem.

Kay and Harald said good-bye; they were going to have a hamburger before the performance. Harald went every night, to check on the house and see that the actors were still playing their parts as he had directed them. Kay sometimes went with him and sat in one of the actors' dressing rooms. "She snorts like an old war horse," explained Libby, "at the smell of the grease paint. You can't keep her out of the greenroom. At college, she was a director." There was one of those silences that come toward the end of a party. A few guests still lingered, not realizing, obviously, that Libby had a dinner date with Nils. "Oh, don't go yet," she urged the woman from the Metropolitan, who obediently sat down again; Libby hated the feeling of a room emptying too quickly, as though everyone were afraid of being the last to leave. It was still light out, a perfect May evening. The greenish-white dogwood grew paler in the shadowed corner; the tall Rhine wine bottles glimmered green and gold on the damask-covered punch table; there was a smell of strawberries and lilies of the valley in the room—Nils had brought her a little bunch. Ida was ready to go, with her black satchel; Libby paid her off and in a fit of spring madness told her to take the rest of the *pâté* home. "You are generous," said Nils. "With your maid and your friend. The Liebfraumilch girl." So he too had noticed Polly's display of bosom. Libby laughed uncertainly. The way he had said "generous" made her slightly uneasy. The Metropolitan Museum woman leaned forward. "Speaking of Liebfraumilch, do any of you recall that amusing Tintoretto in the National Gallery? 'The Milky Way'? Such an unusual conceit." Everyone looked blank. "When will we be alone?" Nils murmured into Libby's ear.

This happened sooner than Libby had anticipated. All at once, the other guests, seeing him whisper to her, got up and left. One minute they were there, and the next they were gone. He turned to her. "I'll get my wrap," she said quickly. But he seized her hand. "Not yet, Elizabeth. Why do you let them call you that horrible nickname?" "You don't like it?" "I like Elizabeth," he answered. "I like her very much. Too much." He pulled her to him and bent back her head and kissed her. Libby responded; she had dreamed of this moment so often that she knew just how it should be—her head falling back, like a chalice, to receive his lips, her nostrils contracting, her eyes shut. Nils's lips were soft and warm, contrary to her imaginings, for she always thought of him in a ski sweater, fair and ice-cold, his blond hair windswept under the peak of his cap. The thin skin of his face was very tight-drawn, over reddened high cheekbones, and she would have supposed, with all that outdoor life, that his lips would be hard and taut. He brushed his mouth back and forth gently over hers. Then he tilted her chin, looked into her eyes and kissed her passionately, taking her breath away. Libby staggered back a little and released herself. "Elizabeth!" he said, and again he pulled her to him and kissed her very gently, murmuring her name. In a minute —or hours, she could not really tell—she could feel his large teeth pressing hard against her closed mouth. She broke away, staggering back a second time. She tried to laugh. "Quiet," he said. She pulled the chain of the big brass table lamp, for it was getting dark, and leaned against the table, supporting herself with the palm of one hand while with the other she nervously pushed back her hair. He came and stood beside her, encircling her shoulders with his arm, so that she could rest against him, her forehead brushing his cheek; he was four inches, she reckoned, taller than she was—a perfect difference. Standing like that, at rest, Libby felt utterly comfy; time slipped by. Then he slowly turned her to him, and, before she knew it, he had his tongue in her mouth and was pushing it against hers. His tongue was very firm and pointed. "Give me your tongue, Elizabeth. Give me a tongue kiss." Slowly and reluctantly, she raised the tip of her tongue and let it touch his; a quiver of fire darted through her. Their tongues played together in her mouth; he tried to draw hers, sucking, into his mouth, but she would not let him. A warning bell told her they had gone far enough. This time he let her go of his own accord; she smiled glassily. "We must go," she said. He ran his beautifully manicured hand up and down her arm in its long tight taffeta sleeve. "Beautiful Elizabeth. Lovely rippling muscles. You're a strong girl, aren't you? A strong passionate girl." Libby felt so flattered that she allowed him to kiss her some more.

Then he went and pulled down the blinds and led Libby toward the sofa. "Come, Elizabeth," he said disarmingly, "let's read some poems together and drink some wine." Libby could not resist this; she let him take the *Oxford Book* from her poetry shelf and pour them two brimming glasses of Liebfraumilch from a fresh bottle, which he uncorked. He came and sat beside her on the sofa. "Skoal," he said. "Rhine maiden!" Libby giggled. "Shakespeare," she said unexpectedly, "died of an overdose of Rhenish wine and pickled herring." Nils looked through the book, frowning; Libby's favorite lines were underscored, and the margins were peppered with exclamation points and question marks. "Ah, here it is!" he cried. And he began to read aloud "The Passionate Shepherd to His Love":

"'Come live with me and be my Love,/ And we will all the pleasures prove. . . .'" Et cetera; Libby felt a tiny bit embarrassed; that poem was such a chestnut—she had known it by heart since she was sixteen. When he had finished, he leaned over and kissed her hungrily. "Oh, but I wager you don't know the answer, sir," she said laughing and extricating herself. "'The Shepherdess Replies.' Sir Walter Raleigh." And she began to recite from memory. "'If all the world and love were young,/ And truth in every shepherd's tongue . . . / Then these delights my mind might move/ To live with thee and be thy Love.'" Her voice faltered as he gazed at her. ". . . 'Thy coral clasps and amber studs . . .'" How did it go? The upshot was that Raleigh, speaking for the shepherdess, refused the shepherd's kind invitation. "Give me the book," she begged. Nils demanded another kiss in payment—a longer one. She was limp when he let her have the book. His hand stroked her hair as she thumbed through the index, looking for Raleigh; the pages, irritatingly, stuck together. She tried to ignore his hand, which had reached the back of her neck and was toying with the collar, and concentrate on finding the poem. All at once, she heard one of the snaps at the back of her dress open.

At that faint sound, all Libby's faculties stood alert; her spine stiffened. Her eyes goggled. Her Adam's apple moved as she swallowed. She realized he was planning to seduce her. The book fell open of its own accord on her lap. This must be the Continental approach. Those barons and counts used maneuvers so obvious that you would not think they would try them. Oh, poor Nils, how he was dropping in her estimation. If he only knew how old-fashioned he seemed! Another snap surreptitiously opened. Libby could not decide whether to laugh or be angry. How to show him his mistake, without hurting his feelings, so that they could still go out to dinner? Her senses had stopped fluttering, like a clock ceasing to tick; her blood was perfectly mute. As if he were aware of the change in the temperature, he turned her head to him and stared into her eyes. Libby swallowed again. When he drew her to him and kissed her, she kept her teeth gritted. That ought to give him the hint. "Ice Maiden," he said, reproachfully. "That's enough, Nils," she said, trying to sound more friendly than she felt. She plunked her feet firmly on the floor, closed the book, and started to get up. But suddenly he had her in a vise of iron and bore her backward on the sofa. "Kiss me," he said roughly. "No, not that way. Give me your tongue." Libby thought it wiser to comply. He was frighteningly strong; she remembered with horror having heard that athletes had uncontrollable sex urges and something, too, about Scandinavians being the most ferocious Don Juans. Who had said that—Kay? This kiss actually hurt her; he was biting her lips. "Please, Nils!" she cried, opening her eyes wide, to see his eyes staring at her like two blue pinpoints and his lips drawn back across his teeth like a wild animal about to charge. He had changed into a totally different person, very cruel-looking. Libby would have been fascinated if she had not been so scared. He was holding her down with his body, while his hands sought to caress her. The more she wriggled, the more determined he got. As she struggled, the snaps opened at the back of her dress; a hook tore loose from her brassière. Then she heard a fearful sound of ripping material—her brand-new dress bought at Bendel's spring sale! With one hand, he tore the bodice open, clear away from the sleeve, which remained dangling on her arm; with the other, he held her pinned down by her wrist, which he twisted when she tried to move. He buried his head in her neck and started pulling at her skirt.

Libby was moaning with terror. She considered screaming for help, but she had never spoken to the people in the other apartments, and she could not bear to be found by strangers in her torn clothes and general disarray. Dimly she thought of Polly and those lodgers, who would have rescued Polly in a second if anybody had attempted anything. She wondered if she could faint, but what might not happen while she was unconscious? The doctors at Vassar used to say that a woman could not be forced against her will. They advised girls to kick a man in his testicles or jab him there with your knee. When she started to try that, aiming with her knee at what she hoped was the right place, Nils gave a crowing laugh and slapped her lightly across the face. "Bad girl." The transformation of Nils was the most painful aspect.

"Are you a virgin?" he said suddenly, stopping right in the middle of his fell design. Libby nodded speechlessly. Her only hope, she now felt, was to throw herself on his mercies. "Oh, what a bore!" he said, half relaxing his hold. "What a bore you are, Elizabeth!" He grimaced. "Libby, I should say." With a shake, he disengaged himself. Libby had never been so hurt in her whole life. She lay there, gulping, in her ruined dress, looking piteously up at him out of her big, brown affrighted eyes. He pulled her skirt down roughly over her glove-silk bloomers. "It would not even be amusing to rape you," he said. And with that he rose from her sofa and calmly went into her bathroom. Libby was left alone with the *Oxford Book of English Verse*. She could hear him go to the toilet without even running the water or shutting the door. Then, whistling, he let himself out of her apartment. She heard the latch click and his step on the stairs, and that was that.

Libby tottered to her feet and headed straight for the mirror. She looked like the Wreck of the Hesperus. Moreover, she was hungry; he had not even waited till after dinner. And she had let Ida take the *pâté*. "'You are generous,'" she said to herself in the mirror. "'Beautiful Elizabeth.'" Her feelings were in the strangest turmoil. Nils, of course, could not have meant that she was a bore; he had to vent his chagrin at finding out that she was a virgin. His code as an aristocrat had made him stop then. It was the code that was a bore to him. He wanted to rape her and go berserk like the old Vikings. At least that would have been something dramatic and conclusive. She would have lost her honor. But she would have found out what it was like when a man did it to you. Libby had a little secret; she sometimes made love to herself, on the bath mat, after having her tub. She always felt awful afterward, sort of shaken and depleted and wondering what people would think if they could see her, especially when she took herself what she called "Over the Top." She stared at her pale face in the mirror, asking herself whether Nils could have guessed: was that what made him think she was experienced? They said it gave you circles under your eyes. "No," she said to herself, shuddering. "No." Perish the thought. Nobody could guess. And no one would ever guess the shaming, sickening, beastly thing that had happened, or failed to happen, this evening. Nils would not tell. Or would he?

Priss Hartshorn Crockett was nursing her baby. That was the big news. "I never expected a breast-fed grandson," said Priss's mother, laughing and accepting a martini from her son-in-law, Dr. Sloan Crockett, the budding pediatrician. It was the cocktail hour in Priss's room at New York Hospital—terribly gay. Over the weekend, Sloan stopped in every afternoon and shook up martinis for visitors. He had done his residency at the hospital, so that he could get ice from the diet kitchen and generally break the rules.

"You never expected a *g-grandson*, Mother," pointed out Priss with her slight nervous stammer from the bed. She was wearing a pale-blue bed jacket, and her thin ashy hair was set in waves; the student nurse had done it for her that morning. On her lips, which were dry, was a new shade of lipstick, by Tussy; her doctor had ordered her to put on lipstick and powder right in the middle of labor; he and Sloan both thought it was important for a maternity patient to keep herself up to the mark. Priss, whose personality was confessed to be rather colorless, looked unreal to herself sitting up in bed all bedecked and bedizened—like one of those New York children dressed in furs and trailing satins and their mothers' slippers to beg in the streets at Halloween. Little Ella Cinders, Sloan called her, after that funny in the paper. She would have been more comfortable in the short cotton hospital nightshirt that tied in back, but the floor nurses every morning made her struggle into a satin-and-lace "nightie" from her trousseau. Doctor's orders, they said.

The nurses treated Priss as a special pet because she had been in Obstetrics and Gynecology three times with miscarriages before she had made the grade. To be sure of coming to term this time, she had quit her job with the League of Women Shoppers and stayed in bed or on the sofa for the first five months of pregnancy—her uterus was retroverted. Even so, in the last month she had had a kidney complication; they had rushed her to the hospital and fed her intravenously till the inflammation went down. But now, as Mrs. Hartshorn said, the nativity had been accomplished. Glory be, on the Feast of St. Stephen, the day after Christmas, Priss had been brought to bed with a seven-and-a-half-pound son; delivery had been normal, though labor had been protracted—twenty-two hours. Her room was full of holly, mistletoe, azaleas, and cyclamen, and there was a little Christmas tree by her bedside. The child was to be called Stephen, after the first martyr.

He was in the nursery now, behind the plate-glass window at the end of the corridor—roaring his head off; his feeding time was six o'clock. Priss was drinking an eggnog, to help her lactate; liquids were very important, but she had lost her taste for milk during pregnancy, doing nothing and having to force herself to drink that quart a day that the doctors insisted on if she were not to lose her teeth building the baby's bones. Now, to tempt her, the nurses flavored her milk with egg and sugar and vanilla and gave her fruit juices on the hour and ginger ale and Coke—every kind of liquid but alcohol, for if she drank a martini, Stephen would have gin for his dinner.

Sloan rattled the ice in the silver shaker and chatted with Priss's brother, Allen, who was down for the holidays from Harvard Law. Those two were great friends, both being staunch Republicans, unlike Priss and Mrs. Hartshorn. Liberalism seemed to run in the female line: Mrs. Hartshorn and her dead husband had had a running battle over Wilson and the League, and now Priss and Sloan were at swords' points over Roosevelt and socialized medicine. It had been a red-letter day for Sloan and Allen when the Supreme Court killed the Blue Eagle and put Priss out of a job. Working for the League of Women Shoppers had never seemed as exciting to her; it was more like a volunteer thing, which had made it easier for her to resign to have Stephen.

Priss had been good about that, though she missed her work and fretted about finances, since Sloan was just getting established in practice (with an older pediatrician), and they had depended on her salary for cigarettes and concerts and theatres and contributions to charity and their library membership—Priss was a great reader. Her mother could not help very much, because she still had her two youngest in college (Linda was at Bennington), which was quite a bit for a poor widow woman, as Mrs. Hartshorn gaily called herself, to swing. She had been sending Priss her maid, the faithful Irene, to do the housework mornings, and most evenings Lily, the cook, would nip over with a casserole for Priss to heat, so that Sloan would have one good hot meal, at least, in his daily round. When Priss came home from the hospital, Irene, who had had children of her own, was to move in for two weeks and sleep on an army cot in the baby's room (the dining room as *was*) to save the cost of a practical nurse.

This was Mrs. Hartshorn's present to the young parents; to the newborn himself she was giving an English pram, a mad extravagance, and, come the spring, she was going to send them Linda's old crib, which was shut up in the attic in Oyster Bay, and her high chair and odds and ends, though high chairs, they said, were out now. For the time being, Stephen would sleep in a laundry basket on the baby-carriage mattress—quite a clever idea that Priss had got from a pamphlet on child care issued by the Department of Labor.

"Yes, my dear, no pun intended," said Mrs. Hartshorn to Polly Andrews, who had dropped in to see Priss. Allen guffawed. "Why not the Department of the Interior?" Priss winced at her brother's witticism. "The pamphlet's an excellent home manual," she said earnestly. "Sloan thinks so too, believe it or not, Allen." "Some of your friend Madam Perkins' work?" retorted Allen. In the bed, Priss grew tense, preparing an answer; her lips moved voicelessly, in spasms. "No politics today," said Mrs. Hartshorn firmly. "We've declared a moratorium. Priss has to think of her milk."

Lakey, she went on to Polly, had sent the most exquisite christening robe from Paris, fit for a dauphin—a great surprise, because she had not written for ages; she was doing her doctorate at the Sorbonne. And Pokey Prothero Beauchamp, who had had twins herself the year before, had sent a baby scales, a most thoughtful gift. Everyone had been frightfully kind. Dottie Renfrew Latham had arranged, from way out in Arizona, for Bloomingdale's to deliver a sterilizer, all complete with bottles and racks, instead of the conventional baby cup or porringer. That would come in handy later on, when Priss's milk ran out.

Mrs. Hartshorn glanced at her daughter and lowered her voice. "Just fancy little Priss being the first of your set to do it,

Polly. She's so flat there she's never had to wear a brassière. But Sloan says it's not the size that counts. I do hope he's right. The miracle of the loaves and fishes, *I* call it. All the other babies in the nursery are on bottles. The nurses prefer it that way. I'm inclined to agree with them. Doctors are all theory. Nurses see the facts." She swallowed her martini in a single draft, like medicine; this was the style among advanced society women of her age. She wiped her lips and refused a "dividend" from the silver shaker. "Which way progress, Polly?" she demanded, in a slightly louder voice, shaking her white bobbed locks. "The bottle was the war cry of my generation. Linda was bottle-fed. And you can't imagine the difference. For us, the bottle spelled the end of colic, and the frantic young husband walking the baby all night. We swore by the bottle, we of the avant-garde. My mother-in-law was horripilated. And now, I confess, Polly, I'm horripilated myself."

Her son-in-law pricked up his ears and gave a tolerant smile. He was a tall young man with glasses and an Arrow-collar profile who had worked his way through medical school; his father, an army surgeon, had died of influenza during the war, and his mother was a housemother at a girls' school in Virginia. Priss had met him at her cousin's coming-out party junior year, through another cousin, a medical student, who had been ordered to bring some extra men.

"Medicine seems to be all cycles," continued Mrs. Hartshorn. "That's the bone I pick with Sloan. Like what's his name's new theory of history. First we nursed our babies; then science told us not to. Now it tells us we were right in the first place. Or were we wrong then but would be right now? Reminds me of relativity, if I understand Mr. Einstein."

Sloan ignored this excursion. "By nursing Stephen," he said patiently, "Priss can give him her immunities for at least the first year. He won't be liable to chicken pox or measles or whooping cough. And he will have a certain protection from colds. Of course, in some cases the mother's milk disagrees with the child. You get a rash or stomach upsets. Then you have to weigh the advantages of breast feeding against the negative side effects."

"And psychologically," appended Polly, "isn't the breast-fed baby supposed to have a warmer relation with his mother than the bottle-fed baby?" Sloan frowned. "Psychology is still a long way from being a science," he declared. "Let's stick to measurable facts. Demonstrable facts. We can demonstrate that the breast-fed infant gets his mother's immunities. And we know from the scales that Stephen is gaining. An ounce a day, Cousin Louisa." This was his name for Mrs. Hartshorn. "You can't argue with the scales."

The sound of a baby's crying made itself heard in the silence that followed this speech. "That's Stephen again," said Mrs. Hartshorn. "I recognize his voice. He yells louder than any other baby in the nursery." "Shows he's a healthy young fellow," replied Sloan. "Time to worry if he didn't cry for his dinner. Eh, Priss?" Priss smiled wanly. "Sloan says it's good for his lungs," she said, grimacing. "Develops them," agreed Sloan. "Like a bellows." He drew air into his chest and released it.

Mrs. Hartshorn looked at her watch. "Can't the nurse bring him in now?" she wondered. "It's quarter of six." "The *schedule*, Mother!" cried Priss. "The reason babies in your time had colic wasn't because they were breast-fed, but because they were picked up at all sorts of irregular times and fed whenever they cried. The point is to have a schedule and stick to it absolutely!"

There was a knock on the half-open door. More visitors were arriving: Connie Storey and her husband and young Dr. Edris, who had been Sloan's roommate in medical school. The conversation grew louder, and the room was full of cigarette smoke. Mrs. Hartshorn opened a window and tried to produce a *courant d'air*. What was the point of keeping the infant behind glass if he were then brought in to nurse in a smoke-filled room? "Not to mention our germs," she added, exhaling with a certain complacency, as though her germs were especially vigorous and well-pedigreed. Sloan shook his head. "A baby needs to build up some immunities before going home from the hospital. If he's never been exposed to germs, he gets sick the minute he gets home. I think we overdo the sterility business, don't you, Bill? Just a bit?" "Depends," said Dr. Edris. "You can't impress it too much on the average mother." Sloan smiled faintly. "'Boil baby's rattle every time he drops it,'" he quoted. "Don't you believe in boiling everything, Sloan?"

anxiously demanded Priss. "That's what the child-care pamphlet says to do." "You goop," said her brother. "That pamphlet was written for slum women; by a Vassar graduate, I
bet." "Rattles are out anyway," Priss replied stoutly. "Everyone knows they're unsanitary and likely to break." "A dangerous toy," agreed Sloan. There was a silence. "Sometimes
Sloan likes to play the heretic," smiled Priss. "You should
hear him *épater* the floor nurses." Mrs. Hartshorn nodded.
"A promising sign in a doctor. Inspires confidence," she observed. "Though goodness knows why. We all trust a doctor
who doesn't believe in medicine."

In the middle of the general laugh, a nurse tapped at the
door. "Excuse us, ladies and gentlemen. Feeding time." When
the room was cleared of guests, she closed the window Mrs.
Hartshorn had opened and then brought the baby in on her
shoulder. He was wearing a long white nightgown and his face
was red and swollen; she placed him next to Priss in the bed. It
was exactly six o'clock. "Which one is it tonight, dear?" she
demanded. Priss, who had managed to lower one shoulder of
her nightgown, indicated her right breast. The nurse swabbed
it with cotton and alcohol and laid the baby to suck; as usual,
he made a face at the alcohol and pushed the nipple away. The
nurse settled it firmly in his mouth again; then she went about
the room emptying ashtrays and collecting glasses to take back
to the diet kitchen. "You had quite a party tonight."

To Priss, this sounded like a criticism, and she did not reply.
Instead, she gritted her teeth. The baby's mouth always hurt
her nipple at the beginning, like a bite. Her breasts were very
sensitive, and she hated to have Sloan touch them in love-
making; she had hoped that nursing the baby would get her
over that. People said that nursing was very satisfying, sensu-
ally, to the mother, and she had thought that if she got in the
habit with a baby, she would not mind so much with a grown
man. Though she had not told Sloan, this was one of her
principal reasons for agreeing to breast-feed Stephen: so that
she could give Sloan, who was entitled to it, more fun in bed.
But so far nursing, like most of sex, was an ordeal she had to
steel herself for each time it happened by using all her will
power and thinking about love and self-sacrifice. The nurse
was watching her now, to make sure that the baby was drawing

at the nipple properly. "Relax, Mrs. Crockett," she said kindly. "Baby can sense it if you're tense." Priss sighed and tried to let go. But naturally the more she concentrated on relaxing, the more tense she got. "Bless braces, damn relaxes," she joked feebly. "You're tired this evening," said the nurse. Priss nodded, feeling grateful that someone knew and disloyal, at the same time, to Sloan, who did not know that it wore her out to have company, especially mixed company that sat there discussing her milk.

But as the baby (she wished the nurse would call him "Stephen," not "Baby") commenced to suck rhythmically, making a little noise like a snore, Priss grew somewhat easier. She did not *enjoy* the sucking, but she liked his fresh, milky smell, which made her think of churns and dairies, and his pale fuzz of hair and his warmth. Soon she was unaware of his sucking, except as a hypnotic rhythm; the nurse put the bell in her hand and tiptoed out. Priss was almost asleep when she came to, with a start; Stephen was asleep himself. His little mouth had ceased to tug, and the noise he was making *was* a light snore. She joggled him a little, as she had been taught to do, but her nipple slipped out of his mouth. He turned his round soft head away and lay sleeping with his cheek flat on her chest. Priss was terrified; she tried to turn his head and thrust her breast into his mouth. He resisted; his little hands rose and beat feebly at her breast to push it away. She shifted her position and looked at her watch. He had only been nursing seven minutes, and he was supposed to nurse fifteen to get the milk he needed to carry him through till the next feeding, which would be at ten o'clock. She had been cautioned before not to let him fall asleep. She rang the bell, which turned the light on outside her door.

No one came; she listened; there was complete silence in the corridor. Not even the sound of a baby crying came from the far end at the nursery. They were all being fed, obviously—all but poor Stephen—and the nurses were all busy, giving them their bottles. She was always fearful of being left alone with Stephen and usually she contrived to keep a nurse with her, making conversation. But since yesterday there were two new babies in the nursery and two new mothers to care for, so that Priss had become an "old" mother, who ought to be able to look after herself. But this was the first time she had been left entirely alone; normally the nurse popped her head in the door from time to time, to see how things were going. Priss was afraid the nurses knew that she was afraid of Stephen—her own flesh and blood.

Still no one came; another three minutes had passed. She thought of Sloan, who would be in the Visitors' Lounge with her mother and Bill Edris, talking and enjoying himself; it was against the hospital rules for the husband to watch the mother nurse, and this was one rule that Sloan did not care to break. Perhaps a passing interne would notice her light. She raised her arm to look at her watch again; two more minutes gone. She felt as though she and Stephen were marooned together in eternity or tied together like prisoners in some gruesome form of punishment. It was useless to remind herself that this frightening bundle was her own child and Sloan's. Rather, she felt, to her shame, that he was a piece of hospital property that had been dumped on her and abandoned—they would never come to take him away.

Just then Stephen woke. He gave a long sigh and turned his head, burying it in her breast, and at once went back to sleep again. Priss could feel his nose pressing against her shrinking skin, and the idea that he might suffocate made her suddenly cold with fear. That was always happening to babies in their cribs. Maybe he had already suffocated; she listened and could not hear his breathing—only the loud noise of her own. Her heart was pounding with a sort of stutter. She tried to move his head gently, but again he resisted, and she was afraid of accidentally touching the soft part of his skull. But at least he was still alive. Gratefully, she tried to collect herself and make an intelligent decision. She could telephone down to the switchboard and get them to send help. But two things deterred her: first, her shyness and dislike of being a nuisance; second, the fact that the telephone was on the right side of the bed and she would have to move Stephen to reach it, but moving Stephen was just the problem. She was scared to. Scared of what, she asked herself. Scared that he might cry, she answered.

"Priss Hartshorn Crockett!" she said sternly to herself. "Are you ready to let your newborn baby die of suffocation because you're shy and/or because you can't bear to hear him cry? What would your mother think?" Determined, she half sat up, and this abrupt movement dislodged the baby, who slipped to her side in a little heap, woke up and began to cry furiously. At that moment, the door opened.

"Well, what's going on here?" exclaimed the student nurse, who was Priss's favorite; she was glad it was not the other one, at any rate. The girl, in her blue-striped uniform, picked up Stephen and cuddled him in her arms. "Have you two been having a fight?" Priss replied with a weak chime of laughter; humor was not her strong point, but now that she saw the baby safe in the nurse's strong bare arms, she laughed with relief. "Is he all right? I'm afraid I lost my head." "Stephen's just plain mad, isn't he?" the girl said, addressing the baby. "Does he want to go back to bed?" She picked up his blanket and wrapped him in it; she patted his back to "bubble" him. "No, no!" cried Priss. "Give him back, please. He hasn't finished nursing. I let him go to sleep in the middle."

"Oh, my!" said the girl. "You must have been scared, all right. I'll stay with you this time till he finishes." The baby belched, and the girl unwrapped him and laid him, under the covers, on Priss's breast. "Somebody should have come in to bubble him," she said. "He swallowed a lot of air." She gently slid the nipple into his mouth. The baby pushed it away and began to cry again. He was evidently angry. The two girls— Priss was the older—gazed at each other sadly. "Does that happen often?" said Priss. "I don't know," said the girl. "Most of our babies are bottle babies. But they do that sometimes with the bottle if the holes in the nipple aren't big enough; they get mad and push the bottle away." "Because the milk doesn't come fast enough," said Priss. "That's my trouble. But I wouldn't mind if he pushed a *b-bottle* away." Her thin little face looked rueful. "He's tired," said the student nurse. "Did you hear him this afternoon?" Priss nodded, looking down at the baby. "It's a vicious circle," she said gloomily. "He wears himself out crying because he's famished and then he's too exhausted to nurse."

The door opened again. "You left Mrs. Crockett's light on," the older nurse chided the student. "You should remember to snap it off when you come in. What was the trouble here, anyway?" "He won't nurse," said Priss. The three women looked at each other and sighed jointly. "Let's see if you have any milk left," said the older nurse finally, in a practical tone. She moved the baby's head slightly to one side and squeezed Priss's breast; a drop of watery liquid appeared. "You can try it," she conceded. "But he'll have to learn to work for his supper. The harder he works, of course, the more milk you produce. The breast should be well drained." She squeezed Priss's breast again, then clapped "Baby's" head to the moist nipple. While both nurses watched, he sucked for another minute, for two minutes, and stopped. "Shall we prime the pump again?" said Priss with a feeble smile. The older nurse bent down. "The breast is empty. No sense in wearing him out for nothing. I'll take him now and weigh him."

In a moment the student nurse was back, breathless. "Two ounces!" she reported. "Shall I tell your company they can come back?" Priss was overjoyed; her supper tray appeared while she was waiting for her family to return, and she felt almost hungry. "We've heard your vital statistic," announced Mrs. Hartshorn. "Is two ounces a lot?" asked Allen dubiously. An excellent average feeding, declared Sloan: Priss's milk was highly concentrated, though the volume was not large; that was why the baby was gaining steadily, despite the little fuss he made before meals. Then they all trooped out for the evening, to let Priss have her supper in peace. Sloan was carrying the cocktail shaker; they would not need it any more in the hospital, for next weekend Priss would be home.

Priss picked up the last number of *Consumer Reports*; she was hoping they would have an article on bottled baby foods. She knew she was letting herself slip, mentally, in the hospital; she *lived* on the bulletins the nurses brought her of how many ounces Stephen had taken—they weighed him before and after each feeding. If the nurse forgot to come and tell her, she nearly died, imagining the worst and not having the gumption to ring and ask. The other important event was the regular morning weighing, before his bath, which showed his over-all gain for the day. Nothing but these figures and her own fluid intake interested Priss now; she was always having to ring for the bedpan because of the gallons of water she imbibed. The nurses were awfully co-operative, though they disapproved, she knew (except the student), of her breast-feeding Stephen. They thought Sloan and her obstetrician, Dr. Turner, were balmy. But they too were impressed, *nolens volens*, by the evidence of the scales. The child *was* growing.

If it had not been for the bulletins, Priss would certainly have lost faith. Sloan and Dr. Turner did not have to hear Stephen crying. The nurses and Priss had to hear it. At eight o'clock that night, right on the dot, down in the nursery Stephen started to cry. She knew his voice—the whole floor knew it. Sometimes he would whimper and then go back to sleep for a while, but when he began noisily, as he was doing now, he might cry for two solid hours—a scandal. It was against the rules for the nurses to pick him up; they were allowed to change him and give him a drink of water, and that was all. The babies were not supposed to be "handled." And if they gave him a second drink of water, he might not nurse properly when feeding time finally came.

Sometimes merely changing him would quiet him for the time being. Often the drink of water would quiet him. But not always. A lot depended, Priss had discovered, on when he got the water; if they gave it to him too soon, he would sleep briefly and wake up again, howling. If he woke up midway between feedings, the nurse usually let him cry, after changing him, for an hour, and then gave him the water, so that, tired from crying and with a deceptively full stomach, he would often sleep through until the next feeding. That was the best, for then he was fresh when he was brought in to nurse and would draw with might and main from the nipple. But if he woke up shortly after a feeding, it was horrible: after an hour's cry, he would get his water, sleep, wake up and cry again without stopping—his record, so far, was two hours and three-quarters.

Priss's ear was attuned to every detail of this routine; she could tell when he was getting his water, when the nurse was just changing him or turning him over. She could tell when he fell asleep from sheer exhaustion, by the way his cries subsided and finally trailed off. She could recognize the first sleepy whimperings, and her imagination shared the nurse's hesitation as to whether to pick him up and change him at once or whether to leave him alone, hoping that he would not wake fully. She knew too that one of the nurses (she was not sure which) used to break the rules and pick him up and rock him in her arms; this was indicated by a sudden respite, a fairly long silence, and then a fierce renewal of crying as he was set back in his basket again. She could never make up her mind how she felt toward the nurse who did this: thankful or disapproving.

The nights were the worst. There were nights when, hearing him start at three or four in the morning, she would have welcomed anything that would let him stop and rest—paregoric, a sugar-tit, any of those wicked things. During her pregnancy, Priss had read a great deal about past mistakes in child rearing; according to the literature, they were the result not only of ignorance, but of sheer selfishness: a nurse or a mother who gave a crying child paregoric usually did it for her own peace of mind, not wanting to be bothered. For the doctors agreed it did not hurt a baby to cry; it only hurt grownups to listen to him. She *supposed* this was true. The nurses here wrote down every day on Stephen's chart how many hours he cried, but neither Sloan nor Dr. Turner turned a hair when they looked at that on the chart; all they cared about was the weight curve.

Sloan had warned Priss repeatedly against listening to the nurses: they meant well but they were in a rut. They also liked to think they knew better than the doctor. It irritated him to have Priss dwell on how long Stephen had "vocalized." "If it bothers you so much," he had said to her sharply the other day, "you can get them to give you some cotton for your ears." That was not Priss's point, but she had considered doing what he said because she knew that worrying was bad for her milk supply; the nurses were always telling her that. But she was too much of a liberal to "turn a deaf ear" to a hungry baby; that would be like those people who were blind to bread lines and picket lines. If Stephen howled, she wanted to know it. Moreover, being a worrier, she would *imagine* that Stephen was crying if she had ear stoppers in. Sloan replied that this was ridiculous, but that since she refused to be rational, she would have to suffer.

Poor Sloan was impatient with suffering; that was why, probably, he had become a doctor. But he hid his idealism behind an armor of hardness; otherwise, he could not go on practicing, seeing all the pain he saw. She had often formulated this theory about Sloan when they had words about crossing a picket line or boycotting Spain and Japan ("Little Captain Boycott," he called her, to their friends), but now, in the hospital, it struck her as peculiar that nurses, who heard more crying than doctors did, did not develop an armor against it. And she did *not* think that it was only for their own peace of mind that the nurses had begun muttering among themselves (she had heard them) that they would like to see Dr. Turner spend just one night in the patient's place.

They blamed Dr. Turner, because he was Priss's doctor, but it was really Sloan who had the bee in his bonnet. Lying in bed tensely listening to Stephen's mournful cry, Priss suddenly did not understand why Sloan was so strong for breast-feeding. Was it entirely for the reasons he gave—the medical reasons? Or because he had a stubborn streak and felt that Mrs. Hartshorn, the nurses, and Priss were all against him? Or was it something worse? It crossed her mind that Sloan, who was just starting in practice, might regard her nursing Stephen as a sort of advertisement. He liked to make a point of his differences with dear old Dr. Drysdale, who had taken him into his office and who had practically introduced the bottle into New York society. Dr. Drysdale prided himself on being ultra-scientific, but Sloan said that all that boiling and sterilizing was inefficient and wasteful (not to mention the cost of the equipment), when you could tap nature's resource; the baby could be weaned from the breast directly to the cup. Any mother could nurse, he maintained, just as any woman could keep her weight down during pregnancy—Mrs. Hartshorn had been astonished at how little Priss had gained, even with being on the sofa. Priss had been proud of keeping her girlish figure and proud as Lucifer of nursing Stephen, but now her pride was deflated by the thought that Sloan was using her to prove his theories, like a testimonial in a magazine. And it was true that the tale of her nursing had spread far and wide: everybody and his brother in this wing of the hospital seemed to have heard that poor little Mrs. Crockett, a chestless wonder, was breast-feeding; outside, in the Cosmopolitan Club, her mother's circle were all talking about it. "Well, you've certainly started something!" Kay

Strong Petersen had commented. "Every pregnant alumna who's heard about you wants to nurse."

It was unlike Priss to be bitter, but it galled her to feel, as she did tonight, that she was a party to a gross deception—one of those frauds on the public that the government Bureau of Standards was always out to uncover. At nine o'clock, when the maid brought in her fruit juice, Stephen was still crying, steadily, like a buzz saw; Priss was trying to do a crossword puzzle but could not concentrate. At the opening of the door, the screams from the nursery came louder; a weaker voice had joined Stephen's. The idea that her child disturbed the other infants greatly troubled Priss, though the nurses tried to reassure her: newborn babies, they said, quickly got accustomed to a familiar noise. Still, Priss could not refrain from framing an apologetic sentence to the maid. "Oh, dear, Catherine," she said (she had made a point of learning the maids' names), "do you hear him? He'll wake up the whole hospital." "Hear him?" replied Catherine, who was Irish. "He'll wake the dead. When are they going to let him have a bottle, for God's sake?" "I don't know," said Priss, closing her eyes in pain. "Ah, don't take it so hard," the maid said jauntily, straightening Priss's covers. "He's exercising his lungs." Priss wished everyone would not say that. "It's not my place to ask," said Catherine, moving closer to plump Priss's pillows, "but I've been wondering. What put it into your head to nurse?" Priss felt her neck redden. "Im-m-munities," she stammered. The maid looked at her curiously. "You know," said Priss. "Like vaccination. He can't get any diseases I've had, like mumps or chicken pox or measles." "Always something new," said Catherine, shaking her head. She poured Priss fresh water. "They're always inventing something, aren't they?" Priss nodded. "Would you like your radio on, now? A little music? You won't hear him, over the music." "No, thank you, Catherine," said Priss. "Can I crank you up a bit, Mrs. Crockett?" "No, thank you," Priss repeated. The maid hesitated. "Good night, then, and cheer up. Look on the bright side. They used to say it developed the bust."

Priss could not help treasuring this last remark; she saved it to tell her mother tomorrow, in the brogue, if she could without stuttering. At the same time she had to admit that she had been secretly hoping that Stephen *would* be a bust-developer and she had made Dr. Turner laugh when she asked him anxiously whether she wouldn't need a nursing brassière. Her mood lightened; outside, silence reigned—Stephen must have had his drink of water while she and the maid were talking.

This calm was broken by the head floor nurse, Miss Swenson, who was going off duty. She came in and closed the door. "I want to tell you, Mrs. Crockett, that I'm going to speak to Dr. Turner in the morning. To recommend that Stephen be given a supplementary bottle." The nurse's casual tone did not fool Priss. *A supplementary bottle*—the phrase sounded horrid, as if Miss Swenson had said, "I'm going to recommend a dose of strychnine." The very word *bottle* made Priss bristle, no matter what adjectives were attached. She braced herself against her pillows and prepared to give battle. Miss Swenson went on smoothly, as if she had not noticed the effect of her announcement on Priss. "I know this will be a great relief to you, Mrs. Crockett. We all understand what you've been going through. You've been a wonderful patient, a remarkable patient." Even in her shock, Priss recognized that Miss Swenson, whom she had always liked, was speaking with real earnestness. "But why?" she brought out finally. "The scales . . ."

Miss Swenson, who was in her thirties with blond hair in a bun, came to the bedside and took her hand. "I know how you feel, my dear. Torn. Most nursing mothers cry when I have to tell them that I recommend a supplementary bottle. Even when the child is failing to gain weight. They want to keep trying. You're exceptionally brave not to break down." "You mean this happens often?" asked Priss. "Not very often. But we have one or two younger doctors who like to have the mothers nurse as long as they're able. Not all the mothers agree, of course. There's still a prejudice against breast-feeding, especially—and this will surprise you—among ward patients. They feel that a bottle baby is socially superior." "How interesting!" Priss exclaimed. "And we see that same attitude with our Jewish private patients. Even when they have plenty of milk, and the doctor encourages it, they don't want to nurse; they have the idea it's lower East Side." "How interesting," Priss repeated thoughtfully. "Oh, being a nurse one sees a great deal. And the class differences are quite extraordinary.

For example, on a surgical floor you'll find that all the female private patients and many of the male private patients after an abdominal operation have post-operative urinary retention. While in a ward of Negro men you won't get a single case. It's simply a question of modesty; the upper class has been trained to feel embarrassment about the lower part of the body and after an operation when the abdomen has been opened, their inhibitions get to work and they can't urinate."

"Fascinating," breathed Priss. She often wished she had studied sociology. But she did not want to be distracted from the main point. "Do higher-income women have a lower milk supply?" She did not like to use the words *upper class*. Miss Swenson avoided answering this blunt question; probably she was afraid of depressing Priss with the thought that her case was statistically pretty hopeless. She looked at her watch. "I want to explain the supplementary bottle to you, Mrs. Crockett." To Priss's surprise, she found that this phrase no longer sounded like a death knell. "But if he's gaining the right amount . . . ?" she protested, nevertheless. "He's an unusually hungry baby," said Miss Swenson. "Your milk is quite adequate from a nutritional point of view, but it doesn't give him enough volume. What I suggest, Mrs. Crockett, is this. After his six o'clock evening feeding, starting tomorrow, we'll give him a small amount of formula in a bottle. Your milk supply is at its lowest then, I've noticed. At ten he gets enough volume from you to hold him. On a full stomach he'll sleep through till two; so will you, poor girl. In fact, with the supplementary bottle we may even be able to train him, before you leave the hospital, to sleep right through till six in the morning, so that you'll have an unbroken night. We like to do that anyway for our mothers, before they go home; once the baby has the habit of the two o'clock feeding, it's hard for the mother to break it herself. A baby works like a little clock, and we like to have it set right before the mother takes over."

Priss nodded. How wonderful, she thought, of the hospital to plan ahead for the mothers. None of this would have been possible a few years before. "If he's still fretful, even with one supplementary bottle," Miss Swenson went on, "we may have to give him more. Some babies take a supplementary bottle after each time at the breast. But in Stephen's case I don't think this will be necessary. You may even find that your flow of milk increases, once Stephen is more comfortable."

When Miss Swenson left, Priss was a changed woman. What impressed her, she said to herself, was the empirical spirit here, the willingness to try without prejudice different methods and *mixtures* of methods till they found one that worked, which was often a compromise, like the New Deal. She was sure Miss Swenson was a Democrat. She was so relieved that Sloan had got his training here, instead of at Columbia and Presbyterian. This hospital, she mused, half fancifully, was like an up-to-date factory: no baby was sent out until he was in good working order, tried and tested and guaranteed to run without friction for at least the first few months. Why, they even gave demonstrations, for mothers who were not lucky enough to afford an Irene or a practical nurse, on how to bathe a baby and bubble him and fold his diapers, and the ambulatory mothers who wanted to were allowed to go into the diet kitchen and see the formulas made! And these new babies who ate and slept regularly, on a schedule, like little clocks, as Miss Swenson said, were going to grow up into a new kind of man, who perhaps (it did not do to be *too* optimistic) would no longer want to make wars and grab property. And nowaday everything was being so easy for those babies' mothers: the infants were trained to the toilet in the very first months, by just being set gently on the potty when their regular time came, and as for washing diapers, there was this new thing called Diaper Service that came every day with fresh diapers and took away the soiled ones in a sanitized can.

That night Stephen broke all his previous records—three solid hours, from 3:00 A.M. till 6:00. Dr. Turner, when he came into Priss's room the next morning, scolded her for the circles under her eyes and advised her to put on some rouge. But he was very sweet about the bottle, acting as though Miss Swenson's suggestion was what he had decided to prescribe himself, after looking at the chart. The weight curve, he said thoughtfully, was not the whole picture. Priss did not remind him that he had said the exact opposite, standing in the same spot, two days before, on Saturday. He departed humming, having picked one of Priss's roses for his buttonhole.

The fly in the ointment was Sloan. She was afraid he would

see red at the words *supplementary bottle*. Dr. Turner promised
to talk to him; if *she* did it, Priss thought, she would find herself
stammering and using some sickly euphemism like "Tonight
Stephen is going to get some formula for dessert." It was odd
how hospitals got you talking that way. One thing Priss was
resolved on: neither she nor anyone else was ever going to talk
baby-talk to Stephen. Or use expressions like "Wee-wee" or
"Number Two." She had not yet decided what to say instead.

At lunch time, Sloan appeared; he was angry. A muscle
twitched by his eye. He was more angry at Dr. Turner and the
nurses than he was at Priss, whom he treated as an innocent
party. They had high-pressured her, he said, into accepting the
bottle. "But, Sloan," she argued, "it does sound like a good
idea. Stephen will be getting the best of both worlds, don't
you see?" Sloan shook his head. "Prissy, you're a layman.
Turner's a woman's doctor. When you leave the hospital, he
doesn't follow through. Except for your check-up. He doesn't
see what happens when a child that's been nursing starts getting a bottle. Neither do these maternity nurses. That's what
the pediatrician sees. Every darned time." He sat down in the
armchair and ran his hand through his blond hair; Priss saw
that he was truly upset. "What happens, Sloan?" she said gently. "It's simple," he said, wiping his glasses. "When a child
gets an ounce of formula, without half trying, from a bottle,
he stops nursing so eagerly from the breast. Why should he?
The child is a reasonable being. When he stops sucking for all
he's worth, the mother's milk supply goes down. Then they
give him another 'supplementary bottle.' Then another. Within
a week he's getting a bottle with each breast-feeding. At that
point he starts rejecting the breast. Too much trouble. Or the
pediatrician steps in and calls a halt. If the mother's milk is
down to an ounce a feeding, it's not worthwhile to go on. Especially with the headache of boiling the bottles and the nipples and making the formula for six daily feedings—it's a
duplication of labor. I tell you, Priss, if Stephen starts on a
bottle tonight, you won't be home a week before your milk
gives out, and you'll have a full-time bottle baby!"

Priss nodded meekly. She seemed to have no mind of her
own. In no time, he had convinced her that it would be all
over with her nursing if they gave Stephen that bottle. Why, it

would be like starting him on drugs or liquor; right away, he would get a taste for it. She saw what Sloan was fighting and how Miss Swenson and Dr. Turner had deceived her. For herself, she felt sad and beaten, as though she had lost her reason for living if she could not nurse Stephen. It was silly how much she had counted on it. "Does it make that much difference, Sloan?" she said earnestly. "Haven't you and I got a wee bit hipped on this nursing?"

"No," he said, in a dead voice. "It doesn't make so much difference. We wanted to give Stephen the best possible start, that's all. If you'd been able to nurse him even a month or two . . ." "I'm sorry," said Priss. "It's not your fault," he said. "It's this damned hospital. I know them. They wouldn't let you try. You would have come through with flying colors. Just one more day would have done it. Two more days." "What do you mean?" "Stephen would have settled down and stopped crying for the moon. Your milk supply has been building. Look at the chart. That's what I told Turner. Nobody here has the guts to go through with an experiment. A baby yells and they hand him a bottle. You can't make any progress in medicine unless you're willing to be hard. It's the same with your friend Roosevelt and those soft-headed social workers in the White House. The economy would have recovered by itself if they'd left it alone, instead of listening to the whimpers of the down-and-outs. Recovery! There hasn't been any recovery. The economy is sick and pumped full of formula." He gave a sudden boyish laugh. "Pretty good, that, wasn't it, Prissy?" "It was funny," she said primly, "but I don't admit the comparison."

"Good old Priss," he said fondly, still pleased with his pun. "Never give an inch." "What did you tell Dr. Turner?" she said. He shrugged. "What I just told you. He said it was no use trying to experiment under present-day hospital conditions. The nursing staff is against you. It's a conspiracy."

"What do you mean, Sloan, exactly, when you say 'experiment'?" "To prove that any woman can nurse," he said impatiently. "*You* know; you've heard it a hundred times." "Sloan," she said coaxingly, "be fair. Stephen cries about ten hours a day."

Sloan raised a finger. "In the first place, ten hours is exaggerated. In the second place, what of it? In the third place, the nurses pick him up and fuss over him when he cries." Priss could not answer this. "Of course they do," said Sloan. "So that naturally he cries some more. Already, in the second week of life, he's learned to cry to get attention." He folded his arms and stared, frowning, at Priss.

"We'll fix that," he said, "when we get him home. You're not to let Irene pick him up, except to change him. Once you've established that he's not cold or wet, back he goes in his basket." "I agree with you utterly," said Priss. "I've already had a talk with Irene. She understands that babies are treated differently now. But what about the bottle?" "He'll get one supplementary bottle," Sloan said. "For the time being. When we get him home, I have a little idea to try."

Priss felt a chill; he alarmed her. Ever since she had been in the hospital, her feelings for Sloan had been undergoing a change. Sometimes she thought she was not in love with him any more. Or perhaps it was a thing that happened to many women: now that her baby was born, she felt divided in her interests. She had begun to see that she might have to defend Stephen against Sloan, and the more so because Sloan was a doctor and therefore had a double authority. She found that she was checking what Sloan said against what the nurses said, against what the Department of Labor pamphlet said, against *Parents' Magazine*. When Sloan declared that the baby should sleep in an unheated room, she was amazed to find that the Department of Labor agreed with him; the nursery in the hospital, of course, was heated. There was a side of Sloan, she had decided, that she mistrusted, a side that could be summed up by saying that he was a Republican. Up to now this had not mattered; most men she knew were Republicans—it was almost part of being a man. But she did not like the thought of a Republican controlling the destiny of a helpless baby. In medicine, Sloan was quite forward-looking, but he was enamored of his own theories, which he wanted to enforce, like Prohibition, regardless of the human factor. She wondered, really, whether he was going to make a very good pediatrician.

"What's your idea, Sloan?" she asked, trying not to sound anxious. "Oh, a thought I had." He got up and strolled to the window. "I wondered how Stephen would do on a three-hour cycle." Priss's eyes nearly popped out of her head. "The four-hour cycle isn't sacred, Prissy," he said, coming to her

bedside. "Don't look so severe. Some of the new men are trying a three-hour cycle. The point is to find the right one for
the individual baby. All babies aren't alike, you know." Priss
pondered the implications of this, which did not sound like
Sloan exactly. It occurred to her that he had been doing some
homework in the latest medical journals. "Obviously," he went
on, "you can't try out the three-hour cycle in a hospital; the
routine isn't geared to it. You'd have all the nurses up in arms.
But if a baby's unusually hungry and cries a great deal, it can
easily be tried at home." Priss's heart was touched. She took
back everything she had just thought. He had been worrying
about Stephen too, though he had not showed it. Probably he
had been reading far into the night. But, like all doctors, he would
not admit openly to having made a mistake or even to having
changed his mind. "It's even simpler, Priss, with the breast than
it would be with the bottle. You could give him the breast
every three hours for a week or two, then revert to the four-
hour schedule. The main thing is to have a regular cycle, whatever the length of the intervals." "But would I have enough
milk?" The vision of Stephen leaving her breast hungry eight
times a day was rather daunting. "Your milk ought to be stim-
ulated by nursing more frequently," he said. "Anyway, I'd like
to try it." Priss could not see the harm, provided her milk held
out. But she felt it her duty to put a last question. "You're sure
you're not turning the clock back? I mean, the next thing
would be feeding the baby every two hours and then every
time he's hungry. And before we knew it, we'd be back to
Mother's day." Sloan laughed. "Or Grandmother's day," he said.
"Don't be silly."

You would never guess what happened after Sloan left. Priss
had just finished giving Stephen his afternoon feeding when
she got a telephone call from Julie Bentkamp, another classmate, who was an editor of *Mademoiselle*. Julie had heard from
Libby MacAusland, who was now a high-powered literary
agent, that Priss was nursing her own baby. She thought that
was very exciting and she wondered whether Priss would like
to write an article on how it felt for *Mademoiselle*. Priss said
that she couldn't think of it; she was sure it was against medical
ethics for a doctor's wife to write a piece like that. A few minutes later, Libby herself rang up—the same old Libby. She said

that if Priss wrote it, she was positive she could resell it to the *Reader's Digest*. "You could write it under a pseudonym," she pointed out. "Though personally I should think Sloan would welcome the advertisement. Let me call him and ask him." "Doctors don't advertise," said Priss coldly. "That's just the point, Libby." Priss was annoyed; this was the "high-pressure salesmanship" that she hated. Who could have told Libby, she asked herself—an idle question. What she feared was that Sloan, if Libby got at him, instead of being stuffy, would urge her to do it; she tried to imagine old Mrs. Drysdale, Dr. Drysdale's wife, writing such a thing even when she was young. . . . "I'll ask Sloan for a drink," Libby went on. "Now that he's a lonely bachelor. With Julie. I'm sure we can talk him into it. You should see Julie now; she's a knockout." "If you d-dare, Libby—" cried Priss. "The thing is," said Libby, "you must be sure to put in your bust dimensions. Not in so many words. But you have to let the reader know that you're not a perfect thirty-six. Otherwise the reader would miss the point." "I understand, Libby," said Priss. "And put in that you were Phi Beta Kappa at college and worked for the government. If Sloan agrees, of course, they'll run a picture of you in the contributors column." "*I'm not going to do it*," said Priss. "I only know how to write reports on economics. My style is too dry." "Oh, I'll rewrite it for you," said Libby airily. "I'll do all the descriptive parts and the emotions, if you want. If you just tell me honestly what it's like." "*I'm not going to do it*," Priss repeated. "Under any circumstances." "You can have a nurse for six months with the profits if we sell it to the *Reader's Digest*. A nanny with a cap—do they wear streamers?—to take the baby to the park . . ." Priss held the receiver away from her ear; finally there was a silence. Then Libby's voice resumed in a different tone. "Why not?" Priss hesitated. "It's in poor t-taste," she stammered. "I don't see that," said Libby. "I don't see that at all." Her voice grew louder and louder. "Is it in poor taste to talk about it? Why, it's the most natural thing in the world. In Italy, the women do it in public, and no one thinks a thing about it." "I'm not going to do it in public," Priss said. "And if it's so natural, why are you so excited about putting it in a magazine? You think it's unnatural, that's why." And she hung up the telephone. It *was* unnatural, she said to herself forlornly. Accidentally, she had put her finger on the truth, like accidentally hitting a scab. She was doing "the most natural thing in the world," suckling her young, and for some peculiar reason it was completely unnatural, strained, and false, like a posed photograph. Everyone in the hospital knew this, her mother knew it, her visitors knew it; that was why they were all talking about her nursing and pretending that it was exciting, when it was not, except as a thing to talk about. In reality, what she had been doing was horrid, and right now, in the nursery, a baby's voice was rising to tell her so—the voice, in fact, that she had been refusing to listen to, though she had heard it for at least a week. It was making a natural request, in this day and age; it was asking for a bottle.

POLLY Andrews and Gus LeRoy had been having a love affair for nearly a year. She still lived in a furnished room-
and-bath and went to work every morning at Medical Center,
and he shared an apartment with another man just around the
corner—a book designer who, like Gus, was separated from his
wife. Every night after work Gus came to Polly's for drinks,
unless he had to go out with an author, and after drinks she
cooked them dinner on her hot plate. Afterward they went to
a movie or to a meeting about the Spanish Civil War or silicosis
or the sharecroppers or they played Polly's phonograph, but
every week night he went home to sleep because it was simpler
that way—he had his shaving things there and his pipes and
the manuscripts he was reading; it did not disturb him if the
book designer had women in the other bedroom, so long as
Gus could have his corn flakes and coffee the next morning in
his bathrobe without having to make conversation with a third
party.

Saturdays he worked till noon, but they had Saturday afternoons together, to go for walks in the Italian section or in
Chinatown or to the Hispanic Museum or the Barnard Cloisters. Coming home, they usually marketed, if Polly had not
done it Saturday morning; Gus would buy wine on University
Place, and they would walk past Wanamaker's with bags of
groceries all the way to St. Mark's Place and cook in Polly's
landlady's kitchen if the landlady and her husband had gone to
their weekend cottage in New Jersey. Or else Gus would take
Polly to a French or Spanish place for dinner and dancing.
Saturday nights, he stayed at Polly's, in her narrow bed, and
Sunday mornings they had a late breakfast together and read
the papers. Sunday afternoon he spent with his little boy, taking him to the Bronx Zoo or to ride on the Staten Island Ferry
or climb up the Statue of Liberty or walk across the George
Washington Bridge or visit the Aquarium at the Battery or the
Snake House in the little zoo on Staten Island; it was Polly
who planned their expeditions, but she would not go along.
"Not until we are married," she said, which always made Gus

chuckle because the phrase sounded so old-fashioned, as though she were refusing him her favors until she had a wedding ring. But that was the way she felt. So Sunday afternoons Polly saw her old friends, and Sunday evenings, when Gus brought young Gus home, he stayed for a glass of beer with his wife and afterward fixed himself a sandwich in his kitchen. Sunday night, they had agreed, was his "night off" from Polly, which she used to do her laundry and wash her hair.

It was Sunday night now, and Polly's underwear, stockings, and girdle hung in her bathroom. In the living room her English ivy and Delicious Monster had just had their weekly bath too, and her blouses were pinned to a stout cord festooned across her window; she was brushing her long damp hair with an Ogilvie Sisters hairbrush and rubbing it with a towel. On another towel a white wool sweater was stretched out to dry. Doing her laundry, Polly had found, was a working girl's cure for depression, and Sunday nights she was depressed. The soapsuds, the steam, the smell of damp lamb's wool, the squeak of her clean hair gradually made her feel, though, that somehow it would "all come out in the wash." If she ironed six white blouses in her landlady's kitchen, mended her stockings, and started on a diet to lose five pounds, Gus would decide that they could not wait any longer to get married.

Five afternoons a week, before coming to Polly's, he had an hour with his psychoanalyst. The psychoanalyst said it was a principle of analysis that the patient should not change his life situation while undergoing treatment; this would upset the analytic relation. Therefore Gus had not done anything about getting a divorce. When he was "ready" for a divorce—the analyst's expression—he assumed he would go to Reno for six weeks. But Reno divorces were expensive, and Polly did not know how Gus was going to pay for one, when his savings were being spent on psychoanalysis and half his salary was made over to his wife for temporary maintenance and child support. Polly had her doubts too that Gus's wife would agree to give him a divorce. She had promised him one when he was finished with his analysis, but Polly suspected that she and the analyst were in cahoots to wear him out by attrition. He had been in analysis three months when he met Polly at Libby's May wine party, and the analyst was quite taken aback when he heard they had started a serious relationship—he felt that Gus had broken his promise. As if a man could control falling in love!

Polly's family did not have an inkling of what was going on, but her friends guessed there must be a married man in the picture because she was so silent about how she was spending her time. The theory was that it must be one of the doctors at the hospital. Polly was reticent about their love, not because she was ashamed but because she could not bear the thought of advice and sympathy. The only people who knew for certain were the people who could not avoid knowing: the book designer, Polly's landlady and her husband, the two lodgers, and Ross, her Aunt Julia's maid, who had been in the habit of dropping in evenings to give Polly "a hand" with her knitting or sewing. Not even Miss Bisbee, Gus's secretary, knew. Polly would not go to literary cocktail parties with Gus ("After we're married," she said), partly from a dread of meeting Libby but mainly from that same sense of propriety that made her balk at spending Sundays with little Gus and his father, so long as his father and mother were man and wife. Polly hated questions— the questions young Gus would ask and the questions his mother would put to him, the questions her appearance at cocktail parties would solicit from the people in Gus's office. "When are you going to get married?" was what everyone immediately wanted to know when they saw a girl and a man in love. It was what Ross had asked, straight off, and Mr. Schneider, who did not believe in marriage, and the landlady, who belonged to a nudist group in New Jersey, and Mr. Scherbatyeff. And a truthful answer to this question led everyone at once to ask another one, as if in a single voice: why was Gus going to a psychoanalyst? What was the matter with him?

It was a question that, strangely enough, no one had ever asked about her father, when he had been "put away" in Riggs, poor darling, though her father's disease had a name—melancholia —which would have made it easy to answer queries. If only Gus had talked to himself or refused to talk or engaged in weeping fits or what the doctors called bizarre behavior, no one would have asked what was wrong with him! But the trouble here was just the opposite. Polly could not see that there was anything the matter with Gus. He was one of the most normal men she had ever met, at least to the naked eye, which was all she had to judge with. No loathèd melancholy or black bile or antic disposition. He liked to dance cheek to cheek and play tennis and drive a car—he had an old Hupmobile jacked up in a garage in Brooklyn. Like most New Englanders, he was cautious with the pennies, but he always went to the best shops when buying presents—he had given Polly a beautiful handbag, some carved lapis lazuli earrings, and a soft blue sweater from Brooks Brothers; every week, practically, he brought her flowers, and when they went out to dance on Saturday he bought her violets or a camellia. On the other hand, he did not care what he wore; he had two rather threadbare suits bought off the rack at Wanamaker's, a tweed jacket, flannels, and some bow ties. He had Blue Cross hospital insurance and went to the dentist three times a year to get his teeth cleaned. He watched his waistline and checked up on young Gus's visits to the pediatrician, who was one of the best younger men in the city, like Gus's analyst, who had been Brill's favorite pupil. Though he was only thirty, he was a second father to his authors, very patient in listening to their troubles and getting them lawyers, theatre tickets, discount books, an apartment, a secretary, a girl friend—whatever they needed. He had been active in starting the unit of the Book and Magazine Guild in his office, though he could not be a union member himself because he was considered part of management. He smoked union-made cigarettes when he did not smoke a pipe and tried to look for the union label on whatever he bought; unlike Priss, however, he was a secret believer in name brands, like Arrow shirts and Firestone tires and Teacher's Highland Cream and Gillette razors. He could not be persuaded by the consumer movement that something at half the price was just as good. It tickled him to watch Polly mix her powder and cold cream at home, to save money; she failed to count the cost of her labor, he pointed out.

His liking for name brands was what had sold him on Communism years ago, when he graduated from Brown spank into the depression. Shaw had already converted him to socialism, but if you were going to be a socialist, his roommate argued, you ought to give your business to the biggest and best firm producing socialism, *i.e.*, the Soviet Union. So Gus switched to Communism, but only after he had gone to see for himself. He and his roommate made a tour of the Soviet Union the summer after college and they were impressed by the dams and power plants and the collective farms and the Intourist girl guide. After that, Norman Thomas seemed pretty ineffectual. Gus never took any notice of the little splinter groups, like the Trotskyites, which Polly's friend Mr. Schneider, across the hall, belonged to, or the Lovestoneites or the Musteites—every big movement, he said, had its share of cranks. Yet he had not joined the Party when he and his roommate got back. He did not want to hurt his father, the owner of a job-printing business in Fall River that had been in the family for four generations. The LeRoys were respected by the mill-owning families whose wedding and funeral announcements, visiting cards, dance programs, "Keep Off" signs, and foreclosure sale notices they had been printing since the Civil War; in their shop below the presses on Main Street, they also sold school supplies, Christmas cards, Valentines, and gift-wrapping paper. If Gus became an active Communist, those flinty millowners were perfectly capable of boycotting the LeRoy shop. Besides, the American Communists did not seem to Gus as responsible as the Russian ones. Instead, he married a Party member—a Jewish girl he had met on a double date at a dance at Webster Hall; she taught the first grade at a downtown progressive school.

Kay Petersen, Polly knew, would say that Gus's attraction to Communism—and in particular to Communist women—was a sign of emotional instability. But Polly herself did not think so; she could not see the Party as the Scarlet Woman in Gus's life. Moreover, he was phlegmatic in his sympathy. He never took part in demonstrations or marched in May Day parades or referred to the police as Cossacks; the only part of the *Daily Worker* he read was the sports page. He did not argue with the infidels, including herself, and in fact did not seem to care about spreading the faith, unlike poor Mr. Schneider, who was always trying to convert her to Trotskyism and just now was extremely exercised about the Moscow trials, which he brought up every time he met Gus on the stairs. They were too far away, Gus said, to judge the rights and wrongs of—history would have to decide. To him they seemed insignificant in comparison with the war in Spain, which was something he was really excited about.

He was busy commissioning books on Spain—an anthology of Loyalist war poetry, a picture study of the International Brigade, a new translation of *Don Quixote*. He had tried to get Hemingway to do a book on El Campesino, but unfortunately he was already signed up with Scribners, and Vincent Sheean, his other idea, did not answer his cables. He hoped for a great novel to come out of the Abraham Lincoln Battalion, and at one point this winter, when they were recruiting, he decided to join up himself and slipped off during his lunch hour to have a physical, without even telling his analyst. The picture of Gus as a brave volunteer in a beret appealed to Polly; she thought he would have made an excellent officer. But when his wife heard about it (he was going to leave his life-insurance policy to take care of Gus Fourth), she accused him of irresponsibility. In Gus's case, she said, enlisting would be an escape mechanism, which would make his action politically invalid. According to her, he was unwilling to finish his analysis and instead was running away from his real problems, which concerned her and their son, and incidentally who was going to pay the child support while Gus was fighting the Fascists or hanging around cafés in Madrid? Hearing this, Polly was sorry for his wife, in the same way that she was sorry for a person like Libby, who was always lying to herself. But then, trying to be fair, she wondered whether it was really the money or whether the money was not an excuse his wife gave herself for worrying that Gus might be killed; perhaps his wife in her way loved him more than she did, who would be quite willing to let him risk his life for a cause.

Polly sympathized warmly with the Spanish Republicans and when asked about the reason for her allegiance, she would answer smiling, "I'm a Basque." This was a reference to the fact that there was a Catholic strain in Polly's ancestry; on her mother's side she was an Ayer and related to Lord Acton. Politically, she and Gus were opposites; her heart hastened to the losers in any battle, and she loved small sects with quaint doctrines, like Döllinger's Old Catholics, who denied the infallibility of the Pope, the Dukhobors, who went to Canada to escape the Czar's military service, the virtuous Anabaptists, the

Chassidic Jews, who danced and leapt for joy in Polish villages; she championed "lost" races like the Basques, with their mysterious language; she was partial to extinct and extirpated species, like the passenger pigeon, on which she had done a paper for Zoology. Not since Bonnie Prince Charlie had she cared so much for a cause as she did now for the Loyalists in Spain. She and Gus were both very generous with contributions to the Republican war effort, though Gus gave for airplanes and Polly gave for ambulances and medical supplies. Normally, she said smiling—that is, in peacetime—she was a pacifist, but in Gus's place she would have volunteered, and she was surprised he had listened to the analyst, who told him that he would be more useful to the Spanish cause in New York than in Madrid. This might be true, but Polly could not imagine consenting to weigh yourself in the balance like that, as though you were an ingot you were hoarding. It was this side of Communism that Polly did not cotton to.

But if Polly was surprised that Gus had listened to the analyst, she was more surprised that the analyst had talked to him. "I thought they weren't supposed to give you advice," she said frowning. The analyst, Gus had told her, was utterly neutral; he only listened to the patient and asked an occasional question. The patient was meant to interpret himself. "That's the theory," Gus answered. "But he's a human being," he explained. "If he sees a patient about to commit suicide, naturally he steps in, as a human being." "I should think he would step in as a doctor," Polly said mildly. Gus shook his head. "Unh-unh," he said. "That's what they have to watch out for. The patient's always trying to involve the analyst, qua analyst, in an unorthodox situation. To coax him out from behind his barrier. But the analyst has to stay behind that barrier—Rule One. If he can't, he has to terminate the analysis. But the patients are cunning as hell. Dr. Bijur might figure, for instance, that my signing up with the Lincoln Battalion was just a trap to get him interested in my personal decisions. A play for attention." He wrung his eyebrows. "Christ, Polly, maybe it was. Maybe I was just playing soldier." "But were you?" cried Polly. "I believed you. Weren't you sincere, Gus?" "How do I know?" said Gus, spreading his hands. "Good Lord!" said Polly. There it was again, that curious thing, of treating yourself as if you were a dense, opaque object. Or as if you were not you but someone else, whose motives you could only guess at. Was this strange, flat objectivity what was the matter with Gus or was it an effect of the treatment?

She did not pursue the subject. Rule Two, she knew, was that the patient was not supposed to discuss his illness with his friends or family, and this was almost the longest conversation she and Gus had ever had about his analysis—since the very first one, when he had broken it to her, after they had already slept together several times, that he was going to Dr. Bijur. Polly was a conscientious girl and she would no more have tempted Gus to talk to her about his analysis than she would have pressed sugar on a diabetic, and the result was that she was totally in the dark about what to him, no doubt, was the most vital part of his life. For if it were not the most vital part of his life, why would he be going to talk for an hour a day about it to a stranger?

In retrospect, Polly sometimes wondered whether she would have let Gus come up to her room and make love to her if he had told her ahead of time he was "in analysis." He had told her he was married and living apart from his wife (which she already knew anyway from Libby), but not a peep about the analyst. Polly could see why; at first he did not know her well enough to tell her, and when he did know her well enough it was because they had been to bed together and then it was too late for Polly to have any choice. The die was cast, for, having let him love her, she loved him. But *if* she had known beforehand, she doubted that she would have lost her virginity with an "analysand"; she would have been afraid to.

Polly had always known that sex would mean a great deal to her. That was why she had been leery of men. She could tell from conversations with other girls in college that necking did not shake them to their foundations the way it did her when she was engaged. Several times then, she had nearly gone the limit, as they used to call it, but something had always saved her—once a campus policeman but mostly the boy himself, who had scruples. When she had broken her engagement and had to go to the infirmary, it was sex principally that tortured her. After that, she had firmly suppressed her desires, to the point of avoiding movies with kissing in them; she did not want to be "aroused." She decided she wanted a cool, starchy independent life, with ruffles of humor like window curtains. They told her she had a sweet nature, and she made friends easily, as she could get birds to eat from her hand. Having considered her own case carefully, as well as the hereditary "taint," she concluded that she had best live for friendship, not for love or marriage. She saw herself in later years, large and soft, as an abbess, framed in a wimple, or as an Episcopal deaconess tending the altar, dusting the organ, and visiting the sick of a parish. As it happened, she was an unbeliever, but time, she supposed, might remedy that. Her immediate danger, she saw, was that she was on the verge of becoming a "character," and she resisted being pasted, at twenty-six, which was not yet old, in an album. Already some of her friends were treating her as a "find" they had pounced on in a thrift shop—a slightly cracked piece of old china.

It was true, she did not care for people with drive or those most likely to succeed, which had made her rather a misfit at Vassar; the only way she could like assured, aggressive girls like Libby and Kay was to feel sorry for them. She was horribly sorry for Libby, to the point where she could hardly bear seeing her; Libby's red open mouth, continually gabbling, was like a running wound in the middle of her empty face. But Libby had no suspicion, of course, that there was anything about her to pity, which was just what made her pitiable; *she* thought she was sorry for Polly and was doing her a favor every time she made some imposition on her. If Polly stopped seeing her, then poor Libby would have no one to imagine that she was being charitable to, because Libby could not be charitable to anyone who was really miserable but only to someone like Polly who was quite happy as she was. But this being quite happy as she was, alas, was what made her a "character" in the eyes of her incredulous friends; the Andrews family were regarded as eccentric because they had lost their money and survived. Polly could laugh at this notion, but for most people, evidently, it *was* eccentric or possibly a pose to be jolly when your money was gone. And to wear your aunt's old Paris clothes, made over, with a twinkle, was original, though Polly did not know how you were expected to wear them—in the deepest gloom? If Polly had come to prefer the company of odd ducks, it was possibly because they had no conception of oddity, or, rather, they thought you were odd if you weren't. Mr. Scherbatyeff, for example, looked on Libby as an incredible phenomenon and kept asking Polly to explain her.

There was only one point on which all Polly's acquaintances, odd or not, agreed, and that was that she ought to be married. "You pretty girl. Why you no marry?" said the iceman, adding his voice to the chorus. "I'm waiting for the right man," said Polly. And this, despite the wisdom she exercised on herself, was secretly the case. If she made it difficult for him to find her, that was part of the test he had to pass. "How are you going to *meet* anybody, Polly?" her classmates cried. "Living the way you do and never going out with a soul?" She was familiar with the arguments: that the way to meet a man was through other men, that you did not have to love a man or even to like him a lot to agree to go to dinner and a theatre with him, that he only wanted your company, which was little enough to give. But Polly's own strong desires made her doubt this, and she did not think it right to start a relation you were not prepared to go further with; it did not seem to her honest to use a man to meet other men. So she had stubbornly refused all attempts to arrange male friendships for her—the extra man invited to dinner and prodded into gallantry. "Dick will take you home, Polly. Won't you, Dick?" "No, thank you," Polly would interpose. "I'll take the First Avenue bus. I live right next to the bus line." Even Mr. Schneider and Mr. Scherbatyeff had been guilty of similar efforts; a series of young Trotskyites had been produced by Mr. Schneider, to meet Polly and drink a glass of "schnapps" in his room, while Mr. Scherbatyeff had served up a nephew who was learning the hotel business in Chicago. Above all, Polly had declined to be coupled with Libby's awful brother, known as "Brother," who was always eager to take her out.

"It is your pride, little girl, that makes you act so," said Mr. Schneider one evening when she had reproached him for trying to find her a "man." "Maybe," said Polly. "But don't you think, Mr. Schneider, that love ought to come as a surprise? Like entertaining an angel unawares." The deep cleft in her chin dimpled. "You know how it is in mystery stories. The murderer is the least obvious suspect, the person you never would have guessed. That's the way I feel about love. The 'right man' for me will never be the extra man specially invited for me. He'll be the person the hostess never in her born days would have chosen. If he comes." Mr. Schneider looked gloomy. "You mean," he said, nodding, "you will fall in love with a married man. All the other suspects are obvious."

Sure enough, it had been like that with Gus. "You two are the *last* people," Libby had said the next day, "that I would have expected to hit it off. Did he ask you out again?" Polly had answered no, truthfully—he had only taken her phone number—and Libby was not surprised. "He's awfully hard to talk to," she remarked. "And not your cup of tea at all. I've been thinking about you, Polly. You're the type older people find attractive. Older people and other girls. But a man like Gus LeRoy would be blind to your looks. That's why I nearly went kerplunk when you walked out of here with him last night. You might not think so to talk to him, he's so quiet, but he's the *dernier cri* in publishing; you should see the authors on his list. Authors that are personally devoted to him and that he could take with him tomorrow if he left Ferris. Of course a lot of them are Communists; they say he's a secret Party member and has orders to bore from within at Ferris. But, like it or lump it, some of our best authors are Communists this year." She sighed. Polly was silent. "Did he talk about me?" asked Libby suddenly. "A bit," said Polly. "Oh, what did he say? Tell me all." "He said you were doing awfully well as an agent. I think he used the word 'crackerjack.'" Libby was disappointed. "He must have said more than that. Does he think I'm attractive? He must or he wouldn't have come to my party. I'm afraid I rather neglected him. Did he mention that? I had eyes only for Nils. You know, the baron." She sighed again. "He proposed last night." "Oh, Libby," said Polly, laughing, "you can't marry the ski jumper at Altman's! I hope you refused." Libby nodded. "He was in a rage. Berserk. Will you promise not to repeat it if I tell you what happened?" "I promise." "When I turned him down, he tried to rape me! My new Bendel dress is in ribbons—did you like it? And I'm a mass of bruises. Let me show you." She opened her blouse. "How horrible!" said Polly, staring at the black-and-blue marks on Libby's thin chest and arms. Libby rebuttoned her blouse. "Of course he apologized afterward and was no end contrite." "But how did you stop him?" said Polly. "I told him I was a virgin. That brought him to his senses at once. After all, he's a man of honor. But what a Viking! Lucky you, out with Gloomy Gus. I don't suppose he even tried to kiss you?" "No," said Polly. "He called me 'Miss Andrews' with every other sentence." She smiled. "Poor fellow," she added. "Poor fellow!" exclaimed Libby. "What's poor about him?" "He's lonely," said Polly. "He said so when he asked me to have dinner with him. He's a nice, solid man and he misses his wife and child. He reminded me of a widower." Libby raised her eyes to heaven.

Polly was telling the truth. She had begun by being sorry for Gus. And the way he had called her "Miss Andrews" all through dinner had amused her—as though there were a desk between them instead of a restaurant table. That desk, she had fancied, was part of him, like an extra limb or buttress; he had a special desk voice, judicious, and a habit of tilting back in his chair that had immediately made her see him in his office. He had told her, as a joke on himself, the story of Libby fainting on his carpet. "I thought the girl was starving, Miss Andrews, so help me God." He looked ruefully from under his eyebrows at Polly, who burst into laughter. "When did you find out different?" she asked finally. "Not for quite a while. Her boss told me, as a matter of fact. Seems the MacAuslands are among the powers-that-be in Pittsfield. Is that true?" "Yes," said Polly. "They own one of the principal mills. That's how I first knew Libby. My family live in Stockbridge." "Mill owners?" Polly shook her head. "Father was an architect who never built anything except for his relations. He lived on his investments till the crash." "And now?" "Mother has a tiny income, and we have a farm that we work. *They* work," she corrected herself. "And what do you do, Miss Andrews?" "I'm a hospital technician." "That must be interesting. And rewarding. Where do you work?" And so on. Exactly, Polly thought, like a job interview. This whole desk side of Gus, which impressed Libby, had touched Polly's heart. She sometimes felt she had fallen in love with a desk, a swivel chair, and a small scratchy mustache.

Still, to fall in love with a desk and be presented with a couch was daunting. She often now tried to picture him on the psychiatric couch and failed. Did he smoke his pipe and fold his arms behind his head? Or did he chain-smoke cigarettes, dropping the ashes into an ashtray on his chest, as he sometimes did in bed? Which voice did he use—the desk voice, which creaked like the creaking of the swivel chair, or a softer, lighter voice that matched his boyish smile, slim ankles, soft red lips, and the ingenuous way he had of wrinkling his nose at her, bunny-like, to signify warm affection?

When he had first told her about the analyst, his voice had trembled, and there were tears in his eyes. He had got out of bed, wearing Polly's Japanese kimono, a relic of Aunt Julia's Oriental travels, which came down just to his knees; nervously, he lit a cigarette and flung himself into her armchair. "There's a thing I've got to confess to you. I'm being psychoanalyzed." Polly sat up in bed, clutching the sheet to her in an instinctive movement, as though a third person had entered the room. "Why?" she demanded. "Oh, Gus, why?" Her voice came out like a wail. He did not tell her why, though he seemed to think he had. What he told her was how he had happened to start going to the doctor.

It was all his wife's idea. After Gus had walked out on her, because she had been "running around" with a Party organizer, Esther—that was her name—had decided she wanted him back. She had tried all the old methods—tears, threats, promises—without shaking Gus's determination not to return home. Then one day she came to see him in his office in a calmer frame of mind and with an entirely new proposal, which was that they should both go to analysts, to see whether their marriage could be saved. To Gus, after the scenes he had been through, this had seemed a reasonable offer, and he was struck, above all, by the change in his wife's attitude. She pointed out that analysis would help her in her work with children; quite a few of her fellow-teachers were being analyzed for no other purpose than that, and the school principal strongly recommended it for the whole staff. It would probably help Gus too, in his work with authors, make him better able to deal with their conflicts, so that even if he and she decided to divorce when they were finished, they would have gained a great deal from it professionally. Gus told her he would think it over, but before she left his office he had already resolved to give it a try. He too would have liked to save his marriage, on account of little Gus, and his hopelessness about it had been based on the notion that neither he nor Esther could be changed. If he had not been hopeless, he would have gone back long ago, for he missed Esther and there was no one else in his life. The idea of gaining an "insight"—a word Esther used freely—attracted him too, Polly could see; he was grateful for the insights of Marxism and, manlike, was eager to add a new tool to his thinking kit.

All this Polly understood. What she could not understand was why he kept on going to the doctor now, when there *was* someone else in his life. Now that he no longer had a doubt about divorcing Esther, why didn't he stop? Was it because of the promise he had given? But if so, that implied to Polly's mind that there still was a possibility that the analysis might return him to Esther, all mended, like some article that had been sent for repair. Or was he continuing to go, as she sometimes felt, from sheer inertia? Or because the doctor had discovered something seriously wrong with him, as when you went to get a cavity filled and learned you had a huge abscess?

Gus had asked her if she minded that night when he had broken the news. "Of course not," she had answered, meaning that she loved him just the same and always would. But in fact she did mind, she had found. It gave her a very unpleasant feeling to have Gus come to her every day "fresh from the couch." She wished he could have his "hour" in the morning, before work, or at lunchtime. This way, she could not help wondering what they had been talking about, whether it was her, horrible thought, or Esther, horrible thought too. She hoped it was about his childhood; it was all right if it was about his childhood. The odd thing was that he never seemed shaken or upset when he arrived from the analyst's; he was always as matter-of-fact as if he had come from the barbershop. He was much more excited on certain Fridays when he got excused from the analyst to audit a meeting of the Book and Magazine Guild. In his place, Polly was sure she would have been in turmoil if she had just spent an hour ransacking her unconscious.

Or indeed her conscious. Gus was not allowed to read Freud while he was in analysis (another rule), but Polly in her lunch hour had been perusing the literature available in the psychiatric section of the Medical Center library. Though the psychiatrists at the hospital were violently anti-analytic, at least they had the books of Freud and his principal followers. She was trying—rather slyly, she felt—to find out which of the neuroses or psychoneuroses Gus could be suffering from. But he did not seem to fit any of the descriptions of hysteria, anxiety hysteria, compulsion neurosis, anxiety neurosis, character neurosis. He was most like a compulsion neurotic, in that he was set in his ways, punctual, and reliable, but she noticed that he did not do any of the things that compulsion neurotics were supposed to do, like being sure to step on the cracks of the sidewalk or *not* to step on them, as the case might be. On the other hand, anxiety patients had difficulty making decisions, and it was true that Gus had been of two minds about enlisting to fight in Spain and had vacillated a bit about leaving his wife. But a real anxiety patient, according to the books, was one who could not make up his mind whether to take the B.M.T. or the I.R.T. to work, for instance and Gus always took the bus. Moreover, with all the neuroses, the patient's sexual life was supposed to be disturbed. Polly had no point of comparison, but Gus's sexual life, so far as she could see, was completely unruffled; he was always eager to make love and seemed to have had a lot of practice, for he did it very authoritatively and had taught Polly how with great tenderness, like a man teaching a child to fly a kite or spin a top or button its buttons—he was obviously a good father. It was bliss, Polly thought, making love with him.

The more Polly read and studied Gus, the more convinced she became that the only thing wrong with him was that he was spending $25 a week going to a psychoanalyst. And she asked herself whether that could be a disease, a form of hypochondria, and whether you would have to go to an analyst to be cured of it.

But if she could not match dear Gus, like a paint sample or snippet of material, with any of the charted neuroses, the opposite, she found to her dismay, was true of herself. She seemed to be suffering from all of them. She was compulsive, obsessional, oral, anal, hysterical, and anxious. If her sexual life was not disturbed now, it certainly had been. A sense of guilt transpired from her Sunday-night washing ritual, and she allayed her anxiety by the propitiatory magic of ironing and darning. The plants on her window sills were the children she could not have. She was addicted to counting; she collected buttons, corsage pins, string, pebbles, hat pins, corks, ribbons, and newspaper clippings; she made lists, including this one, and was acquiring a craving for drink. The fact that she viewed this alarming picture with humorous fascination was itself a very bad sign, proving a dissociation from herself, a flight into fantasy and storytelling from an "unbearable" reality. The whole Andrews family, Freud would say, lived in a world of myth.

Joking aside—and there were times when, reluctantly, she had to put joking aside—Polly realized that she was in a deplorable state. Whatever the clinical name for it. Sunday nights she knew that she was terribly unhappy. Again. Love had done this to her, for the second time. Love was bad for her. There must be certain people who were allergic to love, and she was one of them. Not only was it bad for her; it made her bad; it poisoned her. Before she knew Gus, not only had she been far, far happier but she had been nicer. Loving Gus was turning her into an awful person, a person she hated.

That person came to a head on Sundays, like a boil, because Sundays Gus saw little Gus and his wife. She was perfectly concious of the connection, unlike the patients she read about who could not seem to put two and two together. She was jealous. On top of that, she was conscience-stricken, for, to be truthful, she did not approve of divorce where there were children. Unless the parents came to blows in front of them or one of them was an evil influence. Look at what her own mother had suffered from her father. And yet they were together. Esther had committed adultery repeatedly and she did not sound like a pleasant woman, but Gus had loved her enough to have a child by her. If Polly were not the "other woman," she would advise Gus to go back to her. At least on a trial basis. No, that was equivocating. Forever.

At that word, Polly's blood ran cold. She wrapped a dry towel round her damp head and began to darn a hole in the toe of a stocking. It was not she who had asked Gus to marry her, but the other way around. Yet that was no excuse. She was acting like Cain in the Bible and pretending that the divorce was Gus's business and she had nothing to do with it; she was not Gus's keeper. But she was. She told herself that it had never entered anyone's mind but Esther's that Gus should go back to her. That was not true, though. It had entered Polly's. Not all at once, but gradually. During the week she forgot about it, but on Sundays, when Gus was not there, it came creeping back. As if, once she had entertained it, she could never turn it away. And in this it behaved exactly like a temptation. She longed to tell Gus about it, but she was afraid that he would laugh at her or perhaps that he wouldn't. This thought was her Sunday secret. And the whispering of conscience (if that was what it was), far from directing her mind to good resolves, made her still more jealous—just short of the point where she mentally slew little Gus. Here something stayed her hand, always, and instead she slew Esther and lived happily ever after with little Gus and his father.

Polly put down the darning egg. She went to the window and felt her blouses to see whether they were dry enough yet to iron. They were. She wrapped them in a towel and coiled up her hair and stuck two big pins through it. If she ironed, she said to herself, Gus would call to say good night to her, as he sometimes did. She had come to feel that this call was a reward she earned, for if she moped and did not do her ironing or mend her stockings and step-ins, often, as if he knew, he did not call.

She had discovered a sad little law: a man never called when you needed him but only when you didn't. If you really got absorbed in your ironing or in doing your bureau drawers, to the point where you did not want to be interrupted, that was the moment the phone decided to ring. You had to mean it; you had to forget about him honestly and enjoy your own society before it worked. You got what you wanted, in other words, as soon as you saw you could do without it, which meant, if Polly reasoned right, that you *never* got what you wanted. Practically every other Sunday Polly gaily found she could do without Gus if she had to; climbing the stairs with a stack of blouses still warm from the iron, she would feel quite happy and self-sufficient and think that it might be almost a deprivation to get married. And she wondered if Gus, a block away, puttering around his kitchen, smoking his pipe, listening to the news on his radio, was thinking the same thing. Whether they were not, really, a bachelor and an old maid who were deceiving themselves and each other about the urgency of their desire to mate.

But this was the *other* Sunday. Tonight she needed him and so probably he would not call. It was late, and the house was still. She pondered knocking on Mr. Schneider's door, to ask him to keep her company in the kitchen while she ironed. Though she had banished the bogeys for the time being, the prospect of the lonely kitchen, in the basement of the house, and of the labor of putting up the heavy ironing board seemed infinitely wearisome to her. And she was afraid of being alone with her thoughts there, out of the protection of her own four walls.

Yet if she summoned Mr. Schneider, he would be bound to start talking politics with her, and this, she felt, would be disloyal to Gus. If it were not the Moscow trials, it would be the war in Spain. Mr. Schneider was hipped on a group called the "Poum" and he also favored the Anarchists, both of whom, according to Gus, were sabotaging the war. But according to Mr. Schneider, it was the Russian commissars who were sabotaging the revolution and thereby losing the war to Franco. Mr. Schneider said the Communists were murdering Anarchists and Poumists, and Gus said they were not and if they were it was because the others were traitors and richly deserved their fate. Polly could see how Gus as a practical man would logically support the Russians, who were the only ones who were sending help to Spain, but she could not control her instincts, which went sneaking over to Mr. Schneider's side of the argument. Besides, Mr. Schneider was a better arguer than she was, who could only repeat lamely what Gus told her, which meant that Gus was worsted by proxy every time she let Mr. Schneider get started. Gus saw no harm in letting Mr. Schneider "blow off steam," but Polly felt it was wiser to avoid the occasions of sin, for the truth was that she half liked listening to Mr. Schneider go on. It was a kind of eavesdropping, hearing what the party did not want people like herself to hear. Listening to Gus and then to Mr. Schneider describe the same set of events was like looking at the war in Spain through a stereopticon—you gained a dimension, seeing it from two sides. This was her justification for listening, and she thought that if someone like Mr. Schneider could get Roosevelt's ear it might persuade him to lift the embargo, for if the Americans sent arms, then the Russians would no longer be in control. But really she was not so much interested in the fine points of the Spanish Civil War as in Gus, and what Mr. Schneider gave her, without meaning to, was another perspective on him. In this perspective, Gus appeared credulous—"the Stalinists and their dupes," Mr. Schneider was fond of saying. But if Gus was a dupe, she ought not to want to know it.

Yet wanting to know was consuming her. She blamed the psychoanalyst for that. It was the psychoanalyst who had made Gus a mystery man, at least to her, and often, she suspected, to himself. The idea that there was another Gus who came out like a ground hog every afternoon at five o'clock was becoming more horrible day by day. At first she had minded the psychoanalyst because he was an obstacle to their getting married; now she hated him because, the longer Gus went, the more she speculated about what passed between the two of them. She was sure Gus told the doctor things he did not tell her. Perhaps he told the doctor that he was no longer so keen on marrying her or that he dreamed every night of Esther—how did she know? Or perhaps the doctor told him that he *thought* he loved Polly Andrews but his dreams proved he didn't. He could not be going to an analyst all this time unless he had a "conflict," but what was the conflict between?

Most of all, though, she hated the doctor because, thanks to him, she had seen things in herself that she hated. If there was another Gus, there was also another Polly. Not only a jealous Polly who engaged in murderous fantasies, but a suspicious, spying Polly. The worst was that itch to know. When she mentally slew Esther, she was not unduly disturbed, because the real Polly would not kill Esther even if she could do it by cosmic rays or by pressing a button. But the real Polly would give anything to be present, in a cloak of invisibility, in Dr. Bijur's office. Why did she *have* to know? Feminine curiosity. Pandora's box, the source, according to the Greeks, of all the evils in the world. Bluebeard's closet. Yet Pandora's box at least had been primed with genuine troubles, nasty little winged creatures that she let loose on humanity, and Bluebeard's closet had been full of bloody corpses—the moral of those tales was that it was best to remain in ignorance. Polly did not approve of that moral; no science major could. It was another fable, she feared, that fitted her case—the story of Cupid and Psyche. Gus on the analytic couch, all innocent trust, was the sleeping Cupid, and she was Psyche, with her wax taper, trying to steal a look at his face, though she knew it was forbidden. What had Psyche expected—an ugly monster? Instead, she saw a beautiful god. But when the hot wax of her curiosity seared him, he woke up and flew away sadly. The moral of that story was that love was a gift that you must not question, because it came from the gods. What Polly was doing, to her sorrow, was like looking for the price tag on a priceless present. The penalty was that love would leave her. But she could not stop; that was the trouble with sins of thought. Once Psyche got the urge to see what Cupid looked like, she was done for, poor girl; she could not keep from wondering and speculating between his nightly visits—he came at the end of the business day, just like Gus. It showed gumption, Polly thought, on Psyche's part, to take a candle and get it over with.

For her own part, she wished she could say "Choose between me and the analyst." But she could not. She was too soft and pliant. Besides, she had kept hoping that the analysis would end soon. But lately, as though by reverse serendipity, she had been hearing stories that cast a new light on that. Kay Petersen knew a woman who had been going eight years. Why, at that rate, when the wedding bells rang, Polly would be too old, practically, to have children, and Gus would be on home relief. The only bright spot Polly could see was that Gus's savings would run out before long. Analysts, apparently, did not extend credit; they were worse than the telephone company and Consolidated Edison put together.

Cheered by this thought, Polly went softly down to the kitchen and put up the ironing board. In his room, Mr. Schneider had begun playing his fiddle. She was in the middle of her third blouse when the phone rang on the landing. It was Gus. He wanted to know if he could see her for a minute this evening. Polly unplugged the iron and hurried up to her room to put on lipstick and powder. Before she had time to do her hair properly the doorbell rang. He kissed her, and they climbed the stairs together.

"Looks like a laundry," he commented, entering. "You've been washing your hair." He approached her, sniffing, and dropped a kiss on her topknot. "Smells good," he said. "Nice shampoo." "Camomile rinse," said Polly. She poured them each a glass of New York State sherry. He glanced around her room. It was the first time he had been here on a Sunday evening. She waited, wondering why he had come; he did not take off his tweed topcoat but walked to her street windows with his glass, looked out idly, and pulled the shades.

"I had a talk with Esther this evening." "Oh?" "We talked about my analysis." "Oh?" The second "Oh?" was more cautious. Had he come to tell her that he and Esther had decided to call off the analysis? "She asked me how it was going. Hers is going great. She dreamt she went to her analyst's funeral. 'You're telling me,' he said, 'that the analysis is finished.' Next week she's having her last hour." "Well!" said Polly brightly. Gus coughed. "My own news wasn't so good, Polly. I had to tell her I was blocked." He fingered the avocado plant that Polly had grown from a seed. "Oh," said Polly. "Blocked?" He nodded. "What does that mean, exactly?" "I don't dream," he said, flushing. "It's funny, but I've stopped dreaming. Completely." "Is that so serious?" "It's a hell of a note," said Gus. "But why? There are lots of people who don't dream. I remember a girl at college who used to pay me to wake her up in the morning yelling 'Fire' to make her dream for a paper she was writing on Freud. That was part of Student Self-Help." She smiled. Gus frowned. "The point is, Polly, if I don't dream, I've got nothing to say to Bijur." "Nothing?" "Nothing. Literally. Not a damn word."

He drained his sherry despondently. "Every day it's the same story. I go in. 'Good afternoon, doctor.' I lie down on the couch. 'Any dreams?' says Bijur, picking up his notebook. 'No.' He puts down the notebook. Silence. At the end of fifty minutes, he tells me the hour's over. I hand him my five bucks. 'So long, doctor,' and I leave."

"Every *day*?" cried Polly. "Just about." "But can't you talk about something else? The weather. Or a movie you've seen. You can't just lie there without making a sound!" "But I do. It's not a social occasion, honey. You're supposed to dredge up stuff from your unconscious. If I don't have a dream to warm the motor, I'm stuck. I can't start free-associating in a vacuum. So I just lie there. Once last week I fell asleep. I'd had a rough day at the office. He had to tap me on the shoulder to let me know the hour was up."

"But you can free-associate to *anything*," said Polly. "The word 'fire' for instance. What does it make you think of?" "Water." "And water?" "Fire." She could not help laughing. "Oh, dear." "You see?" he said darkly. "That's what I mean. I'm blocked." "Have you tried talking about not talking?" "Bijur suggested that. 'Why do you suppose you refuse to talk?' he asked me. 'I don't know,' I said. End of conversation." He grimaced. "I've never liked the idea of talking to somebody who doesn't answer, who just sits there behind you, thinking."

"How long has this been going on?" "About a month. Longer, off and on." Polly's face crinkled into smiles. "If you only knew what I'd been imagining!" "About my analysis?" She nodded. "I never thought I'd tell you. I was afraid you talked about me." "Why should I talk about you?" "Well, I mean, sex . . ." said Polly. "You goop," said Gus tenderly. "The patient doesn't talk about real sex. He talks about sexual fantasies. If he has any. I haven't since I was a kid." He paced about the room. "You know, Polly, what's wrong with me? I'm not interested in myself." "But Gus," she said gently, "I think that's an admirable thing. Doesn't everybody strive for self-forgetfulness?" She was about to say "Look at the saints" and corrected herself. "Look at Lenin," she said instead. "Did he think about himself?" "He thought about the masses," Gus answered. "But frankly I don't think much about the masses either. Not in those terms." "What *do* you think about?" she asked curiously. "Sales conference. Dust jackets. Bookstore reports. Agents. A talk I have to give to the League of American Writers." He brooded.

"I don't think your doctor ought to take the money," she said virtuously. "It's unethical." Gus shook his head. "According to him, it's all grist to the mill. He told me that when I wondered whether I shouldn't quit—stop wasting his time. He said most patients expressed their resistance through talking. I express mine by silence. But my silence, he claims, is valuable. It shows the treatment is working and I'm fighting it."

Polly lost patience. Seeing Gus so upset and so humble

made her angry. She asked the question she had resolved never to ask. "Tell me," she said, trying to sound casual, "what *are* you being treated for? What's supposed to be the matter with you? What's its name?" "Name?" He sounded surprised. "Yes," prompted Polly. "'Compulsion neurosis,' 'obsessional neurosis,' 'anxiety neurosis'—one of those." Gus scratched his head. "He's never said." "Never *said?*" "No. I think maybe it's against the rules to tell the patient the name of what's the matter with him." "But aren't you curious?" "No. What's in a name, anyway?" Polly controlled herself. "If you went to a doctor with a rash," she said, "wouldn't you feel entitled to know whether he thought it was measles or prickly heat?" "That's different." Polly tried another tack. "What are your symptoms, then? If I were writing your chart, what would I put down? The patient complains of . . . ?" Gus seemed suddenly irritated. "Get the hospital out of your mind, Polly. I went, I told you, because Esther and I agreed. Because our marriage had broken up, over my jealousy. Esther wanted a free relationship; I couldn't take it."

A feeling of alarm came over Polly. "Oh," she said. "But that's natural, surely?" He knitted his brows. "Only in our culture, Polly. You understand, don't you, that there's a conflict in me between Fall River and Union Square?" "There is in almost everybody, isn't there? I mean of our generation. Maybe not exactly Union Square." She hesitated. "What if there were nothing the matter with you, Gus? What if you were just normal?" "If there were nothing the matter with me, I wouldn't be blocked, would I?" He sat down wearily. Polly touched his shoulder. "What did Esther say?" He closed his eyes. "She said I was sabotaging the analysis. Because of you." "So she knows about me." "Jacoby told her." That was the book designer. Gus opened his eyes. "Esther thinks I'd unblock if I stopped seeing you for the time being."

Polly stiffened. Her first impulse was to laugh; instead, she waited, warily watching Gus. "The way Esther looks at it," he went on, flushing, "I'm throwing a monkey wrench into the analysis to keep from getting well. Because the part of me that's weak and evasive clings to you for support or refuge. The fact that you work in a hospital makes me see you as a nurse. If I got well, I'd have to leave my nurse." He looked at her inquiringly. "What do you think of that?" "I think," Polly said with a tight throat, "that Esther ought not to practice medicine without a license. Isn't it up to Dr. Bijur to tell you these things, if they're true? He should be the one to recommend that you stop seeing me for the time being."

"He can't, Polly. He's my analyst. We've been over that before. He can't advise me about my life-decisions. He can only listen when I report them." "At least," remarked Polly, "this will give you something to talk about in your next session." "That's a nasty crack," said Gus. "Have I deserved that, Polly?" He wrinkled his nose appealingly. "I love you." "But you've already decided, haven't you?" she said steadily. "You're going to do what Esther says. That's why you came to see me to-night." "I wanted to talk to you about it before I saw Bijur. And I have a lunch with an author tomorrow. But I haven't decided anything. We have to decide this together." Polly folded her hands and stared at them. "Hell," said Gus. "I don't suggest I believe what Esther said. But I might be game to try it as an experiment. After all, she knows me pretty well. And she has a good head on her shoulders. If we agreed to stop seeing each other for a week or so and I unblocked, that might prove something. And if I didn't unblock, that would prove she was wrong, wouldn't it?" He smiled eagerly. "She knows you *very* well," observed Polly.

"Hey!" he said. "That isn't like you, Poll. You sound catty, like other women." "I am like other women." "No." He shook his head. "You're not. You're like a girl in a story book." He looked around the room. "That's how I always think of you, as a girl in a story book or a fairy tale. A girl with long fair hair who lives in a special room surrounded by kindly dwarfs." For some reason, this friendly allusion to the lodgers was the thing that undid her. Tears streamed from her eyes; she had never thought he liked the two "dwarfs." "And that's why you're going to let me go," she said. "Because I'm part of a fairy tale. I'm unreal." She brushed away her tears and poured herself another glass of sherry.

"Whoa!" he said. "I'm not going to let you go. This is just a temporary tactic. In the interests of the over-all strategy. Please understand, Polly. I made an agreement with Esther, and she's going to hold me to it. If I don't finish the analysis, no divorce." "We could wait," she said. "You could quit the analysis and we could wait. Living in sin. You could move in here or we could find another place." "I couldn't do that to you," he said emphatically. "You weren't built to live in sin. I would never forgive myself for what it'd do to you." "Is that Union Square speaking?" "No, that's Fall River. Granite Block." She smiled mistily. "So you do understand," he said. "And you know I love you."

Polly reflected, turning the gold-speckled glass in her hand. "I know. I must be crazy, but I know. And I know something else. You're going to go back to Esther. You think you're not, but you are." He was struck. "Why do you say that?" Polly waved a hand. "Little Gus, the party, the psychoanalyst. You've never really left her. To leave her, you'd have to change your life. And you can't. It's all built in to you, like built-in furniture. Your job too. Your authors. Jacoby. I've always known we'd never get married," she added sadly. "I don't belong with the built-in furniture. I'm a knickknack."

"Are you condemning me, Polly?" said Gus. "No." "Is there something you think I should have done different?" "No." "Tell the truth." "It's just a silly thing." She hesitated. "Nothing to do with us. I think you should have listened to Mr. Schneider about the Moscow trials." "Oh for Christ's sake!" said Gus. "I told you it was silly," she said. "No, Gus, listen. I think you *should* go back to Esther. Or I *think* I think you should." What she meant, she supposed, was that he would be doing the right thing, for him, but that she wished he were different. A better man or a worse one. A few minutes ago, she had suddenly realized a fact that explained everything: Gus was ordinary. That was what was the matter with him.

He was looking at her piteously, as if he felt naked before her eyes; at the same time, she observed, with surprise, that he still had his topcoat on, like someone who had come on business. "It's been awfully tough, Polly," he burst out. "These Sundays. You don't know. With the kid always asking, when I bring him back, 'Are you going to stay this time, Daddy?'" "I know." "And Jacoby, with his drawing board and his dames. Not that he hasn't been damn decent." It was a minute before Polly recognized that he was taking her at her word: he was going home. As soon as he could with honor. And he was glad and grateful, as if she had "released" him. This was not what she had meant at all; she had meant that sometime in the future, eventually, he would go back. "I've loved you so much," he said. "More than anyone, ever." He sighed. "'Each man kills the thing he loves,' I guess." "I'll be all right," she whispered. "Oh, I know *that*," he said loudly. "You're strong and wise—too good for me." He turned his head and looked around the room, as if in farewell to it. "'Like the base Indian threw a pearl away, richer than all his tribe,'" he muttered into her neck. Polly was embarrassed. They heard Mr. Schneider tune up his fiddle again. Gus kissed her and gently disengaged himself, holding her at arm's length, with his hands on her shoulders. "I'll call you," he said. "Toward the end of the week. To see how you're doing. If you need anything, call me." It came to her that he was going to leave without making love to her.

This would mean they had made love *for the last time* this morning. But that did not count: this morning they did not know it was for the last time. When the door shut behind him, she still could not believe it. "It *can't* end like this," she said to herself over and over, drumming with her knuckles on her mouth to keep from screaming. The fact that he had not made love to her became a proof that he would be back; he would remember and come back, like someone who has forgotten some important ceremony, someone who has taken "French leave." When the church clock struck one, she knew he would not come; he would not disturb the house by ringing the bell so late. Yet she waited, thinking that he might throw pebbles at her window. She undressed and sat at the window in her kimono, watching the street. Toward morning, she slept for an hour; then she went to work as usual, and her sufferings, as if punching a time clock, did not begin again until after five.

On the way home on the bus her mind automatically started to make a market list—bread, milk, lettuce—and then stopped with a jerk. She could not buy food just for herself. But if she did not buy food, this said that she knew Gus would not come tonight. And she did not know it; she refused to. To know it was to let fate see that she accepted it; if she accepted it, she could not live another minute. But if she bought food for two, this told fate that she was counting on his coming. And if she counted on it, he would never come. He would only come if she were unprepared. Or would he come only if she were prepared? With her lamp trimmed like the wise virgins? Christianity would tell her to buy food for two, but the pagans would say, "Don't risk it."

Getting off the bus, she stood in front of the A & P while other shoppers brushed past her; she was glued to the spot. It was as though this decision—to market or not to market—would settle her whole future. And she could not decide. She took a few steps down the street and turned back uncertainly. She read the weekly specials in the window; they had oxtails at a bargain, and Gus liked oxtail soup. If she made oxtail soup tonight, it would be ready for tomorrow. But what if he never came again? What would she do with the soup? Oxtail soup with sherry. She had sherry. Supposing she were to compromise and get eggs? If he did not come, they would do for breakfast. At the word "breakfast" she let out a little cry; she had forgotten about the night. She read the specials again.

It occurred to her that there was something familiar about this panic of indecision, as if she had experienced it before, quite recently, and then she remembered. It was those cases she had read about in the hospital library—the anxiety patients who could not make up their minds about what to buy for dinner or which subway line to take to work. This was what it meant, then, to be a neurotic. To be a neurotic was to live, day in, day out, in a state of terror lest you decide the wrong thing. "Oh, poor people!" she exclaimed aloud, and the pain of her own suffering turned into an agonized pity for those others who had to endure steadily something she had only experienced now for a few moments and which was already unendurable. A beggar came up to her, and again her will was paralyzed. She wanted to give him money, the money she would have spent in the A & P, but she remembered that Gus frowned on giving money to beggars, because charity, he said, helped perpetuate the capitalist system. If she disobeyed Gus's will, he would never come tonight. While her mind veered this way and that, the man went on down the street, shuffling. He had decided for her. But this thought made her act. She ran after him, opening her pocketbook, and stuffed two dollar bills into his hand. Then slowly she walked home. She had given the money freely, on a quick impulse, not as a bargain, and she did not expect any result from it.

Under her door was a letter for her. She picked it up, not daring to look at it, for she knew it would be from Gus. She took off her coat and hung it up, washed her hands, watered her plants, lit a cigarette. Then, trembling, she tore open the letter. Inside was a single sheet of paper, a short letter, in hand-writing. She did not look directly at it yet but put it on the table, glancing at it sidewise, as if it could tell her what it said without making her read it. The letter was from her father.

Dear Polly:

Your mother and I have decided to get a divorce. If it suits you, I would like to come to New York and live with you. That is, if you are not otherwise encumbered. I could make myself useful, do the shopping and cooking for you. We might look for a little flat together. Your mother will keep the farm. My mental health is excellent.

Your obedient servant and loving father,
Henry L. K. Andrews

IT was an ill wind that blew nobody good. Had Gus not decided to go back to Esther (and he did, the following week), Polly would have had to turn her father away. In fact, if the letter had arrived on Saturday, instead of Monday, she would have been in a terrible quandary. On Saturday there was still Gus. What *could* she have done? Probably she would have telephoned her mother and begged her to keep her father on the farm—not to rush into a divorce. Or she might have suggested mental treatment. The irony of this was not lost on her from the very first minute. She took cold comfort from the thought that, thanks to Gus, she could wire her father to come ahead. On hearing the news, everyone took for granted that her parents' separation must have been a dreadful shock to her, but the sad truth was that all Polly felt then was a wan gratitude that her father was coming. It was with a start finally that she remembered her mother and wondered how she was taking it.

Long afterward, Polly admitted that it had all worked out for the best. She was happy, living with her father, far happier than she had been with Gus. They suited each other. And his arrival, three days after his letter, was occupational therapy for her—just what a doctor would have prescribed.

Mr. Andrews himself, when he got off the train, was in fine fettle—a small white-haired old man with a goblin head and bright blue eyes; he was carrying a case of fresh farm eggs, which he would not entrust to the redcap, and a bouquet of jonquils. He had not been so well in years, he declared, and Kate was well too, never better. He attributed it all to divorce —a splendid institution. Everyone should get a divorce. Kate already looked ten years younger. "But won't it take a long time, Father?" said Polly. "All the legal side. Even if Mother consents." But Mr. Andrews was sanguine. "Kate's already filed the papers and served me. The process server came to tea. I've given her grounds, the best grounds there are." Polly was slightly shocked at the notion that her father, at his age, had been committing adultery. But he meant insanity. He was delighted

with himself for having had the foresight to be loony and to
have the papers to prove it.

Low-spirited as she was during the first days, Polly was
amused by her father. She was startled to hear herself laugh
aloud the night he came; it was as if the sound had come from
someone else. She told herself that she was going through the
motions of living, now that she had someone to live for, but
before long she found she was looking forward to coming
home from work, wondering what they would have for dinner
and what her father had been up to in her absence. He was
immensely proud of the divorce and talked about it to everyone, as if it were some new process he had discovered, all by
himself. For the time being, Polly had taken for him a room on
the third floor; on weekends, they were going to look for an
apartment. But then Mr. Andrews had a better idea. Having
made friends with the landlady, he persuaded her to turn the
top-floor rooms into an apartment for him and Polly—the
lodger in the one that was rented could move downstairs to
Polly's place. He designed the new apartment himself, using
the hall to gain space and to make a little kitchen, long and
narrow, like a ship's galley. All spring and early summer he and
Polly were busy with the remodeling, which did not cost the
landlady very much since Mr. Andrews gave his services free,
did some of the carpentry himself (he had learned at the work-
shop in the sanatorium), and found a secondhand sink and
plumbing fixtures in the junk yards he haunted, looking for
treasure. Polly learned to paint, well enough to do the bookshelves and cupboards; she sewed curtains from old sheets,
with a blue and red border, the colors of the French flag, and
she got to work with upholstery tacks and recovered two of
the landlady's Victorian chairs.

The apartment, when it was finished, was delightful, with its
old marble fireplaces and inside shutters; if Mr. Andrews and
Polly were ever to leave it, the landlady could rent it for much
more than she was charging them. Carried away with his success, Mr. Andrews wanted to redo the whole house into
apartments and make the landlady's fortune—a project Polly
vetoed, thinking of Mr. Schneider and Mr. Scherbatyeff, who
could not afford apartment rentals and would have had to
move. Mr. Andrews had to content himself with the plan of

making Polly a little winter garden or greenhouse for her plants, outside the back windows, which had a southern exposure; he wanted this to be Polly's Christmas present and spent a good deal of his time at the glazier's.

The change in Mr. Andrews amazed everyone who knew him. It could not be just the divorce, his sister Julia said, nor dear Polly's good heart and youthful spirits. Something else must have happened to Henry. It was Polly's mother who provided the information, during a visit she made to New York, where she stayed with her ex-sister-in-law on Park Avenue. "They changed the name of his illness, did you know that, Polly? They don't call it melancholia any more. They call it manic-depressive psychosis. When Henry heard that, he felt as if he'd been cheated all these years. He'd only had the 'depressed' phase, you see. He cheered up extraordinarily and began to make all these projects. Beginning with the crazy notion that we ought to get a divorce. At first I went along with it just to humor him. You know, the way I did when he insisted on being baptized into the Roman faith by the village curé and then baptized all you children himself. I knew those baptisms were otiose, since you'd all been christened as infants in the Episcopal church. Well, I assumed the divorce bug would pass, like the Romanism bug. But he got more and more set on it and on coming to New York. So I finally said to myself, 'Why not? Henry may have a good idea, after all. At our time of life, there's no earthly reason to stay together if we don't feel like it.' And I've been a new woman myself ever since." Polly looked at her mother, pouring tea at Aunt Julia's table. It was true; she was blooming, like an expansive widow, and she had had a new permanent wave. "Excuse me, madam," said Ross, who was passing biscuits, "but why couldn't you and Mr. Henry just live apart, the way so many couples do?" "Henry said that wouldn't be respectable," replied Mrs. Andrews. "It would be like living together without marriage— living apart without a divorce." "I see," said Ross. "I never thought of it that way." She gave Polly a wink. "I can run the farm much better myself," Mrs. Andrews went on to Polly, lighting a cigarette and oblivious of Polly's blush. "With just your brothers' help. Henry was always interfering, and he's never cared for domestic animals. He was only interested in his pot herbs and his kitchen garden. Now that he's gone, we've bought some Black Angus and I'm going to try turkeys for the Thanksgiving market—I've been to see Charles & Company and they took an order. If Henry were there, he'd insist on Chinese pheasants or peacocks. And peacocks are such an unpleasant bird! Quarrelsome and shrill."

"Do you mean that Father is in a 'manic' state?" "I suppose so, my dear," Mrs. Andrews answered comfortably. "Let's only hope it lasts. He's not giving you any trouble, is he?" "No," said Polly, but the next day she had a talk with the second psychiatrist-in-charge at the Payne Whitney Clinic, whom she had known as a young resident. She often had to give metabolism tests to manic-depressive patients, but she had not known that her father's "melancholia"—which she connected with "*Il Penseroso*" and with Dürer's engraving—was part of the same syndrome. In her experience, the manic patients were frequently under restraint, in straitjackets, and she was amazed at her mother's unconcern.

Yes, said the young doctor, Mr. Andrews' behavior did indeed reveal some of the typical manic symptoms, but in a mild form. It was possible that a trough of depression would follow, but, given the mildness of the manic elation, it need not be severe. At her father's age, the cycle often lengthened or abated altogether. "How old is he?" "About sixty." The doctor nodded. "After the climacteric, many manic-depressive patients spontaneously recover." Polly told him her mother's idea: that her father had changed his symptoms when he learned the new name of his disease. The doctor laughed. "That isn't possible, is it?" said Polly. "With these nuts anything is possible, Polly," he declared. "Insanity is a funny thing. We don't really understand anything about it. Why they get sick, why they get well. Changing the name may make a difference. We've noticed that now that we no longer speak of dementia praecox, we get fewer dementia-praecox patients. It tempts you to think sometimes that all mental illness has a hysterical origin, that they're all copying the latest textbooks. Even the illiterate patients. Could your father be hysterical?" "I don't think so," said Polly. "Though he used to cry a lot. But very quietly." "Would you like me to see him?" Polly hesitated; she was feeling greatly relieved, without knowing why. "You might come for sherry some afternoon. Or for Sunday lunch, if you're off duty. Very informal. Father's a good cook and he loves to entertain."

This was true. Polly's social life had become much more active since her father had been sharing an apartment with her. The chief problem was restraining his expenditures. He had discovered the new A & P self-service market and was an enthusiastic patron, confident that he was saving money with every purchase he made. He shopped in quantity, saying that it saved time; the big economy-size package appealed to him; he took advantage of "special offers" and never missed a sale. He was also fond of the Italian fish and vegetable markets on lower Second Avenue, where he bought all manner of strange sea creatures and vegetables Polly had never seen before. Every Sunday at lunch they entertained, using chafing dishes Aunt Julia had put away as old-fashioned, and the guests sometimes stayed the whole afternoon, playing games or listening to the phonograph. Polly now had great trouble finding time to do her laundry and wash her hair.

Shortly after his arrival, Mr. Andrews had taken up ping-pong; as a young man, he had played tennis very well, and now he had found a bar on First Avenue with a long back room where there was a ping-pong table. Every day he played with the "regulars" and on Saturday afternoons he would take part in tournaments, in which he insisted that Polly play too. In this way, she met a number of young men, some of whom would turn up for Sunday lunch or for her father's Friday-night bouillabaisse. The guests often brought a bottle of wine. When Mr. Schneider came, he brought his violin. Or there would be a chess tournament, which Mr. Scherbatyeff presided over. "I hear you have a *salon*," Libby said enviously on the telephone. "Why don't you invite me? Kay says Norine Blake says you and your father are the *succès fou* of the year."

But the red-letter day in Mr. Andrews' life was the day he became a Trotskyite. Not just a sympathizer, but an organizational Trotskyite! It was Mr. Schneider, of course, who was responsible. Once the apartment was finished, Mr. Andrews had time to kill while Polly was at the hospital, and behind her back Mr. Schneider had been supplying him with reams of books and pamphlets about the Moscow trials. At first her father had found them heavy going; he had never taken much interest in politics, being a pessimist in the tradition of Henry Adams. But his attention was slowly fixed by the element of mystery in these trials—her father had a passion for puzzles, rebuses, mazes, conundrums. He concluded that Trotsky was innocent. The figure of the whiskered war commissar wearing a white uniform and riding in his armored train or reading French novels during Politburo meetings captured his imagination. He demanded that Mr. Schneider recruit him to the Trotskyite group. And unlike the village curé in France, who had required him to take instruction before being "received," the Trotskyites, apparently, had accepted him as he was. He never understood the "dialectic" and was lax in attendance at meetings, but he made up for this by the zeal with which, wearing a red necktie and an ancient pair of spats, he sold the *Socialist Appeal* on the street outside Stalinist rallies. He proselytized at Aunt Julia's tea table and at his ping-pong bar.

Polly was embarrassed by her father's behavior; she felt that his style of dress and upper-class accent were giving the Trotskyites a bad name: the Stalinists would laugh at this "typical convert" to the doctrine of permanent revolution. And just as Gus had not made a Stalinist of her, her father could not make her a Trotskyite. She felt that neither Mr. Schneider nor her father would be so enthusiastic about the Old Man, as they called him, if he were actually in power. She did not approve of revolutions, unless they were absolutely necessary, and she thought it peculiar, to say the least, that her father and his friends were eager to make revolutions in democratic countries like France and the United States instead of concentrating on Hitler and Mussolini, who *ought* to be overthrown. Of course, as her father said, it was pretty hopeless to make a revolution against Hitler for the time being, since the workers' parties had all been suppressed; still, it seemed rather unfair to penalize Roosevelt and Blum for not being Hitler. Fair play, replied her father, was a bourgeois concept and did not apply against the class enemy. Polly would have been horrified to hear her parent talk this way if she had thought he believed what he was saying. But she was sure that he did not, and furthermore the idea of his "seizing power" made her smile, it was so unlikely. She wondered whether the Trotskyites were not all a little touched. "Do you belong to a cell, Father?" she asked him, but he would not say, claiming that he was under discipline. It struck her that becoming a Trotskyite had merely given him one more thing to be snobbish about. He now looked down his nose at Stalinists, progressives, and New Dealers, as well as on the middle class and the "moneyed elements," whom he had always derided. Some of his worst prejudices, she told him, scolding, were being reinforced by his new adherence. For example, coming from Massachusetts, he had a plaintive aversion to the Irish, and he was elated to hear that Marx had called the Irish the bribed tools of imperialism. "Look at that bribed tool of imperialism!" he would whisper, of the poor policeman on the beat.

Eventually, of course, he learned about Gus ("That Stalinist," he called him), from Mr. Schneider or Mr. Scherbatyeff or the landlady—Polly never knew exactly. The people in the house believed that Polly had sent Gus away when she knew her father was coming, but Polly was too honest to let her father think that she had sacrificed love to family duty, and one night she told him the true story. The fact that Gus had been unequal to getting a divorce increased Mr. Andrews' contempt for him. "Are you still pining for that Stalinist publisher?" he asked, if Polly was quiet.

Polly no longer pined, but she felt that her fate was sealed the night she got her father's letter. Fate had sent her father as a sign that it would be kind to her so long as she did not think of men or marriage. Gus had called her, as he promised, at the end of that first week; when the buzzer had rung, Mr. Andrews had gone to the telephone. "A man wants to talk to you," he reported, and Polly, feeling weak, went to the phone on the landing. "Who was that?" said Gus. "That was my father," said Polly. "He's come to stay with me." There was a long silence. "Does he know?" said Gus. "No." "Oh, good. Then I guess I'd better stay away." Polly said nothing. "I'll call you again next week," he said. He called, to say that he was moving back to his apartment. "Is your father still there?" "Yes." "I'd like to meet him some time." "Yes," said Polly. "Later." After he had hung up, she remembered that she ought to have asked him if he had "unblocked."

Once he had moved, she lost hope of running into him on the street some morning or evening; his own apartment was on the other side of town, in Greenwich Village. Yet she wondered about this hope, for she remembered, quite clearly, the thrill of fear that had gone through her when her father had called her to the telephone. *She had been afraid that Gus would tell her he wanted her back.* If he had, what would she have done? At the same time, paradoxically, she still felt their love affair had not quite finished: it lived somewhere underground, between them, growing in the dark as people's hair and fingernails grew after their death. She was sure she would meet him again somewhere, some day. This presentiment too was tainted with dread.

When her father became a Trotskyite, she took a defiant pleasure in the thought that the two might meet—on opposite sides of a picket line. And her father's side would be the *right* side. She imagined her father trying to sell him a copy of the *Socialist Appeal* outside some rally for Spain. Gus would shake his head brusquely, and he would be *wrong*, because he was afraid to read what the other side said, and Mr. Schneider was not afraid to read the *Daily Worker* from cover to cover every day. If it came to the picket lines, she was a Trotskyite too.

But when the two did meet, it was not in the political arena. It was in the ping-pong bar one Saturday afternoon. Polly, luckily, had stayed home to listen to the Metropolitan Opera on the radio. "I met that Stalinist," Mr. Andrews said, coming home with a shopping basket full of groceries. "LeRoy. Beat him two sets out of three." Polly was pleased; she would have hated it if Gus had beaten her father. "What was he doing there?" "He came in with a chap called Jacoby, another Stalinist. A book designer. Your friend has taken up ping-pong to lose weight, he says. They're probably infiltrating that bar." "How did you know he was he?" said Polly. "I didn't. He knew I was I." He laughed gently. "I'm well known there. Eccentric Henry Andrews. Decayed gentleman. Used to play tennis with Borotra. Now lives with his beautiful daughter, Polly, on East Tenth Street. Trotskyist agent and saboteur." "Oh, Father!" said Polly impatiently. "You think they came there because of you?" "Of course." "Did you talk about politics?" "No. We talked about you." "You didn't—?" Mr. Andrews shook his head. "*He* brought you up. He asked if I had a daughter Polly. Then a great many other tiresome questions.

How were you? What were you doing? Did you still have the same job? Were you still living in the same place? I told him your mother and I were divorced." "What did he say?" "That it must have been a shock for you." "What did you think of him?" "Ordinary," said Mr. Andrews. "Sadly ordinary. A dull dog. Not a bad fellow, though, Polly. He took losing well, at any rate. I think he was in love with you. That makes him worse, of course. If he dropped you because he was tired of you or wasn't really attracted, I could sympathize. But this poor chap is a dangerous neurotic."

Polly laughed. "So you saw that, Father. I never could. He always seemed so normal." "It's the same thing," said her father, putting the groceries away. "All neurotics are petty bourgeois. And vice versa. Madness is too revolutionary for them. They can't go the whole hog. We madmen are the aristocrats of mental illness. You could never marry that fellow, my dear. He probably knew that himself."

"I can never marry," said Polly. "Nonsense," said Mr. Andrews. "I intend to find you a husband. For purely selfish reasons. I need a son-in-law to support me in my old age. I don't want to crawl back to Kate." "You'll stay with me. I'll take care of you." "No, thank you, my dear. I don't want to be the companion of an embittered old maid." Polly was hurt. "If you sacrifice your youth to me, you'll be embittered," said Mr. Andrews. "Or you ought to be. But if I find you a nice husband, you'll be grateful. Both of you. You'll keep a spare room for me and take me as a tax deduction."

Polly bit her lip. When her father used the word "selfish," he was speaking the truth. He was selfish; both her parents were selfish. Loving him, she did not mind. Selfish people, she felt, were more fun to be with than unselfish people. If her father had been mild and self-effacing, she would have hated living with him. Instead, he was mild and self-willed. He liked contriving little surprises for her and doing her little courtesies, but it was he who planned their life, like a child playing house. He was hard to circumvent, once he had an idea in his head, and he was quite capable of gently forcing her to marry to provide a home for his old age. And in fact he had a point; she did not know how else she would be able to support him. She could not give him back to her mother—the divorce had taken care of that. It was not that she felt "saddled" with him; only she did not see how her salary would keep both of them in the style her father liked or how she would ever earn a great deal more than she did. Mrs. Andrews helped by sending eggs and poultry from the farm—"my alimony payments," her father called them. Aunt Julia helped; she had given them bed linen and blankets and, as usual, she gave Polly clothes, which Polly and Ross fixed over. But with her father on the scene, Polly had less time for dressmaking and moreover she needed more dresses; if people were coming, he would not let her appear in just a blouse and skirt—"Put on something pretty," he would say. That he was thinking of her and not of himself made his thoughtlessness harder to bear.

It was the same with the household money. Every week Polly gave him an allowance, and every week he overspent it and had to ask her for more. And again it was not for himself, but for treats for her and their friends. Knowing him, as the autumn days passed, Polly grew afraid of Christmas. She had decreed that all their presents had to be homemade, and by that she meant little things like penwipers. During her vacation, on the farm, she had made jellies out of crabapples and mint and thyme and rosemary, which she intended as presents for their friends and relations, and she was going to make her pomander balls again; at work, she was knitting a muffler for her father and for her mother she had bought a length of cerise jersey, on which she was sewing bows of colored velvet ribbon for an evening scarf—she had got the idea from *Vogue*. But to her father "homemade" meant that greenhouse, which he declared he was going to putty together with his own hands; he claimed at first that the sun would heat it, but lately he had been deep in conference with a plumber about how to maintain a temperature of fifty degrees, night and day. And of course he justified it all as an economy: Polly would have flowering plants from cuttings all winter long for the house, and they could force hyacinths and crocuses for Easter to give their friends. In the long run, it would "pay for itself," an expression he had grown attached to.

Polly did not want that greenhouse, much as she loved flowers, any more than her mother would have wanted peacocks, and she was trying to divert Mr. Andrews' inventive powers to making simply some glass shelves that he could run across the window like a plant cupboard. Mr. Andrews said that was a commonplace of modern design, and in the end, Polly supposed, she would have to ask the landlady to put her foot down. She hated to go behind her father's back, but that was what young Dr. Ridgeley said she must do when it came to money matters.

They had talked again about her father, after Jim Ridgeley had come to lunch one Sunday, and he had asked her, straight off, whether Mr. Andrews had become very openhanded lately. This, it seemed, was one of the signs of the onset of a manic attack. It would be wise, he suggested, to close her charge accounts and to warn tradespeople against giving her father credit. Polly did not have any charge accounts—only a D.A. at Macy's, and besides, she felt Jim Ridgeley was looking at her father too clinically. He did not understand that a person who had had an independent income for most of his life could not grasp, really, what being poor meant. Polly grasped it, because she was "a child of the depression," but her father still felt that prosperity was just around the corner. That was why, to him, the "economies" he made were a kind of play—an adventure, like when the power failed in the country and you used candles and oil lamps and drew your water from the well. Her father, in financial matters, always expected the power to come on again. This was a delusion, but a delusion shared by many people, including, Polly noted, quite a few of her classmates.

As for the delusion that spending was saving, this too, Polly observed, was quite widespread; all the advertisements tried to make you feel that. Many people too, as they grew older, became obsessed, like her father, with bargains. No matter how much money they had. Aunt Julia had reached that stage and was always buying useless articles because she had seen them at a sale. Every January, for example, she "replenished" her linen closet at the white sales, even though the sheets and towels and pillow cases she had bought the previous January had never been used. Yet Aunt Julia was perfectly sane.

Except for a big item like the greenhouse, Polly excused her father. It was not his fault that two could not live as cheaply as one. Their problem, she decided, was to find another source of income. Last week, she had gone to the Morris Plan and

borrowed some money on her salary, and the experience had
frightened her. She felt as if she were taking the first step
downward into vice or ruin. The interest rate shocked her and
confirmed her instinct that there was something actually immoral about the transaction—a kind of blackmail; the interest,
she sensed, was hush money. No questions asked. And in fact it
was to avoid questions that she had gone to the Morris Plan
people, whose ad she had seen on the bus. She could have
asked Aunt Julia, but Aunt Julia would have exacted "a serious
talk" from her, wanted to see her budget—where was the money
going?—and would at once have started blaming her father.
And supposing his carelessness about money *were* a part of his
illness, he ought not to be reproached for it, Polly felt—only
protected. She did not mention the loan to him.

But how was she going to pay it back? To pay it back, they
would have to spend even less than they had been doing, but
the reason for the loan was that already they were spending
more than their income. Aunt Julia's Christmas check would
not make up the difference. There were so many little things
that added up: when they had calculated the rent on the apartment, they had forgotten that, with an apartment, they would
have to pay the gas and electricity too.

Polly had been casting about in her mind for ways of supple-
menting her pay. She thought of needlework or of marketing
her herbal jellies and pomander balls through the Woman's
Exchange. She and her father could make plum puddings or
fruit cakes. But when she figured out one day at lunch the
profit on a jar of rosemary jelly that would retail, say, at twenty
cents a jar, she saw that with the cost of the jars, the sugar, the
labels, and the shipping, she would have to make five hundred
jars to earn $25, and this on the assumption that the fruit and
herbs and cooking gas were free. She tried the pomander balls.
What could they retail for? Fifty cents? That was too high, but
it took her an evening to make six of them, and there was the
cost of the oranges and the orris root and the cloves and the
ribbons, not to mention the sore thumb she got from pushing
in the cloves. It would be the same with needlework. For the
first time, she understood the charms of mass production. Her
conclusion was that it was idle to think that a person could
make money by using her hands in her spare time: you would

have to be an invalid or blind to show a profit. She had a vision of herself and her father, both blind or bedridden, supported by a charity, happily weaving baskets and embroidering table-cloths. Useful members of society.

For weeks she had been preoccupied with money-making schemes. She sent in solutions to the contests in the *Post*. She asked her father whether he would like to dictate a cookbook to her, giving his favorite French receipts; Libby could market it for them. But the notion of sharing his receipts did not appeal to her father, and he did not like Libby. She wondered whether, if someone gave them the capital, she and her father could open a small restaurant. Or whether she could make a cucumber skin cream and sell the formula to Elizabeth Arden. She glanced through the alumnae notes of the Vassar magazine for inspira-tion, but most alumnae described themselves as happy with their "volunteer work" or heading a Girl Scout group; a few were doing part-time teaching, one was a cowgirl, and one was walking dogs. It occurred to her that her father might be called to do jury duty, which made her smile; he would be such an unusual juror. This led to the picture of him as a professional mourner—but did they have them in America?—or a member of an opera claque. He could sit in the evenings with children, for he was a very good storyteller: why had no one thought of that as an occupation? She could quit her job, and he and she could hire out as cook and chambermaid.

These visions, Polly recognized, were all utopian, when not simply humorous. But when she tried to think more practically, she was appalled by the images that crept into her mind. Just now, on this Saturday afternoon, when her father had been talking to her about marriage, a picture of Aunt Julia's will ap-peared before her. They were gathered together, the relations, in Aunt Julia's library, the corpse was in the drawing room, and the lawyer was reading her will to them: Henry Andrews was the chief beneficiary.

"I wouldn't count on Julia," her father said quietly. Polly jumped. He had this uncanny faculty—which Polly had ob-served in some of the mental patients in the hospital—of sitting there silently, reading your thoughts. "Julia," her father went on, "is a queer one. She's likely to leave everything she's got to a charity. With a pension to Ross. The Animal Protection

Union. Or the Salvation Army. To be used for Santa Claus uniforms." He gave his plaintive laugh. "In my opinion, Julia is senile." Polly knew what her father was thinking of. His sister had always been a temperance woman, because of the history of alcoholism in the family; her uncles and all her brothers, except Henry, had succumbed to the malady. But until recent years she had served wine at her dinners, even during Prohibition, though she herself drank only ginger ale. The law, she said, did not extend to a gentleman's private cellar. But since repeal, illustrating the Andrews' perversity, she had banned wine from her table and served ginger ale, cider, grape juice, and various health drinks described by her brother as nauseous; he insisted that he had been served coconut milk. "Throughout the meal." Her latest crime, however, was more serious. She had emptied the contents of her husband's cellar down the sink in the butler's pantry. "I might have sold it," she said. "I had the man from Lehmann appraise the contents. It would have brought me a pretty penny. But my conscience forbade it. To have sold it would have been trafficking in death. Like these munitions-makers you read about—profiteers." "You could have given it to me," said Henry. "It wouldn't be good for you, Henry. And anyway you have no place to keep it. You know yourself that fine wines deteriorate if kept in improper conditions." In fact, Ross had saved a number of bottles of Mr. Andrews' favorite claret and brought them down to Tenth Street, but Mr. Andrews was incensed. "It was typical of Julia," he said now, "to have the cellar appraised before scuttling it. I wouldn't be surprised to learn that she had several different appraisers in. To enter her virtue in the ledger at the highest bid. It will be the same with her will. There'll be a long preamble explaining what she intended originally to leave to her survivors and explaining that she finally decided that it would not be good for them to have it. 'My husband's money brought me a great deal of unhappiness. I do not wish to transmit this unhappiness to others.'"

Polly smiled. She hoped her father was right, for if he was, she would be able to forget about Aunt Julia's will. Counting on it was close to wishing for her death. Not that Polly had done that, but she feared she might if things got very bad. Or even if she did not, it was still wrong to see the *good side* of the loss of a relation.

"No," said her father. "I must find you a husband. Invest my hopes in grandchildren—not in the death of an old woman. Though I still trust that I can get her to leave a small legacy to the Trotskyites." "You're crazy," said Polly, laughing. "You can't seem to get it through your head that Aunt Julia's a Republican." "I know that, my dear," said Mr. Andrews. "But Julia has been convinced by what she reads in the papers that we Trotskyites are counter-revolutionary agents bent on destroying the Soviet Union. Walter Duranty and those fellows, you know, have made her believe in the trials. If what they write wasn't true, she says, it wouldn't be in the New York *Times*, would it? And of course I've added my bit. The Trotskyites, I've assured her, are the only effective force fighting Stalin. Roosevelt is playing right into his hands. And Hitler has his own ax to grind." "You're a crook, Father," said Polly, kissing him. "Not at all," said her father. "It's true. And I've saved Julia from being a fascist."

This conversation, by entertaining her, made Polly forget her worries for the moment. That was the trouble with her father. When she was with him, she could not remember to worry. And when she did remember, it was with a start of fear at the thought that she could have forgotten. At night she had terrible dreams about money, from which she would awake sweating. Once she dreamed that Christmas had come and the whole apartment had turned into a greenhouse as big as the Crystal Palace because she had forgotten to tell the landlady to countermand it. Another night she thought that she and her father had become nudists because he said they would economize that way on clothes, and an Irish policeman arrested them. But at the hospital one day she found a solution to their troubles. It was a solution she had never thought of because, like the purloined letter, it was staring her right in the face. She was taking blood for a transfusion from a professional donor, and the thought popped into her mind: "Why not I?" That week she sold a pint of her blood to the laboratory. The next week she did it again and the week after. She was sure it was not dangerous; professional donors did it all the time, and the internes sometimes did it. Besides, she was unusually healthy and well nourished this year because her father was an excellent dietitian—she was bursting with iron and vitamins, and if she looked anemic, it was only that she was naturally pale. Yet she told herself that it would be wiser, in the future, to make her donations at Bellevue or at another laboratory, where nobody knew her, so as not to cause talk among her colleagues. The next time, though, she was in a hurry, for it was the week before Christmas and she had used her lunch hour to buy candy canes and paper to make chains for Christmas-tree decorations—her mother had sent them a tree from the farm. So she went to her own laboratory as usual, saying that this would be the last time.

That day, as luck would have it, she was discovered by Dr. Ridgeley, who had come in to look at a patient's blood sample. "What are you doing?" he wanted to know, though he could see quite clearly from the apparatus, which still hung beside the couch where she was resting, as you were made to do after giving blood. "Christmas money," said Polly, smiling nervously and letting her clenched fist relax. His eyes got quite big and he turned and went out of the room. In a minute, he came back. He had been consulting the records. "This is your fourth donation, Polly," he said sharply. "What's the trouble?" "Christmas," she repeated. But he thought it was her father. "Did you do what I told you?" he said. "Shut down your charge accounts? See that he doesn't get credit?" "I don't have any charge accounts. He doesn't use credit."

"That you know of," said Dr. Ridgeley. "Look here, Polly. Allow me to put two and two together. If I see a manic patient and meet a member of his family selling her blood in a laboratory, I conclude that he's been on a spending spree." "No," said Polly. "We're just short of money over the holidays." She got up. "Sit down," he said. "Your father, my dear girl, is severely ill. Someone ought to see that he gets treatment." "Goes to the hospital, you mean? No, Dr. Ridgeley." She refused to call him "Jim" now. "He's sane, I swear to you. His mind is completely clear. He's just a little bit eccentric." "These spending sprees, I told you," he said impatiently, "are symptomatic. They indicate that the patient is way up on the manic curve. The next stage is often an outbreak of violence, with megalomania. Commonly with a sense of mission. Is your father interested in politics?"

Polly paled; she was dizzy, which she tried to attribute to blood loss. "Everyone is interested in politics," she muttered. "I'm not," said Jim Ridgeley. "But I mean, does he have some special angle? Some pet formula to save the world? A discovery he's made in recent months?" To Polly, this was magic. "He's a Trotskyite," she whispered. "What's that?" he said. "Oh, don't be so ignorant!" cried Polly. "Trotsky. Leon Trotsky. One of the makers of the Russian Revolution. Commander of the Red Army. Stalin's arch-enemy. In exile in Mexico." "I've heard of him, sure," said Jim Ridgeley. "Didn't he used to be a pants-presser in Brooklyn?" "No!" cried Polly. "That's a legend!" A great gulf had opened between her and this young man, and she felt she was screaming across it. In fairness, she tried to remember that a year ago she too had probably thought that Trotsky had pressed pants in Brooklyn; a year ago, she had been almost as ignorant as this doctor. But this only made her realize how far she had traveled from her starting point, the normal educated center, where Jim Ridgeley doggedly stood in his white coat, and which now seemed to her subnormal and uneducated. Yet he had guessed her father was a Trotskyite without even knowing what one was. She began explaining to him that the Trotskyites were the only true Communists and that, right now, they were in the Socialist party. "You've heard of Norman Thomas, I hope." "Sure thing," replied the doctor. "He ran for President. I voted for him myself in '32." "Well," said Polly, relieved, "the Trotskyites are part of his movement." As she spoke, she was aware of a slight dishonesty. The Trotskyites, she knew from her father, had entered the Socialist party "as a tactic"; they were not really Socialists like Norman Thomas at all.

He sat down on the leather couch beside her. "Be that as it may," he said, a phrase Polly disliked, "they're a small sect with a mission. Is that right?" "In a way," said Polly. "They believe in permanent revolution." And in spite of herself, she smiled. The doctor nodded. "In other words, you think they're nuts." She tried to be honest. Forgetting about her father, did she think Mr. Schneider was a nut? "On many points, I think they're right. But on that one point—permanent revolution—I can't help feeling that they're a bit out of touch with reality. But that's just my idea. I may lack vision." He smiled at her quizzingly. "You have wonderful eyes," he said. He leaned forward. For a startled moment, she thought he was going to kiss her. Then he jumped to his feet.

"Polly, you ought to commit your father." "Never." He took her hand. "Maybe I feel strongly because I'm falling in love with you," he said. Polly pulled her hand away. She was not as surprised as she ought to have been. In the back of her mind, she feared, she had been angling to make Dr. Ridgeley fall in love with her; that was why she had consulted him about her father! Just like other women, she had had her eye on him, having guessed that he liked her quite a bit. Sensing nothing but that about him (she now admitted), she had "thrown herself in his way." But now that she had heard what she had been hoping to hear, she was scared. She wished he could have said something different; he sounded like the hero of a woman's magazine story. The idea too that she had probably been using her poor father as a pawn to lure this young man forward made her smile disgustedly at herself. At the same time, inside her, an exultant voice was crowing, "He loves me!" But then another voice said who was Jim Ridgeley after all, what did she know about him? Her father might say that he was sadly ordinary—another Gus. The proof of this was that he could talk of love and of putting her father in an asylum in one and the same breath. She gave him an icy look. "If you won't do it," he said in a different tone, "your mother should." "She can't," Polly answered triumphantly. "You forget. They're divorced." "Then the nearest of kin." "His sister," said Polly. "My Aunt Julia." He nodded. "She's senile," said Polly, in that same tone of childish triumph. She did not know what had got into her, some mischievous demon that was prompting her to lie. "And your brothers?" "They'd never do it. Any more than I would. You'll have to give up, Dr. Ridgeley." "Stop playing," he said. "It's a dangerous game." "*My father is not dangerous*," said Polly. "You leave him alone." "He's dangerous to you now," he said gently. "You shouldn't be giving your life blood for him." "I suppose you think I have a father complex," she answered coldly. He shook his head. "I'm not a Freudian. You feel protective toward him. As if he were your child. This may be because you haven't yet had any children."

Suddenly Polly began to cry. He put his arms around her, and she pressed her wet cheek against his stiff white coat. She felt completely disconsolate. Nothing lasted. First, Gus, and then on top of that her father. She had been so happy with him and she would be still, if only they had some money or if he were just a *little* different. But it was true, he was like a child, and gradually she had got to know that, just as gradually she had got to know that Gus would never marry her. But she ought to have faced facts in both cases from the beginning. She had welcomed her father because she needed him and had deliberately not noticed his frailties, just as she had done with Gus. And with her father, there was probably a little element of trying to be superior to her mother: *she* could make him happy, if her mother couldn't. This meant she had given in to him, where her mother had had the strength not to. They should *never* have taken the apartment, her mother could have told her that; that was the beginning of the *folie de grandeur*. She could not control her father; she was inert. The same with Gus. If she had given him a strong lead, he would have married her.

"I had an *awful* love affair," she said, still weeping. "The man threw me over. I wanted to die, and then my father came. I thought finally I had a purpose in life, that I could take care of him. And now I can't seem to do it. It's not his fault; I just don't earn enough for the two of us. And I can't ship him back to my mother. And I won't put him in an asylum. He really and truly isn't certifiable. You said yourself he might 'spontaneously recover.' Of course, I could go to my aunt. I guess that's what I'd better do."

"Go to your aunt?" "Ask her for money. She isn't senile. That was a lie. And she's very rich, or used to be—nobody really knows how much she has left. But you know how funny rich people are about money." "That might solve your problem temporarily," he said, sounding like a psychiatrist. "But you must face the fact that your father may get worse. What will you do with him when you marry, Polly?" "I can't marry," she said. "You know that. At least, I can't have children, with my heredity. I've come to terms with that finally. It would be selfish to have children—wicked."

"Was it wicked to have you?" he said smiling. Polly rushed to her parents' defense. "They didn't know, then, about my father's melancholia. That happened later." He still smiled, and Polly saw the point. Would she wish not to have been born? Unhappy as she was, she could not say that. Even when she had wished to die, she had not wished never to have been alive. Nobody alive could do that. "What strange set ideas you have!" he said. "And you a medical technician. It isn't as if you had a family history of idiocy. Or hereditary syphilis." "I always thought," said Polly, "that from a scientific point of view I ought to be sterilized." "Good God!" he replied. "What bunkum! Where did you learn that?" "At college," said Polly. "I don't mean the professors taught it in class, but it was sort of in the atmosphere. Eugenics. That certain people ought to be prevented from breeding. Not Vassar women of course"—she smiled—"but the others. I always felt like one of the others. There was a lot of inbreeding in my family—people marrying their cousins. The Andrews' blood has run thin." "'The blood of the Andrews,'" he said, glancing at Polly's arm, where a pad of cotton still lay at the point the vein had been opened. "I'll prove to you that I have confidence in the blood of the Andrews. Will you marry me?" "But we've never even had a date," protested Polly rather speciously. "You don't know me. We've never—" She stopped herself. "Been to bed," he finished.

"All right, let's go to a hotel. You call your father and tell him you won't be home. I've got my car outside. We'll have dinner first and a dance. Are you a good dancer?" Polly feared this was a "line" he used with all the young nurses and technicians, and yet if he asked them all to marry him, how did he edge out of it afterward? He was quite good-looking, tall and curly-haired, and that in itself suddenly made her suspicious. In real life, it was only homely men who fell in love with a bang and did not leave you to guess about their intentions. He had a breezy manner of talking that she was at a loss to interpret; it *might* come, she told herself, from dealing with sick people. "Are you always such a 'fast worker'?" she asked teasingly, taking the tone she took with her father in his headstrong moments. "No," he said. "Not with women. Believe it or not, I've never told a woman I loved her before. Or signed 'Love' to a letter, except to my folks. And I'm thirty years old. Naturally, now that it seems to have hit me, I don't want to waste time." Polly's misgivings lessened. But she laughed gently. "'Waste time,'" she chided. "How long do you imagine you've been in love with me?" He looked at his watch. "About half an hour," he said matter-of-factly. "But I've always liked you. I picked you out when you first came to the hospital." So she had been right, Polly said to herself. Her confidence increased. But she was frightened now in a new way. He was different from Gus, straightforward, and she liked that, yet she found herself wanting to parry his onslaught. He was all too eager to commit himself, which meant he was committing *her*. But at the same time his hurry made this whole conversation seem unreal to her, like a daydream. "But we have nothing in common," she started to object, but this sounded rude, she decided. Instead she said, "Even if I were to marry, I could never marry a psychiatrist." To her surprise, she discovered she meant this, from the bottom of her heart. Looking for what was wrong with Jim Ridgeley, she had found it, alas. A psychiatrist would have a desk side even more wooden than Gus's; indeed, she had already noticed signs of it. "Good," Jim Ridgeley said promptly. "I'm going to get out. It was a mistake I made in medical school. I thought it was a science. It ain't. I'm leaving here the first of the year." "But what will you do then?" said Polly, thinking that if he left at the first of the year, she would miss him. One side of her was resolutely ignoring his intention of marrying her. "General medicine? But you'd have to start all over again, with your internship." "No. Research. There are discoveries to be made in treating mental illness, but they won't be made in the consulting room. They'll come from the laboratory. Brain chemistry. I have a job lined up with a research team; I share an apartment with one of them. You can work with us too—as a technician. There's no future for you here." "I know that," said Polly. "But what attracts you about mental illness, Jim?" "The waste," he said emphatically. "Of human resources. I'm impatient." "I can *see* that," she murmured. "Then I suppose I have a bit of the do-gooder in me. Came by it naturally. My father's a minister. Presbyterian." "Oh?" This news was pleasing to Polly; it would be nice, she reflected, to have a minister in the family. "If you like, he can marry us. Or we can go down to City Hall."

The more serious he sounded, the more Polly tried to joke. "And what about *my* father?" she said lightly. "You can use him as a guinea pig, I suppose. To test out your brilliant discoveries. He could be my dowry." He frowned. Already, she said to herself sadly, he was starting to disapprove of her. "He can live with us and keep house," he said shortly. "Do you mean that?" "I wouldn't say it otherwise," he answered. "And after we're married, I can keep an eye on him. To tell the truth, Polly, I think most of our patients would be better off at home. The Victorian system was better, with mad Auntie upstairs. More human. The fault lies mostly with the families. They want to get their mad relation out of the house and into what's known as 'the hands of competent professionals.' *I.e.*, sadistic nurses and orderlies. The same with old people; nobody wants old people around any more." "Oh, I agree!" exclaimed Polly. "I like old people. It's awful, the way they're junked, like old cars. But if that's the way you think, why did you say he should be committed?" "The difference between theory and practice. I didn't like the idea of your being alone with him." "*He's not dangerous*," repeated Polly. "They would never have sent him home from Riggs if he were dangerous." "Nonsense," he said. "Most homicidal lunatics who go berserk and murder ten people are found to have been just released from a mental hospital. Your father was let out of Riggs because you had no money to keep him there. If you had, he might be there still." "You're very cynical," said Polly. "You get that way in psychiatry," he answered. "But let's grant that your father isn't dangerous; you probably know more about it than a doctor. He may still be dangerous to himself. If he dips into a depressed phase. He was suicidal at one time, wasn't he?" "I'm not sure. He talked about it, and Mother was afraid." "Well." He looked at her; his eyes were like him—a light brown, with surprising green flecks. "Maybe," he said, "I told you to commit him partly to see what you'd say." "Oh!" exclaimed Polly. "You were testing me! Like a fairy tale." She was disillusioned. "Maybe," he repeated. "It's a habit you fall into as a doctor. Watching for the reflexes. But I already knew what you'd answer. I knew you'd say no. I think what I wanted to see was whether I could scare you." "You did," said Polly. "No, I didn't. Not fundamentally. Nothing could persuade you to distrust your father. You're not a distrustful girl." "Oh, but I am!" said Polly, thinking of how she had been with Gus. "I *know* my father, that's all."

Polly found she had agreed to marry Jim without ever being

aware of saying Yes. They did not go to a hotel that night; they had dinner and danced, and he took her home. They kissed a long time in his car in front of her apartment. When she went upstairs, finally, she still did not know whether she loved him or not. It had all happened too quickly. But she was relieved that she was going to marry him, and she wondered whether this was immoral. In the old days, people used to say that gratitude could turn to love—could that be true? She had liked kissing him, but that might be just sex. Sex, Polly had concluded, was not a reliable test of love. What bothered her most was the thought that she and Jim had so little in common —a phrase she kept repeating anxiously to herself. Outside the hospital, they had not a single common acquaintance. And as for those old friends, the characters in books—King Arthur and Sir Lancelot and Mr. Micawber and Mr. Collins and Vronsky and darling Prince Andrei, who were like members of the family—why, Jim seemed hardly to recall them. When she mentioned Dr. Lydgate tonight, he confessed he had never read *Middlemarch*—only *Silas Marner* in school, which he hated. He could not read novels, he said, and he had no preference between Hector and Achilles. At least both Jim and she knew the Bible and they both had been science majors, but was that enough? He was more intelligent than she was, but he had not had a Vassar education. And she was insular, like all the Andrews. Why else would they have kept marrying their cousins if not to share the same jokes, the same memories, the same grandparents or great-grandparents even? What would Jim talk about with her brothers, who were only interested in farming now and either discussed feeds and beef-cattle prices or swapped lines from Virgil's *Georgics*, the way other bumpkins swapped dirty stories? They would have bored Polly stiff if she had not known them all her life. And then there were all the old cousins and second cousins who would come out of their holes for her wedding at the smell of champagne. Not that she would have champagne; Aunt Julia's greatest "sacrifice" had been dumping the champagne she had been saving for Polly's wedding. What would a psychiatrist make of the whole Andrews clan? Polly's mother still described *her* feelings on meeting them as a young bride from New York. "Your father and I," she now said, "have never been compatible. I was too normal for Henry." But no one would guess that, seeing her on the farm dressed in overalls with a finger wave in her majestic coiffure. These thoughts had never troubled Polly when she had dreamed of marriage with Gus, which proved, perhaps, she decided, that she had never believed in that marriage. This time, she was trying to be realistic.

When she came in, her father, who was a night owl, was still awake. She felt sure he would notice the change in her, though she had combed her hair and put on lipstick in the car, and she was reluctant to confess to him that she had got engaged in a single night. Luckily, his mind was elsewhere. He had been waiting for her to come home to tell her, as he said, an important piece of news. "He's going to get married," she exclaimed to herself. But no; he had got a job. In a thrift shop on Lexington Avenue, where he was going to be assistant to the manageress, who ran it for a charity. The pay was not much, but he had only to sit in the shop afternoons and talk to customers; he would have his mornings to himself.

"Why, that's wonderful, Father!" said Polly. "How did you ever get it?" "Julia arranged it," he said. "Julia's on the board. The position's usually kept for 'reduced gentlewomen,' but she lobbied me through. I believe I'm being exchanged for a club membership. 'Henry knows wood' was her slogan." "That's wonderful," Polly repeated. "When do you start?" "Tomorrow. This afternoon the manageress explained my duties to me and itemized the stock. A preponderance of white elephants. The stuff is all donated." "Is it all bric-a-brac?" said Polly. "By no means. We have second-hand furs, children's clothes, old dinner jackets, maids' and butlers' uniforms. A great many of those, thanks to the late unpleasantness." This was his name for the depression. Polly frowned; she did not like the thought of her father selling old clothes. "They come from the best houses," he said. "And there are amusing French dolls and music boxes. Armoires, *étagères,* jardinieres. Whatnots, umbrella stands, marble-topped commodes. Gilt chairs for musicales. Gold-headed canes, fawn gloves, opera hats, fans, Spanish combs, mantillas, a harp. Horsehair sofas. An instructive inventory of the passé."

"But what made Aunt Julia think of finding you a job?" "I asked her for money. This spurred her to find work for me so that, as she nicely phrased it, I 'would not have to beg.' Had I asked her to look out for a job for me, she would have told me I was too old." "Was this one of your deep-laid plots?" "Quite the reverse. But now that it's happened, I find myself pleased to be a breadwinner. I've joined the working class. And of course Julia plans to exploit me." "How?" "Well, 'Henry knows wood.' I'm to keep a sharp eye out in the event that a bit of Sheraton or Hepplewhite pops in from an attic. Then I'm to set it aside for her quietly." "You can't do that!" said Polly firmly. "That would be cheating the charity." "Exactly my sister's design. As she confided to me, 'Some of our younger members have no notion of the value of old furniture.' Through another of her charities, she says, she picked up a rare Aubusson for a song." Polly made a shocked noise. "But where is it?" Mr. Andrews laughed. "In her storeroom. She's waiting for its former owner to die. It might be embarrassing for Julia if the lady dropped in to call and found the rug underfoot." "But why would anyone give a rare Aubusson away?" "The revolution in taste," said Mr. Andrews. "It's the only revolution they're aware of, these ladies. Their daughters persuade them that they must do the house over in the modern manner. Or they say, 'Mother, why don't you buy a flat in River House and get rid of some of this junk? I warn you, John and I won't take a stick of it when you die.'"

It occurred to Polly while he was talking that if she had known this afternoon that he had found work, she might not have sold her blood at the hospital, and in that case she would not be engaged at this moment. It was another of those kinks in time or failures to overlap, like the one that was responsible for her father's being here now. The idea that she had nearly missed being engaged terrified her, as though *that*, not this, were her real fate, which she had circumvented by accident, like those people who *ought* to have gone down on the *Titanic* and for some reason at the last minute did not sail. This fear showed her that already she must be in love.

The announcement of Polly's engagement did not surprise any of her friends. They had always known, they said, that there was "somebody" at the hospital. It was only logical that Polly should marry one of the young doctors. "We were counting on it for you, my dear," said Libby. "We all had our fingers crossed." It was as if her friends wanted to rob her of the extraordinariness of her love. The implication was that, if it had not been Jim, it would have been Dr. X in obstetrics or Dr. Y in general surgery. And it could never have been anybody else. She had made the great discovery that Jim was good, and this filled her with wonder—most good people were rather elderly. Yet when she tried to communicate this to others, they seemed bewildered, as if she were talking a foreign language. Even her mother did not appear to understand. "Why, yes, Polly, he's very attractive. And intelligent, I expect. You're very well suited to each other." "That's not what I mean, Mother." "I suppose you mean he's a bit of an idealist. But you were bound to marry someone like that. A worldly man wouldn't have attracted you."

Only Mr. Schneider and the iceman seemed to feel as she did. The iceman wanted to be assured that her *fidanzato* was "a good man." Mr. Schneider went further. "I understand what you are feeling," he said. "As Socrates showed, love cannot be anything else but the love of the good. But to find the good is very rare. That is why love is rare, in spite of what people think. It happens to one in a thousand, and to that one it is a revelation. No wonder he cannot communicate with the other nine hundred and ninety-nine."

What did surprise Polly's friends—though not Mr. Schneider —was that Mr. Andrews was going to live with the young couple. One by one, her group mates appeared to advise her against this—Pokey Beauchamp made a special trip by plane up from Princeton. Dottie, who was in town with her husband for the theatres and staying at the Plaza, went so far as to talk to Polly's mother. Even Helena Davison drawled a warning over cocktails in the Vassar Club lounge. Priss Crockett came to lunch in the coffee shop at the hospital. As a pediatrician, Sloan, she said, was terribly opposed. "When you have children, you will have to think of them. Supposing your f-father—?" "Goes mad again," said Polly. "Would that be so terrible for them, Priss? He was mad off and on when we were children, my brothers and I." That was different, Priss allowed; in those days, people did not know any better than to expose young children to mental illness—Polly and her brothers had been lucky, that was all. But even if Mr. Andrews were normal,

Polly's friends thought she would be making a terrible mistake
—a mistake that this generation, at least, had learned to avoid.
You did not have your relations to live with you if you wanted
your marriage to succeed; it was the one thing on which you
put your foot down. Opinion was unanimous on the point. If
Polly wanted to fly in the face of experience, she was practically
dooming her marriage from the start.

"And you mean to say your doctor *accepts* it?" the young
matrons of Polly's circle cried, shocked. "Yes," said Polly. This
astonishing news planted a grave doubt in her friends' minds.
"If he really loves you," argued Kay, "I should think he would
want to be alone with you. Wild horses wouldn't have persuaded Harald to share me." Polly did not reply that rumor
had it that she and Harald were on the verge of breaking up.
"What would you suggest I do with my father?" she demanded
quietly instead. "Why can't he live with your aunt Julia?" "He
doesn't like her," said Polly. "But she has a *huge* apartment,"
said Kay. "He could have his own quarters. And servants to
look after him. He'd be much better off than crowded in with
you. What are you going to do with him when you entertain?
At your aunt's he could have a tray." In her ignorance, Polly
had thought that you "lived happily ever after," unless your
husband was unfaithful, but the Class of '33 seemed to feel that
you could not relax for a minute in your drive to make your
marriage "go." Polly was quite willing to make sacrifices, having learned to do so in a big family, but that was not what her
classmates meant. It was very important, they thought, for a
woman to preserve her individuality; otherwise she might not
hold her husband. "At least," remarked Libby, "you're not
going to take him with you on your honeymoon?" "Of course
not," said Polly impatiently. But soon Polly's mother wrote,
anxiously, wanting to know whether it was true that Henry
was going to accompany them on the honeymoon—Louisa
Hartshorn had heard it at the Cosmopolitan Club.

The only person who was deaf to the general concern was
Mr. Andrews, who had taken it for granted from the outset
that he would live with the newlyweds. For him, the problem
was architectural: finding an apartment that would house the
three of them and not cost too much to fix over. He was looking at railroad apartments on the upper East Side, near Jim's

laboratory; he had seen one on the top floor of an old-law tenement where it would be possible to make skylights to introduce light into the inner rooms. They were going to be married in the spring—on the farm, the plan was; Jim's parents would come from Ohio, and his father would perform the ceremony. It was Dottie's hope that Mr. and Mrs. Andrews might be reconciled by the occasion and make it a double wedding. "Your father could be Jim's best man, and your mother could be your matron of honor. And then vice versa. Terribly original." She twinkled. "Don't you love the thought, Polly?"

When Jim heard this, he told Polly that they had better be married right away at City Hall and get it over with. Polly agreed. So as not to hurt anybody's feelings, they did not even take her father as a witness. They were married by a magistrate, and that night they went to Key West for their honeymoon, sharing a lower berth. From the station they sent telegrams announcing what they had done. Polly's friends were greatly disappointed that they had not had a chance to give her a shower or any kind of send-off. But they understood that a gay wedding, under the circumstances, would have been more than she could bear. The group was awfully sorry for Polly and would have sent her a floral tribute by telegram if only they had known her address. But naturally she and Jim were lying low, enjoying the last days the two of them would have alone together ever, probably, in their lives. In Dottie's suite at the Plaza, a few of the girls and their husbands drank a toast to her *in absentia*. "To her happiness!" they said loyally, clicking glasses. She deserved it if anyone did, the girls affirmed. The men's sympathies went to Jim Ridgeley, whom they did not know, but as Brook, Dottie's husband, continued to refill the champagne glasses, they concurred among themselves that he must be an odd gent to take a situation like that lying down.

13

EARLY one morning in March Polly appeared at the Payne Whitney Clinic, Woman's Division, to give a metabolism test to a mental patient who had been admitted the night before. When she came back from her honeymoon, she had stayed on at the hospital; she hoped she might be pregnant, since they had taken no precautions. If that were the case (and it was still too early to be sure), there would be no point in starting a new job that she would have to leave in October. Jim came to the hospital every day and had lunch with her in the staff dining room, where they held hands under the table. In the evenings Polly's classmates were busy separating them at a series of "fork suppers" given in their honor. Having joined the ranks of the married, Polly and Jim were not permitted to sit together, but had to balance plates on their laps at opposite ends of a room. These parties, at which everyone was half a couple and lived in an elevator building, gave Polly a vast sense of distance. All the husbands, it went without saying, were "doing awfully well" in fire insurance or banking or magazine work, and her classmates, except for a few rebels, who were not necessarily the same rebels as in college, were "taking their place in society." Yet there were nights when Polly felt, watching them and listening, that she must be the only girl in the Class of '33 who was happy.

It was plain to Polly that many of her married classmates were disappointed in their husbands and envied the girls, like Helena, who had not got married. In June the class would have its fifth reunion and already it had its first divorcees. These hares were discussed wistfully by the tortoises of the class. It was felt that they at least had "done something." Norine Blake's divorce—she had gone to a ranch outside Reno and now called herself "Mrs. Schmittlapp Blake"—had earned her a place of renown in alumnae affairs equal to that of Connie Storey, who had become a model for Bergdorf, or of Lily Marvin, who dressed windows for Elizabeth Arden, and outranking poor Binkie Barnes, who was working as a C.I.O. organizer, and Bubbles Purdy, who was studying to be a preacher.

Within the group itself, only Libby had made her mark. Kay, once so vital, had ceased to be a pace setter. Last year rumor had had it that she, who had been the first of the class to be married, would be the first to be divorced—quite a record. But she was still toiling at Macy's as a junior executive in personnel, and Harald was still writing plays that were as yet unproduced. From time to time, he had a job as a stage manager or a director of a summer theatre, and Kay's family was helping them in their hours of need. Opinion at the fork suppers was divided as to whether Kay was a drag on Harald or vice versa. No one had seen them recently, it seemed, except Dottie, who had made a point of it this winter, and Helena, who had had them to dinner at the Savoy Plaza when her parents were in town. The two of them, Dottie reported, were now running with a fast, poker-playing set, where she was known as "Mrs. Pete" and Harald as "Mr. Pete"; the women were older than Kay, had deep, drawling voices, and called all the men "Mr.," including their own husbands. The game was dealer's choice, and it cost a quarter to open; Harald was a real gambler, but Kay was just a greenhorn who held her cards so that anyone could see them and had a craze for deuces-and-one-eyed-Jacks-wild. For her part, Helena told Polly that her mother, who was a great amateur diagnostician, had announced that Kay was on the edge of a nervous breakdown.

"The patient is quite refractory," the nurse warned Polly that morning in the corridor, as she unlocked the door. "She may not co-operate." The woman in the bed was Kay. She had a huge black eye and contusions on her bare arms. At the sight of Polly in her starched white coat, she burst into copious tears. She was comparing their positions, Polly realized with sympathy, trying to remember whether she had ever seen Kay cry before. Rather than ask questions, which might have upset Kay more, Polly got a washcloth and bathed her swollen face. When she saw that Kay, contrary to what the nurse had said, did not offer any resistance, she found her pocketbook in a bureau drawer, took a comb from it, and gently combed her hair. She did not offer her a mirror because of the black eye. In a few moments, Kay's sobs subsided; she sat up. "What are you going to do to me?" she asked curiously, eying Polly's big cylindrical tank. "I've come to give you a basal metabolism test, that's all," answered Polly. "It doesn't hurt." "I know that," said Kay impatiently. "But I haven't had any breakfast!" This protest was so like Kay that Polly was reassured. To her surprise, except for her appearance, her friend seemed completely herself. "You'll have your breakfast afterward," she told her. "We give these tests on an empty stomach." "Oh," said Kay. "Heavens, I'm glad you're here! You don't *know* the terrible things they've been doing to me, Polly." Last night the nurses had taken her belt away from her. "I can't wear my dress without a belt." They had taken her nightgown sash too ("Look!") and they had tried to take her wedding ring, but she would not let them. "We had a frightful struggle, practically a wrestling match, but then the head nurse came and said to let me keep it for the night. Score one for me. After that, they made me open my mouth and looked in to see if I had any removable bridges, though I'd already told them I hadn't. If I had had, they probably would have yanked them out. I must say, I was awfully tempted to bite them." She gave her loud Western laugh. "I wish now I had." She glanced quickly at Polly for approval—which Polly feared was a very bad symptom. Kay was *proud* of battling with the nurses, as if she thought she were still a student standing up to the Dean or Prexy. Did she not understand about straitjackets? It was almost as if she did not grasp where she was. Then it occurred to Polly that Kay was simply embarrassed. "I gather," Kay went on in a different tone, "that they think I want to commit suicide. They keep peering at me through those slats in the door. Did they expect me to hang myself with my belt? And what was I supposed to do with my wedding ring?" "Swallow it." Polly's answer was prompt; she thought the nurses would have done better to explain to Kay. "That's just routine," she said, smiling. "They take away everybody's belt and wedding ring. I'm surprised they let you keep yours. And all the rooms on this floor have peepholes." "Like a jail," said Kay. "'Judases,' don't they call them?" Tears came into her eyes again. "Harald betrayed me. He put me in here and left me. He pretended it was the regular hospital."

"But what happened? Why are you here?" "First tell me where I am." "You don't know?" said Polly. "I suppose it must be an insane asylum," Kay answered. "Though the nurses keep saying, 'Oh no, dear. Nothing like that. It's just a place for nervous people to rest.' I made *such* a fool of myself last night when they brought me in here. I asked where the telephone was, right away. I felt like talking to somebody. They said there were no telephones in the rooms. So I said, 'Why not?' but they wouldn't give a reason. I ought to have guessed then, but instead I decided that this must be some cheap wing of the hospital, a glorified ward, and that Harald had put me in here to save money—you know how he is. Then I asked for a radio, and they wouldn't let me have one. 'Why not?' I said. They alleged that it was against the rules. That was *very* peculiar, I said: I had a friend who had had a baby right here in New York Hospital a year ago, and *she* had had a radio. I remembered it distinctly." She grinned. "They must have thought I was crazy. Right after that, they took my belt away." "They do think you're crazy," Polly interposed. "You're in the Payne Whitney Clinic. It's a private mental hospital, attached to Cornell Medical Center. This is the admissions floor, where they sort the patients out."

Kay drew a deep sighing breath. She closed her eyes. "All right. Now I know. I had to hear it from somebody to believe it." "But tell me how you got here," urged Polly softly, stroking her friend's bent head. Kay opened her eyes. "Will you believe me?" she said. "Somebody's *got* to believe me." "Of course, I'll believe you," said Polly warmly. She had come to the shocked conclusion that there must have been some mistake —as sometimes happened in hospitals. Petersen was a common name, at least in the form of "Peterson," which was the way it had been spelled on Kay's chart. How awful if Kay had come in with an appendix and they had sent her here through a mix-up! But that left the black eye to be explained. "It was Harald," said Kay dully. "He beat me when he'd been drinking. When was it? It seems so long ago, but it must have been yesterday morning. Yes, yesterday morning." "He was drinking in the morning?" "He'd been out all night. When he came in at seven in the morning, I accused him of being with a woman. I know it was silly of me, to accuse him when he'd been drinking. I ought to have waited till he was sober." Polly checked a laugh; Kay's self-criticism was always revealing. "But I was a bit hysterical, I guess. We'd had some people in for cocktails, and we all got quite high. Then when they left, about seven-thirty, and I was making dinner, I needed a cucumber pickle for a sauce. So I sent Harald out to get one at a delicatessen, and he never came back. I realize it was stupid; I could have used India relish. But the recipe called for a cucumber pickle. Anyway, he didn't come back till morning. I ought to have pretended to be asleep—I see that now. Instead, I confronted him. I said he'd been with Liz Longwell—you don't know her, but we play poker with them. She was Bryn Mawr, '29, and her husband's away, trying a case in Washington. Whereupon Harald said he was tired of my dirty mind, and he hit me. You know, I saw stars, the way they do in the funny papers. It was silly, but I hit him back. Then he knocked me down and kicked me in the stomach. What should I have done, Polly? Picked myself up and waited for him to be sorry the next day? I know that's the right technique, but I haven't got the patience. I jumped up and ran into the kitchen. He ran after me, and I picked up the bread knife. I purposely didn't take the carving knife because he'd just sharpened it and I didn't want to scare him too much. Just enough to bring him to his senses. I waved it and said, 'Don't you come near me!' He knocked it out of my hand. Then he pushed me into the dressing room and locked the door. I waited there for a while, trying to get control of myself and hear what he was doing. Finally, I heard him snore. It never occurred to him that it was getting late and that I had to go to work. I knocked on the door; then I pounded; then I took time out to put on my clothes and pounded some more. I was crying and sobbing. And not a sound came from the other room; he'd even stopped snoring. I couldn't see through the keyhole because he'd left the key in the lock. He might have been dead.

"Finally I heard the doorbell ring. Two elevator boys were there, asking what was happening. Harald got up and talked to them through the door, telling them to go away. But they could hear me crying inside; I couldn't stop." "Oh, poor Kay!" "Wait!" said Kay. "You haven't heard what happened next. The elevator boys went away, and the next thing I knew the police had come. Harald opened the door, as cool as you please. He'd lain down on the bed in his clothes and after that little bit of sleep he must have seemed sober, though he had liquor on his breath. The police came in—there were two of them—and wanted to know what was going on. I was so terrified I'd stopped crying. But then through the door I could hear Harald telling them that we were rehearsing a scene from a play."

Polly caught her breath. "Did they believe that?" "At first they didn't. 'We'd like to hear your wife's story,' they said. 'She's dressing,' said Harald. 'When she's dressed, she'll confirm what I'm telling you.' Then he offered to make a pot of coffee, which was an excuse to get them to follow him into the kitchen. He put on the percolator and left them there at the table in the dinette. Then he came into the living room and quietly unlocked the dressing-room door. 'Are you almost dressed, darling?' he called. 'Some gentlemen from the police want to talk to you.' I had to make up my mind fast; I knew he was counting on me to back him up and the very thought that he could, after what he'd done, made me mad. But I had to help him. After all, he has a police record, though they didn't seem to know that. I washed and put on a lot of powder and came out. This black eye didn't show then. I backed up his story. My husband, I explained to them, was a playwright, and I'd been trained as a director; we were doing a scene from a play he'd written."

"What did they say?" "First they said it was a funny time of day to be rehearsing a play, but I explained he'd been working late at the theatre—the elevator boys had seen him come home—and that I was doing the woman's part with him before going to work at the store. Then they asked to see the script. I was sure we were done for. But Harald—I must say this was masterful of him—thought very fast and whipped one of his old plays out of the cupboard. At the end of the second act there's a violent scene between a man and a woman. He handed it to the lieutenant, open at the right place, and asked whether he'd like to hear us do it. The lieutenant said no. He read about half a page; they finished their coffee and left, telling us not to rehearse again in a residential building. 'Hire a hall,' said the lieutenant, with a big wink at me. Harald promised them tickets to the play when it was produced."

"You must have carried it off very well, Kay," declared Polly admiringly. "That's what I thought," said Kay. "But as soon as they were gone, instead of thanking me for saving him from being arrested, Harald started abusing me again. He said that as usual I'd got everything twisted and that it was he who saved *me* from being arrested. Did I deny having attacked him with a butcher knife? It was a bread knife, I told him. 'A small point,' said Harald. When I said that I'd just waved it, he smiled in his superior way. 'You should have seen your face, my dear. It's a sight I'll never forget. "I met Murder on the way. It had a face like my wife Kay."'" "Did he really quote Shelley?" Polly marveled. "Was that what it was? Yes, he did," Kay replied, rather proudly. "Harald is awfully well read. Anyway, he said that if I didn't remember lunging at him with the knife, I was suffering from amnesia and ought to have psychiatric treatment. At that I started crying again; it seemed so hopeless to argue with him. I ought to have just gone to work, realizing that he was tired and still under the influence of liquor. But I cried and cried, which gave him an excuse to say I was hysterical. He put on his hat and coat. He was going to Norine Blake's, he said, to see if she would let him sleep a few hours in peace in her bedroom—she still has the same place she used to have with Put. 'If you go to her, I'll never forgive you,' I said very dramatically, barring the way. He just stood there and looked at me, up and down. This was more of my insane jealousy, he said. I had sunk so low as to suspect my best friend. 'Doesn't that tell you something, Kay, about yourself?' Well, I did feel rather cheap, though I hadn't meant sex. I'd never suspect Harald of sleeping with Norine—she's not Harald's type. But I was jealous of his going there—giving Norine a chance to tell everybody that Harald had come to her because at home I didn't give him any rest. To me, that was more disloyal than adultery. But he went just the same, saying that he would send Norine over to calm me down—I could hardly accuse him of fornicating with her if she were with me. I didn't particularly want to see Norine but I agreed that she could come.

"In a little while she turned up and said that Harald had begged her to quiet me, that he was frightened by the state I was in. I admitted that this wasn't the first fight we'd had; we've been fighting all the time lately." "Has he beaten you before?" asked Polly gravely. "No. Well, yes. But a long time ago, and I've never told anybody about it. Norine said that I ought to go to a hospital for a few days to get a complete rest; I couldn't rest so long as Harald and I were cooped up in this two-room apartment. If I would rather, she said, I could come and stay with her. But I didn't want to do that. She's such a terrible housekeeper, and besides it would be like a proof that Harald and I had separated. She made tea, and we talked, and at lunchtime Harald came back with some sandwiches from the delicatessen. That made me think of the cucumber pickle and my sauce, and I started crying again. 'You see?' Harald said to Norine. 'At the sight of me she bursts into tears.' I didn't explain about the pickle, because Norine would have thought I was crazy, sending him out because of a recipe. She thinks my cooking is compulsive. We talked all afternoon, and they convinced me that I ought to go to a hospital, where I could just rest and read and listen to the radio. Then when I was rested, Harald and I could decide what we wanted to do about our marriage. The thing, though, that really settled it was my hospital insurance. As soon as Norine heard I had Blue Cross, she was on the telephone, checking up with her doctor about whether I could use it if I had a private room. He said yes, if I paid the difference. So before I knew it, she had it all fixed up for me to go to Harkness. I didn't *want* to go to Harkness; New York Hospital is so much more attractive—I loved the room Priss had with those rough-weave yellow curtains and pure white walls; it had such a modern feeling. Harald said to humor me, and Norine called her doctor back; he told her he didn't practice at New York Hospital but he could get another doctor to admit me. We waited, playing three-handed bridge, till they called and said they had a room for me. By that time, it was night. I packed a bag, and Harald took me in a taxi; when we asked at the main door, they rang up and sent us around to this other building. We thought it must be an annex. Harald brought me in and went into an office to fill out forms while I waited in the lobby. A nurse came and took my bag and said that Harald could go now; the doctor would see me in a minute, and then I'd be taken to my room.

"By then, I was looking forward to it; I did feel awfully tired, and at the thought of a milk shake in bed and an alcohol rub and nurses looking after me and not having to get up in the morning, I was glad that Harald and Norine had persuaded me. Maybe it would help to get away from Harald for a little while, though he could come in the afternoon and make cocktails, like Priss's husband—you remember. Sitting there in the lobby, I was just beginning to wonder where the gift shop was and the florist and the circulating library when a tall doctor came out of an office to talk to me. He seemed awfully curious to know how I'd got the black eye. I laughed and said I'd run into a door, but he didn't get the joke. He kept on pressing me till finally I said, 'I won't tell you.' I didn't see why he should know what had happened between Harald and me. 'We shall have to ask your husband then,' he said. 'Ask him!' I said, sassily, and I rather wondered what Harald would say. But by then of course Harald was gone. The doctor had the nurse take me upstairs into this depressing room, so drab, with no private bath, no telephone, no nothing. I decided, though, not to make a fuss then, but to go to bed and ask to have my room changed the next morning. While I was thinking that, the nurses got to work and searched me. I couldn't believe it. They went through my pocketbook too and took my matches away. If I wanted a cigarette, they said, I would have to get a light from a nurse. 'But what if I want to smoke in bed?' Against the rules, they said; I could only smoke in the lounge or if a staff member was with me in my room. 'I'd like a cigarette now,' I said. But the nurse said no; I was to go to bed immediately. By this time, of course, I'd caught on to the fact that this couldn't be the regular hospital, but I kept getting these shocks. I was determined not to let them scare me but to act as naturally as I could. When the nurse left, I climbed into bed and was just starting to read the morning paper, which I'd never got around to, when suddenly the light went out. I told myself it must be the bulb and I rang. Eventually the nurse opened the door. 'My light's out,' I told her. 'Can you fix it, please?' But it seemed she'd turned it out herself, from a switch outside the door. I told her to turn it on again, and she refused. So there I was, alone in the dark."

Polly squeezed her hand. "All that was routine," she said. "For the admissions floor. Until a psychiatrist has seen a new patient, they take precautions." "But I saw that doctor last night." "He wasn't one of the regular psychiatrists. Just a resident, probably, on night duty." "Why was he so inquisitive

about my black eye? That's the part I still can't understand."
"The assumption is that any injury is self-inflicted. When you
wouldn't answer him, he thought you were trying to hide
that." "But why should I want to give myself a black eye?"
"Patients do," said Polly. "Or they may get one throwing
themselves in front of a car or down the stairs or off an em-
bankment. When you see the psychiatrist this morning, after
you've had your breakfast, you must tell him the truth about
your eye. Even so, he'll probably want confirmation from
Harald." "Confirmation from Harald!" Kay repeated indignantly. "What if he were to lie? Anyway, I don't want to see a
psychiatrist. I want to get out of here. Right away." "You can't
get out," said Polly. "Until you see a psychiatrist. If you tell
him the whole story, he may be able to release you. I'm not
sure, Kay. You'd better send for Harald right away. I'll phone
him as soon as we get this test done. I'm afraid that if he committed you, he will have to take you out himself. Otherwise,
the procedure's rather long." "Harald committed me?" cried
Kay. "He must have," said Polly. "Unless you committed yourself. Did you?" "No." Kay was positive. "That must have been
those forms he filled out in the office," she said. The two girls'
eyes dilated. "But that means," Kay said slowly, "that he knew
what kind of place this was when he left me." Polly did not
speak. "Doesn't it, Polly?" Kay urged, her voice rising. "I said
to you just now that he betrayed me. But I didn't mean it, I
swear. I thought we *both* thought it was part of the regular
hospital." "Perhaps," suggested Polly hopefully, "Harald didn't
realize what he was doing." "No." Kay shook her head. "Harald never signs anything without knowing exactly what it is.
He prides himself on that. He always adds up the bill himself
in a restaurant and makes the waiter tell him what each item is.
Sometimes I could go through the floor. And he reads all the
fine print in a lease. So he knew." She sank her chin in her
hand; her black eye stood out livid in her face, which had
slowly drained of color. She looked gaunt and old. Polly
glanced at her watch. "Come!" she commanded. "Let's do
your metabolism. Afterward, we can talk."

Polly wanted time for reflection. While Kay was breathing
into the big cylinder and she herself was watching the gauges,
the room was still. She was very worried for Kay. The grim

thought flitted across her mind that Harald, for some reason of his own, wanted Kay out of the way for a period and had deliberately put her in here, using Norine as a cat's paw. Or could Harald and Norine be lovers who were plotting Kay's destruction? But such things did not happen in real life, not any more. And what could they gain by such a maneuver? Grounds for divorce? But if Harald wanted a divorce, Kay would surely give it to him.

Almost worse was to think that Harald and Norine had persuaded themselves that Kay really was a mental case. They might have chivvied her in here with benevolent intent. If Harald imagined he was acting from laudable motives, poor Kay was a cooked goose. Remember the bread knife, Polly shuddered. A man who could convince himself that Kay was dangerous could readily convince a psychiatrist—the burden of proof rested on the patient, and how could Kay prove what had been in her mind?

But there was another possibility, a more cheerful one. Supposing Harald had had no notion of putting Kay in Payne Whitney but when he found that this had happened, through some administrative mistake (which Polly might be able to check up on), he had signed the commitment papers as a sort of sardonic joke? That would be quite in Harald's style. Polly nodded to herself. She could just imagine him yielding to a prankish impulse and signing with a flourish while raising a baleful eyebrow and mentally shaking an owlish forefinger. But in that case he would surely be back this morning to take Kay out. He might be here already, waiting downstairs, with a bouquet, to move her grandly to that room with the rough-weave yellow curtains.

This idea relieved Polly's mind. Given Harald, it was the most natural explanation. She smiled. It occurred to her that the whole thing was a little bit Kay's fault; if she had agreed to go to Harkness Pavilion, she might be listening to a radio now while a student nurse rearranged her pillows and offered her a mid-morning fruit juice with a glass straw.

The metabolism test was finished. It was an unexpected boon to be able to tell Kay that she had a perfect score. The figures worked out to zero, which was extremely rare. No doubt this explained her energy. Her organism was in absolute balance. Polly knew that this was not a proof of sanity; nevertheless, she felt it was a good omen. And Kay glowed as if the machine had paid her a compliment. "Wait till I tell Harald!" she exulted. Polly must be sure to impress on him that Kay was the first patient in all her experience to score zero.

While the maid was serving Kay's breakfast, Polly slipped out to inquire whether Harald, by any chance, was waiting downstairs. The nurse said no message had come through. "Call and check up, please," said Polly. "Mrs. Petersen is an old friend of mine." She went back into Kay's room. In a moment, the nurse appeared. "No, Mrs. Ridgeley." "No, what?" said Kay. "No, I don't have a ten o'clock appointment on my calendar," Polly lied quickly. Since Kay had not shared her hope, there was no reason for her to share her disappointment. "I'm going to call Harald," she said. "Wonderful," Kay answered, putting jam on her toast. The result of her basal metabolism seemed to have restored her natural optimism. "We're feeling better this morning, aren't we?" said the nurse. "Finish up, dear, and I'll help you dress."

There was no answer at Kay's apartment. All the better, Polly said to herself; Harald must be on his way. Nevertheless, she called Jim at his Center and told him briefly what had happened. He promised to come early and stop in to see Kay before lunch. "If she's still here, of course," appended Polly. "She'll be there," said Jim. "Now don't be cynical," said Polly. In her room, Kay, wearing a brown dress, which did need a belt, was packing her bag. "Did you get him?" she said. Polly explained that he must be on his way to the hospital. The nurse winked at Polly. "Mrs. Petersen doesn't seem to like us here," she jested. "She'd rather go home to hubby." "She doesn't want me to pack," Kay said to Polly. "I've been explaining to her that it's all a mistake. I'm meant to be in New York Hospital." The nurse smiled delicately. What Kay did not know was that one of the commonest delusions among the patients was that they were here through a mistake. "I'll be running along now, Mrs. Ridgeley," the nurse said. She turned to Kay. "Mrs. Ridgeley has her own work to do. You mustn't keep her here talking." Polly came to Kay's support. "I'll stay with her a few minutes," she said. "Her husband will be coming to take her out." "I *see*!" said the nurse, with a slight sniff. She evidently felt that Polly was erring in encouraging the patient's false hopes.

"He really will come, you think?" said Kay, when they were alone. "Of course," said Polly. She lit cigarettes for them both. They looked at their watches. "He ought to be here in fifteen minutes," Kay said. "If he'd just left when you called." "Twenty," said Polly. "It's a five-minute walk from the First Avenue bus." "Maybe he took a taxi." They smoked. Kay's volubility had deserted her, and Polly's attempts to introduce impersonal topics failed. They were both concentrating on Harald and willing him to come soon. Kay picked up yesterday's paper, to read Lucius Beebe. "Harald's met him," she said. Suddenly they heard screams from the far end of the corridor and the sound of running, rubber-soled feet. "Oh, my God!" said Kay. "It's nothing," said Polly. "One of the patients has got 'excited,' that's all. The nurses will take care of her." "What will they do?" said Kay. "Send her upstairs," said Polly. "The violent wards are up above, on the seventh and eighth floors. When a patient in isolation shows signs of improvement, they send her down here on trial, to see how she does with the group of new patients. But quite often she has to be removed. That's probably what's happening now." They could hear sounds of a scuffle. "Will they use a straitjacket?" Kay wanted to know. "If they have to," said Polly. They listened. A new voice, closer to Kay's room, had begun to howl like a dog. More feet came running, and Polly could distinguish the heavier tread of a doctor or of a male orderly from the violent floors. Kay clung to Polly. They heard a man's voice give an order. Then all was quiet. "Do they have padded cells up there?" Kay whispered. "Yes," said Polly. "I think so. But I've never been up." She was inwardly furious, for Kay—why had this had to happen this morning? Jim was right when he criticized the hospital for what he called the bedlam on the admissions floor; it was callous to bring the very sick into contact with people who were tottering on the brink of sanity. New patients with nothing more than a mild nervous breakdown or very young, almost children, were terrified by what they heard and saw in their first days. Polly had just been given a living illustration of this; Kay was still trembling. "I remember at college," she said, "when we used to visit the state asylum for Psych. I never thought then—" Her eyes filled with tears; she did not finish her sentence. "Polly!" she said. "What if he tells them I'm crazy?"

But Harald had not come when, at the end of half an hour, Polly had to go. The nurse came to say that she was wanted right away in the main building for a blood analysis. "Go ahead," said Kay. "I'll be all right. I've got some books to read." Polly lingered. "I wish I could leave you some matches. . . . But I don't want to get you in trouble. . . . If the psychiatrist comes—" She broke off. What she had started to say was "Be careful." Instead, she said, "Don't worry. Whatever happens, Kay, Jim will be here before lunch." Kay nodded and produced an unconvincing smile. She watched Polly pack up her equipment. "Go on," she said. "What are you waiting for?" Polly wheeled her tray out the door. The corridor was empty. All the doors were ajar; the other patients must be at morning exercise. There was nothing else to do—those were the regulations—but Polly felt horrible doing it: "Am I my sister's jailer?" said her conscience. What were those lines in Dante's *Inferno* that her father recited when they locked him up in Riggs? "*E io senti chiavar l'uscio di sotto/ all'orribile torre.* . . ." She took the key and locked Kay in.

On the other side of the door, Kay heard the key turn and knew that Polly had turned it. She did not blame her. She did not even blame the perfidious Harald. Soon in her office, she supposed, Polly would be trying to call him. But Kay had lost hope that he would answer. Probably he had not spent the night in the apartment; he was with a woman somewhere. Nor did she think he would turn up at the hospital. The thing she had been dreading for five years had happened: he had left her. Not the way other husbands did, after long discussions and lawyers and dividing up the furniture. She had always known that Harald, one day, would simply disappear. Neither she nor his parents nor anyone who had known him would ever see him again. He would surface, like a submarine, in the Middle West or South America with a different identity. He had been a mystery to her from the beginning and he would vanish mysteriously into nowhere. To leave her locked up in a mental hospital, like somebody tied up in a closet by robbers, would be just the kind of thing he would relish. Eventually, she supposed, she would have to have him declared dead, and he would relish that too. She could hear the cock's crow of his laughter, like that of the Pathé rooster, coming from the four corners of the earth.

And to the day she died, she would never know whether he had been unfaithful to her. She would not even have that last satisfaction. To deprive her and tantalize her was his whole aim. She had tried to bind him with possessions, but he slipped away like Houdini. If he left her, he would not even take his typewriter, which she had got him for Christmas at a discount. That was another thing. He knew she admired him and wanted him to be a success, but he circumvented her as if on purpose. Sometimes she felt that he was postponing being a success till he could wear out her patience; as soon as she gave up and left him, his name would mock her in lights.

She had really thought of leaving him. Last year Norine had had a pet plan, that they should both hitchhike to Reno. Norine said that if Kay gave Harald his freedom, it would liberate his creative energies. The idea had half tempted Kay, as a glorious sacrifice, though she had insisted they go on the train. But she did not tell Harald for fear he would agree, which would take all the zest out of the project. Then Harald had said to her, smiling, one night when they had company, "I hear, Kay, you're planning to divorce me." And again she had been unable to tell whether he would have minded or not. He had had an air of being secretly amused, but, question him as she would, she could never make him say what was funny, if there *was* something funny, about her wanting to get a divorce.

Probably he did not take it seriously because he thought she loved him. There he was making a mistake. She had loved him at first, she reckoned, but he had tormented her so long with his elusiveness that she did not know, honestly, now whether she even liked him. If she had been sure of him, she might have found out. But things had never stood still long enough for her to decide. It sometimes struck her that Harald would not let her be sure of him for fear of losing his attraction: it was a lesson he had learned in some handbook, the way he had learned about those multiplication tables. But Kay could have told him that he would have been far more attractive to her if she could have trusted him. You could not love a man who was always playing hide-and-seek with you; that was the lesson *she* had learned.

Well, Harald might say, if that was so, why was she grieving? Why did she feel now as if her heart was broken? Kay tried to answer this question. She was grieving, she decided, for a Harald-That-Never-Was, not for the real Harald. But if she lost the real Harald, who was not such a muchness, she lost her only link with the Harald-That-Never-Was. Then it was really finished—her dream. She lay on the bed, thinking. There was something else. She had always despised failures, but if Harald had left her, she was one.

At eleven-thirty there was a knock. A young psychiatrist with glasses had come to talk to her. "We were hoping to see Mr. Petersen this morning," he said with an air of disapproval, so that Kay felt she ought to apologize. He took notes while she told him her story. When she had finished, breathlessly, and was waiting to hear his verdict, he sat for a few minutes in silence, riffling through his notebook. "Why do you place such importance on your belt?" he suddenly demanded. "The night nurses reported that you first became very unruly when they asked you to give it to them. And I have a note here that you spoke about it to Mrs. Ridgeley too and to Mrs. Burke, the day nurse." "Polly told you that?" Kay exclaimed, hurt and bewildered. "Mrs. Ridgeley wondered whether we couldn't make an exception and give you your belt back. But of course, as Mrs. Ridgeley should know, we can't make an exception until we've seen your husband." Again he looked at her accusingly, as if it were her fault that Harald had not come. "It's not my fault—" she began. "Just a minute," he said. "I see that you've used the expressions 'his fault,' 'my fault,' and their equivalents thirty-seven times in the course of our talk. I wonder if you'd like to give me your thoughts on that." Kay was dumbfounded. "I don't understand," she said. "I was promised that when I saw a psychiatrist, I could go to the regular hospital." "No one in authority could have given you such a promise," he replied sharply. "I'm afraid that's your own phantasy, Mrs. Petersen." Kay flushed. It was true that Polly had only said maybe.

The psychiatrist frowned at Kay's suitcase. "I wanted to avoid this discussion," he said. "Which will be quite unprofitable for both of us while you're in a state of great emotional tension and your judgment is affected. You're in no condition, just now, to make an important life-decision. You have a black eye, which you claim your husband gave you. I have no way of knowing whether this is true. In any case we're better equipped here to take care of you than they are across the way. There seems to be nothing wrong with you physically except the eye. We'll begin tests later on in the day to make sure; in the course of your stay here you'll have a thorough medical and dental check-up. But you appear to be in good health. The regular hospital is designed for patients who are physically ill. It's not a rest home or a sanatorium. If you feel you're not in need of psychiatric treatment, you can go home or go to a hotel."

"All right, I'll go to a hotel," promptly retorted Kay. He raised a finger. "Not so fast. *If* your husband consents. Let me be open with you. You can't leave here till we've had a talk with Mr. Petersen. He committed you last night, and we would be negligent if we released you on your own say-so. After all, we know nothing about you. And on your own account you did threaten your husband with a knife." Kay opened her mouth. "I don't say you are dangerous," the doctor intervened. "If we thought so, you would be on one of the violent floors. You are here for your own protection, believe me." "But what if Harald never comes?" The doctor smiled. "That seems very unlikely. Don't go borrowing trouble, Mrs. Petersen. But I'll answer your question. In that eventuality, the head of the hospital, after making a careful study, can release you if he thinks it's warranted."

"And if Harald insists I stay here?" "I think you and your husband, with our help, will reach a harmonious agreement about what's best to be done." These words chilled Kay's bones. "But supposing Harald contradicts what I've told you?" "We have experience in getting at the truth." "And if you believe me, instead of him, will you let me out?" "Under those circumstances, the head of the hospital can release you." "I demand to see the head of the hospital!" "Dr. Janson will see you in due time." "When?" For the first time, the psychiatrist looked human. He laughed. "You're certainly a persistent woman." "I always have been," Kay agreed. "Tell me honestly, do you think I'm insane?" He considered. "Frankly," he said, "you've made a favorable impression on me." Kay beamed. "That is not to say," the psychiatrist warned, "that you don't have severe emotional difficulties. Possibly of an hysterical character. My advice to you is to relax. Have a good lunch and get to know the other patients. You'll find some of these women very interesting. They come from good homes too. Some of them are highly cultured. Later in the afternoon you can have hydrotherapy—you'll enjoy it. And you can go to art class or weaving. Do you like to work with your hands?" Kay did, but she refused to admit it. "Kindergarten," she said scornfully. "Our other patients—" began the doctor. "I'm *not* your other patients!" interrupted Kay. He got up. "Good-by, Mrs. Petersen," he said coldly. She had not meant to sound so rude. He closed his notebook. "When your husband comes, I'll be happy to have a talk with him. And I'll see you tomorrow." "Tomorrow!" He nodded. "I shall strongly recommend your spending at least another night in the hospital. Even if the interview is completely satisfactory." He removed a metal rod from the pocket of his white coat. "Excuse me," he said and tapped her knee. Her leg jerked. "Just a formality," he said. "Your reflexes are normal, as I expected." He shook hands. "Oh, one thing. Mrs. Ridgeley is much concerned about you. I've given permission for Dr. Ridgeley to see you when he comes." He went out briskly.

When Jim Ridgeley came, Kay was in the dining room with the other patients. The psychiatrist had left orders that she was to join them in the lounge for recreation before lunch. Immediately, a squabble had broken out as to which of them was to sit next to Kay at table, which the nurse in charge had settled by placing her between a grey-haired woman, who said she was a manic-depressive, and a pretty girl of about Kay's own age, who told Kay she had been brought to the hospital in a strait-jacket. "I was on the seventh floor for a long time; now I'm better," she confided. "My husband's coming to take me home soon." At this a noisy towheaded girl burst into loud laughter. "She hasn't got a husband," the grey-haired woman whispered to Kay. "He's left her." Across the round table from Kay sat a catatonic with a boyish bob; she was the only one whose face did not move a muscle when Kay, replying to a question, announced that she was here through a mistake. Some laughed;

others looked anxious. "You mustn't say that," the pretty girl whispered. "Even if it's true. They'll never let you out if you say that. They may even send you back to the seventh floor."

Just then, Jim Ridgeley put his head in the dining room. "Hello, Kay," he said. He surveyed the women at the several tables, who were eating their soup, and nodded to those he recognized. He looked cross and rumpled. "Have Mrs. Petersen's lunch brought to her in her room," he said to the nurse at Kay's table. "I want to talk to her." "Oh, no fair!" shouted the tow-headed girl. "Dr. Ridgeley's *my* sweetie," said a fat woman, clowning. "Why have you left me, Dr. Ridgeley?"

He hurried Kay into her room. "This is a crime," he said. "They have no business keeping you here." He was late because he had been arguing with the psychiatrist who had seen Kay. "What did he say?" "In a word that he couldn't 'take the responsibility' for your release. He wants to pass the buck to Harald, who of course can't be found." "Have you tried?" "Polly's been trying all morning. She finally sent him a telegram. If he doesn't show up this afternoon, I'm going to send out a police call for him." His anger surprised and pleased Kay; she had forgotten how it felt to have a champion. The last champion she had had was her Dads, back home.

"Look here," said Jim. "It's not going to be easy to get you out of here unless Harald co-operates. If I were still on the staff, I could swing it. But I'm not, and my departure wasn't a popular move. They're standing on technicalities. Harald could sue them, I suppose, if they let you out and you murdered him." He laughed. "That's the kind of reasoning. Old Janson is a fussbudget. They can't get the idea that a mental home isn't a healthy place for a girl who's upset. They love it here themselves." He studied Kay. "If it weren't for that shiner of yours, I'd pass you out with me as a visitor." Kay looked up from her lunch tray in alarm; she had a strong feeling for legality. "Polly said you were impulsive," she remarked. He nodded. "Let's think," he said. "Your father's a doctor, is that right?" "An orthopedic surgeon. But he's in general practice too." "Supposing I phoned him?" said Jim. "He could hop on a train tonight. They'd certainly release you to him." "But it takes three days to get here," objected Kay. "Anyway, I couldn't bear it. That Dads should know. If he thought I was in a place like

this . . ." Her tears started again. "Or if he heard about the
black eye and the police . . . It would kill Dads. He thinks
our marriage is a big success and he just worships Harald."
"From afar, I assume," Jim remarked dryly.

"I've always been Dads' favorite child," Kay continued,
wiping her eyes. "He trusts me completely. And I've made him
believe in Harald." Jim stood looking out the small barred
window. "What exactly do you find to believe in?" he asked,
not turning around. "Why, he's a genius," said Kay. "I mean, if
you knew the theatre—" She broke off. "Doesn't Polly think
he's a genius?" she asked anxiously. "She hasn't said," Jim answered. He swung around to face Kay. "You know, Kay, there's
one point on which I question your sanity." "Harald," she
supplied in a low voice. He sighed. "I suppose you love him."

"It sounds more interesting that way," Kay answered candidly. "But I don't think I do. In a way, I think I hate him."
"Well, that's refreshing," he said. "Of course, I hardly know
him, Kay. But if you hate the guy?" "Why don't I leave him?"
One reason she never confided in anyone was the fear of having to answer this question. But perhaps a psychiatrist could
help her. "I can't explain," she said miserably. "Do you think I
could be a masochist?" He smiled. "No. Even Hopper—the
psychiatrist you saw—was struck by your 'lack of affect' in response to your husband's brutality." "He believed me then!"
exclaimed Kay. "That means a lot to you," he commented
sympathetically. "Were you given to lying at one time?" Kay
nodded. "Awful," she said. "But only to build myself up. Or to
get something I wanted." "But you'd never bear false witness
against your neighbor." "Oh, no!" she said, shocked. "And
I've reformed. Ask Polly. The thing is—I might as well tell
you—Harald isn't very truthful. And I've had a reaction against
that. Maybe it's just a reaction against Harald." He reflected.
"Do you think your marriage could be a sort of fish story?"

Kay met his eyes. "How did you guess?" she said. "I suppose
it is. Could that be why I can't run out on it? If I did, everybody would know it was a failure. You don't realize, Jim, I'm a
sort of legend in Salt Lake City. 'The girl who went east and
made good.'" "'Made good'?" "By marrying Harald. The
theatre. It all sounds so glamorous to Mums and Dads and the
girls I went to school with. You see, I wanted to be a director

myself. Or an actress. But I really have no talent. That's my tragedy."

Jim looked at his watch. "See here, Kay. Everybody's at lunch. I'm going to try to pass you out. Nobody knows you're a patient except the staff on this floor. You walk down the hall with me to the elevator. If we meet a nurse, O.K.; I'll turn you over to her. If we don't, we can make a getaway. The elevator men are all friends of mine. You'll have to leave your suitcase. Polly can bring it later. Where's your coat? I'll carry it till we get in the elevator."

Kay's methodical nature was jarred by the interruption of her train of thought; now that she had started, she was eager to go on discussing Harald. But Jim's enthusiasm caught her for a moment. Polly was lucky; he was quite a knight-errant. "I can't let you do that. Why, it might get you disqualified. They'd be furious when they found out I was gone." "Baloney. They'll be relieved and grateful, for a *fait accompli*. Besides, we can let them think I forgot to lock you in and you walked out on your own initiative." Kay made a grimace. The thought of taking the blame for what was solely his idea did not appeal to her. To be publicly rescued was one thing, but to figure in the records as an escaped lunatic was another. "No," she said stiffly. "I don't want to run away. I want to leave with flying colors. With the hospital acknowledging their mistake." "You don't know hospitals," said Jim. But he saw he could not persuade her. She feared she was a disappointment to him—would Polly, in her place, have agreed? Kay strongly doubted it.

He stood up, looking frustrated. He was a man, she could tell, who liked to get things done. "We'll have you moved off this floor at least," he said, setting his jaw. And he explained to her that the hospital worked by a system of promotion. The patients graduated from one floor to the next, going downward. The star patients, those who were pronounced "convalescent," *i.e.*, almost ready to leave, were on the fourth floor, which was more like a college dormitory. The windows were not barred; the patients were not locked in; they were allowed to wear their belts and wedding rings and had regular visiting hours; they could turn off their light when they wanted, and the only rule was—just like college—that they could not smoke in their rooms. As he painted this picture of privilege,

Kay brightened. "Do you really think you can get me on the fourth floor?" "This afternoon. Providing they have a bed." "You mean I can skip the fifth? Do they let patients do that?" "Not as a usual thing. But this isn't a usual case, is it?" Kay smiled happily; she had always wanted to skip a grade in school, she confided.

Sure enough, within a half hour, the nurse came to move her to the fourth floor. Unfortunately, the other patients were in their rooms, napping, so they could not see her go. Kay tried not to savor her triumph and to think, rather, with sympathy of those she was leaving behind, who would be months, probably, getting the double promotion she had achieved in a single day. Yet she could not help preening herself on this very point as she sauntered down the corridor. It was only the memory of the pretty girl that made her feel a little bit sad.

Her new room was very much nicer, though it too did not have a telephone and the walls were an institutional tan. Unpacking her toilet articles, Kay decided that she would not mind staying in Payne Whitney if only her sanity were established. At four o'clock she had an appointment for a general medical examination; tomorrow morning she would see a gynecologist. And it was all "on the house," said the new nurse, who had dropped in to get acquainted. At five, Kay would have hydrotherapy. The patients were kept pretty busy in the daytime, but in the evenings they played bridge until it was time for their hot chocolate or Ovaltine. There was a ping-pong table; twice a week they had movies, which the male patients were taken to also. The hospital had a beauty parlor, and occasionally there were dances. Frankly, said Kay, it would give her the creeps to have a male patient for a partner. The nurse agreed, but the women, she said, were a lovely group—she would hate to see them go home.

Just before supper, Harald was announced. Immediately, Kay started to tremble. "You don't have to see him, dear, if you don't want to," the nurse told her. But Kay declared she was ready. She promised herself not to cry and not to accuse him, but the first words that sprang from her lips were "Where have you been?" In answer, he handed her a florist's box, from Goldfarb's, containing two red camellias, her favorite flower. He had not come because he had been unable to face her after what he had done. He had been walking the streets. He had seen the dawn come up on the East River, and all day he had been roaming the city, thinking about Kay.

Kay fought down her desire to believe him. The day of reckoning, she told herself, had come; she must not let herself be bought off by two camellias. "You committed me," she said coldly. "Didn't you?" Harald did not deny it. "But how could you? How *could* you?" "I know," he said, groaning. "I know." He could not explain what had made him do it. "I was tired," he said. "Obviously there'd been a mistake. But there we were, and it was late. If I hadn't signed, where would I have taken you? They had a room reserved for you here. And they told me it was just a formality. An acquiescent devil inside me wanted to believe that. Ha!" When he had left the hospital, he had stopped in a bar and then had gone home and slept for a few hours, anesthetized, but his conscience had waked him, and while it was still dark he had gone out into the streets. He had walked the whole city and twice crossed the Brooklyn Bridge. Standing on a pier in the North River, he had considered shipping on a freighter as a seaman and disappearing for good, into the Canal Zone or Australia. "I knew it!" cried Kay. Then he had walked to the Bronx Zoo and studied the apes, his ancestors, in the monkey house—then back, to Wall Street, where he had watched the ticker tape. He raised his right foot to show her the hole in his shoe sole. Finally he had taken the subway to Fifty-ninth Street, stopped at Goldfarb's, and come here. "Have you eaten?" Kay demanded. He shook his head. "Did you see the psychiatrist?" "Yes, my poor girl; I've made a full confession. You can leave whenever you want. *Mea culpa.*" He was silent for a moment. "The psychiatrist told me, Kay, that you refused to give up your wedding ring." He took her hand and gently pressed his lips to the gold-and-silver band. "I accepted that as a sign that some day you might forgive me. Was I wrong?"

This was the most abject apology she had ever had from Harald; Kay could not believe her ears. It almost made it worthwhile to have been shut up in an institution. "Tonight?" she said. "Can I leave tonight?" "If you wish. And you're not too tired." Kay hesitated. She remembered that in the morning she had an appointment with a gynecologist. And she was curious to see the other patients. Now that she was here, it seemed a pity, in a way, not to stay. "I saw a catatonic schizophrenic this morning," she announced. "I sat across from her at lunch. It was fascinating. She was completely rigid and had to be fed like a doll. And there was this pretty girl next to me who looked completely normal but they'd brought her in in a straitjacket. She liked me. They fought over which ones should sit next to me. As if I were a new girl at school." Harald smiled. "What else did you do?" "I had hydrotherapy. And a medical exam. I talked to Polly's husband." She felt herself color. "He wanted me to escape. And, oh, I have to tell you about my metabolism. . . ."

Harald listened. There was a discreet knock on the door. "Supper in five minutes, Mrs. Petersen." They started. "What should I do?" Kay said. A vague sense of disappointment came over her at the thought of going home; it was like having to leave a party too soon. "Would you like to stay here for the night?" said Harald. She deliberated. She did not want to hurt his feelings. "We agreed you needed a rest, you remember," he encouraged her. "And you can't go to work until your poor eye heals. Anyway, you've asked for a week's sick leave." "I know." "Your Blue Cross covers psychiatric hospitals. I made a point of finding out in the office. If I were you, I'd stay here a week or two. You can have daily talks with the psychiatrist. It's all included in the treatment. With your background in psychology, it ought to be fruitful for you. It'll give you a tool you can use in your personnel work, to study the other women here. And you may get a line on yourself." "But there's nothing wrong with me," said Kay. "I thought that was established." Her willingness to stay in the hospital was rapidly diminishing when she heard Harald proposing it. "Jim Ridgeley said it was a crime I was here," she said hotly. "Oh, please, Kay, no reproaches!" replied Harald. "If you can't forgive me, simply say so and I'll go." Kay caught herself up; she did not wish to drive him away. "I'd stay," she said cautiously, "if it was understood that I wasn't a mental case like these other people. I don't mind talking to the psychiatrist if it's clear that I don't really need to. I mean, of course everybody needs to, but . . ." She floundered. "But everybody doesn't have Blue Cross," supplied Harald.

Kay tested him. "If I say no, will you take me home?" "Of course." "All right, I'll stay," she decided. "Then I'd better go and have supper. You'll come tomorrow, won't you?" Harald promised. "In any event," he remarked, "the psychiatrist will probably be wanting me." "Wanting you?" Kay bridled. "They like to get other points of view on the patient. Incidentally, he'd like to talk to a few of your friends. Shall I have Norine come in the morning? She can drop in to see you afterward. And who else? Helena?" Kay stared at him. "If you tell my friends," she said, "I'll kill you." Hearing what she had said, she clapped her hand to her mouth. "Of course I didn't mean that," she gasped. "But I beg you, Harald, don't tell Norine. Don't let her talk to the psychiatrist. I'll do anything you want if you keep Norine away from here." Heavy sobs began to shake her. "Oh, don't be childish," Harald said impatiently. "Save it for the psychiatrist." This brutal tone, so soon after his apology, cut her to the heart. The nurse knocked again. "Are you coming to supper, Mrs. Petersen?" "She's coming," Harald answered for her. "Go wash your face. Good-bye. I'll see you tomorrow." The door shut.

Slowly Kay pinned the camellias to her dress. She reminded herself that she was free to leave. It was her own choice that she was staying. Unlike the other patients, she had never for a minute been out of her mind. But as she advanced to the dining room, a terrible doubt possessed her. They were using psychology on her: it was not her own choice, and she was not free, and Harald was not sorry—the psychiatrist had coached him, that was all.

14

Priss Crockett, who brought Stephen to play in Central Park every morning, was surprised one June day, when she arrived pushing the stroller and followed by Stephen, to see a familiar figure seated on a bench with a baby carriage. It was Norine Schmittlapp, wearing a smart pair of slacks and black sunglasses. The hood of the carriage was down, and on the carriage mattress, which was covered with a rubber sheet, lay a naked infant, male. Priss halted; it was "her" bench Norine was occupying. She was uncertain whether Norine would recognize her; it must be five years since they had met. Norine had changed; she had put on weight and her hair was blondined. "Hi," said Norine, looking up briefly. "Join us. This is Ichabod." She joggled the baby carriage. Her tinted gaze sought out Stephen, who was pulling an educational toy along the walk. "Is that yours?" Priss presented her young. "Say how do you do, Stephen, to the lady." She did not know how to introduce Norine, who evidently had remarried. Norine shook Stephen's hand. "Norine Rogers. Glad to know you." On her engagement finger was a huge diamond in a platinum setting, and the baby carriage was an English model with a monogram. "Do you come here every day?" she asked Priss.

They were neighbors, it seemed. She had just moved into a brownstone, between Park and Madison, that she and her husband had bought; Priss's apartment was on Lexington and Seventy-second. "But you're lucky," said Priss enviously. "You must have a back yard. You don't need to come to the Park." She herself found it quite a chore, mornings, to push the stroller all the way from Lexington and get back in time to put Stephen's baked potato in the oven for a twelve o'clock lunch. Norine said that her back yard was still full of glass bricks and cement-mixers. They were doing the house over, putting in a ramp where the stairs had been and a wall of glass bricks on the street side. Priss realized that Norine's house must be the one the whole neighborhood was discussing; she wondered what Rogers Norine could have married. "My husband's a Jew," Norine threw out. "His people changed the name from Rosenberg. Do you mind Jews? I'm mad for them myself." Before Priss could answer, she continued, talking in the rapid-fire way Priss remembered, as if she were dictating a letter. "Freddy's whole tribe converted. When they changed their name. He's a confirmed Episcopalian. I was hell-bent to have him go back to the old Orthodox faith. With a prayer shawl and phylacteries. The real Mosaic law. The Reformed rite is just a nineteenth-century compromise. But an Orthodox Jew can't marry a shiksah." Priss was surprised to hear this. Norine nodded. "They frown on exogamy. Like the Papists. The Episcopalians have a taboo on divorce; Freddy's minister wouldn't marry a divorced woman. So we got a Lutheran pastor in Yorkville. Freddy's parents expected to see a framed picture of Hitler in the dominie's parlor." She laughed. "Are you interested in religion?" Priss confessed that she was more interested in politics. "I'm burned out on politics," said Norine. "Since Munich. My passion's comparative religion. Society is finished if it can't find its way back to God. The problem for people like us is to rediscover faith. It's easy for the masses; they never lost it. But for the elite it's another story."

Her eyes fixed on Stephen. "This your only offspring?" Priss explained that she had had a series of miscarriages, but she still hoped to have more children, for it would be sad for Stephen to grow up as an only child. "Adopt some," said Norine. "It's the only way. If the elite can't breed, it has to graft new stock or face extinction. Do you know that the Vassar graduate has only 2.2 children?" Priss was aware of this statistic, which had caused concern in alumnae circles—Vassar women were barely replacing themselves while the rest of the population was multiplying. "What does your husband do?" Norine demanded. "He's a pediatrician." "Oh," said Norine. "What school?" Priss began to tell her where Sloan had been trained. Norine cut her off. "What school of thought. Behaviorist? Gestalt? Steiner? Klein? Anna Freud?" Priss was ashamed to say that she did not know. "He's a medical doctor," she said apologetically. Then she essayed a personal question of her own.

"What does *your* husband do, Norine?" Norine chuckled. "He's a banker. With Kuhn, Loeb. He comes from old money-lending stock. From Frankfurt originally. But they had a Diaspora and they're scattered all over the place. The black sheep

of the family became a Zionist and went to Palestine. They
never mention his name. Freddy's parents were trying to pass,"
she went on somberly. "Like so many rich German Jews. They
sent him to Choate and Princeton, where he had a searing experience with one of the clubs. When the club found out
'Rogers' was 'Rosenberg,' he was asked to resign." Priss made
a clucking sound, to which Norine replied with a short laugh.
It was as if this incident gave her a peculiar kind of relish.

Priss glanced at little Ichabod, who, she observed, had been
circumcised, and felt guiltily glad that Stephen did not have a
Jewish father. It struck her, awful as it sounded, that if you
wanted to give your child the best start in life, you would not
marry a Jew. But Norine, she supposed, was dauntless on his
behalf; Priss felt in awe of a person who could fasten a name
like that on a baby. "Aren't you afraid he'll be called 'Icky' in
school?" she said impulsively. "He'll have to learn to fight his
battles early," philosophized Norine. "Ichabod the Inglorious.
That's what the name means in Hebrew. 'No glory.'" She
rocked the carriage.

"How old is he?" "Three months." Priss wished Norine
would lower the hood of the carriage; she feared the mid-
morning sun was too strong for his little head, which had
scarcely any hair yet. "Isn't he awfully young for a sun bath?"
Norine scouted the thought; she had been exposing him to
the sun daily since she had brought him home from Mount
Sinai. Nevertheless, she slightly lowered the hood, so that his
face was in the shade. "It's O.K. here," she observed content-
edly. "No nursemaids or English nannies. The place I was yesterday, they made an awful stink because he was nude. They
were afraid their starchy girls would get ideas from his little
prick—weren't they, Ichabod?" Her big hand patted his penis,
which stiffened. Priss swallowed several times; she glanced uneasily in the direction of Stephen, who, happily, was chasing
his ball in the grass. She was always terrified of arousing Stephen; she hated retracting his foreskin when washing him,
though Sloan said she should, for hygienic reasons. But she
would almost rather he was dirty than have him get an Oedipus complex from her handling him. Lately, without telling
Sloan, she had been omitting this step from his bath.

"Have you got a watch?" Norine asked, yawning. Priss told

her the time. "Are you nursing?" she asked, stealing an envious look at Norine's massive breasts. "My milk ran out," said Norine. "So did mine!" cried Priss. "As soon as I left the hospital. How long did *you* nurse?" "Four weeks. Then Freddy slept with the girl we had looking after Ichabod, and my milk went on strike." Priss gulped; the story she had been about to relate, of how her milk had run out as soon as they gave Stephen a supplementary bottle, was hastily vetoed on her lips. "I ought to have seen it coming," Norine went on, lighting a cigarette. "We hadn't had real sex together for a coon's age. You know how it is. At the end of your pregnancy it's *verboten* and it's *verboten* for a month after the kid's born. Freddy got very randy. And he felt he had a rival in Ichabod. Then we hired this Irish slut. Straight off the boat. She was a cousin of Freddy's mother's waitress. A real Mick. Eyes put in with a sooty finger and no sexual morals. In the old sod, she'd been sleeping with her uncle; she told me that. Naturally Freddy couldn't keep his hands off her. She had a room next to the nursery, where Freddy slept on a cot; I kept Ichabod in bed with me at night—it bushed me to get up for those 2:00 A.M. feedings— and Freddy said he disturbed him." Priss was sorely tempted to put in a word of guidance—did Norine not know that under no circumstances, not even in a crowded slum home, should a baby be permitted to sleep with an adult? But her shyness and fear of stammering impeded her. "Freddy," Norine continued, "was sneaking into her room. I found out when I was making her bed. There was Freddy's semen on the sheet. What got me was that she hadn't had the grace to use a towel. I pulled the sheet off the bed and confronted Freddy with it while he was eating his breakfast and reading the *Wall Street Journal*. He said it was partly my fault. Instead of treating her like a servant, I'd waited on her hand and foot, so that she felt she had a right to sleep with the master: she was just as good as me. Making her bed, for instance. It was up to her to make her own bed. He's right; I'm no good with labor. He had to put her out of the house himself. While he did, I washed the sheet in the washing machine; he said I should have left it for the laundress. We quarreled, and it affected my milk."

"They say a shock can do that," said Priss. "But at least Ichabod got his im-munities." Norine agreed; the damage, she said absently, would be psychic. She reached into the carriage and found a rubber pacifier, which she thrust into his mouth. Priss gazed at this article, nonplused. "Is that to keep him from sucking his thumb?" she asked. "You know, Norine, pediatricians today think it's better to let them suck their thumbs than try to break them of the habit. What I did with Stephen was distract him gently every time he put his thumb in his mouth. But that p-p-pacifier"—the word seemed to stick in her throat —"is awfully unsanitary. And it can change the shape of his mouth. You really ought to throw it away. Sloan would be shocked if he saw it. It can be just as habit-forming as thumb-sucking." She spoke earnestly, amazed to see a girl of Norine's education so ignorant. Norine listened patiently. "If a kid sucks his thumb," she said, "it's because he's been deprived of oral gratification. He needs his daily quota of sucking time, and he can't get it from the bottle. So you give him a rubber tit. Don't you, Ichabod?" She smiled tenderly at Ichabod, who indeed wore a look of bliss as he drew on the rubber teat. Priss tried to avert her eyes from the spectacle. For a child to find heaven in a dummy breast was the worst thing she could think of—worse than self-abuse. She felt there ought to be a law against the manufacture of such devices.

Stephen approached the carriage. "Wass sat?" he asked curiously. His hand went out to touch the pacifier in the baby's mouth. Priss snatched his hand away. He continued to stare eagerly, evidently interested by the noises of content Ichabod was making. "Wass sat?" he repeated. Norine removed the pacifier from the baby's mouth. "You want to try it?" she said kindly. She wiped it with a clean diaper and offered it to Stephen. Priss swiftly intervened. She reached into the stroller and drew out a lollipop wrapped in waxed paper. "Here!" she said. "That 'pop' belongs to the baby. Give it back to Mrs. Rogers. This is yours." Stephen accepted the lollipop. Priss had discovered that a system of exchange worked very well with him; he would docilely trade a "bad" thing, like a safety pin, for a "good" thing, like a picture book, and often seemed to be unaware that a substitution had taken place.

Norine observed this little drama. "You've got him trained," she said finally, with a laconic smile. "I suppose he's trained to the toilet too." "I'm afraid not," said Priss, embarrassed. She lowered her voice. "I'm at my wits' end, honestly. Of course, I've never punished him, the way our mothers and nurses did, when he has an 'accident.' But I almost wish I could spank him. Instead, I've done *everything* you're supposed to. You know. 'Observe the time of day when he has his movement and then gently put him on the toidey-seat at that time every morning. If he doesn't do it, take him off, without any sign of displeasure. If he does do it, smile and clap your hands.'"

Norine had touched on her most sensitive point. As the wife of a pediatrician, she was bitterly ashamed that Stephen, at the age of two and a half, was not able to control his bowels. He not only made evil-smelling messes in his bed, at naptime, but he sometimes soiled his pants here in the Park, which was why she sought out this isolated bench, rather than take him to the playground. Or he did it—like last weekend—in his bathing trunks on the beach at the Oyster Bay clubhouse, in front of the whole summer colony, who were sunning and having cocktails. Sloan, even though he was a doctor, was extremely annoyed whenever Stephen did it in public, but he would never help Priss clean Stephen up or do anything to relieve her embarrassment. Last weekend, for instance, it was her young sister Linda who had come to her rescue when Stephen had got away from her and capered down the beach with his full bathing trunks. Linda had captured him and carried him into the clubhouse, where she helped Priss by washing out his pants while Priss washed him. Meanwhile Sloan had sat under an umbrella ignoring the whole episode.

Afterward he had told her that she and her sister had made an unnecessary hullabaloo. Yet it was the only sphere where he could say she had failed with Stephen. He did not wet his bed any more; he ate his vegetables and junkets; he was obedient; he hardly ever cried now, and at night he went to sleep at his appointed time, surrounded by his stuffed animals. She could not see where she had erred in training him. Neither could her mother. Together, they had retraced the whole history, from the first mornings she had set him on the new toidey-seat strapped to the regular toilet. Immediately, he had changed the time of his movement. It jumped from nine o'clock to ten to seven and all around the clock, with Priss and the young girl she had had helping her chasing it in vain. Whenever they judged, from his expression, that he needed to "go," they would clap him on the toidey, so that he would associate the two ideas. But no matter how long they lay in ambush for him or how patiently they waited once he was on the seat, usually he disappointed them. Often, as soon as they took him off, he would do it in his crib.

When he was smaller, Priss had tried to think that he did not understand what was wanted of him, and Sloan had authorized her to grunt and make pushing grimaces, to encourage him to imitate her. But her grunts produced no results except to make her feel foolish. She tried leaving him on the toidey alone, so that he would not suppose it was a game the two of them were playing. She tried leaving him there longer, but Sloan said five minutes was enough. On the rare occasions when—by pure chance, it seemed to Priss—he "performed," she moderated her pantomime of approval, so that he would not sense it as a punishment when she did not smile or clap.

Sloan's belief was that Priss's nervousness was to blame, just as it had been with her nursing. "He senses your tension when you put him on the toilet. Relax." Yet Sloan himself would have been far from relaxed if he had had to clean up Stephen's bed when he had fouled his toys and stuffed animals. Sloan always said that the right way was to avoid even the appearance of censure when that occurred. "Just be matter-of-fact. Act as though nothing had happened." But that would be a lie. By this time, Stephen must know, though she had never reproached him by word or sign, that she did not really like him to do Number Two in his bed. In fact, it had become clear to her that not only did he know but enjoyed the knowledge. Particularly on a day when she would lead guests to his room after a luncheon party and find that "it" had happened. Seeing the ladies flee from the scene of the crime, he responded with gurgles and crows. Priss suspected there was a streak of rebellion tucked away in Stephen, which expressed itself by thwarting her in this particular way. As if he had read a handbook on pediatrics and knew that this was one naughty action for which he could not be punished; instead, he could punish her.

This thought was too morbid to be discussed, even with her mother. Could a two-and-a-half-year-old plot and carry out a scheme of revenge? And for what? Alas, in her darkest moments, Priss feared she knew. For the bottle he had got too late, for the schedule he had been held to, on the minute: six, ten, two, six, ten, two. Perhaps even for this "sucking" Norine talked about that he had missed. For never having been picked up when he cried, except to have his diaper changed or be given a drink of water. For the fact, in short, that his father was a pediatrician. Everyone, including Mrs. Hartshorn, who had begun as a skeptic, now exclaimed over how well the new regime had worked; they had never seen a two-year-old so strong, so big, so well behaved and self-sufficient. Priss's friends, when they came to dinner, were amazed to observe that Stephen went to bed without any discussion. Priss sang to him; he had his arrowroot cookie, his drink of water, and his kiss. Then he was tucked in, and out went his light. He did not call out to have it turned on again or ask for his door to be left open. "He was trained as an infant," Sloan would say, passing the hors d'oeuvres. "Priss never went in to him, once he'd been stowed away for the night. And we accustomed him to noise. He's never had a pillow." Not one of Priss's friends could match that; they had tried to follow the broad principles, but they had weakened on some detail, with the result that their young disturbed the parents' cocktail hour with pleas for drinks of water, light, attention generally; they were afraid of the dark or had food crotchets or refused to take naps. The point, Sloan said, was to have the force of character to stick to the system absolutely, except in cases of illness or on trips. Stephen had got a good start in life because Priss had never compromised. This was what Priss endeavored to think herself, encouraged by her friends' admiration. Yet at times she furtively wondered whether when Stephen made messes in his pants he was not getting his own back for being alive at all.

"I hope you'll be luckier than I've been," she said sadly to Norine. "Have you started toilet training yet? Sloan has a theory that we waited too long. If you begin early enough, he says, there's no reason a baby should be harder to train than an animal." Norine shook her head. She did not plan to train Ichabod. He needed the fun of playing with his own excrement, just as he needed sucking. "When he's ready to use the toilet, he'll ask for it. Probably when he starts nursery school. The pressure of the group will encourage him to give up his anal pleasures. You'll find, when you put yours in nursery school, that he'll make the great renunciation." She did not plan to wean Ichabod either—that is, from the bottle. He would wean himself when he was Stephen's age, and, if he did not, *tant pis.*

"Where in the world did you get such ideas?" Not, Priss was certain, from a reputable pediatrician; Norine must have got hold of some quack. They were based on anthropology, Norine explained. Scientists had been watching the habits of primitive peoples and drawing valuable conclusions. The Pueblo Indians, for instance, who were the *crème de la crème* of the Indian world, did not wean their children till they were two or three years old. Most primitive peoples did not bother about toilet training at all. "But they have no toilets," said Priss. Norine nodded. "That's the price of our culture. If you have a flush toilet, you make a fetish of it. Have you read Margaret Mead? A great woman, that."

Needless to say, Ichabod was not on a schedule. He created his own schedule. He was picked up whenever he cried and was fed "on demand." "What about baby foods? Are you going to give him baby foods?" Norine did not know. But she was against feeding a baby a restricted diet. "Babies are tough," she said. "They'll choose their own diet if you offer them a variety of foods." Priss said that she thought girls today were perhaps making it too easy for themselves by opening a jar of baby food, instead of puréeing fresh vegetables at home and pressing beef in the ricer for beef juice. The question did not appear to interest Norine. Indeed, the discussions that raged in pediatric circles—how soon to start orange juice, evaporated milk versus Borden's, bottled baby foods versus homemade, enemas versus glycerine suppositories, the merits of Pablum, the new three-hour feeding schedule for hungry babies (Priss and Sloan had pioneered that!)—seemed never to have reached her ears. Ichabod, she repeated, would make his own decisions; already he had shown a taste for Italian spaghetti—she made a practice of offering him scraps of food from her plate. She did not possess a baby scales or a bathinet. He was bathed in the washbasin. She stared reflectively at Stephen. "How old is he? Three?" "Two and a half next Saturday." Norine pondered. "In his day, of course, you were still hipped on scales and clocks and thermometers. The age of measurement. God, it seems a long time ago!" She yawned and stretched her big frame. "We had a late night last night. Some Jesuits for dinner. And somebody playing the drums. Then Ichabod burned the candle at both ends."

Priss girded her loins for combat; it was plain to her that Norine was talking through her hat. "The age of measurement is just beginning," she said doughtily. "For the first time we're establishing norms. In all fields. You ought to keep up with the latest developments. Have you heard about Gesell's studies at Yale? Finally we're going to have a scientific picture of the child. Gesell shows us what to expect in terms of achievement of a one-year-old, a two-year-old, a three-year-old. When he publishes his findings in p-p-popular form, every mother will have a y-yardstick."

This time Norine smothered her yawn. "I know Gesell's work. He's a fossil relic of behaviorism. His daughter was '35." "What does that prove?" demanded Priss. Norine declined to argue. "You still believe in progress," she said kindly. "I'd forgotten there were people who did. It's your substitute for religion. Your tribal totem is the yardstick. But we've transcended all that. No first-rate mind can accept the concept of progress any more." "You used to be such a radical," protested Priss. "Don't you admire some of what Roosevelt is doing? TVA, rural electrification, the Farm Resettlement Administration, crop control, Wages and Hours. Granting that he's made some mistakes—" "I still am a radical," interrupted Norine. "But now I fathom what it means—going back to the roots. The New Deal is rootless—superficial. It doesn't even have the dynamism of fascism."

"Does your husband agree with your ideas?" "Does yours?" retorted Norine. "No," Priss had to admit. "Not about politics. We're at daggers drawn." Right now, they were quarreling about Danzig; Sloan did not care if Hitler gobbled up the whole of Europe—he was for America First. "The old Vassar story," commented Norine. "I leave politics to Freddy. Being a Jew and upper crust, he's profoundly torn between interventionism abroad and *laissez faire* at home. Freddy isn't an intellectual. But before we were married, we had an understanding that he should read Kafka and Joyce and Toynbee and the

cultural anthropologists. Some of the basic books. So that se-
mantically we can have the same referents." Priss wondered
that Norine should have left out Freud. "Most of Freud's out
of date," Norine declared. "He was too narrowly a man of his
place and time. The old Austrian Empire, with its folkways, he
took for a universal culture. Jung has more to say to me. And
some of the younger post-Freudians. Not that I don't owe a
lot to Freud."

Priss, who had always been planning to read Freud some day
when she had the time, felt relieved and disappointed to hear
that it was no longer necessary. Norine, she presumed, knew
about such things. She sounded almost as if Freud were dead.
Priss had a flutter of anxiety that she might have missed reading his obituaries in the papers; she seemed to have missed so
much. "Of course," Norine was saying, "between Freddy and
me there's a deep cultural conflict. Our Vassar education made
it tough for me to accept my womanly role. While Freddy, as a
Jew, instinctively adopts the matriarchal principle. He wants
me to reign in the home while he goes to the counting-house.
That's great, as far as Ichabod goes; he doesn't interfere with
my program and he keeps his mother muzzled. Freddy's philo-
progenitive; he's interested in founding a dynasty. So long as I
can breed, I'm a sacred cow to him. Bed's very important to
Freddy; he's a sensualist, like Solomon. Collects erotica. He
worships me because I'm a goy. Besides, like so many rich
Jews, he's a snob. He likes to have interesting people in the
house, and I can give him that." She broke off and gave vent to
a sigh. "The trouble is— The trouble is—" She dropped her
voice and looked around her. "Christ, I can say it to you. You
probably have the same problem." Priss swallowed nervously;
she feared Norine was going to talk about sex, which was still
Priss's bête noire.

"The trouble is my brains," said Norine. "I was formed as an
intellectual by Lockwood and those other gals. Freddy doesn't
mind that I can think rings around him; he likes it. But I'm
conscious of a yawning abyss. And he expects me to be a *Haus-
frau* at the same time. A hostess, he calls it. I've got to dress well
and set a good table. He thinks it ought to be easy because we
have servants. But I can't handle servants. It's a relic, I guess, of
my political period. Freddy's taken to hiring them himself, but I

demoralize them, he says, as soon as they get in the house. They take a cue from my cerebralism. They start drinking and padding the bills and forgetting to polish the silver. Freddy goes all to pieces if he gets served warmed-over coffee in a tarnished pot—he's a sybarite. Or if the table linen's dirty. He made the butler change it last night just as we were sitting down to dinner. I never noticed it myself; I was too busy discussing Natural Law with those Jesuits."

"You can go over the linen and the silver in the morning," Priss pointed out. "Before you have a dinner party. Take out everything you're going to use and check it." Though a Phi Beta Kappa, she had never had any trouble with her part-time maids, who usually came to her through her mother. Brains, she thought, were supposed to help you organize your life efficiently; besides, she had never heard that Norine had shone as a student. "I know," answered Norine. "I've been trying to turn over a new leaf, now that we have a new house. I start out with a woman who comes to massage me and give me exercises to relax. But before I know it, I'm discussing the Monophysites or the Athanasian Creed or Maimonides. The weirdest types come to work for me; I seem to magnetize them. The butler we have now is an Anthroposophist. Last night he started doing eurhythmics." She laughed.

"You really feel our education was a mistake?" Priss asked anxiously. Sloan had often expressed the same view, but that was because it had given her ideas he disagreed with. "Oh, completely," said Norine. "I've been crippled for life." She stretched. Priss looked at her watch. It was time for her and Stephen to leave. Norine rose too. "Ichabod and I'll keep you company." She pinned a diaper on her offspring and covered him with a monogrammed blanket. "*Pour les convenances*," she said. Together they crossed Fifth Avenue and walked along Seventy-second Street, wheeling their children. The conversation became desultory. "When did I see you last?" Norine wondered. "Was it at Kay's?" said Priss. "The year after college?" "That's right," said Norine. There was a silence. "Poor Kay," said Priss, dodging a grocery cart from Gristede's.

"Do you ever hear from her?" asked Norine. "Not for a long time," said Priss. "Not since she went out West. It must be over a year." Mutely, Priss reproached herself for not having written. "I see Harald sometimes," Norine volunteered in her uninflected tones. "Oh. What is he doing?" "The same. He's back on his feet again. He took Kay's breakdown and their separation pretty hard. God, how that man suffered!"

Priss hesitated. "But was it really a breakdown? Polly Ridgeley —Polly Andrews; you remember her—always says it wasn't. That she got worse in the hospital." "Did you see her there?" asked Norine somberly. Priss had not. "I did," said Norine. "The doctors sent for me right away. To get a line on her. I was supposed to be her best friend. When I went to her room, she was completely withdrawn. Told me to go away. She had persecution delusions that focused on me. The doctors felt there was some Lesbian attachment. It's a funny thing about paranoids; they always feel they're being persecuted by a member of their own sex. Who's really their love-object. When I finally got her to talk, it turned out she felt I'd betrayed her by discussing her with the psychiatrists. She didn't seem to bear any grudge against Harald, though he went there practically every day for an interview. He was lacerated with guilt because he'd treated her like hell toward the end, not understanding that her aberrations were clinical. The layman never realizes that about a person he's close to."

"But what was really the matter?" said Priss. "*I* understood that she went there through some sort of mix-up and stayed because it was a rest home where she could work things out, away from Harald. I gathered he was pretty much at fault." "That was the cover story," said Norine. "They never settled on a final diagnosis. But a lot of basic things were the matter. Sex. Competitiveness with men. An underlying Lesbian drive that was too firmly repressed. Thwarted social strivings. She made it at Vassar with you people in the South Tower. But she never could make it again. So she transferred all her ambitions to Harald, and the insensate pressure of that was too much for him. She was killing the goose that ought to have laid the golden eggs. And all the time she was driving him to make money, she was ruthlessly undercutting him because of her penis-envy. Plus a determination to punish him for not giving her a vicarious success. Harald saw it all better himself after a couple of sessions with the doctors. I cleared up a few points for them and I got Put, my ex-husband, to go around and talk to them too. He was brilliant on the subject of Kay's spending money. He gave an unforgettable picture of her delusions of wealth. Comparing the way she lived with the way we lived, though Put was working and Harald was practically on the dole."

"Don't you think," said Priss, "that the depression had something to do with it? If she'd married Harald when the economy was normal, he would have had work, and their standard of living would have corresponded with their income. Kay's false p-p-premise was assuming that Harald would have full employment. So she contracted debts. But that was a common pattern. And the theatre was slow to feel the effects of Recovery. If they'd married a little later, there would have been the Federal Theatre. But the idea of a works program for the arts didn't come till '35, unfortunately. Roosevelt was very late recognizing the need for job security for artists and performers."

"So you see it as an economic tragedy." "Yes. The high divorce rate in our class—" "With the New Deal as the *deus ex machina*," interrupted Norine. "Arriving too late to supply the happy ending." She chuckled. "You may have a point. As a matter of fact, Harald's working with the Federal Theatre now. If Congress doesn't kill it. Just when he's got his chance as a director." Priss's brow wrinkled. "I'm afraid Congress *will* kill it, Norine. Poor Harald! He does have bad luck. It's uncanny." She shivered in her seersucker frock. Norine agreed. "Potentially, he's a great man, Harald." They had reached the corner of Seventy-second and Park. "Poor Kay!" sighed Priss again, resolved to write to her this afternoon while Stephen was napping. "It was medieval of Macy's to fire her because she'd had a breakdown. It ought to have been treated as ordinary sick leave. And then to be dispossessed from their apartment, on top of that." "Macy's gave her severance pay," observed Norine. Priss shook her head sorrowfully, putting herself in Kay's place. No wonder, she thought, Kay had yielded and gone back to Utah when her father came to get her; everything in the East had failed her. "Her whole house of cards . . ." she muttered, staring down Park Avenue.

"Why don't you come home with me?" Norine suddenly proposed. "We'll have some coffee." "I have to get Stephen's

lunch," explained Priss. "We'll feed him," said Norine hospita-
bly. "We've got a lamb chop around somewhere and some
lettuce. Can he eat that?" Priss was tempted. At home she too
had a lamb chop and fresh spinach and his potato waiting to be
cooked, and she had made him tapioca this morning with fluffy
egg white. But she was flattered to discover that she had not
bored Norine and a little tired of the monotony of her life.
Since she had given up her job, before Stephen was born, she
seldom saw anyone "different." "We have three cats," Norine
said to Stephen. "And a basket full of kittens." This decided
Priss; animals, she felt, were important to a child, and Sloan
would not let them keep one in the apartment because of
allergies.

Norine's house had a red door. Workmen were still finishing
the wall of glass brick. Inside, a ramp, freshly painted, ran up
to the upper floors. A gaunt manservant in shirt sleeves appeared to wheel the carriage, with Ichabod in it, upstairs. This
arrangement seemed to Priss very practical: bumping a carriage
up and down stairs was a nuisance and to leave it blocking the
entry was a nuisance too; then too when Ichabod was bigger
he could not fall down a ramp. She was impressed by the
house, which struck her as comfortable; it only looked strange
from the street, and you could say that the other houses were
out of step, not Norine's. The thing that surprised her was that
Norine could have a house like this and be against progress at
the same time. But Norine explained that it was "classical
modern."

In the living room, which was on the second floor, two walls
were painted dark red; the glass bricks from the street let in a
filtered light, and a short inside wall of glass bricks half shut off
a bar, which was trimmed with chromium. There were round
glass tables with chromium trim and big cream-colored fleecy
sofas. Great glass bowls were filled with dogwood, which
proved, on closer examination, to have paper flowers stuck on
the branches. In the library there was a big phonograph, a set
of drums, and a white piano, like in a night club. Large balloon
brandy glasses, containing the dregs of brandy, still stood on
the piano. The rooms were lit by indirect lighting, hidden in
troughs, and the floors were covered from wall to wall with
very thick cream-colored carpeting. Everything was expensive

and in what Priss recognized as "good taste." It was only that to Priss, who was small, all the furniture seemed very large—giants' furniture. When Norine settled her at one end of a deep sofa in the living room, she felt like Goldilocks in the biggest of the three bears' beds.

Stephen had been led away by the manservant, to see the kittens, who lived in the laundry on the ground floor. "Coffee will be here in a minute," said Norine, planting herself at the opposite end of the sofa. "Unless you can't stand it reheated." She placed a big glass ashtray, like a tub, between them, opened a cigarette box, took off her sunglasses and shoes. "They'll keep Stephen downstairs," she said. "Now we can talk." She crossed her legs under her in the black linen slacks. "Maybe you'll be surprised to hear that I was madly in love with Harald. For four years. I never let it interfere with my relation with Kay. I married Freddy when I saw it was hopeless. It had always been hopeless, but I kidded myself." She spoke in a dry voice, smoking rapidly, and rocking herself back and forth on her haunches; her lethargy had vanished. "We had a few rolls in the hay years ago—nothing much. Then for him it was over: Harald is like that. But he kept coming around, as a friend; he made me his confidante, told me all about his other women. Did you know he had other women?" Priss nodded. "Did he ever make a pass at you?" "No. But he did at Dottie. After she was married. He tried to make an assignation with her." "Women were necessary to him," Norine said. "But I thought I was special. I figured he was laying off me because of Kay, because he respected our relationship. Every now and then, he used to undress me and study my body. Then he'd slap my flank and go home. Or off to some other woman. Afterward, he'd tell me about it. Whenever he slept with a woman, he told me. What he didn't tell me, though, was about the women he didn't sleep with. I wasn't the only one, I found out. He went around town undressing his old flames and then leaving them. Just to know they were available. Like somebody checking stock. And all his old mistresses were in love with him. At least all the ones I knew. Harald has great charisma. He could have been a monk."

The gaunt butler came in with a tray on which were two outsized coffee cups, a tarnished silver pot, and a cream and sugar service. The sugar was wrapped in paper marked "Schrafft's." "I can't get used to being rich," Norine sighed. "I always take the sugar they give you home with me when I have a cup of coffee at Schrafft's counter. But the help can't be bothered to unwrap them. Freddy is mortified." The butler withdrew. "Perkins!" Norine called after him. "Empty this ashtray, will you?" He took the big tub and brought a fresh one. "I have to keep after him about that," Norine said. "Freddy's hell on emptying ashtrays. It's funny, anything he's touched he wants to have taken away and washed."

Priss had become conscious, during this conversation, that the back of her skirt was damp and getting damper. She moved from one buttock to the other, shifting her weight. Then she touched the cream-colored cushion. It was distinctly wet. At the same moment Norine explored the seat of her linen slacks. "Oh, God!" she said. "They've done it again. They must have washed these cushions with soapsuds while I was out. Freddy's giving everybody here a washing complex." She laughed. "Freddy's father got an attack of rheumatism the other night from the damp slip cover he sat on in the dining room." Priss stood up; her skirt had a great wet stain. "Perkins!" Norine went to the door and called downstairs. "Bring us a couple of bath towels, will you?" The butler came in with two huge monogrammed towels and spread them at either end of the sofa for the two young women to sit down on. "Thanks," said Norine. Perkins left. "Tell me"—she turned to Priss—"do you say 'thank you' to a servant? Freddy says you're not supposed to thank them; waiting on you is their duty." "You don't thank them when they serve you at table," said Priss. "But if they do some special errand for you, like bringing those towels, you do. And you usually say 'please,'" she added discreetly, "if you ask them for something special. I mean, you might say, 'Will you serve Mr. Rogers the roast again?' But if you asked a maid to bring you a handkerchief or your pocketbook, you'd say 'please.'" "That's what I thought," said Norine. "Freddy's wrong. I guess I'll have to get *Emily Post*. At my grandmother's, I remember, we always said 'please' and 'thank you,' but they were German—my father's people. The help was like part of the family. I don't know the rules of New York society like you."

Priss was embarrassed; she was sure that Freddy knew as much as she did. It was just that Norine had failed to understand the fine points. The butler reappeared. He murmured something in Norine's ear. "Oh, O.K.," she said, glancing in Priss's direction. "Do something about it. Please." "What did he say?" asked Priss, feeling that it had to do with her. Perkins waited. "Stephen shat," Norine said casually. Priss leapt to her feet, turning all the colors. "I'm coming," she said to the butler. "Oh, I'm so sorry!" "Perkins can tend to it," said Norine, firmly reseating Priss on the sofa. "Or Ichabod's nurse'll do it. Just have his pants washed out and put a diaper on him," she said to the man. Too willingly, Priss gave in. Stephen's disgrace and the strange past tense of that word, which she had never heard used before in regular conversation, even in the present (let alone by a woman and before a servant!), had left her giddy. Could that be the right form, she asked herself curiously. It sounded like "begat" in the Bible—archaic. Her mind, blushing for itself, tried out other possible past forms.

"Where was I?" said Norine. "Oh, Harald. Well, I was mad about him. But he was fixated on Kay. I never could grasp that, exactly. All the psychiatrists at the hospital would say was that was a 'certain bond.' 'Mutual dependency.' Harald always talked about her vitality. He thought her aggressive drives were connected with the Life Force—he's never outgrown Shaw. Do you think she's more vital than I am?" Priss did not want to answer this question. "Kay has a great deal of energy," she said. "And she had a great belief in Harald. Don't you think that was the principal thing? And then—I don't want to be unkind, but Kay was the family breadwinner." "Harald could have had a dozen rich women," declared Norine. "And I would have scrubbed floors for him myself. Or worked as a waitress or a taxi-dance girl. It was no sacrifice for Kay to punch the time clock at Macy's. She liked it. While I was ready to sacrifice everything."

Tears came into her tawny eyes. "Oh, don't say that, Norine!" begged Priss, touched by these tears almost to the point of confidence herself. She did not recommend sacrifice, having meekly given up her job and her social ideals for Sloan's sake. It was now too late, because of Stephen, but she was convinced she had made a mistake. Sloan would be far happier himself if

she were where she longed to be—in Washington, as a humble
cog in the New Deal, which he hated—and he could boast of
"my Bolshevik wife." He had been proud of her when she was
with the N.R.A., because she had had gumption, and now
even that was gone.

"Yes!" said Norine, with conviction. "And I'd still sacrifice
everything. All Freddy's shekels." She looked bleakly around at
her possessions. "You don't mean everything," said Priss firmly.
"What about Ichabod?" Norine lit a cigarette. "Christ, I'd
forgotten Ichabod. No. You're right. I've given hostages to
fortune. *A* hostage. Harald would never take on another man's
kid." She gave a hoarse cough. "And he's not partial to the
Chosen People. To him, Ichabod is a little Yid." Priss was
shocked by Norine's language; perhaps it was different when
you were married to a Jew; perhaps that gave you a sort of license, the way Negroes could call each other "nigger." But it
made Priss highly uncomfortable. She set her coffee cup down.
Norine smoked in silence, evidently despondent. Priss regretted having come home with her; the invitation, she now recognized, had just been a pretext to talk about Harald. Like all
acts of self-indulgence, it had left Norine now, probably, wishing she hadn't. Responsively, Priss's own conscience stirred;
she felt she ought not to have brought Stephen to this strange
house. Sloan would disapprove. The Lord knew what they
would be giving Stephen to eat downstairs—something bad
for him, no doubt. And he would be late getting home for his
rest.

"I wonder," she said politely, "if we could take a peek at
Stephen. He's not used to strangers." Her conscience smote
her again for having let these people clean him up. What if
they had told him "Bad boy!" as so many ignorant servants did
with children? Yet a few minutes ago she had been almost
hoping they had. Norine got up promptly. "Sure," she said.
"Tell me one thing first, though." Her cigarette cough rattled.
Priss could not imagine what was coming. Norine stared down
into her eyes. "Do you think Ichabod looks Jewish?"

Again Priss did not know how to answer. Ichabod was too
young to have a hooked nose; his eyes were still the color of all
babies' eyes—a dark slate blue; his skin was dark, but that
might be from his sun baths. It was true that he seemed

somehow different from other babies. He was unusually long, Priss had observed, and this gave him a look of melancholy, like an exhausted reed. There were circles under his eyes, and his little features were slightly drawn. There was no doubt that he appeared to be a child marked for a special destiny, as they said of the Jewish people. His nakedness also gave him a kind of pathos, as though he were not just a baby but a small forked zoo specimen of the human race. But the fact that he bore no resemblance to Stephen at his age did not supply an answer to Norine's question, even had Priss been willing to give it. The real thing was, she was not sure what Norine wanted to hear.

"He doesn't look like you," she said truthfully. "Perhaps he's like his father." Norine produced a large framed photograph of a dark, curly-haired, rather handsome, slightly plump man. Ichabod did not look like Freddy. "He looks like himself, I guess," Norine summed up. They went down the ramp. In the kitchen, they found Stephen, wearing a diaper, the butler, a cook, three big Angora cats and a basket of kittens. Stephen had finished his lunch, except for a slab of chocolate cake, which he had left on his plate. "He doesn't seem to want it, ma'am," the cook said to Norine. They were all gazing at Stephen in astonishment. Priss apologized. "He doesn't know what it is. He only knows graham crackers and animal crackers and arrowroot cookies." "Cookie," said Stephen. "Animal cacka." Just then, in the doorway appeared a very pretty blonde young woman in a low-cut thin blouse that showed her breasts; she wore a pleated pastel skirt and high-heeled shoes. "Hi, Cecilia," said Norine. She turned to Priss. "This is Ichabod's nurse." The girl was carrying Stephen's underpants and yellow sunsuit. "The pants are still damp," she said. "But I've ironed the sunsuit dry, Norine. Do you want me to put it on him?" "I'll do it," said Priss hastily. When the girl had bent down to help him, Stephen had put a hand out to touch her breast. He still eyed her as his mother dressed him. "Wass sat?" he said, pointing. Everyone but the butler and Priss laughed. "He's precocious," said the girl, hugging him, which gave Stephen the chance he wanted. He plunged his hand into the neck of her dress. "Watch out," chuckled Norine. "Cecilia's a virgin and a Papist." Priss removed his hand. She looked around for something to give him, lest he start to cry. There was nothing but the slab of cake; the stroller was upstairs. She broke off a piece of cake and divided it in two. One piece she put in her mouth. "Look! It's good," she said, chewing. Reluctantly, he drew his eyes from the bold nursemaid and imitated his mother. Soon he was greedily eating chocolate cake, from a Jewish bakery, with fudge frosting.

15

AFTER that, Priss chose a new location in the Park. Though she sometimes passed the house with the red door, she took the other side of the street and she did not see Norine again till Kay's funeral. Then more than a year had passed, a terrible year, and everything had changed. The war had broken out. Lakey had come back from Europe. France had fallen; the *Luftwaffe* was bombing England, and Kay was dead, at twenty-nine. It was a beautiful July day, like the June day of Kay's wedding, and once again the scene was St. George's Church, on Stuyvesant Square. This time the service was being held in the church itself; there were too many mourners to fit in the chapel. The organ was playing "And all our flesh is as the grass" from the Brahms Requiem Mass, and the undertakers had carried in Kay's casket, a very simple one. It stood at the altar covered with white baby's breath and white zinnias. The rector himself was officiating.

Kay would have been happy about that, her friends knew. They had worked with might and main to get her buried as an Episcopalian. Mrs. Hartshorn had finally arranged it by speaking to Dr. Reiland, an old family friend. She pointed out that Kay had been married in his church, which ought to entitle him to give her the last rites. Before that, Polly's Aunt Julia had talked to *her* rector at St. Bartholomew's, and Pokey, from the country, had telephoned St. James's; Helena had got a friend who was married to the son of the rector of St. Thomas's to intercede. It was amazing how sticky these ministers could be about burying a person who was not a church member.

Kay's father and mother would arrive too late for the ceremony; in this warm weather you could not wait too long. On the long-distance, they had told Helena to have their daughter cremated, and they would take her ashes home—they were very bitter. But Helena was certain that Kay would have hated that, and she had telephoned back to say that her friends would like to arrange a church ceremony for her, if her parents would agree. Whatever Kay would have wanted, her father said; probably her friends knew best. That was bitter too. Yet the group were sure they were doing the right thing. Kay had grown away from her parents; they had not seen eye to eye at all while she was out West, and it had hurt them when she had insisted on coming back to New York after the divorce, though she had a home with them. But they had staked her, which was sweet, just as now they had wired the funeral parlor with an authority for Helena to act. How sad that Kay had not found time—that was what her father said—to write them a single letter in the month before she "went." Naturally, if she had known, she would have.

At college the group had had long discussions of how you would like to be buried. Pokey had voted for cremation with no service at all, and Libby had wanted her ashes scattered over New York Harbor. But Kay, like the rest, had been for regular burial in the ground, with a minister reading the funeral service over her—she loved the "I am the Resurrection and the Life" part (actually that came in the church service, not at the open grave), which she used to recite, having played Sydney Carton in a school dramatization of *A Tale of Two Cities*. And she hated embalming; she did not want to be pumped full of fluid. In Salt Lake City, she used to go out with a boy whose father was an undertaker, she had once confided, blushing for it, to Lakey, and he had showed her all the grisly paraphernalia. How like Kay it was to have such violent preferences, her friends agreed. After all these years—seven, since graduation—the group could still remember exactly what she liked and what she despised. And she had never grown older and wiser.

This had made it easy for them—sad to say—to get her ready for the funeral. It was the first time they had ever done anything like that. When somebody close to them had died, it had been an elderly person, and they had had nothing to do with the arrangements. They did not know the first thing about laying out the dead. But since Kay was divorced from Harald and her family was not here, they had pitched in. To begin with, they had had a frightful struggle with the undertaker, who had wanted to embalm her when he had got her body from the police, and Helena had had to telephone a lawyer to make sure they were within their rights. To fly in the face of convention turned out to be so much trouble that in the end it seemed hardly worthwhile. But Mrs. Hartshorn had helped and Ross and Mrs. Davison, who had been in the Vassar Club lounge when it happened and Kay went hurtling down from the twentieth floor. Luckily her fall had been broken by a ledge on the thirteenth and she had landed in an awning, so that she was not smashed to bits; only her poor neck had been snapped. And luckily too Mrs. Davison had been there—she had come down from Watch Hill for a meeting of the board of the English-Speaking Union—to claim the body and have Helena get in touch with Kay's parents.

They had laid her out in Helena's studio apartment on West Eleventh Street, which seemed the most suitable place, since Helena was still single and besides they had been roommates. The undertaker had disguised her bruises, but they would not let him make her up to "look natural." Kay had never used rouge. They had gone through the closet of her room at the Vassar Club, looking for the right dress—there could be no question of her wedding dress, and in any case she had thrown it away long ago; she had never liked that dress with the white fichu. Holding up her clothes (many of which could have stood a stitch or two) on their hangers, they could not make up their minds. Lakey, with her clear intellect, cut through their indecision. Kay would like to be buried in a new dress, of course. The others could not imagine shopping for a dead person, but Lakey took one of Kay's dresses for a sample and went straight off to Fortuny's and bought her an off-white silk pleated gown—the kind the Duchess of Guermantes used to receive in. Then the others remembered that Kay had always longed for a Fortuny gown, which she never in her wildest moments could have afforded. Kay would have loved the dress and loved having Lakey buy it for her. They put her old gold bracelet on her bare arm; she had never had any other jewelry but her wedding ring—she hated costume stuff. Helena looked for lilies of the valley for her—they used to pick them together in the woods by the Pine Walk—but of course their season was over. Mrs. Davison had a very nice thought; she closed Kay's eyes with two early Christian silver coins, which she sent Helena out to find at a collector's.

There had been a great deal to do and in such a short time. They had had no idea how complicated the last arrangements

were, particularly when the defunct had been, like Kay, a
stranger and a sojourner. Finding a funeral plot. Pokey, very
generously, had donated a grave in her family's plot, which
would have pleased Kay too, to lie among all those Livingstons
and Schuylers. Notifying everyone who had known Kay. Putting an item in the newspapers. Choosing the psalms and the
lesson and the prayers with the minister; Helena and Mrs.
Davison had taken care of that. Choosing the hymn. There
were so many decisions to make. The flowers; they had determined to have only natural flowers of the season, nothing floristy. But that was easier said than done; the florists were bent
on selling you wreaths and acted as if you were trying to
economize when you said no, like the undertaker when you
refused embalming and held out for a simple coffin. Kay would
have liked a plain pine box, but that was absolutely unthinkable, apparently. Then making up your minds whether to have
the casket open or closed in the church. They finally agreed to
have it closed, but that those who had known Kay best and
wanted to see her could come to Helena's place before the
undertaker's people arrived. Helena served sherry and biscuits
to those who came. Again that had involved decisions: sherry
or Madeira, biscuits or sandwiches. The girls were reluctant
even to think about such things as sandwiches (open or
closed?), but the older women were firm that Helena had to
offer what Mrs. Davison called funeral meats.

You found that you got obsessed with these petty details.
They were supposed to distract you from your grief. In fact,
that was just what they did. You caught yourself forgetting the
reason you were doing all this: because Kay had died. And the
relief of finally arriving at a decision or having it taken out of
your hands, as when Lakey got the dress, made you feel positively gay, till you remembered.

It was curious, too, the differences in people that came out
in the face of death. You hated yourself for observing them, at
such a time, but you could not help yourself. For instance,
Mrs. Hartshorn and Ross were wonderful about dressing Kay,
even the most awful part—putting on her underwear; she had
been delivered "prepared for burial" (which they supposed
must mean eviscerated), wrapped in a sort of shroud. And
Polly calmly helped them, which was understandable, proba-

bly, because she had worked in a hospital. But the others could not even stay in the room while it was happening. When Ross came into the living room to ask a question—should they put a brassière on Miss Kay?—they felt sick. It was a hard question to decide too. It seemed against nature, somehow, to bury someone in a brassière (fortunately, Kay had never worn a girdle), and yet, as Ross pointed out, the Fortuny gown was clinging. In the end, they told Ross to put her brassière on.

The girls were interested to see that Mrs. Davison, who was a wonder in a supervisory capacity and never flinched mentally from a fact of death, felt just as they did about handling a dead body. She stayed in the living room with them, leading the conversation, while Ross and Mrs. Hartshorn and Polly "did the necessary." "I wonder, Helena," she said, "that you did not have the undertaker's people dress her. That's what they are paid for. 'From each according to his capacities.'" Frankly, the others wondered too, now that they grasped what it entailed, but they had taken a dislike to the undertaker with his clammy voice and his rouge pots. Yet undertakers were necessary members of society—how necessary, the girls saw only now.

Even with Kay in the next room (that was another thing), the group could not help being covertly amused by Mrs. Davison, who was a card and knew she was a card, they suspected. Clad in her billowy black dress, with an onyx brooch, she chatted sociably of cerements and winding sheets, now and then drawing an apt quotation from her reticule or loosing a dark shaft of humor. "If only Kay could have been here," she declared, shaking her head, "she could have run the whole show for us, dontcha know."

As long as there was anything to do, Libby did not appear. Nor did she offer to help with the expenses, which the others had divvied up. She had been married, last summer in Pittsfield, to a best-selling author of historical novels whose books she had been handling; only Polly had gone to her wedding, which took place in the family garden, with an Elizabethan pageant and Purcell played on recorders in the gazebo. On the morning of the funeral, she came breathlessly for sherry and biscuits, wearing a black toque and a long chain she described as a chatelaine. She did not think the Fortuny dress was Kay's color and was full of curiosity to learn what Lakey had paid for it. And as if sensing the group's disapproval, she proceeded to put her foot in it still more. "Now, girls," she said, hitching forward in her chair and examining a biscuit, "tell me. I won't tell a soul. Did she jump or fall?"

Mrs. Davison laid a restraining plump hand on Polly's arm. "You may tell everyone you wish, Elizabeth. Indeed, I hope you will. She fell." "Oh, I know that was the police verdict," said Libby. Helena started to speak. "I have the floor, Helena," said Mrs. Davison. "After all, I was the last to see her alive. Not an hour before. I invited her to have coffee with me in the lounge after dinner. I was always partial to Kay. And as I told the police, she was in excellent spirits. Her mind was perfectly clear. We discussed Mr. Churchill and the air raids and the necessity of a draft in this country. She spoke of an interview she expected to have for a position with Saks Fifth Avenue. Kay had no intention of taking her own life. If she had not 'done time' in a mental institution, the question would never have been raised."

The young women nodded. That was what was so unfair about the whole thing. And if Kay had not been cleared by the police, she could not have had Christian burial. She would have had to lie in unhallowed ground.

"You might say, Elizabeth," Mrs. Davison continued gravely, "that Kay was the first American war casualty." "Oh, Mother!" protested Helena. "That's a ridiculous way of putting it." But in a ridiculous way it was true. Kay had been airplane-spotting, it seemed, from her window at the Vassar Club when somehow she lost her balance and fell. She had had two cocktails before dinner, which might have slightly affected her motor reactions. To those who had been seeing her regularly since she had come back this spring, the manner of her death was a shock but not a complete surprise. She had become very war conscious, like many single women. As her friends could testify, she talked a great deal about air raids and preparedness. Ever since the invasion of the Lowlands, she had been saying that it was just a matter of days before America would be in the war. She was convinced it would begin with a surprise enemy air attack; Hitler would not wait for Roosevelt to arm and declare war on him. He would send the *Luftwaffe* over one night to wipe out New York or Washington. If she were in Hitler's place, that was exactly what she would do. It was the whole principle of the blitzkrieg. She knew an air force officer who said that the Nazis had long-range bombers—Hitler's secret weapon—that were capable of making the flight. They would probably concert it with a submarine attack on the coast.

The fact that America was neutral did not mean anything. Norway and Denmark and the Lowlands had been neutral too. She was keen on the idea that Mayor La Guardia should start air-raid drills in New York and impose a blackout. She wanted to be an air-raid warden, like the ones they had in England, and she was urging the Vassar Club to get pails of sand and shovels and start a civilian defense unit. She bought a radio for her room, and someone had given her a deck of Air Force silhouette cards, which she was studying to familiarize herself with the various plane shapes. When she was not listening to the radio or arguing with isolationists, she was scanning the skies.

This new craze of Kay's had amused her friends when it had not saddened them. Even Priss, who was active in several committees to get America into the war on the Allied side, did not believe Hitler would attack America. She almost wished he would, to goad the American people into action. Her fear was that the war would end this summer—how much longer could the English people hold out alone?—with Europe enslaved, while America sat back and did nothing. Or sent too little and too late, as it had done with France. Priss had nearly lost her mind while France was falling; she too had been glued to the radio. She had made Sloan get a portable to take to the beach at Oyster Bay. And now every hour on the hour in the city she turned on the news, expecting to hear that Churchill had capitulated or fled with the government to Canada. This dread, in fact, was in everyone's mind. All the while they were getting ready for the funeral, Helena had the radio turned on low, for fear they would miss a bulletin. For the rest of their lives, they thought, whenever they remembered Kay, they would remember the voice of the announcer recounting the night's casualties. Only Mrs. Davison had hope. "Mark my words, the English people will never surrender. As I say to Davy Davison, it will be another Spanish Armada." But Kay, with her positive character, had already left England behind and was planning the defense of America. What had saddened her friends was that her interest in what she called Hitler's timetable was so obviously a rounding on Harald, who had become a fanatical America Firster and was getting quite a name for himself speaking at their rallies. If only Kay could have forgotten him, instead of enlisting in a rival campaign. Still, her zeal of preparedness had given her something to live for. What a cruel irony that it should have caused her death!

The maid who did her room at the Vassar Club told the police that she had often seen Kay craning out the window and warned her against doing it. "Yes, Elizabeth," said Mrs. Davison. "I questioned the maid myself. And I measured the window. A girl of Kay's height could easily have lost her balance and gone out. As I pointed out to the police, her radio was on, and she had left a cigarette burning in the ashtray by her bedside. A very dangerous habit. But no young woman who was going to kill herself would do it in the middle of a cigarette. Evidently, while she was smoking, she heard a plane's motor or several motors and got up to lean out the window. I believe I heard the motors myself as I was glancing through a magazine in the lounge. But everything was driven from my mind by the sound of that crash. I can hear it now." She took out a handkerchief and wiped her eyes.

As the group took their seats in the church, they looked around in surprise at the number of people who were already there. It was almost a crowd and more were still arriving. There was Kay's former supervisor at Macy's and a whole delegation of her fellow-workers. Mrs. Renfrew had come from Gloucester, to represent Dottie. Mr. Andrews was there, with his sister, the famous Aunt Julia, and Ross. Libby and her husband. Lakey and the titled friend who had come back with her from Europe—the Baroness d'Estienne. Pokey and her husband were there, and in the pew just ahead, Polly and Helena were astonished to see Hatton, the Prothero butler. "Hello, Hatton," whispered Polly. "Good afternoon, madam. Good afternoon, miss. I'm here to represent the family. The Madam sends her condolences. And Forbes begs to be remembered." It was quite a society funeral, which would have delighted Kay.

Connie Storey ambled down the aisle and took a seat next to Putnam Blake and his third wife. "Quite a turnout, Mother," said Mr. Davison approvingly. "Kind of a vote of confidence." Polly picked out Dick Brown, that old friend of Harald's, whom time had not been kind to. Jim Ridgeley slipped into the pew beside Polly. "Do you know all these people?" he asked Polly. "No," she whispered back. "I'll be damned!" he said and pointed out the psychiatrist who had treated Kay at Payne Whitney. "Those look to me like some of the old patients," he said, indicating three women together. Mrs. Davison nodded to the secretary of the Vassar Club. Priss recognized Mrs. Sisson, whom she had sat next to at Kay's wedding. Other classmates appeared. An army officer with wings over his pocket took his seat. "I believe Kay was quite thick with him," Mrs. Davison confided to her husband. Helena nudged Polly. There came Norine, dressed in complete black with a veil; she appeared to be pregnant, and in a sort of sling that was suspended from her shoulder to her hip and joggled as she walked, there hung a small child; his bare legs and feet protruded from this species of pouch or pocket as if from a pair of rompers. "My smelling salts!" exclaimed Pokey in audible tones. "What is that, a kangaroo?" said Mr. Davison coarsely. "Hush, Father," reproved Mrs. Davison. "It's Ic-chabod," said Priss. "But what in the world—?" whispered Polly. "It's the latest thing," muttered Priss. "I read about them in a government pamphlet. They're meant for busy mothers who've nobody to leave their babies with. And the child's supposed to get reassurance from the warmth of the mother's b-body." Norine took a seat next to Dick Brown. She placed Ichabod on her lap by shifting the sling. "What's the idea of the papoose?" he said. "You squaw woman?" Norine nodded. "I want to give him the experience of death." "I see," he said gravely. "Early. Like mumps."

The ripple of astonishment that had gone through the church at the apparition of Ichabod subsided as new arrivals came in. Polly recognized Kay's former maid, old Clara, who ran a funeral parlor in Harlem. Mrs. Flanagan, Kay's pet teacher, who had been head of the Federal Theatre, came in with her former assistant. "I never thought she'd come!" exclaimed Helena. The altar was completely banked with flowers.

The organ stopped. The rector came in and took his place behind the casket. The congregation stood up. "I am the Resurrection and the Life, saith the Lord: he that believeth in me, though he were dead, yet shall he live, and whosoever liveth and believeth in me shall never die." Lakey felt a tear fall. She was surprised by her grief. The sole emotion she had willed herself to feel was the cold fierce passion that this funeral should be perfect, a flawless mirror of what Kay would find admirable. For herself, she hoped that when she died some stranger would tie a stone around her neck and throw her in the sea. She loathed insincere mourning and, rather than mourn insincerely, she would have preferred to have her eyes put out. Another weak tear dropped. Then she noticed that heads were turning. Furious with the others, she quickly looked too. Harald, wearing a dark suit, had entered and taken a seat at the back of the church. How like him, she said to herself icily, to make us turn around to see him. Polly and Helena peeked too. They had feared he would come. And of course he had a right to be here, though they had not invited him, just as he had a right to kneel down, while the rest of the congregation was standing, and bury his skull-like head in his hand, seeming to pray. Yet they too were incensed.

In the slight pause that preceded the reading of the first psalm, everyone in the church, even those who did not know him, became aware of the presence of Harald. It was as if a biased shadow had fallen on the assembly. If you could have an evil sprite at a funeral, reflected Helena, like a bad fairy at a christening, that was Mr. Harald Handfast. She set her small jaw. She did not understand why his sour mana made her milk of human kindness curdle. There was no further harm he could do Kay. A strange phrase crossed her drawling mind. Harald was "taking the joy out of Kay's funeral."

With a slight uneasy appraisal of the congregation, as though his practiced eye had taken cognizance of Ichabod and Harald as possible centers of disturbance, the rector started the first psalm. "Lord, let me know mine end, and the number of my days. . . ." There was a rustle and creaking. Some of the mourners remained standing; others sat down; others knelt; still others compromised between sitting and kneeling, crouching forward on the pews. Polly decided to follow Hatton, who had seated himself. He was one of the few persons in the church, she mused, who would know how to comport himself at a funeral. She thought of Kay's wedding and how young and superstitious they had all been that day and how little they had changed. She herself again had the crazy fear that some hitch might develop in the proceedings, which now would cause the rector to decide that he could not bury Kay after all. But there *had* been some peculiar features about the wedding, and there was nothing peculiar about the funeral, or was there? The peculiarity was only Harald's presence. He ought not to have come. But by coming he had made everything they had arranged—Kay's dress, the old Roman coins, the music and flowers, the liturgy itself—seem silly and girlish. "He is Death at her funeral," she said to herself.

The second psalm began. Polly bent her head and concentrated on Kay. The fondness and pity that had flooded her while dressing her inert body came welling back. She considered Kay's life, which had not been a life but only a sort of greeting, a Hello There. The girl who lay in the casket was finally the heroine of the hour. The rest had been nothing, a vain presumptuous shadow. "In the morning it is green and groweth up; but in the evening it is cut down, dried up, and withered," intoned the rector. *That* was appropriate and not just to her poor, shattered end. Polly was certain that Kay had not killed herself, though she had been very unhappy in the hospital when the psychiatrists had made her face the advisability of a separation from Harald. She had all but had a real nervous breakdown at the thought of having to be "nobody" instead of the wife of a genius. But if, like a suicide, she had imagined everybody grieving over her, she would be satisfied now. "I love you, Kay," Polly whispered contritely.

When the rector launched into the *De Profundis*, Priss felt Helena and Mrs. Davison had overdone it; three psalms were too many. And they had chosen the longest epistle for the lesson: St. Paul to the Corinthians, I:15. The words were beautiful, but she was worried for Ichabod. Knowing what she did about Norine's views of toilet training, she feared he would have an accident. With all the flowers the church was very close; it was surely her imagination, but she would have sworn that either he *had* or else Kay—. It was useless to look at Pokey; she had no sense of smell. The congregation was getting restless, nodding and whispering to each other as they recognized familiar quotations in the lesson. "Thou foolish one, that which thou sowest is not quickened, except it die." "*Si le grain ne meurt*," Priss heard Lakey murmur to her companion. ". . . For the trumpet shall sound, and the dead shall be raised incorruptible, and we shall be changed." "Handel," Mrs. Davison reminded her husband. "*The Messiah*." Priss noticed that Polly was crying hard, and Jim was squeezing her hand. Lakey was crying too—tears, Priss thought, like crystal drops, ran down her rigid face; her teeth were set. Priss wished the lesson would stop talking about "corruptible." "O Death, where is thy sting?" Pokey gave her husband a big nudge. "I never knew that was where that came from!" Suddenly Priss found herself thinking of the worms in the graveyard; a sob shook her.

It was an embarrassment to Helena when the hymn came, one of her mother's favorites, Number 245: "He leadeth me." She herself had wanted to have Bach's hymn, from the Passion Chorale: "O Sacred Head surrounded by crown of piercing thorn." But her mother said the other was more inspiring, which meant that it sounded like a revival meeting under canvas. She knew all the words by heart and did not even feign, as Helena did, to make use of the hymnal. Her big breathy voice, off key, competed with the organ. With the last lines, Mrs. Davison let all the stops out. "E'en death's cold wave I will not flee/ Since God through Jordan leadeth me." Helena dryly pictured God assisting her mother by the hand to cross the River Jordan, and she feared that everyone in the church had been furnished with the same tableau. Yet her mother was a complete agnostic, like the majority of the mourners. She did not believe in a future life for Kay, so what was there to be inspired about? Nothing. Helena's realism forbade her to cry. Who was there to cry for? Kay? But there was no Kay any more. That left no one to be sorry for that Helena could see.

They knelt down to pray. Suddenly it was over. The congregation found itself on the sidewalk, disbanded, and the undertaker's men went in to get the coffin. Libby wondered why they had not had pallbearers; it would have been much more impressive. And she thought the casket should have been left open. Spying Connie Storey, she rushed off to greet her. She was not going to the cemetery, and Connie, who was a working woman too, might like to share a taxi with her. Tonight, before she and her husband went out, she meant to write down her impressions of the ceremony. It had been almost unbearably moving.

Cars had been ordered to take everyone to the cemetery who wished to go and did not have a car of his own. They were lined up outside the church behind the hearse. Helena had the list and was checking it off. No provision had been made for Harald. He could have gone with Norine, except that Norine was not going, thank Heaven; it was a miracle, everyone agreed, that that youngster had not acted up during the service—he had nodded wearily on his mother's lap. Harald stood on the sidewalk, alone and enigmatically smiling. "Jim and I can take him in our car," volunteered Polly. "One of us *has* to speak to him." Helena was less Christian. "My mother will invite him. She has 'an open mind.' Let her do it." But Harald had approached Lakey. "May I ride with you?" they heard him ask. Lakey had a smart bottle-green European two-seater waiting at the curb. "I'm sorry," she said. "I have no room for you." But the Baroness excused herself. "If you do not mind, Elinor, I will not go to the interment." "Very well," said Lakey to Harald. "Get in. Can you drive?" Harald took the wheel. As the cortege began to move, the mourners saw the green two-seater dart out ahead of the hearse. "What do you bet he makes advances to her?" said Polly tearfully. She and Jim and Helena and Mr. Andrews were in the Ridgeley Ford. "Let us hope he does," said Mr. Andrews mildly. "I understand the Baroness packs a pair of brass knuckles."

The return of Lakey on the *Rex* had been a thrilling event for the group. They had gathered at the dock one April morning to meet her, seven strong. Kay had been alive then of course, just back from Utah, and Dottie had fitted it in with a vacation trip to Bermuda. The idea of surprising Lakey by meeting her in a body had been Pokey's; Pokey was unconscious of the passage of time and scoffed at the thought that Lakey might be different. Some of the others had misgivings, though, as they watched the gangplank being lowered. They were afraid Lakey might have outgrown them. She was almost bound to find them provincial after the professors, art historians, and collectors she had been living among in Europe. The return addresses on some of her letters and post cards suggested, as Helena said, that Lakey had been "broadened"—she always seemed to be staying with important people in villas, *palazzi*, and chateaus. The last time she wrote, to say she was coming home because she thought Italy would be in the war soon, was from the house of Bernard Berenson, the famous art critic, in Settignano. Lined up on the dock, straining their eyes for a glimpse of her, preparing their hands to wave, the more sensitive girls were conscious of being a staid settled group with husbands and children at home, for the most part; Pokey now had three, and Polly had a little girl.

When they saw her come down the gangplank, with her swift, sure step, her chin raised, in a dark violet suit and hat and carrying a green leather toilet case and a slim furled green silk umbrella, they were amazed at how young she looked still. They had all cut their hair and had permanents, but Lakey still wore hers in a black knot at the nape of her neck, which gave her a girlish air, and she had kept her marvelous figure. She saw them; her green eyes widened with pleasure; she waved. After the embraces (she kissed them all on both cheeks and held them off to look at them), she introduced the short, stocky foreign woman who was with her—someone, the girls took it, she had met on the crossing.

On the pier, there was a long wait for Lakey's luggage. She had dozens of suitcases, thirty-two wardrobe trunks, beautifully wrapped parcels tied with bright colored ribbon, and innumerable packing cases containing paintings, books, and china. On her customs declaration, she was a "returning foreign resident," which meant she did not have to pay duty on her personal and household belongings. But she had masses of presents, which, being Lakey, she had declared, and she was an interminable time with the customs man and the lists she had made out in her large, clear, oblong writing. There was nothing the group could do to help, once her luggage was assembled, and they did not like to stare at the contents of the trunks and suitcases the man directed her to open, yet even Pokey's eyes bugged at the quantities of underwear, handkerchiefs, nightgowns, peignoirs, shoes, gloves, all wrapped in snowy tissue paper—not to mention dresses, hats, scarves, woolen coats, silk coats, beautifully folded and in tissue paper too. This impressive array—yet she did not have a single fur coat, Libby reported— made the girls think awkwardly of schedules, formula, laundry, diapers. They could not spend all morning on the pier. As they waited, restlessly tapping their feet (you could not smoke), they realized that the Baroness, who had finished with customs, was waiting too. She seemed to be with Lakey and was not very friendly to the girls, who tried politely to make conversation with her about conditions in Europe. She was a German, it transpired, who had been married to a French baron; she had had to leave France in September when the war broke out. Like Lakey, she had been staying in Florence, but she did not know Libby's aunt in Fiesole. Every now and then she would go over and say something to Lakey; they heard her call her "Darling" with a trilled *r*. It was Kay who caught on first. Lakey had become a Lesbian. This woman was her man.

Slowly the group understood. This was why Lakey had stayed abroad so long. Abroad people were more tolerant of Lesbians, and Lakey's family in Lake Forest did not have to know. It was a terrible moment. Each girl recognized that she was, they were *de trop*. They had made a fearful *gaffe* in coming to welcome Lakey with open arms, as if she belonged to them, when plainly she belonged exclusively to the Baroness. They could not help gleaning that the two of them would be staying together at the Elysée Hotel. Lakey, the Baroness said, in reply to Kay's blunt question, was going to Chicago for a brief visit to her family. After that, she would look for a place in the country, outside New York. "Something very qu-i-et," said the Baroness. The girls got the point. Lakey wanted to be alone with the Baroness, undisturbed by neighbors and old friends. Or at least that was what the Baroness wanted.

The girls eyed each other. They had had the day planned. Pokey's family's chauffeur was waiting outside to drive Lakey to her hotel and install her. Then later they would all meet for an elegant lunch. Afterward, each girl wanted to be the first to show Lakey her apartment, her husband, her child or children. Except Kay, who had nothing to show her but who therefore felt she had the best claim on her. Now they did not know whether to jettison these plans completely or to proceed with them and include the Baroness. They did not know whether to be discreet about this relationship or open. What did Lakey want? Would she like them to go away? Perhaps she would never forgive them for surprising her like this at the dock. By instinct, the group turned to Kay, who, with her experience in the theatre, ought to be able to tell them what to do. But Kay was nonplused. Her open face clearly showed her disappointment, chagrin, and irresolution. It occurred to them all that Lakey, who had always been frightening and superior, would now look down on them for not being Lesbians. On the other hand, she had seemed truly glad to see them.

Studying Lakey with the customs man, they asked themselves, in silence, how long Lakey had been a Lesbian, whether the Baroness had made her one or she had started on her own. This led them to wonder whether she could possibly have been one at college—suppressed, of course. In the light of this terrible discovery, they examined her clothes for telltale signs. It was a Schiaparelli suit she was wearing; Kay had asked that straight out—she had guessed it was a Schiaparelli. "Schiap makes all Elinor's clothes," the Baroness had remarked, and they had watched that nickname, casually pronounced, take the wind out of Kay's sails. Lakey had on silk stockings, quite sheer, high-heeled calf shoes, a green silk blouse with a ruffle. If anything, she looked more feminine than before. With the Baroness you could tell, though she did not have a boyish haircut or a man's tie; she wore a heavy tweed suit, service sheer stockings, and pumps with Cuban heels. Yet it was odd to think that the Baroness had been married and Lakey had not.

As soon as Lakey was through with the customs man, she had solved their difficulties with the utmost naturalness. She accepted the offer of Pokey's chauffeur to take her and the Baroness to the hotel. As for lunch, she sent the Baroness off to the Metropolitan Museum, telling her to eat in the cafeteria: it would introduce her to America. "Maria is a bear," she said, laughing. "She growls at strangers." She had lunch with the group herself and that evening she invited those of them who were free and their husbands to have cocktails with her and the Baroness in the Monkey Bar of the hotel. That, the girls found, was the pattern. If it was an occasion when husbands would be present, the Baroness came; otherwise Lakey was on her own.

Once the group understood the convention by which the Baroness was "my friend" like a self-evident axiom, their stiffness relaxed. Gradually, in the weeks that followed, the Baroness unbent too. Far from snubbing the group because they were not Lesbians, she seemed to find it a point in their favor. It was only of Kay, living alone at the Vassar Club and divorced, that she appeared to be suspicious. The group was surprised to find that both Lakey and Maria were strong anti-fascists. They would not have expected Lakey to be so human as to have common garden political sympathies. But she was more human in many ways than they remembered. The other surprise was that she liked children. The very thing the girls would have thought a Lesbian would be contemptuous of— their maternity—was a source of attraction to Lakey. Having brought a lovely set of Italian embroidered bibs for Polly's baby, she would put one on her and feed her in her lap whenever she came to the apartment. To Priss's Stephen, she had brought a prism and a set of antique toy soldiers; she liked to tell him stories and finger-paint with him. And when she went down one weekend to stay with Pokey at Princeton, she visited the stables and played Hide-and-Seek with the twins. She loved to do cutouts and make jumping mice out of her huge linen handkerchiefs.

Both she and Maria were very practical. They knew a great deal about food and dressmaking and were interested, for instance, in designing a new kind of maternity dress for Polly, who was pregnant. Maria had studied nursing, which, it seemed, was quite common among the European aristocracy, going back to the days when the lady of a castle had to prescribe for the peasants and take care of the wounded in war. The fact that none of the group, except Polly, could cut out a dress or make a bandage shocked Maria, as if they were barbarians.

It was astonishing, but within a month some of the girls found themselves talking of "having Lakey and Maria to dinner," just as they might speak of a normal couple. When she and Maria finally took a big house outside Greenwich, Polly and Jim and Kay and Helena all went out to stay with them.

Yet side by side with this the group felt, with one accord, that what had happened to Lakey was a tragedy. They tried not to think of what she and Maria did in bed together. Only Kay claimed to be able to picture their "embraces" with equanimity. They liked Maria as a person; if only she could have finished in a tail, like a mermaid! The same with Lakey, who in fact resembled a mermaid, with her large green eyes and white skin. Polly and Helena, who had became close friends now that Helena lived in New York, had tried to discuss the question as dispassionately as they could. They could not escape the gentle sense that the relationship these two had was perverted. One sign of this was the Baroness's jealousy. Maria was very jealous of both men and women—indeed, of all strangers. She carried a revolver her husband had given her and had made Lakey buy two ferocious watchdogs. And now there were these brass knuckles that Mr. Andrews had somehow learned about! It was too easy to picture Maria using them on any man who would try to save Lakey. And the word, save, was indicative. On the one hand, there were Lakey-and-Maria, as you might say Polly-and-Jim, a contented married pair; on the other, there was an exquisite captive of a fierce robber woman, locked up in a Castle Perilous, and woe to the knight who came to release her from the enchantment. But it was possible to see it the other way around. Supposing it were Lakey, the inscrutable, intelligent Lakey, who had made poor Maria, who was not very bright, her prisoner and slave? The fact that it was possible to reverse the relation like an hourglass was what the girls found so troubling. In the same way, it troubled them to wonder which one of the pair was the man and which the woman. Obviously, Maria, in her pajamas and bathrobe, was the man, and Lakey, in her silk-and-lace peignoirs and batiste-and-lace nightgowns, with her hair down her back, was the woman, and yet these could be disguises—masquerade costumes. It bothered Polly and Helena to think that what was presented to their eyes was mere appearance, and that behind that, underneath it, was something *of which they would not approve.*

Harald and Lakey were driving very fast across the Queensborough Bridge. He wanted to go to a bar before putting in an appearance at the cemetery, and Lakey had agreed. "Who arranged that comedy?" he asked, turning to glance at Lakey's profile. "You mean the funeral," said Lakey. "What would you have done?" Harald did not answer. "You have to bury a body," said Lakey. "Or cremate it. You can't simply put it down the incinerator or out with the trash." He meditated. "If there's difficulty in disposing of a body," he observed, "that suggests there's been foul play. I was given the impression back there in the church that the belief was that *I* had done away with her." Lakey patted the knot at the back of her neck. "She killed herself of course," stated Harald. "Why?" said Lakey calmly. "Sheer competitiveness," he answered. "For years I've been trying to kill myself, ever since I've known her." Lakey looked at him for a minute steadily; his face was quite haggard. "She decided to show me how to do it. *She* could do it better. On the first try." He waited. "You don't believe me, do you, you inscrutable idol. You're right. I've never seriously tried to kill myself. It's always been a fake. Fake suicide attempts have been the Petersen specialty. And yet I honestly wish to die. I swear that to you. If we could just go off the road." He pulled the wheel sharply to the right. "Stop that," said Lakey. He righted the car. "And she," he said, "*she* had the gall to kill herself and fake a death-by-accident." "How do you mean?" "That air-plane spotting. The silhouette cards. Having the maid see her at the window and warn her. Those were clumsy plants. A crude alibi. So that we'd believe she'd lost her balance." "How do you know all the details?" "From Mama Davison. We had a nice little chat on the phone." "But why would she want to fool us?" Harald shrugged. "Her parents, I suppose. That se-nile 'Dads' she talks about. Or maybe she was ashamed to confess so ostentatiously that her life was a failure. 'Everyone would know.'"

Lakey studied this man, whom she had never liked, and said nothing. Her intention was limited to getting to the cemetery without having him kill them both in a dramatic effort to show her that he had the courage to commit suicide. He was a good driver; she had let him drive deliberately to test him. She had a certain curiosity about him, which she would like to satisfy, and she was aware that he had a curiosity about her.

"'The Madonna of the Smoking Room,' he said. "It's funny, but I never picked you for a sapphic. And yet I have a good eye. When did you start? Or were you always that way?" "Always," said Lakey. His imprudent questions shaped a plan in her mind. "The 'group,'" said Harald, "must have been in quite a 'tizzy' when you finally showed your colors. God's bowels, how tired I was of the 'group' before I was through!" "They're dears," said Lakey. Harald turned his head and lifted an eyebrow. "Did you say they were dears?" "Yes," said Lakey. "All but one. Libby is a *mauvaise fille*." "A woman's taste," said Harald. Lakey smiled. "My friend, the Baroness d'Estienne, is enchanted with them. She loves American women." "Christ's body!" said Harald. "Yes," said Lakey. "She says American women are a fourth sex."

Harald glanced at her again. "'Always,' you said. That means when you were in college." His eyes narrowed. "I suppose you were in love with the 'group.' All seven of them, excluding yourself. Collectively and singly. That explains it. I never understood what you—a girl with a mind—were doing in that *galère*." He nodded. "So you were in love with them. They were pretty to look at when nubile, I grant you. Why, you had a regular seraglio in that tower of yours. Kay always said that you turned hot and cold, picked them up, dropped them— they never knew why. But they were *fascinated*." He imitated their collective voice. Lakey smiled. "It's true, I had favorites."

Harald stopped the car in front of a bar. They went in, and he ordered a double whisky for himself and a single for Lakey. They sat in a booth. "Five minutes," said Lakey. "You don't have to worry," he said. "We can see the cortege pass." He downed half his whisky. "Who were your favorites?" he said. "No, don't tell me. I'll guess. Dottie. Pokey. Kay. Helena." "Not Helena," said Lakey. "I like her now, but I didn't care for her in college. She was like a homely little boy." "Polly?" said Harald. "I was a snob," said Lakey. "Polly was on a scholarship and doing self-help. One felt she was going to seed." Her delicate dark eyebrows winced. "One was so callow then. I don't like to think about it. Girls are brutal." Harald finished his whisky. "Were you in love with Kay?" Lakey cupped her chin in her hand. "She was lovely in her sophomore year. You hadn't met her then. On the Daisy Chain. Like a wild flower herself. It's a kind of country beauty I'm particularly fond of. Very paintable. Who might have done her? Caravaggio? Some of the Spaniards? Anyone who painted gypsies. Or mountain people. She had a beautiful neck, like a stem. And such a strong back and tapering waist." Harald ordered another whisky. His face had darkened.

"She was thick-skinned," he said. "It amused me to hurt her. To get some kind of response out of her. And after I'd hurt her I felt tenderness for her. Then she'd ruin that by trying to drag some concession out of me. She was literal, always wanting me to be sorry in words. I don't know, Lakey; I've never loved a woman. I've loved some men—great directors, political leaders. As a kid, I loved my father. But living with a woman is like living with an echo, a loud echo in Kay's case. That voice of hers got on my nerves. Meaninglessly repeating what it'd heard. Generally from me, I admit." He laughed. "I felt like some lonely captain with a parrot. But at least she had a kind of integrity. Physically she was straight. She was a virgin when I took her and she never wanted anybody else. Or anybody else's ideas." His voice grew husky. "That meant something. A chronically unfaithful man has to have a faithful wife; otherwise it's no marriage. And Kay never found out I was unfaithful to her. I can boast of that, Lakey. She occasionally suspected, but I always lied to her. Faithfully." He laughed again. "But her jealousy wrecked everything in the end. It was unreasonable." "What do you mean?" "I never gave her anything to be jealous of. I protected her. Whenever I slept with a woman, I made sure Kay could never find out. That meant I could never break clean with them. No matter how fed up I was. Like that wench, Norine; you saw her in the church. A real blackmailer. She had the goods on me; in an idle moment I played the beast with two backs with her. For years I had to keep her hoping, so that she wouldn't be moved to tell Kay. That was weary work. For which Kay repaid me with hysterical accusations. Christ, I was only seeing her for Kay's sake." Lakey gave him a level look of scorn and disbelief. "Christ, don't be conventional," he said. "I don't expect that from you. You and I understand each other. I might have loved you, Lakey, if you weren't a lover of women. You might have saved me; I might have saved you. You can't love men; I can't love women. We might have loved each other—who knows? We're the two superior people in a cast of fools and supernumeraries. At last we meet to match swords. Let's duel in her grave, shall we?"

Just then out the window they saw the hearse go by. Harald tossed off a drink at the bar. They got into the car. This time Lakey drove. Listening to Harald's wild talk had disgusted her; she concluded that he was utterly specious. She was ashamed of the curiosity she had felt about him. To be curious about someone opened you to contamination from them. But she was still determined to play him a trick, to take a revenge for Kay, for women, and most of all for the impudence of his associating himself with her. She had no pity for Harald. Swinging the car into line behind the funeral procession, she waited for the question he would ask. "To be superior," he said, "of course, is not only a prerequisite for tragedy; it *is* tragedy. Hamlet's tragedy. We are forced to lower ourselves in our commerce with dolts, which sometimes gives us a feeling of hollowness, as if it were we who were hollow, not they. Could Hamlet love the daughter of Polonius? Could you or I 'love' Kay? Of course there was her body." He nodded at the hearse. "To think that I've known it!" He gave a quick side glance at Lakey. "Your 'love' for her, I assume, was purely platonic." Lakey looked straight ahead. "And yet," said Harald, "that's hard to believe, considering her mind. You must have wanted her, didn't you? Did she reject you? Is that why you 'dropped' her?" "I was tired of her," said Lakey truthfully. "I used to tire very easily of people." "You haven't answered my question," said Harald. "I don't propose to," said Lakey. "You're impertinent." "*Did you sleep with her?*" said Harald violently. Lakey smiled, like a lizard. "You ought to have asked Kay," she said. "She would have told you. She was such an honest girl at the end. Very American, Maria thought." "You're rotten," he said. "Completely rotten. Vicious. Did you corrupt the whole group? What a pretty picture!" Lakey was content; she had forced this dreadful man at last to be truthful; the fact that he revealed a hatred of "abnormality" was only to be expected. "What a filthy Lesbian trick," he said. "Not to fight openly but to poison the rapiers." Lakey did not point out to him that he had poisoned them himself. Her conscience was clear. She had made a little pact with herself to speak only the exact truth and insinuate nothing. Moreover, from her point of view, which he did not consider, poor normal Kay would not have sinned by being her prey instead of his. Far better for her, in fact, for

Lakey, she hoped, would have been kind to her. "You're a coward," Harald said, "to spread your slime on a dead girl. No wonder you hid yourself abroad all those years. You ought to have stayed in Europe, where the lights are going out. You belong there; you're dead. You've never used your mind except to acquire sterile knowledge. You're a museum parasite. You have no part of America! Let me out!" "You want to get out of the car?" said Lakey. "Yes," said Harald. "You bury her. You and the 'group.'" Lakey stopped the car. He got out. She drove on, following the cortege, watching him in the rear-view mirror as he crossed the road and stood, thumbing a ride, while cars full of returning mourners glided past him, back to New York.

BIRDS OF AMERICA

"... to attempt to embody the Idea in an example, as one might embody the wise man in a novel, is unseemly ... for our natural limitations, which persistently interfere with the perfection of the Idea, forbid all illusion about such an attempt. ..."

To Hannah

Winter Visitors

IN the Wild Life Sanctuary, the Great Horned Owl had died. The woman who showed the Palmer Homestead, on the edge of the woods, remembered the event distinctly: he had passed away the winter before last. Peter Levi, a college junior, swallowed this news with a long gulping movement of his prominent Adam's apple; grief and shock choked him. "You have to expect changes," he heard her say in a sharp tone, as he turned away from the doorstep, unable to speak. The old witch knew he was blaming her for the knockout punch she had just given him, standing calmly in her white shoes on the doormat that spelled out "WELCOME," her hands on her hips. Until she spoke, he had supposed that the owl was still somewhere about, cruising in the woods, a noiseless shadow, hunting his prey. The idea that he could have "passed away" like any senior citizen had not crossed Peter's mind. Revisiting the great bird in his tall outdoor cage littered with owl pellets of hair, claws, and bones was a treat Peter had been promising himself from the moment he heard from his mother that they were coming back to Rocky Port for the summer; it almost made up to him for the fact that she and his divorced father had agreed that he could not go to Mississippi with the Students for Civil Rights group. His mother, left to herself, might have let him go, but his father, who was more realistic, decided that Peter was too unsure of himself with people to take part in the program. Peter felt the *babbo*'s criticism was validated by his behavior this afternoon.

Instead of simply knocking and asking what had happened to the owl, as he had planned when reconnoitering the house from across the road, he had paid the price of admission (Adults, $.50) and let himself be conducted through the homestead before he dared pop the question and at the last had nearly chickened out, for fear the woman would think he had been *using* her for his own stealthy purposes, which were antagonistic to old paneling and original floorboards. Peter, a philosophy minor, was an adept of the Kantian ethic; he had pledged himself never to treat anyone as a means ("The Other

365

is always an End: thy Maxim," said a card he carried in his wallet, with his driving license, vaccination certificate, and memberships in SNCC, CORE, and SANE), and yet because of his shyness, which made his approaches circuitous, he repeatedly found himself doing exactly that. It was only a kind of wild loyalty to the owl that had disgorged the question from his lips just as she was about to shut the door. If he did not ask now, he prodded himself, he would *never* find out. It would be no use asking in Rocky Port, where no one knew anything, and he could not come back here to inquire, for that would put his present visit, already suspicious ("Funny a boy your age should be interested in antiques"), in a still more bizarre light. Yet if he did not find out, it would be as if he did not *care*—another horrible sin. When he finally did ask, addressing her on the stoop from an inferior position on the lawn, it was in a casual, preppy voice. "By the way, could you tell me what's become of the Great Horned Owl they used to have over there in the Wild Life Sanctuary?" How could he hope to fight for civil rights in Mississippi when he did not feel he had the *right* to ask a simple question in "neighborly" New England? The *babbo* knew best.

Except in the classroom and of people he already knew outside it, Peter loathed asking questions. When he was little, he could not bear to have his mother stop the car and call out to a native for directions. "They won't *know*, Mother! *Please* go on!" Prevention being the best cure (Peter was fond of adages), at a very early age he became a whiz at map-reading, sitting on her right on a cushion; Peter the Navigator, his stepfather in the back seat used to call him. He had never outgrown the feeling that a quest for information was a series of maneuvers in a game of espionage. In a library, rather than apply to the librarian, he would loiter about till he discovered where the card catalogues were kept and then trace the book he wanted to its lair through the Dewey Decimal system—Melvil Dewey, on his school lists, figured as a Great American, outranking Eli Whitney and the inventor of the McCormick Reaper. In a museum, he learned how to use the plan posted near the cloakroom while he was still in the first grade and would be tugging his mother toward "Armor" before she could question a guard. Similarly with a new A & P supermarket, whenever he and his mother moved; he raced about quivering like a magnetic needle till he found the bearings of Tide and tapioca and Grape-Nuts. He could always smoke out the toilets, hers and his, in filling stations and restaurants.

When he was young, the game was easier and more fun, because no one noticed him; a child, he observed, possessed a natural camouflage and could blend into the social landscape —a corollary of Peter Levi's Law that normal adults were not interested in children. But now that he was an adult himself, in all but the right to vote or marry without his parents' consent, he had become suddenly visible, and the surreptitious pursuit of information had become not only much more difficult but also associated with a kind of anguish, whose source was a notion of duty.

This afternoon, for example, when he found the cage in the woods empty and derelict and the wire netting torn, he at once knew that he would have to *do* something about it and he could not tell whether this was the cause of the anger he felt spurt out of him or whether that fury was a pure primary reaction to the fact that the marvelous bird was gone. He had slunk out of the sanctuary and sat down at the entrance under a tree labeled "Buttonwood," where he noted that a house across the road, set back on a hillock, had a sign on the lawn: "Open to the Public." Then he saw the manly course that was open to *him*: inquire of the owl's nearest neighbor. He was scanning the small-paned, brown-shingled redoubt when a curtain twitched in a downstairs window; a counter-spy was watching him. "Now or never," he said hoarsely, cawing like the Raven. The word *never* usually got results. Another magic formula, which he used to ward off discouragement after failure, was "Once more unto the breach, dear friends." He was inclined to think of himself as a collection of persons who had to be assembled for any initiative.

He ought to have thanked the woman for telling him but he could not. Still swallowing hard, he bolted across the stubbly lawn to where his motorbike was parked. The screen door slammed. In a minute it opened again. "Young man! You didn't sign the guest book!" Starting the motor, he pretended not to hear her. This was the only satisfaction he could chalk up for the afternoon. She had not got him to sign! He had spotted the book, open, the moment he entered the homestead and had cunningly diverted her attention with a purchase of postcards, which were now in his jacket pocket. The total expense, including admission to this waste of shame, was $.65. The owl's blood money. Peter, who was thrifty, decided to enter the sum as a reward he had offered for knowledge of the bird's whereabouts. "I am a propitiatory person," he chanted, to the tune of his sputtering motor, as he chugged home. He could already hear his mother's cheerful voice, probably emanating from the kitchen, wanting to know if he had seen his friend the owl. The word *friend* stabbed him in the guts; he pictured himself in Mississippi, hanging about a county courthouse or a garage or general store, trying to learn, without directly asking, what had happened to a missing Negro friend. . . . Moreover, he knew that his mother would feel almost as badly as he did when he had to tell her the owl had croaked.

Coming back to Rocky Port, to strengthen his roots before going abroad, was just one radical blow after another, as far as Peter was concerned. "Guess you'll notice changes," the village chorus greeted him. Or, in fugue, "You won't find many changes." Peter always answered "Yes" to the first of these challenges and "No" to the second, wondering why the local *amour-propre* should keep twanging so insistently on the theme of change. The changes Peter noticed were not those the storekeepers and the mailman seemed to be alluding to. He was not even aware, till duly admonished, that the Portuguese had built a new Catholic church, replacing the old one, which the Yankees now said had been "charming"; his mother had had to point out to him the new Sugar 'N' Spice Shop and the new Bait & Lure Shop and the new Corner Cupboard and the Lamplighter and the second art gallery and the hand-lettered signs advertising merchants and realtors that swung on curly iron brackets at the turn-off to the village, replacing the old "commercial" billboards. He did observe that most of the houses had sprouted little historical notices, bordered in yellow, also hand-lettered and with ampersands and wavy dashes, telling when they had been built and who had lived there or kept a school or a tavern or a marble yard there. The house his mother had rented, painted a dark colonial red, bore the date 1780, and Peleg Turnbull, a ship's chandler, had kept a shop in the front rooms. One of Peter's mother's first actions had been to find a hammer and remove the placard stating this. At once there came a written protest from the landlady, to which his mother answered that this epidemic of historical notices reminded her unpleasantly of the colored quarantine signs of her childhood: "Measles," "Mumps," "Scarlet Fever." Yellow, she thought, had been measles.

"Quarantined by history," Peter remarked in his slightly hoarse voice, backing up his mother's stand. But really he was attached to history, provided it stayed still. Now that the point had been called to his attention, he rather missed the old billboards as well as the neon storefront signs. Except in the field of civil rights, he was opposed to progress in any direction, including backwards, which was the direction Rocky Port seemed to be heading in, and wanted everything in the sensuous world to be the same as it had been when he was younger. To be precise, when he was fifteen, nearly four years ago.

That was when he and his mother had first come to Rocky Port, in the fall, out of season; she had rented a house near the water, in the "wrong" section of the village, where the Portuguese lived. From his bedroom window, he used to watch three cormorants that stood on pilings in the cove and he had been counting on seeing them again on his return. He had three sentimental journeys planned: the first to the cormorants, the second to the Great Horned Owl, and the third to a hidden waterfall up in the back country. To date, he had had two disappointments. Number One, the cormorants were gone. The first evening, while his mother was wrenching off the placard, he had hurried down on foot, past the laundress' house, to where they used to live. A single boring gull sat on one of the piles; that was all. He kept coming back to look at different times of day, pretending to be taking a stroll. But it was no use. They were gone. And nobody but he and his mother seemed to be able to recall them.

"You mean gulls, don't you, Peter?" his mother's new friends said. "No," he said. "Not gulls. I *know* gulls." "Can he mean the Arctic Tern?" "He means cormorants," said his mother. Then at a cocktail party, given at a house on the harbor, he met a retired admiral whose small hawk face he remembered. "The cormorants? Sure, son," said the admiral, who came from the South. "They're nesting now in Labrador. They'll be back in the fall." "I won't be here then," said Peter. In the fall, he would be in Paris, taking his junior year at the Sorbonne. For the first time, he felt sad at the thought. He could not understand, either, how he could have forgotten that cormorants migrated, when he had spent hours in the reference section of the village Free Library, identifying the three black birds, uncertain to start with whether they were the Double Crested Cormorant or the Common Cormorant, which was a lot rarer. He was worried that he might be losing his memory. To cheer himself up, he decided that some fall he could come back here and find them again, when he was through with college and the Army. Maybe on his honeymoon. "The cormorant's life span?" said the admiral. "Hell, son, maybe ten, fifteen years. Those three damn birds have been here winters as long as I have. Now let's see. I retired in '58. . . ." It was clear to Peter that the admiral was just gassing to cover up his ignorance; like most of the people here, he was not interested in getting to the bottom of anything. He began to talk vociferously, waving his short pipe, about the ages attained by ships' parrots, in an argumentative tone that Peter was coming to recognize as the cry of the Rocky Port species, mature, male, which always sounded as if its assertions were about to be contested by another species—foreign or black. Peter felt he would not welcome a heart-to-heart with the admiral on the topic of integration. Yet this chat, he feared, was on his summer calendar, as predictable as Fourth of July fireworks or the appearance of a spring robin on a Rocky Port lawn. Despite that, he rather liked the old man, first for remembering the cormorants, second for remembering him, and third for surviving unchanged from that other year.

That year had a special value for Peter because that year he got the wish he used to make on every baby tooth he put under his pillow to dream on: to live in a little house in New England with his mother by themselves. He had never liked California; he missed the winter. He hated his stepfather's garden in Berkeley, with roses and daffodils and tulips and irises all blooming at the same time, so that there was never anything to look forward to. The only birds that appealed to him there were the hummingbirds. He hated the desert; he

was convinced that it was the product of some nuclear ca-
tastrophe that had befallen an earlier race of scientists. He declined to consider Death Valley a part of Nature. Peter was
strongly in favor of Nature, and he was against modern physics
for interfering with Her.

His stepfather was in the physics department of the University of California, a very valuable man; he had helped bring
heavy water to England from the Continent during the war.
Peter had always imagined Hans carrying it in his suitcase
through customs. He was a refugee, like Peter's own father.
The difference was that Peter's father, who taught history at
Wellesley, had left Italy for political reasons and not just because he was Jewish, while Hans might still be pottering in his
laboratory in the Fatherland if he had not been born a Jew.
Peter's mother was not Jewish. He had heard his aunt say that
her sister had a "thing" about Jews, which he hoped included
him. Peter slightly preferred his own father to Hans, but he
tried to think that this preference was impersonal, like preferring the seashore to the mountains or breakfast to lunch: he
liked the East better than the West, Italy better than Germany,
history better than physics. Personally, Hans was genial, and
the *babbo* was bad-tempered. Peter always felt wicked when he
would place his baby tooth under his pillow, to dream of running away with the fair Rosamund (called "Rosie" by Hans),
and then wake up the next morning to find a silver dollar that
he knew Hans had put there. Silver dollars were one item Peter
approved of in the West. In the end, when the wish came true,
he was quite sorry for Hans, who had agreed to a "trial separation." Coming east on the train, four years ago, come September, the gladder Peter was at the thought that he and his
mother were alone at last, the sorrier he felt for Hans, who had
waved them off at the station.

Four years ago, he was deeply in love with his mother. He was
a tall boy with a long nose and gaunt features—the picture of
his father at the same age, except for his eyes, which were gray,
like hers. He often stared at himself in the mirror, but for the
opposite reason from Narcissus; it was *her* eyes he gazed into,
captive in his Jewish face. He had known for a long time about
the Oedipus complex; his stepfather used to tease him with

"And how is young Oedipus?" But he did not think that, on balance, he would like to sleep with his mother, only to be with her where there were no other people. He was sure that despite what she said she would marry again, and he would have a new set of stepbrothers and stepsisters, probably. All he asked of the gods was a year with her. Already he realized that this year, when he was fifteen, would be the last year of his childhood; at sixteen, he would be a youth and lose his innocence. He had seen it happen to his stepbrothers.

Peter wanted to grow up; he did not plan to be a Peter Pan. But he felt that a halcyon interval was owing him, particularly because of the divorce, which required him to spend the summer with his father, so that only the school year, the darker part, belonged to her. Because of school and "activities," he hardly ever had her to himself, unless he was sick, and unfortunately he got sick mostly in the summer. When he was little, she used to read to him at bedtime, but now he was too old for that. Holidays—Christmas and Easter—were allocated by Hans to family trips. On weekends, Hans was always home. That was the way the ball bounced. The fact that his mother did not love Hans as much as she did Peter made her always anxious to "include" him in all their projects. Knowing his mother, Peter often felt that it would have been a lucky break for him if he had been her stepchild, instead of the wormy apple of her eye.

Yet she must have had it in mind all along to "make it up" to Peter when she was free. Then it would be his turn. Though she was reticent about personal things, Peter guessed there was some sort of promise between them, which involved, on his side, being patient. It did not surprise him when she told him that she and Hans were parting. Each of her marriages, Peter pointed out to her, had lasted seven years—a Biblical span. She had never counted, but he had. Nor had there ever been any question for Peter but that she was living in exile out there in corny California; when the two of them finally cut and ran, it would be back to New England, their real home. The only problem was where.

She put that up to Peter; he could choose, providing it was not an island. He picked Rocky Port. It looked lonely—a thin finger of land pointing out to sea, far from a main highway.

She laughed when he showed it to her on the map. "Define a peninsula, Peter." A body of land almost entirely surrounded by water, from the Latin *paene insula*, an almost-island. Peter laughed too. Then she protested that they did not know a living soul in the vicinity; nobody she knew had ever been to Rocky Port. But that was how he had plotted it, dismissing Cape Cod, Vermont, commuters' Connecticut, and hesitating over the Massachusetts North Shore, which attracted him but where they would be likely to get visits from the *babbo*. Peter had calculated the driving time from Wellesley to Ipswich; he was not taking any chances on a renewed romance between his parents.

It worried her that he might not find friends of his own age in such an isolated (there was that word again) village. But this was the last year, Peter explained, that he would *want* to be solitary; next year, he would be interested in girls and parties. Up to now he had always lived in an academic community, even in the summer, because the *babbo* invariably vacationed with a lot of other professors. It was the last year too, he argued, that he would be allowed to be by himself with birds and animals unless he planned to be an ornithologist or a zoologist. A young boy was expected to like animals, but he would have to be forty before he could watch them again without somebody watching *him*. Hearing the desperation in his voice, his mother capitulated. Besides, she had told him he could choose.

In her place, Peter would just have gone there, without further research, but his mother was trying to reform from being a "hopeless romantic," in the words of her sister. She got the state guidebook out of the college library and looked up Rocky Port; she found the name of a real-estate agent in a directory of realtors and sent off a letter with their specifications, asking about schools and transportation. She signed it "Rosamund Brown," her own name, which Peter would not have done, even though he was glad that she was giving up Hans's moniker. He would have liked them to live under an alias.

The agent, a Mrs. Curtis, wrote back immediately with listings and asked if she were *the* Rosamund Brown; if so, she had some of her records. Peter's mother was a professional musician. "But my records are all out of print!" she cried. She was always surprised and touched when someone remembered her, because she had not played a recital or in a real concert for years—only for fun with a University chamber group. She had given up the concert stage when Hans was summoned to Berkeley; California was too far from the center. Peter could tell that she took the realtor's letter as a wonderful, strange omen; she was being recalled to life. For his part, Peter took the omen as bad. If his mother had a fan in Rocky Port, it was no longer virgin territory. The place was probably full of artists and writers and music-lovers generally; he ought to have been put on guard by the elm-shaded streets and the Greek Revival doorways in the photographs in the state guidebook. He was relieved to learn from the agent's second letter that the artistic colony closed their houses early in September.

"I'm afraid you'll find it rather bleak," Mrs. Curtis wrote apologetically. "After Labor Day, we go 'back to Nature.' The little house you're interested in is in rather a 'slummy' section, but it has a lovely view and you'll be quite by yourselves. There's no television set, I'm afraid, for your son, but there's a good working piano. I realize that isn't the same as a harpsichord, but you can probably 'make do.' The kitchen is fairly well equipped; I imagine that, like so many of our musical artists, you like to cook wonderful things. Your son can walk to the old Rocky Port high school on the harbor; the grand new consolidated high school on Route 1 isn't finished yet—politics. Do I understand you won't have a car? Would you like me to have the piano tuned?"

His mother, as always, was her own piano-tuner, and they did not have a car, that fall. Both cars had stayed with Hans, which Peter, on the whole, was glad of, for it limited his mother's movements. When his bicycle finally came by Railway Express, with the harpsichord and the clavichord, he mostly left it in the cellar, because she did not have one. Instead, they took walks together, which they had never done in Berkeley. Every clear evening they walked down to the point, past the abandoned lighthouse and the boarded-up whaling museum, to see the sun set; this was their daily contact with the natives, who came in their Fords and Chevrolets for the same reason. It was a local ritual, like the lowering of a flag. They watched the fishing boats come home; the pink sky was full of gulls. Then they would wend their own way back to supper, past the plastics factory and the Doric bank and the Civil War cannon in the square. At home, the cormorants would be standing on their piles, three black silhouettes in the paling light; they never came to the lighthouse point. They never mixed with the other birds—a fact that struck Peter from the beginning.

He decided they were sacred birds, an unholy trinity. Standing on their dark piles in the water, they had an evil, old, Egyptian look; gorged, their black wings spread to dry in the sun, they resembled hieroglyphs or emblems on an escutcheon. In their neck was a pouch that bulged when they had been fishing. They did not swim or float on the surface like other birds but darted through the water in a sinuous, snakelike way. He had never seen them squat or sit. They were always erect, spread-eagled; not sedentary—vigilant. They seldom moved, though they occasionally gave a flap of their wings or a turn of their long serpentine necks. They usually stood facing away, surveying the cove like sentries, or, in profile, commanding the open sea, but sometimes he would come back from some private sleeveless errand to find that they had wheeled about and were facing him in glistening formation. Unlike the shrieking terns and squawking gulls, they did not utter a sound. This stillness and fixity were what made them seem so horribly ancient, Peter thought, as though they preceded time. That and their snaky appearance, which took you back to the age of flying reptiles. Moreover, their soundless habit gave their slightest movement the quality of a pantomime; from his bedroom window, he could pretend he was watching a drama of hieratic gesture.

He did not know why he connected the cormorants with his mother and their flight back to Nature's bosom, but if he could have had a seal ring made (he was still a sealing-wax addict) in memory of that year, it would have been incised with three cormorants—his sign. His mother said they made her think of the three black-cloaked masked Revenges at the end of the first act of *Don Giovanni*: Donna Elvira, Donna Anna, and Don Ottavio. Peter agreed. There was that about them too. Three pouchy pursuers, storers-up of grudges. He wondered about their sex. Were they father, mother, and son? Or three brothers? The last of their race. In one bird book he had read that only a few hundred Common European Cormorants were left in North America. There must be even fewer now than when the book was written. Unless, of course, they were protected.

The Great Horned Owl seemed very old too, nearly extinct, with its immobile dilated pupils and its long nightgown of ruffly feathers. He was exceptionally pale for his species, cruel-looking, and very big. Peter's mother almost thought he must be an Arctic Horned Owl because he was so pale. They had come upon him like an apparition in the chill solitary woods, having discovered the Wild Life Sanctuary in the course of a Saturday walk. The Boy Scouts, they decided, must have marked the trails with visual aids pointing to squirrels, autumn foliage, and owls—ordinary screech owls, not this great tufted tigerish creature. And someone, a very brave Scout, must have captured him and put him in the home-made cage nailed to a tree and labeled "*Bubo Virginianus*—Great Horned Owl"; someone must feed him field mice and whatever other sacrifices he regurgitated in the form of those hairy pellets. But they never met a Scout or any other human being in the sanctuary.

Besides the trails through the woods and the captive owl in his tree-house, it had a log cabin with educational exhibits of pyrites and quartzes and shells and stuffed birds and stuffed animals and butterflies and amusing insects like the Walking Stick. There were wild-flower and fern charts on the walls. It was the kind of place where you would expect to find a custodian to reprimand you or get you to join the Audubon Society, but it was empty except for the taxidermic presences in the glass cabinets. To come on it, swept and garnished, in the woods was spooky, like the story his mother used to tell of the ship *Marie Celeste*, which was found afloat in mid-ocean in apple-pie order, with mess tables set and ovens still warm and not a hand aboard.

Nobody Peter and his mother met in Rocky Port had ever visited the sanctuary or could say who ran it; they thought Peter and his mother were talking about the *bird* sanctuary, which was something different, a desolate state preserve of dunes and marshes and jackpine, where couples went to make love. Mrs. Curtis took Peter and his mother there in her car one Sunday morning, and they did not see a single worthwhile bird—just beer cans and the remains of campfires. It seemed funny to Peter that there should be *two* sanctuaries in the locality and each, as it were, unaware of the other, like two people that had not been introduced. Mrs. Curtis could not explain it. If Peter wanted to find out more about *his* sanctuary, she advised him to sign up at school with a Nature Study group. The manual training teacher was the one to see; he would know all about it. Peter refused the suggestion. He did not want his relationship with Nature organized and managed for him.

Indeed, he liked the mystery surrounding *his* sanctuary and the fact that he and his mother were its only (visible) initiates. Exploring, they found a dark stream, stepping-stones, mallards, a pond. By Christmas, his mother said, the pond would surely freeze over; she promised to buy skates at the hardware store and teach him to skate. They could use the log cabin as a shelter to thaw out their feet. Already a black frost had come; the autumn leaves had fallen, and you could identify the deciduous trees only by their shapes. With the end of daylight-saving time, the afternoons were shortened; when they left the sanctuary, it was almost night. In the dusk sometimes, from the road home, they would hear a ululating cry, and Peter would hoot back. He knew from his reading that Great Horned Owls bred in snow and ice; it worried him that the lonely hooter did not have a mate. The idea occurred to him to let him out of his cage, which would not be hard; his mother, who was fearless of authority, would help him. Selfishly, too, Peter longed to see him fly, just once—the drifting flight the books described, like a big moth coasting overhead.

But then Peter would be *responsible* for the sequel. What if the owl, weakened by captivity, was unequal to liberation? It might starve, left on its own in the woods. Alternatively, the predatory killer, freed, might make a holocaust in the wild-life refuge. Peter thought with anguish of the pine grosbeaks he and his mother had seen, almost tame, in a wild apple tree on Columbus Day; he imagined their rosy bodies all red with gore. A sanctuary was meant to be *safe*. He recognized with a sad Hello the classic conservative arguments as they passed through his head—arguments for not meddling with the *status quo.* A silent shadow, like the shadow of the hunting bird, fell across his happiness. He wished he had never thought of releasing the owl in the first place. Now that the notion of change had glided into his mind, he could not just accept the bird's being there as natural. It had to be *justified*. Perhaps he was simply getting bored, but it no longer gave him much pleasure to engage in a staring match with the barred and striped prisoner—a game that, in any case, his mother deplored. When Armistice Day came, he rejected her offer to bring a picnic to the sanctuary. "Let's take in a movie," he said in a sullen voice.

His mother was bewildered; he often hurt her by his unwillingness to explain himself. It would have killed him to tell her that he was depressed by his lack of guts about the owl; she did not even know that he had been weighing the question of setting him free. He loved her too much to confide his weaknesses to her. He preferred discussing hers, which were obvious.

For example, she had gone and bought him a large illustrated *Birds of America*, to replace (in *her* mind) the little blue Peterson guide that had been left behind in Berkeley. Peter was quite happy using the reference section of the Free Library, even if they did not let you take the books home—it was good training for his memory. He enjoyed being resourceful, living off the land, like a hunter, not always having to buy things in a store. Moreover, he considered the gift a placebo. He disapproved of her habit of leaving their possessions behind whenever she got a divorce; she had done the same thing with his father.

He particularly objected to her leaving the phonograph with Hans, who never remembered to change the needle. He and his mother had long arguments about this on the train coming east; he loved arguing with his mother, who was quite intelligent, he used to tell her, for a faculty wife. A house that had a piano would surely have a phonograph, she said, and when she found she was wrong (the real-estate agent, *Peter* said, would have *mentioned* a phonograph), she went and bought a cheap stereo portable. "Did it *have* to be stereo?" Peter groaned, homesick for their old mono set. He disliked being offered substitutes. At least she had brought along some of their records—those she called "Peter's," like the Haydn Hunting

Horn, which bayed, *he* thought (his mother said no), like a lost hound in the woods, and Handel's Water Music, which bubbled and gurgled. But Peter had not been able to reason her into taking any of the art books or the eleventh edition of the Britannica. "Hans doesn't want it, Mother. He says it's completely out of date in all the sciences." "We'll advertise for another," she said, soothing. "If we take it, he'll miss it."

Peter did not applaud his mother's "noble" side. Naturally, he would have hated it if she had stuck Hans for alimony, but it would have been a *kindness* to Hans, in Peter's opinion, to take the espresso pots and half the sheets and towels, to speak only of the baser items, instead of borrowing the sheets they were now sleeping on from Mrs. Curtis and drinking awful coffee from a dripolator. The least his mother could do for Hans, if she was going to leave him, was to give him some petty cause for grievance, something that would lay her open to criticism in the Faculty Club. Instead, she had been "perfect," taking only her mother's silver and Peter's baby cup and fork and spoon and every Christmas present Hans had ever given them, naturally—so as not to hurt his feelings—no matter how useless or hard to pack. The result was that it was Hans who was open to criticism, sitting out there with two cars in his garage and cupboards full of china and linen and glasses and kitchen stuff, while she, innocent and good, was "roughing it" with chipped plates and corny glasses with mottoes and taking the bus to the nearest town twice a week to buy groceries in the supermarket. His mother, he decided, was being so good she was bad, and this worried him.

She must want Hans to feel that an *angel* had left him, which meant, according to Peter, that she wanted Hans to still be in love with her. If she was really eager for Hans to "get over" her, she should show him her worst side. Like letting Peter pinch the old German binoculars that were hanging in the hall closet in Berkeley and that Hans never used because he could not bother to take off his regular glasses.

She claimed that you had to pay for freedom by being ready to give up everything. It was ignoble, she said, to latch onto property, even if it was partly yours. OK, but every week she bought something that was a duplicate or reasonable facsimile of some article she had left in Berkeley. Like the stereo set or cake racks or an iron griddle for flapjacks. This jarred on Peter morally, as well as on his bump of thrift. To buy the same things over again, even if you needed them, was not his definition of renunciation.

This being alone with her with the leisure to study her faults was a great pleasure to him. Peter loved America, and his mother's shortcomings were exactly those of the country; they could be summed up under the heading of extravagance. That formulation he owed to the *babbo*, who often held forth on the theme to other academics. Puritanism, the *babbo* said, was an extravagance, like Prohibition; Americans were logicians with no idea of limit. Peter's father loved America too—which tended to puzzle Americans, Peter noticed. He always liked to hear the story of his mother's first meeting with his father, at a party in New York toward the end of the war—she was studying musicology then at the Mannes School and working with Landowska. After the party, they walked down Park Avenue, and she said to him "But what do you like about America?" since most refugees she had met were musicians who were pining for the cafés they had come from. Peter's father thought. "I like the American birds." She said this was what had made her fall in love with that dark, scowling man. "It was such a funny thing to hear. Instead of 'I like your tall buildings' or 'I like your long-legged women' or 'Your democratic institutions.'" "But what did he mean?" Peter always asked. His mother was not certain. "Maybe he just meant they were different from the ones he knew."

Now that he was a full-grown male, Peter thought he understood the *babbo*'s gambit. With her light-brown hair and gray eyes and rosy skin, his mother was like an American bird—the rose-breasted grosbeak, for instance, modest and vivid. His father had been paying her a compliment. And probably, like a lot of Europeans, he was fed up with what he knew and wanted to meet another human species, which at least would be *different*, like the birds of the New World. "*Mi piaceva il suo candore*," he said to Peter one summer, as if grudgingly, when Peter was drawing him out. Peter had taken this to mean that the young Rosamund, like the Father of her Country, could not tell a lie. Now that he knew Italian better (he was taking Italian Lit. at college as part of his Romance languages major), he knew that *candore* was the usual word for naïveté.

The *babbo* used to say that Peter's mother was the first girl he met who was what he called a "real American," meaning a descendant of the old Puritan colonists. To an historian, Peter guessed, that might have been pretty exciting, and the more so because her forebears out in Ohio had taken part in the opening of the West. A Boston deb could have bored the *babbo*, but Peter's mother came from pioneer stock that had settled in Marietta from New England after the Revolutionary War. The fact that she had been very pretty was a point his father did not mention. Nor did he recall having said anything about birds the night he met her. According to him, he had told her that he liked her name: Rosamund Brown. Peter liked her name too; it reminded him of a Thomas Hardy poem she had once set to music and which had a refrain: "Dear Lizbie Browne." When he was small, he could not connect "Brown" with himself; he felt much more like his father than like her, to the extent of always thinking of her as a Gentile. That was why her faults pleased him, like an unfamiliar kind of marking or speckling.

At his present age, he looked on the fair Rosamund with cooler eyes. He loved her still, but he was no longer in love with her. He had become cautious about her, mistrusting her consistent sweetness and unruffled temper. She was too good to be true, he discovered. Like all older people, she betrayed. Besides, her faults were no longer unfamiliar. He recognized them in himself. Her zeal to please had set him a bad example; it had made him placatory. Her scruples in him had become irresolution and an endless picking at himself that was like masturbation—a habit he had not completely outgrown and which seemed to him ignominious, even though both she and the *babbo* had said it was natural in puberty; on that score, he felt, they had given him a wrong steer. Moreover, her good qualities (she was generous, to a fault, he acknowledged dryly) did not inspire imitation. Rather the contrary. Everyone, he had observed, around the fair Rosamund turned into an ogre to protect her from herself. With his nineteenth birthday coming up, he admired his father for having the strength of his defects (something Peter would never achieve, thanks to her training, alas) and viewed his mother with a kind of ironic sympathy. But when he was fifteen, he was living in a childish world of magic, where his mother was the stranger and his captive.

While he was in school, she practiced or analyzed pieces on the clavichord, working out the fingering; he gathered this was quite hard. She was preparing an all-Elizabethan lecture-recital to go on a tour of colleges. That was how she had got started, when she had left Landowska's master classes. Her field used to be early English music; she talked about it to college audiences and illustrated her talk on the harpsichord. Later on, she gave recitals and played with a group. His aunt told him confidentially that his mother was a better musical scholar than she was a performer. Remembering this, Peter wondered whether she would ever make the grade again. He hoped she knew that that music of olden time was not so much of a novelty as it had been in her day, right after the war. He did not let himself dwell on what would happen to *him* if her tour finally materialized. She could not play at colleges, obviously, during summer vacations, which was the time he would normally be with his father. And if she went away in the school year, who would stay with him? He was too old for a sitter and too young— public opinion would say—to stay by himself; he would not want her to get into trouble with the SPCC. Hans would have come in handy, but now there was no Hans.

When he was little, it seemed, before they were divorced from his father, he used to start crying at the sight of the truckers who were coming to take the harpsichord. He had learned that this meant that his mother was going away again. The *babbo* and his nurse could never persuade him that she would come back. Once when he was holding onto the harpsichord's legs, to keep the movers from taking it (he must have been about four, he guessed), his father had picked him up and spanked him hard; he remembered his mother crying, which made his father even angrier. "*Ricatto!*" he shouted. "Blackmail! The boy must get used to it. He should be glad you are an artist!" Peter's nurse would not tell him what that funny word, *blackmail*, meant; later he heard it quite often and always applied to himself.

When he was little, Peter hated his father for (as he thought) making his mother go away when she did not want to. He did not believe her when she explained that she *liked* having people listen to her music. If she liked it, why did she and his father argue about it? Why did his father yell at him if he disturbed her when she was practicing, while *she* was always glad to stop and get him a cookie or an animal cracker? Why had he overheard her, pleading, in his father's study, "Have pity, Paolo" (the fair Rosamund talked like one of her madrigals when emotional). "Let me cancel the concert. This is killing me"? He had gone and got his toy gun and pointed it at his father: "You let my mother stay home!" His mother always said, now, that she was grateful to his father for having made her go on with her concert appearances. He ought to be grateful himself, he guessed, for not having been permitted to tyrannize over his mother. But *would* it have been so bad for him if she had laid off the concert stage for a couple of years, till he was old enough to understand what it was all about?

That fall in Rocky Port, he was reconciled, he thought, to his mother's career for practical reasons. They were living off capital, which he gathered was some sort of sin. If she did not take alimony, she would have to earn some dough. But the day was still far off, he assured himself; it would be months before her program was ready, at the rate she was going. He had nothing to worry about so long as she was still tinkering with the clavichord. When she started working on the harpsichord, that would mean she was really rehearsing. He knew this because she had told him so. He did not understand much about her instruments, except that you could not do *mains croisées* on the clavichord because it had only one keyboard. But the point of *mains croisées* escaped him. Nor did he follow her when she talked about things like figured basses and *continuo*. He did not regard her seriously as a musician, because she was his mother; besides, the only music he liked much, in his heart, was opera.

He did not mind an instrument like the hunting horn or the trumpet in *The Messiah* ("the trumpet shall sound . . . and we shall be changed"; his mother said that was a musical pun) that made him think of a solo voice. If he had been able to play himself, he would have been a trumpeter. But that would have to wait for his next incarnation. On his eighth birthday, he had learned the awful truth. Kindly Hans gave him a child's violin; Peter found it at his place at breakfast, and he saw from his mother's stricken face that it was a surprise to her too. "You think he is too young, Rosie?" Hans queried anxiously. The next thing Peter remembered, he was standing by the harpsichord, singing a scale as she struck the notes for him. "*Ach!*" said Hans. Hans had not noticed, till then, that Peter was tone-deaf. Or at least, as his mother put it, he did not hear intervals well enough to play the violin. He could be trained, she said, to read music and appreciate it; no one was *really* tone-deaf. He could learn to play the piano, which did not require an ear and would teach him something about music. "You can have piano lessons for your birthday instead," she said gaily to Peter. But Peter did not want that. He wanted the little violin, which Hans, an Indian giver, took back to the store. In revenge, he would not listen to the childish music like *Peter and the Wolf* that Hans brought home to instruct him. When he got interested in opera, he always started the record *after* the overture. He refused to be broadened by going to concerts with Hans and his mother, and though he had recently admitted the horn family to his friendship, he drew the line there. He would not let his mother buy him more Haydn or Handel; he suspected her of using the Hunting Horn and the Water Music as the opening wedge.

Yet sometimes in Rocky Port, when he came home from school, he would hear the clavichord tinkling in her bedroom upstairs and he would shut the front door quietly and listen, imagining that this was a fairy-tale house with the miller's daughter upstairs spinning a room full of gold for the king, her husband. For the first time, he "got" this courtly music. Before disturbing her, he would fetch some wood and build a fire in the fireplace, making a fanciful design of logs and kindling. He would have liked to get ice and fix her a drink, but she disapproved of children's serving as bartenders to their parents—a custom Hans, who liked his *schnapps*, had tried to introduce on the grounds that it was American.

Of course, it was American, but his mother would not admit it. She had her own notions of what was American, going back to her own childhood. Reading aloud to children in the evening, Fourth of July sparklers and fireworks, Easter-egg hunts, Christmas stockings with an orange in the toe, popcorn and cranberry chains on the Christmas tree, ducking for apples at Halloween, shadow pictures on the walls, lemonade, fresh cider, picnics, treasure hunts, anagrams, checkers, eggs goldenrod, home-made cakes, muffins, popovers, and corn breads, fortune-telling, sweet peas, butterfly nets, narcissus bulbs in pebbles, Trillium, Spring Beauty, arbutus, lady's-slippers, cat's cradles, swings, bicycles, wooden ice-cream freezers, fishing with angleworms, rowing, ice-skating, blueberrying, hymn-singing. Her family had been mostly doctors, judges, and ministers; when she was in grade school, she had learned to play the organ in her grandfather's church. Her first professional performance was substituting for the organist when he was drunk one Whitsunday morning—when he was drunk he always wanted to play "We Three Kings of Orient Are."

She was strong for the traditional and whenever she made an innovation, it became part of the tradition, something that had "always" been. Like chess, which Hans had introduced, or Peter's Monopoly game. On the other hand, certain items of Americana were never admitted to the fair Rosamund's canon. They included ketchup, trick-or-treat, square-dancing, sailing, golf, skiing, bridge, and virtually anything in a can. Also Christmas-tree lights and those colored Christmas-tree balls you bought in boxes. Peter had got her to confess that out in Marietta in her childhood they had had balls and lights on the tree as well as ketchup in the pantry. But he did this only to try her. He too preferred the tree as it had "always" been, with everything on it edible except the paper chains he cut and pasted and the star he used to make, with her help. He was averse himself to sailing and skiing or at least to the smooth types who went in for them, and she had persuaded him, empirically, that home-made chili sauce was better than the bottled ketchup his peer-groupers poured on their hamburgers, just as she had converted him to the doctrine of the home-made cake by teaching him and his school friends in Berkeley to bake in her kitchen on Saturdays—first a cake made with a mix and then a real one; their mothers, he estimated, had not necessarily thanked her for this proselytizing work. As for being a bartender, back in Berkeley he had accepted the deprivation, agreeing that it was nauseating to see little kids shaking up Martinis for a smirking crowd.

In Rocky Port, with just the two of them, it would have been different, he thought. But he guessed she was bothered by the old Oedipus business there. Somebody had warned her or she had warned herself that she should never let Peter take over the offices of a husband, which meant that he could not make drinks or put out the lights for the night or unlock the house door when they came home from a trip together. He was allowed to set the table and sometimes to help her with the dishes; on Sundays he could make scrambled eggs for their breakfast, because he had always done that; on Saturdays occasionally he could bake a cake—ditto. But if she had a drink before dinner, she did not even like it if he joined her with a Coke. Too connubial, he supposed. After he had done this a few times, she discontinued her nightly Scotch before the fire. That was her way (a sacrifice) of edging out of an awkward situation. Her plight called forth Peter's chivalry. He rescued her, perceiving that she as an adult needed a pleasure that he did not share. Shortly before dinner, after their sunset tryst, he would take a Coke from the icebox and repair with it upstairs to his room. "Why don't you have a drink, Mother, while I hit the homework?" Thus she knew the coast was clear. He would stay at his desk till he heard her rattling things in the kitchen, which told him that she had had her grog. Then he would come down and lounge in the kitchen doorway, watching her with critical comments while she cooked. It would never occur to her to do as most kids' mothers did and bring her drink to the kitchen.

Her problems in keeping him at a filial distance amused him and made his heart swell with tenderness—the same tenderness he felt for those laborious creatures, birds and animals. Watching her fend him off, he was also reassured for the future. She would never "encourage" a suitor, if Peter's experience was an index. And yet how had it happened that Hans had subtracted her from his father?

He could always get her goat by calling her by her first name. "Stop that, Peter! Stop it, this minute!" "Why should I, Rosamund?" he would say, in a clowning voice. "Rosamund, give me a reason." It was as if she were being tickled; she laughed but really she was scared. His mother, he decided, was dressed in a little brief of authority that she was afraid would slip off. She was firm about being treated as his parent and no nonsense. After supper came the Children's Hour; they would sit by the fire and talk. Sometimes she mended. Or they would both read. If the night was clear and still, they would go out and look at the stars. He was teaching her to find the simpler constellations from his old star book—a present from Hans. If it was not a school night, he could vanquish her at chess. At nine-thirty, on school nights, he would start upstairs for his bath. Once he was in bed, she would come and open his window and kiss him good night on the top of his head. After he was asleep, she set the table, he supposed, for breakfast, measured and sifted flour for flapjacks or muffins or whatever, put out the garbage, lowered the thermostat, went around turning out lights, drew a bath. This night self of hers was unknown to him; he never heard her go to bed. In the morning, the first thing he knew, she was shutting his window and opening the curtains to let in the light. Usually, she was dressed and she was always in a good humor, which he was not.

That year, he did not masturbate. He had kicked the habit, temporarily, because of her. It did not seem to him democratic to give himself that solitary bang when she was all alone in her bedroom or downstairs in the kitchen getting things ready for his breakfast. It had been all right, from that point of view, when Hans was around, but it was not all right now. Peter, his family said, was a born Solon on points of equity; the *babbo* never tired of telling a story Peter hoped was apocryphal: about how he had worried about chattel slavery when he was in the first grade and had announced to his teacher that it was "a good idea, but quite mean." His fair-mindedness made his mother hope that he would be a judge, like her father. His birthday was under the sign of Libra, and family legend had it that as a child his passion was weighing things on a toy scales, which he toddled around with like an attribute of Justice. "Peter ponders," said his mother. One notion he had pondered, while still quite young, was the accepted idea that grownups should work while children played. "Your work is to grow, my boy," Hans used to tell him. Peter could never buy that. It was not a just division of labor. Still less could he "play with himself" when his mother, thanks to him, was not even going to parties. After a while he was not in the mood.

They were living a life of virtue, or so he believed. That year he equated virtue with happiness, still ignorant of Kant's teaching. From a Kantian angle, he now recognized, nearly everything he did or refrained from doing in Rocky Port was outside the moral law, strictly speaking, since he was obeying not Duty but Inclination. Being helpful, chaste, minding his mother was a pleasure in those circumstances, where the well-tuned clavichord gave the pitch; he no longer sighed over his homework, though he missed Hans's help with his algebra. Nor did he groan at getting up in the morning, for his rising was a daily ceremony like the cormorants' toilet, which he could watch from his window while he pulled on his clothes. From his present vantage point, he could confirm that he had been living not just in a fairy tale but in a paradise, in which his love for his mother coincided with his love of Nature and of the austere New England landscape. That was why he had that sense of homecoming or repatriation. And one of the features of the Earthly Paradise (which made it preferable, in Peter's view, to Heaven) was the absence of others.

Winter was in the air, described by the postman as a cold snap; Peter's favorite stars, the Pleiades, were so clear in the frosty night that he had seen the Lost Pleiad. Yet except for the tradespeople, the postman, and sundry ministers of grace like Mrs. Curtis, Peter and his mother still knew no one in Rocky Port. Peter was on terms with his classmates, but he had deliberately made no friends. He did not want to invite anyone home, as though it would break a spell.

He liked to fancy that he and his mother were pioneers, exploring a wilderness unknown to the aborigines. This notion gained support not only from their lack of friends and of a car and a television set but also from the ghostly music of the clavichord, from an American history course he was taking, and from the meals his mother dished up. Having left her cookbooks behind (naturally), she had bought an old Fannie Farmer in the village junkshop. This gave her the idea of cooking American, at which Peter to start with had raised an eyebrow. American in his experience meant steaks spread with charcoal seasoning, frozen corn-on-the-cob, shredded lettuce with "Russian" dressing, "Hawaiian" ham and sticky pineapple. In Berkeley, he had been proud of his mother's disdain for the prevailing cookery. For a while there, she had had a game of cooking the foods of the countries Peter was studying in geography or whose stamps he was collecting in his album—his favorites had been black beans (Brazilian) with orange slices and Persian chicken with rose water. For Hans she had made Tafelspitz and German and Austrian desserts and for Peter her old Italian stand-bys, such as green *lasagne al forno*—he used to help her roll out the sheets of *pasta* for it and hang them up in the kitchen like dish towels. In contrast to this, an American diet would be pretty monotonous; he hoped she was not going to ask him to dig a barbecue pit. She told him to wait and see.

Peter waited. They had pot roast and New England boiled dinner and fried chicken and lobsters and scallops and bluefish and mackerel and scalloped oysters and clam chowder. They had Cape Cod Turkey, which some people said was salmon but his mother thought was baked fresh cod with a stuffing. They had codfish cakes and corned beef hash and red flannel hash and chicken hash (three ways), spoon bread and hominy and Rhode Island jonnycake and country sausage with fried apple rings and Brown Betty and Indian pudding and pandowdy and apple pie and cranberry pie. Before the first black frost, she bought green tomatoes and made jars of pickles. They stole quinces from a bush in the yard of a closed-up captain's house with a widow's walk, and she put up quince jelly. Peter was ready to admit that he had never had it so good.

His mother turned everything she did into a game—with rules, of course. The rules of the Rocky Port kitchen were that every recipe had to come out of Fannie Farmer, had to be made entirely at home from fresh—or dried or salted—ingredients, and had to be, insofar as possible, an invention of the New World. Pennsylvania Dutch dishes were permitted, but *gnocchi*, they sadly agreed, although in Fannie Farmer, did not get under the wire. Noodles but not spaghetti. A dish, his mother decided, did not have its citizenship papers if it had been cooked in America for less than a hundred years—discriminatory legislation, Peter commented.

In case of dispute, Peter was assigned to go to the library

after school and look up, for instance, when the Portuguese had first come to America, not counting Magellan: late nineteenth century, imported as cheap labor to work in the cotton mills of New Bedford and the North Atlantic fishing industry. His mother thought she was opposed to progressive education, but in fact she was a natural progressive educator. Because of this cooking bee, he learned about the Irish potato famine, and the '48 revolutions in Germany, and the depressed price of wheat in Sweden in 1886—a peak year of Swedish immigration into Wisconsin and Minnesota. German Jews had begun coming in large numbers after '48, so that on the length-of-residence principle, as he slyly remarked to his mother, she should be making *gefüllte* fish and matzoth balls. Those dishes, she quickly replied, were not in Fannie Farmer, which proved they had not been assimilated, unlike Irish stew—chauvinism, said Peter, getting a rise.

Mixes, obviously, were out, as well as frozen foods. Canned tomatoes were allowed, because housewives had "always" put them up, and an unexplained exception was made for canned bouillon. Portuguese bread was allowed, because, his mother said, it belonged to the locality, and it would be stupid to eat store bread under the circumstances. She would make French toast but not "French" pancakes. Lunches did not count. Peter could have tuna fish with store mayonnaise and Campbell's vegetable soup with the alphabet in it and salami and yoghurt—whatever he wanted. For lunch, his mother usually had bouillon, an apple, and milk.

The game was not as easy as it sounded, since the Rocky Port market leaned heavily on its frozen-food chests, and there were few fresh vegetables to be had, even in the supermarket in the neighboring town. They had onions and carrots and potatoes and cabbage, red and white, in various forms and leeks and broccoli (which Peter questioned) and beets and squash and spinach (though not the bag kind) and fried and scalloped tomatoes. His mother rang the changes on apples and pears and quinces and dried prunes and apricots; she made ambrosia, using fresh coconut, and "snows" and soufflés and puddings and cobblers. They had nuts and what the grocer called rat cheese. There was a lobster pound on a wharf just down the street, and Peter learned to boil the lobsters himself; his mother would not hear of his bisecting them alive for broiling, though he guaranteed her that was a more merciful death.

Getting fresh fish was a problem, despite the fishing fleet. It was easier for a gull. Finally his mother found a fisherman who sold her striped bass and mackerel and bluefish and codfish and smelts; she waited outside the back door of his house to get it, like contraband, which reminded her of her father's stories of Prohibition and the moonshiners who had stills in the woods and came up before him as a judge in federal court. In the grocery store, she bought salt codfish in funny wooden boxes with a sliding cover that Peter used afterward for his stone and shell collections. "When I was a girl, I kept buttons in them," she remembered.

This made her think of the artistic button collections housewives used to show at county fairs when she was a girl, and this, in turn, made her think of the oil paintings done on cigar-box covers—views of the Rhine—German farmers gave her great-grandfather, a country doctor. "In those days, Peter, nobody threw anything away. They tried to think what they could *do* with it or *make* of it. Waste was considered a crime. 'It's a crime to throw that away,' my grandmother always said. What that really meant was that you were stupid if you couldn't find a use for something. Like burying fishbones in corn hills when you were planting, the way the Indians used to do. Or making potpourri of old flower petals. Or patchwork quilts. People were conservationists, like Nature."

Peter could not imagine, she said, what America had been like in those days, at least for the comfortable classes, which included carpenters and house-painters and streetcar conductors. Already it had been changing when she was a girl. It had only been in the summers, when she and her sister went to their grandmother's farm, after their mother had died, that she had really seen the old America, which she connected with the speckled foxglove in her grandmother's yard. In the winters, in Marietta, where she had grown up and gone to college, it had not been so different from now. Just the difference between radio and television and between short-play and long-play records. She smiled at Peter for idealizing the days of radio.

But in the war years, she said, America had become more pastoral, more the way it had been in the farmland. That was because of the scarcities. Nobody could get help; the girls were all working in the war plants. You had to do things yourself. Rationing made you economize. People walked again because of the gasoline shortage. Old wood- and coal-stoves came out on account of the lack of fuel oil. Meat and canned goods were going to the Army. She had liked the war years. Peter thought maybe because that was her youth and she had got away from home. She and her sister came to New York in '42 to study at the Mannes School; that same year, she started with Landowska. Peter, who kept relentless tabs on her birthdays, knew that she had been twenty-one then. They had had what she called a dumbbell apartment—two big rooms with a narrow connecting passage. Back home, their stepmother had planted a Victory Garden, and every week in the summertime huge boxes of vegetables, packed in damp newspapers, arrived by Railway Express—their stepmother was too patriotic to waste fertilizer on flowers, which did not help the war effort. His aunt was impatient with these shipments and wanted to dump them in the garbage. But the fair Rosamund distributed string beans and cucumbers and squashes to everyone they knew; she studied cookbooks and stayed up late in the warm summer nights (that was before air conditioning) pickling and preserving in big crocks and Mason jars. She gave the results as presents or bartered them for sugar coupons. They hitchhiked to the seashore, where they dug clams and gathered mussels. A painter on Fire Island taught her to mushroom in the pine woods. Her grandfather, the minister, kept bees in the parsonage yard and he sent them fresh honey. Peter was sorry he had not been alive then. The way his mother described it, the war sounded like an idyl. He filed the thought away in the Two-Sides-to-Every-Question compartment.

Excited by her sessions in the Rocky Port kitchen, she told Peter tales of her girlhood, of phosphorescent wood and fireflies and prodigious snowmen. He heard about her ancestors and the old Northwest Territory, which had been organized in Marietta, the first settlement in the state. He was glad to know that the Ohio Company had prohibited slavery in the territory way back in the eighteenth century. She promised to take him, some day, to Marietta, where he had not been since he was a baby; it had been an Enlightenment capital, full of educators.

The streets had been given classical names, such as Sacra Via, which had greatly pleased the *babbo*, who in a fit of enthusiasm had wanted to have Peter christened by his great-grandfather. But his mother said no; a Jew could not do that in the year 1945. Peter was surprised to hear that the old parts of Marietta were in a Classic Revival style that looked in fact a lot like Rocky Port. He had imagined Ohio as an inland California.

His mother—like many musicians, she said—had a remarkable memory, and she never repeated a story, except as an encore, just as, this fall in the kitchen, she never repeated a dish. Peter was keeping score. She had not yet had a failure despite inadequate equipment, which led her to swear sometimes, especially when she was making a piecrust, using a wine bottle for a rolling-pin. "The poor workman blames his tools, Mother," he would tease her, leaning against the kitchen door.

They often discussed why they felt so at home in New England. It could not be just the Doric columns and peristyles and pediments, in his mother's case, or the fact that Peter had been born in South Hadley, Massachusetts—his father had been teaching at Mount Holyoke then. Could there be such a thing as racial memory? But if so, why was that memory selective? Why "remember" New England rather than Florence or Palestine, neither of which drew Peter at all? Maybe there was a collective American memory of white meeting-houses and village greens that you acquired at birth or naturalization. New England was the promised land, even for those who had left it behind or who had never seen it, except in the movies. His mother said that was because New England *looked* like the ideal America that you studied in civics; it looked republican, with a small *r*.

Going to school every day, Peter was well aware that he had not left Berkeley and the Radiation Laboratory totally behind. It did not need Preparedness Drill to tell him that. He had only to look at his classmates, many of whom would leave school at the statutory age of sixteen to go to work in the plastics factory or at the nearby submarine base. But his mother had more illusions to shatter. Since she seldom talked with anyone except an elderly storekeeper, she could believe she was living in the past. It was a storekeeper who delivered the blow. The village hardware store did not carry bean pots.

"How extraordinary, Peter! The man says they don't make them any more. Do you think that can be true?" She was always asking him wide-eyed, troubled questions like that one, to which he could not possibly, at his age, know the answer; it was a kind of flattery, applied to the male ego. The only bean pot Peter was familiar with was pictured on a can. But he saw that for his mother this was a truly upsetting discovery, tantamount to finding that the American Eagle was extinct. She was even more ruffled when she returned from her weekly shopping trip with the report that the two hardware stores in the neighboring town did not carry bean pots either. "Don't get any call for them," one shopkeeper had told her. The other said, "Try the antique store, lady. Two doors down." "Can you imagine that, Peter? How do you explain it? Why, when we left your father—how long ago was it?" "Eight years." "Eight years. That isn't such a long time, is it? Well, eight years ago, every hardware store in New England had bean pots galore. Just the way they had seeds and onion sets and tomato plants in the springtime. Do you suppose that if I took the train to Providence . . . ? I could go to the Brown Music Library while I was there. . . ."

"Can't you use a casserole, Mother?" Peter was trying to be helpful, but his mother looked at him in horror, as if he were a changeling. "What a question!" she said. He did not blame his mother for caring about things like bean pots in the face of a general indifference; indeed, he loved her for that. On the other hand, he could not share her sense of shock and loss, just as he could not respond, except lamely, when she told him someone he had never known had died. In the end, Mrs. Curtis gave them her bean pot, which she had been using as a vase for a bouquet of dried grasses. "You can keep it, my dear. I haven't baked a bean in twenty years. How nice that you're going to do it for Peter!"

Mrs. Curtis herself, an eldritch old person, ate most of her meals in the Portuguese diner; Peter had often seen her there when he stopped by for a hamburger. "We must do something for her, Peter," his mother repeated. He guessed what was coming: Thanksgiving. The two of them could not eat a whole turkey between them; they would have to have guests or do without. Peter was torn between gluttony and his reluctance to have company. His mother, he suspected, would not be satisfied to have just Mrs. Curtis. She would want to ask all her descendants too. He had nothing personal against Mrs. Curtis' descendants; one of her grandchildren, a girl, he talked to at school occasionally. Nevertheless, his heart hardened. Mrs. Curtis would be bound to ask them back. She had already been telling Peter about "a few friends" in Rocky Port who were dying to meet his mother. He foresaw a series of musical evenings.

On the other hand, he was familiar with his mother's attachment to Thanksgiving as a day of bounty. In Berkeley, every year she had rounded up all the lonely hearts available on the campus—plus a wheel or two (the fair Rosamund was transparent), so that no one would suddenly glance around the groaning board and ask himself what they all had in common. As long as he could remember, wherever he and his mother lived, there had been company present when she struck up the hymn "We GATHer toGETHer to ASK the Lord's BLESSing," which she said was an old Dutch resistance tune from the time of William the Silent. Adjuring himself not to be selfish, Peter hit on a compromise. "Why don't we ask Aunt Millie to come up from New York with her brood?"

His mother was touched by the suggestion; she knew that Peter did not particularly care for her sister. Her delight made Peter ashamed. Was she all that lonely? Maybe she was just eager to show their new household to somebody; women were like that. He found that he himself was rather looking forward to taking his cousins for a walk in the sanctuary and showing them the cormorants on their piles. "'It is not good that man should be alone,'" Mrs. Curtis had hissed at him the other day in the library.

Nature rewarded Peter for thinking of his mother. Two days before Thanksgiving, an apple tree in the yard across the street uncannily burst into bloom. Although a confirmed atheist, he could not help seeing this as a blessing conferred especially on their household; the Lord was making a covenant with Peter the Levite. The blossoming tree was Aaron's Rod—what else?—the sign that the Lord had picked Aaron to be high priest of Israel and set him apart, with the tribe of Levi, from the others. Aaron's Rod, if Peter recalled right, had put out almond blossoms overnight; the Lord was a craftsman who worked with local materials—almonds in the desert, apples here. It occurred to Peter that this was only the latest of a series of rather broad hints that he and his mother had been led to Rocky Port to work out a special destiny. He was too modest to suppose that he was the Messiah, but he might be a precursor, a sort of pilot-project in the wilderness. He did not confide the thought in his mother, who, after all, was a Gentile and outside the Law. But he knew that she was marveling too.

The house across the street was boarded up for the winter, like the other shuttered houses on the water; out of season, no one passed this way except the mailman and the newsboy on his bicycle, delivering the morning paper, and now it was barely light when the folded paper was pitched onto the porch. So that the mystery of the flowering apple tree, like that of the owl and the cormorants, was being enacted just for the two of them, in Nature's private code. The mailman, when he passed —bringing a Thanksgiving card with a turkey on it from Hans to Peter—could offer no explanation. He had never heard tell of an apple tree in these parts blooming at Thanksgiving; he guessed it was a Freak of Nature. "Radio says snow," he added, and, sure enough, on Thanksgiving Day, while they were all at table, with Millicent's husband carving, the promised snow came. The whole family rushed to the window. Across the way, snowflakes were gently falling on the tender green leaves, rose-red buds and pink-and-white shivering blossoms. "Quite a production," said Millie in her ironical tones.

"Hey, kids," she ordered, "go and get your cameras. Did you put in color film?" Peter groaned to himself. He watched with savage hate while his cousins stole the apple tree with their clicking Kodaks. "Have you got it?" said his aunt. His cousins had it in their little black boxes. The graceless meal resumed. Peter's uncle put a drumstick on Peter's plate. With her eyes, his mother warned him not to say he preferred white meat. Later that afternoon, just before dusk, someone tapped Hello on the window. It was Mrs. Curtis and all her family come to see the apple tree. His mother had *shared* the secret. The fire was burning in the hearth; outside, it was still snowing. "Ask them in," commanded Millie. "Peter, go open the door."

In a minute, the little house was full of windbreakers, scarves, and galoshes. Millie's husband was in the kitchen, mixing drinks. Peter's Coca-Cola supply was decimated. He was sent upstairs for his Monopoly set. His chess set, where he had been working out a chess problem, was commandeered by his uncle to play with Mrs. Curtis' son-in-law, who did not know any better than to open with the King's Rook's pawn. Peter's fire was re-laid, with the logs placed upward, teepee style. And his mother stood smiling on the scene, murmuring with her sister, whom an evil day—which answered to the name of Peter Levi—had brought to Rocky Port.

His aunt, who was older than his mother, took pride in her ability to "size up" situations; she had the brusque, brutal air of a person detailed to cut Gordian knots. All through the day, she had been interrogating Peter about himself, his mother, and their relations with the Rocky Port community. She had established that Hans still wrote to his mother and that his mother probably answered. Her dry blue eye had inventoried the house, checking off the chessmen, the prism that hung in Peter's window, Handel's *Messiah* on the phonograph, the bird book, the star book, the tree book, the bean pot, the music on his mother's clavichord, the clothes in his mother's closet. At table she had noted the home-made cranberry jelly molded in the shape of a heart (there were duplicate tin hearts in Berkeley and in the *babbo*'s kitchen in Wellesley), the corn bread and walnut stuffing, the green tomato pickle, the mincemeat tarts with home-made vanilla ice cream that Peter had been stirring every half hour in the refrigerator trays. She had learned that the turkey was a fresh-killed local bird and how much his mother had paid for it. She had taken stock of the cormorants and assessed the woodpile. It was as though these separate items "hung together" in some derisory pattern, like a stitched sampler—Rosamund's folly.

From time to time, she wagged her Clairol-tinted head confidentially at Peter, in token of despair—as when she ascertained that his mother had *walked* to the turkey farm to pick out the bird—and his aunt Millie was such a consummate spectator that he felt himself pulled into a box seat beside her, watching their private life—his and his mother's—unfold, with the embarrassed sense that it was, as Millie would say, a "performance." Not real, footlit, with stage snow outside and stagey food on the table, against a painted backdrop of old-time New England seascape. With shame, he saw himself through her eyes as conned by his mother into a storybook romance, which they lived on a daily basis—he licked his lips, mortified to admit it—and not just when they had company. The fact that his mother made his breakfast every morning, instead of simply leaving corn flakes and frozen fruit juice and chocolate milk for him, became a hideous confession as his aunt sweated it out of him. He was guilty of being less average than his cousins, and that was his wicked mother's fault.

Peter could well see that his aunt, behind a façade of good nature, was jealous of her sister. His mother was a musician, while Millie worked for a music publisher. When they were girls, his mother had been feckless and dreamy, and Millie had been the practical one, but now his mother had a passion for work, and Millie was shrewd and lazy. His mother had a glowing girlish skin, which she scrubbed with soap and water, disobeying her sister's warnings, while Millie's creamed skin sagged. Most of all, Peter guessed, his aunt was jealous of his mother's "hold" on himself, which she could not reproduce on her own uninteresting progeny. But jealousy had made her watchful, and Peter, a veteran observer, his mother's privileged critic, could not help responding to the prose in his aunt's view of them. What were they doing here anyway, playing house together, a growing boy and a woman nearly forty, who was old enough to be his mother? Millie's common sense was the Tempter in the Garden. He fell. "Peter, go open the door." What could he do but obey?

She had come in the nick of time to set things right; that was what she plainly thought. Aunt Millie always acted like that, whenever she paid a visit—as though her coming was providential. With her tinted hair, she reminded Peter rather of King Arthur's trouble-making sister, Queen Morgan le Fay. A fairy tale needed a bad fairy; he ought to have considered that before. She had arrived tugging at her girdle and waving her stout wand of disenchantment. And when she left, everything was blighted. "You feel gloomy because you ate too much, Peter," his mother told him as he helped her wipe a mountain of dishes. But Peter knew he was not wrong. The next morning, the apple blossoms were blasted, and the tree, he was afraid, would never get up the strength to bloom again in the spring. He blamed this on his aunt and he was not the only one. "You brought winter with you," Mrs. Curtis had shot at Millie, like a sudden accusation, after her second drink. Thanksgiving, as Peter saw it, had been his last day of grace. After that, he paid his debt to society. The following week, they went to dinner at Mrs. Curtis' house. They began to meet people. Thanks to Millie, the sluices opened, and Rocky Port rushed in.

Yet the reality did not live up to Peter's forebodings, which alarmed him, as though his early-warning system had been misled by a flight of birds. Unless he was softening up, their new acquaintances were not a threat. Behind their fanlight doorways was a fog of amnesia, induced, he thought, by alcohol, which flowed in Lethean streams from the liquor store. The worst thing they did was repeat themselves, playing the same dulled record; for years, nobody had bothered to change their needle. They did not have the energy to get up a musical evening. The admiral, who did crewelwork, and his wife, who painted china, were the most strenuous members of the community.

The men drove about in their cars, dressed like hunters or trappers, in boots and mackinaws and fur caps, to visit their frozen-food lockers. Their wives offered Peter's mother lifts to go marketing and invited Peter to view television. The few men in his mother's age-group were already paired off, and their cars would be recognized if they tried to take her to the bird sanctuary and make a pass. There was no danger here that Peter could see. Being a musician, his mother could not hit the bottle. True to her promise, she bought them skates; when it snowed again, their own footprints and the tracks of birds and animals were the only trails leading in and out of the still woods. Peter's uneasiness subsided; he let her go out to dinner without him and did not lie awake listening for her step on the porch. One afternoon, as he was coming home from school, he thought he heard the *harpsichord* playing, but when he opened the door, the music had stopped. His mother was talking on the telephone, and he guessed he might have been mistaken.

They arranged to go to Millie's for Christmas, so that they did not have their tree. Now that they were acquainted in Rocky Port, his mother said, they would never be allowed to have Christmas by themselves. It would be considered unfriendly. Peter did not argue; he accepted the lesser evil and besides he would not mind seeing New York, he thought. But it would have been fun to chop down their own tree in the woods. He found it queer to think that for the first time since he was a baby he would not be popping corn over the fire and watching her string those chains, like red and white beads, of popcorn and cranberries alternating, that festooned her lap and trailed over the carpet, while the long white thread in her needle turned pink from the cranberry juice. He would not be helping her gild walnuts or make gingerbread men, putting in the raisins for the face and buttons himself. He pictured last Christmas in Berkeley and felt homesick, unexpectedly, for Hans, heavy-footed on a ladder, hanging candy canes on the green branches. He was acquiring a distrust for holidays.

Christmas Eve, on Riverside Drive, he hung up his sock with his cousins. Millie's tree had balls and lights and nothing edible on it at all—not even a gold-wrapped chocolate coin. They were lucky, he told his mother, it was not dyed. From his aunt and uncle, he received—guess what?—a camera; his aunt's presents were always pointed, like the baseball mitt she had once sent him, to tell his mother that he should take an interest in athletics. From the fair Rosamund he got a pair of field glasses, which was what he had been fearing. He would rather have bought them himself, second hand, in a pawnshop; his mother was not good at picking out articles like bird books and field glasses—her idea was to get the most expensive. She also gave him a seal ring with the head of some Greek worthy, tickets to *Carmen* at the opera, and *The Seasons* by Haydn.

On Christmas Day, there was a party. Millie had invited some of his mother's old gang: her agent, the chamber group she used to play with, the head of a record company. *E così via*; his aunt did not need to explain the principle of the party to Peter—he got it. She was master-minding her sister's comeback. His mother had a new dress, and Millie took her around and made her talk to all the people who could "do something" for her; there was a man from the State Department in charge of cultural exchanges and an old society lady who gave recitals at her house. Peter, who helped make drinks, got sick on Martinis and was taken to the bathroom by a friendly woman who said she used to be his mother's page-turner. He retched most of the night, and his aunt philosophically put a basin by his bed; it was time he stopped being babied, she told his mother, who wanted to call a doctor with a stomach pump. When they finally got back to Rocky Port, there was New Year's Eve and New Year's Day eggnog. Then at midyears, he failed his higher algebra.

On receipt of the news, the *babbo* drove down from Wellesley and talked gloomily about college boards. As a pedagogue, he was hipped on college admissions statistics. "You ought to have looked into the schools before coming here," he said sharply. "I talked to your sister. She tells me the boy is not even getting Latin now." It was true, the Rocky Port high school did not give Latin; Peter's aunt had wormed this out of him during Thanksgiving dinner. "He will never get into Harvard now," the *babbo* said tragically. He sounded very angry with his mother. It was just like old times, Peter thought, listening from his bedroom. The *babbo* had already been mad at her, it transpired, for leaving Hans and coming here. Why could she not have waited another year, till Peter had finished algebra? "I find it very upsetting to have you back here in New England," he grumbled, slightly lowering his voice. Peter's mother ignored this. "New England has been good for Peter. He feels at home here. You always said he was a zoophile. It's extraordinary what he's learned this fall about Nature."

"Nature!" the *babbo* shouted. "Nature! Don't be a goddamn fool! Nature is an anachronism. Does the boy have companions of his own age? Your sister tells me that he has not made a single friend. Can he qualify for any college from this high school? Or do you expect him to join the labor force at seventeen? When you are serious, we may begin talking again." Peter's mother remained silent. His father burst out. "And what will he do when you go on tour? Have you thought of that?"

Upstairs at his desk, Peter pricked up his ears for his mother's answer. But he could only catch the word "problem"; her voice had sunk too low. "You have not thought," he heard his father sum up. "That is like you, *cara mia*. A creature of

impulse. But don't forget that I am paying the boy's bills."
This was tough on his mother. She hated being reminded that
his father was contributing to his support—which seemed
perfectly just to Peter but not to her, because she had left his
father. "What do you want me to do, Paolo? I've taken this
house for a year. Do you suppose, if I could find a tutor . . . ?
He really has a very good mind." He heard his father's step;
the door to the living room was closed softly. One of the *babbo*'s principles was that a child should never be praised in his
own hearing.

So that before he knew it, they had shanghaied him into
boarding-school without even asking his consent. When Peter
was summoned downstairs, it had already been decided. His
father knew a school that specialized in "the boy of uneven
attainments," that is, the boy who had failed one or two subjects. It was not far from Wellesley. While his mother made tea,
his father telephoned to the headmaster to find out if there was
a vacant place and when he learned that there was, he ordered
Peter to pack. His mother served tea, not making conversation, from shame, Peter knew, and because she was afraid that
if she talked she would cry. She just looked at him across his
father like somebody trying to exchange signals over the head
of a guard. He knew her excuse: that the divorce decree gave
his father control over his education. Finally, she spoke up.
Peter would have to have a haircut and name-tapes on his
clothes; he could not go, just like that. But his father was being
a man of action—the old "*cosa fatta capo ha*" stuff. If Peter
drove back with him tonight, he would be able to start the
new term tomorrow; his mother could see about name-tapes
and things of that kind later. If he needed further outfitting in
a hurry, the *babbo* could take him to Boston one afternoon
after classes.

It was dark when they drove off; they were going to have
dinner on the road. His father would not even let his mother
fix them supper. "But when will I see him again?" Peter's
mother cried out in the doorway, as though she had not taken
in, until that minute, what was happening. "Go in the house!"
his father yelled. "You will catch cold." "Yes, go in the house,
Mother," Peter said, with pity. It was not her fault he had failed
algebra; he had brought this on himself. "At least put on a

coat." But she stood there, clasping her chest, under the wan porch-light, till his father impatiently promised to arrange for Peter to come home soon on a weekend, providing the headmaster gave a good report of him. She must not come to the school, which would upset Peter; the *babbo* would drive over himself every Sunday to take him out to lunch and check on his progress.

Peter waved farewell to his mother; he blew a kiss, which probably she could not see. He thought of her alone with the tea dishes and the preparations for the supper he would never eat. "Tell the cormorants I'll be seeing them!" As his father let out the clutch, it came to him that in fact he had not seen those three fishy characters for several days. Maybe longer. Or could it be that he had ceased to notice them—which meant that, without knowing it, he no longer cared? No wonder his father had come, like black retribution, to take him away.

In school, he tried not to brood about his mother. If he acted unhappy, they would probably not let him go home till Easter. He signed up for the chess team and appeared on the hockey field. At night, he wrote her short amusing letters and sealed them with his seal ring. The only animal at school, aside from a few chickens, was the headmaster's dachshund, to which he gave perfunctory pats whenever their paths crossed. The headmaster said he was making a good adjustment.

On Lincoln's Birthday, which that year made a long weekend, he was allowed to go home. His mother came to fetch him, driving Mrs. Curtis' car. It was a beautiful bright blue morning. She had brought a picnic lunch and Peter's field glasses, which he had forgotten. On the way back to Rocky Port, they stopped to eat in a glen up in the back country where they had never been. That was the day they found the waterfall, using a geodetic map Mrs. Curtis had left in the glove compartment. Peter circled the spot on the map, so that they would be able to locate it again when he came home for Easter.

But then, in the car, his mother broke the news. *She was giving up the house in Rocky Port.* The man from the State Department (Peter remembered?) that she had met at Millie's Christmas party was going to send her abroad with a chamber-music group. Their regular harpsichordist had had an automobile accident. His mother would have to be in New York to rehearse with them, and Mrs. Curtis had been very understanding and helpful about finding another tenant to finish out the lease. By a lucky coincidence, a house had burned down in Rocky Port just the other night, and the owners were looking for a place to live while they rebuilt it. It made an ideal arrangement. So that at Easter-time ("Think of it, Peter!") she would be in Rome, playing, and he could fly over and be with her for his spring vacation. The *babbo* had agreed.

Grimly, Peter recognized another of the fair Rosamund's substitutes. It struck him that his being in boarding-school just now was a great convenience for his mother. As she babbled on, flushed and excited, he felt himself turn into *another person*—possibly a man, if they were made of stone. Cruelly, he wondered how long, exactly, she had known about this tour. "When did you get the invite, Mother?" "Oh, just the other day. Last week." He watched her cheek redden, as if she guessed what he was thinking. "I thought I wouldn't write you about it but save it to tell you when you came." He stared at the road. "Who set the fire?" he inquired. "What fire?" "The house that burned down so *opportunely*," he said with an acid smile.

Her hands, in leather and chamois driving-gloves, tightened on the wheel. For a moment, he relented. "'I suspect Mrs. Curtis in the verandah with the kitchen matches,'" he proposed lightly, alluding to their old game of Clue. She patted his bony knee. "You don't mind, do you, Peter? I thought since you were in school anyway . . . And Easter isn't so far off. I thought you'd *like* to go to Rome. After all, you've never been abroad." "That means we'll never come back to Rocky Port, doesn't it, Mother?" "I don't know, Peter. How can I say? Maybe in the summertime." "But I'll be with *babbo* then." "Not all the time. Now that you're in school it wouldn't be fair for him to have you the whole summer. We'll have to divide you." "In what proportions?" he said coldly.

He studied his mother's profile. A tear trembled in her eye. If he were on a jury, he might give her the benefit of the doubt. Probably it was true that she had just got the official invitation. But wasn't it likely—more than likely—that she had been sounded out, some time back, through her sister? Maybe on

Christmas Day even, while they slugged him with Martinis. Then his father's visit would have been a charade enacted for his consumption. If he had not failed algebra, they would have found some other pretext. Once they had him in school, they could do what they wanted. If he ran away, the headmaster would have him tracked with bloodhounds, which had already happened to another kid.

He endeavored to reason with himself. Had his mother ever lied to him before? The stone man answered cynically: not that he *knew* of. He felt his sanity totter. If the fair Rosamund was false, then his whole life, up to now, was a deception, and if she was not false, he was batty. He found himself wondering about the other harpsichordist's automobile "accident." Did his mother have an alibi? He giggled sardonically to himself.

His mother's head turned quickly in his direction. "Pay attention to the road, Mother." Supposing he were to take her, step by step, over the history of the offer, demanding times and places. "Was it mentioned to you at Christmas, Mother? Think back. Take your time." But what if she confessed? He would not want to hear it. And actually the details did not matter. What mattered was that she was *glad* he was in boarding-school, so that she was free to go to Europe. And he was not glad; that was the difference between them. Maybe she had not arranged to put him there; maybe she was on the level. But now that it had come about, she was profiting. All she cared about, he thought with contempt, was that her conscience should be clear.

In their house, everything looked strange. Her instruments were gone, and there was a large blue trunk open in the living room; she had bought it at the junk shop and painted it. His shirts and socks and underwear were packed, with name-tapes sewed on them; she was giving him the stereo set, to take back to school with him, and the records she called his, which now, he noted, included *Don Giovanni*, *The Messiah*, and one of her own old recordings that was a present to her from Mrs. Curtis. In the kitchen, she had live lobsters waiting for him to cook.

He went up to his room. The prism was no longer in his window, and all his books had been packed. The white linen window curtains and white crinkly bedspread had been sent to the laundress. He looked out at the cove. It was low tide.

Some gulls were squawking around the slimy piles. Standing at his window, he felt no curiosity about the absence of the cormorants, just as he felt no curiosity about what his mother, downstairs, was whipping up for dessert. He could ask her when she had seen them last, but he doubted whether she had troubled to keep track of them after he had gone. She liked birds but she was not really interested in them.

He was curious about something else. He went to the head of the stairway. "Tell me, Mother," he called out, "did the headmaster know you were going to Europe?" "Yes," she called back. He did not know why *this* should be such a body blow, considering everything. He ought to have sensed it was strange that they would let him go home after only eleven days of captivity; he should have asked himself the reason for this mark of favor. Now he knew.

Four years later, as a hoary ghost going on nineteen, he had amnestied his parents for putting him in boarding-school. Within their limitations, they had been right. If he had stayed at Rocky Port High, he could never have made a halfway good college; he saw that. Of course, it had solved all his mother's problems to have him in school, but she would not have done it for that motive. Not she. If the offer had come *before* his father's visit, she would have fought off the suggestion of boarding-school like a person refusing to listen to temptation. But a temptation was something attractive; that, for Peter, was the sad part. Though his mother had been sorry when he had been carted off, it was because a sort of promise had been broken, and she always hated that. But she regretted it for *him*, not for herself. As the *babbo* kept telling him, "You must not forget, your mother has her own life."

Yet from his present perspective, he could recognize that his parents had done the natural thing, being what they were. His mother's departure for Europe and his own departure for school had been on Nature's schedule for the sub-species they belonged to—white, middle-income intelligentsia. His parents had been responding to a deep instinctual drive of their class, for which he forgave them as individuals, his father somewhat more than his mother. At this late date too, he at last understood why the cormorants had failed to materialize on that

February weekend to receive his Hail and Farewell. He was probably right in thinking that he had not seen them since sometime during exam week, toward the end of January. There was a natural explanation. They had simply migrated south when the thermometer dropped and had doubtless been living in New Jersey.

The Battle of Rocky Port

PETER's mother had warned him that Rocky Port might be different after four years. For that matter, he was different himself, and so was she. Three years ago, in the fall, she had married again—an art historian this time, a Gentile from Massachusetts, a nice guy. He was divorced, with three little kids, who lived mostly with their mother, like Hans's offspring. Peter had met him in Rome, when he went over that Easter, and guessed immediately that "Bob" would be his new stepfather. Bob had a grant to do a book on Mannerism, and he took Peter and his mother to see a great many churches, which Peter quite liked, to his surprise, for he did not like the word *Mannerism*. But the churches he liked best, it turned out, were by a madman called Borromini and were Baroque.

He was resigned to his mother's marrying, since he was in school. He was not a dog in the manger but more like the fox and the grapes. Now he divided his summers between his parents; his father had finally bought a house on Cape Cod, and his mother and stepfather tended to spend their summers in Europe. Last summer, they had taken a house near Perugia, and Peter had studied for a while at the University, in the school for *Stranieri*. It had been very hot; the level of the courses had been low, and he would have preferred to be with his father on the Cape. There was not much Nature in Italy; the peasants had shot most of the bird population, and Peter missed the American brooks, ponds, and woods. What he had liked chiefly in Umbria were the black-eyed milk-white oxen, which made him think of Io after she had been turned into a cow.

"Why can't we go back to Rocky Port?" he asked every year when summer plans were discussed. His new stepbrothers and stepsister used to copy him. "Why can't we go to Rocky Port?" Now his demand, so long on file, had suddenly been acceded to, and he knew the reasons. To cushion the blow about Mississippi and to give him a good memory of America, which he could take with him to Europe, where he would be on his own for the first time. His mother had sacrificed her Italian summer to be with him; his stepfather was in Siena for six weeks, working. So that once again he and his mother were alone with her instruments, and he found he was glad.

This year, they had a car, as well as his motorbike. Their old house had been sold to some middle-class types and painted another color. The "historic" house they were now renting was on the best street, shaded by elms and maples. It had four original fireplaces, a hedge that Peter had to clip, and two bathrooms. In short, like most Americans, except the poor, they had got richer in the interim. To Peter's slight astonishment, his mother had made a success. She had played behind the Iron Curtain and in India and Japan and South America—everywhere but Africa, just about. Her records were in the college music shop, with her picture on the cover in a low-necked dress, and his roommate, a music addict, had asked him for her autograph. His stepfather, who taught at NYU, was a recognized authority on Mannerism, which had been "in" for several years now. He lectured, authenticated, published, and he was always getting grants and fellowships for research and travel. There was nothing wrong with this that Peter could put his finger on; a society that starved art and artists would not, he guessed, be preferable. His mother was making an effort to live as she had always done—only somewhat better. Except when she was in Europe, she still did her own housework; she would not travel first class, unless the government was paying for it. She mended and sewed and gave lessons, free, to young musicians. She did not mind playing *continuo* with a group whose work she respected, and every now and then she gave a benefit to help refugees from Franco or for some other worthwhile cause. She was an easy target for composers who dedicated pieces to her, which she then had to perform. Everyone, especially her sister, told her she was doing too much—a thing she liked to hear. In fact, to Peter, who refrained from saying it, both she and Bob seemed tired. He believed her when she said she was looking forward to Rocky Port as a respite from seeing people. This summer, with his help, she was going to be anti-social.

That ought not to be hard, Peter thought. Right away, of course, they were invited to cocktail parties and they went. His mother said that if you accepted the first invitation and stayed just a short time, people would be satisfied to leave you alone—you had done your duty. Besides, she was curious about the artistic colony Mrs. Curtis had mentioned who were alleged to spend their summers here. But this was one of the changes that had to be expected, apparently. Museum directors, *New Yorker* contributors, Metropolitan Opera songsters, fashion photographers, makers of woodcuts, food-writers, *Reader's Digest* editors were extinct in the area, though their names were still mentioned, as on a village honor roll, like the World War II tablet opposite the Portuguese church. Some, it appeared, had died at an unstated date; others had been divorced or just "gone away." Those who still owned houses—chiefly Victorian churches that had been turned into studios or dwellings —rented them for high prices and were living in Rome or on a Greek island.

By contrast, the phantom crew Peter and his mother had met four years ago was still in evidence, more or less intact, beaming on his mother: "Well, hello, Stranger!" Their number had been increased by new recruits. The great change in Rocky Port, it seemed, was the multiplication of what were now known as All-Year-Rounders. "Are you Summer or All-Year-Rounder?" Peter was asked, in no idle tones, as he made his maiden appearance at a Rocky Port function. If you answered "Summer," he discovered, you were supposed to say it with a sigh. The All-Year-Rounders did not welcome summer people, except as proselytes. "Come on, boy, you get your pretty mother to buy some property here. Rocky Port needs you." "'Uncle Sam needs you,'" Peter muttered, lifting an eyebrow. "Maybe they don't like it here," a woman suggested, teetering. "What have we got to offer?" "Oh, we like it," said Peter hurriedly. "But my mother has to be in New York. Because of her music. And my stepfather teaches there." "You're never too young to retire and start living," a man interposed. "Look at me." Peter looked. The man, though the worse for drink, did not appear to be more than forty; he was wearing a pair of flowered Bermuda shorts. "He used to run a coal-mine," a deep-voiced woman who ran the bookshop explained to Peter. "Came up here on a yacht and fell in love with the place. Never went back. People here have more leisure to do the things they really enjoy. *Culti-ver leur jardin*. They want to get out of the rat-race."

He had never heard this expression actually used before, except by teen-age cynics, but it was common, he found, among the Rocky Port *gratin*. According to themselves, they were all escaping from the rat-race. "Poor Jack has to go back to the rat-race," a young woman who used to be a model sighed, of her husband, a lawyer for breakfast foods. Fortunately there was now a regular air service to New York, and a new thruway had been built, cutting the driving time by fifteen minutes.

Peter was startled to meet this kind of American on the native soil—the kind he had seen in Europe and instinctively disbelieved in: women who said "wee wee" and were on the prowl for "the little girls' room," corporation executives with corporations who were either going to vote for Goldwater or considered him "too extreme," couples with cruisers and sea-skis who were belligerent about "Veet Nam," couples who announced "We're three-Martini men, ourselves," couples who served drinks in glasses marked "Wood Alcohol—Your Poison." In Europe, his mother used to say that this kind of American was manufactured for export only; you never saw them at home. But here they were in Rocky Port, assembled for shipping. "My husband and I spend every winter in Positano." It was his first contact, he realized, with the American bourgeoisie *in situ*.

"Stay away from them. They're Birchers," a voice hissed in his ear at his second cocktail party. It was Mrs. Curtis, tapping on his elbow, to detach him from an elderly couple he had just been introduced to. "Sorry?" "Birchers," she repeated impatiently. "The John Birch Society." "Oh." He stared at the harmless-looking pair who had been offering to bring him together with their granddaughter; they lived in the house on the water where the apple tree had blossomed—he had been going to tell them about it, in case they didn't know. "Is there really a branch of John Birch here?" he whispered, to Mrs. Curtis; he had pictured them mostly out West, like bad men in a movie, wearing Stetson hats. "Ha ha," she answered darkly, shaking her small round head with its white Dutch bangs. "Where do they meet?" "No one knows. They're underground." Inwardly, Peter scoffed. He did not want to believe in a hidden network of reactionaries; that was McCarthyism in reverse, he felt. "But if they're underground, how can you be sure who is or who isn't a member? I mean, do you have any evidence, Mrs. Curtis? Those people I was talking to, they didn't sound like crackpots. Maybe they're just regular Republicans." "They have their private atom shelter. Stocked with French wines. At the bottom of their garden." She nodded her white head, with determination, three times. After this, Peter was ashamed that whenever he saw the elderly couple, arm in arm, approaching, he crossed to the other side of the street.

Having seen the lay of the land socially, his mother decided that they ought to take expeditions, get to know the geography better. She went to the county seat and bought a surveyor's map, which she turned over to Peter. The first thing they were going to do was find the waterfall again and swim in the pool at its foot; she loved icy water. But the map, Peter discovered, though printed last year, was already an historical curio. The new highway construction had altered everything; the map bore only a dreamlike relation to the bulldozed countryside. Road numbers had changed, and the old Indian trail, which he had counted on to get his bearings, had melted into the thruway. He could see the waterfall distinctly in his mind's eye. You followed the Indian trail, which was a secondary road, to the edge of a state forest; then you turned left, going by a lake or a reservoir, till you got to the glen. There the road became impassable, but you saw blue blazes painted on trees and leading into the woods. You parked and started hiking. He remembered the spot exactly; a jay had flashed by. Eventually you came to a slippery walk with a rusty iron railing that led up to the waterfall. Beside the dark pool at its bottom there had been an overturned blue canoe. But now, with the roads changed and leaves on the trees, everything looked different. New little houses had toadstooled; they passed a trailer camp. They drove about in circles, misled by landmarks that appeared to be familiar. They stopped to listen, thinking they heard the sound of rapids. They argued. Peter suggested climbing a tree, as in the jungle. Finally his mother said they must give up and ask Mrs. Curtis if she still had the map Peter had marked. But Mrs. Curtis had junked her old maps when the thruway approached; like many elderly people, she was a new broom. The cobwebs were in her memory. She had no recollection of a waterfall up in that neck of the woods. "You must mean Pierce's Mills. There's an old milldam there, with a falls. Used to be a cheese factory too." "We've seen Pierce's Mills," his mother said. "That's a *village*, Ellen. This is a *forest*." "You don't mean the old granite quarry?" His mother looked at Peter. Why remind Mrs. Curtis that it was she who had told them about the waterfall in the first place?

They tried again, twice more. They found a Boy Scout camp on a lake; they found a reservoir. They found a remote village called Green's Falls. But the glen was lost. The waterfall was lost. His mother kept stopping the car at every crossroads and asking, but no one could help her.

She took the loss of the waterfall harder than the owl's death or the absence of the cormorants. After all, she said, waterfalls did not die or migrate in the normal course of Nature. She felt it as a deliberate blow at her sanity. To console her, Peter suggested blueberrying. Back in the Free Library, he had been reading the old state guidebook, done by the WPA before he was born, and been amused by descriptions of the roadside flower-stands tended by farm wives and of happy urchins selling blueberries from house to house. The flower-stands were no more, but there must still be blueberries in the thin, second-growth woods. In the stores, you could buy only big tasteless cultivated blueberries shipped from Maine. Instead of just setting out on their own with pails and saucepans, his mother had to inquire where the best blueberry patches were. They were in copperhead country, she was told. She would not go and she would not let Peter go either. He accepted her veto, just as he had accepted the veto on Mississippi, having pondered the problem of the rights of parents. Until he was twenty-one, his life did not belong to him; he was in debt for it to his parents. He did not have the right to risk it without their consent, as long as they were reasonable. If he died at nineteen from a copperhead bite, he would feel awful for his mother, especially since the *babbo* would say it was her fault. And the fact that he would be dead and not able to stand up for her would make him more reprehensible. Anyway, blueberrying without her would not have been much fun.

In recompense, they picked water lilies from a slightly noisome pond. Peter watched baseball games on the village diamond.

One day, they drove across the state border to an herb farm, where she bought herbal teas and plants of perfumed mints and geraniums to put in their window boxes and where they saw a hummingbird and a lot of goldfinches. Another day, picking pink mallows in the marshes, they saw a flight of Snowy Egrets or immature Little Blue Herons—without his field glasses, he could not be sure which.

Summer had brought to light a beach club and a golf course. There was a drive on to put them up for membership in the club. Four years ago, Peter could never have made it, because the board had been "stuffy" about Jews. "Nobody named Levi would have even been considered. No matter who your mother was." "The Virgin Mary was a Levi," Peter remarked stiffly. It irritated him to have to listen to briefings about discrimination, which inevitably had a smug tone, whether the speaker was for excluding Jews or not. "Really? Isn't that fascinating? I must make a note of that. Just in case some of the old fogeys try to blackball you." But that, it seemed, was unlikely, if they had the right sponsors; the club had been integrating. Last year a lovely Jewish family had finally been accepted and were able to swim and play tennis there, though of course they had their own tennis court and their own heated swimming pool, thermostatically controlled, which they had built before they had been let in. The club had come "a long way" in a very short time; only two years ago, a Jewish boy, brought as a guest, had been asked to leave the dance floor by the club president. "Is the same guy still president?" Peter wanted to know. Well, in fact, yes; Rome was not built in a day. But Peter and his mother would not have to worry if they brought Jewish house guests for a swim; no one would say a word. The club might be a bore for his mother, but it would be Peter's chance to get to know the young people. There were dances every Saturday night and movies on Wednesday. Peter could swim and play tennis and perhaps even sail, if some of the youngsters with boats would take him on as crew. Thursday was barbecue night; his mother might like to bring steaks or hamburgers and cook out on the beach over the communal fire with the others, which would smooth Peter's path. . . .

Peter's interest in this proposition was nil. There was a perfectly good public beach down at the point. Every evening, just before sunset, he and his mother swam there; he would dive from the raft with his former classmates, most of whom were working in a war plant, having been deferred by the Army. From the raft, he could watch the natives—who were not the same as the All-Year-Rounders—assemble in their cars to watch the sun set. Then he and his mother would drive home, wrapped in beach towels, to change. He would light a fire and pour them each a glass of sherry. At such times, he was happy.

He accepted the fact that he would not get to know any girls this summer; the club recruiters had been right on this point. If he did not belong to the club, he would not meet the local younger set, short of nodding to them at parties. Occasionally, on the beach, he would strike up a conversation with girls he had known in high school, who were working in the plastics factory or clerking in a store; quite a few were married and had a baby. But these proletarian girls had even less allure for him than the girls in pony-tails driving Volkswagens. They were not interested in civil rights, even to argue against them. They simply did not care what happened to the Negro. It was not their fault; they had not had his opportunities. The civil-rights fight, he recognized, was a luxury for most of the whites who engaged in it; his classmates who had gone to Mississippi had had their fares and expenses paid by their families, just as though they were going on field period. If he was free (as he hoped) from prejudice, unlike his contemporaries on the raft, this was owing largely to his parents, who in turn had had "advantages." He was trying to think clearly this summer, before going abroad, about himself and his country. The native girls on the beach would have been glad, evidently, to "date" him, because he was from "away," but he could not date a girl who was not interested in civil rights—which meant, in practice, a girl who had not been to Smith or Wellesley or Swarthmore or Antioch or some other upper-middle-class school. If he had gone to Mississippi, it would have been the same; the Negro girls he might have gone around with, like the ones he used to see last winter, would have belonged to a "leader group"—otherwise, they would not be in the civil-rights movement. Their fathers would be mostly ministers and doctors and teachers and musicians, just like his own parents.

Sexually, he was pretty much a prisoner of his class, and he wondered if it would have been different had he stayed in Rocky Port High. Maybe he would not be still a virgin. Right now, he was content to stay home nights with his mother, reading and working on his French; he could quite well wait for mid-August to see girls, when he would go to his father on the Cape. And he did not feel he was missing anything if she went out to dinner by herself.

Whenever she went out to dinner, she returned despondent. It was not the people so much (she had found a few she liked), as what she had to eat. Four years ago—she remembered distinctly—a meal had begun with soup or oysters or lobster cocktail or an avocado with Roquefort dressing. *Something*. But now, it seemed, after large basins of Martinis-on-the-rocks (a drink she considered parvenu, as opposed to the classic Martini), you sat right down to the main course or it was served to you on your lap. Nobody alluded to the vanished first course; it was like a relation that had died and could not be mentioned. "How do you account for that, Peter? Do you suppose it died a lingering death? Or did it happen all of a sudden, like a stroke?" "Probably a mercy killing," said Peter. "Why don't you ask somebody, Mother, if you really want to know?" "How can I? Who would I ask? It would have to be someone who still served it, and I seem to be the only one." "You'd better lay off it yourself, Mother." "Why?" she said, indignant. "We've always had a first course. Why should I change? They have just as much time for cooking as I have, these women. More." "That's just the point, Mother," he groaned.

Peter hated it when she sent him around to borrow muffin tins or cake racks or a flour sifter. Nobody had them; nobody used them any more. "You don't get the picture, Mother. You're out of touch. Americans have stopped cooking. You embarrass them." "Nonsense. In New York, all my friends cook." "'New York is not America,' Mother. Old adage." In the very first days, she had drawn attention to herself by giving Mrs. Curtis a list of things that were missing in their kitchen that she considered *essential*, underlining the word, such as pie tins and a breadboard. There was practically nothing in the cupboards, she said, but drinking equipment. Their landlady, a Goldwater stalwart, had taken offense; she refused to supply any more kitchen stuff unless his mother restored the historical notice to the house front. The situation was deadlocked. His mother said that a house without a griddle or a strainer, not to mention pie tins and so on, had no claim to an historical placard. She refused to buy the equipment herself, on the ground that the house had been rented "furnished," except for linen and silver. In the end, Mrs. Curtis, who still liked his mother, took up a collection from people's attics. The arrival of these items was watched by their red-faced landlady from her house across the street. Peter's mother considered this a triumph, but to his mind it was a draw.

His mother's kitchen-shower included a number of items she had not asked for; *e.g.*, a butter churn, a preserving kettle, and an old wooden ice-cream freezer with a rusty crank. His mother lit up. She was going to make ice cream at once, in their back yard, for Mrs. Curtis' grandchildren; Peter could crank. She found rock salt in the hardware store. The owner was curious as to what she planned to do with it; folks here used it, winters, to melt the ice on their sidewalks. She explained. That night, she had a note from the landlady, protesting the use of rock salt in her garden—which was just a flagged terrace without a blade of grass to be damaged, as his mother pointed out in her reply.

The contest between the two had become a sort of sporting event, watched by the community with a certain impartiality of which Peter felt his mother was not wholly aware. The liberals were for his mother, because she was a novelty in the Rocky Port summer scene and was furnishing amusement at no cost except to herself. The Old Guard was for the landlady, because his mother was an interloper who played an outlandish instrument under the stage name of "Brown," though it was known on good authority that she had been born Rosie Bronsky on the Lower East Side. But on the issues, it ought to have been the other way around. His mother's sympathizers, Peter noticed, were not rushing to follow her example, and among the landlady's supporters there were probably a few old ladies who could still wield a rolling-pin. Be that as it might, his mother was the only avowed reactionary in cooking in Rocky Port, and this was bound, Peter feared, to make her unpopular even among her chums in the end.

She made a share-cropping deal with Mrs. Curtis, to harvest her currants. She and Peter were going to pick the currants, make jelly out of them, and give Mrs. Curtis half. Four years ago, his mother had bought jelly glasses in the grocery store. Now, the storekeeper shook his gray head emphatically. "Don't get any call for them." It was the bean-pot motif, developed. With jelly glasses, naturally, paraffin had gone. And Mason jars with rubbers. "Haven't had a call for them in years, ma'am. Don't know as they make 'em any more. Guess you notice changes." "Yes, I do," said Peter's mother coldly. "It's not his fault," Peter whispered, excruciated.

She was going to make jelly, she said, gritting her teeth, if she had to buy store jelly and dump it down the sink, to use the jars. The thought of this waste sickened Peter; he would rather have gone scavenging in the town dump for old mayonnaise containers. Fortunately, jelly glasses and paraffin were found at the county seat—the glasses covered with dust and cobwebs like some vintage wine.

Then she decided to make watermelon pickle, saving up the rinds in huge quantities in the kitchen, using every available pan and cover to keep the flies off. Peter, who had never heard of this delicacy, could not believe the result was going to be worth the trouble. She bought screw-top jars and procured the magic ingredient—calcium oxide—from a druggist ten miles off. "Mind if I ask what you want it for, lady?" the druggist said. Peter's mother froze. "Why? Is it poison?" "No, 'tain't that. I was just wondering. Haven't had a call—" "I know," she said. "I'm going to make watermelon pickle." The druggist smacked his lips. "That's a real old-timer. Hadn't thought of that . . ." "I'll give you a jar," said Peter's mother, with her usual impulsiveness, moved to spread the gospel.

The fisherman they used to go to had moved to Florida, and she could not find fish anywhere that was not filleted, though a number of quaint shingled fish shops with sawdust on the floor had opened in the area, selling "real New England clam chowder" in cans, bottled Tartar sauce, lobsters, cooked, to take home, lobster meat, and canned Chalet Suzanne lobster bisque; in the supermarkets, the fish was frozen. The only fresh fish on the whole coast seemed to be pale, boneless, skinless flounder, "ready to fry." "There are other fish in the sea," she commented. "What happens to them?" The clerk in the fish shop was offended. "Couldn't tell you that, ma'am." "Am I wrong," she demanded, "to want a whole fresh fish—with head and bones—on the seashore? Is that asking too much?" "Don't get any call—" Peter's mother put her hands to her ears.

She could not get a fowl from the butcher—only roasters and fryers and chicken-in-parts. "Folks here don't make soup like they used to. Don't have the time for it. Guess we're kind of spoiled," the butcher summed up, with a complacent gray grin, twiddling his thumbs in his apron. "You are," she retorted.

"Maybe *you're* spoiled, Mother. Only a few rich people with cooks can afford the kind of food you like." "*I* like!" she exclaimed. "What about you, Peter? Anyway, the things you can't find here are the cheap things. Like smelts and cod. A fowl is cheaper than a roasting chicken, and you get soup from it too. Then you can make something with the leftovers the next day. Why, the cook we had in Umbria could get three meals for four people out of a hen. I admire that. Economy is a contact with reality, Peter. I love reality. I hope you always will too." Her light voice trembled with seriousness. She meant what she said, deeply, but he could not help trying to calculate how much she had spent on gasoline scouring the countryside for jelly glasses.

Anyway, it was not just food, she said. What about buttons? She could not find buttons for Peter's shirts at the village notions store, which was full of New England souvenir items, such as whaling ships in bottles. "Button man hasn't been through in a coon's age," said the stout woman behind the counter. "Don't you think you *ought* to stock buttons?" Peter's mother said earnestly, putting it on a moral plane. "Supposing I didn't have a car to drive to the nearest town to get them? Or I couldn't afford the bus fare? What would I do?" "Search me," said the woman.

Peter was worried. He wished his stepfather would come home. People in the stores had begun to stare, nudgingly, at his mother, and not because she was pretty or famous. She was looking older this summer, and most people in the stores did not know or care that she was *the* Rosamund Brown. It might have been different if she had ever played on television. He offered to do the marketing for her, to take her out of the public eye. Then he saw for himself what she meant. It was unnerving to cross out item after item on the lists that she gave him—not available. And he made a discovery of his own that shocked him: he was unable to buy plain yoghurt, one of his favorite foods. He could choose between prune and strawberry. The clerk in the Portuguese market, which he patronized in preference to the Yankee market when he did the shopping himself, explained to him that plain yoghurt was a "slow mover." That, in two words, was the trouble. He and his mother were wedded to slow movers.

"Is a country store just a distribution point?" she exclaimed. "In that case, it would be better to have socialism. State stores, like in Poland and Hungary." Peter frowned. His mother, ever since she had played behind the Iron Curtain, sounded as if she was getting soft on Communism. In politics, he took after his father, who was still a mainstay of the anti-Communist left. "We still have political freedom," he reminded her. "I wonder," she replied, "what political freedom means here now. Take this election, Peter. Hasn't it come down to a choice between prune and strawberry?"

Peter laughed hoarsely. She was right in a way. "Still, Mother, you do think it's important that Goldwater should be defeated?" She sighed. "I suppose so. Still, I'd like to be able to vote for Norman Thomas, the way we did in the old days. Or Darlington Hoopes! Now the Socialists aren't even on the ballot." Peter nodded. The good old days! He remembered starting second grade festooned with Darlington Hoopes buttons that he had made his mother procure for him at Socialist Party headquarters in Boston—she had not been able to find them in Holyoke. But he did not encourage her political nostalgia. In November, she might write in Norman Thomas and throw away her vote. Since he was too young to vote himself, he had to trust her to do it for him. It seemed to him that the issues were more important these days than when the Socialists had been running.

Sometimes she divined ahead of time, when she was making her list, that some product like buckwheat flour was going to be unobtainable and she would leave it to Peter to choose between Aunt Jemima and nothing. But sometimes she was rocked back on her heels. He came home one morning to tell her that salt codfish in those wooden boxes with the sliding covers was not to be found—what should he do? "Did you ask, Peter?" "I looked. It isn't there." "Impossible!" She struck a violent blow on the harpsichord. "I'll go myself. Probably they've changed the packaging. When will you get over being so shy, Peter?" He loped along beside her down the main street. She waited her turn at the check-out counter and put the question. A peculiar expression crossed the Yankee store-keeper's face—something between a twinge of guilt and a smirk of satisfaction. Peter's mother closed her eyes. "Don't tell me." "Yep! They ain't making that any more. That is 'a thing of the past,' ma'am." He rubbed his hands on his apron. "I can sell you frozen codfish cakes, ready to fry—very tasty. Of course, you pay a mite more; you have to expect that." "It's not the same," she said, her voice quivering. She leaned over the counter, staring at the grocer like his mercantile conscience. "You realize it's not the same, don't you?" "Oh, I wouldn't say that, ma'am. No, I wouldn't say that. You put on some ketchup and you won't notice a mite of difference."

"Give up the fight, Mother." The news that tapioca, except in instant form, was "a thing of the past" too made him feel old, a weary Rip Van Winkle returned from a drive-in bowling alley. In this sinister summer of race riots, church-burnings, civil-rights workers vanishing in Mississippi, in New York, a cop, off duty, shooting to kill at a Negro kid, the fact that tapioca, his old love, had kicked the bucket ought not to matter. Yet if he said that to his mother, she felt he was abandoning her.

It disturbed him to see her so irritated by everything. He had always thought of her as equable. He could not accuse her of being a superficial person, but it was at least arguable, he thought, that she was reading too much into the minutiae. She acted as if the difference between sliced bread and unsliced was the difference between wrong and right. He wondered if she was getting near the menopause. For the first time in her life that Peter could remember, she had begun—what an irony!—to have cooking failures. Not when they were alone, but when they had company. And being what she was, she had to apologize. "Just serve it, Mother. Don't say anything. They'll never know." Glumly, he watched her trying to turn her battle with

Rocky Port into a game, laughing at her misadventures and writing with amusement about them to his stepfather—letters she sometimes let Peter read. It sounded funny when you read about it. Yet he feared that—also for the first time in her life— she did not see herself as others saw her.

For himself, he invented a different game—taking the Goldwater stickers off people's cars. He worked at night, selecting his target before dark came. He burned the trophies in the fireplace when his mother was out; if he told her what he was doing, she would be bound to boast about it, and he would find himself fleeing from Rocky Port with a price on his head —intimidating voters, which he hoped he was doing, was a federal crime. His most daring exploit was getting the huge streamer off the bumper of their landlady's Buick, which she kept parked under a street light directly across the way. He needed a confederate to engage her on the telephone in the back hall while he did the job. She slept in the downstairs front bedroom, with a shotgun, supposedly, by her side. "Hell, son," said the admiral. "I'd have done the same thing at your age. Down South, I was a Republican before I could shave, which was like being a card-carrying Communist. Now, with this race business, I'm kind of leaning toward Goldwater myself. Guess I'm part of the white backlash." He agreed to act as a decoy, however, and to get his wife to invite Peter's mother to a lecture, to keep her out of the way. He and Peter set their watches together and worked out a code for Peter to signal with a flashlight when the deed was done. Failing Goldwater stickers, Peter removed "Ausable Chasm" and "Desert of Maine" from the bumpers of passing tourists.

These puerile activities gave direction, of a sort, to his summer and led him to make friends with the admiral, who had lost a son in the war. He was the only older WASP Peter knew, except his mother, who still had some pioneer spirit. The old man was disgruntled with the modern world, and Peter could almost forgive him, in view of his Tennessee origins, for being prejudiced against Negroes (which the admiral denied), because he was prejudiced against so many other groups and persons, regardless of race, creed, or color—*e.g.*, social workers, J. Edgar Hoover, and the CIA. Peter was hoping to influence him, before the summer was over, to stay at home, come

November, rather than vote for Goldwater; he was one of the mass of "Undecideds" who were a headache to pollsters and political scientists. Peter could sympathize with a pollster who got the admiral in his sampling. He himself had just about decided to class him as a visceral fascist when he learned that the old man and his wife and Mrs. Curtis constituted the local chapter of a Ban-the-Bomb organization.

The admiral, known as "Reb" for rebel—his sobriquet at Annapolis—had a hammock and a telescope on his back porch, from which he viewed the stars. He knew the coast well—the many islands, islets, points, coves, harbors, inlets, salt marshes —and the shore and sea birds. He was a student of the hurricanes that came this way in the fall. Before he had had his heart attack, two years back, he had been vociferous at town meetings. Now he puttered about, smoking his pipe, doing crewelwork, helping his wife with her Gift Shop, slyly drinking snorts of whiskey, and making horrible curries. What pleased Peter in the admiral was that he resembled the element he had lived in—salty, shifty, protean, like the Old Man of the Sea. He was the only All-Year-Rounder whose former occupation you could guess after a short conversation. He had a small, mean mouth, a hoarse sea bird's voice, and was reputed to be violent when drinking.

The admiral boasted of being unwelcome at the beach club, which had only let him in, he said, because it was "traditional" to accept naval officers. The word *tradition* was often heard at Rocky Port cocktail parties, usually on the lips of a woman with blue hair or a fat man in Polynesian shorts. The village was protecting its traditions, Peter was repeatedly told, as though Rocky Port were a sanctuary full of banded birds threatened with extirpation. He wondered what had been handed down to these people that they thought they were safeguarding—besides money. There was nothing distinctive about Rocky Port's institutions or way of life, unless it was the frequency of gift shops selling "gourmet" foods, outsize pepper mills, "amusing" aprons and chef's costumes, bar equipment, and frozen croissants, "just like in France." "Taking in each other's washing," the admiral declared. Probably they deserved credit for maintaining their houses and keeping the streets swept. The fact remained that Rocky Port was a

museum and, like all museums, Peter's mother said, best when
it was all-but-empty and you could hear your footfalls echo.
They should never have come back in season.

Still, there was one traditional event, everyone told them,
that capped the summer and was unique to Rocky Port; you
would not see anything like it at Watch Hill or Weekapaug or
Saunderstown. This was the annual celebration of the Battle of
Rocky Port, where the British had been defeated in the War of
1812. It was a two-day affair in which the whole community
participated, man, woman, and child—a typical old-time New
England jamboree. Normally, Peter would have gone to his
father in mid-August, but his departure was postponed for the
sake of this celebration, which the *babbo*, as an educator, could
hardly deny him. It began the fifteenth of August with an
Historic Houses and Gardens tour, under Garden Club auspices, that drew crowds from as far away as Providence. Next
morning, there was a parade, led by the Portuguese Holy
Ghost Club, which had a brass band; that afternoon, there was
a fair on the village green for the benefit of the town churches
and charities, with games, ponies, a cake sale, rummage, a sale
of secondhand books, and stands of vegetables, flowers, and
fruits.

This was the sort of event his mother rose to. If the locals
had had any sense, Peter thought, they would have put her on
the program committee. She would have been happy to tell
fortunes, look up old martial airs and arrange them for the
band, contribute a button collection—cutting them off her
own clothes, if necessary; she would have organized a needlework contest, made pinwheels, donated jars of pickles and
jelly, helped sew costumes, put Peter to work painting mints
with vegetable colors. It was a disappointment that she was
only asked to bake a cake for the cake sale to benefit the Free
Library. "Can't I make a pot of beans for one of the other
charities? And a freezer of ice cream?" she said to Mrs. Curtis,
who had come to sign her up for the cake. "I'd love to,
wouldn't I, Peter?"

"I know you would," said Mrs. Curtis, patting his mother's
hand. "But it won't be necessary, my dear." The ice-cream
concession, she explained, was given to a commercial company
—the same people who handled the sale of Coca-Cola and

hot dogs. "I don't understand," said Peter's mother. "You can still use some home-made ice cream. Peach, I thought. And baked beans have become a sort of novelty. What are the other women making?" Mrs. Curtis looked sidewise at Peter; some bad news, he surmised, was going to be broken to his mother. "It's like this, Rosamund. The company won't sell hot dogs and ice cream for us unless they have the exclusive concession. Doesn't pay them unless they handle all the refreshments. Our charities farm out the stands to them on a percentage basis." "You mean that's *all*? Commercial ice cream and hot dogs?"

"And cakes to take home. That's the way it is." Mrs. Curtis turned to Peter. "I was afraid she was going to take it hard. It's kind of a shock at first. Why, I remember the time when we used to have potato salads and chicken potpies and clam pies. Rice salad, lobster salad, macaroni salad. Yes, and baked beans and home-made ice cream. Peppermint was a great seller. Boston brown bread. Oatmeal bread. Date bread. Always a lot of baked goods. You can get women to bake when they won't do anything else. Point of pride with them. Sex, I've always thought. Getting a rise out of the batter."

"How long has this been going on?" Peter's mother interrupted. "Well, it's quite some time now. Seems to me the Red Cross started it, with the store hot dogs. Somebody had a relative with Howard Johnson's, it might have been. They came in with their stoves and their frankfurters and rolls and then they cleaned up after themselves. Saved a lot of trouble. The other organizations caught on—the Visiting Nurse and the Community Fund. Pretty soon we were all doing it. Sort of a trend. In the old days, people rushed around the first thing after the parade to get that one's chicken pie or the other one's lobster salad. Then when you ran out, the ones who came late were sore. Felt they'd been cheated. Old Mrs. Drysdale, up in the big house, used to send down a pot of bouillabaisse every year, made by her French chef. Always caused bad blood. This way, it's more democratic. The Catholic church was the last to fall into line. They had their own refreshment stand up till '63. Oh, let me tell you, the priest cracked the whip over those women! A real Simon Legree, that one was. Preached against Adlai because he was a divorced man. And they followed him like sheep. It was 'Mrs. Rodriguez, you'll make your Parker House rolls,' and 'Mrs. Santos, you'll make your Southern fried chicken'—no excuses accepted. But the Church couldn't hold out forever, with the tide running the other way. Pope John, you know."

Peter and his mother eyed each other sadly. She cleared her throat. "What kind of cake should I make, Ellen?" "Whatever your heart desires, dear. Chocolate's always safe. My husband used to like a marble cake. I guess I don't have to tell you not to use a mix." His mother brightened. "Is that a rule? How nice!" "We have the Catholics to thank for it," Mrs. Curtis said. "'Nix on Mixes,' Father Cassidy—that's the new one— told the women, right from the pulpit. Threatened them with the confessional. Those priests like to eat." "Are the Papists running the fair?" Peter wanted to know. "If they won't use mixes," said Mrs. Curtis, "we've got to keep in line with them. We don't want them to sell their cakes ahead of ours, do we?"

"Why just cakes?" said Peter. "Why not pies? You ought to diversify." "A good pie is hard to make," said Mrs. Curtis. "They say it's a lost art." "You can't even buy pastry flour in the grocery store," put in Peter's mother. "Can't you?" said Mrs. Curtis absently. "Well, times change. There's talk every year of cutting out the cake sale, as more trouble than it's worth. A lot would give the money and more not to have the oven on in this hot weather. But the majority clings to it. We get people coming every year just for the cake sale. It's traditional."

"'Let them eat cake,'" said Peter. He tried to imagine the contented masses on the village green. "What games do they have?" "Well, we used to have archery. Broad jump. Potato races. Weight-lifting. But now it's pretty standardized. Mostly throwing rings over the necks of Coca-Cola bottles at ten cents a throw. You win one of those dolls. That's all a concession too. The men come from outside and give us a cut of what they make. Times past, there was one that brought a shooting-gallery, with ducks. But it comes to the same thing if you just throw rings at bottles."

When Mrs. Curtis had gone, Peter's mother said that the fair sounded rather commercialized. Perhaps they had better not expect too much of it. He was too old to ride a pony and if he wanted a hot dog he could go to the diner. She did hope he would enjoy the parade and the Historic Houses and Gardens tour. Or would he rather skip the whole thing and go, as originally planned, to his father on the Cape?

The offer went to his heart. He could not accept it. If he walked out on Rocky Port now, he would be walking out on her and her foundering values. Even if his presence embarrassed her, he had to go down with the ship.

She knew that old houses did not greatly interest him, that he disliked crowds and would probably feel self-conscious standing in line to view flower-arrangements done by Garden Club ladies, although he liked *her* flowers and botany and had giant plants crawling around his college room. But he knew how much she was looking forward to the garden tour, having been deprived of a garden herself this summer. The yard in back of their house was all flagged, with no place for flower beds—only for garden furniture and a "service area" containing garbage cans. Less maintenance, the landlady stated, and it made a nice setting for cocktails. All summer his mother had been picking wild flowers for their parlor in the woods and marshes, and Peter could understand her enthusiasm at the prospect of seeing what she called "real" flowers growing in beds and borders. Remembering the acres of armor and miles of mummies she had traversed with him when he was little, he made a resolution not to be bored; it was no good resolving not to *act* bored, as he had learned in Italy.

Those old New England gardens could be marvelous, she told him, especially in seaports. You discovered rare plants and shrubs that ships' captains had brought home from the Orient. Flowers that were in Shakespeare and Keats and that must have traveled from England in the form of roots, slips, bulbs, and cuttings, with the early settlers. Old-fashioned roses. White double narcissus and poppies that bloomed every year on Memorial Day. Spicebush, lemon lilies, a kind of Persian lilac that smelled of Necco Wafers. A plant called Beauty Bush and one called Sensitive Plant that winced when you touched it. Old ladies' flowers like heliotrope and verbena and pinks. Hollyhocks, self-seeded, against white picket fences. A great deal of honeysuckle, privet, and box. Sundials, arbors, trellises, an occasional gazebo. Dogs' gravestones. It was a pity that the tour was so late in the season; most of the perennials, except phlox, would be finished. But the annuals ought to be particularly brilliant. Something in the sea air or light brought out the colors of zinnias and pale lemon African marigolds. She only hoped there would not be too many dahlias.

On the morning of the great day, she was up early, wearing a pink linen dress. She told Peter to put on his seersucker suit and shine his shoes. At nine, the sky clouded over. A few drops of rain fell. The mailman reassured her. "Radio says fair. Paper says fair. That rain don't mean a thing. It's just the weather." At eleven, in fact, it stopped raining. His mother put on a large straw hat, and they took their places in line, outside the first house on the tour. Their landlady, who was an officer of the Garden Club, was selling tickets. "I'm going to *speak*," whispered Peter's mother. "Lovely day, after all, Mrs. Hills," she said pleasantly. The landlady sold them two tickets, which would also entitle them to tea later in the day. "Did you lock up after you?" she said curtly, making change. "I never lock up," said Peter's mother. "Well, I'm warning you. Strangers in town." "But a stranger is just someone you don't know, Mrs. Hills," his mother said, in a friendly tone. "And don't want to," retorted the landlady, handing her a program. "You get another element these days. Riffraff from the towns. Only come to rubberneck. Never known what it is to own beautiful things and take care of them." "My son can go home and lock up, if you're really concerned," said his mother, who was evidently determined not to spoil the day by a dispute.

When he returned, his mother was studying the program, printed in red and blue type on thick white paper and decorated with an American flag rippling in the breeze. "A Stroll into the Past" was the title. Peter counted the stars in the flag; there were sixteen, which he supposed was historically justified—his father would know. On the back of the program was a little map of the village; each "open" house had a number. Peter scrutinized it. In their old neighborhood, he noted some small letters: *a*, *b*, and *c*. "Portugee gardens," he heard Mrs. Hills explain to a pair of out-of-towners. "Houses aren't shown." She pointed to the bottom of the program, where there was a section headed "Gardens Open." They belonged to a Mr. Antone Silvia, a Mrs. Rose Santos, and a Mrs. Mary Lacerda.

He and his mother began the tour with "a typical sea-captain's house of an early time." Two hostesses were directing traffic through the small, rather dark rooms. Visitors dressed in their best clothes jostled each other to stare at highboys, low-boys, duck-footed tables, carpets, china cabinets, silver, pewter, ancestral portraits, faded family photographs, keepsakes, which were exciting more curiosity than the flower-arrangements tagged with red and blue ribbons and the architectural features described in the program. "Please don't touch!" a voice rapped out from time to time, as someone fingered the china or looked for the hallmark on the silver. Peter was surprised by the number of middle-aged men in the throng. It was hot, and there was a strong smell of furniture polish, overlaying a slight moldy smell of old upholstery. Someone had forgotten to take down the Christmas mistletoe in the parlor doorway. "Tacky," was his mother's verdict. While she lined up to look at the flower-arrangements, he tried to take an interest in the books on the library shelves. The most recent acquisitions he could find were Winston Churchill's war memoirs and *Peyton Place*. His mother beckoned. "Let's go." In the garden, there was less congestion. They looked around. "Has there been a drought or something?" Peter wondered aloud. The only evidence of gardening he noted was a compost heap. "Ssh!" said his mother, peering at the program. "Come, let's find 'Aunt Mary Chase's roses.' It says here they were planted during the Civil War." They followed a flagged walk that led, past some bushes, to a "service area." They retraced their steps. His mother asked someone. "There!" A spindly rose with two faded blooms was leaning against a trellis. She swallowed her disappointment. "What a shame it's so late in the season! Those old varieties of roses never do much after June. It looks as if these people"—she glanced again at the program—"had rather let their garden go. But in spring it must be lovely, don't you think so, Peter? Look, they had peonies and lilies of the valley. And that must be iris." "Where?" said Peter. She indicated some yellow foliage. "They ought to separate them," she said absently. "Those are violets," she went on, tapping a leaf with her foot. "Probably just ordinary wood violets. Oh, see the quinces!"

"Come on, Mother." He led the way out. They tried "a fine example of a prosperous shipowner's dwelling." Peter found

Winston Churchill's war memoirs, *The Carpetbaggers*, and the
bound files of the *National Geographic*. "But there aren't any
flowers!" his mother whispered, in the garden. She exaggerated, but not greatly. It was the same all along the line. Here
and there, shrubs and hardy perennials were still gamely
blooming, survivors of another era, like Longfellow's *Poems*,
which they discovered propping up a small-paned window.
Hydrangeas, phlox, funkia, yucca—his mother named them
off. Lilac bushes, indestructible, stood in the dooryards, surrounded by suckers. You could infer from latticework where a
rose arbor had been and make out designs faintly traced by
decimated box. Raised oblongs in the arid lawns, like graves,
testified to former flower beds. "That must have been a strawberry patch!" his mother cried, pointing. She found some old
yellow roses. But there was hardly an annual or a biennial to be
seen, except in the yards of the Portuguese section, where
zinnias and dahlias were growing in uncontrolled abundance,
like the children of the poor. Elsewhere, as Peter commented,
old Mother Nature seemed to have taken the pill.

His own mother kept apologizing. "I'm sorry, Peter." "Why?
It's not your fault." She cheered up slightly in Gardens *a*, *b*, and
c, which were attached to two-story frame tenement dwellings.
Mr. Antone Silvia had potted red geraniums and white ruffled
petunias and transplanted ferns from the woods. Mrs. Santos
had scattered seeds of every kind broadcast: cockscombs, zinnias, kitchen herbs, dahlias, cosmos, calendulas, marigolds, asters
—a riot, remarked Peter, of bloom. Mrs. Lacerda had roses
and dahlias. "The darling Portuguese!" they heard a young
woman in tight turquoise pants exclaim to her companion in
Mr. Silvia's small neat grassy plot. "They have a green thumb
but no taste. Don't you love them? Red, white, and green—
you can *see* Tony thinking out his colors. I always make a pilgrimage to Mrs. Lacerda's funny garden, and she brings me a
rose in her hot little hand. It was such a clever idea to have
them in the Garden Club. We were afraid they'd notice the
difference between their gardens and ours. Not at all, my dear.
Totally unaware of it."

Peter's mother's laugh made the young woman jump. "Take
it easy, Mother." She had already drawn attention to them by a
display of mirth back in one of the houses when he suggested

that maybe the reason they did not see more flowers growing was that they had all been picked for the flower-arrangements. She seemed to want people to listen while she gaily read aloud from the program: "An arrangement of flowers and/or foliage in an old tea-caddy or canister." "A doorstep arrangement of wild flowers and/or foliage in a stoneware container." "An arrangement of roadside material featuring one or more seashells." He did not see what was so funny, and neither did the rest of the auditory. "Well, come and look, Peter." Then the light broke.

Tea-caddies, ironstone tureens, Lowestoft dishes, seashells, and (naturally) bean pots were filled with "wild material," which, translated from Garden Club parlance, meant weeds. Among them, Peter recognized some old friends. Cat-tails from the marshes, Queen Anne's lace, beach peas, Black-eyed Susan, Bouncing Bet. His mother said it had been like that in every house so far. He decided to start keeping a tally. According to his final count, the commonest "flower" in this unusual flower show was Queen Anne's lace. Bouncing Bet scored second—"so versatile," he heard a woman say. There was also a multitude of field and beach grasses unknown by name to him but which belonged, his mother said coldly, on a hay-fever chart. Here and there, combined with this wild material, were a few roses and/or blue hydrangeas, some stalks of delphinium, a gladiolus. The visitors filing through seemed lost in admiration. "Look at that, will you, sweetheart," an earnest man in a yachting blazer said to his wife. "It shows what you can do with just one rose."

An exception was the contest set by their landlady: "An arrangement of red, white, and blue flowers in an old pewter container. CHAIRMAN: Mrs. Frances B. Hills." The prize winners here had used conventional flowers, like larkspurs and petunias. His mother said this must be because few weeds came in patriotic colors. A debate was going on. Some argued that "Honorable Mention," who had used Queen Anne's lace, field asters, and devil's-paintbrush (which to Peter's eye was orange), ought to have had first prize. A man stood up for the awards. "To me, they look bright and colorful." "Floristy," his wife told him. And that indeed was the case. The scandal reached Peter and his mother at the diner, where they were eating their lunch. "You folks hear what happened?" said the waitress. It was all over town: the first- and second-prize winners in Mrs. Hills's contest had been disqualified; they had bought their material from a florist in Westerly. The truck had been seen delivering.

At tea at the house of the Garden Club president, Peter and his mother, in search of a friendly face, found the admiral chuckling to himself on the terrace overlooking the harbor. "They've confessed," he said. "Been asked to resign from the Garden Club. If Frances Hills had her way, they'd be stood in the pillory. 'Collapse of public morality.'" He munched at a thawed frozen sandwich from the Corner Cupboard and spat out a sliver of ice. "Seems as though they could make a sandwich at home." "Did you *see* the flower-arrangements, Reb?" The admiral nodded. "Did the whole tour. Paid good money for it. Only flowers worth seeing came from the florist." He sourly recalled the days at the War College when he had grown giant dahlias. "They'll have instant flowers next." "A weed is an instant flower," Peter's mother pointed out. The admiral chortled. "The country's going to hell, sweetheart. Fellow came the other day, tried to sell me an atom-bomb shelter made of compressed marble dust. Claimed it was a new industry, helping unemployment in the area. The Great Society! I tell you, I'm swinging more and more to Goldwater."

Peter's mother started to argue. "Goldwater is *worse*, Reb. Look at his foreign policy. And he runs a *department store*. At least Johnson taught school." Peter took his mother's empty teacup and glided toward the dining room. The admiral sounded like a fascist, and his mother sounded like a Communist, and they were the two people he liked in Rocky Port. Mrs. Curtis in his view was too fey to count politically. He approached the tea table, where Mrs. Hills was pouring. "Young man, why don't you wait and let other people be served before you? This is the third time you've been through the line. Don't you get enough to eat at home?" Peter replied non-violently. "It's for my mother."

He went back to the terrace and reported the exchange. The admiral laughed. "Steer clear of her, son. She's kind of inflamed today. Having that happen at her contest. Never at her best anyway in an election year." He turned to Peter's mother. "You know, the other night somebody took the Goldwater streamer off her car. I think she suspects young Peter here." He winked at Peter. "Why, that's the most unjust thing! Why should she suspect Peter?" She set her cup down, as though to take action. Peter met the admiral's eyes, slightly hooded, like a hawk's. The old man shook his head. He gently pulled Peter's mother to her seat. "Let be, honey. Let's you and I go on discussing politics. Now I voted for Adlai in '52 and again in '56. I never liked Ike. . . ." Peter wondered whether the admiral was too old to make passes. And if he made a pass, should the fair Rosamund yield if he promised to vote for Johnson?

The next morning, before the parade, a policeman came to their door. Their landlady wanted the historical notice put back on the house front immediately, before the parade started. With so many visitors in town, interested in historic houses, Peter's mother, she claimed, was depreciating the value of her property. "Says she gave you a written request to nail the sign up where it was more than a month ago." Peter's mother took a stand in the doorway. "I'm sorry, but I've rented this house, and there's nothing in the lease that requires me to carry advertising on it." The policeman rubbed his foot on the Welcome mat. "Come on, lady. Mrs. Hills has the law on her side. Selectmen say every old house in Rocky Port township has to have one of those boards." "If she has the law on her side, let her sue me. Excuse me, officer; I'm busy." She started to turn away; she was making seven-minute frosting for her cake for the fair.

"Not so fast there, lady," said the policeman. "I'm talking to you." She pushed open the screen door impatiently and came out onto the doorstep. The policeman backed up, bumping into Peter, who had been watering the herbal geraniums in the window boxes. Some water from the watering-can spilled onto the policeman's uniform. A little crowd was gathering under the elms and maples: tourists hung with cameras and a few paraders in period costumes with muskets. Because of the parade, the street had been cleared of motor traffic. In front of the Holy Ghost Club, the band was tuning up. "Selectmen say—" repeated the policeman in a louder voice. "Is that a town ordinance, officer?" Peter heard his own voice croak.

Mindful of his civil-rights training, he was making a simple request for information; that was what you did when met by a sheriff and his deputies at a county line. "Pipe down, Buster," the cop said. Behind him, Peter saw a tourist hold up a light meter. "My son asked you a question," said his mother, as the camera clicked. "And his name is not Buster." "That's enough out of you too, lady." The band struck up "Yankee Doodle." "Come on, Missus, let's have a little co-operation. I got a parade to handle. I give you five minutes to put that board back."

That was a tactical mistake, Peter estimated. His mother could not hammer the placard back with all these clowns watching her. Across the street, he observed their landlady surveying the scene from her bedroom window. "Or let Buster do it," emended the cop. Peter looked to his mother for guidance. In his opinion, it would be wiser to comply. The cop was flustered and ignorant, probably, of the law—something he would be unwilling to betray in front of so many witnesses. You were supposed to see your opponent as a human being and avoid making him look foolish in public. "Why don't you go in the house and talk it over, Mother? Maybe you can come to an agreement." "I'm afraid that's out of the question," she said coolly. "There isn't any board. I burned it." Peter gulped. It was her bridges she had just burned; the sign was stored in the basement. "I used it for kindling. By mistake." She smiled defiantly. The cop could see she was lying—she seemed to want him to. "Did you report this careless destruction of property?" "No." "Why not?" "It slipped my mind." The cop sighed. "Lady, I'm going to have to ask you to walk along to the police station."

"I'm sorry, I'm frosting a cake." In the crowd, someone laughed. "Don't give me that," the cop said. "Step along now." "Have you got a warrant?" Peter asked quietly. The cop's eyes narrowed. "Let's see your draft card, buddy." Peter slowly put down the watering-can, balancing it on the window box. The cop prodded him with a finger. "Let's see that draft card!" "Don't you touch him!" his mother cried. Another policeman elbowed his way through the onlookers. "What's going on here? Clear the street, folks. You're holding up the parade." Encouraged by the reinforcement, the first cop gripped Peter's arm. "All right, you! Let's have it!" Before he could restrain her, his mother picked up the watering-can, which was still half full, and poured the contents over the cop. "I advise you to cool off," she said between her teeth.

Owing to these events, they missed the parade as well as the fair on the green. They were in the village jail, waiting to be charged with disorderly conduct, resisting arrest, and assaulting a police officer. An elderly attendant locked Peter in a cell, while someone went to fetch the matron to lock up his mother. They had not been booked because there was no one to book them; the police force was busy supervising the festivities. There was no one in jail but the two of them—not even a cockroach. In the distance he heard the band. Finally it stopped and was replaced by a loud-speaker. He knew that lunch-time must have come because he was hungry—they had taken away his wristwatch when they searched him.

The jail fare proved to be hamburgers from the Portuguese diner, with plenty of ketchup, delivered by Margery, the waitress, Peter's old friend, who, it transpired, moonlighted as matron in the lockup. She let herself into his cell, handed him his tray, lit a cigarette, and combed out her beehive hairdo. "I remembered how you liked them—rare, and I made your mother's rare too." What she had not remembered was that they preferred mustard. Peter was relieved to glean that his mother had not said so. "Gee, thanks, Margery; I mean . . ." He hesitated, unsure of how to address her in their changed relationship.

"Go ahead, call me Marge," she said. "I can get you seconds, if you want." He wondered what he should do about tipping her; they had taken away his money too. "Don't give it a thought, Pete. It's a pleasure. Anyway, the town pays my time here, and it makes a change. Don't happen often that they send for me. We rarely get a woman in jail. Last one was a murderess. Police caught her, where she was hiding out in Rocky Port. She was wanted in Hartford for an axe-murder. Geez, Pete, it come as a shock to me to see your mother here. A lady like her. You never know these days, do you? Nobody told me. Just 'You're wanted as matron, Marge.' I didn't even have time to slip off my apron."

"Neither did my mother," Peter remarked dryly. Margery nodded. "You don't have to tell me. Geez, Pete, I had to search her. Right down to her panties and hose. A lady like her. Just the same as a hooker. But like I told her, the law says I have to do it. I can't go against the law." "You mustn't buy that," said Peter. "If anybody feels a law is unjust, he ought to disobey it." "You mean like Prohibition?" Peter had not thought of the analogy. "Actually, I was thinking of segregation. Or marching without a permit. I didn't mean it was unjust that you had to search my mother." "I was just doing my job," Margery retorted. "Like I told her. But, God, it broke my heart. Skin like a baby, she has. Geez, Pete, what are things coming to?"

Peter did not know. Though he could not nurse his mother's wrongs with the same woeful relish as the jail matron, he agreed that she did not belong in "a place like this"—as Margery kept calling it, shaking her head. In fact, his cell, which slept four, had a toilet, and a window box filled with white and purple petunias. Conditions were pretty good. Nevertheless, it shocked him to think of his mother, who was very modest, being stripped by a wardress. He asked himself what was the difference between Margery and a hospital nurse—his mother would be stripped in a hospital as a matter of course. The evident difference was that in a hospital his mother would be a private patient. What was biting Margery was that his mother was getting the common-criminal treatment, while statistically she was an uncommon criminal. It seemed to be otherwise with him. His age, he assumed, made his being in a place like this appear more natural.

While Margery went to fetch his dessert, he pursued his thoughts. Whatever others might feel, he regarded his own presence here as wholly unnatural—fantastic. He could not believe that Peter Levi was in jail in good old Rocky Port. Down South, it would have been different: you went there knowing that you might be arrested; you went to bear witness. Just as the *babbo*, who had done time in Mussolini's prisons, had felt that he "belonged" there because he opposed fascism. You belonged in a place where you had chosen to be. But this morning's adventure had had a horrible, unreal, automated character from the outset. For one thing, it had all happened so fast, like a car accident. One minute he was peacefully watering the geraniums and the next he was aiming a feeble left at a policeman's jaw. His reason felt aggrieved; what had happened did not make sense in the general scheme. It was like that time, last fall on the Cape, when he had swum out too far and lost his wind: the thought that he might be drowning, all alone in the unfriendly ocean, while his family was sunning on the beach, had appeared to him as a sort of gross insult—the last straw, really. He asked himself now whether this stubborn sense of personal immunity, like the sense of personal immortality, was a bourgeois trait.

Another point was needling him. "*A lady like her.*" He confessed that it had gratified him to hear Margery say it. He was glad that somebody in this madhouse recognized that his mother was gently bred, a gentle person. But what would Margery say of Mrs. Hills, who was not a hooker either, if she landed in the clink? Did Margery know the difference between his mother and Mrs. Hills or was she just evincing class prejudice? In that case he ought to have corrected her instead of silently consenting. As an egalitarian, he ought to be repelled by the survival of feudal notions among the "lower orders"; yet in his heart he had been humbly thanking Margery for not confusing his mother with an axe-murderess from Hartford. This meant, he guessed, that he was uncertain of his own values and needed a friendly waitress to confirm them. But maybe in a democracy that was the way it should be; his mother was a "lady" by Margery's consent.

The afternoon went by. Solitary confinement, he discovered, did not promote a Socratic dialogue with yourself. You got bored. He practiced the conjugation of French irregular verbs, sang his favorite arias to himself ("*Se vuol ballare, signor contino*"), and endeavored to guess the time from the length of the shadows cast by the bars on his floor. He supposed he had the right to ask for a lawyer and make one telephone call but he felt no inclination to exercise those rights. Sooner or later, he and his mother would be sprung. No doubt their friends outside were working on that now. The syrup for his mother's frosting must have boiled away on the stove. Had anybody turned off the gas?

"So you're in the brig, son." Peter was dozing when the admiral was admitted to his cell. He had brought Peter's pajamas, bathrobe, and toothbrush, and a stack of magazines. "Am I going to have to stay here all *night*?" Peter cried out, forgetting to think of his mother. "Isn't anybody posting bail or anything? Listen, sir, tomorrow I have to go to my father." The admiral soothed him. He and Mrs. Curtis had been to see a lawyer, who had called up a judge at the county seat. They could not be released on bail until they had been charged before a magistrate. He delved into his old black satchel and brought out a thermos of Martinis and some cake, wrapped in foil, from the fair. "Here's something to brush your teeth with. You can eat the cake later." He poured Peter a Martini into the thermos top.

"Here's how it is, son. The judge and the lawyer-fellow say to go slow. The lawyer's in there now, talking to your mother. His advice is not to insist on being charged. Doesn't do, in a little place like Rocky Port, to stand up on your hind legs and yell for your legal rights." "Amen," said Peter. The old man looked at him shrewdly. "From what I hear, your trouble, son, was that you thought you were down South." "I guess that's true." "Down South," said the admiral, "with all this agitation, the sheriff knows the law. All the fine print. Has to, if he's going to use it against you. The police up here haven't had the opportunity. Never come up against any civil-rights workers." Peter laughed feebly. "Still, even up here, they must know about habeas corpus," he objected. "Sure," said the admiral. "After twenty-four hours, the lawyer can get a writ. But it won't come to that. Point is to give the police a chance to think it over. The chief of police won't be happy when he finds he has a celebrity in the brig. Once your mother's charged, she's likely to have to stand trial. Papers will get hold of it, and the police won't want to drop the case, because that'd make it look as if they were in the wrong. She could turn around and sue them for false arrest. None of that would do Rocky Port any good, or your mother either. When an artist gets to fighting with the police, the scuttlebutt always is they've been drinking. Kind of a natural conclusion, in my experience. Bottoms up, boy." Peter downed the Martini.

The admiral refilled his cup. "After supper, the judge is coming over for the fireworks. He'll have a session with the chief of police. But that'll be kind of late. Fireworks don't start till ten o'clock." "Fireworks?" said Peter wanly. Nobody had told him that the annual celebration ended with a fireworks display. "Looks as if you'd have to miss them. But you'll be a free man in the morning. The judge will appreciate it if your mother sends him one of her albums. Chief of police maybe too." "The payola," muttered Peter.

The admiral weighed anchor after watching Peter finish the second Martini, which he did not really want. He looked at the cartoons in the *New Yorker* and could not get the point of the jokes. A mood of bitter dissatisfaction took hold of him, which he declined to blame on the wormwood he had consumed. He was nauseated by society. It occurred to him that the old man had tried to get him drunk on purpose so as to keep him from insisting on his right to a trial. His mother, he assumed, was taking the lawyer's advice, and he was angry that he had not been consulted. They *ought* to stand trial, he considered. The charges were true. And what was their defense? That a policeman had called him "Buster" and asked for his draft card. He laughed sullenly to himself. If there was any justice in Rocky Port, they should be lucky to get off with a suspended sentence.

He tried to get his thoughts in order. Naturally, he was opposed to cops' throwing their weight around. But that was how they were. And if that was how they were, they ought to be consistent, handing it out equally to the famous and the infamous. He did not think there was any clause in the Constitution that entitled a citizen not to be called "Buster." That, apparently, was a privilege. He was free to resent the way the cop talked to a person he considered nobody, a weedy member of the draft pool, but the cop, in fact, had a duty not to know *who he was.* Peter was ashamed of his mother for letting them talk her into taking advantage of her celebrity and ashamed of the admiral for bringing liquor into his cell and breaking the rules—it was against Kant's teaching to pretend to be a law unto yourself. His mother's celebrity, as a matter of fact, was exactly what had got them into trouble; she was used to being flattered by people like Margery who "knew" she played the harp. If the cop had "known" that, he would have handled her with deference, which in turn would have satisfied her ego. So that in some depressing way the whole thing boiled down to a misunderstanding, which the cop would probably pay for.

The old jailer came and took away his dinner tray. Night fell.

Peter put on his pajamas and brushed his teeth with some salt he had saved from his dinner. He washed. These familiar night-time actions made him lonely for his mother. He remembered how she used to tuck him in when he was little, tell him his story, and bring him his glass of water. All at once, he felt contrite. He should never have made her come back to Rocky Port. He took back his harsh judgments. Obviously, a celebrity was in a position to demand courtesy from the law; she would have been wrong if she had not made an example of herself. A cop ought to fear that every nobody was a possible somebody or had a relation who was. This one would think twice before calling the next kid "Buster" or "buddy," even a kid from the wrong side of town—as Margery said, you never knew these days. Forgiving all his enemies, he fell asleep.

He had forgotten where he was when he heard someone unlocking his door. The jailer beckoned. "You want to see the fireworks?" He led Peter down the corridor and up some stairs, out to the back of the jail, where there was a raised porch with some rocking-chairs. His mother was already there, in a dressing-gown and mules, smoking a cigarette with Margery. She hugged him. "Isn't this fun? We're having an adventure, Peter." He sighed. That was her way, when he was little, of characterizing some gruesome mishap, such as running out of gas in the desert ten miles from the nearest ghost town. They watched the rockets and the Roman candles. His mother was happy, giving litle cries of pleasure as the fireworks bloomed, like big flowers in the sky, and groaning when they fizzled, until the jailer cautioned her not to make noise.

Peter realized that he was happy too. He and his mother were jailbirds, like Thoreau. True, they were getting preferential treatment, but probably Thoreau had got preferential treatment too. Small worries crossed his mind. He had left his motorbike in the back yard, with the gate unlocked; he hoped nobody would steal it. His father might be angry if he was late arriving at the Cape; he was never one to listen to an excuse. But Peter could not get really alarmed. He felt safe, with his mother, in this clapboarded jail; it had a cosy, small-town Yankee atmosphere. Quite near at hand, he heard an owl hoot. His mother whispered that the fireworks were *exceptionally* good. "They don't change much," said the jailer. "Ain't much new you can do with a rocket or a Roman candle." They were lucky, he added, to have a box seat. "Couldn't have picked a better night, ma'am, you and the boy, for getting yourselves in-carcerated. This town-jail porch is the ideal spot"—he pronounced it EYEDEEL, with equal stresses—"for watching the fireworks down there on the point." The rocking-chairs, which had held so many cops' bottoms, creaked.

To Be a Pilgrim

URING his first weeks as a student in Paris, Peter moved several times. The Embassy had given him a list of approved French families that took boarders, but he did not want to live with a French family. For the moment, he did not want to shack up with an American family either and baby-sit in exchange for his room and board, though this idea appealed to him more; he liked children. But if he stayed with Americans, he would never improve his French.

Until he landed at Le Havre, he considered himself fluent in French. Against his parents' advice, he had brought his motorbike, refusing to be separated from it, as though, said his mother, it were the fleet of fire-trucks he had slept with as a child. Owing to the motorbike, he had traveled by boat, whereas the other students in his group were traveling by charter plane. On the voyage, every day he had gone down to the hold to visit his trusty old steed, which, thanks to the New York Mafia, had a broken headlight, like a blind cyclops' eye. According to his well-laid plans, he would be reunited with it on the dock and speed off for Paris, checking his suitcases and book bag through on the train: a two-pronged assault on the capital. On the boat (an American bottom; Peter was supporting the dollar), the baggage-master had assured him that all he would have to do, after seeing the bike through customs, would be to gas up on the pier and take off. On the pier he would find an agent to handle the shipping of his baggage, but Peter distrusted agents; his travel motto was "Do-it-yourself." He had his route mapped; his first stop was going to be Rouen, to inspect the remains of the cathedral and the church of St.-Maclou —he had decided to be interested in art this year.

But on the dock the French scored their first victory over Peter Levi, famed linguist. He heard himself say "*De Le Havre*," instead of "*Du Havre*," to the porter he had hired to guard his motorbike while he took his bags to *Expéditions*, and immediately his forces were thrown into confusion. He was routed by an enemy tactic he came to know well: they lay patiently in ambush, waiting for you to make a mistake; then they sprang. Confident of the difficulty of their terrain, they could afford to let you forge ahead for a paragraph without offering any resistance—time was on their side. As soon as those two little words (*"De Le"*) plopped from his lips, everything changed, as though, *knowing better*, he had pronounced a sort of negative password.

The porter, who only a minute before had been chiming *"Oui, monsieur"* and *"Parfaitement,"* suddenly shifted to sign language. The burden of his pantomime seemed to be that Peter should surrender his trusty steed to another porter while the first one carried his bags. Resigning himself to a double tip, Peter agreed. *"On est en France, Pierre,"* he said to himself. But you could not buy off this enemy (there ended the second lesson); not even money spoke to the French.

Before his eyes, the motorbike was seized and wheeled away while his captive bags were hustled off in another direction—toward the boat train, he realized, gulping. He stood swallowing his saliva, uncertain which to trail. The porter with the suitcases turned around and beckoned angrily with his head for Peter to follow. All at once, Peter grasped their maneuver. They were trying to put him on the boat train! He ran after his suitcases; the motorbike had vanished into the madding crowd on the platform. *"Essayez de comprendre, monsieur,"* he pleaded, catching up with the original porter. *"Je vais à Paris en vélomoteur. Je ne voyage pas avec le train."*

The man halted. "Ticket!" he shouted in English, bringing his face close to Peter's, so that it was impossible not to smell the morning wine on his breath. Peter launched an appeal to himself for a little calm. He spoke as slowly as he could, putting a pause after each word like a language-teaching tape. *"Je n'ai pas de billet. Je vais à Paris en vélomoteur. Rendez-moi mes bagages, s'il vous plaît."* "Ticket! Ticket!" repeated the porter peremptorily. Some Americans at the train window looked down at Peter and smiled. He was dressed for the road in leather helmet, leather jacket, khaki pants; strapped to his back was a canvas pack containing his pajamas, clean underwear, shaving stuff, toothbrush, goggles, Band-Aids, the green Michelin guide to Normandy, road maps, the *Plan de Paris*, candy bars for energy, and a French-English pocket dictionary. "He wants to see your ticket," a woman called out from the train.

At that moment, an ally appeared on the platform, smoking a small cigar—a young salesman of pharmaceuticals who used to drop in, slumming, at the tourist-class bar. "What's your problem?" he said in a thin, snappy voice; he was a blond former druggist from Berkeley who made the trip, cabin class, twice a year on business. Peter explained. He wanted to send his *baggage* by train and get his *motorbike* back. The salesman summoned a man from Cook's. The verdict was that Peter's baggage could not travel unaccompanied on the boat train. "But I can send it by express or freight, surely?" Did Peter have an address in Paris where it could be delivered? Peter's only address was "Care of American Express," and he hesitated to say this in front of the man from Cook's. "Better hop on the train," said the salesman. "Play it their way." "But my motorbike!" The motorbike was already in the baggage car (where else?). The porter claimed this was what the gentleman wanted. "*Mais je vous ai dit cinq fois, monsieur—*" Peter started to expostulate. The salesman cut in. "Give him his check for the bike," he said to the porter. "And get a move on with those bags. The train's due out of here in five minutes. Find him an empty place. Second class. Do you want the smoking or the non-smoking?" "I don't care," said Peter. "Non-smoking, I guess." To Peter's surprise, the porter dug. He complained, in French, that all the places on the train were reserved. "Baloney!" said the salesman to the porter. "There're plenty of seats down the line." He patted Peter's arm. "You're all set now. See you soon. And let me give you a little guidance. Never try to speak French to these froggies, even if you know how. They lose their respect for you."

Unstrapping his pack in the compartment, Peter compared this advice with the advice he had received from his father, which was never under any circumstances let a French person trap you into speaking English—they lost their respect for you. Pensively, he took off his helmet and felt in his pocket to make sure his bicycle clips were still there.

Once the train got moving, Peter was filled with gloom. The auspices looked bad. Not only had his project been frustrated and his mount shot from under him, but he had suffered a failure of nerve in the face of French civilization. The fact was, there still would have been time, probably, to get his motorbike off the train. Instead, he had let the salesman arrange the terms of his capitulation and had actually felt grateful to him. The reason was not far to seek. He had been afraid of being left by himself on the pier, in the midst of all those French, trying to do something unconventional like express his stuff to Paris. He guessed he had had an attack of agoraphobia, which was as common as the trots, they said, among American tourists. To tell the awful truth, he now wished he had traveled with a group.

On the boat, he had been expecting to meet some fellow-students in tourist class, but there were only a few married Fulbrights with babies, who were not interested in a kid his age. The only other student he found was a Wellesley girl in first class who had graduated last June, a former pupil of the *babbo*'s; unfortunately, she had got off at Cobh. Most students nowadays, the purser told him, traveled by air, unless they came with their parents. The word *nowadays*, after Rocky Port, was poison to Peter; it made him feel like the Last Rose of Summer blooming wanly on D deck.

Staring out the window at the vanishing oil refineries of Le Havre, Peter wished he knew where he stood about being an anachronism. On the one hand, he admired Don Quixote, who had replaced Sir Pellias the Gentle Knight as his hero when he had to "outgrow" King Arthur and the Companions of the Round Table and the nightly story he told himself of marrying the Damsel Parcenet. At college he had done a paper on the role of Rosinante in Cervantes' thought for his gen ed course, and he had named his motorbike Rosinante as a pious act. He had bought it, second hand, with his savings freshman year, at a time when others were getting sports cars, and he had brought it to Europe, he supposed, because everybody at home made fun of his attachment to it and of the curious (they said) idea he had that somebody might steal it—according to his father, it was its own best insurance against theft. On the other hand, unlike some of his classmates, he could not swallow Burke and neoconservatism or Plato's Philosopher King; nor could he wear waistcoats and grow an Edwardian mustache. He was a weirdie without conviction, cast in the part by others, just as, in school plays, he always got the clown's bells, because of his long nose and reedy build; his first year in boarding-school, they had made him be Jaques in *As You Like It*, "weeping and commenting upon the sobbing deer." Shake-speare was coarsely punning, their English teacher explained: a "jakes" was the Elizabethan word for toilet, like "john" today in girls' schools, and Monsieur Jakes (guffaws) was a "wet blanket." Peter had never told his mother that for a while the kids there used to call him Jakes ("Jakes, have you been to the john?"), though he had not been really picked on for some reason—quite mysterious, considering that he hated athletics and that boys at that age were beasts.

At college, there was a Peter Levi myth, a girl on the Cape who had a brother in his class told the *babbo*. He was regarded as a master of one-upmanship, it seemed, and he even had im-itators, when the last thing he craved was to start a fashion. His roommate freshman year, a shallow character who owned a Porsche, had congratulated him warmly on the motorbike, telling him that it was a "great" ploy. It was not a ploy, of course. His aunt Millie had been nearer the mark when she said the motorbike was his mother's punishment for not hav-ing got him a dog when he was little. He had given it a new paint job (Mahogany) this summer in his father's barn on the Cape and he often bought it presents: a padlock, a rear-view mirror, a bicycle pump, wicker side-baskets. He knew they were presents because he never spent any money on himself if he could help it—the bicycle clips were his father's contribu-tion. And it was true too that he was loyal to the motorbike because it was old and unsteady; he would not have felt the same toward it if it had been new, any more than he would have wanted a pure-bred puppy; it was old dog-eared dogs he used to follow on the street and try to pat. He had once brought a stray mutt home, but Hans, who had asthma, was allergic to dog hair, and when they could not find the owner, it had to be taken to the pound. Maybe the motorbike was Peter's animal helper, but if so, that was something he tried to keep dark. He had been ashamed of visiting it so often on the voyage and, just now, when he hurried back to the baggage car to check up on it, he had been ashamed to meet the salesman checking up on his cases of samples.

He ought to despise himself, he knew, for worrying all the time that the bike might be stolen. He hated hearing Americans talk about being robbed and gypped abroad. His room-mate freshman year, whose parents had a villa at Antibes, used to assure him that every beggar in Europe was a millionaire; it was a known fact, he claimed, and only suckers gave them money. This maniac traveled with his currency in his shoes. Other kids Peter had met when he was in Italy were always insisting that they had had their traveler's checks stolen in some place like Harry's Bar in Venice; they hid their money under their mattress or the rug and were constantly counting it to see whether the chambermaid had taken any. Or they were fighting with a taxi driver because they did not realize that the night rate was different from what they paid in the daytime. They got these ideas from their bourgeois parents, obviously.

Peter's parents had erred, he thought, in the opposite direction. They had drilled into him the principle that to accuse a servant or a cleaning-woman of stealing from you (or breaking your toys) was just about the worst thing you could do. On this they were in perfect accord. If Peter came to his father crying "Somebody took my ball," his father would shake him and shout "*L'hai persa! L'hai persa!*" In fact, he had not been allowed to think that *anyone* stole, except professional robbers in masks. His mother just laughed when he told her there was a kleptomaniac in his dormitory in school. He had tried to be grateful for this training when he compared it with what his schoolmates were getting, but there were times, especially at school, when he felt his parents had lived too sheltered a life. After all, he used to remind them, there *was* such a thing as theft; the stork did not carry dollar bills away in its beak. Now he saw their point. It was worse to be suspicious than to be robbed. He would not want to live with an insane person like his ex-roommate as his constant companion, and your constant companion, alas, was yourself.

Still, he could not help worrying about the motorbike. That was different, he told himself, from worrying about a bank roll. Property was theft, his parents were always quoting, to get his goat—his mother had copied it from his father, who used to be an anarchist before he settled down. Now even his stepfather said it. But if one of them had listened sympatheti-cally, instead of scoffing at his worries, he might not have this complex now. In a sense, it was their fault. Peter chewed his lip. He had caught himself trying to pass the buck. What was biting him now had nothing to do with his parents. He was angry with himself for having betrayed a kind of promise he had made to the motorbike, to ride it through thick and thin to Paris.

Peter was alone in the compartment, though some hand baggage was piled on the racks; doubtless, whoever owned it was fraternizing. Outside in the corridor he could hear Americans talking. Their favorite sport, he had observed, was confiding their itineraries in detail. "Then we fly with SAS to Copenhagen, where we get the ferry to Malmö and pick up a Volvo. . . ." "Frank leaves his medical congress and meets me in Seville, where we join a tour for three days. . . ." "We rent a Citroën *deux-chevaux* in Paris and drive it to Zurich. There we turn it in and get the Lufthansa flight to Munich. . . ." "In England we buy a Morris Minor and take it back on the boat with us. We spend one night in Bath and another at the Mitre in Oxford. Harold's cousin married an English girl; they have three lovely children." The voices, whoever they belonged to, were always middle-aged and pursy. Peter had noticed this on the boat. He wondered what Americans had talked about before they became the Affluent Society.

It had not been a lively crossing. Of his cabin-mates, one was a native-born federal employee from Washington who gave him a play-by-play preview of his hoteling, one was a Persian who spoke no English, and the third was an elderly Polish racist from Chicago who was booked from Paris on LOT to visit his daughter near Poznan. Over his nightly beer in the bar, Peter listened to stenographers and receptionists talk to each other and to the barman; he learned where they had bought what they were wearing and how much they had paid for it, what movies had been shown on their previous crossings and who had played in them, their European programs with arrival and departure times and identification of carriers. The girl from Wellesley had invited him up to first class, which he had expected to be more glamorous. But the only difference he could see was that the people there wore more jewelry and had different hours in the swimming pool. The conversations were just the same: exercises in total recall of the travel graph. When Peter was unable to pinpoint his movements on his earlier trips to Europe, he felt apologetic, just as he did when he admitted that he did not know where he would be staying in Paris. It sounded like a ploy.

The train was now in open country. He saw cows and big barns and apple orchards and, for the first time in his life, mistletoe actually growing, great springy balls of it, which he first took for giant birds' nests perched on the apple branches. His spirits brightened. He was in druid territory, and he looked around hopefully for oak groves. His favorite Norse god, Balder the Beautiful, an Apollonian figure, had been slain by an arrow made of mistletoe wood from the sacred oak. He jumped up and got down his book bag and took out the French tree book, a present from his stepfather—*Arbres et arbustes de nos forêts et de nos jardins.* He found *le gui,* but only its picture and its Latin name. Then he remembered. There was a Latin proverb about it. Mistletoe was a pest carried by the missel-thrush in its turds. The orchards that flashed by, hung with these strange, shiny, pagan ornaments, might be dying. He could not see any apples on a lot of the trees—a troubling allegory, he decided. Nevertheless, he was so excited by the marvel that he opened the door of his compartment and signaled to two girls who were standing in the corridor. "Mistletoe!" he said. "Look!" The girls looked. "Oh, yeah, yeah. Well, whaddya know! Thanks for telling us. Say, have you heard when this train gets to Paris?"

They had not really seen it, Peter thought. They had just said Yes to be polite. Like the Rocky Porters, they were not curious. If they had been interested, he would have showed it to them in the tree book and explained about the turds. But it was not worth the effort. He hoisted the book bag back onto the rack. "These are my people," he said to himself with a sort of pang. In a few days, probably, he would be homesick for these flat or furry voices.

Being an American, he was coming to think, was like being Jewish, only worse: you recognized "your people" everywhere in their Great Diaspora and you were mortified by them and mortified by being mortified; you were drawn to them, sorry for them, amused by them, nauseated by them. Not only that. They spotted you as one of them, infallibly, just as Jews could always spot other Jews, even when they had had their noses fixed and changed their names. On the boat, for the sake of privacy, he had been playing Peter the Hermit, his nose in a French book, his feet in espadrilles, and his upper half in a striped Italian jersey his stepfather had brought back from a market stall in Siena; in the swimming pool, when raked by somebody's toenails, he said "*Oh, pardon!*" or "*Scusi!*" according to his mood. The Americans were not fooled. "You're an American, aren't you? That's what I told my girl friend. This English fellow thought you were French." In the lounge before dinner he played chess in French with the Persian, who knew the French names of the moves and pieces, and the little kids who drifted up to watch the game were soon calling out to each other, "Say, this guy's an American! Let's be on his side!" It was no good trying to speed them on their way with "*Via, bambini,*" or "*Foutez le camp.*" For them, he was as American as Mom's macaroni or a Swedish meatball.

It was worse than being Jewish, Peter felt, in the sense that nobody was excluding you and you made your own ghettoes around Army bases and in "exclusive" hotels abroad, eating your own version of kosher like his table-mates on the boat, who were always clamoring for ketchup and suspecting their steak of being underdone, or like the dinner-jacketed clowns in first class who had to have sour cream and chives on their Great Big Baked Potato and acted martyred if the meat they were getting was only U.S. Choice instead of U.S. Prime. Being a Jew gave you a history of martyrdom that at least was old and dignified. If you were a Jew, you were "one of the chosen," while an American was just a Philistine. Jews were told by non-Jews that they should be proud of their heritage, steeped in tradition, et cetera; that was one of the mixed blessings of being Jewish. But nobody told an American how great it was to be him. You could not be proud of being an American, not any more. Peter took his mother's word for it that you could when she was young. Now, even the insensitive type, like the pharmaceuticals salesman, was bluffing when he put out the Stars and Stripes. On the boat, every American Peter met asked the same question—in lowered tones—when they heard he was going to Paris as a student: "Aren't you afraid of anti-Americanism?" Peter could not figure out why they treated this query as a top secret, looking around to make sure nobody heard them ask it.

He had resolved not to think about anti-Americanism while in Paris. The fear that people might be prejudiced against him was not one of his weaknesses. Some of the students in his group had been asked by a sociologist to collect instances of discrimination against them as Americans, but nobody had asked him to do that, fortunately. If they had, he would have given them a blast. As though anti-Americanism were a disease, like anti-Semitism, that could be studied scientifically by some government agency. These kids were actually going to be paid for finking on waiters and landladies—like getting a bounty from the state if you sent in muskrat skins.

Peter did not blame the French or anyone else for not liking America after what had been happening last summer while he sat getting a tan in Rocky Port. Just being white, he thought, did not make him guilty, but it was one strike against him, like original sin, which was not your fault and yet had to be paid for—he had been sending contributions from his allowance to CORE and SNCC and he would have mowed lawns in Rocky Port and donated the proceeds if anybody had had a lawn left to mow instead of a flagged terrace or what they called "ground cover." He was not a civil-rights hero; on the other hand, to be fair to himself, he was not a racist murderer, and he felt a sympathy for his country, which had to look at itself in this ugly mirror every night on television.

The *babbo* had given him a good briefing on this, in his study on the Cape, the day before the boat sailed. Peter trusted his father when he said that America was not going fascist; his father did not even think Goldwater was a fascist—the historical conditions for fascism were not present. This meant that it was all right still to register with your draft board and have a passport and defend your country in argument when some French egghead tried to tell you that all Americans were conformists or that university education was restricted to "the Pullman class." His father was worried about America this summer but he felt there was hope. He said Peter should not be too much influenced by his mother's pessimism. It was a mistake to think that Communism was better because it did not have a television culture; that only meant that Communism was backward, and a television culture, when it came, would be much worse in a totalitarian state, where dissent was not possible. Peter was relieved to hear this view put forward; his own faith in America had been shaken by Rocky Port, which the *babbo* dismissed—too easily, perhaps, not having spent the summer there. "Your mother always liked those old resorts. Snug harbors. It is no good crawling back into the American womb. It has had a hysterectomy." He laughed. Peter looked at him. "Be serious, *babbo*," he said plaintively.

Maybe it was childish, but Peter wanted to give his country a hand abroad. Of course, there was nothing he could do that would wipe out the civil-rights murders in Mississippi and the bombings and church-burnings and assorted atrocities. In fact, if he realized his plan of being a model student, kind and courteous to all, far from straightening the French out about the U.S., he would really be deceiving them as to what a lot of Americans, maybe the majority, were like. The thought of serving as a sort of whitewash had been preying on his mind; he could never have confided it to anyone but his father, because it sounded conceited.

The *babbo* nodded. He said the scruple was typical of the Anglo-Saxon mercantile conscience, always fearful of giving a false impression to the foreign buyer. "You are like my students at Holyoke when I first came there—all those pretty girls wearing big glasses. 'You musn't get the idea the average American thinks the way I do, Professor Levi.'" It was not up to Peter to worry about whether he was truly representative. At best, as a quality export, he might create a little good will for his country, which was badly in need of it. Peter was right to take his mission seriously; he and his young friends had an important role to play abroad. He must not be ashamed, for America, because he was a minority: five just men would have saved Sodom, if Lot had been able to find them. The main thing was to be himself; if Peter was true to himself, nobody could be misled, for nobody could suppose that such an unusual boy was a standard American product. "'To thine own self be true . . . thou canst not then be false to any man,'" Peter had muttered, pleased and confused by the compliment. Every father, he guessed, was a Polonius when he sent a son abroad. He wondered whether he himself was a prig, like

Laertes, who had probably been anxious to counter the rotten reputation of Denmark with the Parisians of his day.

In hard fact, Peter was less apprehensive about anti-Americanism among the French than about anti-Americanism in himself. Ever since he had left the native shores, he had been having violent bouts of it, followed by bouts of remorse. It was a thing, like malaria in the tropics, that you caught abroad, evidently; at home, he was drawn to the man on the street or behind the gasoline pump. He would have thought that by this time—it was his third trip to Europe—he would have built up immunities to the bug. But it was not so. Halfway to Paris, in an already weakened condition, he had a bad attack. The other occupants of his compartment returned—three stout old ladies in crêpe blouses and woolen skirts who were part of a tour of retired grade-school teachers from the Middle West. Peter had seen them on the boat tied up in those orange life-jackets during lifeboat drill. The rest of the tour, he now gleaned, was in the adjoining compartment with their tour director, who had met them at Le Havre. They had never been in Europe before and already they were beefing.

Peter tried not to listen; he unpacked the *Plan de Paris* and started to chart his course from the station to the Left Bank. But he could not help hearing what they were discussing. One of them had broken her bridge that morning on a toasted English muffin. She was the stocky, white-haired one, resembling a bulldog, in a blue blouse, with a silver-and-turquoise brooch, looking like a Navajo trophy brought back from the Southwest. She had saved the remains of the English muffin—a hardened leathery criminal—as evidence against the steamship company.

Peter felt thankful that no Asian or African student was sitting in his place. He believed in the American public-school system and he had a good memory of the older women who had taught him fractions and long division and *Ivanhoe*; he had liked them nearly as well as old female librarians and much better than most professors and masters in private schools. But now his point of view seemed to have suffered a sea-change. The voices of the trio were loud and argumentative. *Of course* Miss Lewis was entitled to compensation, it was her *duty* to teach the steamship line a lesson, the whole tour was behind her, et cetera. As for their tour director, they could not understand that man's attitude. He might have taken a *little* interest, out of common courtesy; he might have *looked* at the bridge, to see if it could be soldered together, instead of acting as if it would bite him. That was what he was paid for. That was what they paid him for, wasn't it? They could visit museums and churches without his help. Their travel agent ought not to have given them one of those Hungarian refugees, not even French, more of a glorified guide than a real tour director; a real tour director was supposed to be *handy*.

The old woman fished in her purse and pulled out something wrapped in Kleenex. Peter had a horrid view of the bridge—some yellowish teeth and very pink gums, backed with metal and with little metal hooks at either end. One of the hooks was broken, and three of the teeth had come out; they were wrapped in a separate piece of Kleenex. The exhibit passed from hand to hand. On request, the old woman opened her mouth wide, divulging some grisly stumps, and fitted the appliance into place, while her companions, in turn, peered at the result. All three acted as if Peter were not there. One of them, who had bifocals, gray hair, big pearl earrings, and a gray blouse, suddenly clicked her tongue. "I wonder now . . . I've got some Fasteeth in my beauty case." While Peter watched, she reassembled the denture, sprinkling it with some white powder—a fixative, he supposed—which she shook from a little blue can onto the artificial gums. "Try that, Miss Lewis. Put your denture back in, dear, and grit your teeth. Let it set for a couple of minutes."

Resuming her seat, she "included" Peter with a tap on the knee. "You're an American boy, aren't you? That's what we thought. 'An American boy is sitting in our compartment,' I told Miss Lewis. 'We won't have to stand on ceremony with him.'" Peter groaned to himself; between Americans abroad, there could be no secrets, apparently. "It isn't the first time he's seen a lady's denture, I bet." This was the third teacher, a red-faced jolly one, with popping eyes, like big Bing cherries; she wore a pink blouse and a lot of pink glass jewelry—probably she had taught the first grade. She gave Peter a wink, as though false teeth were part of a woman's mystery, like knickers or bloomers or whatever they wore where she came from.

"As a matter of fact, it is," Peter said hoarsely. Then he feared he had given offense. "There was a poet who came to college to give a reading," he volunteered. "His false teeth kept whistling, and he yanked them out and dropped them in the glass of water on the lectern. The audience gave him a great hand. But I wasn't there. I was in the infirmary." "My! Isn't that interesting? Was he one of those modern poets?" "Yes," said Peter.

"You can open now, Miss Lewis." The old woman unclenched her jaws. "There!" said the gray-haired teacher. "She won't be able to eat, of course. But cosmetically it's more attractive, isn't it?" She took out a pocket-mirror. "Smile, dear!" There was a clink of china and metal as the denture fell, rattling, against the patient's lower teeth. Peter gagged sympathetically; he was afraid she was going to swallow it. He heard a choking noise. But she reached in and grabbed it in time. "Drat!" she said, as the loose teeth scattered on the floor. Peter got up and chased them for her on his hands and knees. "Your pearls, madam," he said with an awkward bow, trying to lighten what he felt must be a dark moment for a woman, even an old woman. Down on the dirty floor, he had put himself in her place. It was no joke to break your teeth on your first day in Europe. It was no joke to be old and crumbling like masonry.

"I've got the name of a French dentist," he offered. "Maybe he could help you out. I'm going to him eventually to get my teeth cleaned. Our family dentist in New York recommended him." "I want an American dentist, young man. Isn't it aggravating that our tour director doesn't know one? You'd think he'd know a thing like that. He's paid to know a thing like that." She salivated angrily as she spoke; her toothless upper gums spat.

"You see"—the gray-haired teacher in bifocals smiled—"Miss Lewis doesn't want some mercenary French dentist to go and make her a whole new bridge. That's a long job, and we only have the week in Paris. She wants this bridge soldered together temporarily, to get her through the trip. But if she goes to one of these French dentists, chances are, as soon as he sees she's an American, he'll try to take advantage of her."

"Do you have any evidence for that statement?" Peter was tempted to ask, but he let the missionary opportunity pass, not, he hoped, from cowardice, but because he had made a rule recently not to bait people who were too old to change. Instead, he remained stiffly silent. "Well!" said the jolly one. "*I*'m the lucky girl! I brought along a spare plate. My daughter warned me. The bread in Europe is so *chewy*, she said. My son-in-law lost a gold inlay on their last trip, and the food kept packing in. 'Mamma,' my daughter told me, 'you go and get Dr. Edwards to copy your old plate in plastic.' It's wonderful what they can do with plastic. Just feel how light that is." Another toothsome exhibit, wrapped in gauze, made the rounds.

Peter averted his eyes. He sat hunched in his corner—Peter Levi, noted misanthrope. He did not even have the recourse of looking out the window; he had given up his usurped seat when the teachers came in. If he went out to stretch his legs in the corridor, it might be taken as a snub—despite appearances, Americans were sensitive. He listened while the retired educators kicked around the proposition that people over here took such *poor* care of their teeth: the school children did not get milk; they were not taught dental hygiene; there was no fluoridation program; and the wine they drank gave you tartar. No wonder dentists here were still in the dark ages. To Peter, this did not follow. He would expect countries with *bad* teeth to have *good* dentists. Like America.

He decided to give them a shock. "My father used to think all Americans had false teeth," he blurted out. "You know, like movie stars. My father's Italian," he added lamely. The teachers laughed. "Isn't that typical? The ideas these folks get about us!" Peter did not join in the merriment, though he had to admit that at home when the *babbo* told the story it was as a joke on himself. "I hope," said the gray-haired one severely, "you're going to try to give your relatives over here a better picture of the U.S. You talk like you were American-born. Is this your first trip to Europe?" "No," said Peter curtly, feeling that he had dealt out enough information. Then he repented. "It's my first trip to France. I mean, except for a couple of days at St.-Tropez when I was younger. I drove up from Italy with my family, and we took the boat at Cannes. The *Cristoforo Colombo*. But I've never been in Paris before."

Indeed, he had never arrived alone in a big foreign city before; someone had always met him. The sense of the difference hit him. No one would be waving to him from the platform, as the train pulled in. No one would hug him, crying "Peter!" No one would waft him off in a cab to a hotel, pointing out monuments on the way. No one in fact would know he was there.

If these old teachers did away with him, it would be quite a while before he was missed. Only his faithful motorbike would be waiting for him in the station, unclaimed. When his parents did not hear from him, eventually they would cable the Embassy, but by that time the trail would be cold. His heart lurched at the thought that for the first time in his life he did not count, *i.e.*, nobody was counting him; he was nobody's chicken. Not even God's, because there was no God. If a universal roll call were decreed tomorrow, there would be nobody to mark Peter Levi "Absent." This meant that *pro tem* there was no Peter Levi, except in his own mind. It was a creepy idea, like solipsism in philosophy. He would only begin to be real again when he had an address and people started checking up on him.

But supposing when he arrived he could not find a place to stay? Foolishly, as he now felt, he had not listened to his parents and made a hotel reservation. He had wanted to be free to do a little touring en route if the spirit moved him; on the map he had marked a place called St.-Wandrille, near Rouen, where there was an old Benedictine abbey—some Catholic convert had told him the monks there took pilgrims for the night. He liked the pious notion of being a pilgrim, sleeping in a monk's cell and hearing them chant the plain song when he woke up with the birds. He saw himself in some old woodcut with a humble scallop shell—his dinner plate—and a pointed pilgrim hat with another, tiny scallop shell on the crown, hitting the trail of Saint Jacques. Or as a young knight in home-made wattled armor like Sir Percival of Gales (the darling son of his poor widowed mother), seeking shelter from a kindly hermit. Or crossing the Seine on a rude ferry; he had checked a *bac* on the map near the abbey and pictured the rustic ferryman, a giant Christopher, pushing off with his solitary passenger for the other shore. But now the sense of adventure, which he had opposed to his parents' prudence, had abandoned him. Unhorsed, he did not feel errant. Instead, the responsibility of finding a hotel room in an unknown city weighed on him like some vile duty that he would like to shirk.

"I suppose you spoke Italian in your home." They were questioning him again. "When did your folks come to America?" "My father came during the war," Peter answered shortly; he was too dejected to pick up the conversational ball. Besides, if these old educators could not figure out from that datum that his father was an anti-fascist exile, he was not going to tell them. Let them think his father was a Wop immigrant instead of a Wop emigrant—who cared?

In any case, maybe he should have said "My father's an Italian Jew," just in case there were anti-Semites present. People of Jewish "extraction" (the word reminded him of the Rocky Port kitchen with flannel jelly bags dripping in concert) ought to be willing to declare themselves, but Peter often forgot. What he disliked about being Peter Levi was that there was so much to explain. He almost wished he had been born Pinkus Levy in Flatbush—a self-evident proposition. Technically, he was an Italo-American on his father's side, which would not have been so bad if his father had been what was meant by an Italo-American, instead of being a professor and a Jew, which would not have been so bad either if he had been what was meant by a Jew, instead of being, primarily, an Italian, since his part of the Levi family (a Triestine outfit) had been assimilated in Florence for generations, and, growing up in a Catholic country, the *babbo* had a lot more in common with the Jesuits, whom he hated, than with a rabbi, whom he knew nothing about.

As a Jew, Peter was a farce; the proof was that nobody had ever given him a rough time on that account. He was grateful to his last name for saving him the labor of telling people he was Jewish; on the other hand, like many labor-saving devices, such as dishwashers, it made almost more work in the end. There was no easy way to get it across that he was only a half-Jew. He could not send out announcements saying that his mother was a Christian or wear half a yellow star on his coat-lapel. In other times or climes, he would have had no worries on this score: under the Nuremberg Laws, he would have counted as a Jew, while in Israel he would count as a Christian, since what mattered to them was your mother—he did not know how he would fare in the Arab states.

Maybe it was not important anyway to set the record straight. To point out that you were "only" half-Jewish although your name was Levi made you feel like a recreant. Yet it was part of being an American that, once you got started, you felt impelled to tell all the people all the truth all the time. His college tutor, a stupid Freudian, had advised his mother that Peter had an "identity problem." But *he* was quite clear who he was; the problem was whether it was necessary to clear up other people. His tragedy, he had decided, was that his every move in this domain seemed to require a lengthy gloss. *E.g.*, in his school, which was trying to be liberal, he was told that he could be excused from the headmaster's course in Christian religion—a low blow to Peter because he was quite interested in Christian religion. When he said No, thanks, he would like to take the course, his attitude seemed natural to him but not, he discovered, to the headmaster or to the other kids, who thought he must be nuts to go to a class he could get out of. The headmaster made him write out his reasons for taking the course and did not accept that being an atheist was a valid one, till he heard from the *babbo* about all the dominies on the fair Rosamund's side. From the kids' point of view, Peter was practically a scab. They envied a certain Weinstein, who was allowed Yom Kippur and Rosh Hashana off, and a Catholic kid named Ryan, who even got excused from chapel. Peter would have been glad to belong to some religion that got you out of athletics, but he enjoyed chapel—it was the only peaceful moment in the school day. Looking back, he concluded that taking Christian religion must have been his first, innocent ploy.

One of the attractions of Europe for him was that he would not have to go into all this with the native population. In Europe, you did not have to have antecedents if you came from the New World. You were an American, and that was it.

"Does your mamma make the real spaghetti?" the jolly teacher wondered. "Spaghetti with meat sauce!" She sighed. "Out in Kansas we don't get the real Italian food. My daughter told me it isn't the same at all." "My mother usually makes it plain," Peter replied cautiously. "With just butter and cheese." The three women turned a joint suspicious stare on him. "Yes," he said. "You'd be surprised. A lot of Italians eat it that way. You watch when you're in a restaurant. What they like is the *pasta*. Your daughter probably had it *alla bolognese*. Or *al ragù*. Sometimes my mother makes it with *pesto*. Like in 'mortar and pestle.' That's Genoese. You take basil and parsley and garlic and pine nuts and cheese and pound them in a mortar with olive oil. It's green." He ground to a halt, reminded of Peter Levi's Paradox: most people did not care to be taught what they did not already know; it made them feel ignorant.

"Well, live and learn! What else does your mother make? Those pizza pies?" Peter hedged. "She's got a pretty big repertory." A little bird with an olive branch in its beak was telling him to avoid Italian words and phrases since he could not avoid pronouncing them correctly. "A few years ago, when we lived in New England, she had a jag of cooking American."

"Isn't that nice now?" They softened. "I guess she was trying to please you. Give you the same as your friends had, in *their* homes. You must have a very smart mother." "Yes, I have," said Peter, drawing a deep breath. He seemed to have been elected It in a game of Twenty Questions where the players were meant to finally discover that their modest train companion was the son of Rosamund Brown, the famous harpsichordist. Whom they would never have heard of. But that was not the point. The point was, if he did not give them a clue or two, he would be meanly concealing information that these women, as his fellow-Americans, were somehow entitled to, even though, when they got it, they would feel disappointed—all that work for nothing. Having a celebrity in your family gave you an unfair advantage over people who did not guess you had a celebrity in your family. If the teachers were to find out afterward that he had had this ace in the hole, they would think he had been laughing up his sleeve at them. In common decency, he ought to help them out. If it had been a real game of Twenty Questions, at this juncture he could have given them a weary hint: "Look, you haven't *asked* me if my mother is Italian."

"Where did you attend high school?" The gray-haired one rapped out the demand. "In Massachusetts." Peter hedged again; he felt embarrassed to admit that he had gone to a private school. "I mean, that's where I graduated." Then he mumbled the names of his previous schools: Rocky Port High, junior high at Berkeley. "Your folks moved a lot," the teacher commented. "It's a wonder you weren't put back a class." Old Miss Lewis nodded. "Always hard on a transfer." "Have you got lots of brothers and sisters at home?" asked the jolly teacher kindly.

"Well, yes and no." Peter licked his lips. "My parents are divorced." Though divorce was common as measles in the U.S., he could feel himself turning red. "So that I have quite a few stepbrothers and -sisters. And a half-brother and -sister on my father's side. But I'm my mother's only child." Of all the facts about himself, this business of divorce and step-parents was the one that, for some reason, he hated most to talk about. But of course it had to be the one that came out most naturally in the course of a casual conversation. If you were under twenty-one, oldsters always asked you if you had brothers and sisters; it made them feel benevolent.

As he had feared, silence followed his revelation. Probably the teachers were pitying him for his "broken" home. In fairness to his parents, he ought to explain that he *liked* the net effect of serial monogamy: being an only child and still having a flock of kids around of whom he did not have to be jealous, as he would have been, certainly, if his parents had gone on breeding together when he was little. But the average American, he had noticed, looked skeptical when he said he approved of divorce for parents; they seemed to think he had been indoctrinated. He decided to pipe down. If he went on talking, he would be bound to disclose that his mother had been divorced *twice*.

There was still an hour to fill in before the train got to Paris. Outside in the corridor, two transistor radios were playing. Peter would have been glad to read or sleep or practice his French argot, but the teachers obviously felt they could not let the conversation die at the point it had reached. "My!" said the jolly one. "You've got a lot of books there! Are you over here to study?" Peter answered that he was taking his junior year at the Sorbonne, under a supervised program; lots of colleges had them. Someone, he reflected, could make a fortune with a small, battery-powered tape-recorder, designed for travel, that would play back standard answers when asked a standard question, such as "Will you be taking your courses in

French?" "How big is the Sorbonne campus?" "Will you live in a dormitory?" "Do they have fraternities and sororities?"

"Of course you've got a place to stay in Paris." Peter swallowed. "No, I haven't. My plans are sort of fluid." He laughed weakly. "I thought I'd just cruise around and find a cheap hotel room. Back home, you could sign up to live with a French family, but I couldn't see doing that." The teachers stiffened. "Don't you know that Paris is *jammed* at this time of year? Our travel agent says there isn't a *bed*. Why, our tour has had its reservations for months! What were your folks thinking of, not to get you a hotel room?"

"My mother wanted to. She kept telling me Paris was crowded. But I wouldn't let her. I . . ." The argument he had given his mother was that he was not sure, exactly, when he would get to Paris. But that, he recalled with a jolt, was ancient history now. Incredibly, he had nearly forgotten the premise of his reasoning: the cherished idea of visiting Normandy en route. For a minute, his guard had been down. If he had not caught himself in time, it would have all come out about the motorbike and his defeat at the hands of those porters. The very thought of being *here*, penned up with these nosy old women, when he might have been *there* in solitary splendor, musing in a cathedral like Henry Adams, made his throat tighten. It was as though his plans had died young and he was traveling with their coffin. No one, he resolved, was going to prise out of him this unspeakable chapter in his history—not even his mother, when he wrote to her tonight.

The teachers were waiting. He cleared his throat. "Well, you see, I've got a principle. About not being forehanded. A lot of this compulsive planning, if you get what I mean, is just a way of trying to stay ahead of the next guy. Be smart and reserve in advance so that when some dumb guy shows up, you've got the priority. I mean, it's OK probably for older people—people your age—and women with little babies, but for somebody my age it's repulsive. Either there are enough rooms to go around, so why bother with all the early-birding? Or there aren't enough rooms to go around, so why not take your chances with the rest of humanity? Let the other guy be first. Live dangerously."

"Well, young man," observed old Miss Lewis with unexpected force, "you talk like a real American. It's nice to meet a boy these days that doesn't expect to have everything done *for* him, from cradle to grave. Not afraid to rough it, are you? Did you learn that in your Scout troop?" "Well, no," said Peter. "I never was a Scout. As a matter of fact, I got it from my father, probably. He used to be a philosophical anarchist. They believe in mutual aid. There's a whole book, very interesting, by Prince Kropotkin, about mutual aid in the animal world. And they think that nobody really owns anything as long as there's a scarcity. I mean, take the jacket I'm wearing. I treat it as if it were mine, but it doesn't really belong to me as long as somebody else doesn't have a jacket. I just sort of have it on loan. It's the same with a hotel room."

The gray-haired teacher looked at him sharply through the upper half of her bifocals. "Out West, where we come from, there's a fair share of mutual aid. We call it being neighborly. In Kansas, you could sleep in a barn or a hayfield. Or in most folks' spare bedroom. Folks are pretty nice, that way, to strangers. But Paris isn't Kansas—from what I hear anyway." Peter grinned. "Yeah, I've heard that too." "So what will you do, if you don't find a hotel room? Have you considered that?"

Peter had been considering it. "They say you can get arrested and spend the night in jail." He gave another weak laugh. "Actually, that isn't as bad as you might think. My mother and I spent the night in jail this summer. Of course that was back in New England." "Speeding." The jolly teacher nodded. "Those state troopers in New England are something fierce, my daughter says." Cravenly, Peter decided to let this pass. "My mother says that in London if you can't get a place to sleep, you just go to the police station, and they lock you up for the night. Only you have to get up early. In Paris, I could sleep under a bridge. With the *clochards*. Those are the French bums. But I guess they might not accept me. They have a pretty tight organization. I wouldn't mind being a wandering scholar. Like in the Middle Ages. They were sort of intellectual tramps."

"Oh. We thought you were dressed kind of funny. That pack and all. Miss Lewis thought she saw you with a motorcycle back there on the pier." "Must have been two other guys, ha ha," Peter said. His resistance stiffened. He was not going to feed their hungry curiosity. Anyway, it was not a motorcycle. If they did not know the difference, *tant pis* for them. "We thought maybe you might be one of those Beatniks you hear about." Peter was slightly offended. "I don't smoke pot, if that's what you mean. And the Beats usually have beards." "That's what I said, girls!" exclaimed the jolly teacher. "And they don't wash either. I said, this young fellow washes. And he's had his hair cut not too long ago." Peter flinched. "Samson Agonistes," he muttered.

The teachers ignored him. "Back home," said the jolly one, "he could go to the Travelers Aid in the depot. But I don't guess they have that over here." "The Y? Time was, a young fellow could always get a room there for a dollar. Is there a Y in Paris, I wonder? What about a church group? Young man, are your folks Catholic or what?" Peter gulped. Here was his opportunity. "I guess they're 'what.' My father is a Jew. But he doesn't have any religion." "We're Methodist Episcopal ourselves," said the gray-haired teacher briskly. "But to us you're a fellow-American, regardless of creed or color. Why, we may have a Jew for president if Barry gets in." There was a silence. She gazed out the window and clicked her tongue. "Wouldn't you know it? It's raining. Our first day in France. Now how are you going to look for a room in a downpour like that?" Peter glanced at the streaming window-panes.

"Please," he said, "let's drop the subject, if you don't mind. I'll be OK. This is just a shower. I can wait in the station till it blows over." Their worrying was contagious. He was starting to panic. He reminded himself that he and his mother and his step-father had arrived in St.-Tropez that time without a reservation and he had said they would find rooms and they had. But maybe that had been a fluke. He thought sickly of the population explosion. According to the Wellesley girl, three thousand U.S. juniors were slated to hit Paris this fall. She claimed to have read it in a magazine.

The teachers consulted in undertones. Bifocals put an end to the caucus. "Young man, we've been thinking. We have a nice clean hotel near the station. Our travel agent back home swears by it. We've each of us got a good-sized room to ourselves. Two of us could double up for the night and let you have the spare room. That'll give you a chance to look around."

Peter's Adam's apple bobbed. "Golly!" he said warmly. "Golly, that's nice of you!" It was true, what refugees like his father said: Americans were a kind people. Peter tried to imagine any European he knew, starting with the *babbo*, being glad to sleep two to a bed so that a college kid who was dressed kind of funny would have a place to lay his head. But Americans were like that, especially the ones from the heartland. His mother might do it, coming from Marietta. Still, she was relatively young. It was harder, Peter knew, for old people, who were generally poor sleepers, to share a room. The cockles of his heart moved. O brave new world! As he used to tell his mother, you should not judge a book by its cover.

At the same time, a cynic inside him warned him to take it easy. He could not figure himself joining a tour of old grade-school teachers from Kansas or wherever. That was the catch: the helping-hand type of American was usually not the type you wanted to see a great deal of, abroad or at home. And they were the type that would not take No for an answer. If he refused, the teachers would assume it was because he was bashful or afraid of putting them out and keep pressing him till he agreed.

"It's awfully kind of you—" "Not at all. Not at all." They smiled, showing gums and dentures. "We Americans have to stick together." But that was not it. They were doing themselves an injustice. If he were a foreigner, they would be just as determined to help him out. Like a lot of people, they were embarrassed by doing a good deed and felt they had to find a lousy reason for it.

"Well, thanks," he said. "But the thing is, I have to be on the other side of town. Near the Sorbonne. Tomorrow I have to register and all that. You know, buy books for my courses and check in with my professors. Stuff like that." He was aware that this did not sound convincing; he could have used a few lessons from the *babbo*, who was a master of invention when the need arose. "Well, then, why not leave that pack and those grips of yours at our hotel for the time being? You can go out and scout around then. If you find a room, well and good. If you don't, we're glad to accommodate."

Peter did not point out that he could check his bags at the station. He sought a more gracious argument. "I thought I'd park my stuff with the other students in my group. They got here yesterday by plane, and we're supposed to sort of keep in touch. I would have come on the plane with them, but my mother doesn't like me to fly." He had hit the right note. "Well, why didn't you say so? The way you were talking, we pictured you as all alone in the big city. If your friends are here already . . ." He was free. There was no way they could ever find out that his group's charter flight was not due to arrive for a week. Even if it crashed and they read about it in the paper, they would have no reason to associate it with Peter.

He was appalled by his line of thought. Accepting the loss of his classmates, like a giant pawn sacrifice, if only he could be safe in his corner. As soon as he got to Paris, he would turn over a new leaf. They were now in the suburbs. Fifteen more minutes, he reckoned. He went to the toilet. Coming back, he found the teachers buttoning up their coats. They had taken down their hand baggage. As his eye traveled upward to inventory his effects, he became aware of his leather helmet, where he had tossed it on the rack. He froze. It seemed hardly possible that the teachers could have failed to see it while taking down their stuff. The chin strap was dangling through the spokes on the rack. His mind raced. How could he explain what this distinctive piece of headgear was doing there, if they were to ask him, which they might do any minute? He was carrying it for a friend? He wore it to protect his ears because of a mastoid operation? "'Never apologize, never explain,'" he muttered to himself. But whoever said that had never been subjected to several hours' direct questioning by a team of elementary-school teachers. Admit the truth? That would entail further explanations: he would have to say *why* he had disclaimed possession of a motorcycle. And in fact his reasons for doing so now escaped him. Maybe he was a psychopath and just getting to know himself, removed from the context of home and school. The helmet stared at him. He tried looking the other way in the hope that it would become invisible. Finally a feeble answer suggested itself. "I guess somebody must have left it there," he could hear himself croak, in his mind's ear. "That guy you saw on the pier. Maybe I'd better take it to the Lost and Found." Somewhere outside a cock ought to be crowing. But now that he was prepared, the three Norns did not call on him. They were pinning on corsages of sweet peas that somebody had sent them to the dock at Le Havre. Still, they appeared friendly. They smiled. Maybe they had not noticed the helmet after all.

Gratitude made him remorseful. They had offered him their bed. In the light of that, his own secretiveness and mumbling reserve looked shady. He had been acting like a miser, hoarding his gold. He was unable to *give*. Too late, he recognized that he ought to have accepted their invitation. At least left his bags with them while he went around looking for a hotel. Even now he could volunteer to take the old lady to the dentist. In his place, Don Quixote would have jumped at the opportunity. But Peter felt too embarrassed. If Miss Lewis had been disguised as a beggar-woman or a ragged refugee, it might have been different, he told himself. Anyhow, he would have plenty of other chances to be a model American, once he was in Paris and free of his compatriots.

But of course he was not free, as he quickly discovered in the station. He was trapped by all the lies he had told. He had been assuming that it would be simple to lose his train-companions in the howling mob on the platform. But he took the extra precaution of letting them get off first, while he lingered in the compartment, pretending to be strapping on his pack. As a final safety measure, he stowed the helmet, *pro tem*, in his book bag. As soon as the coast was clear, he would get a porter to take his bags ahead to the checkroom and hurry down the line himself to claim his motorbike. Once his bags were checked, he would speed off on his motorbike to look for a hotel room. The chances of the teachers' seeing him, from the top of some tourist bus, were one in several million. And even if they saw him, they would not be able to make a positive identification —a cycling outfit made you look like a hundred other guys.

Reassuring himself, he counted up to fifty and then peered out the window. At the rear of the train, outside the baggage car, the teachers were gathered, with the rest of their tour and their tour director, supervising the unloading of their suitcases. There seemed to be an argument. He quickly withdrew his head. He decided to count up to a hundred. Sweat broke out on his forehead; he was wilting in his leather jacket. He craned his neck out the window again. A motorbike was being lifted off the train. The teachers were coming his way. Ducking, Peter urged himself to be patient. No one could steal the motorbike as long as he was here watching.

The crowd on the platform was thinning. From his coign of vantage, effaced against the wall, he saw the teachers go by. He stood up and breathed easier. In only another minute, they would have disappeared through the gate. Unless they stopped to talk to somebody they knew. He was alone on the train, he presumed. And now he discovered fresh grounds for alarm. What if the train backed out of the station with him aboard? The car he was in gave a jolt. "*Descendez, monsieur. Descendez!*" a train official called out from below. "*Vous êtes à Paris.*" "This is the end of the line, buddy," an American voice said. Peter slung his book bag around his neck. He adjusted his pack, picked up his suitcases, and limply descended from the train. His patience had been rewarded: there was no sign of the teachers. Nor, he became aware, of his motorbike. Outside the baggage car, the platform was empty, and the baggage-car doors were shut. The unthinkable had finally happened.

As if in a dream, he heard himself shouting. "*Au voleur!*" Words he could not have imagined himself uttering and which yet sounded strangely familiar, as though he had read them in a story or a play—which he had, he recognized several hours later: it was the shriek of poor old Harpagon, the local Shylock —Stop, thief! Nobody answered him; they stared and shrugged. He moderated his pitch. "*On m'a volé mon vélomoteur!*" Tears and perspiration were running down his face. Suddenly the train official and several porters all talked at once. "*A la douane, monsieur! Vous le retrouverez à la douane. Il faut passer par la douane.*" They were pointing at some vehicles that had been whizzing past, loaded with trunks, crates, and suitcases. He descried a wheel and a bit of mahogany fender. "*Voilà votre vélomoteur!*"

Peter blinked. He still did not understand. Where were they taking it? "*A la douane!*" repeated the train official impatiently. "Customs!" "You have to go through customs," an American voice said. "There's a big hall in the station where you wait for your baggage. Then an inspector comes and looks at it." "But I've already *been* through customs. At Le Havre. *Monsieur!*

J'ai dédouané déjà—au Havre." It was the same story. They refused to listen. "You went through *immigration* at Le Havre," the American said. "This is customs." Peter shook his head stubbornly. He knew what he had done. Finally he dug. Customs for boat-train passengers was in Paris. He was a boat-train passenger. Q.E.D. Sighing, he repaired to the customs hall, which was still milling with angry people. Someone's baggage was being searched—the Persian. "They're looking for hashish," he heard a woman say. He retired to a corner and sat down on his big suitcase to wait his turn.

Soon he heard voices he knew. "Hoo hoo! Hoo hoo!" They were still around. The whole tour had spotted him and was heading in his direction. "Here we are! Are you having an *awful* time getting one of those inspectors? My! We've been here for hours, seems like. You just come right along with us. Our tour director will help you. Here, Mr. Kormendi, will you get that man to mark the young man's bags too?" Before Peter knew it, he had gone through customs a second time. "Now what you need is a taxicab. Mr. Kormendi will show you where you stand in line for one. We're going to walk, ourselves. Our hotel is just across the way. Here, Mr. Kormendi, tell that porter to come back and take the young man's bags to the taxi line." Peter said he was planning to go by subway. "I have to economize." "Well, let Mr. Kormendi show you where you get it. He might as well make himself useful." Peter started to say that this would be too much trouble, when the tour director, a tall fat man with protruding teeth, resembling a hare, interposed in a guttural accent. The young gentleman would not be permitted in the Métro with so much baggage. If the ladies wished, he would be glad to accompany their young friend to the taxi queue.

Peter drew a deep breath. Across the hall, the motorbike was standing. On its fender was a chalk mark made by the inspector this morning at Le Havre, which meant that it would be easy, he supposed, for anyone to walk off with it. If he allowed himself to be put in a taxi, he would never see it again probably. "Excuse me a minute," he pleaded. "I think I see somebody I know." And in fact his sweat-drenched eyes had caught sight of the pharmaceuticals salesman, like a natty mirage, proceeding toward the exit with a porter and his cases of samples. "Hi!" called Peter. "Why, hi there!" said the pharmaceuticals salesman. "I was wondering what had happened to you." He stared at Peter and the conclave of teachers. "Say, you look kind of white!" "Can you give me a lift?" said Peter quickly. "To the Left Bank." As the salesman told him afterward, he could see right away that Peter was on the verge of fainting; having been a druggist, he was familiar with the signs: glassy eyes, cheesy color, profuse sweating. He did not ask any questions. "Why, sure," he said. "Sure. I've got a car meeting me. Happy to drop you anywhere you want to go." He tipped his hat to the teachers. Peter gave a feeble wave of the hand in their direction. "Thanks again. Don't let me keep you any longer. I've met this friend."

Half an hour later, he was in a Caddy '62. In his wallet was a check for the motorbike, which had been left in the *consigne* at the station, and he was being deposited at a hotel on the Left Bank that catered to the American Air Force. While he waited in the station bar, munching a ham sandwich and drinking a restorative cognac, the salesman had fixed it up for him. It had only taken a couple of phone calls. There was an Air Force general, it seemed, that he had helped out once with some penicillin for a base in the south of France. The general was glad to return the favor. This hotel, which was not too far from the Sorbonne, was reserved for the military in transit and their families. Civilians not connected with the service were not supposed to stay there. But if you knew somebody, they could usually find you a slot.

Peter listened wanly. He had tacked from Scylla to Charybdis and he no longer cared. When the salesman had said that he knew a cheap hotel on the Left Bank, he had omitted to specify what kind of hotel it was. A man of action, he shot off to telephone, while Peter, the man of reflection, was left to await results. When he reappeared making the V-for-Victory sign, it was too late to jib. The starch had gone out of Peter. Without experiencing any special surprise, he allowed his liberator to check the motorbike ("Take my advice and sell it; it'll always be a headache") and "fill him in" about the hotel they were bound for. It was not the Ritz, said the salesman, but the room should be fairly clean, and you did not have to tip. Peter was going to pass for the general's wife's nephew. He must be sure to remember that when he checked in with the sergeant at the desk.

From the back seat of the Cadillac, Peter looked out the rain-splashed window. This was Paris. Tonight—"to make it legal"—he and the salesman were going to have a drink at the Crillon with the general. Later, after dinner, they might go on to the Lido. Peter did not protest. He had stopped protesting. He was floating, like a human shipwreck, on a tide of good will. It was no use fighting against it. If he could only hold out long enough, the tide would recede and leave him to his own resources. All he had to do was avoid further entanglements. The virtue, he argued, of a military hotel was that they would kick him out after a couple of nights. Meanwhile, in the words of the salesman, the tab would be minimal. He would be able to take a shower and maybe, he told himself, crossing his fingers, the sergeant would let him keep his motorbike in the cellar. He wondered where his family had ever got the idea he was obstinate.

Epistle from Mother Carey's Chicken

Dear Ma:

I have finally found an apartment. It's on the fifth floor (American sixth), which is good exercise for me. One room, "furnished," plus a separate jakes and a sort of bird bath. I've bought a student lamp, which helps. It has a radiator, but the heat hasn't come on yet; the furnace is in the landlady's apartment, and she doesn't feel the cold. She has let me have some sheets and a so-called blanket, which I took to the cleaner's. Still, it's better than those hotels I've been staying in. Did I write you from the one where they had six Japanese acrobats sleeping on the floor in the room next to me? Contortionists, I assume.

I'm glad to be on my own, making my bed and sweeping. It's good to do a little physical work, and you feel less lonely in your own place, with your stuff unpacked. Also, I never could solve the tipping problem. That was the good part of that military hotel on the rue Littré. But in those other fleabags, where the *service* was *compris* theoretically in the price of the room, I was constantly on the horns of the dilemma. I mean, being an American and getting money from home, I felt I ought to tip the chambermaid even if the other inhabitants didn't. "From each according to his abilities." You know. But then I figured that if I tipped, it was scabbing on the others, who didn't have the dough. Being *prepotente*, the rich American youth. Buying the red carpet. And if I crossed the chambermaid's palm, I did get more service, I found out. In one hotel, every time I started to go to the communal toilet, down the hall, she would rush ahead of me—"*Un instant, monsieur*"—and clean it with one of those filthy hard-rubber brushes they have, all caked with excrement, and when I thanked her, she backed out, curtseying: "*A votre service, monsieur.*" It was on account of that I moved. It got so I was lurking in my room, waiting for her to leave the floor so that I wouldn't get this special treatment I seemed to be paying for. If the other inhabitants had to use a dirty, stinking toilet, why should I be the exception? In fact, it was her job to clean the toilet.

On the other hand, when I didn't tip, I felt like a cheapskate. Because of the way I've been brought up, I guess. It's all your fault (ha ha). I tried asking myself what Kant would do in my position: "Behave as if thy maxim could be a universal law." If my maxim was not to tip because the next guy didn't, that would be pretty hard on the chambermaids of Paris, I decided. So, if he was true to his philosophy, Kant would tip. Of course he didn't have to face the issue, never leaving Königsberg. But you could also argue that tipping made it tough on the non-tipper (which I could produce some empirical evidence for), and therefore Kant might be against it. If I understand him, he is saying that an action should be judged by its implications, *i.e.*, if everybody did what you are doing, what would the world be like? Well, a world in which every student gave a five-franc gratuity weekly to the woman who cleaned his room would be OK, but what about a world in which every *other* student did it? Maybe the categorical imperative is not the best guide for Americans abroad. When you think of it, the rule of thumb about tipping is just the opposite of Kant: watch what everybody else does and do the same.

I never could make up my mind whether tipping or not tipping was more cowardly in the circumstances. Maybe any action becomes cowardly once you stop to reason about it. Conscience doth make cowards of us all, eh, *mamma mia*? If you start an argument with yourself, that makes two people at least, and when you have two people, one of them starts appeasing the other.

Anyway, I've found this apartment. It will only cost 30,000 old francs a month, plus the utilities (there's a gas hot-water heater over the bathtub) and a small donation to the concierge at New Year's. The place has its drawbacks but it's a lot better than the *chambres de bonne* a lot of kids rent in the mansards of old buildings. You ought to see those rooms, like a series of doghouses under the eaves, where the maids used to be kept. No heat or running water, the usual foul toilet in the hall, and a common tap with a rusty basin underneath where you go to fill your pitcher and empty your slops. No bathtub or *bidet* on the whole floor; I guess they expected the maids to be dirty. The advantage is that, being high up, you generally have a nice view, through a slanting skylight. There are whole families— mostly Spaniards and Algerians—living in some of those holes.

It's an education, looking for an apartment. Quite a few French families want to rent you a room where you share a bathroom and toilet with them and maybe have the use of the kitchen to make your morning coffee. They call it an apartment. You waste a lot of time that way, answering ads. They won't admit on the telephone that the place doesn't have a separate entrance—*une seule clef*. At first I didn't know how to say that and if I said *une seule porte*—like *una porta sola*— they'd say, "*Oui, oui, monsieur, une seule porte.*" Even when they get the idea, they pretend to be surprised, as though a separate entrance was something unheard of and the only reason you could want one was to give orgies or sell your body to French queers.

I got my present pad through the grapevine. The desk clerk at my last hotel knew about it and told the owner I was *per bene*. The putative heating is included in the rent, and there's a two-burner hot plate and a few chipped dishes and a coffeepot. I can wash the dishes in the bathtub. The only thing is, there isn't much light. It looks out on a shaft that goes down to what they call a *courette*, where the garbage cans are kept. But I'll be here mostly in the evenings and anyway the days are getting shorter, as the landlady pointed out. *I.e.*, when I get up in the morning and come back in the afternoon it will be dark outside anyhow. She had fixed the place up for her son, who was a student; hence the amenities. There are even some home-made bookshelves. It is on a landing, up a few steps from the service entrance of her own apartment. I have to use the service stairs.

At night, the big main door on the ground floor is locked at ten o'clock. If I come in after that, I ring for the concierge to push a button that opens the door. The signal is six short rings; otherwise, she won't open, in case I might be a *clochard* or a burglar. The Parisians spend a lot of time worrying about burglars and prowlers. In those hotels I was staying in, the chambermaid, on receiving a tip, would immediately start warning me about the other denizens—they stole. "*Méfiez-vous, monsieur.*" I was urged to be sure to lock my door when I was inside and to put my watch and money under my pillow while I was sleeping. I found this quite unpleasant. It made me look at anybody I passed on the stairs with a sort of smutty curiosity, as though they might have it "in them" to be a thief. Like wondering whether a woman you see waiting on a corner could be a prostitute. The French are a suspicious people.

But in fact there's a lot of theft in those Left Bank flops. You would be surprised. In one place I was staying—on the rue St.-André-des-Arts—a kid had his typewriter taken, a new Olivetti. It turned out that it wasn't even his; he'd borrowed it from a girl friend who typed manuscripts for a living. He reported it to the police, but they just shrugged. Too common an occurrence in that precinct. The way this kid, who was Dutch, reconstructed it, somebody must have lifted his key from the board downstairs, while the desk clerk was elsewhere (half the time in those hotels there's nobody at the desk; you have to ring a hand-bell to get somebody to come), and gone up to his room and helped himself. The Dutchman wanted the police to search all the rooms; he reasoned that it had to be someone in the hotel, who had heard him typing. But the police told him that whoever stole the typewriter would have gone out and sold it right away. They even implied, when he started making a scene, that he might have sold it himself and then reported that he had been robbed.

Then I heard about a Swedish *au pair* girl, in that same hotel, who left her gold watch in the communal bathroom in the soap-dish; when she missed it, ten minutes later, it was gone. An American girl found her crying on the stairs and went with her to the police station. "My golden watch!" she kept saying. You'd think that thieves, being hard up themselves, would have a fellow-feeling; I mean, steal from people who could afford it. But of course people who can afford it stay in hotels where the clientele is "above" stealing watches and typewriters. I guess the world is a vicious circle.

I think I will like Paris better now that I'm no longer a member of its floating population, which can be fairly sordid. The food, at my age level, is fairly sordid too. There are a few *foyers* with a table d'hôte, for students, that are not so bad, but they're crowded and when the novelty wears off they're not a great improvement on eating in commons at home, except that you can have wine. The bread and croissants are great, of course, but the French don't know how to make a sandwich. And I miss salads and orange juice and tuna fish. They hardly ever serve vegetables, except French fries. There's nothing here to compare with the spinach in the Automat, for instance. And I miss the stand-up bars in Italy, where you can have a healthy snack and a *cappuccino*. What I like best in the restaurants here is the *crudités*, but you can't sit down and order *crudités* and a glass of milk; you have to be force-fed with the entire menu. Sometimes I just have a dozen *praires* (which are cheaper than oysters), standing up, on the street, for lunch.

I've started doing my own cooking, with a vegetable binge. No icebox, needless to say, in this apartment, but that doesn't matter with the present room temperature. Besides, the French, like the Italians, only buy what they need for one day. I had a shock, though, yesterday, when I went to do my marketing at the Marché Buci—that big outdoor market, near the Odéon. At one stall, I asked for a carrot, and the *type* refused to sell me one. He said I had to buy a kilo. Like you, dearest Ma, I started to argue. I wanted to know why. How it would damage him to sell me one carrot or one apple or one pear. I explained that I didn't have an icebox and that I was just one person. "*Ça ne me regarde pas,*" he growled. Finally we compromised on a pound. That's quite a lot of carrots for a single man. While he was weighing them, I got into conversation with an Italian, who had been watching me and smiling—very nice, about the *babbo*'s age, an intellectual. He said that in Italy not only would they sell you one carrot but divide it in four. According to him, this only proved that Italy is a poor country, while France is a rich country. I said the Italians had more heart than the French, even if they gyp you sometimes. The French *grudge* gypping you, Mother. Maybe, I said, people in poor countries had more heart than people in rich countries. After all, Poverty used to be represented as a Virtue. I hadn't noticed any statues of Poverty on French churches.

By the way, did you know that most of the statues on the churches here had their heads chopped off? In the French

Revolution. And in the Wars of Religion, this Italian told me. But he agreed that Dame Poverty was not seen as a Virtue in France, which he seemed to think was a good thing.

After I had bought a pound of carrots, three cucumbers, a pound of tomatoes, a pound of onions, and a huge cooked beet, we went to a café around the corner, near the statue of Danton, and continued the discussion. He thought it was funny that an American should idealize poverty, and when I told him that in America you could buy one carrot even in a supermarket, he seemed skeptical. Perhaps in the Negro sections, he said. No, I said, anywhere. It was a free country; you could buy as much or as little as you wanted. I had to admit, though, that as far as I knew you couldn't buy one cigarette at a time, the way you can in Italy. And I realize now I ought to have mentioned those carrots in plastic bags, which sort of bear out his point. It's odd they slipped my mind.

Anyway, he explained that in Paris you could buy a single carrot or onion or lemon in a *grocery store*. That's different from a market. Only in a grocery store you pay more than you would pay if you bought the carrot at the market. But since you can't, the point is academic. I said maybe students who lived in the quarter could get up a pool to buy a kilo a day of vegetables and fruit at the market and then divide it up. Take turns doing the shopping. He said I was defining a co-operative.

It sank me to learn that I'm too small an economic unit to take part in the French way of life. I love those street markets —so colorful—and I'd counted on haunting them every day after school with my *filet*. What's the point of being in Europe if you have to line up in a grocery store, which is usually part of a chain, just like at home? This Italian said not to be discouraged: I could still buy fish and meat and cheeses at those market stalls, and in time, if they got to know me, the vegetable- and fruit-sellers might relent; I could become "*l'américain du Marché Buci*."

When we parted, he asked me to come around to his place some evening for dinner; he has kids but much younger than me. If I go (I'm supposed to call him, since I have no phone), it will be the first time I've been in a French household, except that he isn't French. He left Italy under Mussolini, like the *babbo*, and his wife is Russian.

Unfortunately, I haven't made many contacts here. In my course in French civilization, we're all foreigners, obviously. The only student I've had any real talks with is a Norwegian named Dag, who is a sort of Marxist troll. He wants me to go to Poland with him during Christmas vacation. There are some Smith girls I met at a place called Reid Hall where they have supplementary classes, in English, but they stick pretty much together. I asked one to go rowing with me the other day on the lake in the Bois de Boulogne, but her afternoons are all sewed up with her peer group doing art appreciation at the Louvre. On Saturdays and Sundays the lake is too crowded.

I don't see how anybody gets to know any French students, unless they have a letter of introduction. I've tried going to cafés where they're said to hang out, but they're mostly full of Americans who have heard the same rumor. And if they aren't full of Americans, nobody will talk to me. I've actually gone as far as asking for a light. The place to find French students is at the movies. They seem to spend all their time there.

That reminds me. Did you know that you're supposed to tip the usher in a French movie house? I didn't know and got hissed at by the woman the other day when I went to see an Antonioni flick. All the students in the vicinity stopped necking and turned to ogle me as I stumbled into my seat. I gather I was being called a *"sale américain,"* but if she knew I was an American, she might have enlightened me about the local customs. It must happen all the time with foreigners. But I suppose that's what makes her mad. Usually when I'm in some place like a stand-up coffee bar, I watch what the other customers do and follow their example, but in a movie house you're literally in the dark. This little incident wrecked the film for me. I hardly saw Monica Vitti because of the rage I was in. The picture was half over before I finally grasped what my big crime of omission had been. Then it was too late to rectify it—at least without getting stared at some more. Besides, I couldn't see how much the other customers were giving. In case you want to know, it's a franc on the Champs-Elysées and fifty centimes in the little places. The clerk at my hotel told me.

At home I never thought I was much of a conformist. But I now see that I was without knowing it. I did what everybody else did without being aware I was copying them. Here I *mind* being different. Being abroad makes you conscious of the whole imitative side of human behavior. The ape in man. The tourists have it better. I don't sneer any more when I see them being carted around in those double-decker buses with earphones on their ears. I envy them. They've all told each other who they are and where they come from, and to the French they're part of the landscape, like the Tour Eiffel—nobody notices them, except other tourists. Here nobody knows who I am, as a person, which is all right with me, but I can't fade into the foliage either. If I still had Aunt Millie's camera and were willing to carry it, it might make me invisible to the French. Just another tourist. It occurs to me that that's why, unconsciously, the men are all draped with cameras and light meters and the old women have their glasses slung around their necks—to show they belong to the species, tourist, which allows them to disappear as individuals.

You were right. I haven't used the motorbike much. Last Sunday, I took a run out to Senlis, to look at the church, which is older than Notre-Dame. I think I like Gothic, at least here in France. It reminds me of the forests these people came out of—druidical. The church in Senlis has a greenish light, as if you were in a sacred wood, with stone boughs meeting overhead in the bosky side aisles and the deambulatory—all that interlacing and those bent perspectives. They treat stone as if it was pliant, like branches. And the choir is a sort of clearing in the forest. While I was there, to complete the illusion, a swallow flew through.

The other afternoon I took the Métro and a bus and went to see St.-Denis, which is the first important Gothic in France, right in the middle of a working-class suburb. Unfortunately, I picked the wrong day, so that I couldn't see the choir, where the kings of France are buried; I didn't mind missing them, but the choir is the original Gothic of the Abbé Suger. Probably Bob knows about him. Next Sunday I'm going to Chartres, but I'll break down and take the train, I guess. It's easier than riding Rosinante through the Sunday traffic. That would be quixotic.

Everybody I meet advises me to sell the motorbike. For one thing, it constitutes a parking problem. They don't have parking places for two-wheeled vehicles, the way they do in Rome and Perugia. Which I guess is another proof that France is a rich country, while Italy is a poor country. And if you park it by the curb you can get a ticket. For the last couple of weeks it's been left in the court of an apartment house near that military hotel, where there's a concierge whose dog I've made friends with. But I can't keep it there indefinitely; being out in the open isn't doing the new paint job any good. I hardly ever ride it in Paris, except to go to the Bois, rowing, to keep myself in shape, and that time I wrote you about, when I went chestnutting in the Parc de St.-Cloud. I'd been hoping the concierge in my apartment building would let me park it in the cellar, but it turns out that the cellar is divided up into individual *caves*, locked and padlocked, that belong to the individual tenants, and I'm not entitled to one. Anyway, they're very damp; you can't even store a suitcase in them without its growing whiskers.

If I knew somebody who had a house in the country, I could store it with them for the winter. But I don't. That salesman who helped me out said I should advertise it for sale at the PX. The general could fix it up so that I could post a notice on the bulletin board. Maybe if I did that, I could find it a good home. By the way, the general said his wife could get me anything I wanted at the PX: cigarettes, liquor, canned stuff. It appears that she could even get me a typewriter for one-third less than you have to pay (I quote) stateside. They had me to dinner with their teen-age daughter.

What do you think about the ethics of using the PX? I don't mean for liquor or cigarettes. But it might be nice to have some tuna fish and peanut butter. And they carry Danish milk there. I can resist the edibles, though. What really tempts me is the idea of a typewriter. And possibly a steam-iron to press my clothes. The PX store is supposed to be for the military and Embassy personnel only; you have to have a card to get in. But the general says the regulations are aimed at preventing PX-buying for resale, which is unfair to the local economy. I wouldn't be hurting the local economy if I bought a typewriter at the PX because I wouldn't get a typewriter at all unless I got it there. Which I guess proves that I don't *need* a typewriter. The same with the iron. I can worry along without them. Which presumably answers my question.

I think *you* would be against buying stuff at the PX because you wouldn't want to be the kind of person who loaded up at the PX. I agree there's something *antipatico* in the idea. When I went to the general's apartment for dinner, I got a taste of PX-living. We had a big canned American ham, which the general carved with an electric slicer; it was baked with Dole's pineapple and brown sugar and with it were canned potato balls and frozen peas and lima beans, followed by American vanilla ice cream and Hershey's chocolate sauce and FFV cookies. They thought I might be homesick, they said. Before dinner, I had a shot of Jack Daniel and afterward Maxwell House coffee, made in an electric percolator, and chocolate mints. The wife kept announcing the brand names, like those butlers you see in the movies calling out the names of the guests. After dinner, we listened to rock 'n' roll on their hi-fi set. And they showed me all over the apartment; the kitchen was like an appliances salesroom or an ad for Revere copperware. They even get their light bulbs from the PX.

They feel that having all this junk around is a political act; they're a sort of showcase of the American way of life for the general's French colleagues at SHAPE or wherever he is. The wives, said Mrs. General, would give their *eyeteeth* for her outsize General Motors refrigerator, not to mention her pop-up toaster, her electric knife-sharpener and can-opener, her washing-machine and dryer, her floor-waxer, et cetera. I blushed for her when she said that, but possibly she's right. Possibly the locals do envy them their easy access to all these goodies, symbolized by the PX card. What shocked me was learning that even little kids have PX cards. Their daughter has had one practically from the time she could walk.

Do you remember that Navy wife we knew in Berkeley who kept asking you whether you didn't want to share a big double-breasted turkey with her? She used to get them at the Commissary somewhere in the Bay Area. I remember you saying coldly that it sounded like a double-breasted suit. She was always after you to get on the gravy train with her and she was hurt when you always refused.

The same way you would never buy anything at a discount house, though you liked Sears, Roebuck. I used to ask you what was the difference, and you said that buying at Sears,

Roebuck was economical but buying at a discount house was greedy. But I think you liked Sears, Roebuck because it was traditional; your grandmother had "always" bought lawn-mowers and sprinklers there. Sears, Roebuck, to you, was the "old" America where people had lawns and wore mail-order underwear in the winter. If you'll excuse me for saying so (I've been examining the roots of my thinking lately), you confuse the ethical and the aesthetic. Of course you may be right, in a sense. When Kant asks what would the world be like if everyone stole, that may be at bottom an aesthetic question. What would the world *look* like?

I'd like to talk this over with somebody, but who? When I first studied the categorical imperative, I thought, like a lot of laymen, that it was the same as the Golden Rule. Don't steal from your neighbor because you wouldn't want him to steal from you. But the motive there is selfish. Sort of an imaginary deal or bargain: how would *I* feel if somebody stole *my* pocketbook? I'm projecting my petty self-interest outward. The categorical imperative is purer, like a theorem in geometry. Presented with the question Should I steal or Why shouldn't I steal, Kant tells me to contemplate a world of thieves disinterestedly and accept it or reject it. If I reject it, that means that I don't care for the over-all picture, regardless of where I might figure in it. But then, you might say, ethics boils down to a question of taste. Only, with Kant taste isn't relative. He assumes that everybody, the thief included, would reject the picture of a world in which everybody stole. Because the picture is self-contradictory. He was trying, in fact, to take the taste out of ethics, to base ethics on a universal agreement that would spring from a common recognition of what is evident. The way philosophers have always been trying to take the taste out of aesthetics.

Pragmatically, nearly everybody, at least in the Western world, agrees that the Parthenon is beautiful. It isn't a question of taste, like Mannerism, for instance, which you can get to like, the way you do olives. Kant's ethics, as I see it, is a beautiful structure, based on a law of harmony and inner consistency, that in its way resembles the Parthenon, while yours, Mother, if you'll excuse me, is more like olives. Caviare to the general. Your ethics is based on *style*, which never has to give a consistent reason why it is the way it is. And if an outsider looks for the reason, it is likely to be historical: I mean that somebody like Louis XIV introduced a certain shape of armchair, which a select few can recognize. Purely contingent.

You shudder at the thought of a double-breasted turkey because a single-breasted turkey is classical. Your style would be compromised if you joined the herd around the PX-trough. But you can't persuade anyone else to abstain unless they love you and want to be like you. You saw that in Rocky Port. In your way, you are an exemplary person, but the common man can't imitate you, although you think he ought to. It's as if Mozart said to Salieri, "Why not be like me?"

You are an accident, Mother, which for some reason you don't want to recognize. Let's say a happy accident. But you can't legislate. That's your great weakness, and you know it. You want your whim or prejudice to be a universal law. Maybe all artists are like that; they feel they are the *end* of some teleological chain. I'm coming to the conclusion that art is incompatible with democracy. If I want to be a democrat, it's an awful handicap to be the son of an artist. I will have to reject you, if I can. Because—to put it bluntly—you are a snob. Without wanting to be one. You can't help it.

For instance, you don't really want to vote for Johnson, because, you say, he is "common." Doesn't that show that your whole way of looking at things is permeated by archaic caste notions? If I argue that Harry Truman was common, you say no, he was ordinary—a fine distinction. I guess an ordinary person is a common person you approve of. Then you say you don't like Johnson's face; it's crafty. Well, I just looked that word up in the dictionary. It comes from craft, the artisan's skill at twisting his material. Which proves how we still despise the artisan, the guy who had to work with his hands.

It isn't just you. Our whole vocabulary is rotten with feudal distinctions. Look at *villain* or *clown*. Those were just words for peasants. Then think about "O what a rogue and peasant slave am I!" Do you know what *rogue* meant? A beggar. Being a prince, Hamlet couldn't think of any worse things to call himself. And Hamlet is an ethical person. The vocabulary of ethics, once you start to think about it, is more foul and retrograde than any other kind of talk. We say an action is low or base or mean or boorish, which are all synonyms for vulgar, *i.e.*, characteristic of the common people. As opposed to noble, gentle, kind, meaning aristocratic. And people who don't use these terms—at least in their own minds—for the most part haven't even entered the realm of the ethical. They don't give a damn whether an action is noble or ignoble, princely or beggarly; they live for their gross desires. There's no vocabulary for a democratic ethics; even words like *free* or *frank*, which you would think were sort of yeoman words, actually meant belonging to the ruling class. I suppose in Russia *proletarian* is still a term of praise, but the proletariat there—in theory—*is* the ruling class. Why can't we find words to express a classless ideal? Do you remember, when I was about six, an old Russian Social Revolutionary came to see the *babbo*? He had just escaped from somewhere, maybe Siberia or a DP camp, and he said, "I would like to make a little money. In the most dignified and democratic way possible." This made you both laugh a lot, and the *babbo* used to tell it as a story, but I couldn't see what was funny about it. In fact, Mother, what *was* so funny? Unless you were just laughing at him for his ignorance of the ways of the capitalist world. I would like to meet that man now.

It seems to me that if my generation is serious it will have to reform language. Get rid of its hoary increment of prejudice. Like those French Jacobins chopping off the heads of statues. Around Paris, they've been restored, I read in the guidebook, by Viollet-le-Duc. On Notre-Dame, for instance, you have to look twice to see that the kings of Judah on the façade are just plastic-surgery paste-ups. But outside of Paris, they say, you get the full effect—rows of headless bodies on the church fronts. I saw some the other day in the Louvre. A massacre. This gory gallery made more impression on me than practically anything I've seen. Apostles and saints reduced to stumps. Or bunches of drapery. I never grasped before what the French Revolution meant. An Italian—even a half-Italian and a half-Jew like me—can't help feeling revolted by these hacked-up groups in defenseless stone. It goes against the grain. My balls ached in sympathy. For Mother Church, I guess, and her poor bleeding trunk. What a change to wander into the peaceful Italian rooms, where nobody had harmed a hair of that boy Baptist's head! I love Donatello. Italians, unlike the French, are still a *family*. Maybe because they weren't ever a nation. Or because they inherited the Roman *pietas*, which was reverence for ancestors. I will have to mull that over. But I felt it very strongly with this Italian yesterday—as if he were my long-lost uncle. And I gather he reciprocated. The funny thing is, he is a half-Jew too—a tall guy, slightly bald, looks like a patriarch. His name is Bonfante. But his mother, believe it or not, was a Levi. No connection, apparently. She came from Ancona.

We talked about the Terror, and he advised me to read a book by Salvemini, on the conditions that led up to the French Revolution; he is going to lend it to me. I told him I thought the French had a *faible* for decapitation. After all, their patron saint is Saint Denis, who was beheaded, and you keep seeing statues of him carrying his head in his hands like a jack-o'-lantern. An anticipation of the guillotine. Bonfante said the guillotine was just a rationalization of an old inefficient process. I said that applied to the gas chambers, and he had to admit I was right.

But afterwards I thought that maybe those French mobs had been logical in wrecking the symbols of the old régime. Those decapitated statues shook my democratic complacency; whoever did that meant business. Only they didn't go far enough. They should have chopped off the head of language while they were at it. That was the point, of course, of changing the names of the days and months and starting the calendar over. But they needed a bigger purge; no more *ci-devant* words. Only words that pointed to something like *tree* or *house*. Is that the idea behind English linguistic philosophy? I guess you wouldn't know. Instead of devouring its own children, the Revolution should have killed off its parents. They would have had to abolish all past literature and art, including the *lumières*. Grinning Voltaire *and* the Holy Virgin. Possibly music too—all those masses and madrigals and stately minuets. Smash the pianos and harpsichords, unstring the violins. Into the cannon foundry with the knightly trumpets.

Naturally, this might have been offensive to me if I had been alive then—after all, I hate to lop off the head of a dandelion. But if it had been done in 1789, possibly I'd be able to think clearly today. I feel awfully confused now, as though my mind were a pool that looked transparent till I started stirring up its muddy depths with a stick. This could be the effect of being away from home and becoming a "rootless cosmopolitan." I've never felt before like a foreign particle. And since I haven't anybody congenial to talk to, I am talking to myself. Tonight is the first chance I've had to *sfogarmi*, to get rid of that bottled-up feeling. Don't show this letter to anyone. Please.

You know, you and the *babbo* always said I was an egalitarian. That used to embarrass me, but it's true. I've got this bug about equality. And now I'm in the place where the whole thing started, where you see *Liberté, Egalité, Fraternité* frowning at you in gold letters from the faces of public buildings. They even have it on the fronts of *churches*, sometimes stenciled and sometimes cut right into the stone. As though some kid had gone wild with a rubber stamp that it got for its birthday. The handwriting on the wall, only it's printed in big Roman letters. This must go back to the Revolution, when the churches were turned into powder-magazines or temples of Reason or Glory. Funny that in all these years nobody erased it; I wonder if the Germans tried during the Occupation. Out, damned spot. You would think the guidebooks would have a word to say about this revolutionary slogan, which hits every tourist in the eye, but they pass it over in silence, just as if it was one of those obscene graffiti you see in the Métro. OAS or A BAS LES JUIFS.

I've decided that may be why the Parisians are so sullen and why they drink. They thought of equality first. My theory is that equality is a sort of poison; once it got into the human bloodstream, nobody could eliminate it. It just stayed there, corroding us. I mean, it might have been better if nobody had ever thought of it in the first place. But they did, and once they did, it should have been thought *through*. Which never happened.

When you consider that mankind lived for centuries without this idea's ever seriously entering anybody's mind! It never occurred to Socrates or Plato or any of the old philosophers. The idea of *everybody's* being equal, not just Athenians or free men. You could say it occurred to slaves and people like the Ciompi in Florence; naturally it would. But it didn't get into the thinking of the people *on top*, the reasoners and legislators. Not till the eighteenth century. Yet you couldn't say that Socrates or Pericles was stupid or a blind supporter of an oligarchy. The idea of equality was like that play about the man who came to dinner. It was "entertained," and then we were in the soup. Pardon the unintentional pun.

Equality, of course, is that specter Marx was talking about, the specter of communism, which is still stalking around, haunting the globe, without ever having been *embodied* anywhere. It's still two-thirds of a ghost. At home, in spite of the Constitution, we don't have real political equality, and the Russians don't have real economic equality—far from it. One would lead to the other, logically, or so people suspect: that's why the white Southerners are afraid to give the Negro the vote; the next thing he would be asking for would be a decent job. And if the Russian workers got consumer goods, they would soon be asking for the vote.

I have made a discovery, Mother! Whenever in history, equality appeared on the agenda, it was exported somewhere else, like an undesirable. In the eighteenth century, when the idea began traveling around Europe, it was shipped off to the New World, where there was more room. But pretty soon, as the East got crowded, equality became sort of smelly and was sent out West, in a covered wagon, to the wide-open spaces, so that back home people could forget about it for a while. In your generation, Roosevelt made a few gestures in the direction of equality, until World War II came along and took priority. In my generation, the idea has drifted South and joined the civil-rights movement, where it's stirring up trouble. So a new move is indicated, on the principle of "Keep moving, buddy." Maybe into space, if there isn't another world war. Space will be the new frontier, full of homesteaders: opportunity beckons, enlist in space. But the problem will arise there too; the colonists on Mars or the moon will want equal rights with the world or a universal one-hour week or something. Then there may be another migration, into the Milky Way. But finally humanity will have to face the specter, unless it decides to commit suicide instead, which it might. We may agree to blow ourselves up, like a man who knows he's suffering from an incurable disease.

If the race would try equality once, then we might find out that it worked. Let everybody keep hands off and give it a fair chance. Which the French Revolution never had. Or the

Russian. Not even dear old Castro. And if we found out that it didn't work, OK. We would stop being *haunted* by it.

Let me give you a little parable. In olden time a man who lived in a big house and wore a fur cloak felt superior to a ragged man who lived in a hovel. And the reason was simple: a tautology. He felt superior *because* he lived in a big house and wore a fur cloak. That was all there was to it. If he was charitable, like Good King Wenceslas (your favorite Bohemian), he could take a few sticks to the peasant in his hovel at Christmastime. But Good King Wenceslas was a *saint*, and besides it was *Christmas*. And, being a saint, he didn't doubt the justice that had put him in his palace and the other in his forest-hut. That was where God had assigned them, for some unfathomable reason, and the difference in their degree made the poor man grateful for the king's goodness. Inequality was natural on this earth, though there might be some surprises in Heaven.

Today, though, King Wenceslas would feel guilty because he lived in a palace. It would prey on his mind. If he was a reactionary, he would think he had to justify his accommodations by showing that he had the *right* to them, that he was superior, either by birth or by get-up-and-go to the peasant down the road. He could argue that there was no use turning his palace over to the peasant, who would only wreck it, keep the coal in the bathtub, etc. In short, he would have to find some social doctrine or "law" that entitled him to be where he was. Appeal to some imaginary tribunal that would *award* him the palace.

If King Wenceslas today was a liberal, with the peasants solidly behind him, he might become president, like Kennedy, and his wife could make the White House more palatial and have artists, like you, Mother, to perform. As long as he was on the peasants' side, he could feel OK, relatively, about retaining the palace and furs. And the more royal and dynastic he was, the more, probably, he would argue that Society needs Symbols, etc. A liberal King Wenceslas, strangely enough, seems to sleep better than his reactionary uncle.

But nobody today really feels comfortable inside his own skin. The poor feel guilty for being poor, and the rich feel guilty for being rich. The poor are afraid that it's not an accident that they are poor but that there is something ghastly wrong with them, while the rich are afraid that it *is* an accident that they're rich. The over-developed countries feel guilty toward the under-developed countries, and the under-developed countries feel ashamed of standing in line for a handout. You can measure the change in King Wenceslas' thinking by the fact that a hundred years ago a country was *proud* of being rich. I guess no country was ever proud of being poor. Unless a masochistic country like Poland or Ireland?

Last winter, while I was working for civil rights, I worried about being a guilty white liberal. Today I'm not so much bothered by that. I have it in a better perspective. Aside from the fact of not being able to help being white, I have come to the conclusion that working for civil rights is a good thing in itself, even if I do it to bribe my conscience. A lot of the churches and abbeys in France wouldn't have been built if kings and nobles hadn't been trying to purge themselves of blood-guilt. Hospitals too. I send part of my allowance to civil-rights causes, which lets me stay on the sidelines or in the cheering section. If a person feels guilty, it's better to pay a recompense. Be your own redeemer. Take our friend the admiral. If he sent a few guilt-dollars to the NAACP or the Urban League or the Brotherhood of Sleeping Car Porters, he would be a lot easier in his mind. He acts so defiant because he's secretly ashamed of his/our treatment of the Negro. He knows he's wrong. It strikes me that our whole country is secretly ashamed, for being rich and white, and this may make us dangerous.

Possibly I ought to feel ashamed myself, because I'm not giving my whole time to civil rights, though I claim to believe in it. But I don't look for excuses for being here studying in Paris. That's a decision I've made, a conscious act of my will, and I notice that I don't repine much over anything I've done *consciously*—you have to accept the choices of your will in a sporting spirit. *Cosa fatta capo ha*, as the *babbo* says.

What is biting me here in Paris is something different: *being who I am* at this juncture in history. I sense myself as irrelevant to practically everything: this room, this street, this city, this world, this universe. Except to you and Bob and the *babbo*. I'm just an epiphenomenon of your joint history—a wandering footnote. It's only in connection with you people, who formed me, that I make a semblance of sense.

You remember how in King Arthur everybody keeps saying

to an errant knight, "Tell me thy name and thy condition." Whereupon he tells, and they search his wounds and give him a bath of tepid water. It would be nice to be errant in a story-book where your fellow-knights recognize you when you say who you are. I am slightly attracted to that Smith girl I mentioned because she can place me, like somebody looking in a file: her cousin used to spend the summer in Rocky Port, and her mother met you once in New York, *e così via*. In fact, she's quite boring and middle-class, though pretty; she actually said, "It's a small world, isn't it?" But when I'm around her, I feel slightly more real. She knows my name and my condition.

You may think I'm wandering from the theme of equality. But I'm not. A person has to assume, especially if he's studying philosophy, that he has a common world with the rest of humanity. Not just the common world of sense data and a common receiving apparatus but a common *inner* world—his mind, which he uses like a laboratory to conduct experiments. As soon as you start to philosophize, you predicate a common world. A basically democratic world, in which Socrates and the slave boy, obeying the command of reason, arrive at the same conclusion. There can't be such a thing as an aristocratic philosophy; once philosophy starts getting exclusive, like neo-Platonism, it turns into a cult, with secret doctrines and initiates.

Then, bang, here in Paris, I find I'm really isolated. Not only don't I share a language (my French is lousy, to my great surprise) with most of the people I see, or a social background, or a political outlook, but we don't have in common the most elementary rules of conduct that I thought were shared by our whole sub-species. In a minute I will tell you what I mean. Those cheesy hotels. Perhaps dormitory life should have prepared me for the shock. But I must have been lucky in school and college. No, Mother, I don't mean stealing or homosexuality. Do you know why I *had* to get an apartment? Why I had to retreat into my present private world? Something I've already spoken of. Those communal toilets.

It started in that military hotel. Every morning when I went to move my bowels, after waiting my turn, I found the bowl all smeared and streaked with excrement. Sometimes the previous user hadn't bothered to flush it at all; there would be those turds in the bowl and a smell, naturally. I would flush and open the window to air the place out before sitting down; the seat was often still warm from the bottom of the last guy who had defecated. It made me nauseous, but I said to myself that these were Air Force men: maybe you had to expect that they would have been toughened up, living in barracks.

But when I moved, it was the same. There were the same oily streaks of evil-smelling shit on the porcelain; sometimes the bowl would be all splashed, even the underside of the toilet seat would be splashed, because the last occupant had had diarrhea. You know; the Paris trots. If it turned out that I only had to pee (squeamishness was making me constipated), I would find myself in a quandary: whether to carefully clean off the filth with that rubber brush and wash the underside of the toilet seat with wet toilet paper or just to pee and flush and walk out. Well, I never could bring myself to accept the second alternative. I *had* to clean up for the next person. Even though I felt there was something degrading about stooping, literally, to do it. And the smell would make me gag, unless I held my breath. How did you ever stand it, Mother, washing my diapers? I remember (or did you tell me?) that when I had done Number Two, you always washed them out yourself before sending them to the diaper service. I wonder if everyone did. And, if I recall, it was years before I was housebroken.

Anyway, while laving the "lavatory," far from giving myself a merit badge for public service, I felt furtive. What would anyone think if they found me? Actually once a girl did find me, swabbing away with toilet paper; in that hotel, the john door didn't bolt. She hastily withdrew. At least she couldn't know that it was somebody else's shit I was laboriously removing. That was what I told myself when I met her afterwards in the hall.

I couldn't understand why I should have this complex about being caught in the act. Was I afraid of what a wig-picker might say? Or embarrassed at being a Boy Scout? I tried to examine my motives. Was I cleaning up somebody else's shit for fear that the next person would think it was mine? There might be an element of that, I admitted. But if I had been promised that nobody would see me issuing from that toilet, I would still have cleaned it. I would have cleaned it if I knew that the hotel was going to be demolished five minutes later by a hydrogen bomb.

Of course, Mother, I could have left it for the chambermaid. Or rung the bell and asked her to do it. One morning, in the hotel on the rue de la Harpe, while I was hovering in my room, waiting for the coast to be clear, I heard someone go into the toilet and then come right out again, banging the door; resolute steps marched to the hall telephone, and a voice, speaking good French, told the management to send somebody up instantly to clean the toilet on the fifth floor, it was filthy, disgusting. . . . Probably the whole floor was listening, and pretty soon the chambermaid came running. I fell in love, abjectly (and maybe I wasn't the only one), with the owner of that voice—it was a woman, that was all I ever knew. She must have checked out that same day.

But I could never have emulated her. Lack of courage, I suppose. Plus the feeling that I would rather be a menial myself than assume that some other menial should take work like that in her stride. That was why it disgusted me that that chambermaid I mentioned should leap to the task with alacrity just because I had tipped her. At that point I had the right to think that if she could do it for me, why not for everybody?

The worst of those hotels, though, was realizing that some of my predecessors on the hot seat had been girls and women. That killed me. Knowing *that* about them. I would see a plump little Irish girl come tripping out of the toilet and go in and find her excrement waiting in the bowl, practically steaming, like horse turds. In my last hotel there was an old Englishwoman on my floor that the desk clerk said was a writer; I used to hear her typing sometimes in her room. If I saw her returning from the jakes, I would turn around and postpone answering the call of Nature, so that I wouldn't have to follow her in and compromise her dignity. It was compromised enough, I felt, by her having to run the gauntlet every morning to attend to her needs: between 8:00 A.M. and 9:30 A.M., in that circuit, every door on the corridor is stealthily ajar, and the inhabitant is crouched like a runner to make the dash down the hall when he hears the chain pulled.

Actually it got so I was using the toilet in American Express every time I went for my mail and urinals on the street and in cafés. I developed a horror of identifying the faeces I was finding every morning in the bowl; I preferred them to remain anonymous. Finding pubic hairs in the communal bathtub never bothered me particularly.

If this is the way things are, Mother, how am I going to be able to take the Army? I don't mind latrines, which are sort of natural. What's horrible to me is the combination of (relatively) modern plumbing and beastly squalor. But animals are more dainty. They hide their turds whenever they can. Except herd animals like cows and sheep. Well, horses. But that was what I kept thinking: how much more fastidious animals were. I remembered how I used to say that I preferred animals to people, which worried you.

Don't imagine that I was living on some Parisian skid row. Or in some of the Beat hotels, which at least might have been amusing. All my places were on the fringe of respectability. The clientele was mainly students who looked as if they came from middle-class families, where presumably you're taught not to be physically offensive to others. The way you taught me. You taught me so long ago that I feel as if I'd always known instinctively to clean the toilet after myself. *I.e.*, to look and see if it was necessary. Something I did automatically, without thinking about it, like brushing my teeth in the morning or using a handkerchief or a Kleenex when I had to blow my nose.

After a while, I began to speculate about my fellow-residents. So far as I could tell from the evidence, the majority either didn't mind leaving traces of themselves or else didn't notice. They just went in, did their business, and exited, pulling the chain, without waiting to see whether the water flushed. But how was it possible not to notice the traces of the guy before you and, noticing, not to react? Could humanity be divided into people who noticed and people who didn't? If so, there was no common world.

That thought really depressed me. If there was no agreement on a primary matter like that, then it was useless to look for agreement on "higher" principles. And I couldn't help feeling moral about it—judging my predecessors in the toilet in a highly unfavorable way. A shitty lot. I was glad I was different from them. I mean, that there was *somebody* around that had a better standard of communal living and that that somebody happened to be me. But if I really believed in equality, why was I glad to be the exception? I ought to feel sad and in fact I did—both at the same time.

I guessed I had finally found what was making me so furtive about my one-man sanitation drive—it was undemocratic. I actually began to worry that the guy or girl who came after me, finding the toilet practically sparkling and a fresh breeze blowing in, would resent the implied criticism of the prevailing mores. On the other hand, I hoped I was starting a trend. Like you, Ma. You're always hoping people will copy you, giving them little object-lessons. You think you're not but you are. Along this line, I went to the Prisunic and bought a can of spray deodorizer; at that point I was staying in a hotel where the facilities had no window. I left it beside the toilet, and somebody promptly stole it. What for?

In reality some of the other denizens did get irritated with me. Because I took so long. They would bang on the door or rattle the knob. But flushing and then waiting for the tank to refill and then flushing again takes a little while; with those old toilets, you can't hurry it. Not to mention the actual cleaning and airing. Then I would weigh the need of the person outside against my own desire to do the job right. Some days there would be layers of faeces, like geological deposits—the bottom one hard and dry and scaly and practically impossible to scrape off without Ajax or Dutch Cleanser, which naturally was not supplied. If I was feeling energetic and nobody was waiting to get in, I would clean the brush too, to the best of my ability.

Do you think I could be slightly deranged? It was as if all those rituals were a sort of apology on my part to the rest of the world. An apology for being what I am, the kind of young pharisee whose mother has taught him to clean the toilet. As though I was willing to *slave* for my values to excuse myself for holding them. Yes. It occurs to me that I must have got this from you. Which is why I feel I can harangue you on this malodorous theme.

But maybe it was not such a bad thing, finally, my initiation. Like the bishop washing the feet of twelve selected paupers from the Old Men's Home—do you remember, we saw that in a town outside Rome at Easter-time four years ago? A lesson in humility. Only that was rather a token performance; the old men's feet, we noticed, were clean to start with. The trouble with me is that I check my helpful impulses—giving up my seat in the Métro, for instance—when I notice that nobody else does it. My greatest weakness is the fear of appearing ridiculous. Or is that just because I am young? If I saw an old man painstakingly cleaning the toilet, I would respect him for it. Maybe my bug about equality is just the shame of being different. I will have to think about that.

Dear Ma, I am getting sleepy. Forgive this gloomy epistle. I've omitted the things I like in Paris. Above all, the sky. It's always in motion, with clouds racing across it, which is exhilarating, a real Olympian combat. You hardly ever see that at home. Or in Italy. When I'm depressed, I climb up to the Pantheon and look at the sky.

How is the *babbo*, by the way? Have you heard from him? He keeps writing me with anxious offers of advice and help. Telling me to look up people he used to know twenty years ago. As if I could. One of his suggestions was that I should call Malraux. To get him to talk to my professors. And he sends me the names of cheap restaurants that no longer exist. One thing, according to him, that I must be sure to do while I am here is have an affair with a Frenchwoman. . . .

Much love to Bob. Are there any art books he would like me to get him? How is the campaign going? Dag and I are going to watch the election on TV at a café. I think the French would secretly like Goldwater to get in—to prove that America is the way they imagine it.

Love to you, Mother, from your errant son,

Pierrot le Fou

Peter was taking his plant for a walk. This morning the sun was out, for a change, and he was cutting his class. He carried it, swaying, in its pot down the flight of steps, his private companionway, that led from the rue Monsieur-le-Prince to the rue Antoine-Dubois—a mew populated by cats where Brigitte Bardot had lived in *La Vérité*. He was a past master of short cuts as well as circuitous ways; though he had not yet traveled by sewer, he liked to pretend that some implacable Javert was trailing him. He came out onto the boulevard St.-Germain, greeted the statue of Danton, and stopped to look in the windows of the bookshops selling medical textbooks, colored anatomical charts, and dangling cardboard skeletons.

This uninviting merchandise exercised a gruesome attraction on Peter, who, if he could believe his family, was a known hypochondriac. The quarter where he had elected to live was dominated by the dark carcass of the old Ecole de Médecine, around which, like suckers, had sprung up a commerce in surgical equipment, wheel chairs, orthopedic pulleys, sputum basins, artificial limbs, as well as these bookstores containing yellowing treatises on every disease he could imagine himself catching, including *le grand mal*. The main School of Medicine had moved to a modern building on the rue Jacob, which was why he seldom saw students around here—only an occasional browser leafing through dusty textbooks; it was as if his whole neighborhood had been put up in formaldehyde, like gallstones or those crusty corns and giant bunions he sometimes studied in the half-curtained window of a corn-cutter over near the Carrefour Bac.

At the traffic light, he decided to turn up the rue de Tournon, his favorite street, and walk on the sunny side; there were too many hurrying pedestrians on the boulevard St.-Germain, making it hard for him to clear a path for the tall plant with its crowning glory of pale new leaves unfurling like little umbrellas. It was a member of the ivy family, as you could tell from its name—Fatshedera—although, unlike the English clan, it did not creep or clamber but stood upright. He had bought it at

Les Halles on a Friday afternoon; at five o'clock the public was let into the weekly potted-plant market, after the florists had made their selections. It pleased him that in Paris there was a "day" for every kind of thing, as in the first chapter of Genesis: Friday at Les Halles for potted plants and Tuesday for cut flowers, Sunday morning, on the quai aux Fleurs, for birds; there was even a dog market somewhere on Wednesdays. The Parisian apportionment of the week made him think of Italy, where articles of consumption were grouped, amusingly, into families resembling riddles, as, for example, the family that included salt, matches, stamps, and tobacco (bought from the *tabaccaio*) or the chicken family that included eggs, rabbits, and mushrooms; his father liked to remember a store in Rome that carried pork in the winter and straw hats in the summer.

The plant-seller had warned Peter that the Fatshedera did not like too much light—which should have made it an ideal tenant for his apartment. But after a month's residence there, looking out on the air shaft, it had grown long, leggy, and de-spondent, like its master. Its growth was all tending upward, to the crown, like that of trees in the jungle. The leaves at the base were falling off, one by one, and though he had been carefully irritating the stem at the base to promote new side-ward growth, it had been ignoring this prodding on his part and just kept getting taller, weed-like, till he had finally had this idea of taking it for walks, once or twice a week, depending on the weather. It did not seem to mind drafts, and the out-door temperature on a sunny day in late November was not appreciably colder than the indoor temperature *chez* him. He thought he was beginning to note signs of gratitude in the in-valid for the trouble he was taking; a little bump near the base where he had been poking it with his knife seemed about to produce a stalk or pedicel, and there was a detectable return of chlorophyll, like a green flush to the cheeks of the shut-in. He spoke to it persuasively—sometimes out loud—urging it to grow. So far, he had resisted giving it a shot of fertilizer, be-cause a mildewed American manual he had acquired on the *quais*—*How to Care for Your House Plants*—cautioned against giving fertilizer except to "healthy subjects." That would be like giving a gourmet dinner to a starving person—the old parable of the talents.

How to Care for Your House Plants was full of housewifely pointers that appealed to his frugality, like the column he used to enjoy in the Rocky Port weekly *Sentinel* where readers exchanged recipes for removing berry stains from clothing and keeping squirrels out of the bird-feeding tray. He wondered what dull adventures it had had before coming to lodge on his bookshelf: had it traveled from Montclair to Stuttgart to Châteauroux in the trunk of some Army wife, along with *The Joy of Cooking*, "Getting the Most out of Your Waring Blendor," "How to Use Your Singer," and instructions, with diagram, for carving the Thanksgiving turkey? Obedient to its recommendations, he had started some dish-gardens in his Stygian lair from dried lentils, slices of carrots, and grapefruit pips, setting them out in saucers under his student lamp, equipped with a seventy-five-watt bulb—his landlady had confiscated the 150-watt bulb he had put in originally. Every day he moved the positions of the saucers, so that they would share the light equally, determined not to show partiality in the vegetable kingdom, though already he preferred the lacy carrot. These dish-gardens reminded him of the primary grades: the avocado and grapefruit plants on the broad window sill the class used to water, the acorns he used to hoard, and the interesting fear (which his mother had finally scouted) that a cherry stone he had swallowed would turn into a tree branching out of his mouth.

All children, he guessed, were natural misers and sorcerers; the progeny of his new friends, the Bonfantes, were impressed and delighted by his dish-gardens when he invited them to tea in his apartment. He promised to start them some in their kitchen window from bits of carrots and the eyes of potatoes, and he entrusted them with a sprouting garlic clove, with instructions to keep it in their clothes-closet and gradually bring it out to the light; in the spring, it would have little white bell-like flowers—he did not see why garlic, though not specifically mentioned in *How to Care etc.*, should not act like any other bulb. They wanted to know whether this was American, like the jack-o'-lantern he had made them at Halloween, and Peter said it was. He was the first live American boy Irène and Gianni had ever seen, and they asked him many questions, such as: was it true that Americans ate with their feet on the table? Their conception of America was a blend of Wild West and asphalt jungle, and they listened with doubtful wonder to the stories Peter told of white wooden houses, ponds, waterfalls, skating, clamming, ice-cream freezers, blueberries, corn-on-the-cob—one of his mother's rules for telling stories to children, which she had learned as a child from her father, was always to put in something good to eat.

If he was going to keep up his strength, he felt he had to keep in close touch with his other mother, Nature, while abroad, and, overcoming his shyness, he had asked the young woman at the Embassy in charge of student exchanges whether there was anything like a bird-watching group in Paris. To his surprise, when he returned she had the answer typed out on a sheet of paper: he could join a group called Les Jeunes Ornithologistes de France, which met alternate Sundays for field trips during the fall and winter at a Métro or railroad station. Last Sunday at 10:00 A.M., Peter had been on hand with his field glasses and the *Guide des oiseaux d'Europe* at the meeting-place—a Métro station near the park of les Buttes-Chaumont, which was a part of Paris strange to him, beyond the Gare du Nord. He waited, studying the subway riders as they mounted the stone steps and trying to decide, from their markings and plumage, whether they could be young ornithologists. He was on the verge of speaking to a youth in a red hunter's cap who was hanging about the entrance too until he bethought himself of flashing the bird book, spy-wise, as a signal—no reaction. When the group finally appeared, of course they were unmistakable because of their field glasses and hiking boots. Peter was disappointed that there were only five, all males, and all but one quite old; he had been hoping for a Papagena among them, but few girls, even at home, cared about watching birds.

Nevertheless, he had enjoyed the morning, in the gray northern light of the park, which consisted mainly of steep bare rocks, the buttes it was named for, and was traversed by a cindery railroad track. Not a good place to see birds, he would have thought, except sparrows. It was a sparse, scrubby working-class park without amenities—only a little artificial lake, drained for the winter, and a non-functioning artificial waterfall. Yet he had ten new birds listed in his notebook when he boarded the Métro for home—one uncommon. It was his first experience of going on a bird walk with a group, and he recognized that compared with these briskly striding, sharp-eyed Frenchmen, he was no ornithologist. He was always the last to descry a feathered friend, even an easy one like the *rouge-gorge*, the American robin's plump red-breasted little cousin. He kept losing his place in the bird book while trying to correlate the picture with the description; when he actually identified a bird—a tit, for instance—he could not find it in the index, where it was listed, naturally, under *Mésanges*. If he got his field glasses focused on a *pic-épeiche*, or woodpecker, in flight, the group would be closing in on an *accenteur mouchet*, or hedge sparrow, lurking in a thicket. All this bore out the *babbo*'s theory that Peter did not have the makings of a real naturalist—he only liked Nature, which was not the same thing.

He tried to follow the *ornithologistes'* talk. Today's expedition, he gleaned, was not to look at birds for fun, the way he conceived it, but to verify a scientific suspicion. They were agreeing that a park like les Buttes-Chaumont, on the edge of industrial Paris, had turned into a first-rate bird station. Migrating birds were stopping off more and more in the city as the city spread; they were seeing certain birds this morning that had not been sighted in Paris in fifty years. The idea gave Peter a ray of hope: one of the side-benefits of megalopolis would be that if you lived long enough you could see flocks of evening grosbeaks in the Christmas tree at Rockefeller Center. Every cloud had a silver lining. As the old haunts of birds were transformed into sinister housing developments, linked by murderous highways, the city would become an aviary.

At noon, the bird men had gone home to their Sunday dinners, and with them—a strange fact—the interesting birds vanished too, which seemed to show that Nature, like any performer, was dependent on her audience. Huddled in his sheepskin-lined jacket, Peter sat on a bench, eating a sandwich he had made—a cynosure for common sparrows. With his Swiss pocketknife he providently cut some moss to take back to the Bonfante children as a nest for their sprouting garlic clove; he had been worried about finding them some suitable organic material that would hold moisture without becoming waterlogged. On the whole, he felt content. In his wallet was a receipt for a year's dues—ten francs—that he had forked out at his own insistence to the group's bald-headed leader, which would entitle him to receive regular notices of field trips and slide lectures. Because it was already late November, they had not wanted to accept Peter's money. He could be their guest, they said, for the last two field trips of the year; Sunday after next, they were meeting at the Gare Montparnasse, to go to Trappes and study some waterfowl on the ponds. He could join, if he was still interested, in January, after the holidays. But Peter had persisted.

After they had gone, he took out the receipt and looked at it. It was dated January, 1965—next year. So he had been their guest after all. The rush of warmth to his heart made him realize that this was about the first time he had had occasion to feel grateful to a French person. In fact, the *ornithologistes* seemed to belong to a different race from the French he had been running up against on his daily beat. They had been helping him out all morning, silently indicating birds to him, finding him the right page in his book, supplying the English name of a bird when they knew it, pausing for him to catch up if he fell behind—Peter on his solitary bird walks had been in the habit of stationing himself in ambush and waiting, whereas these men strode ahead purposefully, as though on a military patrol. They acted as a unit, rapidly collating their data; there was no disagreement as to what they saw—as though no possibility of confusion could exist—and nobody tried to see *more* birds quicker than the next man, which had been Peter's tendency when in company with the fair Rosamund, who, he feared, had sometimes let him see birds ahead of her, thus admitting a competition between them.

Munching a Golden apple, he had a glimpse of a great International of peaceful naturalists, to whom technological change was only interesting insofar as it affected the habits of another species. Being a Sunday ornithologist could put you at one with the universe, since whatever happened was bound to produce data, and *any* data were bound, by definition, to be interesting to a specialist. The sight of all those "winter visitors" from the finch and thrush families here in Paris had greatly excited the old *ornithologistes*, as well as the young kid with them, but seeing crows or nothing would have excited them too. If science were still a matter of observing and classifying ancient orders of beings—some of them, like the woodpeckers, already observed by Aristotle—he would like science, Peter thought. Maybe he might have "found himself" if he had been born in old Linnaeus' time; alas, everything seemed bent on demonstrating that he had come into the world too late. He remembered Hans telling some inoffensive botanist at the Thanksgiving feast that the descriptive sciences belonged to the age of the curio cabinet: taxonomy, useful in its day, had no place in the curriculum of a modern university, where biology and genetics were acting *on* Nature, like modern physics and chemistry, disturbing its inmost processes, forcing it to answer questions, smashing its resistance. Suiting the action to the word, Hans had banged thunderously on the dinner table, upsetting the gravy and spilling several glasses of Napa Valley wine.

Peter, aged circa thirteen, had not wholly followed the dispute; he had thought taxonomy was taxidermy and supposed that Hans was inveighing against cabinets of stuffed birds and animals. But he had understood his stepfather's general drift and felt a quivering sympathy for mute, innocent matter, pummeled and interrogated by Hans and his fellow-scientists, whom he pictured as a sort of Gestapo. His resentment of physics had immediately embraced biology, not to mention genetics and every "improved" seed strain developed by an Iowa hybridist from some monstrous mutant. He wondered what the plant world had looked like before all this unnatural marrying and crossing had begun—doubtless better, though his mother possibly had a point when she said that experiment ought to have halted with the invention of the hybrid tea rose; up to then, she approved. She was always trying to draw the line, her personal high-water mark, across the history of achievement and avoid being a total reactionary: in the home, she said, a good place to stop would have been with the flush toilet and the vacuum cleaner. In front of Peter, she did not add Tampax, but he had heard her say it to her sister.

Ornithology, he now concluded, must be one of the few descriptive sciences extant. You simply watched birds and did not try to change them biologically. At least he had never heard of anybody crossing a nightingale with a parrot. Birds in nature were left to themselves, apart from human interference. The most you might do was band them or coax them to show themselves, with birdhouses and trick devices like the hummingbird feeder. He had had one in Berkeley and he now asked himself whether even that decoy had not trespassed a limit; feeding a hummingbird from a tube containing two parts water and one part sugar was possibly habit-forming. What he liked about birds and animals, moths and stars, was precisely their remoteness from himself, their independence and solitariness. He loathed the satellite hanging like a suspended baseball in the night-time sky—*il pallone americano*, the Italians in Perugia used to call it, when he was at the school for *Stranieri*. The satellite was a foreigner too, butting in on the celestial landscape. Furthermore, it had a boring orbit, like American tourists abroad, while the real stars and planets turned and wheeled in the patterns men had named after gods, animals, and utensils.

Plants were different. People had been "cultivating" them, like acquaintances, from earliest times, feeding them and caring for them in gardens, so that they had become attached to the human family, as though they were pets or livestock. His present stepfather had copied out a sentence for his mother last summer from a book he had been reading in Siena on Byzantine aesthetics: "Mortal man was put into the world to be the husbandman of immortal plants." That summed up the relation quite well, Peter reflected this morning, as he gave his dependent plant its airing: he had been allotted the duty of caring for the Fatshedera, which, barring accidents, should outlive him—so far as he knew, only annuals and biennials in the plant world died a "natural" death.

His mother might say he had no business to try to keep a plant in his apartment. Certainly the Fatshedera would have been happier in nature, wherever it basically came from—the Far East, he supposed. But he could not set it free, for it would die if he abandoned it. He was responsible for it, though no Plant Welfare League would intervene if he were to neglect it. Besides, it was making a minuscule contribution to the air of Paris. He had read an article in the *Figaro* on air pollution (some doctor had taken a rat from the laboratory and exposed it on the roof of the Opera House; it was dead in twenty-five minutes), which said that Parisians could help by growing plants on their balconies and window ledges: by inhaling carbon dioxide and exhaling oxygen, they acted as cleansers. Whenever Peter took his tall Fatshedera walking, he felt there was an exchange of benefits; in return for the light it received, it purified the atmosphere like a filter. He did not mind the centaurish figure he cut—half-man, half-vegetable—as he strolled along, the plant overtopping his head; often when he performed an *action*, he noticed, he lost his fear of visibility; he disappeared into the gest.

He examined a printer's window on the rue de Tournon. Printing, as a trade, attracted him; bookbinding too—there was a bookbinder he liked to watch working on the rue de Condé. He had been thinking a lot lately about what he would do with himself when he was through with college and the Army. He was sure he did not want to become an academic, though that was where his language major was leading him— straight into teaching, unless he took the State Department exams for the foreign service. He would have liked to have been a consul in Persia a hundred years ago, studying the native flora and fauna and Oriental religions and writing long reports home on the shah's court intrigues, but he could not see himself in a modern office building issuing visas, promoting U.S. foreign policy and the interests of Standard Oil, and rotating back in two years to Washington for reassignment—in the old days you were consul for twenty years or for life. His ideal career choice would be an occupation that kept him outdoors, like archaeologist or forester or explorer, yet everything in his background was pushing him to be some sort of scribe, if not a pharisee. His father said these were daydreams and not vocational drives: if Peter were serious about wanting to spend his life in the open air, he would have enrolled in a School of Forestry or worked as a logger one summer or dug up Etruscan remains. . . . The *babbo*, Peter had to admit, was a shrewder prophet than his mother, who fondly saw him in a tropical helmet or excavating the skeleton of some Mycenaean warrior when she did not see him arguing before the Supreme Court.

His vocational aptitudes were an old bone of contention

between his parents. To his mother, every schoolboy "interest" —especially when she did not share it—was proof of a wonderful talent to be fostered: for ornithology, ichthyology, entomology, astronomy; she let him bring home a series of chameleons from the circus to roam about the premises, in case he might be gifted for herpetology. To his father, who disliked meeting eels, escapees from Peter's leaky aquarium, on his way downstairs to breakfast, all these hobbies were only an excuse for squandering money; he had vetoed the idea of an aviary, to be constructed in his back yard on the Cape as a summer project for Peter—if the boy cared about ornithology, he pointed out, he would have been dissecting the dead birds he found during school vacations, instead of giving them funerals.

In Paris, Peter had been dreaming of becoming a binder or a printer, though these trades not only kept you indoors but were probably worse for your health than teaching in a classroom, where at least you were on your feet all day in front of a blackboard. He would have enjoyed operating a clandestine press in the Maquis and showering the country with broadsides and leaflets, but there was no Resistance any more except in uncongenial places like the Vietnamese mangrove swamps, and in the U.S. you could not become a printer unless you had an uncle or a father who belonged to the printers' union.

He turned right into the rue de Vaugirard, passed the Senate, and decided against going into the Luxembourg Garden today. Instead, he headed toward the rue de Rennes, where there was a café frequented by some Swedish girls who went to the Alliance Française. As he approached, he heard strange noises—the sound of rhythmic chanting, mixed with honking—coming from the rue de Rennes. He hurried on. At the corner he saw what he took at first to be a parade and he wondered whether today could be a national holiday that he had failed to hear about. All along the wide street, householders were lined up on their balconies, some with brooms and dusters, watching a procession of young people marching abreast and chanting; they were carrying broad streamers and placards with slogans written on them that he could not make out. The traffic on the street had stopped; buses and cars were blowing their horns. Simultaneously with Peter's arrival,

a police car appeared at the intersection, and some gendarmes
descended in a body, wearing dark-blue capes that swirled as
they moved, giving the scene a festive look. Peter realized that
he was witnessing a demonstration, such as he had read about
in history.

More gendarmes were running up the rue de Rennes,
rounding the corner by the municipal pawnshop and blowing
their whistles. Ahead of them came a second wave of marchers,
shouting and singing. Moving to the curb, Peter made out
what was written on one of the billowing streamers. He felt
slightly let down. It was only a student demonstration for
better housing at the Cité Universitaire. The police were trying to break it up. He could hear them growling at the demonstrators, who laughed and jeered back. Behind Peter, in the
glass-enclosed terrace of the corner café, people were standing
on chairs to get a better view. At the far end of the street, near
the Montparnasse station, he could see still more police, alighting from a Black Maria, and he grasped the strategy: they were
trying to hem the students in.

The crowd on the sidewalk was augmenting; those behind
were beginning to shove. A very tall blond boy in a turtle-
necked sweater and tight gray thin jacket edged in next to him
on the curb; Peter was starting to be concerned for the safety
of his plant. "*C'est beau, hein?*" said the boy, surveying the
spectacle. The police had moved in on the marchers, in sa-
lients, swinging their capes. Mentally, Peter compared this airy
ballet to the behavior of the police at home, hitting out with
nightsticks; for the first time, he approved thoroughly of the
French. They had made an art of it, he decided, as he watched
a line of students break and scatter as the graceful capes
descended. In these fall maneuvers between youth and authority, the forces were evenly matched, the students having the
advantage of numbers and the police, like matadors, that of
dexterity. If he had had two free hands, he would have applauded. He slightly lowered his plant, so as not to obstruct
the view for those in his rear.

As he did so, he heard a discordant sound of disapproval or
derision, like the American raspberry; a policeman on the
pavement whirled around and stared at Peter and his neighbor,
whose face wore a sleepy, ironical smile, like that of a large pale

cat. In a moment, the sound was repeated, and again the policeman whirled; the tall boy's drooping eyelid winked enigmatically at Peter—he was a strange-looking person, with high cheekbones, a snub nose, and colorless beetling eyebrows that seemed to express perplexity. Peter, who liked to play the game of guessing nationalities, decided that he could not be French. A Russian, maybe, whose father worked at the Soviet Embassy? Then the boy spoke, in a slow, plaintive voice. "Jan Makowski. University of Chicago. Student of Oriental languages. Pleased to meet you." He had a strong demotic Middle Western accent. Peter introduced himself. "I thought you were Russian," he said. Makowski stuck out his lower lip, as though considering the accusation. "I'm of Polish origin," he said stiffly. "Born in Warsaw. My old man 'chose freedom' when I was a kid. I went to grammar school for a while here, but he couldn't make it in France; we just about starved. Now he teaches political science at Chicago. Full professor." "Same here!" cried Peter. "I mean my father's a professor and he used to be a refugee." Makowski did not appear to find this an especially striking coincidence. "This is great, isn't it?" Peter continued, looking around him. "Compared to those Cossacks back home, I mean. This is more like a game. Everybody here is having a ball."

"You think so?" Peter followed the other's frowning, derisory gaze. The line of students with the streamer had reformed. The *flics* charged them, striking right and left with their capes. A line of blood appeared on the cheek of one of the students; a second student fell to the ground. Peter could see no sign of a weapon and he looked at his neighbor, who stood with folded arms, for enlightenment. The police struck again. Then Peter understood. There was lead in those pretty blue capes; he had read about that somewhere, he now recalled, disgusted at his own simplicity. The students were counter-attacking, ducking the flailing capes. He could distinguish three principal battle-points in the confusion. Makowski nudged him. They watched a boy aim a kick at a cop's balls; the cop caught his foot and swung him around by the leg, then let him drop. There was blood on the street. Behind Peter a woman was calling shame on the police. A flowerpot came hurtling down from a high balcony—possibly by accident. Two policemen rushed into the building. Peter's hand tightened on his own clay pot; he selected a target—a tall red-haired gendarme who would make an easy mark. Then wiser counsel—if that was what it was—prevailed; his grip relaxed, and he started to get the shakes. His hands were sweaty. He might have killed a man a few seconds ago—the cop or even a student. "Peter Levi, Murderer." The thought was strange to him and not unimpressive, though scary. He glanced curiously at Makowski, judicious, with curled lower lip, by his side, a mere scowling spectator. Nobody but Peter himself seemed to be particularly *involved* with what was going on. Clerks in their bright blue *blouses de travail* had left their counters and lined up on the sidewalk to watch; concierges, with their mutts, were standing in their doorways; shopkeepers, concerned for their property, were pulling down their iron blinds.

The students broke and began to run, pursued by the police. A youth was passed, headlong, from cop to cop, and deposited in a Black Maria that had pulled up on the corner, just beyond a flower-cart, at the Métro entrance. The police were working fast. "*Nazi!*" yelled someone behind Peter at a *flic* who was tripping a student. Two *flics* pushed past Peter and seized the offender, a young kid of about sixteen. When he resisted, they slugged him. "*Nazi!*" "*Nazi!*" Peter turned his head but he could not locate where the voice or voices in a funny falsetto were coming from. People were looking in his direction; he asked himself whether his plant could be acting as an aerial. Then he noticed that Makowski was slightly moving his lips. A ventriloquist! He wondered whether the Pole was crazy, playing a trick like that in a crowd, where he could get innocent bystanders arrested. "Cut it out," he muttered.

Now the demonstrators were darting through the throng, wherever they could find an opening, dropping their streamers and placards as they fled into the side streets, into the Métro, into the Magasins Réunis up the block. And instead of just letting them go, the police were hunting them down, aided by embattled concierges and their shrilly barking dogs. They were piling everybody they could catch into the Black Marias. Hungry for prey, they began to grab foreign students coming out of the Alliance Française, youths coming up from the Métro and blinking with surprise in the sunlight. As far as Peter could tell, their idea was to arrest anything that moved in the area between the ages of sixteen and twenty-five. He supposed that he and Makowski owed their immunity to the fact that they were stationary.

What shocked him, as an American, was that the demonstrators, once captured, showed no signs of civic resentment. They did not go limp, like civil-rights workers, but hopped into the paddy-wagons without further protest; it was as if they had been tagged in a game of Prisoners' Base. In the paddy-wagon on the corner, the majority were laughing and clowning; two were playing cards; one, with a bloody kerchief tied around his head, was reading a book. Only the Nordic types from the Alliance Française were giving their captors an argument, which appeared to amuse the French kids, as though being a foreigner and falsely arrested was funny.

Detestation for all and sundry was making Peter nauseous. The Rights of Man were being violated, in the most elementary way, in broad daylight, before the eyes of literally hundreds of citizens, and nobody was raising a finger to help. At home, if this had happened around Columbia, say, there would be dozens of volunteer witnesses telling the cops to lay off, threatening to call up the mayor or their congressman or the Civil Liberties Union; at home, citizens were aware that there *was* such a thing as the Constitution. It came to Peter that he and Makowski, having watched the whole disgusting business from the sidelines, could *do* something about it. They could write a letter to the *Monde*, as *témoins oculaires*, and if the *Monde* would not publish it, they could take it to the *Herald Tribune*. Or they could go to court and testify in the students' defense, assuming there was a trial or some sort of hearing; he was ready to swear that the demonstration had been completely peaceful until the police had used violence to break it up and he could swear too that several of the kids now in custody had not been among the marchers—the police had just arbitrarily seized them and roughed them up when they resisted. His heart thumping with excitement, he carefully memorized the features of two of the most vicious cops, so as to be able to make a positive identification. At the same time, his shyness made him hesitant of approaching the group in the Black

Maria, to promise his support, as though a wall of glass separated him on the sidewalk from them, a few feet away, as though he would be *intruding*. A weird kind of politeness was gluing him to the spot. He put the question to Makowski. "Maybe we should give these guys our names and addresses."

But Makowski did not agree. He thought it was a lot of shit that he and Peter had a duty to offer themselves as witnesses. "Of course the *flics* are sadists. *C'est leur métier.* The French take that for granted. You can't squeal about 'police brutality' in a court here. Everybody would think you were a fink." His voice took on a note of whining, offended logic, as though Peter's proposal caused him physical pain. "Besides, you're a 'guest of France.' Remember? You don't interfere in a family quarrel unless you want your head busted. These French kids would spit on us if we stuck our noses in. They know how the system works: if they behave themselves and keep their mouths shut, the cops will hold them a few hours and then let them go. It's *entendu* that they don't start yelling for a lawyer or claiming the cops have hurt them." With foreign students, it was more serious; foreigners were forbidden to take part in political activity. "Those dumb Swedes and Germans in the *panier à salade* don't dig it but they're about to be deported." "Deported?" Peter gulped. Of course, said Makowski; it happened all the time. The foreigners in the lettuce-basket were just unlucky. If you were a foreigner and got picked up in one of these *bagarres*, you were automatically thrown out of the country.

Peter was incredulous. "Thrown out of the country?" he scoffed. "Without a hearing or anything? But these guys from the Alliance Française have an alibi. They can *prove* they were in class when the march was going on. You're nuts!" But Makowski only laughed. He indicated two blond bespectacled giants whose heavy boots and white wool socks were protruding from the Black Maria. "Twenty-four hours to leave the country!" "Just like that?" cried Peter, who was starting to be convinced. A craven fear for his own tenure on the rue Monsieur-le-Prince entered his bones; in his mind, he slowly tore up the letter he had been writing to the *Monde* and consigned it to the ash can of history. "Just like that," said Makowski. "They relieve you of your passport, and you get it back at the airport. I tell you, it happens all the time. That's why I kept my cool just now. It gives me kicks to bait the police, but France has other things to offer me, and I want to stay a while longer. You know?" Peter supposed he meant women. Feebly, he continued to argue, unwilling to submit to the dictatorship of Makowski's view of things, which, Peter clearly saw, would deprive him of his freedom of action. If you want to be your own master, his father used to say, always be surprised by evil; never anticipate it. Then he thought of his Norwegian friend, Dag. "I couldn't figure out what had become of him. We had a date to watch the election on TV, and he never turned up. His landlady claimed he'd gone back to Norway. Finally I heard a rumor he'd been deported. He was great on attending rallies at the Mutualité. I guess that's what got him. Poor guy."

Makowski was unsympathetic. He knew Dag's type—a law-abiding Scandinavian. They made the big mistake of always carrying their passport and their *carte de séjour*. Involuntarily, Peter's hand flew to his jacket pocket to make sure his were still there. "Mistake?" "That only makes it easier for the police to deport you," Makowski pointed out. He had a whole theory based on his discovery that the French were a lazy people. "If a *flic* asks me for my passport and I hand it over, I simplify his job. He passes it on to his boss, and they rubber-stamp me out of the country like a piece of second-class mail. But if I tell them my passport's at home, they have to figure out what to do next. Send me to get it and trust me to come back? They're not that dumb. Or send an *agent* with me to where I live, which is probably six flights up in some crummy *mansarde*? Nine times out of ten, they'll weigh the headaches involved against the relative ease of just letting me go, with a warning to watch it in the future."

Peter listened with amazement to the wily Pole's exposition, which sounded irrefutable, like so many statements coming from the East. This was quite different stuff from what they told you at the Embassy, where they advised you to stay glued to your documents and to carry a hand-printed card in your wallet saying "I AM PETER LEVI. IN CASE OF ACCIDENT NOTIFY . . ." —a creepy self-advertisement that Peter could not bring himself to pen, even as an exercise in calligraphy. Yet he wondered how his companion, whose age he estimated at twenty, could know so much more than seasoned American officials. A tendency to boastfulness was becoming more and more evident in Makowski, as Peter, his foil, became meeker and meeker; it was an effect, he noticed, that he seemed to have on people. He was ashamed to think of the mole-like life he had been leading: since he had left his hotel, nobody ever asked *him* for his passport, except when he was cashing a traveler's check at American Express—something Makowski, he supposed, would not be caught dead doing. "Number One, they're lazy," his mentor continued. "Number Two, they're interested only in their next meal. If you put those two facts together, you've got this country in the hollow of your hand." He scowled at the distant clock on the Montparnasse station. "Have you noticed—there are hardly any clocks in this town? They hate to give away the time, free." Peter laughed. He had made the same observation himself. "Ten past twelve," said Makowski. "The fun here is over. In five minutes, the *flics* will be knocking off for lunch, and Allee-Allee-Out's-in-Free." Appearances bore him out. The Black Marias at either end of the block were still waiting, with open doors, and Peter could still hear an occasional far-off police whistle shrill all by itself like Roland's horn, but the householders on the rue de Rennes had retired from their balconies, shutting their French windows. On the street the traffic was running normally again, the curious crowds had dispersed, and noontime lines were forming at the bakeries. The two cops on the corner were stamping their feet and looking at their watches. Peter's own feet were cold. "You want to have a beer in the café here?" he suggested.

But Makowski was late already for a date with a girl at the Flore. "Why not join us? We can pick up another chick." Peter was strongly tempted, but he had his plant to take home; he could almost feel it shivering in the autumn wind. Besides, in some crazy way, he felt he *owed* it to the group in the Black Maria not to leave the scene while they remained in duress, able to watch him depart. *Somebody* had to hang around, just as a matter of courtesy. "Maybe later," he said. "If you're still there."

Makowski loped off to the bus-stop. Too late, Peter realized that he had forgotten to ask him for his address, which meant, he guessed, that he was gone beyond recall. He was not sure how much he really liked the Pole, but obviously they had something in common as hyphenated Americans of an uncommon kind: *accidentals*, they would be called in the bird book. A 95 was coming. He watched Makowski get on, not waiting his turn, of course, but charging past a line of people that had been standing there patiently. Peter was spared the pain of grimly noting their reactions, for just then a small dark student came darting out of a building chased by a concierge with a broom. Peter recognized one of the leaders of the march. His pursuer, an aged Nemesis, was screaming for the police to apprehend him: he had been hiding in the service stairway, she panted, and he had done p.p.—"*Oui, il a fait pipi dans mon escalier de service!*" Immediately, a new throng materialized, laughing and passing the word along, as the boy dodged into a doorway. What floor, a joker demanded. "*Le sixième, monsieur,*" she answered with dignity, resting on her broom and regaining her breath; the gendarmes advanced. "*Il n'était pas pressé,*" an old man in a tweed overcoat said, winking, to Peter. "*Il n'était pas pressé, hein?*" the old man repeated, to a workman in a coverall. More people came, pushing and shoving, and the criminal profited from the confusion to race out, zigzag adroitly between them, and spring with a bound onto the bus, which had started to move as the traffic light turned green; the ticket-taker, like a trained confederate, had quickly released the chain barring entrance to the platform. The boy ducked into the interior of the bus.

The police were slow in reacting; they stood as if mystified on the sidewalk, evidently not grasping where their quarry had got to. Then whistles blew. The cop on the next corner waved to the bus to halt. Peter ground his teeth. It was a tricky intersection, where three streets met—what the Romans called a *trivium*—an ill-omened juncture. And there were cops, all of a sudden, on every corner. From where he stood, he was unable to see exactly what happened next, but in a minute the forces of order were dragging the tall Pole to the lettuce-basket.

At first, Peter was simply stunned. It seemed plain to him that everyone except the stupid police must see that they had got the wrong boy. Yet no one moved to interfere. The concierge of the violated building stood nodding with satisfaction as Makowski was tossed into the paddy-wagon. A wild conjecture passed through Peter's head: could Makowski be doing a Sydney Carton? The Poles were alleged to be quixotic. In any case he decided to wait till the bus had crossed the boulevard Raspail, bearing the small demonstrator to safety. Then he counted twenty and approached a gendarme. To his surprise, he did not feel his customary worry about making mistakes in French; the words came out as though memorized ahead of time from a phrase book for the emergency, and in the back of his mind he recalled with interest the saying of Kant: the moral will operates in man with the force of a natural law.

"Pardon, monsieur l'agent; je peux témoigner pour mon compatriote. Il n'a pris aucune part dans la manifestation. Il ne s'est pas caché dans l'immeuble de madame. Il était à côté de moi, tout le temps, sur la chaussée, en simple spectateur. Et il ne ressemble en aucun détail au jeune homme que vous cherchiez."

The gendarme he was addressing had been joined by two others. Silence. They seemed to be waiting for Peter to continue. But he had stated the facts: Makowski had been standing next to him on the sidewalk during the entire demonstration; he did not bear the slightest resemblance to the suspect they were after. *"C'est tout,"* he added hoarsely. *"Croyez-moi."* The kids in the Black Maria had slid forward to listen. Makowski was smiling strangely. Peter became aware that he had said "pavement" when he meant "sidewalk." *"Je veux dire le trottoir."* Without warning, he had started to tremble violently; he saw the Fatshedera quaking in his hand and realized that he was having an attack of stage fright. It was like the time he had played Jaques in school and had had to lean against a tree in the Forest of Arden and all the scenery shook. He had not grasped at first why the audience of boys and parents was laughing—*"Sembrava un bosco di pioppi tremoli,"* was his father's comment: "A Forest of Aspens." It came to him now that all these people were staring at him dumbstruck because he looked weird with his tall companion-plant; the cops probably thought he was a "case."

"Demandez aux autres si vous ne me croyez pas!" he cried, getting angry. *"Tout le monde ici peut confirmer que je dis la vérité!"* He was not the sole witness to the fact that Makowski had not budged from the curb; there were the flower-seller on

the corner and the newspaper-vendor in her tarpaulin shelter
—courtesy *France-Soir*—and the butchers in their bloody
aprons. They had all been standing there like stage extras or a
speechless chorus, contributing local color. "*Qu'il parle bien le
français!*" a voice murmured behind him. Peter disregarded the
flattery. He was going to insist that the cops take his testimony.
"*Voici mon passeport et ma carte de séjour!*"

A shower of membership cards, guarantees, and certificates
fell to the pavement as he searched wildly in his wallet for his
carte de séjour, which to his chagrin was not in his passport; he
hugged his plant awkwardly to his body to free a hand. Bystanders picked them up and restored them to him; a young
lame girl offered to hold the Fatshedera: "*Quelle belle plante!*"
The senior gendarme, who seemed to be a sergeant, took the
documents and slowly looked them over, frowning at the membership in the Jeunes Ornithologistes de France. "*Qu'est-ce que
c'est que ça?*" He found the *carte de séjour* folded into the yellow health certificate. He studied it. Then he tapped all the
documents into a neat pile and handed them back, together
with Peter's passport. "*Bon. Merci, monsieur. Tout est en règle,*"
he said. "*Allons-y!*" he shouted to the driver of the Black Maria.
The motor started. Peter gasped. They were not going to
release Makowski! Apparently he was supposed to count himself lucky that they were letting *him* go free. He gave an inar-
ticulate howl of despair.

In back of him, someone coughed noisily. He heard a
hoarse, deep female voice. "*Il a raison, messieurs. L'américain
vous dit la vérité. L'autre n'y était pour rien. Qu'est-ce que vous
faîtes là? C'est une honte.*" It was *les Journaux* in her leather
apron and thick sweaters. Peter had always bought the *Times*
and *Tribune* from her when he lived in the hotel on the rue
Littré; *ô juste ciel*, she recognized him! He felt a lump in his
throat. He had *made* it; he was finally "accepted" by old Mar-
ianne, *la France*. And now other "popular" voices were joining
in, muttering and grumbling, *les Fleurs*, a window-washer, an
old lady with a cane. "*Soyez raisonnables! Qu'est-ce que cela vous
fout? Après tout! Un peu de calme! Ce sont des enfants!*"

The police sergeant appeared to reflect. His subordinates
were watching him. "*Vos papiers!*" he said to Makowski. And
of course Makowski did not have any. "*Et alors?*" said the

policeman sharply. That settled it. This was France, after all (the Embassy was right), and, regardless of any specific charge, not having your papers was prima-facie evidence that you were up to no good. The attitude of the bystanders confirmed this. "*Il n'a pas ses papiers. Zut!*" A collective shrug disposed of the Pole, whose broad face had assumed a plaintive, aggrieved, innocent expression, as though he could not dig what this fuss was all about. You would think he was some hayseed who had never heard of a travel document. Peter himself experienced an appreciable drop in sympathy. What a clown!

The doors of the Black Maria were shutting on the heap of sprawling kids. Peter's conscience jabbed him. "Makowski!" he yelled. "Jan! Don't worry! I'll go tell the Embassy. Right away. I promise." "Stay out of this, Peter Pan!" the Pole's voice answered rudely, adding an obscenity that made Peter hope that these French did not understand English. He fell back a step, feeling his neck turn red. It came to him that, insanely, Makowski held him *responsible*. Doubtless he had counted on the *vérification d'identité* taking place later, in relative privacy, at the station-house or wherever, when the cops had had their lunch and were in a good humor. But now it was *public knowledge* that he had been picked up without any papers.

Peter declined to swallow Makowski's tales of mass deportations; that could not happen to American citizens, he felt sure. But in the face of those closed black doors, his confidence was eroding. The tumbril's engine started. He realized that he did not even know where they were taking Makowski now. The spectators on the corner would not commit themselves. "*Sais pas.*" "*Ah, non, monsieur, je ne saurais pas vous le dire.*" "*Peut-être à Beaujon?*" "*C'est pas mon affaire. Demandez aux gendarmes.*" But Peter—the old story, he guessed—felt a horrible diffidence about asking the *flics* outright. The window-washer came to his rescue. "*C'est pas la peine, mon gars. Ils ne le disent jamais. La police, vous savez . . .*"

The Black Maria's motor was still idling. Once it bore Makowski off, Peter might never be able to find him in the maze of French bureaucracy. With sudden resolution, he banged on the door. A policeman stuck his head out. Peter asked if he could accompany his friend, as a witness. "*C'est pas un taxi, monsieur,*" the policeman retorted, slamming the doors. In the interior, Peter could hear raucous laughter. "*Alors, arrêtez-moi!*" he shouted. "*Foutez-moi la paix,*" came the grumbling reply.

It was typical of the French that if you asked them to arrest you, they would not help you out. In his fury, he thought of a ruse. All he had to do was open his mouth and say "*Nazi!*" and every *flic* in the *quartier* would spring on him. He would not even have to say it very loud. He swallowed several times in preparation. At home, among his peer group, he could speak lightly of the cops as fascists, but now, to his astonishment, his vocal cords felt paralyzed. As in a nightmare, his mouth opened and closed. No sound came out. Yet it was not from fear, as far as he could determine, but from a profound lack of inclination.

His father was always giving people the drill if they used the term *fascist* when, according to him, they should have used *conservative* or *repressive* or just *brutal*: if you kept throwing that term around, like the boy crying "Wolf," as an expression of simple dislike, you would be unable to recognize real fascism when and if it came. Peter could not recall all the "objective criteria" that the *babbo* said had to be present to justify a diagnosis of fascism but he felt certain the French police would not qualify.

Yet there was more to it than that—some squirming aversion in *him*, related maybe to delicacy. Actually, he was unable to imagine circumstances in which he would find it easy to call *anybody* a Nazi, including Hitler probably. If you called Hitler a Nazi, he would not mind, obviously, so what would be the use?

A *flic* in a blue cape had emerged from the corner café, where presumably he had been telephoning or answering a call of Nature. He barked out an order to the driver. Peter heard the clash of gears. It would be hopeless to chase after the police-wagon. Even if it had to stop for the traffic light at the next corner, he would be incapable of keeping up for more than a block, hampered as he was by his plant. Then in the distance he sighted a taxi coming up the rue de Rennes. He dashed into the street to flag it down, foreseeing, as he waved, that the driver might decline to follow the *panier à salade*; they loved telling you No. Closing his eyes, he recited one of his magic

formulas: "Perseverance, dear my lord, keeps honor bright."
"*Attention!*" someone called.

The police-wagon shot backward. Peter jumped out of the
way. His heel struck the curb behind him; his ankle turned,
and his long bony foot got caught in an opening in the gutter.
He lost his balance, tried to right himself, throwing out his
arms. The Fatshedera was sliding from the crook of his elbow.
Endeavoring to catch it, he fell. As he did, a ringing, explosive
sound reached his ears, seeming far away; it was the clay pot
shattering on the pavement. Somebody was helping him up.
They were asking if he was hurt. He stole a glance around.
Moist black dirt and reddish shards and slivers of the pot were
scattered all over the street and sidewalk; the plant was lying in
the gutter with its whitish root system exposed. *Les Fleurs*
carefully picked it up and wrapped it in a newspaper. "*Tenez,
monsieur.*" She handed it to him. He thanked her. She meant
well, he assumed. But he had seen the crown of pale new leaves
lying a yard away, like a severed head, near the Métro entrance.
Some passer-by had already stepped on it, leaving a green
smear on the sidewalk.

The Black Maria, naturally, had made its getaway, after putting him *hors de combat*. If Peter had not leapt aside, would the
hit-and-run driver at the wheel have jammed on the brakes in
time? According to Dag, a lot of "traffic accidents" were really
engineered by the Deuxième Bureau. If the cops killed a person while giving him the third degree, they just stretched the
body out on the *autoroute* on Sunday and called it a highway
death. Shaking, Peter sat down on the top step of the Métro
entrance and buried his head in his hands. His ankle hurt, and
pulling down his sock, he found blood where he had scraped
it. Maybe he would get blood poisoning and croak. He ought
to find a pharmacy and buy some Mercurochrome, but at this
hour they would all be closed probably. The butchers had
taken in the meat, and the fruit and vegetable merchants along
the rue Notre-Dame-des-Champs were covering their produce. *Les Journaux* was bending over him, wondering if he was
all right. He got to his feet. "*Votre plante,*" she reminded him.
He picked it up. In his mind, he mimicked his mother's consoling voice: "Never mind. We'll get another, Peter." Aloud,
he cried out "No!"

While he was sitting there, nursing his ankle, a vile temptation had visited him, whose source was that artful Eve, his parent. There was an amusing plant he had read about in his manual, known as Dumb Cane, a member of the Dieffenbachia species; the stem, when chewed, paralyzed the tongue. If he were to whip over to Les Halles this afternoon and look for one . . . ? Today, as it chanced, was Friday. He thrust the thought from him. He would have no more plants in his Stygian kingdom, no substitutes, successors, or duplicates, and as for the Fatshedera, he would not take it home for decent burial: he would junk old Fats here at the scene of its decapitation—good riddance. Yet a last trace of humanity remained, he was sorry to perceive, in his hardened heart. He could not perform the committal in plain view of *les Fleurs*, whose stubby chilblained hands had wrapped the grisly trunk in *France-Dimanche*: she would be sorry for her trouble. He would have to wait till he found another trash-basket.

Actually, he disposed of it on American soil, in a wastebasket at the Embassy, where he went to report Makowski's arrest to a bureaucrat in the consular section who could not have cared less. "If you students take part in street demonstrations, there's nothing we can do to help you. It's strictly against regulations for American citizens to meddle in French politics." "He *wasn't* taking part in a demonstration," Peter protested. "You just wrote that down yourself in your notes. He was standing on the curb, next to me." The official frowned over his notes. "Ah yes, so you said. I see it here. Well, all I can tell you is the next time you see a march or a demonstration, walk rapidly in the opposite direction. Don't linger there to gawp. For one thing, you may get hurt. A few years ago, during one of their protest rallies, some bystanders were crushed to death in a Métro entrance. Luckily there were no Americans among them."

Silence followed. The man fiddled with some papers on his desk. "You mean you won't do *anything*?" Peter said finally. "Is that the Embassy's policy?" "Consular policy," the man corrected, "is opposed to taking unnecessary action. Your friend's case isn't as unfamiliar to us as you appear to think. Ordinarily the French police hold these people a few hours, to teach them a lesson, and then let them go." "Yeah," said Peter.

"I've heard that too. But I've also heard that they deport foreign students they pick up, just like that, without a trial or investigation or anything. Actually, it happened to a friend of mine." "An American?" "Well, no." "Just as I thought. It's rare," he went on in a musing tone, "that they deport an American unless he's been up to some mischief. Odd as it seems, they discriminate, if anything, in our favor. One of those little diplomatic mysteries. It may have something to do with the balance of payments. Every one of you students, you realize, who stays here getting money from home and spending it is hurting the dollar."

From the wall, the photo of Lyndon B. Johnson looked at Peter with eyes of reproach. The official leaned across the desk. "And are you sure that this Makowski is a naturalized citizen of the United States?" "I'm not *sure*. I only met him this morning. But he talked like an American." "Didn't you see his passport?" "That was the whole trouble! I *explained* to you. They were just going to let him go when it turned out he'd left his passport at home." "He didn't describe it specifically as an American passport?" Peter sighed. "No. Why would he? Imagine anybody saying 'I left my U.S. passport at home this morning.' I mean, that would imply you had several passports."

"I'm not here to engage in semantics with you. And under the circumstances, I don't see how we can help you. We can't intervene without more information than you've been able to furnish. You have no idea of the number of inquiries we get about you students. Usually from parents, wanting us to find out why Bobby hasn't written. If we called the police and the hospitals about every Tom, Dick, and Harry, we'd have no time left for normal consular business." He got up. "Run along now. If your friend doesn't turn up in a day or two, come back and see me. That's the best I can offer."

"Great!" said Peter bitterly. "You haven't understood the point. I don't know his address. So how can I tell if he turns up or not?" "You can find him at the Sorbonne, I suppose." "He's not at the Sorbonne. He's at the Institute of Oriental Languages. And tomorrow is *Saturday*. The Embassy will be closed. By Monday he might have been deported. They give you twenty-four hours to leave the country."

His hoarse voice broke. Some secretaries looked up. In a

minute, he supposed, they would call the Marine guard to remove him from the chair in which he remained sunk, feeling
too weak and dejected to dislodge himself. He remembered
that he had not eaten since morning. Then the man reached in
his pocket and spoke in a kindlier tone. "I tell you what you
do. Here's a *jeton*. There's a pay phone in the corridor, by the
cashier's window. Call the Commissariat of the arrondissement
where this *bagarre* took place and ask if they're holding your
friend. The Commissariats are listed in the front matter of the
telephone book. Then come back and tell me the result."

"There won't be any result," said Peter, getting reluctantly
to his feet. "You don't know the French, sir, the way a student
does. It'll just be a waste of a *jeton*. Can you figure me trying
to spell Makowski to some half-crocked police sergeant? 'Marie
AnatolKléberOscarWashingtonSuzanneKléberIrma'?" He gave
a hollow laugh. "If *you'd* call, it would be different. They *listen*
to somebody with authority." "On your way," said the man.
"Right through those doors."

It was just as Peter had prophesied. "They hung up on me,"
he reported back. "I think they recognized my voice." For the
first time, the official cracked a smile. He chuckled. "Oh, Jesus!"
he said. Still overcome by merriment, he pointed to the chair,
and Peter obediently sat down. He failed to get the joke, but it
did not matter. He knew he had crossed the Rubicon. He
watched the man pick up the telephone. "*Monsieur Dupuy, s'il
vous plaît . . . Bon, j'attends. . . . Allo, Jacques? C'est nous
encore. Pas mal. Et vous-même? Oui, c'est ça. Une petite bagarre.
Comme d'habitude. Vous êtes au courant? Un certain Makowski,
étudiant . . .*" He doodled on a pad. "*Ah, bon, bon. Merci. A
la prochaine fois, Jacques.*" Jan Makowski, naturalized U.S. citizen, born in Poland, had been released at 3:50 P.M. after verifi-
cation of his papers.

Peter guessed Makowski had scored after all. He left the
Embassy in a good mood. In the end, the vice-consul (he had
given Peter his card) had seemed glad that somebody had
prodded him into being somewhat nicer than he customarily
was. It was funny how people never remembered the well-
known fact that virtue was its own reward but had to keep
discovering it as a novelty. In the garden, he paused to pay
homage to the seated statue of Ben Franklin in his wide bronze

rumpled coat. He liked the patron saint of inventors sitting mildly amid the ornamental shrubbery. He looked home-made, like the funny Stars and Stripes still waving over the Embassy's portal. Some English ivy was climbing up his pedestal.

Peter took the lay of the land. Outside the gate, two gendarmes were walking up and down. In the driveway, a chauffeur sat at the wheel of a big black Embassy car. But nobody was paying attention to Peter in the gathering winter dusk. He advanced stealthily toward the statue, taking his time. With his trusty pocket-knife, he cut some long shoots of ivy. When one of the gendarmes glanced his way, he had already stored the booty in his sheepskin-lined jacket; the heart-shaped leaves of the Fatshedera's creeping cousin were nestling in his bosom. *Hedera helix* rooted easily in water, and then you could plant it in earth. Satisfied by this act of vandalism committed on U.S. property, he sped toward the Métro station. The idea that a new resident of his apartment had been acquired free of charge and at some slight personal risk compensated him for the passing of the old one. Life had to go on. Actually, in the place of one sickly specimen, he could have a whole lusty tribe, in pots, trained on strings to climb up his walls and turn his room into a bower. Offering his second-class ticket to be punched by the ticket-taker, he felt like Prometheus, with a gift of green fire. The punishment, he expected, would come later, in the guise of a *crise de foie* induced by the unhealthy French diet.

Round Table, with the Damsel Parcenet

A HARUSPEX peering into the entrails of the sacrificed traditional bird would have warned one Petrus Levi to beware
of divisive controversy on the feast of Thanksgiving. Holidays,
as he ought to know, were unlucky for him anyway. Instead of
obeying the summons to partake of turkey 'n' trimmings with
the other waifs assembled by the general's wife, he would have
done better to stay home with the door bolted holding no
communications. Holidays brought out the worst in everybody; the Last Supper, terminating with the Agony in the Garden, was par for the course. As they handed over their coats to
the Spanish maid in the vestibule of the general's pad in
Neuilly, the motley crew viewed each other with a natural suspicion. Besides the male strays, readily identifiable in their un-
wonted ties and sports jackets, there were a functionary from
the Embassy and his family who had inescapably put the finger
on Peter in the close confinement of the elevator ("I guess we
all want the fifth, don't we?"), a tall fresh-faced girl with long
American feet, an Air Force wife minus a husband, and some
middle-aged French reactionaries, military, with their unattractive daughter, who were supposed to be getting a free
glimpse of real American hospitality. After the vast repast, preceded by bourbon and laced with sparkling Vouvray, they all
had to go and play softball in the Bois.

There were fourteen at table, which led Peter to speculate
that one of their number had been recruited at the last minute
to take the jinx off. The general normally was a fairly affable
guy, with a white fat baby face, black eyebrows, and a peculiar
haircut, shaved on the sides and standing up on top in short
black bristles, which made him look like a convict. He was attached to NATO, Peter gleaned today, and was an expert on
supply and procurement. His wife, named Letitia (pronounced
Leteetia by her husband), was small, Southern, and friendly.
"Can I sweeten your drink, honey?" was her usual soft refrain.
None of the guests, it appeared, had met each other before, and
some were meeting the host for the first time. His daughter
led them up. "Dad, this is Jay Williams. Dad, this is Roberta

Scott." "Good to know you, Jay. Good to know you, Roberta.
Glad to have you with us." Peter he greeted by his last name,
which perhaps indicated a promotion. "How's it going, Levi?
Have you sold that motorbike yet?"

If this had been an All-American get-together, conversation
might have found its natural level, albeit low. But during the
cocktail period, just as people were starting to relax, daughter
Jean, prodded by the Frenchwoman, initiated a tour of the art
in the apartment from which, like lifeboat drill, nobody was excused. Freighted with drinks and cigarettes, searching furtively
for ashtrays or frankly using a trouser-cuff or the wall-to-wall
carpeting, the straggling troops inspected Korean graphics and
Puerto Rican oils, Japanese ivories, Taiwan scrolls, Spanish fans,
German beer steins, Italian majolica, hanging on the walls or
installed in cabinets with interior lighting—the general, needless
to say, had served in all those places on the U.S. defense perim-
eter and enjoyed a perfect recollection of the circumstances of
each purchase, with emphasis, naturally, on the haggling.

Then, at table, his wife actually *explained* the principle of
Thanksgiving to the French. "It isn't a social event with us,
you see. It isn't exactly a family event either, like Christmas,
which I always think should be for the children. It's the day
when we Americans—oh, help me, Chuck—as we thank God
for our blessings try to gather under our roof some of our
fellow-countrymen who might be lonely or homesick. And all
over the world, Americans are sitting down to the same meal
the Pilgrims ate: turkey and fixings, giblet gravy, creamed onions, mashed turnips or rutabagas. . . . Why, I'd feel like a
heretic if I served duck or Rock Cornish. Though I was reading the menus in the *Herald Tribune*—" "The stranger at the
gate," interrupted the general. "Yes, thank you, Chuck! I was
coming to that. We always make sure to have some foreign
guests with us. Last year, when we were back home at the
Academy, we had this lovely Japanese couple." "It's just a harvest festival, isn't it?" Peter said, tired of feeling like the Hundred Neediest Cases reduced to capsule form. As far as he
could see, what was happening was that Americans were giving
loud thanks for being Americans, and, as the hostess said, this
was going on all over the world concurrently—allowing for
the time difference; the orgy had not yet started in New York.

To Peter, slightly drunk, the meal seemed like a grotesque parody of his mother's annual bounty. The general's wife had the same idea as his mother, only his mother was more refined about it. Identifying with the French couple—whom he disliked on sight—he could not help seeing it as a gross and stupid debauch. Yet "Leteetia" was a perfectly nice woman, according to her lights. She had made that awful speech like a nervous recitation; maybe service wives abroad got directives from the Pentagon on what to tell the natives about Thanksgiving. The poor creature looked exhausted, having no doubt spent the morning basting the turkey with her bulb-baster. The rouge stood out on her inflamed cheeks. The work she and daughter Jean, who seemed to have a good relationship, had put into the food and the table setting, down to the last nut-cup, was begging pathetically for notice. The art that conceals art, Peter reflected glumly, was not an American specialty. With his thumbnail, unobtrusively, he peeled off the price-tag from his hand-crafted napkin.

As for "Chuck," he was in a critical mood. He ordered the carving-knife back to the kitchen to be sharpened and dismissed the autumnal centerpiece, which was obstructing his view, to the sideboard. Listening to the rasp of the combination can-opener and knife-sharpener in the pantry, Peter surmised that they had had a family difference this morning. Had the general been issuing the invitations, he suspected, there might have been fewer under-age deadheads on the list.

If you could ignore the commercials, the food was not too bad. Frankly Peter would not have guessed that the turkey was frozen, from the PX, if the hostess had not announced the fact with what he supposed was pride. In her place, he would have omitted the marshmallows from the candied sweet potatoes, but he approved of the hot Parker House rolls Jean had baked herself this morning, and the colonial stuffing spiked with brandy was OK. The dinner plates, with the Air Force Academy coat-of-arms, were duly warmed in a sort of electric blanket on a tea-wagon at the hostess' left. It was not her fault that, on this of all days, one of the waifs she had collected proved to be a vegetarian.

"Dark or light, Roberta?" queried the general, spearing a slice of breast on the point of his antlered knife. His daughter was holding out a plate destined for the tall girl on Peter's right. "I won't take any, General Lammers." It was as if an infernal machine, quietly ticking, had been planted in the room. The appalled general looked at his wife. He set down the carving-knife. "*No turkey?*" "But honey, you didn't eat your shrimp cocktail either!" moaned Letitia. It was true, Peter realized: his neighbor had left a neat little pile of shrimps in her monogrammed glass goblet and eaten only the lettuce ribbons and the chili sauce. But the significance of it had escaped him. "Is it Paris tummy, honey? We've got just what you need. Jeanie, dear, run and get the Vioform from my medicine cabinet." "She's a vegetarian, Mama," said Jean. "I forgot." "Oh, come *on*," said the general. "This is Thanksgiving!" His white hands, with black hairs on the knuckles, played impatiently with the carving implements. The girl held her ground. "No, thank you. I won't. Really." The rest of the company looked away. He essayed playfulness. "I'm in command here. Mess Sergeant Jean, hold that plate where I can reach it." "She doesn't *want* any, Dad. Don't force her." "Pshaw!" He laid the slice of breast on the plate, which was already heaped with onions, mashed potatoes, sweet potatoes, and so on, placed there by his wife at the other end of the table. "Take that to the young lady."

Now everybody was watching her, some, like Peter, covertly. She had a long nose and short boyish-cut hair that rose in a crest over a "noble" brow. Her eyes were gray, somewhat close together, and she had large appealing ears that reddened easily, as if people were talking about her, which might well be the case. She wore a gray dress made of wool, with a round white collar and a string of pearls, which had been appraised with care by the Frenchwoman, who had eyes like a customs inspector. Peter searched his memory for when or how he had met this dauntless girl before. Maybe in another incarnation. She looked like the title of a book the *babbo* was fond of recommending: *The Protestant Ethic*, but with pink cheeks and a shy grin. If he put a tricorn on her head, he could picture her as a revolutionary patriot dumping tea into Boston harbor. He felt sure he had seen her portrait, maybe in male attire, in the American Wing of the Metropolitan Museum or in some history textbook.

"The stuffing, Chuck. Give Miss Scott some stuffing." The girl opened her thin pink lips as if to protest, then bit the lower one and said nothing. Her plate was returned to the head of the table. The general spooned some stuffing onto it and, taking possession of the gravy boat, rapidly ladled giblet gravy onto her mashed potatoes. "There!"

As her desecrated plate came back, she and Peter exchanged a dismal look. Catching the distress signal, he quickly passed her the cranberry jelly and looked around for olives and celery. "Here, have some." Angry with the general, he gulped down his Vouvray. Nobody would convince him that "Chuck" was just insensitive, incapable of understanding that his own food habits might not be acceptable to the entire human race. Or that he was hurt by the girl's rejection of the sacred fowl, though that no doubt played a part. Unless Peter had gone stir-crazy in his solitary cell on the rue Monsieur-le-Prince, at the head of the table sat a vicious sadist wearing the jovial mask of hospitality. He had seized that gravy boat like a weapon in hand-to-hand combat. No wonder they had made him a brigadier general—at least that mystery was solved. Peter wished he had the strength to pass up the turkey himself, when his turn came, as an act of solidarity. But there were always others to consider, in this case Letitia, who had been toiling harmlessly in the kitchen.

As an animal-lover, Peter, if he was consistent, should have been a vegetarian too. In Perugia he had been nauseated by those poor crumpled little birds the Italians loved to serve—the brain, believe it or not, was the choice morsel. Bob, ever the logician, had pointed out that those larks and thrushes, before being shot, had lived "free as birds"; compare that to the existence of a battery chicken. This had not persuaded Peter to eat *uccelletti* but it had interfered with his enjoyment of broilers. Yet whenever he had feebly tried to interest himself in a naturist diet of fruit and raw vegetables, he had come up against his juvenile gluttony. He could live without steak and chicken, he had decided, but he doubted his present ability to forgo lobster and tuna fish. What he had not taken into account was the social pressures he would have to resist. He would need to be a hero, he now saw.

His other neighbor, a blue-eyed leathery lady with long

earrings and gray hair cut in a fluffy bang, was waiting to engage him in conversation. During the first course she had been filling him in on the fact that her husband had left her for a German girl he had picked up hitchhiking on the *autoroute*. She now recaptured the thread. "Letitia thinks I ought to go home to the States. But what the hell? I've gone to all the trouble to learn French, why *shouldn't* I stay here? He doesn't own Paris. He wants a divorce, but if I give him a divorce, they'll take away my PX card and my QC privileges. You can smile, Peter, but to me it's a tragedy. Twenty years as an Air Force dependent, and tomorrow, if I let him have his so-called freedom, the guards at the PX will tell me 'Sorry, ma'am, we can't let you by. That card has expired.' Civilians don't dig what it means to us. Chuck and Letitia can entertain lavishly because, between you and me, they don't buy a thing on the French market. Not even a stick of celery."

Ordinarily Peter would have felt sorry for this coarse-grained Donna Elvira. Maybe she loved the guy and was ashamed to mention that; it was odd what people were ashamed of, sometimes the best part of themselves, which they looked on as "weakness," he guessed. But now though he kept an ear politely bent in her direction, his eyes slid to his right. Roberta Scott had not succumbed to the appetizing slice of breast in its casing of crisp brown skin. Instead, she was eating carefully around it: the onions, the rutabagas, the sweet potatoes, the Ocean Spray cranberry jelly. She avoided the mashed potatoes polluted with gravy and the stuffing contaminated by animal fat and juices during its stay in the oven. He followed the progress of her fork as it constructed fortifications against the giblet gravy, which ran between the banks of vegetables, lapped at the base of the tottering tower of jelly, divided into rivulets, and finally congealed. Peter was fascinated by these maneuvers. It was like watching a game of Jackstraws or a kid on the beach building a sand-castle as the tide was coming in. Others were stealing looks too. Only the general, content with his petty tactical victory, disregarded what was happening on her plate.

"Somebody ought to tell her parents!" interjected the gray-haired lady, tracing Peter's wandering interest to its source. "Did you ever see anything *like* that? Look how thin she is." Actually, in Peter's estimation, Miss Scott was in the pink of condition, compared to the fat sallow French girl in a two-tone taffeta blouse and to Jean, who today had a stye. She might be underweight, but her eyes were clear, and her breasts made two modest rounds under the thin wool of her dress. An image jumped into his mind of a healthy well-cared-for animal. Her long nose, made for sniffing and scenting, would be cool to the touch, and her hair invited stroking, like a shining pelt. She had gone to Bryn Mawr, he ascertained, and was working at the Institut Pasteur. She must be around twenty-three because after Bryn Mawr she had done a year of medical studies in Philadelphia, where her family lived. It was not hard to picture her as an interne, in a white coat, with a stethoscope.

Meanwhile the carnivores lifted forks that appeared to have grown heavy with their cargo of turkey and trimmings. They wiped grease from their mouths, quaffed wine, sought elusive food particles between their teeth with their tongues or a furtive fingernail; the older women's lipstick smeared. This Roberta did not seem to be wearing lipstick and she was not drinking her wine. That did not long escape detection. "Don't you *drink* either, Miss Scott?" said the hostess, in a voice like the wringing of hands. "I used to sometimes. But I don't really like it." "Not even *wine*? But you're in *France*." "I know." "A glass of milk then?" It turned out that she did not drink milk either. "For Christ's sake, Leteetia," said the general. "Let's hear about something else."

He got up and filled glasses all around, but since Roberta Scott's was already full, indeed brimming, there was nothing he could do about it. He sat down heavily in his place and fixed his light-green eyes, like two probes, on the girl, searching out her secret. "Roberta, Roberta," he chided. It could not be denied that this fasting vestal was putting quite a crimp in the festivities. "*Vous êtes un trouble-fête, mademoiselle*," the Frenchwoman said with a thin pretense of pleasantry. "What is that in English?" "A wet blanket. I know it," Roberta said seriously. "I'm really sorry, Mrs. Lammers." "Don't give it a second thought, sugar. Just enjoy yourself in your own way. If *you're* happy, *we're* happy." That of course was a lie. They would not be happy unless she conformed to their definition of enjoyment, which meant that she would have to be miserable to satisfy them.

Yet if she were old and decrepit or dying of stomach cancer or just unattractive, they would leave her in peace. The fact that she was cheerful and appealing, though not everybody's pin-up, was what threw them into disarray. Peter did not except himself. One part of him—he hoped a small fraction—had been backing the general in that contest of wills. He admired her force of character, but why *come* to Thanksgiving dinner if you were determined not to eat like the rest of the tribe? She could make an exception, just once, to be polite. On the other hand, if she started breaking her rule to please other people, she might as well give up being a vegetarian, he supposed. She had a right to eat and drink whatever she wanted. The trouble was, when she started exercising that right in public, she infringed on the right of the rest of the company to have a good time.

Take him. Like the other castaways, he assumed, he had been looking forward to the occasion, spot-cleaning his jacket, shining his shoes, drinking a liter of milk to line his stomach, hesitating over the choice of a tie. As the hostess had indicated, it was no fun to render thanks all by yourself in a crummy restaurant, which was the only kind a student could afford late in the month on his exhausted allowance. Now he felt like a dipsomaniac cannibal.

Her best solution, he meanly concluded, was to become a hermit. The Middle Ages had the right idea: anybody who wanted to mortify his flesh retired from the world to do it solo. She ought to live in a hut in the forest of Fontainebleau, eating wild berries and honey and wearing a shift made of bark. Even there, strangers would come to look at her, probably, and try to feed her, the way they did with animals in the zoo.

"How do you stand on honey?" he said abruptly. She turned her head, puzzled, chin drawn in, like a bird registering interrogation. "I mean," he said, goading, "it's cruel, isn't it, to take honey from bees?" She pondered. "I suppose it is," she said, knitting her brows. "I never thought about it. I'm not a strict vegetarian, though. With me, it's not a moral thing. When you study medicine, you learn not to worry too much about the sacredness of life. You have to experiment on animals in the laboratory. Anyway, golly, where do you draw the line? A tree is alive. How do we know it isn't conscious when we chop it down? It bleeds just like a human. I just know I feel better if I don't eat meat and some other animal foods."

On hearing that it was not a "moral thing," Peter felt immediately relieved, which was odd. He hoped she was telling the truth and not merely trying to make him feel comfortable in his carnivorous soul. The general's wife broke in. "Is this a health fad or what, honey? What made you decide to take up vegetarianism? I don't mean to be intrusive, but tell us, do you really think it's cruel to kill animals?" So it was not only him. Even the general, who was carving seconds, paused with his knife in mid-air to await the verdict.

The girl repeated, in substance, what she had just been saying to Peter. He wondered how many times a week she had to respond to that query; in short, how often she was invited out to meals. In restaurants, did the waiters ask her? He ought to make her a present of his idea of a pocket tape-recorder that furnished standard answers to standard questions. But she did not seem to mind explaining herself at length. He noticed that, unlike most people, she spoke in paragraphs—somewhat breathlessly.

"To answer your other question, Mrs. Lammers, I really don't know what made me take up being a vegetarian. You could call it a health fad, I guess. But I've had a sort of 'thing' about meat ever since I was little. They had to coax me to eat it. Then in boarding-school I overcame my prejudice. You know how hungry you get in school. The same in camp. And at home I have three younger brothers who aren't too fond of vegetables. My mother has to plan meals to suit the majority.

"But finally in college I started to think for myself. I got to understand body chemistry and I realized that I was being poisoned by what I was eating. Literally. I would keep falling asleep in my after-lunch class; they gave us our heavy meal at noon. Senior year I skipped lunch and ate carrots and peanut butter and dried figs in my room, and right away my marks in Latin—that was my two-thirty class then—went from C-minus to B-plus. But then I lost weight. I wasn't getting enough calories. So when I came to Paris this fall, I saw that here was my chance to experiment. They have these terrific vegetables in the markets, and I found an apartment with a kitchen, where I could cook all sorts of messes. For me, that was real independence. Freedom, golly me!"

"Liberty Hall," said the general. "It's small, but it's home. What I'd like to know, is there some theory behind this? Anything to do with cholesterol?" This year, Peter had observed, all the *croulants* were talking with bated breath about cholesterol, as if it were some new weapon in biological warfare aimed at shortening their lives. The exception was his mother, he was glad to say.

Cholesterol was not really the point, said Roberta. If you eliminated animal foods from your diet, naturally you eliminated animal fats also, thus reducing the cholesterol level in the blood. "But the way vegetarians see it, a low-cholesterol diet based on lean meat, poultry, and fish may be almost as harmful to the body as a high-cholesterol diet. Man is descended from herbivores. His organs weren't designed for the absorption of animal flesh. We don't know when he became a hunter and an omnivore but we know that the habit isn't natural to the order of primates, with the exception of some of the baboons. Why, some people actually claim that it's a flesh diet that's turned man into a killer of his own kind! He has the tiger's instincts without the tiger's taboos. Of course that's only a hypothesis. One way of testing it would be for humanity to practice vegetarianism for several generations. Maybe we'd find that war and murder would disappear."

"Do they have vegetarians in Russia?" the general demanded, emerging from a mental tunnel with a cunning look on his face. Nobody could enlighten him. Roberta guessed that most vegetarians in Russia had been Doukhobors and had emigrated to Canada a long time ago. Peter was interested in the Doukhobors. "They were fantastic," he said. "Completely nonviolent. They not only refused military service, they wouldn't even take up arms against wolves and bears. I read—" The general, with a chuckle, cut him off. "Say, Roberta, why don't you go to Russia and make some converts? That's the place to test your theory. Organize a vegetarian movement." "Don't tease her, Dad." "I'm not teasing. I'm serious. If she has a plan for changing human nature, let her tell this Kosygin about it. He's her boy. 'Everybody turn vegetarian or get sent to a slave-labor camp.'" "Don't listen to him," cried

Letitia. "Why, if you went there and tried to spread the message, they might arrest you as a spy." "'Anti-social element,'" muttered Peter. The general snorted. "'*Might*'! You bet they would. They're not interested in eliminating Ivan's fighting instinct. But in the States we've got a vegetarian party on the ballot. That shows the difference, doesn't it? Did you vote Vegetarian, Roberta?"

"I think you mean the Prohibition Party, General Lammers," she said mildly. "Actually, if you want to know, I voted for Johnson. I'm not a crank; at least I hope not. I don't believe you can legislate reforms in people's habits. It has to be voluntary. Of course it's hard not to want to make converts when you see the change in yourself. I *feel* so much better physically and mentally since I gave up animal foods. It's amazing. My motor reactions are quicker. I need less sleep. There's a big improvement in my attention-span. It's not just a subjective thing. Even my French teacher notices a difference. I honestly think my IQ must have gone up by several points."

"Well!" summed up the hostess. A pall settled again on the banquet, which was looking more and more like a replica of Belshazzar's Feast or the dream of the great king, his father, who was put out to eat grass. The *convives*, if Peter was a fair sample, had now started to worry about the damage they had been inflicting on their brains.

He stared at the huge drumstick bone, like a fossil remain, on his plate. A junior from Northwestern offered a ray of hope. "You've got to remember evolution. If eating meat was bad for man, he wouldn't have survived. Or he would have kicked the habit back in the Stone Age. Man evolved as a flesh-eating higher animal. Maybe he's more intelligent than the apes *because* he became a meat-eater."

"Hear, hear!" said the general. "Well, Roberta, you've certainly given us food for thought, ha ha. What about booze? Are you going to tell us that monkeys don't use fermented beverages?" The girl calmly declared that she had given up drinking *for pleasure*. "You'd be surprised. Truly. I have a much better time now than when I drank cocktails and wine. I like the taste of wine, but just one glass made me sluggish and torpid." "But you smoke," loyally prompted Jean. "Oh yes. And I drink coffee and tea. Lots."

She had a high cheerful sturdy voice, somewhat childish for her age, as if she had been used to living with deaf people. It was true that her assertions were falling on deaf ears. In this group of skeptics, nobody would buy the idea that her abstemiousness was just an innocent form of hedonism, which was the conclusion you would be driven to if you accepted her explanations. In fact, Peter did not buy it himself. If she smoked and drank coffee, it was just protective coloration—the homage virtue paid to vice. He bet she did not inhale.

On the other hand, he recalled, there was the precedent of Epicurus. "There was Epicurus," he said, addressing the center of the table. "What about him?" "Most people don't realize he was an ascetic. I did a paper on him for a course in ethics. He lived on barley bread and cheese and water because he thought the simple life was the way to achieve happiness, which he considered the *summum bonum*. Naturally nobody would believe that. Instead, they believed all the lies the Stoics spread about him being a gourmet and lecherous with women. So now Epicureanism means just the opposite of his teaching. But Roberta"—he stumbled—"I mean Miss Scott, is a real Epicurean. She puts pleasure ahead of virtue, and nobody believes her because they identify pleasure with gross sensual satisfaction." Everybody, including Miss Scott, was gazing at him in wonderment. "Epicurus cultivated serenity of mind. He died with great fortitude of the stone," he concluded.

"The stone!" shrieked the hostess. "Do you mean gallstones? But that's cholesterol!" Peter was not attending. As when he had delivered a short harangue in class, his own distant words roared in his ears like the pounding of the sea in a conch shell. Then slowly he began to pick up fragments of the surrounding chatter. "But what about your proteins?" "Vitamin A?" "Not even *cottage cheese?*" "Green noodles." "But if you eat noodles, you're eating eggs, aren't you?" "Don't you find it hard in the restaurants here? You never see a vegetable except in the markets. I always wonder what they do with them." Peter recognized the languid voice of a Princetonian major in government studies. The clamor of agreement betrayed the anti-French sentiment ever ready to be mobilized when Americans in Paris got together. And as happened with anti-Semites merrily fraternizing, nobody at the table seemed to remember that there were French people present. "I mostly eat in Italian restaurants," the girl said, when the chortles had died down. "They don't mind if you only take spaghetti with tomato sauce and salad and fruit. At home, when I cook for myself, I use the *Yoga Cookbook*."

"I use that too!" cried Peter, who had bought his second-hand along the Seine. "It has some great recipes." "Fantastic. Where in the world did you find yours?" Peter told her. "The guy let me have it for a franc." "Me too!" she exclaimed, her eyes widening. "Isn't that funny? Quai des Grands Augustins. I bargained." "Me quai Voltaire." "Do you have a Waring Blendor?" Peter did not have a Waring Blendor. "Golly, you ought to get one. They're terrific for vegetable soups."

Peter thought anxiously of his mother, who refused all traffic with blenders and mixers; at that moment, in New York (9:00 A.M. Eastern Standard Time), she was doubtless pressing chestnuts or something through a sieve. "Jean can get you one at the PX," the girl went on kindly. "You save a lot that way." "Thanks. Maybe I'll do that." He must be out of his mind. His landlady would never let him have a blender, even if he were willing to scrap family principles and acquire one, and it would be a hard thing to hide in what passed for his closet. Yet could he ask this glorious crank to dinner and use a food mill? It came to him that he must be falling in love, but would she deign to notice a reedy college junior?

According to his mother, there was no such thing as unreciprocated love. Love was something that happened between two people. It was not a solitary affair. But even if that dictum could be trusted, he was not sure that it applied to him. *After adolescence*, the fair Rosamund had stipulated. Maybe he had not finished adolescing. He still had that croak in his voice.

A piece of pumpkin pie had materialized before him. Assuming that egg and milk had gone into its composition, he hardly dared turn his eyes to his right. His own appetite had left him; he shook his head to a scoop of vanilla ice cream. But Roberta Scott was eating the pie. She must be hungry. Her nut-cup, he observed, was empty. Silently he exchanged it for his full one, which he had been saving for her—a present.

"Maybe you'd like to come to supper some night at my place. I could make some spaghetti and salad." She considered this for nearly a minute, putting down her fork and chewing her lower lip; she had a way of looking you steadily in the eyes when you had made a remark, such as he had encountered among very poor people the summer before last in Umbria. "Why, yes, sure, I'd like to. Thanks a lot." A friendly eager smile replaced the clouds of perplexity on her features. "Next week?" he said boldly. "What about Tuesday?"

But even as he spoke he became aware of a pervasive silence. The general was on his feet and tapping on his glass for attention. He was going to offer a toast. To a character called Benjy, aged about eighteen, who had passed most of the meal in speechless obscurity. Peter had been introduced to him in the elevator. "We're Leonard and Alice Burnside, from the Embassy, and this is our son, Benjy. Benjy, put that cigarette out and shake hands." At table his wine intake had been monitored by his mother—a big crinkly-eyed woman with dimples in a magenta wool dress. Now, amid general astonishment, wriggling and pale, he was elevated to star billing. "Is it his birthday?" someone wondered. But it was not Benjy's birthday. The kid was volunteering to take up arms for his country. That was what the clinking of glasses was about.

Glances of disbelief passed among the other young males at the table, numbering three: Peter, the boy from Northwestern, and the ultra-WASP Princetonian, who bore the curious name of Silvanus Platt. They listened to Benjy's mother explaining to the French colonel that her son was so sold on the Vietnamese war that he could not wait to be drafted. "*Il s'est rallié aux couleurs.*" "*Il a devancé l'appel,*" absently corrected the Frenchman. "*Je vous félicite, jeune homme. Et vous surtout, madame.*" He raised his glass.

The mother drank to her son. "It was Benjy's own decision. 'I've got to go, Mom,' he said. Leonard wanted us to refuse our consent. Though he's only Benjy's stepfather. 'Let him wait till he's drafted,' Leonard said. But I couldn't say no to Benjy. I never have been able to. I guess I've spoiled him. But he's my only child." Her face, which might have been pretty when she was young, crinkled and puckered like a wide seersucker bedspread.

During all this, her son had not opened his mouth except to engorge pie and ice cream. Benjy's worst fear, she went on, giggling, was that he might be sent to Germany, instead of out there, where the fighting was. At that point, the kid gave tongue. "Yeah," he said. "That's right."

Actually, Peter felt a revolted pity for Benjy. As transpired somewhat later, the kid was a "problem" who had not been able to get into any college or find a job and had been hanging around Paris collecting traffic tickets while driving the family car—food for powder, in the words of Falstaff. Yet it would be surprising if he passed his physical, he was so awful and pathetic. His hobby was collecting matchbook folders. On the mental plane, the only message that had got through to him was anti-Communism. He wanted to be able to kill Viet Cong. And his parents, probably, were letting the poor creep volunteer in the hope that the Army would make a man of him—passing the buck to the Pentagon where they themselves had failed. That woman must know that she was in line to be a Gold Star mother unless the war stopped.

Slowly it came to Peter that, contrary to what you would expect in such a milieu, Benjy's parents were far from being proud of the patriot they had fledged. Even if he came back covered with medals, he would not get the fatted calf. To hear his mother tell it, she spent most of her time on her knees praying for peace. "Though Benjy doesn't like me to. He hates it if I go into some little church and light a candle." "Yeah. I want to get some of those gorillas first." "*Guerrillas*, please, Benjy." She gave the *l*'s a Spanish pronunciation. "He used to think they were real gorillas," she explained, with a little gurgle of a laugh. "He got that from listening to the radio." "I guess a lot of people make that mistake," the general said easily. "Well, here's luck to you, Ben." He handed the boy a large non-Cuban cigar. "Hope you see some action if that's what you want. In an 'advisory' capacity, of course." He chuckled. From Benjy, a strange ack-ack sound issued; like a kid playing machine-guns, he crouched in his chair, taking aim. "Here they come," he said, "in a human-wave assault!"

Silence followed. Even Chuck appeared somewhat embarrassed by the potential hero in their midst. "I guess Ben saw too many World War II movies when he was younger," he suggested. "The little yellow men in the jungle." "That's what I used to say to Leonard," the boy's mother chimed in. "'I don't see why the Embassy keeps showing those old war movies. They ought to think of the effect on the children.' Didn't I say that, Leonard? And now look at the result. All he can think about is human waves and sharpshooters hiding in coconut palms and assassins in black pajamas."

"Holy cats, Mom," said Benjy, puffing on the general's cigar. "You sound as if I was a freak or something. Isn't a guy supposed to want to fight for his country?" That was the sixty-four-dollar question. "Personally I want to stay alive," said Silvanus Platt. "How about you, Jay?" "Me too," said the boy from Northwestern. "Me too," said Peter, though in fact he was not sure that this ought to be his prime aim. "Wouldn't you rather be dead than red?" said Benjy. "No," said Peter. "Practically nobody would, when it comes down to it. They just think they would. All those Poles and Hungarians would be committing suicide if that idea was true. Anyway, this war isn't stopping Communism, so far as I can see. It may even be helping Communism by making people hate Americans."

To his surprise, the general nodded. "This is the wrong war in the wrong place, the way I look at it. Nothing will suit the world Communist conspiracy better than to have us send a land army to get bogged down in those mangrove swamps. It's a diversionary tactic as old as war. The sooner the U.S. winds up its business out there, the happier all concerned here at NATO will be. We know where the main enemy is located—at the same old address, the Kremlin, Moscow. The day the U.S. lands ground forces on those Asian beaches, it surrenders Western Europe to the Red Army."

Peter had not thought of it this way. Still, he was interested to hear a militarist espouse getting out of Vietnam. "But won't Johnson have to face some pretty rough domestic criticism if we just pull out our advisers and leave the South Vietnamese to cope?" wondered Jay Williams. "For Christ's sake, I said 'wind it up.' Hanoi has to come to its senses. We could knock out that little country with one punch tomorrow. You fellows know that as well as I do. *They* know it."

At these words, suddenly, the party got rough. Practically everybody started shouting his opinion. The Frenchwoman was shrilling about Foster Dulles and the chronic "*lâcheté*" of the Americans. Always too little and too late. The betrayal at

Dienbienphu. Suez. Her husband, more tactful, sought to divide the blame. The French had betrayed too. The Left. Mendès-France. Geneva. He barely stopped short of attacking General De Gaulle, his own commander-in-chief. A parliament of fools was in session. Roberta Scott put her hands over her ears. "But what would you have us do now, sir?" said Silvanus Platt smoothly. "Granting that you're right in your analysis. That's all water over the dam now. Where do we go from here? How do we persuade Ho Chi Minh to call it quits?"

"*Mais la bombe, bien sûr,*" the colonel answered, throwing out his hands. "*Une seule suffirait.*" "Atomic or hydrogen?" Peter inquired coldly, getting in return a pitying look. "*Atomique, naturellement. N'exagérons pas.*" But the general was not convinced that an atomic bomb on Hanoi would do the trick. You had to think of world opinion and what the Russian response would be. If you decided to use the bomb, it might make more sense to drop it on Peking, before the Chinese got theirs. That would give Ho something to think about, and the Russians would scarcely object. "*Ces Chinois s'en foutent,*" said the Frenchman. With the manpower they had, an atom bomb would be just a flea-bite.

"You have a point," conceded Chuck. Still, on the whole, he did not favor dropping atomic hardware on Hanoi. "We can do it with conventional stuff, if we have to." "But why should it be necessary, sir?" said Silvanus Platt. "Wouldn't a clear warning suffice? As you say, they know we have the wherewithal to wipe them out tomorrow." "Yeah," said Benjy. "But they don't think we'll use it. We've got to *show* them." "Benjy!" "*Mais votre fils a raison, madame,*" said the Frenchman. *Le pauvre papa* Khrushchev had been willing to listen to reason; when Kennedy threatened, he understood. But these Orientals were fanatics. . . .

"We can't bomb Hanoi!" Peter burst out. "I mean, it's impossible for us to do a thing like that." "Why not?" said Benjy's stepfather, a bald man who had something to do with trade or economics. "I don't say I favor it necessarily. I just want to know, why not? I was in the Air Force. We bombed Germany." "OK, OK," said Peter, feeling weary. "I agree, we had to do that. Though maybe I would have been against some of those raids if I'd been alive then. I think you can draw a line between bombing military targets and bombing civilians." "The Nazis didn't." "But they were *Nazis*! For Christ's sake, that was the point, wasn't it?" "What's so sacred about a civilian?" said the general. "If he's working in a factory making war goods? Grow up, boy." "I think Peter's right, Dad," said Jean. "We have to be *better* than our enemy." "I agree," said Benjy's mother. "We *are* better than our enemy!" shouted the general. "I haven't finished what I was saying," objected Peter. "Let him talk, honey."

Peter started again. "So we bombed Germany. And Hiroshima and Nagasaki. My generation was born with that on its conscience. My mother says I started kicking inside her when Hiroshima happened." "If it shortened the war, it was worth it," interrupted the general. "Saved American lives *and* Japanese lives. And if we hadn't bombed those dear German civilians, the Nazis would have had the bomb ahead of us. Put that in your pipe and smoke it." "Chuck!" "Don't you think Truman could have dropped one teensy atom bomb on a deserted atoll?" said the woman on Peter's left in dreamy tones. "That would have given the Japanese a chance to surrender when they knew what they were up against. If they didn't surrender then, it was their own responsibility." "'His blood be upon us and upon our children,'" muttered Peter. "Maybe that might have been the best way, Helen," said Mrs Lammers soothingly. "But one man can't think of everything, you know, especially with a war on. We were certainly all grateful to President Truman when it was over. Now let's go into the other room and have some coffee and let Peter Levi have his say."

"OK, skip Hiroshima. We'll never agree about that. About Germany, I'll even concede that maybe our saturation-bombing helped shut down the gas ovens, though my father claims it was the opposite—it stiffened German morale. But anyway the Nazis were bombing England, which was our ally. The North Vietnamese aren't bombing anybody." "Just minding their own business, eh?" said the general. "Are they helping the Viet Cong or aren't they?" put in Benjy's stepfather, getting excited. "Have you heard about infiltration? And atrocities? Civilians— women and children—ruthlessly murdered. Grenades tossed into theatres and other public places. Assassination of teachers and local officials." "Standing operating procedure," said the general, nodding. "Poisoned arrows," said Benjy. "And those punji stakes dipped in shit that they make traps out of. They don't abide by the rules of war." "Beheadings. Kidnappings. Standing operating procedure," repeated the general. "Do you approve of that kind of stuff, Levi?"

Peter groaned. "No." He was starting to feel sick. The general followed up. "Maybe you think it's all U.S. propaganda?" "No, I guess not. I guess those things happen." "*Happen!* Somebody does them. Somebody directed from Hanoi. Directed, supplied, and instigated. We have documentary proof and plenty of it. Now how are you going to put a stop to that?" "I don't know," said Peter.

He was getting the worst of the argument. Across the living room, Roberta Scott had her chin sunk in the palm of her hand, like a statue of Dejection; no help there. And the irony was that he had charged into the debate partly to curry favor, on the theory that a girl like that, from Philadelphia, was bound to be a dyed-in-the-wool Quaker. "Go ahead," insisted the general. "Give us your ideas. We're listening." Peter's head was buzzing. It was like an exam nightmare. He tried to recall things Bob and his mother had said, things he himself had said, during the Goldwater campaign, which already seemed so long ago, like a Golden Age of clarity. And he remembered his father telling his mother that Peter might make a good judge but he could never be an advocate.

Put on the spot, he could not think of a single alternative to the unthinkable, which was bombing those frail little people in conical hats. The slogan "land reform" floated into his ken, like a beat-up slug of printer's type. Give the South Vietnamese peasants something to fight for—a stake in their government? But even if land distribution was possible, it would take a long time and might not end the war but actually intensify it, assuming both sides became equally determined—had anybody ever considered that?

"We should negotiate," he said at last. "Great. Hear, hear," said Mr. Burnside. "I couldn't agree more. But how are we going to get talks going? It takes two to negotiate. We're ready and willing to sit down and talk, but Hanoi claims there's nothing to talk about. We just withdraw our support and let the Viet Cong take over. Simple." Peter licked his lips. "But isn't that what we're saying ourselves? *They* should withdraw *their* support. Why should we have the right to demand that and not them? It's more their country than ours." "So you favor a Commie takeover," said the general. "No! But if I had to choose between that and bombing them, I guess I'd be for that." "So you favor it. You kids might have the guts to say what you think, instead of pussyfooting. Lay it on the line." "Maybe there wouldn't be a takeover," said Peter, voicing his deepest wish. The general gave a bark of laughter. "Oh, God, friend, where have you been all my life?"

The other youths, with the exception of Benjy, had been silent for a long time. It was impossible to tell on whose side they were now, apart from the question of their own personal survival. Roberta Scott was studying some little ivory chessmen on the table beside her; she looked as if every word spoken were making her unhappy. "It's inconceivable!" Peter cried. "Don't you see that? Doesn't *anybody* see that?" "What's inconceivable, honey?" said Letitia. "That we'll bomb North Vietnam. If we do that, I think I'll kill myself." "Is that a promise or a threat?" said Chuck, kidding. "Hey, take it easy." "Why are you getting so worked up?" said Donna Elvira kindly. "I don't like the idea myself, but it wouldn't be the end of the world, would it? What's so special about bombing Hanoi?" "They can't retaliate," said Peter, letting his breath out with a long sigh. "And that's *why* we'd do it. To prove to them how powerful we are. If we thought they could retaliate, we wouldn't."

Roberta raised her eyes and met his. She nodded. "Yes. Golly, yes." "Since when is superior weaponry a reason for not using it?" inquired Chuck. "This is war, not a horse race, buddy." Peter had had enough. Tears rushed to his eyes. "You don't give a damn about your country, you stupid patriot. You don't care *what* it does. Or about its fair name. I *love* America or what I used to think was America. Listening to you, I don't recognize it any more."

To his amazement, nobody moved to throw him out of the apartment. "I think Peter needs a little fresh air," Letitia said quickly. "We all do. Let's get our things on and go out and play softball now. It gets dark so early these days. Though we ought to be grateful to French Daylight Saving. . . ." Still chattering, she was guiding him to the bathroom. She turned on the cold-water tap. "You just put this damp washcloth on your eyes and you'll feel better. We gave you too much bourbon. I always forget that it's a hundred-proof." "I'd better go home now," said Peter, applying the cold cloth to his burning face. "I'm sorry I was rude." "Just a good clean argument, honey. Good for the digestion. You'll forget all about it when you've had some exercise. I know Chuck will. Between you and me, it kind of got under his skin to see that girl refusing to touch her food. I saw that right away. He's such a wonderful host, loves to entertain."

Peter nodded. "Tell me the truth, Mrs. Lammers. Are we going to bomb Hanoi?" "I don't know, Peter. I wouldn't know a thing like that. Chuck wouldn't either. He was just talking off the top of his head. Got carried away. And that Benjy upset him too. We've known him since he was a toddler, when we served with the Burnsides in Madrid. They're *beside* themselves with worry. When you see a boy like that *wanting* to go out and get killed in that crazy war, it makes you wonder. Underneath, Chuck would a lot rather see him sign up for the Peace Corps. I want you to believe that."

"OK, I believe you, Mrs. Lammers." Peter rested his head against the cold tiles of the bathroom wall. "Chuck agrees with you more than you realize. But we just can't walk away, can we? I mean, we have a commitment. If we walk out, our allies right here in NATO will start wondering whether they can trust us. There would be all these repercussions that the ordinary person doesn't think about. You *are* for the NATO shield, aren't you?" As she took the washcloth from his hands, she darted an anxious glance into his eyes.

"I guess so," said Peter. He was not sure what he thought of NATO. His father said it was a necessary evil, which you could say about a lot of things without their becoming good. Still, as long as there was no fighting going on here in Europe, Peter found it hard to take an interest in NATO, one way or another. Which was possibly reasoning in a circle, since if there were no NATO, there might be fighting. Your opinion, he supposed, depended on your assessment of Russian intentions. But he did not want to use his brain any more this afternoon, if he could help it.

Out in the Bois, as Letitia had predicted, he felt somewhat better. He was on Chuck's team, and though he struck out his first time at bat, in the field he was fairly fast on his feet. The stars were the long-legged Roberta, in the pitcher's position, and the big Mrs. Burnside at bat. The French colonel, surprisingly, was an agile shortstop and outfielder and fleet on the bases. Benjy was terrible. He would never survive basic training, even if he passed his physical; his nicotine-stained fingers were all thumbs, and he panted noisily, trotting after an easy fly.

A small crowd of French children gathered to watch *les Américains* and to chase an occasional ball. Peter found he was enjoying himself and even enjoying the sense of being an American, as, waiting his turn at bat, he explained the game in French to the kids. Then in the fourth inning, running after a line drive into left field, he found he had the hiccups. Taking part in the national sport, on top of the national bird, had been too much. He tried holding his breath and swallowing accumulated saliva, hoping they would pass before anybody noticed. Instead, they got worse. When Chuck waved him in at the end of the inning, he was hiccupping so loudly, like a drunkard in a play, that the French *gosses* began to imitate him, whirling around, jerking, and making burpy noises. He could not even get his breath to tell them to scram.

Various remedies were suggested: drinking from the wrong side of a glass, hanging his head and counting to a hundred, getting a sudden shock. He went in search of a drinking-fountain. Needless to say, this being France, none materialized, though he walked for half a mile; the lake where he used to go rowing, polluted, naturally, rose before him like a cruel mirage. Chuck was at bat when he reappeared in their midst. "Hic!" The general, making a foul tip, glanced at him with annoyance. Benjy offered to go with him and try to find a café.

When they had finally found one and Peter had drunk four glasses of Evian while holding his breath, the hiccups subsided. But then he had to wait for Benjy to finish a Pernod he had ordered. "Would you like to smoke some grass?" said Benjy, feeling in his pockets. Peter shook his head. "Let's get back to the ball game." But it was a long way from the café. By the time they got to the Bois, dusk was falling; the little meadow where they had been playing was empty, and all the players had fled. Peter was bitter. "Wouldn't you think they would have waited for us? Hiccups can be a serious thing. Christ, there've been cases of people who've had them for a year and finally kicked off!" "Yeah. I read about one of those." "And that girl is supposed to be a *doctor*! Well, a medical student anyway. All she was interested in was pitching. What about the Hippocratic oath?" "Still, you're OK now, aren't you?" "But they don't *know* that." "I see what you mean. You can't rely on most people, that's for sure. That's what appeals to me about the Army. The buddy-system. Like today. You had it bad in the windpipe, and I stuck by you. You'd do the same for me."

Just then a voice called "Hi!" Jean had waited for them. She emerged from a sort of copse. "Mother was worried about you. She said to take you to the American Hospital if your hiccups hadn't stopped." "I'm OK now, thanks. It was nice of you to wait, though. What happened to the others?" "Benjy's parents went home. And Roberta had to go to a concert." "Oh . . . She didn't leave any message?" "Why, no. But she agreed with Mother that you ought to go to the American Hospital. They could give you an anti-spasmodic, she said." "She didn't say anything about dinner?" "Dinner? Gosh, can you still eat?" "I don't mean now. I asked her to dinner next week. A vegetarian repast." "Isn't that great of you, Peter! Do you know how to cook?" "Yes." "I love cooking myself. What kind of dishes can you make?" "Oh, *you* know, spaghetti. . . . At home I used to bake cakes, but here I don't have an oven."

The three started walking through the landscaped wood. Peter could see that if he was not careful he would be entertaining Jean for dinner soon. And smoking grass with Benjy. Those two seemed to be his real friends. A final hiccup issued from his craw. "Oops!" Jean giggled. "Dad is a card. He thinks you can cure hiccups by will power. That's what he said, just now." "And Roberta, what does she think?" "She claims they're a medical mystery. Doctors don't know what causes them or why they go away." "Like love," said Benjy, astonishingly. "Something in your chemistry that you can't control. Yeah." They continued pensively walking in the direction, they hoped, of a Métro station. For a while they were lost in the wood.

Leviticus

I F it had not been for his draft status, Peter would have quit the Sorbonne. He was bored by his classes, which, being for foreigners, were on a childish level, like the course for *Stranieri* at Perugia. The lecture hall, thronged with humanity, was plunged in hyperborean darkness. True to form, the French were hoarding the electricity; the professor, doubtless under orders from the Ministry of Education, never turned on any lights, so that you could not take notes or draw pictures to alleviate the tedium. There was practically no ventilation, and when he could not get a place on the window sills, Peter chose to sit on the floor, unable to stretch his legs without prodding somebody's bottom but hopeful that the air was purer down there.

It was not just *him*, as he tried to make clear to his family; the other 1,999 foreign kids segregated in French Civilization felt bored and gypped too. In fact, the Left Bank was full of American drop-outs, not bothering to show up at classes any more, since nobody took attendance and their supervisor, if they had one, could not be more indifferent. At the end of the year, there was going to be an exam, which the majority infallibly failed, but even if you failed, you could get a "certificate of attendance" from the professor—a meaningless document that only meant you were registered.

Most of the kids Peter knew were resigned to writing this year off as a total loss, academically, whether they did any work or not. Quite a few were switching to the Alliance Française, where at least they got practice in speaking; at the Sorbonne, all they gave you in "intensive French" was grammar, and the professor did all the talking. But the kids who made that move could be ordered to report straight home for a physical, if their draft board wanted to get tough. You rated a student deferment by being enrolled in a recognized college or university, and going to the Alliance Française, though it actually taught you something, was like going to the Berlitz School at home or taking a correspondence course, as far as Selective Service was concerned. Up to now, as it chanced, General Hershey had not gone fishing in the draft pool of juniors abroad. But there could always be a first time.

Nobody's parents understood the score here. They could not use their imagination and realize that if a bunch of young aliens were isolated and ruthlessly exploited by a chauvinistic French university, naturally they lost all incentive to study; it was the same as in the schools in Harlem. The Sorbonne was only interested in collecting the tuition. As Dag had kept pointing out, it was no accident that the French Civilization class was scheduled for 8:00 A.M.: they *wanted* the kids to cut it, for the simple reason that two thousand were registered for the course, while the hall seated five hundred. Dag was convinced that the curriculum had been devised by the French tourist industry to lure under-age foreign suckers to Paris. And he meant that literally. No wonder the poor methodical Marxist had got deported back to Norway; he had tried to expose the system to everybody he talked to, like the Enemy of the People.

But parents thought their kids were throwing away a wonderful opportunity. His stepfather wrote that he had counted thirty-seven negative words and expressions in Peter's last communication, which was only a page and a half long. In Bob's reckoning, "finally" was a negative, as in "My landlady has finally turned the heat on," "I have finally got a library card to work in the Bibliothèque Nationale," "The packages you sent finally came," "A French girl finally spoke to me in a café yesterday. She wanted to know the time." Reading over his letter, which Bob had enclosed, marked with blue pencil, Peter had to agree that the omission of "finally" would have given some of those sentences a more positive thrust. Evidently, he was bidding for sympathy, which his parents were unwilling to give. Self-pity in the eyes of Bob and his mother was a disgusting habit; if you were sorry for yourself, they would not be sorry for you—a duplication of labor, Bob claimed.

The *babbo* wrote that if Peter was unhappy in Paris, he might transfer next semester to a provincial university like Nancy or Montpellier. And he wondered why Peter had not investigated the special "first year courses" the Sorbonne gave to qualified foreigners; he had heard them well spoken of by the French department at Wellesley. Though he did not thank his father for discussing his private affairs with the stupid Wellesley women, for a while Peter accepted the reproach. He too wished he had applied for one of those courses, instead of joining the mob in French Civilization. Yet from what he gleaned, there was no cause for envy. What his father did not know was that those courses were mass-produced too and on a patronizing freshman level, as you could divine from the name if you thought about it; the lectures were just as moth-eaten, there was no class participation, no assignments were given, not even a reading-list, and the exam, when they finally sprang it, bore no relation to what the professor had been talking about. Every year most of the Americans flunked ignominiously, which was probably how the French had planned it—a national hecatomb.

In retrospect, he concluded that the real ploy would have been to get permission to audit lectures by one of the star professors at the regular Sorbonne or the Hautes Etudes and then take an exam or write a paper for his tutor back home; that way, he could have imbibed some genuine French culture and mingled with French students, at least in the sense of being in the same room with them. But you had to be pretty "motivated"—his adviser's jargon—to attempt that and, not being enrolled, you risked being cracked down on by your draft board just as much as though you were hanging around playing the pinball machine in cafés or looking at old movies at the cinémathèques.

If he wanted to be sure of his student deferment, it was better to stick it out in French Civilization, going through the motions of studying for credit. That, at any rate, was the cynical advice they handed out at the Embassy; some guys in the class had asked. In short, stay in your slot. You might have to do your junior year over when you got home, but in the Affluent Society your parents would go on supporting you until you finally graduated and take you as a tax exemption. If they complained, you could point to the silver lining: you would be in the Class of '67 instead of '66, which would keep you out of the Army one more year. By that time, the war in Vietnam ought to be over.

Like most people his age, he guessed, Peter had a profound wish not to be killed. He was no different from those other guys at the general's Thanksgiving brawl. Though sorry for anybody who had to die in Vietnam, he faced with equanimity the idea that some unknown draftee—maybe even a Negro— should bite the dust instead of him.

He could see in principle that student deferment was a bad form of discrimination, that Selective Service—page Darwin— showed middle-class society red in tooth and claw, but just the same he had his education to finish. Would a nut like his mother want him to volunteer or go to jail as a C.O. or what? She and Bob were opposed to the war, which was why they had finally voted for Johnson. Yet in their letters they had begun to say that he was reneging on his promises, not trying to achieve peace but plotting for a bigger war, now that the election was over. Give him time, Peter urged. At least wait for January, when he would deliver his message to Congress. He *must* have meant what he said about American boys not dying for Asian boys. Even the general, after all, was against landing troops, and as for bombing Hanoi, that was just the Air Force mentality.

For his own part, despite his bibulous statements that afternoon, Peter was not sure exactly how he stood on the war. In reality he worried about what would happen to India, which used to be one of his favorite countries, if the Americans let the Communists take over Indochina. The best hope seemed to be some compromise, whereby the UN, maybe, could step in and supervise an armistice. That was what Roberta thought; when he had called her at the Institut Pasteur and asked her to dinner, she had invited him instead to a concert, and afterward they had had a coffee. She had a lot of faith in U Thant.

He himself derived cheer from the reminder that if you stopped paying attention to these problems, they tended to get solved. Like Laos, which had had him sweating when he was sixteen, or the Berlin Wall. Even the Congo seemed to have simmered down, now that everybody was concentrating on Asia. It was the same as when you had a headache: you could make it go away by stimulating a pain in some other part of your body—your big toe or your crazy bone. He owed that prescription to his mother.

But since she and Bob were so excruciated by the Vietnamese war, shouldn't they be glad that Peter had his II-S deferment?

They were glad selfishly, he assumed, but the fair Rosamund would never like being glad just selfishly. He could count himself lucky that she was not on his draft board; if she were, it might be the sacrifice of Isaac all over again, minus the ram. It would have been interesting to have Isaac's point of view on that episode—something the Bible left out.

Recently he had decided that mercenary armies had made a lot of sense. He still believed in non-violence as a technique of persuasion, but there were some situations that persuasion did not cover. As the *babbo* said, what if Gandhi had been up against Hitler? Unless you were an all-out pacifist, you recognized that *somebody* had to bear arms, and why not somebody who had heard the call, like that poor nut Benjy? Instead of training every young kid to be a killer, it would be more moral, as well as more practical, to restrict the job to specialists. But ordinary twenty-year enlisted men, not just the officer caste, ought to be rewarded by society for the risks they ran, the way Iroquois Indians, who were sure-footed, got big money being high-construction workers—there were some of those *Peaux-Rouges* right here in France; he had read an article about them in *L'Express*. If he were in Johnson's place, he would abolish the draft and finance military training for qualified recruits by taxing people like his parents who could afford it and had children between eighteen and twenty-seven. Anybody over a certain income level who wanted to keep his offspring out of the Army—and ballplayers and prize fighters and movie stars and Pop singers—would have to pay the price, so that the guys who volunteered to do the fighting would earn, say, what an automobile worker brought home on Friday night. What an instructor or a section man got would not be enough to make getting killed attractive.

If he had the energy, he would send his plan to Johnson. He had another plan, along the same lines, to submit to socialist countries. That would be to give people who had degrading jobs like street-cleaners and sewer-workers or shoe-salesmen the highest rewards in the economy. In Paris, it was almost always Algerians, he noticed, that you saw sweeping the streets with those brooms made of twigs or laying sewer pipes. But there was no reason why the dirtiest jobs should be the worst paid. It ought to be the opposite. He was amazed that nobody but Peter Levi had thought of something so simple. And apart from the sheer equity of the arrangement, which was breathtaking in its neatness, like the Fool's Mate, it had another good feature: the materialists would rush down into the sewers, where they belonged, and artists and scientists and scholars would not be corrupted by money, as they were under the present system, even if, like his parents, they failed to recognize it.

He was hurt by the reception his idea got from his friend Bonfante, who as an old revolutionary ("*Papa, c'est un révolutionnaire; il a combattu dans le maquis,*" Irène explained proudly) ought to have been serious about it. Instead, Arturo, whom he found sweeping their apartment, was overcome with glee, laughing almost wolfishly as he wielded the dust-pan; his bald head was tied up in a red bandanna, and he wore a woman's ruffled apron over his trousers, which made Peter feel like Little Red Riding Hood visiting her grandmother. When Arturo had finally moderated his amusement and made a pot of *espresso*, he explained that Peter was too young to understand the relation between money and power. When a new class enriched itself, as had happened with the bourgeoisie before the French Revolution, it proceeded to seize power. What Peter was proposing, without knowing it, was a dictatorship of the proletariat. That was the big joke.

"Your ditch-diggers and sewer-cleaners would be the new rulers. The old Roman proletariat. Not even Marx's factory-workers." "But why should they want power?" Peter said sulkily. "You mean they wouldn't be satisfied just to have the Cadillacs and the weekend *dachas* and sturgeon dinners at three-star restaurants?" "If a Cadillac has no prestige, who wants it? When a worker is paid better than his boss, he will be the boss tomorrow. When the English king, Charles, lost his revenues, because of progressive inflation, he lost his head too."

Peter did not see that a dictatorship of humble sewer-cleaners would be any worse than a dictatorship of fat Party bosses. "They would not be the *same* sewer-cleaners," Arturo pointed out. "The profession would become overcrowded, and the weak would be pushed out. They would be forced to become actors or ballet-dancers—professions without prestige." He gave his high Italian laugh. "What is degrading is not the job, Peter, but the pay attached to it." A surgeon's job was just as revolting as a plumber's. Maybe more so. In the Middle Ages, a surgeon and a barber were one and the same person and rewarded accordingly. "But that proves my point!" cried Peter. "It shows that society can change its mind about the value of a person's work. I guess sewer-cleaners are just as necessary as doctors." "Soon it will all be done by machines," Arturo promised. "When socialism achieves an advanced technology, no one will clean the sewers or sweep the streets."

Arturo always invoked technology as the great solvent when they debated about the future. Europeans were idealistic about machines because they had not had to live with them. The Bonfantes were too impecunious to have a car or television or a washing-machine; they boiled their laundry on the stove. Arturo wrote a financial column for some provincial newspapers, which Peter guessed did not pay too well. He knew all about the stock market and interest rates, but he did not even have a bank account. Elena kept what money they had in postal savings—the next thing to a stocking. Their apartment was in an old decrepit building, over a printing shop, and the presses often shook it, rattling the pictures on the walls. Everything in it was old-fashioned: their Model-T Frigidaire, which also rattled and made midget ice cubes, like a toy; their claw-footed bathtub, which they had bought at a *Démolitions*; their ancient modern art; Arturo's pre-war electric shaver; their gramophone and scratched monaural-78 records. Gas pipes for the old gas lighting fixtures had never been removed when electricity was installed and they crawled about the walls like lianas in a forest. Elena's mother, who had lived with them till she died, had covered every surface with Russian shawls, cushions, throws, and heavy draperies; they had pretty silver, some of it broken, that had come with her from Russia too, like the record of Chaliapin singing *Boris Godunov*, to which Peter was much attached. Her parents were Social Revolutionaries and had to leave Russia with their few unworldly possessions when the Bolsheviks took over.

The most modern implement they possessed was an old vacuum cleaner, which Peter now noticed lying in a corner. He wondered why Arturo had been using the broom. There was a strange amount of dust in the room. Elena was at her job at the Mazarin Library, and the *femme de ménage* was sick. The vacuum was *en panne*, Arturo thought: every time he had used it lately, it had seemed to lack power. "Maybe I can fix it," said Peter, picking up the threadbare hose. He had often vacuumed for his mother in the dear dead days in Rocky Port, and Arturo, though fanatically tidy, was not much good with tools. Peter flipped the switch, and a cloud of dust and grit arose. In fact, the machine was blowing accumulated dust out of the bag into the apartment. "Why, you've been working it backward!" he exclaimed. "*O la la!*" said Arturo, crestfallen. Elena and the children had been right when they claimed that each time papa cleaned the place, it seemed to get dirtier. . . .

The manifest irony of this little *contretemps* put Peter in a better mood. Adjusting the suction, he ran the vacuum vigorously over the floors and rugs while Arturo meekly followed him with a feather duster, cupping his ear with his left hand to hear over the hum of the *aspirateur* as Peter held forth, from his wider experience, on the contemporary technological crisis. Maybe it would be a good thing, Peter shouted, if machines took over the more malodorous functions of society, such as getting rid of the garbage. That was already a *fait accompli* in large sections of America; he described the Disposall gadget his stepmother had on the Cape, which had practically eliminated those grisly trips to the dump. Of course you still had the cans and empty bottles to cope with, but eventually humanity might find some means of dealing with tin cans and old automobiles, besides making sculptures out of them. One solution might be to stop eating out of cans and driving automobiles, but that was too much to hope for in the present state of enlightenment. In any case, he was willing to admit that the Disposall made a real contribution to human happiness, although at the moment of installation in the Wellfleet kitchen he had argued with his stepmother that she would do better to keep a pig.

But each new invention, as far as he was concerned, ought to be viewed with suspicion until it could prove its innocence. In his ideal world-state, a patent office, staffed by moral philosophers, would replace the censors, scrutinizing applications for new processes and gadgets and deciding whether their ultimate effects would be good, bad, or neutral. Merely neutral would be kept pending for a period of years, on probation. Under a system like that, detergents, for instance, could never have reached the market.

Arturo rubbed his eyes. "*Détergents? Qu'est-ce que c'est que ça?*" Typically, he did not even know what they were. Peter flew out to the kitchen and returned with a bottle of washing solution. "*Ça!*" "*Mais c'est du savon!*" "'Soap'!" exclaimed Peter with a pitying laugh. "You're using detergents every day to wash the dishes without even realizing it. Probably your *femme de ménage* buys them. Over here, you're not aware that detergents are fouling up the rivers and poisoning the fish. In America at least we're aware of it. This horrible sludgy foam piles up in lakes and streams, killing all the wild life; it doesn't dissolve the way soap does. Pretty soon all the waterways and the ocean will be choked unless we can stop it." Arturo raised a shoulder. "*Là, tu exagères un peu, mon ami. Quand même!*" The ocean, he felt, would last out his time. "'*Après moi le déluge,*'" observed Peter. "*Qu'est-ce que j'y peux faire, moi?*" Arturo protested. The capitalists were to blame for manufacturing the stuff. "But you don't have to buy it," said Peter. "You could tell your *femme de ménage*. All she has to do is read the fine print on the bottle. My mother and stepmother use only Ivory now or old-style soap powders. You can't wait for a revolution to stop the manufacturers. You have to educate the consumer. The trouble is, detergents are taking over. In a little while, it may be hard to find regular soap in a store. I heard the other day that the PX doesn't carry Ivory Flakes any more."

Arturo appeared bewildered. The significance of Ivory was lost on him. "You know about chemical fertilizers," Peter firmly continued, "and what they're doing to the soil." "*J'en ai entendu parler,*" Arturo replied. "*Mais je ne suis pas exactement au courant.*" He laughed apologetically. There it was. Bonfante had no idea of what technology was actually doing, except in the field of weaponry, where, being anti-American, he was fairly well briefed. He knew about second-strike capability, but he and Elena had never tasted frozen food probably; he had never heard of a TV dinner, never seen a car graveyard, never walked on a tree-shaded street where he was the only pedestrian, not counting dogs. . . .

You could not convey to him the tragedy of a nice little village like Rocky Port, where "exploitation" was not the point at issue. If you mentioned that the laundress there had two TV sets, he thought you were trying to prove something favorable about the American way of life. Whenever Peter started describing the changes that had overtaken his old home in the space of only four years, he rapidly lost his audience. It happened again this afternoon. "Listen, Arturo. It's important." Arturo listened, blinking his eyes, which, strangely for an Italian, were a bright blue—the eyes of an old brigand. He was making an effort to comprehend, but gradually his eyes glazed over. He only brightened when Peter made reference to bomb shelters. He nodded. "*Ils se préparent pour la troisième guerre mondiale.*"

All at once, Peter was overcome by a tremendous feeling of love. He was talking, he realized, to a totally innocent person, like some uncorrupted Papuan of the eighteenth century discovered by Captain Cook. A "good European" so far removed in time from Disposalls, Mixmasters, thermostatically heated swimming pools, frozen-food lockers, thruways, U-Hauls that even if you drew him diagrams he would never get the picture. And like some untutored savage presented with the white man's firewater, he responded with approval to the mention of instant tapioca (*"Très bonne idée"*) and sliced bread. That there were no passenger trains any more in a large part of the U.S., that you could not buy a whole fresh fish on the seashore or a button in a *mercerie*, he simply did not believe: "*Tu plaisantes.*"

Arturo had his column to mail, and they walked together to the post office on the rue Danton. They discussed postal service. "*A New York, ça fonctionne très bien, à ce qu'on dit.*" Peter laughed; his friend's information was characteristically out-of-date. "It *used* to be good, I guess. Now, there's only one delivery a day uptown, where my mother lives." "*Incroyable!*" muttered Arturo. "*Ici il y en a trois.*" He walked along in silence, shaking his head.

For the first time today Peter had really made him wonder. It turned out that he knew a lot about the history of mail. For instance, in the War of 1870, the French had used pigeons to carry letters on microfilm and, more fantastic, they organized a regular service of postal balloons, which the Germans tried to

shoot down with telescopic-sighted Krupp guns—only netting
five balloons, while more than three million letters got through.
"So they invented air mail!" exclaimed Peter. "As far back as
that!" "*Bien sûr.*" Efficient and uniform free public mail delivery had been one of the great progressive achievements of
bourgeois democracy; hence the stress in all the capitalist
countries on the reliability and swiftness of the post. "'Not
rain nor snow nor sleet . . .'" quoted Peter. "It says that on
the post office in New York." The fact that there was only one
mail a day now in the center of world capitalism satisfied Arturo that the system was coming apart. "Down in Wall Street,
I think they have two," put in Peter. "And in the middle of
town, where the big banks and offices are. But a lot of people,
even my mother, use messenger service if it's something important." Arturo nodded. "*C'est très significatif, ce que tu dis
là.*" The U.S., like an old man in his dotage, was reverting to
infancy, *i.e.*, to private messengers to carry the post. The public
sector was breaking down. According to Arturo, that would
account too for the disappearance of trains—another produc-
tive achievement of bourgeois democracy in its phase of expansion. "Trains aren't nationalized in the U.S.," objected
Peter, who was nevertheless struck by his friend's reasoning.
He would be glad to be convinced that capitalism was kicking
the bucket in its headquarters, the United States, so long as it
was a natural death.

They passed a big *marchand de charbon* coming out of his
subterranean lair all sooty, like Pluto, with a sack of coal on his
back. "*Je viens chez vous ce soir,*" the black giant said to Arturo.
He delivered wood for their fireplace. They were called *les
bougnats*—why, Arturo did not know—and were said to come
from the Auvergne, like wet nurses from the Morvan. "*Les enfants adorent ce bougnat.*" Peter could understand that. When
he was young, he confessed, he had liked the idea of infant
chimney-sweeps—small agile black demons clambering down
flues. His mother had read him a book called *The Water Babies*,
about a chimney-sweep named Tom who fell into a brook; he
could not remember the rest. He had been sad when she told
him that they did not exist any more, on account of child-labor
laws. "*Les enfants-ramoneurs,*" agreed Arturo. In his childhood, he too had liked the idea. "*Oui, c'était pittoresque.*" He

made a sudden grimace of disgust. He pointed to the *bougnat*. "*Un ivrogne.*" They were all drunkards, he said, because of the unhealthy conditions they worked in. Soon there would be no more *bougnats*—survivals of injustice and inefficient specialization. "Won't the children miss them?" said Peter. Children could not miss what they had never known, replied Arturo shortly.

Peter disagreed, thinking of blacksmith shops and barber poles and those country fairs his mother talked about. He felt sorry in advance for his children, who would never see the *stoppeuse* darning in the window on the rue de Grenelle or the gilders with their golden signs or the lens-grinder with the big eye over his shop or the cobbler with his wooden shoe.

He pointed to a palette hanging over the emporium of a *marchand de couleurs*. "Nice." Bonfante gave a somber laugh. He asked whether Peter could guess why the palette was there. "For advertising, I suppose. I never thought about it. Does there have to be a reason?" "*Oui! Il y a toujours une raison.*" The explanation was that until the Third Republic the masses had been illiterate. You would not find such quaint signboards in *les beaux quartiers*, but here, where the poor lived, a few had survived. "*Saintes reliques de l'analphabètisme du peuple!*" He wrinkled his nose and stuck out his lower lip, the way all Italians did when they smelled something, morally nauseating. "*Mon cher, il faut toujours se méfier du pittoresque. Ça pue.*"

Peter groaned. It was bad enough to know that everything he liked was doomed to disappearance without feeling obliged to be glad about it. And perforce that should include Bonfante. If he were capable of modernizing, he would be living in some skyscraper in a housing development and driving a new *deux-chevaux*, instead of standing here on the corner tall and gaunt, with his bare bald head, like one of the nicer prophets in the Old Testament, his overcoat flapping in the wind, his chin sunk in his old plaid muffler. He would never even be motorized. This fall when he had started driving-lessons, they had flunked him out of the auto-école.

When they parted, Peter felt another onrush of love. Maybe it was hopeless to shake Arturo's faith in technology. Yet he had to keep trying. A world in which nobody could work except a machine would be horribly boring, he thought. He could not understand why the only people, besides himself, to see this were a few artists, who were prejudiced by the fact that they worked with their hands and enjoyed it. If the right to work became the privilege of a few, which might happen with automation, that would be just as unjust as having leisure the privilege of a few. What was good about the Middle Ages was that everybody had worked: the knight fought, the peasant plowed, and the lady cooked and made simples. Even a cat had a job—of catching mice. In a rational society of the future, the machine could have its allotted sphere, since it was here, as people said, to stay. Only it should be kept in its place. There would be no reason for everybody to write crummy poems or paint ghastly pictures, in order to feel creative, if they had the possibility, stolen from them by machines, of making something useful.

In an incautious moment, he had advanced this thought to his adviser, a sociologist hight Mr. Small, who was probing him for his views on progressive education. Peter thought every child, starting in grade school, should be sent to learn a real trade, like shoemaking, under a master shoemaker, instead of fooling around with finger paints or making ceramics. The old guilds and corporations, with their distinctive dress and the system of masters and apprentices, had been an attractive feature of the Middle Ages, in his opinion; of course there was not much "upward mobility"—only a cycle of replacement and renewal, as happened in the animal kingdom with individuals in a species.

"What interests me about birds and animals is that individuals don't count with them. That's one thing I've learned this year. It ought to be obvious, but I never thought about it before." Mr. Small industriously leafed through Peter's file. "I don't find zoology among your subjects." "No. But you see I belong to this bird-watching group. We go out on Sundays. Birds don't have personalities, except tame ones. They only have collective personalities, like the hermit thrush or the cuckoo or the thieving jay. Or goldfinches, which are gregarious. Maybe you don't grasp the implications of that. But if I didn't have what's called a personality, I wouldn't mind death."

"You think about death a great deal?" "Well, yes. Everybody my age does, I guess, if you can judge by poetry. And of course there's the draft. Anyway, it seems to me that in the past people had less personality and were happier for it. They were more like animals, more natural. I mean, it's natural to die, after all. Rulers had personalities, like Charles le Téméraire or Saint Louis, but most people merged with their occupation and even took their names from it, like Miller or Baker or Skinner. My name, for instance, means priest. I would have been born a priest, literally —the way a bird is born to be a fisher or a fly-catcher."

"You're anxious about the career choices open to you," Mr. Small noted, gazing out the window. "The junior year abroad is often elected as a decision-making device. A retreat and period of stock-taking. The individual is 'closed for inventory,' in business parlance. You're confronted with a bewilderment of choice, the concomitant of an open society. This naturally produces anxiety and evidently, in your case, a wish to regress to a closed, traditional pattern. Your rejection of individual freedom is so extreme that it leads to the fantasy of becoming an animal."

Peter gulped. "You can look at it that way, I guess. It's true, I have this thing about the past. But I always have had. It didn't come on just now. And it's partly because I care about the future. I don't mean mine. I mean humanity's. I keep thinking all the time about the direction we're going in and trying to figure out escape routes. Don't you get scared occasionally?" An eerie blaze lit up Mr. Small's little green eyes; his pale-red lashes blinked angrily. "Scared? I can't think of a more challenging time to be alive in for an American. All the options are open. No society in history before our own has given so-called mass-man such opportunities for self-realization." "To me, everything is closing in," argued Peter. "If I were a Russian or a Pole, at least I might have the illusion that things would be better if there was a revolution. Or even gradual evolution. But here evolution just means giving everybody more of the same. Take a simple example: the Paris traffic." "Use the Métro." "I do. Or I walk. But I can't help worrying about those people stuck in cars."

It was true. Some unkind fairy, finding his brain unemployed, must have set him the gruesome task of coming up with a solution for every current woe. And the Paris traffic problem was a much tougher nut to crack than the reorganization of society. So far, each of his *idées géniales*, such as the common ownership of all vehicles within the city circumference—you picked up a car, free, when you needed it and dropped it when you were through at one of a series of underground parking lots—ran up against some vested interest or was liable to abuse. "Go on." "Well, every time I see a traffic jam, my mind automatically starts milling out plans to offer General De Gaulle or the mayor of Paris, if there is one. For instance, they could prohibit trucks from delivering except at night-time. That would help some. But then the trucks would keep people from sleeping. . . ."

"Have you ever considered having psychiatric treatment?" "No." Not waiting for Mr. Small's gaze to return from its bourne—the distant dome of the Panthéon—Peter donned his jacket. "Excuse me. I just remembered. I have an appointment." Small watched him fumble with the zipper-fastening. "Very well. But keep in mind that the learning-process is not conducted exclusively or even mainly in the classroom. You come to me protesting that the instruction is boring. Well, widen your contacts with people. Talk to them in cafés, in museums, on the street. Don't brood in your room about the world's problems. Meet them, face to face. If you can come out of your protective shell, you'll look back on this year's experience as richly rewarding."

"Ha ha." Peter laughed sourly to himself this afternoon, recalling that *dialogue de sourds*. In fact, a lot of the kids here used words like "rewarding" and "enriching," as though they were writing paid testimonials to "My Junior Year Abroad." Some, like the Smith girl, whom he still occasionally saw, figured that France was teaching them to appreciate America. "It's been very educational," she repeated in a cold smug little voice when complaining about French boys (they wanted her to pay her share if they asked her out), about the bad manners of postal employees (they made her lick her own stamps), about her landlady, whose only interest in her was collecting the rent ("She doesn't think of me as a *person*"). Many insisted that they were learning all by themselves to enjoy art: "Paris has so many opportunities, Peter." As though they had never heard that there were art galleries and museums at home, most of them free to the public, unlike the Louvre, which made the big concession of giving half-rates to students.

Others were bugged on the cinémathèques, like Makowski, who spent his days at the rue d'Ulm and the Palais de Chaillot discovering old American movies. "You can do that in New York," Peter remonstrated, "at the Museum of Modern Art." Peter was tired of Makowski, who had somehow obtained his address and kept dropping around to take a bath or go to the toilet, where he would camp for hours; he lived in a *chambre de bonne*. In principle, Peter did not mind being treated as a comfort station, except that Jan gave nothing in return. When Peter begged him to go to Autun with him one weekend to look at the sculptures of Gislebertus, Makowski could not miss a Buster Keaton movie that was playing on Saturday night. He had practically stopped going to his classes at the Institute of Oriental Languages, saying that he got more language-training eating at Chinese restaurants.

The principle seemed to be that the less you got out of your courses, the more you claimed to be soaking up on the side. It was pathetic, really; even the types who had given up totally on French and passed all their waking hours at the American Center on boulevard Raspail and engaging in oyster-eating contests with each other on the day they got their allowance felt they were getting an education. At nineteen or twenty, Peter supposed, nobody, least of all an American, could face the idea of having made a bad investment of a whole year of their lives.

Yet they had a point; old Pangloss, his adviser, had a point about the so-called learning-process going on independently of any actual studying. Whatever his parents might think, he had made some progress here, for which he could thank Bonfante rather than his moldy classes. The only "intensive French" he got came from Arturo, who would not let him talk Italian with him. He was also picking up some basic Russian from Elena. And if, in the higher realms, he could observe a little growth in himself, he owed that to the Bonfantes, who were real intellectuals, he decided, unlike the academics he had been exposed to most of his life.

There were times when he could not help contrasting Arturo and Elena with his own parents, all four of them. Take that little thing called "respect." Up to now, the only respect he could remember getting had come from tiny children. His parents would be amazed if they saw the way he was deferred to in the Bonfante household. More than that. "*On t'aime, Peter, tu sais,*" Bonfante had told him today, his bright eyes softening, when they finally parted at the entrance to the Cour de Rohan; evidently he feared that he had hurt Peter's feelings. Peter had to admit that he found a declaration like that "supportive." When the *babbo* hurt his feelings by not taking him seriously, he was never even aware of it: "Why is the boy sulking?" he used to shout at his stepmother.

Still, a person had to be careful about letting anything positive that happened to him abroad influence him negatively about his own country and his home or homes. For one thing, the positive was so rare here for a foreigner that you felt like falling on your knees and kissing the hem of the garment of anybody who was kind to you, like the girl in the post office (he had been telling Arturo about her) who put new string for him on the messy Christmas package he brought to the window to mail to New York. Coming on an oasis in a desert made you tend to depreciate the well-watered pastures at home.

He entered his building. The curtain moved in the concierge's loge. A veinous hand extended. "*Votre courrier.*" There were four letters for him. One from his mother, one from his father, one from his former roommate, and one in a strange handwriting, with a Paris postmark on the envelope. He opened it. An invitation to sing Christmas carols next week at the house of some people whose name he did not recognize. On the bottom was written: "At the kind suggestion of Miss Roberta Scott."

His heart nearly stopped. He had made up his mind to go to Rome for Christmas, to get away from Paris and its clammy, unhealthy climate at least for a couple of weeks. The Bonfantes were taking their kids to ski in the Savoie during the *vacances scolaires.* That meant that if he stayed here he would be all alone over the holidays. He could make a call to his mother from the central post office on Christmas night, and that would be it.

If he went to the carol-singing, which was scheduled for the twenty-second, he would have to give up the project of riding his motorbike down through Provence and along the Riviera to Italy; he had studied the route on the map, to skirt snow-covered mountains, and, allowing for sightseeing, it looked as if it might take him a week to reach Rome at this time of year. Of course he could go by train, in a *couchette*, second class, again breaking a vow to the motorbike, but probably it was too late now to get a reservation—the Bonfantes had had theirs for a month. Every Christmas, they said, as soon as the schools closed, there was a mass exodus from Paris.

Even if he could get a place on the train, there was something else to consider. What if Roberta was staying here through the holidays instead of going off with the mob? He had not seen her now for nearly ten days. It would be madness to forgo the chance of having her all to himself in the empty city. The Institut Pasteur, where she worked, might not even *have* vacations. He halted on a landing and drew a deep breath. He felt the promise of Rome crumbling, like the plaster on the walls of the exiguous service staircase, and almost wished he had never got the invitation. At least he would have been spared what Mr. Small, he supposed, would call the decision-making process.

If he could just be sure that Roberta would be staying here, he would gladly renounce Rome. Obviously, he could call her up and ask her, and, if she said no, he would shoot over to American Express and try for a *couchette* on the train that left the twenty-third. That would be the rational approach. He fingered a *jeton* in his pocket, started slowly back down the stairs, vacillated. His whole upbringing fought against a rational approach. To boldly find out and act on the finding would be cheap. As his mother always said, you had to be willing to sacrifice. . . . But *how much*? Furiously, he ground his teeth. Nobody ever told you the specifics; you were just urged not to play it safe, Peter. He continued the ascent to his apartment.

At this stage in his life-history, Roberta's company ought to be worth more than all the churches of Borromini and the Sistine Chapel. Except that he could count on the Sistine Chapel's being there, which was more than he could say for Roberta. He would be glad to play it safe if he knew what safe was. If some friendly jackdaw were to fly down his airshaft with her pocket agenda in its bill! It was a case for a supernatural agency. Maybe he should consult his horoscope in the evening paper. Hating this bargaining his soul was doing with itself, he decided to toss a coin.

Joy to the World

IN his fifth-floor stronghold in the Albergo dei Re Magi, Peter put his eye to the keyhole and took a quick reconnaissance. The door of the WC, diagonally across from his room, was now ajar. He sped out of his room, shutting the door behind him without stopping to lock it, though he had left his wallet on the bed. There was not a second to lose. Even as he shot across the hall, other doors could be heard opening. If he had stopped to lock up, as the maid was always warning him to do, someone might have got there ahead of him, despite the favorable position his room occupied.

It was the same story as in those hotels in Paris. His day started with the race to the *gabinetto*; when he heard the ancient chain pull, he was on his mark. Followed the Herculean clean-up after its last tenant, only here he had to do it with sheets of thin slippery yellowish toilet paper, no brush being furnished. The big difference was that now he had a nice view through the open window of the red-tiled roofs of Rome and of plants growing in pots on neighboring balconies. Across lines of bright laundry, he could even see the pale moth-brown angels with folded wings, like life-jackets, on the strange bell tower of Sant'Andrea delle Fratte. Afterwards he could saunter out and have a *cappuccino* at the coffee-store opposite the Propaganda Fide, buy an orange and a sugar bun, and go back for a second *cappuccino*.

So that he was glad he had not let himself be discouraged by American Express: no *couchettes* available, first *or* second class. Sitting up all night on the ordinary slow train, he had fortified himself with the maxim of William the Silent, which he recited to the clacketing of the wheels: "*Il n'est pas nécessaire d'espérer pour entreprendre, ni de réussir pour persévérer.*" He did not know how the person they called "Guillaume le Taciturne" came to be part of French Civilization, but he gave a good mark to the professor for introducing the class to that thought. Part of the night he stood in the corridor, having relinquished his seat to a Frenchman with a hideous baby. When he unclosed his gummy eyes for the nth time, it was the dawn of

Christmas Eve; Italian officials were saying *"Buon giorno"* and asking for his passport and if he had any contraband. He was home.

Multas per gentes et multa per aequora vectus. Although it was a corny thing to do, after a late Roman supper of the traditional eels, he followed the crowd into midnight mass at Santa Maria Maggiore, by the station. They had a supposed relic of the Bambino's crib that the priests carried in procession, and some wonderful mosaics around the high altar were all lit up and shining like a holy fire. Near where Peter stood was a confessional box in which you could tell your sins in Esperanto. Afterward he lost his way and got swept along by another crowd, coming from the Aracoeli. Among these humbler worshippers were big dogs and a little goat, which he patted. He saw the statue, on horseback, of Marcus Aurelius and met the bagpipers from the Abruzzi, dressed like real shepherds, making their wailing music and passing a collection-plate. Returning to his hotel, he felt too excited to sleep.

The night porter, whom he woke up to get in, told him about a solemn mass at dawn in the church of Sant'Anastasia, at the foot of the Palatine; she had the same birthday as Jesus. He showed him how to find it on a map. It was another long walk. When Peter finally hit the sack after breakfast, he had not been to bed for two whole nights. That way, at least, he had circumnavigated Christmas. Waking up late that afternoon, he found it was already dark outside, since in Italy they did not have daylight saving in the winter. Moreover, it seemed to have rained. He put in a call to his mother and mailed his letters of introduction in the post office at San Silvestro, resigned to passing a solitary weekend on account of tomorrow being Saturday.

Incredibly, they all clicked. It was as if the lemons, cherries, oranges, and bells came up, one after the other, in some miraculous slot-machine attached to his telephone. Bonfante's sister invited him to lunch twice in her apartment; she was married to a professor at the University. A *contessa* who was an old friend of the *babbo*'s invited him to lunch too, with a pair of English pansies; she lived in an historic *palazzo*, and her men-servants wore white gloves. Another friend of the *babbo*'s took him to a dinner *in piedi*, which meant a buffet supper, on the

Via Appia Antica; that night he learned to do the twist. An art scholar Bob knew showed him through the *restauro*, where craftsmen dressed in white like surgeons operated on damaged frescoes, paintings, and sculptures. Everybody acted so sorry when they heard he had spent Christmas day alone, sleeping ("*Se avessimo saputo!*"), that he decided for the future to pretend he had not arrived till Christmas night.

It was an ill wind that blew nobody good. He now felt almost grateful for not having come on his motorbike. He would not have had room in his pack for the two changes of clothes with accompanying haberdashery that at the last minute he had stuffed into his suitcase. Even so, he had had to buy a new pair of too-wide black shoes on the Corso and he was thinking of taking the *babbo* up on the offer of a new suit. His father claimed to know a tailor here who could make him one in forty-eight hours for the price of a ready-made at home. He had instructed Peter not to let them put in any padding and to charge it, evidently suspecting that if he sent a check, Peter would just add the money to his savings and do without the suit. Or get a secondhand one at the old-clothes market near San Giovanni in Laterano, which in fact Peter had been eyeing —why squander a lot of *fric* on something that would hang uselessly in his closet once he got back to Paris? On the other hand, he had spilled *pasta* and Chianti several times on his gray flannel, and the talcum powder and salt they sprinkled on him did not wholly remove the spots.

His mother, too, on the telephone, had asked him about clothes. "But I won't *need* any, Mother. You sound as if I was going to have a Papal audience. What am I going to do with a lot of white shirts? All I have on my program is sightseeing and taking in a few movies." But it turned out that she was right. The Romans *were* hospitable, and Italian men, he had to admit, whatever their age and condition, wore dark suits, white shirts, and dark ties when invited out in the evening. He wondered what they put on, to mark the difference, when somebody died.

His mother wanted to know what had made him change his mind about the motorbike. Of course she was happy that he had, on account of icy roads, but she said that it did not sound like him to listen to the voice of reason. "It's too long a story,

Mother. I'll tell you some other time." "And, dearest, I don't understand why you didn't leave Paris sooner, since the weather there is so grim." "Neither do I," said Peter. "Hey, Ma, this is long distance! Let me say hello to Bob." Bob was inquisitive too. "What kept you so long in Paris? Was it the Smith girl or the beautiful vegetarian?" "Lay off," said Peter. "I had a lottery ticket, I had to study, I had a date with a Christmas carol. Pick the one that suits you." He was not going to confess that he had been holed up in dreary Paris all those extra days, as it turned out, *for nothing.*

He still writhed when he thought of the fool's paradise he had carefully constructed that had fallen ignominiously to pieces at the first contact with reality. Taking "*Qui ne risque rien n'a rien*" for his motto when actually the gamble had been all inside his own mind. On the creeping train, he had plenty of time for mortification. The only comfort he could find in contemplating his downfall was that nobody but himself knew how high he had been flying. Yet that was clammy comfort. If the sole witness to your disappointment was yourself, it indicated you were a weakling or, at best, a nut. Nobody could split his sides laughing at you but nobody could feel sorry for you either.

He could laugh, but without pleasure, at the picture of himself buttoned into his flannel suit, engraved invitation in his pocket, hopefully ringing a doorbell on the rue de Lille and then walking through a garden with statuary to a house with all the windows lit up. His boats were burned, except for a little life-raft—the assurance that at least he would see her at this songfest, and that, he had decided, was worth waiting for, whatever happened next. On purpose, he was late, so as not to be stuck with total strangers, and as his feet crunched on the gravel path he was chanting "*Auprès de ma Blonde*," for which he had invented some new words: "What would you give, my darling, to have your loved one home? I'd give the Sistine Chapel and Buónarróti's dome. The coins in the Trévi Fountain, the Pórta Pincíana walls. An ice cream at Rosáti's, the Villa d'Este falls." And all the while, the one eventuality that had not entered into his calculations was awaiting him, like death biding for Achilles at the Scaean Gate. She was not there.

Yet he had come to the right place. In a big high-ceilinged

room with French windows and heavy white draperies, he found a number of compatriots whom he had already met at a rally of Americans in Paris for Johnson, an organization about which he was having second thoughts; he wished he had back the tithe of his October allowance he had donated to the cause. Trying to quell his apprehension (she might be late or have gone to the bathroom), he shook hands with a corporation lawyer, a trustee of the American Hospital, two bankers, a minister, a management consultant, an author of a famous book he had seen the movie of, a Negro actor, a travel agent, a guy from the American Center, a professor who was writing a book on De Gaulle, and some miscellaneous women in glittering dresses; this, he guessed, was the infrastructure of what they called the American liberal community—plus the hostess' French teacher.

The hostess, a tall thin nervous blonde in a long gray velvet dress that matched the walls, was passing out mimeographed programs with the words and music and urging the guests into a small white music room that contained nothing but an expensive-looking clavichord, a music stand, and two gilt chairs. "Is everybody here?" she kept asking, tapping on a list. "Harry, is everybody here?" Her husband consulted *his* list, on which with a small gold pencil he had been putting little checks. He was tall too and wore a dark-gray velvet smoking jacket, gold-rimmed glasses, and a tie that looked like a stock. It came back to Peter that this guy had passed the hat for the Johnson outfit; he was a fund-raiser for an international church group. "I count one to come still. Shall we begin?"

In the general move forward, Peter found he was stepping on the hostess' skirt. While he was apologizing, the doorbell chimed three times. He gave a cry of relief. "Hey, that's her— Roberta!" "Roberta?" the woman said, still inspecting the damage to her train, on which Peter's foot had left a large damp print. "You mean Bobbie? But she's gone away. Didn't she tell you?" "Gone away? For *good*?" "No, no. Just for the holidays. She and her friend have a fascinating itinerary worked out. They're going to do Romanesque abbeys in Burgundy. Not just the obvious ones like Vézelay and Cluny but the little *recherchés* ones." "I guess she'll go to Autun," Peter said glumly. "Oh, surely. Do you know Gislebertus?" "Only from a book I had." For Christmas, he had sent his mother his copy of *Gislebertus, Sculpteur d'Autun* and some pans and a conical sieve called *le chinois* from the Samaritaine. Envy added to his sense of betrayal. He loved the little raisin-eyed people in that book, especially one of the Magi who looked like Harold Macmillan and a tiny brave naked warrior with a big dagger riding into combat on a gigantic bird.

The hostess was giving her cheek to the new arrival to be kissed and making purring noises. "So naughty of you to be late. Mr. Levi, here's another friend of Roberta's. Silly, do you know Peter Levi?" Peter recognized the heavy eyebrows and thick silken eyelashes of Silvanus Platt. "Hi."

"Will everybody put out their cigarettes, please?" With an ill grace, Peter let himself be lined up among the basses. He considered that he had been tricked into coming here. The invitation had not specifically said that Roberta would be present but it had certainly left itself open to that construction. Nor did he like the idea that the Princetonian, who sang tenor, had been seeing her unbeknownst to him.

His old antipathy to music-lovers refueled. There was no Yule log burning merrily in the living room, and he saw no sign of refreshments. Instead of pictures on the walls, they had gray blown-up photographs of prints of antique instruments. "Less is More" appeared to be the house rule. Everything was gray, black, or white. The hostess blew into a recorder, and the host tinkled away inaudibly on the clavichord—his wife's Christmas present to him. On the program, the words of the carols had been written out in olde Elizabethan spellyng with ampersands, which reminded Peter sourly of Rocky Port. He did not know any of the carols they had exhumed from library stacks and he could not read music, not that it mattered, since he was unable to stay on key. Most of the other carolers seemed to be in his situation. It made him think of those awful mornings in chapel when the headmaster decided to stir things up by posting a new hymn.

He would almost rather be lending volume to "O, Come, All Ye Faithful" or "Silent Night." It struck him that these rich amateurs needed somebody like his mother or Richard Dyer-Bennet to instruct them in the art of the possible. When they had carols at home or at his aunt Millie's, the sisters always included a few that everybody knew, like "What Child Is This?" which had the same tune as "Greensleeves," and "I Saw Three Ships Come Sailing In" and "Once in David's Royal City"—Peter was partial to hymns and carols that had Jews in them.

The purpose of tonight's exercise was obscure to him. If the hosts wanted to play a duet, why couldn't they do it by themselves, instead of recruiting a lot of supernumeraries and giving them sheets of music to hold in their hands as stage-props? The whole occasion was like a long-drawn-out punishment of Tantalus. He guessed there had been a fatal decision to do something "different" this year, which any child could have told them was playing with fire when it came to something like Christmas. Peter felt defrauded not only by the unfamiliar carols but by the tree this couple had, which was trimmed with glass icicles, transparent glass balls, and white roses and carnations that were distributed, when the program finally ended, to the guests according to sex.

At that point, the host ladled out some mulled wine which, the hostess explained, ought really to have been warmed with a hot poker instead of being heated up on the stove. People like that, Peter had noticed, seemed to think that knowing the right way of doing something excused you for doing it the wrong way, as though knowledge was all that mattered. Installing the carnation in his buttonhole, he decided that this could not be more different from the general's home atmosphere, and yet it seemed just as American, in a sinister way he could not define.

He was surprised that this pseudo-worldly pair knew Roberta well enough to refer to her as "Bobbie" and not so surprised that they knew Silvanus Platt, whom the hostess addressed as "Silly" and sometimes "Silly Boy." Peter hated to think what it must have been like for the poor guy in school. Tonight he was wearing a paisley waistcoat and a pocket watch with a gold chain on which hung a Phi Beta Kappa key. Maybe it was his father's, or he had bought it at a pawnshop. Even at Princeton, nobody could earn one before the spring of his junior year, and for that you had to burn the midnight oil, whereas Silvanus' specialty, it appeared, was burning the candle at both ends.

He was prattling to the hostess about girls, ski resorts, night clubs, poker, somebody's wine cellar. Peter was getting ready to make his escape when he heard the name Bobbie. Silvanus could not understand why a vegetarian teetotaler would want to do a tour of Burgundy, of all places, where the whole point was eating and drinking. To be fair, the same thought had crossed Peter's mind. "Food for the soul," the hostess said, puffing on a cigarillo. "You wouldn't dig it, Silly. Darling Bobbie has this *béguin* for the Romanesque. So pure and grand and austere." "But why does she have to go to Burgundy? Isn't there Romanesque around here?" "Nothing to write home about. Use your eyes, darling. Of course there's Normandy. Jumièges, which has some delicious Carolingian bits. And that one where they have the plainsong." "St.-Wandrille," supplied Peter. "But what's great here in the Ile-de-France is the Gothic. Have you been out to St.-Denis? You can see right there where it originated. And you don't have to have a car or anything." "Bobbie wouldn't *look* at a Gothic cathedral," said the hostess with a little laugh. "All those fussy crockets and overloaded gables."

"I *like* Gothic," protested Peter. In fact, one of his plans, if Roberta had stayed here for the holidays, had been to take her to look at Amiens, which, according to a book he was reading, was the Gothic Parthenon. To learn that she was a zealot of the Romanesque was another bad surprise. He felt a loyalty to the Gothic, which he regarded as his personal discovery, and the fact that there was a lot of it around, readily accessible to the modest Paris-based day tripper was an additional merit in his eyes. He had nothing against the Romanesque, as his love of Gislebertus proved, but a girl who could be unfair to Gothic cathedrals was not likely to care for Peter Levi, with his tall attenuated form and crazy soaring pinnacles. "You do?" said the hostess with a thoughtful air. "One has to see Chartres, of course. Marvelous. But Harry and I aren't so *emballés* by church architecture. We're mad on *châteaux*."

Peter remembered his mother saying that you could divide people into those who liked churches and those who liked *châteaux*. She meant the guided-tour kind where you admired the furniture, not ruined castles with dungeons, which you could visit by yourself. According to her, social climbers, even those claiming to be interested in art, got rapidly bored by churches unless they had lots of loot in them in the form of gold, marbles, and precious stones. She had a point, Peter decided, listening to this woman briefing Silly on the *hôtels particuliers* of the Marais. In his mind, he sketched a Last Judgment, with a Weighing of Souls: two little *château* people, resembling the hostess and her husband, were sitting in a balance pulled down by a horrible demon, while in the other basket he and his mother, light as eggs, were mounting upward, tenderly claimed by an angel holding the scales.

The party was breaking up. A servant opened the door to the dining room and then hastily closed it. No boar's head was forthcoming. A long table with twin candelabra was set for two. An insane thought struck Peter. All was not lost. What if he were to go to Autun tomorrow, on his own? It was as good a place as any to spend Christmas, and he had a fair chance of running into Roberta, provided he stayed put. She was bound to visit the cathedral, and he could entrench himself there with his binoculars. A guy could spend a week studying the tympanum and the capitals without getting too bored or (he hoped) catching pneumonia.

Silvanus, who had his coat on, was proposing they go eat some oysters. "OK, but wait a minute." Peter turned to the hostess. "Thank you for a nice time," he lied. Then he took the icy plunge. "I wanted to ask you something. About that tour Roberta and this girl are doing . . . I might be in Autun myself next week some time. . . . On my motorbike. It would be fun if we could make connections. I thought maybe you'd know what her plans were, more or less. I mean, is she going to Dijon first or . . . ?"

Something was wrong. The woman was looking at her husband and lifting a penciled eyebrow. "I haven't made up my mind yet," Peter continued, hedging. "There's this Pole who thinks he might come with me. But I might go to Rome instead. Though they say the trains are pretty full." The woman eyed her husband again. She made that purring noise. "Go to Rome, darling." Other guests were waiting to say good-bye. "Have a scrumptious Christmas." "See you at Klosters." Peter tried again. "About Autun—" The host put his oar in. "My wife says go to Rome. And my wife is a wise woman." He held out Peter's coat. Peter took umbrage. "I don't get it. What's the mystery? Why shouldn't I see Autun if I want to?" The woman gave her husband one of those shall-we-tell-him glances. "Of course you can see Autun. But you might be *de trop* right now. Don't look at me that way, Harry! After all, it's not a secret." She spoke loudly and defiantly, thrusting her pale head forward almost into Peter's face. "Bobbie isn't with a girl. She's with her *petit ami*."

"Cynthia," her husband sighed. She whirled. "I have a perfect right to tell him. Bobbie's my goddaughter. I'm her mother's oldest friend." "That's a funny reason, darling." "It's not!" "Well, thanks," put in Peter hastily. "Thanks a lot really. I wouldn't want to butt in. It was just an idea anyway. I can go to Autun some other time." "*Of course*," soothed the woman, resuming her social mask and turning to look at herself in a long mirror as though to make sure she had it on straight. "Probably I'm over-protective about Bobbie. But her friend is French and a little bit stuffy. He might not be pleased to have an American boy on his trail. Like one of her younger brothers." "'Sister, sister,'" said Silly Boy, "'what's that naughty man doing in your bed?'"

"Come on," urged Peter. "Let's go." He had no desire, not even a morbid one, to hear any more. But Silly was curious, so they had to stand there, with their coats on, listening to the gory details. The *petit ami* was a research doctor, separated from his wife. And Roberta's parents knew. "I imagine they expected something of the sort when they sent her over here. At home, she'd had an unhappy love affair with some man who lived on peanut butter and stood on his head." "Apple butter, darling." "Are you *sure*?" "Oh, absolutely." "Well, anyway, this young doctor couldn't be more normal and *comme il faut*. Does the *chasse à courre* on weekends. Bobbie's always been a passionate athlete. His not being divorced is a convenience, really. If she wants to go ahead with her career, she'll have another two years of medical school and then internship. And then the residency. It's a terribly sensible arrangement. If it lasts, she can do her internship at the American Hospital. None of the complications of marriage and the inevitable childen."

"Yeah, it makes sense," said Peter. Actually, to his stupefied brain, it made no sense at all. In his private order of credibility, a Roberta *dépucelée* ranked far below the Virgin Birth and the Immaculate Conception. If she had not been a virgin unspotted when he had met her at the general's on Thanksgiving, then he would swear no more oaths. But maybe even then she had been bedding down with this doctor. Maybe it had already happened with the headstander. His imagination balked at the thought, just as it had declined when he was little to picture his parents doing it; he preferred to think that he had originated in a cabbage leaf.

Yet had he not hoped to deflower Roberta himself? He was no longer sure. If he had, the hope had been founded on the sheer unlikelihood of the proposition. Hoping against hope seemed to be the only course open to him where sex was concerned. Imagining his own initiation by some practiced hand was repugnant. He did not want to be a hapless Adonis pursued by a hot-breathing Venus; rather, a pure mortal youth loved, while he slept, by a chaste Immortal, like the moon stealing down on Endymion. While feverishly dreaming of trapping the maiden in his snare, he had not once thought ahead to the act that presumably—what else?—would reward his devotion. His mind had drawn a veil. It was true that he had had a mild curiosity about her breasts, but really he had been enamored of her as a radiant totality that included her Waring Blendor and her nutty food ideas; if he had had to pick some part of Roberta that summed up the whole, it might have been those flags of color in her cheeks.

He did not know whether this was natural or whether it was not just another illustration of his being a grotesque anachronism. In movie houses he was always embarrassed to see couples pawing and nuzzling each other, on or off the screen. All he knew of love's raptures came from reading poetry, and the poets, like him, usually did not let their imagination stray much below the waist unless they were rejected and angry. Yet it looked as if the world had changed. To listen to most guys talk today, all they were interested in was some girl being "stacked" and whether or not they could "get laid" by her.

Peter had only fitfully had such coarse thoughts himself and then about streetwalkers or unattractive girls reputed to be pushovers. And when he had them, he was ashamed, since they violated the great commandment he still carried in his wallet:

"The Other is always an End: thy Maxim." If a woman was a tool for obtaining gratification for your tool, she could not be an end. Of course that was the whole logic of prostitution: you used them as a means of getting laid, and they used you as a means of getting dough. So that you could say that it all squared off there, in a sordid realistic way. And if a girl wanted sex and you wanted it too, that could be a deal, he supposed. But in those arrangements, he suspected, one party was usually cheating.

If memory was not lying to him, the *most* he had imagined with Roberta was taking her to Amiens on the train, taking her out to Trappes and showing her the moor hens and the field-fare in the winter ponds and hedges, maybe taking her skating on one of the big rinks, feeding her jasmin tea in his apartment and toast with rose-hip jam—little extensions of his confidence that implied no fell design. Yet as he walked with Silvanus toward St.-Germain-des-Prés, he discovered a strange thing. His love had died on the spot. One swift blow had done it. And he did not feel half as much anguish as when his plant had bit the dust. Only anger with himself and a sense of wasted time. Now he would have to begin all over, trying to find an interest in life beyond the daily grind. It was depressing not to have anything to look forward to any more. True, that had been his state when he had met her, so that he was only back where he had started. Yet there was a limit to a person's resilience. To be repeatedly sent back "home," like a man in parcheesi, by a single throw of the dice, could finally make you resign. Let the others play. Instead of going through the weary ordeal of trying to get to Rome, which would probably disappoint him, he could cable his family to send him an airplane ticket to New York. One-way.

In the café, over their second dozen oysters, annoyance with the virtuous Roberta began to surface. "Frankly, can you swallow that story? Do you see her checking into a hotel room with a man? After all, they ask you for your passport. Don't forget that." Silvanus nodded. "I would have bet anything she was a virgin," continued Peter. "Me too." "The fact that they travel together doesn't necessarily prove anything. Maybe they sleep with a sword between them." "The guy is French, remember?" "But I *saw* her about ten days ago. We went to a concert. She seemed just the same. You know, sort of fresh and wholesome, like an American apple." "The one the doctor ordered, ha ha. But she really was a nice dish." Silvanus fetched a sigh. "I took her out once myself. Skating." "Oh?" "That's all. We had fun. And she paid her own admission. There aren't too many attractions in Paris-after-dark for a vegetarian health fiend." "But that was what was so *misleading*," said Peter. "You assume that if somebody's a puritan, they're a puritan all the way down the line. You'd think you had the right to assume that." "Girls are funny." "Maybe being a vegetarian is the explanation. A person's physical nature has to find *some* outlet. A girl that doesn't drink or eat meat and butter and stuff is available for sex, no?" Silvanus shook his head. "In my experience, you have to get them a little high the first time. Not loaded, because they might be sick, but high."

Peter remained silent. He was thinking that if he went on a strict vegetarian diet, he might be able to lose his own virginity. "You can usually tell," Silvanus went on, "when a girl will. I mean, when a nice girl will. I can't stand tramps." "How do you tell?" "Oh, there are lots of little ways. Sometimes I study them when they come out of the Alliance Française. . . . Some of those Swedish chicks are virgins. Contrary to what you hear."

They ordered a third dozen oysters. Silvanus was having Belons, and Peter was sticking with Claires. "Silvanus—" "Call me Silly, if you want. I don't mind. In fact I'm learning to love it. It disarms the opposition. If you can get a woman to call you Silly, you're in. Especially an older woman. 'Oh, Silly, don't do that!'" He mimicked a female voice. Peter sought another topic. There was a question he had been wanting to ask. "What kind of a name is Silvanus?" "It comes out of the Bible—the Epistles. He was one of Saint Paul's disciples. It's another name, most likely, for Silas, in Acts. There were a lot of Congregational ministers in my father's family, way back, and in each generation we have a Silvanus. People think a name like that is a handicap. They're so wrong. In the first place, it helps you develop an armor early. Second, it makes the general public remember you: girls, headmasters, professors, party-throwers. Third, it makes the whole world feel sorry for you. 'How could your parents have been so cruel as to give a tiny child a burden like that to carry through life?'" Peter gave a weak assenting grin. "Fourth, it's a conversation-starter. If somebody you meet asks you your first name and you say 'Peter,' that's the end of it. No mileage. But if they ask *me* my name, it's an opening for me. Right away, like you, they want to know what kind of a name is that, and we're off."

"Don't you ever get fed up with explaining it?" "No. Why should I? It's less of a drag to repeat something you already know than to try to think up some boring fresh gambit. Anyway, I vary it a little. I haven't given you the bit about Silvanus, Roman god of woodlands, hence 'sylvan.' My uncle Sylvy goes to town on that, reciting Vergil and Horace. '*Horridi dumeta Silvani* . . .' It's a ball. Then there's the bit about Silas being maybe one of the authors of the Gospels." "I never heard of that." "Neither have most people. But you're interested, aren't you?" "Well, mildly. Go on." "No, I just wanted to show you the possibilities. At some point, the other person, if it's a girl, chimes in with 'Don't you think children should be allowed to choose their own names?' Or 'I love the name "Ermentrude," but I wonder if I'd have the courage . . .' Did you notice the time when we ordered these last oysters? 'Silvanus,' if you include 'Silly,' is usually good for a fifteen-minute chat."

Peter burst out laughing. He was warming to this boy, who reminded him of someone, though not physically. He searched his memory. Someone he knew quite well, he thought . . . Then he got it. It was himself. As he might be in the fourth dimension, turned inside out. Or reincarnated. "I think a lot," explained Silvanus. "Though I'm not meant to be very brainy. My brother Barnabas got all the gray matter in the family. But I analyze situations and work out strategies. And I study people. While I'm talking to them, I'm watching their reactions to me. I couldn't do that if I was self-conscious, like you. You have to practice to develop your armor."

"You're a funny guy," said Peter. "Let's see each other when I get back." "Where are you going?" "To Rome, I guess. Would you like to come along?" "I've got to go to Klosters. With Cynthia." He raised his eyebrows suggestively. "You mean that woman tonight? But she's old enough to be your mother!" "Hardly. She may be old enough to be somebody's mother, but *my* mother is *old*." "Doesn't her husband suspect?"

"So what? He's probably used to it. She says he's impotent. They're 'like brother and sister.' Though they all say that." "But weren't you talking to her about girls tonight?" "I make a point of that. It lets her know I'm a free agent. You know, just a butterfly flitting from flower to flower. And it makes her feel brave and generous. Actually, she's rather a tightwad. Or maybe it's him. She comes from one of those breakfast-food families—Grape-Nuts or Ralston's, I forget. But they play poor little church mice, squeak, squeak. In Klosters they have a rather grand chalet. Bobbie stayed there. But I don't expect Santa Claus will put much in poor Silly Boy's stocking. No Cartier watches or diamond cuff links. Something thoughtful, for his soul. *Timeo Danaos et dona ferentes*, as my uncle Sylvy says when he goes to stay with our rich cousin. They're paying my air fare and sending a car to meet me, which is a help, but then there are the tips to the servants and my own wee thoughtful presents. . . ."

"You shouldn't go," said Peter, "if you dislike that Cynthia as much as you give the impression." "Do I sound as if I disliked her?" "Yes." "It's so hard to know what one feels, really. But in cold, cruel fact, I confess I'm going for the skiing. It's my first crack at the Swiss Alps. I couldn't pass that up, don't you see? Then I have this dream. . . ." "What's your dream?" prompted Peter, looking at him with curiosity. Silly crossed his fingers; he knocked on wood. "To get taken on as a ski instructor," he confided. "You're kidding." But Silly was serious. "A guy I know put me on to it. The thing is, you have to connect with some English-speaking group that wants lessons. The instructors up there only know how to talk German, so it's an opportunity for an American to cash in. Unbelievable!" He sighed. "With my room and meals free, I could clear maybe a hundred and fifty dollars. This guy knew another kid who did it last year." And unlike this other kid, Silly had experience. He had been a ski instructor before once in Vermont; a family had hired him to teach their children. But it was easy; anybody could do it that understood the fundamentals. The problem was really contacts. Harry and Cynthia would have to fix it so that he could meet the English and American crowd. "I haven't told her yet. She says she wants to be 'quiet.' I've got to make her give a party for me, right away, when I get there. She has to see how important that is for me." He wiped some little beads of sweat from his forehead. "But don't the people who go to a fancy place like that already know how to ski?" "Yes, but there always have to be first-timers, who want to make it socially. They feel out of it, not knowing how to ski and not knowing the language. That's where my English comes in. I can organize them in a class. It's a question of finding them before they sign up with another group. You can give private lessons too, if you get known. Rich guys and women who need some special attention."

Peter listened dubiously. It seemed clear that this far-fetched project was close to Silly's heart. Maybe kids on their own over here got that way when they overspent their allowance. To deter him was probably impossible, yet Peter felt he should try. Perhaps it was his own pessimistic nature, but he was convinced that nothing would materialize for poor Silly up in those Alps but sorrow and disappointment. Even if he could connect with a job, the woman would find means of keeping him away from it. She had looked tough and selfish, Peter thought, and she was not paying Silly's expenses to have him gamboling on the slopes with other women and girls. In Paris, he might be a free agent, but in a chalet he would be her plaything, like a talking doll.

He pointed that out. "Yes, I know. It could turn out like that. I told you it was my *dream*. The old fairy gold. And if the weather should suddenly get bad, it could be a grim little house party. They play cribbage, and Harry does petit point. And they believe in keeping the heat way down and wrapping themselves in shawls. If they turned up the thermostat, somebody might think they were Americans." He became extremely dejected. In Peter's private book of Leviticus, there was a special law for parents and other moral teachers which he was forgetting: never throw cold water on an enterprise unless you can offer an alternative. "Listen, Silly," he suggested, "why don't you go to Switzerland on your own? You could get taken on as a ski instructor just as well in some other center. Then you'd be independent, don't you see? The fact that you haven't told her shows you're worried yourself about how she'll react. You could go to Saint-Moritz or . . . What are those other ones?" "Gstaad, Davos, Zermatt." "Yes, why not one of those?

You could post notices in the hotels. 'Experienced American gives skiing lessons.'" He hoped he was sounding persuasive. It was not easy. His ignorance of winter sports, except skating, was deep and principled. Personally, he would much rather be drafted into the Army than arrive seeking employment in a mountain village packed with sunburned skiers who knew not Peter Levi. But Silly was manifestly different. He knew his way around.

"It's too late. I promised. Besides, I'm stony. Really stony." Peter reflected. A man of words and not of deeds was like a garden full of weeds. "I can lend you some dough, if you like. I have plenty. You can pay me back out of your profits. And, listen, you don't need to take a plane. There are trains. And if you don't land a ski-instructor job right away, you might be able to wait on table. Or baby-sit. A lot of families take their kids with them to the *sports d'hiver*." "Thanks. I can baby-sit in Paris if I want to." His voice was dry, and he was regarding Peter with something like pity—or was it simple amusement? —from behind that fringe of eyelashes. Peter saw that he had made an error in strategy: the battle for Silly Boy's soul was over. He did not know why he had wanted to reclaim the foolish youth, unless he felt he had "good stuff" in him, as the headmaster used to say about some hopeless delinquent. Without further discussion, they rose. Silly covered a yawn and wound a long white cashmere scarf around his neck. They had paid the bill. "Thanks, honestly, for the offer of the loan. It was a nice thought. My ransom." "Well, have a good vacation anyway." "You too. I can't wait to get on those slopes and pick up a tan. Fresh air and exercise!"

In Rome there were fresh air and exercise, as well as churches, fountains, hills, domes, sword-brandishing angels, *palazzi*, clocks, bells, and friendly inhabitants. Investigating Rome, Peter was happy. It was a nice town to walk in, despite hazardous traffic, and, on his father's recommendation, he had bought himself the T.C.I. guidebook, in Italian, from a pushcart near the Porta Pia that specialized in secondhand guides. He was philosophical about overcast skies and the few drops of rain; they made him appreciate the brilliant days in between, when the sky looked like a tent of pale-blue silk stretched over a circus of gravity-defying shafts, towers, lanterns, flying statuary.

Imperial Rome did not interest him greatly, but he liked the early Christian churches, especially Santa Maria in Cosmedin. In the Piazza Navona, he loved the stalls set up for the Befana with candies and toys and crib figures of the animals and the shepherds and the Magi; there were dolls of knights in armor and beautiful ladies like the Queen of Night and Harlequins and Franciscan friars and, naturally, tanks and spacemen and bombers in plastic, which would eventually no doubt take over, but it had not happened yet.

He made a pious pilgrimage to San Giovanni dei Fiorentini and he looked in on San Luigi dei Francesi, where the priests were French. He visited the ghetto, entering by a street with a name like the Wailing Wall—Via del Pianto. It was not the Jews, though, that were meant to be weeping but the Virgin Mary, in a little hidden church around the corner. The guidebook said she was crying on account of the stubborn *Ebrei*, who would not recognize her son as their saviour—he was glad to see from the kosher signs that they were still holding out, because when they were converted, it would be the millennium, and the world would come to an end. Nearly everywhere he went, he met the bagpipers from the Abruzzi, and everywhere, like an aura, there was the inviting smell of roasting coffee.

In Rome, he never got lonely, he found; there was always somebody eager to start a conversation and to compliment him on his Italian: "*Come parla bene!*" And waiters and countermen and sacristans, like the old woman who sold him his breakfast orange, all wanted to hear him say that their country was beautiful. "*E bella l'Italia, signorino?*" "*Si, si!*" At night in his room, he studied the guidebook, preparing the next day's expedition. This gave him a purpose in life; he could hardly wait for the morning to get up, run the gauntlet to the toilet, shave, and foray out. His hotel, it turned out, was in Borromini territory, which he took as a sign; he was resolved to see all the master's works and he was succeeding, though some were hard to get in to, with peculiar visiting hours or keys to be hunted down. "*E chiuso! E chiuso!*" a voice would bawl from a neighboring top-story window. But in Rome, unlike Paris, they

eventually relented, just as in Rome they would let you stay in
a museum till closing-time.

The only drawback about dear cracked Borromini was that
so often you had to see Bernini, his cruel worldly rival, beside
him or combined with him or sneering at him, as in the fountain in Piazza Navona, where the Nile was supposed to be
covering its face so as not to have to look up at the "top-heavy"
façade of Sant'Agnese and the Plate shuddering and raising its
hand to keep it from falling down, like those joke photos of
tourists holding up the Tower of Pisa. Peter hated Bernini and
made the sign of the figs at him whenever he could, unobserved. He personally could not find anything to object to in
the proportions of Sant'Agnese, except that the saint's statue
with her finger pointing to her breast was perched on one end
of the front balustrade rather than in the middle: where were
the other "errors" that Bernini found so laughable? He bought
a jumbo postcard of the piazza and sent it to Bob, with an
arrow pointing to the church and the message "What's wrong
with this picture? Please inform. Peter."

He was starting to acquire catalogues, postcards, large glossy
reproductions; he invested in a pocket history of architecture,
a pocket-mirror to look at the ceiling of the Sistine Chapel, a
pocket engagement book, a notebook in which to scribble his
reflections. He even wished he had a camera with him. Or that
he had been taught how to draw. Though he used to chide his
mother for extravagant purchases of postcards, telling her she
should rely on her memory, he now felt heartsick when at
Anderson's they could produce only one measly reproduction
of the marvelous bird angels nesting in the vaults of San
Giovanni in Laterano. He had hoped to find a whole flock of
particolari to choose from, to remind him, back in Paris, of
the morning he discovered that fantastic aviary of cherubs and
nearly fainted with pleasure.

If it had not been for Borromini, Peter was not sure that he
would have liked the Baroque and he wondered whether he
did not like *him* for what somebody like Bob might consider
the wrong reasons—because of the downy pennate creatures
he put everywhere, standing in belfries and nesting in vaulted
ceilings, hiding in egg-and-dart moldings, pretending to be
columns, peeking down from pediments. Borromini must have

loved wings, since he usually gave his angels two pairs, like little garments, one folded and one open. And he loved stars,
vegetables, leaves, acorns, flowers. Peter got attached to the
dainty rhymes of concave and convex that seemed to be the master's "language" and to the ribbony movement of plaster around
windows that reminded him of his mother's boiled frosting as it
swirled from her knife onto a birthday cake. He sensed coded
messages coming from Mother Nature in the giant heads of the
stern-eyed falcons (they had breasts like women) surmounting
pillars on Palazzo Falconieri and in the acorns that hung like
earrings on the Sapienza and on the Propaganda Fide, piercing
small holes in its stone flesh. The guy had a strange sense of
humor. Yet Bob said he had committed suicide.

When he looked at Borromini, instead of thinking about
space and "volumes," Peter had the feeling he used to get from
fairy tales: that the world was in constant metamorphosis.
Capitals and columns were turning into vegetable and bird
forms; doors and windows were faces with ears. Invariably, he
was the only visitor to those hidden chapels and oratories—as
if he was the sole member of the human species who, led by
some croaking frog or talking raven in the shape of an ancient
custodian, had ever been introduced into those zoomorphic
interiors, which were buried, like the kernel of a walnut or the
secret of life, inside a neutral brown, hard-to-crack shell. Nobody would guess, for instance, that the vast Propaganda Fide,
bustling with missionaries, across from where Peter had his
morning *cappuccino*, concealed the little cenacle of the Re
Magi, though the name of Peter's hotel was a sort of password,
if anybody stopped to think. Even the light that streamed in
there seemed to be a visitor guided by a special angel.

When Bob's friend Sergio was taking him to lunch, at a
place called Il Buco, Peter broached the subject: where could
he find a good book on Borromini? He had been reconnoitering the bookshops to no avail. Naturally there wasn't one, at
least that Sergio knew of, unless Peter read German. He
seemed surprised by Peter's interest. Like most older people
(he was thin, elegant, and fortyish, with wrinkled laughing
eyes), he began digging for a motive. Was Peter planning to
study architecture? Was he taking a course in the Baroque?
That a layman could "just like" Borromini sounded pretty

evasive; it was the same as with watching birds or keeping a plant in your room. A full explanation was called for, though if a kid was interested in cars, nobody asked him if he was planning to be a garage mechanic. When Peter ticked off the churches and chapels he had been visiting, Sergio threw up his hands. "*Come mai? Un ragazzo di dicianove anni!*" He could hardly believe that a nineteen-year-old with no training in art would simply look under "Borromini" in the guidebook and follow up the page references—seventeen, to be exact. "*In Francia ti piaceva il barocco?*" Peter had been unaware that there was such a thing in Paris as the "Jesuit style"—the French name, it appeared, for the Baroque—and did not think he had seen any examples of it. "*Ma certo. Les Invalides!*" And the church of the Sorbonne, for that matter, which was practically in Peter's backyard. "*E un capriccio*," summed up Sergio, who in reality liked Borromini himself. A restless genius who came from the north and had not fitted into the Roman Counter-Reformation picture. His filiation was Gothic, and if Peter wanted to trace his influence, he should go to Turin. . . .

Hearing the word *Gothic*, Peter experienced a funny thrill. The short hair, newly clipped by a barber, rose lightly on the back of his neck, and he shivered. It was a moment of confirmation. The *principium individuationis* had affirmed itself in the seemingly chaotic perceptions of that *flatus voci*, Peter Levi. There was a *reason* underlying his old predilection for Borromini which, independently of any instruction, had brought about an act of recognition, just as had happened to him with St.-Denis and the Abbé Suger. His choices were stemming from an inner unity, a Tree of Knowledge branching in him. Contrary to what he always feared, the objective world and Peter Levi were in touch with each other. He existed, he was real. If asked to write a paper on "Gothic Elements in the Borrominian Structure," he could not point to any. But they were there, art historians knew about them, and his soul had felt their presence. The hair on the back of his neck subsided; he supposed this was the closest he would come to having a mystical experience. Seeing him shiver, Sergio was afraid that he might be catching a cold. The Roman winter was treacherous; you had to be careful about sitting on the Spanish Steps in the sun.

Peter laughed. He knew he was not going to get sick in Rome; he had too much to see and in such a short time. Feelings of power and mastery coursed through him. He accepted a *grappa* on the house. Leaving the restaurant, he realized that the thing tourists always talked about had happened. He had fallen in love with Rome. When and if he loved a girl really, it would be something joyful like this. And Rome was reciprocating. As his mother said, it took two.

That afternoon, when the stores opened, he went shopping. He picked out an umbrella for Elena Bonfante and a bold striped tie for Arturo, pink gloves for his mother's birthday, and a handkerchief for his landlady. He stopped in at the *babbo*'s tailor and had his measurements taken. In the Piazza Navona he had a stand-up coffee and a chocolate *tartufo* and chose some crib figures of shepherds and the Three Kings to be distributed to his half-brother and -sister and the Bonfante children.

Everything seemed cheap here, in comparison with Paris. In restaurants you could eat just one course if you wanted or take half an order of *pasta*. Moreover, they were nice about cashing checks at American Express. In the post office at San Silvestro, they had typewriters, free, for sending cables on which, with two fingers, Peter tapped out short letters home. At San Silvestro, they wrapped up his packages, at practically no cost, for mailing to America, and the public scribe sewed a dangling button on his raincoat. He left his watch to be cleaned because in Rome he did not need it; every quarter of an hour, wherever you were, a half-dozen church bells sang out the time. In the market, he bought *tuberose* for the kind plump signoras who invited him to meals, and when he climbed on a trolley bus with them, during the noon rush, the other passengers would smile and make room for him, so the flowers would not get crushed; everybody commented on the fragrant smell ("*Che profumo!*"), as though he were making a donation to the general happiness.

In the narrow streets of Vecchia Roma and in Trastevere, he saw scabby palaces and tenements and plenty of poor people, but this did not upset him the way it would have in Paris. On sunny days, caged birds swung from windows, women sat mending in their doorways, workmen making deliveries sang.

Watching a handsome woman drawing water from a fountain, he did not stop to think that this meant she had no *acqua corrente* where she lived. He guessed it was true that poverty seemed more acceptable in warm countries.

The world's problems did not clamor at him for solutions here. When he passed the Senate in Palazzo Madama (*notevole facciata barocca*) or the Chamber of Deputies in Palazzo Montecitorio (*iniziato nel 1650 dal Bernini*), it was hard to remember that there were legislators inside fighting. *Ars longa vita brevis* was a truth that could not be argued with in the Eternal City, where the monuments were big and the inhabitants rather small and grasshopper-like. He endorsed the *apertura alla sinistra* without feeling too hopeful about what it could accomplish. The very fact that the Roman poor seemed so exceedingly numerous compared to the Roman rich made you doubt that land reform or redistribution of wealth could do much to change what looked like a natural state of affairs.

The *Messaggero*, which he read in preference to the *Corriere* and *La Stampa*, was short on what were known as current events and long on the *cronaca* of local stabbings, shootings, poisonings, suicides, frauds, burglaries, arson, as well as national scandals involving adulterate wine, milk, olive oil, building cement; it also featured avalanches, train wrecks, floods, explosions, and ordinary traffic deaths. Each day on finishing the paper, Peter marveled that there was anybody left around to read it, except the police and the fire brigade. He was amused by the thrifty Roman house-painters, who at work wore hats made of folded newspapers, shaped like children's paper boats, from which stared gruesome headlines: BRUCIATO VIVO, STRANGOLATA, IL MOSTRO DELL'AVENTINO. He would be sorry to get back to a town where nothing much seemed to happen but world news and addresses by General De Gaulle.

That was not how the Romans felt. They envied him for living in Paris. To them, it was the main stream. It startled him to find that an American kid domiciled on the Rive Gauche was welcomed here as an authority on what was taking place in the headquarters of fashion, art, music, theatre, NATO, avant-garde politics, and *le nouveau roman*. He was expected to bring the word on hair styles, the Salon de l'Automobile, Althusser, who Sartre was dating, Britain and the Common Market, poor old

Khrushchev's fall. Examined by the *contessa* on structuralism and Malraux's cultural offensive, he began to wonder whether he had actually been living in Paris, so much seemed to have been going on there that he knew nothing about. At the same time, being an American, he was supposed to be up on the Berkeley Free Speech movement, President Johnson's cardiograms, the Alliance for Progress, did-the-CIA-kill-Kennedy? Above all, Vietnam. What was the public sentiment on peace negotiations? Troop commitment? Bombing Hanoi?

"But I haven't been home since early October," he repeated. "All I know about America is what I read in the paper." They read the papers too and more attentively than Peter did—that was obvious. "*Questo Mario Savio, com'è?*" To the disappointment of the Roman academics, Peter had no firm position, one way or the other, on the free-speech controversy. "Berkeley is horrible," he explained. "One of my stepfathers used to teach there. You have to swear a loyalty oath. It's like a great big factory. I guess it's natural that the students would finally rebel." But Bonfante's brother-in-law, who had met a professor from Berkeley last year at the American Academy, was receiving weekly bulletins that he wanted confirmation for: would Peter agree that the student organizers were using neo-fascist methods? Peter could not help him. He was almost ashamed to say that his father, in his letters, had never mentioned the topic. "Wellesley's a long way from Berkeley, you have to realize."

When pressed about civil rights, he was more in touch. But not enough. His questioners were sure that, living in Paris, he must have met James Baldwin. "No. Our paths never crossed." "*Strano. A Lei non interessa il problema dei neri?*" "*Sì!*" What was strange to Peter was the assumption they made that, in his place, they *would* know James Baldwin and Samuel Beckett and Graham Greene and the widow of Richard Wright, not to mention Professor Lévi-Strauss and Professor André Chastel and a cross-section of French students. For them, Paris was a city of opportunities, of lost opportunities as far as Peter was concerned. His only score, in their eyes, was meeting an American general, which was the part of his Parisian experience he would soonest have done without. "*E cosa diceva del Vietnam, questo generale?*" "*Stupidaggini.*" He refused to enlarge. Among these curious, albeit "concerned" Italians, he felt a certain protective loyalty to his country, and to quote some of the general's utterances might help make them come true, like a bad dream told before breakfast.

That insane news-hunger was the only side of the Romans with which he could find fault. It continually amazed him that people privileged to live in this wonderful ocher- and tangerine-colored city of cypresses, fairly frequent blue skies, art, and parasol pines should be so concerned with information feed-in, storage, and retrieval re the darkling plain he had been inhabiting and was fated soon to return to. He supposed it was in their tradition—"*nihil humanum mihi alienum puto*"—but to him they were most human when, like the *Messaggero*, they concentrated on the *cronaca*. As his time grew shorter, he sought asylum in the Vatican, having finished his Borromini itinerary. In the Sistine Chapel, he could be safe from nine until closing-time.

A Sibylline Interlude

O N the day after New Year's, Peter sat down on his accustomed bench, just outside the marble screen, facing the Delphic Sibyl. This would be his last crack at the Michelangelos, since he planned to leave on Tuesday. Sunday the museum would be closed, and Monday Sergio was taking him in a car to Frascati, to see a villa with the ultimate Borromini. The place was already packing up with guided tours. He recognized the busload of Germans who had invaded his hotel the night before and monopolized the toilet since shortly after dawn. But he had learned not to be bothered by the crush of humanity and the horrible Babel of tongues; his most recent acquisition was a pair of ear-stoppers. In the summertime, he understood, the crowds were a lot worse; the room actually stank. The thing to do then, he guessed, was to carry your private Airwick. Modern society provided its own antidotes, if you were resourceful enough to apply them in emergencies not dreamed of by the manufacturer.

At this season, though, for ten minutes at a time the chapel would be almost empty, as though a tide had receded; the throng would rush off into the Stanze di Raffaello. When the Sistine Chapel was full, the "School of Athens" was practically deserted, and vice versa. An oceanographer might be able to chart these human tides and currents, which had a strange regularity of ebb and flow. During one of the longer ebbs, this morning, as Peter trained his pocket-mirror on the vault above, stopping now and then to consult his books of reference, he became aware of a short, vaguely familiar figure sitting on a bench against the entrance wall, beneath the Prophet Zechariah: Mr. Small, his adviser, but wearing the beginnings of a reddish beard, a turtle-necked jersey, baggy pants, boots, and a duffle coat. He looked like one of the older Beats on the Spanish Stairs.

Peter for a minute was not sure it was him, and the professor gave no sign of recognition. Maybe that was understandable. From the point of view of the other, each of them was in disguise. In their previous encounters, *he* had been unshaven, tieless, in his sheepskin coat, whereas Small had been wearing a tweed jacket, a woolen necktie, and loafers. Now Peter was attired in the *babbo*'s new suit and had recently had a haircut and a shoeshine. It was as if they had exchanged clothes, like Leporello and Don Giovanni.

Peter wondered whether he ought to speak. His adviser might be ignoring him on purpose. He might be here in Rome on some squalid adventure. Mysteriously, he was not looking at the frescoes; he was making notes on a pad. Every time a new tourist or group entered, he scribbled. You would have thought he was taking attendance. Now his eye was roving over some Italian schoolgirls led by their priest in a cassock. Humbert Humbert had been a professor too. But the little girls moved on, into the inner chapel, and Mr. Small's scrutiny turned to some elderly American women with glasses around their necks. Maybe he had a rendezvous here, and the other person was late. Golly, what if he was working for the CIA? They met their contacts in funny places.

Eclipsed behind a mass of turbaned Indians surrounding a lady guide, Peter considered this hypothesis. If you could believe Makowski, at least half the American professors doing "research" abroad were on the CIA payroll. He said one of them had tried to recruit him to write weekly reports on pro-Peking activities in the Institute of Oriental Languages. When Makowski ("for kicks") made up his mind to play along, two agents took him, blindfolded, in a car to an apartment in the suburbs with the shades drawn, where they gave him a lie-detector test, which he flunked. That was the most believable part of the story, Peter had promptly decided, but now he began to wonder. . . . Makowski's assignation with the Spooks had been guess where? At the Cluny Museum, in front of the "Lady and the Unicorn."

In the doorway, two young U.S. Air Force men, with crew cuts, seemed to be asking directions. Then they shouldered their way forward to the "Last Judgment," which they stood contemplating, their hands on their hips. The professor followed in their wake and edged himself onto a bench at the far end, beneath the Prophet Jeremiah. Peter rose to get a better view. For all he knew, the Sistine Chapel, on account of Michelangelo, might be a well-known pick-up point for foreign queers. If he spoke, it might embarrass his adviser. On the other hand, it might be a kindness to let him know he was observed. Collecting his gear, Peter quickly installed himself opposite, below the Libyan Sibyl. "Hi, Mr. Small."

The professor raised his small pale eyes. "Why, it's Levy!" he cried. "For the Lord's sake, what are you doing here?" He appeared pleased and surprised to meet Peter, who politely took out his ear-plugs and joined him on the other bench. "Come out and have a smoke." Peter shook his head. "This is my last day here, and I don't want to lose too much time. You see, it was closed yesterday, on account of the holiday. And this morning I was late because of some Germans in my hotel." "Germans?" "They moved in on the toilet so that nobody else had a chance. There's only one toilet to the floor, and they had a big guy standing guard outside it. So I had to wait for American Express to open. It's around the corner from where I'm staying. But I found out they keep the cans there locked. Some stupid new rule. You have to ask a clerk for the key." Mr. Small evinced sympathy. He asked some questions about Peter's hotel. Then he started taking an interest in the T.C.I. guidebook and the *Itinerario Pittorico dei Musei Vaticani*, which had slid from Peter's lap to the floor. The professor picked them up and examined them. "Where did you find these?" he asked sharply.

Peter began to tell about the secondhand-book cart, but Mr. Small, as though dissatisfied with this explanation, leafed through them frowning and pulling curiously at the red and green ribbons that were marking Peter's place. You would think he had come upon some undecipherable Roman papyrus or scrolls from the Dead Sea. The T.C.I. volume with its folding maps and plans appeared to fascinate him. "It's just the ordinary Touring Club guide," Peter felt obliged to point out. "They have them for all the big cities and the different provinces. Like the *Guides Bleus* in France, only these give you better information." The professor read aloud the date on the copyright page. "Nineteen-forty! Lordy me, couldn't you find something more contemporary?" Peter had not noticed how old his treasured guide was. "'*Ristampato giugno 1957*,'" he said, reclaiming it. "My mother used to go around with a pre-war Baedeker and a guy called Augustus Hare."

Mr. Small leaned his head back and let his eyes rest on the ceiling. "I never carry a guide or a map. Of course I'm a very visual person. If art doesn't say something to me directly, without mediation, I'm not interested. When I visit the Sistine Chapel, I don't need all that fine print to tell me what I've been experiencing. Wonderful colors, beautiful forms, marvelous light. You ought to get rid of that portable reference shelf. And these crowds here, contemporary, constantly changing, are just as exciting as any fresco." The word *contemporary* was high on Peter's aversion list, and it seemed to be a favorite with people who weren't. The fact that his adviser thought he was being helpful did not lessen Peter's annoyance. He hated being told how he could save his labor, which nine times out of ten only showed the other person's ignorance. "You haven't really seen the Sistine Chapel unless you've studied it," he objected. "You just think you have. I made that mistake myself when I came here with my mother a few years ago. But there's an awful lot going on in that ceiling. Like those *putti* holding up the pillars. You don't notice them at first. They sort of emerge if you sit here long enough, like animals that will come out if you wait in the woods without making any noise. And those other *putti* on the tablets beneath the Prophets and the Sibyls. Look at that scowling one, under Daniel. He's having a tantrum. That's what's so great about books. They make you see things you might have missed on your own. There are two kinds of *putti*, one flesh-colored and the other marble-colored. And they have different personalities."

Needless to say, Mr. Small had been unaware of any *putti*. He had not even observed the *ignudi*, those heroic pagan youths with laurel wreaths and prominent penises of whom Peter was particularly fond and who, to his eyes, practically whirled off the ceiling at you, like naked athletes playing a game of Statues. To cover up this oversight on the part of his adviser ("*Where?* . . . Oh, yes, of course"), Peter started discoursing about the spandrels. "See those triangles, over the windows. They're supposed to show the ancestors of Christ. But there must be more to it than that. To me there's something sad and almost sinister about them, sort of crouching in the shadows or just staring ahead into space. As though the light of Genesis had gone out or dimmed, like a bulb fading.

Look at that young mother there, just above us, next to Jeremiah. Between him and the Persian Sibyl. She's got on a pale-green blouse and a yellow skirt. Well, she's cutting her skirt with a big shears. Why? For that, you'd have to know the story, and these books I've got don't tell it. So if I want to understand, I need *more* books, don't you see? Like the Bible." He offered his adviser the mirror. "Can you make out the scissors? The other day a lady let me use her opera glasses. I forgot my binoculars in Paris."

Mr. Small handed back the mirror. "Primitive people often cut up their clothes as part of the mourning ritual. I believe it is still customary among orthodox Jews." "I bet you're right! Hey, you've got it, Mr. Small! What do you suppose she's mourning?" "Perhaps the Babylonian Captivity. 'By the waters of Babylon.' But there's no need to look for literal meanings in these accessories. We're not interested in those old Bible tales; probably Michelangelo wasn't either. He had to put them in to satisfy the Pope and his court. What he really cared about, being an artist, was form, line, color. For him, the whole cycle might as well have been an abstract design. Why make a puzzle out of it?" "You're so wrong, Mr. Small," said Peter, his voice rising. "Michelangelo wanted to *say* something. I haven't got the whole message yet, but it's there. If my stepfather was here, he'd agree with me. He teaches history of art. Maybe it was different in your day, but now they put a lot of stress on the iconography." He felt slightly ashamed of invoking authority in a discussion, but Mr. Small seemed to be tickled by that feeble blow below the belt. He gave an indulgent laugh and stretching his arms wide embraced Peter in a sort of half bear hug, as if to say they were buddies despite their difference of opinion. "I'm aware of the new academicism. Entrenched interest groups resent the boom in museum attendance, the availability of cheap reproductions and color slides. They can't accept the fact that art is now within the reach of the masses. In consequence, as one might expect, there's a drive on to restrict the understanding of art, if not the actual experience, to a tiny coterie of privileged specialists and cultured dilettantes. They'd like to turn this wonderful spectacle over our heads into a private field of research, their own little hunting preserve —'Trespassers Keep Out.' Why, if they had their way, they'd

institute screening procedures at all the great museums, to bar
the vulgar public!"

The idea in fact had crossed Peter's mind. Looking down
the chapel, he saw the usual maelstrom. Every corner was occupied by dark serried groups, reminding him of flocks of
starlings, drawn up in formation around their leader. When
they moved, a new flock settled. In the middle of the room,
well-to-do Americans stood with their individual cicerones.
On the bench Peter had left, one old man remained stationary,
having fallen asleep—his white head nodded and jerked. A
mother carried a tiny baby wrapped in a yellow shawl and
sucking on a pacifier. In its father's arms, another baby cried.
On the far side of the *cancellata*, a German in *Lederhosen*
opened a tripod stool and sat down where he could watch the
lady copyist copying a Botticelli. There were nuns, priests in
skirts, priests in trousers—cassocked priests, for some reason,
favored a folded-arm pose when studying the frescoes. On the
raised platform, for the pope's chair, some student types were
lying, using their coats for pillows. Every now and then a custodian in a gray uniform with gold buttons would clap his
hands loudly to make them sit up. A girl in a tight sweater who
looked as if she had gone to Bennington paced around with
long gliding steps, her hands clasped behind her back and her
long straight hair tossing, like the "lost" heroine of some
neurotic ballet. A sort of permanent hum rose from the chapel
—from so many people reading aloud from guidebooks and
brochures—and competing with this natural human-hive
sound were bossy guides rapping for attention: "*Links, Gemälde
Paradiso, recht, Inferno mit Teufels.*" Along the walls, open
compacts and hand mirrors flashed. People squinted, shaded
their eyes, massaged cricks in their necks, bumped into each
other. Two vague soft old ladies attached themselves to an
English-speaking tour. "Do you folks mind if we listen in?
We've wasted a whole half-hour here looking for the Michelangelos and we can't seem to find them." A student sat up and
laughed coarsely. "Christ!" "Christ, yourself!" said Peter. "They
probably expected to see statues. Why is that so stupid? In case
you don't know, he was a sculptor, primarily." He turned to his
adviser. "If I don't wear my ear-plugs, I keep getting into arguments. That's the effect this mob has on you." The confused

incessant movement and medley of tongues made him think of an air terminal where half the flights had been delayed. The Seers above looked down on a sort of Exodus or final Judgment of the tribes and peoples. Whatever Mr. Small thought, some authority, in Peter's opinion, was going to have to separate the sheep from the goats.

"I know screening sounds repulsive, but we do it in colleges, don't we? You must do it in your own seminar when you limit the class to fifteen or whatever." Mr. Small retorted that soon all education would be conducted by TV; the small handpicked class, a vestige of the age of privilege, would be swept away. Peter groaned. "All right, then put all the art on TV too. Maybe eventually that will cut down on attendance, like with night baseball. But I can't wait for that. I want to be able to look at art, live, now, while I'm young, before the Army gets me. Won't you even admit there's a problem? And actually it's not so bad here as in some other museums, though the noise is worse. At least most of the stuff is on the ceiling. Think of the 'Mona Lisa' in the Louvre. It would take a giraffe to see it. Hey, maybe you could invent a periscope!"

At that point, the custodian at his little desk shushed them. "*Per piacere, signori!*" "OK, see you later, Mr. Small," Peter said hastily. He supposed the guides had the right to lecture at the top of their voices to the droves who were paying to be herded around by them, whereas he and his adviser, being unpaid, had a duty to be quiet. Mr. Small, however, was anxious to pursue the conversation. Peter yielded. "I guess we'd better get out of here, though," he suggested. "By all means do," a woman's voice interposed. "Why are such ruffians admitted?" she went on in a loud whisper, evidently misled by Mr. Small's slummy appearance and bearing out his description of the attitudes of the once-happy few. Peter led his adviser into the Borgia Apartments, which were usually empty. It puzzled him that this rather disagreeable teacher should be so eager to talk to him, unless he was just lonely, not knowing any Italian and without even a guidebook for company.

But Mr. Small, it turned out, had method in his madness. He wanted to poll Peter for a study of tourism he was doing. "Tourism? You mean like here?" "The idea surprises you, does it? And yet tourism is all around us, a central fact of our

mobile civilization, so much taken for granted that nobody
has stopped to ponder on it." That was so, Peter reflected. He
supposed statistics got collected somewhere on how much of
their income tourists spent abroad, what carriers they used,
and so on. There were stories with tourists in them, poems
with tourists in them, Steinberg cartoons with tourists in them.
But if he were asked, now, to draw up a reading list on the
subject, not a single "general" title, he realized, would come to
mind. Not even a magazine article in some place like *Harper's*.
If he had seen one, he would have read it. Maybe Mr. Small
was right that most people carried in their heads a "stereotype"
of the tourist that it might be a good idea for research to
dispel.

What was really peculiar, though, and worth a study in itself
was the fact that this rich research territory had not already
been prospected. Even if the stereotype summed up all there
was to say—that the average tourist was an omnipresent inse-
cure guy slung with cameras and carrying drip-dry suits on
hangers in a plastic bag—that did not normally deter sociologists, who, as the *babbo* said, could only "discover" things that
everybody knew anyway. Peter would like to hear a Marxist explanation of the fact that a world-wide industry feeding millions of mouths—billions probably if you counted automobile
workers, workers in aircraft plants, luggage-manufacturers,
Eastman Kodak, Agfa, Zeiss, all the makers of film and cameras, doctors giving shots, manufacturers of life-jackets and
throw-up bags, authors and publishers of travel books, whoever it was that made passports—had been overlooked by the
so-called social disciplines until Professor Beverly F. Small
came along and "happened" to have this brainstorm while sitting at the Deux Magots one Sunday morning idly watching
the crowds and eating a croissant.

Like Newton under the apple tree. No wonder he was pale
and excited. A foundation, naturally, was interested in the
project and paying his expenses for a "dry run" in Rome. On
the basis of that, he expected to get funding for three years'
research. At Easter, he would fly to Athens and cruise around
the Greek islands. "Hey, that's great, Mr. Small! You don't
need a helper, do you?" But his adviser had to be alone during
the early stages of a project; he would be using his vacations to

lay down guidelines for his students, who would take up the work next fall. In the fall, he hoped to fix it with his university so that he could travel with his advanced class on an extended field period. Or he might have to arrange a leave of absence.

The financing sounded like the easiest part. If his grant ran out before the study was finished, it should be easy, he explained, to get additional subsidies from countries like Spain and Portugal, which needed more background on tourist-expectations in developing their reception facilities. Other backing should rapidly become available for a study of this magnitude. In Paris, he had been talking with some of the lesser airlines—Air India, Air Afrique, Aer Lingus, and the like: whatever he and his students discovered about the travel pattern would redound to their advantage in planning and promotion.

"India! Africa! Do you think you'll visit the game reserves, Mr. Small?" His adviser, who now resembled a mushroom, would certainly get a good tan. A doubt crept into Peter's mind. "You don't think you're trying to cover too much territory? Maybe you should concentrate on something small. Like a Turkish fishing village that's been written up in *Holiday*. Find out what happens." Mr. Small snorted. Villages were crawling with *au pair* sociologists doing interminable "careful" investigations of the type Peter mentioned. "The impact of modernity on the folkways! All trivia! Who cares what happens in a village? Now that we have the computer, research must take broad new free forms. CinemaScope. The wide screen." As he had explained in a memo to the foundation, the structuring of the study should emerge from the data itself; it was important to avoid methodological traps that determined the findings in advance. "For the present, I'm feeling my way, using aleatory techniques." *I.e.*, so far, he had just been going around Rome with a tape-recorder, interviewing people at the Trevi Fountain, on the Spanish Stairs, at American Express and Alitalia. This morning he had had his first setback. The Vatican guards had made him check the tape-recorder at the entrance, together with his camera and briefcase. "Isn't that the limit? I couldn't convince them that a tape-recorder is an essential piece of modern scholarly apparatus. They simply kept pointing to the checkroom and repeating '*Guardaroba*,' as if they knew no English—a familiar dodge, of course." He had then sought to telephone to the cultural attaché at the Embassy, to get him to use pull, but first he could not find a telephone and next he could not find a *gettone*, and finally the cultural attaché was giving a lecture to the Rotary in Siracusa.

"You wouldn't come out and talk to the guards for me, would you, Levy? I gather you understand some Italian." He gave Peter's arm a pleading little squeeze, as though he was a blind man deprived of his Seeing Eye dog. "It wouldn't do any good," said Peter, resolved not to go on this stupid errand. "If this was a state museum, they just *might* let you by with it. But the Church is tough. You have to have all sorts of permissions to take photographs or do anything that's not in the rules. I know, on account of my stepfather. They don't like art historians or tourists, really. To them, they're sort of sacrilegious. That's why they give them a hard time. Haven't you noticed all those signs—'*Questo è un luogo sacro*'—outside churches, about being properly dressed? And honestly I don't think they'd care for the idea of interviews in the Sistine Chapel, Mr. Small. Why don't you do it outdoors, on the street? Catch people when they're leaving?"

Mr. Small supposed he could. But tourists leaving a museum were likely to be in a hurry. He needed a relaxed, informal atmosphere. It worked out best when an interview "grew" out of a seemingly casual conversation: "What are you doing in Rome?" "Where are you from?" "Do you have family here?" and so on. This was going to be a depth study, he emphasized, not the usual superficial survey made in airports. To Peter, Mr. Small's scientifically framed questions sounded suspiciously like the ones he had been answering ever since he left his native shores—with those old schoolteachers, for instance, on that gruesome train ride from Le Havre. And in his eyes Mr. Small's costume and sprouting beard, which he wore, he explained, so as not to look like a professor, far from putting a passing tourist at his ease, might suggest he was sidling up for a handout or selling contraband.

In fact, right here, the guard had his eye on them. The gloomy Borgian Sibyls' Chamber (*affreschi di scolari del Pintoricchio molto ritoccati; fu in questa sala forse che Cesare Borgia fece uccidere il cognato*), hung with Flemish arrases like the closet where Polonius eavesdropped, seemed to oppress Mr.

Small with its musty reminiscences of conspiracy. Whenever the guard glanced in the doorway, the professor lowered his voice and bent close to Peter as though the walls had ears. He talked feverishly of the shattering of precedents his undertaking involved. "I'm prepared for attacks, naturally, from the academic Mafia. Some of the small minds in humanistic studies will have their knives out. That's the price one pays for having a certain charisma. Even at the foundation questions have been asked about the utility of this kind of research and the deployment of tax-free resources for fresh ends and novel approaches. In my university I can expect talk of sinecurism, based, as usual, on envy." "Yeah, I can imagine."

Peter chortled. He had to hand it to Small. When he thought of poor Bob, who was forced to spend a certain number of summer hours in hot libraries and dusty archives when drawing an allocation for studying some obscure Mannerist painter, he felt a certain delight in the picture of his adviser, free to lie on a beach all day long or submerge in a snorkel—*anything* he did could not help contributing to his knowledge of tourism, and the less he exerted himself, the more his knowledge would broaden. Eventually he would have to write up his findings or get his student myrmidons to write them up for him, but that was a long way off, and before he was through he might be looking into moon travel.

"Have you thought of getting a shopping and souvenir subsidy?" "What do you mean?" "Well, you know, to buy Swiss watches and Japanese cameras and Florentine leather. All that junk that tourists bring home with them and try to smuggle through customs. The idea of loot is pretty fundamental to the tourist experience. So you should have an expense account to go shopping yourself to learn how it feels." Mr. Small took offense. "Do you find something amusing about tourists or about making a serious study of them?" "Both, I guess, a little." "But you're aware of the importance of the phenomenon?" "Oh, yes." Peter sighed. "And I know I'm part of it." "Such humility is becoming. I feared you might be one of those snobs who distinguish between class tourism and mass tourism."

Peter flushed. "Well, I have to admit I like tourists a lot better in units of one or two than in units of thirty or fifty. But the difference doesn't have to be based on dough. I mean, you see young couples or boys and girls roaming around by themselves who don't look all that prosperous." A sturdy young girl with blond pigtails and bare chapped legs raced through the room and up the stairs. "Take her. She comes every day. She's Dutch or German and spends most of her time with the Blessed Angelicos, I think. I saw her once in Piazza Navona with a knapsack. To me, she's a 'class' tourist." Mr. Small dismissed the northern maiden with an impatient gesture. "Tourism today is a mass industry serving a mass market. The fact is finally being recognized, and adjustments are being made: improvement of mass carriers—planes, ships, and buses—expansion of hotel and camping facilities, introduction at key points of super-restaurants with self-service. The single tourist unit, as you call it, will soon be as outmoded as the coach-and-four. Even the upper crust will travel in groups on yachts, private planes, and the like. No one will be able to reserve individual space. All block booking."

"I can imagine," said Peter, who had his private crystal ball. "But this process you're describing, won't it be self-defeating in the end? Isn't the whole point of travel to have a change of scene? With those giant hotels and cafeterias, every country will look the same. I've been thinking about those Germans in my hotel. They haven't heard anything since they got there but German and broken German. They'll have lunch in some place where '*Man spricht deutsch*' is advertised, and their guide will tell them in German about the catacombs. They probably won't even have to change into Italian money. Their beds and meals will be paid for in advance, and they won't tip the waiters or the chambermaid. They might as well stay home and have a plate of deep-freeze spaghetti and see the Sistine Chapel on television."

"We don't know yet why people travel, Levy. Nobody so far has examined the question culturally and sociologically. Economically we do know something. Package tours for lower-income groups, on the balance sheet, are proving to be more profitable for the host nation than the old de luxe tourism engaged in by the higher brackets. Even the fancy hotels aren't turning away package tours these days. It's the same as with any commodity handled in bulk. They're easier to process in and out."

"I don't see that. Most tours don't stay more than a couple of nights, maximum, in a town. Tomorrow morning, when those Germans leave, my hotel will have to change all their sheets. With the single tourist unit, like me, who's a slow mover, the hotel only has to change the sheets once a week."

This argument caused Mr. Small to give one of his sudden effusive little hugs. He went back to the question of tourist motivation. What caused several million Americans to leave their homes annually to seek out other scenes? "In what way is this culturally determined? What part is played by economic factors, education, social background, geographical distribution, ethnic origin? And how are these, in turn, related to the length of stay abroad? What about 'repeaters'? Statistics, of course, can help us. For instance, it now seems to be established that a far higher percentage of U.S. tourists in Asia comes from the Pacific Coast than from the Eastern seaboard. Isn't that intriguing?"

"I think I could have guessed it." "Guessed it, yes. But to *know* it! For example, I can form a hypothesis as to what brought you to Rome at Christmas-time, which might have served well enough for an old-time writer of fictions. Say a disappointment in love. But as a sociologist, I must make no facile assumptions." He took out his ball-point. "Of course the reasons immediately apparent to you may not be the real reasons or only the tip of the iceberg. Undoubtedly, there's a certain amount of atavism in the travel pattern. Rome, as the center of the Christian world, evidently acts as a magnet during the Christmas and Easter festivals for people of long-standing Christian orientation, even though they may be unaware of the Papal city as the New Bethlehem. Tourism tends to confuse itself with the traditional pilgrimage to the holy places. But we can exclude that in your case since you're Jewish, I assume."

"Half. But the other half went to midnight mass on Christmas Eve. You may have something there about the atavism. I'm not religious or anything. My feet just took me. But let me tell you something else strange. Really strange. I don't know whether you noticed, but in the Sistine Chapel, on the left-hand wall, there's a fresco by Signorelli and Bartolommeo della Gatta. To the left of where you were sitting. Right above

and behind where I was, though I guess you didn't see me.
Well, every day I've been sitting on that same bench, trying
not to look at anything but the Michelangelos, so as not to get
distracted. Of course I move around some but I always come
back to that bench. Then the last time I was there, I had this
weird feeling, as though I ought to turn around. Like a tap on
the shoulder. And what do you think? Behind me, over my
right shoulder, in that Signorelli fresco, I saw a nude youth
with golden hair, wearing a sort of locket and a red scarf
around his loins. Do you remember him? He looks like a tender captive. All the other figures have clothes on." Mr. Small
did not remember the ephebe. "OK, if you go again, look at
him. Do you know who he is, according to the guidebook? The
personification of the tribe of Levi. That's how we pronounce
the name in our family, actually—the same as in 'Levite.' Not
'Levy.' So he's my Renaissance cousin. You know, idealized and
pagan, like a young god or martyr ready for the sacrifice. The
title of the fresco is 'The Testament and Death of Moses.' Do
you think it could be atavism that made me sit down on that
particular bench, under my archetype, till I had to finally turn
around and meet his eyes? He has a tear, like a cast, in one eye,
as though he was crying, but maybe the picture is damaged. Or
maybe he's naked and crying because he has no property. The
Levis weren't allowed to own land."

"Curious," said Mr. Small, taking an extensive note. "You
should read your Jung." Then he brought Peter back to the
weary subject in hand: why he had chosen Rome for his winter
holiday. Of course Peter could not answer. If he knew why he
had come to Rome, his inner self and mainspring would have
no more secrets from him. All he could think of was Borromini
and the Sistine Chapel. "Nonsense," said his adviser. "Those
are your ostensible reasons, pretexts you gave your family to
justify your trip. There are plenty of fine museums in Paris, for
anyone who takes the trouble to stroll through them. Let's dig
a little deeper. I think you said you'd been here before, with
your mother. Did something significant happen to you on
your earlier visit?" "Borromini and Michelangelo." "Bob" had
happened to him on his earlier visit, but he had not come back
to see Bob, so why bring him in? "Yes, yes! You convince me
that they are meaningful to you emotionally. But why?" "I

don't know." "Let's take the Sistine Chapel. Was there some particular feature that stood out in your memory?" Peter sighed. "OK, the Delphic Sibyl."

Mr. Small's ball-point flew. "Does the figure remind you of anyone? A girl? Or a boy perhaps? You know Michelangelo's proclivities?" "A girl." In fact his favorite Sibyl did remind Peter slightly of Roberta but also of his pensive mother, whose arms were muscular from playing the harpsichord. "Unusual that a clothed, asexual figure should excite erotic fantasies in someone your age." "I didn't say erotic," Peter replied stiffly. "And to me she's the height of girlishness. Miss Nature before she got to be Mrs. I love the Prophet Isaiah too. I suppose you think he's effeminate, with that raised eyebrow and drooping hand. To me, he's young Jewishness in a pure, refined state, the way we were before the Diaspora. Intellectual beauty, like in that poem by Shelley."

"'Before,' 'before,'" Mr. Small chided. "It's curious that you show so little interest in the 'Last Judgment'—a much more powerful and gripping design, to my mind." "The 'after,'" said Peter, with a wan grin. "I agree, it doesn't appeal to me much. I like Genesis and the Prophecies." He thought he had made a nice discovery: it was the Prophets and the Sibyls who upheld the whole structure by their mass, weight, and volume. *E.g.*, the old gaunt Cumean Sibyl, in her white cap, bent over her green tome, with an arm like a blacksmith's and gnarled fingers gripping the pages. They were bigger than the other figures, as if to show that their vision of the Redemption surpassed any temporal event. Maybe that was Michelangelo's Platonism, the Ideas being greater than their puny reflections on the wall of the cave. By contrast, the newly emerged Eve, praying, was just a stumpy little fetish. Peter was not sure how the *ignudi* on their pillars fitted in, but they must be another *redeeming* feature, contributing to the uplift, a triumph of something natural over something else. Buonarroti saw plenty to be redeemed in the pitiful sequel to the magic bright moment of the Creation of Man, with God's forefinger passing the spark to Adam's, to call him forth from the deep of His intention. A plan that started with the separation of light from darkness and ended with the drunkenness of Noah left you feeling that the Almighty might have been wiser to stop with the Creation of the

Fish. And the four big vengeful spandrels in the corners carried mysterious and sinister messages: David finishing off the fallen Goliath, Judith and a maid tiptoeing out with Holofernes' head on a platter, Haman being nailed naked to a tree, the Children of Israel in the coils of fiery serpents. Every one of those barbarous episodes, when you thought about it, was an execution. Yet the Prophets and Sibyls, intent on their books and scrolls, were apart from all that, and the sun, when there was any, lit up their garments, which made you know there was hope. Michelangelo must have known that a morning finger of winter sunlight would touch the yellow mantle on Daniel's right knee weather permitting as long as the frescoes lasted. Every time Peter considered that he felt joyful, as when somebody kept a promise.

"Well, let's go on. Based in Paris, as we've established, you had a variety of travel options. Was Rome your first choice?" "Yes. No, I take that back. A while ago, I had the idea of going to Warsaw with this Norwegian I knew. I'd like to see a Slavic country in the snow. Then that fell through; he got deported. Later, I was toying, for about a half an hour, with going to Autun." "*Autun?* Why in the world?" Peter told him about Gislebertus. He was not going to mention the faithless Roberta, even if it was omitting something important. "You seem unfocused," Mr. Small commented. "All over the place. No clear line of direction. Why are you so art-oriented, all of a sudden? The last time I saw you, you told me you were interested in entomology. Something about becoming a bug."

It was typical of adults that they seldom remembered anything straight about a younger person, which showed their real lack of concern. "It was birds," said Peter. "Oh, sorry, what was I thinking of?" "'The Metamorphosis,' by Kafka." "Jove, you're right. Have you read it?" "No. But I know the plot." Mr. Small kept straying from the subject, but possibly that was part of the strategy of a depth interview. Peter grew impatient. He had resolved to go without lunch to study the little spandrels above the lunettes, but already he was behind schedule, and it was a gray morning. On a day like this, the light faded fast in the chapel; after one o'clock it would be too dark to make out those dim, shadowy figures waiting, if that was what they were doing, for the Advent.

"Would you mind if I went back now to the Sistine Chapel?" "Sure, go ahead. Just let me ask you a couple more questions. Have you had any contact with other Americans here? The Beats, for instance?" There was a sudden, bated eagerness in that last "offhand" query, which made Peter wonder if the whole interview had not been leading up to it. It was funny how older people got excited by thinking about the Beats, as if they were some new kind of pornography. "No," said Peter. Mr. Small was disappointed. He had hoped Peter might help him; it turned out that one of his main purposes in Rome was getting to know them better. Amazingly, in Paris he had already picked up quite a few in the Place de la Contrescarpe, near where they had their pads. "They gave me a lot of data. Fascinating stuff. I have it all on tape. Some of course were unwilling to be drawn out, taking me for a member of the Establishment. In Paris, with my Embassy and academic connection, I had to be somewhat circumspect. The place to find their counterparts, they told me, was on the Spanish Steps. Anywhere else that you know of?" "American Express. Maybe Cook's. You could put an ad in the Rome *American*."

Mr. Small shook his head reproachfully. Advertising his purpose would defeat it. Unobtrusive, in his drop-out disguise, he hoped to be accepted by the kids in Piazza di Spagna and gain their total confidence. "It's like any anthropological field trip. You have to talk to them in their own language and respect their value system. Some of them are extraordinarily attractive, as human beings. Last night, I smoked grass with a diversified group and collected their stories." Peter grinned, thinking of Sherlock Holmes in the opium den. "Weren't you afraid of getting stoned, Mr. Small?" "It's fairly simple to simulate inhalation. What's meaningful for them is the communion-rite. Sharing the 'joint.' The feeling of brotherhood. 'Man.' Isn't that beautiful? Not 'Mister.' 'Man.'" "Did you tape them?" "Not yet. We just sat around and got acquainted. Later they'll feel more comfortable, and I can use my machine. I want to be introduced to the pads where they live. They have this idea of community, both sexes intermingled, few or no possessions. I'd like to get that on film. In Paris, I found them camera-shy, like many primitive peoples. My little Minox created the suspicion that I might be the 'fuzz.'"

Actually Mr. Small's findings were not devoid of interest. Peter saw that he was going to have to give up on the spandrels. He looked at his watch. It was too late even to catch a sustaining bite in the priests' bar in St. Peter's, which was one of his favorite refuges. Sergio had steered him to it. You went through a corridor to the left of the transept, as if you were going to the Treasury; then you came to a room all paneled in intarsia, with stars and flowers, and you opened a small door on the right, just like in *Alice in Wonderland*—if nobody had told you, you would never suspect there was a door in that wall. Inside, there were always a lot of priests, the trousered type, drinking beer, but they also served sandwiches and Campari-sodas. Around noon, though, they closed. He knew another secret passage, which he had found on his own, in the Stanze di Raffaello. You walked through a little door marked "Leo X" (the password) beneath the "Incendio del Borgo" and discovered nice clean toilets. On Mr. Small's expressing a desire for the men's room, Peter was now able to conduct him there. For once, he had impressed his adviser. "Why, it's a regular labyrinth," he commented. "Goodness me, how do you get your bearings?" Then he wanted to eat, and Peter, feeling hungry, consented. He had blown the day anyhow. They ransomed the tape-recorder and camera and took a taxi to a *trattoria* in Trastevere Mr. Small had been told about. As might have been predicted, it was full of American tourists, which did not bother Peter but put Mr. Small slightly out of countenance. "I don't see anything 'typical' about this," he said fretfully, as they waited in line. "I suppose it's been discovered." "Who told you about it?" "The cultural attaché." Peter shrugged. "Well! Anyway, you can tape them." "Too noisy." "Go on about the Beats," Peter urged, when they were finally shown to a table. It amused him that his adviser had been studying the migrations of the Beats as though they were salmon or birds. He had even picked up some of the lingo you came across in bird books and Nature Study columns.

The way he put it, few of the Beats were sedentary; they moved on, usually with the onset of winter to warmer climes, and always driven by the need of drugs, which were the same to them as the food supply. There was a whole colony of them, for instance, now established in Nepal, and yet nobody could explain how word passed between them as to where they should forgather next. They appeared to respond to a common "urge" which had a destination coded into it, like an airplane ticket.

Peter laughed. "You mean they have flyways." Mr. Small nodded. What he expected to learn from his research was that tourists in general had flyways. If these could be charted and shifts in schedule and direction predicted, it would be extremely interesting. Already data were being collected at unexpected posts of observation; for instance, Breton peasants made an annual note of the first spring tourists as they did of the return of the swallows—in due course such data would be stored in computers for analysis. The Beatniks were the clearest example of the post-industrial wanderlust and the easiest to investigate, because of their manner of dress, which made them conspicuous, their herding habits, and their dependence on narcotics. Any change in the narcotics laws, any slight relaxation or stiffening in enforcement, produced immediate population shifts among them: an exodus or an invasion.

Something similar could be observed with homosexuals, who were also readily identifiable by their dress, voice, and so on. They too had a herding habit and could be found at certain familiar stations at certain times of the year. They were sedentary, Mr. Small understood, in Capri, Venice, Tangiers, Athens, Taormina. "Amsterdam," supplied Peter. "Oh?" "From what I've heard, anyway." Mr. Small made a note. "I wasn't aware that they congregated so far north. One might be able to look into that during tulip-time." Many of them were nest-builders and, unlike the Beats, they generally traveled in pairs. They were gregarious at their meeting-places, but while in transit each individual pair tended to eschew the company of other pairs. You would not find them banding together, like heterosexual similars, to charter an airplane or a bus. Their migrations too could be understood in terms of the food supply, if that was interpreted in a broad sense to mean readily available adolescent boys. And again, as with the Beats, the food supply was dependent on police attitudes, reflecting of course the attitudes of the community.

The behavior of these deviant minorities, scientifically probed, ought to throw considerable light on the whole tourist phenomenon. A striking parallel could be detected between hostile community reactions to Beatnik or homosexual colonies and hostile community reactions to campers, trailer aggregates, and the like. Commonly one fraction of local opinion encouraged the influx of the outsiders, for evident commercial motives, while another fraction sought to expel them, often on the pretext of sanitation. Moreover, among the so-called invaders themselves, you found a most interesting tendency to identify with the host community and its xenophobic prejudices, to the extent that individuals and even whole groups in the tourist population manifested anger at the presence of other tourists.

"That's it!" cried Peter, looking up from some noodles *al burro* he was winding around his fork. "You've got it in a nutshell, Mr. Small. There's a logical contradiction in the whole tourist routine. The dragon swallowing its own tail. Or maybe I mean a paradox. 'Oh God, tourists!' you hear them moan when they look around some restaurant and see a bunch of compatriots with Diners Club cards who might as well be their duplicates. Sort of a blanket rejection that, if they sat down and analyzed it, would have to include themselves. Only nobody does. They can't. Instead, in the Sistine Chapel, you start thinking of reasons why *you* have the right to be there and all the rest don't. The only tourists you don't look on as gate-crashers are solitary art-lovers you can put in the same class as yourself. Like that Dutch or German girl we saw. But if she was multiplied, I'd start to hate her, I guess."

It came back to Peter that Mr. Small himself had not been too pleased just now to find other Americans here. Nor would he put it past him to have a Diners Club card. But when he dared glance across the table, the professor was fiddling with the tape-recorder, which he had quietly moved into position. His head was cocked over it, and he was listening to Peter with an encouraging smile. "Beautiful!" he said, patting Peter's arm. "Just give me that bit about the Diners Club again." The crowd in the restaurant had thinned out. "Oh, I forget," said Peter. "You hear the same stuff all over the place. Like this morning in American Express, there were these women talking to the clerk. 'Pompeii, isn't that awfully *touristy*?' We saw them again in the Sistine Chapel, with a guide. You know what they decided about the ceiling? Too 'busy.'"

Mr. Small put his ear to the machine again. "Lovely! Just go right ahead. Don't be diffident. Forget about the machine. Pretend you're talking to me directly." "OK. Can't you see that it's to the interest of everybody, including tourists, to discourage tourism? Not counting travel agents, naturally, and other parasites. But to the interest of tourists most of all. The inhabitants, so far as I can see, mind tourists less than other tourists do. I don't mean because they make a profit on them. The inhabitants sort of enjoy tourists, up to a point. They lend a little variety."

"Go on." "Well, the nice thing about travel is the chance to be by yourself in an unspoiled, pristine setting. Or with one person you like a lot. Isn't that the principle behind honeymoons? In English freshman year we read some of Dr. Johnson's *Lives of the Poets*, and it told about how Milton traveled through Italy in the company of a hermit. That must have been just about ideal." Mr. Small smiled. "You mean, have I considered the drawbacks? Lousy inns and bedbugs? Would I really want to go back to that? I guess maybe I couldn't, on account of my conditioning. But people can take more than they think. Look at the Army. If a guy can accept hardship because he's drafted, he ought to be able to stand a little inconvenience to go some place for fun. I mean, I sat up all night on the train to get here, and it was a lot more rewarding than being strapped in on a plane. In comparison, you could say it was an adventure."

"Air travel was once considered an adventure." "Maybe I would have liked it in those days. Now the only adventure you can have in a plane is when it crashes into a mountain. Everything's all upside down. To have a novel experience today, you wouldn't hop in some jet just off the drawing-board, would you? No, you'd ride on a mule or a camel or go up in a balloon. Being in one of these old crumbling cities on your own is like being the first white man or whatever to walk in a virgin forest. Or like coming out of your house in the morning after a big snowfall and almost hating to make the first human footprint. My generation doesn't have experiences like that very often, which is why we come abroad, I guess. There isn't much unspoiled Nature around any more, and the places where people like poets used to look for it—the mountains and the seashore—are all jammed up with humanity and bottle-caps. So arriving in a strange town by yourself, with just your guide-book for a compass, is the nearest equivalent we can find to being alone with Nature, the way travelers used to be in the Age of Discovery."

Peter paused and chewed a mouthful of salad. He did not want to sound like a misanthrope in front of the tape-recorder. "You can't blame the multitudes for wanting sun and swimming and fresh air. Nobody should have a monopoly of that. If office- and factory-workers get vacations, they have to have some place to go. Beaches and resorts should belong to the public, even if it mucks them up. But there has to be *something* left to explore. To give you the illusion that you're blazing a trail, although you know that thousands of others have been there before you."

"Have you ever thought of camping in the north woods? If you want real Nature, that's it. Absolutely untouched. The rangers in the park see to that. No hunting or fishing, no swimming, no dumping, put out your campfires, bring your own firewood and your grub. My wife and I used to do it every summer with the kids. Our only contact with civilization was the chief ranger's radio." Peter made a noncommittal noise. To him, this sounded more like an al fresco meeting with Big Brother than like communing with the infinite. "Is your wife in Paris?" "We're divorced. One of those things. She envied me my relationship with my students. She's basically a cold person, and I'm a warm person." "Oh. Well, I guess those pack trips can be fun. I've never tried. But I went bird-watching once on the Appalachian Trail. I remember the scary feeling when night started coming on fast. I thought I could hear it stalking me in the woods. To me, Nature has a scary side even in the daytime, with twigs and branches snapping at you. Sort of an underlying menace. I suppose, out camping, you can sense that pretty often." Mr. Small misunderstood. "Nothing to be afraid of. The trails are well marked; no fear of getting lost. And if you come down with an appendicitis, a plane will take you out. Sometimes at night you hear bear, but there are always other campers in the next cabins. All you have to do is holler."

Peter returned to his theme. "If you love someone, you

want to be alone with them. The same with art. There ought to be churches and museums where you don't have to meet gangs of tourists, where you can just sit and contemplate. You can't do that any more unless you're on the track of some nut like Borromini that the average person hasn't heard of. If I follow up on the logic of that, I'd decide never to see any of the famous masterpieces, because it's so horribly frustrating to get there and *not* see them."

"Still, you seem to have managed." Peter shook his head, thinking with bitterness of the spandrels, not to mention the lunettes. "Only a little, really. And only by being tricky. Listen, I heard about this rich *studioso* who gets driven by his chauffeur every morning to the Sistine Chapel at nine o'clock and leaves at nine-fifteen. That way he outwits the crowds. I wouldn't want to be him. Yet maybe in time I'll be like that— studying all the angles, to get my cut of the available art. That's what the modern world leads you to." He sighed. "Mr. Small, how can a person be for peace if he's never experienced a feeling of peacefulness? For that you need to be alone and enclosed in something vast like the ocean. An element bigger than you are that will still be there when you're gone." "The stars in those north woods. Remote universes, yet you feel you can reach out and touch them." Peter could not deny that the stars communicated the feeling he had described. Or had at any rate before *il pallone americano* had muscled in on the firmament. "I was thinking of Rome. In Rome, the inhabitants don't intrude on your thoughts, any more than the fish in the ocean. They're part of the element. But mobs of tourists are just garbage dumped here by planes and sightseeing buses, with the guides and storekeepers diving for them like scavenger gulls!"

The Recording Angel in the black box was taking note of his words, he recalled. "If you want me to say I'm part of the garbage, OK, I agree. I'm fouling up the element. When I'm in the Sistine Chapel, I hate my fellow-man. There's something basically wrong with a situation like that. If a guy is in the presence of beauty, he should be having noble thoughts. That's what finally made me get the ear-plugs. Not just to tune out on those ghoulish guided tours but to keep from having evil thoughts about them. 'Avoid the occasions of sin' is one of my father's recipes. He got it from the Jesuits."

"Do you accept democracy, Levy?" Mr. Small shot out the question like a district attorney moving in for the kill. One minute he was giving those encouraging little pats and ingratiating hugs, and the next he had you in the box, as though he was his own stool pigeon. Peter essayed a soft answer. "I always thought I did. But there are some things you can't slice up evenly, like that baby in the Judgment of Solomon. I'm coming to the conclusion that the rules of democracy work better when there isn't too much cash around. The way it used to be in Athens. If we could only get back to that . . ."

"'Barefoot in Athens.'" His adviser's pale foxy eyes regarded him with pity. Peter read his thought. He began to get angry. "All right, so they had slaves. Jefferson had slaves. Don't you think I know that? But just the same, democracy, the way I see it, is something civic, involving a little free space. There's nothing democratic about huge herds of travelers stampeding for the same point. If it's a herd instinct that tells them to converge on the Sistine Chapel, that instinct ought to be redirected to something more appropriate, like a football stadium!"

"Appropriate to whom? What makes you so sure that the Sistine Chapel is appropriate as an end for you and not for the masses?" "It's obvious," said Peter, no longer caring that he had shifted his ground. "You saw that mob scene this morning. They don't even listen to their stupid guides, who half the time tell them everything wrong anyway. Mostly they're bored stiff and yawning, because they had to get up early to join their tour. Instead of looking at the frescoes, they're peeking at their watches. This professor I know says it's the same at the Uffizi in Florence in the summertime. You know what I think? A tourist ought to have to pass an entrance exam to get to see the 'Mona Lisa' or the 'Last Supper' or the Sistine Chapel. It's the only way."

"The '*only*' way?" Mr. Small appeared amused. "Honestly," said Peter. "I've given a lot of thought to it. Prohibiting tours would help, at least in the winter, which is when most of the old folks come, because they get the off-season rate. Or you could restrict tours to certain hours of the day, but the trouble is there aren't so many hours when the light is good. Or you could have one day a week when only tours would be admitted. That might be more fair. But I realize that even a measly half-measure like that wouldn't have a chance under the present set-up. Under capitalism, you can't have the mildest reforms, because art gets milked for profit like everything else."

"Would it be better under Communism?" "Well, at least there wouldn't be any American Express." "What about Intourist?" "Actually I was thinking more of socialism. You'd make more museums for the people and distribute the art around more in the provinces. But still you'd have a problem. So you'd educate the public to see the rationality of an entrance exam. If a person passed, he'd get a card that would admit him to all the three-star attractions, like the 'Mona Lisa' and so on. And if he didn't, there'd still be a lot of art to look at. Then, so as not to weight the scales in favor of intellectual people who were good at passing tests, you could have a lottery too. Prizes would be books of tickets entitling the winners to see, for instance, twelve masterpieces of their choice. Like rationing during the war: a guy might want to use up most of his tickets on the Sistine Chapel and skip the 'School of Athens' or whatever interested him less. I forgot to say that under my system schoolchildren could get in without taking any test. The little kids that come to the Sistine Chapel with their priest or teacher always have a ball. I love to watch them, looking up at the ceiling with big round black eyes and twirling around like tops till they're dizzy. They point and ask questions. '*Una sibilla, cos'è?*' If the priest is any good, he shows them the *putti* playing, and they wonder if they're angels. '*No. Sono fanciulli, come voi. Giocano.*'"

Peter spoke rapidly, ending with a nervous laugh. A sarcastic smile glimmered on his adviser's features, and Peter feared it might refer to a fact he had just noticed himself: his plan had an Achilles' heel. Under socialism, *i.e.*, in an ideal republic, just about everybody would be able to appreciate art, so that there would be no reasonable basis for exclusion, and the museums would be even more packed than they were now.

But Mr. Small had failed to observe the hole in his reasoning. The sneer on his face had another referent. Abruptly he turned off the tape-recorder. "Enough of this modish drivel," he said. To Peter's disbelieving ears, he launched into a defense of capitalism, which was the best system yet invented—or likely to be invented—for technological progress and an equal distribution of goods. "Of course it's flawed, but what human system isn't? Don't tell me socialism hasn't been tried yet! We've had it in all its varieties, mixed and straight, and look at the record. Take a good hard look." And he began to hold forth about something he called the market-mechanism, which worked (with some correction) like the mills of the gods, to spread the wealth, remedy social injustice, multiply choices, advance basic research, apply technology to formerly insoluble human equations. The way he described it made Peter think of one of those mixers the fair Rosamund hated that did everything but chew your food for you.

"Wow!" said Peter. "You surprise me, Mr. Small. I thought you were some sort of far-out radical. Like a tribune of the people. I couldn't understand how you could reconcile the ideas you seemed to be for with wanting to work hand and glove with airlines and reactionary governments." "Those terms have no meaning for a contemporary mind. In my youth I was fond of them too, during a brief romance with that mythic animal called democratic socialism. Today there's no excuse for that kind of ignorance, when any reader of the newspapers can see that Right and Left, if we must use the old vocabulary, have so clearly changed places. Yet the glib slurs on capitalism remain fashionable.

"Capitalism, if you were only aware of it, has shown itself to be the most subtle force for progress the world has ever known. In its post-industrial phase, an insidious, awesome force. Boring from within the old structures, leveling, creating new dreams, new desires, and having the technical know-how and the dynamism to satisfy them. You're living in the midst of a vast global revolution originating in the United States and you seem not to take the slightest interest in it, except to go through some feeble motions of dissent. From your ivory tower, you look down disdainfully on that revolution and pretend to yourself that you'd welcome it if it bore the name of socialism. I can assure you that you wouldn't, my friend. 'Socialism' is your alibi for rejecting the real progress capitalism has made, the leveling you abhor, if the truth were told. 'Garbage,' you said just now, in a moment of outspokenness which no doubt you regret. That was your epithet for the common man."

"Hey, you misunderstood me! I don't think those crowds are garbage in their natural setting. It's the processing that does it to them. That's the word *you* used. The same with real garbage. Before it's processed into that state, it's just food—plain healthy food. And if you take out the tin cans and compost it back into the soil, it will be food again." "Why don't you meet the argument instead of taking refuge in childish verbal fencing?"

"I'm not going to argue with you, Mr. Small. I feel too tired. Just listening to you makes me exhausted, and I'm not saying that to be rude. To have any real discussion, we'd both have to go back to the letter *a*. And honestly you're too old for that. I'd rather have an argument with somebody I share a few assumptions with. Maybe you're right about capitalism being a revolutionary force. Sure, it can produce abundance, but abundance of what? I admit it's bringing about changes. But those aren't the changes my generation wants. If capitalism is so great, what has it done for civil rights?"

"Christ! You privileged kids are all alike. You despise the common man, as long as he's white. But you suddenly love the Negro. If CORE had been holding a caucus this morning in the Sistine Chapel, you would have slavered with joy. All right, I'll tell you what capitalism has done for civil rights. The market-mechanism plus technology has brought the black man off the fields and into the cities. North and South. In the cities you got overcrowding, slums, unemployment, welfare, rioting —an explosive situation produced by the restructuring of agriculture. But out of that miserable crowding, those festering slums, the civil-rights movement was born. Your field nigger, as they called him, never knew he had any rights. The whole thing is an urban movement generated by the dynamics of post-industrial society. If it had been left to you, the black man would have stayed on the land forever, close to Nature, peacefully farming or share-cropping. Which means he would have remained an Uncle Tom!" He struck his fist into his palm with a smack that made Peter jump.

"That's a good point," he acknowledged, swallowing several times. "I never thought of it that way. I guess I only looked at one side of the picture. To me, the slums were bad." Mr. Small grew more affable. "You might say the ghettoes with their high crime rate and juvenile delinquency were a high price to pay for the returns, so far, in actual civil rights gained. But change is often seen as costly in the immediate perspective. Capitalism in time will eradicate the slums because it can't afford them. Slums mean under-consumption; it's as simple as that. I can promise you that in the foreseeable future, with automation and full productivity, the remaining pockets of poverty will be wiped out in the U.S. We will look back on the ghettoes as the inevitable way-stations on the highway of development."

"Yes. Maybe." Now that the meal was over, Peter was disinclined to stir up any more debate. It was strange that, unlike the original Dr. Pangloss, who had a sunny outlook, his descendant was of a variable temper, hard to forecast and seldom *sereno*. Dr. Pangloss' insulation from reality had made him a good traveling companion, but Mr. Small's personal plexiglass bell evidently caused a kind of itchiness or inflammation that kept him irritable and peevish—Peter would not have cared to go through the Lisbon earthquake with him even to be in on the happy ending of seeing him hanged by the Inquisition. Maybe the idea that all was for the best was harder to hold onto nowadays, and a guy like Small had to be satisfied with thinking that *he* was for the best, brimming with good will and faith in the market mechanism all the time that really, if he only knew it, he was stewing in doubt and rancor. He had a higher I.Q., Peter estimated, than Candide's companion, and perhaps that was part of the problem.

Now he played a few sentences back on the tape-recorder, listened as if to music, and lovingly replaced the cover. He seemed so tender with that instrument that Peter wondered if it was new. "Don't mistake me, Peter. I'm not insensitive to your *Angst*. I have my own ambivalences toward this abrasive new society we're making. 'The world is too much with us; late and soon, Getting and spending, we lay waste our powers.' Yes. Nor do I see remedies in the foreseeable future for the sheer increase in man's numbers, though I'm confident they will be found. I believe in man." It occurred to Peter that Mr Small had been successfully analyzed. That might be what was the matter with him. He leaned across the table and touched Peter's arm. "I know you reject the insights of psychiatry. But if this solitude you speak of is so important to you, perhaps you ought to try some of the mind-expanding drugs. My 'Beat' friends may have something to teach us. With drugs, they don't need the manufactured experience of art. Every 'trip' is a tour of the unexplored resources of consciousness. We should ponder the semantics of that word. What if they've found the answer to the very real dilemma of tourism you've posed? A partial answer, anyway. They perhaps show a greater adaptiveness to the mobile environment we live in than those of us, like you, who persist in the traditional patterns. And their solution, in due time, will be within the reach of every housewife, every old person. There's no doubt in my mind that pot will quite soon be legalized and marketed through the normal channels at an acceptable price. The cigarette industry, in trouble over cancer, will perceive the opportunity. There's your market-mechanism, don't you see, with its inherent thrust forward, to open new vistas, resolve old problems!"

Peter laughed. "'Skip that trip up the Nile. Turn on with a Camel.' Yeah." Feeling no acute eagerness for this alternate future either, he added up his share of the bill and put down a thousand-lire note. "Oh! The bad news! Shall we split it?" Peter had had no notion of splitting, since his adviser had consumed a *bistecca fiorentina*, a half-liter of wine, and a *cassata siciliana*, while he had had noodles, a salad, and a small San Pellegrino. But some affluent people were like that; they never noticed, when they offered to divide the bill, that they had had the more costly items.

"Let's see," said Mr. Small. "It comes to about three thousand lire. You put down another five hundred, and I'll leave the tip." Peter, who had hoped for some change from his original contribution, felt himself turn red. "The service is included. See, there it is." He pointed to the item on the bill, trusting that this maneuver would inspire his adviser to make a detailed cost breakdown. "Oh, fine," said Mr. Small, ignoring the bill and waving to the waiter. "What do I give him extra?" "Oh, a couple of hundred."

The waiter was waiting. Peter felt himself in a familiar sort of quandary. Leaving aside the selfish motive of his depleted funds (with the five hundred lire and his rightful change he could buy his supper at a counter and part of his breakfast too), he asked himself whether he did not have a friendly obligation to set his adviser straight. If Small, afterward, were to realize his mistake, he would wish Peter had spoken up. An honest person should always be glad to be saved from cheating another person, especially a younger one. If it was Peter, he would want to be told. But Mr. Small was not Peter—that seemed to be clear—and there were people who would rather walk around with their fly open than have anybody tell them about it. His mother, for instance, always got mad if he said her slip was showing. "Don't you want to know, Mother?" "No." Money, he guessed, could be an even more sensitive area in the adult soul. And Mr. Small might have alimony to pay and maintenance for his kids—he had not revealed how many. Would it be cowardly to take the easy course and fork over the five hundred lire? Or Christian? Was deciding to be "Christian" just an excuse for being a coward? He wondered what that contemporary sibyl "Dear Abby" would advise. "Gently draw the error to your companion's attention"? But that "gently" was a typical sibylline evasion. There was no gentle way of telling somebody he was rooking you.

Peter's hand went slowly to his wallet. Then he remembered the foundation. Mr. Small must have remembered too. "By the bye," he said, "would you mind telling the waiter to bring the check back? And have him mark it 'Paid.' I'd like to have it for my records." In a second, Peter got it. The guy was planning to collect from the foundation on Peter's lunch as well as his own, which would put him not just even but ahead of the game. The fact that he avoided the term *expense account* showed that he had some shame left. But not enough. He had dug his own grave. In it, the worm turned. "In that case," said Peter, "you'll want separate checks, won't you?" He spoke to the waiter. "*Faccia due conti, per favore. Scusi.*" The man somewhat grumpily redid the addition. As Peter pocketed his change, his eyes avoided Mr. Small's. It was better not to gloat over a fallen adversary. Victory was sweet, but the wise man did not seek to savor it.

Outside the restaurant, undeterred by the heavy equipment hanging on straps from his shoulders, Mr. Small managed a final effusive embrace. Then he held Peter at arm's length. "What a wonderful day we've had together." It was hard for

Peter to imagine that this affectionate burbling person had tried to gyp him on the check. "Wait just a minute, Peter. Stay there!" He darted across the piazza, the tape-recorder bouncing against one hip and the camera against the other. In a minute he came running back, having found a local passer-by who was willing to take their picture. Extracting the Rollei from its case, he hung it around the man's neck, showed him how to use the viewer and press the button. After some experiment, he posed himself and Peter, arms linked, against the background of a fountain. Peter faced the camera, feeling the snug pressure of the professor's arm, undeniably "warm," upon his and trying to fight off a sense of total unreality. If today was to figure as a sentimental *ricordo* in Mr. Small's memory book, then one of them had to be nuts. "*Un sorriso, per piacere.* Smile, please, misters." Mr. Small had already obliged. Peter forced a peaked grin to his own lips. He nodded. He was a snob. He preferred most art to most people. He was guilty of juvenile coldness and non-participation. When he had not *shared* whatever the sociologist thought they had experienced, the least he could have done was consent to an equal division of the check.

Two-thirds of a Ghost

COMING back to Paris, with his soul refreshed, Peter encountered a "disagreeable" he had managed to erase from his memory—the *clochards*. In Rome, there were no *clochards* because the Italians were not vinous. One of the world's problems you could ignore there was alcoholism. In the street you seldom saw a drunk person, not counting foreigners. In Rome, there were only ordinary beggars, mostly cripples on church steps and ragged gypsy women with babies in their arms that his ex-roommate claimed were rented. You forked over some *spiccioli* as a matter of course, and the strays, if any, that preyed on your conscience were the homeless, hungry cats.

In Paris, regular beggars were rare and hung out mainly in the subway. He met one—a blind man with an accordion—on his way home, when he had to change at the Gare d'Austerlitz stop, and, keeping to Roman habits, he searched for a donation among the small coins in his pocket, though it meant putting down his heavy suitcase, which at once became a traffic obstruction. To the sundry "*Merde, alors!*" hurled at him by the jostling throng, he replied mechanically, "*Ta gueule.*" In Paris, beggars almost never thanked you, and he was startled to hear the blind man call out after him something that sounded strangely like "*Merci!*" "*De rien,*" Peter mumbled. "*Monsieur!*" the man reiterated, rapping on his begging-cup. Eventually Peter dug. In his confusion, he had dropped some small lire along with the one-centime pieces into the plastic cup, and the blind man, by touch evidently, had detected the fraud. He was angry. Peter put down his suitcase again and fumbled in his pocket; he had no more French coins. He drew a crumpled five-franc note from his wallet—a dollar. The man smoothed it out and felt it carefully, as though it might be counterfeit. "*Ça va,*" he said finally.

This little incident assured Peter he was home. Only in France, he guessed, would a subway beggar, on getting a handout, act like an incensed storekeeper presented with a wooden nickel; he was probably lucky the guy had not called the police. Yet when he thought it over, he found less cause for mirth. The blind man had made sense. If a person gave charity, it was because he decided he owed it, maybe not to a particular individual but to the other half of humanity, and the creditor had the right to expect the account to be settled in the coin of the realm. Just the same as a storekeeper—why not? French logic had punched holes in Peter's philanthropy, which seemed to have been based on the rotten assumption Beggars can't be choosers. Of course it had been an "innocent" mistake, yet not all that innocent underneath. Peter knew he would not have been so careless with the merchants in the Marché Buci. He ought to be glad to be back in this unsentimental country, where icy reason had its temples and everything taught him a lesson.

But the *clochards* were something else. Making his way home that night, along the Boulevard St.-Germain, from the Bonfantes', where he had delivered his offerings and been persuaded to stay for supper, he stumbled over one sleeping on the Métro grating. They did that in the winter to keep warm; often, near the Odéon stop, between the rue St.-Grégoire-de-Tours and the rue de l'Ancienne-Comédie, there would be two or three dark shapes stretched out or huddled on the big iron ventilator grill, which they treated as a hot-air radiator. Normally he picked his way with care to avoid them or even, like the bad Levite in the story of the Good Samaritan, walked on the other side of the street. But tonight he forgot.

His foot trod on something soft and yielding, which stirred under him. He let out a yell of horror. He was walking on what seemed to be a human stomach, but it could be a pair of breasts. The creature was all wrapped up, like a bundle, in a sodden piece of cloth that might once have been an overcoat, and he could not tell its sex or find its face. At least it was still animate. He heard its voice mutter. Then it turned, stretched, settled itself in a more comfortable position; a head had thrust out, and under the street light he had a glimpse of a gray unshaven jaw. Apparently no vital organ had been crushed by being stepped on, but how could he be sure? Alcohol was an anesthetic; in the old days they used it when performing operations—Lord Nelson was crocked when they amputated his arm after Tenerife, or was it while he was dying, at Trafalgar? An awful sour smell came from the recumbent form; on the grill, a few feet away, lay an empty wine bottle.

Peter picked it up and took it to the trash-basket on the corner. If it was left there, somebody could trip on it and hurt themselves. On second thought, he went back and retrieved it. The guy must have paid a deposit on it, and in the morning he could get a few centimes back for the empty—enough for a cheap cup of coffee maybe. Overcoming his repulsion to touching the inert, stinking heap, he thrust the bottle firmly beneath its arm. The *clochard* responded with a hugging, cradling motion, as though the *gros rouge* was a baby. Disgusted, Peter turned away.

It was no use calling the cops to take the bum to a hospital, in case there might be internal bleeding. The gendarmes just laughed if a foreigner tried to get them to do something merciful about a *clochard*. That had happened to Dag, who found one slumped over the wheel of a car in the entrance to his building and thought it was somebody who had had a heart attack. And even if Peter were able, which he doubted, to haul the body home for first-aid, his concierge would probably hear him and bar the way; she had a complex about *clochards*. He started walking toward the *carrefour*, endeavoring not to quicken his steps. He felt furtive, like a motorist leaving the scene of an accident. Every few paces, he turned to look behind him. When he reached the intersection, the *clochard*, to his relief, was stirring. The shapeless hump rose with slow laborious movements like a dinosaur emerging from primeval slime and wove off in the other direction down the boulevard, holding the bottle and, for good measure, Peter's new carryall, which he had used to transport the Bonfante presents and which he could not remember having dropped.

What a reception committee! He felt so weak and sweaty that he could hardly make the stairs leading up to his street. Between the beggar and the drunk, he seemed to have run the gauntlet in some fiendish initiation rite. His heavy boots were slippery from the bum's vomit, and he sat down, holding his breath, and cleaned them with his handkerchief, which he then threw away.

After this, for a while, he encountered *clochards* everywhere, looming in his path, clutching at his sleeve, shuffling past him to a *zinc* or a *pissoir*. He wondered if they could be a form of DT's and instead of snakes or pink elephants he was seeing bottle noses, red rheumy eyes, purple veins, laceless shoes stuffed with newspapers, torn flapping overcoats, and layers on layers of indeterminate clothing stained with wine, spew, mud, and snot. He saw these apparitions zigzagging out of bars, sitting and lying on public benches, fumbling in the morning garbage, staggering along sidewalks, leaning against lamp-posts, propped in doorways, collapsed on the Métro steps, occasionally panhandling, and always at night extended on the various grills, grids, and gratings through which the hot stale breath of the Paris underground lung system was exhaled into the atmosphere, as though Paris itself was a vast unhygienic Russian stove on top of which snored these muzhiks in their bast and rags.

On his walks, he took to counting the grids in his neighborhood that might serve as their night-time couches; he would not have imagined there could be so many, square and rectangular, of diverse sizes and patterns—not just Métro ventilators, he came to realize, but ducts from bakery ovens, conduits from every kind of infernal furnace and combustion-unit sending up blasts of contaminated air. Unless you had a special interest like his or were walking with a girl wearing high heels, which were likely to get caught in the grillwork, you would never notice they were there.

He became conscious, too, of the number of empty bottles lying around in the *quartier*, on sidewalks and in gutters—flotsam warning him of the vicinity of some human wreck. He could not rid his mind of the subject. In the Métro, he watched to see whether anybody but him was reading the anti-alcoholism propaganda and taking it to heart. Where he used to ask himself whether women he saw on street-corners might be prostitutes, his speculations now anxiously turned on whether young workmen tossing it back at a *zinc* might not metamorphose tomorrow into *clochards*. What made a heavy drinker turn into a derelict was a mystery, he guessed, and for a born hypochondriac like himself this rendered the sickness more scary, like multiple sclerosis; you never knew where it might strike. He did not quake on his own behalf (when he drank too much, he got sick, which his aunt said showed he could never become a drunkard) but altruistically, which was worse. He began to look with prophetic dread on crones in the *épicerie* with a pair of Postillon bottles tucked into the bottom of their shopping baskets, husbands of concierges, waiters with trembling hands, the oyster-opener across from the Deux Magots, the customers in Nicolas, even priests.

At least he did not have to worry about his concierge. Though she occasionally lifted a medicinal glass with her aged *copines*, the bottle of nice wine he had given her for Christmas (acting on a bum steer from his father) was still standing on her buffet, like an altar ornament, next to a vase of yellowed "palms" from Palm Sunday and some framed tinted photographs of her relatives and Queen Fabiola. In fact, she had a horror of *clochards*, and if anything could cure him of his own obsession, it was listening to Madame Puel on the topic.

She read about their misdeeds in a concierges' newspaper and exchanged atrocity stories with her pals along the street. To judge by her accounts, her broom and mop got more exercise driving out the poor wretches she found asleep in her hallway than in their normal functions. As the nights got colder, she tightened the rules of the building. The big front door was locked at six o'clock, and when Peter came home after ten, it was not enough now to ring six times; he had to announce himself, which he hated, as he passed the *loge*. "*Levi*." If the tenants expected a guest after that hour, they had to come down themselves and open, by pre-arrangement. Yet despite these new security measures, the *clochards* somehow slipped in, almost, Peter felt, to Madame Puel's satisfaction, as though their breaching her defenses sharpened her relish for battle. Just as she seemed to enjoy telling him, by way of a morning greeting, "*Votre camarade a laissé la porte ouverte*," meaning, usually, Makowski, who often failed to close the front door when he left, though not as often as she pretended.

Sometimes when Peter got home she was lying in wait for him in her bathrobe and *bigoudis*. "*Levi*." To break the monotony of hearing his name issue from his own lips, he now and then used a falsetto or a sepulchral bass. He loathed it when her door unlocked before he could get past. "*Ah, bon soir, Monsieur Levi. J'en ai chassé un déjà vous savez. Une femme.*" Like his mother with a mouse-trap, she kept score. One triumphal night, when the people on the fourth floor left were having a party, she caught three in a row.

He wondered if Madame Puel guessed how miserable it made him to hear about these things and often he suspected she did. She thought he was "soft" on *clochards* because he had dared ask her one icy day what harm it would do to let them sleep in the hall or in the service stairway. "*Ah, monsieur, vous parlez. C'est pas un asile, notre immeuble.*" Who was to clean up their filth after them? "*Vous, Monsieur l'Américain, ou moi, l'employée?*" Fresh from his matins in the Re Magi toilet, Peter allowed that he could do it. The beldame laughed. He would not get the opportunity. It was easy for him to talk. Up there in the mansard, what did a strong young man have to fear from those *salauds*, while she, an old woman, on the ground floor in her *loge*, a widow, could be murdered in her bed?

Peter begged her to try to make distinctions. A *voyou* was one thing, but had a *clochard* ever knocked off anybody that she knew of? In his observation, they were too far gone to hold a bottle, let alone a weapon. "*Vous dites,*" she replied. About a week after this chat, he was surprised, at breakfast, by her rapping at his door. He could tell something important had happened; it was the first time she had been to his room—she used the elevator to reach the other tenants and left the back stairs to be swept by a slave on Saturdays. She was breathless, having made the rounds of the house. But she would not take a cup of coffee or even, at first, sit down. He had asked her, had he not, what harm a *clochard* could do? Could he guess what she had found last night on her third-floor landing when she had chased one of *them* out of the elevator? Peter could not guess. "*Deux mégots, Monsieur Levi! Vous vous rendez compte?*" In her withered palm, she held out two cigarette butts. "*Voilà!*"

Peter nodded. He could see her point. The whole old fire-trap building could have gone up in smoke. But how could she be sure that the butts had been left there by the man she chased? "*C'était une femme,*" she corrected. "*Toujours la même.*" Earlier, Madame Puel had smelled cigarette smoke and crept up the front stairs to investigate. But seemingly there had been nobody, and she had gone back to bed. The way she reconstructed it, the woman, hearing a noise, had hidden in the elevator. Then she had fallen asleep, and her body had slumped against the elevator door. That was how Madame Puel had found her, at 2:00 A.M., when a nurse on the fourth who worked nights had walked up, because the elevator was stuck, and seen what she thought was a cadaver inside.

It was lucky, said Peter, with a compassionate shudder, that the *clocharde* had not set fire to her clothes and burned up, trapped, in the elevator. Unlucky for *her*, thought the concierge; a creature like that was better off dead. Then at least she could not be a threat to others. For herself, Madame Puel did not care. "*Mais vous, qui êtes jeune, qui avez la vie devant vous . . . Et tous les autres, avec leurs familles, leurs distractions. Griller dans un incendie, c'est pas gai.*" She stared at the cigarette butts in her hand and let them drop on Peter's table. "*Eh bien, voilà. Je suis venue vous le dire. C'est tout.*" QED.

Looking into her parched ancient face, Peter had no recommendations to offer. It was pointless to argue that the old run-down building ought to install individual buzzer systems, like in the United States (the skinflint owner would rather collect the fire insurance and retire to the Côte d'Azur), and the joke he considered making ("I suppose you could put up 'No Smoking' signs") seemed inopportune. To his surprise, poor old Madame Puel, now that her point was proved, had become nicer.

"*Je suis bonne catholique, Monsieur Levi. Je sais bien que ces salauds sont des êtres humains en quelque sorte. Mais j' suis pas le Christ.*" It was no pleasure, she assured him, to have to drive them out night after night, but that was her job. "*J' suis payée pour ça.*" When her little dog had been alive, it had been a different story. He barked fearlessly at all intruders. In his day, the building was a fortress; no *clochards*, peddlers, or other unauthorized persons dared set foot in it. But then he nipped at the mailman, and they made her put "*Chien méchant*" on a placard hanging on the *loge* door. "*Chien méchant! Figurez-vous. Quelle honte.*" For *her*, Peter assented sympathetically. But the dog, after all, could not read. Madame Puel tossed her head; her nostrils flared. Boy had *sensed* the shame of it, and, shortly after, he had died. Of mortification. "*Mon vieux compagnon.*" Her eyes filled with tears. Boy had been the building's protector for nearly fifteen years, poor fellow, and all the thanks he got were objections to his barking—not even a marker in the dog cemetery. And now she had taken his place. "*Un chien de garde!*"

She was nothing but a watchdog. And everyone held it against her. "*Vous aussi, Monsieur Levi.*" "*Mais non!*" protested Peter, though of course she was right. He *had* held it against her, but he would not any more. "*Je comprends,*" he added. "*C'est une grande responsabilité.*" He went to the hot plate and put on water to make her a fresh cup of coffee. "*Ah, comme vous êtes bon! Toujours si gentil avec moi et courtois. Vous, un étranger!*" She wiped her eyes. He tried to think how to say in correct French that he would like to have known her dog.

It was human nature, he supposed, that as soon as she recovered she would start attacking *clochards* again. They threw up; they were incontinent; they had vermin; they stole. And if you let one stay, the next night there would be four. They were clever and tightly organized. "*Comme les juifs,*" murmured Peter. And yet maybe it was true. It might even be true what anti-Semites said about Jews sticking together and if-you-knew-one-you-had-to-know-their-friends. Making exceptions was usually a poor idea, he found; it was the same principle as "Just one won't hurt you."

You had to be willing to let the exception *be* the rule. And for that you would need to be Jesus Christ, as Madame Puel said, or a "*Parfait,*" like the Cathars in Languedoc he had been reading about, who thought the whole temporal world was a creation of Satan.

The worst, Peter decided, was the casuistry people practiced in going along with the temporal *status quo*. Even if, like the concierge, they had no choice—the way the world operated—but to give some unfortunate the bum's rush, they could not leave it at that. They had to *talk*. She had convinced herself, for instance, that drink made *clochards* insensible to the cold. "*Ils ne sentent rien, Monsieur Levi. Ils ne sont pas comme vous et moi.*" She really seemed to think that was a proved scientific fact. But if they did not feel the cold, why did they hole up in her elevator and in her entry hall? It never occurred to her to put the two things together.

Most of the American kids here had the same attitude. Some were actually obscene enough to give them the hotfoot, in a spirit of scientific experiment, to see if they would react.

Among the guys and girls who sat around at the American Center, there was a lot of shocked discussion and comparison of notes. The *clochards*, they decided, were a wholly different species from Bowery bums, tramps, hobos, or any other kind of floater or hopeless drunkard they knew. Like Peter, they could not get over finding them underfoot at night. "Aren't there shelters or anything, for Christ's sake?" It bothered them that the *clochards* would not behave normally, like American bums, who sidled up with a hard-luck story and asked for a handout. Instead of begging for dough to make a phone call to their sick old mother in Metz, the *clochards* just glared at them from wild inflamed eyes, like filthy prophets. And when, infrequently, they asked for money, it was more of a brusque demand than an appeal.

Some of those American nuts were avid to draw them out, get their life stories—no doubt to pad out their boring letters home. "They won't talk to me," a girl mourned. "I've tried and *tried*." "They're French," said Peter. He would never have dared venture more than a "*Bonjour*" to a *clochard* himself. To him it was unthinkable to want to ferret out the history of a down-and-outer: "What brought you to this, my good man?" He occasionally dropped a franc on some comatose form and then fled, as if he had committed a trespass. Like most of the other kids, he guessed, and like Madame Puel, he was afraid of *clochards*, the way people were afraid of snakes, even though they knew they were harmless. The pain these bums gave him was moral.

He was ashamed of being so ignorant of a subject that was so much on his mind. But the data gathered by his peer group came chiefly from café waiters and added up to the fact, if it was one, that the *clochard* community was a microcosm of France: you could meet all kinds among them, *agrégés*, doctors, actresses from the Comédie-Française; the distinguished toper with the baby carriage who went around the *quartier* collecting rubbish was a former banker. . . . But that was what the census-taker would note in any hell, *e.g.*, Dante's. That they lived by selling the rubbish they collected and on sponging—mainly off each other—was somewhat more informative, though it left you wondering why, if they were capable of organizing, they did not go a step farther and arrange some minimal housing—even discarded pup tents or sleeping-bags.

According to Silly Platt, who was an authority on *clochards*, Peter's question showed he had not grasped their psychology. "They don't feel the cold the way we do." "That's what my concierge says." "She's so right. They feel it up to a point but not enough to do anything constructive about it. In fact they'd *rather* mess up the hall of a building that somebody has just swept or wallow in their puke on the sidewalk. Have you ever seen a bear's wallow? Guck they like to roll in. That's what these bums go for. They're animals. I gave one half a franc the other day ('*Donnez-moi; j'ai faim*'), and when he leaned over to thank me, sort of bowing, he threw up on my shoes. It's really crazy. He must have thought he was showering me with gratitude. And I watched another one on the Boul Mich. He was shitting down his pants leg. Right in broad daylight. And he just staggered on with this smile on his face, as if the oily stuff slithering down his leg and leaking on the sidewalk was perfume. Guerlain Number Two." "*Basta*," said Peter, gagging.

He was only half persuaded that Silly knew whereof he spoke. "You don't think they do it more as a revenge on society?" "You make it too complicated. If you just look on them as animals, they won't bother you any more. Actually I get sort of a kick out of them." Silly was an authority on several aspects of French life, high and low. He had figured all the angles and liked to live dangerously. A few days after classes started, Peter had run into him on the Métro platform, preparing to ride first class on a second-class ticket. He had some old punched first-class tickets in his pocket, in case the *contrôleur* passed through the car, checking up. "Come on!" Reluctantly, Peter boarded. He had never been in first class before.

"Watch this!" said Silly. "I'm going to have some fun." Obediently, Peter watched a middle-aged Frenchman in a beret who was sitting on a *strapontin* opposite them. Silly's penetrating gray eyes were drilling holes in him, compelling him to look up from his newspaper and meet that transfixing gaze. The man gave a wondering glance sidewise at Peter, turned back to his paper, then peered out again. Meanwhile Silly's orbs did not waver. To Peter's astonishment, the man accepted the challenge. Their eyes crossed swords. It was a

staring match. Finally the Frenchman's eyes dropped. At the
next station, muttering, he got off. "I make them get them
down," announced Silly. "Get what down?" "Their eyes, don't
you see?"

He selected another victim and went through the same
performance. "I always win. The guy that starts has the advantage." "But why do you do it?" "To test my will power.
Watch!" This time it was a youth about their own age, sitting
with his mother. He was harder. Silly leaned slightly forward.
"Get them down, get them down," he was murmuring, like an
incantation. Then the mother caught on. She nudged her son.
"*Jean! Qu'est-ce que tu fais là?*" That did it. "Watch now.
They'll move." Sure enough, the woman, with an angry look
backward, led the boy to another part of the car. "It's more
amusing when they retreat right off the train. Like that first
guy in the beret. You could tell it wasn't his stop."

On the Champs-Elysées, after Silly had turned in an airplane
ticket, they went to a café. Peter was curious about the expression "Get them down." It was a sort of code, Silly guessed, for
getting the French down. "If you don't practice all the time,
they have the upper hand, don't you see? They're one up on
us, knowing French. You have to stay in training." This
eyeball-to-eyeball exercise, he explained, was just one of the
power games he made a point of playing with the French, especially shopkeepers. "They always expect the foreigner to
yield first. When you don't, they're at a total loss. Completely
off base. It's crazy." The thing was never to accept their rules;
invent your own.

For instance, the markets. "You know that old gag about
making you buy a kilo?" Peter groaned. "God, yes." "You
don't mean you still go along with it?" "All the French do,"
argued Peter. "We're not French! We're Americans!" "OK,
but I don't see how you get around it." "I have a system. Listen." When he went marketing, Silly never took more than a
few francs along. He looked over the vendors' merchandise
and decided what he wanted to buy. "Say it's cabbage. I take
two francs out of my pocket and tell the guy, 'Give me two
francs' worth. That's all the money I have.'" "And it works?"
Not only did it work; he got more for his money that way.
"Look. If four oranges weigh out at two francs and twenty-five

centimes, they let me have them for two. They're not going to take a slice off the fourth one. It never fails." Peter felt torn between admiration and envious skepticism. He relaxed a bit when he heard that Silly did his shopping on the rue Mouffetard. He doubted very much that Silly's system would function at the Marché Buci.

Instead of debating that, he asked what had happened in Switzerland. "You were right," Silly admitted. The ski-instructor job had not materialized. But he had got a good tan and really scored playing poker. Moreover he had met a fantastic French girl who had invited him to her home in Versailles. "I'm getting around quite a lot now, as a matter of fact." He had been given hospitality in a number of "homes," which Peter translated to mean rich French people's houses. "How do you do it?" said Peter. "I mean, get to know them—any kind of French?"

Naturally Silly had a system. "Have you noticed that I never wear a watch?" He did that on purpose so as to be able to ask for the time. Also, he did not carry a lighter or matches. "But what use is it if they give you a light or tell you what time it is? In my experience, a hand just delivers a box of matches, and that's it. No words wasted. Honestly, I've been going to the same café near where I live since I got here, and not even the waiter speaks to me."

"You should circulate more. And when somebody French gives you a light, don't just say '*Merci*.' Start talking. Don't wait for them to make the move. And once you have your opening set, you have to be ready with the follow-up. Plan ahead, like in chess. All the time be thinking about how you're going to shift your chair around to pull it up and sit down at their table. In fact when you come into a café look the terrain over and pick the table you want to be next to. Not a group that's practically finished and getting ready to pay the check. Not lovey-dovey couples. Never Americans, because they'll try to pick *you* up, and that's fatal."

"Fatal?" "For both sides. If an American girl picks me up, it's because she's decided I'm French. They want to meet French boys, to practice French on them; American boys vice versa. And older American tourists just want to pick your brains for restaurants and night clubs. Or they have a daughter who's a student who'll be joining them. American girls bore me over here. I make a point of not knowing any, if I can help it. I mean the student crowd. They're a drag. You should do the same. The idea is to be stripped for action."

The advice was wasted on Peter, but it was nice of Silly to give it. Peter could not help liking him for the candid way he shared his know-how and elucidated his ploys. Like the Phi Beta Kappa key he wore, which he had rented from his brother, Barnabas. "But isn't that sort of dangerous? If you run into a real Phi Beta Kappa, won't they start asking embarrassing questions?" "And do what? Call the police? It's just another icebreaker, don't you see? Everybody that's been to college knows right away that I'm too young and giddy to be a real Phi Bete. So they get interested in how I came by it, and I tell them. I'm not really fooling anybody. And the French, who don't know what it stands for, can't wait to have their curiosity satisfied."

He evidently thought that Peter was an unsuccessful opera-tor in need of a helping hand. As a former fellow-sufferer, he sympathized with Peter's shyness, as though this condition made them a single person, like in those testimonial ads for curing baldness that showed the same head before and after. This was a mistake that Peter could not bother to clear up. But though he did not feel much like Silly and would rather remain in his shell than grow what the guy called "armor," it was sur-prising how much they had in common. Even in politics they were not so far apart. Over here, Silly felt more liberal, he re-vealed, though he expected he would revert when he got back to Princeton and the government-studies routine. He was more conscious of poor people here. His father, who was a town planner, kept him on a tight budget, and it interested Peter to learn that Silly, except in his dress (he was wearing a golden corduroy suit and another flowing cashmere scarf), was even more economical than himself. He lived with five other kids in an apartment near the rue Mouffetard, sur-rounded by Algerian cafés where knife fights went on. There was a kerosene stove for heating, but it was so cold you could see your breath. The toilet out in the hall they shared with three other people, and girls were afraid to go to it, on account of VD. They had rigged up a portable shower in the living room, where Silly slept on a cot between blankets, without sheets, to save on laundry. By cooking his own meals, he could get along, he figured, on $1.75 a day, if he had to.

Amazingly, he liked animals, and they discussed going to the zoo at Vincennes together, when it got slightly warmer. Silly had studied zoology and he had a bear he called "his" in the menagerie at the Jardin des Plantes. Whenever he was depressed, he went and visited the bear. He also liked motorbikes, but his father had made him sell his before coming over. If his aunt would send him the money, he might buy Peter's.

Peter's heart leapt. "Would you like to come and see it?" Together they went to Makowski's place, where they inspected the motorbike and powwowed about the draft and Vietnam. The stolid, somber Pole did not take to Silly Boy, who had a lighthearted theory that the U.S. and Hanoi were merely playing poker: Hanoi had all its cards face up on the table, which gave it an advantage, because the U.S. did not want to uncover its hole cards but was gambling that Hanoi would cave in without "seeing" the U.S. royal flush of bombers and Marines. "And what will happen when the crunch comes?" "There won't *be* any crunch. It's a game, see." He knew a girl's father who worked in the Quai d'Orsay. The Russians were in a deal with the U.S. to fold up the game and deliver Hanoi to the peace table. At a new Geneva Conference. It was shaping up right now. Makowski did not believe it, and if there was such a deal it would be a sellout to Communism, just like in Eastern Europe. Silly said no, Vietnam would be neutralized, like Austria. Both players would get their ante back.

When they left Makowski's room, Silly said he was sorry that he could not bring Peter to his apartment. They were having problems. The other tenants were circulating a petition to have them bounced out on account of the noise they made and the parties they threw. His roommates took it seriously, though to him it was a laugh. He thought it was a sort of feather in his cap to have brought the neighbors to the point of petition and assembly. "But pro tem we can't invite anybody. Anyway, the place is a mess."

Peter found Silly, as a companion, a welcome relief from himself. His hyperactive brain, unlike Peter's, seemed to work full time for his airy will. It did not go looking for trouble. Silly's will, Peter estimated, could not be farther from the moral will of Kant, yet there was something innocent and childlike in its operations. If other people were means to him, they were also in a strange way ends. He did not even seem particularly ambitious underneath his patter. "My father really worries that I might become an opportunist," he confided, which made Peter laugh. "You mean you think I am one already?" Peter was not sure. "Paris is my chance to test myself, don't you understand? Have you noticed how many mirrors there are here? Oh yes. It's fantastic. You should try counting. Frenchmen look at themselves all the time. I feel I was predestined to come to Paris. I have to find myself. Put myself together out of all those bitty reflections I see in their eyes." Peter laughed again. "That would make you a mosaic, Silly."

Following this he heard no more from Silly. It was typical of that butterfly to vanish after a seemingly serious heart-to-heart and a pending deal on the motorbike. But Peter had other things on his agenda: the Wellesley girl had written that she was coming to Paris; Roberta had written and asked him to tea; his mother wrote that she might be passing through Paris around Valentine's Day on her way to play in Poland and wanted him to find her a hotel. . . . The groundhog had failed to see his shadow, so spring might be on winter's traces. When his allowance came, he thought of inviting Silly to join him in another oyster-eating orgy—this time *chez* him. He had acquired an oyster-opener. But since they both had no telephone, he procrastinated.

He met him next at the dentist's, when he kept an appointment to have his teeth cleaned, for which a reminder card had been sent: Monday, February 8; 10:00 A.M.; 33 boulevard Malesherbes. Peter had almost not showed up, after the night he had spent, the grimmest in his life. But because his mother was coming, he made himself obey the summons. When he came into the dentist's waiting room, with the morning papers under his arm, he was crying, and the last person he would have wanted to find, reading *Anesthesia Progress*, was Silly Boy Platt.

The night before, on a premature busman's holiday, he had taken in a horror movie—the ten o'clock show. Coming home, he had noted the usual *clochards* on the Métro grating. All was quiet at the concierge's when he passed. Then, on the second landing, he found it—what looked like a human puddle in the weak light of the *minuterie*. Mechanically, he circumvented it and continued his climb. He had seen that it was a woman, rolled up in a brown coat resembling a horse's blanket. That checked out. He felt no surprise, only a horrible weariness. His head was nodding up and down in recognition of the event. This had been waiting for him, he should have known, like a big package with his name on it: Peter Levi, Esq., Noted Humanitarian. In fact, it was overdue. A man's character was his fate—Heraclitus. Old Atropos had taken his measurements as if for a suit of clothes. All afternoon, while he peacefully watched birds in the Yvelines, the plot against him had been thickening.

Nevertheless, he went steadily on, up another flight. Then his steps lagged. He halted and considered. So far as he could tell, the rest of the building was asleep. Waking Madame Puel, to get her to cope, was not a possibility, despite the pleasure it might give her. Also eliminated was kicking the poor bum out himself. He could not. The alternative was what he was already doing: leave her down there on the landing and pursue his course to bed. To him, it was cold and drafty, but to her, it was doubtless cosy, compared with the street. She had the coat over her and probably a lot of filthy sweaters underneath. In the morning, she would be stiff, but it would not take her long to get oiled again.

Till morning, nobody could find her. Madame Puel would not be prowling up the service stairs, and even if that happened, she could not know that *Peter* had seen the bum and failed to react. The woman could have crept in after he had gone to bed. Maybe when that night nurse came home, tired, she could have left the front door ajar. There could be lots of explanations.

The *minuterie* went off. In the dark, its natural element, the voice of conscience bayed. A Peter Levi law said: Do not do what thou wouldst not be known to have done. If an action tempted you to disclaim it, you had better think twice. He thought, groping along the wall for the light button. The pale light came on again, showing him the worn splintery stair treads. Highly inflammable. And of course it was the same *clocharde*, the heavy smoker. It had to be. He acknowledged the other alternative that had been picking at his sleeve, like a person waiting to be recognized.

Even when she opened her bleary eyes, the drunk woman did not understand what Peter wanted. His French did not get through the fumes of alcohol to her. He tried pointing upward and making encouraging signs, but her brain could not grasp that they were going to his apartment. At last he had her upright, and they started climbing, he leading the way and beckoning to her to follow, like Eurydice. She was younger than he thought at first—maybe only in her late thirties—and her features, though blurry, were soft and still feminine. She smelled of tobacco and sour stale booze, but at least she had not vomited recently. On the fourth-floor landing, she fell down, and he had trouble getting her to her feet again. She broke away from his grasp and began rolling heavily down the circular stairs. The last flight was an uphill battle all the way, with the *minuterie* constantly going off and plunging them into darkness. She took advantage of the dark to crawl away. Also she made quite a lot of noise. He was afraid his landlady would wake up. This showed him that his law needed some revision. There were times when you would not want to be caught performing a *good* action. While embarrassment played a part in his desire not to be discovered in the act of dragging a *clocharde* up to his apartment, his main motive was the fear that somebody would prevent him from carrying out the project. It was strange. Even now, the wish closest to his heart was that this female shambles would melt away, like a bad dream he might still wake from, yet at the same time, contradictorily, she had become an assignment he was determined to complete. And a big element in his determination was the resistance he could count on meeting in others, which in fact he was already meeting in the inert object herself.

Unlocking his door and switching on the light, he saw that she was cowering, afraid to come in and afraid, he guessed, to run away. The glazed terror in her eyes told him clearly that she expected *him* to murder *her*—a realization that made him laugh dourly. Maybe a female *clochard* had reason to shrink from "normals," and his reassuring smiles, far from accomplishing their purpose, might be scaring her stiff. He could be a grinning sex maniac. Nevertheless, having looked around the room, she consented to come in.

He fixed her a place to sleep on the floor, next to the radiator, using his sheepskin-lined jacket and a chair cushion and praying that she would not be sick. He rolled up some sweaters for a pillow. Then he led her into his toilet and shut the door. When she failed to come out, he knocked. No reply. Eventually he went in and got her and propelled her to the bathroom with a clean towel. Again she did not emerge. For her, these were hiding-places. He found her huddled in the little bathtub. She had not washed. He guided her back into the living room. "*Voici votre lit, mademoiselle.*" For some reason, he could not call her "*madame.*" Then he showed her his own bed, to make it clear that she was safe. She responded only to signs, and the few thick unintelligible words she mumbled from time to time seemed to be addressed to somebody who was not him. After that, he got out a partly full bottle of wine and poured her some in a glass. He gave her a piece of stale bread, which was all he had, and some cheese. She drank the wine and stretched out her glass for more. "*Après.*" He pointed to the bread and cheese. "*Pain.*" Then to the wine bottle. "*Puis vin.*"

So long as this dumb show went on, it was not so bad. But finally the time came when he had to turn out the light. In the dark, he slipped into the bathroom with his pajamas, to get undressed and washed. On reflection, he decided to sleep in his pants and jersey, taking only his jacket and shoes off. He could not tuck himself in, like a good little boy, in his nice clean pajamas, while the woman lay on the floor in her dirty ragged coat. It did not seem right, even, to brush his teeth.

From his bed, he was unable to tell whether she was awake or not. She hacked and hawked repeatedly, with a smoker's cough, but perhaps she did that in her sleep. The hawking made him feel sick, especially when it turned into choking and a long-drawn-out noise like retching. He put his head under the blanket and covered it with a pillow. He could not smell any vomit, but the window was open. He wished he had a flashlight so that he could creep across and make sure that she had not puked over the landlady's cushion. But if she had, what could he do? The only thing was to go to sleep and forget about it till morning. But he could not fall asleep, though after about an hour the *clocharde* was finally quiet.

He recited all the poems he knew and reviewed the Sistine ceiling. Then as he started to drift off, a terrible thought hit him. She might wake up and start smoking. After all the fresh air he had had today, if he dropped into the arms of Morpheus, he might never know the difference. In bringing her up here, he had never thought of that. It meant that he had only transferred the problem several stories higher. She might still set her clothes on fire and burn up the building. It was no great consolation that he would be among the first to be incinerated. He thought sadly of Madame Puel. She would never forgive him if she died on a widow's pyre.

He tried to remember what you did to put a fire out. You were not supposed to use water but smother it with blankets. But he had only one blanket. He should have taken the woman's matches before he turned out the light. Now it was too late. If he woke her now, it might frighten her. He tiptoed across the room and put an ashtray beside her. Yet that was inadequate precaution. He saw what he had to do: stay awake and keep vigil, like the Dutch boy with his finger in the dike. He did not believe that you had a duty to yourself or maybe even your family, but you owed something to a unit as large as a building.

These anxieties were giving him a perverse craving to smoke himself. In the toilet, he lit up. It had a tiny skylight, which he opened, so that the cigarette smoke would not filter under the door into the living room and put ideas in her head. But this stratagem destroyed his pleasure. He threw the cigarette into the toilet and flushed it away. There was an awful groaning and clanking of water pipes, which he feared might alert his landlady; he had strict orders never to pull the chain after 1:00 A.M. When he came back to bed, the *clocharde* was snoring and making a gurgling noise herself.

Now that sleep was forbidden him, of course he got sleepy. But just as he was slipping into oblivion, a massive depression laid him low. It was the *clocharde*. A sort of swampy miasma was coming from her that he could sense, like something physical. She was poisoning his good deed.

He sought to analyze the bitter melancholy rising in his soul like heartburn. OK, you were not meant to do good actions for *enjoyment* exactly, but they ought not to be so positively repugnant that you had to hold your nose morally while performing them. And that was just how he felt. Instead of being glad that he had helped somebody out, inexplicably he stank to himself. The only moment, he could honestly say, that had given him any pleasure was when he got her to eat the bread and cheese. Yet that was when he was teaching her, with a primitive little reward system, not to be a *clocharde* at least while she was in his apartment but to obey his house rules and drink her wine with food. Act like a fellow-creature. In short, she was only bearable for the few false minutes when he kidded himself that he was reforming her. But he had failed with the clean towel.

It had been a hideous mistake to share his four walls with misery and indigence even for one night. In fact he had no business bringing her here, unless he meant to keep her, which of course he did not. The sole ray of hope was that this cruel and unusual punishment could not last long. In the morning she would scram. She had stopped snoring. Maybe she too was counting the minutes till dawn. She would be no more eager than he was to repeat this experience. On that he would take a bet.

Yet the worst was that, even furnished with hindsight, he did not see what else one Peter Levi could have done than exactly what he did, which made the mistake in some crazy way irreparable. He could walk away from the problem in the street but not in his own building. The problem, as they said, had come home to him. He supposed he might have given her some money for a hotel—bribery.

Madame Puel had hit the nail on the head. "*C'est pas un asile, notre immeuble.*" In the Great Scheme of Things, the building had not been intended to be a *clochards'* dormitory. But what could you do when some *clochards* were insensible to the Great Scheme of Things and refused to *know their place*?

There was no solution. Silly's advice, to look on them as animals, did not meet the problem at all. Tossing in his sheets, Peter was feeling a nauseous repulsion which he would certainly not feel toward an animal. Between himself and this woman was an immeasurable distance that proximity of breathing accentuated.

A sense of solidarity which alone could have justified his action was simply not there. If there had ever been any doubt, now he knew for sure that whatever happened to him in the way of degradation, he could never be a *clochard*. In fact it was much easier to picture himself, if ostracized by his fellow-men, in the form of a stray cat running from Madame Puel's broom.

As a stray cat, all bones and fur, he would be sympathetic to himself, whereas for himself as a *clochard* he would feel an ungovernable antipathy. Yet where was the difference? If a *clochard* had fleas, a cat had fleas. The stink of human urine was not any worse than the stink of cat pee. And as for a *clochard* becoming a permanent charge if you gave them money or fed them (which some of the kids at the American Center alleged), the same could be said with more probability of an animal, which, once you fed it, was fairly certain to return. Finally, the nervous fear that human presence was inspiring in him had no rational basis: the danger of bodily attack was infinitely less than the danger of being scratched or bitten by a crazed beast.

Yet somehow she had him on the defensive, as if being himself was a form of hypocrisy. He was bracing himself against a latent aggression he sensed in her wild dirty hair and general foulness. He sorted out his thoughts. The menace was not to his person but to his sovereignty in the little kingdom he had constructed—his nest of Borromini angels, plants, books, *espresso* pot, student lamp, the drawing he was making, from nature, of a leaf. It was not these things, as *things*, these bits of organic and inorganic materials, toward which he felt protective. If a kitten or a puppy destroyed them, he would be reconciled to the havoc, since the animal was part of Mother Nature —his and Kant's respected friend. However a puppy in your room acted, you could brush your teeth and put on your pajamas.

If this *clocharde* seemed more alien to him than any brute creature, it was just *because* she shared with him, supposedly, a moral faculty that animals did not have, and this moral faculty in man was a regulatory instinct that kept him in balance with the natural things of the world, which were good without putting out any effort. But it was hard to believe that there was any such universal moral faculty when you had a proof to the contrary a few feet away from you. If it was not the *clocharde's* choice that she had got into this grisly state, then there was no freedom of the will, and if it *was* her choice, of which tonight he felt convinced, then the will's objects were not the same for everybody. Either way, everything he cared about fell to pieces. As for the great "Know yourself," after tonight, he would rather not. It was no use pretending that there was common humanity in *him* when all he could think of in the midst of his philosophizing was how many minutes still had to pass before dawn would come to his rescue.

Some time before dawn came, in fact, he fell asleep. When he woke, it was already light out; the improvised couch across the room was empty. There was a trail of urine going toward the door, which was partly open. She had stolen his outside brass doorknob, of all things, and he wondered how she had managed it. Did she carry tools? Otherwise his possessions were intact.

Fate had more in store for him. There was the news in the morning papers awaiting him in the kiosk at the Madeleine, as he slogged to it, drenched from a downpour. All across the front page of the *Herald Tribune* in giant black letters: U.S. PLANES BOMB NORTH VIETNAM BASE. So it had happened, but he refused to believe it yet; he had to see it in the New York *Times*. But the *Times* international edition was sold out, and he took the *Figaro*. 49 AVIONS U.S. (*ayant décollés de trois porte-avions*) BOMBARDENT DES INSTALLATIONS AU NORD DU 17e PARALLELE. JOHNSON AUX FAMILLES AMERICAINES: "ORDRE DE REGAGNER LES ETATS-UNIS." It was in the *Times* of London too. There was no escaping it, any more than he could have eluded the *clocharde* once he found her in his path.

On top of everything, the dentist found a cavity. "Blue Monday," he said waggishly in his Berlitz English. When Peter got out of the chair, Silly was waiting for him. He had been reading the papers Peter had left and he looked pale. "It's bad," he agreed. "But maybe it's just a one-shot thing. They say it's a reprisal." Peter shook his head. "Why would Johnson order American families home then? Your 'poker game'!" "Well, yes. Johnson betrayed us." "Our country! And we're part of it. I said I'd kill myself if we did this and I'm still alive."

"Let's go to the zoo," urged Silly. "It helps usually." "OK." They decided to visit the menagerie at the Jardin des Plantes. "We'll see my bear," said Silly. "That will cheer you up. He's such a nice neat bear. He rakes the leaves in his den."

In preference to the Métro, they took a bus. After last night, Peter could not stand any more confinement. He sat with his chin slumped on his chest while Silly tried to make conversation. "That poor guy Benjy, remember? He willed me his PX card." "You mean he's dead?" "No, no. That was only the expression he used. But now probably he's had it. We'll send regular troops; what do you think?" "Yes." "But you and I don't have too much to worry about." "Why?" "On account of our French, don't you see? Because we can speak French, they won't send us into combat. Even if they draft students like in World War II. They'll keep us back of the front lines, in Saigon, doing liaison with the high-up Vietnamese. I added that up last summer, when Goldwater was making his pitch." "I won't go," said Peter. "But how? Unless you're a Quaker or join the Peace Corps or something?" "I don't know but I won't, that's all."

They watched Silly's brown bear for a while, but he was not raking any leaves. "'*Ursus arctos Linné*,'" read Peter. "Aristotle talks about him." For a moment this made him feel better; at least a few of the things of the world were indestructible. The bear acted sad and somnolent; his fur was a dirty tawny brown like an old worn coat. "Probably he wants to hibernate. But the zoo-keepers won't let him. He has to entertain the public." "I'll pep him up," said Silly. He started aiming peanuts at his nose. The animal's red lower lip came out like a shoe-horn, and they saw his teeth and small tongue. Silly thought of a new sport. He aimed the peanuts just outside the bars, so that the bear had to put his paw out to pull them in. "Hey, quit that! Don't you see that sign?" DANGER in yellow capitals was posted on the bear cage. "He can't reach me." "Anyway, it's cruel," objected Peter. "No, it isn't. It's a game. I always play with him. He loves it."

Peter felt quite relieved when they finally left the bears' den. Though he had been wishing to die all morning, he did not want a bear to get him. In the avalanche of events descending on him, that would be excessive. He proposed that they go explore the labyrinth at the other end of the park. But it was not a real maze, which he had been hoping for; they climbed up a little hill and saw an old armillary sphere and a weather vane. It was easy to find their way out. Going back to the menagerie, they passed a curious exhibit: a cross-section of a giant sequoia, donated by the State of California, through the American Legion, to the *Anciens Combattants de France*, 1927. Standing on its side, the sequoia slice looked like a ringed target, with shiny copper markers stuck into the widening rings like metal flags, noting mammoth occurrences in world history corresponding with the tree's age at the time they happened: the Birth of Christ, the Destruction of Pompeii, Charlemagne, the Landing of the Pilgrims. Peter laughed bitterly. "They should bring this up to date. 'February 7, 1965. Uncle Sam bombs small helpless nation.'" "Maybe the start of World War III," suggested Silly. "You saw: Kosygin is in Hanoi." "I don't care if it's World War III," said Peter. He did, but that was not the point.

Silly wanted to visit the monkey house. Peter objected. "Let's look at some of the trees and plants instead." It struck him that the closer Nature got to the human, the uglier it could be. You could hardly find a plant that was not beautiful, even if in a strange mottled way, but there were plenty of hideous simians. He wondered if it could happen that one morning he might wake up and find that trees, plants, and flowers did not seem beautiful to him any more. That would have to be the end of ethics. It might be starting to happen now. To his horror, the botanical garden had a derelict, desolate appearance, and the rows on rows of denuded plants with their pale-green identifying markers reminded him of a cemetery. "Did you know that Linnaeus tried to get a job as a gardener?" "Oh?" "Nobody would hire him," said Peter.

Silly was still pleading for the monkeys. They compromised. Peter would look at exotic birds, and he would look at gorillas and baboons. At an entrance gate, they were stopped. Without realizing it, they had left the paying section when they went to see the labyrinth. So if they wanted to come back in, they would have to pay again. Silly put up an argument. If the attendant did not let them in free, they would crawl under the fence. To Peter's astonishment, the gatekeeper let them pass.

They walked by a pond of aquatic birds. Peter recognized

some Common European Cormorants drying their wings on the rocks. It was cold and dismal. Scattered about the run-down grounds were strange neglected little wooden huts trimmed with stars and circles and looking as if some crazy Russian or Finn had made them up out of a fairy tale—witch housing, with a *renard famélique* pacing the dooryard. They came to the swans, which were floating down a dirty stream or canal. Some were waddling on their flipper feet across the grass. "Hey, a black swan!" said Silly. "Let's feed him." Leaning over the wire fence, he coaxed the swan to approach. They both put peanuts on the iron fence-bar and watched him crack them in his coral-red bill. A white swan with a banded leg came up. Silly tried to engage it in a staring match, but the swan after a minute turned its head away and flapped its wings rather crossly. He tossed peanuts between the two birds to get them to compete.

Wearied of playing witness to this, Peter ate a few peanuts himself. In his pocket, wrapped in a Kleenex, was a brioche he had bought for breakfast and been unable to eat. He consumed part of that. He did not know much about swans, but it seemed to him that they were becoming quarrelsome, and he grew irritated with Silly for stirring up needless strife among these captive creatures now noisily bristling their feathers. "Leave them alone. Let's go." But Silly was having fun. As a counter-move, Peter tore up his brioche and whistled to the black swan to come to him. Diverted, the bird drew near. It slithered its neck along the ground like an uncoiling garden hose, causing some sparrows to scatter. Instead of throwing the crumbs, Peter held them out, to see if it would eat from his hand. "'*Qu'ils mangent de la brioche*,'" he said. Then he felt a sharp pain in the fleshy part of his palm, the part bounded by his life line. The bird had struck at him savagely. Before he could pull back, he felt another gash, in his forearm, and a third. He heard his voice screaming "*No!*"

Reeling away from the low iron fence, he flung up his other hand to protect his face. It faintly surprised him that the swan did not take wing and continue the attack. Silly supported him to a bench. Blood was trickling from his hand and staining his shirt-cuff, but when he nerved himself to examine them, the gashes did not seem as deep as he expected. Silly had thought it was an artery. "Or a vein anyway. Should I try to make a tourniquet?" "No. It'll be OK. But I think I'd like to go home now." He accepted Silly's offer to take him in a taxi. They wrapped his hand and wrist up in their handkerchiefs, which were clean, thanks to the dental appointment.

Silly left him at his door and sped on to a pharmacy for Mercurochrome and Band-Aids. Fortunately, Madame Puel's door-curtains were drawn. Peter could not face her now. He did not want to answer any questions that might arise about the doorknob. When Silly appeared with supplies, they laved his wounds with a whole bottle of Mercurochrome and applied the Band-Aids. Silly wondered whether they should call Roberta. "No." He fixed Peter some coffee and went to a café and brought back sandwiches and hard-boiled eggs, which he insisted on paying for. He was still blaming himself. Then he remade Peter's tousled bed. "You'd better try to sleep now."

Peter was in a bed, which he suspected was in the American Hospital. He could not remember anything clearly about the last few days. The last he could recall was the swellings in his armpits which had convinced him, when he studied them in his mirror, that he had bubonic plague. They were just like the buboes Boccaccio described with pungent detail in the *Decameron*. Now he asked himself whether he was in a private room or in an isolation ward. He could not guess how he had got here or when. Had he turned himself in or had somebody brought him? He had a faint recollection of leaving class some morning in the middle of a lecture. He thought he would remember riding in an ambulance.

His bed was cranked down flat. There was nobody around now. But there had been a great many people in his room quite recently, he believed. Doctors and nurses and, if he was not mistaken, the Bonfantes, who had looked rather awed. But if the Bonfantes had been here, he could not have the plague. He felt that Silly Boy had been around too and maybe Roberta but he was not sure. Some of his visitors must have been imaginary. He assumed he had been delirious and even now he could tell he had a fever. He drank some water through a glass straw from a glass on his bedside table.

He tried to think back carefully. It seemed as if he had fallen

down on a tiled floor that might have been in a hospital bathroom. After that, a total blackout. Reaching under the hospital
nightshirt, he explored his armpits; the buboes appeared to be
gone. Then his lucidity faded; he lost the order of his thoughts.
Somebody was taking his temperature and feeling his pulse.
But before he could ask her anything, she went away. When he
opened his eyes again, he was pleasantly surprised to see the
Delphic Sibyl. He recognized her immediately; she was wearing that green peaked bonnet. She must have come to tell him
something, and he had the feeling that she had tried to before,
some other day. But while he waited eagerly for her to unroll
the prophetic scroll she was holding, she began smiling on him
with extreme tenderness and was replaced by his mother, who
also had a roll of paper in her hand, which opened up into a
valentine.

She bent down and kissed him. "Well, Peter," she said
fondly, pulling at his forelock. "You've had quite an adventure." That insanely cheerful sentence proved she was real—the
fair Rosamund coming out of her bower to interrupt the Delphic Sibyl. Now he would never know what was in the message.
But at least she could tell him where he was. He was right: it
was the American Hospital. He had come in with a bad infection; the Platt boy had brought him. It actually was Valentine's
Day; he had been here since Friday. "But what happened?"
"They gave you penicillin, and you went into shock. Somebody should have realized you were allergic to penicillin."
"Who?" Peter began to feel suspicious. He was not aware of
having any such allergy. She was covering up something.
Maybe he was dying. He reflected. He must be wrong. If he
were dying, Bob would have come too. And his father would
be stalking up and down, wearing a black frown and a black
suit, looking for somebody to blame, preferably his mother.
Sitting up, he imitated his voice: "'Didn't you *know* the boy
was allergic to penicillin?'"

"You must be feeling better, Peter. In fact that's what *babbo*
said. But I don't think you ever had it. Just Aureomycin and
those things. They don't give penicillin to children usually."
"But what was the matter, that they gave it to me now? I
thought I had the Black Death." His mother gave her gay laugh.
"Swan bite, dearest. Don't you remember? You were bitten by a

black swan. Just like a person in a myth." "Swans don't bite, Mother. They strike with their bill." "I prefer swan bite." This insistence made Peter feel tired. "They're extremely dangerous," his mother went on. "The doctor told me they can break an arm with one blow of their bill. You might have had a fracture too. The Platt boy says it was his fault." "It was. But never mind. What did I have—rabies?" "I don't think swans are rabid, Peter. The doctor didn't mention that. A heavy infection, he said." Peter nodded. "Polluted water. But I washed the wounds out well with Mercurochrome. Every day." "So the doctor told me. You looked like a fire-engine. But you could have used a gallon of Mercurochrome, and it wouldn't have helped, he said. Mercurochrome is only good for superficial cuts, Peter." "Did you know that?" "Not really."

Peter's head was aching. She touched his forehead. "You still have a little temperature. You'd better not talk any more. I'll sit here and read." "Have you been here before, Mother?" "Yesterday. I came from the airport. You were delirious then." "Am I really going to be all right, Mother? Tell me the truth." "Absolutely, Peter. By tomorrow, your fever should be gone. But you'll be weak for a few days. On top of everything else, you fainted in the bathroom, from the penicillin, and may have had a slight concussion." He lay back. "Oh, God!" he cried, remembering. "Are we still bombing those Vietnamese?" She nodded. Tears of rage rolled out of his eyes. "I hate us." "They claim it's only military targets." "Do you believe that?" "No." "Have we hit Hanoi?" She shook her head. "So until that happens," said Peter, "we can feel it's all OK, eh, Ma? They get us used to it by slowly increasing the dose. So we build up a tolerance."

She smoothed his pillow and persuaded him to lie down. In a minute, he started up again. Everything was coming back. "Is the State Department sending you to Poland?" He could see from her face that it was. "You'll have to cancel." "Oh, Peter, you exaggerate. It's just music. Music isn't political." "You know better than that, Rosamund." "But I can't, at the last minute. If I'd known before . . . A performer can't do that." "You have to, Mother. Believe me."

For a while, they did not talk. He actually dozed. Then a maid brought in his supper tray and cranked him up. "It's your first meal," his mother said, smiling. "But I hear you had quite a lot of company. Finally they put a 'No Visitors' sign on your door." "Who was here?" "The Scott girl. She's delightful, Peter. And the Platt boy, of course. What a strange creature! I used to know his father, in New York, before I was married. In fact he was one of my suitors."

Peter was too weary to reflect on the dynastic implications of this. If his mother had married Silly's father, who would he be? He saw that the fair Rosamund was hoping to divert him from the ukase he had issued and he did not mind being diverted, because he knew that in the end she would yield. She needed a little time for the point to sink in. What shook him was that it should have taken her nineteen-year-old son to make plain to her that there were things she could not do. And how had Bob let her get this far on the State Department tab? Peter pitied them both and his mother especially. She had no authority for him any more.

"Who else was here? Come on, keep the ball rolling, Mother." "I think your adviser came." "Did they let him in? God, I hope not." His mother was not sure. "Some just left their names. You seem to have made an extraordinary number of friends. You've been holding a regular levee here. Your concierge is very concerned about you, by the way. She sent you a Get Well card. Here it is." Peter looked at the card. "Oh? You went to my apartment?" "I'm staying there. I hope you don't mind." Actually Peter was glad. He could count on her anyway to water the plants. "It's strange, your doorknob was stolen. How do you account for that, Peter? And the Platt boy didn't lock up when you left. The concierge thinks a derelict must have been sleeping in your room."

Peter gulped. He wondered what his mother would do if the *clocharde* returned while she was there. The thought afforded him some disconsolate amusement. It would be interesting to see *her* tested. But that was unfair, since he would have left her the problem as a legacy. Moreover, to do her justice, she was the only adult he would trust to understand the story of that night. But today was not the moment. Instead, he decided to tell her about the visit of *la Delfica*. "How marvelous! What a nice delirium!" She looked rather proud, as though her son had made a three-star acquaintance. "I think you must have had several imaginary visitors. All your helpers and hinderers. Yesterday you were talking very volubly." "I had a few." "Who were the others? Tell me." Peter shook his head. "Oh, please, Peter!" "No."

He had remembered. A shivery sadness crept through him; he pulled the sheet over his head. He did not want to talk any more. "Please go away, Mother, for a little while. Call up and cancel your ticket. I want to think."

The visitor had been sitting quietly at the foot of his bed, waiting for Peter to wake up—a small man, scarcely five feet high, in an unbuttoned twill jacket with a white stock. It looked as if he had been there quite a while. His hair was curled in sausages and powdered—or was it a periwig?—and fastened behind with a gray bow. He was in the prime of life; around his bright vivacious eyes were crow's-feet, which showed intensive thought. Peter knew him at once, and he evidently had known Peter for a long time, though this was their first meeting. Breaking with his lifelong habit, he had come all the way from Königsberg because Peter was sick. He was making a double exception, since, Peter recalled, he always shunned sickrooms.

"When you were young, you wrote an ode to the West Wind," Peter said, to show how lovingly he had collected every fact about him. "*Theory of Winds*," the little man emended. "Of course. How stupid! I'm sorry. The way I feel, my brain gets things a bit confused. Actually, I've never read it." "It doesn't matter," said Kant. "And you were for the French Revolution," prompted Peter. But that was not what his mentor had come to talk about. "I was thinking of you yesterday," Peter went on, not letting the visitor speak in his excitement at having him here. "I guess it was yesterday. In the Jardin des Plantes. Something our professor said you said about the beautiful things in the world proving that man is made for and fits into the world and that his perception of things agrees with the laws of his perception. It sounded better when he read it in German." "'*Die schönen Dinge zeigen an . . .' Ach, ja!*" Kant bowed his head and sighed.

"Excuse me, sir, you have something to tell me, don't you?" The tiny man moved forward on the counterpane and looked Peter keenly in the eyes, as though anxious as to how he would receive the message he had to deliver. He spoke in a low thin voice. "God is dead," Peter understood him to say. Peter sat up. "I *know* that," he protested. "And you didn't say that anyway. Nietzsche did." He felt put upon, as though by an impostor. Kant smiled. "Yes, Nietzsche said that. And even when Nietzsche said it, the news was not new, and maybe not so tragic after all. Mankind can live without God." "I agree," said Peter. "I've always lived without Him." "No, what *I* say to you is something important. You did not hear me correctly. Listen now carefully and remember." Again he looked Peter steadily and searchingly in the eyes. "Perhaps you have guessed it. Nature is dead, *mein kind*."

CANNIBALS AND MISSIONARIES

*To Rowland
and to the memory of
Will Scarlett*

Dites donc, ma belle,
Où est votre ami?
Il est à la Hollande,
Les hollandais l'ont pris.

One

"BLESS, o Lord, thy gifts to our use and us to thy service; for Christ's sake. Amen." Excited as a kid on the day of his confirmation, the Reverend Frank Barber raced through the grace and drank his orange juice. His gaze embraced his family, whose sleepy heads had slowly returned to an upright position. One chair at the long table was vacant. His eldest, he saw, had already finished his breakfast and taken his plate, cup, and saucer to the pantry. A crumpled embossed yellow paper napkin and an empty orange juice glass marked his place. "He's gone to get the car," said young Helen. Among his manifold blessings, the rector of St. Matthew's, in lovely Gracie Square, was able to count garage privileges, extended as a courtesy to the church, over on York Avenue—a brisk seven-minute walk, great for chasing the cobwebs. He twirled the Lazy Susan in the center of the table and chose a medium-boiled egg from the basket. The eggs wore snug felt hats in the shape of roosters —a wonderful idea, he always thought: they kept the eggs warm and guided your selection, dark blue for medium, yellow for soft.

He was elated that his fledglings had all got up and dressed themselves—though it was Saturday; no school—to see him off on his mission. "Gosh, it's so darned early, it's practically dark out," he marveled. On the table candles burned in two silver candelabra, a gift from the vestry for his and "old" Helen's twentieth anniversary last July. On the sideboard stood four more candles, in saucers, that the youngsters had brought in from their rooms; they were pitching in to conserve electricity, on account of the energy crisis. In the fireplace a wood fire was lit (Frank, Jr., had brought the logs down in a U-Haul from the Dutchess County wood lot of a parishioner), and when the rector had arrived in the dining-room, "old" Helen had been bent over it in her wrapper, toasting English muffins on two forks, her face pink and her hair, pinned up in a knot with a single blond bone hairpin, starting to escape.

"I made the orange juice," announced young Helen, who had a round face and long fair silky hair like her mother's, "while my cruel brothers watched. Well, to be scrupulously fair, they set the table last night." "She *counts*," protested Matthew, the youngest, who was fourteen. There was a cell of women's libbers in the sixth form at her school; in her brothers' judgment, they were making a convert of her. Young Helen tossed her hair. "Matthew knows perfectly well that I'm doing a serious study of the woman-hours expended in this family. It's a social science assignment." John, aged sixteen, raised a finger for silence. "Members of the congregation, peace! Just think, tomorrow the Reverend Frank will be in Persia. And none of us, except Mother, has even been to Europe." "Iran," corrected his brother. "And it'll be the day after tomorrow, for Father," added young Helen. "Remember the time difference." "I like to think of it as Persia still," John said.

"But *they* don't, John," the rector interposed. "We have to respect their feelings. It's their country. Like 'black.'" He shook his head, recollecting. "We've all learned our lesson on that." "Did you really call black people 'Negroes,' Father?" Matthew wanted to know. "Everybody did, Matthew. Except the ones that called them 'niggers.' You're too young to remember." He himself could remember "colored"—what a coon's age ago that seemed! He gave a rueful chuckle and emended the worn old phrase to "raccoon's age": with oppressed minorities, he guessed, you kept *re*learning your lesson.

"But if it's their country," said John, "why are you going there to butt in, like a missionary?" "That's a good question, John. But I don't know that I can answer it now. Time's a-flying. Or, rather, I'm a-flying." His wife and children groaned. "Don't try to slide out of it with one of your puns, Father," said John. "If the Shah is torturing and executing people, that's an old custom in his country. If the opposition got power, they'd do the same to him. I mean, isn't this 'ad hoc' committee of yours just trying to be a salesman for Western democratic merchandise? And why pick on Persia, particularly? Why don't you look into Ethiopia and Uganda too while you're at it?"

Frank observed that his wife was waiting for his answer. She stood watching her brood and her challenged mate from her sentry post at the sideboard, the coffee-pot in her hand and her head to one side, like an alerted bird. He was on trial, he reckoned. She took the young ones' questions more to heart than they did: out of the mouth of babes. But he knew that John was only probing, testing out his father's ideas. The boy, who was the only dark one and wore big glasses, was his father's favorite and his mother's too maybe. They said you should love them all equally, yet even Our Lord had sinned in preferring *His* John, the Beloved Disciple, to the other eleven, who, unless human nature had been different then, must have been jealous of seeing him like that with his head in the Saviour's bosom—had that been Judas's problem?

Removing his mind from Judas, whose problems he often sought to understand, Frank tried to sum up succinctly why he *was* going to Persia—oh, shoot, Iran! Certainly not for a joy ride. "After all," continued John, "the Shah is basically on *our* side. If you want my opinion, that's why you're going, really. I mean, you're so darned liberal that you're sort of perverse." Frank's face lightened. He jumped up and hugged the boy. "You're right, John! You're right! I'm perverse. I never thought of it that way. But isn't that being a Christian? Jesus was perverse. Everybody thought so, even His disciples." He threw back his head and laughed in delight while his family looked on with forbearing smiles. Then he went around the table, giving them each a hug and saving a special squeeze for "old" Helen, who was four months pregnant—they were still keeping it from the children, who were likely to ask what had happened to his strong position on planned parenthood and the population explosion.

The buzzer from downstairs sounded. Frank, Jr., must be getting impatient. Outside the dining-room windows it was morning now, and the January daylight filtering through the marquisette curtains made the candlelight look pale and trembly. The six cocky egg hats lay in disorder around the table. It was time to go. Frank blew the candles out, not waiting for Matthew, who as the youngest had the right, to go around with the snuffer.

Taking a last look around the cosy room, the bright focus of his family life, he strode to the dark vestibule, where his big gray suitcase, his briefcase, and his light overcoat were waiting. At this season, it would be fairly cold (median, 38°) and dry in Teheran, according to their "bible"—the 1913 *Encyclopaedia*

Britannica, in which the boys had done research for him on the trip. So much of the article was out of date (the *Columbia Encylopedia*, in one volume, which the children used for their homework, was current, thank the Lord), but he assumed that *Climate* had not changed greatly. When it came to *Fauna* and *Flora*, he was less easy in his mind: ". . . about four hundred known species of birds" had floored Matthew, the family ornithologist, and he had insisted on lending his father his field glasses. The rector hoped the boy was not in for a disappointment. The only oil mentioned in the entry came from "the castor-oil plant, sesame, linseed, and olive." They had all had a good laugh over that, not stopping to think that the oil wells of modern Iran might have done something to the 1913 bird population. It was Frank, Jr., too readily a kill-joy for his brothers, who had pointed that out.

The *Britannica*, which had come down from the Canon, Helen's father, was getting to be a bone of contention in the family. Frank, Jr., wanted them to buy the new, University of Chicago one—the clerical discount would bring the price down—and Frank, Sr., was beginning to agree, for reasons that this *flora* and *fauna* doubt had brought home to him: the other three, like Helen, Sr., loved reading aloud from the old set, but it was giving them a false picture of the world. They were still dreaming, on his behalf, of the country described by "Ed. M.": "The Anglican mission has its work among the Nestorians of Azerbaijan." "The flamingo comes up from the south as far north as the region of Teheran; the stork abounds." "It is a strange custom with the Persian ladies to dress little girls as boys, and little boys as girls, till they reach the age of seven or eight years; this is often done for fun, or on account of some vow—oftener to avert the evil eye." It was the same problem he faced over the new prayer book, which Helen and the children still rebelled against, preferring the hallowed old words. But prejudice, to Frank's mind, was the greatest affliction you could pass on to your children, and a prejudice in favor of the past, though it looked innocent, could lead them to reject the good in modern society, along with the bad, which of course existed too.

He had been wondering whether, once he got home, he could arrange to have the *Britannica* have an accident—not a fire, because of the history of intolerance linked to book-burning, but a little flood, say, from a leaky radiator—when Helen had gone to the hospital for her lying-in. Such criminal temptations, in a good cause, were familiar to him. Back in '68, he would not have objected to having a draft-card burned in his church, before the altar, though in deference to the vestry he might have offered the sacristy as an alternative.

It was quarter of eight. In the vestibule, the children, suddenly childish, surrounded him. "Your plane isn't till ten. Why do you have to go so soon?" Young Helen wound her arms around his neck. He understood. The Barbers were not used to air travel—they were too numerous—and at the children's age you could not keep news stories of plane accidents and hijackings from them. Maybe John, with his questions just now, had been begging his Dad not to go. Frank's conscience, normally good, all at once misgave him. It pictured Helen to him as a widow with four dependent youngsters and another on the way. As the statesman-philosopher wrote, he that has wife and children has given hostages to fortune. There was a lot to be said, in the end, for a celibate clergy. Because, as a man of God, he *had* to go, darn it; he could not let his family ties stand in his way now. Helen, his tall mainstay, sent him a signal over the heads of the children: be off.

Frank cleared his throat, in which a lump was rising. "We have to stop for Gus first—didn't Frankie tell you?—at the Commodore." The name Gus seemed to act on them like a tranquillizer; the retired Bishop of Missouri, a stout old man in his eighties, was their summer neighbor in the Adirondacks—they had hiked the Indian trails with him and sailed with him on Lake Champlain. He was Frank, Jr.'s godfather and he had christened young Helen. "Oh, well. You'd better hurry then, Father. The Bishop will be on the sidewalk—do you want to bet?—with his watch in his hand." They giggled. How volatile young creatures were!

John took his father's suitcase, and the three rode down with him in the elevator. Helen, in her pink tailored wool wrapper, remained behind. The wife of the pastor of the venerable old Gracie Square church had to be careful. Pewholders lived in the building, and if she went down with him to the lobby as she was, the next thing you heard she would have been on the street "undressed." Scandal-mongering was one of the little crosses of the profession, and the Episcopalians, for all their "worldliness," were as bad as the Baptists.

For travel, under his spring overcoat, he wore a gray tweed jacket, flannels, white shirt, and a big maroon-and-white polka-dot bow tie that Helen had tied for him this morning. He never used a vest, too buttoned-up and reminiscent of the cassock; on vacations he sometimes put on a chamois waistcoat that had come down, like the *Britannica*, from the Canon. In his suitcase were some pre-tied bow ties in loud colors and energetic designs that the younger boys teased him about, two changes of suit (one dark), several changes of socks and under-wear, a pair of black shoes, his slippers, tartan bathrobe, and pajamas, and his clerical dickey and collar. In his briefcase were light reading-matter, an extra bridge consisting of two upper left bicuspids and a molar, extra eyeglasses, Matthew's field glasses, two heavy folders of documentation on "Torture and Illegality in Iran," a shaving and toilet kit, the *Book of Common Prayer*, and his old pocket Bible—in a Moslem country, he did not think he could count on the Gideon Society.

He was a tall man, with a large loose-limbed frame, pale skin, gray widely spaced eyes behind big loose-fitting horn-rimmed glasses, and gray-blond springy hair cut in a style conciliating a crew cut with a pompadour. In his college days, he might have been a footballer, though his movements now were somewhat awkward and flailing. His clothes, his glasses, his necktie, arms, and legs hung on him at a variety of angles, as though unset-tled by a wind of change. At his waistline he had to fight the battle of the bulge: the priestly calling, though not exactly sedentary, gave a busy rector little regular exercise beyond genuflection and marching down the aisle at a measured pace behind the teetering cross while trying to keep step with the choir and the servers.

His eager boyish features, as if to compensate, were extremely active. They wore, for everyday (excluding funerals and sick calls), several galvanic changes of expression racing from inquiry to bewilderment to joyful comprehension, marked by increas-ingly vigorous nods. A receptive person, the Reverend Frank, a listener rather than a talker. His ear was perpetually stretching to catch messages from the outer world, which often gave him the air of a deaf person, though his hearing was good. He was also a great waver, a sender-out of greetings, as from a large craft to smaller vessels sighted in the distance. This morning, despite his preoccupation, he had already, from under the canopy of his building, perceived a neighboring janitor, a delivery boy, the stationer from around the corner, and his arm, flung up, had flagged them, transmitting salutes.

"Come on, Father," interceded Frank, Jr., from the wheel of the car. "This is a No-Standing zone." He was nineteen and destined for the ministry. His deep voice had a nasal honking sound not well suited to the pulpit or the intoning of the liturgy; unfortunately the defect had only become evident when his voice changed, and by that time his life-decision had been made. He was small and narrow-featured, with a long probing nose—different from his brothers and sister, who were tall and favored their parents. This morning, to take his father to the airport, he wore a blazer with his old school shield, blue button-down shirt, necktie, and flannels; his straight yellow hair was cut short and its cowlick subdued by water. Only his feet, in high sneakers and long for his general size, betrayed a kinship with the other three, now grouped on the sidewalk, the boys with sweetly tousled locks and slightly stooping, which gave them an air of benevolence, and all of them dressed in jeans and several layers of frayed sweaters.

As a new pewholder had exclaimed to Helen, the Barbers were an "ideal family": "Your children are straight without being square. You must give us your recipe." In his parents' eyes, that was not quite true of Frank, Jr., who was indeed what they called square nowadays but slightly off plumb. Though he was a wonderful son and a fine human being, he was at present his father's chief worry, because of that voice and some tense aggressive mannerisms that, again, raised a doubt as to whether he really had a pastoral vocation. Given his sincere religious feelings, which abided no questioning, he might have been better off as a monk, the rector sometimes thought. A conventual discipline of early rising, fasting, prayer, and penance was an option that the Episcopal communion, perhaps short-sightedly, was ceasing to offer as an alternative to missions and parish work; it would distress but not surprise his father if one day the boy were to go over to Rome.

On the other hand, the rector surmised, not for the first time, studying his son's gaunt profile as the car headed down Park, he could be worrying about masturbation—a natural habit at his age, but he might feel it was a barrier to holy orders. Frank had had many good talks on the subject with troubled acolytes who did not dare open their hearts to their parents. At home, though, he was a parent himself in his children's eyes, he guessed, despite his efforts to make them look on him as an older, understanding friend. The other morning at breakfast, finding just the three boys at table, he had tried to start a discussion on what Jesus would have said if a disciple had come to Him with Onan's problem ("'Let him who is without sin cast the first stone'" had been John's amused response), but instead of turning into the good free-wheeling exchange he had hoped for, the conversation had died in its tracks. The two younger boys had had a giggling fit, and Frank, Jr., giving them a searing look, had asked to be excused. That was a mistake the rector was not going to make again: offering reassurance, as he ought to know, could look like prying to a kid who was already in doubt about himself. Helen thought that Frank, Jr.'s trouble, if he had one, would clear up, like his occasional acne, as soon as he found a nice girl to get engaged to. And as for the voice (women, bless them, were so down to earth), she thought maybe an adenoids operation . . .

She and Frank had agreed, in last night's pillow talk, that he ought to discuss Frank, Jr., and his vocation with the Bishop. The good old man had a lot of human wisdom, and Frank was looking forward to the long plane trip as a chance to draw him out on all sorts of matters that had been on his mind—the reforestation of the ministry, for example, the big issue that was facing the Church today and of which the question of Frank, Jr.'s vocation was only a tiny facet. Where was the Church going to find young men with deep spiritual convictions who at the same time were not mixed up and withdrawn or, to put it mildly—which was Frank, Jr.'s case—not able to deal with people on an ordinary parish level? And this raised the question of the Church's real mission in modern society.

Making another survey of the set profile beside him, Frank decided to transfer to the back seat when they reached the Commodore; that would give the Bishop a chance to get "reacquainted" with his godson on the way to Kennedy. Last summer Gus had been complaining that he had hardly had a glimpse of "young Frankie," who had gone off to work in a wilderness camp in Maine and had come back just before Labor Day with a home-made haircut, a nose ulcerated from sunburn, a cold, and what looked like a severe case of malnutrition. The youngsters had lived on wild berries, clams, seaweed, tree mushrooms, a few fish they had managed to trap, and—they were practicing survival techniques—roast slugs. The Bishop had been shocked to hear of that, till loyally reminded by the Barbers in chorus of the Baptist's diet of locusts.

There the good soul was, as predicted, on Vanderbilt Avenue, at the entrance to the Commodore, standing in the street, red-faced and with his gold watch open in his palm. An old leather suitcase with foreign hotel stickers stood beside him. Frank waved and leapt out of the car. "Gus, dear friend!" "Frankie, my boy! And young Frankie!" Behind him waited a hotel porter holding the familiar black umbrella with the cherrywood handle and a big book bag made of needlework. It had been stitched by Rachel, the Bishop's beautiful wife, whom the children did not remember because she had died of cancer when she was only fifty, the year young Frankie was born. But they knew her from her pictures, which were all over the Bishop's house, in wood and silver frames, and John had guessed that she was the reason for Gus's unshakable faith in the hereafter—a place that he often talked about, as though it were Burlington, where he usually went for the winter.

This morning he was dressed in a thick three-piece tweed suit and, over that, a Burberry. Gus was something of an Anglophile, and most of his gear went back to the trips he used to make with Rachel in the British Isles after his retirement more than twenty years ago. They had bought that house in the Adirondacks and fixed it up, and then, just like that, a month after Frank, Jr.'s christening, she had died—a photo on "her" piano in Gus's parlor showed her holding the baby in her arms in his christening robe; she was wearing a long-sleeved light-colored dress almost like a wedding gown.

Frank saw to stowing Gus and his precious bag and umbrella comfortably in the front seat, with a lap robe over his chunky knees. He was moved, between tears and chuckles, as always happened when he saw the Bishop after an interval. Gus had ordained him, out in Missouri (which the old man still called "Missoura"), when he got out of Harvard Divinity School; he had made a liberal of him, and now it was the name Augustus Hurlbut high on the list of the "Committee of Inquiry into Iranian Justice" that had caused him to add his own when approached by the young Iranian, Sadegh, one Sunday after Holy Communion. It was the first Sunday in Advent, a day of promise for Christians, and he had been preaching on the ordination of women—a cause Gus too supported, bless him—with a text from, of all people, St. Paul. Romans, xvi, 1: "I commend unto you Phebe our sister." Obviously, with that good fight behind him, he had been in a receptive mood when the slight dark velvet-eyed young man—whom he had noticed, thanks to his new bifocals, from the pulpit—came up to him as he stood in his freshly starched surplice shaking hands and receiving congratulations at the church door: "An inspiring sermon, Rector." "Thank you for your courage, Rector." "Frank, you were cute to take St. Paul." Gus's spirit had been very much with him while he prepared the sermon, and the old man's doughty name, materializing on Sadegh's list, seemed a sign from the Lord. The irony of it was that Gus at that stage, as it turned out, had not even been contacted, and when the Iranians did get to him they used Frank's name.

Confronted with this circumstance, Sadegh had theorized that a first letter had been lost in the mails, which was possible, since the Bishop was not always prompt about having his letters forwarded when he closed up his house at Thanksgiving. He postponed making out a change-of-address card, just as he postponed having his pipes drained, hating to take definite leave of what the children called "Rachel's shrine." But even if that were so, it did not explain everything: Sadegh and his friends were still not out of the woods.

For his own impetuous signature, Frank took some of the blame on himself. On that Sabbath morning, he recollected, as his eye had traveled down the list—which included a leading Jesuit, a rabbi, a senator, a representative, all good names—in the back of his mind he had wondered that Gus, at his age, had agreed to go. But instead of being alerted by the anomaly to at least call Gus in his winter quarters in Burlington, he had let it dictate his own decision: if Gus could do it, so should he.

Now he felt no resentment. He had spent enough years in committee work to know that a pious hook needed to be baited before being lowered into the small reservoir of men of good will. To get any kind of group together to fly at its own expense to some remote corner of the earth to do the Lord's business was never an easy undertaking, he imagined, and Iran was a long way from being a Biafra or a Pretoria. Though Sadegh's briefcase contained a fair number of clippings, they were mostly not current and mostly in French. The mimeographed statement accompanying them spoke of "a total news blackout," which was no great exaggeration, as Frank's own example demonstrated. The whole Barber family took a keen interest in current events, particularly those concerning human rights and oppressed minorities, yet until Sadegh had come up that morning after divine service Frank had had no awareness that the Shah was doing anything worse than giving big wasteful parties for the international jet set while his people lacked food and housing. "No more idea than the man in the moon!" he had emphasized at lunch afterwards, as Helen stood carving the roast. "Did you know, John? Did you, Helen?" And the whole family had shaken their heads. That showed what these young Iranians were up against, and he reminded himself of it whenever in his dealings with them he found himself lacking in patience.

He understood, too, that men who worked on behalf of such causes were men of passion rather than strict principle. They were also, in this case, he gathered, young and inexperienced men. Maybe some group back in Iran was directing them, but he sometimes suspected that they were acting pretty much on their own, living on modest allowances from their families, who had sent them here to study. They did not even have the wherewithal to pay a printshop for a proper letterhead. He could never learn where they lived or how many of them there were. The telephone number Sadegh gave him kept changing, which probably meant he could not pay his room rent. Yet he was always neat and well dressed. It was all a brand-new experience for the rector, and this morning, with his air ticket (Return "OPEN") and his virgin passport in his inner breast pocket, he forgave in advance any further corner-cutting he might encounter in the organization of the trip.

Sadegh's list, as Frank had reluctantly come to realize, was protean in the extreme. Each time Frank asked to see it, it had undergone an unexplained metamorphosis. Father Hesburgh had dropped from sight and turned into a woman college president; a former Solicitor General had appeared and disappeared; the congressman had gone; there was still a senator, though not the same senator; in Paris, a Spanish monsignor and other European "personalities" would join them. As for the rabbi, Frank simply could not make it out. "Is Rabbi Weill coming? Is it *definite*, Sadegh?" "Oh, yes, possible." "No, not possible. *Sure*." "Yes, surely possible. Definite." He had tried to impress on Sadegh and his shadowy friends the importance of having the group be truly representative, and it still disappointed him that they had been unable to see the urgency of including a black—Julian Bond or one of the young ministers in the Southern Christian Leadership Conference. But in any case a rabbi was vital. If he had known Rabbi Weill personally, he would have put in a call to him; his temple (Reformed) was in Denver. When he had thought of calling him anyway, Helen had counseled against it. "You mustn't let these young men *use* you, Frank. You're such a born organizer. But let *them* manage their committee." If only, Frank reflected, they knew how! But about the rabbi, she was right, probably; these inter-faith things could be tricky.

Yet he *liked* Sadegh and the other young man, Asad, who sometimes came with him, and so he could not help trying to steer them out of what he sensed might be heavier water than they counted on. Last week, for instance, he had proposed, with some forcefulness, that the group meet in New York ahead of time, to get to know each other and discuss the program of action. Sadegh and Asad had agreed, with corresponding enthusiasm, yet somehow it had never come about. Now there was nothing to do but wait for whatever surprises the airport was going to produce. If the American wing of the International Committee turned out to consist of the Right Reverend Hurlbut and the Reverend Barber, it would not be the greatest of surprises.

Luckily, the good Lord had given him a sense of humor. But something else bothered him that could develop into more than a joke at his and the Bishop's expense. The fact was, he had no notion of how they were going to gain access to the Shah's prisons and his law courts. He supposed someone had a plan; in Paris, where they were to stay overnight, they would be met by lawyers, Sadegh promised—a Belgian and a don from Oxford who had a chair of jurisprudence. But had it occurred to anyone that the group might be thrown out of the Shah's territory or clapped into jail or, worst of all, denied entry when they descended in a body from the plane? When he had put the question to the young Iranians, he had been assured that this could not happen, but he wondered how they knew. He wondered too whether their mystifying vagueness about details was due to a failure in communication: had they understood *any* of his questions?

"Hey, Father," called Frank, Jr., from the front seat. "Is there going to be some guy with you that speaks the language?" This too had been on Frank's mind, but he dratted his son's lack of diplomacy. The last thing he wanted was to share these mundane worries with the Bishop: old people were prone to become fearful at the slightest suggestion of uncertainty. Thus he had seen no reason to tell Gus that Sadegh and his friends had borrowed his name without his permission; the main thing was that Gus, when finally approached, had accepted, so where was the sense of exciting him about an understandable peccadillo when they were halfway to Kennedy with Teheran as their agreed destination?

The Bishop had turned his head, which was round as a pumpkin and partly bald, in order to catch the answer. Frank considered. At one point, Sadegh had talked of a Cambridge don who spoke several of the native dialects, but then no more was said of him, and he seemed to have been replaced by the jurisprudence don from Oxford. "I'm not totally clear on that, young Frank. We can pick up an interpreter there if we need to. No problem." But there certainly was a problem, as the Bishop was capable of guessing. In a police state any interpreter was almost sure to be a spy, and Iran seemed to qualify as a police state, though any substantial evidence to the contrary would be welcome, at least to Frank. He had an inspiration.

"Through the Embassy," he shouted. The old man nodded. "Or through the Church, Frankie."

Frank felt moved again. The Bishop's serene faith was a rock. And how could he himself have forgotten the Church in his reckonings? Maybe the Anglicans no longer had a mission to the Nestorians of Azerbaijan, but the Church would be there in one or more likely a dozen of its myriad forms—in these oecumenical days it made no great matter which. Of course he had known it, in his soul, if not in his mind. He had brought along his clerical gear to be able to take divine service should the need arise. That was an old habit with him, virtually automatic whenever he packed a bag. But though he never thought about it consciously, it presupposed on his part a profound conviction that wherever a man of God went, there would be Christians and an altar. Unlike Gus, however, who was a seasoned traveler, he had failed to picture the Church as a source of material help.

A pastor in that largely Moslem community, if he did not speak the language himself, would be bound to have native speakers in his flock, along, Frank supposed, with Exxon and Shell representatives, who were in need of God too. And if the pastor was a true shepherd, he would greet with joy his brothers in Christ come to look into torture, summary executions, and trials that were a mockery of justice, which he could *not* but know about granted that even a quarter of the tales in Sadegh's folders were facts. No minister of the gospel, even the most lukewarm, one of Paul's famous Laodiceans, could be unaware of the abominations suffered in those prisons not just by political hotheads but by dissident Moslems protesting the repression of their faith. In fact, there was no excuse *not* to know; prison-visiting was a duty laid on the clergy.

Frank gave an inward start. How strange that he had overlooked that point, when he imposed the duty on himself (Helen was supportive) twice a month throughout the year. Including summers: he was grimly familiar with the inside of every correctional institution in their own and neighboring counties right up to the Canadian border and he had been taking Frank, Jr., along, to instill the habit, ever since the boy had discovered his vocation. Cast your bread upon the waters: he saw himself and the Bishop in their dog-collars being introduced into the Shah's prisons by a clerical accomplice and experienced a sense of deep and sweet relief, as though a balm had been applied to all the vexations of the journey—those foreseen and those as yet unforeseeable.

He cautioned himself not to let his natural hopefulness run away with him. SAVAK, the Shah's secret police, would scarcely have the same sociable attitude as the New York State wardens and guards, who knew him and young Frank and joshed them about searching the hampers of books and magazines they carried: "Any knives or other weapons, Reverend?" But the cloth was the cloth pretty much the world over, and even brutal men, men with something to conceal (who were not entirely lacking in New York State houses of correction), were more inclined to try to deceive it, pull the wool over its eyes, if he could use the figure, than to refuse it entry to the premises. And once you were inside, it was surprising how the prisoners would talk to you, sometimes with the aid of winks and hand gestures if a guard was present. In this age supposed to be irreligious, there was more healthy fear of God and also trust in Him than the laity reckoned.

A happy torpor came over Frank. His chin sank to his chest; he dozed. A doubt shook him awake. They were nearing Kennedy; Gus and the boy were silent. Misgiving as to his own purposes had gained entry to his mind as he cat-napped and was now demanding his full attention. John's questions at the breakfast table might have been a time-bomb, he guessed. The point John had been getting at, stripped of youthful trimmings, went to the heart of the matter: did the Church, *qua* Church, have a role to play in an affair of this kind?

Frank had pretty well resolved that—he had thought—with himself, in the time available to him, what with the pressures of departure added to normal parish work, the children out of school over the holidays, extra morning and evening services, choir rehearsals, the Girls Friendly pageant, extra sermons to prepare for the Nativity and the Circumcision (Epiphany, blessedly, had fallen on a Sunday), distribution of presents to the needy, and the darned crèche and parish-house tree to set up. But two minds were better than one, and he had been counting on picking Gus's brains in the plane today over a sherry or a bourbon (Gus's preferred tipple) on the theology of what they were up to. The subject, as he roughly saw it (he found outlining helpful in his thinking), was really a sub-head under the larger topic of the Church's task in modern society. Gus, he hoped, would play the devil's advocate, bringing up arguments *against* this jaunt they were on and all the other good causes they had crusaded for; then they could change sides, with Gus assuming the defense. Frank had been looking forward to a far-reaching, hard-hitting discussion, like the old midnight bull sessions in Divinity School, that would probably not settle everything but be wonderful mental exercise and maybe useful for a sermon.

In fact he already had a pertinent sermon in the works— based on a contemporary reading of the Book of Jonah—which he had started composing in his head, from force of habit, during his spare moments. In the barber's chair yesterday and last Saturday while watching a game of touch football played by the St. Matthew's men's club against St. George's. Actually, he would not be needing it until his return ("OPEN"), but it was always well to have a sermon ripening, in prudent reserve. None of it yet was on paper; some bits, though, he knew by heart, and he might try them out on the Bishop if the plane was not too crowded. . . .

"How many of us here this morning are Jonahs, who, having heard the divine call to betake ourselves to a place far from our homes—or perhaps merely to a less favored part of our city—to prophesy or, as we might say today, to bear witness, disobey the voice of God, which to us is the voice of conscience, and take ship for a different destination?" "No, the parallels are not perfect. The city Jonah was commanded to preach against was a wicked and flourishing city, whereas the call we hear may order us to go, if only in spirit, to very poor and wretched parts of the world, which some of us may feel are less sinful, on the whole, than the part of the world we would leave. Today the voice of God may speak to us from the columns of a newspaper, from an advertisement in a magazine, from an image on our television set. . . ."

There was no need to belabor that. The congregation would understand that he was talking about Vietnam and Cambodia and South Africa and, closer to home, East Harlem. But now a section was coming that might give them new food for thought. "We may not know, today, how to recognize the call that came to Jonah. It is not always that clear and easy. There are false calls, just as in scripture there were false prophets, and perhaps poor Jonah—let's give him the benefit of the doubt— took the voice he heard for a false voice.

"We must also try to distinguish—and this is particularly true for us in holy orders—a secular call from a spiritual call. Both may be valid but they are not the same. The Bible has taught us that the spiritual has precedence; a secular need, however great, must yield to it. This indeed is a prominent article of Jesus' teaching, though not always of His practice. We see Him, as you know, in the company of the underdog, the underprivileged. But does His sympathy for these lowly ones reach out only to their spiritual part? No. Do not let yourself be deceived. The transcendent Jesus is also a warm human being. He is present at the Marriage of Cana, where there is not enough wine to go around, and, instead of accepting this unfairness of distribution as inevitable and foreordained, He *makes* wine. When He preaches to a hungry multitude, He *makes* loaves and fishes. Even more interesting, he does not offer any *spiritual* comfort, any pie in the sky, to the leper who comes to Him saying 'Lord, if thou wilt, thou canst make me clean.' He cures the man and sends him on his way. Which shows that a fleshly need did not always have a low priority with Jesus; far from it. I dare to think that a secular need equally in our day may take on a sacred character, may cry out to Heaven for remedy. Our Lord is no longer on earth today, and the day of miracles in the old sense is past. Instead, we have our own latter-day miracles of science and technology, capable of feeding and healing the multitude if we will only use them rightly."

So far, pretty telling, although the point ought to be made that poverty had been inevitable in Jesus' day, owing to primitive methods of production; this explained His doctrine of Christian resignation—appropriate in its time-frame but now in need of updating. The whole passage could be expanded when he sat down with pencil and paper. And he would have to look up the words from St. Matthew in the revised version; when drafting a sermon in his head, he fell back, perforce, on King James, which memory—like Helen and her three young allies—was always eager to supply. But he never let details get between him and a powerful idea, such as the one his inspiration had been working toward. Experience had shown him that he might lose it if he did not swiftly clothe it in words.

"And what of civil rights, you may ask, dear friends. And the right to a fair trial and to speak our minds openly? Don't they belong to the political rather than the religious sphere? Yes and no, depending. If the craving for justice and equality was put in our hearts by God (you will not tell me they came from the devil), and in all our hearts to the same measure, then it is God's business that this yearning of the spirit be recognized as belonging to all alike and be loved in all alike. . . ."

That was the real meat of the sermon, and he had been keen to hear Gus's reaction to it. It was a ground-breaking argument for the pastorate's joining in activities (exemplified by today's mission) still looked on by many, in the Church and outside, as extra-curricular. An overwhelming argument, he had thought. But somewhere along the way he had lost sight of Jonah. This morning, while shaving, he had been wondering how he could work Jonah back in. "We in the ministry, like the prophet Jonah, have accepted a special function of attending to the Lord's business, wherever and whenever it calls us. But the world is a bigger, more complex place today than it was in Jonah's time, while we, poor mortals, are still man-sized, like the prophet. We evidently cannot answer, with holy alacrity, *all* the calls that come in to our spiritual switchboard. Not long ago, for instance, on the first Sunday of Advent, the beginning of our Christian year, a young Iranian came up to your rector, after divine service. . . . What was I to tell him, dear friends? That because he was a stranger and we had our own vineyard to tend, his call, though seemingly urgent, must be placed on 'Wait'?"

Jerked awake, like Saul struck down by the questioning Saviour on the road to Damascus, Frank now had the awful suspicion that "Wait" might indeed have been the right answer. He watched the airport Hilton go by and was assailed by a crowd of tardy second thoughts. He was no longer proud of his sermon draft, which to his mind, more uncertain with every passing second, appeared as self-serving. The unfortunate switchboard metaphor pointed to what looked like a basic unwillingness to think through the question of their mission: "Those figures of speech are cop-outs, Father," John had told him. "You bring in astronauts and space modules when you don't want to say what you mean." Frank now admitted the charge. To somebody of his democratic temperament, he guessed, the idea of greater and lesser as applied to other people's emergencies was troubling. Yet a man doing the Lord's business had to budget his outlay of himself.

He asked himself whether a warning—or a sorrowful reproach—could really have come to him from on high as he dozed. Or was the sinking feeling in his stomach due to unseasonably early rising and an undigested breakfast? If God had spoken in his ear, it would be something completely outside his experience. Gus was on close terms with his Maker and seemed to converse with Him intimately as a friend, but Frank, while envying this, attributed it to Rachel's loss. He himself, though he had been granted perfect faith, had never had a direct intimation of the divine presence, not even during the religious crisis that had shaken him up when he was sixteen and led him from the high-school debating squad into sacred studies. On the other side of the coin, inner division, soul struggle, likewise was outside his ken, except as he observed it in parishioners who came to him for guidance. And his only real acquaintance with the pangs of remorse was when he had hurt one of the children's feelings and sought to repair the damage—easier, he often found, in a united family than mending a broken toy. He tried to be a good man and a good pastor and was content to know God, and love Him, through the liturgy and through His commandments.

Yet now it was as if God had deserted him; this too was a new sensation for Frank. The divine guidance on which he relied, confident that it was there, though invisible, steering him on the right road, was suddenly noticeable by its absence. He no longer felt directed but, instead, irresolute as a pinball hesitating on the board. There remained natural reason, which God, who had furnished it, would expect him to use. If it was too late, as he guessed it was, to draw back from this enterprise, he could still be clear with himself on it and gain, maybe, a new perspective.

In short, to come swiftly to the point (Frank, Jr., was

braking as he approached the turn-off for the airport), could it be rightly said that he and the Bishop were answering a call of the kind that had come to Jonah or were they merely acting as world citizens carrying out a secular task? In his own mind, Frank noticed, he had been referring to it as a "mission," which implied, he guessed, an apostolate. But possibly that was bad doctrine. An old-time prophet sent by God on this errand would have aimed at the Shah's reclamation. Yet he and the Bishop (if he could speak for Gus) had no intention of appearing before the monarch, as early Christians, to say nothing of the old-time prophets, would have done. They were going as mere "observers" and practically by stealth. It was probably far-fetched, under modern conditions—screening, security, protocol —to think of securing an audience with the sovereign. But if they failed to make an effort to convey God's displeasure to him, would they not be guilty of Jonah's sin?

There was a big hole—Frank now forced himself to recognize—right in the middle of that confounded sermon. Jonah's sin. It was not just disobedience. His wilfulness had a strange motive. The fact was, Jonah did not want Nineveh to repent. The reason he ignored the Lord's command, indeed did his best to escape from it, was that he was afraid that Nineveh *would* and so avoid God's punishment.

To tell the truth, Frank had never been able to understand Jonah's personality structure. But it was as clear as could be in the Bible that his governing passion was to see Nineveh destroyed, rather than saved. He was a stubborn cuss, with a one-track mind. Being in the whale did not teach him anything. When he finally did preach in that iniquitous city (since the Lord by then had him in His grip), he effected a conversion that any hellfire preacher would envy. The king "arose from his throne and laid his robe from him and covered him with sackcloth and ashes" and ordered his people to turn from their evil ways and "the violence that was in their hands." So the city was saved. But Jonah was angry with God for sparing it. He sat under his gourd-vine and reviled. Why? Narrow, sectarian Judaism maybe: clannish jealousy of the Ninevehites, who were Gentiles. It almost looked as if Jonah did not want his God to be a true Christian.

There was a lesson there for Frank and Gus. "The violence that was in their hands." Change Nineveh to Teheran, and the meaning was clear: for His business, God had no need of "observers"—He knew about the torture and the illegality. What He held out to sinful men was redemption, and for that He needed bearers of His Word.

The car had drawn up at the curb in front of Air France: Frank, Jr., was opening the trunk. In the back seat, Frank sat with his head in his hands, alleging a touch of migraine. He was still thinking. No minister today, he reasoned, would aspire to make converts of Mohammed Reza Pahlavi and Nassiri, his secret-police chief. But a man of God, possessed of the living faith, would hope to bring them to serve God in their own way, as good Moslems, and obey His commandments. Naturally, he and the Bishop, unlike Jonah, did not desire their destruction, whatever Sadegh and his friends might feel on that score. Yet for Christians the mere absence of evil wishes toward a wrongdoer was not enough. As unafraid Christians, they ought not to be satisfied with conducting an investigation and when they were safely out of the country announcing the results at an airport press conference—Asad's idea—in Athens or Paris.

That still might be very much worth doing (Frank was not prepared to gainsay it), but where did the Church come in? If he and Gus did not want to open themselves to the charge of abusing their sacerdotal function, they should go as private citizens, with no handles to their names. Yet without the mantle of their calling, they were no different from Joe Zilch, in short useless to the Iranians. It was a dilemma, all right.

Taxis behind them were honking. Making signs of apology and conciliation, Frank hastily descended from the car. Gus was standing by their baggage, waving his umbrella to attract the attention of a disappearing porter. He looked fresh as a morning rose, all primed to go, without a backward thought, apparently. Still, it was one thing for Gus—who was retired— to be flying off to far lands, and another for Frank, rector of St. Matthew's, charged with the administration of the sacraments and the maintenance of Christian values in the broad community of New York. Of course he had his curates; he had considered them when making his decision. They could run the show, as they did anyway when he was taking his vacation. If he was not back by Ash Wednesday, they would get some useful practice in preaching Lenten sermons.

Yet an uneasiness still gripped him as he stood on the walk eyeing the jet-liners taking off into the overcast sky. It came home to him that, like Jonah, he might be taking evasive action and setting sail for Tarshish when Nineveh, behind him, was where the Lord meant him to be. Would he be cast, he wondered, into the belly of the whale? He thought of the children's fearfulness about air travel—so manifest to him this morning—of Frank, Jr., who had gone to park the car. How would he react when he learned that his mother was pregnant, with his father on the other side of the world and having no fixed date of return? Frank's long-standing doubts about Sadegh's competence returned, combining suddenly with his other doubts and anxieties to make him wish from the bottom of his heart (he refrained from praying) that something would yet happen so that they would not have to go.

Unworthy man, he chided himself, could it be that he was plain afraid? Having bitten off more than he could chew, he might finally be recognizing it at the airport, of all places, where retreat was cut off. But if it was unmanly fear, not the voice of conscience, that was assailing him, he was all the more obliged to quell it and abide by his commitment. There was no time left in any case to peer into his motivations or decide what, if anything, he was nervous of. He must take the plunge briskly, as he used to urge the young ones gathered shivering on the lake shore for the first dip of the season: the water always felt chillier to those who hung back, wetting a toe and getting cold feet. He could not let Sadegh down.

Gus's freckled old hand was testing the weight of Rachel's book bag, which had been placed on top of the others for fear it would get dirty or crushed. No skycap was in sight. If Gus were to have a little heart attack . . . ? The dear soul had been warned by his specialist against lifting anything heavier than a shopping bag of groceries. If he were to try to carry that bag himself, which would be like him, it could not do him any serious damage. But a few palpitations, enough to rule out the trip for both of them—no question but that Frank would have to take the patient home . . . ?

The crazy thoughts that came to you in stress situations, as if planted in your mind by the devil! It made a modern man wonder whether it was not a mistake to doubt Satan's real existence. But of course, thanks to good habits, the "Get thee behind me" followed in a flash; he had hardly felt the brush of temptation before he took the bag firmly from the old man's grasp and set it back on the pile. They had a few minutes, he admonished, before check-in. A porter would surely come. Or he would find one of those carts, like the ones they had in the supermarket. But now a new dastardly thought came to tantalize him. If the flight were to be canceled? They did that quite often these days, on account of the fuel crisis, if the plane was not full. He was certain somebody had told him that. Frank shook his head. It would be only a reprieve. His apple-cheeked old friend had his timepiece out again. "The others ought to be here, Frankie. Should I go in and have a look?"

Frank was slow to reply. If the rabbi was not there, *or* the Senator, if nobody on this blamed committee was there, *then* they would be free to go home. It would be God's will. The prayer he had not let himself pray would be answered. But if he sent Gus inside to reconnoiter and any *one* of the promised four was there, there could be no turning back. This was something, Frank decided, that he did not yet want to know. As long as he did not know, he could still hope.

"Never mind, Gus. I see a porter." In fact a skycap was wheeling a cart down the walk toward them. Preceded by their baggage, Frank and Gus went through the door. At the Air France counter for Economy class, Sadegh was waiting, alone.

To his astonishment and moral relief, Frank's instantaneous reaction was anger: faced with the fact that the committee to all appearances consisted of Gus and himself, he could not contain the oath of disappointment that sprang to his lips. "God damn it, Sadegh, you *promised*!" How little the human heart knew itself! He had sinned in mistrusting his own willingness, nay, eagerness, to fight this good fight. Now that their fine, broad-based crusade was dissolving into thin air before his disbelieving eyes, he could have wept for the pity of it. There was a lesson there of some kind: to use a homely comparison, it was like tossing a coin to decide whether to go hiking or take out the canoe; often you only learned that it was heads you really wanted when the other side, tails, showed its face.

Two

B*on vol*," Aileen Simmons wrote on one of the green-printed cards distributed by the hostess; upon reflection, she added "*Service aimable*." On the line *Effectuez-vous ce voyage pour Affaires* □ *Tourisme* □ *Autres motifs_____*? she had placed a check after *Autres motifs*, without becoming more specific. Her occupation she had given simply as "*Educatrice*." "*Recteur d'université*" sounded a bit pompous for the president of a women's college, and the presence of the other kind of rector, across the aisle, made her hesitate to assume the title. She would have liked to see how those men of God described themselves and what they would put next to "Other" as their reason for taking the flight—like good monolingual Americans, they would use the verso, obviously, provided for English-speakers. Aileen's bump of curiosity was well developed, and it interested her, as a one-time social historian, to note how other people responded to polls and questionnaires, which for her were always a puzzle, like a multiple-choice test.

The problems of identity posed by forms to be completed were one of the perplexities of travel for a thinking reed. The majority seemed to know who and what they were and expressed it swiftly, in block letters, but a worry bird like herself could pore for half a minute over "Domicile." She never knew whether to give her tax residence, which was Fayetteville, Arkansas, her home town, or Sunnydale, Massachusetts, which was the home of Lucy Skinner College and her semi-real residence. Then, on leaving a country, she often forgot which she had decided to put down on entering, thus making herself a mystery, she supposed, to compilers of statistics if those entry and exit forms were kept and ever actually compared.

A person named Aileen, more commonly spelled Eileen, must have started out in life with an identity crisis, she reckoned, and Simmons was frequently written as Simons—she had learned that when looking herself up in *Who's Who*: "SIMMONS, see also SIMONS." In her passport her eyes were "blue," but in her old passport they had been "gray," and her height in the current one had been officially corrected from 6′ 3″ (a comical erratum of the U.S. Passport Office) to 5′ 3″. Her hair, which had had a gray or graying interval, unrecorded in a travel document, had returned to a shade she called for brevity's sake "light brown." She answered to "Dr. Simmons," "President Simmons," and, by preference, "Miss Simmons" or "Simmie." She did not care for "Ms."

She was a chameleon, she imagined. The minute she stepped into a French airplane, she was talking French with the crew, not because she was a Francophile but because she knew how, having done two years of graduate work in French universities and lived with French families. She exercised her French, as she kept up her tennis, whenever the occasion presented itself —in restaurants, chiefly, but also in meetings with her French department staff and at dinners she gave for visiting *conférenciers.* When teased, she always said she was amortizing Senator Fulbright's investment; she had been an early Fulbright scholar, at Montpellier and Strasbourg. In Strasbourg, she had also learned German, which she kept up by listening to records of *lieder* and Mozart and Strauss operas (she loved music) but she no longer tried to speak it with Germans. In Mexico, one summer, she had picked up some Spanish.

As a girl, she had hoped to be a linguist and travel widely, but her Southern accent was a handicap. She carried it over— pure Arkansas, phoneticians said—into whatever tongue she studied, which meant she could never have taught a language at the college level. History had been a *pis aller* for her, but her real field, she had soon discovered, was administration. Here her being Southern, as well as *petite* and a woman and single, was an asset; she was a friendly, outgoing chatterbox and knew how to manage people.

Her seat companion, she noticed, had not filled in the green-printed card. She had completed her landing-card and tossed the other, which was optional, with a sort of disdainful shrug onto the vacant seat between her and Aileen. She was one of those tiresome new young women, evidently, who resisted all attempts at classification and codification, as though they represented designs to "co-opt" her into the prevailing value framework. She was not going to be helpful to Air France by consenting to be an item in their information-storage system, which must answer, Aileen assumed, to some rational need in the planning of flights, though, come to think of it, she was not sure how it served the company to know whether a passenger was traveling for business or for sightseeing or for "other purposes"—she listed some: death in the family, love, health, crime, though crime, if it paid, ought to come under "Business" surely?

Aileen's mind was fond of playing games with itself when it could not find a partner, using whatever materials came to hand; this was the good luck of having been poor as a child with scarcely a new-bought toy in the house. Only rich children were bored; she had pitied them when she had them in class and still did, though with less forbearance, when they came to her now in her office with their dissatisfactions. Her seat companion's casual clothes and indifferent manner marked her as having been one of them—even though, by now, she had probably broken with her "filthy rich" parents: as a rising star of the "new journalism," she could afford that luxury. She had yawned and slept throughout most of the trip, rebuffing the Air France meal and the list of things to buy and the earphones for the movie and yesterday's *Figaro*, accepting only two cups of tea, without sugar, despite Aileen's warning that it would be eleven o'clock at night when they got to Paris, too late to get even a sandwich from room service at the hotel. She was now studying herself, rather angrily, in the mirror of an old Louis Vuitton travel case and jerking a comb through her dark short springy hair which finished in a frizzy bang over her high forehead and in which Aileen had detected with interest two gray threads. On an impulse, Aileen leaned over. "Tell me, honey, how would you sum up, if you had to, our reason for being on this flight?" She was prepared for this advance to be rejected, like all her other overtures, including the kindly hint that it would be wise to take those boots off—the elegant skin-tight things she wore, all the way up the calf, were bound to make the feet swell. But this time the dour young woman smiled. "Interference with the internal affairs of another country?" she suggested. Aileen laughed. At least she had broken the ice.

The hostess came through, collecting the Air France cards. The rector, in the aisle seat, handed his and the Bishop's over, duly filled in, and thanked the girl for the flight, just as though she were a real-life hostess. "I'm glad you enjoyed it, sir." "And our compliments to the pilot," added the Bishop. "I will tell him, sir." And probably she would; the human equation still counted in a 707. Aileen's heart warmed to the two courteous Episcolopians (as they called them back home); they were her idea of old-style American liberals and not afraid of a good time either. Before lunch, they had had a couple of bourbons, and the Reverend had got slightly high, shaking his head in ceaseless wonderment and then going off into roars of laughter that shook his whole body, like somebody being tickled. When he relapsed into gravity, he was the picture of the "concerned clergyman," all frowns and thoughtfulness, as though the fall of a sparrow had suddenly registered on his radar screen, reminding him of his duty to care. Aileen had had a bourbon herself and half a bottle of wine with her meal, which had made her want to talk, so that from her window seat she would lean across her uncommunicative fellow-traveler and address remarks and questions to the Reverend, before she finally got up—when the imprisoning tray was taken away— and circulated through the plane.

But they did not like to see you drifting down the aisle or perching on the arm of a seat. She had been sent back to her place when the "turbulence" announcement came over the loud-speaker, and after that they had shown the movie, which she had watched without the earphones, trying to analyze what was happening and who the characters were. If she had had it to do over, she would not have elected the window seat, so confining; nor would she have chosen, necessarily, to be across from the clergy. Yet in fact she was glad they were along and glad they were somewhere close by, accessible to waves and smiles and a "Cheers" as she raised her bourbon glass. During the film, when the plane was dark and quiet, she could hear the Reverend's loud carrying voice quoting from Scriptures —the Book of Jonah, it sounded like. Though she had been a hard-shell agnostic ever since leaving high school and disliked everything about organized religion except the old Methodist hymns, today it comforted her to feel that her spiritual welfare must be of interest to two experienced males, just as it would have relieved her to know that a doctor was on the trip, though

she hardly ever caught anything more than a cold when traveling or a touch of "Paris tummy," for which she had pills handy
in her purse.

The pair inspired trust, particularly the nice ruddy old Bishop,
whom she had liked on sight when he appeared in the departure lounge. She had not been so sure at first about the Reverend, in his bow tie, semi-crew cut, and loafers—a masquerade
that failed, transparently, to disguise his calling. He was carrying a swollen briefcase and a worn tapestry hold-all that looked
as if a doting helpmeet or the Altar Guild had stitched it. The
peppy "collegiate" tie had worked itself around to a 45-degree
angle, butting against his chin. He had set down the bags to
straighten it and adjust his large glasses, appearing utterly dis-
traught as he stood like a lost parcel in the middle of the
lounge, seeking someone to claim him. Discouragement and
vast perplexity were written all over him, and no wonder—as
she told them later, this was the most *unstructured* committee
she had ever in her whole life come across.

    She had hurried right up to them, in her Southern way.
"You two must be Bishop Hurlbut and the Reverend Barber."
The Bishop had let out a chuckle. "Well, Frank, you see? She
knew us without our dog-collars." Then he had taken her
hand. "And your name, my dear?" "Aileen Simmons. Lucy
Skinner College." He nodded. "We nearly worked together.
You came onto the ACLU board the year I stepped down.
And where is your home, may I ask?" He had noticed her accent. "Down your way, Bishop, originally, and I still go back
most summers." "Missoura!" he cried, his dark-brown eyes
lighting up. "Think of that, Frank!" "Over the border. Arkansas. Fayetteville. But we know about you down home." That
was a tiny white lie: maybe the older folks in Fayetteville were
familiar with "Gus" Hurlbut's exploits as Bishop of Missouri
back in the thirties (hadn't he said "God damn them" from the
pulpit preaching against some mine operators?), but she had
only come to hear of these ancient jousts up north—as a matter of fact, a few weeks ago, from her Professor of Religion,
who had brushed her up on Frank Barber too.

    "Fayetteville. Simmons." The Bishop seemed to be search-
ing his memory. He shook his head. "And your mother's

name?" "Burdick. Catherine Burdick." "Bless me. She knew my Rachel. She used to visit down there, at the University. She talked of a family named Burdick." "There are lots of Burdicks in the area," said Aileen. "But at the University," the Bishop insisted. "Rachel Mackenzie, she was then, before her first marriage." Aileen knitted her brows as if thinking. Her maternal grandfather had indeed had a connection with the University: he was the campus policeman. She was not ashamed of the fact but she doubted that her mother, who had clerked in a feed store, could have known the Bishop's "Rachel" as a girl. To go into this at the moment would only disappoint the kindly old man, so bent on establishing a bond, and it was possible that her mother had been kin to some Burdicks at the University. Most of those Southern homonyms were cousins, if not kissing cousins.

The Reverend finally had had the good sense to interrupt; her genealogy could wait. He wanted to know whether she had seen a rabbi anywhere. "I don't know as I could spot a rabbi," Aileen said, with irritation. "Do you mean there's one joining our group?" Two religious men were already a sufficiency. And there was still a monsignor from Spain in the offing, according to what she had been told. "Oh, Lord!" said the Reverend, sighing. "The mysterious east. So our friend Sadegh didn't tell you. But I understood him to say, just now, that the rabbi's wife was here. When I asked him if the rabbi had come, he said 'Mrs. Weill is upstairs, in the departure lounge. She waits for you.' Isn't that what you heard, Gus?" The Bishop said that his hearing was not as sharp as it had been. "Maybe your rabbi is a woman," Aileen suggested. She watched the Reverend turn this over in his mind. The thought that temples and synagogues might be accepting women for the rabbinate, while his own church tarried, would be uncomfortable for him to accept.

"I was only joking," she told him. It had been naughty of her. Having consulted *Who's Who* and the *New York Times Index*, as well as her Professor of Religion, she was aware of the rector of St. Matthew's (Harvard, D.D.) as an enthusiastic position-taker, most recently identified with the ordination of women, and the impulse to tease him on that sore subject had been as natural as breathing. But he was in too much of a flurry to recognize a joke. She resolved to be more careful in the future; the fact that she knew "all" about him, starting with his birth date (two years before her own), full names of wife, parents, and children, was a temptation to her mischievous side to use its advantage over the poor minister, who knew no more about her, probably, than he did about this missing rabbi.

But who was the rabbi? What brain had he sprung from? In self-protection, Aileen made it a rule to be well armed with facts about any group she agreed to join. This applied most forcefully to omnium-gatherums such as today's delegation. As president of a leading women's college, she was asked in practically every mail to serve on a committee, sponsor a meeting, endorse legislation, sign an appeal, so that she had to pick and choose between contenders for her sympathy: "What suitors have we got this morning?" her PR man would say, riffling through her "In" box. So many of the demands were worthy and (if the unfeeling man only knew!) tore at her heartstrings. But no matter how virtuous the cause, it was the company her name would keep, if only on a letterhead, that she was obliged to bear in mind. In her position, she had to be especially wary of being tarred with a "leftist" brush; thanks to the wicked war in Vietnam, many of the old fellow-travelers had got a foot back into the door of liberal organizations, and the newer "movement" people, with youth's short memory, did not seem to care.

She had explained all that to the Iranians. This committee, she had pointed out, was in an unusually exposed position; in passing judgment on the Shah, it would be open to the charge of furthering Soviet penetration into the Middle East, which meant that its acts and membership, as well as its financing (she was glad to know they were all traveling at their own expense), must be above suspicion. She thought she had made that perfectly clear.

Yet here she was now, with her bags checked to Paris, being informed out of the blue that a rabbi of unknown provenance, whose surname she had not even heard properly, had been added—and his wife too, apparently—to this tiny committee, which would have to live and work together in a closed foreign environment under the eye of the secret police. It was true that a rabbi these days was unlikely to be pro-Soviet, but if he was over forty and a joiner, he might well have sponsored some Soviet-American Friendship rally or signed the Stockholm Peace Appeal. . . . And a pro-Zionist rabbi would be just as much of a liability, given the tone of the Shah's pronouncements on Israel. Another point, minor in comparison, but not negligible: supposing he and his wife were orthodox and ate kosher? Had anybody thought of the problems that would create? An administrative mind learned to pay attention to such things, which counted when strangers of different backgrounds were thrown together, as Lucy Skinner's experience with the Black Muslim girls could tell you.

He might be Reformed, of course, and have a clean liberal record, but Aileen should have been allowed to check up on that herself, at her leisure, and while there was time to reconsider. *Who's Who*, for a starter, could be quite revealing when you knew how to read between the lines. Now, if he turned up, there was nothing to be done. You did not resign from a committee—because the organizers had misled you—at an airport, on the brink of departure.

She felt incensed with the Iranians but also with herself: she had been *lax*. In a way, it was understandable. They had come to her with a letter from an old friend in the drama department; before he went to Lincoln Center, where he was now, he had worked in the Persian theatre on a grant. He vouched for the group of young rebels; he had known several of them personally and their families. They were not Communists; quite the contrary. They belonged to the conservative opposition and objected to the Shah on moral and traditionalist grounds. He himself had been greatly disturbed by the reports of torture he kept hearing while in Iran and he urged Aileen to do something to help: "Go dig out the facts, darling. And the country is enchanting." Aileen had always trusted his judgment and she recognized his thinking in the list of names the young Iranians showed her, with stars opposite those that were "definite." She agreed, with one exception: "Reston won't do it," she said, and of course she was right.

Yet she ought not to have left it there. She knew that. Several times, in fact, she had been on the verge of telephoning the Reverend Barber, whose number she had found in the

Manhattan directory, but then she had reflected that it was Christmas and he would be up to his neck in church doings, hard to catch at his office (she was reluctant to call him at home), and, besides, she herself had been frantic over the holidays, flying back and forth to chair two round tables, look in at the MLA meeting, talk to a Boston alumnae group—it had been as much as she could do to buy some clothes at the sales for the journey.

None of that, though, was the real reason. The truth was, she would never have said yes in the first place except for her insatiable travel urge and the monotony of the New England winter. Teheran was dull, they said, but there were wonderful remote spots to visit if she could take a little time off from the committee: Naqsh-i-Rustan, Takht-i-Jamshid, Cyrus's tomb at Pasargadae, Isfahan. . . . Once those breath-taking pictures had taken shape in her imagination (with some assistance from *The National Geographic* in the library basement), she had been unwilling, she reckoned, to hear any fresh facts about the committee that might cause her to think twice: she *had* to see the "Cube of Zoroaster," Darius's palace, the graves of the Sassanids, and the rock-hewn tombs of the Achaeminid kings.

To tell a little more truth (it was wise to be candid with oneself), there had also been the promise of getting to know the Senator, a handsome man in his photographs and recently widowed. She saw them flying to Shiraz over weekends and renting a car to explore the country together, picnicking in the ruins; the others would not be interested in antiquities, probably, and, if some were, they could come along, sharing the expenses.

"A rabbi is so darned important," the Reverend was stating, as if to himself. He had sunk down on a bench opposite her while the Bishop had gone to the men's room. Aileen made no comment. Instead, she voiced her own worries. "They should be calling our flight any minute now. What do you suppose has happened to the Senator? He was meant to be coming in on an early plane from Washington." "Oh?" That was news, evidently, to the Reverend, but, unlike him, she had not been *totally* remiss. Last week she had had her secretary call the Senator's office in Washington; his chief aide said that Iran was certainly on the boss's calendar and asked the girl to tell

President Simmons that the Senator was looking forward to meeting her. This had given her the right, she thought, to call again, and yesterday the same aide had said that, yes, he was booked this morning on a flight to Kennedy. But it was typical of Miss Meloney, in many ways an excellent secretary, that she had not thought to find out *what* flight. It could have been late or canceled. But unless you knew the flight number there was no way of checking up. "Mr. Barber, do you think you could just go downstairs and ask Mr. Sadegh if there's been a message?"

"Sadegh has gone," said the minister. Aileen let out a wail and fell back in a heap on the bench. Unbelievably, while the two clerics were checking in, the Iranian had made a phone call and "discovered" he had an appointment. So he had asked the minister's son for a ride back to town. "And you let them go," said Aileen. Useless to wonder why he had not exercised some parental authority. She turned her stricken face to the Bishop, who had seated himself during this exchange and was rocking calmly back and forth with his big umbrella between his chubby knees. "If the young fellow wanted to make himself scarce, plenty of vehicles were available," he observed.

Aileen felt ready to cry. The Senator was going to be a No Show—hadn't she always had the presentiment? The Iranian, somehow, must have known it or found it out from his phone call. "Then he just couldn't face us and he ran away. Don't you agree, Bishop Hurlbut? Don't you *know* that's what's happened? I vote we go home."

"You may be right, my dear. When you've served on as many duly constituted bodies as I have, you come to expect eleventh-hour defections. But I reckon the Senator would have had the courtesy to have one of us paged here if he missed his plane for some reason. He and I are old acquaintances, though we've sometimes been on different sides of the fence. I made a long-distance call to his office the other day—to check up, don't you know—and his right-hand man told me that Iran was on his calendar all right. 'Glad you called, Bishop,' he said. 'I know the Senator is looking forward to meeting you again.' So, until we have more information, I vote we give Sadegh the benefit of the doubt." Aileen was surprised that a man of his age and reputation for godliness could be so easily soft-soaped. "That only proves that the Senator is a politician," she said.

The boarding sign went on. Passengers started filing into the second section of the lounge, past an Air France official at a high desk. A line formed. The Reverend hesitated. He made another lingering survey of the lounge.

Aileen's attention wandered. A new group of passengers, led by an Air France hostess, had entered from a corridor at the far end of the hall and was moving past the barrier, while the line already formed was halted. First class, naturally; they were being taken straight to the plane. She caught sight of a silvery head, then a tall, erect figure, which turned and scanned the queue and the slowly emptying lounge. The Senator! He was looking for them. Aileen vigorously waved. But he did not see her; she was too small. She reached in her bag for a handkerchief and signaled with it over her head. "Here we are, Senator!" But he could not hear her either. By her side, the tall Reverend was executing crossed-arm motions, like a trainman flagging an engineer. The Senator finally grinned and waved back. Then, making a gesture of helplessness, he moved forward, into the Security section.

"Come on," urged Aileen. "Bishop, don't you think we ought to get in line now?" The minister was still worrying about his rabbi. "Should we have him paged on the loudspeaker?" "'Rabbi and/or Mrs. Weill'?" suggested the Bishop, amused. Aileen clapped her hand to her head. Her earrings bounced. "Heavens, I thought you said 'Weiss,' Reverend. There's a *Miss* Weil over there telephoning. Or she was, a few minutes ago. But she pronounces it 'Vile' and spells it with one *l*. I was so concerned about the Senator that I didn't see the connection." She laughed to cover her confusion in making the admission, which was true but came out sounding lame, like a lie.

It was the clerics' turn to be *bouleversés*. Now they knew how it felt to hear casually, on the dawn of D-day, that a new element had been added to the troops. Open-mouthed, they looked to Aileen for explanations. "A journalist. She writes for *The New Yorker*. And *The Atlantic Monthly*." "*The Atlantic*." The Bishop nodded. "Sophie Weil." "Why, yes!" exclaimed the Reverend. "I read an article by her only last month. On Oman, was it?" Brazil, the Bishop thought. Either or both, Aileen said. "Miss Weil gets around. Brazil was another torture story." "Right! Right!" cried the Reverend. "I remember that too. Wonderful stuff!" It was as though the good religious man had totally forgotten about the "importance" of the rabbi.

"Well! I guess that clears up the mystery. Not Sadegh's fault, really. Just a little communications breakdown. The rabbi in Denver couldn't make it and instead we'll have Sophie. Coincidence of names. But why did he say 'Mrs.,' I wonder?" He shook his head. "Between ourselves, Miss Simmons, didn't you find him kind of hard to pin down sometimes? As if there was no real, frank, open exchange . . . Of course, his English! But I guess our Iranian won't be so fluent either." He bubbled on joyously.

"I didn't meet Mr. Sadegh until this morning," Aileen said. "At the check-in counter. He had Miss Weil with him, and we agreed to be seat mates. It was Mr. Asad who came up to Sunnydale to talk to me, with another young man. And we spoke French. If you mean, did they misrepresent this committee to me, no, I can't say they did, Reverend, not really. They didn't tell me a rabbi was coming, but then, apparently, you were mistaken about that, don't you think so, Bishop? I must say, Mr. Asad might have let me know sooner that a journalist would be joining us, instead of leaving me a note last night at my hotel. But then, as I understand it, she isn't to be part of our committee or sign any statement we may release. She's going along as a reporter, on an assignment. . . . Isn't that so, Miss Weil?"

Aileen's seat mate, a tall dark long-nosed young woman wearing a long suede coat, had silently come up. "Let me introduce you to the Bishop and the Reverend. I was telling them that you're going to be with us but purely as a reporter. Mr. Asad and his friends made the arrangement with you. Or was it with your editor?" Aileen raised her head brightly, prepared to listen, as she did at assemblies when presenting a student speaker. The young woman turned to the two clergymen. "It was my own idea. I've known Asad for ages and when he told me the other night about your committee, I decided I wanted to go along. I guess I ought to have cleared it with all of you, since you're the ones concerned. . . ." This was Aileen's opinion; the Bishop and the Reverend, however, were making chivalrous noises of dissent. "But there wasn't time, and the Iranians, you know, are so frightfully vague. I wasn't sure how many of you there would be or how to reach you." Lucy Skinner College was not exactly a needle in a haystack, Aileen reflected. But she only nodded, as if in thoughtful accord, as she listened to the breathy voice addressing itself gravely to the two men, who were nodding also.

"Did the Senator make it?" Aileen pointed; you could still see the back of his head in Security. "Terrific," the girl said. "I suppose they kept him in the V.I.P. pen." Aileen gave a little cry; she had not thought to ponder the implications of senatorial privilege. "Does that mean he'll be traveling first class while the rest of us stay in Economy?" Miss Weil looked at her curiously. "What difference does it make?" The men too were gazing at Aileen, as if in wonderment. "Well, I mean," she protested, "we're a group, aren't we? We have an agenda to discuss. We ought to elect a chairman. Don't you think so, Bishop?" Before the old man could answer, Miss Weil declared, with a stifled yawn, that there was no cause for worry: the Senator could not ride first class unless he had paid a first-class fare. "The V.I.P. lounge is just a courtesy." "But how do you know that?" Aileen said plaintively. "You sound so sure, honey."

In the line, the Bishop counted heads. "Five, with the Senator. But, Frankie, shouldn't there be six?" "The rabbi," Aileen reminded him. "But no"—she corrected herself—"Miss Weil is the rabbi, isn't she?" "Somebody's missing," announced the Reverend. "Don't you have a list?" Aileen said sharply. "Doesn't any of us have a list?" Miss Weil spoke up. "There's meant to be a professor with you. A Middle East specialist. From Buffalo." "Bless you!" cried the Reverend. "Right! Right! Lenz, that's the name. I must be losing my mind. You'll think we're a woolly lot of liberals, Miss Weil. With Sadegh disappearing and everything, I plain forgot about him. Lenz. Victor Lenz. Sadegh told me to add him. I have his career data here somewhere." Inexcusable. But then Aileen recalled having seen the name herself, on the emended list they had sent her during the holidays. She had found one reference to him in the *Readers' Guide*—an article or review in *The New Republic*—that she had not had time to follow up. "Well, we can't wait for him," said the Bishop. "We may find him on the plane."

But as they moved ahead, toward the barrier, a little blond man, unshaven, in a long dark overcoat, took a boarding-card from his teeth and accosted Aileen. "President Simmons? I met you once at a panel discussion. But you wouldn't remember me, I know. I asked a question from the floor. Bishop Hurlbut, Reverend Barber, glad to know you. Sorry I can't shake hands." So this apparition was Lenz. In his left hand was an open basket that held what looked like blankets and some canned goods; a man's purse and a long trailing scarf were slung around his neck; a folded tabloid protruded from an overcoat pocket; and in his right hand was a cage containing— surely?—an animal. "Sophie Weil," Aileen indicated, when no one else spoke. "Lenz. Victor Lenz. My pleasure." "Is that a cat?" said Miss Weil.

The professor nodded happily. "Sapphire, my Persian." He crouched down and spoke to it. "Yes, Sappho, nice Sappho, mustn't be scared." "You don't mean to say it's going with us?" cried Aileen. "Coals to Newcastle, yes, you may wonder. But I couldn't leave her with the nasty vet, could I, Sapphire? We came down on the bus yesterday. Domestic airlines can be tiresome about animals. But we got to bed late, and Sapphire forgot to wake me this morning. So we nearly didn't make it. I don't suppose any of you knows where to get a drink here." The smell Aileen had been noticing could not be the cat, then. In fact the professor reeked of stale alcohol.

"There must be a drinking fountain somewhere," volunteered the Reverend, stepping out of line and looking around him vaguely. The official at the barrier snapped his fingers. "Please, ladies and gentlemen! *S'il vous plaît, messieurs et dames!*" "You can get a drink of water on the plane," Aileen heard the Reverend telling the professor, as the matron frisked her for weapons.

But the retired Bishop of Missouri had a keener eye. On boarding the aircraft, he halted and from one of the pockets of his thick tweed suit he brought out a good-sized silver flask. "For medicinal purposes," he said, offering it to the professor. "Get yourself a paper cup."

Aileen had questioned the Bishop's wisdom in offering a hair of the dog to somebody so evidently in need of it. It would be the last straw, she thought, if the committee were to find itself with a problem drinker, as well as a cat, on its hands. Iran, being Moslem, was dry, presumably, but that did not apply to foreigners, not in big cities, and anyway alcoholics were cunning, adept at procuring bottles and hiding them like squirrels. The Bishop and the Reverend no doubt had experience in dealing with drunkards, and perhaps they could be trusted to handle Lenz, should he start picking fights with the secret police, for instance. . . . It was not up to her to keep a watch on him; yet the habit of supervision (she had been a dean, for her sins, and before that a registrar) and foreseeing eventualities was hard to throw off.

But before she could ponder the matter, a diversion had occurred. While they were filing through first class on their way to Economy, a large pale ringed hand had gone out to intercept the Bishop: "Gus! My dear man! How lovely!" And "Charles!" the Bishop had responded. The reunion had been cut short by the steward, chivying them on to where they belonged, past the Senator, who was already installed in his shirt sleeves in the first row of Economy, with his glasses on, and papers spread out all around him—they had given him a whole block of seats to himself. He jumped up and shook hands, explaining with a smile and a pained twist of the dark eyebrows that he had work to do: he would be stopping by for a chat as soon as his "desk" was cleared. "Did our friend fix his glittering eye on you?" he said to the Bishop.

Then they were scarcely airborne when the same hand, followed by a snowy cuff, had parted the curtain that divided the sheep from the goats and the man called Charles had peered in: a long white papery face, long nose, dark eyes, dead black hair. After some debate with the steward, he was allowed to come through. He stood in the aisle, holding both the Bishop's hands in his and proclaiming his delight in a high "English" voice that caused passengers in the rows ahead to turn about in their seats, as though anticipating a show. The fluting tones, rising to a rooster's crow, suggested deafness or its social equivalent to Aileen.

He was an old man, nearly as old as the Bishop but extremely well preserved, like a thin dried haddock. The raven hair was his own but certainly dyed, and his face was powdered with

talcum. He wore a suit of coffee-colored silk, with many flaps
and pockets, that looked as if it had been made for a planter in
Java before the First War, an elegant soft shirt, and a beige
waistcoat; on his feet were black silk socks and long shoes the
color of old-time stove blacking. He fitted a cigarette into an
ivory holder, and his jewelry consisted of monogrammed gold
cufflinks, a plain heavy gold ring, like a man's wedding band
but worn on the right hand, an antique ring with an intaglio
cut in some pale gem, and the latest thing in costly wrist-
watches. And he was on his way to Teheran.

"On a *tour*. Can you imagine it? I'm part of a first-class
package." The Bishop's response, inaudible, could be inferred
by anybody who was curious. "You too, dear boy? Isn't that
glorious? I shall certainly play hookey." Charles's tour was tremendous value, Economy class heard: first-category hotels,
chauffeured limousines, archaeologists serving as guides, delicious food (they *said*), all included with the air fare, for less
than it would cost Charles to dine out for a week in New York.
Aileen was aware of a general stir in the public that perhaps
represented envy. Nobody was paying attention to the hostess
in the aisle demonstrating the inflation of the life jacket. "Trust
the rich to find a bargain. I had no *idea*. In my poky way, I
thought package tours were what my plumber takes. But I
shall pay the price in socializing. My millionaires are up there
drinking alcohol already. Full of Republican sound and fury.
You should have seen the faces when I spoke to Senator Carey.
Charming man. You would think, wouldn't you, that collectors
would be more civilized. That living with beautiful things
would rub off on them. A total fallacy. By the bye, have you
talked to the Senator? There in the front row; magnificent
head. I suppose he's bound for Paris to attend one of those
'meetings' politicians today go in for. I found him rather taciturn, I must say. You know he lost his wife."

Charles remained oblivious of the commotion in the aisle
caused by the news he had just disseminated, which was sending autograph-hunters forward with menus to be signed.
"Such a joy to see you, my dear. And how splendid to know
that we shall be together on the plane tomorrow. Sensible of
you to go tourist class. The rich are only tolerable in their
own settings. Those dreadfully named Bloody Marys they're

engorging. So menstrual, I always tell them. Well, as a good Democrat, I shall have a split of champagne with my lunch."

The Bishop must have warned him that others were listening. Disappointingly, for a time nothing further could be heard. Aileen had resigned herself to yesterday's *Figaro* and was scanning the Classifieds for items of interest when Charles again became audible, expressing concern for the Bishop's health. "You're dressed much too warmly, dear fellow. These carriers are always overheated. You'll catch cold, and that will be tiresome for you. Light-weight summer suits, I find, are best for plane travel, in this natural color. It shows the dirt less than the dyed silks, despite what people tell one. Then I always travel with a shawl or two as well as a light overcoat. And you must be careful about the sun, even in winter out there. We shall have to find you a proper broad-brimmed hat. Felt, not a Panama, mind you. The tomb-towers, as you'll see, can be damp."

He had no suspicion, evidently, of the Bishop's mission "out there." The thought that any motive other than site-seeing could be operative had not crossed his mind. Aileen wondered how those two could ever have come to know each other; maybe ADA, she speculated. But if "Charles" was such a Democrat, why was he traveling with a group of rich Republicans? "Collectors," he had said. She got up to go to the ladies' room, edging past Miss Weil and giving a little wave, as she went, to the Bishop.

When she came back, with her hair fluffed out under her turban and fresh mascara, the Bishop was waiting to introduce them. "President Simmons, my old friend Charles Tennant. Won't you join us, Miss Simmons?" "Well, just for a minute." She took the vacant place between the two ancient men. Against the wall, near the serving-pantry, the Reverend was talking happily with a hostess, who was getting the drinks cart ready. "Charles is bound for Iran too," the Bishop explained. "So I gathered," said Aileen. "Did I hear you say something about collectors, Mr. Tennant? Is it a tour of *art* collectors you're with?"

It was an archaeological tour got up by a band of "proud possessors" who were discovering Iran as it threatened to make itself scarce. The energy crisis was responsible for bringing them together on a common carrier; normally they would have chartered a plane or flown in a baby jet belonging to one of their companies—two of the men in the party were company directors. The poor dears saw this as their "very last opportunity" to tour the famous ruins, visit the museums, and explore some of the new digs before the Shah raised the price of oil again. There was a curator from the Fine Arts Museum with them, who was hoping to interest them in financing new excavations—an unlikely eventuality, Charles considered. "You mean the *Boston* Museum," Aileen decided. "But why? Are you all from Boston?" She ought to have remembered that the museum was renowned for its oriental section. "Dear me, no," said Charles. "We're from New York and Pittsburgh and Cincinnati and Hartford and Worcester—the dark satanic mills." "Charles lives on Mount Vernon Street," put in the Bishop. "He has a crackerjack oriental collection." "Almost nothing from Iran, alas. A few Khabur bits and pieces I picked up fifty years ago. No, our little curator is the only knowledgeable member of our party. Like some of the ladies, I've been 'cramming' for the journey."

He turned to Aileen. "You must come to tea one day if porcelains interest you." Then he gave a screech. "But you have some lovely Chinese work in your museum!" "You *know* our little museum?" Better than she did, she perceived, as he named a "hare's fur cup" and some "priceless *blanc de Chine*" that she could not picture to herself—ages ago, in her predecessor's time, an alumna had left Lucy Skinner a lot of *chinoiserie*. "Those people with you, are they important collectors?" she said.

"*Je regrette, monsieur . . .*" The steward was telling the gentleman that he would have to return to his own class; the hostesses were about to serve drinks and needed the aisle clear. The Reverend was waiting to reoccupy his seat. "Well, that was nice!" Aileen declared, when Charles had gone. "Bishop, do you know what a hare's fur cup is?"

Back in her place, she had slowly grown pensive. The wine at lunch, probably, had done it. True to his promise, the Senator had come by, on his way back from the men's room, for a short chat. But Miss Weil had chosen that moment to sit up and take notice (she had seemed utterly deaf to Charles's incursion), so that the conversation, inevitably, was three-cornered. The Senator reported that Sapphire had lunched on salmon from the hors d'oeuvres course cut up and heated by the hostess and had declined a bowl of milk. The professor and the cat had the bank of seats opposite him, which appeared to amuse the Senator. Aileen did not dare ask him whether Lenz was continuing to drink; Miss Weil, she could not forget, was a journalist. . . . And when Aileen returned his visit, just before the film-showing, Lenz himself, shaved at last, was very much in evidence, with the caged animal beside him and a blonde hostess bending over murmuring "*Minette, minette.*" The Senator was calling him "Victor" and dispensing a fund of cat stories. Then came the turbulence announcement, and she had to climb over Miss Weil again and wearily strap herself into her corner.

It had been a strategic error not to elect to sit by herself. She had wanted to take the young woman's measure, and the New York–Paris leg of the journey, she had estimated, would provide an early occasion. But almost the reverse had happened. She knew no more about Miss Weil and her intentions than when she had boarded, and the journalist, if she had cared to listen, had quite a lot of "material" on Aileen. It was sensing that girl beside her, like a silent criticism, that was inducing her to feel defensive about herself. Though she was not at all what they called "a calculating person"—much too outgoing and open to sudden impulse—she would not like a stranger to see, sometimes, the little reckonings that were going on in her head. And they showed sometimes, she feared, giving those who did not know her a bizarre impression. For instance, before lunch just now she had asked Charles too many questions —perhaps even the Bishop had noticed—which did not sound totally idle. But when she heard that there was a group of art collectors bound for Teheran up in first class and then in the next breath Lucy Skinner's art gallery was mentioned, she could not help making a connection. Now her brain was considering how she could get at them and find out *what* they collected, which was natural in somebody who had to be concerned with gifts and bequests, while a contrary thought chain was leading her to wonder how she could avoid them if they turned up at Zoroaster's Cube or the wall tombs of Naqsh-i-Rustan when she was with Senator Carey. She could not stop herself from *thinking*, any more than the average person, on being shown 2 and 2, could avoid making 4.

Her fault was only an unusual degree of mental activity. The curse of intelligence. Stupid people were unconscious of their slow-moving thought processes. But take Charles's plain gold ring: a mind like hers could not fail to perceive immediately that it was on the "wrong" hand and be aware of what conclusions to draw. Though he must be nearly eighty and queer in every sense, there he was, a man and unmarried. With a fair share of worldly goods. If he owned a house on Mount Vernon Street and collected porcelains, he could not be, as she had first thought, some kind of gentleman guide. She could not be blamed if in the forefront of her idling mind these facts were turning over, along with the notation that she was fifty this year and single.

For some time now, ever since her *affaire* with the head of the classics department had ended, she had been looking at men from that angle. To her shame, even the Bishop had passed through her head this morning. The deterrent was not the dead wife, so hard to replace, or his age, but the fact that he was too sweet: when he died, she knew she would suffer. She did not *mean* to be sizing up old men; it was almost cruel. But so few men of her own age were available. Most men of her own age were either married or queer. A married man could always turn into a widower, but a queer remained a queer, though an old one, if you had some interests in common, might prove to be your best hope, assuming he was no longer very active sexually—a women's college would not offer many fleshly temptations. Yet what if she were called upon to be the first woman president of Harvard or Yale? In that event, a homosexual consort would be a liability.

Her bald approach to this topic seemed to distress her friends. "Honey," her PR man said, "you shouldn't talk that way in front of me. I'm a *man*. You shouldn't even talk that way to yourself. You got to leave something to fate." But Aileen had no trust in fate. She preferred to see this as a problem for study, researching the field of "availables" in the same spirit as she leafed through scholarly publications in the hunt for a candidate with the right qualifications for an expected vacancy in one of the departments. And with luck she might kill two birds with one stone; that was how she had found her classicist, an excellent teacher and a grass widower. But then, when he was settled in, with a nice house and a top salary, his mercenary wife had returned to him. Divorced men were a mirage: they either went back to their wives or married someone much younger, the way they would turn in an old Buick for a new Volkswagen.

She was not the kind married men left their wives for; she had learned that cruel lesson in her thirties. So her choice ought to lie between widowers and bachelors, which was not a bright outlook, given the known facts that most wives outlived their husbands and that most bachelors were disguised halves of a homosexual couple.

She ought to have married when she was young, but then she had not wanted to. She had prized her independence. Making her own way up the academic ladder, she did not fancy adding the burden of a husband to be carried along; the Ph.D. candidates she met in the graduate-school mills and in the cafeterias and faculty dining-rooms of small Southern colleges were far from enticing *partis*, and the deans and department heads had their careers already made and would never forsake tenure as well as their wives and children to follow her north when the call came.

The typical academic married too early; as a student, she had taken note of this classic mistake and made up her mind to learn from it. A woman had the advantage of being able to discard an outgrown spouse without being bled for alimony, but even so, casting off a husband who had become too small for you, like a child's pair of shoes, was bound to be painful and exhausting. Aileen was careful with her energy, which she kept for her career, her family, and her friendships. From the little experience she had had of it, she wanted no truck with remorse.

If it had not been for her family, she might have married nonetheless—the inevitable childhood sweetheart, who was still in Fayetteville and a doctor. But her family gave her the emotional nourishment and sense of belonging a woman needed. She was close to her brothers and sisters, all settled in

Fayetteville, and truly loved her mother, an intelligent woman (even if she had only a high-school diploma) from whom she had got her brains. Once her Papa had died, her Mamma had wonderfully grown and developed, politically as well as culturally—she had been in the local anti-Vietnam-war movement, written regular letters of support and advice to Senator Fulbright, and at the age of seventy-one had got on a bus to Washington to march in a demonstration. Aileen had been helping her family ever since she had left home. In the summers, she insisted on paying her keep, though her mother now was reasonably well fixed, with her father's life-insurance and the widow's benefits she drew from the federal government—Papa had been a mailman. Mamma owned the house free and clear, rented rooms to students during the term, and occasionally gave a hand to her former boss, who was now eighty, with the accounts and inventory in the old feed store, which had expanded into a big hardware and housewares business and was mainly run by his daughter.

It would not have surprised Aileen if her Mamma had married again; she had gentlemen friends who sat on the porch or in the "den" with her and took her out riding on Sundays. At seventy-six, she did not feel too old for sex, apparently: she had had it with Aileen's father right up to the end, she confided, and still "missed him that way." But you did not need to get married for that, fortunately. There was always somebody who wanted to sleep with you, Aileen had found. That was one of the surprises of middle age—she would never have imagined when she was young that if you put some perfume on and left your room door on the latch in the Statler Hilton during the MLA meeting, a distinguished Russian specialist would come gliding to your bed. It had happened just this Christmas.

As Aileen saw it, sex gave a woman only two problems. Contraception was no longer a worry, thanks to the menopause, which she had completed, with gratitude, last summer, but, as that problem had receded, the other—taking care with whom you did it and where—had become more acute. Permissiveness did not extend to older females—even Mamma was criticized if she pulled the shades when entertaining—still less to older heads of female institutions. Most married men could be relied on for discretion; they had their own motives for concealment. Nevertheless she had made it a rule not to be tempted by a member of the faculty, no matter how attractive, and in the case of a visiting lecturer to respect the prohibition laid down for students—not on college property. Her classicist had been an exception. The first time, it had happened in her house, and the next morning, before the maid came, she had had to wash the sheet and iron it by hand—taking it to the laundromat would have been too risky. After that they had met in Boston hotels.

In general nowadays she kept sex for vacations and the professional conferences that figured more and more on her calendar. Some of her nicest memories were of "stolen" interludes during forums and panels with interesting men whom she never expected to see again. And if sometimes their paths did cross a second time, at another round table, there was seldom any further question of sex. Yet she remembered and, meeting their eyes in the course of some boring presentation, she knew they remembered too.

Thanks to her mother, she did not have to feel tied to Lucy Skinner. Mamma had made a home for her. She had her room, with her familiar things; her old trunks were stored in the cellar; in the den were her photograph albums. There were files of her correspondence in the attic, her doctoral thesis, programs of seminars she had attended, with the papers that had been read. Her summer dresses were waiting for her, hung up in bags, with lavender. But that was another thing: her mother was getting on. When she went, Aileen would be alone, with no center to her life. A room at one of her sisters' with full-grown children under foot would not be the same at all. It was Mamma's fault that she had never been domestic. She had mastered a few French and Mexican recipes for entertaining, and her sisters had taught her to iron. But housekeeping was Mamma's sphere, so that Aileen had not been able to develop her own touch and style, except in clothes. The President's house at Lucy Skinner bore few marks of her occupancy beyond some gay pillows she had scattered about, for students to sit on the floor on, some old prints of French cities, and her record collection. Buildings and Grounds supplied flowers twice a week and arranged them—she did not have Mamma's "hand" with bouquets—and the china and glassware she used reflected the taste of old Miss Smith, her predecessor. Even if Aileen had known how, she would not have tried to make the impersonal house homey.

She spent most of her time in her office, surrounded by the clacketing of typewriters and the ringing of telephones in the anteroom. At night, when she was not invited out to dinner or entertaining officially, she would eat in one of the student dining-halls or sit down at a table in the college snack bar, where a group would immediately join her. She dropped in on classes, films, exhibitions, lectures, and could usually be counted on to rise in the audience, wrapped in a bright shawl, and ask the first question. After college events, she would have students and faculty in for drinks. These habits had made her popular; Miss Smith, a shy academic woman, had been almost a recluse.

No one would have guessed—she thought—that underneath her liveliness was an awful fear of loneliness. Though she had been living by herself for nearly thirty years, she was seldom, in practice, alone. If she had to be alone for a whole evening, she poured herself a bourbon, listened to the news, telephoned, played the phonograph. She had lost the feeling she had had as a girl that a book could be a companion, which meant that she read less and less. She hated silence and sitting still and when she sank into meditation (as now perforce, on the plane), her thoughts were a kind of noise she kept going in her head. But she was getting a bit cracked, she feared. After a few drinks recently, playing *Carmen* one night, she had danced all by herself, clicking a pair of castanets she had brought back years ago from Mexico and stamping her heels, forgetful of how grotesque she would have looked if anyone had peeked in. Fortunately, the President's house was in an isolated position, on a hillock.

Late at night often, she would pick up the telephone and call her mother or one of her sisters; with the time difference, they would not be asleep yet. This lifeline to Arkansas, at arm's reach when all else failed, had made her neglectful of the fact that her youth had gone while she was looking the other way. Of course fifty today was not old. There were examples of women older than herself who got husbands: George Eliot was sixty when she married Mr. Cross. But George Eliot was an exception for whom the laws of probability did not count. Aileen knew herself to be no such awesome phenomenon; lacking fame and a big brain, she was subject to the ordinary hazards of competition: unlike George Eliot, she was not even exceptionally homely, which had probably been some sort of advantage. Men were not afraid of ugly women. On the other hand, she lacked the *je ne sais quoi* that came from having been a beauty; she was betwixt and between, even though her appearance had benefited from the sharpening that age and wiser make-up had brought to her features, and she had kept her pert figure. In any case, at fifty, whatever you looked like, you could not expect a *coup de foudre*; time and proximity were necessary. But meanwhile you were being crowded not only by your coevals, entering the market via death or divorce, but by the oncoming generations, who were not looking for marriage necessarily—which made it doubly unfair.

Sophie Weil, for instance. Calmly deciding to attach herself to their group, she had never given a thought probably to how Aileen as the only woman would feel. Now they were two, and Aileen's chances of "making time" with the Senator were reduced to a forlorn hope. With a glamorous journalist in her thirties available for a "flirt," he would not have a minute for a still attractive female of his own age—four whole years younger, actually. Unless he was a very unusual politician, he would soon be eagerly carrying the sullen *New Yorker* correspondent's suitcases and deploying his Irish charm. And the meanness, the waste, of it was that the girl had no need of a silver-haired widower for a husband; if she was like most of her kind, she would be opposed to the entire concept of marriage, and it would not cross her mind that she was standing in the way of somebody who felt otherwise. To her, it would be inconceivable that a fifty-year-old educator could be any kind of rival.

So that made one motive less for the voyage to Teheran. Nevertheless Aileen found herself slowly cheering up. Eliminating the Senator from her computations meant that she would be relieved of the labor of devising strategies to throw herself in his way: maneuvering to sit next to him on tomorrow's flight, lurking in the hotel lobby to catch him as he alighted from the elevator, arranging to have herself appointed the group's chairman so that she would have occasion to stop by his room on committee business, leave little notes in his box. . . . If she could swallow her disappointment now, she would be spared a host of future disappointments and humiliating setbacks. She could enjoy the time in Iran as a working vacation that might even benefit a few of her fellow-men. Not waiting for the movie to end, she opened Asad's folder and switched on the overhead light. The awful torture-descriptions made her wince as she thoughtfully turned the pages, underlining the paragraphs that seemed most promising for the committee to follow up.

It was extraordinary how altruism, a decision to focus on others, could put you at peace with yourself. Aileen was accustomed to thinking of herself as a good person (while always resolving to be better) but lately she had been having some doubts. Her quick sympathy with the Shah's victims reassured her: cruelty appalled her, and that was the main thing to watch out for in yourself—any tendency to be insensitive to suffering, if it was only a headache. Cruelty, she had read once, was the only sin a modern mind recognized as such, and she went out of her way therefore to be considerate, which was the reason her staff loved her. And want of consideration, when she observed it in someone else, could afflict her like the drilling of a tooth.

Even in little things, like her neighbor's lofty rejection of the Air France questionnaire—"*Aidez-nous à vous mieux connaître*"—which somebody had taken trouble to frame. It had actually hurt her to watch, out of the corner of her eye, as the green-printed card was tossed as if derisively onto the seat between them. She had been indignant for the card, which, like Aileen, was only asking for some innocent information: "Help us to know you better."

The pathetic fallacy at work! Cards did not have feelings. In the disdainful gesture she must have sensed a rejection of her middle-class self and her values, among which was the duty to be helpful and do as you were asked when no possible harm was involved. By her offhand act, Miss Weil was scorning Aileen for having filled *hers* out. But that scarcely explained—or did it?—the positive hatred Aileen had felt well up in her, almost like a physical thing. And now it was rising again as she tried to concentrate on the folder. "*Pig*," she said under her breath, using one of *their* epithets. "Stupid, arrogant pig."

It was not the first time this had happened to her recently. In her office, she would watch poor harmless stolid Miss Meloney, who adored her, and catch herself thinking "Bag!" or even "Old bag!" though Miss Meloney was younger than she was and a virtuous spinster, so far as Aileen knew, and the only connection there appeared to be was that the secretary, too broad in the beam already, had the habit of bringing her lunch to her desk and wrapping the unfinished morsels—a half-eaten browning apple or a mustard-oozing sandwich—in one of those plastic tissues called "Baggies," a package of which stood next to her typewriter. She had come to hate Miss Meloney and did not know why. The sole therapy she knew for that was to hug her a great deal and smile warmly whenever she caught her eye and send thoughtful little things to the poor girl's mother, who was a shut-in.

Yet where was the common factor between Miss Meloney and Sophie? Perhaps it was just her time of life and having a silent female body so close to her in a confined space. But there had been other signs of a growing divergence between her behavior and her feelings, which she found quite upsetting, especially as there could be no question of altering one to match the other: she could not change her feelings, and if she stopped sending Miss Meloney's mother presents or struck Miss Weil, it might make her a whole person but not a person she would like better. Her best hope was that actions might occasionally prompt the appropriate emotions: a hug could sometimes make her feel warm. She would try to remember that with Sophie.

The No Smoking sign went on. The plane was starting its descent. "Paree!" she called to the Bishop, who was peering out the window. Then, distinctly, they heard a hostess scream. Aileen closed her eyes tight. They were being hijacked, she supposed. She heard someone running down the aisle. A hostess raced past. A male voice was shouting angrily. Aileen peeked through her fingers. The pilot, or the co-pilot, was standing in front of the curtain that shut off first class. She could not see a hijacker. Then, toward the front, someone laughed. A word was passing along. "*Le chat!*" "It's a cat."

"Sapphire," needlessly explained the Reverend. "Keep your seats, please!" the officer ordered. "Everyone be seated. *Attachez vos ceintures.*" The hostesses and the steward were chasing the cat up and down the aisle.

Aileen rose half out of her seat to see what was happening. It looked as if the animal might have escaped into first class. "But *why* did he let it out of its cage, Reverend? Mr. Lenz! How could you do such a wicked, dangerous thing?" "*Asseyez-vous, madame! Et vous, monsieur, retournez à votre siège!*" Paying no heed, Lenz was creeping down the aisle, making coaxing sounds. The cat was hiding, as they did when they were frightened. "*Regagnez votre siège,*" repeated the steward, not adding "*monsieur*" this time. "*Dépêchez-vous.*" A hostess came by, looking under the seats. "*Minou, minou,*" she wheedled. "Here, kitty, kitty," essayed the Reverend. "I guess it doesn't understand French," he added to the hostess with a foolish laugh. "Oh, sir," she replied, "you do not imagine the trouble that gentleman has made. He have taken *minou* from her box and hold her on his knees. I tell him he must not do that; it is forbidden. But he say the cat is crying. I have to call the steward. Then when no one is looking, he take her out again." "Totally irresponsible!" Aileen declared. "You are right," said the hostess. "And *en plus* he smoked in the toilet." Aileen clapped her hand to her head.

Sophie's boot was exploring the floor. Her long arm reached down. "Why, it's Sapphire; hello, Sapphire." She scooped up the blue Persian and set her on her lap, rubbing her cheek against the long fur. "We must find you some catnip." The passengers applauded as the hostess came to retrieve the now purring animal. The crew took their places against the wall. There was a bump, and the flight was over.

On the bulletin board, after they had cleared immigration, the Reverend discovered a message addressed to Senator James Carey et al. LOOKING FORWARD TO MEETING YOU AT HOTEL EIGHT A.M. BREAKFAST. VAN VLIET DE JONGE CAMERON. The Senator held up the missive. "Does anybody have a guess as to how many persons that is?" It could be three or two or just one. He was laughing. "Come on, et al." Nobody knew. As they waited for their baggage he took Aileen's arm. "Kind of a funny committee, isn't it?" he murmured. Her eyes flew up alarmed and met his. Was he thinking of quitting? But no; he was just sharing his amusement with her. He would be a set-up for anything that tickled him, as she ought to have known.

Outside, a long black car from the Embassy was waiting for him. He conferred with the chauffeur. "Bishop, ladies, step in." He clapped the Reverend on the shoulder. "You go up in front, Rector. Sapphire and I will hop a taxi with Professor Lenz." "Victor, please, Senator." "OK, Victor, so long as you keep calling me Senator." His deep soft laugh was still audible as the chauffeur closed the doors of the limousine and they drove off into the night. "A charmer, eh, Frankie?" commented the Bishop. Aileen glanced at Sophie Weil's profile, trying to read the expression there. That he should have chosen a cat in preference to either or both of them to ride into Paris with showed how elusive of commitment he would be. She sighed. "A dreamboat. As we used to say down our way, Bishop Gus, remember? Tell us, what was his wife like?" The Bishop obliged.

Three

I N fact, Van Vliet de Jonge Cameron was two persons. They rose from a round table in the hotel dining-room to greet the Americans. Cameron had been drinking tea for his breakfast, which went some way to prove that the Oxford don promised by Sadegh had actually been delivered and stood holding a chair for Miss Simmons. He was a small, out-at-elbows, taciturn Scot, somewhere in his late forties—"painfully shy" was the diagnosis. "Had a good night?" he shot out and, unable to face the Yankee return fire, beat a retreat into silence, which he only broke of his own free will to ask permission to light up a pipe. Van Vliet de Jonge had been drinking *café au lait* and lit a cheroot. He was a handsome, strong-jawed, hazel-eyed, high-colored, talkative Dutchman, dressed in a whipcord suit of eccentric tailoring, with a long, well-cut, flaring jacket that had an unusual number of pocket flaps and sleeve buttons; for a tie, he wore a pale scarf folded like a stock in some ancestral portrait of a magistrate or town councilor. It was his birthday, he announced, in a cheerful voice with the sound of a tenor horn in it, and he offered a round of schnapps: he was thirty-eight years old and had already been twice a deputy in Parliament, had a Javanese wife who was a lawyer, like himself, and three children.

While the waiter waited, the majority reached a consensus of Too-early-in-the-day. The Bishop surprised them by accepting a calvados: his doctor recommended an eye-opener for dilating the arteries and, as a matter of fact, it was his birthday too this morning. The conjunction of birthdays could not fail to be felt as significant—a favorable auspice for their journey. Cameron relented, taking a small whiskey; the Senator followed; the rest raised their coffee-cups, and a toast was drunk. "We must get you a *cake*!" Aileen said with determination. "How many candles, Bishop Gus?" Eighty-three, the old man admitted, shaking his round white head. "And one to grow on," the Reverend added, bringing a pair of tears into the Bishop's eyes, which caused the others to look away sympathetically: did he doubt, poor man, that he would live out the year?

"How old is Sapphire, I wonder?" mused the Senator, creating a welcome diversion. "In human terms, I mean." "Sapphire?" Van Vliet's cigar paused alertly in mid-air; his comprehension of English was good. It was a relief too to have someone on the mission who had an ear cocked for detail. "A cat," Miss Simmons told him. "She and Professor Lenz—the other member of our delegation—must be having breakfast in their room." "A scrumptious blue Persian," declared Miss Weil, abruptly rising. She was dressed this morning in a brown turtle-neck jersey, a long string of beads, and a skirt. They watched her cross the lobby, pick up her suede coat from on top of her suitcase, and vanish into the street.

There were six left at table—a quorum. The small dining-room was empty except for themselves. "Should the meeting come to order?" inquired Miss Simmons. "Do we have any business to transact?" The rector cleared his throat. There was the business—he hated to remind them—of Monsignor Lopez de Mayo: where was he? A long story, answered Van Vliet de Jonge, but the short of it was not to expect him. "Mohammed should be here soon. He may explain. There seems to have been a misunderstanding." The Americans nodded. "Well, I can live without a monsignor!" declared Aileen. "Can't you, Bishop? Can't you, Senator Jim?" The Senator grinned. "It's our friend the rector who feels the need. But from what I gather—excuse me, Reverend—if we poke around the cat-houses in the neighborhood, we can probably raise a cardinal." Aileen gave a shriek of accord. The hotel, as they could hardly avoid noticing the night before, was on the edge of the red-light district. The only excuse that she could find, in all charity, for having been put here—stained tablecloth at break-fast, dust under the beds—was that it was convenient for get-ting to and from the airport, being close to Châtelet, or—as the indulgent Bishop put it—from his window, by stretching, you could see the spire of Sainte-Chapelle.

"Oh, what the heck," said Frank recklessly. "I sign off on the monsignor. We're having such a wonderful time without him. Isn't this *café au lait* great?" As he helped himself to sugar, a cloud the size of a man's hand passed across the beaming expanse of his features. He had remembered torture and illegality.

Having discovered a birthday in common, they began, as

strangers do when thrown together in a novel circumstance, to seek other matching data in their life histories, like players at gin rummy seeking to fill out a run or three of a kind. Senator Carey and the Dutchman were both lawyers; in addition, they had both been at school with monks—the Senator's Benedictine and the Dutchman's Dominican—and both held elective office. The Senator was still a Catholic, but Van Vliet de Jonge had disposed of his faith back at Catholic University in Nijmegen. The Bishop and the rector and Aileen had Protestant upbringings as a *trait d'union* with Cameron, who had been Church of Scotland, in other words a Presbyterian, which led Van Vliet to dilate entertainingly on the politics of Calvinism in Holland. Sophie Weil and Lenz, had they been present, might have found that they shared the Jewish faith, though with a name like Lenz you could not tell: he might equally well have been born a Catholic or a Lutheran. Van Vliet had served with the Council of Europe in Strasbourg and knew the street where Aileen had lived as a graduate student. Strasbourg brought up the subject of storks, which reminded Van Vliet of the herons' nests in the tree-tops of his garden in a suburb of Amsterdam. Reverting to the stork, Senator Carey wondered how it had displaced the cabbage-leaf as the explanation of where babies came from: was it a German carryover? He had had a German grandfather by the name of August on his mother's side, which was Bishop Hurlbut's case as well.

The rector had been wearing a look of deepening perplexity. "Excuse me, Professor Cameron, but aren't you a lawyer too? That would make three." "A lawyer? Dear me, no." Frank persisted, sensing a semantic obstacle. "But you're a professor of jurisprudence. With us, a professor of law is a lawyer. Isn't that right, Senator?" "With us too, I believe," Cameron said. "But I'm not a professor of jurisprudence, you see."

The rector fell back in his chair. He stared despondently at the Bishop and shook his head as if it had grown too heavy. "We've been misled again, Gus." "Sorry," said Cameron, swallowing. "Awfully sorry to disappoint you if you were expecting a jurisprudence man. I can drop out if you like." Apparently they had all been eyeing the poor fellow accusingly, as if he were an impostor. "Don't think of that," hastily begged the rector. "We're all in this together." He took counsel with himself and sighed. "Maybe we should have a vote on whether to go ahead or just throw in the sponge. Which I'd certainly hate to do. But these young Iranians—let's be honest with ourselves—don't seem to have our Western conception of the truth. I won't bore you with the details, Mr. Cameron and Mr. De Jonge—well, there was a rabbi they promised us who never showed up, and now the monsignor. . . ." "And Sophie," prompted Aileen, but on getting a quizzing look from the Senator she let the Reverend continue. "The kindest interpretation we can put on it is that they've tended to take shots in the dark, and the question is, do we want to proceed with what may be, darn it, a wild goose chase."

The Bishop leaned forward. "Easy, Frankie." He turned to Cameron. "And what *are* you, then, sir? What is your field of work?" "I'm a simple historian, I'm afraid." He was the author of a textbook on Pakistan after the Raj. Problems of decolonialization were his special interest. But he had done some recent work on Iran, touching mainly on the Shah's "white revolution" and his offensive against the mullahs and the bazaar. The whiskey seemed to have finally loosened Cameron's tongue. "To be sure, I know some law. Local law, that is. The historian has to, just as he has to have some acquaintance with the languages." "You know Persian?" The rector was visibly cheering up. "New Persian. And some of the dialects, in a sketchy sort of way. I've had Indo-Iranian languages as a hobby ever since I was a laddie. And I did a stint in Afghanistan before I was called to Oxford." "So you *are* at Oxford, then," Aileen summed up, nodding her approval. "That part was right." "Oh, yes. But you mustn't think I'm a professor. With us, that implies a chair. I'm just a humble lecturer." "So what do we call you?" "Dr. Cameron, if you want to be formal. But my name is Archibald—Archie." The rector chortled. "I guess we can pardon you, Archie, if your arch-sin is not being a lawyer." "There *are* some legal niceties in what I've published," said Cameron thoughtfully. "I can see how a confusion arose." There was no further question of disbanding. "Why, he's an *expert*, Reverend," marveled Aileen. "We're so lucky to have him with us."

The getting-acquainted process went forward in the lobby, where, having paid their bills, they sat surrounded by their suitcases waiting for Van Vliet's Mohammed, who lived in some student complex in an outlying part of town. Their Air France–UTA plane left at eleven-thirty from Charles de Gaulle; had they only thought of it, they might have checked their main baggage there last night. Although some had counted on the early rising to do a little sightseeing, it was now felt to be too late for even a short stroll. At nine-thirty, they began to be anxious and to consider leaving a message for Mohammed, in case he had overslept—there was no way of checking since he had no telephone, naturally. He could follow them to the airport with Sophie, unless she reappeared soon. Lenz could be summoned from his room; he was getting dressed, the Senator testified, or had been an hour ago.

Cameron demurred. Mohammed, he pointed out, was bringing them a voucher with their hotel reservations; they had better wait. "We can dispense with that, Frank," declared the Bishop, who had commenced to pace the floor with his watch out. Old people were fidgety about departures, and Frank, who had seen it in his parishioners, was moved to reflect that the fear of missing a conveyance—a train, a bus, or Elijah's chariot—played a large part in their thoughts. Seeing the old man's eagerness to be off, the others exchanged nervous glances; he was red in the face and fuming, as if on the verge of explosion. Senator Carey intervened. "The hotel situation is tight there, Gus. My people from the Embassy were amazed last night to hear that our party had got space. The hotels are packed with munitions salesmen. Same all through the Middle East, they say." Homeopathic medicine, Van Vliet noted appreciatively: anxiety, in a small dose, applied to anxiety. And in fact the Bishop subsided, sinking into an overstuffed chair.

At nine-forty Mohammed was there, with a stiff blue folder containing the voucher, further documentation, and a list of names and addresses in Teheran. In every respect, the Americans decided, he might have been Sadegh's twin brother, except that Sadegh's folders were green. With characteristic zeal, he had a fleet of taxis ordered; the first was already outside. But there was no hurry, Mohammed said: the driver had made a mistake—they were meant to be here at ten. Meanwhile, the porter could start taking out the baggage. "*Tout le monde a son visa, j'espère.*"

Aileen clapped her hand to her cheek. The others were nodding, and of course she had hers, obtained well in advance from the consulate in New York during the Christmas holidays. But Lenz, who still had not come down? And Sophie? There was no reason to be alarmed on her account; her kind of journalist (Senator Carey agreed) knew about visas. Lenz was something else, though. The visa requirement had probably not crossed his mind. And anyway where would he have got one? It would be strange if there were a consulate in Buffalo.

"You'd better ring his room, Reverend, and ask him," commanded Aileen. "And tell him to hurry. Tell him the taxi is here." There might still be time to pass by the Iranian consulate; if the Senator went along with him and used rank, a tourist visa could be issued in five minutes. "*Monsieur Asad—oh, pardon!—Monsieur Mohammed, où se trouve votre consulat?*" She might have known. It was in the Sixteenth, on the avenue d'Iéna—back in the other direction. But assuming they left now, and assuming there was not too much traffic, they could allow fifteen minutes, even twenty, for the detour and yet be at the airport by ten-forty. Once they had the visa, all they had to do was get on the *périphérique*. How fortunate, as it had turned out, that the taxi had come early.

"Isn't human nature strange, Bishop Gus? I don't take to Mr. Lenz one bit—I guess none of us does really—but here I am worrying about how we can get him his visa. When I ought to be grateful to the hand of Providence if it's stretched out to keep him here. You just know he's going to drink and make trouble, Mr. Van Vliet. The best thing that could have happened to our committee would have been to have him overlook that little formality. Now that we have wonderful Mr. Cameron, we don't need another Middle Eastern specialist, who probably doesn't know ten words of the language anyway. Utterly unreliable, that's how he is, you'll see. And yet I want desperately to help him out of the foolish trouble he's made for himself, don't you, Senator Carey? Is it just being American and neighborly, do you think? I wonder if there isn't something more universal at work. As if in these few hours we've become an organic community, like a living body, and if one part gets cut off, all the others feel it . . . ?"

Victor's room did not answer, the rector reported. Aileen

threw up her hands. "Where can he have got to? He's found some low *zinc*, I'll bet anything." His key was not in his box but of course it could be in his pocket. "Strange that I didn't see him go out, though. In the dining-room, where I sat, I had my eye on our bags and the door the whole time. And since then, we've all been here in the lobby. Are you sure you rang the right room . . . ?" She checked her watch with the clock behind the desk. "Well, if he turns up in five minutes, and sober, he can still pass by the consulate." "But it's Sunday, my dear," said the Bishop gently, interposing a word.

"*Sunday!* You mean the consulate will be closed?" She wheeled on Mohammed, forgetting in her agitation to speak French. "It's not *possible*. They *must* work Sundays at your consulate. They're Moslems." Mohammed shook his head; the office was closed. He might have mentioned that sooner in-stead of letting her run on. When she had wanted the consul-ate's address, did he suppose it was to put in her memory book? And why had none of the others seen fit to remind her that it was Sunday, since they all seemed to have known it? "We weren't privy to your thoughts," said the Senator.

In the midst of this, Sophie entered, breathless, through the revolving door, bearing a ribboned box from a pastry shop. The cake, of course. "I couldn't find candles," she explained. That was why she had been so long. But she had two votive tapers from a church in her handbag. "Did you steal them or pay?" The Senator was teasing, but she considered the ques-tion gravely, knitting up her brows—like a child, Van Vliet de Jonge thought. She had put two francs in the box and yet felt like a thief. "Quite right," said the Senator. "They're conse-crated." "I know." Under her long arm was a magazine with a girl in a knitted cap on the cover: *Elle*. She offered it to Van Vliet: it had a nifty horoscope column; on the plane the birth-day boys could read what the stars had to tell them. But she had chosen the wrong moment. The rector took the cake box from her and placed it out of view on a side table. "Professor Lenz has disappeared."

The second and third taxis were now at the door. It was decided that the Bishop, with Dr. Cameron and the rector, should take the first one, immediately, to the airport. The others could give Lenz five minutes more, and if he was still missing, the second taxi would take Aileen, Van Vliet, and the Senator. Sophie volunteered to remain, with Mohammed.

Contrary to what might have been assumed, the dispatch of the first group did nothing to relieve the uneasiness of those remaining. For one thing, their shrunken numbers—they were only four now, not counting Mohammed—gave them a woeful look of having been abandoned, thus bearing out, Van Vliet noted, Aileen's theory of a "community." For another, now that the Bishop was out of the way, they could speak freely. "Do you think he could be dead up there?" Aileen asked before a minute had passed. "You always read about foreigners dying in sordid Paris hotel rooms." She shot a telling glance at the dusty rubber plants and unemptied ash trays in the lobby. "His color was *awful* yesterday. Like whey, as my Mamma says. Maybe one of us should go and knock on his door." "If he's dead, how will that tell us?" said the Senator. Nevertheless, he strode across the lobby and pressed the elevator button.

"If he has gone and died and on Sunday too, what a nuisance," Aileen continued. "One of us will have to stay, that's all." "Mr. Barber is the obvious candidate, isn't he?" Sophie suggested with a small smile. Aileen's face cleared momentarily. "How true. What else can the clergy do for us but marry us and bury us? Still, would it be right to go on to Teheran without him? The Bishop certainly wouldn't want to." The Senator's deep laughing voice called out. "I don't know about Victor, but the elevator has bitten the dust."

Sophie looked at the clock. "You three had better go on. I'll wait here with Mohammed. We can send the concierge up on foot with a pass-key, just to ease our minds. When you check in, ask for a message." "Well . . ." said Aileen. "It's true, Sophie, you're not one of the committee." After a moment's wavering, she followed Van Vliet and the Senator through the revolving door, reappearing promptly on the next rotation. "I have an idea. In case he still turns up. Will they maybe give him a visa at the airport in Teheran? Ask Mohammed what he thinks. A friend of mine once . . ."

The question was rendered moot by the appearance of Lenz from the carpeted staircase. He had been stuck between floors in the elevator, and a chambermaid had let him out. He was carrying the cat-container, and the maid followed with his baggage. And he had his visa. He showed it to them, folded into his passport, seeming surprised but not offended at the general stupefaction. He could not know (Van Vliet reflected, pondering the gravity-defying power of ideas to stand unsupported by evidence) that his co-nationals had been fully persuaded that he was visa-less and half-persuaded that he was dead.

Till now, it had not occurred to any of them to ask whether the cat needed papers. "Well, I'm not going to worry about that detail," said Aileen, seating herself in the taxi between Van Vliet and the Senator, then turning around to peer out the back window to make sure the others got off. As the third taxi began to move, a clerk came running out of the hotel and signaled to the driver to stop. Lenz had forgotten to pay his bill, naturally. Aileen called to their own driver to stop too. Lenz had dismounted and seemed to be arguing with the clerk about the bill, angrily indicating some item with his forefinger. "They're trying to charge him for Sappho," estimated the Senator. In the third taxi, where Sophie was waiting, a large dog had sat up in the front seat beside the driver, contributing his bark to the affray while his owner held him back. He must be trying to leap over the seat at the caged cat in the rear. "Do you say it's raining cats and dogs?" asked the Dutchman. "Or dogs and cats?" Aileen screamed. "Let's go. I can't stand it. I'm a wreck. Look! Now he's going to wait for his change." Lenz was still on the sidewalk, the dog was still barking and growling, and a fourth taxi was pulling up, when Aileen and the two men drove off.

Nevertheless, the entire party reached the airport with a few minutes to spare. Alighting from the moving belt, Van Vliet and Aileen found the Bishop and the rector in the departure satellite talking with two ladies wearing mink coats and an old powdered man in a wide-brimmed black hat whom Aileen gaily greeted as "Mr. Charles." Cameron was on the level below exploring the duty-free shops, where Lenz had stopped off too. Mohammed had been said good-bye to at the check-in counter, having earned a merit badge by remembering the cake and going back to fetch it in a fifth taxi, for which Sophie had succeeded in reimbursing him. At the head of the moving staircase, the Senator was surrounded by young admirers bound for Moscow, whom he had introduced to Sophie; a joint autographing session was in progress. Everyone was present or accounted for.

Yet Van Vliet, studying the scene from a solitary banquette where Aileen had left him, felt puzzled, like a new boy in class observing a network of relationships to which he has no clue. The old gloved party leaning on an ivory-headed stick and the mink-draped ladies—could they possibly be members of a committee of inquiry? The briefings given by the Iranian youths had left many questions unanswered. He had sensed a possible mystery in the group's financing; although he was paying his own way, he was entitled as a lawyer to wonder whether outside funds were not being supplied. Could the expensive-looking trio be what the Americans called "angels"? Van Vliet did not like it. He signaled to Aileen, who detached herself and came hurrying to his side. "Those people—are they with us too?" She laughed and patted his arm. "After this morning, you can believe anything, can't you?" But he was not to worry; they were just millionaire art collectors—part of a tour—on their way to visit archaeological sites in Iran. There was no connection, except that "Mr. Charles" was an old friend of the Bishop's. "You wouldn't guess he was an American, would you?"

Van Vliet would not have. His visual ideas about Americans were derived mainly from the movies. Though he knew England and the English well, he had not met many live Americans before this morning. He discounted the NATO generals he had shaken hands with while inspecting maneuvers; the military, like the armies of tourists who came to view the tulips, offered an unreliable index to a country's national character. In the taxi he had confessed his ignorance. Senator Carey of course was familiar to him from Dutch television as a leading dove in the Senate and he was a type, like Adlai Stevenson in the previous generation, that Europeans thought they understood. But the rest of the American delegation were novelties to a Dutchman, he admitted. If the pastor brought back memories of Harold Lloyd in *The Freshman*, no contemporary analogy for him in movieland presented itself. And there were no Old World equivalents that Van Vliet could find for these curious American liberals. The exception was the young woman, the journalist, whom he felt he knew. "Our Sophie!" Aileen cried. "Why, she's the 'new journalism'—the latest American thing." "We have many of her in Holland, believe me," Van Vliet assured her. "Dozens of Sophies, dear me!" She gave a sharp tinkle of a laugh. "Then we don't have to warn you that she'll be making all of us characters in the piece she's writing."

Van Vliet nodded; he had taken account of that prospect at breakfast. "Well, of course, you're a political man. But the sweet old Bishop and the rector don't seem to have grasped the implications at all." "What implications?" Van Vliet said blandly. "Why, of having her along with us. They can be *devastating*." The Senator threw back his silver head and laughed, savoring his amusement as if it were a rich morsel of private food for thought. "You're used to 'exposure,' Senator," Aileen insisted. "But it's hurting, for the rest of us, to see our little foibles and mannerisms *faithfully* reproduced on the printed page. Like all our 'new' journalists, Mr. Van Vliet, Sophie Weil has a phonographic ear. That's the way they're trained nowadays. I don't mean it against her personally. Just to give you an example, there was a young man from one of the news magazines who spent five days on our campus. I had him to breakfast and dinner and I don't know what all. Then I found spread out in the magazine word for word all these things I'd told him, the way you would a friend, about myself and the problems we had at Lucy Skinner. I know he didn't see anything wrong in what he did. He *liked* me, I could tell. Of course my press man wrote a letter. But there are things you can't reply to. Like comparing my voice to Martha Mitchell's. She's from my home state, Mr. Van Vliet: Pine Bluffs, Arkansas. But they talk differently over there. And such a cruel description of my appearance: 'a sprightly weight-watcher' with 'an incipient double chin.'" She arched her neck. "Well, if you're used to that in Holland, you'll survive. We all will, of course. What I really fear is that more space will be given to us and our squabbles and divisions than to those poor torture victims." "I think we're kind of dull," said the Senator, perversely offering a ray of hope. "Unless the Reverend gets oecumenical with those Mohammedans, we're not likely to provide much copy."

"Why does he laugh so much, that long fellow?" Van Vliet inquired. "We Americans are great laughers," said the Senator. "You mean 'tall,' not 'long,'" corrected Aileen. That was a common Dutch mistake, which Van Vliet went on making, though he had been patiently set right by dozens, perhaps hundreds, of native English-speakers. His retort was to give the two a lesson in how to pronounce his surname in the correct, Dutch way. "'Fan Fleet,'" essayed the Senator. "Sounds like a name for a strip dancer." Van Vliet surprised them by catching the allusion. He was aware of Fanne Foxe. "In Amsterdam we read the *Herald Tribune*." "Does that 'van' mean you're noble?" Aileen wanted to know. The "van" in Holland, he had to explain, as so often to English people (the French and Spanish never asked), was not like the German "von." It was not a *particule de noblesse*. And "de Jonge"? No, that did not prove blue blood either; there were lots of "de Jonge"s tacked onto ordinary Dutch surnames. "Not even gentry," summed up Aileen in a regretful tone. "Sorry. I'm a commoner." "Well, aren't we all, Senator?" she sighed, making the best of it.

His Christian name, he told them, was Henk. "Oh, I like that!" she cried. "Is it short for Hendrik?" It had been once, but now it was a regular given name. "Like Harry with us," said the Senator. "They nearly named me that till one of the relatives thought of 'hari-kari.'" "What were your people, Senator Jim?" "Farmers." "But they must have been well-to-do if they sent you to a monastery to study. How long were you there?" "Four years of high school. Then I went to the seminary." He winked at Henk. "Your turn." To Van Vliet's amusement, the persistent little woman obediently turned his way. "And you, Mr. Van Vliet, do you come from a long line of lawyers?" "My father was a judge." The Senator's terse style was catching. But he lacked the heart to hold back something half the Netherlands could tell her: his paternal grandfather (1865–1935), also a magistrate, had been the author of fifty-seven popular novels—Adriaan Van Vliet de Jonge, once a household word. "Oh. Are they translated?" "Into German, two or three. We Dutch have a hermetic literature."

"But you're a poet yourself," interposed the Senator. Van Vliet was impressed. First-rate staff work, he conjectured with envy; it was never like that in The Hague. Aileen was excited. "You mean a *known* poet?" "Two impressive volumes of verse," said the Senator. "Nearly cost you your seat in Parliament." "How did you find all that out?" exclaimed Aileen, evidently envious too. The lazy-voiced man smiled. "You forget there's a Dutch Embassy in Washington. The ambassador is a friend of mine, as it happens." Aileen seized both men's arms. "The Senator writes poetry too! I know I read that somewhere. But he calls himself a 'Sunday poet,' so he doesn't publish. Another tie between you two. You mustn't laugh. Something like that—bonding—can be vital in situations of stress."

Van Vliet looked at her with greater attention. Bright wary eyes, sharp nose, soft chin—a little hawk's face. He had been taking her chatter as no more than a bad habit or a screen to mask pervasive anxiety—she was single ("Miss") and getting on. But her last words and her grip on their arms suggested that the little predator was feeling a specific alarm. Did she imagine the Shah was going to jail her? Van Vliet smiled at the innocence—or, rather, ignorance—of such a foreboding, which he could easily dispel.

None of the Americans, he gathered—except their most junior, Miss Weil—had ever taken part in an enterprise of this kind. Europeans were more used to putting their noses into the affairs of foreign police states. Before he went to Parliament, he had worked with Amnesty and sat in on trials in Spain; in Bolivia he had taken depositions from terrorized witnesses and their families. More recently, when the Dutch had raised the question of the Greek colonels in the Council of Europe, he and a Socialist deputy had been empowered by their parties to fly to Athens and try to substantiate the stories of torture and murder in the regime's prisons and penal colonies. To say it in all modesty, their mission had been rather successful: if the colonels had not fallen as a direct result, their government at least had been censured by the Council for violation of human rights as specified in the charter. A small victory, typically Dutch-sized and won by Dutch perseverance. More relevantly, neither he nor his fellow-deputy had been molested by the colonels' police. They had been obstructed but not harassed, and he did not think they had owed their immunity to their status as members of Parliament of a NATO country.

The worst this group could expect would be that they would be followed. Or that at midnight, when they arrived, they would find that their hotel reservations had vanished without a trace. Van Vliet did not share Cameron's faith in Mohammed's voucher. He assumed that the young man's organization would have been infiltrated by Parisian agents of SAVAK, who would have informed Teheran of the committee's make-up and intentions in the fullest possible detail. Unless (he reflected) poor Mohammed's network was largely imaginary, which would not be promising for the hotel voucher either.

Van Vliet was not an apprehensive subject; he had his portion of the national phlegm. Accommodations, he felt sure, would be found, one way or another, if necessary through the pastor's church or the Senator's connections with the Embassy —the Dutchmen of the Queen's Embassy would have been long since abed. Yet SAVAK engaged his interest; his imagination, though a tranquil organ, was active. Riding beside Aileen on the escalator and again on the long moving belt like a flattened *montagne russe* bearing them up to the departure satellite, he had taken note of two dark men—one mustached—who seemed to be sticking too close for comfort and who were speaking a language that might well be Iranian. Then he had reined in his fancy: a plane going to Teheran would naturally have Iranians aboard. In any case, he did not mind being watched by secret policemen, who were easily shaken off when a real need arose; during dull moments in unfree countries, he had been able to amuse himself by picking them out in a courtroom or in a crowded café.

He did not invite Aileen to join him in that pastime as they sat together waiting for the boarding announcement. He was sympathetic to women and their gift for worry, which was curiously random in its objects, he had found in his legal practice. Perhaps the idea that the dread SAVAK could possess ubiquity had not crossed her mind. He would have liked, as a matter of fact, to have a look at his horoscope while they waited—*Elle*'s astrologer was an amazing fellow, often cited by his wife after a session at the hairdresser's. But considering his present companion, he overcame the impulse to take the magazine from his briefcase. She would be bound to read over his shoulder and, not content with Capricorn, leap ahead to her own sign—a risky procedure for one on the brink of a momentous undertaking and as susceptible as she. Van Vliet sighed. On his birthday, he should have the right to consult with the augurs while the day was still young, but chivalry, he supposed, was enjoined on him.

Besides, he had taken a liking to Aileen and he now followed her willingly when, on the pretext of locating an ash tray, she set out on her own job of espionage, stalking the first-class passengers who had cornered the two clerics. "I have an idea those women are former parishioners of the Rev's." Waving her cigarette as a *laisser-passer*, she drew Van Vliet forward, bobbing in and out of the small crowd, till they had reached a listening-post. "Did you hear that? 'Reverend Mr. Barber.' Not 'Reverend Barber,' 'Reverend *Mr.* Barber.' It's one of the clues those social people drop to let the rest of us know who they are." Her confederate showed puzzlement; there was some drama afoot, evidently, that he was failing to appreciate.

Aileen elucidated. St. Matthew's was a fashionable New York church, right on the edge of a slum, naturally. "And Reverend Barber is a fashionable preacher?" Henk re-examined the "long" dominie with the happy protruding ears and twisted bow tie and concluded that fashion in America must have to wear a democratic disguise. "Well, he *was*," said Aileen. "He got to be *too* fashionable, intellectually, for his Gracie Square flock. He invited a black revolutionary to preach from his pulpit one Sunday, and his front pews left him in a body and went over to St. James's, on Madison Avenue. These are some of the front pews, I'll bet." Van Vliet felt suddenly bored. In Holland, he told her, such "happenings" in churches were commonplace, only there it was the Catholics, following *aggiornamento*, who staged trendy masses, with guitars and rock music and student hippies and schismatic Marxists mounting to the pulpit to sermonize. "They have ships' biscuits"—he stifled a yawn—"that they pass in a basket for communion and a chalice of wine that goes from hand to hand. There's a movement to make it a beer tankard—in Holland, why not?" She nodded. "Sort of love feasts. We have that too. But this black revolutionary at St. Matthew's demanded reparations from the churches. It was all in the papers. Millions of dollars, just like war reparations. Do you have that in Holland?" Before Van Vliet could answer, she had made a silencing gesture. "*Au revoir*, dear impetuous Mr. Barber. We shall look for you in Naqsh-i-Rustan. So nice to find you again, and in mufti, after all these years." "'Mufti'!" snorted Aileen, as the woman moved off at an unhurried pace. "You see, I was right." Van Vliet did not understand her interest in following this encounter, nor indeed where her true sympathies lay. He would have liked, though, to know whether the Reverend's church had paid reparations and, if so, how many guilders. But the plane was boarding.

It was a 747 this time and less than half full. They would be able to stretch out, after lunch had been served, and sleep or meditate till quarter of five, local time, when they were supposed to arrive in Tel Aviv—their only stop. They had agreed to sit together in the well-named (said the Senator) Salon Rouge, the middle cabin of Economy, where smoking was permitted. That little sacrifice on the part of the non-smokers would enable the group to visit back and forth without disturbing other passengers, and yet each would have a bank of two or three seats to himself. When nap-time came, the Bishop and he could lie head to head, the Reverend pointed out, all a-marvel at the discovery. He had never ridden in a jumbo jet before. Lenz, of course, was the non-conformist. Where the others were spread out within conversational range through the center portion of the cabin, he had elected to be up front beside the movie screen, and found himself next to an Israeli couple with a baby in a swinging bassinet-thing that the hostess fitted into place—an arrangement that was not going to suit Sapphire, he objected, appearing suddenly in the aisle in his long flapping overcoat when he ought to have been strapped into his seat belt.

His cat, he said, was sensitive to noise, and what was an infant doing in a section reserved for smokers? "Isn't that the parents' business?" a voice behind him demanded, and for a moment, as Lenz swung around, it looked as if there might be an incident. He was persuaded to return to his place by the steward's promise that after take-off he and the cat could move.

But he had to be near a door, he stipulated, pausing on his way. "Near a door?" "Because of my claustrophobia." Someone tittered. "You can go into the Salon Jaune, sir," calmly said the steward, indicating two seats by an exit door in the front of the cabin behind. That suggestion did not please Lenz either: too close to the serving-pantry, and Sapphire was sensitive to cooking smells. "Well, sir, I cannot help you then. We cannot ask that family to move. They have reserve that place. It is near the toilets. And anyway, sir, they go only as far as Tel Aviv." "Go back and sit down, Victor," called the Senator. "We want to take off."

Ahead, the young orthodox couple (cute as two pins, it was decided; the husband wore a beard in ringlets and a black hat) seemed impervious, luckily, to the controversy; the bassinet placidly rocked. "You must excuse our friend," the Reverend told the steward, when Victor was finally out of earshot. "Do you have this type of problem often?" "Very often, sir. Especially with gentlemen. They do not wish to sit near a baby." The Bishop nodded. "'Suffer the little children.' We humans are funny animals, aren't we? Why, bless me, if the plane had been full, our Victor would be feeling no call to be choosy. But with all these empty seats to pick from, he'll never find one that suits him. There's a moral there, surely." "Explicate that, Gus," begged the Reverend, but the old man's rumbling tones were lost like the Sibyl's utterance in the sudden roar of the engines.

When the No Smoking sign went off, Van Vliet lit a Batavia twist. With a careful turn of his head, he established that the two dark men he had wondered about were directly behind him, on the aisle. After a moment's reflection, he unfastened his seat belt and moved across to join Aileen. If he did not join her, he considered, she was likely to come over to him—an invitation to eavesdroppers if there ever was one. In the middle bank of seats, the Senator, just ahead of her, had already stretched out, in his shirt sleeves, with his arms folded behind his head on two pillows and did not look ready for company. Cameron, a difficult conversationalist, was puffing on his pipe by a window on the Senator's left. The Bishop and the Reverend, in front of the Senator, were minding the Lord's store, reciting the service for the day—the first Sunday after Epiphany—with the Bishop taking the responses. Van Vliet recognized the Anglican rite, which the Americans called Episcopalian. The droning of voices took him back to his school days with the monks in Brabant.

In choosing Aileen, Van Vliet was obeying his good angel. While the plane was gaining altitude, he had made up his mind to pair off with President Simmons, since there was bound to be pairing in a group of this kind. He did not enjoy being unfaithful to his wife, but it happened on trips if he did not take precautions. The Weil girl—actually a woman; he estimated her age at thirty-four—was the occasion of sin to be avoided. His aversion to bright young women journalists (one of the Dutch lot had pursued him from Schiphol to Athens, with the full backing of her editor, at that time, but no longer, his friend) might fail him, he feared, in her case. She had a tense, brave way of talking, in short, breathless spurts, and an arresting face, like a Byzantine icon—Cameron had produced the comparison this morning, watching her come in with the cake. At present, she was sitting alone, in the row ahead of Cameron, by the window. As he stood up to take the lay of the land, he had picked out the curly black head leaning against the seat back's bright red antimacassar. She put up a hand to cover a yawn, and he admired the long spatulate fingers and the stretch of the long olive neck.

He set his jaw. If he left her alone, she would gravitate to the Senator or vice versa. The lines of force were predictable in these situations. He was vain of being a good-looking, well-set-up male and did not envy the American his two meters —a tall Dutchman was a gross error of Nature. In age he had the advantage of fifteen to twenty years. In mother-wit, they were about equal, he reckoned, and he suspected he was a truer poet. But in power—irresistible to some women—the leader of a minority fraction in Her Majesty's Staten-generaal was Thumbling by comparison, which would make a contest interesting to the permanent spectator in himself. He pushed away the thought: the challenge to his virility represented by a formidable U.S. lawmaker was temptation in its most infantile form. Besides, he had no doubt as to who would win; as in a fairy-tale, he had only to wish it.

He heard the rector beginning on the lesson for the day. "I beseech you, therefore, brethren, by the mercies of God, that ye present your bodies a living sacrifice. . . . And be not conformed to this world, but be ye transformed by the renewing of your mind." The shoe seemed to fit. Making a wry face, Henk crossed the aisle like a Rubicon and left the field to Carey. The die was cast. Aileen would help divert him from the other while posing no danger herself. On that score, as a male, he felt confidence. He had no sexual interest (it was cruel, but he could not help it) in women who had passed the age of child-bearing—which no doubt made him a "sexist," as somebody like Sophie, if he bedded her, would be quick to tell him.

Aileen looked up with a smile. "Mynheer Van Vliet! So you've come to talk to me!" She snatched up the long scarf she had unwound from her coppery hair and patted the seat beside her. On her lap was an archaeological guide to Persia, which the Bishop had passed back to her. "'I'm too old, my dear, for ancient history, and we have other work to do in that unfertile soil.' That was his presentation speech. Isn't he dear?" Van Vliet took up the book, which was the property, it seemed, of "Mr. Charles." On second thought, he set it aside and went to retrieve his briefcase, reminded of the blue folder he had put in it with the list of names and addresses in Teheran. He could not leave that lying about. It occurred to him, moreover, that in view of a possible search at the airport, he would do well to commit the contents to memory and flush it down a toilet in Tel Aviv. There was also *Elle* with the horoscope, which he ought to consult soon, if only to repay Sophie for her trouble. "Oh, dear, do we have to *work*?" Aileen lamented on seeing the briefcase. He made a silencing motion. He had heard Dutch being spoken.

Behind Aileen were a tow-headed young man and woman. He directed her attention to them. "Dutch!" he whispered. Aileen turned around. "What about it?" Van Vliet drew a hand across his eyes. No foreigner would understand. It always struck him as droll, almost uncanny, to find Dutch people outside of Holland, where they properly belonged—as though they were toy people who had stepped out of the tiny see-through box they lived in with their Queen and their princesses and Prince Bernhard and Klaus and the tulips. In a poem he had tried to express the idea of Holland as an imaginary country, invented by a travel author or satirist-turned-children's-storyteller, in which he himself, poor Henk, was fated to be born and sit in a scale-model parliament and write despairing verses which nobody but another Dutchman could pronounce or understand. Being Dutch was a comical predicament, more grotesque even than being Swiss. *They* had watches and weather clocks and cheese with absurd holes, in the place of dikes and windmills and outlandish pipes, but at least they had Alps as a trademark instead of a flat country like the medieval picture of the world, which had not had scientific credibility since Columbus and the navigators.

No rational mind in this century could believe in Holland as a real place—where but in animal farmland could the Prime Minister be a Mr. Owl?—and finding Dutch people outside, in the real world, was a threat to any Dutchman's sanity. Besides, on practical as well as ontological grounds, Van Vliet did not care to be picked out like a straw from a heap by unknown sharp-eyed compatriots who had the advantage of knowing *him*. "Van Vliet de Jonge! Did you see him?" the pair behind him would be telling each other. In a small country like Holland, where the main verticals were television aerials, it was too easy to be a celebrity. As leader of a new, left-of-center grouping, he was unavoidable in most living-rooms, including his own. Behind the famous uncurtained window panes, as he drove home in the black night, he met himself seriatim in brilliant Philips color, a gesturing household dummy, framed in the box. In his real body, he could not stop at a gin shop for a glass of genever or eat a herring from a street stall without causing a mild stir of recognition. In the extended family of the Netherlands, with its characteristic long memory, that was only to be expected; before he had been the deputy, he had been the scion of his father and his grandfather.

But abroad he was nobody, which was also to be expected. A few years ago, a Dutch company had taken a poll in France and Britain and found to its own surprise that the vast majority of newspaper readers could not identify the Prime Minister of Holland, the aforesaid Mr. Owl's predecessor. Tested on other figures, older people remembered Queen Wilhelmina and, if politically conscious, Spaak—a Belgian. To be somebody and yet nobody was a typical Dutch irony, which Van Vliet when abroad preferred to relish alone and unrecognized over a dish of tripe or an *andouillette* in a bistro, pondering the sayings "a fish out of water" and "a big fish in a small pond," with a melancholy flare, typically Dutch also, of the long nostrils, in his case, by luck, finely cut.

He had studied the Netherlands countenance and its register of expressions like Narcissus staring into a pool and decided that that widening of the nostrils, amounting to a sniff often in women, expressed a deep humor, in both senses, of the national soul but probably could be traced—half of him was a materialist—to the once widespread habit of snuff-taking and to the watery atmosphere that had been irritating the sinuses for centuries. You would not find it in Germans, even those nearby ones of the Rhineland. The nose and nasal passages were the seat of Dutch mental life, and the slow peristaltic intake of the nose-holes, as of a pensive digestive tract, had doubtless been a factor in developing the cheerful horn-blare of the Dutch voice, distinct from German gutturals, rasped from the throat, just as the Dutch language was distinct from German and not, as some fools insisted, a humble country cousin on the order of *Schwyzer-dütsch.*

Being Dutch, he sadly recognized, was turning into a fixed idea with him, to which each and every experience seemed to be referring maniacally, and like any poor madman sensing himself pursued, he could not hope to find comprehension in foreigners. He heard Dutch voices over his shoulder, and "What about it?" this woman said, without sympathy. The Senator, for his part, on hearing American spoken behind him, would reach for his Parker or his Waterman—no complexes there; he was used to finding a *landgenoot* under every bush. Americans had the snugger delusion of taking their country for the world.

Now she was quizzing him about the "Dutch elm disease"— some kind of tree plague, he gathered, widespread in England and America but utterly unknown in Holland, which of course she did not believe. "I'm sure it started in Holland. All your lovely elms. Our campus has been *decimated.*" With a commiserating glance at the expressionless young people behind him, for whom English must be a second language, he abruptly disengaged himself and took a turn in the aisle to regain his equability. He would never convince her that tall healthy specimens of *ulmus campestris* extended their branches a few meters from his house; she would tell him they were oaks. But she was only trying to show a friendly interest in his country and could not know that to a Dutchman it was irritating to be lumped with tree beetles, "Dutch treats," "Dutch uncles," wooden shoes, the royal family, bicycle-pedaling ("Is it true that you've all taken to your bicycles to solve the energy crisis?" "No"), and so on. On meeting a French parliamentarian, would she be reminded of frogs' legs and "French letters"?

He put his nose into the rear cabin and noted the sparsity of passengers: uneconomic for Air France, he would have thought, to keep these big planes flying during the off-season. In the pantry, he watched the hostesses preparing the drinks cart. Continuing his tour of inspection, he drifted forward to the toilets. Lenz had made his peace with the Jewish baby and was entertaining it with Sapphire's mouse. All seemed to be well. On his return, he found that Aileen had profited from his absence to move next to the Senator, now sitting upright and reknotting his tie. Sophie was absorbed in the *Monde*. He took a seat next to Cameron, who declared himself ready for a whiskey. As they waited for the cart with its freight of bottles to be wheeled up the aisle, conversation was laborious. Van Vliet regretted the loss of Aileen. He tried Scottish separatism —there were interesting parallels with Holland's Frisian minority problem—the don puffed and nodded. He mentioned a talk he had given to the Oxford Union on Surinam independence; Cameron was sorry to have missed it. "My line of country, you know." There was a long pause; he drew on his pipe, evidently expecting his companion to continue unassisted. But Van Vliet's natural volubility was failing him; this was Sisyphean work. "You were saying?" prompted Cameron. Van Vliet raised a finger. He thought he had heard a scream come from the service area.

"Oh, drat that cat!" Aileen exclaimed from the bank of seats opposite. "Those poor stewardesses! He's gone and let her out again." Cameron stiffened. "What? What? Oh, the cat; I see." The Bishop leaned back. "We had quite a saga coming over. Professor Lenz allowed his pet out of its cage. They hate the confinement, don't you know. But she led us a merry chase. Up and down the aisle and under the seats before they could locate her. You never saw such a to-do. And now history repeats itself. Well, we must bear with Clio, an old lady with one foot in the grave, eh, Dr. Cameron?"

A hostess went forward with a determined step, ignoring the passengers' questions. "She's gone to complain to the pilot," Aileen announced. "The pilot yesterday was furious. You'd think that man would have more consideration. He's only making it harder for other people to bring their cats into the cabin with them. Most airlines make them travel in the hold. But just because Air France is nice enough to let them ride with their owner, he abuses the privilege. And now the rest of us have to wait for our drinks till they catch that pesky animal." Understanding that a cat was at large, other passengers in the vicinity were stirring, to peer circumspectly under the seats, but no one was taking action. Lenz, up front, seemed to be sitting tight. "Why doesn't he *do* something?" Aileen cried. "And where have those hostesses got to?" With a small screech, she pulled up her legs. "She's under here somewhere, I know it. Didn't you feel her slip by then, Senator?" The Senator shook his head. Aileen examined a violet stocking for damage. "Isn't anybody going to try to catch her?" she demanded. "Are we all afraid of a cat? I know I am. Did you see those claws yesterday? I don't want her jumping in *my* lap." "Here, kitty, kitty," coaxed the Reverend obediently, patting his own lap. "Here, pretty puss." There was no response. "I don't see her," he apologized. "Old Victor ought to bell her," comfortably remarked the Senator, declining to be enlisted in a chase.

Van Vliet and Cameron chuckled. They had seen neither hide nor hair of a blue Persian but were agreeable to the consensus that one was prowling about; indeed, Van Vliet could almost have sworn that a minute ago he had felt something furry brush past his trouser leg. "She's holed up somewhere, I'll be bound," said the Bishop. "Wonderful how they can make themselves small when they want to. My Rachel had a Maltese, couldn't abide the sound of a vacuum cleaner—" "Yesterday Sophie found her," Aileen interrupted. "Sophie! *You* look! Please!" The urgency in her voice surprised Van

Vliet, yet he mentally seconded the motion. The pantry area was hidden from view by a partition, but his ears told him that activity back there had been suspended. Aileen had been right: for some nonsensical reason, no drinks were going to be served while the state of emergency lasted. And he had been looking forward to a glass.

Ahead of him, Sophie slowly unfastened her seat belt, set down the paper she had been reading, and, half bent over, her narrow shoulders hunched, went creeping along the aisle. "You! Back in your seat!" a male voice shouted, in a harsh, heavy accent. Van Vliet's head turned with a jerk. At the rear of the cabin stood the pair of dark men who had been sitting behind him. The shorter and plumper had a submachine gun which he was aiming on a long diagonal in Sophie's direction; the taller, with the mustache, had two grenades slung from his belt. Behind them peered two hostesses. They were being hijacked.

Sophie's head came up. "Me?" Her bang and forehead appeared, followed by her wondering eyes. Then she must have seen the gun. Ducking for cover, she moved up the aisle, hitching along like a centipede, while the gun kept pace with her. A strangled voice inside Van Vliet pleaded with her to hurry: as in a nightmare or at a film, he could only watch—no sound came from his throat, merely a series of swallows. Across the aisle from him, Aileen had her hands to her ears, and her eyes were closed. It occurred to Van Vliet too late, when the poor girl had edged back into her place and was tremulously refastening her seat belt—a strange security measure, surely, to take under the circumstances—that he might have interposed his own body between her and the gun barrel. The realization shook him till a defense lawyer broke in to argue that flinging himself on top of her as she passed would only have succeeded in pinning them both to the floor.

Nevertheless, that he had failed to have the thought was somewhat humiliating. A sense of slight disappointment in himself merged with a sense of disappointment in the whole event. The hijacker, seeming satisfied, had lowered his gun, and the captain's voice came soothingly over the loud-speaker: passengers were to remain seated until further instructions; if everyone stayed quiet and obeyed orders, no one would be hurt. On behalf of himself and the crew, he apologized for the inconvenience. Van Vliet smiled to himself at the inadequacy of this formula, yet as he analyzed his reactions, it seemed to him that Air France had found the *mot juste*. He was conscious chiefly of irritation, as at an untoward interruption, such as might be produced by a power failure or a tiresome visitor. The irruption of these men and their weapons was bound to be time-consuming, and as a busy person he already felt robbed of precious hours, which might turn into days.

He was also mystified, which added to his vexation. His instincts had been warning him that their committee might be followed, in fact accompanied, by the Shah's spies—nothing could be more normal. And the event was busy proving him right, so that in some childish way he was pleased. Yet why this farce of a take-over? Perhaps he was still in shock, and his mind was not working well, but to him it made no sense. If SAVAK's aim was to frighten off the committee, they ought to have waited till Teheran, where with no danger or "inconvenience" to the rest of the passengers he and his companions could be seized and loaded at gun-point onto an outgoing plane. Then, like one coming out of anesthesia, he remembered the Tel Aviv stop. Palestinians, not Iranians? The thought, dawning as a mere notion, brought him sharply to attention. He raised himself slightly in his seat and out of the corner of his eye he took fresh stock of the gunner, who had moved to the center of the cabin.

Beside him, Cameron spoke up. "Rather a bore, this, don't you find? One reads about these bloody things but one doesn't expect them to happen to oneself." Van Vliet concurred. "Palestinians, do you think?" Cameron supposed so. "One can't be sure of course till one hears them speak in their own language. Do you know any Arabic?" "No." "Pity. Neither do I but I can recognize the phonemes—the noises they make, you know." Van Vliet wondered why it was a pity. "You mean we might learn what they have in mind? But are they likely to talk much in front of us?" "No," patiently said Cameron, "I was thinking that if we knew their language, we could open a dialogue with them." The idea of Cameron's opening a dialogue with anyone should have been funny, but Van Vliet, from the depths of his ignorance, was prepared to be respectful. "No chance that they might be Iranians?" Cameron turned his head. "Hardly. Your Iranian's facial features and skin color set him off from the Arabs. Although there's some Semitic admixture in the southeast. Anyhow, the Shah's opposition doesn't go in for hijacking. Rather indolent chaps, on the whole."

Van Vliet felt relieved that at least he had not voiced his conviction that SAVAK must be at the bottom of this—absurd of him to have held to it with such stubbornness, when other, less egocentric, explanations lay so ready to hand. And he supposed he ought to be grateful to the hijackers for having furnished Cameron, finally, with a congenial subject. No doubt, like so many British academics, he was a reader of thrillers and detective fiction. In a cautious undertone, he speculated on the provenance of the weapons: the gun, he decided, was an American make, and gun and grenades must have been introduced into the cabin—into a lavatory, most likely—through collusion with the cleaning staff. "Mostly North Africans here, as you know, like the dustmen." He tapped out his pipe. "Where do I think they're taking us?" He spread out the book of flight maps provided in the pocket of the seat ahead, and his pipestem silently indicated the possibilities: the Libyan desert, Aden, the Syrian desert, Oman. "Depends on whether they've received training in terrorism and are executing a mission in complicity with their sponsors. If they're an As-Saiqa commando squad, for instance, they got their guerrilla training in Syria, and Syria will have to accept them. If they trained in Libya, we can expect a welcoming committee of Khaddafi's people."

In any case, on landing, the pilot would be handed the usual list of demands. "Release of their comrades from Israeli prisons, indemnities, the lot. If our two friends are linked with a serious guerrilla network, we can count on some rough moments." His burry voice dropped still another register. Van Vliet could barely hear him over the hum of the engines. His ear caught the words "brutes" and "hostages," and his gaze followed Cameron's, which was directed meaningfully toward their right. "The Senator?" Cameron nodded, with an air of satisfaction, like one who has brought a seminar to a triumphant conclusion.

Van Vliet frowned: that implied that the hijackers knew that the Senator would be on the plane. Perfectly possible, Cameron declared. On the other hand, the selection of this particular flight might have been fortuitous. "These bully-boys, like as not, are acting on their own and don't have the foggiest notion of how to proceed next. Palestinian hotheads deciding to do their wee bit in harassing air traffic to Israel while lining their own pockets. On that assumption, they boarded the first plane for Tel Aviv that their confederates—or confederate—could smuggle arms into. Sunday being Sunday, most of the regular cleaning staff would be having a lie-in this morning, leaving the coast clear. If what we have here is a nasty pair of free lances, the passenger list is of no interest to them. We're a parcel, to be turned over with the plane on delivery of x thousand pounds."

Weighing this second hypothesis, Van Vliet grew more cheerful. Far better to be in the hands of men directed by the profit-motive than in those of idealistic terrorists. He re-examined the machine-gunner, a short, fattish, gloomy young fellow who looked, in fact, more like a clerk or the policeman Van Vliet had first taken him for than like the gaunt Palestinian extremists whose photos appeared from time to time in the press. It seemed encouraging also that there were only two. Guerrillas taking over a giant plane would be more numerous, he reasoned. Ransacking his memory for precedents, he regretted that he had not paid closer attention to the hijacking phenomenon before meeting it in person. He had indistinct but unreassuring recollections of captive planes zigzagging about in the sky at the direction of a lone gunman seeking a host country that would promise him and his booty asylum. There had been an occasion in America when the hijacker had simply bailed out with his packets of dollars and taken to the woods. But that, if memory served, had been mountain country. He doubted that such a solution would be feasible in Arabia Deserta with its parching sands.

Having stated the problem, Cameron lit a second pipe and disappeared, like a deity, in a cloud of smoke. The machine-gunner, as though restless or bored with his assignment, strolled forward, picking up an illustrated magazine from one of the seats as he went. He stood at the front entry with the magazine in his left hand, leafing through the pages and raising his eyes occasionally. The grenade-carrier was no longer to be seen. Then, as if the plane had re-entered the everyday world, the hostesses appeared with menus and the drinks cart. "Are they on the house?" jested the Senator. His deep easy voice, breaking into the general hush, caused a movement of disapproval, as though he had committed an act of irreverence in church. "I can't tell you, sir," said the girl. "Would you like me to ask the steward?" "Never mind. Just give me a split of that champagne." He laid a hand on his neighbor's. "What would you like, Aileen?" When his turn came, Van Vliet took a single whiskey. But others were asking for doubles, pointing in dumb show at the miniature bottles of spirits; the Senator's awful daring had evidently made them tremble lest any convivial noise coming from them be interpreted as disrespect. Cameron, bolder, raised his whiskey glass. "Well, Dutch courage, eh?"

Van Vliet looked at his watch. If they were on course, they should be crossing the Alps. He was starting to take a serious interest in their destination. But he could not see down from the window without getting up from his seat. The Air France map indicated that the plane should be heading southeast; he tried without success to take his bearings from the sun shadows. It was his impression that they had changed direction slightly. A smell of warm food was coming from the pantries: a choice of chicken chasseur, he had learned from the menu, or *boeuf bourguignon*.

The meal, though, was slow in coming. Some passengers were ordering fresh drinks. Half of them would soon be drunk, Van Vliet estimated, which no doubt suited the hijackers' book. As alcohol did its work in releasing inhibitions, the cabin grew more vocal. They watched a hostess go forward with two trays. "Well, finally!" said Aileen, leaning into the aisle. In front of her stood three empty miniatures of bourbon. "I'm famished, aren't you, Mynheer?" When no further trays immediately followed, a grumble of protest became audible. Van Vliet's stomach, to his shame, was adding its own growl. A hostess came by, collecting glasses. Aileen tapped her sleeve. "*Mademoiselle! S'il vous plaît!* Can you tell us why a few people up there have been served while the rest of us have to wait?" "Cool it," advised the Senator, raising a pained eyebrow that sent a message of deepest sympathy—women!—to the also-suffering Van Vliet. Aileen swung about. "I'm not complaining. I just want to know. *On a le droit à savoir, je suppose.*" "It is a special order, sir," said the hostess, ignoring Aileen's upturned face. "When they book, that family have ask for our kosher service." There was a muffled explosion of laughter. "Kosher, yet!" said a voice. "Fantastic!" murmured Van Vliet. "Fantastic!" He shook his head. The Senator, he observed, was seizing the opportunity to put a low-voiced question to the girl. "May be, sir. I am not permitted to discuss the *détournement* with passengers. But you will have your luncheons soon. It is just that we serve the kosher diet first, since it is separate."

Van Vliet sighed. He would not be sorry if the energy crisis reduced Holland to the bi-plane and the glider. Even in so-called normal circumstances, he disliked being confined in an elephantine flying object while passengers and crew enacted a fantasy of ordinary earth life in its more anodyne aspects, the sole allusion to the un-earthly facts of the case being the life-jacket demonstration, which, he suddenly recognized, had been omitted from today's program—an oversight attributable to the hijacking, he supposed.

As he was lifting the foil from his *boeuf bourguignon*, a note was passed from the Senator. "Will they show us the movie? Your guess." Van Vliet gave an appreciative laugh and handed the note to Cameron, who frowned and drew out a pencil. "Unlikely," he wrote back. "If you have in mind that darkening the plane would give us our chance to overpower them, these chaps will see that too. Unless they're utter fools. Which should not be excluded. We must get word to the personnel to be ready to show the film as usual." Just then the aircraft veered. There could be no doubt about it. The pilot was banking and turning left. Van Vliet eyed Cameron, whose bushy eyebrows went up. They were heading north.

Four

"Do you have anything that might serve as a weapon?" Senator Carey stared at the new message from Cameron. He laughed and wrote out an answer: "Hell, no. I went through Security." Actually, he had a weapon on him—a multi-bladed Swiss Army pocket knife his wife had given him for his birthday when he was a young first-term Congressman (committees: patents and coins) with half-soled shoes, one suit, and lethargic political expectations. Since she had died, he carried it as a relic of her and of a time of relative innocence—those camping trips they used to take in the August recess instead of touching base with the voters in the district. It had served him mainly to gut fish for the frying pan he had given her, but you could kill a man with it. He felt no urge, however, to encourage Cameron in his fantasies of resistance. The Scot, he reckoned, had had "a good war" and was thrilling to the call of the pibroch again.

James Augustine Carey had had a moderately good war himself, having enlisted at nineteen in the U.S. Navy's air corps and seen considerable action as a navigator in the Pacific theatre. In flying school he had failed mysteriously to get his "wings"—the instructor blamed it on lack of ambition—but in fact he was quite capable of piloting a plane and had proved it more than once when the pilot beside him was wounded or hung over. They had made him a lieutenant, j.g., six months before the War ended and sent him back to teach celestial navigation to cadets. "And a star to steer her by!"—he was as out of synch with what a flier had to know nowadays as a rusty car-crank stowed in the trunk of a Mustang. Never mind; he was still able to estimate distances and wind vectors and roughly plot the course the pilot was now on. Should the pilot and the co-pilot be killed or incapacitated during this adventure, he could probably, with God's help and some coaching, assume the controls and bring the big jet down.

He trusted it was not going to come to that. This frolic had all the earmarks of a routine hijacking, no more noteworthy than a Georgetown mugging except in the venue and the size of the haul, whose worth to the lawbreakers he estimated at up to half a million dollars—a fair price for the return of the plane and the crew and passengers intact. A low-risk investment of time, nerve, and manpower, if the two could bring it off, and there was no reason visible to him why they should fail to—no sign of a security guard aboard (Air France, he understood, had a policy of not carrying any), which disposed of the possibility of a shoot-out; the crew was being cooperative, and the underwriters, as usual, would pay.

If no one rocked the boat, the affair should proceed as smoothly as any normal jet flight. He hated these big planes and the whole soft sell of air travel, designed to persuade the passenger that he was not in a thoroughly unnatural position, several thousand leagues above ground with his heart in his mouth, but instead lounging in a dream-like movie auditorium with a drink in his hand and soft music playing in his ears. He liked a real plane, without amenities, a basic tool of transport that made you conscious of the extraordinary *fact* of flying, with its peril and discomfort. Hijacking, for a while, had made jet travel a little more suspenseful, but now the reality had pretty well leached out of that, though the journalists still tried to make it sound like a bated-breath business with an open-ended plot. Today's "ordeal"—as it would be described—ought not to last longer than a few hours, most of which would be spent dully at an airfield, deprived of information, while negotiations went on. Waiting, characteristically, would be the main chore.

Barring accidents. And among potentials for accident, there was the human factor, represented today by the impetuous Cameron, with his fond daydreams or—more accurately—pipe-dreams of hand-to-hand combat. Responses to seizure had not yet been programmed to the point of total automatized consent, and in any group of passengers you might find individuals, usually of middle age, still programmed to resistance. Such individuals, of course, constituted a menace to the collective.

Yet there was a wee drop of Cameron in the blood of most active males. At any rate, in himself Jim Carey had already noted a certain curiosity about the morale of the hijackers and the state of readiness of their weapons, joined with a sneaking curiosity as to his own morale and his state of fitness. Not only had he asked himself whether he was capable, should the worst happen, of bringing the plane down, but he had been letting his mind go back to the training in jiu-jitsu the Navy had put him through more than thirty years ago. He wondered whether the art of judo, which he had been pretty good at, was something that came back to you when occasion arose, like being able to ride a bicycle, or whether it got away from you, like Latin or playing the piano at social events. It had occurred to him as he watched lunch being served that the gunner could be disarmed by a couple of determined men with seats on the aisle and a concerted strategy, one to trip him as he passed and the other to get hold of the weapon. This had been a disinterested speculation; his own seat was not on the aisle but cut off from it by the small bulk of Ms. Simmons. Among the males in their party with aisle seats, he eliminated the Reverend, a man of peace, and Victor, up in front and hence incommunicado. That left only the Dutchman, an alert fellow, who must have done his military training. He did not rule out the handsome, long-legged Sophie, once she regained her presence of mind—he could picture her in khakis as an Israeli girl-fighter on patrol at some border kibbutz.

In any event, the problem was not the gunner, but the grenadier. That x quantity in the equation was now out of sight, back by the serving-pantry presumably, but Jim Carey had had a view of the small deadly engines, the Queen of Hell's pomegranates, hanging from his belt, brief but sufficient to persuade him that the pin of at least one had been pulled. Any jarring contact, even a bad landing bump, could send him and everybody in the vicinity to Persephone's domain. *Assuming the grenade was active.* On the other hand, the grenades might be dummies. In the history of hijacking, there were plenty of episodes in which water pistols and other toy weapons had served to hold a plane at bay. Unfortunately, there were also episodes featuring real weapons, in the hands of psychopaths and suicidal terrorists. These men did not look to Carey like a kamikaze squad, but appearances might be deceptive—as he was postulating of the grenades themselves, which *looked* dangerous and could well be harmless. Nevertheless, they deterred, like a nuclear capability.

At least they deterred Carey. His curiosity, though aroused, was satisfied to exercise itself in the abstract; he felt no real need to know. Cameron, he expected, was on a different track: he must be taking as a working hypothesis the conviction that the grenades were inoperative or just irrelevant to some Boy Scout ethic of action. Carey scrawled a fresh note on a paper napkin and sent it along. Van Vliet de Jonge read it as it went by him. He nodded. "'Who steals my purse steals trash,'" Carey had written. "Keep your shirt on." Only money, filthy lucre, was at stake, after all. And it was not as if the raiders were after Cameron's life-savings, which perhaps were worth defending at knife-point. It was corporate money, "covered" by insurance, whose transfer to the hijackers' pockets nobody could feel as touching him personally in a vital spot. Except in terms of envy: a hard-working lecturer in history or, for that matter, a U.S. Senator might well see red at the thought of a fortune acquired with so little honest sweat. But that was a daily occurrence in the board rooms and offices of government procurement; Cameron could not be ignorant of the facts of modern business life.

No doubt there was a principle somewhere to be discerned in this affair that a righteous man might be inclined to do battle for—resistance to the tyranny of arms or the right to travel unharassed and unimpeded. But this right in fact was a fringe benefit of paid-up membership in the shrinking Free World and even in England, its cradle, only a couple of centuries old; to "go unarmed unharmed," as the saying went, had been far from the rule on the American frontier. Freedom of travel was conceded today in only a residual part of the globe and there hedged about by passport and visa formalities which had been unknown in most of the "civilized" world up to the First War. If air piracy represented a reversion to an age of lawlessness, when nobody could count himself safe outside his own door, it had also reintroduced illegal searches, which Americans (Carey spoke for himself and a few of his colleagues in the Senate) had begun by resenting and had quickly got used to, evidently preferring their personal safety to their constitutional rights.

As a constitutionalist, Carey was unhappy about the fact of being hijacked, to which there was no constitutional or democratic reply. Having submitted to an illegal search at the airport, he was now submitting to force while consoling himself with history and philosophy, whereas, in his mind—and not merely as a male animal, in his gut—he believed that force should always be resisted. By hook or crook; in his interior citadel, if nowhere else, James Augustine Carey ought to be saying no to power-at-the-end-of-a-gun-barrel. Yet here he sat, staring at a slab of Nesselrode pudding, and the unaccustomed sensation of lacking power was disagreeable, for there was an implication of consent. But rushing to improvised arms, even if that were feasible, would be an over-reaction, also damaging to the self-respect. Moreover, there were others to be considered. They had the right, surely, not to be blown sky-high—for once the figure was appropriate—as the result of a unilateral decision to meet force with force. An opportunity for taking a poll seemed unlikely to present itself, but if consulted, an overwhelming majority of the passengers would vote to sit tight. Your majority's chief wish was to stay out of trouble; few, if any, battles would ever have been fought if the choice had rested with the troops.

In the past, history indicated, warlike tribes had been known, and courage, if you could believe the chroniclers, could be roused by oratory. But today the citizenry grew up fearful, every man-jack a non-interventionist. Only kooks, far out on the Right and Left, were ready to take up arms for what they believed in, which was why the Founding Fathers' wisdom in assigning the power to declare war to the Congress, rather than the Executive, had been short-sighted—they had relied on a nation of minute-men. Roosevelt had had to con the people and their elected representatives into the Second World War, and Johnson had followed suit, manufacturing his own Pearl Harbor in Tonkin Gulf to get a blank check issued to him for the war in Vietnam. While Carey had approved of the first commitment and disapproved of the second, he could see that deception had been needful in both cases if intervention was what was desired, and he had often wondered whether Kennedy's handling of the missiles crisis would have been endorsed by the country if a draft of his intentions had been submitted in advance to a vote.

Cameron, evidently, was looking to *him* now to exercise leadership, and he did not care for the assignment. Vetoing hare-brained counter-insurgency schemes was easy enough, but the alternatives were not clear. Short of supine acceptance, there ought to be some middle course, involving the arts of persuasion or mere watchful waiting on opportunity, generally glimpsed too late. And it was not just Cameron who was turning to him for leadership. He sensed that he had been "elected" by his own group—and probably by a fair number of others who had got wind that he was aboard—if only to set the tone. It was mainly a question of style. Whatever he did, or failed to do, would be on the record. It was a "moment of truth" which he would have been glad to evade. But he was too experiencd politically to ignore the sensation, stiffening his spine like a chilling yardstick thrust down his collar, of being a model in a showcase: "SENATE DOVE KEEPS HIS COOL. Asked how a liberal legislator felt on being hijacked, Carey quipped 'There ought to be a law.'"

It irritated him to surmise that others were looking to him for guidance when, like the rest of the human cargo, he lacked the first requisite—information—on which to base a line of conduct. He was used to being briefed on any matter likely to confront him, but now no aide sat by his side to whisper in his ear or pass him a folder of vital statistics on air piracy. Of course if he were feeling inventive, he could easily devise some innocent-seeming experiments to assess these men and the lengths to which they were willing to go. But he was not feeling inventive, and the trial balloon he had idly sent up half an hour ago with his jape "Are they on the house?" had signally failed as a temperature-taker. The gunman, if he had heard, made as if he hadn't, like old Father Peter in study hall deciding not to let himself be provoked by a solitary humorist in the back rows. And Milady Simmons was still displeased with him for his ill-timed—as she saw it—levity. "What made you want to tease that poor hostess? She's scared to come near us now. You saw how she trembled when she tried to open your champagne. Why, Senator, I think you're perverse."

The passing of notes made her nervous too. "Be careful. They'll see you. They'll think you and Mr. Cameron are up to something. We don't want to make them jumpy." As she spoke, the gunman crossed in front of the movie screen and came slowly down the aisle. "He's going to make you show him what you've been writing. Oh, my God!" Carey grinned. "Shall I swallow it?" With his teeth, he tore a shred from Cameron's original missive and carefully chewed it. The machine-gunner passed by. Aileen opened an eye. "He's gone. *Please* don't try to bait them any more, Senator. You act as though this was a game. Don't you take anything seriously?" From beneath her penciled brows came a sidelong measuring look. "I never wanted to believe the stories they told—" "How I lost the nomination to McGovern." He had heard that music before. "Don't sneer. I always defended you. I said you were just being honest. But students who worked for you in Miami said you were *impossible*. You quipped and clowned when delegates asked you questions instead of taking clear stands." "My positions were known," retorted Carey. "Anyway Nixon would have clobbered me. I would have rather it happened to George."

In fact he took the hijackers as seriously, he thought, as they deserved. Since they were neither Westerners nor Africans nor Orientals, they were Arabs, one could reasonably assume. No doubt they believed they were furthering the cause of Palestinian liberation—that hornet's nest Israel had idiotically stirred up for herself when she elected not to give back the occupied territories. The only puzzle was why a French airliner had been chosen as a target; since France was a friend to the Arab cause, Air France was regarded as a "safe" company to fly with. If that was no longer so, a cleavage might be opening in French-Arab relations which no one in Washington was yet aware of—something to do, perhaps, with Mystère and Mirage deliveries. Or could France be quietly resuming shipment of parts to Israel? Seen in that light, this morning's take-over could possess some real interest; he asked himself whether the Dutch parliamentarian was considering these implications too.

On the other hand, this pair might be low-grade members of the North African underworld without awareness of the political significance of seizing a French plane. In their ignorance of larger stakes, they would have been expecting to be received with military honors in Tripoli or Damascus when in fact their arrival could only be an embarrassment. The sudden change of course, just now, favored that hypothesis; indeed, there could be no other explanation for the pilot's executing a U-turn midway to Rome than that the Arab capitals, queried by radio, had refused the plane clearance to land. For the past ten minutes—Carey checked his watch—they had been proceeding north-northwest and must now be re-crossing the Alps. It seemed odd, though, that the gunman showed no loss of aplomb. Carey could only conclude that the change of course had been negotiated with the invisible grenadier, who was probably in command of the operation and in touch with the pilot by inter-com. Unless, up front, there was a third hijacker? Across the aisle, the Scot and the Dutchman were again bent over a map. Carey scratched his head. It almost looked as if they were returning to base—Charles de Gaulle airport. But for what reason? Feeling the first trace of misgiving, he listened but could hear nothing amiss in the regular pulse of the engines. Refueling? Unnecessary, unless their next stop was to be Moscow, and the Russians did not take to hijackers. A radar failure?

The stewardesses collecting the lunch trays were giving out no flight bulletins. "I don't know, sir," said the girl, as Carey handed over his. He retained the glass of Evian—his throat was dry. The mystery was thickening, like the cloud cover outside. If it was De Gaulle they were heading for, the pilot ought to be starting his descent. But they were still at cruising speed.

A wild surmise—Erin—entered his mind. Improbable, he sharply told himself, to the last degree that this pair could be linked with breakaway IRA terrorists and be seeking a hideout on a remote farm in Galway to barter the plane and its passengers against a package composed of Bridget Rose Dugdale, the Price sisters, and the usual Palestinian guerrillas held in Israeli jails. He must have had one too many last night with his friends from the Embassy. Only an Irishman, or a hungover half-Irishman, could summon up such a bogey from the ancestral peat fires. Granted, it was no secret that ties existed between those boyos and Palestinian guerrilla units, who were training them (as if they needed it!) in terrorist techniques and supplying them with arms. But no boggy meadow or field could take a jumbo jet, and an attempt to land on a small hidden airstrip, if such existed in the Irish Republic, would result in gruesome casualties, if not certain death for all concerned. Were the hijackers to put forward such a crazy demand, the pilot would have to dissuade them and, if he failed, let them shoot him rather than carry out their orders.

Carey sighed. He repented last night's conviviality. Since Eleanor had died, he had been resorting to drink, mainly from boredom and because he was sleeping badly. If it had not been for their religion, they would have divorced long ago, and yet now he missed her. His punishment, he supposed, for not having believed her when she used to tell him "When I die, you'll be sorry." In her last illness, she had finally stopped saying that, perhaps from lack of conviction; a pity she could not be here now to enjoy her triumph or, to be fair to her many virtues, seek to console him for the loss of her.

She drank herself, like most senators' wives, but for him she had been jealous of booze: "It takes you away from us." Jealousy made her exaggerate his attachment to the bottle: "The curse of the Irish; if it weren't for me, you'd be an alcoholic." He had never been more than a sporadic drinker, while campaigning or, precisely, to get away from her after a tiresome quarrel, and in the Senate he could count as abstemious, but now he had to accord her a certain skill in divination. He rarely went to bed totally sober these days, and this morning he had broken his own golden rule—not to add alcohol, even a beer, to a hangover. The double birthday, however, had imposed a celebratory glass, and the champagne he had ordered for the panache. He had not finished it and had felt no temptation to follow up with wine. Actually, to be fair to himself, last night's over-indulgence had been venial, mainly a matter of late hours, and excused by the prospect of a dull journey to Teheran. He had counted on a restorative snooze all the way to Tel Aviv, but first this little woman had come to jaw with him, then there was the false alarm on Victor's cat, and finally the hijackers had burst on the scene. If he had known he was going to be hijacked, he would have been better prepared, he hoped, but then, as the Church taught, the wise virgin always had her lamp trimmed.

In the seat ahead, he noticed, the Bishop was dozing—a display of holy sangfroid he envied. But if he himself were to take forty winks, it would only contribute to his Luciferian legend. "*Perverse!* Why, let me tell you, that man slept right through a hijacking. As soon as he saw what was happening, he ordered a bottle of champagne, and the next thing I knew he was snoring. I don't deny his intelligence or his charm, when he wants to use it, but would you want him in the White House? I mean, in a nuclear crisis . . ."

Jim Carey supposed it was his fate to be type-cast as a semi-bad apple. Being good-looking played its part in that. "He certainly is a *handsome* man," Eleanor's father, a mortician, used to comment whenever the tall law student, then known as Augie, came to take her out in his ancient salesman's coupe—a grudging professional concession that the suitor would make a nice corpse. Yet being handsome had never hurt the Kennedys or Stu Symington—no sulphurous additive suspected there. He was a better Catholic than any of the Kennedys, though few, outside his confessor, would believe that. But when he made a retreat, which he still did occasionally, it went on the debit side: the inference drawn by the gossip columns was that he was a "spoiled priest." In his last try for the Democratic nod, his backers had implored him, for Christ's sake, to stay out of monasteries; if he needed a rest from the world, he could find some island in Maine and commune with Nature— the "spoiled priest" canard was turning off not only Jews and Protestants but Catholics. When he ignored the advice and slipped into a Benedictine monastery for a weekend—with the Secret Service, assigned to him by law as a candidate, camping in a motel opposite so they could check on the monks' fire-escapes —his chief speech-writer went over to Shirley Chisholm. No great loss; he could write his own speeches. But he did not care for the golden handshake the scribe gave him on quitting: "I have great respect for Senator Carey's moral courage, but the guy doesn't want to get elected. I guess what he wants is for somebody to hand him a crown."

He could not deny having been a seminarian. His aunts and mother had seen to that. But they had not foreseen Pearl Harbor. He had enlisted in the Navy's air corps that same Christmas (to be exact, St. Stephen's day), from a mixture of motives—patriotic reflexes, a desire to avoid the draft, a desire to avoid the priesthood, from which the "sneak attack" had intervened providentially, he felt, to save him. As a seminarian, he might not have been drafted, but if his draft board had let him stay on and be ordained, he would have ended up in the

Army as a chaplain—an unappealing prospect to a youngster who had been a state-wide athletic star at Saint Ben's. Besides, coming from a farm area, he had always wanted to go to sea or fly an airplane, and the Navy offered both. The choice between God and country had not involved much wrestling with his conscience: God would still be there when Hitler and the Japs had been defeated. And God had surely not meant him to be a priest. At the outside, a monk though never an abbot: often a bridesmaid but never a bride, he might have risen to be Master of Novices. But he could not have taken the discipline, unless self-imposed by the so-named scourge. Among religious callings, being a hermit might have suited him best; a loner, not a team man, was his image. And when he had started out, in the winter of '68, preaching his campaign in the New Hampshire wilderness, he had actually thought of Peter the Hermit leading his *paupères* in what was known as the first act of the first crusade. Like Peter, he had come on strong in the first act, and then the barons had moved in to take over, and he was left by the wayside with a tiny band of ragged zealots by the time they reached the Holy Land, i.e., the convention.

His arch-sin and political crime was lack of humility. It was why he could never have been fitted for the monastic life, still less for the parish circuit, though he might have starred in the confessional. In politics, on the cocktail circuit, it was a crime he was drawn and quartered for every four years during the hunting season for presidential "hopefuls." Back in the home territory, the folks did not seem to mind—the older ones still remembered him as an end on Saint Ben's famous unbeaten high-school eleven and a crack third baseman on the spring nine. Even so, as he had heard his campaign workers say, it was a miracle that such an arrogant guy kept getting elected and re-elected to the House and then the Senate; some of it could be explained by the law of inertia, but the *first time?* Some said he owed it to Eleanor, a born campaigner and particularly effective with women's groups, but most argued that it could not be all the wife, which coincided with his own view. He was proud but not vain, and each time the returns came in showing him out in front, he began by suspecting a miscount. True, it was a Democratic state with a mixed German and Irish population and a Farmer-Labor tradition, but the machine had tried more than once to unseat him in the primaries and never even come close. Natural causes, Eleanor included, were insufficient to account for the phenomenon, and he too was inclined to consider it a miracle, proof of a Divine intention that for its own inscrutable reasons had chosen him to be a legislator rather than a small-town lawyer and weekly poet for the county newspaper.

Or an actor. At Veblen's old school (where he had enrolled under the GI bill after the War), the head of the drama department had urged him to take a screen test, but Carey had thought he was too old and his mouth was too small, like a woman's. The truth was, he did not care to be an idol. Yet there was an actor somewhere in his make-up, along with the priest and the ballplayer and versifier; he was a vocational mongrel or alley cat for all his royal ways. Like his only friend in the Senate, old Sam Ervin (now, alas, retired), he was a Shakespearean and resorted mischievously to quotation. During the uproar in the '72 campaign over the question of homosexual marriage, he had fielded queries from the audience with "'Let me not to the marriage of true minds admit impediment.' Next?" He supposed he must project a saturnine image from the depths of a private melancholy unfathomed by his conscious intellect. Though he was a ready laugher and chuckler, news photographers liked to catch him in a brown study or with an eyebrow that appeared to be wincing in cerebral pain. His silver hair (hereditary; his father had been snow-white at thirty) lit up the paradoxes of his public personality by contrasting with his soft, smooth features, unlined except for the amused wrinkles around the eyes, so that he looked like a Drama School performer made up for the role of a senator. And in fact he was detached from his simulacrum, though not totally out of sympathy with it. Like a finished actor, he observed himself playing his part and made critical notes; he was rarely satisfied with a performance and distrusted audience reaction.

According to Eleanor, his greatest liability was his unwillingness to "throw himself into" whatever he was doing. "You make it so obvious. Some part of you is just standing there coldly and watching." She was right, though "coldly" was a typical editorial injection—compared with most of his colleagues, he was an incinerator. It was something else that tempered his commitments; whether he was interrogating a witness before one of his committees or sub-committees or receiving a delegation of dairy farmers or "meeting the press" on the tube or simply copulating, there was always a playful element. It was in sports and games, as she noted too, that he was most serious and concentrated. "Anybody watching you play softball would think you really cared." But sports were playful by definition except to the pros; you could "give yourself" without equivocation to pitching or a game of poker, whereas in politics and so-called interpersonal relations, amusement was a necessary solace, like a boon companion you brought along to keep you honest.

On the other hand, he was accused of "having too high standards." He himself could never make out whether they were too high or too low—his expectations of humanity were slim. If it were not for God's grace, all would surely burn—he had no trouble in believing that. Yet God's grace was meant to be "sufficient" to each and every occasion, and on this cardinal point he doubted: judging by the evidence, there was not enough of it available for present-day needs. It was supposed to be limitless but perhaps it was running out like the underground reserves of coal and oil on this unhappy planet. A good man, like Pope John or this old Bishop, was now a museum wonder, and Jim Carey, as a born-and-bred plains democrat, could not help regarding that as a suspicious circumstance.

Since he had left the seminary, he had never taken much interest in the question of whether he himself was a good man or a bad man; that was the Lord's business, not his, to tote up. The sin of pride, in his private experience, was unconquerable: curb it here and it reared up its head there. God, who had made him intelligent, would have to allow for the incisiveness of judgment that went with it. He lacked charity. If he loved anybody, it was God, the only person to whom he could talk, who angered him (unlike his human associates, who, for all their efforts, could never fully rouse his ire), who made him happy in the contemplation of His handiwork, who filled him with a longing for union and abandoned him during long intervals. Maybe his mistake was to expect God to approve of him for his truthfulness, the only quality in himself he greatly valued. The theologians, his confessor reminded him, had not numbered that among the virtues. In their catalogue (lifted from Plato, as his confessor had forgotten), there were only prudence, justice, fortitude, and temperance. He feared he saw what his spiritual mentor was getting at. Since nothing could be concealed from Him who knew the secrets of all hearts, honesty was no virtue in His regard, and a man who laid claim to truth-telling was very likely committing the old Greek sin of hubris, aspiring to dispense a commodity that only the gods possessed. In short, his dry candor, so attractive and yet so disturbing to his adherents, was only another form of satanic pride.

President Simmons was nudging him. He opened his eyes. Across the aisle, the Dutchman's right hand was up and signaling for attention. "Please, Teacher! Can I go to the toilet?" Some nervous snickers were heard. "What the mischief?" exclaimed the Bishop, waking up. After a suspenseful moment, the gunman accorded permission. The deputy, looking now somewhat sheepish, made his way to the toilets; it was not easy to saunter with an AK trained on your back. "Whatever possessed him?" said Aileen. "Why couldn't he just *ask*? Don't you legislators ever grow up?" "He was testing," said Carey. "Like inserting a straw in a cake. You must have seen your mother do it."

The deputy, Carey estimated, must be using his promenade to get the lay of the land. It would be interesting to know what the grenade-carrier was up to, and from the vantage-point of the toilet block both the serving-pantry and the cabin behind could be inspected. But before Van Vliet could return with whatever facts he had collected, a collective gasp directed Carey's attention forward. In the entry from the first-class cabin, a tall elegantly dressed figure stood leaning calmly on a cane. "Mr. Charles!" whispered Aileen. "So I see," said Carey. In the far aisle, the machine-gunner, intent on the rear toilets, had not noticed the new arrival. As the frail old party came abreast of him, he swung about, startled, and moved to block the way. Muttering something—an Arabic curse or an order?— he thrust the gun-barrel into Tennant's fawn-colored waistcoat, which covered a slight gentlemanly paunch. "Nonsense," they heard Tennant reply in his high piercing voice. "I don't propose to return to where I belong, as you call it." He made a deterring motion with his cane. "Don't be frightened, my dear fellow. I have no intention of harming you. I have a long-standing sympathy with the Arab cause. And if you shoot me, you will simply waste your ammunition on an eighty-two-year-old non-combatant. I am quite prepared for death. My affairs are in order, and I've already begun divesting myself of my worldly goods."

He gently deflected the gun with his elbow. "Come, let's not fence about. We both know you're not going to shoot me." Lifting his head, like a rooster getting ready to crow, he addressed a stage aside, or confidential parenthesis, to the cabin at large. "I sensed *immediately* that something was wrong. Engine trouble, I feared, when I noticed the plane was veering about, but then a little bird told me it was a hijacking. Not a word of sense to be got from the stewardesses, of course. So I decided to come back and investigate. When the steward tried to interfere, then I *knew*, and he admitted—he had to; it was obvious—that there'd been a *détournement d'avion*. Now, if you'll just let me by—I believe I see my friends back there."

The gunman let him pass. Settling his waistcoat, he lowered himself into Van Vliet de Jonge's seat. He sighed. "So much nicer, if one is going to be hijacked, to be among friends, one's own kind." The Dutchman came back from the toilet. "Oh, dear me, were you sitting here? I'm afraid we haven't met." Aileen did the introductions. "Van Vliet de Jonge . . . ? That rings a far-off bell. Adriaan van Vliet de Jonge. The novelist. Now utterly forgotten, I suppose." "His grandfather," supplied Aileen. The old man sprang up. "How delightful. My dear boy, I *knew* your grandfather. Charming man, and so very kind to me. I was only a lad, you see. Before the First War, in Germany. I was doing my *Wanderjahre*, with my tutor. A house party, it was, in the Rhineland, near the Dutch border. I wanted to see Zutphen, in your country, where Sir Philip Sidney fell, and your grandfather arranged to take me. I believe Hugo von Hofmannsthal was staying in the house too. He had no idea of Philip Sidney's falling in Flanders. Between ourselves, I don't think he knew who Sidney *was*. When I happened to speak of the Countess of Pembroke—'Sidney's sister, Pembroke's mother'—he asked whether she was a guest in the house. But your grandfather knew. He gave me one of his books, translated into German. Splendid writer. Harvard has it now, inscribed to me of course. As I indicated to our captor, I'm divesting myself of my possessions. Two strapping young men came from the Lamont and packed up my library. Next I must part with my porcelains. At the end of one's journey, one must travel light, don't you agree?"

"You missed something, Mr. Van Vliet," interposed Aileen. "The most thrilling scene. 'I am quite prepared for death,' he said. With a gun-barrel right in his stomach, he coolly stared that hijacker down. *Chapeau, Monsieur Charles.*" The old man gave a delighted whinny of a laugh. "Well, you see, I have so little to lose. I mustn't expect to live forever, must I, and in Boston one is mugged at every corner. Then one can't get staff any more, so that at times one feels quite ready to shuffle off this mortal coil. But you mustn't let me usurp your seat, Deputy."

It was not his seat, the Dutchman explained. "I was sitting back there, in fact." He looked around with a perplexed face. "There's room here," put in Sophie Weil, turning. Before the old man could rise, she was swinging her long legs aside to let Van Vliet de Jonge pass. Jim Carey flexed an eyebrow. He had been wondering how long the handsome hazel-eyed deputy would resist this other call of Nature.

Cameron and Tennant were now seat-mates—an ill-matched pair. "A sword cane?" came the screech after a spell of quiet. "Dear me, no. In my stick collection, I have a few examples, but this isn't one. I don't believe they're permitted in airplanes. Quite right too. I should drop that line of thought if I were you. Had I been carrying a sword cane, I should have had far less moral authority with our friend up there. Unarmed, unharmed, I always say. Look at your London bobby." They heard Cameron mention a "duty to resist." Tennant cackled. "What a strange notion! I'm quite comfortable and enjoying myself, aren't you? But everybody to his own taste. If yours runs to deadly weapons, they supply razor blades in the lavatories, as I recall."

The Dutchman and Carey exchanged smiles. It was a long time since an airplane had carried complimentary razor blades, probably not since the advent of hijacking. But the Bishop's toilet kit would be well stocked, surely, with Gillette steel, perhaps even with an old-fashioned straight razor and a strop to give it an edge. In fact, Carey mused, a resourceful man would see this crate as an arsenal. The glasses they gave you these days were plastic, but the wine bottles were still made of glass; apparently Cameron had never been present at a bar-room fight or he would not be asking for better than a jagged broken bottle. Or, coming on an opponent from behind, you could garrote him with a leather shoelace, such as the Bishop was wearing in his stout brogues. What to do, however, about a live grenade in an enclosed space?

"Are all of you charming people traveling together?" the fluting voice inquired of Aileen. "Dr. Cameron and Deputy Van Vliet de Jonge too? I see. Now don't tell me. I must put my thinking cap on. What can you have in common that's taking you to Teheran or is it Tel Aviv?" He counted on his white ringed fingers. "My old friend Augustus Hurlbut, the Reverend Mr. Barber (St. Matthew's, isn't it?), Senator Carey . . . Why, you must be a committee!" He looked around him triumphantly. "I see I can take silence for consent. A bishop, a senator, a parson, the president of a distinguished college. Tinker, tailor, soldier, sailor. A Dutch parliamentary leader, a don from the British Isles. A trouble-shooting young woman journalist. It's as plain as Pikes Peak. What you lack, if I may say so, is a rabbi." In the seat ahead of Aileen, the Reverend had one of his fits of merriment. He slapped his knee. With an air of contented malice, Tennant continued. "Now what can your committee be up to? Are you off to quiz Golda, poor dear? No, I remember. We agreed to meet in Teheran, didn't we, Augustus? Ah, yes, well." He sighed. "I fear I can guess your business. And the Shah started out so well. Charming man, I'm told. But a visionary, always so dangerous. And he fell under the influence of that dreadful vizier of his." "Nassiri," said Sophie. "That's it, his secret police chief! A thoroughly wicked person. My dear, the shocking things they do to those young men in prison, some of them from excellent families. Well, you know better than I, naturally. That electric grill. They slide those young bodies into the device and *toast* them. A friend in England sent me a clipping on the subject which quite put me off my feed. It came in the morning mail, which I open while I wait for my toast to pop up. I couldn't *look* at an

English muffin." "St. Lawrence on the gridiron. Old idea," said Carey.

"How clever of you, James. Yes, with all our technology, we're relapsing into barbarism. One sees the proofs of it all around one. Sheer medieval savagery. I shan't live to see the dawn of a new Renaissance." "That was damned barbaric too," growled Cameron. "Yes, one can't deny that. But there were compensations—glorious art and literature. The main enemy of civilization—you'll excuse me, Augustus—has always been religion, the spirit of fanaticism. Hunting down heresy, those dreadful dogs of the Inquisition, St. Dominic's hounds, that one sees in the cloister of Santa Maria Novella. Today we find them amusing. We don't stop to think that we ourselves are living in a new age of wars of religion. Persecution of unbelievers. One thought one had seen the last of that with Hitler."

"And Stalin?" demanded Aileen. "Quite right, dear lady. One ought to have known. But I confess that for a long time I simply refused to believe in the horrors of the Soviet camps. I opposed the cold war on principle and then, you see, I belong to a generation that taught itself not to accept atrocity stories. The 'rape of Belgium.' Now one wonders whether Kaiser Willy's troops *weren't* impaling babies on bayonets and crucifying nuns." His shrill ululating laugh caused Carey to wince and duck his head.

Though he had known Charles Tennant for years, he had seldom felt entirely easy in his company. By now, thanks to death and retirement, Carey had moved up (he reckoned) to second or third on Charles's senatorial mailing list for regular advice and remonstrance—Charles never wrote to a newspaper but to selected members of the upper house, presidents, secretaries of defense and state. Those voluminous, closely penned "epistles" on pale blue monogrammed stationery usually wound up, Carey assumed, in the burn bag, which was a pity because Charles, while long-winded, was a sharp old bird and moreover had "done his homework," as was evidenced by the quantity of heavily underscored enclosures clipped from technical journals, the *Times* of London, *Stars and Stripes*, the *Guardian*, *Barron's Weekly*, stockholders' reports. He was never without a silver clipping tool resembling a small pen and had a horror of photostats. As a moderately active legislator, Carey could rarely do justice to that hand-crafted correspondence (if only Charles had learned to use the typewriter or would dictate to a secretary!), but he kept a fair amount of it in a file he had marked *Vox Populi*. To his credit, the far-sighted old liberal had been an early opponent of the war in Vietnam; he boasted that his reproaches to Kennedy on that subject, though uncatalogued in the Kennedy Library, dated back to '61. And on the day Carey announced himself as an anti-war candidate against Johnson, a check from Charles W. Tennant on the State Street Trust was in the mail. "Accept a thousand 'iron men' for your 'war chest.' Gratefully . . ." Dated October 7, 1967. Carey would not forget that. When, rising from a doubtful seat and half-attainted stall (for he was taking some flak from the home front and from his old enemies, the columnists, who had hit on the word "lackluster" for his performance), he went into New Hampshire that brave winter, he would frequently find Charles, wrapped in layers of scarves, shawls, and steamer rugs, seated in a front row of the hall—generally a chilly high-school gymnasium—with a box lunch containing chicken and watercress sandwiches, a large damask napkin, and a silver Thermos of his cook's bouillon on his lap. A somewhat unwelcome cynosure of attention, as was his antique Armstrong-Siddeley stationed outside, with a chauffeur at the wheel. "All that guy lacks is finger bowls," one of the young campaign workers had commented. "What would you call him, Senator?" "A philanthropist, I guess," Carey had said shortly. "Can't you persuade him to stay away, Jim?" Eleanor had entreated. The old hedonist's shrieked observations on "the quality of life" (meaning the hotel accommodations) in rural New Hampshire were being poorly received in the hall. "'I know not the man,'" Carey had cited sardonically. "No. I won't."

But in today's flying auditorium Charles's unabashed, intrepid old voice was tempting Carey to deny him—thrice over—if only he could. Though he was normally immune to social embarrassment (a female complaint, he considered), doubts as to the threshold of tolerance of less sophisticated passengers could not be repressed. Without ill will, with remorseful affection even, he wished their visitor would go back to first class, where, whatever he thought, he belonged.

"So you plan to spend your time in that lovely country investigating torture in the Shah's jails. And I shall be with my millionaires' tour. As Lenin said, 'From each according to his capacities.' Dear me. I must say I've felt a qualm or two about my little jaunt. Mind you, I haven't *seen* the toaster thing, but there can hardly be so much smoke without fire, can there? But then I said to myself that one would become a total shut-in if one let moral considerations dictate one's travel plans. I suppose one could still permit oneself to visit the Scandinavian countries, though there's so little to see there. And your delightful country, Mr. Van Vliet de Jonge, with its splendid museum and attractive people. The Dutch have been much maligned by their neighbors; I've never found them in the least stolid or phlegmatic. But France, Italy? Thoroughly corrupt and police-ridden, and in France you have shocking discrimination against the foreign labor force. No wonder, I say, that they have all these tiresome strikes. England? Well, one has one's friends there, but there've been some quite off-putting disclosures about English prison conditions. And I'm told that Scotland Yard—can that be true, Dr. Cameron?—uses the third degree." He laughed. "No, a peep into Portugal and perhaps into Greece, now that the colonels are gone, and then one would be forced to go virtuously home." "Hear, hear!" came a mutter from the rear, causing Charles to turn around, smiling amiably in all directions like royalty acknowledging applause. Nevertheless he slightly lowered his voice.

"I did draw the line at the colonels, but, between ourselves, my digestion was grateful for a holiday from the nasty Greek food and wine. As for Iran, well, I said to myself that it's no wickeder probably than Spain, where my liberal friends go in droves. And what would I accomplish for those poor young oppositionists by staying home? It's not as if the Shah were dependent on tourism to make ends meet, is it? I am not such a noodle as to fancy that my depreciated dollars could make the slightest difference to him. Then, too, I said, that were I to meet him, which is not beyond the bounds of possibility, I would give him a piece of my mind. 'Look here,' I would say—"

Carey softly groaned. Nobody was censuring the old duck for clinging to the pleasure principle in the few years he had left. Amnesty International would surely get its tithe from the sybarite's holiday that in his own mind he ought to be renouncing—Charles paid up regularly for his venial sins. And as for the Shah's getting "a piece of his mind," that could be forecast with utter certainty if an invitation to the palace were to be issued. No one within earshot today would expect Charles, wherever he found himself, to show a lack of gumption. But Charles was not going to meet the Shah, at least not immediately—a point that in the flush of victory he seemed to be overlooking.

Indeed the fact of that victory—and of Charles basking like a lizard in the glory of it—was starting to worry Carey. The more he pondered it, the less he liked it. The old man's naughty venturesomeness had been rewarded. He had got his way. With every captive eye watching, the hijacker had backed down. But to anyone familiar with power and its vagaries, it was obvious that consequences could be in store. Another passenger, encouraged by Charles's success, would "try something," and the hijacker would over-react, to prove himself.

For the first time, Carey felt distinctly uneasy. He had a bodily premonition of danger, such as he had known once or twice—and with justification—in the navigator's seat with an unseasoned pilot beside him, though now he could not sense, glancing about, in what quarter trouble might be lurking. He felt confident of his power to deter Cameron, who anyway was well fenced in by Charles and his lolling walking-stick. And he trusted Van Vliet de Jonge, a political animal like himself, to have the right reflexes if an emergency were to present itself. But he would feel far happier were he posted commandingly in an aisle seat to restrain any untoward moves. He meditated asking Aileen to change places with him. Yet the slightest stir among the passengers was capable, if he was right in his foreboding, of producing a volley of gunfire.

He looked at his watch again. "Jesus!" he swore. They must have already overflown Paris. He would not feel easy till they were on the ground somewhere. Once they were on the ground, the likelihood of an incident within the plane would be minimal, or so his instinct told him. Outside, the police (in what country's uniforms?) might surround the plane and, if negotiations broke down, try to take it by storm. But that would be a whole new ballgame, which the passengers would have to sit out in the grandstand, waiting for the result to declare itself.

Charles's zestful prattle had finally died down. Next to Sophie, Van Vliet de Jonge had turned his head and was scrutinizing the seats in back. He looked mystified by whatever he saw there. A note was passed along from him—addressed, surprisingly, to "Miss Symans." She opened it and turned her head too, studying the rows behind. She frowned. "Something wrong?" inquired Carey. "Well, no. But it's strange. He wants me to tell him whether some young Dutch people who were sitting back there were a figment of his imagination. Here, read it." He put on his glasses. "You have to know the context," Aileen explained. "He has this phobia about being Dutch. How they have a secret language and how Holland is an imaginary country. I didn't follow it all too well. But when he sees Dutch people, I mean outside Holland, he gets a haunted feeling, as if they were a mirage." Carey laughed sympathetically. "But the strange part is, Senator Jim, that young couple isn't there any more. Isn't that weird? Of course I don't *know* they were Dutch. I just took his word for it. I didn't pay too much attention to them. If you asked me, I couldn't describe them. But I could swear there were two young people sitting behind us, and now that whole row is empty." "Probably moved," said Carey. "Yes, but where to? I don't see them anywhere back there. Still, as I say, I might not recognize them if I did." "Well, reassure him. Tell him you saw them too." Aileen ruminated. "I suppose he missed them when he had to go to the men's room." Her sharp eyes flew open wide. "I'll bet that's *why* he went to the men's room! The secret language. He wanted to pass them a message that nobody but a Dutch person could understand. Like a code. He had some plan in mind and needed their help."

Carey held up a hand. The pilot was starting his descent. Overhead, the seat belt signs flashed on. In a few minutes, they should be able to see land below. Now, short of a crash, nothing could happen, Carey decided: the passengers were concentrating on the windows, trying to make out where they were. He held his lighter to Aileen's cigarette. "You'd better have one too," she told him. "It'll be our last for days maybe. They'll never let us smoke on an airfield." "'For days'?" he said quizzingly. "Come on, it's not that grim. The plane and the crew are all these fellows need for bargaining purposes. The odds are, they'll let the passengers go. For them, we civilians constitute a headache." She stared at him. "A 'headache'? Why, Jim, with you aboard and the Bishop and the deputy, they've captured a real prize. Don't you think these men know that?" He reflected. "No. I don't believe they studied the passenger list." She shrugged. "Even if they didn't know in advance, by now they must realize." "How?" "Senator Carey! Do you recall giving out your autograph to a whole pack of students back in the airport lounge? Do you think you were invisible? If I saw you, these men must have. And you had Sophie giving out autographs too. Don't tell me a hijacker wouldn't be interested. Why, this is the most important international hijacking that's ever happened. Those millionaires up in first class are just the meringue on the pie."

The plane emerged from the cloud cover. A patch of water was sighted, but then a swirl of fog came in. No visibility, Cameron reported from his window. The pilot had decreased speed. "Oh, God, what now?" said Aileen. "Holding pattern," explained Carey. "Could be the fog. Or could be the pilot negotiating with the control tower for permission to land. Or could be he's just waiting his turn." "Wouldn't you think that at least we'd have priority?" Aileen exclaimed, irritably stabbing out her cigarette. Then a rift in the fog opened up. Van Vliet de Jonge rose in his seat, like a rider in stirrups. "Holland!" he called out. "*Nederland!*" Tears of laughter were running down his handsome ruddy cheeks. The fog closed in again. The plane continued to circle.

The cabin was still, as if holding its breath. Then, without warning, with Mother Earth so near, pandemonium erupted. They heard a cat's furious cries, a man's angry yells, a metallic clatter as of something falling. From the rear, two shots rang out. The plane lurched, and the lights went dim. When they came back on, passengers were ducked down in their seats; the Reverend had assumed the fetal position. Carey looked back to where the shots had come from. By the serving-pantry, a tall fair-haired young man with big round spectacles stood holding a rifle; behind him was a fair-haired young woman, wearing glasses too. There was no sign of the grenadier. Up front, the machine-gunner was half-kneeling on the carpet, reaching toward his weapon somewhere ahead while clutching his leg and groaning. Further down the aisle lay a ball of bleeding blue fur. Beside it, Victor was weeping.

As Carey sought to understand this frozen scene, the young man raised his rifle and took aim. Sapphire's back arched; she rose into the air and visibly died. Crouched next to Carey, Aileen was moaning hysterically. "Why did they have to kill Sapphire? *Why*, Senator Jim? Beautiful, beautiful Sapphire. Oh, how cruel, how terribly cruel." "To put her out of her misery," Carey said, putting an arm around her. "You could see she was horribly wounded. I don't understand who did that." "'Who did that?'" cried Aileen. "Why *he* did!" Carey's eyes turned to the machine-gunner, who was picking himself up and retrieving his gun; he was ashy and his plump figure seemed to droop. "No!" Aileen cried, sobbing. "Not him. *Him*." Carey's eyes went to the young fellow with the rifle. He could not sort this out. "The Dutch!" Aileen exclaimed impatiently. "Those two. Him and the girl. I thought I didn't remember what they looked like. But of course I did. I recognized them right away, the minute I heard the shots and peeked over the seat."

Carey supposed he was being exceptionally dense. "You mean, when he was shooting at *him*, he hit Sapphire too, by accident. She was in the way." "He wasn't shooting at *him*. Don't you see, they're all on the same side! The Dutch and the Arabs. They're a gang." He could not follow this reasoning. In his own mind, he had concluded that the tow-headed young man was a security guard or maybe an Interpol agent—there could have been a tip-off on this morning's operation. On Aileen's side, though, spoke the fact that the hijacker, strangely, had been allowed to repossess his gun; he held it with one hand while with the other he pulled up his trouser-leg to examine his calf, which was bleeding. "Yet *somebody* shot our friend there," protested Carey. "Look. Surface wound, probably. I guess they aimed to disable him. Shoot at the legs—good police principle." Aileen shook her head. "Nobody shot him. That was Sapphire. She clawed him. So they killed her." She began to sob again. "Oh, poor darling Sapphire. She gave her life for us."

This was an exaggeration—her Southern fancy tearily doing its embroidery. Yet in the main Aileen's reconstruction of the event and cast of characters was exact, as was swiftly demonstrated when the plane touched down. "Schiphol," declared Van Vliet de Jonge, with a doleful countenance, as the fair strapping fellow and the girl strode ahead to first class, leaving the scowling young Arab with the machine-gun in charge. Almost at once, over the loud-speaker, they heard a woman's voice speaking excellent Nordic English: passengers were to remain in their seats with their seat belts fastened; in due time, a cold snack would be served; those needing to use the toilets were to raise their hands and permission would be given but no paper was to be put in the bowl. Soon a steward came by, distributing extra blankets; the lights dimmed. Outside, dusk was gathering. It was four in the afternoon; they had been in the plane five hours.

As though to help pass the time, the steward, finally, was willing to answer questions. He confirmed that Victor had released the cat from its container but he could not say for what reason. Possibly the animal had been crying. Then he did not know whether the hijacker had kicked the poor cat when it crossed his path, causing it to strike back with its claws, or whether the cat had struck out at him first, sensing an enemy. He favored the latter notion. "*Les chats, vous savez, c'est une race mystérieuse. Très sensibilisée. Surtout les chats pur-sang. On leur prête des pouvoirs occultes.*" Aileen wailed softly. The Bishop blew his nose. There was a silence. "But what happened then, steward?" Charles demanded. "One would like to hear." Badly scratched and perhaps also bitten by the animal, the hijacker had dropped his weapon; that was the metallic clatter they had heard, as the gun struck the chromium of a seat frame. "And the Dutch?" prompted Aileen. "Dutch?" The steward had supposed they were Germans: "*anarchistes de la bande Baader-Meinhof.*" The deputy ruefully set him straight. "*Des hollandais pur-sang, je vous assure.*" At the moment of take-over, it appeared, they had moved in concert with the Arabs and seized the two cabins behind—the woman had a small pistol in her blouse. When the machine-gunner had let his weapon fall, the grenade-carrier must have summoned them. He had been holding two stewardesses in the strategic serving-pantry block at the center of the plane. "*C'est le chef de la bande, paraît-il.*"

Cameron leaned forward. "How long would you say the

gun was lying there before the other thugs intervened? One minute, two?" "Perhaps half a minute, sir." "Umm. Pity Lenz didn't seize the gun while he had the chance." Aileen concurred. "Especially when you think that that was what Sapphire *intended* him to do. She gave him the opportunity, and he failed." "You mustn't attribute design to a cat," put in Sophie sharply. "They have a brain the size of a minute." "Pity the creature wasn't rabid," mused Charles with an elfin grin. "'Rabid'?" said the steward. "*La rage*," said Aileen. "Oh, sir, that has been taken care of. We have given the pirate an anti-tetanus injection." Carey's eyebrows went up.

They wanted to know what had been done with the body. If they stood up, they could see it, still lying in the far aisle, the steward said. The hostesses had wanted to clean the blood off its fur and put it in a box for its master. But the hijackers had refused; they intended the corpse to be left there, as an example. "What monsters," said Aileen. "Don't you think we might ask the Bishop to say a prayer for her?" "No," said Carey.

He wrapped himself in his blanket, pulling it up over his eyes. When he opened them, it was night outside. In the shadowy dimness of the cabin, he perceived Victor, huddled in his long coat, kneeling in the far aisle by his cat's side, keeping vigil. The deputy was awake too and watching. "Antigone," he whispered. Carey nodded.

He had dropped off to sleep again when two figures, one holding a flashlight, appeared—the mustached grenade-carrier and a stewardess. They went along the aisles, stopping here and there to tap a half-awake passenger on the shoulder. It reminded Carey eerily of school dormitory inspection or of the awful night-time summonses that were wont to rouse the men in sick bay. "*Prenez vos affaires. Vous pouvez sortir*," the stewardess was murmuring as she went. The exodus had begun. Up front, the Israeli couple with their wailing baby were being ordered to get a move on. "Out! *Raus! Weg*," the grenadier barked. From the rear cabins, men, women, and children were filing past with their hand baggage, some still struggling into their coats. A woman had forgotten her umbrella. "Later, *madame. Maintenant vous sortez*." Aileen started to rise. "*Pas vous, madame*," the stewardess intervened. So they were separating the sheep from the goats. As the last camera-laden straggler passed through into first class, the lights went on full. Carey saw that he and his party were alone in the cabin. Victor had retreated to his place, up front. Nine little Indians, counting Charles.

In the serving-pantry there was a sudden bustle. The hostesses came forward with trays. The grenadier, yawning, undid his bristling belt and tossed it on a seat like a discarded stage prop. He settled himself and accepted a tray.

Five

A VOICE was speaking to Van Vliet de Jonge in Dutch. They were still at Schiphol. Outside it was full day. He looked up into the pale green eyes, enlarged by thick lenses, of the young man who had shot the cat. "You sleep too soundly, Deputy. Come along now. We want a chat with your honor." They knew him, of course. As he had been saying, Holland was a small country. For his part, he knew the accent of Groningen—not the once-moated city, but the dour, grudge-holding province. This was a lad from the grim Northeast, reared—one could be eighty per cent certain—in a "black stockings" sect of the deepest Protestant dye. The bad teeth, half-bared in a tight sarcastic smile, bore it out: the *gereformeerde kerk* looked on dentistry as devil's work. Henk adjusted his scarf and reluctantly rose. These harsh signs of election did not bode well for a Brabanter from the sweet Catholic land "below the rivers"—current political preferences and class rancors aside.

Mounting the spiral staircase to the second story, in the cockpit he found the Air France captain, his co-pilots, and yesterday's grenadier, now armed with a very realistic large pistol. The hulking northlander—Roodeschool? Stadskanaal? —dismissed the second co-pilot and took his place in the swiveling "navigator's seat" with his back to the instrument panel and his rifle across his big knees. The gunwoman, wearing a woolen peasant blouse and a miniskirt, brought in a tray with five cups of coffee and retired, presumably to guard duty in the adjoining first-class cabin. The interview was brief. Six minutes later, he was back in his place beside Sophie, who was energetically combing her hair.

The talk had gone rapidly, in English—the common language, it transpired, as at any international meeting. He and his friends were hostages. He would be treated as group leader and held responsible for its full cooperation. During the night, negotiations had begun with the criminal government in The Hague. "Why not with the French criminals at the Quai d'Orsay?" Van Vliet had inquired, in Dutch. The question had been ignored. Nor had he been able to discover what demands the hijackers were making. For the moment, they merely wanted a plane, to be supplied by the Dutch, to fly to their next destination with the hostages. "Your government, Deputy, has refused." It was not his government, he objected, with a measure of truth. "Your fraction is the accomplice of the ruling social democrats," retorted the gunwoman, reappearing in the doorway with her coffee-pot. "If Van Vliet de Jonge's fraction voted against the American stooges, they would fall." As this was a fact known to everyone in Holland, he had not denied it. Nor did he feel moved to point out—what would surely be of no interest to these people—that the consequence of such an action would be a government of the Right.

Still, if the Prime Minister—or, more likely, the Minister of Defense—was refusing to give them a plane they craved, it was hardly his fault. In any case, they were knocking at the wrong door. It was the French they ought to have been dealing with. That the 747 was now on Dutch soil was immaterial. Permission to land must have been granted at the request of the French ambassador; that was probably why the pilot had circled so long yesterday, while the request was being considered. Yet between the hijackers and France's representative no dialogue had been opened, though messages had come last night from the control tower that he was at the airport and ready to talk. At least so the co-pilot intervened to say, wearily, out of the corner of his mouth, glancing backward at Van Vliet, as if for help with these intractable people. Van Vliet turned to the rifleman: "*Is dat waar?*" "A ruse," replied that one, with contempt.

Van Vliet shook his head. He was mystified. Why pick on the Dutch? The French, he remarked, were in a position to send them any aircraft they wanted, in exchange for the one they were holding. Even the latest model of bomber, if that were their heart's desire. "*Bien sûr,*" the pilot concurred. "*Mais soyons sérieux. Plutôt un DC-8.*" In any event, as he had been telling the air pirates, they were exhausting themselves here to no purpose; he had only to return them in the Boeing to De Gaulle, where their demand would be studied. "This option does not interest us," the Arab air pirate had answered.

More than once during this puzzling conversation, Van

Vliet had tried to steer it into Dutch. Each time this had brought a scowl from the Arab, which yielded, at any rate, one piece of information: perfect trust did not reign among the confederates. It was the young woman who chiefly roused his curiosity. Was she the northlander's sweetheart or did she "belong" to the Arab? Or was she—despite the coffee service —their boss? If he could have got her to speak Dutch, he might have the first elements of an Identikit portrait. But not only would she not speak it, when she heard *him* speak it to her comrade-at-arms, she put on a blank face, as though waiting to be supplied with a translation. If he had not overheard the pair of them yesterday talking Dutch behind him (unfortunate that he had heard but not listened!), her show of ignorance might have convinced. She was fiercely determined, evidently, not to admit by a word or sign that she shared a mother-tongue with the enemy.

Yet for what reason, unless because he was Dutch, had he been selected as go-between or interlocutor? Were they un-aware that Senator Carey was aboard? It now indeed looked as if yesterday's exploit had been based on a tip-off that a catch of notorious liberals—"your group"—would be on the Teheran flight. Mindful of SAVAK, Van Vliet de Jonge had told no one of the trip except his family and one trusted associate and he assumed that the others too had been reasonably discreet. Yet obviously there had been a leak. The young Iranians in Paris may have innocently boasted of what was afoot to their fellow-students, who would include the usual anarchists and PFLP zealots. Even more probably, the tip had come from SAVAK. Had he not cheerily estimated, in what now seemed another incarnation, that SAVAK's spies would have seen to it that this committee did not arrive unannounced in Teheran? But prevention was the better cure. What could be more fitting than that a "black" secret police should transmit a full Interpol description, down to the flight number, of an incoming party of pinks to a squad of red terrorists? Two birds with one stone, if all went well, that is to say badly. In an hour or so, the Shah and his murderous vizier would be rubbing their hands as they followed the current episode on Iranian television. Still, even SAVAK's information system, being in some degree human, was necessarily imperfect. Since the committee itself had not known, till it met itself yesterday at breakfast, who would be in the party, it was possible that Carey's identity was not yet known to the hijackers.

Eventually, Van Vliet supposed, they would think of conducting a passport check. But at present their attention was centered on the exaction of a getaway plane. Now he understood why he had been summoned: they were looking to him for counsel. "Have you told my government that you have a Dutch parliamentarian aboard?" To his amazement, they had not. "Tell them," he advised, shortly. He knew his countrymen. The stubborn fellow at Defense would resign rather than give up a single training glider *so long as no Dutch interest was involved*. To be told that Prince Philip or the Pope of Rome was among the captives would not budge him. Henk, however, was another story. As it happened, he was a good friend of the Minister's (during a late session they often lifted a glass in the parliamentary bar), but even a mortal enemy, if he sat in the Tweede Kamer, was a vital piece of Holland worth at least a Fokker Friendship to the old boy. "Say that you are holding a member of Her Majesty's Parliament," he had reiterated. Yet, watching the faces cloud over, he saw that he had failed to convince them.

He could not fathom their reluctance. How could it harm their cause to let it be known that a Dutch deputy was aboard? The psychology of terrorists was evidently a closed book to him. Did they fear that the police would storm the plane to free him? He could easily have shown them that the effect on his government would be quite the opposite—an increase in caution. But: "We have heard enough from you." The discussion was over. It was as if an instinct, impervious to reason, warned them against revealing the smallest fact to the enemy, who might find a means to profit.

In a strange way, he was disappointed. Returned to his seat, he felt crestfallen. No doubt it irked him as a lawyer to give sound advice and perceive that it would not be followed: he had begun to look on these malefactors as his clients. Yet, beyond that, there was in him a persistent desire to be helpful, even when this helpfulness, if allowed to have its way, would further some project for which he had no great sympathy. In the present case, an antipathy: he had a distaste for hijackers and hijacking which the interview just terminated had done nothing to modify. Nevertheless, he had found himself "identifying" with these poor brutes—*kapers*, as his countrymen called them, from the old word for privateers—or, rather, with the problem they confronted: the procurement of an escape plane from his old friend and parliamentary colleague. Since he had at once seen the problem's solution in the card at their disposal—himself—it had seemed urgent to get them to play it, and his failure at persuasion was somehow profoundly saddening.

He had a love of solutions and a sometimes fatal generosity in offering them. A footnote in his country's annals might one day tell how in the year 1972, when parlous elections had left Holland without a majority, the radical deputy Van Vliet de Jonge had gone to the Queen with a truly beautiful formula of his own devising to allow Mr. Owl, his political opponent, to assume the reins of government. Like a proud child speeding to the sovereign with the year's first *kievit* egg—a Dutch rite of spring. Juliana was still grateful to him; Beatrix too. He had declined his due guerdon—a post in the Cabinet. And he had no regrets: "*Paete, non dolet,*" as the Stoic's wife said, passing him the sword she had plunged into her Roman heart.

He foresaw no regrets today were the hijackers, thanks to his coaching, to finally get their plane. True, he and his fellow-hostages would be winging off with them on the next leg of a journey which was not bright with promise. But his cerebral part would feel satisfied to have broken a deadlock by the simple application of reason. The alternative was sitting it out here in dreary confinement while each side sought by threats or deceitful promises to sap the other's morale. Since immediate release seemed not to be in question, his preference, on balance, was for a change of scene.

In this, he knew, lay the best and the worst of him: disinterested, eager absorption in the thickening plot of his time and place that went with a certain lightness, not to say levity, of commitment. If he was not small-minded, neither was he—as the palace believed—"large-souled." His attempt to be helpful to the *kapers* could hardly be laid to brotherly love. The feeling that moved him was more like the friendly impatience of a bystander watching a game of bowls. A prompting instinct, such as caused his eyes, during a debate in the House, to drop to his neighbor's half-penciled-in crossword puzzle while the gallery waited for him to claim the floor. At the journalists' *Kring* in Amsterdam, he would stop in late at night, to sit behind the chess players, move on to the match at the billiard table, lend an argument to a literary dispute. Adversary situations drew him, but his interest span was short. Though his life might be at stake, his lively brain was unable to enlist in a heavy-breathing contest between hijackers and lawful authority; he was outside it, above the chessboard, looking down the bishop's diagonal, swiftly noting openings and opportunities, foreseeing moves for either side. In short, like Senator Carey (or the reputation Carey bore), he was an intellectual and political dilettante, lacking the qualities of leadership.

Already wife and children, his dear vested interests, were becoming remote; they belonged to *out there*, beyond the portholes' range of vision, like blips flitting across the radar screen. If Durgie was watching television—which often she did not—they must be anxious or envious. Were they ringing Air France to ask whether *pappie* was listed as a passenger on the big plane they could see on their set? There had been several flights yesterday from Paris to Teheran. And Air France's line, it went without saying, would be busy or unresponsive. Yet from his perspective, as two-thirds of a ghost, his family and the little alarms he might be causing them seemed ghostly themselves, diminished in reality. He could not enter into their feelings, even by conjecture, and his greatest pang of remorse, on their account, came from the thought that he might have bought flight insurance at one of those vending machines at the airport. He had never been inclined to do that and always wondered at the provident souls who could—a safe landing must give rise to mixed emotions in the insured one—but the next time, he now vowed, he would: for ten francs, roughly eight guilders, Durgie might hit the jackpot. Catching himself, he laughed shortly. "The next time"! As a matter of fact, he did not recall seeing such an infernal machine at De Gaulle yesterday; perhaps they had gone out, like complimentary razor blades in the toilets, when the *kapers* came in.

Meanwhile the others had gathered some news of their own. During his absence, the talkative steward had come by; the crew had heard that the first-class passengers were about to be released. "Did those fellows tell you anything about that?" the Bishop called out. He was the only one of the group to seem spry this morning. In the toilets, the electricity was *kapot*, so that the water-closets would not flush and the outlets for electric razors were inoperative. But the Bishop had shaved, with an old-style razor evidently; Van Vliet noticed a curl of shaving cream near his capacious ear, the deafer one. On Carey's chin, there was a dark stubble that matched his mercurial eyebrows. The pastor must have tried to use the Bishop's blade, as some still bleeding cuts and white styptic-pencil marks bore witness. Charles had applied a thick dusting of powder. Victor was sleeping, finally, beneath his overcoat and a heap of blankets, his head burrowing in a pillow. The heating too had ceased to function, and it was cold in the cabin. But the Bishop, in his thick tweeds, was comfortably dressed for the occasion.

In answer to the old man's question, Henk could only shout that negotiations were going on for a Dutch plane: no mention had been made of first-class passengers. But he could report that they were still there; in the "lounge," he had seen them, being served Bloody Marys. A cry went up. Here in Economy, they had had nothing but some weak coffee the steward had brought. "Not even a Danish," sighed Sophie. "Did they give them breakfast up there too?" Aileen demanded, giving his shoulder a peremptory tap. Van Vliet could not say; he had noticed what the Americans called "nibbles" on the service wagon as he edged past, but that information, he decided, was better kept to himself. Angry patches had appeared on Aileen's sharp cheekbones; the little jaw had tightened. He was not especially hungry, and what was gnawing at this poor woman's vitals, he surmised, was principally social envy. It would do none of them harm to miss a meal. Moreover, he would feel a little ashamed, as a well-nourished man, to mention a need of food to hijackers who represented, at least in their own minds, the famished of the earth. Yet if negotiations were going to drag on, the hijackers, he judged, would do well to ask for something to eat for the hostages—a compassionate service the Dutch would not refuse.

A few rows ahead, the young woman now stood on guard, her pistol stuck into the bosom of her blue embroidered blouse. It was up to him, probably, in the interests of general harmony, to voice the suggestion. He cleared his throat, preparing to raise his hand. It went up slowly. He found he had no appetite for making a plea on behalf of these, on the whole, too corpulent bellies. Sophie looked at him inquiringly. But the gunwoman's eyes flicked past his feebly waving hand—she was not going to give him even the briefest attention—and he let it fall, like a flag of surrender. "She didn't see you," said Sophie. "No." He was a craven and grateful to be spared.

Then, by good fortune, the Bishop remembered the cake. He lifted it out of its box, on its paper-lace doily, cut it with the Senator's pocket knife, said grace, and distributed slices. They ate while the hijacker dourly watched, stroking her pistol. "Why, bless me," said the old man. "She may be hungry too." He wrapped a generous slice in his pocket handkerchief, and Sophie bore it forward. "What is this?" said the recipient in a loud, suspicious tone. "Well, it *was* a birthday cake," said Sophie. "Would your friends like some? There's plenty. We must just save a piece for *him*." Her nod indicated Victor, supine under his coverings. "Get back to your seat," replied the hijacker. Without further comment, she slowly ate the cake. The Bishop's gesture had not had any noticeable softening effect.

Once the crumbs had been cleared away, time hung heavy. There was nothing to do but guess about what was happening, and Van Vliet was the best authority the group possessed. "Is your Cabinet meeting?" Sophie wondered. Not the full Cabinet, he thought, but an emergency task force: the Minister of Justice would have been the first to be alerted; he would have called the Prime Minister, the Minister of Defense, and the Minister of Foreign Affairs; they must have met last night and again this morning. "Where?" At the Ministry of Justice, probably, so as not to give the affair undue importance. He himself wondered about the Queen. Had she been told yet? And Bernhard? The consort, he explained, had a keen interest in planes and flying; in addition, he had the title of Inspector General of the Armed Forces. "Does that mean his ideas will be listened to, because he's the Queen's husband? I thought you had a constitutional monarchy." Van Vliet was not prepared to dilate, just now, on the role of the monarchy in present-day Holland. "The Queen is listened to. Like her mother. She's respected, as a person, and strains to be progressive." But the consort, who had the outlook of a business man, was something else. His ideas, if he were to offer any, on what attitude should be taken toward the hijackers, would be conveyed to the Defense Minister and duly tabled, with thanks. "But why the Defense Minister? Why should the armed forces have a voice? When I picture Mr. Schlesinger and the Pentagon, it scares me silly." The vision of his starchy and punctilious friend in the role of Dr. Strangelove was amusing, but Van Vliet saw he had to be patient with this bony, beautiful American who construed everything on the hated paradigm of her own government— "the military industrial complex."

Because, he gently explained, an escape plane, if it were to be furnished, would have to come from the armed forces. "Not KLM?" Certainly not; the decision being weighed was a decision of state, to be implemented from national defense stocks, which could only be drawn on with the Defense Minister's consent. "It touches his budget, you see." A screech announced that Aileen had been listening. "You mean they'll transfer us to a military plane?" "Affirmative," said the Senator. She bridled. "Why, I never heard of such a thing!" Her head turned, looking to others to share her outrage. What did she expect—Prince Bernhard's private plane?

He felt suddenly depressed. The boredom of confinement was beginning to tell. Hell, as Sartre said, was others. Outside, there were no signs of action. The big plane sat by itself, as if in quarantine, evidently because an explosion was feared. Somewhere there must be fire engines, police, ambulances, cameramen, but nothing was visible but the empty tarmac; he could not even make out in which direction the terminal lay. Yet from time to time he could hear other planes taking off; the ordinary course of life had not stopped in deference to the piteous exception.

"Mynheer Van Vliet!" Aileen again. She had been thinking about those art collectors up in first class. "Don't you think you ought to *tell* these people who they are? It's not fair— honestly, is it?—for them to be let go while we sit here with a price on our head because some of us, like the Senator, are celebrities. We have an important job to do, in Iran— doesn't anybody remember?—and they're just idle rich." Carey's pained glance met Van Vliet's. "For Christ's sake, Aileen, change the record." "The Senator doesn't agree," she persisted. "But somebody ought to let them know, before it's too late, that they have better fish to fry than us. It wouldn't hurt those millionaires a bit to be held for ransom. They could hand over their Giorgiones and Titians and priceless hare's fur cups—it's all loot anyway." "Damn it!" begged Sophie. "Keep your voice down." Aileen surveyed the gunwoman. "She's not listening. Besides, I don't care if she does hear. As a revolutionary, she ought to realize the social implications of holding us prisoner while useless members of society go free. I mean, it isn't as if they were invalids or children. I don't see why they should be entitled to my compassion. There has to be some scale of values. We should tell these liberation fighters or whatever they call themselves that holding this committee as hostages is giving direct aid to the Shah of Iran."

Van Vliet noticed that Sophie beside him was quivering. "President Simmons, I don't understand you," she exclaimed, turning around and speaking in a low trembling voice. "Are you prepared to buy our freedom in exchange for information we can furnish, or think we can furnish, on some helpless fellow-mortals? People we don't even know. What gives us the right? The word for that is delation." The vials of Sophie's scorn, emptied on the older woman, produced no effect. Aileen appeared to consider before replying and, when she did, her tone was tranquil, as though she were interviewing a delinquent student in her office. "I don't feel it would be a betrayal, if that's what you're implying, Sophie. Most of us have made sacrifices to join this committee. We've invested our time, our power of judgment, and even our savings in this work. Our loyalty should be to that, surely, rather than to a tour of millionaires with whom I, for one, have nothing in common. Perhaps you feel you have. But I don't want to insist. Shall we put it to a vote?"

"Unnecessary," observed the Senator. "You've rendered the question moot." He nodded toward the hijacker, who was heading with a rapid step toward the first-class cabin. She spoke into the inter-com, and in a minute the shorter Arab, the one with the submachine gun, replaced her on guard. It looked as if Aileen had played the informer with determination and success. And Van Vliet could not wholly dislike her for it; he felt a kind of pity for the democratic demon in the little woman that had been roused to fury by the news of Bloody Marys ahead. Besides, she had sinned to no avail, probably, if benefit to herself had been her motive: the millionaires' loss was unlikely to be her gain. Instead, thanks to her intervention, both groups now qualified to be held as hostages, which meant that the hijackers would be requiring a roomier getaway craft.

Shortly, as if to test the thesis, a bus drew up. Cameron, from his window, was the first to sight it. First-class passengers were indeed being released. But Cameron's view was obstructed by a wing; he was unable to see much more than the feet and legs of some of the lucky ones and the duty-free shopping bags many were still carrying. Soon, though, the gunwoman showed her face again and beckoned to Van Vliet. He was marched once more up to the cockpit, past the first-class cabin. Many seats were now empty, but some contained passengers: Aileen's "millionaires," manifestly, to judge by the display of camel's hair and crocodile and the American tongue being spoken. The cabin was in disarray, strewn with abandoned newspapers and magazines. One lady appeared to have fainted and was being given smelling-salts by a stewardess as Van Vliet was hurried up the stairs.

How the winnowing out had been effected, he could only conjecture—probably with the aid of the crew's manifest; the tour would have been booked as a unit, he supposed. His politician's eye swiftly canvassed them—he noted the two minked women whom he had seen talking with the pastor in the departure lounge and who, he now perceived, were mother and daughter. The sexes were about equally divided; the median age was perhaps fifty, and altogether they numbered eleven. With "Mr. Charles," still back in Economy and dozing, that gave a total of twelve and, with themselves, twenty. Plus the crew. Quite a party. On the whole, he was not sorry that Aileen had "fingered" the collectors; misery loved company, and their own band of liberals could stand some diversification. Still, a last-minute increment of eleven, more than doubling the number of hostages, must be demanding some serious readjustment in their captors' thinking. He would be surprised if they had not sharply debated among themselves about taking on the additional burden. Cupidity, in St. Paul's words, was the root of all evil; the temptation to take on the collectors might have sowed the first seeds of disunity—not necessarily a welcome development.

In the cockpit, the tall northlander and the co-pilot, wearing headphones, were testing a recording device, while the Arab was busy with his grenades and a coil of wire, which he ran along the entry partition, as if readying the plane for demolition. In these menacing conditions, Van Vliet was to make a tape, he learned—in Dutch, to be relayed by radio to his government, urging prompt compliance with the latest demand. It was interesting that they were not inviting him to make a direct broadcast—a sign of mistrust he found flattering to his courage. He was curious to hear what the "latest demand" consisted of, and, true to form, the confederates hesitated. "Tell him," said the woman finally. "His knowledge cannot hurt us." The Groningener complied. They wanted a helicopter capable of transporting thirty persons. "And your lying government has answered that it does not have a helicopter of such dimensions."

Van Vliet inwardly whistled. "It is not a lie," he remarked, after a moment, concealing his surprise. Having served on a parliamentary committee of liaison with the armed forces, he could assure them that no helicopter in the Dutch squadrons had a capacity of more than ten persons. "Can we believe this?" "Yes." From their faces he saw that they were accepting his word and he pressed his advantage. Why a helicopter? Why not a regular plane? "This is not your concern," the Groningener told him. "You will simply make the tape as we instruct you." But this meant then that The Hague was aware that he was their prisoner. "Our guest, Deputy," corrected his compatriot, with a tight-lipped smile. "So you told them?" "We confirmed that you were on board."

The inference was clear. Durgie, watching television or opening her morning paper, had feared for him. And he was glad, he fondly recognized. The wise girl must have telephoned to the Prime Minister's wife, who was her friend: "Elisabeth, tell your husband. I think Henk is in that plane." "We have confirmed," resumed the *kaper*. "But the fascists have asked for proof. So we send them your voice." "Why not my ear?" Van Vliet quipped. "All in good time, Deputy. For the present, we shall let them hear your melodious voice."

Van Vliet considered. The strange thought struck him that what his government must really be asking for was proof that he was alive. A tape could not supply that. On receiving it, the cautious legalists in The Hague would feel justified in asking for further evidence, thus prolonging the wait. "If you will allow me, I will read first from the morning's weather report. You will have had it, surely, from the control tower." The *kapers* looked at each other. "That will be helpful," the woman agreed in a grudging tone. It would be too much to expect thanks.

He spoke to the recording instrument in the pilot's box, announcing the winds and the morning's temperature and the prediction of fog. Next he attested that he was Van Vliet de Jonge, that he and his fellow-hostages were unharmed and receiving correct treatment. But their continuing safety, he had been assured, depended on the delivery of a helicopter of the type already specified no later than 2:00 P.M. Interference with its fueling and departure would not be tolerated, and attempts to "tail" it would have serious consequences: "My greetings." To his own critical ear, he sounded brainwashed, like the Patricia Hearst girl or an American POW bowing from the waist. But no variation on the prescribed text was permitted. His suggestion that he might take the occasion to appeal for some food for the hostages was vetoed; the Arab explained that the authorities could seize the humanitarian pretext to introduce a paralyzing gas into a sandwich container or coffee-urn. Only in regard to the two o'clock deadline had they agreed to a modification. Their original deadline had been noon. They did not say—and he did not inquire—what horrors lay in store if the deadline was not met. But the methodical wiring of the cabin had lent insistence to his argument that his government, typically slow and ponderous in its deliberations, would need more time.

This was a fact, but there was another pertinent fact that second thoughts caused him to withhold. On hearing the text read to him, he had been strongly tempted to offer a bit of advice: "When you next speak with the control tower, you must tell them that you believe my government when it says it doesn't have such helicopters. But then remind them of the NATO air forces." Then he had buttoned his lips firmly, forcing that counsel back. It was true that the big German brother, across the border, had helicopters capable of holding at least fifty; only last fall, with a pang of small-country envy, he had watched squads of specialists emerge from them during NATO maneuvers. But were he to voice the suggestion, as a terse word to the wise men in his government, he would have become the hijackers' ally; worse still, he would appear as such to the ministers in session. The hijackers might be sadistic enough to invite him to make it *in propria persona* on their tape. If he declined, they might shoot him, though that would be an imprudence at this stage, which would cost them a bargaining card (a fair Jack of Diamonds) with Her Majesty's government. But whoever's voice print was on the NATO reminder, Den Uyl and the rest would recognize the brain of Van Vliet de Jonge behind it, and he was too cowardly, he discovered, to face the judgment those good fellows would pass on him. To appear as privy counselor to a ruthless gang of terrorists was different from his cherished picture of himself, and he wondered whether the crisis was not opening for inspection a split or fatal crack in his character like a hidden "fault" deep in geology.

In any case, the Cabinet did not need to have the NATO air forces recalled to its memory. His stiff-necked friend at Defense was well aware of those big whirring birds nested on the other side of the Rhine. Having been told that a Dutch parliamentarian was among the captives, he must be already overcoming his resistance to borrowing from the German neighbor. In the gloomy conference chamber at Justice, he would make the decision, swallowing his national pride in a single gulp. In his mind's eye, Van Vliet already saw the convulsive movement of the spare gullet and prominent Adam's apple as it went painfully down.

But then argument was likely to be needed to convince the fellow-ministers—Dutch statesmanship required that all sides of every question be examined with due care, and the greater the urgency the more your stubborn Lowlander refused to be hurried—and still lengthier argument to convince the partner at Bonn that a loan under the circumstances was appropriate. "*Bitte, sagen Sie mir*, how does NATO enter?"—had Holland's defenses, perchance, been penetrated by a Warsaw Pact force? If the German Defense people wanted to be sticky, they could declare it their duty, *ja, sicher*, to consult the supreme NATO command, i.e., the American general in Brussels, who in turn would have to consult Washington. And if Den Uyl, foreseeing all this, were to appeal directly to Schmidt, in the name of good social-democratic relations, to get him out of this pickle, Schmidt would no doubt agree to do the favor, resigning himself to eventual questions in the Bundestag. Even then there would remain matters to be chewed over: for example, whether German pilots familiar with that class of helicopter could be borrowed from the base in Aachen—better not, in view of the risks; in Den Uyl's place, Van Vliet would ask for Dutch volunteers.

At best, assuming that Helmut was in his chancellery, in a positive mood, and available to speak to Joop, the "decision-making process" would surely take an hour or two, to which must be added the flight time from Aachen, another hour— a giant helicopter would not be much speedier than an automobile. And already it was ten o'clock. Counting up the hours of uncertainty lying ahead for his unfortunate government, Henk rested his head on his seat back and softly groaned. He deeply repented the vagary that had sent him winging off to Iran and left the group in The Hague (assembling even now, he supposed, to listen to the obviously dictated tape) in the humiliating quandary of going next door with hat in hand to save "the esteemed delegate's" skin. He felt a sympathy, bordering on love, for his friend at the Defense helm; the others would disperse to their various departments, but his ordeal would not end till he knocked, once again, on the neighbor's door, returning the borrowed craft like a housewife's cup of sugar. In comparison, Henk recognized, his own state of mind was tranquil. Whatever was going to happen was beyond his control. No lives depended on his decisions. Ideally irresponsible, a captured pawn, he could only muse and conjecture.

In his absence, he discovered, a silver flask of whiskey, belonging to the Bishop, had been circulating. The good man had saved some for him. He swallowed the last dram and let his mind run on the interesting question: why a helicopter, why not a regular plane? The answer could only lie in the terrain that awaited them. Either a small air-strip—"liberated" from some innocent flying club—with too short a runway to take even a Friendship, or else an open field or stretch of pasture. On the screen of his memory, he sought to project the countless films on the war in Vietnam he had watched on television; brushing aside MIGs, B-52s, falling bombs, bomb craters, screaming peasants, napalm canisters, napalm victims, at length he saw the big American "Hueys" descending on rice fields, i.e., on soft marshy ground. A small helicopter could land in a jungle or on a mountain top, but the big fellows had needed space.

The Senator no doubt could tell him for sure, or Sophie from her time as a war correspondent, but it was a quirk he treasured in his character to think out a problem whenever possible unaided, using only his memory and his reasoning power, as though he were the last human on earth. . . . So (he reflected, closing his eyes) the presumption was that the gang's prepared hideaway was not in a mountainous or even hilly area, not tucked away in a narrow secluded valley, but, rather, in flat country. The flying range of helicopters excluded desert sands—there were none in Europe, mercifully—and populous farm areas could be ruled out because of inquisitive neighbors. Flat terrain, sparsely inhabited. He considered the empty plain of Apulia, the huge tableland he had inspected one splendid late August while leading a Common Market delegation to the Agricultural Fair in Bari—the Fiera del Levante, it had been called. To wake up in that somber country would almost repay being a hostage: he could compose a Horatian ode. But the whiskey on an empty stomach must be addling him. Antique Apulia was nearly as distant as a stork's winter quarters in Africa. A wide lonely northern beach, such as had served for commando operations during the Second War? He rubbed his jaw. No. Hardly at this season. All along, he had perceived, like a looming fatality, that Holland was going to answer the bill of specifications. Holland, of all places, and the Dutch pair would have known it. Not the industrial tulip fields, or the thickly populated south and center, not farm-rich Friesland either, but the polders. Most likely, the New Polder. Flevoland: Eureka! He let out a cry. "What's the matter?" said Sophie. The jubilant sound issuing from him had contained a measure of pain.

The others were turning to him too. "Anything wrong?" said Carey. "Are you all right, sir?" inquired the Bishop. He was all right, Van Vliet supposed—at least not all wrong. Everything fitted. He knew at last why they were here. But how could he tell these people that tonight they would be sleeping on a polder, when none of them, probably, knew what a polder was? Some kind of mattress, most of them would think. As usual with foreigners, he would have to explain that a polder was land reclaimed from the sea. They were on one now: Schiphol. The word meant "ship-hole." The airport occupied what was formerly a wet marshy hole, made, according to legend, by a sinking ship. Wherever they looked, there had once been water. A hundred feet below them sails had billowed, and naval battles had been fought. A good third of Holland, you could say, was nothing but a collection or accretion of polders. That was why there were dikes. And, once upon a time, windmills. Nowadays their duties were performed by pumping-stations, draining off salt water so that the sea floor could be filled in and leveled and afterwards maintained in a dry state. Over the centuries, aided by a natural silting-in process, Holland had been encroaching on the sea's territory. Or, as your Dutchman liked to say, it had been "won back" from the sea.

"Jolly interesting," said Cameron, peering out the window. "Must say I never knew the extent of the operation. Though of course I'm familiar with the Zuyder Zee project." That was not a polder, Van Vliet de Jonge pointed out; in a sense, it was the opposite—a man-made lake. But from the Zuyder Zee project, polders had resulted. Cameron nodded. "Increased your arable land area." That indeed was the point. But they were slow to perceive the relevance; arable land was not created overnight. Once the sea floor had been pumped dry, it had to be de-salted, then planted with grasses for sheep-grazing. Eventually, when the sheep had done their work, it would turn into farmland, indistinguishable from the rest of Holland.

"Wonderful engineers, your people," the Bishop summed up. "Now what leads you to think that these people will be taking us to a polder, as you call it? Funny word, by the way, isn't it? Any connection with poltergeists?" "A poltergeist, Gus, is a noisy spirit," remonstrated the Senator. "From the German, *Polter*, meaning uproar, plus *Geist*." The Bishop smote his head. "I'm old, James, forgive me. I must be losing my German, along with my teeth and my wits. And years back, don't you know, I had occasion to look into poltergeists. There's a school in the Church that thinks they're true cases of diabolical possession. We had a parish in the diocese—in Joplin, it was—where they claimed to have one of those prankish spirits in the organ loft; struck up ribald tunes in the middle of a baptism or when the Altar Guild was doing the flowers. Rector wanted to exorcise it with bell, book, and candle. Well, I had to put my foot down. Turned out in the end, wouldn't you know it, to be the organist's wife. My Rachel sensed it right off, the minute she laid eyes on her. 'There's your poltergeist,' she said." "Sex!" interrupted Aileen. "She was sex-starved. I expect your organist had been too busy pawing the choir boys to take care of his spouse's needs. We had a case like that at Lucy Skinner. Malicious mischief in the chemistry laboratory. Buildings and Grounds caught the woman at it. An instructor, frustrated lesbian. We had to let her go, of course. . . ."

Van Vliet de Jonge waited. "The polders," the Bishop recalled finally. "You were going to tell us, sir?" Now that he had their ears again, Van Vliet proceeded. Northeast of Amsterdam lay the two most recent examples, popularly known as the Old Polder and the New Polder, both creations of the North Sea wall or dike, which had transformed the Zuyder Zee into a fresh-water lake. The "old" one dated back to the thirties, though work on it had been halted during the War and the Nazi occupation; it was more interesting than the "new" one because it had incorporated an island—pre-war maps still showed it that way, surrounded by water, in the middle of the "Southern Sea"—with an old fishing town and trees and what was for Holland a hill, on which stood a little church that now housed a so-called shipwreck museum. But it could hardly be interesting to the hijackers, for the simple reason that it was settled, though as yet somewhat sparsely in comparison with the rest of Holland. Whereas the New Polder, to the south of it, was virtually empty—virgin territory populated mainly by shore birds. The New Polder—Flevoland—was Holland's Alaska. Roads had been laid out, an industrial town-complex projected, and a small airport too, if he recalled right, but, except for the roads, all that booming development was still a blueprint on the drawing-boards of the planners. Factories, cinema, shopping-center, art gallery, angular modern church lay in the future; the sheep had vanished, but cows had not yet taken their places. Here and there, barns, with typical orange roofs, had gone up or were in the process of construction from prefabricated elements, but the spick-and-span homes and bright flower gardens that would follow were no more than a prophecy, borne out by occasional surveyor's sticks in the sedgy waste. When he had last driven through, with his family on a Sunday, bird-watching, they had noted a few isolated new farmhouses—pioneers. By now, other enterprising colonists, encouraged by government subsidies, would have made the trek and set up house under strictly uniform rooftrees as prescribed in the specifications of the central planning authority on holdings limited by law to thirty hectares: "About seventy-five acres," supplied the Senator. "The wide open spaces." And in such a dark-green-frame, neighborless house, with clothes-pole staked outside, like a settler's claim, the *kapers'* confederates were surely installed with arms and provisions to withstand a siege. . . .

"Do you believe it?" Aileen exclaimed, turning to her neighbor. "Sounds reasonable," said the Senator. "Can't think of a better explanation of why they should be wanting a chopper." He had only one objection: if a hideaway had been set up on this New Polder, why had the pilot, following the take-over, continued on a southward course, in the direction of Rome and North Africa? Van Vliet had considered this too. His answer, not wholly satisfying, was to conjecture that the polder had been prepared as a fall-back position: the hijackers' original hope had been to be welcomed in Libya or Algiers probably. Perhaps there had been disagreement among them, the Dutch pair from the start favoring the polder solution, where familiarity with the terrain and the ways of the "host" government would give them ascendancy, while the Arabs, naturally, plumped for North Africa. "Will we ever know?" sighed Sophie. "If we come out alive," Van Vliet promised her. One of his main interests in survival, he found, was precisely to know the peripeties of the drama. He did not want to die in a state of mystification.

Gradually the group fell silent, as though overcome by despondency, hitting them one by one like a powerful drug. Each sat with his private thoughts. As he brooded, Van Vliet's nostrils made out a faint new smell. The cat, he feared: Sapphire. Before long, she would stink to high heaven. And what if he had been wrong in his expectations, what if the German helicopter did not come after all? By an act of will, he refrained from looking at his watch. But it must be almost noon; in The Hague and Amsterdam, deep church bells would soon be ringing. Two hours left. The common word "deadline" was taking on an uncommon significance. He thought of Faust. At two o'clock, punctually, if the helicopter failed to materialize, would the execution of hostages begin?

He heard the Bishop loudly clear his throat and hoped he was not going to lead them in prayer. But instead of addressing the Saviour, he was turning to Henk. "You mentioned a shipwreck museum, sir. Why don't you tell us about that? It will help us pass the time, don't you know." Henk groaned at the old man's simplicity: the last thing they should be wanting was to make time pass swiftly. But the others were nodding; like children at bedtime, they were ready to hear a story. A fairy-tale, laid in polderland, whose herald or bard he had become. "Please," urged Sophie. "Entertain them. They're scared, and you talk so well." "The Arabian Nights," remarked Carey. "Right on, friend."

Henk obliged. The Zuyder Zee museum, to give it its proper name, on the former island of Schokland, though intended for scholars and specialists, had become a popular excursion spot for Dutch families; his children preferred it to the Tropical Museum, Rembrandt's House, the Torture Museum in The Hague, and even to Aartis, the famous Amsterdam zoo with Prince Bernhard's new elephant house. It was the children who had named it the shipwreck museum. Though the cases contained all kinds of archaeological materials recently dug up on the island, what interested them was not the bones of prehistoric animals or neolithic axes but the finds made when the pumps had dried out the sea floor. Carcasses of sunken ships had been uncovered, ribbed hulls and bony masts, curving prows like necks; 156 vessels had been yielded up by the Zuyder Zee. On the hilly grounds, overlooking what was now fresh water, entire gruesome specimens—lessons in ship's anatomy—were on display. It was as though a blanket had been drawn back from Father Neptune's bed to disclose a marine graveyard. The skeletal ships had gone to eternal rest, like the ancient Egyptians and the Etruscans, with their familiar household objects for company: cooking utensils, tableware, saws, bolts and nails, cannonballs, pipe-bowls, shoes, buckles, buttons. "Doubloons?" suggested Sophie. Henk did not recall any in the showcases—probably the Nazis had got to them first—but there were Dutch coins of course in plenty, some surprisingly recent, with Queen Wilhelmina's portly head. And a curious find had been the skeleton of a drowned fisherman with coins lying beside it—circa 1600—that must have fallen out of a trusty breeches' pocket slowly eaten away by the sea.

"Shoes, you said," mused the Senator. "Wooden, of course?" "Isn't this wonderful, Gus?" cried the pastor. "The romance of the sea. Full fathom five." Van Vliet de Jonge shook his head. The interesting thing about the shipwreck museum, he confided, was its lack of romance. The detritus of a commercial people brought to light by the pumps belonged to the same industrious family as the pumps. The long salty immersion had failed to effect a metamorphosis into something rich and strange. The shards of crockery and rusty pieces of metal were stoutly recognizable, still, in their function of use-objects—as though a sumptuary law of the lowland sea had decreed against extravagance of form or fancifulness of hue in the changes wrought by the element. "Why do you keep putting your country down?" Aileen objected. She was sure there must be wonderful old Delft patterns on the china. Van Vliet shrugged. Sailing ships had not used Delft but rough earthenware and wooden bowls, as was known from the characteristically detailed inventories that had gone down with them to a watery grave. The contents of Davy Jones's locker, as laid bare by the Dutch engineering genius, ran to such "finds" as a cargo of late eighteenth-century codfish, tidily decapitated for the market.

"Sailors' knitting needles?" hazarded Carey. Van Vliet turned in his direction, startled. Here was one who understood. Their minds were meeting, as if in connivance, over the heads of the others. "Any trace of a captain's parrot?" "I should hardly think so, Senator," put in Cameron. "Bird bones and feathers would decompose quite rapidly in salt water."

"Have you written a poem about that museum?" Aileen wondered. Again Henk was startled; her perceptions were sharper than one would have guessed. "The Mariner's Knitting Needle" was one of the best-known pieces in his first collection of verse. "Recite it for us, why don't you?" "Oh, yes, do," they struck up, in choir. But he found himself demurring. He was hesitant to make his poetic self known to the other man in the presence of all these *figurants*. "Then the Senator can give us one of *his* poems," Aileen went on. He met Carey's eyes. No. The spark that had passed between them was male in gender and private. "He writes in *Dutch*, dear lady," reproved Mr. Charles. "Like his grandfather." There, of course, it was, the always valid excuse of his hermetic language; mournful experiences had taught him the truth of the saying that poetry was untranslatable. "Well, recite *something*," said Aileen. "Don't you know any poems in French or English?"

Van Vliet was tempted. In his well-stored memory, ready to hand, lay a poetic prose fragment on the shipwreck theme. By the Japanese poet Bashō (1644–1694), in an English rendering. The poet had made a journey to the eastern provinces of *his* islands; he stood on a precipice looking down to the shore of the Inland Sea, where a famous battle had taken place, in which the young lord Yoshitsune had vanquished the Taira, and all their people had perished. Standing on the historic precipice, the scene of Yoshitsune's downhill rush, the poet pictured the ancient battle and the splendid finery of the warrior court sinking to the sea bottom. On the mournful promontory of Schokland, Van Vliet had more than once declaimed the passage to Durgie and the children. Now he raised his head and began. "'The great confusion of the day, together with other tragic incidents of the time, rose afresh in my mind, and I saw before me the aged grandmother of the young emperor taking him in her arms, his mother carrying him on her shoulders, his legs pitifully tangled in her dress, and all of them running into a boat to escape the onslaught of the enemy. Various ladies of the court followed them, and threw into the boat all kinds of things—rare musical instruments, for example —wrapped in sheets and quilts. Many things of value, however, must have fallen overboard—imperial food into the sea for the fish to feed upon—'" Suddenly, he could not go on; a lump had come into his throat and tears to his eyes. "'The compacts,'" Carey's rich voice prompted: "'. . . and ladies' vanity boxes on to the sand to be quite forgotten among the grass.'" Van Vliet resumed: "'This is probably why, even today after a thousand years, the waves break on the beach with such a melancholy sound.'"

There was a soft clapping of hands. The Bishop wiped his eyes. Henk's were now dry. He was moved by the fresh proof of a kinship with the American Senator but more confirmed than surprised. In the back of his mind, he must have wagered that Carey would know the Japanese poet too. He had brought out his bit of Bashō—from "Travels of a Well-worn Satchel"—like a broken coin or a single earring in an old tale, on the bold premise that Carey, if he cared to, would produce the earring's mate, the other half of the coin. And it had happened; the brothers, long separated (had Henk, the cadet, been stolen at birth by a *kabouter* and spirited to Brabant?), had recognized each other across the gulf of an aisle. Yet the witnesses of their mutual recognition, far from being wonderstruck by the marvel, seemed to feel that it was only natural that two poet-legislators should be acquainted with the same "secret" author and go on spouting him together like "To be or not to be."

The wonder came from another source. Unnoticed, the Arab guard had moved closer during the recitation. He now touched Van Vliet's elbow. "I hear this poem before. Yes. Many times. From a Japanese comrade—Japanese Red Army." Old Tennant was the first to recover his wits. "You know Japanese? How clever of you. Such a difficult language. We used to go there, porcelain-hunting, my friend and I, between the wars. Staying in the charming Japanese inns, where they took such good care of us—" "No," interrupted the Arab. "He translate." "Into Arabic? Dear me!" "English. Japanese know only English. Not Arab tongues, not French." "*Vous êtes francophone, monsieur?*" Aileen asked, adopting a social tone too.

"Yes. No. For us, French is colonial tongue." His face darkened. "And you, Deputy, how you know this poem? My comrade love it very much. He love this Yoshitsune." The gaze turned on Van Vliet was accusatory. In the face of that scowl—and of the submachine gun swinging from the plump shoulder—he felt unable to explain how he had come into possession of the "poem," which in fact was a travel sketch in prose. From the Arab's point of view, he had stolen it, he supposed, in his character of colonialist. And actually he could not remember where and how he had acquired the little Penguin Classic, with a wash drawing of Bashō, wearing a sort of nightcap, on the cover—probably in an airport bookstall. "How you know it?" the Arab repeated. In his terms, of course, he had the right to ask; he had established his own claim to those lines—they had come to him, by inheritance, from a comrade-at-arms. With compassion, Van Vliet pictured the circumstances: a training camp in Lebanon or Syria, tents or improvised barracks, long, cold desert nights, the moon, a homesick Japanese youngster wrapped in a burnoos or army blanket, chattering of a feudal warrior-hero betrayed, in the end, by his wicked half-brother. He looked for a soft answer to turn away wrath. The gruffness and fat were misleading; this was a youth, not a full-fledged man. "I think I must have found the book in a shop." Diplomatically he avoided the mercantile word "bought." "And you must not be surprised. We Dutch are a curious people and we are curious about Japan, which has much in common with Holland." "Sea people," said the Arab, nodding. "Sea people are imperialistic. River people not so much." Having laid down the general statement, he showed his white teeth in a large, quite friendly smile. Contact had been made.

"And your comrade?" asked Sophie. "Where is he now?" "In prison," the Arab said curtly. "They torture him." The pastor made a clucking noise indicative of sympathy. "Who?" "The Israeli." "Come now," Aileen protested. "The Israelis don't torture prisoners." "You ought to qualify that, Miss Simmons," put in the pastor, with a quick inter-faith smile for the Arab. "We don't *know* that they don't." Charges to that effect, he reminded her, had been made by the Syrians before the UN. "Charges aren't proof," she retorted. "I'll take the Israelis' word any day over the Syrians'." "I'd *prefer* to take their word," said the pastor. "I guess we all would. I mean, as a Christian, I don't want to think that anybody is torturing anybody." "What does that *mean*, Reverend?" Aileen said irritably. "Why 'as a Christian'?" The Reverend gave one of his boyish laughs. "Heck, I'm all tangled up. What I'm trying to say is that if we do incline to take the Israelis' word, it's not because we don't believe the Syrians." "Then what *is* it, man?" exclaimed Cameron. The Bishop held out an oar to his floundering disciple. "Frank means that our faith teaches us not to be over-ready to believe the worst of our fellow-men, whoever they are. In charity, until we know more, he would like to give the Israelis the benefit of the doubt."

The Arab had moved off—out of hearing, Van Vliet trusted. He wished the Americans would close the debate or adjourn it sine die. But Aileen, like a wailing echo, persisted. "I never heard that the Israelis were torturing Japanese prisoners, did you, Senator Jim?" "Let's leave it that they're just torturing Syrians—all in the family. You'd like that better, wouldn't you? And now be quiet, can't you? Our friend's flash point may be lower than you guess."

Van Vliet's fondness for the Senator was increasing by leaps and bounds. Aileen and the dominie, in their obliviousness, were illustrating the worst of what he had heard of the American character. A people given to argumentation, someone had said. And, whatever the subject, the debate was always between themselves—as though only their own opinions counted—and was settled when they reached a conclusion or simply got tired, as the world had watched them do in Vietnam. At least Sophie had held her peace; perhaps, being Jewish, she lacked the authority to pontificate conferred on the others as a birthright. No one had asked him his opinion, but his work with Amnesty had convinced him that all prisoners were tortured; the difference was one of degree. Prison itself was a torture, and especially excruciating to violent revolutionaries of today's school, who lacked the patience of the old revolutionaries; they could not accept incarceration as a stage, like puberty, in their political development. This young gunman, for example, would never be able to "mature" quietly, pent up in a Western jail while awaiting trial by authorities whose legitimacy he did not recognize. To him and his comrades, detention was per se unjust.

In that context, the committee's "mission" to Iran must appear as the height of frivolity—in the stern eyes of actionists a punishable offense. For this young hijacker, surely, the Shah's crimes against humanity were of minimal interest in comparison with the *fact* of his comrade's detention in an Israeli jail. Not to mention the honor roll of other comrades ripe for liberation: the Price sisters, held by the English, Andreas Baader, Ulrike Meinhof, Gudrun Esslin, confined in Helmut's cells, the adjutants of "Carlos" in Giscard's hands. . . . And no committee of Western liberals felt the call to investigate their conditions of detainment, though the courtroom in Stuttgart was only an hour's flight away. Instead, as the hijackers would see it, the conscience of the West was busy looking the other way, at the mote in the Shah's eye.

Henk was not sure he saw it in quite that light himself. But they had a point. One might not concur in the notion that violence in self-ordained hands was above the "bourgeois" law, but did it follow that agents of terror had forfeited all their human rights when they treated themselves as sacred instruments? That indeed seemed to be the prevailing assumption in liberal-minded circles. The capture of a terrorist could hardly be expected to produce universal grief, yet the usual reaction "Good riddance," of which he too had occasionally been guilty, had its own barbarity.

As for the charge of frivolity, you could find considerable evidence of it in this ill-starred expedition. To be honest, he had been aware from the start that curiosity had played a leading part in his decision to join: the lure of the bazaars, carpets, miniatures, minarets, rose water in the cookery, Shiraz, Persepolis if there was time. Curiosity too about the Americans— where did such a group fit in their system?—desire to know Carey in a working relationship; speculations about the Shah and his consort. And he had probably hoped for a poem or two as a by-product.

Yet he felt no strong urge to condemn himself for impurity of motives; if a good deed was able to embrace a few stolen pleasures, so much the better. He was no Calvinist. Besides, in the committee's defense, it could be argued that liberal observers could not be present in all the world's jails and courtrooms simultaneously; unlike God, the liberal was limited by ubiety. Nevertheless, why pick on the Shah? If the truth were known, Henk feared, Reza Pahlavi's enormities had been chosen for this group's attention not just because he had an attractive country with an agreeable winter climate but for a still less pardonable motive: his regime was an easy target. Every good soul was opposed to torture, but it suited the Western soul's book to be able to attest to it in a distant land ruled by an oil monarch who was neither friend nor foe. A foe would not admit your committee, and to find fault with a friend would give pain. If your committee were to find evidence of torture in Israel, it would meet with little sympathy for its "courage" on its return. And if it failed to find evidence, it would be accused of conducting a whitewash. For liberals, the Shah was ideal; only his ambassadors would write angry letters to the newspapers. And his victims, always described as youths of good middle-class families and of respectable political antecedents, were ideal victims from a liberal point of view—guilty of nothing more than advocacy. The only embarrassment, for the committee, would be to discover a few terrorists among them—unlikely, as domestic terrorists were executed there with great promptitude.

Henk sighed. Involuntarily, he looked at his watch. Fifteen minutes before one. He hoped that these young bandits were not going to become his surrogate conscience for the duration, however that was to be reckoned, in hours, days, or weeks. It occurred to him that he might be experiencing in his own person a thing he had read about with slight disgust in the newspapers: the incredible tendency on the part of hostages— bank tellers, air stewardesses, motherly middle-aged passengers —to "see the good side" of their kidnappers: "They behaved to us like perfect gentlemen," "He was as sweet as he could be." Some carried it to the point of actually falling in love with them; he remembered the Swedish bank employee who greeted her release by announcing her engagement to the leading criminal. Henk would not say that his own symptoms were in any way amorous. Nor did he think that he was in the process of being converted to a terrorist outlook: observing terror at close quarters, he felt more than ever the futility and waste of it. But, being at close quarters, he could not fail to glimpse their point of view, which caused him to turn about and look at his own party with freshened eyes.

Yet he was feeling something else: pity for the hijackers. Their brief life-expectancy moved him as he studied the moony countenance of the machine-gunner, the soft baby-fat cheeks and incipient dewlaps. Within a year, in all likelihood, this boy would be dead; prison would only be an unwelcome reprieve— if held too long, he would hang himself. There were no active middle-aged terrorists or grizzled retired terrorists. He was a warrior, born to a short life, like the sulky Achilles or his friend's idol Yoshitsune. And, whatever he had been taught in his training camp, he would not really expect his ideas to live after him. Today's arch-revolutionaries had no faith in a future life for their ideas; it was gone, like the Christian faith in God's design.

If, thanks to this calfish specimen, Henk's own days or minutes were now numbered, at least he had had his full share of life's rewards and amusements. The fact that he had just celebrated, after a fashion, his thirty-eighth birthday (where, by the way, was that magazine with the horoscope?) suddenly seemed rather indecent, an actuarial disproportion that was like being overweight in a time of world hunger. And the pity he felt for the *kapers*, even that brute of a woman, was sharpened by irritation with the sheer folly of their enterprise. The optimum result they could hope for would be to gain the release of a few fellow-terrorists, to engage in more hijackings, daring raids, and kidnappings—a vicious circle, for most would be shot or returned to jail. The ransom money they might extort could only serve to finance a new round of suicidal operations; unlike the normal criminal, they knew of no other use for it. A food distribution, were they to include it in their demands, would turn into a grotesque scene from Brueghel.

Could reason make them see the vicious circle they were spinning in? That they were all doomed to violent and pointless extinction, on the model of their hero, Che? They would hardly be open to dissuasion at this stage. It would be pointless to make the effort, even if he were summoned again. A plea coming from him addressed to their own self-interest would not be recognized as such, however feelingly it was expressed.

But later a time might come. If they got their helicopter and were put down with their freight of captives on the lonely polder, a new chapter could open. Under those circumstances, it might not be impossible, for example, to "reach" the machine-gunner, evidently the most susceptible member of the team. Bashō, as had been demonstrated, was the soft spot in his warrior's carapace. The cluster of tender sentiment surrounding the poet and the Japanese guerrilla might be the point of entry.

If the youth was responsive to poetry, in principle he was salvageable, though it was true, Henk sadly recalled, that here in Holland some of the worst SS men had been lovers of Rilke and Hölderlin—his father, the magistrate, had cited the fact ironically when he had gone to witness against them at their trials. Still, poetry, as a frail *trait d'union*, the thin edge of the wedge, was a hope—the only one available. That Henk had been led by a queer chain of coincidences to recite those lines could be taken for a sign from Heaven, showing him the right way. But the plump gloomy boy, however open to softer influences he might prove to be, was subordinate to the others. Even if he could be gently detached from them, at night as he stood watch, how in fact could he help? He had only the one weapon. And should one aim after all at corrupting a minor? That was what it would amount to. Henk shook his head, feeling distaste for the train of thought he had been pursuing. Once again he despaired.

Sophie gripped his hand; he raised his eyes. The woman was standing in the doorway, her pistol peeping from her blouse. She had an announcement to make. A light meal was going to be served. As soon as they had eaten, the prisoners were to gather their hand baggage and proceed to the first-class cabin, where disembarkation would take place. A helicopter was standing by. "And Sapphire?" asked Victor hoarsely, speaking for the first time today; there were cake-crumbs in his two-day-old beard. "You will leave your cat," said the woman. "The hostesses will dispose of it. And you will not be needing the carrier."

Before Van Vliet de Jonge left the cabin, he retrieved the copy of *Elle*. In captivity he would have time, finally, to peruse his birthday horoscope. But in the aisle the young Arab abruptly took the magazine from him and stood frowning at the cover, which showed a pretty blonde girl wearing a blue-and-white crocheted cap—the winter sports number. His eyes slowly rose and met Van Vliet's with a look of childish mischief—was he inviting the deputy to a hand-to-hand struggle for possession of a French cover girl? Then with a grunt, as if to denote relinquishment, he handed the fashion magazine back. His white teeth flashed in a broadening, still mischievous smile as he helped himself instead to a cigar from the deputy's pocket.

Six

HUMAN nature, they decided, was contrary. One would have supposed that they would have been grateful for practically any change, anything to break the monotony— more than a day in the jumbo at that point without even a cribbage-board. Yet the first-class hostages had not welcomed the arrival of a slew of hostages from Economy in their midst. Utterly unannounced: up to the minute the curtain had parted and that procession had filed in, one had thought one was alone in one's glory; it had stood to reason that when the separation of the sheep from the goats had taken place, eons ago, the whole Economy contingent would have been released. So that it had been a shock to see these people appear and to learn that one was going to have them for company on the next leg of the journey, for no sooner had they made their appearance than the loud-speaker had blared: everyone was to collect his belongings and stand ready to board another aircraft.

But then a long wait had followed, and in the interval one had had time to sort out who was who, more or less, among one's future companions. The gangling, bow-tied minister (Lily knew him from ages back) had got himself quite a name for being the worst type of bleeding heart—sad for his sweet wife and family and for his church, which was paying the price; nobody had a pew there any more. The stout tweedy old party with him, who looked quite a dear really with his apple cheeks and his "brolly," had been a bishop somewhere out west, but he was tarred with the same brush: he had been close to Eleanor, it seemed, though Franklin could never abide him. And dear silly Charles, turning up like a bad penny after his "slumming" tour; one forgave him because one was used to his prattle. He was a nice old thing at heart, wouldn't hurt a fly. He knew what it was to live with beautiful things. But clinging to him was a little rouged woman with dangling earrings and a screechy voice who could not stop talking—some sort of menopausal cause-person probably that he had picked up for his sins on one of his pinko boards. And there was a red-eyed unshaven creature draped in a filthy scarf and with a basket of cat food and "kitty-litter" who was evidently one of the flock; he had helped himself to several miniatures of vodka from the serving-pantry as he went by, and the steward had just shrugged. What the lot of them had been doing on a flight to Teheran was rather hard to imagine; there was nothing in that part of the world but oil and archaeology, and neither, one would think, was their dish of tea.

But it fitted that that Senator Carey was with them, a maverick even in his own party. He was a well-groomed man at any rate, rather actorish like so many of his trade but handsome in a theatrical way. He probably used a rinse on that silver hair and dyed his eyebrows. And of course he would be odoriferous of toilet lotion—the Irish in him coming out. He was exchanging witticisms with a younger man, quite handsome too, with a trench coat slung over his shoulders and got up in a flaring whipcord suit coat that must have been "bespoke"; he wore a folded-over scarf for a tie and did not seem like an American. With them was a tall, frowning girl with a long Jewish nose that Beryl said she knew—another lefty, needless to say. Bringing up the rear had been a short bristly man, who looked like a professor, with a pipe. Most of them could have done with a freshening-up in the lavatory.

Luckily, though, there was room in the helicopter for the two parties to keep their distance. Beryl, right away, had wanted to fraternize, but Lily, exercising a mother's rights, had made her stay put. Until they had actually laid eyes on the "whirlybird" they were going to have to board—quite a feat for a woman of Margaret's girth—they had been fearing a tight squeeze. Some of the ladies had armed themselves with atomizers from their toilet cases to ward off odors, and clever Mrs. Chadwick had improvised quite a pretty fan from the Air France menu. But there was space, and to spare, for everybody, including two of the cabin crew. The steward told them that the giant helicopter had been flown in from Germany (West), which was the reason for the long delay, but Harold Chadwick was sure it was an American jobbie—they did not make them that size over here. And one certainly need not have worried about lack of air. In fact, it was awfully drafty. Noisy as well; you could hardly hear yourself think. Johnnie Ramsbotham, who was up front, had kept shouting at the pilot to ask where they were bound for, but any answers he might have got were lost in the din of the propeller-blades. The stewardess—the nice one, with the smelling-salts—had no idea where they might be going. Lapland, it felt like, from the interior temperature. The high-colored, strong-jawed fellow in the whipcord seemed to know; he was standing up, rather dangerously, and pointing out landmarks to the Senator.

But it was useless to call out and ask him; he would not be able to hear. That was the disadvantage of having stayed with one's own group, leaving a no man's land of empty seats in between. Johnnie, who was a sailor and knew how to take his bearings, thought they must still be over Holland. But they had not seen any windmills. And not a sign of a landing field. That had made poor Harold anxious, as the sun was already setting. He flew his own plane, so he understood these things. According to him, the pilot would not dare to put down in the dark, just like that, without ground flares to guide him. They could count on half an hour of light after sunset; after that, they would have to find a proper landing field or crash.

It was unnerving to have to hear that, considering all they had been through already; it would be the last straw to die at this point in a common ordinary plane crash. So far, except for the little curator, everybody had been amazingly brave, treating it as a lark and fortifying the inner man with drinks; Helen Potter was quite tiddly. They had agreed to be philosophical about their baggage—Air France could keep it for them in Amsterdam, hopefully under lock and key—you could hardly expect hijackers to be interested in whether you had your nighties or clean shirts. On seeing the new additions to the party, the men, typically, had been concerned about rations: wherever they were headed for, there would be a great many mouths to feed, and the lefties, they feared, would get the lion's share. Foresighted Johnnie, before quitting the jumbo, had stuffed his pockets with Air France candies from the tray. Still, it would not hurt most of the males to tighten their belts a bit; they could make believe they were at one of their "fat farms." Yet now, with dusk gathering, all the bravely hidden worries peeked out.

First, the mystifying fact of having been singled out as "hostage material" (Beryl's funny phrase) when the rest of the first-class passengers had been sent packing. "Do we look so prosperous?" Johnnie had innocently wondered. Well, obviously they did. Johnnie Ramsbotham was one of the two hundred richest men in America. But how could the hijackers know that? Unless Charles had been naughty. The old tease loved to talk about "my millionaires" and "my Republicans." Of course he would never stop to think that hijackers too had ears. And next there were the collections, which was the point that they all— multi-millionaires or just making ends meet—had in common. Could a little bird have told the hijackers about those? Helen's Vermeer was famous, and she had been generous—or foolish— enough to share it with the public by letting it hang on loan in a show for one of her charities. And Harold's Cézannes were in all the books. Johnnie collected only sporting art, but his Stubbses and Degas were worth fortunes, not to mention his Dufy sailing subjects and his great Ward. As for Lily, some authorities thought her English water-colors, though fewer in number, were every bit as fine as Paul Mellon's.

Then of course there was the "couple" little Mr. Walton, the curator, had included on his own say-so—they were of his ilk, evidently. They had joined the tour at the airport, having driven up from their villa in the south of France: that was in the winter; the rest of the time they lived in Duxbury, outside of Boston. No one knew yet what they collected. Prints, one might guess, since, to judge from their battered attaché cases sporting ancient hotel stickers, they belonged to the category of "more taste than money." But prints, these days, were "in" and could fetch enormous prices. Eventually one could ask.

Yet even if the hijackers had somehow got wind of this tour of collectors, how could that serve their purposes? All those treasures were back in America, protected by the latest burglar-alarm systems and fully insured. Nobody traveled with their valuables these days. Years ago, Wintie Thorp, before he became a vegetable, used to take his Byzantine ivories with him on the steamer to Europe and set one up in his hotel dressing-room every morning on the shaving-stand, so that he could look at it while shaving, start the day right, but there were no old-fashioned steamers any more and no shaving-stands, unless maybe at Claridge's, and Margaret had sold the collection—*too* portable. Today someone feeling the pinch and having been stung once too often at Sotheby Parke Bernet might hand-carry a little pair of icons or a Book of Hours to Christie's in London for appraisal, but if the insurance company knew about it, the premiums would be prohibitive. Of the present group, only Charles, apparently, could not learn to move with the times; he insisted on wearing that intaglio ring—crystal, with "*amor fati*" incised in it—that he said had belonged to some Lord Acton, and if you turned out his pockets you would be bound to find a few of his "trinkets," a rare Babylonian shekel or a sweet little Twelfth Dynasty Horus. At least his fabulous porcelains were safe with his couple on Mount Vernon Street. So that the collections should be the least of anybody's worries now; there was no earthly reason to fear on their behalf.

And yet she did, roared Margaret, and doubtless they all did in their hearts. The penalty of owning great works of art, or even itsy-bitsy ones, was that the minute anything out-of-the-way happened, your thoughts flew to them like a mother bird to the nest. Most of the time, unless you were showing the collection to visitors, you hardly *saw* the master works hanging on your walls or mounted in cases, the way you ceased to hear a clock ticking after awhile—it was something about the attention-span. That was why experts advised one to keep changing their positions. If Helen looked at her Vermeer more than once a week, it would be unusual; her maid, dusting the frame with a special soft brush, spent more time, probably, "communing" with it than she did. It was a privilege to be a domestic in a house like that, where practically every stick of furniture was signed by a great cabinet-maker; they said beauty was contagious if you were exposed to it long enough, but sometimes one wondered—look at Harold. In any case, rub off on you or not, beautiful things were a heavy responsibility. Worse than children, who eventually grew up and found their own way. Whenever you went off for a weekend, or even downtown to the hairdresser, a part of you stayed home with your treasures, and your first thought, on opening the door after an absence, was to make sure they were still there. They said you could store them in a vault, like your jewelry, when you went away, but what was the point of having beautiful things if you had to keep coming home to blank spaces on the walls and a constant traffic of bonded moving-men on the carpets? Then there was the burden of caring for them, seeing that they had the right temperature and humidity, protecting them from the sun, making certain that they were dusted, or not dusted, as the case might be. At least, unlike an animal, they did not have to be exercised.

Lily, by the bye, had a funny story about this bolshie minister when he was a curate. She had had him to one of her musical teas—that was when she still had the house on Fifth Avenue —and in those days there was a little Augustus John in the morning-room that had come down to her from an aunt. People always asked to see it, because of the subject—Churchill's beautiful American mother—though it was a flashy thing and she finally put it up for auction. Anyway, that day there was a new butler, and when this Reverend Mr. Barber turned up, just out of Divinity School, he asked him "Where is the John?" In an undertone, because the music had already started. So the butler said "Here, sir," and showed him to the toilet. The curate was so mortified that he went in and did his business and turned tail and left. Lily only heard later, from the butler, what had happened. "He asked me for the john, madam, and I directed him."

"I don't know why Mother insists on telling that story," loudly complained Beryl, an overweight child in her late thirties who was always picking quarrels with Lily. For weeks, they gathered, she had been refusing to come on this tour and then, characteristically, changed her mind at the last minute—such a bother for Lily, who had to pull strings with the Iranian ambassador in Washington, so that the girl could have her visa in time. He could not have been more charming, and yet Beryl would not even write him a little note of thanks. Now she was tickled that they had been hijacked; it had "made" her winter, she announced. She would say anything of course to be different, but perhaps in a pitiful way it was true. Her life with Lily in that apartment was rather barren; she had so few interests of her own and refused to share in her mother's: she had hated art from the cradle and had her own queer little collections of inartistic objects, such as antique false teeth and poison labels for medicine bottles—quite amusingly arranged, it had to be admitted; she had the family knack.

If only she had not had that figure problem, which was not glands but plain over-eating—stuffing herself to fill an aching inner void—she could have been rather stunning. She had a real porcelain complexion (proof of perfect elimination, considering what she ate!), which she had to disfigure with big circus patches of rouge. Her hair was thick and naturally blond, and she wore it in a wide Dutch bang that came down to a point in the middle over the family nose—a twenties style called the "Sweetheart" that she had found in some cheap magazine. Her best feature was her eyes, bluer than Lily's and glittering like sapphires, which too often she hid behind huge dark glasses, as though she thought she was Jacqueline Bouvier or a film star. And she would not let Lily dress her. Instead, she had a passion for "separates"—billowy skirts and assorted bright-colored blouses that recalled whole choruses of buxom villagers in an opera. Johnnie commented that Beryl's outfits always looked as if she had bought each item in a different Thrift shop and then thrown them all together in a hopper. For the flight she had not wanted to wear her lovely long mink—Lily's Christmas offering. Instead, there was a cherished junk-fur jacket dyed a brilliant blue that she had planned to put on over slacks. Lily had had to insist, and now, in this freezing cabin, Beryl could be grateful.

Her trouble, of course, was that she dressed to get attention, from men, obviously (the idea that women dressed for other women certainly did not apply in her case), and she succeeded; that is, she made herself conspicuous, which was not hard, given her size. She might have taken a leaf from Margaret's book, but Margaret was all in scale; her height and deep booming voice carried her weight, and the mannish *tailleurs* she wore (always Captain Molyneux) made her look redoubtable, like a monument, which would stand out naturally in a crowd. You could not call the Statue of Liberty conspicuous. And nice men, as anyone could have told Beryl, did not care to be seen with conspicuous women, while the other kind, who would have been attracted anyway by her inherited wealth, seemed to find her an embarrassment themselves in the long run. An heiress who looked like something out of the five-and-ten (there had been Woolworth money, be it said, on Joe's side) and would not be caught dead in a smart supper club, only the lowest of low dives, must be a chore to run about with, even in Mother's chauffeured old Rolls. At any rate her "pashes" were always letting her down, and she cried in her bedroom and had orders sent in from the drugstore, rejecting Lily's trays. Naturally, as with the clothes she set her heart on, she was fatally drawn to men who were crude and common, men who were bound to hurt her. It would not be beyond Beryl to set her cap at one of the hijackers before this was over. The young Arab was *rather* interested; that was clear already. Mohammedans admired fat women, and that milk-white skin and yellow hair had an appeal for the dark-skinned races, as poor Lily had reason to know: a few years ago, there had been a Negro delivery boy who was learning to play the trumpet, but when Beryl had paid for enough lessons he had got a job with a band and skipped out. Even undesirables had their sticking-point—surprising but true. And, however one viewed her appearance, Beryl could be impossibly rude and overbearing.

Yet she could be a sweet child too. Johnnie, who liked to spar with her, was convinced that she was still a virgin. It was a case, he argued, of arrested adolescence; one of his wives had been the same—you could see it in their chubby upper arms. If she could just cut loose from Lily's apron-strings, she would mature fast, he thought; as it was, her mind had developed, but her body had not kept pace with it. As proof that she had a head on her shoulders he would cite the fact that she had never played around with drugs; she was still in the milkshake stage and did not even like alcohol, except gin alexanders and sweet liqueurs. If Beryl's sitting-room, as Lily maintained, had a permanent sweet reek of marijuana—damned hard to get out of the draperies, as Johnnie knew from his own progeny's "dens"—it was only her friends smoking the weed. Milkshakes and crushes and a yen to be different from Mamma, that was all that was the matter with Beryl. She held it against Lily that they were rich (though Lily only had her widow's portion); that seemed to be the chief grievance, which Johnnie said he could understand—he had faced the problem himself as a young man. She would have to learn to live with it, like everybody else, and stop feeling that it was a "curse" and her mother's fault. No wonder, though, that she had got a kick out of being hijacked. "Serves us right," she had repeated, back in the

Air France jet, with a triumphant shake of her yellow locks. "*C'est bien fait pour nous,*" she had proceeded to translate, beaming up at the plump young Arab. "*N'est-ce pas, monsieur?*" But the wary youth had had the grace to be evasive. "*Sais pas, madame.*"

Well, doubtless it was lucky that someone in the party, for whatever disloyal reason, was enjoying the experience. Beryl's total fearlessness, you could say, was good for the general morale, which needed some bolstering now that the drinks had worn off. The little curator was shivering in his thin coat; if it had not been for that constant whirring noise, one could surely have heard his teeth chatter—the stewardess ought to have thought to bring some Air France blankets along. And the sun was rapidly setting. They watched it sink like a plummet off to the left of the "chopper," as Harold called it. To the left and slightly astern. So they were heading northeast. In the glass bubble, beside the pilot, the big tow-headed Teutonic hijacker —they had decided to nickname him "Hans" and his girl friend "Gretel"—was leaning forward and scanning the ground. Were they nearing their destination? The pilot flew lower. He hovered. But below there was no sign of life, nothing to be seen but a ruler-straight highway running through flat unimproved land. No cars, no houses with lights in them, even though they had passed big pylons that must be for electricity. After a long pause, seemingly for inspection, the pilot continued on course, flying low above the empty highway. Far off to the left, where the sun had set, there was a gleam that was probably water, and on the right there appeared to be water too. They must be skimming over an island or a peninsula. Beside the road there were thick bushes and small, evenly planted leafless trees and what might be ditches for drainage or irrigation, but only an occasional shadowy structure that could be a house or a barn—in the gathering dusk, it was hard to tell. Yet there were no animals about, not a single cow or a sheep. "What the hell?" said Henry Potter, speaking his first word in several hours.

All at once, some lights went on below—lanterns, probably, for they were moving back and forth, as though signaling. In reply, the pilot put on his landing-lights. The "chopper" came slowly down, grazing the tree-tops. It landed. Right in the

middle of a four-lane concrete highway. And they were expected to get out. The side-doors opened. "Welcome to
Flevoland!" said the cheerful fellow in the whipcord. He had
jumped off first, without a by-your-leave, and stood helping
the others to descend. He gave a hand to the creaky old Bishop
and then aided Margaret Thorp, who managed to look majestic despite her vast circumference as she was hoisted by the
steward and the stewardess into his extended arms. Beryl leapt
off quite nimbly, like the equestrienne she had been in her
teens, and turned back to assist her mother. The "wife" of the
couple—Warren's friends—helped the older "husband."

Meanwhile the team of hijackers stood by, grinning contemptuously at these simple displays of courtesy and doing
nothing themselves to be useful. Beyond the bright circle
made by the helicopter's landing-lights, other figures could be
seen, armed with rifles. Until everyone was out of the helicopter, they too merely watched, making no move. One had the
impression they were counting the hostages. The crew, as was
proper, stayed aboard till the last and occupied themselves
with the hand baggage; impatient looks passed among the hijackers as overnight cases from Gucci and Hermès were carefully lowered. "Hans" snapped his thick fingers and shouted at
the crew to hurry up, setting an example by seizing a Louis
Vuitton case and hurling it to the pavement—in the stillness,
you could distinctly hear the sound of breaking glass. Then the
rest of the baggage tumbled out in a heap, followed by the
steward and the stewardess and the co-pilot, who was in military uniform, like the pilot. This was a military aircraft, evidently, which helped explain the lack of amenities; Harold said
it must be used to carry paratroopers. The pilot was taking his
time, methodically collecting papers and checking the equipment; he passed a Red Cross kit down to the stewardess.
"Hans" barked an order; the lights went out, and the pilot
scrambled down.

In the thick dusk, you could hardly make out anything. The
lanterns of the reception committee had been shaded or
doused. Impossible to tell where one was or how many of
these lurking figures there were. All one knew was that one
had been dumped without explanation on a highway that
seemed to run through an absolute wilderness. Perhaps vehi-

cles would appear to take them on the next lap of the dreadful journey—cars or, more likely, a truck. Yet, whichever way one looked, there was no faint beam of approaching headlights. They heard footsteps receding, twigs snapping, and the rustle of reeds or underbrush. Were they going to trek on foot with what was left of their worldly goods to some robbers' den in the woods? Or could a motor boat be moored waiting to receive them? The water they had observed argued for that, but the thought of exchanging *terra firma* for still another unreliable element was more than reason was willing to entertain. They waited.

At last Charles—bless him—took it on himself to confront the skulking gang, whose forms could barely be discerned in the murk. "Well, my dears," he screeched, "I presume you don't plan to keep us all night on this public thoroughfare. We'd be grateful if you'd show us promptly to our accommodations. This evening damp is most unhealthy; one could easily take a chill, you see, and you don't want to turn your 'hospitality room' into an infirmary, do you?" He gave that crowing laugh. A soft, gurgling sound like a suppressed giggle came from the plump young Arab, who added a friendly nudge of his weapon at Beryl's ribs. Gretel was unamused. "You will not move from this place till we tell you. Your comfort is of no interest to us at this time. You will remain here under guard of the Palestine Liberation Army." In other words, Beryl's friend, the fatted calf, whom they had named "Ahmed," and the older one with the mustache, whom they had decided to call "Abdul." Gretel's harsh voice continued. "And if any of you is so foolish as to 'try anything' during our absence, one of your number will pay the price." She strode through the group of captives, surveying them with a swiftly produced, pencil-sized flashlight, as though taking her pick. The choice fell on the Bishop. "He will come with us." Whereupon she and Hans simply melted away into the shadows, along with their band of accomplices and the helpless old man, whom they had deprived of his brolly. They ignored the murmur of shock that rose from the hostages, and the rector's loud pleas to be taken instead (the Bishop, it seemed, had a heart condition) got only a grunt from Gretel. "And no smoking!" Her "parting shot" was delivered from somewhere in the bushes with terrifying accuracy. "Put that pipe out!" A pipe rattled to the pavement. Dear Gretel must have eyes in the back of her head.

Absurd of her, though, to think that anyone would try to escape. True, the two Arabs did not look very fit and might be overpowered by sheer force of numbers, but where did one take it from there? Quite apart from the horrid threat to shoot the Bishop—surely that was what she had implied?—at the slightest false move from the others, it would be madness to strike out into this unknown terrain in mid-January and with no proper footwear to boot. By now it was pitch-dark. The hostages' eyes, still not adjusted to the blackness, could hardly distinguish the shape of the giant helicopter a few yards away. Tomorrow it might be another story. They would be able to see the lie of the land and take their bearings from the sun. Now fog was swirling in; no guiding stars were visible overhead, and not a glimmer of a rising moon. The most they could be sure of was that this sinister, deserted spot was somewhere near the sea. "Why, for all we know, it might be the Faroe Islands," declared Lily. "My God, Mother!" Beryl chided. "Didn't they give you any geography in that finishing school of yours?" "I was speaking figuratively," said Lily. "And you know very well that Saint Tim's is not a finishing school. It offers an excellent education." Good marks for Lily! In these trying circumstances, she could have been forgiven if she had mentioned the string of schools and colleges that Beryl had been asked to leave.

The luminous dial of Johnnie's watch—the latest thing in digitals—showed 6:02. Unbelievable. It felt more like midnight. And a good half-hour anyway must have passed since they had been left standing here in a huddle like cattle, but there was no way of telling, as nobody had thought to check the time when they landed. Or had the pilot noted it in his log? In the stillness, they could hear the occasional toot of a foghorn and the cry of a night bird, hawk or kestrel. Then, in the distance, a rustling and skittering that was surely animals, squirrels or rabbits or weasels, depending on the latitude. Finally a few in the party with sharp ears became aware of another sound, dull and regular, as of far-off pistons. "Do you hear that?" Harold Chadwick whispered. His wife listened. "Yes. What on earth can it be, Chaddie?" He did not know. For some reason, that rhythmic mechanical sound, in the absence of any of the normal noises of civilization, was very unnerving, like the pulsing of an infernal engine. "Sounds like a pump," said Henry. But as they all listened, it stopped, and the night became utterly silent. Then it resumed.

"It *is* a pump." That was the man in the whipcord again; his pale scarf, folded like a stock, could just be made out. In a body, the first-class hostages turned to him; all the carefully built little social barriers came down, as of course they had to in an emergency, with everyone standing here chock-a-block. He talked with quite a strong accent, difficult to place, but he sounded like a person who was very sure of himself. What they were hearing, he said, was a pumping-station. They were in Holland. And he was Dutch himself, naturally. "But I thought you said 'Welcome to Flevoland' or some name like that," protested Beryl. She was right; it *had* been somewhat misleading. But "Flevoland," it seemed, was the name of this part of Holland. From a lake which used to be here in Roman times that the Romans had called "Lake Flavus," meaning yellow.

"I'll be darned," said Johnnie. "What happened to the lake?" Well, that was a long story, said the Dutchman, and then proceeded to tell it, as people always did when they said that. But it was interesting and gave them something to think about besides the state of their extremities and the clammy fear that was starting to creep over them like the fog. The temperature was close to freezing, and standing on the icy concrete was an ordeal, especially for the women in their thin shoes. The group was at a loss as to how to interpret Gretel's injunction not to move—did it mean stay glued to the spot or could they take a few steps to stretch their legs instead of just shifting from foot to foot?

Anyhow, to hear the Dutchman tell it, the Roman lake and the land around it had been gradually taken over by the sea; then in recent times the process had been reversed. When the Zuyder Zee had been closed in from the North Sea, the old lake bottom had been drained and made into a "polder." The highway underfoot ran along a raised dike, which was part of the system that kept the water out. But it was fresh water now, not salt—the Ijsselmeer, pronounced something like "ice," he said. And this whole place they were on was a polder. "Land reclamation," said Johnnie. "Now I get it. We're on your 'Oost Polder.'" Johnnie was amazing; one would think that he never read a book and cared for nothing but his pictures and sailing and horses, but one forgot that his financial interests brought him in touch with all sorts of remote places and people, so that he could be a mine of the strangest information. It would not be surprising if one of his companies had been researching these polders for investment. And once Johnnie got hold of a fact, it stayed with him. It was stored away in his memory for when it might come in handy. Like tonight. The Dutchman, you could tell, was pleased as Punch to meet an American who knew something about his country. If the circumstances had been more normal, one could have expected an exchange of visiting cards. As it was, they traded names. "Van Vliet de Jonge." "Ramsbotham."

The reason the area was so empty was that it was all new land, ready for development. The water they had noticed to the east of them was a lake with brand-new artificial beaches for tourism. A few miles to the north, an airport was under construction. There would be some light industry in the new towns, but Flevoland's 52,000 hectares would be used mainly for cereals, sugar beets, potatoes, and dairy-farming. "What about timber?" said Johnnie. "4000 hectares," answered the other. "About 46,000 will be in agriculture." Harold interrupted. He had had his fill of this discussion. What interested him was whether the hijackers were going to make them sleep in the chopper. The Dutchman doubted it. He supposed their hideaway would prove to be a farmhouse—a few had already been built, well set back from the road. "You may have noticed one or two from the air." A farmhouse, he guessed, and a barn, too, had been taken over and got ready by their confederates. "Hopefully," said Harold, with a short laugh. "Jesus, how many are we?" "Twenty-four, with the pilots," said the Dutchman. "You've got it all at your finger-tips, haven't you?" retorted Harold, who was clearly in one of his rude moods. He was someone who was sensitive to being left out.

"What makes you so sure anyway that it's this so-called polder of yours that they've brought us to?" "Why, he guessed it hours ago, back in the plane, didn't he, Senator, didn't you, Mynheer Van Vliet?" That was the little Economy class woman with all the rouge. "And now this pumping-station proves he was right. On a newly drained polder, he explained to us, the pumps run day and night. Maintaining the water level."

"How interesting, Mr. Van Vliet," said Lily. "Do tell us what made you guess." "Exercise of reason," spoke up the Senator. "Plus being Dutch. When they asked for a helicopter, he had all the clues in his hand." "Clues?" "Sure. The flying range of helicopters and their capability of landing in rough terrain without a runway gave him his coordinates. And being Dutch, he was aware of polder country—wide open spaces with hardly any folks around. In easy flying radius of Schiphol. Your ordinary passenger plane couldn't have put down here. Well, maybe a Piper Cub. But for that we were too many, as Father Time said." "'Father Time'?" Lily sounded alarmed. "*Jude the Obscure*, Mother. Didn't they have that on your reading-list at Saint Tim's?"

Margaret took up the questioning. "Thank you, Beryl. Now I wonder if this gentleman will enlighten us a little further. Can you tell us, sir, how these Germans and Arabs came to be acquainted with your uninhabited polder? Is it a matter of general knowledge?" Well, you could have knocked them over with a feather: "Hans" and "Gretel" were not German; they were Dutch. "You'll have to think of some new names for them, Mother," twitted Beryl. "And you don't know any Dutch names, I bet." "Naming the animals," observed the Senator, in his dry way. "Try 'Rip' as in 'Winkle.'" "But Hans *is* a Dutch name," declared Helen. "Remember *Hans Brinker or The Silver Skates*? Mary Mapes Dodge. How I doted on that book. But I forget what his dear little sister was called." "Well, give us some Dutch given names, Mr. Van Vliet," ordered Margaret in her measured my-good-man tones. "Maarten, Willem, Adriaan . . . Liesbeth, Henriette . . ." "*Saskia!*" interrupted Helen. But who would want to call a hijackeress after Rembrandt's glorious young wife? Mr. Van Vliet was thinking. "For him, you ought to have a Groningen sort of name. Gerrit . . . ?" "Never mind this name game." Harold's voice was raised again. "What I'd like to hear is how our friend here knew the gang had asked for a helicopter."

Harold had a point. In first class they had not been told a word about a helicopter or any other kind of getaway plane.

How was it that Economy seemed to know such a lot while first-class passengers had been kept totally in the dark? "Very simple. The hijackers told me," cheerily replied Mr. Van Vliet and-whatever-the-rest-of-his-name-was. Again the first-class hostages could only gasp. This man had been in the terrorists' confidence and was brazen enough to admit it. It was a horrid sensation to feel that you might have a Judas in your midst. Finally Charles, the old know-all, had the goodness to explain. Mr. Van Vliet de Jonge was a deputy in their Parliament. "The leader of his party, I believe. I knew his grandfather. Charming man. His party is in the ruling coalition, you see, and since our captors were negotiating over the wireless with the Dutch government, it was only logical that he should be chosen as intermediary. Which in turn permitted him to learn some of their demands."

"Of course, Mother," cried Beryl. "Don't you remember? There was a man they took up to the pilot's cabin. Twice, I think. That was Mr. Van Vliet de Jonge, obviously. But you people never notice anything. If you saw him, you probably thought he was another hijacker. By that time, you were all drunk anyway like most of your generation. Except Mrs. Chadwick—'just a little unseasoned tomato juice'—who was fainting." "Manners, Beryl," interposed Johnnie. "Keep your shirt on. Unlike you, honey child, the rest of us were under a strain. And, now that you mention it, I do recall somebody's being hustled up those corkscrew steps. But I didn't take much notice. And you're right: just about then, Eloise fainted."

When he stopped, one was almost grateful for the dark. As if to bear out Beryl's allegation, a distinct smell of alcohol was reaching their nostrils. It must come from the Vuitton case that had been thrown down with such violence; a bottle of whiskey must have broken—more likely, a pair of bottles. Still, Beryl's outburst, whatever the foundation in fact, could not be dismissed as easily as her protector, Johnnie, seemed to think. To accuse your mother, in public, with strangers listening, of having been drunk was rather unforgivable. And, on top of that, to do a take-off of little Mrs. Chadwick's la-de-da way of speaking. That was cruel. Actually nobody had been what you would call drunk, except the Potters, and Henry never showed it. When once in a great while he would have to be carried out of his club and entrusted to his chauffeur, it always came as a surprise: one minute he was erect and in full possession of his faculties (as far as could be judged), and the next he swayed and toppled over like a tall tree in a forest. It could happen at any time of day but only in the club—never when ladies were present. He was a gentleman to the core; the men said that when he keeled over it was almost a noble sight, like watching a cathedral pine fall. Unfortunately Helen, who now and then took one martini too many, in order to keep him company, had no head for liquor, which led people to think that she was an alcoholic and a cross for sober Henry to bear, when the exact opposite happened to be the case.

The dark was doubly welcome because it gave them time to think about Charles's revelations, and one would not like the person in question to be aware of it. There was no real reason to doubt that he was a deputy in Parliament, even though somebody like Harold might immediately want proof. Being self-made, Harold was naturally suspicious of those who had less of this world's goods than he had acquired, and right now one could not altogether blame him; the present circumstances, so eerie, hardly conduced to an atmosphere of trust. But the fact that Charles had known this man's grandfather was some sort of testimonial: Charles was awfully well connected. On the other hand, whoever one's grandfather had been did not prevent one, these days, from crossing over to the other side—almost the contrary; a mother could scarcely be sure any more that her own children were not manufacturing bombs in the cellar. What really mattered in a critical moment such as this was not blood or the ability to get elected—look at Carey—but a sense of responsibility. Was this de Jonge a responsible person? That was what one needed to know. He might be everything that Charles claimed, a leader of his party and so on, yet he had an irresponsible air about him—insouciant perhaps was the word. As though the common peril was a matter of no concern. Of course that could be put on. In the morning one would be able to tell better; one liked to *see* the person one was talking to, in order to judge fairly. Now there was only the voice to go by, and the accent, though not his fault, did serve as a reminder that he could speak to the chief terrorists in their own language with no one the wiser.

He was a great talker, clearly, and, without knowing more about him, one could not foresee what he might let drop to these compatriots of his, not necessarily meaning any harm.

It would be wisdom to warn Helen, if one could just draw her quietly aside, not to dream of mentioning her Vermeer to him, which under ordinary conditions would be the most natural thing for her to do were she to find herself traveling with a pleasant-spoken Dutchman. Vermeers, as she ought to know, seemed to have a fatal attraction for art thieves and declared enemies of society. There had been that shocking case, a few winters ago, of the Kenwood House Vermeer. The terrorists had seized the canvas, in broad daylight at gun-point, from the lovely house, partly Adam, just outside London that had been a gift of Lord Iveagh to the public. Then they had cut strips off it and mailed them to a newspaper, just like that Getty boy's ear. They threatened to "execute" it as an act of proletarian justice if their demands were not met by a certain date. Yet what was it, exactly, that they had wanted? Money, naturally, and for some Irish bombers in English jails to go free, and a food distribution, or was one getting confused with the Hearst case? There were so many of these raids and kidnappings, all alike basically, that it was hard to keep the long lists of "demands" straight. In any case, the world had waited, utterly aghast at the barbarity, for the appointed day to dawn, but then the day passed and nothing happened, and eventually the picture was found, not too much the worse for wear, in a London cemetery, propped up against a gravestone. The subject of the painting—a girl in a yellow dress trimmed with ermine holding a guitar—was very similar to Helen's; you could almost speak of a replica, though Helen's was an inch or two smaller and the landscape hanging on the wall behind the guitar-player was different. That was why so many of Helen's friends had thought it was foolish of her to let hers go on show right on the heels of the Kenwood House atrocity; it was inviting a repetition.

Before that there had been the Rijksmuseum "The Love Letter," which was stolen while on show in Belgium and savagely mistreated. They said that had been a professional "heist" but professionals were usually not interested in mutilating priceless treasures—only in collecting the ransom; they had nothing against the pictures as art. Normal criminality was a thing one could understand—the acquisitive instinct we all have, carried to wicked lengths—but the new wave of terrorism let loose on helpless works of art was beyond ordinary human comprehension. That Japanese woman spraying the "Mona Lisa" with red paint to protest the museum hours that she thought discriminated against Japanese workers or women or whatever. It was heartbreaking to read about these sprayings and gougings and hackings, which were all politically motivated at bottom, even if it was only a crazy Australian artist's grudge against Michelangelo for being an acknowledged genius when he could not get recognition himself—so he attacked the "Pietà" in St. Peter's. And you did not have to be a "proud possessor" to feel the hurt of it. The ordinary newspaper-reader, if the truth were told, had trembled far more for the Vermeer when it was threatened than for the Hearst girl or even the Getty boy.

"I have many grandchildren," old Mr. Getty had commented when he let it be known that he was not going to satisfy the kidnappers' demands. He meant that if he paid up for Paul, the gangsters would be encouraged to kidnap the rest of his descendants one after the other. But the remark had been misinterpreted: people thought a callous old man was stating that among so many grandchildren one more or less did not matter. And if you compared the average grandchild with an irreplaceable work of art, that was true in a way, though one shouldn't say it. Helen had many attractive grandchildren, who would doubtless go on breeding and multiplying on the face of the earth, but her Vermeer was one of a kind, or almost. It was like a trust she held for posterity. The pleasure owning it gave her was only the income. Rather, what *had* been the pleasure; the constant increase in burglaries, pushing up the insurance premiums, and now this wave of wanton terrorism were taking a good deal of the joy out of owning beautiful things. But to let them "go public," as business people said of old family-owned companies, was not a solution; your precious works of art were no safer in a museum, as the Kenwood House crime proved. At any rate, Helen ought to be put on her guard. And if tomorrow, after a night's sleep and a chance to look about, a council of war were held, to discuss the situation and size up the chances of escape, it would be fairer to de Jonge to manage to leave him out of it. Or if negotiation, instead, were decided on—one could always *try*—they should be chary of taking him into their confidence. One of their own group, by rights, should be the spokesman, since it was money, to put it coarsely, that would be talking. . . .

Now the moon was trying to show itself, and a few stars twinkled in and out of the clouds. The fog had lifted, and, besides, their eyes had adjusted to the darkness. It had to do with the pupils dilating or else contracting, one or the other—Harold, who had started out as a pharmacist, would probably know. They saw Beryl plump herself down on the pavement; she had plenty of padding but she would ruin her nice coat. The others had found it wiser to stay on their feet and keep exercising their limbs—the Senator was throwing imaginary pitches. The temperature was dropping; you could tell because the pavement was getting slippery—a thin glaze of ice had started to form. Along each side of the road ran a ditch, too deep to see whether it held water. Beyond, there were tall reeds or sedges, and some distance off, perhaps half a mile, in the direction from which they had heard the foghorn, they could now make out a house of sorts, distinguishable by the roofline, and a big looming shed or barn. No lights showed.

Every few minutes someone consulted Johnnie's luminous watch. What had happened to their captors? No one was talking any more. Each seemed to be wrapped in his thoughts. The younger of Warren's two friends had assumed a yoga posture. Helen's head jerked on her neck; she was falling asleep on her feet. At that point, forceful Margaret decided to take the reins in her hands. "Rector," she ordered. "Give us an evening prayer." When he launched into "Lighten our darkness, we beseech thee, O Lord," everyone had to laugh—it was so appropriate. Then, looking around like a chairwoman, she called on Van Vliet to tell them what kind of government his country had. "Wait a minute," burst in Harold. "Don't say it. Let me have one guess. Socialist." He had scored on the first try, which seemed to give him some grim satisfaction, though you would think he would rather have been wrong. "Thanks, Maggie, for asking. Now we know." "Know what?" demanded Beryl.

"Know what?" echoed the woman with the wailing Southern voice. They saw the Senator turn his head to listen.

Dear Lily undertook to pour oil on the troubled waters. "There are socialists *and* socialists, Harold. One has to know which kind." "There's only one kind," retorted Harold. The Senator gave a brief laugh and went back to pitching. Johnnie came to Lily's aid. In his understanding, he said, Holland was something like England—what they liked to call a "welfare state," with the Queen and Labor. "And isn't Holland in NATO?" ventured Lily. "I feel sure I read that somewhere." "You're thinking of Belgium, Mother." But Lily was right. Indeed Holland was in NATO, Mr. Van Vliet assured them. And he tiptoed over to the "whirlybird" and tenderly patted the little tail-propeller. "The NATO shield." Even Harold had to chuckle when the humor of it was explained to him. The "chopper" was part of the NATO defense screen. Mr. Van Vliet's government had borrowed it from the Germans. To oblige a team of international terrorists. "A crazy world," summed up Lily's rector-as-was.

But after that "light moment," despondency returned. Seven o'clock came and still no sign of the main hijackers. "Abdul" and "Ahmed" were talking in low voices. Maybe they too were getting worried. Harold wondered why Dutch planes had not started looking for the party. "Christ, our course could have been plotted by radar. They ought to have pinpointed where we are. By now we should have heard some action overhead." But the partly covered sky was silent, and a new tooting of foghorns indicated a very obvious reason: no search plane would undertake a mission in this weather. "I'm scared, Chaddie," said Eloise. In fact they were all growing frightened. Older people could perish of exposure if left standing here all night. And the odor of whiskey still emanating from the Vuitton case was tantalizing, to say the least. What a pity that Henry had not packed his private stock more carefully.

If another half-hour were to pass in this vain waiting, some initiative would have to be taken. Everyone might decide to move in a body back into the helicopter, where at least there were seats and some shelter. Or start a bonfire—there were those leafless young trees along the road that appeared to be poplars; the men could tear branches off, although the wood

might be too damp to burn. But first one would have to convince the two Arabs, who must be freezing themselves, to let
them disobey Gretel's order; perhaps Beryl could try.

Life was full of irony. The last thing one would have expected was that one would find oneself longing for Hans and
Gretel to return. Why were they staying away so long? Had
something dreadful happened back there in that house? The
conspirators might have got into an argument and killed each
other in a shoot-out. Or blown themselves up while wiring the
place with explosives. But then one would have heard the
noise. The wildest conjectures must be passing through every
mind, though no one dared voice them. It was like being left
by one's nurse as a child in the park with one's pail and shovel
and told to stay put till she came back. The fears that rose to
assail one when she did not appear for hours and one's little
feet were getting cold! That she had been run over by a car,
that she had got lost in the park, that the bogey-man had taken
her, that she had just walked off on purpose and was never
coming back. That sense of utter abandonment—it was odd to
feel it now. And the same fear one had had then of disobeying
by going to look for her. Nurse, as one knew now, had simply
been off with some young man and when she came back, she
was cross that one was frightened and made one promise not
to tell the Missus. Well, most of us have had such experiences,
and they leave a mark.

Of course the situations were not parallel. One had usually
loved Nurse. One had wanted her never to leave. While if one
was sure that Hans and Gretel had disappeared for good, it
would be bliss beyond belief. It was the doubt that was so
harrowing. Rather than remain a prey to useless guessing and
imagining, not to mention desperately hungry and chilled to
the bone, almost anybody, actually, would prefer to see their
scowling faces. It was normal to be silently pleading for them
to come back soon: "*Please*, Hans and Gretel, where are you?"
And the Bishop, too, of course. How strange to have almost
forgotten about him.

Seven

I T would be an exaggeration to say that these people had never been so glad to see anyone in their lives. More exactly (Sophie estimated), no sound of footsteps had ever been so welcome to them as the purposeful tread advancing almost in march-time—the leaders had changed their footwear and were wearing thick boots. All too soon, naturally, they were perceived again in their true colors—hardly had they shown their faces when it was obvious that the leopard had not changed his spots. Absent, they had been idealized: it was curious how, within the mere space of an anxious hour or so, the group huddled here had succeeded in forgetting what their captors had been like. Apprehension as to what was coming next would have been the rational emotion. Instead, if her own feelings were an index, the nearing steps of the *kapers*, heralded by a distant snapping of twigs, had evoked simple gratitude: they were a rescue party.

Their return meant food, shelter, sleep, possibly a blanket—civilization. At any rate, to Sophie: she had been picturing the shadowy house off there as a sort of canteen or mess, with cauldrons of hot soup, bread, Dutch cheese, coffee. She had not eaten a full meal for seventy-two hours. And for the older people, people of her parents' age, all this must have been much harder. She was hungry, and her legs, encased like sausages in these elegant leather boots, had lost all feeling. Yet as a journalist she was familiar with rough assignments—she had humped about in army trucks and slept in a cave alongside guerrillas eager to be interviewed; she had lived for days on a diet of black beans and rice—and furthermore she was thirty-six, still young. The older people, with their hardening arteries and poor circulation, not to mention proneness to worry, could only be objects of compassion to someone so junior and so far ahead in experience. For their sake, she tried to picture army cots in the house or barn or at least rows of mattresses; if this was to last long, sleep would become essential for keeping a steady head. For her, hay or the floor would do, if only she could get these boots off—a razor, she feared, might be required.

She felt sorriest for the art collectors. A millionaire's life was no preparation for the trials of being a hostage. Perhaps, in the light of present-day trends, they should be getting special training courses to harden them up for the eventuality. But in fact the collectors had borne up remarkably well, and she wondered whether her parents could have equaled them—they had the double handicap of being semi-rich and Jewish, which taken together seemed to soften the fibre. These super-rich Wasps had been lambs on the whole: no complaints, no moans, just the stately silliness proper to their station in life. The only black sheep among them had been the quarrelsome man with the Midwestern accent and the younger wife; it was hard to imagine what art he collected—cock-fighting subjects? On the fringe, as if not quite accepted among the super-rich, was a pair of queens with the usual age difference between them. They were bearing up well too, considering the fact that they *were* on the fringe. She tried to guess what the parched old one collected—the other probably cooked, drove the car, and generally catered—prints, she thought: Beardsley first impressions, Klimt, Cocteau, Japanese erotica.

The fat girl, Beryl Somebody, Sophie remembered from school; she was the one who had appeared in the sixth-form year with a trunkful of incredible clothes that she had cut to pieces with a pinking shears on a dreary Sunday afternoon in a fit of misery or boredom while her roommate looked on. It was easy to sympathize with the act, which had contrived to get her expelled—a thing that almost never happened at Putney and caused her to stand out in the memory as someone who had put Mrs. H.'s progressiveness to the supreme test. She deserved a commemorative plaque, really, for exposing the hypocrisy of the place. It had been odd to find her again, traveling with her mother and dressed in a long lustrous matronly mink coat but otherwise not much changed from the old Beryl. She was still fat and flaxen with made-up electric blue eyes that blinked like a china doll's and still a disciplinary problem, or so it sounded. Sophie saw that she could not have changed greatly herself, for it was clear that Beryl remembered her too. "Hi, there," she had muttered over her shoulder as they were boarding the helicopter. Later they might have a chat, dormitory style, when Sophie's boots were off and the older generation would be snoozing, having taken its Valium or sleeping-pill.

But something was wrong with that picture. They were not going to be bedded down yet. And where was the Bishop? The hijackers had not brought him back with them. The realization seemed to steal over the whole group of hostages in the course of an instant, as though they were one body that had been nudged to attention. What had this pair done with the nice old man? Near her, eyebrows shot up, making points of interrogation; shrugging shoulders replied in dumb show. Nobody, Sophie supposed, wished to be the one to ask, partly for fear of learning the answer but mostly for fear of angering their hosts —if that was the right word for these redoubtable people. In any case, for the moment the leaders were unapproachable— they were over by the helicopter arguing heatedly with the pilot; their voices were raised—and the Arabs, though available, could claim not to know. If other members of the band had come back with the leaders, they were waiting silently in the bushes.

Sophie told herself that there could be an innocent explanation for the Bishop's disappearance, and no doubt her fellow-hostages were telling themselves the same thing. He might be asleep, for instance. Yet this sop she was offering her conscience for not speaking up—"Where is the Bishop?" she was free to shout, or "Please, where is Bishop Hurlbut?"—failed to be effective, since from long experience she recognized it as a sop. She sensed in herself a reluctance to antagonize that she knew too well, a disabling reluctance for someone in her profession. She had proof of her physical courage and the courage of her pen, but spoken words, for her, were different. It was not mere dread of offending a powerful person but embarrassment: she did not like to ask a point-blank question when the anticipated reply, or evasion, was something only a prosecuting attorney could pounce on with joy. She had given long thought to this subject; was it tact or shyness or femininity that inhibited her? She was sure that if she had had the bad fate to interview Nixon, she would have helped him cover up, at least while she sat in his office under his shifty eye. Poor girl (she sighed to herself), she wanted to be "clean." She always pitied confessors, who in their stuffy intimate boxes had to hear and wash away such a lot of dirty sins. And tonight, added to that squeamishness was a plain, weak, selfish desire not to incur the special hostility of "Hans" and "Gretel," as the collectors were calling them—naming the animals, the Senator had observed. She was the only Jew, she guessed, in this whole caboodle; why should it fall to her to speak up?

But the parson, thank God, had recognized his duty. They watched him approach the Arab guard and secure a permission, apparently. Then he brought out a pocket handkerchief —plaid, but in the dark it could pass for white—and holding it up as a truce flag he manfully crossed the open ground to the helicopter, where the second pilot had joined the loud debate. Two flashlight beams played over the tall missionary form. "He's asking," Simmons marveled. "I wouldn't have the courage; honestly, would you? But then he has to. Being his brother's keeper, I mean." "He's getting the bum's rush," commented Harold. It was true. In two shakes of a lamb's tail, the parson was hurtling back toward his companions; a rough final shove from the older Arab caused him to slip on the icy pavement— he fell. "I guess they mean business," he said, trying to laugh as he picked himself up. He applied the flag of truce, groaning, to his shin. But it was only a scrape. "And so what did they tell you?" Sophie demanded. "Nothing. Not a darned thing. She just gave me a piece of her mind for butting in. Quite a scold, she is. A regular martinet." Soon the woman herself strode up, as if to enforce the lesson poor Mr. Barber had got. The dispute with the pilots—whatever it had been about—seemed to be over. But something had left her in a vicious humor. "We are not here to answer your questions. We are not accountable to you swine. You were ordered not to disperse, and one of you has disobeyed. Now you will form a line, quickly. We have no time to waste."

The erect old collector reached for his wife's dressing-case. "Here you are, Helen. Margaret, my dear, where's yours?" "Drop that case!" exclaimed the woman. "And form a line, I said." "But we need our things," protested Harold's wife. "Our night things, don't you see, so as to go to bed." She might have been explaining matters to a child, Sophie thought.

"'Beddy-bye,' '*do-do*,'" the mincing voice went on. "Forget *do-do*, Mrs. Parasite," said the woman. "You are going to be put to work." "Me?" "Some of you. All of you. We will decide." What work could she mean? Uncertainly, the hostages lined up and faced the two confederates. Like confused recruits, they did not understand the order and were too frightened to ask more. All that was clear to Sophie was that the leaders were making a selection. They went down the long line using their little flashlights like methodical probes. After a brief appearance the moon had gone in again, and the last few stars were covered. The dancing rays of light made the dark seem darker. Sophie was glad to know, anyway, that she had Henk on her right side and on her left Jim Carey, who laced his fingers firmly in hers and murmured "Whatever's coming, let's the three of us try to stay together." On his other side was Simmons; a faint shriek came from that quarter. "He was *feeling* me, Jim," the wailing voice confided. "What part of you?" asked the Senator. "I guess you'd call it my biceps," she admitted, raising a laugh. "Auschwitz," muttered Sophie, not finding this very funny. Paranoia, perhaps, but it did seem to her that a Nazi-style sifting of those fit to work was going on. What would they do with the others—kill them or save the ammunition and leave them to die of exposure? She asked herself what it meant that neither of the two had bothered to test *her* muscles. Again she considered the fact of being Jewish: did that classify her as fit to work or the opposite? Hunger was making her light-headed. If she was slightly delirious, that would account for the somber imaginings that were assailing her— her own special pink elephants; her parents had got out of Frankfurt early, but distant relatives from the French branch had died in the ovens. "Fall out," barked the woman. Sophie jumped. "Ahmed, take him away." It was Charles the woman was speaking of. How shameful to feel relief.

Yet the elimination of Charles threw a new and terribly clear light on the Bishop's disappearance. In a flash the confusion in her head was replaced by hyper-lucidity. The old and the unfit. "Take him away"—a code expression, most likely, on the model of "the final solution" or "Waste 'em" in Vietnam. At the same time, in another part of her mind she was finding it wildly comical that "Ahmed's" name was Ahmed. And in still a different compartment, her brain was working on a hideous new theory: the Bishop had died of a heart attack, *or* they had killed him, and they were picking a burial squad. Sophie could not stand it. "I'm going to *demand* that they tell us. If they won't say where he is, it means they've done away with him." "What good will it do us to know, Sophie?" Carey said gently, stroking her cold fingers. "It *always* does good to know," Sophie said passionately, pushing his hand away. "No talking there!" shouted the man's voice. A flashlight was turned in their direction. In its path Sophie distinctly saw—unless it was a hallucination—a figure carrying a shovel crossing the road. Her knees began to buckle. "Henk!" she appealed, in a whisper. He was not there. It was like waking up from a bad dream and finding the place beside you empty. But he had merely stepped forward, without saying a word. The leaders saw him. "Back in line there, Deputy. Take your place."

He was not going to obey. He stood there quite coolly (she could tell from his profile and the tilt of his chin), his head thrown back as if idly contemplating the sky. As she watched, he calmly folded his arms and continued to gaze upward, like the musing figure of a poet in a German Romantic painting— all he lacked was a black cloak wrapped around him. Sophie smiled; in this half-minute she had grown uncannily calm herself. No doubt it was the advent of real danger that had done it. She ought to tremble at his daring; instead, she was content —perhaps the true word was "thrilled"—that he was standing his ground.

If Henk did not move, she reasoned, they would come over to him themselves. The odds were that they would not shoot him unless they had to. A little plume of white vapor, like smoke, came from the nostril she could see and made her think of a bull-god snorting. And of course he was not a political animal for nothing; the bold strategy was working. First the man and then the woman materialized from the shadows, drawn as if by a magnet or by common, normal curiosity—an underrated force of attraction. Henk shifted his head in their direction, like somebody who thought he had heard visitors. The man said something in Dutch. Henk answered with a word that sounded like "Nay." Stepping up rather too close to him, the woman pointed her flashlight into his face. He

ignored it and started talking to the man. Then he made an
irritable gesture, as if to ward off the beam of light, like a
buzzing fly, from his eyes. The man's hand suddenly closed
over the woman's; he clicked her flashlight off. His own he
kept pointed at the pavement, lighting up patches of ice. Henk
continued. "He's asking about the Bishop," Sophie murmured
to Carey. "I heard him say '*bisschop*.'" They strained their ears
to follow. Carey caught the words "*oud man*," which must be
"old man." But as the rapid exchange went on, they could pick
up less and less. Their German was not much help; the pronunciation was too different. The recurring "Nay," a nasal
sound, was evidently "No" or "*Nein*," and the woman kept
interrupting with what sounded like "*haast hebben*," which
might be kin to German "*Die Hast*" and English "hurry."

If so, she was not the only impatient one. From the far end of
the line, the unmistakable voice of Harold called out. "What's
going on? What are you telling them, de Jonge?" He must have
received a cuff or a sharp poke from an Arab gun butt, for there
was a loud grunt and he subsided. The discussion in Dutch
went on. The word "helicopter," however spelled, was being
pronounced. Sophie turned quickly to Carey. He had got it too.
He emitted a soft whistle. She could not guess what he was
surmising, but for her part Sophie had just had a sudden joyful
suspicion. Was the Bishop going to be evacuated, as an act of
mercy—"medevac," the Army would have called it in Vietnam
—and Charles too? "Bishop," "old man," "helicopter," even
"*hebben haast*"—it all added up to that. As for the work-detail
the leaders had been choosing, that could be for ordinary
chores; collecting firewood, for instance, or KP—nothing would
make her happier now than to be set to peeling potatoes, especially if she knew that an ailing old cleric and his ancient crony
were going to be flown out. She blessed Henk for his gift of
persuasion. The hulking man, she estimated, was more than half
convinced; at least he was listening and nodding his head up and
down, as if pondering. And the woman was staying out of it.
Her restless flashlight was on again, playing over the pavement.
Sophie's eye absently followed it. She froze. Lying by the edge
of the road were *two* shovels.

"Nay," Van Vliet was saying. Just down the row, another
voice, pleasanter than Harold's, intervened—Beryl's mother.

"Dear Mr. Van Vliet, don't argue with them. You're only making them cross. Let's just do as we're told and get it over with." "Can it, Mother. We're not meant to be talking, don't you realize that?"

But Henk answered, and the big fellow did not stop him. Sophie tried to listen, but her attention kept wandering. Had no one else noticed the shovels? She touched Carey's sleeve and pointed. He shrugged. He was more interested in what Henk was saying—something about being a lawyer and advice being his profession. Could she be wrong in the dire conclusion she had leapt to? Leaping to conclusions was a bad habit with her. Wouldn't they be spades rather than shovels if a grave was to be dug? She ordered herself to listen. Henk was telling the hostages in English what he had told the two leaders in Dutch. "They have said that they are not accountable to us. In strict power terms that is true. But I counsel them that it is in their own interest not to keep us in ignorance when they need our cooperation." Sophie bridled. "Cooperation?" she muttered to Carey. What did that mean? They were in a no-choice situation; they *had* to cooperate. He was a charming, absurd Dutchman, over-trained in coalition politics. Nevertheless, she reminded herself, softening, he was brave, and for that she owed him some attention. Slave labor, he was saying, was always inefficient. "That is known from the camps. But in the gulag there were millions, so the low productivity of each individual unit was unimportant; in the scale of things it did not matter." Why was Henk telling all this to the hostages, half of whom could not care less? Then slowly she understood: he was really addressing himself to the *kapers*, taking advantage of having the floor to repeat an argument that he had been making in camera. It was a parliamentary trick, to use an attentive gallery to make your point sink in, as though doubling the size of the audience doubled the force of your words. And possibly it did. "Here tonight," he continued cheerily, "the labor force is very small. Perhaps thirty persons. They need the full productivity of thirty persons and therefore they must pay for it." "'Pay'? That's a bit stiff, isn't it, under the circs?" The collector called Ramsbotham laughed in a worldly way, as if he thought poor Henk quite mad or in need of a business education. Henk took his meaning. "I am not a 'simple,' as we say in Dutch. No.

Ask yourself a question. What have our friends here got that we haven't?" "Guns," yelled Harold. "Evidently," said Henk. "But what else?" No one knew. "Information," answered Henk. "They must pay us in information."

"Your Bishop is alive," the woman said abruptly. "He has not been harmed. No one will be harmed at this stage of the operation that behaves himself. He is too old, simply, for the work, and we have told him so. He will only be in the way." "The work?" echoed Beryl's mother. "You will see," said the man. "Now fall out, madam. Fall out again, funny old gentleman." That was Charles, who had slipped back into line— doubtless to hear better. "And you, Deputy, fall in."

It ought to have been plain as a pikestaff. It was a question of moving the helicopter. Henk had guessed it before they told him. Jim Carey had guessed it. That was the "work." As soon as the fog cleared, or in the morning at the very latest, search planes would come looking for them. That man Harold had been griping, half an hour ago, that none had come yet. The helicopter would have to be hidden. It could not be left standing here all night in plain view.

That *of course* they could not leave it parked on the highway was a fact of life too obvious to have escaped Sophie's attention; she would have had to be a total idiot not to see that. But she had given no consideration to the mechanics of its removal; when they were ready, the pilot, she had assumed, would taxi it off the road to some nearby hiding-place. All that would have been thought through. But in the dark she had failed to notice something that the men had seen at once: the helicopter did not have wheels; it had skids. Yet why claim the dark as an excuse? The truth was that she had not used her eyes, while the men had. And even if at some point she had vaguely taken note of the skids, she would probably have failed to grasp the implications: without wheels, the craft could not taxi. Having to hear that explained to her now, jointly, by Henk and Jim made her blush for herself as a journalist. She would fire herself had she been here on assignment, charged with "covering" the event. She hated imperceptiveness, most of all in herself. And being a woman, alas, had something to do with this particular lapse from grace; women did not think about machinery.

Henk said that the hijackers themselves had failed to notice the skids at Schiphol. They had become aware of them here. And right away they had got angry at the pilots. But it was not the pilots who had flown the aircraft in from Germany. They were Dutch Air Force men and the Germans who had brought it had turned it over as it stood, complete with the operations manual for the Dutchmen to figure out. Still, commented Sophie, you would think that these Dutch would have *mentioned* the skids while the helicopter was still at Schiphol and it would not have been too late to change them. No point, Henk retorted: there was not a set of wheels in Holland that would fit this model. His placid tone irritated her; she wanted blame to be assigned. Then why in the world, she said crossly, did the Germans send one with skids? Henk shrugged. At this time of year the craft was probably used for paratrooper training exercises on snow and ice; when the order came down from the Ministry, nobody at the base had thought to put on wheels. Very natural, too, said Carey. "These birds should have sent their specifications along. Hell, they might have got pontoons." The two men laughed. Being males, they found the quandary amusing.

So, since the helicopter could not taxi, it was going to have to be pushed or pulled. The road was icing up nicely, Carey estimated, testing it with his feet. "But that's impossible," Sophie protested. "Why can't the pilot fly it to wherever they want it to go?" That was the idea of the *kapers*, Henk said. But the pilot had refused. The argument just now had been about that. "You could hear it all?" said Carey. "Enough," Henk said, "to seize the drift. Or do you say 'catch the drift'?" "'Get the drift,'" said Sophie, feeling quite impatient. "But go on. Why did the pilot refuse?" "Not enough room for maneuver," answered the Senator. "If he took it up and tried to turn it on a dime in these conditions, there'd be a fair chance of a foul-up." "And he was unwilling to take the chance," observed Sophie. "Why didn't they ask the co-pilot if he was so afraid?" Henk said that the co-pilot had agreed with the pilot. "These fellows are Dutch and stubborn." He held up a finger, recommending quiet. Over by the helicopter, the argument with the pilots had resumed. And no wonder, Sophie thought. A fresh survey of this band of hostages ought to have convinced them that the job could not be done by manpower—sheer madness even to consider it. "They are telling that the helicopter is the property of the German air arm," Henk reported. "And they say the Royal Dutch Air Force has responsibility for this property." "Kind of funny," said Carey. "I mean to be harping on property and responsibility when you want to make an anarchist see your point."

Then all at once the discussion was over. The big hijacker and the co-pilot were underneath the helicopter, looking up at something. The pilots had won their point. Carey said he was not surprised. On balance, he guessed, the hijackers could not have been too eager to see the helicopter take off with the Royal Dutch Air Force at the controls. "Nothing much to prevent them from flying it back to Schiphol, wouldn't you say, Henk? Then good-bye getaway craft." "But why do they *need* a getaway craft?" Sophie demanded. "Psychological," said Carey, and let it go at that. The pilot was now inside the helicopter. From the bottom he was letting out a long cable. "Standard equipment," said Carey. "A hoist, they call it. Used for making drops and pick-ups normally. He has a winch in there that's operated by a motor." He had been a flyer, Sophie remembered, in the Second World War. The cable unwound and lay on the pavement, in coils, like a thin black snake. "But I thought we were going to push," said Sophie. "They'll try the hoist for now," Carey said. "But I expect the time for pushing will come."

The lazy voice broke off. Suddenly there was a great deal of action. It was as though a whistle had been blown. First, the male hostages were quickly separated from the women and formed into a squad, which was set to work unwinding the cable. Then, from the periphery, four new figures appeared. All were dressed in windbreakers and baggy pants, but one might be a woman—she was too far off still to tell. Two stayed by the cable, watching it play out, and two ran off to a point several yards up the highway. They had brought lanterns with them, and now you could see better. But without Carey to brief her, Sophie felt at a loss. She could not make out what was happening, exactly. The pair up the highway was shouting in rapid German. "*Ja!*" "*Nein,*" "*Doch, das stimmt,*" "*Nein. Es stimmt nicht.*" Eventually it dawned on her: they were looking for a tree to fix the cable to. But the trees along the road were just big saplings—willows, Sophie thought, and she tried to remember from her parents' property whether willow was a soft wood or a hard wood. There could not be any full-grown trees anywhere here; the polder was too new. In the thicket were only tall bushes. And along the road no telephone poles. Nothing stout and fixed to anchor onto. And no hope of a big jutting rock; the land was perfectly flat—level sea-bottom. She was not surprised that Carey had sounded skeptical. Yet the confederates, apparently, had found a tree, several yards further up the road, that they thought would suit the purpose, for one of them called out "Jeroen! *Ja, ja! Hier!*" and the tall Dutch hijacker—they were big, Henk said, in the fen-lands he came from—went up to consult with them. Then an order was given, and the hostages hoisted the cable onto their shoulders and marching in step, spaced out in single file, carried it up the road till the order to halt came. The frieze of toiling figures with the cable stretched between them looked curiously like a chain gang silhouetted against the night sky.

The end of the cable reached, but there could not be much slack, because a wait followed while the men tried to hook it to the tree trunk, cursing in a babel of tongues ("*Merde!*" cried the voice of Henk). Finally the laborers fell back. There was a sound of cranking and groaning as the winch turned and the cable tautened. The helicopter moved. It was proceeding on a diagonal to the highway's edge. The problem, of course, was the skids. The thin glaze of ice on the highway was uneven, and halfway along the great hulk seemed to balk. You could hear the skids scrape on the pavement. "Halt!" called the co-pilot and went over to inspect.

There was a consultation. No damage seemed to have been done, and the hijackers, apparently, had been prepared for a setback. An emollient of some kind, Sophie guessed, was needed to grease the skids; the ice was too patchy. She thought madly of Dutch butter. But mud, it seemed, was the answer, and there was no shortage of it in the ditch beside the highway. That was where the shovels fitted in.

Now the women were put to work. Pails were produced, and two groups were formed, one to carry the pails, which "Gretel" was rapidly filling, and the other to apply the contents by hand to the stretch of pavement in front of the runners. The new confederate, who was in fact a woman, pale, thin, German, and young, seized the second shovel and followed Gretel's example. While this was going on, the men took places at the rear of the helicopter, to start pushing when the word came—they would push in concert with the turning winch. Having lost—or wasted—so much time, the hijackers were now in a great hurry. But the pails were small, almost like children's pails, and the mud was cold; actually there were splinters of ice in it. Sophie's hands ached, and she looked with pity at the manicured fingernails of Harold's wife, which showed a blackish red in the lantern light. In Sophie's view, it would have made sense to let the hostages use a shovel to smooth the mud onto the pavement rather than have them slather it on like cold cream with their bare hands. But the shovels were reserved for the use of Gretel and the other. Rather than trust the captives with them, they leaned on them during pauses to watch contemptuously, like forewomen, while the feeble carriers bore off their dripping loads.

At length the leadership was satisfied with the slippery state of the pavement, and the pilot resumed his place. The winch turned, the men pushed, but, instead of advancing, the helicopter was sliding backward. The cable was pulling the tree, which slowly rose, turned a sort of somersault, exposing its roots, and was dragged along the road. A sound of clucking came from the women. "Sheer vandalism," Sophie's nearest neighbor pronounced. "Don't you agree? When one thinks of the money this government must have spent planting those trees . . ." Yet they were going to try again, with another tree—still frailer in appearance, Sophie considered. She rather sympathized with her neighbor: before they were through, they would have ripped up every tree in the area. But at least this next one, unlike its predecessor, had not been weakened by a first assault. And the hijackers this time were trying a new strategy. A rope was brought from the helicopter and tied to the tree trunk. The workers were redistributed. Males, both hostages and hijackers, were assigned to pull on the rope, to hold the tree steady when the winch started its counter-pull, while the women, all of them, were to push the helicopter from the rear. They practiced, then "One, two, *three*!" the fen-land giant counted. The cable tightened. The helicopter moved forward. They had done it.

But the job was not yet over. The ditch they had been digging in constituted a new hazard. It was not very wide; nevertheless there was the danger that one of the skids could slip into it and tip the helicopter over on its side. "Jeroen"—at any rate they now knew his name, which rhymed with "shoon"; was it Dutch for "Jerome"?—stood with his hands on his hips, studying the ditch. He measured the skids and shook his head. Then he called to Ahmed, who brought him a small ax, of the kind used for cutting firewood. Seizing it in his huge hands, he set to work to chop branches off the young willows till he had enough to fill in the ditch at the point the helicopter would cross. Here there was no question of using the winch. Again the women got behind to push; in front, the work-gang of men pulled on the cable. Without gloves, their hands slipped; it was hard to get a purchase. But the bed of twigs and branches was wet and slimy; in half a minute the helicopter was across.

Now there was less hurry. Even though the helicopter was still visible, it was not blocking the road to a truck or car that wanted to pass—there must be maintenance men at that pumping-station and if they worked in shifts, some could be arriving or leaving at any hour of the night. This highway must connect with the mainland, where people lived, and to Sophie it was a miracle that no vehicle so far had appeared. And if one had, what would the hijackers have done? Taken whoever was in it prisoner, she supposed. But then the car would have to be hidden too. At any rate it would have had wheels. And if the night-shift worker had had a family, wouldn't somebody have given the alarm when he failed to come home? All the time they had been pushing and shoving she had been worrying, she realized, that a car would come before they finished, and now that that danger no longer mattered much—in the dark a driver would be concentrating on the road and not looking to see what was beside it—she pushed the damp fringe back from her forehead and breathed easier.

There remained the thick underbrush to be dealt with. A sort of path or track, she noticed, already ran through it, and the vegetation was crushed and trampled in places. But the track was too narrow for the helicopter to pass. It would have to be widened. Otherwise, she guessed, the rotor blades might get tangled in the tall reeds. Or some other damage could befall its vital parts. Fatigue was making her unmechanical brain even more hazy: in Vietnam she had ridden in dozens of helicopters and actually come under fire from the ground once, yet now she could not even remember where their engines were exactly. But she was right about widening the path.

While the teams of hostages rested and the men mopped their brows ("Wonderful exercise!" she heard the minister proclaim), Ahmed busied himself with the ax. His progress along the thicket's encroaching edges was maddeningly slow, and behind him he left masses of snarled reeds and prickly branches, which the others, following in his wake, had to clear away. Carey, walking beside her and watching the young man's clumsy efforts, was manifestly losing patience. "Here, let me have that," he said and proceeded to cut a clean swath, rapidly felling bushes on either side as he went. There came a piercing whistle. "Put that ax down!" It was strange how these people, though they must be even more tired than the hostages, could be so alert. They must have their wits about them to be instantly conscious of the deadly-weapon potential latent in an ax or a mere shovel.

Or was it not, rather, dim-witted on their part to be so fiercely suspicious? One thing they were incapable of divining, it seemed, was the impulse to be helpful common to most Americans—other people had it but not to the same degree. In America, if you were not born with it, they taught it to you in school. Carey's was just a reflex reaction to the sight of incompetence; it hurt the American farm boy in him to watch somebody use an ax that badly. Nor was it only the Senator. Sophie had noticed that the task of moving this oversize helicopter to safety had produced something like a team spirit even in the bystanders. Once indignation over the tree-uprooting had subsided, there had been a quick shower of advice, to which Simmons of course had contributed but also the queenly mammoth they called Margaret: "You will have more traction, I think, Harold, if you shift your position somewhat more to the right." More remarkable: a pair of pale yellow gloves had been silently tendered to the cable-pullers, relayed—too late, as it happened—from Charles, banished to the shadows but evidently taking an active interest. And now poor Ahmed had managed to cut his thumb; instead of letting it bleed, the Air France stewardess promptly came forward with her first-aid kit. These little occurrences touched Sophie. Of course it was in the stewardess's training. And of course Ahmed was by way of becoming everybody's pet hijacker. But something more was at work, Sophie felt—an endearing, irrational, human tendency to make common cause. Nothing could be more foreign to the hostages' self-interest than the project of hiding this helicopter.

Finally the path was declared to be wide enough. Ahmed's place had been taken by a gaunt new Palestinian even less adept. "I guess in the desert they don't get much use for an ax," summed up Carey. Henk had gone ahead merrily at the wood-chopper's side, and now he reported what he had been able to see: a typical gabled Dutch farmhouse, two stories high, and near it a barn in construction—it lacked one wall and a roof. The helicopter was ready to move. There was no need for fresh mud; the ground here, being marshy and half-frozen, was naturally slippery—a point the pastor had demonstrated by another sorry tumble. There were also, Henk said, crusted remnants of a snowfall in the open space around the barn, where the helicopter would obviously go. From now on the job would be easy. And in fact that was so. The only difficulties were interposed by the pilots. The track was still on the narrow side—either thanks to Ahmed and his successor or because the hijackers had not wanted to make it too wide, in case it would be noticeable from the air—and to keep the helicopter straight on course, free of interference from protruding briars and branch-ends, seemed to have become a point of honor with the flyers, who from time to time shouted "*Halt!*" and brought everything to a standstill, as though a few scratches on the German paint job would matter. It was their training, Sophie supposed. But the *kapers* were humoring them, and the helicopter made it to the barn.

Urging it in, finally, was the simplest part. It really looked as though Providence were working on the hijackers' behalf. That the barn lacked a wall and a roof could not have been better for their purposes. If the roof had been on, the helicopter could not possibly have fitted under it, and the open side was a made-to-order portal. The unfinished barn was a perfect berth; you would almost think it had been designed by a builder to function as a hangar. And lying around, as though in readiness, were sheets of builders' tar paper and a carpenter's ladder. It was quick work for the more able-bodied hostages, following the northlander's instructions, to climb up and fit the tar paper loosely over the top, like a tent, resting on the outspread blades. When the job was finished, the lanterns were put away, and everyone stood back to admire. As though at the command of a stage electrician, the moon came out, to provide a ghostly lighting. Standing back, you would never know that a helicopter was garaged here unless you were directly in front, facing the open side. And from the air, that would not matter; from the air, the illusion would be complete. A search plane would see only a typical barn in the process of construction, and the tar paper might have been laid over the top to keep the damp out. No jungle camouflage, Sophie decided, could ever have been so naturalistic. "A light blanket of snow would add a touch," commented Jim. He himself was a wet blanket, Sophie told him. Her legs had regained feeling, and she momentarily forgot being hungry in a general glow of satisfaction—Veblen's pride of workmanship, it must be, though her own part had been small.

The other hostages, too, had been reanimated; interest had shifted to the dark farmhouse and what it might contain by way of amenities. "Will there be a toilet?" Simmons wondered. Beryl's mother was hoping for a "bathe"—even a sponge bath. The men's thoughts ran to food and heating: better not be counting on steaks, though, and Ramsbotham understood that Holland had an oil shortage. Henk, as the authority, was besieged with eager questions: would they heat with gas maybe, how many rooms in a farmer's house, any hope of a frigidaire? For these poor souls, merely naming those "necessities of life"—warmth, food, running water—even with cautious pessimism, could not fail to bring on a mood of anticipation. "Will they let us get our things now?" said Harold's wife.

Certainly by now they had earned a good night's rest and something hot to eat. But the hijackers did not see it that way. From their point of view, there was still work to be done. Obviously the path that had just been widened would have to be restored to at least a semblance of its earlier state, so that from the air it would look as if nothing more than a builder's truck had used it, to bring in materials. They could not just quit and go to bed. With reluctance, Sophie conceded that, and Jim Carey, beside her, was nodding his agreement as the leader, leaning against the barn wall, went down the list of tasks that remained. A squad of hostages was to collect sedge, lopped-off branches, and so on, to fill in the sides of the path. The uprooted tree was to be put back in place and all traces of disturbance cleared off the highway. To Sophie, it was as if a stage were about to be set, with the hostages as scene-shifters, and she asked herself whether so much verisimilitude was really necessary—could there be an element of sadistic enjoyment? "And our toilet cases?" prompted Harold's wife, whose chief interest probably lay in her eight-hour cream. Curious, though, that the hijackers had omitted to mention the detail of the hostages' "things"; now that the helicopter was gone, the pile of cases on the highway was the most conspicuous item for miles around. The question annoyed Gretel. "We have not forgotten, Mrs. Moneybags. A squad will be assigned to place them in the ditch until we are ready." That was a cruel blow; some of the women gasped and some emitted piteous bleats. Sophie caught Henk's eye. He cleared his throat. "*Neen!*" he called out. Again he was going to come to the rescue. Over by the barn, he talked rapidly to the two in Dutch; Sophie watched his gestures—he seemed to be counting on his fingers, as a demonstration of something. And almost at once Jeroen was making an announcement: for "compassionate reasons," a group of hostages would be permitted to collect their "hand baggages" and proceed to the house; the others would finish the work.

"How did you pull that off?" inquired Carey when Henk was back among them. "Yes, how?" said Sophie. "I said that here are too many persons. For them, it must be dangerous. And most are not needed." Whenever he had been speaking Dutch, she noticed, his English got worse, as though he were trying to be his own interpreter at some summit meeting—he had pronounced "said" as "sayed." Or was it a sign of strain? He was certainly a gifted negotiator.

It was the first-class passengers who reaped the immediate

benefit. With the exception of Beryl and the curator, they were being sent off to bed, which was only fair, Sophie thought: most of them were well past fifty. It was a relief to see them set forth, guarded by two Arabs and clutching their cases. "But *I'm* fifty," cried Simmons. "Why should they be privileged?" "You don't look it, Aileen," said Carey. "Let them have their shut-eye. Be good now and stay with us liberals." "But they'll eat up all the food, Jim." Nevertheless, she complied. In a minute she was helping him pick up branches.

As it turned out, everyone's baggage was promptly transported to the house. The steward and stewardess saw to it, and the pilots lent a hand. They did not forget the Bishop's umbrella or his old carryall—his dead wife's needlework. The squad working on the path smiled as they watched the young pilot go past with the treasured possession. "Gus'll be happy as a clam to see it again," the minister redundantly said. "Did he love her so much?" asked Simmons. "Or only after she was dead?" In the moonlight Sophie saw Carey wince. "Cult of relics," he said, roughly pushing a heap of briars into position.

Their labors were almost over. The final chore was to remove all the skid traces from the highway. In Sophie's opinion, this was overdoing it. The *kapers* were succumbing to a perfectionist temptation, unless they were plain brutes. And in their place she would have advised water, carried from their hideaway if necessary, rather than a broom. She and Beryl were alone on the empty road. They had relieved the young museum man and the silent Scottish don. The tree had been replanted, the path had been "landscaped" to the limit of possibility, and most of the weary workers had been allowed to go to the house. Only Henk and Jim remained, waiting loyally by the road's edge and strictly forbidden to help. Somewhere nearby, the leaders were keeping watch. Eventually they would come with their flashlights to assure themselves that Beryl and Sophie had not shirked. To shirk was certainly tempting, with one broom between them and the skid tracks half frozen in places. They could have used a shovel as a scraper; instead they had only the feet God had given them. Kicking at a lump of ice, Beryl hurt her big toe. Sophie commiserated, grateful, now, for her boots. Both would greatly like to know how it was that the two of them had been specially elected to perform this senseless last task by themselves. "Why us?" wondered Beryl. Sophie suspected that it was because the gang was punishing her for being Jewish but she decided not to say that; anyway, it did not explain Beryl. On that point, however, Beryl had her own theory. "Ahmed likes me," she said. "That's why."

Suddenly Sophie was bone-tired, too tired, she feared, to be able to eat. And tomorrow, she expected, would be worse, even if they were fed, because tomorrow there would be nothing to do but wait. She took the muddy broom from Beryl and gave a ferocious swipe. As she did so, Beryl's head turned. They heard the sound of a plane's motor. It was flying low. A searchlight was playing over the highway perhaps half a mile off and coming nearer. They saw a flare drop. "Cripes," said Beryl and ducked. Automatically Sophie let go of her broom; she crouched. A strange thought crossed her mind. "If it sees us," the thought said, "we are lost." She scrambled toward the road's edge, looking crazily for shelter.

"Down!" the man's voice commanded from somewhere in the underbrush. Clearly he could not see that the order was superfluous. "Down, both of you," said the woman's voice. "Into the ditch." "She loves that ditch," muttered Beryl. The icy, muddy trough was the last hiding-place either of them would have chosen; nevertheless they obeyed. Sophie hoped at least that Henk and Jim would be there, too, but they must have been told to hide in the bushes. She was by herself with her one-time classmate, the two of them crouching down, with their feet in the gelid mud. "Does she remind you of Mrs. H.?" Beryl said, under her breath. "Ssh!" said Sophie. She had remembered something. The broom. She had left it lying on the road. She asked herself whether Gretel realized that. Maybe she could not see it from where she had taken cover. Sophie straightened up and peered out. The searchlight was still some distance off, making broad sweeping arcs; she had time. Her heart raced; her knees shook, as if the plane was "enemy" with a load of bombs to release on her. She crept out. "Get back!" called the man's voice. Sophie did not answer. She inched along the highway on her hands and knees—dirt on her suede coat no longer mattered—till she could touch the tip of the broom-handle; then she pulled the broom toward her and fell back with it into the ditch. "The broom," she explained, idiotically. Beryl gripped her filthy hand. "Shake, sister." All at once, Sophie remembered a funny thing about her at Putney: the time she had told the whole form that she was changing her name to "Aventurine" and expected them all to call her that.

Now the plane was directly overhead. Another flare was dropped. Next to her, Sophie could feel Beryl holding her breath. Impossible that the plane would not see them as a motionless pair of shadows in this blinding light. The pilot was making sweeps, yet what interested him seemed to be farther up the road. Did the replanted tree look peculiar? She remembered reading a background story—was it about the Moors murders?—which said that aerial photographs could show where a grave had been dug from the way the soil looked even when the turf had been carefully replaced. Now even Beryl's breathing seemed to her too loud; she could not rid herself of the queer feeling that they could be overheard by the plane. Yet the pilot could not have noticed anything suspicious, for he had turned away from the road, in the direction of the dark house and the barn. It was safe now to peek out. He dipped, and the searchlight prowled. The peaked roofline of the house showed clearly, a quarter of a mile away. Sophie wondered what the hostages inside were feeling. She pictured Harold trying to signal from the roof. But apparently the pilot was satisfied that there was nothing there but "a typical Dutch farmhouse." In a minute the plane veered back to the highway. It went on, still flying low, toward what must be the mainland. The sound of the motor gradually died away.

The scare was over; bodies popped up, as if resurrecting, and stretched their limbs. Nothing could be heard but the distant pumping-station, the sudden rustle of bird wings, and low human voices, still pitched to an undertone. The flare petered out; everything returned to normal. Or so to speak. "'Beddy-bye,' eh?" said Carey, and no one contradicted. As he took her arm to steady her on the homeward path, Sophie could not help feeling that she had proved quite a heroine in the broom episode—courage and initiative under fire. Yet she fought back the urge to mention it, since on the one hand objectively there had been no "fire," as a sane part of her giddy mind must always have known, and on the other the whole adventure, insofar as it was one, was best kept between herself and "Aventurine." What would the Bishop think if he heard that single-handed and without prompting or duress Sophie Weil had foiled a powerful search plane intent on learning their whereabouts? And that she was unrepentant and unregretful, though she could not say why. He would pray for her maybe.

Eight

URING the night, a thin snow had fallen. The temperature
stood at –1° Celsius. The sky was empty; no plane had yet
come snooping. From the air, in any case, nothing unusual
would be noticed: a typical new farmhouse painted dark green
in the Frisian way, its eastern window panes glittering in the
rising sun, the sloping roof tiles a shiny fresh orange. Outside
the main door swung a clothes-yard on which laundry hung,
the only sign of habitation. Fifty meters off, there would appear to be a barn twice the size of the house in construction,
loosely roofed over with tar paper or plastic sheeting and
lightly blanketed with snow. Beyond, stretching to the horizon
and broken only by the gleam of a canal, lay ploughed fields
marked by frozen furrows like the deep wrinkles of a weath-
ered *boer* face—on the ridges the earth color showed through
where the wind had swept them bare. Around the house were
dainty bird tracks but as yet no human footprints. Later the
men would be led out in pairs to pee and move their bowels, if
able, close to the back shed; the women would use the downstairs toilet for the time being—the toilet permission would be
revoked were a breach of discipline to occur. From the air, the
house should appear to be occupied but not unduly, not beyond the norm of four to six persons warranted for a settler's
family.

On this day in reality it held thirty-two. Eight guards, twenty-
four prisoners, which made an acceptable ratio: for every three
imperialists, one people's army soldier. In the kitchen the Air
France personnel was preparing a morning meal of bread,
cheese, cold ham, butter, and coffee. The same meal had been
distributed the night before, with the addition of pea soup and
herring. If the hostages were to become constipated on this
diet, it made no matter: fewer trips under guard to the outdoors and fewer stinking turds deposited. For this reason,
prunes had been struck off the list of military supplies required.
The logistics of this phase of the operation had been reviewed
in depth; no detail of housekeeping was too small to be passed
over. These people, it must be remembered, were prisoners of

war. In engaging an enemy the less left to chance, the greater your flexibility in meeting the challenge of the unexpected under whatever form it might arise—"For want of a nail," as the proverb said.

Now, thanks to good planning, on this Tuesday morning, precisely forty-four hours after the launching of the assault, the innocent-looking farmhouse was an arsenal, stocked to the rafters with arms and ammunition, sandbags, explosives, canned and dried foods, smoked meat and fish, legumes and cereals, dairy products, blood plasma—all the matériel needful for a sustained auto-defense. The dwelling stood isolated, in open ground, without neighbors. As yet, no tree or shrub, which might afford cover, screened it from the wind. Any force seeking to approach would be seen immediately, at any rate by daylight. On the side away from the barn ran an entry road visible along its whole length from the big kitchen window, no doubt for the housewife's convenience; the underbrush that might have obstructed a sweeping view had been cleared and stacked in piles. The thicket near the highway on the barn side extended only a few hundred meters of protection. As noted in the initial study, the position had one small drawback, unavoidable in this terrain: the dwelling lacked a cellar, which might have been used for storage and for punishing disciplinary offenders. On the other hand, in the utility room, which occupied the shed, there was a big deep-freeze chest, and the kitchen had a frigidaire, ample shelves and cupboards and old-style bins. Outside the rear door were a chicken coop and a rabbit run. The welfare state was kind to its kulaks.

This rich farmer's house boasted eight rooms: on the ground floor, utility room, kitchen, family living-room, and *beste kamer*, plus a lavatory off the entry hall, containing shower and toilet; upstairs, the parents' room, two rooms for the children, playroom, and bathroom with tub and toilet. Above, reached by a ladder, was an attic. These *boers* had a washing-machine, a color television, a floor-waxer, a dish-washer, and central heating, fueled by oil—earth gas, the Netherlands' bragging retort to the Arab oil "boycott," had not arrived at the polder. The cookstove ran on propane. In addition, these folk had a tractor, fueled by petrol, and a new family automobile—a Ford Fiesta —as well as bicycles. On Sunday morning, bright and early, the

Fiesta had carried the farmer and his butterball wife and four children to Schiphol, with six round-trip tickets (four half-fare) to the Balearics for a two weeks' winter vacation in the sun. Besides the *dreck* of capitalist technology, the family had a real eiderdown on the matrimonial bed, a child's crib painted with traditional Hindeloopen designs, and, in the *beste kamer*, genuine old-time oak-framed samplers embroidered with Old Testament mottoes, an *erfstuk* Reformed Bible bound in leather, with silver locks, a vase of peacock feathers, and three oriental carpets, one of which Yusuf declared to be genuine and at least fifty years old.

The Palestine Liberation Army had been impressed by this farmer's style of life. That was one of the negative side-effects of the decision to lease a pioneer house on the new polder as a base of operations. The Arab comrades should have been armed by their revolutionary training to resist the crude seductions of the welfare state. What they saw here, they should know, was window-dressing. The upper peasantry of the "advanced" countries of the West were a privileged caste, the same as the trade unionists, poisoned by the crumbs that fell to them from the rich man's table. All these social elements were the bribed tools of imperialism, in Marx's phrase—some of the old prophet's insights were still useful. One had thought that Hussein and Ahmed, at least, as "guest workers" in the kitchens and streets and sewers of Paris, would long ago have been demystified. They had seen with their own eyes the realities of class and race behind the façade: the HLMs and bidonvilles of Giscard's police state, alias *la belle France*. Their social origin was petty bourgeois, but in their political activity as emigrants they had shared the "quality of life" of the sweated underproletariat and did not need to be taught how to hate.

Yusuf, by contrast, was a greenhorn, detailed to the present mission from his training camp in Syria; he was an expert in explosives but still innocent of the inner workings of bourgeois democracy on its home ground. In view of that, it had seemed wiser to withhold him from the first and most dangerous phase of the operation. His physical courage was guaranteed by his Syrian sponsors, but the take-over of an airplane was a more serious affair than raiding a kibbutz or blowing up a hotel. A direct strike at the vital organs of the West called for a more seasoned militant than Yusuf, on arrival, proved to be. After a preliminary screening, in Frankfurt, it had been decided to defer him for service on the polder, where he would be able to make himself useful and profit from instruction from the other comrades. He had been conducted to a safe house in Aachen, issued a new false passport and identity papers, provided with a haircut, a suit of clothes, and a solid pair of shoes. Three days ago, with the German comrades and Carlos, the Uruguayan, he had crossed the border at Maastricht. The signal from Paris had come. The following noon, Sunday, the operation would begin; at that time the support elements arriving from Germany should already be in place, with concise directions for preparing the farmhouse to receive the commando and its prisoners, whose number was still unknown.

Coordination had been excellent. There had been no difficulty at the border with Yusuf's papers, and the trunk of the car had not even been opened. Twenty-four hours later, it might have been another story—with the capture of the plane a general alert could have gone out. Yet, despite the good functioning of the time-table and the accurate deployment of the reserves, it now looked as if there might have been an error of judgment on the human level, insofar as Yusuf was concerned. Too little was known about him; his language capacity, in particular, had been overestimated by the Syrian contact—the only Western tongue familiar to him was a rudimentary English he had picked up in a Zionist carpet factory. Inspection this morning showed that he had carried out his assignments creditably: the house had been correctly wired, the remaining stocks of explosives stored in a dry place—the choice of a flour bin was commendable. But he had no reading skill, and, once his work was completed, time, it seemed, had hung heavy on his hands.

This was a restless *knabe*, Elfride reported, and, like so many of the *fedayin*, curious, full of questions needing clear answers, which, because of the language handicap, she had been unable to give him, she feared. In the end, he had passed his Sunday silently roaming about the house, doing his laundry in the washing-machine, and watching the children's hour program from a German station on the farmer's television: Snow White and the Seven Dwarfs. On Monday he had counted the piles of starched linen sheets in the housewife's cupboard and walked over the farmer's fields. Horst and Carlos had not known what to do with him.

With the appearance last night of Ahmed and Hussein, his tongue had loosened. But Ahmed, who had his own weaknesses, was more concerned with his cut thumb—wondering whether he should not give himself an injection of blood plasma from the frigidaire—than with their comrade's political education. Like Yusuf, Ahmed and Hussein seemed bewitched by the kulak's living space and by the signs of wealth they pointed to, eagerly chattering in Arabic. Encouraged by Yusuf and his childlike excitement, they had reverted themselves to an infantile level. It became clear that there was an irritating residue of gullibility in all three comrades. Yusuf had showed them his discovery—the shower—and they got into it together, giggling and splashing each other, as though they had never met a hot-and-cold shower before. Then, having been assigned to the big bed, they climbed under the eiderdown, which they fingered with awe, tucking it tenderly under their chins, when a mature political reaction, as Greet commented, would have been to slash the old fetish through with a knife and let the feathers fly. The whole disheartening performance was like an advertisement of the benefits of capitalism. Did the sleeping patriots dream of this fat land of milk and honey, where the merry peasant had "never had it so good"?

Jeroen felt discouraged. Seated at the kitchen table, he spat out a morsel of ham onto the paper plate in front of him. Then he sought to be fair. There was a reverence for property here, he realized, that no bourgeois could possibly feel, and it would have to be treated with care or the Arabs could become problems. He was touched by it in a way, remembering himself when he had first come to Amsterdam as an apprentice electrician and looked with wonder at the great houses on the canals and the pictures in the Rijksmuseum. It had been a feeling close to worship and had made him ask whether he should not become an artist, dedicate himself to a thing he thought he saw represented here, which he had called to himself "*waarde*." This "worth" or value, he imagined, was what the liberation fighters were seeing in the farmer's housing, which was causing them, still this morning, to open their dark eyes wide, as though they had been given a vision of paradise.

An oriental paradise, he thought to himself, shaking his head, and hoped the idea was not racist. A regular Garden of Allah, sumptuously carpeted, for it was the *beste kamer*, he perceived, that affected them most strongly—they would tire of the shower-bath and the washing-machine. Except for the couple's bedroom, the remainder of the dwelling was more like a "contemporary" suburban villa than an agricultural worker's home. The manipulative hand of some firm of Amsterdam architects—planners for the state—was crudely evident in the family room, where the new television throned and a stack of religious newspapers seemed to wait for banishment. "Picture" window, rough plaster wall with "sculpture" pattern, false ceiling beams, synthetic-tweed floor covering, indirect lighting panels—Jeroen was sadly familiar with this alienating mass-produced *rommel*. He had installed the identical panels and fixtures in city housing developments for workers and could look back on the shame of it as a step in his own development. Here they would name it "polder style," and where the wild sedges now grew there would be a landscaped house lot, ornamental shrubbery, a weeping willow, a rock garden, possibly a pool. But the couple had respected the old concept in furnishing the parlor.

Crossing the magic threshold, the three Arabs stared at the housewife's collection of well-watered plants blooming on window-sill and tables before the shining plate-glass window, at the framed tinted photos of the ancestors, at the harmonium in the corner, at the doilies and antimacassars, at the vase of peacock feathers; they stood silent before the deep-toned carpet, apparently the real one, that hung on the round window-table and they stepped softly, as if fearful of leaving a footprint, on the thick carpets that lay on the waxed floor.

Jeroen had watched their nostrils sensuously take in the characteristic Dutch *beste kamer* smell, of furniture polish—the good old *boenwas*, guaranteed pure from the hive—mixed with the moist hothouse fragrance of flowering plants, with a strong sniff of lye, and a damp, slightly moldy odor of upholstery fabric exuded by a rarely opened room. Yet it was pointless to explain to them, as Greet was doing, that the room was never used except for marriages and will-readings and maybe sometimes the Sabbath. That could only heighten the value of the room in their eyes; what they sensed here was something sacred. The *beste kamer* was a religious shrine, a holy of holies, with a ceremonial carpet serving as altar cloth; the predominant smell of soap and beeswax was the odor of sanctity. If it was used for everyday, it would no longer be a place of worship. To demystify them, it would be necessary to show them what god was being worshipped here and at what cost of blood and grinding toil to their brothers.

It was true that such a room occupied valuable space in a house and had no practical utility. But a mosque had no practical utility. And in Jeroen's view, which differed sharply from Greet's on this point, a revolutionary should not try to set at naught the experience of something higher, called "transcendence" in philosophy. He did not accept the position, typical of orthodox Leninism, that the philosophers had been sheer obscurantists; some of their terms, if reinterpreted and purged of ruling-class overtones, pointed to truths that the revolutionary should embrace as his own. There was a potential in man for rising above—in other words, transcending—gross material concerns that the revolutionary by his act and example sought to bring to full life in every human creature, while the bourgeois and the bourgeois revisionist sought to strangle it at birth, above all in the working masses but finally, perforce, in themselves. The argument of practicality, which Greet was invoking to disabuse the Arabs, could make no impression on them since it was essentially a bourgeois argument.

Moreover the childish reverence they showed for this standard Dutch kitsch had to be understood and allowed for in context. It reflected the oppression and deprivation of agricultural workers in their homeland. That such a house should appear to them as a palace told the whole story of imperialist exploitation of the "backward" peoples. To let oneself be impatient with the comrades' wonderment would be a fault, mirroring one's own sense of superior social development. Greet despised the *beste kamer* of her middle-class parents as the ultimate symbol of Dutch hypocrisy; to profane this farmer's parlor was seen by her as a revolutionary necessity—she was insisting, for instance, that they go back on the promise they had given to water the housewife's army of plants. With all that Jeroen did not sympathize. He had no especially vengeful feelings toward his hard-working parents' humble best room with the big black Bible and the wheezy old harmonium; the clambering "Busy Lizzies" on the window-sill, industriously flowering without care or nourishment, the lowest of the low among house plants, had been a bright joy of his childhood. To leave this woman's innocent plants to droop and die as an act of revolutionary justice would be a kind of slow execution painful to witness and, far from setting the Arabs an example of disciplined class behavior, would only confuse and hurt them. Their development in these matters should be allowed to find its own way without undue prompting or correction. Regarding Ahmed and Hussein, it had been a mistake, plainly, to assume that the lessons learned in Giscard's France would be seen to apply to the Netherlands; the West was a hydra, bearing many heads, which had to be struck off separately, even though the trunk of the beast was one and indivisible.

The fact was that Den Uyl and his allies were cleverer than their brothers of the Right. They were able to take in the working class with their skilful propaganda, which consisted not in empty slogans but in social measures speaking for themselves and to a certain degree incontestably. A revolutionary would err in saying that there was large-scale poverty in Holland and naked oppression of minorities, that the aged were harshly neglected—Jeroen's own parents, drawing their state pension and health benefits, were living proof of paternalistic "favoritism" to the old. That the pension policy was a ruse to induce early retirement and withdraw a section of the work force from the labor market, thus masking real unemployment, did not alter the facts. The noisy protests of the Right, howling against "confiscatory" taxation and blind to its own interests—in reality so well served by Den Uyl and Company—helped sustain the fiction. It was only in foreign policy that Den Uyl and his gang regularly gave their game away: was it not openly boasted that staunch little Holland was the "best friend" of Israel and the U.S. imperialist warmakers? Hand in glove with the imperialists, as their trusted lackey, Den Uyl could afford a crocodile's concern for human rights in General Pinochet's Chile and the moribund Franco's Spain. On the domestic scene, the multi-nationals flourished through shameless bribery and corruption, while land-reclamation projects, such as this polder, kept alive the national myth of sturdy self-help. That the Communist Party had no influence and the only real opposition came from the Right and the fanatic confessional parties demonstrated how effective the simulation of socialism had been. Even the Indonesians, after a period in unpublicized camps, were consenting to be "absorbed" by their former colonialist masters. Should one blame Arab patriots, born and raised in the teeming bazaars, if they were not wholly immune to the subtle indoctrination of this farmer's housing?

They were also impressed—and for the same reasons, rooted in history—by the extent of the farmer's fields. After walking them yesterday, Yusuf had concluded that they must comprise fifty hectares already ploughed, with about five, including the house lot, still unimproved. He had said to Elfride that the man here must be a big landowner, an exploiter. She had told him no, correctly. Lying to the masses was always a mistake; one had to explain and carefully expose the underlying contradictions. Being a German and unfamiliar with Dutch agrarian patterns, she could not say whether this farmer owned the land or rented it from the state, but in the end it came to the same. Narrowly speaking, he was not an exploiter, since it was clear that he used machinery rather than the labor of landless peasants to work it, yet, in a broader sense, as an instrument of imperialism, he was exploiting the resources of the Third World, in his very tractor and the diesel that fueled it, the rubber tires of his automobile, the copper-derived chromium of his wife's appliances, the nitrates of his fertilizer, and so on. On the other hand, it would be stupid to pretend that he and his wife, by Dutch standards, enjoyed great prosperity; there was too much evidence here to the contrary, though some of it might not be visible to a Palestinian eye. Even the word "kulak" was probably misplaced. In terms of the Dutch class structure, these were not moneyed people. The new furniture consisted of "suites" purchased no doubt at a discount house; there were no books, and the only picture was a cheap reproduction of a Rembrandt self-portrait tacked up in the children's playroom. Very likely the man was still paying out to the usurers of the loan companies on the car and the tractor. His wife made her own and the children's clothes, as an old Singer in the couple's room testified. But in Yusuf's eyes, a sewing-machine was a sign of affluence—another contradiction springing from historical unevenness.

The clearest proof, however, that this family's circumstances were relatively modest was the way they had jumped at the offer to vacate the premises for a two-week period. It had perhaps not even been necessary to throw in the vacation in the Balearics. Probably they would have been glad to move in with relatives on the mainland—the woman had her people in Kampen. So Jeroen had contended, but Greet, though not denying it, had argued that the cost factor must be weighed against the temptation the couple might feel to "look in" on their tenants—some trivial pretext could always be found. She did not trust the woman; to her mind, it was worth a thousand guilders for the group to have the assurance that the creature was out of Holland, safely lying on a beach and coated with sunburn lotion, during the crucial first phase of the operation. Doubtless she had been right; Jeroen knew it was inconsistent for a revolutionary to have, like him, a penny-pinching mentality inherited from peasant forebears of the deepest "black-stockings" dye.

Besides, Greet had to be deferred to for the remarkable vision she had shown in proposing the polder as a base. From the start they had all seen that for a strike of this magnitude a fall-back position would have to be prepared, since the usual ports of call, though sometimes curiously open to commercial hijackers, could not be counted on to receive a people's army commando and its prisoners of war—this was one of the sad results of factional division within the liquidation-of-the-Zionist-entity forces. That among the people's prisoners an American senator would figure made it all the more likely that a "diplomatic" attitude could be expected from the Arab capitals, to say nothing of Havana, where this senator was regarded, simplistically, as some kind of friend. Hence it had been essential to develop a serious alternative, not dependent on the whims and opportunistic calculations of national leaders, and it was Greet, at the December meeting, who had had the genius to think of the polder. Like every creative idea, it had got a lukewarm reception to begin with; all sorts of "practical" objections were raised, particularly by the German comrades. But then Jeroen himself had caught fire, and, before the meeting was over, the whole planning council was converted.

After that, a familiar law of momentum took over: the more the comrades studied the polder, the less interest they showed in the original list of sanctuaries which were to be tried before falling back, as a last resort, on a substitute. By a swift overturn, comparable to a revolution, almost overnight and yet without anyone's conscious decision, the last became first. When finally, after cautious reconnoitering and consultation of a geodetic map, this particular farmhouse had been pinpointed as most suited to their purpose, it was as if they could no longer, willingly, reverse direction, any more than a snowball rolling downhill could change course. This, at any rate, was Jeroen's analysis of the phenomenon as he looked back from today's perspective on the stages, unrolling as in a slow-motion film, from doubt to total commitment the plan had traversed. From here, like any process when looked at backward, it appeared foreordained, never to have been in doubt. Yet at the final meeting in Paris, on the eve of the great day, it had still been voted that on take-over the pilot would query the "sympathizing" Arab capitals for permission to land. But more as a matter of form—if his sense of that meeting was correct—and as a brotherly concession to the Syrian arms-suppliers than in any serious expectation of a favorable response. Jeroen did not like to think, now, what his reaction would have been if an Arab capital had surprised them. Bitter regret, surely, for the time and work and study that had gone into the polder alternative—not to mention the air fares and the rent money and the Majorca hotel outlay—but, beyond that, for Jeroen and perhaps for Greet too, there would have been almost an artistic disappointment.

Already, while it was still a blueprint, they were proud of their idea, of its simple clean lines and undeniable originality—it owed nothing in its conception to any of the current models of revolutionary strategy. The Japanese Red Army comrades, Wadi Haddad and his PFLP contingent, even the matchless "Carlos" could only admire. And in the captive Boeing, Jeroen had needed all his schooling in indifference to keep an impassive face as they monitored the radio for answers which were strangely slow in coming, while the plane flew steadily south-ward and, on the polder, if all had gone well, the farmhouse stood ready and waiting. To sit dully, by contrast, in the Libyan desert, while Khaddafi's people bargained for you would have been a sorry comedown; in fact such a prospect had become unthinkable to Jeroen, and not merely because the most pre-dictable outcome would be "administrative detention" in a Benghazi jail.

Working out the details—the bothersome minutiae, each of which required a separate inspiration to resolve—he had fallen in love with the plan. He had watched it grow under their hands, change and develop, meet and encompass obstacles or else leap over them. The sense of it as a work of art had grown in him, and not a solitary work of art fashioned by a bourgeois dreamer out of lifeless materials but an active, vital collabora-tion in which even the farmer and his wife and red-cheeked children played a part, albeit an unwitting one. They were the local materials to be worked in, as your architect used brick or fieldstone, according to availability, and they were also the "local color," the *oud-Hollands* camouflage serving as your disguise. And insofar as they were a part of the medium you worked in, the resistance they offered to your design had to be calculated and incorporated as an element in the overall pic-ture. In short, they were a challenge, and here again it was Greet who had responded creatively.

The problem presented was simple, and yet everything hung on it: how to approach these people with an offer to "borrow" their property that would not excite their suspicions. Suspicion was inbred in farm-dwellers—a reflex set in motion by any novelty, by the mere sight of a stranger. Yet to take over the house by force was an option ruled out by the circumstances; violence applied prematurely would abort the whole design. Some stratagem was needed that would disarm the pair as effectively as a weapon and yet have an innocent, indeed attrac-tive appearance. Something familiar to them in their everyday life, something they would welcome as it crossed their thresh-old. A fistful of money would not do it; the sight of money in quantity would be too unfamiliar. To find an "open sesame" was not so easy; the others were almost ready to give up and look for another stronghold when Greet hit on the answer:

television, of course. They would pose as a television crew doing a story on the polder.

No one doubted that this at last was the solution—an answer so obvious that it might have been overlooked, like the television aerial on the roof of the dwelling over which the eye passed without taking notice, any more than of a chimney. And the event had proved her right, as if it had been programmed: the knock on the door, footsteps inside, a pair of blue eyes peering out the window, cautious unbolting of the door, inspection of the four persons standing outside, carrying cameras and sound equipment, quick glance at the small truck parked in the entry road with large stickers "Hamburger Rundfunk" on its sides and rear, removal of apron, smoothing of hair, and "Come in, please, ladies and gentlemen, but kindly wipe your feet." Then, after the inevitable service of coffee, the housewife was ready to hear their proposition.

The truck and the stickers on it must have dispelled any lingering doubt. The stickers had been Horst's idea. Strange how, from the instant that impersonating a television crew was thought of, the details had fallen into place, like iron filings assembling around a powerful magnet. Improvements and minor corrections seemed to derive naturally from the key concept, as if it had a brain of its own. Jeroen, at the beginning, had thought of hand-lettering the trunk with the name of the German station, but Horst had showed him the risk in that if they should happen to be stopped by the highway police— stickers, which could be removed immediately on leaving the farmhouse, served the same purpose and would not be seen to be stickers unless examined close up. Similarly, the original scenario had had them coming from the Omroepstichting. But Jeroen himself had seen the flaw: it would be too easy for the couple to check up with the Dutch feature service; a simple phone call would do it. German television combined the known and the remote. It was watched regularly in Holland, yet to place a call to Hamburg to check up on a polder documentary would be beyond these people. In addition, "Hamburger Rundfunk" had the virtue of explaining the German comrades: Horst was posing as the sound-man, with Elfride as his script girl. Jeroen was the camera-man, and Greet his lighting assistant and the crew's interpreter. The dark-skinned

Yusuf and Carlos would not be seen during the negotiations; they would appear later, when the family's departure from Schiphol had been confirmed by the comrade at the KLM desk.

It had been wonderful how the couple had swallowed the story. "*Dummköpfer!*" said Horst. Yet should one sneer at them for credulousness, considering the inducements to belief furnished by the stickers, the Hamburg license-plate, the paraphernalia of sound-equipment, cameras, cables, blackboard, tripod, light meter, carried into the house by the "crew"? Hundreds of feet of simulated film were turned, showing the husband seated on the tractor, the wife feeding the chickens, the children at play, and so on. An interview with the couple on polder conditions was taped—a genuine one, by good luck, since the woman's final request, when the team was already packing up, was to hear her voice played back.

They had raised fewer objections than had been anticipated in the preparatory study. The man's main concern was that he should be back in time for his spring sowing, which, given the state of the ground, could be as late as February, and he agreed, though with slight hesitation, that work on the barn should be halted when the keys were turned over—too noisy and disruptive for the crew while it was filming. He might have asked why the Germans had chosen the dead season of the year for doing a documentary on polder life—"scheduling" was the only answer Jeroen had been able to think of—but the question seemed not to have occurred to him, and the woman's questions had to do with the sleeping arrangements— were the two couples married?—with the oil and electricity bills and potential damage to the furnishings—who would pay? A generous deposit, to cover, also, wear and tear on towels and bed linen, had sufficed to quiet her.

Her only demur arose over the contract, made out in duplicate on paper bearing the letterhead of the Hamburg station, which Jeroen put in her hands, pleased to have remembered this crowning small touch of verisimilitude. She did not want it, and her man, meeting her eyes, had concurred. For a moment, Jeroen had been dumbfounded. Then he understood: taxes. Obviously the couple preferred to have the deal take place under the table, with nothing on paper to show income received. Putting the contract back in his pocket, he had nearly laughed for joy. This solved the last problem confronting the commando: how to keep the woman from talking. Were she to boast to her kin and neighbors that her house had been chosen by a German network for a documentary on the polder, the place would be surrounded by curiosity-seekers. Even the resourceful Greet had been unable to think of a means, stronger than mere persuasion, of guaranteeing the creature's silence. A reward to be placed in the couple's hands on their return if the crew had been allowed to film undisturbed by neighbors or relatives? But the promise of a reward for silence might sow a germ of doubt: respectable people, the pair might well reflect, did not pay to have no witnesses to their doings. In the group's thinking, that bridge had been still uncrossed when they had arrived at the house that first morning; they were waiting on inspiration. Then the woman's gesture, totally unexpected, of pushing back the contract, did their work for them. There could be no better insurance that the affair would remain quiet than that the couple had their own motive for concealment: cheating the tax man! And this illustrated once again the genius of the central concept: the raw materials of bourgeois life, of their own initiative, sprang forward to collaborate in a revolutionary design aimed at its destruction. Moreover it showed—to descend to the particular—how erroneous it would have been to pretend to come from Dutch television: revenue from Omroepstichting would be automatically reported to The Hague; no motive, then, for silence. Looking back on that series of lucky chances, or narrow escapes, Jeroen felt confirmed in his persistent sense of being guided in this enterprise by an unseen power that fitted everything together, like Hegel's "cunning of reason" or Adam Smith's "invisible hand." He did not yet know the name of this power that was directing him but every now and again he felt its gentle pressure. What had prompted him, for example, to draw up a contract that had seemed at the time a mere touch of artistry, a perhaps wasteful embellishment? And the labor of printing the letterhead had been, in one sense, a waste; yet if he had not been moved to do that, how else could the group have learned that it had no cause for worry in the woman's wagging tongue? It was as if every "artistic" stroke had responded to a logic in the decaying capitalist structure. When a spearhead of revolutionaries brought a plan of subversion to bear on a bourgeois entity, that inner logic, uncannily, started to apply of itself, without priming.

Nevertheless, on Sunday afternoon, while Yusuf was watching *Schneeweiss und die sieben Zwerge* on the *Kinderprogramm* in the living-room and Carlos was napping, Elfride and Horst had passed an anxious hour or so at the kitchen window, alert to the danger represented by the woman's parents in Kampen, only half an hour's drive away. Who knew, after all, what story the daughter had told them? And if the old people were to turn up on an after-church ride with a bee in their bonnet of "keeping an eye on" the property, their failing eyesight could hardly miss the redoubt of sandbags that Carlos had toiled all morning to build, making efficient use of the farmer's potato sacks. But the Sabbath afternoon had gone by without a sign of an interloper. Jeroen, had he thought of it, could have put the comrades' minds at rest. From all the signs, as Elfride, a pastor's daughter, might have noted herself, these people were strict Calvinists, and their parents would be stricter. A born Lutheran from Hesse maybe would not know, but Dutch Calvinists of that persuasion did not joy-ride on Sunday or visit back and forth. In fact, the man of the house, though Elfride and Horst were unaware of the episode, had entered his first objection on learning that they were to fly on the Sunday morning.

Jeroen ought to have foreseen that. When poor Greet, all unsuspecting, came by with the tickets and the hotel vouchers, it had been too late to change. Everything depended on adherence to the schedule, which had the family's departure from Schiphol synchronizing with the Boeing's departure from De Gaulle and following, by eighteen hours, on the crossing of the border at Maastricht by the German-led detail. The man's sudden balking, at that juncture, could have been a real disaster. Luckily, he had allowed Greet and his disappointed family to persuade him to overlook, for once, the observance of the Sabbath: the fault would not be his but Hamburg's for setting an inflexible date. And on the way to the airport, as the woman pointed out, they could get the Gereformeerd service on the car radio.

Aside from this conscientious obstacle—the ultimate close shave—the family had given no real problems. Early Sunday morning, Elfride and Horst had arrived at the farmhouse in the by-now-familiar truck, explaining that the Dutch crew would follow: they had been held up in Amsterdam by trouble with one of the cameras; probably the family would cross them on the road. The woman, at Greet's suggestion, had prepared a list of instructions as to the watering of the plants, the regulation of the thermostat, disposal of the garbage, and so on. The Fiesta was already packed, and the man was worrying about parking it at the airport in a place where it would not be stolen—"too many lawless elements these days," he told Horst in broken German. Then came the transfer of the keys, and for an instant Elfride thought she saw a shade of doubt in the woman's eyes; clearly she would rather have Greet, who spoke her language, to entrust them to—that would be almost like "in the family." The man told her to hurry. Outside, the children, restless and eager to leave, were examining the truck. The older boy was pulling at one of the stickers. He called out something in Dutch. "Look, *moeder*, it comes off!" was what he was saying, plainly. He held up the sticker in his grubby little hand. Elfride caught her breath. She was sure she saw a funny, thoughtful expression come over the woman's face. But Horst was really a wonder. "*Ja, ja*, it comes off," he told the child in German, with a hearty laugh. "Now let's put it back, shall we?" Seeing his good humor, the woman scolded the child. "*Genoeg!*" she said—"That's enough." Then, to Horst, "Excuse it." Whatever she may have asked herself for a fleeting second, the importance of the stickers had not sunk into her mind. The Fiesta drove off, with the children waving from the rear window. In a few minutes, the back-up car waiting with Yusuf and Carlos was able to emerge from a side road off the highway. Supplies and the short-wave radio were swiftly transferred to the house. Werner, the driver, would head straight for the German border. The truck, stolen in Rotterdam, with the false Hamburg license-plate and altered serial number, had no further part to play; eventually it would be found by the police in the parking lot at Schiphol, where the young comrade assigned to fetch it had been instructed to abandon it after wiping off his fingerprints.

Now, two days later, Jeroen sat at the kitchen table before the short-wave set, holding an earphone to his right ear—the hearing of the left had been impaired by a beating he had got in a "Red Youth" demonstration in The Hague. The breakfast service was finished. The Air France people had washed up the coffee-pot and cleared off the paper plates and cups, which would be burned in the outdoor incinerator when the right moment came. He was alone. The kitchen had been declared out of bounds except to the Air France cabin crew and the two Dutch pilots. It had been decided to treat them as neutrals; they were working folk, with the usual pay grievances, and so, in principle, capable of being radicalized—Greet herself was a former KLM hostess, won to the just cause during a siege on the Cairo air-strip. In any case, their services were needed for the preparation and issue of food. Jeroen had elected to make the kitchen their command post because of its size, the unbroken view from the windows, and the privacy it offered during most of the day; it had sliding doors, which could be closed, as now, when important business was being transacted. Moreover, it pleased him to sit in a kitchen.

Werner's voice was coming through, clearly now, from Aachen. Still no news. Irritably, Jeroen put down the earphone and pushed the big set aside: he did not need to be reminded of the time difference; he knew quite well that it was only four in the morning in New York. Of course it was too early to expect a full report on the list of eleven parasites that Aachen had relayed to the comrades there; obviously museums and galleries would not open till ten, which would be four in the afternoon here. But there were other sources; newspapers stayed open all night. The names he and Greet had hurried last night to copy from the first-class passports must be on file in any newspaper "morgue." In that metropolis, surely, there were also students of art, critics of art, professors of art, with links to the movement who could be waked up for consultation. Some relevant information, however incomplete, should have reached the cell in Aachen by this time; the details could be filled in when the museums and art libraries opened.

But the names "Ramsbotham," "Tallboys," "Potter," "Chadwick," et cetera—with home cities added to avoid the possibility of confusion—had produced from New York, so far, only such banalities as "millionaire sportsman," "fat cat," "self-styled philanthropist," "extreme right-winger." Not a word suggestive of art patronage, to the point where Jeroen was beginning to wonder whether he and Greet had not made a mistake. Had they been too impulsive in departing, on their own initiative, from the agreed-on plan calling for the release of all first-class passengers? When they had got wind of a tour of collectors aboard the Boeing, it had seemed, at least to Jeroen, a challenge that could not be refused. Now, however, he asked himself if he and Greet had not over-reacted when she had hurried forward bringing word of "Giorgiones and Titians" belonging to a tour of millionaires traveling in first class: she had heard the little liberal woman say so. But that woman was an exaggerator, as they had since observed. Perhaps these people were not art collectors at all but just ordinary rich people who "owned" a painting or two.

To have seized a group of ordinary rich people, even millionaires, held no interest for Jeroen. Money, though it would have to figure on the list of demands, was the least of the commando's objectives. Furthermore, extorting ransom from a handful of plutocrats would fatally shift the emphasis: a jugular strike based on principle and aimed dramatically at the "superstructure," in Marxian terms, of Western capitalism would take on the appearance of another pinprick hardly distinguishable from run-of-the-mill criminality. Millionaires could pay "a king's ransom" and barely feel it, just as your rich bourgeois, held up on the street, surrendered his purse gladly, unlike the poor man—there was plenty more where it came from. To deal a blow at this society, it was necessary to take from it something it deemed irreplaceable.

That, at any rate, had been the concept behind the capture of the Boeing, known to be carrying an international committee of liberal cat's paws of the energy interests to investigate torture in Iran. The other passengers were of no concern—bystanders or civilians, to be sent about their business as rapidly as possible. "Excess baggage," as Horst had formulated it; for the coup to make its point, the committee must be *seen* to be the exclusive target. Seizing this body of self-appointed just men on an errand of mercy to the Third World struck at the core of the West's pious notion of itself. And to strike not at random but selectively, choosing showcase models of civic virtue whose price was above rubies and whom the West would have to save at any cost or renounce its image of "caring," was, of course, sacrilege. Without sacrilege, as history showed, there could be no terror worthy of the name. And the fact that these good souls were journeying on a patently selfless mission, in Economy class as befitted their social outlook, could be counted on to add to the horror and condemnation the deed would call forth. A reaction of universal shock and outrage was essential to the success of the design. There would have been nothing like it since the Olympic Games "massacre," and those were only athletes.

To the people's ear, the chorus of indignation would have a comic sound, for the West, in fact, set no value on concerned and high-minded citizens except when they could be used to further some purpose of its own. Had this committee perished in a plane crash, Washington, ordering a day of remembrance, would have been relieved, on the whole, to be rid of them, since its anti-Soviet interest required a simulation of friendship with the Shah, despite pressures from business elements hurt by the oil "squeeze" and desirous of a tougher line with him—this conflict of interests, out of which such a committee of innocents would tend to be born, was a typical contradiction of late capitalism.

Yet a pretense of valuing its critics was still essential to the system in its present stage, and the price of maintaining the pretense in this case was going to be rather high. To save these sacred skins, the horrified West would have to accept an exchange: for every just man, four people's army militants, to be released from the imperialists' jails. Having calculated the ratio with an eye to due measure, Jeroen had not believed that they should ask more. To ask more might decide the imperialists to refuse any concessions, on the ground that terror, knowing no bounds, could be met only with firmness. For the commando, there would then be nothing for it but to execute the prisoners.

In the new circumstances, however, that thinking was no longer viable. It had been natural to postulate the release of class-war militants according to a strict ratio, particularly for the German comrades, who had had Andreas and Ulrike in mind and Gudrun and Jan-Carl and the other Werner and

Irmgaard. . . . But that goal, they would have to see, was no longer within reach of the commando. Study of the passports proved that, contrary to earlier and supposedly "sure" information, the venerable prelate from Köln was not among the prisoners—Greet and Jeroen, in the Boeing, had already thought as much—hence, Bonn could sit back and smile at the fantasy of such a demand. Similarly, an American rabbi and Israeli stooge "guaranteed" to be with this committee was nowhere in evidence, so that the Zionist state could smile, too, at any ultimatum calling for the freeing of the Arab brothers it held. Bad luck for the Palestinian army, but it would have to be accepted. The whole position would have to be re-thought, in view of the current actuality, and larger demands conceived. It was a challenge to the imagination to find a truly radical approach. The old formula of a body-for-bodies exchange was too often unproductive, leading to killing for want of a better result. The enemy by his attitude, rather than proletarian justice, dictated your disposal of the prisoners.

In any case, killing was not a choice Jeroen cared to make except as a last resort. Killing the cat had been a botch, offensive to his workman's instinct; he had felt momentary pleasure in the act of taking aim, but using the poor creature to set an example to the passengers had surely been unnecessary. He blamed his nerves, which had been on edge as the pilot kept circling over Schiphol and it had begun to look as if they could not land. Killing accomplished little and with forethought could usually be avoided. As for torture, that was not envisioned. Elfride had been eager to give these liberals a taste of the conditions of detention suffered by comrades in the imperialists' jails. But solitary confinement, as at Stammheim, in a windowless box with a judas-hole and a blinding overhead light burning night and day, was clearly impossible in these living quarters which had not been designed as a prison. Perfect reciprocity—an eye for an eye—was an ideal that the revolutionary with his inferior means could not hope to achieve. Furthermore, the age of most of the hostages and their soft habits of life would make simple detention, with the inevitable crowding and inadequate toilet facilities, a species of harsh punishment that in their case suited the crime.

"Torture" in fact was the word they were already using to

describe having had to sleep without blankets or mattress "like sardines in a can," one lot on the floor of the family living-room and the rest in the unfinished attic—those who had passed the night in the living-room objected to the bad air and those who had been sent to the attic protested the lack of heating. Posted with his rifle at the head of the stairway, Carlos had had to hear their grumblings and their intermittent snores. And now Greet reported that a petition was about to be presented by the pastor asking, on humane grounds, that any who wished it should be allowed to sleep in the helicopter; in the family room they were still disputing over the wording. Jeroen could have told them that they were wasting their breath. It was a rule of guerrilla operations never to disperse your hostages.

In the original plan, of course, excessive crowding had not been foreseen. The addition of twelve from first class to the nucleus of eight liberals was responsible. Yet if these people proved to be important collectors of art, then the difficulties of housekeeping and management created by their numbers would seem slight in comparison to the matchless opportunity their uninteresting bodies represented. If their collections were to contain a single Titian or Giorgione, their presence in the chosen plane constituted a windfall that Jeroen in his wildest dreams would hardly have dared to conceive.

Back in the Boeing, having brought him the incredible news, Greet, woman-like, had cooled in the face of his enthusiasm. All at once, she professed not to see the difference between a collector of paintings and any other Mr. or Mrs. Moneybags. "What causes you to think they are better, pray?" "Not they in themselves," he had answered. "What they have is better. Better than cars or yachts or 'securities.' Maybe not in our eyes but in the eyes of their society." "In *your* eyes, Jeroen," Greet had retorted. "I do not like to see you so excited." And in a moment she had added "I think I am sorry I told you." Faced with that wilful blindness, he had had to make her understand the uniqueness of the opportunity: finding this tour aboard put them within striking distance of dozens, perhaps hundreds, of priceless works of art. How they would manage to get hold of a few of those treasures was not yet clear to him. He would have to think, he had told her. But once they *had* managed it, no demand would be too bold. This society had two talismans: one moral and therefore hypocritical, honored by lip service, and the other material, honored in daily practice and most highly venerated in the form of works of art. In the interior of the Boeing, by one chance in a million, the pair co-existed, even if for the moment the art works were present only nominally, at a second remove. Such a chance would never arise again; if they let the collectors go, they would re-nounce a prize that would not be offered them twice. If they kept them, they ran no extra risk.

In the end, his arguments had persuaded her. The polder house, he had showed her, was one incentive the more, almost dictating their action to them. When again would they possess a stronghold with ample storage facilities, completely isolated and yet accessible by helicopter? It would not even be neces-sary for the helicopters bringing the canvases to land; their cargo could be dropped in the open field. In the event that large canvases were delivered—statuary, unless small, should not be attempted—the barn roof could be finished and insu-lated, which would be a job for the hostages.

Jeroen sighed. Thinking backward, to the great moment of decision in the Boeing, his mind was leaping too far ahead. Doggedly, he pulled the set to him and tried the Aachen fre-quency. Only static. Yet he could not make a serious plan until he knew what the collections, if in fact they existed, consisted of. There was no point in interrogating the prisoners, as Carlos had proposed: they would lie. And if there were no important works of art in the collections, it was hardly worth the effort. Better to get rid of the whole tour, though he could not think how. He would not accept dubious attributions or "school" or "follower" works. And no American stuff. His heart was set on the masters. He wanted Rubens, Rembrandt, Goya, Vermeer, as well as the Titians and Giorgiones, which may have been only a figure of speech. With American buying power in mind, he had been choosing, letting his memory range over the whole history of art. "You have gone back to your old love, Jeroen," Greet had reproached him on the plane. Now she slid open the door and, seeing him with the radio, she said it again. "Back to your first love. Be careful, Jeroen."

The accusation was partly true. In his young days in Amster-dam, when the word "*waarde*" had sounded in his brain, it had not once occurred to him to work to become rich so that he could own a fine canal house with pictures in it. His idea had been to consecrate himself, in poverty like a monk, to the value people called "art" by learning, if possible, to make some of it himself. As though to pay back a debt he owed for the joy his eyes were experiencing in the museums and along the canals. For a time he tried to teach himself by sketching in the Rijksmuseum and eventually also in the Stedelijkmuseum—he still loved Van Gogh as a person and as an artist. He went to night classes in drawing. But then he became interested in his trade union and began to give his evenings to union meetings and slowly he grew disillusioned with art. Next, moving steadily leftward, by a process that now seemed to him logical and as natural as the growth process in an organism, he joined the Party. There he got his only higher education—his parents had put him to work at the legal school-quitting age of sixteen. In the Party, too, he had learned to make prints and to letter; they paid for his going to classes and used his crude work in posters and handbills and sometimes in *De Waarheid*, their paper. He knew it was crude and was proud of that, for now the sole value he saw in art was that of transmitting messages to the people to incite them to action—at election times he painted wooden placards to be placed on the bridges urging the masses to vote for the C.P.N. He hated "art for art's sake," though he accepted the Party's teaching that in a classless society such a wasteful indulgence could finally be afforded. Then he became disillusioned with the Party and turned sharply against it. He saw that he had let himself be deceived: it was merely another part of the system of world-wide oppression— openly as in the Soviet Union or covertly as in Holland, where it served as a willing safety valve for the masses' discontent. He was ashamed of having had his work in *De Waarheid*, which did not tell the Truth, as its name pretended, but just a different set of lies. When he broke, he passed almost overnight to direct action. He became what was called a terrorist.

Now art, even the Party kind of making propaganda, lost all interest for him, except in the sense that a deed was a work of art—the only true one, he had become convinced. The deed, unless botched, was totally expressive; ends and means coincided. Unlike the Party's "art as a weapon," it was pure, its own justification. It had no aim outside itself. The purpose served by the capture of the Boeing was simply the continuance or asseveration of the original thrust; ransom money, the release of fellow-actionists, were not goals in which one came to rest but means of ensuring repetition.

Direct action had a perfect circular motion; it aimed at its own autonomous perpetuation and sovereignty. And the circle, as all students of drawing knew, was the most beautiful of forms. Thus in a sense he had returned to where he had started: terrorism was art for art's sake in the political realm. Some in the movement believed that their action would give rise to a new society, but this belief was an impurity. Jeroen was not even sure that the construction of a just society ought to concern a revolutionary; that dream had been dreamed too often. He thought Trotsky was right in his notion of the permanent revolution, right but insincere—in his day of power his ruthless repression of the sailors of Kronstadt had exposed his real attitude. Revolution, if it was not just a catchword, should mean revolving, an eternal spinning, the opposite of *e*volution, so attractive to the bourgeois soul. For the true revolutionary, the only point of rest lay in the stillness at the center of the circle, just as a wheel rapidly turning on its axis gave the appearance of arrested motion.

Such ideas were deeply troubling to Greet. She did not like to hear him state that the struggles of the Palestinian people were merely a parenthesis, to be closed without regret when they had served their purpose—"Your theories again." She was jealous of his brain, which she regarded as an untrustworthy organ capable of leading him away from her and the others into a foreign sphere. As she sat across the table somberly gazing at him, he could read her mind. She was fearing that his interest in the group of collectors was a sign of softening or backsliding, that he would let himself be diverted by his old passion from the main end. There she was wrong. His "artistic" interest in them was of another sort; he was excited by the sheer beauty of the coup he envisioned. He had seen that they could be *transmuted*; it only needed the Midas touch of exchanging them against their masterpieces to turn their base substance into pure gold. The method of persuasion remained to be studied—whatever was best calculated to convince the collectors to accept the principle of paying their ransom "in kind." He foresaw a two-way airlift: crates of art descending, the "owners" ascending, to be shipped back home or to Teheran according to their mood. The transfer would put an end to the crowding and, far more interesting, it would render the farmhouse impregnable. Once the house contained irreplaceable masterpieces, any notion of taking it by storm would have to be abandoned by the imperialists unless they wished to pass for "barbarians" before the eyes of their entire "civilized" world. At that point, the commando could dictate its own terms and at its own good leisure; there would be no hurry.

Yet in the immediate time was pressing. It might only be a matter of hours before the disguise of the polder house was penetrated. The short-wave radio, indispensable as it was at this stage, was also a danger that had to be reckoned with. If the enemy were to pick up the "pirate" transmissions, the unlicensed frequencies could of course be spotted, and the authorities at both ends, having mapped the bearings, would swiftly close in. Here on the polder, the hostages were a safeguard, precluding an instant swoop, but the comrades in Aachen risked being surprised with their mobile transmitter by a cordon of police. Each transmission was increasing the likelihood of detection. The remedy was to shift to another set of frequencies, but there was a limit to how long that game could be played. Out of regard for the Aachen comrades, communications should be discontinued at the earliest possible moment. Yet to break off contact while New York was still to be heard from would constitute a defeat, and the Aachen cell, so far, agreed. For a while longer, Werner would keep trying and accept the risk, only moving to a neighboring frequency, by agreement, every third hour. The best hope was that the possibility of clandestine transmissions to and from the "criminal band" would be slow to occur to the authorities. And up to now there had been no discernible attempt at jamming—the usual warning sign. Yet unfortunately the absence of interference could read in two opposite senses.

There was nothing to do but stupidly wait. The fact that this morning no plane had yet come prowling overhead was at least a reassurance. The fools might be off on another track.

Every hour the radio announced that an "energetic" hunt for the missing helicopter was in progress but gave no particulars. The evening news on television was bound to be fuller, if only in order to pander to the public's craving for thrills; they might even be shown the "dragnet" of search planes and police with walkie-talkies, or would it be merely interviews with the Defense and Justice ministers and the families of the hostages? Belgian and German radio reported a "security blanket," and of course there was not a hope of seeing a newspaper. As the hours passed, Jeroen grew unwontedly restless. To be marooned here with no news except that doled out by official sources was an experience he had not pictured in his planning. He felt cut off, left out of events and decisions that nevertheless should concern him as a prime actor—hardly, in that respect, in a better position than the hostages, who must be guessing and speculating too.

The final ridiculous touch was to discover this morning that the farm couple had had their telephone service suspended: the farmer had indicated to Horst that there was a coin box down the highway in case the crew needed to place long-distance calls. That was of no significance, so long as they had the radio, but the sight of the dead instrument on the kitchen counter was a sour reminder of the meanness and mistrust in the bourgeois nature, preparing petty frustrations for the foreigner in return for his generosity—what if the "crew" from Hamburg had urgently needed a doctor?

Adding to Jeroen's own frustration was the feeling that the comrades here were showing a certain reserve toward his plans for the collectors. He could count on Greet; she was loyal, in spite of her cavils. And in fairness he could not expect Horst and Elfride and Carlos to immediately share his enthusiasm; not having been on the Boeing, they had learned only last night of the abrupt revision of the program that had raised the number of hostages from eight to twenty. As for the Arabs, they had not yet had the collectors explained to them—there would be time enough for that when New York had pronounced—and had not been moved to ask; for them, the evidence that these additional people were rich was doubtless sufficient reason for their being here. It was depressing, though, that Werner, on being told late last night by radio of the unforeseen development, had responded almost with ecstasy (*"Wunder-bar, nicht? Unglaublich!"*), while those here on the spot had had only neutral comments, as if to say time would tell. Nor had they warmed up appreciably as time had gone by.

It must be the waiting and watching him fiddle uselessly with the radio. Werner, in freedom, had the active part, telephoning New York, and on his own initiative making roundabout inquiries of a famous Aachen collector, who, however, knew only hyper-realism, post-op, post-pop, earth art, and the Americans who collected such *rommel.* Here the comrades were condemned to unemployment; they had nothing to do but eat and stand guard and rebuff the hostages' incessant demands for news.

Inactivity was the problem. From being masters of the situation, they were slipping into a state of dependency and powerlessness in respect to the outside world. The moment they got the information, good tidings or bad, it would be necessary, Jeroen decided, for the commando to assert itself and abandon this cat-and-mouse game. There could be no further need for hiding and waiting, maiden-like, to be found. An announcement from the command post would declare its location—why not? A flag might even be flown, boldly, from the roof. Making one on the Singer from the housewife's scraps of dressmaking material would give the hostages something to do. Some of the present precautions could be relaxed. There was no reason that the prisoners should not be permitted to go for short walks around the house, twice a day, under guard. For aerial reconnaissance to observe them at their exercise could do no harm. Jeroen did not agree that the headquarters should be regarded as a punitive re-education center—Elfride's idea, typically German. Contrary to what she said, it was not his intention to coddle the hostages, but last night's experience showed that given favorable conditions even the most unpromising human material was capable of cooperation.

The evening meal was being distributed when Aachen finally signaled that it was ready to transmit. Horst was monitoring the set, and the stewardess came running to bring Jeroen from the family room, where he stood looking at television. They were showing Royal Navy dredges dragging the Ijsselmeer for the helicopter—good entertainment; a few of the hostages, seated on the floor, were laughing and clapping. From the shadows on the screen, the time would appear to have been early afternoon, now several hours in the past. Just before dark, doubtless at the close of that costly and fruitless operation, a plane had circled over the farmhouse and disappeared into the sunset; the hostages had watched it through the pastor's binoculars. Now the house stood in darkness, except for the family room, lit by the television and a single lamp, the playroom upstairs, where the farm children would be doing their homework, the stairway, and the kitchen.

Jeroen seated himself at the table, fitted the gray rubber earphones on his head, took the pencil Horst was holding out to him, and prepared to write. The message was coming through clearly. The code they had settled on was simple, more like a shorthand used by children in a family to communicate among themselves when elders were listening than like the usual ciphers, which were child's play for the experts to "break."

Horst peered over Jeroen's shoulder as he wrote. "Your prognosis justified. Grandma Potter much better than was first thought. Dr. Van der Meer from Delft in constant attendance, also Dr. Tiziano but the one they call Big George unavailable for consultation. Sheer bosh that she cannot recover. Uncle Widderhintere's condition complicated by history of sporting activity. Keeps Duffy at bedside, also British specialists highly regarded in field, such as Stubbs, Ward, Marshall. The Gas fellow drops in from race track to see patient but Uncle Widder unwilling receive Ed's dancers in home. Since husband's decease, Cousin Margaret has mild religious mania, much attached to the Greek, sees visions in sepia of archangels but enjoys more colorful commerce with angelic monk and Italian primitive types, including older monk called Laurence." The next was unintelligible, then "Chadwick, *sagt Anna, hat 8 grosser kinder. . . .*"

With a sudden motion, Horst turned the radio off; he had heard a plane's motor. They listened. Out the window they could see a searchlight playing. Jeroen removed the head set and yawned. Let them come. He had heard all he needed. With the pencil he beat time to the beam of light dancing across the snow. He hummed an air from the hymnal—an old

Dutch Resistance marching song—and wondered whether he would still be able to pick it out on the parlor harmonium. But Horst had not caught the mood. He frowned at the piece of paper lying on the table. "*Was soll das heissen, Jeroen?*" What the devil did all that mean? His heavy voice was plaintive.

Patiently Jeroen translated the message. There was a Vermeer in the Potter woman's collection, as well as a Titian, but no Giorgione, alias "Big George." In compensation, there was a Bosch. "Widderhintere" was Ramsbotham; he collected sporting art, including Dufy ("Duffy") and Degas racing subjects— no ballet dancers. "Cousin Margaret" was the big woman; sacred art was her field. She owned El Grecos ("the Greek"), sepia drawings by Michelangelo and Raphael (the "archangels"), a Fra Angelico, and a number of Italian primitives, unidentified except for Lorenzo Monaco ("Lorenzo the Monk"). The last passage to come through was hard to decipher, perhaps garbled: "Chadwick, *sagt Anna, hat 8 grosser kinder.*" Eight important pictures, but what? It was good that Horst found the answer. "*Sagt Anna*" equaled "Says Anne": Chadwick had eight Cézannes.

The search plane had completed its mission; the sound of the motors grew fainter as it gained altitude. The others, bursting into the kitchen, did not need to be told that the news was tremendous; they could read it on the faces of Horst and Jeroen. These collectors were the real thing. A Vermeer, a Titian, a Bosch, eight Cézannes—those were sufficient credentials. Yet, as always, there were some—the greedy Greet, in particular—who were not satisfied, who had to know more. What was in the *rest* of the collections? Only four had been summarized. "Elfride, we must speak to Aachen again. They should finish their report to us."

She moved to the set. Jeroen held up a hand. "*Neen.*" Another contact with the comrades, he warned her, was not to be dreamed of at the moment. Supposing the search plane's radio had picked up even a small portion of the last transmission? She had not thought of that. There was a silence. The stewardess put in her head and withdrew. "*Wir haben das Wesentliche,*" Horst said. "I support Jeroen. Now let us have some soup." At the stove, Greet picked up the soup ladle and filled seven bowls: "Ahmed, what are you doing here? You should be on guard duty." She raised her bowl. "Eight Cézannes. I toast you, Jeroen." "To Werner," he corrected. "To the revolution." From now on, he could see, his leadership would be uncontested. Tears came to his eyes. He had proved himself.

Nine

I T was their fourth day of captivity, and their second pent up in this farmhouse. The worst, Sophie thought, was not the crowding and lack of sleep or even the endless guessing based on ignorance but the fact that there was nothing to read. The only books were a kind of farmer's almanac, a children's encyclopedia, and the Bible—all in Dutch, naturally. Last night they had had the distraction of watching television, with Henk doing simultaneous translation, but this morning the screen was an empty gray, matching the weather and their tired minds. In Holland, it seemed, there were never any television programs in the daytime, when people were assumed to be at work—"Very civilized, Mynheer," gamely commented Simmons. "I could do without Barbara Walters, couldn't you, Sophie?" In the kitchen, the hijackers had a radio and they had let Denise, the stewardess, listen to Radio Belge while she was preparing breakfast. A development in the case, she heard, was expected within a few hours; there was a report that a message had been received from the hijackers but as yet no official confirmation.

Henk thought that if there were any real breakthrough, television, exceptionally, would be on the air with photo bulletins; they would not have to wait, like last night, for the evening news to show them that the Air Force and the Navy were still looking for them. In any case, since early morning there had been activity overhead, which offered the hope that their place of imprisonment had been spotted. Military planes passed and repassed, possibly taking photographs, but then flew away without trying to land. From the farmhouse windows the highway was invisible, and the men, when they went out to pee and relieve their bowels after breakfast, had heard no rumble of traffic that would indicate the approach of a rescue force. It was strange that in all this time—Tuesday and nearly half of Wednesday—not even the mailman or a traveling salesman had come up the entry road that led to the kitchen door.

After the milling and confusion of yesterday, the hostages

were settling in, establishing routines alarmingly suggestive of permanence, though they did not see this themselves. Routines gave them a feeling of security, Sophie supposed; the first-class passengers must be used to having their wealth of time organized for them, as on cruises and "cures" and country house-parties. In the parlor today, by general request, Frank had conducted morning service. Now, warming to his role of pastor *cum* cheer-leader, he was trying to pick out Episcopal hymns on the old Calvinistic harmonium, which wheezed and groaned as if in dissent. It was a solo performance; invited to "sing-along," the others only hummed or beat time with a foot and eventually ceased to follow. Margaret, the big millionairess —they were on first-name terms this morning—had installed herself, like one administering a hint, on the horsehair sofa with the green folder "Torture and Illegality in Iran." It should have been reading time—study hall—for everybody, but the blue and green folders were the only fresh reading matter aside from archaeological guides to Persia, an English pocket Bible, *Wild Life of the Near East*, and the *Book of Common Prayer* that the hand baggage had yielded. The news magazines, *Vogues*, and *Harper's Bazaars* they had had with them in the Boeing had exhausted their usefulness during the long wait at Schiphol. In Sophie's carryall was an old copy of *Harper's* with an article by her in it which she had brought along as a credential, but she was too shy as yet to offer it—selfish of her, she feared.

Just beyond, in the family living-room, a checkers game was in progress, with coins for pieces. Using Eloise's manicure scissors, Johnnie was cutting photos from a Dutch illustrated magazine to make a set of playing cards. It was a sign of something maybe that the dread "Gretel"—whose real name proved to be Greet, short for Margaretha—had not seen fit to confiscate the scissors. The two gays from Antibes were playing "I packed my grandmother's trunk" with Beryl and the curator, their suggestion of charades having been rebuffed. Sophie had played it *ad infinitum* on rainy days, which was most of the time, in a Wasp girls' camp in Maine; the idea was to fill the "trunk" with unlikely and giggle-producing articles that each player had to name over in the correct order before adding a new one. Thus, this morning: "Sunpruf cream, a rosary, Muhammad Ali's jock-strap, Odorono, *Les très riches heures du duc de Berry*, Nixon's *Six Crises . . .*" For a while, the Senator had been refereeing but now he was showing Victor a match game, "Cannibals and Missionaries," that had been popular with navy flyers during the War.

Here in the parlor, as Frank pumped out "JEsus CALLS us O'ER the TUmult," those allergic to games in the morning were resorting to conversational gambits to make the time pass. "Are you related to the lovely old rose?" Beryl's mother inquired of Henk. "She means Dr. Van Fleet," interposed Margaret, looking up from her reading. "Of course," said Lily. Her soft blue eyes dwelt encouragingly on Henk. "A pure pale pink climber and a great New England favorite. One doesn't find it any more in the catalogues. Mother had it on a trellis outside the library door of the old house in Yarmouth. Ideal for cutting, like a hybrid tea. I believe there was a Mrs. Van Fleet too." "He spells it differently, Lily," Helen Potter ventured. "With a *V*." "*V* into *F*. A common New World corruption," observed Charles. "We Americans wrote down words as we heard them—phonetically, don't you see? But the great hybridizer, Dr. W. Van Fleet, can hardly have been 'family' to our distinguished young friend. The Dutch connection there would have been remote. His work was done at Bell Station, Maryland. And the family of climbers associated with him were of Japanese origin, the Wichuraiana—not your China teas at all." "Silver Moon," said Helen. "Dorothy Perkins. Now I ask myself who she was." It was astonishing to Sophie how much knowledge such "old money" people hoarded, like string-savers; its value, apparently, lay in its total uselessness and inapplicability to the practical world. "Ah, yes," fluted Charles, as if responsive to Sophie's thought. "Those old dooryard hybrids mean nothing to the rose fancier today. They were 'retired' from service years ago, like a line of automobiles. One cannot guess the reason; your Dr. Van Fleet was extremely hardy and free-flowering. But no doubt if one looked into it one would discover a Marxist explanation. The eternal profit motive." The Bishop, who had been dozing in a straight chair, opened his eyes. "Damn them!" he pronounced, fiercely, and then continued his nap.

Lily seemed disappointed. The hope of "placing" Van Vliet must have been brightening her empty morning. As a practicing lady, she was bent on pursuing connections; in her world, Sophie guessed, everyone had to be related, if only to a rose. The pursuit of connections extended "one's" boundaries; the poor souls did not wish to feel narrow in their outlook. This had led to a quite comical incident with the Tupamaro on the first night. "I am Carlos," he had said, introducing himself to the roomful of hostages he was to guard. At which Lily had risen from her couch of folded mink, as if from her tea-table, to receive him. "Not *the* Carlos!" she had breathed. But he too had to disappoint her. He was not the "most wanted," Number One terrorist, Vladimir Ilych Ramirez, but just *a* Carlos. Lily's graciousness had thereupon abated, but not so that he could *feel* an abrupt loss of interest; the cooling of her manner was gradual, a gentle drop in temperature that only another perfect lady could measure.

Now, to cover her little let-down on having failed to strike a sympathetic chord with the bright-cheeked deputy, she turned to Margaret and lightly tapped the green folder. "Is it interesting?" "Not exactly hammock reading," Margaret growled. Lily spied a second folder peeping out of Frank's briefcase. "May I?" She slowly turned the pages. No one spoke. Henk was studying the Flevoland listings in the regional telephone directory. Helen was dead-heading the housewife's plants, dropping the faded blossoms into an outspread Kleenex. Sophie, her loose-leaf notebook on her knee, was starting to keep a journal —it would be something to read tomorrow. Underneath the plant table, Cameron was busy with pencil and paper constructing a crossword puzzle; he was half hidden, as if in a rich tent, by the oriental rug that hung down over the sides like a tablecloth. At the harmonium, Frank had shifted to "Fairest Lord Jesus."

"Please!" Lily murmured, indicating the soft pedal. Margaret added her august voice. "Reverend Mr. Barber—Frank, I should say—do you intend to keep pumping at that melodeon all morning? Some of us here are musical." The minister jumped up from the stool, apologizing. In the quiet, they watched Lily read. "Have you come to the toaster thing?" Helen asked. Lily shook her head. Helen sighed. "Ghastly." They noticed that Henry was preparing to speak: his gray head and long spare body gave preliminary jerks and nods, like a wind-up toy starting to move—stage fright or alcoholic trembles? "T-toaster, my eye," he finally brought out. "It takes my sainted wife to believe that. I d-dipped into the bloody stuff this morning and, believe me, I could have found a better use for good p-paper outdoors." "Please, Henry!" said his wife. He started, and shook himself, like one awaking, and then began to mumble, nodding to himself. "'Ladies present, Henry.' Must remember, Henry. Very important to remember, Pa always said." The Bishop was watching him with concern. The others averted their eyes. It was an embarrassing metamorphosis. The dignified old beau appeared staggeringly drunk, which was impossible—nobody had had a moment unobserved. Yet in a minute he recovered himself. The thick speech miraculously cleared, and he found his lost train of thought. "Yes, as I was saying, Lily, what I'd like to know is who gets this material out. It's not signed, you'll notice. Means nobody stands behind it. Anonymous hate literature is what it looks like, I'm afraid. People in our position ought to make it a principle never to read anything that somebody hasn't put his John Hancock to. Saves a lot of time too. On that principle, I never look at an editorial in a newspaper. Why should I have my mind poisoned by somebody I don't even know? And from what I've been told the Shah's a gentleman or as near to it as they make them in those parts. Helen and I have letters to him. That should say something."

Henk tapped his head warningly with a forefinger, and Sophie nodded. But the others were going to argue with this lunatic. "Now wait a minute there!" burst out the minister. "You're taking a very illiberal attitude. An ignorant attitude, sir. The Gospels aren't signed, and do you refuse to read them? Do you close your mind to Homer?" "I agree, Reverend," cried Aileen. "Why should we have to listen to this affluent nonsense? Does he refuse to read the Dow Index and the Stock Exchange quotations? They're not signed, but I'll bet he reads them *religiously*. Don't you? Come on, admit it!" "But he doesn't," said Helen. "Henry says a gentleman leaves the financial page to his broker."

"Does he leave it to his butler to shit for him?" called out Victor from the next room. Attracted by the raised voices, a group was collecting in the doorway. Carey stood in the center with folded arms and a look of amusement. Beside him appeared Harold, truculent as always. "What's going on? Was somebody in here talking about climbers?" "Climbing *roses*, Chaddie," said Eloise. "Now they're arguing about some silly report on torture." "What do you mean, 'silly'?" "What do *you* know?" Several angry voices were shouting at once. Ahmed, posted in the hallway, could be heard calling to Jeroen to come from the kitchen. Then Charles raised a pale hand.

"My dears, we do sound like a prison riot. And we don't want to be punished, do we? Although, with all this din, some of us might welcome a turn in solitary. Potter, dear fellow, our companions are a committee to look into these allegations. Or *were* a committee, I should say. No doubt you aren't aware of that. You don't wish to impugn their motives, I'm sure. When and if their report is made, it will of course carry their signatures. You need have no fear on that score. For my part, I haven't had access to these particular documents, but friends abroad, knowing my interests, send me cuttings on affairs of this kind. The electric grill you mention is a matter of record. I believe I have even seen a diagram. One can picture it as a pop-up toaster or as one of those sandwich-like contrivances our countrymen use to carbonize beefsteaks at their 'cook-outs'—deplorable practice and quite carcinogenic, I'm told." A shriek came from Simmons. "Doesn't he slay you?" she said to Sophie. "Yes," said Sophie. It was true that she found Charles a rather frightening personality. He intended to shock, of course, but was it shock therapy he had in mind or some dreadful private joke? In any case, it was working here. The checkers players drifted back to their improvised board, and the bridge-players resumed their foursome: "Two no trump." In the parlor, the discussion moved on to cancer and a supposed cure for cancer. The Bishop produced his flask—a horn of plenty or pitcher of Baucis and Philemon—and offered a nip to Henry, who had begun to shake again. Soon the shakes stopped.

The episode led Sophie to wonder about the effects of deprivation if the present state of affairs were to continue long. What would happen when the Bishop's flask, which he must be replenishing from that hold-all, finally ran dry? Henry might get a rather high-priced cure, for which his wife would be grateful. But what about tobacco—Cameron's pipe, Henk's cigars, her own and Aileen's cigarettes? Most of the hostages were addicts of one kind or another, she supposed. With the older people, if it was not liquor or tobacco—Charles allowed himself a single Sobranie after meals as an aid to digestion—it would be pills. Yet the terrorists, who did not seem to have any of the usual vices or "dependences" themselves, would be in no position, even if willing, to cater to their captives' habits when private stores ran out. This could result in demoralization or, at best, a general fraying of nerves. The solidarity of the hostage group—such as it was—would not be proof against sudden fits of irritability such as they had just seen. With this in mind, Sophie was already rationing her cigarette consumption, so as to be able to share. In her bag were two cartons of Trues, designed to last three weeks in Iran, but in four days, thanks mainly to the harrowing time at Schiphol, one was half gone. Now, however, it should not be too hard to cut down; in these close rooms smoking seemed anti-social anyway. And yet, to her shame and surprise—she was used to thinking of herself as a both contained and generous person—she had felt something close to fury when Beryl, twice, had "borrowed" a cigarette to offer Ahmed. They said that extreme situations brought out the truth of one's character. Another cherished image, she realized, was a picture of herself as fearless which she had come to accept on hearsay: "You're so brave, Sophie." Would she have to discard that too? So far, she thought she could say honestly, she had not been really afraid. But so far nothing really scary had happened, and it was possible that when a test came she would discover, simply, that up to then she "had never known the meaning of fear." She replaced the cigarette—which would have been her fourth since breakfast—in the pack and took up her notebook again. "Eleven-thirty a.m., Flevoland . . ." She wrote on steadily, but there was little to record but her thoughts—only the occasional buzz of a plane overhead, the passage of a solitary heron and a flock of black birds with white bills that Henk said were coots from the Ijsselmeer.

Lily closed the folder and appeared to meditate on the contents. In the circumstances, being a slow reader was enviable:

she had got two hours, Sophie estimated, out of roughly eighty double-spaced pages, which worked out to about two-thirds of a page a minute. She polished her reading-glasses with a chamois and restored them to their embroidered case. "Could the Shah be back of this, I wonder?" "Back of *what*, Mother?" Beryl had got tired of packing her grandmother's trunk and was staring out the window in the parlor. "*This*," repeated Lily, waving a hand. She meant the hijacking, obviously. "Oh, Mother, don't be so stupid. How could the Shah figure?" "Very simply," Henk answered. "The idea is not stupid. Or at any rate I have had it myself." "Me too," agreed Sophie. To anyone with a political head it was by no means improbable that, if not the Shah in person, SAVAK, his secret police, had arranged for their committee to be deflected. As Henk was pointing out, collusion between "red" terrorists and "black" secret police was classical; it went back at least to czarist Russia. But by what route the insight had entered Lily's mind was a mystery. Had they "done" *The Possessed* at Saint Timothy's under an unusually thorough teacher? Sophie sought to imagine Lily in middy and skirt delivering an oral report on the ties between the Okhrana and terrorist circles such as Dostoievsky described in the novel. In any case, the insight, however come by, was impressive in a woman of her background.

But "awfully far-fetched" opined Margaret, and the Reverend concurred, though from a different starting-point, clearly. *She* refused to entertain the thought because it reflected on the ethics of the Shah, and Frank would not harbor it because he did not want to be "over-critical" of the terrorists. Whereas Beryl, more simply, scouted it because it had been voiced by her mother. It was an interesting study in the reception or, rather, non-reception of ideas. And still another factor was at work in these minds, as Sophie slowly recognized—the ineluctable factor of class.

Shah or no Shah, the first-class hostages, on the whole, resented any suggestion that the hijacking could have been aimed at passengers in Economy. They preferred to see themselves as the sole cause. And vice versa. "How can you talk such nonsense, Lily?" boomed Margaret. "I don't give a fig about the Shah, but it was *us* these people were after—no question of it." "But why us, dear?" wailed Lily. "Because we're filthy rich,

Mother; that's why." "The Shah doesn't want our money," pursued Margaret. "He can buy and sell the lot of us. That's why he couldn't be behind this outrage for a minute. But the gang in there was after our money all right. They marked the plane down because they heard we would be on it. No one can tell me otherwise."

"I can, Madam." Cameron's voice, accompanied by a puff of pipe smoke, came like an oracle from under the table. "You confuse two notional sequences. Lack of training in clear thinking, I daresay. Let us separate the two sequences and examine them. Taking the premise that you were the target, I believe we can all agree that the Shah may be exculpated. As you say, he has no need of money, least of all dollars, of which you have a great many, if I can judge by my ears. But this premise cannot be assumed; it is what you started out to prove. Therefore, rightly, it should appear at the end of your argument, as the logical or persuasive conclusion. If we take the opposite premise, that the committee in Economy was the target, then things have another look. The Shah cannot be cleared of suspicion. We may decide that he was the priming agent that set the operation in motion, very likely with funds drawn from the secret-police budget—this was not engineered on a shoestring. The more we consider it, the more plausible it comes to seem that the committee was indeed the target. But again we are assuming what we set out to prove. Moreover, if we affirm that the committee was the target, this leaves us to explain your presence here, just as your belief that you and you alone were aimed at leaves you to explain *our* presence. It might be useful to think in terms of primary and secondary targets. In that case, the simplest hypothesis, and hence the one to be preferred, is that we were the primary target, that is, in essence the Shah's pigeon—though we may have been interesting to these anarchists for other reasons—and that you, *ab initio*, or at some later stage, came to be viewed as a prize in your own right."

"Bravo, Archie," applauded Henk. "Beautiful," said Sophie. "My God!" said Aileen, who had been yawning. "He's going to set that carpet on fire!" In fact a coal from the don's pipe must have singed the rug from under which his bristly head had appeared. There was a smell of burning wool. "Water!" called Beryl.

"Ahmed, quick, bring some water!" "Dear me, no," said Charles. "You must smother it." After a minute, thanks to Charles's recipe, the incipient fire had been put out, leaving only a charred spot.

But the argument smoldered. "The Shah's a red herring," declared Henry. "I haven't seen a shred of evidence that connects him. Just a bee in certain bonnets and logic-chopping." That was true, Sophie reflected. Henry continued, observing that he had the floor. "Let's take a look at what's under our noses. Put yourself in the shoes of these people here." "Who are you speaking to?" said Aileen. "You. You impress me as a bright lady with a tongue in her head. I'd like to hear your opinion. Assuming you were a terrorist, would you hold *you* for ransom or my wife? I've no doubt that you have many fine personal qualities that make you valuable to your associates, whatever you do in life, but let me state it bluntly: what do you *own*?" "Just the clothes on my back," said Aileen, preening. "These old rags from Filene's." "Well, then?"

She pursed her lips and grew serious, as though the educator in her had been called on to address this forum. "I'm important in what I stand for. My name counts. The half-dozen boards and committees I serve on represent the most vital currents in American opinion. I'm a *public person*, Mister Potter. You don't know what that means. Why, right this minute, I'll bet, my picture is on the front page of the *Times*, along with the Senator's naturally, and the Reverend's and Bishop Hurlbut's, I guess. And thousands of my alumnae are deeply concerned for my fate. You can't say that for your wife and her friends. They'll be lucky if their picture is in the society columns, which have blacks and Jews nowadays, in case you don't know it. I'm sorry, Mister Potter, but you don't *mean* anything in the world. And nobody is more on to that than a terrorist. All that these Baader-Meinhofs and so on care for is publicity, being spread over the front page. They're totally indifferent to money; the sensational million-dollar ransoms they demand are just headline-grabbers. Now who is going to get them more publicity, who is the public truly anxious about, our committee or your ridiculous tour? Add to that the fact, which is probably news to you, that they hate liberals even more than you do. Because they're serious and know that we're the enemy. We stand in their way."

Simmons's cheeks were flushed, making a curious color-contrast with her rouge; her eyes sparkled. She seemed earnestly moved, almost to the point of tears, as though the conviction she had of her importance were a religious matter—a cause she was pleading. But the collector group was offended, and the Bishop was shaking his head in sorrow, maybe at the prospect of another rift. Besides, it was unchristian, surely, to tell another human being to his face that he was nobody. Without being a sorrowing Christian, Sophie felt shocked and troubled herself. To her mind, it was a shameless performance, regardless of the truth of the assertions, which in fact somehow made it worse. She smiled comfortingly at Lily, who smiled back. Henry and Helen sat rigid. To make things worse, Beryl decided to weigh in. She turned on the finally silent Aileen. "I know you," she said rudely. "'Thousands of alumnae'! You're 'Simmie.' You were the registrar at Lucy Skinner when they kicked me out. But you didn't have the war paint and the henna then. And you were no flaming liberal. Remember, Sophie?" "I didn't go to Lucy Skinner," said Sophie, glad to be able to stay out of this.

"The laughing cavalier!" suddenly cried Lily. She was indicating Henk. "I *knew* I knew that face. Don't you see it, Helen? A haunting resemblance. If you just add a tiny chin beard and mustaches." "What the hell are you talking about?" said Beryl. "Why, the Hals in the Wallace Collection, darling. The subject must have been an ancestor of yours, Henk." "Oh, Christ," replied Beryl. "Stop trying to create a diversion. Or stop being so obvious about it." Upon this, silence ensued. You could hear Aileen sniffling. At a meaningful nod from the Bishop, Frank installed himself once more at the harmonium and sounded a chord for attention.

"Let's try to sort this out. Does it really matter which of us is more important to these young men and women who are holding us in captivity? We each have our own *kind* of importance. Maybe we're symbols of things they don't like in the world of today. That's what I try to bear in mind. They don't hate me as an individual, I tell myself. They want to change the system of which we're all a part, like it or not. You and I, Aileen, as well as Henry. And I can't say that I blame them, though I may question their methods. Even there we mustn't be too sure. 'I bring not peace but a sword,' our Lord said. But the main fact to remember is that we're all in this together. We don't know why we've been chosen. Indeed, there is some mystery to it, I have to admit, as in God's inscrutable ways. Not that I mean to compare the election that has fallen on us with a divine intervention, although to some of His prophets the Old Testament Jahveh may have seemed like a holy terror."

"Oh, my God," muttered Sophie. But the good man was under a strain. It was not easy to play the peacemaker among these heathen. As for the habit of punning, that must be a tic, like the preaching habit which it seemed to go along with and which was maybe uncontrollable too. The poor fellow had been deformed by an unnatural occupation. "Lordy," he said, "there I go again. I can never resist a pun, my youngsters complain. Yes, but seriously, there may be food for thought there as to how these young folk conceive their mission, that Jeroen in particular. Strict Calvinist home, he confided in me when I was drawing him out. Well. Perhaps we shall eventually learn whether our carrier was singled out on account of the worldly goods of some of us or on account of the place some others of us occupy in the community. As we have been reminded, we have a bishop and a U.S. senator among us. Or chance, if there is such a thing—which as a Christian I'm taught to doubt—may have been responsible for our being gathered in this place together. Our captors may have struck at random, as the fisherman casts his net on the waters unwitting what the catch will be. Some passengers, as we have seen, were thrown back into the sea of ordinary daily life to go about their business like fish of no commercial value. And we have been retained. Whatever the reason behind that, we must look on our being here as a call. A call to deepen our faith and our brotherly love, which may be sorely tested. To extend our experience, launch our frail barks onto uncharted waters. Not everyone has the good fortune—yes, the good fortune—to be hijacked."

He paused, as though prepared for a stir of dissent. But no one contested him. "To be shaken out of his complacency, dislodged from his daily unthinking rut. 'As of old, Saint Andrew heard it, By the Galilean lake, Turned from home and toil and kindred, Leaving all for His dear sake.' That is why I chose the dear old hymn just now. To show us that we have been given an opportunity. Through this unforeseen contact with our captors we can be enlarged." "I like 'unforeseen contact,'" murmured Henk. Sophie giggled. Yet there was merit in the minister's thought, if only it could be freed from the clerical gaiters it wore.

"We will be bigger people for it, if we will only let ourselves. Let us not brood over the mystery that has assembled us in this place or compete for precedence one over the other in our captors' eyes." "Hear, hear!" said Henk, clapping. "Amen," said the Bishop. But Frank had not finished. "Let us, rather, accept it as coming from God, whether we believe in a personal God or merely in some higher force. I am led to think of Jonah—"

"Excuse me, sir." Denise was standing in the doorway. "I do not like to interrupt, but some passengers are wanted in the kitchen. First Mrs. Potter, please." Helen rose and followed the stewardess. Her small pigeon-breasted figure appeared resolute. "'The call,'" commented Aileen. Beryl grinned at Sophie. "Makes me think of being sent for to the headmistress's office." Sophie remembered. In the classroom, when the summons came, nobody ever supposed that the one sent for was going to hear anything good—the best hope was that it would be just a death in the family. It was the same here. Everybody avoided Henry Potter's eye, as if an execution were already taking place. "It'll be Ma's turn next, want to bet?" said Beryl. The smell of pea soup heating in the kitchen provided some wan reassurance. If lunch was about to be served, nothing very terrible could be happening in there. "Maybe they've taken her outside," muttered Beryl. "But why poor old Helen?" spoke up Henry. "Helen *first*," emphasized Margaret. "Don't worry, they'll have the rest of us on the carpet before long. 'Malefactors of great wealth.' Remember? He was the start of all this. I was a girl then, but Father knew it." "That doesn't answer my question, Maggie. Why my wife first? Why not Johnnie?" "Maybe just because we ask that," quietly said Sophie. "The aim of terror is to terrify, isn't it, and the trick there is to be arbitrary, *above* the rules of reason. Logically they should have started with Mr. Ramsbotham. It makes sense because he's the richest and a man. But if they acted logically, that would give us a handle on them." Henk agreed. "Maybe they drew straws, and your wife's was the short one. The point is for their actions to *defy* understanding. They're answerable to nobody and nothing—not even, as Sophie says, to the laws of reason."

"Quite," said Cameron, his head again emerging. "Yet if your conjecture is right, then you *have* understood and even given a name to a principle governing their behavior. That it answers to the name of 'arbitrary' still means that one can subsume it under a general law, in other words conclude that by and large one can expect aleatory conduct from them." "Well, I suppose that's some comfort, Beryl," Lily said cheerfully. Beryl laughed. "Can you define 'aleatory' by any chance, Mother?" "'Dicey.' '*Alea jacta est*,'" supplied Henry, causing Margaret to shake her large head and sigh. "The ruin of a fine mind," she pronounced in a carrying bass aside.

"To understand that there's no understanding what they're up to," Lily mused. "And yet I have the funniest inkling. Maybe I'd better not say it. In case *they're* listening." "For heaven's sake, how?" said Margaret. "These rooms could be 'bugged,'" Lily retorted. "Quite true," said Henk, before Beryl could contradict. "I have been thinking that too." "Well, whisper it, then, Mother," prompted Beryl. "Just a minute!" said Frank. "Let's make assurance doubly sure." He began to play chopsticks energetically on the harmonium. Lily spoke into her daughter's ear. In turn Beryl whispered to Sophie: "The Vermeer." By the time it reached Cameron, it had become "Fear more." But most had understood. Though not as rich as Johnnie, Helen was the star collector: she owned a Vermeer.

The gravity of the first-class faces left no doubt as to the inference being drawn. It was as though Lily had voiced a collective thought that had lain too deep for words. The collectors sat with bowed heads, reflecting. Prompted by the naming of the Vermeer, each, evidently, was considering his own valuables. Even the outsiders were moved to sober reflection, like spectators watching a stranger's coffin pass. "Is it an important Vermeer?" Simmons whispered and, on being assured that it was, fell to pondering. It was not the occasion to tell her that there were no *un*important Vermeers; the parlor was silent, as if it contained mourners. In the next room, the games came to a respectful halt as word of the "inkling" leaked. Sitting with folded hands, Sophie was led to think of the death of Sapphire, she was not sure why. What did Victor's wickedly murdered pet have in common with a Vermeer of Delft except the color blue? Or—more to the point—that each was a rarity, a "pearl" of its kind? If Sapphire had been an alley cat, would she have got the same treatment?

Sophie had no idea of what might be in the rest of the collections, but the mere thought of works of art as legitimate prey for terrorists caused her sympathetic nervous system pain. If they could deliberately shoot a superb Persian cat—there had been *two* shots, she clearly remembered—there must be policy behind it. Sapphire had died as an advertisement of some unusual intention. That strange young man, Jeroen, might view himself and his band as apostles of "desacralization," which would be terror in a pure state, she guessed. In comparison, treating the lives of adult human hostages as bargaining counters seemed like normal, "civilized" warfare.

To her surprise, Henk was winking at her. He tapped his head again. Unwillingly, she saw what he was trying to tell her. To a rational mind, he meant, this was a nutty example of group-think: these people had become *possessed* by the notion that their art treasures were in danger, without asking themselves how that could be or considering it aloud as an objective proposition. They "felt it in their bones," and the feeling was so strong that it had gripped the whole body of hostages, not just the fraction that had personal cause for anxiety. Only Henk, a Dutch skeptic, seemed to be immune. To judge by the silence, everyone else was just as suggestible as Sophie herself.

The first sight of Helen removed any uncertainty. Their bones had been right. The tribunes of the people had decreed that she could have her freedom in exchange for the "Girl in a Blue Cap with a Guitar." Henry's freedom would cost her a Titian. They had wanted the little Bosch, too—hardly bigger than a postage stamp—but mercifully it was on show in Los Angeles; she had a clipping from *Time* to prove it. The group had tried her and passed sentence, payment in kind, from which there could be no appeal. She had begged them—on her knees, literally—to take her whole fortune in the place of the "Girl" but without any effect. Snuffling and wiping her pale eyes, rejecting Henry's effort to quiet her and Denise's smelling-salts, she now took the entire "family room" into her confidence. Around her an eager ring formed, curiosity proving stronger than pity. Ransoming Henry, she told them, would not be so very painful; the Titian was studio work mostly, and she had never cared for the subject. But she would almost rather die, she had decided, than see harm come to the precious Vermeer—in perfect condition, with its wonderful crackle; when its near-replica, "The Guitar Player," had been seized from Kenwood House, she had suffered untold agonies, even though its "execution" by the vandals would have made her own unique. They had given her an hour to make up her mind.

Next Harold was tapped, then Johnnie, then Margaret, then Charles, and finally Lily. "Cheer up, Mother," counseled Beryl. "The pecking order proves that they don't know the value of 'fine English water-colors.'" For a perhaps evident reason the "boys" from Antibes were not being summoned to the bar. "'*Rien à déclarer.*' 'Nothing to declare,'" John, the younger, hazarded with a nervous giggle, as though apologizing for their luck. One by one, with increasing rapidity, the others rejoined their fellows: Harold was supported by the steward; Lily flew to Beryl's arms. Unlike Helen, they were keeping their own confidence. Whatever sentence had been passed on them was not for general consumption. Disregarding the compassionate eyes turned on them, they bunched in desolate twos and threes, like stately crows in a flock of starlings. Helen was finally persuaded to go into the parlor, out of the melee.

If it had been possible, Sophie would have fled the scene. She did not like the position of onlooker. It was obscene, like sitting in perfect health in a surgeon's waiting-room and watching the patients emerge. "They must resent us," murmured Henk. "If they're aware that we're here," said Carey. "Doesn't look much like it." In her own way, Simmons was respectful of their feelings. "We ought to go in and offer Helen our sympathy, don't you think? I was kind of mean back then." "You can try," said Sophie, unwillingly tagging along. The trouble was, it was impossible to sympathize in the true meaning of the word. You could not put yourself in the place of someone who owned a Vermeer—it was not a universal experience. You might be able to feel with a millionaire who had lost all his money; on a smaller scale, it could happen to you. But here the best you could do was to sympathize with the innocent Vermeer itself. To *tell* Helen you were sorry only marked the distance between you and her. But "Thank you, my dear," Helen answered. "I'm sure you mean it."

Soon the service of lunch intervened, breaking up the knots of collectors and generally loosening tongues. Discussion of the predicament of the few spread to the many. The greatest puzzle, it was agreed, was how the hijackers could have learned what was in the collections. "*Attributed* to Titian," they had said to Helen. Amazing. They were even up on the fact that she had arranged to give her Giorgione—pen-and-wash; unique —to the National Gallery. Most people thought it was hanging there on loan. That they knew about Johnnie's sporting art was peculiar too, surely. Stubbs was a "name," but how many hijackers had heard of Ben Marshall? Until a few minutes ago, Sophie had never heard of him herself. "Did you ask how they got their information?" The question was stupid; asking would have been a waste of breath. And not a word had been volunteered, naturally, that would give a clue. Jeroen, it seemed, had had lists in front of him which he consulted, leaving it up to the victim to affirm or deny. Poor Helen had begun by trying to disavow her Vermeer. "But it was all written down there— the size and the tiny restoration and the provenance." A tear fell onto her paper plate. "She could see that he knew," explained Henry.

"But what crime were you charged with?" interrupted Aileen. "I mean, specifically?" "Possession of art works 'stolen' from the people," answered Johnnie with a short laugh. "What can you say to an arraignment like that? That you bought them or had them left to you? To this kangaroo court, that's no defense. They shut you up by reading to you from the damn lists they've got—the evidence, as they see it. I must say, it's uncanny, finding they have it all there in black and white. Shakes a fellow up, almost makes him feel guilty as charged. Especially if he tries to hold anything back. Just to give you an example, I thought they'd missed out on my Degas, and so naturally I didn't call the oversight to their attention. Then damned if they didn't come up with it. Accused me of lack of frankness." Sophie nodded. It was cruel of them, she thought—a refinement of malice to let the collectors "prove" their guilt by denials and evasions and then face them with a full bill of particulars obtained from an unguessable quarter.

The suspicion that someone had informed was inevitable. During lunch it was vacillating between Charles and Warren, the curator. Or so Beryl, who was in on their councils, reported. "Wouldn't you know they'd want to hang it on a queer?" Beryl herself would have liked to hang it on "Simmie," but there was no way: "The hag knows nothing about pictures." The conchie minister, she said, knew about Lily's collection, but that was from long ago: "Most of the things Ma had then have gone on the block." The Economy class hostages had all been given a clean bill of health. "Ma pretends to be glad of it. Maybe she really is. Have you noticed that Henk likes her?"

But if Economy was excluded, it followed that the millionaires had to believe that the culprit was one of their own party or else that a tip had come from an outside source. You would have thought that they would have embraced the second theory, for their own peace of mind, but they were unreasonably slow in coming to it, said Beryl, and only through a process of elimination worthy of Sherlock Holmes. "The finger *can't* point to Eddie and John. They don't know any of us but Warren. And Warren, my God, is just an orientalist. How would he know about Johnnie's stuff?" The logical suspect, among their own number, was Charles, of course. He had come back from his interrogation crowing that he had been "let off scot-free"; his own explanation was that he had persuaded the gang that the few porcelains he still owned were too fragile to be moved unless he packed them himself. Yet it could also mean that he had been "singing" for his supper. "Harold was all for 'confronting' him. Whereupon the others decided that they didn't want to think that of him, really. You know why? 'Because we've known him all our lives.' That's what they call 'being fair.'" "Why don't they suspect you, Beryl?" They ought to, in view of Ahmed, Sophie was thinking. Beryl shrugged. "Because they've known Ma all their lives, I guess."

Anyhow, now they were leaning toward the "outside source"

theory. It supported their faith in having been the sole motive for the hijacking. "This proves it to the hilt," proclaimed Margaret. "Before we ever left our homes, these people knew down to the last brush-stroke what was in our collections. This was planned months in advance, as soon as some revolutionary read in the Museum bulletin about our tour to Iran. But they had to wait till we got to De Gaulle because the security at Kennedy was too tight!" "Idlewild," said Harold. "But you're right; this clinches it. How could they have got the nuts and bolts on my Cézannes in this godforsaken hole? No way. The only puzzler is why they waited so long to spring it on us."

"Shouldn't we be helping Helen to think now?" said Lily, looking at her watch. "She has to decide very soon. But there's so much that she doesn't *know*, that none of us knows. What are they plotting to do with the Vermeer, with all our lovely things? They can't be thinking of bringing them here. I made bold to ask, but of course they wouldn't say. All they said was that if I wanted to return to my family unharmed I must make a tape instructing them to carry out orders for the delivery of my Samuel Palmer and my Turners and Cotmans—they didn't seem at all interested in Girtin, although he was so important. I had no need to know more than that, they told me. Just address the tape to a member of my family and precise instructions for packing and delivery would follow. But, as I tried to explain to them, since Joe died my only close family is Beryl. I wouldn't trust my sister-in-law, dear that she is, to know a Cotman from—"

"Personally I think I'd go along, Lily. That's the way I'm tilting myself. Play at being cooperative. I've pretty well decided to tell them that I accept. And with my Cézannes, I have more at stake. I'll just make one stipulation. That I direct the tape to my lawyer. Whatever I instruct my lawyer, he'll know that I'm under duress, so he'll have the sense not to play for keeps. With a relative you never can tell. My lawyer'll be smart enough to go through the motions of obeying instructions, in the interests of my and Eloise's safety, all the time being damn sure that the government isn't going to let him turn over a fortune in irreplaceable paintings to some reds representing these gorillas. The Treasury or the Attorney General will get a stay or an injunction or figure out some hokey-pokey. An agreement made under duress isn't binding. What do you think, Carey? You're a lawyer."

"I can't advise you," Jim said, rather stiffly. "But I can tell you the law. It's against U.S. policy to negotiate the demands of hijackers. If your lawyer starts negotiating at your instance, he will go to jail." "But he wouldn't *negotiate*. He'd fake and stall till the government stepped in." "It's not up to the government to do your lawyer's duty for him. He's an officer of the court. Of course he could arrive at some agreement with the FBI to seem to play ball with these folks, bait a trap with your works of art or reasonable facsimiles of them. . . . You're familiar with the scenario, surely."

"Well, fine. It adds up to the same, doesn't it? If I accept, I've been a good boy, so far as the gorillas can see. And I'll have gained time. They're not going to shoot me as long as they think they have eight signed Cézannes in the bag. My lawyer'll need proof that I'm alive before he agrees to deliver. Even if they start getting impatient, they'll make up their minds to cool it." Carey sighed. "If you want to address the tape to your lawyer, I see no objection that Jeroen and Company can have. But you'll put your lawyer in a hell of a dilemma. He gets an instruction with your voice print on it. Is he supposed to carry it out or not? Either way, he's placed in a questionable position. Your instruction tells him to break the law. As an officer of the court, his first duty, then, is to report it. At the same time, being your lawyer, he will feel bound to respect the confidentiality of the communication. If we assume that he's scrupulous and reports it, not only does he ignore your express instructions, but he also, by the act of reporting it, frustrates any intention you may have of complying."

The warning was clear, Sophie thought, but she was not sure that Chadwick understood. Jim was being cautious, for reasons of his own, and for the first time she saw in him the quality that had disappointed so many of his followers. Simmons saw it too. "He just won't commit himself. Look at him, Sophie." He sat lounging on the floor, with his back against a wall and his long legs stretched out, and was idly tossing a coin. Sophie admitted that this show of detachment must appear cavalier to the millionaires. Yet the very fact that their treasures were at stake—to say nothing of their lives, probably, if they refused—might excuse his reluctance to pronounce. She wished Henk would say something; Jim's being a U.S. senator could be another element, not necessarily an admirable one, in his reluctance.

"What's the difference between my lawyer and a relative?" Harold demanded in his customary suspicious tones. Carey caught the coin and with his other hand covered a yawn. "Only that the relative is under no obligation to report a criminal communication of this nature. Otherwise the position is the same."

"So do you advise Helen to make the tape?" said Lily, anxiously looking at her watch again. "Sorry. I can't advise you, Lily. It would be improper on my part. I'll say this much." Slowly he got to his feet. "Any of you who agrees to make a tape under the existing circumstances will *not* be regarded as an accessory to a criminal proceeding. On that score, you need have no inhibitions. On the other hand, it would be unwise to think that the making of the tape is the easy way out. Having made it, you may find that you are bound to it. Or that our friends will require a promptness in compliance that you don't envision. Measures of an ugly sort may be taken to induce speed."

"But if we refuse," said Henry, "they'll kill us, isn't that the idea?" The collectors exchanged looks. "We had different impressions," Lily said. "*I* certainly thought so, but some of us weren't so sure. I don't believe the word 'kill' was actually used." "Not to me," said Johnnie. "It was more of a vague menace." Again, of course, no one had asked. "They left it to our imagination," said Harold. "Depends on how much you have." "They were *very* definite, though, about the deadline," Lily put in. "Each of us has an hour from the time he was dismissed. I wonder why." "Prolongs the torture," Henry suggested. "And on our side of the fence, I don't see the possibility of stringing the thing out, playing for time. We must give a Yes or a No." Charles giggled. "Why, by the bye, is it always assumed that time is on the side of the angels?" "Let's make the tapes," declared Margaret, rising. "Where's the harm in it? There's many a slip . . . I shall direct mine to my butler. I've implicit confidence in his judgment. One's children cannot be wholly objective. Remember that, Helen. Your eldest stands to inherit the lovely Vermeer, does he not?"

"No." Helen, who had been pacing the carpet with short unsteady steps, plumped herself down like a stout little bolster on the sofa. "No to *what*, dear?" cried Lily in a voice of alarm. "No, I shan't give them the Vermeer." "Oh, *Helen!*" the ladies reproached her in wailing chorus. "No," Helen repeated with a decisive wobble of her receding, indeterminate chin. "I don't *care* what they promise. Jeroen swore to me that not a hair of its head would be harmed. But I've no right to take his word for it. Any more than if it were a child. The painting will stay where it is, Henry. They can have the Titian if they want."

It became alarmingly clear that she intended to stick to her guns. Henry's reasoning was useless, and Frank could not shake her resolution, though he was feeling it his pastoral duty to try. Like anyone who has arrived at an immense decision, she had a look of being at rest, serene as a rock in the midst of the storm around her. Bearing out the prophecy that they could be "bigger" for their experience, her dumpy form seemed to have gained a full inch and not only in moral stature. It was a matter of posture, doubtless; her small muffin head was drawn up and her chest thrust mildly forward as she sat unmoving in the "place of honor" vacated by Margaret on the sofa. Perhaps she felt proud of the dauntless stand she had taken or pleased to be the undivided center of attention, but, if so, it only showed in a vague, bemused little smile, which she directed at those around her benignly and sympathetically, as though, from her present modest elevation, they were no longer quite in focus.

She did not turn a deaf ear to their arguments and objection but listened politely, with an evident effort at attention, nodding from time to time to show that she was following, as no doubt she did at her club when a lecturer dealt with a topic that was "interesting," although not directly to her. Facing her, Frank had drawn up a straight chair and kept hitching himself forward on it so as to be able to "reach" her. To the audience grouped around them he seemed to be giving a demonstration of his professional skills, like a doctor operating on a patient before a group of students. This was something he could not help, but the audience—or at least Sophie—could not help viewing it as a performance, that is, critically, forgetful of the earnestness of his purpose.

"Helen! You bear the same lovely name, 'torch' in Greek, as my own wife and daughter. Now let's think a little about this Vermeer. In the last analysis, it's a material object, isn't it? Just oil and canvas handled in a certain way that you and I recognize as art. But that's relative, don't you agree? Depending on the culture we've been raised in. I mean, to an Eskimo or a Ugandan, the marks on that piece of canvas wouldn't say a darn thing. 'Beauty is in the eye of the beholder,' as the old saw had it. Well, isn't that pretty much accepted by art historians today? In art, we're responding to a set of conventions, the way we do in our clothes and the food we eat. Some creative spirits want to overthrow those conventions, and I don't say that I altogether blame them, even though I don't always understand what they're getting at. But that's beside the point. The point is that in our society we're making a shibboleth of art. We've learned that there's nothing sacred or eternal in our dress fashions and food habits. We've lived through several revolutions in those departments, with women wearing pants and men carrying purses and our young people cooking in 'woks' and eating raw fish like the Japanese. . . . Well, you know what I mean. But our attitudes toward art are still as rigid as they ever were, paradoxical as that may sound. We reverence art as something sacred, when we ought to be using it for our enjoyment as we do today with our clothes. Modern art hasn't succeeded in liberating man from the fetishism of Art with a capital *A*. We've come to worship a class of objects—paintings and sculptures—and we treat their creators as gods. If we all could be artists, as one day I hope we can, we wouldn't feel that way any more. We wouldn't look on art as precious property to be accumulated by any single person or society. Now, mind you, I think this totemism has a lot to do with the failure of organized religion. Despite church attendance figures, we've let ordinary humanity lose touch with the divine, with God. No wonder that the lucky few among us are tempted to put daubs of oil on canvas in His place. I say 'daubs' deliberately, Helen, to shock you. Remember, we've just agreed that to the Ugandan your Vermeer is no thing of beauty, and who is to say that he's wrong?"

"Yes, thank you, Frank. Very interesting. I know you mean well. And I suppose it's all relative, as you say. I've never cared much for African sculpture, though I know people who have a passion for it." Frank hitched himself forward another inch and made a gesture of entreaty. "Helen! Do you still know your Ten Commandments?" She nodded. "Well, recite me the First, then." "'Thou shalt not make unto thee any graven image,' is that what you mean?" "Yes, dear Helen. 'Or the likeness of any thing that is in heaven above or in the earth beneath, or in the water under the earth.' This terrible experience should bring home to us the good sense of that commandment. Of course what was being enjoined against at that time was the fashioning and worship of idols. Secular art was unknown to the ancient Hebrews and indeed to most of the ancient peoples. And the special genius of the Hebrew religion was that its God was invisible, that is, immaterial, not to be represented or imitated in any material shape or form. The Incarnation, of course, was a radical break with that view of Him. 'And was made man.' Still, I wonder whether the old ban on representation didn't have more true wisdom in it than our own Church, reacting to the Puritan excesses, has been willing to admit. Did Moses foresee that the fashioning of images would be bound to lead to the worship of them? The story of the Golden Calf seems to point that way, doesn't it?"

"My wife's a Presbyterian," said Henry. "You won't find graven images in her church. But you're dead right on one point. She idolizes that Vermeer." Helen still wore her dreamy smile. "Did you ever happen to see it, Frank? It was hanging on show at Wildenstein's. For the Crippled Children. There was always a throng around it, wasn't there, Henry?" "I'm sorry," confessed Frank. "I missed it. I'm so darned busy with church work that I don't get out much to exhibitions any more." "Oh, well, then . . . If you had, you might understand." She was in love with the picture, that was obvious, though the minister did not seem to realize it. Moreover, there was a suggestion of tender reminiscence in her tone, a commemorative note, as though the "Girl" belonged to a distant, enshrined past, too far off now for tears. However the others were interpreting the ultimatum, Helen had clearly decided that she was on her way to a better world, leaving her dear possession behind.

Undiscouraged, Frank tried another tack. "Maybe we make

too much of a cult of originals. Helen has had the privilege of living with one, but if she'd lived with a reproduction instead, nobody could take it away from her. If it happened to be stolen, she could always get another, exactly the same. Whereas when you lose a loved one, say a member of your family, there's no replacement. That's why, Helen, we hold human life sacred; the individual in each of us is one of a kind, loved by the Creator for the divine unique spark in him. Don't let your 'torch' go out. Your life is sacred to me, Helen, as it should be to you. You blaspheme if you think of exchanging it for a mere material possession, a thing whose value may be specious—in the sense of highly relative—as you yourself admit." But the Vermeer was one of a kind; that was the point he himself had just made, even if for him it would have done better to exist in the plural. It was odd that he did not see that everything he was saying about human life applied for Helen, equally—indeed more emphatically—to her "Girl."

"Leave her be, Frankie," gently spoke up the Bishop. "Let her follow her own counsel. We shall pray for you, my dear, and ask the good Lord to soften the hearts of these misguided young people toward you." "Helen Potter!" Jeroen himself stood in the doorway. "Come along now." Henk half rose, as if to intervene. "Stay where you are, Deputy," Jeroen said. "This affair does not concern you. You also, Henry Potter. Your wife does not need your company." With her short teetering steps, she followed him into the kitchen; Hussein with his pistol was at her back. The Bishop wiped his eyes. There went the stuff of martyrs. "Queen Victoria," whispered Henk, gravely approving. In fact there *was* a resemblance to the queen in her later years, something of pudgy royal dignity, that all at once had become visible.

"I suppose I might have offered to take her place," muttered Henry. "It wouldn't have done any good," the others assured him. "She's made her bed," said Harold. "Shut up, you," said Sophie. The door to the kitchen was closed. Outside Hussein stood on guard, his pistol raised. Frank and the Bishop moved their lips in silent prayer. Carey swiftly crossed himself. "I can't bear it," cried Aileen, putting her fingers to her ears. For an eternity they waited.

Ten

WITHOUT any warning, toward the end of the afternoon, the television screen lit up. It was still Wednesday. Yusuf, very helpfully, got to work twirling the dials till the image would stay put. In the box appeared the farmhouse they were prisoners in, shown from several angles and surprisingly close up. The shots had been taken from the air: those military planes that they had heard zooming about this morning; sometimes, annoyingly, a wing got in the way of the picture. It was odd to have a bird's-eye view of your place of confinement, which you had never fully seen with your own eyes—on the night they had arrived it had been too dark. Now they were able to look down on the broad sloping roof—underneath was the drafty attic half of them had been sleeping in—the television aerial, the chicken coop and the rabbit run near the spot where the men peed. From above they saw a crisscrossing of canals and ditches, the highway they had landed on, and the big unfinished barn with its roofing of tarpaulin. Although the snow had melted, the camouflage job was still effective; examining it from a pilot's perspective, even Harold admitted to a certain satisfaction in the result of their labors, what the Sophie girl called "pride of workmanship."

Yusuf had turned up the sound, and Henk, who was found napping on the floor behind the sofa, was rushed to the screen to translate. They had missed the beginning while they were trying to wake him up, but they learned—what they could see anyway—that the long-awaited breakthrough had happened. It was the hijackers themselves who had taken the initiative. They had broadcast a message to the authorities announcing their location; the radio in the kitchen, it seemed, was a powerful short-wave sending and receiving set, which one of the Arabs—Yusuf probably—had known how to rig up to the TV aerial. Henk and Carey said that they had suspected that there would be a "pirate station" in the house—a pity that they had not come out with that sooner, when it would have cleared up some little misunderstandings. Anyway, the authorities, at first, had treated the message as a hoax, with the result that two whole hours had been lost. The message identifying the "command post's" position had come through shortly after two, according to the commentator, and now it was a few minutes past four.

The program, apparently, had started with a full list of the hijackers' demands; that of course would be the part they had missed. But now a spokesman came on the screen recapitulating the chief ones. First, an astronomic ransom—one and a quarter million dollars, half to be distributed among the workers and peasants of Surinam—for the return of the helicopter and its crew. Second, immediate withdrawal of Holland from NATO and breaking of relations with Israel. Third, liberation of all "class-war prisoners" from Dutch jails. Superficially, that one sounded more feasible: in a very liberal country like Holland, there could not be so many. But in fact it could mean anything, depending on the definition: the release of common criminals, for instance, if they were of working-class origin, which obviously most of them would be. The demand, Henk said, would be unacceptable as it stood to his government; several rounds of "clarification" might be needed before the ruling coalition could consider acting on it. Eventually a few fringe elements who by stretching a point could be regarded as political prisoners might be let out: e.g., small groups of squatters who had occupied canal houses and struck policemen seeking to evict them. . . . But in his opinion the *kapers* did not take this demand of theirs too seriously; it was on their list *pro forma*, to satisfy revolutionary protocol. The outcome for the hostages would surely not hinge on it. The same with NATO and Israel: he doubted that the terrorists really expected to change the foreign policy of the Netherlands by their "rhetoric"—his expression—of violence.

More to the point was the final demand: that a small helicopter with a one-man crew be supplied to pick up a bundle of tapes containing instructions from the prisoners to their families on how to bring about their release. This demand had a deadline attached to it. In less than half an hour from now, the pilot was to begin hovering over a designated spot, which would be marked by a flag and lanterns, thirty meters from the command post; at a signal he was to drop a cable. He was not to attempt to land, and any other craft entering the air space during the pick-up would be shot down. The tapes must then be transferred to a long-range carrier and delivered to the families of the hostages; under no circumstances should they be allowed to fall into the hands of the FBI or any other agency of the U.S. imperialist government. Failure to observe this condition would bring immediate reprisals. The Dutch military attaché in Washington would be held responsible for the prompt transfer of the tapes to the parties concerned. Delay or sabotage on his part would be viewed as an act of war, to be answered for in blood by the prisoner Van Vliet de Jonge, whose image in full color now flashed on the screen. . . . As he sat on the floor, fiddling with the knobs, they saw him chatting with the Queen at the opening of Parliament, addressing a crowd, eating a herring at a street stall. Then came some still photos of his wife and their children, poor little tykes—it was a surprise to learn that he was married to a Javanese beauty, slender, with sloe eyes. Henk's family vanished from the screen and were replaced by the Minister of Defense, a funny stiff old socialist, declaring that Her Majesty's government, mindful of the human factor, was bending every effort to meet the conditions laid down in the final demand: a helicopter of the Alouette II type was being dispatched, and a Lockheed Lodestar stood ready to receive the bundle of tapes. With a last sweeping view of the farmhouse, the special broadcast ended. Further news and commentary would be shown on the regular program at eighteen hours fifty-five, five minutes of seven.

As the image of their prison faded from the screen, the Chadwicks eyed each other. It looked indeed as though Senator Carey had known whereof he spoke when he said that making the tapes was not "the easy way out." He had tried to warn Harold in particular against that fatal cocksureness of his. It had been foolish of Harold, foolish of all of them, to imagine that the "*kapers*," as Henk called them, would not do everything in their power to keep the FBI from interfering with their plan. As for "stalling" over the delivery of the paintings ("gaining time"!), from what they had just heard such tactics could cost Henk his life. Harold might not care if Henk was executed, but the others would. He was such good company, their "Laughing Cavalier," and he had a brilliant career ahead of him—they had not understood that till they saw him on television, though Charles had always said so.

No wonder Harold and Eloise were looking doubtfully at each other. After all, if he had not been so brassily confident of the harmlessness of making the tapes, the others might have hesitated. And there sat Helen, the living proof of how wrong they had been to listen to him. Jeroen and Company—so far at least—had wreaked no vengeance on her. She had made a tape with instructions to turn over the Titian as the price of Henry's head. That was all. No one had struck her or furiously twisted her arm. They had simply told her that they would be seeing her later. She had seemed almost let down when she came trotting back into the room. It was hard to believe that the band would give up on the Vermeer so easily; they would surely try again. But two hours had passed, and no new summons had come for her. If anyone had "gained time," it was she. Of course they had other business to occupy them, most importantly the helicopter, which was due any minute if the deadline was really going to be met.

The hostages in the parlor crowded against the western window to watch for it. In the dusk, they saw lanterns moving in the direction of the field. Nothing yet but a star—Venus rising—in the sky. "Watchman, tell us of the night," someone hummed, as a "sick" joke surely, for it was not signs of promise such as had appeared to the Magi that they were awaiting— rather, the reverse in the collectors' case. Still, one could not deny that there was something strangely thrilling in scanning the evening sky for the approach of a visitant from what seemed now like the other world. At any rate, it would be a break in the monotony. For some time, they had been hearing heavy thumps against the house wall: extra sandbags, the men said, being piled up around it in the event of an attack. At last Eloise's sharp ears caught the sound of the helicopter's rotors. There it was, hovering, a midget compared to theirs. They were able to watch the drop of the cable, but, disappointingly, the armed guards with lanterns patrolling cut off a view of the loading. Also it had become dark. They had only a glimpse of an indistinct object swinging upward to tell them that the pick-up was over. The little craft with their voices aboard immediately started to climb.

It was natural to feel despondent when it had disappeared. Only Harold, by bluster, avoided a sinking of spirits. He claimed not to feel that they had just said good-bye to their paintings—he still had faith in the FBI. According to him, the warning on television only meant that the FBI would have to be careful. They knew how to work under cover. If the Dutch tried to keep them out of the picture, they would have their own means. "Why, Maggie's butler could be understudied by an FBI man and not even the other help the wiser. Half the waiters and butlers passing trays of drinks and sandwiches at your red-as-a-rose fund-raisers are FBI plants. Like detectives guarding the wedding presents in monkey suits. If Gerry Ford knows what's good for him, they'll be careful." He patted his trousers pocket, where, one presumed, his billfold lay. The ladies sighed. How far away the time seemed when they were wont to tell each other that Harold and his wife—the first one—were "deliciously common"!

Johnnie shook his head. "No, Harold, my boy. If the FBI gets into it, they'll blow it. Sure as shooting." "Even if it means some of our lives," said Lily, sadly. "I'm awfully afraid you're right. It's a terrible commentary, isn't it?" "I never thought I'd reach the point of looking on the FBI as my enemy," declared Margaret.

"It only needs a weensy change in perspective, doesn't it?" That was Charles, being dreadful again. "A little bird tells me that we're not the enthusiasts for 'law and order' that we were a few days ago. It was that interesting third demand that brought it home to me. Why, my dear, I said to myself, if the whole criminal population of Holland were turned loose— every last cutthroat and child-molester and wife-beater—I'd have no objection as long as it meant that I'd be allowed to journey to Naqsh-i-Rustan with my ears and toes and fingers still safely about me. And since I'm a rational animal and not totally selfish, I hope, I found myself led to question the social utility of prisons. What difference would it make, Charles, I said, if in fact those criminals *were* all let loose? Very little, I concluded. Accepting such a prospect for my own subjective motives, rather than fearing it for society at large, allowed me to regard it objectively—a distinct gain, I always think. Till today, I confess, I'd tended to look on our penal institutions as a necessary evil. And, as for the second demand, can we honestly say that it would be a tragedy if Holland were to leave NATO and suspend relations with Israel? My own answer, I admit, would be prejudiced. As a pacifist, I hold no brief for NATO, and, though I'm not unsympathetic to Israel, I feel she could use a little lesson."

"Oh, *poor* Israel," moaned Beryl's "Simmie." "Would you take away her last friend? Well, I guess I would, if it was the only way of saving our lives. And you have to admit that some of her policies are open to criticism." "You see?" crowed Charles. He was right, one had to acknowledge: things did look different from a captive's point of view. One's dearest principles shrank in importance when weighed against one's freedom, till finally one began to ask whether they *were* so important, after all. Take the example of NATO: would Harold be such a jingo about the NATO forces as the first line of defense against Communism if taking Holland out of the first line would let them all go home in peace? France, come to think of it, he might tell himself, had left NATO years ago and the world had not come to an end.

"Yes," said Simmie. "And I'm starting to wonder about something else. Our famous free press. I know it's good that we have it and vital to a democracy. But in connection with your pictures, I ask myself . . . I mean, what's to stop reporters from interviewing all our families?" "Nothing," said Carey. "We can be sure that it's been done." "Well, then, when this tapes bombshell breaks, won't they be pounding at those same doors again?" Carey nodded. "Mmm . . . I take your meaning." But the others were left in the dark. "Explain," said Beryl. "Don't be so damned mysterious." "No mystery," said Carey. "Aileen means that this time some of the families will shut the door in their faces." "Yes. On the one hand, my Mamma will let them in and tell them that, no, she hasn't received any tape from me. They're bound to believe her. Mamma's a very truthful person. Anyway, in a small town like Fayetteville, everybody would know if she had. The same with your daughter, Jim. They'd seek her out in college, and she'd talk to them, wouldn't she, and tell them no tape? It would be like that with every one of *our* families, but with you people's it wouldn't. They'd refuse to see reporters for fear of saying something out of turn. So it would be easy to narrow it down and know who'd got a tape and who hadn't. Then it wouldn't take a genius to realize that every hostage who made a tape was an important art collector."

"Or just rich, Aileen," said Warren. "Well, the two go together," she retorted and then fell silent, as if the interruption had confused her. "In any case," said the Senator, helping her, "thanks to the press, the FBI won't have much of a problem running down the addressees of the tapes. The reporters lying in wait outside the stately homes will function as pointer dogs. As for watching the families' movements, noting visitors, photographing them, trailing them, the press'll provide those services for Kelley's cops at no extra charge."

The collectors groaned in unison. The families had a right to their privacy in circumstances like this. Though no one, of course, wanted his works of art to be handed over to the *kapers'* accomplices, the thought that the press by its vigilance would stand in the way was very disagreeable. If one was willing to pay the ransom, that should be the end of it; press and government should stand aside till the deed was done. Granted, it was breaking the law, but there were times when the law was wrong.

It was true that great wealth, even relatively great wealth, got one in the habit of wanting one's own way, whatever the cost. Yet it was not an altogether bad habit to have formed. They were right to feel their hackles rise at the very idea of arbitrary interference in an affair that concerned no one but themselves. The paintings were theirs, so they should be free to dispose of them according to their own lights. Obviously, owning a masterpiece was a sacred trust—they all felt that, even Eloise with her pretty-pretty Laurencins—but how that trust should be regarded in an emergency ought to lie between one and one's own conscience. If the rich were staunch Republicans, that was not because they grudged a fair wage and decent medical care and playgrounds and the rest of it to the poor, nor even because they believed blindly in capitalism as the best system yet invented for creating wealth and spreading it to the workman and the small investor, but because they were accustomed to freedom and jealous of having it taken away from them by the government and the prying press. A poor man did not appreciate the value of freedom, never having had much; that was a sad fact and often not his fault.

Yet if one could not help waxing indignant at the prospect of reporters wantonly interfering with one's right to pay up, in another part of one's mind was a little prayer that some outside force—not necessarily reporters—*would* intervene to save the treasures that too weakly one had agreed to sacrifice. Nobody knew *what* he or she wanted, really. For the *kapers* to have their way or not to have it? If they had their way, that would put an end to the torment at any rate. But to see them thwarted, gnashing their teeth like the villains they were, had greater appeal to the fancy.

Rescue, realistically, was the only hope. Of their own accord, the terrorists would not "go away," like a bad dream. A daring raid, under cover of darkness, might do it. Actually, quite a few of the party had been counting on the helicopter for deliverance: it had been tempting to picture a body of paratroopers springing from it heavily armed, overpowering the guards and calling on the leaders to come out of the house and surrender. Such had been his fond fancy, Johnnie confessed; others had imagined canisters of a paralyzing gas as well. But here again did one really desire that? The house was wired, all the way to the rafters, and these people were fanatics. At the very minimum, were a rescue force to land, there would be shooting. The hostages, one might argue, could lie on the floor, out of the line of fire. But there was that "human shield" tactic so familiar from thriller films. To think of one's frail body serving as a buckler for Jeroen's hefty frame made one recognize how inseparable one's interests had become from theirs, bound up together despite the evident differences for as long as this lasted; there was a name for that in biology: symbiosis. No wonder that when the helicopter appeared, it had been a relief, on the whole, to see that it was much too small to carry an army of flying Dutchmen—only the pilot and maybe one passenger could fit into it.

"Sophie," said Johnnie, "you're a journalist. What bright idea do you have for calling the pack off so that our families can do the necessary, if that seems best to them, to bring us back alive?" "The press isn't as unfeeling as you all seem to think," she answered in a low voice, interlacing her long fingers. "On its own, it can behave responsibly when it sees that the public's 'right to know' conflicts with military security or with the safety of individual lives. But it doesn't like to be dictated to or hear from others what its bounden duty is. It might help now, I guess, if an appeal was made to the papers to leave the families alone while negotiations are going on." "But who would make the appeal, Sophie?" asked Lily. "The Dutch, I suppose," said Sophie. "Through the military attaché." But she herself did not sound very convinced. "Surely it would come better from the families?" Margaret said. Probably it would, but how convey the idea to the families? They might think of it for themselves and they might not.

There was a dejected silence. "We're so helpless, aren't we?" sighed Eloise. "If only, over there, they could have the benefit of the thinking we're doing here. We could give them so many pointers." "I have an idea!" Aileen cried. "Why don't you make the appeal to the press yourselves? You could do another tape, with all your voices on it." They all turned to Carey. "Go ahead," he said. "I'm sure Jeroen *et al.* will be happy to air it for you." "You're being sarcastic," said Lily. "Do you mean we shouldn't?" "Suit yourselves, Lily," he answered. "But why so eager to make sure that our hosts get their hands on your pictures? Looks like you want to do their job for them. Kind of an auxiliary fire-fighting team of volunteers standing by with hook and ladder, getting your piece of the action." "But would an appeal *work*?" said Johnnie. Carey supposed it would, for the time being, with the big papers, till some small fry broke the embargo. Aileen burst in. "I've got a better idea. Sophie should do it." "Thanks," said Sophie dryly. "As a journalist you'll carry *much* more conviction," Aileen persisted. "Your colleagues will listen to you when they might not to a lot of millionaires. The voice of privilege isn't their favorite music. But as a fellow-worker, you'll speak directly to their professional consciences." But Sophie refused, point blank.

"Will you do it, then, Bishop?" The old man started. He had not been paying attention. "Do what, my dear?" His ruddy face had a purplish flush. Come to think of it, he had not been looking well since lunch time. "Make an appeal to the press, honey—" "Press?" He stared around the room. "Are there reporters here?" Sweat broke out on his broad forehead. "Hold it, Aileen," ordered the Senator, when he saw that her mouth was open, ready to speak again. He moved over to where Gus was sitting and took his pulse. Then his eyebrows went up. "Get Denise." He was unbuttoning the old man's shirt collar. "Is that better? Can you hear me, Gus?" The Bishop faintly nodded and tried to speak. His jaw worked. "Head." "Your head hurts, does it?" There was a feebler motion of the head and a facial sign like a wink. One eye was wide open and staring. He was having a stroke. As he twitched and fell forward, Frank caught him. "Shall we get him onto the sofa?" "Maybe better not move him," said Harold, joining himself to the purposeful circle around the sick old man. "Let's just take off his shoes." They unlaced the heavy brogues, and Frank chafed his feet in the thick socks. The right foot hung down, a dead weight.

"Stand back!" Denise was there now; she had been in the kitchen preparing supper. Having taken his pulse herself, she said it would be all right to move him, and Frank and Jim, with Harold helping, carried him to the sofa. He was breathing wheezily and seemed to be unconscious. Harold looked over the contents of Denise's first-aid kit and made a face. They had nearly forgotten that he had started out behind the counter, as a pharmacist—he had made his first million by "cornering" some new drug. "Is this all you've got?" he demanded. "I fear so, sir. Would you think to try the adrenalin?" "Are you crazy, woman? The worst thing you could give him. This is a stroke, see?" "There are *medicaments* in the frigidaire, sir." "Blood plasma, yes, plenty," said Ahmed, who had been hovering about anxiously. "*Voulez-vous que j'en cherche?*" Harold hooted. "Counter-indicated, I should imagine, Ahmed," put in Charles. "In my young years, I recall, blood-letting was a favored remedy for apoplectic strokes. Yes, I can still see the jar of leeches in Grandfather's sick chamber. We were in Seville, as it happened, when he was stricken while watching a procession of flagellants." Harold nodded. "Blood-letting would have taken the blood pressure *down*, which is what you have to do with a stroke. Adrenalin and plasma send it *up*." "And icebags," Charles continued, "were applied to the forehead. Could an icebag be improvised, I wonder?" Denise thought it could and hurried off to the kitchen.

Harold went back to studying the bottles and boxes in the first-aid kit. "Aspirin, anyway," he said. "May help some in dilating the veins. At least it'll relieve the headache. You heard him indicate that his head was aching? Normal in a stroke. Often the first symptom. Glucose—could there be any glucose in that frigidaire? But, hell, you'd have to administer it as an intravenous drip. No chance of that. In the old days they went in for camphor injections. . . ."

He had not stopped talking, thinking aloud evidently, when Greet appeared. She studied the Bishop, whose breathing was still noisy, and calmly removed his false teeth. Next she took his pulse. "You should raise his head and shoulders," she commented, letting his wrist drop. She had been an airline stewardess herself—KLM; trust Beryl to have learned that. Her eye went around the parlor with manifest dissatisfaction till it fell on the big Bible with its silver locks. "That will do," she decided. "Place it there, under the shoulders, and you, Pastor, add your coat." She showed Frank how to fold it. "Can he be flown out?" he asked, when his friend had been propped up in what to the layman appeared a rather uncomfortable position. But no doubt Greet knew what she was doing. One could not call her attitude kind, but it did seem very professional. KLM must give them more training than Air France did in handling emergencies. Or could she have taken a nursing course to prepare herself for enlisting in their "people's army"?

"This man cannot be moved yet. When he recovers consciousness, we will see." In her opinion, it was only a mild stroke. He was not in deep coma, and his pulse was better. In any case, he could not be flown out unaccompanied. They watched as her eye reviewed them. If Gus were flown out, what lucky person would be chosen to go with him? Frank was the logical selection, but, as Sophie had said yesterday—or was it only this morning?—that was not how these people's minds worked. The one thing you could wager on was that there would be no call for volunteers.

Harold held up a little ampoule. At last he had found something that interested him in Denise's kit. "Papaverine. Well, well." Greet took the glass container from him and inspected it herself. "A vaso-dilator," Harold told her. "Just what the doctor ordered. Miracle that she's got it. And of course she has the hypodermic." Greet dismissed his notion of a miracle. Papaverine, she said, was often found in flight emergency kits; it was to be doubted, though, that it was much more useful than aspirin for dilating the vessels. But she agreed that they should try it. "He may not be able to swallow aspirin. That girl, I think, is capable of giving an intramuscular injection." But there was only the one ampoule, and if Denise bungled the shot, it would be a great pity. Greet watched her busy herself with the syringe and a little bottle of alcohol. "No. Go to the kitchen and boil some water. I will give the injection myself." When the hypodermic was brought back in a pan of water, with a pair of tongs, she filled it. "Now turn him on his side and bring the trousers down." The Bishop's trousers were lowered, and his capacious underpants and flowing shirt-tail moved to one side, exposing his white buttock—the right one. Greet pressed his ancient flesh firmly between her thumb and forefinger and plunged the needle in. Then he was placed on his back again, with his trousers rebuttoned. Thanks to Denise's butter-fingers, there had been no avoiding a glimpse of his private parts.

Greet stood looking down at him for a minute and again took his pulse. "We have seen from his passport that the age of this man is eighty-three years. Were you unaware, Pastor, that he suffered from high blood pressure? Why have you brought him with you on your 'fact-finding' crusade? He should be in a home for the aged." She turned on her heel and strode out. "We will be giving you the icebag you have asked for."

Not many minutes later, the Bishop stirred. He was conscious and could talk a little, though his speech was impaired. That might be because of the missing dentures, the lack of which he noticed, asking querulously what Frank had done with them. Frank fitted them into the poor old mouth, which drooped on one side so that saliva ran out. The whole right side of his face seemed to be paralyzed, and his speech, though improved, was still thick. At first he did not know where he was and recognized only Frank. Gradually he took in a bit more of his surroundings. He sat up irritably on finding the Bible underneath him and demanded that it be taken away. Yet he knew it was Calvin's Bible, which showed that he was becoming less confused. His color was better, and he was able to swallow some of the liquids Denise fed him, holding his head up like a baby's. He complained of a "fierce" headache—a normal sequela, Harold said—and they brought him aspirin and a plastic sack with ice-cubes in it.

By night-time, he was almost himself again. They had moved him to the other sofa, in the family room, where he could watch television, which he followed remarkably well, considering that he seemed to have grown deafer in the last few hours and that his right eye, now blinking occasionally, was teary. The screen showed the helicopter, landing at a military airfield, and a crowd of reporters being held back by the military police. To the general surprise, he remembered about the tapes and about Helen, too. "Here you are, big as life," he told her. "The good Lord answered our prayer." They were not shown the departure of the Lodestar, if in fact it had actually left. But they saw the Minister of Defense again and clapped for him, like an old friend.

When bedtime came, Gus was tucked in for the night on the family-room sofa. They found his pajamas in his old tapestry carryall and put them on him. It was quite an event for one of their number to retire in proper night clothes, rather than fully dressed. Carlos brought him his own blanket and a pillow. Instead of going to the attic, Denise was to sleep at his feet, with Frank next to her. Just before "lights out," Elfride came in with a warm drink with a sedative in it. Horst had looked in for a minute, and all three Arabs had appeared to wish the old man a good night. Only Jeroen, in all this time, had not showed his face. It was his conscience reproaching him, Frank was sure. Frank was in a buoyant mood, having regained all his "pep" now that the Bishop was out of the woods, as he put it. Gus's stroke, he believed, was going to prove to be the blessed turning-point in this whole adventure. God's grace worked in mysterious ways, and He may have seen fit to try His servant with a little syncope in order to show these young anarchists the human havoc they could wreak through over-immersion in theory. "Over-immersion" was a funny way of putting it.

At any rate, Gus's own heart was touched by the attentions paid him. "You've been so good," he kept repeating in his still quavery voice to everyone who approached him. Well, he was a Christian and supposed to love his enemies, which meant seeing the good in them. In view of that, the others decided not to mention in his presence the little thing that had just happened: a few minutes ago, Helen was turned back as she was mounting the stairway clutching as usual her rubberized dressing-case to freshen up for the night. Her toilet privilege had been revoked. She could go outdoors with the men, Hussein told her, barring the way with the submachine gun he had taken over from Ahmed. In the shock of it, she had said no, she wouldn't, without considering her waterworks or the fact that it was dark outside so that no one would see her. Now it was too late. The single chamber-pot in the house had been placed where the Bishop could use it, and she would not want to do tinkle-tinkle and disturb him.

Thursday was nearly over. Twenty-four hours had gone by since the Bishop's "*attaque*," as Aileen persisted in calling it—she had been talking French a mile a minute with Denise and Jean, the steward. There was no news yet on television, and the radio report was only that "negotiations" were proceeding through the Dutch Embassy in Washington. But on the scene there had been some changes—for the better, on the whole. Groups of hostages had been allowed to go out for walks, under guard and not too far from the house. Only Helen had been kept in, as a punishment, and Gus, on "doctor's orders" —he had taken a few, remarkably spry steps in the family room, refusing Frank's arm, but then had been made to rest.

Outside, since morning, a new sight had met their eyes: a cordon of special police in black uniforms with white braid around the neck drawn up in the fields perhaps five hundred yards off. They were an elite force, Henk said, called the *marechaussee*— something like guardsmen—and were used in state emergencies. According to Ahmed, the people's army had agreed to having them drawn up there, for its own protection. No sooner had the news gone on the air than curiosity-seekers had swarmed into the area. Last night the highway police had set up road blocks; the only cars permitted through belonged to people who lived here or worked in the pumping-station. But that had not stopped polder dwellers and pump men from hiking cross-country to have a look. It was to prevent that, partly, that the guardsmen had been brought in. A warning had gone out, too, against violating the air space immediately overhead. Yet the hostages on their walks today had seen civil-ian planes and a civilian helicopter. Most of them, Henk thought, had been chartered by the press and foreign televi-sion chains, but a few, surely, were taking tourists up for a spin over the area at so many guilders a head. It would not surprise him if a balloon were to appear. In fact, just before dusk, one group of hostages saw a glider. That was Holland, he explained; his countrymen were bound to turn the event into a carnival, with local-color touches. On the military's list of problems would be an invasion of skaters along the canals.

Every one of those aircraft carried photographers, one sus-pected. Frank, who had been allowed to bring his field glasses out with him, was sure he had caught sight of a telescopic lens pointing down at them from the helicopter. It was unpleasant to know one was being photographed by dozens of perfect strangers as one stumbled and slipped along the ruts of frozen fields with one's casual travel clothes looking decidedly the worse for wear.

The deterioration of one's appearance was one of the crosses of captivity that one had to bear with equanimity. They were all in the same boat, luckily, and yet, unluckily, not quite. The men's beards, for instance, grew at different speeds and some were coarser and spikier than others: Charles proved to be virtually hairless in the face except for his eyebrows, while Harold's jaw bristled with a thick pepper-and-salt stubble. Moreover, one had only to look at the men to realize how favored women were in comparison. Even there, though, there were degrees. Eloise, with her mirror and tweezers, managed to be impecca-ble, while Helen was a sight. She had had an "accident," poor dear, during the night, which had left a large spot that still showed, even when it had dried out, on the back of her dress, and all morning she had smelled of urine. One's olfactories could not help noticing, either, that Sophie was menstruating; being older, in these close quarters, had its compensations. The close quarters meant, too, that every little imperfection showed up as if in a magnifying mirror: the gray roots, for ex-ample, at the parting of Aileen's hair, a stye Beryl was getting, the boil on Victor's neck.

All were rumpled, and soiled as to collars and cuffs, though, again, not equally. Some looked "as if they had slept in their clothes," as of course everyone had, but a few were fortunate in the materials they had happened to be wearing. Henry's vintage herringbone seemed to be made of iron, and, until he had been stricken, the Bishop's tweeds had not showed a wrinkle or a spot. Henk's whipcord, too, was very wrinkle-resistant. As for Carey, he revealed his vanity every single night by taking off his trousers and sleeping on them to preserve the crease— like an actor on the road, he said—in his shorts and covered with his overcoat: he slid them under the rug, where they served as a mattress as well. No gentleman born could have done that.

The black-and-white *marechaussee* had field glasses, which they trained on the prisoners and their guards at exercise. To them, the differences in grooming and cleanliness so apparent to the hostages themselves were probably not visible. They would all look the same. But the guardsmen were less interested probably in the presentability of the hostages than in their health and morale, which would appear to be good. If the uniformed men knew the number of the hostages and could count, they might notice that two had not been taken out for an airing and report that to their superiors. But through their field glasses they might see, too, that relations between guards and prisoners were far from ferocious; perhaps in order to leave that impression, the amiable ones—Carlos and Ahmed— had been chosen as "chaperons." Nor would the impression be wrong. Inside the house, too, the atmosphere had lightened, leading one to wonder as to what could be the reason. Frank's theory that Gus's stroke had produced a change of heart had not won many converts; it was so obviously what a minister would like to believe.

During the commotion caused by the stroke, the idea of appealing to the press had been allowed to drop. This morning Aileen had tried to revive it, but she had been unable to compete with the distractions furnished by the cordon of guardsmen, the fresh air and exercise, and the continuing sideshow of airborne photographers and sightseers. With all these fresh sources of interest immediately at hand, they did not have time to worry about what might be happening in Washington and New York. Anyway, asking the press to stay away in a big country like America would be utterly futile if in a little country like

Holland the authorities themselves could not do better than this afternoon's spectacle suggested. Far from being considerate of others' misfortune, people—not just the press ghouls—only wanted to batten on it.

This was borne out by the evening news. On the screen they were shown the line of men in uniform, the barriers across the highway, and, behind the barriers—what they would not have suspected—a throng of cars, bicycles, small trucks, and pedestrians. Merchants were selling smoked eels and herring from booths on wheels to the crowd, and, despite the temperature, there was an ice-cream vendor with cones and Eskimo pies. Some schoolchildren were flying a kite with a long tail. A reporter with a notebook jumped the barrier, and they watched the police chase him and capture him. On the canal next to the highway there were skaters, sure enough, in bright caps and scarves, that the police had to turn back too. It was like a national holiday. "The *kermis*," said Henk.

This day had seemed the shortest of any they had spent in captivity. There had been no further mention of flying Gus out. That thought had fallen by the wayside, like the proposed appeal to the press. Gus himself did not want to hear of it. "I feel a power of good in me, Frankie," he said firmly, meaning —one gathered—that he had been filled with the spirit during his close encounter with the other world and intended to remain among them as the vessel of it. The staunch old soul must believe that the power of good stored up in him could move mountains.

For supper, there were *pannekoeken*—pancakes; Denise had made them as a surprise out of a mix she found in the housewife's larder and fresh eggs from the chicken coop. After supper, there were two "tables" of bridge, played with new cards John and Beryl had cut out and colored, using the children's crayons—the court cards, very amusing, had single eyes and two noses like Picassos. The match game Carey had showed Victor had caught on with some of the others, and a whole circle was concentrating on it. It was more of a puzzle, really: you had three matches representing cannibals and three representing missionaries, and the idea was to ferry them across a river in a boat that held two persons. The cannibals could never outnumber the missionaries at any stage, on one river

3 missionaries who can all row; 3 cannibals of whom only one can row.

A river to be crossed. 1 boat holding two persons.

The cannibals must never outnumber the missionaries on either bank of the river.

AHMED'S
SOLUTION

bank or the other, or the missionaries would be eaten; all three missionaries knew how to row, and there was one rowing cannibal. Ahmed, who was on guard, came up to watch and suddenly put on a scowl. He decided that the game was racist. The real problem, he said, would be to keep the missionaries from enslaving the cannibals through the technology they brought with them, and the fact that the hostages had not seen that for themselves should show them how deeply racism was embedded in their culture. But, having recited his piece, the mercurial creature promptly came out of his sulk, took six matches—twisting the heads off of the ones that stood for missionaries—trotted them rapidly in pairs and singly back and forth across the rug, ending with two cannibals on the final trip and a winning grin on his brown face. He had solved the puzzle! Bravo for Ahmed! "You're the rowing cannibal, Ahmed," the Senator told him, which was a risky kind of compliment. But the budding terrorist was pleased as Punch.

Before long it was toilet-time. Yusuf came on guard and ordered Helen out with the men. By now she was used to the humiliation. Then lights out. They were all hoping to sleep, after their time in the open, breathing in pure air. But it was not to be. The group in the living-room had just settled down when the Bishop's voice called for Frank. From the piteous sound of it they knew at once that something was wrong. They could hear Frank trying to comfort him. But it was not what they thought: Gus was not having a second stroke—he had forgotten the Lord's Prayer. In comparison, that might appear unimportant, but to him of course it was everything. He sounded frightened out of his wits. Before going to sleep, it seemed, he had wanted to say his prayers and all at once he could not remember how the Lord's Prayer began. In the dark now Frank was prompting him. "Our Father . . ." "Our Father," the old man repeated after him. But he could not go on by himself. "Who art in heaven." "Who art in heaven." "Hallowed be Thy name." "Hallowed be Thy name." It was terrible to listen to it. He broke off with a moan and must have put his hand to his head. "Does your head ache?" "No." He wanted to be left alone. There was silence, then he shouted in a terrible voice "My God, my God, why hast Thou forsaken me?" Christ's last words—awful. "There, now, you see, you remember *that*,"

Frank said, in a horrible effort to put cheer in him. "The other will come back in the morning, when you're rested. All of us get these blocks. Often on the things we know best."

From the doorway Yusuf pointed his flashlight into the room. In its beam they saw Gus sitting upright in rumpled pajamas, his fringe of white hair awry. "No, Yusuf," Frank said. "Turn it off, will you, please. We're all right here. Just a little wakeful." At last they heard the Bishop snoring, more wheezily than usual, but not enough, they decided, to send for Greet. During the night, he started up several times calling for "Rachel." He seemed to be asking her, whoever she was, for something. "Where the mischief is it? What have you done with it?" He was getting very excited. "What is it you're looking for, Gus?" Carey's easy voice asked. He had come to sit by him, to spell Frank for a bit. "Can't remember. Whatever it was, she took it away with her and hid it. She's always hiding things from me." "His mind's wandering," said Frank. "No use hoping to sleep till he quiets down again." "Tell her I need it. I have to have it now. I'm too old to put up with her tricks. You never loved me, Rachel. Don't you think I know that? You only loved my love for you." Then he fell to snoring again.

"Oh, my goodness," said Frank. "Do you think he really believed that all those years?" "He had doubts, I suppose," said Carey. "Being a religious man. But if she loved his love for her, she loved him." "Isn't that a sophistry, Jim?" Those nearest could not help listening; it was curious how the word "love" made one prick up one's ears even when one had passed the age for it. "But what about this whatever-it-is he thinks he's lost, Jim? Do you understand what he's talking about?" "His faith, I should think. She took it away with her when she died, and he needs it to meet her in Heaven." The sofa springs creaked. "That's it!" cried the Bishop, wide awake and chuckling. "Leave it to a Papist, eh, James? You darned fool, Frankie. I ordained you and made a good liberal of you, but even God Almighty couldn't make a spiritual man of you."

Some time during the night, the Bishop died. He must have gone quietly, for no one heard him. He was already getting cold when Frank touched his hand and knelt down to pray for him in the first light. There was nothing to do but wait for their captors to come down and take over. It would not be possible to bury him because the ground was partly frozen. Probably the best would be to have his body flown out. His friends could see to getting him out of his pajamas and shaved and dressed. These were labors of love that, by giving them something to do, would help relieve their feelings. Surprisingly, Charles was weeping big tears. But the one closest to the Bishop was not as broken up as one would have thought: Frank merely blew his nose from time to time and shook his head. It was as if he were still shocked or bewildered by the statements Gus had made during the night. In view of those, it was just as well perhaps that the old man had not lingered; he himself would not have wanted to live with his mind gone. And yet it was sad.

At last Jeroen and Greet came in to look at the body. Yusuf had brought them the news, but the only sign of life from them for what seemed like ages was the squawking of their radio in the kitchen. Now that they were here, they were very inhuman in their attitude. They pulled back the blanket and carefully examined the body. Then Jeroen ordered Jean and Denise to dress it—breakfast could wait. He would not let anyone help them and he did not want the body washed or shaved. Nor would he tell Frank whether they planned to announce the death soon—Frank was thinking of Gus's relations. "In our own time and in our own way. You will see," Jeroen replied and walked out. No one had had the courage to ask him what they were to do with the Bishop's things or any of the dozen questions that came to mind.

When the body was dressed and reverently laid on the sofa, Jeroen reappeared. "Sit him up," he ordered. The coins Denise had placed on the Bishop's eyelids fell to the floor. "Now open the eyes." Impossible to imagine what the purpose of this could be. Were they going to take his picture? The next thing they all knew they were being pushed into the parlor—Denise and Jean too. When the door was slammed on them, there was scarcely room to breathe. As they stood there, pressed together, swaying at the slightest motion and bumping into the plants, a rattle of gunfire came from behind the door. Then the door was opened, and they were allowed back into the next room—a privilege they could have done without. The Bishop's body lay slumped forward on the sofa, riddled with bullets.

Along his vest buttons were holes darkly oozing blood. Hussein was recharging the submachine gun. At a nod from Jeroen, Yusuf and Carlos carried the corpse out, dripping blood onto the rug.

"Was he *alive?*" shrieked Lily. Henk shook his head. "So you think a dead man has no blood in him?" Jeroen said, with a peculiar satisfied smile. "Then why have you done this terrible thing, Jeroen?" cried Frank in a voice of anger, which broke into wild sobs. Jeroen went on smiling. "The deputy has guessed, I think." "You had bad news," said Henk. "No pictures," agreed Carey. "Well, that was to be foreseen." He turned to the others. "They must have learned, first thing this morning, that Washington refused." But the others still could not make a connection. "The application of force was indicated," Carey dryly hinted. Henk nodded. Then Sophie saw. "You were going to shoot a hostage," she told Jeroen. "Beautiful!" "And, my dears, they've done so, haven't they?" fluted Charles. "Most economical of you, Jeroen. My compliments. You have seen the use of leftovers in your revolutionary broth." That was a dreadful way of putting it, but at least all now understood. From their own point of view, callous as it sounded, it was providential that the Bishop had died during the night, allowing the revolutionaries to find a "use" for his body. It had saved them the work of having to shoot a live hostage. If he had waited to die until later in the day, one of the people in this room—which?—would already have been executed.

Jeroen stood there listening, neither confirming nor denying. "You will now eat breakfast," he commanded, as Denise entered with the usual "*ontbijt*" on the pastry-board she made do with for a tray. When he was gone, they found that they were hungry: it was well known that death quickened the appetite. While they ate, the television screen lit up. A spokesman from the Ministry of Justice was announcing that a message had been received from the hijackers: a first hostage had just been executed, and the assassins now called for a helicopter to come and pick up the body. It must arrive within a delay of no less than two hours and observe the same conditions as before. The execution was to be understood in the context of legitimate ransom demands accepted as such by the prisoners themselves that Washington had criminally rejected. The identity of the hostage was not known, the spokesman added. Then the Minister himself came on the screen, appealing to the hijackers to take no more lives while Her Majesty's government continued its efforts to find a peaceful solution. No avenue leading in that direction would be left unexplored. That was all.

It left a good deal to be mulled over in the long morning ahead. "No avenue will be left unexplored," for instance—what did that signify? Henk thought it meant that Den Uyl was appealing to the Vatican and to the NATO allies to put pressure on Washington. The announcement that a hostage had been murdered would make his task easier.

"It won't wash," predicted Johnnie. "An autopsy's bound to show that poor Gus died of a cerebral incident." "We don't *know* that," Frank pointed out. "It might have been a heart attack. He had a heart condition, you know." Johnnie kept his patience. "Whatever he died of, it'll be easy enough for the experts to establish that the bullet wounds were sustained after death." "Not so easy," said Harold. "Rigor mortis hadn't set in, you notice. So there'll be no way of fixing the order of events prior to the onset of death. The cerebral accident or heart failure could have been a *result* of the bullet wounds or of just plain fear when he saw the Thompson aimed at him." He sounded like quite a different person when he was in his own element. "He *didn't* see it," objected Henry. "Jeepers, man, *we* know that, but the medical examiners won't. And the fact that we can sit here debating when we witnessed the whole thing shows what a free-for-all the pathologists'll have with the autopsy. Hell, there are likely to be *two* autopsies, one here and one when they get him home. This is Dutch soil, no?" "There will be a *lijkschouwing*, certainly," Henk agreed. "Before the body can be released. And the body may be held, in expectation of a trial, if the cause of death is in doubt. I am not sure of the law." "Well, that's your answer, Johnnie. Meanwhile there's a corpse full of bullets, which will be all the prima facie evidence Gerry Ford needs to get his ass moving on the pictures."

"And yet we know better," sighed Aileen. Others sighed with her. It would be maddening to watch the terrorists get away with their hoax—that was the only word for it—and be unable to speak out and expose the deception. And yet should one be anxious to expose them? As long as they succeeded in palming off the dead Bishop as a live hostage they had ruthlessly shot down, there would be no pressing need, surely, to select another candidate. Not till Washington refused again, and would it, with all those international pressures? It was only one's feeling for the truth that objected.

Frank's missionary mind had been elsewhere. "Don't you think that we should have grounds for rejoicing, as well as sorrow, in what we have witnessed? To me, the most interesting fact is that Jeroen and his comrades were unwilling to take human life." "Unwilling or just kind of reluctant?" said Carey. "Loath," suggested Aileen. But, whatever the shadings, Frank was basically right. There was no denying that Jeroen had chosen *not* to shoot one of their number. And if he was truly unwilling to kill a fellow-creature and kept finding excuses not to—why, after all, had they spared Helen?—then there was no great reason to be afraid of him, which should be cause for rejoicing in itself. Yet in fact it left one strangely uneasy.

Frank might be glad, piously, for Jeroen's immortal soul, but the general reaction—if one could judge by a few comments— was more complex. If they could be sure that this proclaimed revolutionary was incapable of killing anything more than a cat, they would be relieved for selfish reasons, but he would go down in their estimation. Over these days they had formed an "image" of him which they would have preferred to keep intact. He seemed so hard and resolute, yet fair in his own way—an enemy one could respect. And since one was in his power anyway, it was preferable to look up to him. As Margaret said, a Jeroen who was "loath" to take human life was too small for his boots. "Your class still has warrior values," Henk commented, seeming amused. "I don't see it that way, Maggie," Harold objected. "Don't you think we'll have to hand it to him for getting away with murder if he pulls this stunt off?" That was the slick business man speaking, and "murder" was scarcely the appropriate word. Yet it was interesting that Harold, of all people, should come to appreciate a hijacker and precisely for qualities valued in the business world. Of course Jeroen was bright as a button.

It was interesting, too, to learn that one had warrior values. Captivity was bringing out new facets in everyone. On the sad side, Helen, with her poor weak kidneys, had turned into something pathetic and repulsive, like an animal clawing at the door to "go out." The admiration she had won for her willingness to die for her "Girl" had evaporated when Jeroen denied her the privilege. To be fair, that was clever of him. Now even Lily's exquisite manners were finding Helen rather hard to take. In the end, Jeroen would get the "Girl" anyway was the general prophecy.

On the cheerful side, Lily was blooming: there was more to her mentally than had ever been suspected, least of all by Beryl. And Beryl herself was different. But, above all, there was the adventure of getting to know oneself, which was like making a new acquaintance. In the usual social round, there was so little time for that. Until deprivation showed them, they had not realized how many hours they spent changing their clothes, going to the hairdresser, the dressmaker, having the *masseur* or the *masseuse* in. Bathing twice a day, as the men did—in the morning and after squash—took up a good half-hour in itself. Not to speak of shaving and using the sun lamp—Johnnie. Then changing your books at the library or having your chauffeur do it: had anyone ever counted the hours consumed by that? Naturally they all fretted now over the absence of these time-takers and complained of being bored. Yet there *was* the compensation of having, for once, leisure—the last thing, come to think of it, that the so-called leisure class enjoyed—to contemplate one's navel, study one's reactions and those of one's friends, probe into human psychology, which could be disappointing, embarrassing, but also plain fascinating.

This morning, in addition, they could profit from the unusual quiet. With the Bishop dead, games, which tended to become noisy and argumentative, were of course not to be thought of, and Frank could not tune up on that instrument. Out of respect, even conversations were subdued—no shouting matches. And probably there was small prospect of being taken out for exercise, at least while the helicopter was expected.

The Bishop's body, they learned, was in the shed; quite soon, though, the guards would be taking it outside to be ready when the helicopter appeared. As the time drew near, Frank, brave man, asked if he could hold a funeral service. Surprisingly, the *kapers* raised no objection. They would allow Frank and the Senator to carry their friend's body to the field, escorted by Jeroen and two guards. Frank could say the last rites over it, provided that he limited them to precisely five minutes; the mourners were not to attempt to linger but must return at once to the house. At Henk's request, another concession was made: he and Charles could accompany the cortège too and remain for the service. But no one else need apply.

A handful of hostages hurried into the parlor to watch from the window. Most of the first-class passengers, however, felt it more seemly to stay behind. "Eloise, sit down," Harold ordered. "What makes you want to rubberneck?" But Lily, armed with a clean handkerchief and wearing her black cashmere over her shoulders, refused to be deterred. "I think we should all mourn for him. It was so sad about his faith. I'm sure he got it back, though, in the watches of the night." Beryl raised her eyebrows but with a sigh she joined her mother, and gradually others followed till the gloomy little parlor was full.

Frank had left the *Book of Common Prayer*, marked with a red place-ribbon, so that those who wanted could take part in the service. After "I am the resurrection and the life, saith the Lord," he was going to use Psalm XXVII, "The Lord is my light and my salvation; whom then shall I fear?"—very appropriate —and lastly some verses from the fourteenth chapter of the Gospel of St. John, "In my Father's house are many mansions" —very appropriate too. He had timed the selections, pacing up and down: three minutes. That would leave room for the Lord's Prayer—some wondered about the tact of that—and the responses. He was fussed by not having his round collar and dickey with him for the occasion; they were at Schiphol still, in his suitcase.

They watched as the procession came round the end of the house: Carey and Henk as pallbearers carrying the body on their shoulders, followed by Charles and his walking-stick, and with Frank in the lead. The three terrorists stood on the sidelines, their weapons lowered. Despite them or perhaps because of them, it was very moving. Cameron opened the window a crack, and the voices of Henk and Carey could be heard chanting in Latin as they marched along, keeping step: "*Requiem aeternam dona ei Domine. . . .*" They had good strong voices,

Henk's a pure tenor and Carey's a rich baritone. Then the voices faded. The body was set down on the open ground with not even a blanket to cover it; Frank made the sign of the cross and began to recite the Scriptures. He did not attempt to sing, and his voice was too broken to carry. But in the parlor they followed him, some looking on at the book and some reciting from memory. A few simply moved their lips or stood with bowed heads. They could tell when he came to the prayer because the group in the field knelt down by the body, but in the parlor, after a moment of indecision, everyone remained standing. In the doorway, Sophie—hesitant because of being Jewish, probably—finally joined in with the last "Amen."

When Cameron closed the window, most were in tears. Outside, the mourners were turning back to the house, no longer keeping step. Without the body to support and accompany, like an offering, their number seemed to dwindle, and they looked pathetic in those flat fields under the sad gray sky. The illusion they had given while the Bishop was with them of a band of early Christians chanting and professing their faith in the wilderness had vanished; the composition, so like a frieze, broke up, and they could be four hoboes, almost, unshaven, in unpressed suits, heading for shelter in a barn. It illustrated the value of ritual and the need for forms. There were no clods of earth to throw into the grave by way of farewell, because of course there was no grave. Frank had performed the regular burial service, which was the best he could do under the circumstances no doubt, but without grave or coffin this was like a mere sketch, a cartoon, of Christian burial.

Those remaining at the window watched Jeroen stride back to the house and tried to make out what the Arabs left behind were doing. In fact, the pair of them were packing the Bishop for shipment; using what looked like two large potato sacks, they were stuffing the white head and the shoulders into one and the feet into the other. By shaking the Bishop down, they made the sacks meet in the middle, around his waist; then they used another sack to truss the package up and they finished with some rope. During the shaking down, the Bishop's silver flask fell out and went into Yusuf's pocket. Finally, they shouldered their weapons and waited, scanning the sky. The helicopter was strangely slow in coming. There was a general move out of the parlor. Few had the stomach to stay and press Frank's hand, tell him "Very inspiring," and so on, or to witness the Bishop's ascent. Yet those who lingered at the window were rewarded in the end by a touching scene.

It was Sophie who first noticed the big dark bird hovering in the air, almost directly above the Bishop's remains. She grasped Henk's arm. "What is it?" "A gull?" suggested Lily. Henk shook his head. "A buzzard, I think." Carey crossed himself. "Not a vulture?" wondered Lily. "Only in zoos," said Henk. "But it's too *soon*," argued Frank. Henk shrugged. "Maybe. Look!" Another big dark bird, of the same family, had joined the first, hanging motionless with wings outspread. "Buzzards, all right," declared Cameron. "Twa corbies, eh? But it *is* too soon, man, for the creatures to sniff carrion." "They're waiting," said Henk. "He bled, Archie," Carey added. Johnnie reached for the field glasses. "Don't look!" cried Sophie, covering her eyes. "I can't bear it. They're going to strike!"

It must have appeared so to Ahmed, too, for, as they watched, he began to wave his short arms and thrash his body around to frighten the buzzards off. He was acting as a scarecrow to protect the Bishop. Except for the two motionless birds, the sky was empty. Below, far away, was the cordon of guardsmen. The only movement on the ground, as far as the eye could see, came from Ahmed, whirling and waving his arms. Yusuf stood by, doing nothing. Now the birds were turning in a circle above the body. Ahmed picked up a rock and threw it at them, then another. "Why in God's name doesn't he shoot them?" cried Frank. "Saving his ammo," said Carey. Ahmed was aiming another rock upward, with a motion like a baseball pitcher's, when the birds, as if coming to a decision, wheeled about and flew heavily away. The helicopter appeared. Perhaps it was the noise of its rotors and not the angelic Ahmed that had scared the buzzards off. Sophie burst into tears as though from relief and flung herself on Henk, fervently kissing him. Then, still crying, she kissed Jim and Lily. But it was sallow little Ahmed that they would have all liked to hug for showing simple respect for the dead. In their emotion, of course, they forgot the obvious fact that the Bishop would not *be* dead, bundled up in potato sacks and a prey to hideous scavengers, were it not for Ahmed and his ilk.

Eleven

HE was just as glad, on the whole, not to figure in the batch of hostages scheduled for release today or tomorrow, depending. The Congress was still in recess; he had no wife waiting for him; the company here was congenial, and he was curious as to what would happen next. The release of the first lot hung on the delivery of the first consignment of paintings, which were presumably in transit, having left Dulles yesterday in the Dutch diplomatic pouch. Washington must have finally caved in, under the combined pressures of the Vatican, the World Council of Churches, the Archbishop of Canterbury, the Quakers, sundry ambassadors, and the hostages' well-heeled relatives. But nothing in this shifting world was certain; the "qualifying" hostages already eyeing their watches might be counting their chickens too soon. An amusing wrinkle would be if the carrier winging toward them with their El Grecos *et alii* were hijacked by professional mobsters.

Barring the unforeseen, however, a helicopter should arrive within the next twenty-four hours and unload the canvases. The hostages had already been warned that a careful inspection would follow, to determine that the paintings were genuine, corresponding anyway to attested photographs the relatives had been ordered to provide. If the inspection found nothing suspicious, the hostages would be permitted to embark. In short, an on-the-spot horse trade, transacted while the helicopter waited and the national guard looked on.

To give himself credit, Jim had surmised, fairly early, that this was the plan. It made sense. The exchange of flesh-and-blood hostages for painted images, eidola, had a number of advantages that the strategic genius of Jeroen would perceive. In the first place, eidola did not have to be fed. They would take up less space than their owners were doing, and they did not ask questions or require watching. With reasonable care, they would not fall sick. More important, upon their arrival the polder farmhouse would become impregnable. Any thought of taking it by storm in a pre-dawn raid would become un-thinkable to the Dutch authorities, who otherwise might accept the risk to innocent lives entailed. After all, in investing a target, civilian casualties were largely unavoidable, viz., "We had to destroy the hamlet in order to save it." If a hostage or two got killed, it had to be seen in the perspective of the greater good of the greater number. But works of art were a different type of non-combatant, not to be touched with a ten-foot pole by any government respectful of "values." It was in the nature of civilians to die sooner or later, by preference in bed, but also in car crashes, earthquakes, air raids, and so on, while works of art by their nature and in principle were imperishable. In addition, they were irreplaceable, which could not be said of their owners. Once the paintings were here, Jim reckoned, the farmhouse would be safe as a church. Guards could almost be dispensed with; all the authorities needed to know was that within the walls a man was standing ready to activate a fuse.

Finally, the masterpieces would not only guarantee the security of the command post; they would be replacing their owners as hostages. Threats to execute one or all of them would have more powerful leverage than threats to execute one or all of the present company; the very notion of such an infamy would cause a thrill of horror to run round the civilized world. And Henk's unlucky prime minister would find himself in a worse fix than before. Inhibited from resorting to force to dislodge the barbarians, he would be reduced to begging, since what, realistically, did he have left to offer in a peaceful trade-off? Bombarded with ultimata by the enemy, he would be under crossfire from his own troops. On the one hand, he would be told to stand firm against "blackmail." On the other, if he showed undue Dutch stubbornness in the face of a menace to art, he would bear the brand of "philistine" writ in large letters across his socialist forehead; the entire circuit of Philistia would rise to apply the hot iron. The lesson to be derived—well understood by Jeroen—was that paintings were more sacrosanct than persons.

It had been short-sighted of the Dutch not to see that. The use of art as a weapon had been conceded by them to the *kapers* with no perception, seemingly, of the consequences. And yet there were recent precedents, just across the Channel, that should have been instructive—put a terrorist next to a work of art and you got an infernal new chemistry, as scarifying to "civilization" as the nuclear arm. But it had not occurred to The Hague, evidently, that the hijackers would insist that the paintings be flown to the polder. So far as could be judged from television, the reaction of official circles had been one of the purest surprise. But what had The Hague been expecting? To transfer them by armored truck to a New York bank vault in care of the Weatherman account?

The collectors, too, had been unprepared for the news that the paintings were coming here. For days they had been voicing puzzlement as to what the hijackers were going to "do" with their lovely things, as though the only function of a world-renowned painting was to enhance the furnishings of a drawing-room or proceed finally, through a tax write-off, to the wall of a museum, duly labeled "Potter bequest." That, Jim supposed, was immortality to them: a vision of future museum visitors bending to read a label. It had failed to penetrate, apparently, that art was negotiable tender; they were privileged indeed not to have seen their holdings in that cruel commercial light when every secretary knew that pictures were the soundest investment, a hedge against inflation, and so on. Even now, they had not quite grasped that the substitution of their "things" for themselves represented an immense improvement in the *kapers'* position. Instead, they were already worrying about where and how the paintings were going to be kept and pronouncing it "quite insane" of Jeroen to have dreamed of bringing them here, with no humidifiers, no curtains to be drawn against the sun, no proper thermostat to maintain an even temperature. And the poor little Potter woman was still busy wondering why she had not been allowed to die for her Vermeer, unable to accept the idea that any sane hijacker, given the slightest hope of ultimately laying hands on her canvas, would be satisfied to leave her her unrewarding life. Her case, in fact, suggested that it had probably not been necessary for all of them to make the tapes—at any rate not so precipitately.

Now most of the Croesuses would soon be going home, the Potter woman included. The withdrawal of the toilet privilege had done it; following on Gus's funeral, they had revoked Henry's too. When his wife learned that the stately old duffer had been forbidden to go outside with the other males, she had capitulated. Both were on today's list for release, which meant that the bruited Vermeer would be aboard the helicopter when it turned up. The Chadwicks, unfortunately, were remaining; dear Lily and Beryl, too, by way of compensation. The rumor was that these four would be in the second batch; there had been some question or mix-up about the delivery of their holdings.

Like him, Henk and Sophie were content to stay; they were looking forward to seeing the Vermeer unpacked. Jim was curious to see it himself, but he was looking forward more to simple peace and quiet and room to stretch his legs. There was also the fact that supplies were running low; Aileen had told Greet that they should ask for a food delivery as well, and Greet as always had been unreceptive to advice. Aileen said the prisoners should have a Suggestion Box, so that their ideas could get a fair hearing—hard to know whether she meant that seriously. In any case, with eight fewer mouths to feed, the strain on the larder would be somewhat relieved.

Rumor—in other words, their friendly Tupamaro—also had it that tomorrow or the next day the Dutch airmen would be allowed to fly the German helicopter to freedom. If so, that would liberate the barn and reduce the total of hostages to thirteen—a manageable number, though Lily was superstitious about it. It looked as though the ransom money had been paid or promised. There had been no word of it on television; instead, the box had spoken of the expected release of some "*kabouters*" in accordance with Demand Three. It seemed clear that out in the busy world things were moving along nicely, so far, although Greet had voiced displeasure at the *kabouter* announcement. Those were middle-class elements, she said, calling themselves "goblins" and living in a childish fairy-tale of non-violent pranks; to release them was to violate both the spirit and the letter of the important third demand.

Still, the fact remained that eight hostages were fairly certain to be freed within the next hours, which showed that the government's concessions, by and large, were meeting the commando's requirements. Strictly speaking, half the number would have satisfied the terms. Old Charles and Warren and the two "boys" from Antibes had been thrown in as a gift, it would appear. Warren owned no art, and Eddie's collection consisted of erotic prints from near and distant lands—"just a *potpourri*," he explained with a withered smile—while John's only holding was a collection of rare cookbooks. They were going to be set at liberty without any pretense of exacting a *quid pro quo*—an injustice keenly felt by Aileen. The case of Charles and his porcelains was slightly different; they were letting him go on his say-so, and now he was regretting it. "I'm hoist with my own petard, James," he lamented. "I should have dearly loved to stay on with your brave committee, like a rump parliament, to the bitter end. So short-sighted of me. But that gorgon won't hear of it. I don't eat much, I said to her, and my conversation is good value, they tell me. But no. I have made my bed and I must lie on it."

"James" would be sorry himself to see him go. It was a punishment prettily designed to fit the crime, for Charles, of course, had conned them: his porcelains, he had been confiding, were by no means as breakable as he had let on. These people had the art of punishment. It would "kill" Charles to leave now with his "whole" winter ruined, and to see himself separated from the anointed band of liberals seemed to be hurting the most. "Do I deserve to be sent packing with my millionaires, James? Well, I suppose I do. Yet I'd hoped there was a saving difference." Jim was noncommittal; he trusted there was a credit balance in the Recording Angel's books—Charles would have an account marked "Special." But, apart from the wound to his feelings, he was probably well out of this business. Whatever he believed, his age and sybaritic habits did not fit him for a long internment. And, insofar as the future was legible, that was surely what was in store for the communion of saints.

On that subject, "James" had come to have second thoughts. He could not see that the trumpeted arrival of the paintings was going to solve anything. A brilliant coup, a stroke of genius, whatever you liked, nevertheless, when and if it happened, it would be unproductive in terms of final ends. The bleat from the sheared sheep "What will they *do* with our beautiful things?" had merit, on reflection. Unless he planned to open a gallery in the barn, there was nothing Jeroen *could* do with all that art. Well, he could hold it for exchange. Jim had been pointing that out to himself and others as if it were a self-evident proposition, needing no demonstration. But the longer he pondered it, the less reasonable it appeared. Exchange against what, exactly?

Safe-conduct? But that was already assured. Money? But if they wanted money—beyond the "price" of the helicopter—it would have figured in their demands. Having chosen, in lieu of it, "priceless" works of art, they would hardly be satisfied at this point to convert them into packets of currency, however portable. Liberation of comrades in Israeli jails? No doubt they would be glad to see that but they must be aware that it was chimerical—they lacked what Aileen called the "*atouts.*" The fact that a gang in Holland was holding some art works was of no concern to the Israelis. It might be different if the people's army had got hold of the original Ark of the Covenant and Aaron's rod and phylacteries. No. It came down, unfortunately, to Demand Two. And Demand Two was non-negotiable. Den Uyl could not and would not take Holland out of NATO or break relations with Israel at the beck of a terrorist's will. And a demand of that type left no room for maneuver or compromise: offering to cut down the NATO forces by a quarter and being prepared to settle for a third; agreeing to reduce the Embassy staff in Tel Aviv over a period to be discussed. The Netherlands' foreign policy could not be turned around to suit a few gunmen by the present team at bat; that would require a whole new ballgame and some funny new uniforms. What Demand Two, in fact, implied was Jeroen's seizure of power. It would be interesting to know whether Jeroen himself understood that. Did he suppose he could build a power base on a single hijacking?

Jim strolled to the window and stood looking out. For a moment, he wondered whether he ought to discuss this with Henk. But that cheerful nature was already on record to the effect that Demand Two was "*pro forma.*" Jim shook his head. "Think again, Henk," he silently adjured. "Review the bidding and try to explain the pictures." Retracing the steps of his own reasoning, half-praying to find a false one, he arrived at the same starting-point: what end was served by bringing the pictures here? Well, they guaranteed the security of the command post; so far, that figured. It was demonstrable and would be demonstrated in the coming days. But reason could not rest there, although his own had been quite pleasantly doing that, like Aeneas in Dido's arms, till jarred, just now, by a doubt. Impregnability, my friend, he had told himself, was not an end in itself. It must serve an ulterior purpose. For the *kapers* to stay holed up here impregnably for an indefinite period argued a great aim in view.

Staring out at the improbable, man-made landscape, he chuckled. They were plump in the middle of Nowhere. A diverting vision appeared to him, of the polder as Jeroen's crazed kingdom, the farmhouse as his castle, his *feste Burg* (if it was not a sin to quote Luther), and the barn, hung with masterpieces, his royal picture gallery. He would be Lord of the Waters, and the committee would be his serfs, tilling the reclaimed land, making the sea floor bloom, maybe erecting a mountain or two, never to be manumitted, *et in saecula saeculorum*. They would breed, with each other and with their overlords, and produce the New Man. The fancy continued to tickle him, and he did not consider it altogether wide of the mark. Demand Two was irrational, and, if Jeroen did not know that, he was mad.

But would he be having the pictures flown to him, with another consignment to follow, unless he intended to persist in it? Otherwise, having achieved the majority of his ends, he would be calling for a plane to fly him and his cohorts and whatever trophies they desired to keep to an air-strip of his choice, there to prepare himself to strike again and yet again at the "system." Electing that scenario, he would become a hero and a legend and perhaps disappear eventually like Prester John into the African continent. Here he was, instead, resolutely painting himself into a corner, or so it looked, if the decision to return the NATO helicopter was a sign. He intended to dig in for the duration with a skeleton crew of hostages and stand firm on Demand Two. The pictures would make him that much more intractable. The fact of having obtained them against all likelihood, abetted by Providence in the shape of the Bishop's death, was apt to imbue him with a feeling of irresistible strength. The pictures were a misfortune, for unless he ceded sooner or later to the unbudging piece of Dutch reality represented by Mr. Owl, there was no way for this story to end.

Sophie held up a penny. He shook his head. "No sale." His thoughts were too queer and gloomy to worry her with yet. Time would tell, and the exercise of reason could lead a man astray. For example, he had been considering only Jeroen—the brain of the undertaking and *qua* brain transparent, like a chess opponent whose intentions are manifest though the power to counter them may be lacking. But there were seven others among the hijackers who might be developing intentions of their own.

Besides, Henk and Sophie were in love. Analyzing Jeroen and his eventual aims no longer excited them except as a game or pastime which they could take part in as a duet. Love gave them a shorter perspective: seize the day. He wished them well and would be happy for them when finally—today or tomorrow —there would be fewer onlookers. But there was no way for that story to end either. Henk was married; there was no chance here for them to be alone, and afterward an affair was unlikely. Jim could picture a single tryst—*ite missa est*—in a KLM-style twin-bedder in the airport hotel on the day release to real life took place. But of course Henk's wife would be meeting him. Now they could only touch hands as he lit her cigarettes, and he could take her arm on walks. No detail of this "tragedy" (actually an idyl) was missed by the chorus of sympathizers, which professed itself "sorriest" for Sophie, watching openly for her reaction when his wife appeared on television, noting the trembling of her hand when he held out fire for her True cigarettes. The spark that passed between them when their fingers met was likened by one of the chorus to the divine spark passing between God and Adam on the Sistine Chapel ceiling. "Probably friction from the rug," Jim suggested, although privately he did not doubt that the sexual electricity between two such handsome creatures, one at the grave pole of being, one at the merry, could be referred to God's creation.

He could marry Sophie when this was over. The idea had occurred to him, but he was not really tempted. He admired her aquiline beauty and sympathized with her tenseness; it would be a proof of loyalty to Henk and cement this experience. But he knew that he could never marry a journalist without asking her to give up her profession. He could not have a wife running around the world and exposing herself to danger while he sat reading the headlines in the Senate Office Building. A notoriously brave woman was a handicap to a political man. Yet during these last days his mind had been turning on marriage at least semi-seriously for the first time since Eleanor had died. Maybe it was a survival instinct: sketching out a future for himself with a woman by his side "tied him down" to having a future.

Strange as it might seem, he had been considering Lily. Any single man in public life, he guessed, had an occasional pipe-dream of marrying a rich widow. Jim did not blame himself for it, though he feared it sprang from his indolence. As a clever lazy war veteran, he might have had the makings of a fortune-hunter in him, had he not married young. Now, with Eleanor out of the way, he was a "catch," he discovered; his fan mail was replete with offers of marriage, filed under "Matrimonial," in the "Inactive" drawer. Though the thought recurred idly when he contemplated his campaign debts, he put it aside. The woods were full of available widows of independent means, but he could be thankful that his requirements were inordinate—God's grace, he reckoned, at work against the old Mammon. She would have to be pleasant to look at, with the hair color Nature gave her, pleasant-spoken—what his mother used to call a real lady—good company, capable of good works, no friend of the bottle and no enemy either, mature but not too old. There were few, if any, rich relicts answering to that description—St. Bridget of Sweden, who fitted (give or take a few visions), had passed on a long time ago. In short, it was a pipe-dream: Q.E.D. He indulged it, knowing the field: fund-raising dinners had taught him how little in deportment and personal attributes the rich had to offer and how much they demanded in the way of attention for the bounty of a four-figure check.

Yet here was Lily, who filled the bill on all counts and had the additional endearing attribute of being slightly absurd. At first sight he had typed her as an "older" woman, that is, beyond the age, but recently he had been trying to estimate how old she actually was. If you gave Beryl thirty-seven or possibly thirty-eight, then, assuming her mother had had her at the age of twenty, Lily would now be fifty-seven or fifty-eight, scarcely older than he was himself. And society buds in those days

married early, so that she could have been eighteen, fresh from
that social school of hers where they taught Dostoievsky along
with riding-to-hounds, when she went to the altar (Episcopal)
—which would make her nineteen when Beryl was born. Her
skin was still fresh and smooth, except for a few perplexed lines
across her pretty forehead; it was only the gray hair that put
age on her, but he applauded her for not dyeing it, and, hell,
his was nearly white. Nor was she a dim-wit, despite the initial
impression. Her "inklings" were worth paying heed to, as Henk,
too, had observed—she had made quite a conquest of Henk.
That her collector friends and her daughter rushed to correct
her every time she opened her mouth with some dreamy suggestion was an argument for her intelligence. It sounded as if
her associates had been sighing over her for years. He got the
sense, too, that her collection was regarded as a triumph of
taste over buying power, i.e., that she was not quite as moneyed as the rest of them—all to the good; he would not want
to marry a great smelly fortune and its bodyguard of tax-
dodging lawyers. The attraction Lily exercised on him could
have something to do with his feeling for the weaker party in
any confrontation of forces. In her group here, she was a minority needing defense in its right to be heard. Henk had the
same reaction, natural in a democrat, if not in the *demos*.
Which reminded him: in the event of their marrying, something would have to be done about that society accent, which
would not go down at Grange suppers; an elocution teacher
could see to it—the voice itself was a nice soprano. The only
drawback was Beryl.

"Funny bunch, aren't they? What do you make of Lily?"
"Why, I like her," answered Sophie, having duly weighed the
question. "She's much the nicest of them, isn't she? Henk says
she reminds him of some pale pink rose she described that isn't
grown any more. Its name was Van F-l-e-e-t." Spelling that out
seemed to please her. "I'll miss her and Beryl when they go.
But of course they're another world. If we met them again in
real life, we'd have nothing to say to each other, would we?
Except about *this*. Perhaps we should hold reunions, like the
press corps that served in Vietnam. But those things are always
grisly—total flops. You've been through some experience together which gives you the sense that you have something in

common. But when you meet again, you find that you've all reverted to type. The thing that held you together is gone, and you discover that you don't even have the same memories of it. It's better not to try, I think."

She was talking of herself and Henk, obviously. Jim lightly took her hand. "You don't agree with the Rev, then, that some of us can be changed by the opportunity we've been offered?" "He least of all." She laughed. "A few of us maybe *think* we've been altered. But we all have to revert. It's a law of nature. Like in the plant world, with the perennials going back to the original sick magenta. Frightening. Have you ever been to a college reunion? Or a veterans' reunion?" "I'm a politician," he said. "And I'll see *you* again, Sophie." "That's different. We have a *reason* to see each other. We work the same side of the street. It's not a complete accident that we were on the plane together. Your being on that committee was pretty much why I came along. I always wanted to know you. But the rest is fortuitous, mainly. We've been thrown together like marbles shaken in a bag." "And yet connections came to light," he suggested. "You knew Beryl. Beryl knew Aileen. Charles knew Henk's grandfather. And I knew *of* Henk." "You *researched* him," teased Sophie. "I wish I could read his poetry, don't you?" "You could learn Dutch," he said. "When you know German, it's not hard. I find I understand quite a bit."

Sophie smiled. "Remember '*haast hebben*'?" She was dreamy —her first words of Dutch "taking her back," like a yellowed dance program. Then her tone changed. "You never learn a language unless you use it. Anyway, the committee's a unit. And the millionaires are another. Oil and water. I think we deserve credit for having mixed as well as we have. That's Henk, mainly, on our side, and Lily, I suppose, on theirs. They've both been well brought up. But Lily in real life would be unbearably conventional, wouldn't she? Otherwise why would Beryl have declared a revolution?" She had touched on a vital point. "I prefer Lily," he said shortly. "Well, I've known Beryl longer," said Sophie. "But I admit I wouldn't seek her out as a friend. She has no real interests, that's her trouble. Having been brought up in an arch-Republican family, she's rebelled by being totally a-political. And she hates art and books; Lily's a great reader, it seems." Jim pricked up his ears but he only remarked: "Arch-Republican? I should have thought of Lily as a swing-voter." "You know what Henk says?" Sophie went on. "That they're the common-law criminals—the millionaires, I mean—and we're the politicals. Do you see?"

Jim saw indeed. It was an interesting idea. On the model of a Soviet labor camp, the common-law criminals—murderers, thieves, and such—would be serving short sentences, while the political offenders would be in for long stretches, often till their health broke, or in dire cases, like the poet Mandelstam's, till death intervened. In the scales of "people's justice" as weighed out here on the polder, a similar distinction seemed to apply. The millionaires—ordinary pickpockets and highway robbers—would be going home, having paid for their crimes. But conditions for the committee's release, individually or as a unit, had never been "aired" in any communiqué that had reached their ears. Not a *quid* or a *quo* vouchsafed. From time to time, their likenesses appeared on the screen—always Henk and himself—accompanied by the comment "So far as is known, the deputy [or the Senator] is still alive." As in the Gulag, a blanket of silence covered the politicals' fate; for all the world knew, they could in fact be dead. Confronting himself over and over on the screen—mainly on the '68 campaign trail, preaching to the unconverted, suffering the little children—Jim got the eerie feeling that he *had* died, at any rate politically, some time back and was watching the pages of a memorial album turn.

When the collectors were gone, it might be the committee's turn finally to learn what they must give—or see given *for* them—in exchange for their freedom. But the itch to know in Jim's case was far from overwhelming. He feared he could guess. Would their release in fact hang on Demand Two? If Henk was right, it would be artistically appropriate—meet and just in the *kapers'* eyes—for the fate of the "politicals" to be sewed up with that demand, political as a stick of dynamite. Moreover, like Charles's banishment, it would constitute a punishment suited to the crime. Their crime as liberals—he believed he could confess for all—was, *primo*, to support the Atlantic Pact. Critically, and with this or that reservation, nevertheless, *grosso modo*, they were for the "shield." *Secundo*, they were for the survival of the Jewish state; any reservations they had put on record as to

Israel's policies could be shown to stem from the belief that her current behavior was suicidal. To be instrumental in the dismantling of NATO and the ostracism of Israel would be a torture worthy of SAVAK. Perhaps, like the Potter lady with her picture, most of them would rather die than stand by as helpless spectators while such a deal was arrived at in their interest.

Jim pulled himself up short. That would never happen. There was no cause to fear it. But what if constraint were put on them to make a bunch of tapes urging the acceptance of the second demand? That could be in the cards. And what would he do if "invited" to make a tape? An uneasiness took hold of him as he foresaw the argument that might edge him into consenting. It was what he had just told himself for the nth time: that Demand Two was unacceptable. Whatever pleas the eminent hostages might make, Den Uyl and his Cabinet would have to stand firm, stoppering their ears like the sailors of Ulysses. Hence it could do no harm to make a tape. He was *free* to make a tape, in all good conscience, at the bidding of his own intelligence, which reminded him that a hundred tapes could not alter the outcome. So then? His uneasiness only grew deeper. Something in him was opposed to making a tape—perhaps the old Christian yearning for martyrdom or just an addiction to truth-telling. He was wary, with reason, of his brain. Not that it misled him; its assessments were generally dead-right. It was not clouded by self-interest or prone to "rationalization." But it had deterred him, too often, from action by showing him the futility of it. That had happened after Wisconsin. Now it could prompt him to *embark* on an action by the same type of demonstration. He might allow himself to do a distasteful, base thing secure in the private knowledge that it could have no effect. The operative word was "base." It was an ordinary matter of honor. He guessed that an honorable act—or abstention from action—was always needless, wasteful, uncalled for. The requirements of honor had to buck the assessments of intelligence. And in James Augustine Carey, he acknowledged, laziness and intelligence could be accomplices. The easiest thing would be to make the tape.

They were finishing lunch when the pictures came. In custom-made flat wooden cases that fitted their dimensions and were going to be a job to open. In the shed, the hijackers went to work on them with hammers and pliers, and Ahmed promptly smashed his thumb, reopening the six-day-old wound. Chadwick's offer to help had been turned down, but he was allowed to stand around kibitzing. As on the first night, revolutionary discipline had relaxed; the collectors wandered in and out of the shed, expressing anxiety over the paintings that were no longer theirs. They were anxious, more selfishly, over the slow progress of the uncrating; by the time the pictures were vetted, the sun might have set, and the pilot of this helicopter did not want to take off in the dark.

The first case to be opened produced a surprise. The picture that was emerging, to Jim's inexpert eye, did not look like an Old Master. In fact, it was a good-sized Cézanne. Soon Harold's Cézannes, all eight of them, were sharing wall space with a kiddy-car and the family bicycles. Someone had blundered. But they were carried into the family room and stacked against the wall; Harold set them up, one by one, in front of the TV set to be looked at. "Of course you're seeing them without reflectors," he explained. To Jim, they looked like every Cézanne he had ever seen, only more so: there were the apples, Mrs. Cézanne, that mountain near Aix, pine trees with red bark growing in red earth, some pears with more apples and a white pitcher, the card-players, and what Harold said were the first oils of "The Bathers." Jim glanced at Lily. The feeling he was getting of *déjà vu* made him wonder whether they were not high-class copies—had Harold been stung or had that lawyer of his pulled a fast one? She read his thought. "Rather standard, aren't they? But he's not an adventurous collector. You'd almost doubt they were real, they're so 'classic,' so much what one's conditioned to expect. But they are, you know. You see how the paint is laid on, very characteristic. Dear, clumsy Cézanne." "Couldn't draw, of course," boomed Margaret. "Look at that arm." She pointed to a nude figure among the bathers. "Completely out of drawing." Jim was impressed.

A large envelope containing documentation had come with the shipment. Jeroen took a long time studying the photos and transparencies and comparing them with the paintings. While this was happening, a number of the hostages, Jim himself and Lily included, returned to the shed. They were in time to see a long narrow painting of a horse race unpacked. Jim would not have recognized it as a Degas. "Oh, yes," said Lily. "He did a great many of those. I believe he was mad about racing. Lovely, isn't it? Johnnie has an eye. Do you think that's Longchamp—see the stand there? Or did it exist in his time?" "I can't tell you, Lily," said Jim. "I only know Aqueduct." "That's a joke, isn't it?" "Yes." There followed a huge landscape with precipitous gray cliffs and a sunlit meadow below on which sheep, very small, were grazing. "The Ward," Lily said. "Nearly as grand as the one in the Tate." "I like it," said Jim. "Notice the waterfall?" Then came an artist he recognized—Winslow Homer —and another—Dufy—and half a dozen "sporting" subjects: stags locking horns, a lion and a tiger fighting, two boxers in a ring, an archery contest, a horse in a stable with a groom and a cat—Stubbs, said Lily—a game of horseshoes, a horse market at a country fair. "Thomas Hardy," said Jim. "Oh, no, I don't *think* so," said Lily. "Maybe a Morland. Oh, I see, you mean *Hardy*. Yes. *The Mayor of Casterbridge*." That was a good recovery, he thought. He frowned. "What the hell is this one?" Lily put on her glasses and bent down. "That must be a mistake. It's a print. Not very old either. 'Elephants Wading,' it says." "Where's the tie-in with sport?" "I don't really know, Jim. Johnnie's idea of sport can be rather all-embracing. Still, in India, in the old days, didn't the rajahs hunt elephants? I seem to remember that." He saw that if he stuck with this lady he was going to learn a good deal.

Jeroen meanwhile had declared himself satisfied with the Cézannes. The inspection of Johnnie's works was more cursory, to the point of offending Johnnie, who stood by, eager to show the provenances and present photos for comparison. Jeroen, he complained, should not be approving them in bulk like a job lot. The Stubbs Arabian, for instance, would repay examination—the market these days was full of journeyman "Gimcracks" and "Herods" being offered as Stubbses. "Well, I oughtn't to blame him. You have to remember that until recently sporting art was put below the salt—a reaction against Landseer and good old Rosa Bonheur. I was a pioneer, along with Mellon, when I started my collection." "Mellon?" Jim queried. "Paul," Lily whispered. Johnnie was continuing. "People thought those things had no standing as art, belonged in a club or a trophy room. All that's changed, thanks, if I may say it, to my labors."

"He gives this talk," Lily explained softly, "whenever he shows his collection." "Shut up, Ma," said Beryl. Johnnie raced on regardless; he needed no spurring. "I've promoted it with the serious investor the way I would a stock, commissioned monographs, underwritten college lectures. I'm offering my alma mater a Ramsbotham Chair in the Visual History of Sport. The result is, we're beginning to see fakes—the surest sign, of course, of the impetus we've given. Up to now though—here's the funny bit—we've had no success in interesting the collector crowd in dog subjects. Nobody wants dogs except as accessories in a conversation piece or a fox-hunting scene. Though there were many fine artists once upon a time who made a pile in dog portraits. Take old Maud Earl. How do you explain that?" No one had a suggestion. His "job lot" was consigned to the parlor, and he was a free man, cleared for take-off as soon as the rest were ready.

Henry's Titian—a man in black armor—also passed muster. There remained several smallish cases. "Those are Margaret's things, I suppose," Lily said. "Though I remembered the Greco as bigger." When the cases were pried open, a cry rang out. "My Marie Laurencins! Oh, shit, Chaddie, what have those horse's asses done?" There were six of them, and one much like the next: the same doe-eyed misty maidens that Jim recalled from his early days. They were easy to like. In fact, when he was young, Marie Laurencin had been his favorite modern painter. He guessed that was because he had always been able to spot her, like a Stutz Bearcat. He had liked Redon and Rouault for the same reason. But from Lily's little cluck of disappointment, he judged that the artist had "dated."

Margaret's art had been left behind somehow. A quick check with the pilot confirmed that it had not been sent on from Dulles—so far as he knew. Evidently the signals had got crossed: Chadwick's Cézannes had been meant to come in the next shipment, and Eloise's Laurencins had not been meant to come at all. It was reassuring in a way to see that life among the terrorists was just as liable to foul-ups as normal government activity on Capitol Hill. But the alarming discovery was that the Vermeer was missing too. It was definitely not in the helicopter; to satisfy Jeroen, Ahmed and Carlos went out and searched, though there was no place it could be hiding.

Jeroen was angry. For the first time, he let his displeasure show. He did not appear to mind so much about Margaret's stuff; it was the Vermeer that his heart had been set on. He shouted that there was a plot among the imperialists to hold it back. In reply, he was canceling all departures. The helicopter would return empty. "Carlos, tell the pilot he should go." The moment, plainly, was critical. The collectors cowered before the vengeful giant, as if before their eyes he had turned into a cruel ogre. The whole crowd was looking to Henk, as if trusting him to mediate. But abruptly Greet intervened, playing, for her, the unusual role of pacifier. She spoke with Jeroen in Dutch. "She reminds him of the food supply," whispered Henk. They debated. At length Jeroen squared his shoulders, accepting, it seemed, her arguments. "You will go now as promised," Greet announced. "The armed proletariat keeps its word." The Chadwick couple, she said, would replace Helen and Margaret, the total remaining at eight. There could be no question of letting Henry remain behind. "You are to tell the imperialists that this is our last concession. We will tolerate no more delays and evasions."

The sun was setting when they boarded, for first they had to undergo a search, pronounced very humiliating by Eloise, who had been stripped by Greet and Elfride. The point of the search was not clear to those remaining. "Pure sadism" was Aileen's verdict. To prevent the smuggling out of information, Henk thought—a plan of the house, for example, with some indication of the wiring system. Jim could not see that. The collector group on its own was capable of drawing a plan, describing the sleeping arrangements, guessing at the location of the fuse-box, and so on. Henk shook his head. Of the eight that had been freed, only Charles, he reasoned, had wit enough to provide useful information, and Charles would have an over-supply of it, very apt to mystify the authorities. "No, Jim. Our *kapers* are fearful only of you and me. They look on us two as their peers. '*Weerga*,' we say." In his belief, the *kapers* feared that he and Jim, between them, might contrive to send the authorities not only plans and diagrams but political counsel—advice on the timing of an attack, analysis of the leadership structure of the commando, recommendations on negotiating tactics. . . . "Inscribed on the head of a pin?" Jim inquired.

It was true that, in their place, Jeroen would have been doing just about that. Taping tiny spills of paper covered with writing—doubtless in code—to Eloise's underwear. But he himself had not once thought of spiriting out a message of any sort, let alone one of a para-military nature. Nor, evidently, had Henk. There was no need of messages, written or oral. The returning hostages would report that their fellow-captives when last seen were alive and well, which was all that mattered to the families. More significant for the authorities, they would report that Gus had died a natural death. As for hints on negotiation, Jim had none to offer; in the last hours he had come to see the situation as hopeless, barring, as ever, a miracle. Jeroen had moved into a no-win position and apparently did not know it. And if Henk had a clever formula in mind for breaking out of the deadlock, he would have mentioned it. There was no information lying around here that could not be transmitted by direct word of mouth. Aileen must be right; pure sadism was the explanation. Or else it was something the *kapers* read in a terrorist's handbook: frisk captives prior to release.

Jim was struck, though, by the notion—which had not occurred to him—that the *kapers*, i.e., Jeroen, regarded them as their peers. If it meant simply that on both sides there was a sound sense of power and its leverage—Jeroen a gifted tyro and Henk and himself old adepts—the idea, though novel, was not especially interesting. But it could imply something else: a mutual recognition. That tied in with a thought he had been pursuing—till interrupted by the arrival of the pictures—that the situation of a terrorist in terms of achievement of ends was hopelessly circumscribed. He was limited by the *status quo ante* that in principle he was setting out to topple. People liked to say that terrorism "could not really change anything." And unfortunately that was the fact. The demands it was able to see satisfied were demands in keeping with the established value system: turnover of money or equivalent goods, supply of transport, distribution of food to the poor. Even the freeing of the occasional "class-war prisoner" fell considerably short of amnesty and was more like parole; the liberated comrade nine times out of ten was promptly re-arrested, on suspicion of recidivism, i.e., on sight. The same with safe-conduct; it saw the undesirables safely out of the country, at which point they became fugitives with a price on their heads, obliged to take cover in semi-friendly countries where as terrorists they found no employment. All in all, an unprofitable exercise of juvenile energy and imagination. And yet they kept trying.

But what had his own career of bucking the system netted in the long run? A few immediate gains compatible with the *status quo ante* and no fundamental change. He could claim the fall of Johnson and the tempering of the war in Vietnam. But the fall of Johnson had eventuated in Nixon (which had to figure as a debit), and the war in Vietnam would have been winding down anyway. The establishment dipped into its provident fund and gave what it would not feel the loss of to dissent burning its draft card. He had been as much of a millennialist in his hopes as any "misguided" terrorist. Observing that, he laughed, feeling a real fondness for Jeroen. What Greet liked to call the armed politics of the underground—their euphemism, he guessed, for terror—was only the kid brother of minority electoral politics, with the same old Achilles heel.

Coming out of his abstraction, Jim looked around him. Night had fallen, and they were alone with the paintings. Mrs. Cézanne in a blue apron was propped against the TV set, and the Titian "Gentleman in Armor" was opposite, behind the davenport. The ever-silent Yusuf was on guard. Contrary to expectations, the house felt lonely. Maybe Harold was right that the paintings needed reflectors, for the longer Jim stared at them, the more disappointing they seemed. Longer acquaintance was not helping him to see "new treasures" in any of these canvases, as Lily had promised him it would. The contrary, almost, was true. Probably a trained eye was required. He was relieved anyhow that the Marie Laurencins had been sent back to the shed. Johnnie's collection, stacked up in the parlor, he found the most rewarding. There was something to look at in those pictures beyond pictorial "values"; some of them even told a story, or you could make a story out of them, and the animals were great, particularly the "Stags Fighting." He also liked the fact that, as far as he could judge, the horse in the Stubbs, though a breed you did not see now, had its bones and muscles in the right places—Lily said Stubbs had written a book on the anatomy of the horse. By contrast, he was more and more bothered by that arm on one of the "Bathers"; he wished Margaret had never mentioned that it was "out of drawing," for now he could see that himself; in fact it was the only thing he *could* see in the picture.

He had no doubt that he was reacting like a philistine, like the two Dutch pilots, who seemed to be made highly uncomfortable by the pictures, walking up to study them with heavily knit brows, shaking their heads and turning away, then drifting back, unable to resist having another look. Like him, the pilots were more at ease with Johnnie's pictures. Not Yusuf, though. It occurred to Jim, measuring Yusuf's inflexible frown, that he was asking himself whether the chief had not gone loco.

Art had a disquieting power of producing social embarrassment; Jim was familiar with the symptoms in Eleanor. In museums he had noticed that it caused people to make silly remarks and then laugh self-consciously, as if the pictures, which knew better, could hear them. It could not be just ignorance; displays of armor and mummies and natural-history exhibits did not have that effect. And even he was prone to it, for all his self-possession. If you were alone with art long enough, as here—or when he used to wait for a girl he knew on a bench in front of "An Old Woman Cutting her Nails"—you began to get the feeling that it was looking right at you. Like the reproduction in his grandmother's parlor of a trick painting of Jesus whose sorrowing eyes seemed to follow you: the Hound of Heaven. Lily said there was a room in Mantua with a frescoed horse whose eyes moved when you did. Jim had missed that— and a lot else—in Virgil's burg while wandering along the Mincio with the Ninth Bucolic in hand: "*qua se subducere colles incipiunt.*" Fortunately, anyhow, he did not sense the apples eyeing him—what worried him there was that he could not find anything especially clumsy in the way they were painted.

All these ghostly and somehow demanding presences were unnerving in the quiet house. It would be better when Mrs. Cézanne was replaced by the seven o'clock news—live. He found it impossible to ignore them, though, according to Beryl, that was what collectors did. "They hardly ever look at them. Ask Mother." There was some truth in that, Lily admitted.

One of the boons, then, of being a collector was that you felt at home with art to the point of not noticing its presence; it was just part of the furniture.

"If you don't look at the stuff you own, what gives you the right to have it?" Victor. The paintings must have been getting at that touchy customer too. With his sprouting beard and blackheads and the boils on his neck, he looked noisome, as if he were coming to a head; during exercise, he had been playing with the rabbits, and he had rabbit hairs all over him. "The rest of the race isn't all that jaded." "One isn't 'jaded,' Victor," said Lily. "I think one's constantly aware of one's beautiful things—what's the word?—subliminally." "But tell us something," demanded Aileen, whose hackles were also up. "What do you gain as a person by living with your 'beautiful things'? Has it made you any different? Would it make Jim and me any different? Can you pretend that any of that beauty has rubbed off on Harold and Eloise? Why, Harold could be a museum guard, for all the good that being exposed to Cézanne has done him." "Harold's rather a new collector," observed Lily. "And Morgan and Frick?" "But is art meant to be morally improving?" objected Sophie. "Think of Goering." "Well, leave out morals for the moment," Aileen agreed. "Show me *any* result. Really, having been with this tour of yours for a week now, I wonder. . . . I can't see what this vaunted ownership has done for you. Well, all right, there's Charles. I guess it's made him kinkier than he might have been." "They don't claim to be art authorities or scholars, Aileen," Sophie said. "Art authorities would be worse," said Beryl. "Poor Ma's just having fun."

"So art gives pleasure to man, can we agree on that?" said Frank. "It's like God's own delight in His Creation." Lily nodded. "Genesis. 'And, behold, it was very good.' I often think about that." "Come off it," Victor retorted. "Is that why they take schoolchildren to museums? Stop dodging the issue, you folks. We all know in our gut that art educates. In other societies, they're aware of the power it has of speaking directly to the masses, teaching them to be better socialists, better citizens. The trouble is that with us it's fallen into the wrong hands. Forget the speculators. I mean you proud possessors that claim to have a corner in it. This isn't the eighteenth century. The concept of the collector is so rotten by now that it stinks. Why, Yusuf here instinctively has a better appreciation of those apples than all your museum boards. Cézanne painted for *him*; he's been hungry and knows what an apple means." All eyes turned inquiringly on Yusuf, whose scowling features betrayed no interest even in hearing his name. "I want to get this on record," Victor went on excitedly, raising his thin voice and striking his fist into his palm. "In my considered belief, Jeroen and Greet had a great idea in liberating these pictures from their plushy jailers. The more I've seen and heard here, the more I salute them for that."

This harangue, coming from that quarter, caused less of a stir than Victor had probably hoped. "Has he been drinking? Where did he get it?" Aileen whispered. "Why, the man's a common agitator," Margaret exclaimed, not deigning to lower her voice. "Kind of an *un*common agitator," Jim said, behind his hand, to Henk. Lily had overheard. "How interesting that you say that," she murmured. "Why interesting, Lily?" "Well, I don't like to say it, but I had a little theory of my own." "Oh?" They moved behind the TV set. "I rather thought, Jim, that he might be connected with—well, with certain initials. . . ." "You mean—?" She meant CIA.

"What made you think that?" "Oh, little things. He seemed different from the rest of your committee. As if he didn't quite belong. None of you knew him before. Then that mushroom look he has. The man from underground. I don't mean to be snobbish. There are a number of well-connected, brainy men in that organization. In fact, Beryl and I have letters to one in Teheran—a cousin of a cousin. He's quite out in the open, attached to the Embassy. But this cousin said that Teheran was *full* of them, open and not so open. They have a kind of investment in the Shah. That made me wonder, too. Then I couldn't help noticing that Victor drank more than was good for him. They say that's a characteristic of agents. The strain of the life they lead. The constant deception . . . But of course none of that's *proof*."

"No." He pondered. "Have you mentioned this to Beryl?" "Surely not. She'd laugh at me." "Well, don't. I've no more knowledge than you have, Lily, but if what you think is true and word of it gets to the Committee of Public Safety here, well, we could witness a real execution. Or if it isn't true, for that matter." But it *was* true, he felt confident, and it alarmed him for Victor that Lily should have spotted it. His own case was different; he was a pro. It had become evident to him, some time back, that Victor must be an agent. He had all the earmarks. Starting with the cover: half the university specialists traveling around on grants in the Middle East were working part-time or full-time for the Agency. Jim had nothing against that; as long as they confined themselves to information-gathering, they served some sort of purpose. Moreover, it stood to reason that the CIA would try to plant a man of its own on the committee, to observe and report back via the Embassy cable-room or maybe even to obstruct the committee in its work. As far as that went, Cameron could be an MI-5 plant, although Jim doubted it. Britain's interests were not so tied to the Shah, and Archie appeared to be what he seemed: a burry don with no secret drawers about him. Jim doubted, too, that either of them would have been reporting directly to SAVAK, which would have made for an interesting time in the Shah's country, almost as lively as a hijacking. In any case, the hijacking had made the entire question immaterial. Jim had mentioned his thought to Henk, he could not remember when—while they were still at Schiphol, he believed—in confidence, naturally, on a no-action basis. The cat by then had died, and Victor, they agreed, was at present more to be pitied than subjected to any form of ostracism. They had not spoken of it again.

But that outburst, just now, was troubling. If he was trying to curry favor with the people's army—which was certainly what it had sounded like, given the raised voice—Victor must be in a bad state. Somehow, presumably, he must have come to fear that his captors were going to get wind of the CIA link-up. Jim knew how such a fear could grow in a nervous mind; he had clients like Victor years ago when he was still practicing law. Every day that passed, far from calming him, would appear to increase the danger. And he had no one to share his worry with, no one to laugh him out of it, show him that it lacked any basis in reality. . . . Or did it? "Wait a minute, Carey," Jim said to himself. Victor might have reason. That college where he taught in upstate New York might be swarming with envious colleagues only too eager to denounce him to the nearest "underground" news sheet—Jim doubted that Victor was very popular. And a story like that could be picked up and sent merrily out on the waves by an early-morning newscaster who found himself short of hijacking copy. From that point on, world-wide diffusion would depend on the conscience of journalism, often pretty elastic. Anything damaging to the CIA was considered newsworthy these days, whoever got hurt in the process. Hell, the revelation, duly supplemented by CIA denials, could have been carried *already* by the news services. "Over" then to Radio Moscow, and back to Ostberliner Rundfunk, coming home to roost finally on the *kapers'* short-wave aerial, crowing like the Pathé cock.

Jim's imagination, he observed, was quite equal to supplying extra fuel to Victor's, should it stand in need of it. And he had no difficulty in picturing the sequel: the "trial," the confession, the sentence, the bullet-plugged body dumped in the field without benefit of funeral service. The only question was, would poor old Victor have the stamina to wait to be accused? Unable to stand the suspense, he might decide to anticipate the workings of revolutionary justice and accuse himself, claiming to have been "re-educated" by his current experiences. That way, he might hope to be pardoned, though Jim, in his place, would not be too sanguine. To maintain credibility, the *kapers* needed another execution.

As he glanced at Victor, pale and silent, squatting by the sofa, his arms wrapped around his chest, Jim was feeling sympathetic vibrations. What had been passing through his mind was a troop of mere possibilities, but the possible by definition was a thing that was capable of happening. The idea suddenly gripped him that he would have to save Victor. He did not know who or what had made him Victor's keeper. Perhaps it was a caprice—the old bottom-dog business—or Victor's increasing resemblance to a bum calling out the Salvation Army in him. Or his obligation as a senator to a putative federal employee. Anyhow something would have to be done to rescue Victor from the fear he was in, before he did something on his own that was bound to be ill judged.

If only there were some way of getting him out of here . . . That was the best hope. Invalided out maybe? On the next departing whirlybird. He asked himself whether Victor was capable of playing sick. He looked sick enough already—doubtless because of bad conscience and attendant lack of sleep. He was a hysterical type, certainly, and that type was gifted at working up symptoms. With a short inner laugh Jim pictured Victor receiving the stigmata. But of course nothing could be done without his cooperation. Jim sighed. He had no choice but to be frank with him, confront him with his guilty secret or—correction needed—the secret Jim was imputing to him. And if he denied having any problem? Or wept and playacted while admitting it? Jim was not in a mood for dramatics.

To his relief, Victor came clean almost from the start. It was as though he had been hoping that Jim would confess him. "Apologies, Senator, for that goofed-up performance. I figured you'd understand. I was trying to plant the idea that I was getting ready to defect to their side. I thought that if I seemed to be willing to serve in their ranks, they might figure that there was a lot of information I could pass on." He raised his eyes, forcing Jim to meet his look. "Actually, I don't know a damn thing. I only had the one contact, the same one I met every time. You knew right away, didn't you?"

"No. Not right away. I expected there might be a Spook with us but I hadn't yet settled on you. The cat threw me off." "Funny. I thought you knew that first morning on the plane. When you made friends with Sapphire. I decided you were trying to show me you were sorry for me, didn't blame me too much. You're a tolerant guy, Senator." "I'm an indifferent man, Victor. That's my secret. Enough of these boyish confidences. What we want is an action plan. These folks aren't indifferent. Before anything rough happens, you and I have to get you out of here. Do you know how to fake a temperature?"

Victor did, and he could make his pulse race. At once he was full of energy. "When shall we start? Shall I stretch out on the floor now?" Jim interposed a caution. "Let's not tip our hand too soon. We don't want Greet giving you a thorough physical tonight." For the time being, he proposed, Victor should merely let it be known that he was not feeling too well and wanted to be left alone. Victor nodded. "Then tomorrow I can suddenly be worse." "Tomorrow *morning*?" Victor was racing his engine. They ought to be careful with their timing.

Victor should not have to play sick for too long; he was not a convincing actor, judging by the recent performance, and it might overtax his abilities to keep up the pretense. "Let's aim to find out, first, when our pilots are slated to go." The acute phase, if Victor could manage it, should be arranged to coincide, as if providentially, with a helicopter waiting in the wings. "But I already know that," said Victor. "Tomorrow. Carlos said so. They're just waiting to clear the flight landing with the Germans in Aachen."

Tomorrow morning, then, Jim agreed. "Denise can take your temperature and report it to Greet. She'll examine you and order the Royal Air Force to take you aboard. And she won't waste much time in the process. Hell, you might have a contagious disease." The promise of action—*any* action—was enlivening. But Victor, all at once, before he had even started, developed cold feet. A discouraging personality: Jim wondered how the Agency had managed him, but they had experience with unstable types. "Maybe it's too soon, Senator," he argued. "We don't *know* that Dirk and Pieter will be shipping out tomorrow." "We don't. But you just said that we had good reason to think it. And you'll have to be ready to get onstage with your act." Their roles had reversed in the course of a half-hour; Jim was impatient to begin, and Victor was hanging back. "I'm afraid, Senator." "Fine. Let's see your teeth chatter. But don't overdo it for now." Victor lay down on the floor. "I need a bar of soap."

Jim laughed aloud. It was the old army game, popular with draft dodgers till the medics caught on; it had been used in the Navy too, he acknowledged, by scared young pilots hoping to duck out of a mission. A bar of soap was placed in the armpit, secured, usually, by adhesive tape; he had never understood the chemistry of it, but in a few hours the body temperature went way up. "How long will you need to have it there?" "Two or three hours. All night will be OK." "Can you manage without the adhesive?" Victor thought he could if he did not move around much. "But can't you pinch some from Denise's kit?" he wondered. "Better not, my friend, if you think you can get along without it. Adhesive leaves marks." "They come off with ether." "No." Jim was enjoying himself and he was sorry to see his confederate lapse so readily into a state of total dependency. He did not even have soap of his own. Jim passed him a fair-sized bar of Ivory in a Statler Hotel wrapping from his inactive shaving kit. "Laundry soap would be better," said Victor. "Well, you'll have to make do with what's available. Be grateful it isn't Camay."

During the night a hand tugged at him. "Senator?" "What is it, Victor?" "Don't you want to try it yourself? That way, we could be shipped out together." "No. Nice of you to think of it. But two would tax credibility." "Well, you could leave me here." Jim wondered whether he meant that. "Thank you, Victor, but I'm in no special danger that I know of. You're a case all to yourself. Say, what about the pulse?" "Oh. Well, I'd need pepper for that. A *lot* of pepper. I don't see how we could get any. They never give us pepper." "Well, forget it. When Greet comes to examine you, you won't need pepper to make your pulse race." "That's true." It was good to know, at any rate, that Victor had some respect for limits: he could have proposed that Jim raid the kitchen for him. Essaying to fall asleep again, Jim set himself the puzzle of what war Victor had dodged—too young for Korea, too old for Vietnam. Korea, he concluded.

"Do you mind if we talk a little?" Reluctantly, Jim moved nearer, renouncing sleep for a second time. "I want to tell you something. Jim—do you mind if I call you that? My mission in Iran. I was only going to report back to the Agency. I couldn't see how that could hurt your committee. You were going to hold a press conference anyway." Not in Teheran, brother, Jim observed to himself. But he let Victor go on. "You won't believe it, but I *identified* with your committee. I would never have agreed to sabotage what it was trying to do. Like this afternoon. I really hold to what I said about art. I came on strong because I meant it. On that one point, I share the hijackers' credo. It just so happened that I was able to play up to them without compromising my integrity." In the darkness Jim grimaced. "Maybe you *ought* to defect, Victor."

Victor's voice brightened. "Do you think so? It's true that underneath I have an ambivalence about them. But I'd never really fit in. They'd never really accept me." "Victor, the Apostate." "Why do you have to mock, Jim? It's been so fatal to you as a leader. And you're better than that. But I want to go back to what I started to say. When I took the assignment to work my way into your committee, it didn't feel right to me. I can confess that now. I didn't see the harm in it, but it rubbed me the wrong way. Sailing under false colors with a group like yours that I respected. You don't know it, but I'm a scholar in my field. I met Aileen once at a scholarly gathering, though she doesn't remember it. But there was the free trip to Iran, where I could brush up on my subject in my spare time, and then there was the chance of associating with you people on equal terms. . . . Well, you know how it is."

"You were tempted," agreed Jim. "But my conscience must have bothered me finally. Over Christmas, I did some heavy drinking, and, like a lot of compulsive drinkers, I have an allergy to alcohol. I can't handle it. Well, you know what happened. I blacked out in my hotel room and if it hadn't been for Sapphire I would have missed the plane at Kennedy." That detail was new to Jim. "Yes. My unconscious must have wanted me to miss it. Anyway, I've been punished." He waited, as if expecting Jim to complete his thought. "Sapphire?" "Of course. I killed her, Jim." "Strange. I had the impression that Jeroen killed her." "You're mocking me again. You know what I mean. I had no business bringing her. It was my insecurity and selfishness. Because I wanted company, somebody to be with me that loved me, whatever I was or did. She didn't want to come. Sapphire hated traveling, hated the cage. So I let her out." He groaned. "For humane motives, Victor." "Not entirely. I've gone over and over it, Jim. No. She got on my nerves, clawing at the cage and wailing. That began to undercut me. It was a reproach, telling me I shouldn't have brought her. And I was still drinking. When I drink, I can't stand any authority telling me what to do. If I hear of a rule, I'm bound to break it: observe the green light; no smoking in the toilet. All that stewardess had to do was tell me that I should keep '*Minou*' in her cage. *So I let her out.* I tell myself that at least I could have kept her in my lap. Why didn't I? Because I didn't care, really, whether she prowled the aisles and disturbed the other passengers. I *liked* the idea. And that stunt she has—had—of hiding. The manhunt they put on for her. That was really rich!"

"But the second time? With the hijackers?" "I don't remember. Maybe I was half-asleep. And how could I expect a hijacker to shoot her?" His voice rose suddenly, sounding shrill and aggrieved, as though someone was accusing him. That was where examinations of conscience tended to end—in a burst of pitiful anger. The Church was right; confession to a priest, carrying absolution and penance, was wiser. Poor Victor had run the gamut of emotions. The sequel, now, would be tears. No doubt he was right in blaming himself about the cat, but then everyone here, surely, had something to answer for that would make the present event appear like the working of justice. "Let's catch some sleep now," he urged, and returned to his pallet.

He was disturbed, for the last time, by Archie. Oh, Christ. Archie wanted to tell him, while the others were still asleep, that he had slipped a folded plan of the house and surrounding ground, with a sketch of a practicable tunnel, into Eloise's vanity-case, under her powder-puff, camouflaged by a thick layer of face-powder.

Twelve

ENK could have told them not to depend on the release of the big NATO helicopter for the execution of their plan. Morning had scarcely broken when he learned from the downcast pilots that they would not be going today. Carlos had wakened them to say that their departure had been put off indefinitely, and Pieter was taking it hard: his wife in Sneek was due to have their first baby at any moment. Henk commiserated but saw no ground for appeal. The *kapers* must have their reasons. Having consoled the pilots with philosophy—the child would be born anyway—he was startled by Jim's reaction to the news when it reached him finally during the breakfast service. "Jesus!" he swore, and let his cup of coffee spill over on Denise's tray. What was it to Jim that a young father would not see his wife through her labor? Then, during the toilet "break," Jim and Victor enlightened him.

He was glad to be taken—though a bit late—into their confidence. He would have been sorry to be left out. In return, he sought to put fresh cheer into them. Their idea was sound. They had only to be patient and wait for the next opportunity, which might come sooner than they guessed. As material encouragement, he offered to contribute a fresh bar of soap and some snuff, to bring on sneezing. And as it happened, luck was with them. The sparkling film of hoarfrost had not yet melted in the morning sun rays when a small helicopter put down in the field.

Welcome as the sight was to him *qua* duly inducted conspirator, he could not help reckoning the cost to his government of these repeated arrivals and departures. He pictured the Tweede Kamer in late session tonight—the billiard-green leather, pew-like benches and the gallery filled to capacity as his friend at Defense rose beside the Speaker to answer questions from the rightist fractions on the "squandering" of oil reserves during the national emergency to "coddle" a handful of impudent terrorists. And the daily siphoning of the precious fluid—the life blood of the "system"—must be gratifying to the *kapers'* pride. A pity, he thought, really, that no means had been found to convert earth gas to high octane fuel.

The new helicopter seemed to have been expected. It brought a case containing Helen's Vermeer and a small fair man with gold-rimmed glasses, recognizable to Henk at a hundred meters as his countryman. The unexpected was Charles, emerging gleefully from the freight bay and stretching his long legs. "Here I am," he shrilled, entering the family room with unruffled composure despite the pistol at his back. "Don't be tiresome, Hussein. I shan't try to escape." He looked around him happily. "How nice to be back. I always wanted the experience of being a stowaway."

Like many of the old man's boasts, this proved to be somewhat fanciful. To be accurate, he had come as a hitchhiker. "This delightful gentleman, Mr. Van der Kampe—your compatriot, Henk—was kind enough to give me a lift. Yes. We met by good luck at the heliport, when I was feeling frightfully down-at-the-mouth. Scarcely knowing what to do with myself, yet unwilling to turn tail and go home. Mr. Van der Kampe is from your incomparable Rijksmuseum, Henk. We found many friends in common. He explained to me as we chatted that he had been sent for to vouch for Helen's Vermeer. If I divined correctly, the suggestion came from our friend Jeroen. Indeed, one can fancy it as an imperative. Naturally Mr. Van der Kampe was somewhat apprehensive as to the circumstances he might find here. I was able to allay his anxieties, and we became thick as thieves."

Henk's eyes turned to the Rijksmuseum expert, who had remained impassive during this account of himself and his mission. He had set down the briefcase he carried and stood, trim feet together, like a mute exhibit being presented by Charles. Yet surely he understood English—which of the tulip-people didn't? "But how did the two of you come to meet, really?" cried Sophie, voicing Henk's own mystification as she looked from one to the other. "Why, my dear, he recognized me!" The small precise-featured Dutchman gave a small nod. "While I was having a cup of chocolate at the little bar they have. He saw me on television, imagine!"

Henk and Sophie exchanged a smile. They had all seen Charles on television last night. On the seven o'clock news program and, as an encore, at eight. He had actually spoken a few quaint words of Dutch. "You were a hit, Charles," said Jim in his easy tones. "Far outshining the rest. And, yes, I agree, quite memorable. Wouldn't you say, Lily?" "Oh, by all means. The star. We were proud of you." "But where *was* this bar?" Aileen asked. "My dear, I can't tell you exactly. At the military airfield, where we landed." "And they let you stay all *night* at a military airfield?" "I *hid*!" said Charles. Henk lifted a questioning eyebrow; he was acquainted with that heliport. "In the toilet for a time, if you must know. Then there was a jeep that I had noticed standing outside, which became rather chilly, I must say." "An *empty* jeep?" "Oh, no. That would have been careless of them, wouldn't it? There was a young soldier in a greatcoat asleep at the wheel." "And then?" "And then, my dear, let's just say that I have a way with me. In the end, the junior officer in command was most accommodating; you Dutch are so helpful to foreigners. Imagine if one had been in France. The only bother was that he was eager to furnish me transportation to Amsterdam. But I managed to stay put, resorting to what they call 'delaying tactics.' And the young men coming on duty had seen me on television. Some of them asked for my autograph. I expect they thought I was some figure of the stage or screen. In return, they were most informative. I learned that Helen's picture had been left behind. It had stood there all day. Anyone could have stolen it."

He broke off and eyed Van der Kampe, who was examining the Titian with the aid of a loupe. At Charles's prompting ("Do have a look at the splendid Ward they have in the next room"), he moved on into the *beste kamer*. Charles waited. "Well," he continued, lowering his voice, "I was not quite so guileless as I led *him* to believe. Hussein, would you mind shutting that door? At my age, one must be careful of drafts. Thank you. To go on with my story: I was forearmed, you see, by my young informants. Being assured that the picture was there emboldened me to hang on. When Mr. Van der Kampe appeared, one of my young acquaintances, guessing my interest, nipped into the toilet, where I was taking evasive action, to tell me that orders were for that gentleman to embark with the painting. Not being familiar with art matters, he could not say why. But I intuited it and I posted myself at the bar, trusting that a conversation between us would open. When it did, I offered myself as his guide. We agreed that he would pass me off, should the deception be necessary, as a fellow-authority. From our Fine Arts Museum—between ourselves, shockingly weak in Dutch seventeenth century, but who would know that here?"

Sounds from the shed announced that the Vermeer's case was being opened. At a sign from Jim, Henk, drawing Sophie with him, joined Van der Kampe in the parlor. He had no great yearning to fraternize in Dutch with this *landgenoot*, but it was important to Jim to know how long, roughly, the authentication was going to take. In short, how soon he would be returning to Amsterdam. Victor needed to be ready.

Though content to be enlisted in the rescue operation, Henk, on reflection, did not share Jim's sense of Victor's peril, which was based, he thought, on a misreading of the *kapers*' mentality. He doubted that CIA agents in the present circumstances were an endangered species needing protection. Almost the contrary. As the *kapers* would view it, if he read them right, he and Jim, even Sophie, were key imperialist agents operating under the cloak of liberalism and more deserving of execution by a people's firing squad than a rank-and-filer like Victor, were he to be exposed. In the scale of things, Victor would be judged to be a mere tool exploited by the bosses for his language skills and his Middle East credentials, and he had only to confess to be given a second chance. Redemption would be easy, as often happened with informers. To an observer, that seemed obvious. Yet the wretch, being fearful, was unwilling to take the chance. He preferred to be saved by his Great White Father, the Senator.

In any case, Henk was happy to do his share. It would be their first act of subversion. Like a schoolboy, he was almost offended when his snuff was refused. He had agreed, of course, to say nothing to Sophie, and Jim, he noticed, was keeping his distance from Lily this morning. Wisely, Henk considered, for that observant lady was likely to detect his suppressed excitement and remark on it wonderingly in public. One of the conditions of the game of skill they were playing was that anyone not in the secret had to be looked on as a potential enemy.

Entrusted with the vital mission of sounding out Van der Kampe, Henk felt honored and slightly apprehensive. He was

a scout, obliged to step carefully lest an over-heavy footfall or
the crackling of a twig give his purpose away. On entering the
room with Sophie, he had experienced a kind of stage fright;
he swallowed to moisten his dry throat. Danger was an exhila-
rant. He had lost all sense of proportion, he told himself, for
the slight risk they were running was as nothing in comparison
with the permanent danger that surrounded them, whose effect
was mainly depressing. He supposed the difference was that this
danger was of their own choosing—they were courting it, you
might say, like a woman.

Van der Kampe would not say how long it would take him
to pronounce on the Vermeer. He seemed irritated by the question. An irritable fussy little man, the worst type of Nether-
lander, and made nervous, evidently, by the guns—he did not
appear to have noticed the highly visible wiring—and by the
mixed company he found himself in. He was a snob, *natuurlijk*,
and the apparition of Charles in full traveling regalia at the
heliport must have led him to expect better things. "Of the old
school, that one," he said to Henk in Dutch with a pale
purse-lipped smile. The rest he found harder to catalogue.
Mrs. Potter, he understood, would be traveling back with him
in the event that he could certify her painting. Her husband
was standing by in a hotel in Amsterdam—in the bar, Henk
imagined, and not with a cup of hot chocolate. He saw that
the uneasy fellow was taking Margaret, who retained some
semblance of grandeur, for the owner of the Vermeer. "One of
the great old fortunes, my 'guide' let me know." Henk redirected the authority's deferential gaze. "Not *that* lady!" Van
der Kampe exclaimed, shocked. "We're prisoners," Henk reminded him. He felt embarrassed in front of this stranger for
the state of Helen's dress, as if she were an aunt or an even
nearer relation.

Van der Kampe excused himself. He had forgotten their
state of duress. And now he understood (he said) why Henk
had been anxious to learn when he would be returning to
Amsterdam. "You will be wanting to send messages to your
wife and children. By all means. Lose no time, please, in pen-
ning them. I shall be more than glad to deliver them to your
home." Henk felt Sophie stiffen beside him at the words
"*vrouw*" and "*kinderen*." But Van der Kampe's field of vision,

on the whole perhaps fortunately, did not seem to include Sophie. If Henk were to mention that the feminine shape opposite
him bore an uncanny resemblance to the Empress Theodora in
the Ravenna mosaic, Van der Kampe, he supposed, would explain that that was not his "field." "Your address, please, and
may I offer you pen and paper?" Henk reflected. "You *must*
write," said Sophie. For a moment, Henk could think of no
message to send that would not be heavily humorous ("Greetings from Flevoland") or a lie ("I miss you and think of you
constantly"). In the end, he wrote "I am well. I amuse myself
and I send you my love. Greet Elisabeth." "Who is Elisabeth?"
said Sophie. "The wife of Den Uyl." To shake off the thought
of his family, he moved to the window, where he had a good
view of the helicopter. There should be room, he estimated,
for another passenger. Mrs. Potter was a small woman, and
Van der Kampe was not much bigger. With the Vermeer out of
the way, one of them and Victor, supine, ought to fit quite
easily into the cargo bay.

Van der Kampe begged pardon. He had to answer a pressing
call of nature. Unaware of the privilege, he was shown to the
toilet. Leaving Sophie behind, Henk strolled into the family
room. He made an affirmative sign to Jim. The expert, he had
concluded, would make short work of his expertise; he was in
a state of terror that now seemed to be gripping even his bowels. Henk suddenly realized that the man must believe that it
had been an act of great bravery to come here. And in his
vanity he perhaps still suspected that he had been brought here
on a ruse and was going to be held hostage.

Carey was tackling Denise. "Come here, *chérie*. Mr. Lenz
had a bad night. He looks damn sick this morning." "*J'ai vu*,"
she agreed. In truth Victor looked terrible. He lay huddled in
a chair with red spots on his high cheekbones and his forehead
the color of a young Leidsekaas with cumin. "Should we take
his temperature?" Aileen proposed. It was wonderful how
valuable at times an interfering woman could be. Denise's
thermometer read 39.5°. "What's that in Fahrenheit?" someone asked. Sophie answered from the doorway. "103.1." Henk
was pleased to think of a computer with flashing lights swiftly
adding, subtracting, multiplying, inside that noble head. "I
knew those boils were unhealthy," Aileen observed. "Shouldn't

you give him aspirin, Denise? At least he'll feel more comfortable. Temporarily, they'll bring the fever down. Oh, poor Victor."

Jim held up a hand. "Whoa there, Bossie. Not till Greet has a look at him. What do you think, Henk?" Before he could answer, Aileen had reversed herself. "No, Denise. Better not. It could be something serious, and the aspirin would mask it. We might have *known* something like this would happen. Could we ask to have a doctor flown in? When I think of the darling Bishop . . . He might be alive today. *You* ask, Henk. Jeroen listens to you." "It might be more to the point," Jim commented, "to fly old Victor out." "But would they ever agree to that?" Lily asked. "Why not?" said Henk. "They could put him on the helicopter with Van der Kampe." "Now *there's* a thought," cried the Reverend. "*Chapeau*, Henk," said Aileen. "Actually they'd be criminals not to." "They *are* criminals," said Lily. "Still, perhaps one *should* remind them of Gus." "I wouldn't advise it," said Jim. "You don't want to put their backs up. Let them decide for themselves what's to be done. The main thing is for Greet to look at him. And let's not get too worked up, Aileen. He may just have some little bug, a touch of flu." "With 103.1?" Aileen retorted. "Why, we could all catch it!" Ahmed felt Victor's forehead. "*Très malade*," he decided. "Well, go tell your boss-lady," said Beryl.

A distraction, however, occurred as the painting was brought in. Van der Kampe seemed to be still in the toilet. Jeroen himself carried the canvas to the parlor and ranged it against the west wall, where the light was best. In the family room, Victor was helped to the sofa and left to himself while the rest of them crowded in to see the "Girl."

She wore a blue cap—more like a coif—over sandy corkscrew ringlets that looked as if they had just come out of curl-papers; her long full jacket was yellow taffeta trimmed with ermine, and her billowy skirt was white with dark-blue panels. She held a guitar on her lap; she was touching the strings with her right hand, and her head was turned sideways as if she was looking toward someone, maybe her teacher, for a cue. Or else there was a spinet in the next room, and she was both looking that way and listening for a chord to tell her to begin. There was something uncertain in her attitude, and she held the guitar awkwardly. Her high-colored cheeks, stiff curls, and big Dutch nose had a provincial, teenager look. Henk did not think that the "Girl" could have been much of a musician. He felt sure she was a Vermeer, though.

He did not know the painting. He was certain that he had never seen it in reproduction. But it must be very similar to the Vermeer that had been stolen by terrorists in London. That was maybe why Jeroen had been so interested in it: he was copying those Irish extremists or competing with them. Henk remembered the photos and daily news stories in the English press and his own keen concern for "the hostage," whose fate had been more avidly followed than if she had been a live maiden. It was "only" a material object, as the pastor had said of this one a few days back, yet—possibly for that reason— there had been an aura of sacrilege about that riveting event. When a strip of the canvas had been mailed to a newspaper, it had been, for Henk at least, like the martyrdom of a Christian virgin as depicted in his old *Calendar of Saints*—Agatha, his mother's name saint, having her tender breasts slashed off by fiendish pagans.

Sophie was staring at the painting. Her brow was furrowed, and her narrow jaw thrust out in deep American meditation. She was asking the canvas to "say" something to her—something profound and important that it had never told anyone else. Henk waited. "It's a weird thing," she said finally. "It makes me think of old studio photography. She's all dressed up to have her picture taken, and the photographer has arranged the lighting, pulling back that curtain from the window so as to let the sun's rays fall just right on her features. He's adjusted the folds of her dress and tilted her head, running back and forth to the camera to see how she looks in the lens. He's not satisfied; she needs something to do with her hands. But he has an idea: that prop guitar he keeps in the studio. He puts it in her lap and shows her how to hold it. Then he ducks under his black hood. 'Wait for the birdie.' Click."

Henk was amazed. What she had noticed was there, certainly; she had made a true observation about Vermeer. "The *instantané* effect. 'Click,' as you say. You will never find that in a Rembrandt. Rembrandt never 'catches' his sitters in a single flitting instant." "Fleeting," said Sophie. "Rembrandt's sitters, you mean, have been there for centuries, like his trees?" "Something like that. Vermeer, I think, Sophie, is always painting time. That's the meaning of all the musical instruments and the clock in the 'View of Delft.' You know it?" "I saw it once in Paris. At the Orangerie. I noticed the clock too." Henk felt extraordinarily happy. "You are right, this picture is weird," he told her. "*Raar*, we say in Dutch. Because it says to you that it is posed while at the same time it is telling you that it is a snapshot, a split second of arrested motion." "You think that's on purpose?" "Yes. It points to a contradiction. There is pathos in it. The grotesquely overdressed young girl, with the pearls round her neck—" "Do you suppose she could be Jewish, Henk?" He studied the "Girl"'s features again. "The nose," prompted Sophie. "And those dark popping eyes. Plus being overdressed." "All that is Dutch," he consoled her. "We are much like you, Sophie—a merchant race with overdeveloped noses and—"

"Please!" They stepped back. Van der Kampe was finally ready to examine the canvas. He neared it, drew back, got down on one knee and looked up at it. Doffing his spectacles, he took a big magnifying glass from his briefcase and held it close to the canvas, where there appeared to be a signature, then moved it slowly across with his bare eye squinting through the lens. Henk was reminded of the feeling of having a doctor's head pressed against your chest as he listened to your inner organs. The only sound that came from the Rijksmuseum clinician was of heavy breathing as he knelt before the work. Finally he put his cheek to the surface and blew softly.

"He's dissatisfied," whispered Sophie. "Oh, God. Poor Helen." "It's not that," said Henk. "He doesn't like to give an opinion under these conditions." "Because he thinks Helen's life might depend on what he decides," assented Sophie. Henk shook his head. "This gentleman thinks of his career, of his professional standing. As he explained to me, he would normally never consent to do an authentication 'off the cuff,' without the facilities of the Rijksmuseum laboratories." "No talking, please." "Come," said Henk, guiding Sophie into the family room. What he saw there reassured him. There were still red patches on the invalid's cheeks, and Jim and Denise were with him.

In the laboratories—Henk reflected—the painting could be subjected to x-rays, carbon tests, and so on, by the men in white under Van der Kampe's authority; he would never be under the necessity of using his own unaided judgment in making an attribution. No wonder he was so uneasy; physical fear would be heightened by professional fear arising from lack of practice. It was probably years since he had arrived at an independent judgment of a work of art. "Like doctors today," said Sophie. "They're afraid to diagnose a case of chicken pox unless they can send samples to the laboratory. They don't like house calls either. I suppose, for him, this counts as a house call." She pondered.

"But what made him come, then?" Henk gave a short laugh. "His patriotic duty, he would tell us. In fact he's a high civil servant depending—you will smile, Sophie—on the Ministry of Culture, Recreation, and Social Work." "You mean they put pressure on him?" Henk did not know. The most effective pressures on such a type were those he would exert on himself. "They had only to suggest to him that in the event of his refusal they would regretfully have to turn to his younger colleague of the Mauritiushuis in The Hague." Van der Kampe could never permit that. That the other should appear in the world press, not to mention Eurovision, as the Netherlands' leading authority on Vermeer of Delft! Undertaking a dangerous mission in the sensational hijacking case, decorated by the Queen, maybe even receiving a knighthood . . . Sophie nodded. "But if he's so scared for his career, will he give an honest opinion?" "You don't know Hollanders. 'Without fear or favor,' as he would put it." "I wish he'd hurry." "He will not be hurried. Although, as you see, he is burning with impatience to leave. Even in these unsuitable conditions, he is determined to live up to the 'highest professional standard.'"

Jim, too, was becoming impatient. "Can't you light a fire under him? Christ, how long can a man's body maintain an artificially induced 103° temperature?" But Victor's hand was hot, and his teeth were authentically chattering. Henk seated himself at his bedside on the sofa's edge and became aware of an unmistakably soapy smell. It would be wise, he suggested, to get rid of the evidence before Greet was summoned. Victor fumbled in his clothing and handed over a sticky remnant of soap to which a few pale body hairs clung.

In the *beste kamer*, Van der Kampe had declared himself ready to pronounce. Greet ordered the room cleared, leaving herself, Jeroen, Horst, and Elfride in the auditory. In the doorway Henk protested. Mrs. Potter, he argued, had a right to be present and to have a Dutch-speaking witness to translate for her. "And you volunteer, Deputy?" Greet was sarcastic. He was a lawyer, Henk retorted, and there was no one else on hand to represent Mrs. Potter who had a knowledge of Dutch. "The truth is, you are curious," said Greet. Nevertheless she allowed both him and the owner to stay.

Horst shut the door, and Van der Kampe took a stand before the canvas. He had set his briefcase on the harmonium and from time to time, as he spoke, he took neatly stapled documents from it for reference. At his request, to avoid distractions, the Ramsbotham collection had had their faces turned to the wall. Except for the ever-present pistol in Greet's bulging bosom, there were no weapons in the room, and it might have been a seminar for a group of picked students. Charles's walking-stick served the expert as a pointer; all he lacked were slides. From the harmonium stool, Henk translated. There was a small restoration, the speaker indicated, of the left-hand fingers and some signs of an earlier over-painting in the landscape hanging on the wall behind the subject. The glazes were in unusually good condition. Though the signature seemed to have been added by another hand, the painting appeared to be an authentic work of Johannes van der Meer, probably executed in the last years of the artist's life. Possibly on commission from a client familiar with the Kenwood House "Guitar Player" and desirous of owning a work of the same kind. Photos and transparencies were produced from the briefcase and passed from hand to hand. Jeroen accepted the expert's magnifying glass. Beside Henk, Helen preened. "Just what the authorities at home said."

It was evidently not a replica, Van der Kampe proceeded, but might be described as a variation on a theme. The Kenwood House painting (consultation of papers from briefcase), dated approximately 1667, was generally identified with a work known to have been in the hands of the painter's widow following on his death. A picture of like description figured in the Amsterdam sale of 1676. Conceivably, that was the present work. Or possibly the canvas here was to be equated with a work that figured in Lot 4 in the later sale, of 1696, as "A Young Lady with a Guitar." The notion of two closely allied "guitar" works of the master—one believed to have been lost—had often been put forward. Helen nodded.

Van der Kampe offered photostats of documents for inspection and stepped back to the canvas. With the stick, he indicated the source of light, a window on the right almost entirely masked by a blackish drapery, as in a camera obscura, thus permitting the sun's rays—the stick moved—to irradiate the subject's face and upper body and the wall behind her with an effect of stage lighting. This treatment was also found in the "Guitar Player"—Henk obediently held up a photo enlargement—and supported a late date, as did the thinness and fluidity of the paint. In the absence of scientific tests, nothing more could be said. The painting had all the hallmarks of a late Van der Meer, but this could also be seen as a suspicious circumstance. Without chemical analysis of paints and canvas, forgery should not be ruled out. One could postulate a master forger of the nineteenth century, active during the period of Van der Meer's "rediscovery," or a current forger with access, through a clever dealer, to canvas dating from the seventeenth century. The painting was either a genuine Van der Meer of the second rank—a certain lack of freshness was to be noted, deriving possibly from diminished inspiration, often found in near-replicas done to order—or it was the work of an anonymous imitator endowed with undisputable genius. The speaker personally inclined to the first hypothesis, but in any case it was a work of museum quality.

He promptly picked up his briefcase and, gesturing to Horst to open the door, went briskly into the next room. Helen followed him. Her stout little body was quivering with indignation. "'Second rank'! But if it's a forgery it's a work of 'genius.' Oh, no, sir, you contradict yourself!" In Henk's view, there was no contradiction, but Van der Kampe did not dispute that with her. He stood polishing his spectacles, ready to depart. "It's *had* all those tests he speaks of," Helen went on, beginning to sniffle. "And passed them with flying colors." "In the States, madam. But professionally, you see, I cannot take account of that. Were you to offer it to the Rijksmuseum, we should have to submit it to our own testing processes, even though, as I've indicated, I've no personal doubt that it's genuine. Someday, in fact, I should be greatly interested in doing a monograph comparing it with the Kenwood House canvas. I'm quite often in New York, and if you'd allow me to call on you and study it at leisure—" He was stopped by a burst of tears. The pompous fool had forgotten that if his validation was accepted she would no longer have the painting. "Pray forgive me. How tactless of me." He glanced at his watch. "In any event, if you will be staying on a few days in Amsterdam, I shall take pleasure in showing you our Van der Meer archive. Your husband as well. Fascinating insights were gained in our restoration clinic at the time of that unhappy incident—you recall it, of course—the canvas hacked from its frame while on exhibition in Belgium. Irreparably damaged, we feared, when we first recovered it."

"'The Love Letter.' Yes. Quite some time ago." Her mind hopped like a bird onto the new topic. "I always asked myself, did the museum pay a ransom?" "Madam, as a distinguished collector, you know very well that my answer must be a negative. But, as I was saying, it will be an honor, one day when we meet again—" "'When you meet again'!" Margaret burst out. "Why, she'll be going back with you. I gather you've won her her freedom, though you took your time over it, I must say."

Greet looked to Jeroen. "We are satisfied, Mr. Curator," he said. "You and Mrs. Potter will proceed at once to the helicopter. Carlos!" "And you will be going too, old gentleman," Greet ordered quite fiercely, handing Charles his walking-stick. "Carlos, take him along." "Can you wait a minute?" said Aileen. "Victor's sick. There, on the couch." "We are busy," said Greet. "I will look at the prisoner later." "He has much fever, Greet," put in Denise. "*Très malade*," said Ahmed, making his own teeth chatter. "Could you send for a doctor maybe?" Jim said in a meditative tone that won Henk's full admiration. "I guess that aircraft out there might pick one up if a message was sent ahead." "You will leave decisions to us, Senator. We are masters here. I will look at the prisoner, Jeroen." Denise stood ready with her thermometer. Greet shook it down and inserted it roughly under Victor's tongue. "39°." Her thumb went down on Victor's limp wrist, taking his pulse. "Fast. But not so fast as the fever would propose. Is there a history of tuberculosis?" Victor licked his lips, and his eyes turned to Jim, who made a dissuasive motion with his head. Henk agreed: the fewer lies the better. "Not that I know of," said Victor. "*Vreemde*," she said to Jeroen. "She says it is strange," Henk reported. Greet and Jeroen eyed each other. They murmured together in Dutch. Henk crossed his fingers, touching the piece of soap in his pocket. He caught the words "*uit*" and "*weg*." They were telling each other, evidently, that it would be best to be rid of Victor. Henk nodded affirmatively to Jim.

It looked like clear sailing. Only one little reef remained to be crossed: was there room, after all, in the helicopter? When estimating the craft's seating capacity, Henk had overlooked Charles. Van der Kampe, who had been listening impatiently, had his own word to add. He was not prepared to have his return flight compromised by the extra burden of a sick man. "I wish to put my foot down," he said loudly. "What is now proposed is for us dangerous. I do not like it. They have promised me safe-conduct, Deputy. Four besides the pilot is an overload—too many."

"Goody!" Charles cried, with a clap of his hands. "He can have my place." Greet looked to her partner. Jeroen shrugged. More hurried Dutch undertones. She was angry. In a way, Henk sympathized: to let the incorrigible old man stay in defiance of her orders would undermine her whole conception of discipline. But Charles, as he had said, had a "way" with him. Jeroen overruled her. Once again, from the parlor window, they witnessed a departure to freedom. Seeing Victor safely stowed in the freight bay, Henk and Jim breathed easier. "Wouldn't you know, they forgot to search them!" observed Aileen, clicking her tongue.

The following day brought Margaret's collection. No expert accompanied her El Greco "Saint in Ecstasy," her tiny Lorenzo Monaco "Virgin and Saints," her sepia drawings by Raphael and *sanguine* by Michelangelo. Jeroen, however, was satisfied, and they were put in the parlor, replacing the Ramsbotham collection, which was stacked in the shed. "What your museum needs is an annex, Jeroen," Jim commented, as Margaret took her leave. But with Margaret, Charles went, definitively—he had gained only a day of grace. Next to go were Dirk and Pieter and the NATO helicopter, which was pushed out of the barn with surprising ease. Of the collectors, there remained only Lily and Beryl. This, as Henk and Sophie decided long after, had been the happiest time. There was not so much work for Denise and Jean; chicken and rabbit appeared on the menu. The *kapers*' mood was still indulgent; everyone got toilet privileges, and the men were allowed to shave. There were walks twice a day for the entire company, with only one guard, and pairing off occurred as a matter of course: Jim and Lily— on rainy days under the Bishop's umbrella—Aileen and Archie —fast friends by now—Henk and Sophie, and, in the rear, the pastor and Beryl, unluckily not so well matched. The pastor's binoculars were a godsend. Thanks to them and to Henk's in-struction, the hostages learned the shore birds of the Nether-lands; as Lily said, that was something they would have in common all their lives. In the house, Frank conducted morning service as usual, which somewhat appeased his longing to be shepherd to the flock. But when he sought by example to in-troduce grace before meals, the practice was discouraged. There were no more arguments—only lively discussions often lasting till late in the evening and usually touched off by the paintings that confronted them at every turn of the head.

Afterward it was sadder. The departures of Lily and Beryl ap-peared in retrospect to have been the turning-point. It was odd to have Lily replaced by her water-colors, which uncannily resem-bled her. Airy clouds, mountain peaks at sunrise, cottages, ancient bridges, country-church spires, hay ricks, lichened castles, they represented Nature and the works of men in their least terrestrial aspect—they were gentle English "inklings." In their tasteful "neutral" frames, they were ranged upstairs in the children's play-room, and Jim, using the excuse of going to the toilet, frequently went up to look at them. He was communing with her spirit, he said. She had kissed him on leaving and cried a little, producing the chaste handkerchief—still immaculate—that she had used for the Bishop's funeral. Henk and Sophie, trying not to watch, could not make out what her real feelings were. "Come on, Ma," Beryl interrupted. She had already said good-bye to Ahmed and given him her address in New York. With Lily and Beryl, Jean went. Now they were only seven.

The realignment that followed was inevitable. With Jim be-reft of Lily, Henk and Sophie saw no choice but to close ranks around him. Once again, as at the start, they were a threesome, Sophie between the two men. Jim's efforts to join up with Aileen, leaving them alone, were seldom successful. Having "lost" Jim to Lily, Aileen was determined to keep Archie to herself, and Archie, when Jim joined them, tended to detach himself and gravitate toward the also bereft and quite pretty Denise, mismatched with the pastor, who could not speak French. It was jackstraws, said Sophie: when you pulled out one—Lily—the whole house came down. In any case, the re-duction in numbers made being alone in this confined space all but impossible. Lovers lost themselves best in a crowd.

This became cruelly apparent at night, when the lights were turned off. The attic was no longer serving as a dormitory; for sleeping, the hostages were divided between the *beste kamer* and the family room. By Aileen's decree, Sophie was on one sofa and she herself on the other, with Denise curling up in a chair. The men were assigned to the floor, and Henk was far-ther removed in every sense from Sophie than he had been when the room was packed with bodies and they had lain side by side often, sensing each other's breathing as they listened to the older people snore.

Would they ever make love? For his part, he was unable to imagine its happening now, as if on a public stage. Sophie was bolder. The other day she had wistfully mentioned the attic. "Do you think Ahmed . . . ?" She meant would Ahmed let them use it some night when he was on guard. "For a few minutes or all night?" he had answered dryly. Impossible, he had told her, with seven *kapers* bedded on the floor below, the creaking stairs, and the unlucky other hostages waking, per-haps, and missing them. He would not want to restrain himself to a quick noiseless act with Sophie; she was not a whore you went upstairs with while your friends waited below. Finally, it would seem wrong to him to joy in her hungrily when the others were not so favored. It might have been different when Lily was still here. Not that she and Jim, at their age, would have been likely to have a go themselves. But they had formed a kind of couple. No, he would not attempt it and, if he did, he would probably be impotent or at any rate dissatisfied.

Yet when he spoke of a future meeting it was Sophie who drew back. "You could stay on in Amsterdam," he pointed out. "No." On the polder, she said, she would have no scruple, because the polder was a separate world. It could not be mistaken for real life. On the polder, they could love each other and be sure of a clean ending: death for either or both or release, which would cut the thread. She did not want their love to be "messy," that is, clouded by his thoughts for his family, deception, stolen meetings—"the usual when the man is married." She was right, he recognized, as far as Amsterdam went: he was too well known to register in a hotel with her or even to go up in the lift to a room she would be waiting in. And The Hague would be worse. Indeed, thanks to the present adventure, there was no corner in Holland where they could hope to hide. And, once restored to his family, he could not promptly leave them and his work to fly off to meet her in Avila or Assisi or a chalet in the Austrian Alps. But Flanders might be possible.

"Do you know Bruges?" he said. "No. But no," said Sophie. "The people there would know you. Anyway, what would your plan be? To meet me for overnight?" She could stay on, he said, and visit the museums, and he would come back to her. "Bruges is nice. You could even take a train to Gand for the day." "Ghent," she said. "'The Mystic Lamb.' I've seen it. And when you came to Bruges, Henk, what would you do? Leave a friend's telephone number where you could be reached, I suppose. Then clear it with the friend so that he could call you at our hotel in case something happened at home. A government crisis or one of the children sick." He had not sufficiently reflected. Sophie laughed. "I can see you've never had a serious affair. Not overnight, with hotels and friends covering for you." "And you have?" "It sounds so, doesn't it? Yes. But this is different. I think I truly love you, Henk. I wouldn't like to watch you behaving shabbily. To be honest, I think you'd find it quite hard."

Unfairly, he had been angry. Her resistance had struck the vein of obstinacy in him. In the bathroom mirror, he saw that his jaw was set in moody lines of determination. He resented the mention of the attic—a substitute, such as you might offer a child. He was jealous, of course, as well. It irked him that a one-time affair with a married man (or several) should pre-judge her relation with *him*. Yet gradually his irritation sub-sided. He was being wilful himself, he perceived. Moreover, she was righter than he. It was absurd that he should be sad because she refused to meet him in Bruges. The local outlook, after Lily's departure, made nonsense of such a quarrel. As soon debate whether she would accept a rendezvous in heaven —on a cloud—which seemed closer to hand.

Negotiations, he had learned, were at a standstill. Jeroen himself confirmed it, with a curious show of pride. And Jim had not been wrong: they were serious about their Demand Two. That was the sticking-point. Holding valuable live hos-tages and invaluable works of art, Jeroen believed himself to be an irresistible force. He could not see that Den Uyl was an immovable object. "Talk to him, Henk," Aileen begged. But he had already shown the lot of them, point by point, why it was impossible for Den Uyl to agree. Greet had listened in-tently; Henk had felt he was half-convincing her. Horst and Elfride were noncommittal; the Arabs and Carlos could not follow the presentation, and Jeroen calmly smiled. "You will see," he predicted.

It was now a true siege. As in the Middle Ages, the oppo-nents faced each other across a neutral terrain, each counting on the force of attrition to sap the other's morale. Inside the fortress, supplies were running low. But the *kapers*, so far, had declined to ask for a food drop. That would be a sign of weak-ness, Greet told Aileen. There was still flour in the larder, dried milk, a little cooking fat, and some legumes. The rabbits had been sacrificed at the rate of two a week, but the hens were being hoarded, for their eggs, until they ceased to lay. A share of the new-laid eggs was replaced under the hen each morning with the idea of hatching chickens. "How long does it take," Sophie wondered, "for a chicken to be big enough to eat?" Archie had the answer; he had grown up on a sheep farm in Aberdeenshire. Three or four months. That gave them the measure of the *kapers*' determination. In view of this, it was lucky that the farmer had left a good supply of chicken feed. "We'll be eating it soon ourselves," Aileen prophesied. "Not so daft," said Archie: chicken feed was readily digestible, having a high protein content, considerable fat, and roughage. There were no crops yet, naturally, in the farmer's new-planted fields, but the binoculars had shown ducks swimming in the distant canal, and the whir of pheasants had been heard. This inspired Ahmed and Hussein to talk of foraging out for game, taking a hostage along for protection. But the leaders were doubtful about a dispersion of forces. Up to now, this had differed from a medieval siege in that there had been no sorties and no attempt at scaling the ramparts, which were reinforced nevertheless from time to time.

As the unchanging days passed, the hostages came to perceive that the world outside was diminishing in reality for them. Staring fixedly out the parlor window, Henk no longer "saw" the *marechaussee* drawn up in the field. They had become part of the scenery. He supposed he was aware of them all the time "subliminally," like Lily with her collection. If he looked out one morning and they were not there, he would notice them, he hoped, as an absence. Just as he had ceased to pay attention to the air traffic overhead and perceived one day with an effect of surprise that it had stopped; the sky was empty except for an occasional patrol plane. In a parallel development, the world was becoming oblivious of *them*.

On television, the polder "ordeal" figured more and more rarely. The descent of Lily and Beryl, in their furs, at the heliport was a kind of grand finale—though the fond audience in the family room did not guess it—before a curtain dropped. Now nights in a row went by without the obligatory shots of the farmhouse and the accompanying bulletin read by a spokesman from the Justice Ministry. The farmhouse returned briefly to a stellar place on the screen when the *boer* himself and his *vrouw*, back from the Balearics with peeling sunburns, were interviewed in the house of relatives in Kampen. ("The old country," they both called the mainland, where they were staying, which made Henk smile, translating—that was how the polder settlers thought of Holland.) Hearing them tell their tale, the captives, as in a cinema flashback, were able to reconstruct the early part of the story, its infancy, you might say. Its humble birth, in the mind of Jeroen, remained obscure.

The couple's testimony led the police to an abandoned truck with a false Hamburg license-plate in the airport parking lot. This was the first clue, the spokesman explained, that the police had had to work on; there was hope now of finding the gang's accomplices. But the trail, evidently, was cold. The truck—stolen, of course—was shown on an evening program, and then no more was heard of it, or of the *boer*, who had spoken feelingly of his winter wheat crop. The story, like the year, was at a dead point. "I wonder what happened to Archie's tunnel," Jim inquired with a dry laugh one night.

Consciousness of being buried, like a small item in a newspaper, was affecting the *kapers* too. Their fading from the news, to be replaced by other raiders, kidnappers, bombers, could not fail to worry them. To maintain their ascendancy, they would feel bound, soon, to execute a hostage. Or so Henk feared and he supposed that Jim was sharing the thought— Archie too, perhaps. The external signs were ominous: frequent sounds of argument from the kitchen, with Yusuf's voice dominant—sometimes plaintive, sometimes shrill. Present policy, obviously, was being questioned. It was natural that some of the commando—the less intelligent—should be spoiling for an action. Jeroen, heavy-browed and silent, as if marking a withdrawal, was spending more and more time shut up in the parlor with the Vermeer. Ahmed now and then softly knocked and joined him. When on guard, Ahmed seemed depressed.

But executing a hostage would be a mistake, from their own point of view. Henk believed he could show that much to a few of them, at least to Greet and Jeroen. It was not a point of principle, on which Jeroen would balk, but a point of praxis. Having resolved to speak, Henk waited till he could find the two alone. The moment came after lunch on a Sunday—their fourth in captivity, unless he was losing count—when Denise had finished washing up and Carlos, a "friendly," was on guard. Carlos carried his message, and the kitchen door was opened. The pair sat at the table. Greet was darning Jeroen's sock, and his big white foot was bare. The others were above, presumably napping.

"You have something to tell us?" "Yes." He had determined to come straight to the subject, and she had spoken Dutch— from her, a good sign. They had been discussing the execution of a hostage, he told them. They showed no surprise that he knew. It would be an error, he said—a *fout.* "*Waarom?*" That was Greet, not sounding, as so often, sarcastic but as though she were more than curious to know his reasons. Jeroen's reaction could not be seen; he was bending down to put the sock and heavy boot on. If they killed a hostage now, Henk explained, it would be like a signal to the authorities to strike—a pretext certain elements in the coalition would have been waiting for to employ "strong measures." "Van Agt," said Greet, naming the Minister of Justice. "There must be much public pressure," continued Henk. Killing a hostage would clear the way, which had been blocked by Den Uyl's scruples. "They will storm the house. You cannot prevent that." Jeroen held up a hand. "You are right. We cannot prevent that. But there are comrades here who do not believe they will storm it. They say, look at your Bishop. There was no reprisal. To the contrary, we gained our way. You recall that?"

That had been in the early stages, Henk pointed out, when the policy of peaceful negotiations had had the upper hand. "But now it is late, Jeroen. My government is tired; the people are tired. They feel this has gone on too long. But they will be patient and wait a little longer if you do not kill." Jeroen nodded. That was his view, he acknowledged, and Greet's. "But maybe we see that, like you, because we are all Dutch. Though we are enemies, we have a similar political understanding of this country. We Dutch are not fond of bloodshed. Mr. Den Uyl is not fond of bloodshed. We are of one mind on this. But the others . . . Even Carlos." He sighed. Not Ahmed, said Greet. He was loyal to Jeroen; he loved him. But the others . . . Jeroen sighed again. "Because the imperialists did not retaliate when we gave them your Bishop's body, they are sure the imperialists here are weak. If we shoot a hostage, they say, the imperialists will see we are serious and concede us whatever we demand. They say the imperialists will not storm the command post for fear of heavy casualties."

"Among the hostages," Henk corrected. "Again, that was true at the start. But not any more, if *you* kill." Greet interrupted. "They have learned to accept the assurance of casualties. That is the weakness, evidently, of too long confrontation. I have told you so, Jeroen." "And they are stronger," Henk added. "You are only eight. If they lose eight men storming the house, for them it is only unfortunate. But you cannot lose

eight. Even six, even five. Those who do not die will be taken
prisoners. As for us, some will die, but that, too, is only unfortunate. A tragedy, people will say. But that is literature." "They
will not willingly harm the pictures," Jeroen suddenly objected.
"That was true, too, at one time," said Henk. "But no longer,
I imagine. Now, if you force them to strike, they will *hope* not
to harm the pictures. Or only a few."

"So what do you advise? An action is necessary for the comrades' morale." The Arabs, he said, were failing to grasp the
importance of the second demand, the part, that is, concerning
the NATO forces. They were interested only in Israel. "We
will be frank with you, Van Vliet de Jonge. Yusuf has been a
problem. He believes that we deceived him, that we promised
to liberate the Israeli prisoners." "And you did not?" "We saw
this idea was invalid, though I confess we had considered it for
a time. To liberate Israeli prisoners, you must strike directly at
Israel. At the outset we believed that world feeling might be
capable of forcing Israel's compliance. But we came to recognize
our error. Solidarity, even among those of the same interests, is
unnatural in the capitalist world. You saw how Washington
sought to block the agreed-on delivery of the paintings. But
Yusuf is too undeveloped to understand this. He suspects we
betrayed the Palestine liberation fighters to enrich ourselves
with Western art."

In any case, Yusuf was a source of disaffection. He was intent
on revising the demands and on starting to kill hostages to
enforce the one close to his heart. "He has a cousin, you must
know, that the Israelis are torturing." And he had half won
over Hussein. "But the Germans?" That was different, Jeroen
said. The Germans and Carlos, more developed politically,
were in full agreement with the demands as they stood. But
they, too, were arguing that it was time to kill a first hostage.
"So you are outnumbered." "Not altogether. Among themselves, the comrades disagree on the timing and order of the
executions. The German comrades prefer to go slow and to
start with you, Deputy. The Arab comrades would start with
the Jewish woman." Henk felt himself turn pale. "You need
not be afraid," Greet said with a smile. "This dissension means
that we are still masters. But you must offer us a solution."

There was no solution, Henk thought, and, before long,

Jeroen would see that. The woman already knew. Surrender with promise of safe-conduct might still be acceptable to the authorities but not any longer to the comrades, he judged from what he had heard. Some, at least, among them were on a suicidal course. In his clever planning—admirable, the touch of the German "television team" that the *boer* had told of!—Jeroen had overlooked the time factor. For all concerned, this had gone on too long. Nevertheless he pondered. If there was no visible solution, there could be an immediate alternative that would take the edge off their hunger for executions. A substitute could be offered, as in an old story. Instead of a hostage, why not a painting? One not sufficiently "priceless" to seem a flagrant provocation. A Marie Laurencin? As he spoke the words, he felt a strange sorrow, as though he were condemning a frail living thing—a moth or butterfly—to death.

Jeroen and Greet nodded. He had chosen well. "We shall tell the comrades that this is our decision." The door opened. Horst and Elfride entered. "Ah," said Horst in German, "you are instructing the prisoner to tape an appeal? Excellent!" Henk closed his eyes. He had hoped to avoid that stupid imperative. But the Germans, evidently, had been conferring too. They had decided that a plea from the deputy might work as well, for the time being, as an execution; finding him there persuaded them that the other two had come to the same conclusion. Henk shrugged and looked at Jeroen. It could have no effect on The Hague, but, if Jeroen wanted it, he would do it. He had enlisted, he saw, as Jeroen's ally and Greet's in their contest with their own dissident elements. That was the result of having been taken into their confidence; he would do whatever would help them. An hour ago, if ordered to tape an appeal, he would have cheerfully refused, not desiring to sound like a fool or a coward to his governmental colleagues. And when it became known that he had made a tape for transmission—should that be Jeroen's will—his fellow-hostages would be surprised and shocked. They would not have expected that of him. Even if he did not immediately tell them what he had done, there would be no way of concealing the fact from them: tonight he would be back on the screen—still campaigning or talking with the Queen in her feathers at the opening of Parliament—as his craven words were registered on the sound track. He felt sad in advance for Sophie. She would not know what led him to it; that a majority of the *kapers* had been calling for executions was a fearsome thing he must keep from her.

"And what, pray, am I to beg of my government?" Acceptance, of course, of the second demand. "You will add," said Elfride, "that if they fail to give a positive response, acts of justice from our side will commence." Jeroen met his eyes; he, too, shrugged. This must mean that he, too, saw the futility of it. "You will state in your own words what the comrades require." In the end, the tape was dispensed with. With the four standing over him, he sat in a chair and spoke directly to the short-wave radio. Though the idiot words were shaming, when he had finished, he felt satisfied, rather proud. He had been careful to keep his voice light to obviate the suspicion that he had been tortured or drugged.

Horst and Elfride went out. Jeroen and Greet remained with the radio. "You expect a response?" said Henk. "You ironize, Van Vliet de Jonge," Jeroen answered, without hostility. "You do not believe there will be one." "In any case, negative. I have told you why already. Nothing has changed." "I would like to hear again," Greet said. Wearily, Henk repeated the arguments demonstrating the impossibility of the second demand. As he spoke, he felt compunction for Jeroen; if finally he was convincing him, brute force of reason was killing a long-held dream. He was sorry for that; it would have been wonderful if the brave fellow, single-handed and by sheer persistence, could have taken the Lowlands out of NATO. He would have gone down in the national annals like William the Silent or the boy with his finger in the dike. "You have only your will on your side, Jeroen. Den Uyl has reality—the power of circumstances. *His* individual will does not count. You see a battle of wills but you are wrong. It is your single will against the inertia of facts. Holland will not send the NATO forces away unless many facts change and evolve, of their own weight, independently." The woman was nodding. Jeroen only stared at the silent radio. He drew a deep breath. "It is exercise time," he said. "You will go out with the others, Van Vliet de Jonge. And you also, Greet. Everyone must have exercise today. I order it."

Henk's conscience misgave him. Jeroen's voice was dull; there was the lead of despair in it, and his arms hung heavily by his sides. With a violent gesture, he had turned off the radio. It had been wrong to discourage the dream without offering something in its place. "Look, Jeroen, here is another thought. Why not sensibly ask for a food drop? They will accept, because of the hostages, and the mood of your comrades will soften. Hungry men are prone to mutiny. Then we can think together of what is to be done." "He is right, Jeroen," said Greet with a sigh. Jeroen smiled. "Thank you. You are a man of good will. I have seen that. It is a pity that your lot has been cast with the class enemy. Yes, we will consider, as you say, what is to be done. Yet if we give up our second demand, what is left? Nothing." Henk was silent. "You have not killed anyone," he said finally. "That is in your favor." "If we surrender, you imply. . . ." "He implies that the imperialists will allow us safe-conduct out of the country," said Greet. "Since you've committed no capital crime," Henk agreed. "It is likely that they will concede that, yes," said Jeroen. "But to Yusuf and Hussein unbelievable. They have another mentality." "With food, they may be less suspicious," Henk argued. "And you can impress on them that many capitals will be proud to receive your band, now that you are famous." "Thank you. While you are having exercise, I shall be thinking." He moved to the door. "Carlos!"

Only Ahmed remained behind, to be with Jeroen. He would not be dissuaded. It was a sunny cold afternoon. They saw a flock of snow buntings around the house, and in the field near the canal the binoculars showed them mallards walking in pairs, like couples on a Sunday outing. "And it *is* Sunday," cried Aileen. "Isn't that funny? Do you suppose they know it?" Henk welcomed her chatter. "You were in there a long time," Sophie had said to him as he was helping her on with her coat. "What was it?" "I was advising them to ask for a food drop." "Oh, glory. And will they do it?" "I don't know. Jeroen is thinking." They walked briskly in threes and twos—Sophie with Henk and Jim, Aileen with Archie and the dominie, Horst and Elfride with Carlos, Denise with Greet, Hussein and Yusuf bringing up the rear. "We look like a procession," Aileen called out. "It's the first time, isn't it, that so many have been out together. I wonder what it means." Henk wondered too. Any departure from custom had a significance, they had learned. It was the first time, also, that Greet had left the house, and evidently she did not feel easy.

"We shall return now," she announced abruptly, seizing Denise's arm and wheeling about. Cries of protest arose. "Oh, Greet, that's not fair," remonstrated Aileen. "Jeroen *said* we were to have thirty minutes. We all heard him. And we've only been out ten." "Another five," pleaded the pastor. "It's such a wonderful day. You need the fresh air, Greet. It'll put roses in your cheeks." Greet did not bother to answer. With big strides, almost running and pulling Denise along, she was on her way back to the house. "What's got into her?" said Archie. "She's gone white as tallow." "She's jealous of the Vermeer," Aileen said. "Haven't you noticed? She hates it when he shuts himself up with it." But suddenly, as if stampeded, they were all rushing toward the house, Greet in the lead and the Germans just behind her. Henk felt Yusuf's rifle at his back and irritably pulled away. He and Sophie were the last into the shed. As they stumbled in—Sophie's boots were bothering her—they heard a fearful yell: Jeroen. "*Uitstappt!*" "Get out!" "Berserk," estimated Archie. They could not see Jeroen, but those ahead —who could, apparently—were turning back in a rout, choking the narrow entry hall, when the first explosion came. A second explosion followed, then a third. Wood and plaster were falling. As if transfixed, Henk watched the profile of a painted stag's head with a big baleful eye alight on his own head; he brushed it off. His last action—at any rate, that he remembered—was flinging himself on Sophie, to shield her from a huge piece of jagged glass that was hurtling toward them through the air. Then something—a timber or window frame—hit his skull with a loud crack, and he "knew no more."

Envoi

AILEEN and Frank were taking the plane—KLM—to New York. They had been the only ones to survive without serious injury when Jeroen blew himself and the house up. Most had been killed instantly: Jeroen and Greet, Archie and the Senator, the Germans, Carlos, Denise. Two of the Arabs had died from burns before they could be evacuated; the cookstove, run on propane, had caught fire. Ahmed had died two days later in the hospital; his lung had been punctured by a falling joist, and transfusions could not save him. Sophie was in a *kliniek*, having lost an arm. Henk was at home now, still in bed; he had had a concussion and gone into deep coma. For a time it had been feared that his brain, if he lived, would be affected. He had also lost a good deal of blood from splinters of glass that had pierced his neck and hands and had had to be removed by surgery.

He and Sophie had been unconscious and bleeding badly when the military were finally able to enter what was left of the house, in time to put out the fire, which had spread beyond the kitchen to the entry hall and was just licking at the stairway. Frank and Aileen, making their way through the debris, had found the two of them under a pair of children's bicycles before the guardsmen came and had not known what to do: whether it would be more dangerous to move them or to wait for help. They had lifted the bicycles off them and waited, with Frank praying his heart out and Aileen counting to a hundred, while they smelled the smoke and listened to the nearing crackle of the fire. Outside there was nothing but rubble, which had had to be partly cleared before the stretchers could enter. All the pictures had been blown to pieces, except for Lily's water-colors—though sections of the floor had caved in, the upstairs was not much damaged, apart from broken windows. In the yard, even the chickens had perished. Yet Frank and Aileen, though dazed and shaken and temporarily deafened, had emerged with only superficial cuts and bruises. They had been strong enough to visit the mortuary and identify the bodies, and Frank, after a physical, had been allowed to give a pint of blood to Ahmed.

Identifying the bodies had been an ordeal they could not yet describe. Some were horribly dismembered; they had known Jim Carey principally by his silver hair. Yet Jeroen, who had been at the very center of the explosions, as if in the eye of a hurricane, had hardly been touched, so far as one could see. His glasses had been broken, and his chest had been crushed by a beam, but that was not visible under the sheet. On the slab he looked peaceful, though he must have died in a fury of rage, because his orders had been disobeyed.

They had learned from Ahmed what had happened. In the hospital he had been too weak to have visitors, but he had talked to them on the medical helicopter that had come to take the living to Amsterdam. And he must have talked to the police at some point, since the whole story was in the papers. Frank and Aileen had read it in the *Herald Tribune* and in the London *Times* while staying at the house of the U.S. Consul General, who had contrived to keep the press away. They had brought copies to Sophie, for when she would be up to reading about it; the amputation had caused her a great deal of pain, and she was still under sedation. The stories had carried all their pictures and a drawing of the interior of the house showing the wiring system and where the fuses had been. The *Times* had found an old photo of Greet in her KLM hostess uniform, just like the two girls today. But they did not have a good picture of Jeroen.

In the medical helicopter, Ahmed had been very sad. It was not just that so many lives had been wasted, though he was sorry about his comrades and had shed tears when he heard about the Senator, who had encouraged him to recite Arab poetry. Rather, it was that he had wanted to die himself— a warrior's death—with Jeroen. Jeroen, he said, had not decided on the spur of the moment. He had been thinking of it for a long time. He had not told Ahmed, but Ahmed had known. He had come upon him one day in the parlor with the detonator—no bigger than a little pencil—in his hands, sitting there quietly with the Vermeer. But even if Ahmed had not seen the detonator, he would have understood what was in

Jeroen's mind. Greet had begun to guess too, he thought, because she loved him, though with a woman's love, which was more interfering than a brother's. She had always mistrusted the paintings. Bending to catch Ahmed's words, Aileen and Frank had nodded. It must have been a sudden suspicion that had driven her back to the house that fatal afternoon, to frustrate Jeroen's design.

He had planned to die alone with the "Girl" he had fallen in love with—like a bride, Ahmed said. After the others had gone out walking, he had sent Ahmed away too, ordering him to follow them and not linger around the house. But Ahmed had been determined to die with him; it was a privilege he wanted for himself which the others would not share. He had crept back through the front entrance, which no one used, and observed Jeroen's arrangements: the time device ticking to activate the battery, and the sticks of dynamite wired to the joists as usual—Yusuf had tested the wiring, as a matter of routine, that morning. Hiding in the pantry, Ahmed had known that he would not have long to wait; Jeroen would have timed the blast to allow ten or perhaps fifteen minutes for the others to be well away. But Greet, woman-like, had destroyed her man's plan and herself as well. Absorbed in his thoughts, Jeroen could not have noticed them returning across the field. The first Ahmed knew of it, in the windowless pantry, had been the sound of voices, a door banging, and in the same moment, a fierce startled yell from Jeroen. Yelling angrily in Dutch, he had sought to drive them back, out of the house, where they had no business. But they had not understood, losing valuable seconds in mystification, though in fact that had not mattered. It had been too late anyway.

"I can't get that picture out of my mind," Frank confided as they unfastened their seat belts. "Him standing there with that wild look and his arm raised, to expel us, like the angel with the flaming sword, at Eden's gate, you know. It was all so darned Biblical." "Lot's wife," Aileen said. "Greet. Turning around in that field to look back. Lot's wife was disobedient too. A pillar of salt. Could you *face* Greet's remains in that mortuary? Barely identifiable." Frank shook his head to dispel the memory. "I keep thinking of Samson, Aileen. I guess that comes the closest to our big strapping fellow. . . ." "Pulling down the temple," she agreed. "On himself and all the Philistines. But Jeroen didn't *intend* to kill anybody but himself. I think we have to accept that. Himself and the pictures. It was more like suttee in a way."

The hostesses circulated menus. "I still don't understand what drove him to take his life," Frank resumed after a cursory look. Henk, they had discovered, took the blame on himself. When they had visited him—sitting up in bed and mournfully eating a piece of smoked eel—he had told them about his last interview with Jeroen. Even then, it seemed, he had sensed that he was doing wrong to make him see that their enterprise had no future. It was true, but he should not have demonstrated it, not at that juncture, when Jeroen's own people had been turning against him. He had let his love of reasoning carry him away. Frank had tried to reassure him: according to Ahmed, Jeroen was going to blow himself up anyway. Henk had been interested to hear that, but he still held himself responsible; whatever Jeroen's intentions, their talk had been the precipitating cause. "You think you triggered it," Aileen had summed up. He did not take to her verb, Henk had answered, making a wry face, but, yes, he was persuaded that the impulse to sudden action had come from him. Despair—the ultimate sin against the Holy Ghost—had resolved Jeroen, and he had been the source; he had despaired *for* Jeroen, and Jeroen had known it. He had not had the right to take hope away.

"It was peculiar, Reverend," Aileen said now. "I suppose he can't help blaming himself for Sophie's arm. He hasn't seen the poor girl yet, of course. But, aside from that, from the way he talked I almost got the feeling that he *sympathized* with his *kapers* and their project. As though he grieved for them and wished for their own sake that he hadn't disillusioned them. That's crazy. You have to take hope away from dangerous criminals, show them they can't win, don't you?" Frank guessed that was true. "But Henk's conscience may tell him that he should have added some positive suggestion. I wonder myself why they never thought of surrender. Wouldn't that have been the logical thing?" "You've said that before," Aileen reminded him. "But I don't see Jeroen as the type to surrender. Can you picture him marching out with a white flag? And the Arabs were planning to kill us all anyway—the *kamikaze* idea. Henk said so. If Jeroen had tried to surrender, they would have started shooting, don't you see? I wish we'd asked Ahmed about that."

"The *needlessness* of the slaughter," Frank continued after a moment. "I keep coming back to that. It must trouble Henk too. I gather he feels that if Jeroen had been left to himself he might have planned his own destruction better, not to endanger other lives." "He tried. We have to give him that," said Aileen. "He put too much faith in technology," Frank decided. "Modern man. I ask myself, Aileen, why didn't he use a plain old-fashioned gun? That rifle of his. I wish somebody would clarify that for me." Aileen sighed. "Here they come with the cart. Let's order a drink." "You mean I ought to use my imagination," said the Reverend. "But I'm a down-to-earth sort of cuss, if you can believe it of a man of my calling. In temporal affairs I have to have my *i*'s dotted and my *t*'s crossed." "Ahmed explained it," she said. "As much as anyone can. He empathized with Jeroen."

"*C'était un poète, madame*," the poor Arab, very dignified, had told her in the helicopter, choking out the words as he tried to raise himself on the stretcher. They had not realized then what had happened to his lung. He meant, apparently, that Jeroen had designed a poetic end for himself, like a Viking's funeral. He had intended to go down with his ship ablaze. "*Il fallait tout détruire.*" All his plunder. "*C'était un homme du Nord, vous savez. Je l'aimais beaucoup. Je l'ai compris. Même sa deuxième demande.*" To a Palestinian, she could see, NATO was not all that important, but Ahmed had gone along, knowing that to Jeroen his second demand meant everything. "*Mais les tableaux, Ahmed. Pourquoi?*" Like a muezzin, he repeated: "*Il fallait tout détruire, tout sacrifier.*" But Jeroen had loved the pictures, she protested, or at least the Vermeer. Why, then, destroy them? One must sacrifice what one loves, Ahmed had answered. "*Le geste sublime d'un grand révolutionnaire.*" Blood rose to his lips; he spat and before their eyes lost consciousness, falling back onto the stretcher.

The hostess reached across the Reverend and set a bourbon on Aileen's tray, beside a plastic glass filled with ice-cubes. "Civilization," Aileen commented, winking back a tear. "Poor Ahmed. I grieve for him, I must say." She unscrewed the little bottle. "He was the only one in the end who didn't want to kill us. Not counting Jeroen and Greet, of course. *That* was a surprise, wasn't it? I mean, the change in Greet." "We were all changed, Aileen. Don't you sense it in yourself?" She considered. "Not really." She raised her eyes to his and lifted her glass. "Cheers. No, I don't feel changed and, frankly, I don't notice any difference in you. We're the same as ever. Maybe that says something. We're the ones that nothing happened to, physically or morally."

He was startled. His face fell. "That's a harsh judgment, Aileen. And a snap judgment. You'll learn better when you've digested this experience. I'm still struggling to encompass it myself. Maybe we both have a bit of 'survivor guilt,' which in your case leads you to fear that there may be a lack of depth in yourself if you're alive and well when the others—" "There *is* a lack of depth and in you, too. Well, we have to live with that. We're two-dimensional, Reverend." "But, Aileen, surely you feel sorrow." "Not much. Only superficially, like with our cuts. Yet you could say"—she laughed—"that I lost two matrimonial prospects in the great explosion. Did you know Archie was a widower? His wife died of cirrhosis of the liver. An alcoholic, isn't that terrible?" "But who was the other? Why, good heavens, you must mean Jim. A great tragedy, that, and for the country. He had so much to give." "He'd given it," she said shortly. "There was nothing left. It was obvious. That page had already turned."

Frank felt chilled. Women of her age with the misfortune of being childless could have an unnecessarily bald way of passing judgment. They drank for a time in silence. "After lunch," said Aileen, brightening, "shall we look at Sophie's journal? There's not much left of it, but it will help pass the time." Pages from Sophie's notebook had been found in the rubble, blown to the four winds; the authorities had come upon a few, semi-intact, in the rabbit run. They had been turned over to Sophie after Aileen had identified them. "Poor Sophie," Aileen said. "She wanted me to destroy them. But I made her see that they constituted a valuable document. Somebody might want to use them for a history of terrorism or she might use them herself if she decided to write a book about the polder events." "That could be a good project for her," Frank admitted. "If it didn't stir up too many memories . . . With her handicap, I suppose she can dictate." "I told her that. But she wants to be re-educated to do everything with her left hand; she even thinks she can learn to type with it." "They have special keyboards," Frank remembered. "So much is done nowadays to help victims of accidents to adjust to the machines we all depend on." "Well, she's brave," Aileen said. "Wasn't it strange to hear her laugh about the wooden arm she'd get with movable fingers?" Frank thought that she had been on a "high" that day from the opium or whatever it was they gave her: she had also spoken, gaily, of designing bathing dresses for herself that would have balloon sleeves and full skirts to go with them—she had always loved swimming, she told them.

The original of the journal was in Aileen's briefcase. Sophie, on her "high," had offered to donate it to the Lucy Skinner library, and Aileen had taken her up on it. A photostat was going home to Connecticut with Sophie's parents. There was nothing intimate in it, Aileen said; she had seen that when she identified it for the police. It had looked like a mixture of scraps of overheard conversations and Sophie's own thoughts. Many pages had been lost; others were too tattered and stained—with water and probably blood—to be legible to anyone but Sophie. Yet of course it could not fail to be interesting to those who had lived through the events. When the trays had been cleared off, Aileen got it out. "Now here's some conversation." They bent over the sheets.

E.   You never miss a chance to make fun of us for being capitalists.

C.   A missionary to the heathen, that is my role. My upbringing and tastes, you see, didn't fit me for evangelizing the masses.

E.   . . . made his first killing in pharmaceuticals. Squibb bought him out because he had a corner in one of those mycin drugs . . . money he borrowed from friends in local rackets. . . . They had a pool, and Harold was the brains. But if some baby was dying and couldn't get the drug because Harold was pushing the price up?

C.   My dear, it doesn't do to dwell on the origin of a fortune. . . . Some are older than others so that the smell of the buried bodies isn't so fresh. My own small holdings go back to the textile mills—horridly sweated immigrant labor, mostly Portuguese. One could even say that the newer money is somewhat cleaner.

E. (brightening)   Do you really think so? But you have so much culture. It frightens me to hear you talk sometimes. I feel so ignorant and inferior. And I know that Chaddie and I can never catch up. It's no use for him to own the Cézannes and me my poor Marie Laurencins—very unadventurous of me. I ought to branch out but I'm afraid to. Owning them doesn't give us any real satisfaction except for Chaddie's ego. What's the use of owning them if you don't know what to say about them when people come to see the collection. You feel you don't own them at all. You just have them there for other people to look at. Chaddie doesn't have the time of course, but I've been to art appreciation courses in our museum. It's a woman's job to understand art. Division of labor, he says. But I appreciated the pictures more before I took the courses. They only made me feel stupid. For instance, our teacher said that Cézanne was a bad draughtsman and tried to illustrate it with a pointer in that "Man with a Pipe." I couldn't see what he meant and when I went home and told Harold he was furious and said I could drop the course. I guess if I'd been able to tell him why Cézanne was a bad drawer he would have been even madder. When I do learn anything in the class he says I sound like a parrot.

C.   Mmm.

E.   . . . want Harold to turn over the Cézannes to them. They don't care about my Laurencins. Do you think he should agree? No, I shouldn't ask you. For you it's not the same. When I listen to you talk, I have the feeling that you own art with your mind. It won't make any difference to you if you have to turn over your collections. You'll still own them in your head, the way you do masses of things that don't belong to you, that you've just seen once, in a museum or somewhere. But Harold and I wouldn't. If he lets them have the Cézannes, that's it. He'll have nothing to have any pride in any more. Though in a way it would be a relief. Let me tell you, he actually bragged to me because they wanted his Cézannes and not my things. He said it proved he had more taste.

C.   In your Harold's place . . .

"That's all of that," Aileen said. "I wonder when it was. Now here's a different bit."

Mrs. Tallboys (gracious). Are you related to the rose? A lovely
old pink climber. You don't find it any more in the catalogues.
Dr. Van Fleet. Mother had it on a trellis outside the library
door. . . . F-l-e-e-t.

"That was much earlier," Aileen decided. "I'm surprised to see
she was keeping the diary then. Well, you don't need to read it.
We all heard it anyway. What made Sophie write it down? She
seems to have been fascinated by those people. But I wouldn't
think they'd make good copy, would you? But here's something about you. 'F. keeps wanting to have serious discussion
of terrorism.'" But the rest of the page was gone.

"Let's look at her own thoughts. We *know* pretty much what
the rest of us said but we don't know what she was thinking. I
always wondered what was going on in that head." "Should
we?" "I told you, there's nothing private. Not a word about
her and Henk. And, after all, she *gave* me the journal. If it
worries you, we can stop. There's quite a long stretch here
without any stains or torn parts. See, it starts with me."

Aileen's question: what can art "do" for you, can it make
you a better person, etc.? To the second part, evidently not.
Collectors, dealers, museum people, art experts worse class of
person generically than dentists or plumbers, say. Was it always
so? Probably. Isabella d'Este, François Ier, Medici popes. Leave
reasons for this aside for the moment and consider first part of
the question. Does art have *any* effect on person who lives with
it? Yes, it may. "Rub-off" from constant exposure to beauty
can develop taste, e.g., Lily. That is, teach the art of acquisition. The "connoisseur" merely a highly trained consumer.
"Lily has an eye," "Johnnie has an eye," they say of each other.
Eye an organ of appropriation: Charles. A sensitized eye may
make up for slender means; tastefulness substitutes for money.
But all this essentially a circular process—familiar association
with beauty enables one to recognize, i.e., seize on, more of
the same. Ownership of works of a. qualifies a set of well-to-do
persons—at any rate in principle—to be "discriminating"; to
that point, it's educational. *Great* means not strictly necessary,
may even be a handicap: millionaire's eye can afford be "lazy,"
relying on pack of seeing-eye dogs—Berenson, Duveen—to
do work for it. But for collector *some* means or family history

of them v. important. Art and wealth boon companions. Sad but so.

Returning to second half of A.'s question, isn't that part of the reason that experts, dealers, curators, fall into same bag as collectors—like them, snobs, reactionaries, materialists? Even poor Warren has itch for spending names, pathetic triviality. His specialization means corrupting contact w. trustees, donors, etc., as on this journey. Lives "high" when w. his Croesuses, gets familiar, over-familiar, w. butlers, limousines, first-class travel, w'd surely have been presented to Shah & Madam Shah. At home a church mouse and must feel contempt for ignorance of most trustees, donors, he fated to accompany to view treasures. V. bad for character. "Servants of art" form obsequious priestly caste.

Yet perennial association of art and wealth not whole explanation of seeming evil effect of art on moral fiber of its devotees. Visual art (see above) excites cupidity, desire to possess, also touch, finger—my mother a trial on chateau tours; exclusive enjoyment everybody's dream. Strange this should be so? Concerts and stage plays v. different. Communal. Who would want to be sole audience for symphony or stage play? If no one else in hall, w'd be sorry for actors and musicians. But no one wishes to share painting & statuary w. mob of strangers. My ideal: to be alone in Venice Accademia or w. chosen friend. Perhaps problem is that visual beauty always incorporated in an object (Rev. Frank deplores). How share an object between many in limited span of time? Judgment of Solomon. Books? Must be alone—or undisturbed anyway—to read a book. But a book, though an object, exists in the plural; no displeasure felt if others are reading it at identical moment.

Back to A.'s question, first part. Put it another way: can an aesthete ever be a good man? Strongly doubt it. Cf. Kierkegaard on inferiority of aesthetic to ethical. H. says pronounced Kerkegor.

Artist himself not aesthete. Workman, rather. Artists notorious for lacking taste. Able appreciate "hand" of fellow-craftsman or predecessor, but taste prerogative of amateur. Artist often unrefined, rough individual; unlike his product, out of place in collector's salon.

Sophie! Are you saying art is good for nothing? In fact bad, like radium, for people regularly exposed to it? V. bright and clever, but you know better. True, if you judge art by human types attracted by its "aura," you're bound to condemn it. But forget collectors and other parasitic growths on the noble tree.

What about works of art—the Parthenon—that have always belonged to general realm of onlookers, gods, supposedly, and men? Frescoes in churches and statues standing in public squares. Cathedrals. Skyscrapers. Whoever commissioned them —cardinals or Seagrams or the city fathers—by now they're part of the social fabric. Surely they're art as it was meant to be. Sacred artifacts owned by nobody and by everybody that passes by. A lot of them (Chartres) visible from a long way off. But they can be tucked away in a cloister (Moissac) or even in an oratory shown you by an old nun. The point is, they've become assimilated to whole family of natural objects—mountain ranges, harbors, stands of trees—that have settled down to live with us too. Of course they "do" something for human community; they're pillars holding it up. But also living members. Come to be seen often as protectors, esp. in old cities. Like lares and penates of Roman house. Perhaps represent eternity, on account of remarkable endurance. Anyway they "concentrate the mind wonderfully," as Dr. J. said of hanging. And there's no question of taste, fine discrimination, involved. Everyone understands they're wondrous without being told. Cf. the first rainbow a child sees. With them it doesn't matter whether their "owners"—clerics or Union Carbide—notice they're there or pass them by oblivious most of the time. Here "just part of the furniture" no sacrilege as no religion of art involved. Not there to be worshipped by idolatrous possessor but to be lived among by the many. In fact the term "art" may be out of place in this context. Art merely the medium, the element, by which the sacred, i.e., the extraordinary, is conveyed.

Written in another hand across the bottom of the page was "You romance." She must have showed the journal to Henk. The next entry—probably some pages were missing—had no connection with art.

> . . . These very different from guerrillas I've interviewed. Except Carlos. I almost feel I know him. Hussein & Yusuf wary, a bit like some of the Laos I visited in their cave "command post." But more hostile. Of course circumstances different; in Laos I was treated as a "friendly." Bolivia too. And my old friends in the mountains saw themselves as patriots bent on liberating their country—a limited objective.
>
> A. keeps calling "*kapers*" fanatics. Yes, but what does it mean? 90% of the population is a fanatic: look at "Chaddie," who's

less of a collector's piece than I like to think. Frank is a fanatic on keeping an open mind. Wish we had a dictionary so I could see what word comes from. "She's a fanatic for neatness"; same as French *maniaque*. Doctrinal fervor certainly implied, which gives a chill to others. Yet Jeroen not particularly insistent on strict observance except in vocabulary: "imperialists," "people's army," "people's court." Vocabulary his hair shirt. Or monastic "habit." Otherwise quite open to reason. Ahmed a doll. Fanaticism linked to abstinence. Abstention from alcohol, tobacco, sex, forbidden books, forbidden thoughts. *There's* the distinction: H. and J. not madly tolerant but enjoy thinking, take pleasure in play of their minds. Jeroen's hair-shirt vocabulary keeps his mind pure of thought. But he's intelligent, H. says, so must have temptations. But I suspect he takes the urge out in planning; planning comes from his will, and his mind then gets a permit to exercise. True of any puritan; revolutionaries today as the last puritans. Do he and Greet have sex? H. and J. think not any more.

A gap followed; then she was writing about museums.

Problem of art for the masses. Museum = private collection opened to public at certain hours & under certain depressing conditions. Public there on sufferance, unwelcomed, continually watched and chided. Guards' happiest hour ten minutes before closing time when they can start throwing people out. Note difference between this and usual attitude of sacristan or verger, eager to open and explain. Must distinguish between the many & the masses. Many good, masses n.g. Museum is crowd-drawer and conceives mission as such. Attendance figures plotted on rising graph. Growth statistics, cf. industry. Greater growth, less individual member of crowd can see what he came to look at. Most drawn by curiosity anyway; museum promotion, presence of guards, searches, no briefcases or umbrellas, locked cases & cabinets, restraining cords to hold public back all convey thought of museum as fantastic treasure trove. People flock to see treasure.

Since undemocratic restrict attendance to so-called qualified persons, solution would be to get art out of museums whenever possible. Malraux had right idea when he took "valuable" statues out of Louvre and set them up on the grass, where any bus-rider can look at them: traffic jams become boon. Evidently this not possible w. paintings. But lots c'd be returned to point of origin—churches, monasteries, town halls, shrines. Sh'd apply to other works too, e.g., Elgin Marbles. Interesting w'd be to "unmake" Barnard Cloisters, repatriating component parts. Such a reparations policy (aegis UNESCO?) w'd have same appeal as returning Maine to Indians. Suggest it to Senator as campaign plank for '76: promising vote loser. But it w'd be just and bring about much needed redistribution of art works. Not only Europe; Asia & Africa w'd benefit. Could Jeroen add it to demands? All right, a whimsy, but *something* will have to be done soon, as w. pollution. Decentralization the watchword. As for educating schoolchildren, what was wrong with copies and casts?

The other hand had inserted a question: "The horses of San Marco?" And Sophie had put in her answer: "They can stay."

Special problems w. modern art. Went from painter's studio to dealer or straight to collector. Hard to find a "home" to return it to. Artists' studios torn down. But statuary—Arp & Brancusi —sh'd be placed somewhere outdoors, where it can have air around it and breathe. Henry Moore "King and Queen" & other big pieces "naturalized" like daffodils in Hampshire landscape. Why not more "earth sculptures"? America big enough & empty enough to accommodate whole cities of sculpture, esp. in the desert. Great Salt Lake? Dakota badlands. Stonehenge c'd give hints.

Again pages seemed to be missing. Then came two—bloodstained but partly legible—that Aileen remembered watching Sophie write.

Friday. Lily's pictures came today. Show perfect taste, like everything about her, including her name—Tallboys. She was born Bocock, I learned. *Re* her water-colors, I mean not just that they're exquisite in themselves but that they show restraint in her as a collector. Somehow it's proper to collect water-colors—not grabby. Anybody has the right to own a few. Some limit like that ought to have been respected in collecting. Maybe in her case it just a happy accident because she's poorer than the others. Johnnie's collection rather appealing; at least it reflects his interests. But private collections . . . Must go public. Happening anyway. A few c'd be maintained as illustrations of history of taste. Preferably in little castles & hunting lodges . . . But without guards—only guides & not too many. Identification of art with lucre to be discouraged. Then fewer tourists w'd come in bus loads to see it. (Did I write that before?)

Correction. "Art & money boon companions." Holds mainly for easel paintings & things like reliquaries, drinking cups, etc. Things which actually were a species of furniture. Furniture (*meubles*, *meubelen* in Dutch, H. says) movable by definition. Frescoes, monumental sculpture, bas-reliefs, altar panels, town-halls paintings are stable, cemented into place & time. Celebrations, *vide* triumphal arches. Lots carted off in war . . . pillage. But that felt as desecration, contrary to original intention. Whereas church vessels & easel paintings almost "made" to be stolen.

4 p.m. L. and B. left. Still light. Days getting longer.

The remainder of the page and the succeeding ones were badly torn and defaced. "No use trying to read those," Aileen said, unexpectedly bringing her handkerchief to her eyes. "But here she is, still writing about art. Do you want to go on? We'd better hurry. They're going to show the movie."

. . . dissatisfied my distinction mobile vs. stable despite germ of truth. Try art as treasure vs. art as celebration. Easel paintings treasure, hoarded by owner for solitary enjoyment. Cf. Jeroen w. "Girl." Find that disturbing but "Girl" disturbing too. Wonder if I'd want to live with her. She *too* compelling, like "Mona Lisa." Doubt she w'd be "good" for one in long run. "Feasting" one's eyes: miser's banquet. Mme. Cézanne better for soul—piece of Nature. Cézanne atypical as easel painter; hence failure in own time. Yet whole museum effect here uncanny. We forced to live w. paintings. As punishment? "Girl" consummate example of sin of West; fetish of art as commodity—denial of Marx labor theory of value. Troublemaker maybe. Arabs don't like her. Upset by pictures here. Islam forbids images. But what about figures in carpets? Only animals, I guess. Awful no books to consult, but awful we so dependent on books. Punishments inflicted here weirdly suited to our bourgeois crimes: forced feeding w. art, deprivation of books, esp. dictionaries, encyclopedias, histories—West's cabbala. I feel it as lesson.

She appeared to have let several days pass before the next entry.

Today Ash Wednesday, Frank tells us. Fast and pray. We fasting all right; *kapers* too—no distinction made. Must collect thoughts again. Ask self central question: why Jeroen wanted pictures. Well, good "investment" for him; improve bargaining position. But also lend artistry to design—flourish of mockery of capitalist values. Yet much ambivalence in him, surely. Loving the thing you hate. You hate it because you love it. In an evil world—"system," he w'd call it—the beautiful gets ugly, like a fallen angel, and must be cast out if fresh start to be made. Yet God loved Lucifer better than all the others.

Thinking this, I am sorry for Jeroen. Greet too. I almost wish them luck. Idealists, I know, are dangerous, but the claim of the ideal (Ibsen) has to be felt or else. . . . Or else the world, our deteriorating world, will continue on its course by sheer inertia. Inertia is taking over, right here; you can sense it. The effort persists but only of its own momentum, beyond Jeroen's control, I think. He must act soon somehow to end that. And Henk's *marechaussee* out there—the reality principle—don't have to act. Only wait. Oh, dear. What can happen? I w'd give an arm, as they say, if this thing could end grandly, the way Jeroen w'd wish, whatever that is by now.

"Good Lord!" Frank smote his brow. "Very chilling," agreed Aileen. The hostesses had been pulling the blinds to darken the cabin. Now the lights were switched off. "That's all there is anyway," Aileen said. "Do you think that was the last thing she wrote? Well, let's not dwell on it. Too painful. At least she's alive." In the dark, she shook down the sheets of the journal. She must have sensed that Frank's shoulders were heaving, for she waited. Then she went on in her usual bright voice, as if kindly not noticing the fight he had been having with his emotions.

"I was hoping she'd put down more about terrorism, weren't you? She actually fell for it, that's clear from the end. But it would have been interesting if she'd analyzed the state of mind that brought her to that point. Nobody's going to care about her views on art. Pure Radcliffe term paper—all the right references, with the obligatory New Left twist. Poor Sophie. That isn't her field." "What?" said Frank. "Oh, sorry. I was thinking about Gus. It's funny how it hits you. Something about those torn pages set it off maybe. But you were saying that art wasn't Sophie's forte, wasn't that it?" "Never mind, Frank." "No, it's good to keep our brains occupied. But about art and Sophie, I'm really no judge, Aileen. I must say, though, I was impressed by how much she knew. Her European background maybe. This has been my first trip abroad." She gave a little screech and patted his arm. "Better luck next time."

His shoulders heaved again—with appreciation of the joke. "I must remember that, for my youngsters. 'Father's first trip abroad.'" He had not seen the risible side. But he was laughing too hard; she was eyeing him with concern. "Seriously," he continued, "there was another thing. . . . I was interested in what she had to say about idealists being dangerous. That hit home. I'm a confirmed idealist, as I guess you can tell. And to be honest with you, Aileen, I had a sneaking sympathy for Jeroen myself. You're a bit too hard on Sophie there. I never felt that he and I were all that far apart. If his gifts could have been turned to a more progressive purpose—gradual better-ment of the old society . . . Platitudinous, yet how else can you say it? And we shouldn't be afraid of platitudes. But Henk put his finger on it. You remember, the other day when we visited him and he said that Jeroen had fallen into despair—the ultimate sin against the Holy Ghost? That's true of so many of our young people; they're driven to violence by despair. I see it with the blacks; we must act to give them hope, Aileen." "Do you want to watch the movie or sleep?" she interrupted.

David Niven was on the screen wearing a tropical helmet. He seemed to be in Malaysia or Indonesia, having problems with native guerrillas. They had not rented earphones—Aileen said she never did—but they were able to follow the action quite well. They certainly knew about guerrillas, and watching television plays in Dutch night after night had taught them to do without words. It had been good mental training, the Reverend Frank acknowledged, glad to be reminded of the need to count their rewards.

APPENDIX

The Novels That Got Away

SOMEWHERE on these premises in Paris—along with boxes of old Christmas decorations—or in a trunk in Maine there must be the vestiges of two novels I started and abandoned decades ago. It will be no great loss if they are not exhumed. The first, titled "The Lost Week," was inspired by a descent on Truro, on Cape Cod, by Charlie Jackson, the novelist, in the summer of 1945. Spurred on by friends (the subject was "made for me," they thought), I began it there and then in the first heat of amusement. A satire, it was to be, on the literary life and the thirst for fame, just as dangerous to self-respect as the thirst for alcohol; the protagonist was called Herbert Harper. That is about all I remember, though the manuscript ran to 80 or 90 typed pages.

Better than the manuscript I remember the circumstances of taking it and my typewriter at the very end of that summer by a series of trains and a ferry to Yarmouth in Nova Scotia, where I planned to work for a week without interruption in what I pictured as the Evangeline country. I would put up at an inn or a fisherman's shingled cottage and take solitary walks along the beach to freshen my invention. The reality was rather different. My last view of the sea was from the ferry that took me to Digby. Yarmouth proved to be a desolating commercial town containing banks, insurance companies and a movie house. I stayed at the traveling salesmen's hotel (the only accommodation, I think) and rode up in the elevator and down three times a day to the dining room, where I was eyed without much curiosity by the salesmen with their cases of samples at nearby tables. I spoke to nobody, and nobody spoke to me. After a single frightening foray into the businesslike streets in search of the harbor, which I never found, I stayed all day long in my room like a prisoner sentenced to the typewriter. The room was made up while I was below, eating; the waiter brought me my food with scarcely a look or a word. My sole terse exchanges were with the bank clerk who changed my money and the postal employee who took my telegram when I nerved myself to go out a second time in order to plot my escape.

By a turn of poetic justice, this became my own lost week. On my return, no one, I discovered, believed that I had gone all that way to Nova Scotia to get ahead with a novel: My friends were convinced that there had been a romantic episode, a secret tryst. And I had nothing, finally, to show for it, despite the unusual activity of my typewriter, which had been steadily yielding about 10 pages a day at the command of my weakening will. As I packed them into the suitcase, I already "guessed." I had run out of steam. The novel had ground to a halt, petering out in the middle of a sentence, for all I know. I have never looked to see.

Six or seven years later, in Portsmouth, R. I. (having published "The Oasis" and "The Groves of Academe"), I made another false start. This time the action is laid in New York. The heroine is a young married woman known only as Mrs. Harold Husted—no given name. The tone of the writing is brisk; she is a brisk small person with sandy hair. The story opens in midtown on a fine city morning; she is on the street early, perhaps having taken a child to the school bus. There is a description of early morning sights and sounds—the giant iceman emerging from his cellar, the bakery truck delivering, the milkman. Her crisp little nature loves being out among these other early birds, pioneers of the day—birds of *her* feather, she feels them to be. I can recall only one phrase: "weaving a ribbon of newness through the garment (?) of the day."

But almost at once a disagreeable duty imposes itself. She must find an open drugstore and shut herself up in a phone booth to call her lover. He will still be in bed, of course, soggy with sleep, eyelids gummy, voice rheumy and thick. "Honey," he wheedles, sounding plaintive but nonetheless appeasing. She is repelled, as she is every morning when she has to wake him. But if she does not call him now, it will be too late. She cannot do it from her apartment; her husband is there. She has only this quarter of an hour. Often, as today, she is tempted to forgo letting him know when she will be free; she can put her nickel back into her coin purse and go home. But generally she exerts her will, forcing herself to drop the coin and not to be irritated when he answers. If only he could be up *one* morning, just to please her. He *knows* the burden is on her because he must not call her at home.

Yet why does she go through with this chore? It is a mystery to her. Maybe because it *is* a chore, like cleaning the oven, and she feels duty-bound, as a good person, to conquer her aversion. When she is with him, across a lunch table or in his (still) unmade bed, after a while it wears off. But why must she have a lover at all? He is her first, and yet he has become chronic, like a habit.

The manuscript breaks off in the phone booth, that is, at the familiar lowest moment of Mrs. Harold Husted's day: no more ribbon of newness. Looking back, I think I see why I could not go on. This pitiful cramped version of the eternal triangle is too abstract, too neoclassical, to make a novel. We do not need to know more about the lover or about Mr. Harold Husted, the husband, who for some plausible or implausible reason will still be at home at 9 o'clock in the morning. All we need to know has already been told. Actually this is a short story that should have ended (where it did) in the phone booth. If a student gave me the manuscript, I would tell her that. But I also see something that a teacher of writing would not have been able to guess. Clearly, this fragment is a foreshadowing of "The Group." Though little Mrs. Husted's story does not appear there, her anxious but game spirit has carried over.

But those two were not the only novels I started and then gave up. There was an earlier one, much more ambitious, which no longer exists in any file or trunk, having been—as we would say now—recycled. It was to be a story of treason and divided allegiances. The setting was the Reading Room of the New York Public Library. There, on the odd-numbered side, sat a studious person surrounded by stacks of books, doing research on seemingly diverse subjects that would turn out to be the central matter of the novel itself. The time was contemporary: 1942, the middle of World War II. I myself was sitting at an old rolltop desk, painted white, in Edmund Wilson's house in Wellfleet on Cape Cod. Newly installed in the windows were blackout shades. Among the frequenters of "my" public library reading room would be a number of refugees from Hitler.

The book was to contain three separate narratives, three episodes from history, linked by a common theme. The first had to do with Dumnorix and Diviciacus, the Haeduans, a pair of ill-matched brothers who figured in Caesar's "Gallic Wars": one was loyal, and one was faithless. From Caesar's point of view, evidently. For him, as for Miss Mackay, my Latin teacher at Annie Wright Seminary in Tacoma, there could be no doubt as to which was which. Diviciacus was the good Indian, and Dumnorix the bad Indian. But there was a less Roman way of looking at it, which had become visible to me as I grew up. From a Gaulish point of view, the shifty, oath-breaking Dumnorix was a patriot and the honorable Diviciacus was a traitor, an antique Quisling or mustached puppet of Rome. Overtones of current events were meant to be heard, and yet this (as I now feel) was somewhat misleading.

Certainly the story as told by Caesar was equivocal, capable of being read in opposed senses. But could that be said, really, of Vidkus Quisling if you assigned him an imaginary brother (Gunnar) who fought and died in the Resistance? There was only one way in which I, the author, could see *that* pair. Here, perhaps, was the flaw in the novel that caused it eventually to buckle and fall apart: the contemporary parallels were imperfect. To side with Caesar was no hideous crime; Vercingetorix himself had been Caesar's friend until the pivotal moment came; a Romanized Arvernian, probably speaking some Latin, could well have felt somewhat torn, divided within himself.

Something of the kind proved to be the case of the two Indian sachems, sons of Massasoit—King Philip, as he was called by the English, and his brother known as Alexander—whom I began to look into, with the idea of using them as a subplot in the Dumnorix-Diviciacus section. King Philip was a far nobler figure than the crafty Dumnorix, and the story of his rising and bloody defeat was horrible: His head, said the Britannica, "was sent to Plymouth and set on a pole in a public place, where it remained for a quarter-of-a-century; his right hand was given to his slayer, who preserved it in rum and won many pennies by exhibiting it in the New England towns." Yet there was the settlers' side to be considered, too, and the side represented by the "friendlies," who in the end very successfully betrayed him.

At some point, Philip, who had earned the name of a "states-man," must have been of two minds.

In short, I was stretching a point in trying to set up a har-monic with what was then "today." True, Caesar's story of the two Haeduan brothers did have the capacity of eternal recur-rence, causing it to repeat itself over the ages in varying "colo-nial" contexts. But for a Caesar to have a "side," he must be felt to be a force of civilization, progress, order, law, bridge-building; his imperial eagles nesting in the Capitol must be seen to have sharp vision and powerful wings. None of this applied to Hitler, and the refugees who were going to be heard from time to time on the library steps favorably comparing German music, scenery, coffee houses with our native articles were not rent by divided loyalties; they were merely homesick.

There were no real traitors in any of my narratives, whatever I tried to think. But at that shivery time—when a rubber boat from a Nazi submarine came ashore one night on the beach near Provincetown—the figure of the traitor or turncoat had a fascination for literary people, and I suspect I was being guided by a mode-in-the-making. At any rate, I remember having little pangs of territorial jealousy when, not too much later—why did this subject appeal specially to women?—Rebecca West's "The Meaning of Treason" and Elizabeth Bowen's "The Heat of the Day" came out while my novel lay in a drawer; after all, I had thought of it first.

The second episode was to be about Parnell. Here one set of loyalties crisscrossed with a tangled host of others: multiple loy-alties, multiple betrayals. Kitty O'Shea betrayed Captain O'Shea with Parnell, then betrayed Parnell with him; at least O'Shea believed that a child she bore while "wedded" to Parnell was his own. Next, O'Shea, having taken money and a Parliamentary seat for his silence, betrayed Parnell to a prudish public. The faithful Michael Davitt thereupon deserted the "Chief"; Ireland deserted her Leader, who took ill and died, abandoned by all but "Wifey." As Yeats said it, to the music of a street ballad: "The Bishops and the Party/ That tragic story made,/ A hus-band that had sold his wife/ And after that betrayed;/ But sto-ries that live longest/ Are sung above the glass,/ And Parnell loved his country,/ And Parnell loved his lass."

Yet who betrayed whom and what? Ireland was faithless to Parnell, but wasn't Parnell faithless to the cause of Irish liberty, not to mention Gladstone, in evidently preferring the "lass," who in reality was a 45-year-old married woman when the blows began to fall? Moreover, the tragedy had its sordid interludes of trimming, lies and venality: Parnell might have braved the scandal and lived openly with Mrs. O'Shea, maybe married (she had grounds for a divorce), if they had not been waiting for her proper old aunt to die and leave her a large inheritance. Instead, they continued to buy off the untrustworthy Captain O'Shea and were exposed anyway when he upped and filed for a divorce. Only the villain of the piece remained true to his lights. His motives seemed to have been always financial, with revenge as a secondary spur, moving him at long last to action when the main interest was thwarted.

The third episode was hazier in my mind. It would probably have dealt with Wordsworth. The Poet Laureate, Browning's "Lost Leader" ("Just for a handful of silver he left us,/ Just for a riband to stick in his coat."): His repudiation of his youth, of the French Revolution, of Annette, the French girl, and the reputed child of their union that he was said to have disowned.

Yet, since I was thinking of a turncoat poet, I am surprised that it did not occur to me to put in Pound, a bona fide traitor to his country, either as a replacement for poor old Wordsworth or as a modern foil to him. The reason may be that a genuine traitor did not interest me. To me, Pound's politics, to which (it must be said) he was faithful, were a silly aberration; in this sphere, I found him simply a curio, not much different from Lord Haw-Haw or Tokyo Rose. I was incapable of taking seriously the pull of Fascist ideology. In a novelist this may not have been a virtue.

In other words, the novel I believed I was writing had only a remote bearing on the "big" theme I had set myself. This, obviously, was why I could not go further with it. I had no faith in it myself. Yet in any novel (in my experience) there is a crisis of faith for the author. This generally occurs toward the end of Chapter Two, when the first impetus has gone; occasionally in Chapter Three. It happened to me with "The Group," with "A Charmed Life," with "Birds of America." The crisis can last a night or a few hours; with "The Group" it lasted years, during which I put the manuscript aside, thinking I would never go back to it.

There is no use going on till the crisis is resolved. You cannot evade it; you have to face the strong possibility that what you have been carefully writing and rewriting is not a fiction but a hollow lie. If you finally persuade yourself that your suspicions are wrong, you can continue. But another crisis may occur. A moment comes, though, about three-quarters of the way through the book, when you know you are going to finish it; this is the moment when it has gained your belief.

With the initial crisis, a simple rereading, after an interval, may reassure me. More often, notes to myself in the form of questions and answers are required ("What am I trying to say here?" "What's behind this or that incident?" "What makes me give him red hair?"). In short, there has to be a severe critical effort to get behind or underneath the glassy written surface; you laboriously mine your own book for its meaning. It may be that you can find nothing behind or underneath, or else something you do not like. Then you put the book aside. Occasionally, time will disclose to you a meaning or pattern that you failed to find on the first look—time has turned you into a more "objective" reader.

With the public-library novel, this confrontation did not take place. I was too inexperienced. Somewhere in the Dumnorix-Diviciacus part, that is, toward the beginning, I got discouraged and stopped, I had looked ahead and was daunted. What I might have noticed, had I paused and asked myself questions, was that this historical farrago was not about treason but about me. The division between the Haeduan brothers was in myself. I was a natural rebel who was also in love with law. This was my autobiography, and it was not going to change.

Ten years passed. Then all of a sudden I found a use for those by that time yellowed pages. They were salvaged, like old dress material, for "The Figures in the Clock," in "Memories of a Catholic Girlhood." That was where they had always belonged, where in fact they came from. From Annie Wright Seminary and my Latin teacher, Miss Mackay, who for semi-fictional purposes now became "Miss Gowrie." For me, at least, this was a happy ending, for Dumnorix and Diviciacus had been resting uneasily all that time in some half-closed chamber of my mind, turning from side to side like Dante's sick man. Now I had done my best to make them comfortable—Caesar and Vercingetorix too.

But as yet I have not found a good place for Parnell.

CHRONOLOGY

NOTE ON THE TEXTS

NOTES

Chronology

Unless otherwise identified, quotations in this chronology come from a letter McCarthy wrote to Doris Grumbach, the first of her biographers, on February 22, 1966, in which McCarthy included her own year-by-year chronology of her life, with often revealing commentary. The letter is now among the Mary McCarthy Papers in the Special Collections of the Vassar College Library.

1912   Born Mary Therese McCarthy on June 21 in Seattle, first child of Roy and Therese Preston McCarthy. (Father, born in 1880 in Illinois to devout Catholic family, attended the University of Minnesota. Mother born 1888 in Seattle, Washington, to nominally Protestant father and Jewish mother. Parents met in 1910 at Oregon resort and were married in April 1911 despite reservations of both families —Roy McCarthy had a damaged heart and had previously been hospitalized for alcoholism. Mother converts to Catholicism. At first the couple settles in Minneapolis so that Roy can work at his father's grain elevator business, but they move to Seattle when he starts drinking again.) In fall, father begins law school at the University of Washington and paternal grandparents purchase them a house at 934 22nd Avenue.

1914   Brother Kevin McCarthy, the eldest of Mary's three brothers and the one to whom she would remain the closest (later a well-known actor in theater, films, and television), born February 15.

1915   Father graduates with law degree and begins to practice part-time, but by 1917 his heart condition makes it impossible for him to work. Brother James Preston born September 5.

1917   Brother Sheridan born April 26.

1918   In fall, mother enrolls McCarthy as a day student at the Forest Ridge Convent of the Sacred Heart. Family moves to Minneapolis, where paternal grandparents have purchased them a house; on three-day train journey everyone contracts Spanish flu virus. Father dies on November 6 at home of paternal grandparents; mother the next day. McCarthy and her brothers are put into the often neglectful and cruel care of Margaret and Myers Shriver, their great-aunt and great-uncle. Enrolled in St. Stephen's, a Catholic elementary school.

1923   After a visit to Minneapolis leaves her maternal grand-father, Harold Preston, appalled, McCarthy is rescued from the Shriver household and moved to Seattle; enrolled in Forest Ridge Convent school. Brothers Kevin and Preston go to live with paternal grandparents, while Sheridan remains with the Shrivers. Given free range of grandfa-ther's library, and reads Dickens, Tolstoy, and *The Count of Monte Cristo.*

1925   Enters Garfield High School in Seattle; despite continued adventurous reading, she nearly fails all of her courses and after a year will be "removed from the excitement of boys" to an all-girls school, Annie Wright Seminary in Tacoma.

1926   Over next three years will run "away from school once, just for fun, with another girl . . . Acted in many school plays. Wrote 'realistic' short stories and romances rather in the manner of [British historical novelist] Maurice Hewlett which were shown to Miss Atkinson, for her private con-sumption. Took (strangely) cooking course one year, probably because the teacher was young and pretty. Was terrible at it." Loses virginity in the fall of 1926 "in Mar-mon roadster; unpleasant experience." English teacher Dorothy Atkinson, a recent Vassar graduate, encourages her to write short stories. Decides to attend Vassar herself, and begins the necessary three years of Latin for admis-sion.

1928   Has additional sexual experiences with a portrait painter in Seattle; travels to Montana in the summer on vacation with two classmates. "Also knew weird circle of Lesbians, who liked to read Pierre Louÿs aloud. Introduced by friend, 'Ted' (Ethel) Rosenberg, alluded to in *Catholic Girlhood.*"

1929   Graduates from Annie Wright as class valedictorian. Does summer study at Seattle's Cornish School; takes classes in theatre and eurythmics. Meets Harold Johnsrud (born 1904 in St. Cloud, Minnesota), who is "acting in local little theatre and having affair with eurythmics teacher. . . . Went to 'Symphonies under the Stars,' in the stadium, con-ducted by Michel Piastro. Tried to grasp music; failed. Only

responded to names such as 'Sarabande,' 'Scarlatti.'" Enters
Vassar in the fall after once more meeting Johnsrud "on
street of New York first day on pre-college visit with
grandmother and aunt. Only person I knew in New York.
Seemed like fate . . . Love affair began shortly after;
lasted, with very bad vicissitudes in summer of '32, through
college . . . Cruel man, really. Liked to get power through
wounding." The strongest influences on her at Vassar are
Helen Sandison and Anna Kitchel, English department
professors whose aesthetic approach to literary study appeals to McCarthy more than the progressive political interpretations of their colleague Helen Drusilla Lockwood.

1932   In summer, works for art dealer Emmanuel "Manny" J.
        Rousuck in New York. Describes him in a letter to her
        friend Frani Blough as "a nice, sweet, battered soul who
        spends his time skulking about, avoiding the sheriff."
        (Several years later she will fictionalize him as "Mr. Sheer"
        in "Rogue's Gallery," *The Company She Keeps*.)

1933   Publishes essay "Touchstone Ambitious" about the Eliza-
        bethan writer Sir John Harington in *The Vassar Journal of
        Undergraduate Studies*. Graduates from Vassar in mid-
        June and marries Johnsrud at St. George's Episcopal
        Church in New York on June 21; "Wedding very much as
        in *The Group*." Over the next few years Johnsrud is "un-
        employed a good deal . . . Expensive apartment (my
        fault), debts, no money. Did not ask family, except when
        had appendix out." Begins reviewing books for *The New
        Republic*. At the end of the year writes to Frani Blough,
        her old Vassar classmate: "Housework and a book review
        or two are not effective substitutes for sixteen hours of
        classes a week."

1934   Falls out with Malcolm Cowley at *The New Republic* over
        a review of Lauren Gilfillan's *I Went to Pit College*, a mem-
        oir he pressured her to praise. After changing his mind
        about the book, Cowley prints a "correction" to what he
        deems an overly favorable notice by McCarthy, who has
        begun reviewing regularly for *The Nation*. On February 6,
        joins Selden Rodman, Dorothy Parker, Alexander Wooll-
        cott, and others in a demonstration of support for striking
        waiters at the Waldorf-Astoria hotel.

1935   That fall, in *The Nation*, writes most of a much remarked
        upon five-part series about American book reviewing,

"Our Critics, Right or Wrong." Shares the byline with Margaret Marshall.

1936 Gets Reno divorce from Johnsrud on August 11 in order to marry a "young unemployable, John Porter, later died in Mexico, wretched circumstances. Looked like Fred MacMurray. Charm . . . Williams boy, had worked on *Paris Herald*." (McCarthy had marched with Porter in a May Day parade on lower Broadway that year.) In the fall returns to New York, decides not to marry Porter; rents apartment on Gay Street in Greenwich Village. Works again for Rousuck. Develops friendship with James T. Farrell and his wife. In November, attends a book party for *New Masses* cartoonist Art Young, at which she bucks the Stalinist tide by saying that Trotsky deserves a fair hearing. (The Moscow Trials had begun in August.) Soon finds herself being listed on the letterhead of the Committee for the Defense of Leon Trotsky.

1937 Works at Covici Friede publishers and helps Ralph Craig to ghostwrite the memoirs of radio broadcaster H. V. Kaltenborn. Begins affair with Philip Rahv (born 1908 in Russia, a member of the Trotsky Defense Committee who was separated from his wife) and lives with him on Beekman Place ("borrowed apartment rich friends") and East End Avenue. Meets literary critic for *The New Republic* Edmund Wilson (born 1895 in New Jersey) in the offices of the new *Partisan Review*, which proclaims its editorial policy in December: "*Partisan Review* is aware of its responsibility to the revolutionary movement in general, but we disclaim obligation to any of its organized political expressions."

1938 Grandfather Harold Preston dies on New Year's Day. Marries Wilson on February 10; quits publishing job and moves with Wilson to Stamford, Connecticut. "At Wilson's insistence," writes her first short story, "Cruel and Barbarous Treatment." Spends three weeks in New York's Payne Whitney Psychiatric Clinic after a violent altercation with Wilson on June 8, while she is two months pregnant. Wilson claims to have noticed "an acute hysterical condition," but McCarthy receives a diagnosis of anxiety. She refuses Wilson's suggestion that she have an abortion. In August, returns to Stamford and writes for *Partisan Review*. Her only child, Reuel Kimball Wilson, is born December 25.

1939   Accompanies Wilson to Chicago while he teaches in the university's summer term. In late July, McCarthy and Reuel visit her grandmother, Augusta Morgenstern Preston, in Seattle. In October, Wilsons rent house in Truro, Massachusetts, on Cape Cod. Johnsrud, her first husband, dies on December 23 in a fire at the Hotel Brevoort in New York.

1940   In June, the Wilsons move for the summer from Truro to a house in Wellfleet. "Edmund disapproves" of the nearby presence of Philip Rahv and his wife in Provincetown. They return to Stamford in the fall; McCarthy contributes her "Theater Chronicle" to *Partisan Review* and writes the stories for *The Company She Keeps*.

1941   Living in Stamford that winter with Wilson, continues to see psychoanalyst Dr. Richard Frank (she has been his patient since late 1938) until she and Wilson move into the house he buys in Wellfleet that June. "The Man in the Brooks Brothers Shirt" is published in July in *Partisan Review*.

1942   Spends winter and spring with Wilson at the Little Hotel in New York. *The Company She Keeps* is published in May by Simon and Schuster. John Chamberlain, the model for portions of the main character in "Portrait of the Intellectual as a Yale Man," reviews the book in *The New York Times*. Spends summer, as well as weekends during the fall, in Wellfleet; the rest of the time she is in New York, living in Stuyvesant Square. Sees another psychoanalyst, Dr. Abraham Kardiner.

1943   Rents New York apartment with Wilson and Reuel. Back at Wellfleet for the summer and in the Gramercy Park Hotel in New York that fall. Wilson begins writing for *The New Yorker*. Reuel begins kindergarten in New York City.

1944   Spends winter and spring at the Gramercy Park; summer in Wellfleet. Meets Italian activist Nicola Chiaromonte on Cape Cod. Leaves Wilson after a fierce argument in July but then returns by September. "The Weeds," a short story depicting aspects of their marriage, appears in *The New Yorker* in September. She and Wilson live with Reuel on Henderson Place in New York that fall; he attends St. Bernard's School. In the fall, and through early 1945, has an affair with art critic Clement Greenberg.

1945 Leaves Wilson in January and takes Reuel; they live first at the Stanhope Hotel in Manhattan, then at brother Kevin's East 56th Street apartment. Meets Bowden Broadwater (born 1920 in Maryland, he is a recent Harvard graduate and a fact-checker at *The New Yorker*) at the house of Niccolò Tucci the night she leaves Wilson. Spends an "idyllic summer" (until Hiroshima—"everything different after") with Reuel in Truro; Broadwater visits them there. Becomes "close friends" with Nicola Chiaromonte. "Tolstoy. Beach conversations. Reading Shakespeare aloud in a group—a recurrent feature in my life . . . On the beach, I translating Simone Weil's *Iliad or Poem of Force*. Getting sand in my typewriter." Works on, then abandons, a novelette called *The Lost Week*. In September, begins teaching at Bard College (the basis for Jocelyn College in *The Groves of Academe*). Gives a course on "The Modern Novel" that doesn't go past Henry James. Reaches divorce settlement with Wilson in October.

1946 Leaves Bard College after spring semester. Makes first trip to Europe in July. Travels with Broadwater in France and Italy. Moves in with him and his sister that fall on East 57th Street in New York; they marry on December 18 (divorce from Wilson finalized days before). Reuel back at St. Bernard's. In November, criticizes John Hersey's *Hiroshima* in a letter to *politics*, journal edited by Dwight Macdonald.

1947 In February meets, and begins lifelong detestation of, Simone de Beauvoir. Spends summer in Pawlet, Vermont, which will become the setting for *The Oasis*. Broadwater works for *Partisan Review* in the fall. McCarthy inherits $23,250 when Louis McCarthy, her uncle, sells the McCarthy family's grain elevator company.

1948 Teaches at Sarah Lawrence during spring semester. Publishes review of *A Streetcar Named Desire*, declaring that Tennessee Williams's play "reeks of literary ambition as the [Kowalski] apartment reeks of cheap perfume." Writes *The Oasis* and spends summer in Cornwall, Connecticut, seeing some "White Russian friends." Along with Dwight Macdonald, Nicolas Nabokov, Elizabeth Hardwick, Philip Rahv, and other intellectuals, works on the formation of "Europe-America Groups," whose manifesto says they hope "to provide some center of solidarity with and support for intellectuals in Europe . . . in the face of the extreme polarity of Soviet and American power."

1949   *The Oasis* is published in *Horizon* magazine in February and wins the *Horizon* prize of £200 that fall. Rahv, recognizable in *The Oasis* as "Will Taub," threatens a libel suit. Dwight Macdonald ("Macdougal Macdermott") isn't pleased either. Political philosopher Hannah Arendt calls the book "a gem" and her friendship with McCarthy, after an early misunderstanding, takes off. Buys a house in Portsmouth, Rhode Island, with Broadwater. Reuel at St. Michael's School, Newport. In March, McCarthy, Robert Lowell, Elizabeth Hardwick, and Macdonald "infiltrate" the Stalinist-dominated Cultural and Scientific Conference for World Peace at New York's Waldorf-Astoria. They "make anti-Communist speeches from floor . . . amusing event; wrote bad story about it later, never published." Receives Guggenheim Fellowship. In October, revisits Vassar for *Holiday* magazine article ("The Vassar Girl"), which will be published in May 1951. Suffers miscarriage in mid-November.

1950   Living in Portsmouth. In early spring, writes a ten-part article for the *New York Post* on nightlife in New York's Greenwich Village. *Cast a Cold Eye* published by Harcourt Brace and Company (which will publish the majority of the rest of her books); it includes several short stories along with memoir pieces that will later go into *Memories of a Catholic Girlhood*. Begins writing *The Groves of Academe*.

1951   Writes "A Tin Butterfly," which will become part of *Memories of a Catholic Girlhood*. Finishes *The Groves of Academe*. "Reuel at St. George's as a day boy."

1952   Publishes a scathing review ("Mlle. Gulliver en Amérique") in January of Simone de Beauvoir's *America Day by Day*. At a second Waldorf Conference, she "clashe[s] with Sidney Hook, Max Eastman," who had both turned right politically, over the behavior of Senator Joseph McCarthy. *The Groves of Academe* published in February. Begins writing *The Group*. On a train to Missouri, before giving a lecture to teachers, she meets the anti-Semitic colonel who becomes the subject of her essay "Artists in Uniform." Prompted by concern with the state of civil liberties in America, she considers going to Harvard Law School; is dissuaded by Judge John Biggs, chief judge of the Third

U.S. Circuit Court of Appeals in Philadelphia, an old friend of Wilson's. In October, she and Broadwater sell house in Portsmouth and buy one on Cape Cod, which happens to be close to Wilson's home.

1953   Spends early part of year in New York's Hotel Chelsea, often in the company of Hannah Arendt. Seeks start-up funding for a "social, political" magazine to be called *Critic*. "Fail to raise enough money and have run out of money myself, having abandoned novel [*The Group*] for time being." Summers in borrowed house of Helvetia Perkins in Montpelier, Vermont, an experience that will go into her story "The Appalachian Revolution." Having "agreed to stay away from Cape House when Reuel there with Edmund," lectures at Bread Loaf School of English in summer: her talk, "Settling the Colonel's Hash," is a witty refutation of symbol-hunting interpretations of "Artists in Uniform." In fall, goes to the Cape and writes story about accidental injury that Broadwater incurs to his hand. (This becomes the first chapter in *A Charmed Life*.) In October, rents the New York apartment of Alfred Kazin—their mutual dislike will grow with the years—to write "The Appalachian Revolution." Serves as one of the fiction judges for the National Book Award, which goes, with her approval, to Saul Bellow's *The Adventures of Augie March*.

1954   In January and February, "Dottie Makes an Honest Woman of Herself," a version of which will become *The Group*'s third chapter, appears as a short story in *Partisan Review*. Early in the year travels to Portugal with Broadwater; a *New Yorker* travel piece results. Also works on *A Charmed Life*, "having decided to turn it into novel." Maternal grandmother Augusta Preston dies on February 7. Spends summer on the Cape ("Edmund and I now dividing Reuel's vacation") and fall in Rhode Island. Randall Jarrell's comic novel of academic manners, *Pictures from an Institution*, published in June, recognizably depicts McCarthy as "Gertrude Johnson."

1955   Finishes *A Charmed Life* in borrowed villa on Capri. "Bowden and I on poor terms." Travels through Italy and Greece during a difficult pregnancy. Suffers apparent miscarriage in Greece and then a "definitive" one on plane to Paris in June. *A Charmed Life* is published in June. Meets

Reuel in London while doing a program for the BBC. Agrees to Rosamund and Georges Bernier's proposal that she write a book on Venice, where she spends the fall doing research. "Reuel and Bowden return [to] America alone." Goes back to New York in December, the house on the Cape having been sold after Broadwater decides they cannot go back there after *A Charmed Life* comes out; the novel is full of recognizable characters from Wellfleet. In reviewing the book, *Time* calls McCarthy "quite possibly the cleverest writer America has ever produced."

1956   Lives on East 94th Street in New York as Broadwater begins running the library at St. Bernard's school. *Sights and Spectacles*, a collection of her theater criticism, published by Farrar, Straus and Cudahy. Travels to Italy in May to visit Bernard Berenson, the American art historian she had met in Venice. Spends much of the summer in Venice with Broadwater and Reuel. After Broadwater returns to New York, travels to Holland, Paris, and London—where she resumes love affair with British journalist John Davenport that began in Italy. "Crisis on return to New York." Reuel enters Harvard. *Venice Observed* published in November.

1957   *Memories of a Catholic Girlhood* is published in late spring. "Crisis surmounted" with Broadwater. Returns to Italy in May, planning to write a book on Florence, Mantua, and Bologna. Broadwater joins her in Florence in June. "Peace restored" between them when she returns to New York in October.

1958   Back to Europe in May; the Italian book will now be all about Florence and not the other two cities. Joined in Italy by Evelyn Hofer, who takes photographs to illustrate the book, and Broadwater. Reuel spends summer working in Paris. Back in New York in the fall, she and Broadwater assemble *The Stones of Florence*, "layout, pictures, etc. Bowden very good at this."

1959   Resumes work on *The Group* after several years away from the manuscript. In October and November spends seven weeks in Tripoli at the villa of an Italian friend—"rather ideal" for work on the novel. Receives second Guggenheim Fellowship as well as proposal from State Department for lecture tour of Eastern European countries. *The Stones of Florence* is published in October. Arrives in

Warsaw in December, where she meets James West, a U.S. Embassy public affairs officer (born 1914 in Old Town, Maine; West is married with three young children).

1960   Lectures on "Characters in Fiction" and "The Fact in Fiction." The tour takes McCarthy, as well as Saul Bellow, to Poland and Yugoslavia. She continues with speaking engagements in Britain. Arranges rendezvous with West in Paris in March before flying home to New York to collect her possessions. Reuel graduates from Harvard. Returns to Europe and takes apartment in Rome, "with many trips to meet Jim—Zurich, Vienna, France, Copenhagen, even Warsaw—till September or October." Turns the two lectures on fiction into pieces for *On the Contrary: Articles of Belief 1946–1961*, which is published the following autumn by Farrar, Straus and Cudahy. Joins West in Warsaw in October to live "under cover (more or less), like a captive in hideous hotel room with Party emblems on bedspreads, curtains. Hardly went out, and when did tried to lose self in faceless crowd. Under these nervous conditions, started work on *Group* again." Goes to Paris on December 1.

1961   Divorced from Broadwater, in Alabama, on February 14; marries West, just divorced from his wife, in Paris on April 15. Embassy will not allow her to join him at his post in Warsaw until the former Mrs. West departs the city. Suffers slipped disk while waiting in Vienna and spends three weeks in clinic there. Arrives in Warsaw in a wheelchair and is "cured by Polish doctor." Summer in Bocca di Magra, Italy. McCarthy and West spend his fall home leave from the State Department in Stonington, Connecticut. Interviewed for *The Paris Review* "Writers at Work" series by Elisabeth Niebuhr (later Sifton).

1962   After more time in Stonington, as well as Washington, West is made director of information for the new Office of Economic Cooperation and Development (OECD) in Paris. The couple arrive there in March and buy the apartment on the rue de Rennes where they will live for the next quarter century. McCarthy extravagantly praises Vladimir Nabokov's *Pale Fire* in *The New Republic* in June. The Wests summer in Bocca di Magra.

1963   *The Group*, published in August, becomes a major best seller. McCarthy finds the sales "stupefying." The novel is reviewed negatively in *The New York Review of Books* by

Norman Mailer (who nevertheless calls McCarthy "our saint, our umpire, our lit arbiter, our broadsword"), and parodied in the same journal by McCarthy's friend Elizabeth Hardwick, writing under the name "Xavier Prynne." Charles Feldman options the film rights for $162,500.

1964   "The Hue and Cry," McCarthy's defense of Hannah Arendt against attacks on *Eichmann in Jerusalem*, appears in *Partisan Review*. Lectures on Shakespeare in California. The Wests spend Jim's summer home leave in Stonington, Connecticut, with his children. Begins *Birds of America*.

1966   Film of *The Group*, produced by Feldman, directed by Sidney Lumet, and with a cast including Candice Bergman, Joan Hackett, and Elizabeth Hartman, premieres in March. Brother Sheridan dies in October.

1967   Travels to South Vietnam in February to report on the war for *The New York Review of Books*. Doris Grumbach publishes a biography of McCarthy in late spring (*The Company She Kept*), much to the displeasure of its subject, who regrets her candid cooperation. McCarthy and West buy a house in Castine, Maine; they begin spending summers there—often in the company of Lowell, Hardwick, and poet Philip Booth—while continuing to live the rest of the year in Paris.

1968   A second trip to Vietnam in March, this time to the North, results in the publication of *Hanoi*, the second of three short volumes about the war.

1971   *Birds of America* published in summer, her first novel since *The Group*. Noting its extensive considerations of politics, ethics, nature, and the environment, Helen Vendler, in *The New York Times Book Review*, calls it a "fictional essay." In August, covers the war-crimes trial of Captain Ernest Medina at Fort McPherson, Georgia, for *The New Yorker*.

1972   *Medina* appears in book form. Edmund Wilson dies June 12. Considers and abandons a plan to have fellow intellectuals, politicians, and other figures travel to Hanoi during the "Christmas bombing" campaign conducted by the Nixon administration.

1973   In June, covers the U.S. Senate's Watergate hearings, chaired by North Carolina's Sam Ervin, for the London *Observer*.

1974 In February, pays tribute to Philip Rahv, who died the year before, in *The New York Times Book Review*. *The Mask of State*, a collection of her Watergate reporting dedicated to Senator Ervin, published in the summer. *The Seventeenth Degree*, collecting three volumes about the Vietnam War, also published.

1975 Hannah Arendt dies, in New York, on December 4. In McCarthy's obituary for Arendt, she writes: "Hannah is the only person I have ever watched *think*."

1976 Edits Arendt's last work, *The Life of the Mind*, while also composing what will be her own last novel, *Cannibals and Missionaries*.

1979 *Cannibals and Missionaries* is published in October. During her publicity tour for the novel, McCarthy records interview with Dick Cavett and remarks of playwright Lillian Hellman that "every word she writes is a lie, including 'and' and 'the.'" McCarthy had long been repelled by Hellman's Stalinism and mendacious memoirs.

1980 Hellman sues McCarthy for $2.25 million for libel once the Cavett interview airs in January. Gives the Northcliffe Lectures at the University of London; they are published in October as *Ideas and the Novel*.

1982 Returns to Vassar in February as the President's Distinguished Visitor.

1984 Awarded the National Medal for Literature at the New York Public Library on May 3. Hellman's death on June 30 leads to the dropping of the lawsuit by the executors of her estate. The litigation had been expensive and stressful for McCarthy, who on July 16 is operated on, successfully, for water on the brain. On August 26 she receives the Edward MacDowell Medal for significant contribution to American culture.

1985 *Occasional Prose*, a collection of McCarthy's critical writing, published in May. Her papers are acquired by the Vassar College library.

1986 Returns, after nearly forty years, to teaching at Bard College, on the Charles Stevenson Chair of Literature.

1987 *How I Grew*, a memoir of her early years, is published in the spring.

1988   Elected to the American Academy of Arts and Letters and inducted in May. Carol Gelderman's biography, *Mary McCarthy: A Life*, is published in August.

1989   Works on *Intellectual Memoirs: New York, 1936–1938*, which will be published posthumously. Dies in New York Hospital on October 25 of lung cancer; buried in Castine, Maine.

Note on the Texts

This volume contains three novels by Mary McCarthy, *The Group* (1963), *Birds of America* (1971), and *Cannibals and Missionaries* (1979), as well as the essay "The Novels That Got Away." A companion Library of America volume collects the remainder of her fiction: the novels *The Company She Keeps*, *The Oasis*, *The Groves of Academe*, and *A Charmed Life*, as well as all eight of her short stories.

McCarthy began writing *The Group* in Portsmouth, Rhode Island, in 1952, intending to follow eight Vassar graduates from the class of 1933 through the Depression, World War II, and up to 1950. After working on the novel for a year, she put it aside in 1953 to pursue funding for her magazine, *Critic*. However, when she returned to writing in late 1954, she decided to shelve the manuscript, and she carved out two discrete sections to publish as short stories. "The Group" was published in the anthology *Avon Book of Modern Writing* No. 2 (Avon Publications, Inc., 1954), pp. 32–54, edited by William Phillips and Philip Rahv; and "Dottie Makes an Honest Woman of Herself" was published in *Partisan Review*, January–February 1954, pp. 34–52.

In spring 1959, after receiving a second Guggenheim Fellowship, McCarthy resumed work on the novel and revised the previously completed sections; "The Group" became chapter 1, and "Dottie Makes an Honest Woman of Herself" became chapter 3. She completed the novel, having decided to end it at the outbreak of World War II, in Paris in April 1963, and chapters 11 and 12 were published as "Polly Andrews, Class of '33" in *The New Yorker*, June 29, 1963, pp. 23–61. *The Group* was published in August 1963 by Harcourt, Brace & World, Inc. McCarthy is not known to have been involved in the preparation of a British edition, which was published in London by Weidenfeld and Nicolson in October 1963. The present volume uses the first American edition as its text.

McCarthy began writing *Birds of America* in spring 1964, while living in Paris, and worked on it on and off for the next seven years, finishing it in early 1971. The first two chapters were originally published as "Birds of America" in *Southern Review*, July 1965, pp. 644–83. The sixth chapter, "Round Table, with the Damsel Parcenet," was originally published as "Thanksgiving in Paris" in *The Atlantic*, August 1970, pp. 43–52. *Birds of America* was published in spring 1971 by Harcourt Brace Jovanovich. McCarthy is not known to have been involved in the preparation of a British edition, which was published in London by Weidenfeld & Nicolson in 1971. The present volume uses the first American edition as its text.

In May 1974, McCarthy gave a talk on "Art Values and the Value of Art" (later published as "Living with Beautiful Things") at the University of Aberdeen. Her friend Hannah Arendt, who was in the audience, suggested that McCarthy draw on the talk for a novel. She began writing what would become *Cannibals and Missionaries* at the end of 1974 and by February 1975 had completed the first chapter. By December she had completed five chapters, when her work on the novel was halted by the death of Arendt and McCarthy's editing of Arendt's last work, *The Life of the Mind*. She resumed work on her novel in early 1978 and finished it in February 1979. *Cannibals and Missionaries* was published in fall 1979 by Harcourt Brace Jovanovich. A British edition using the same plates as the American edition was published in London by Weidenfeld & Nicolson in 1979. The present volume uses the first American edition as its text.

As an appendix, this volume includes "The Novels That Got Away," which was published in *The New York Times Book Review* on November 25, 1979, pp. 9, 100–101, the source of the present text.

This volume presents the texts of the original printings chosen for inclusion here, but it does not attempt to reproduce features of their typographic design. The texts are presented without change, except for the correction of typographical errors. Spelling, punctuation, and capitalization are often expressive features, and they are not altered, even when inconsistent or irregular. The following is a list of typographical errors corrected, cited by page and line number: 78.20, spiritual race,'; 98.23, Bete; 115.20, corespondent; 120.33, *What is Art?.*; 182.27, MacCollister's; 206.17, bortsch; 261.34, beggers; 317.39, Frankfort; 338.19, Sidney; 499.15, fields; 499.18, *de l'Europe*; 540.37, atrocites?; 560.25, *des*; 578.4, let's; 587.7–8, Kennedy? ¶Above; 612.10, that . . .; 644.30, *mangent la*; 653.1, *dîtes*; 661.22, touseled; 705.37, al.'"; 720.21, *montagne suisse*; 724.29, well-setup; 727.27, shouder,; 764.35, *sèrieux.*; 774.28–29, Groninger; 785.7, "The compacts,"; 816.22, Klimmt,; 821.31, than; 918.19, Book of Common Prayer,; 955.36, 39.5.°; 980.19 and .25, "*C'etait*.

Notes

In the notes below, the reference numbers denote page and line of this volume (the line count includes headings, but not rule lines). Often no note is made for material included in the eleventh edition of *Merriam-Webster's Collegiate Dictionary*. Biblical quotations and allusions are keyed to the King James Version; references to Shakespeare to *The Riverside Shakespeare*, ed. G. Blakemore Evans (Boston: Houghton Mifflin, 1974). For further biographical background, references to other studies, and more detailed notes, see Doris Grumbach, *The Company She Kept* (New York: Coward-McCann, 1967); Carol Gelderman, *Mary McCarthy: A Life* (New York: St. Martin's Press, 1988); Carol Brightman, *Writing Dangerously: Mary McCarthy and Her World* (New York: Clarkson Potter, 1992); and Frances Kiernan, *Seeing Mary Plain* (New York: W. W. Norton & Company, 2000); as well as *Conversations with Mary McCarthy*, ed. Carol Gelderman (Jackson: University Press of Mississippi, 1991), and Sherli Evens Goldman, *Mary McCarthy: A Bibliography* (New York: Harcourt, Brace & World, 1968).

THE GROUP

3.6   Karl F. Reiland] Liberal clergyman (1871–1964), rector of St. George's Protestant Episcopal Church in New York from 1915 to 1936. McCarthy married her first husband at St. George's in 1933.

3.9   Peter Stuyvesant] Stuyvesant (1610–1672) was the last Dutch governor of New Netherland before the English took over and renamed it New York.

4.17–18   old Miss Washburn] Margaret Floy Washburn (1871–1939) was a Vassar alumna and later professor of psychology at the college. Author of *The Animal Mind: A Textbook of Comparative Psychology* (1908).

4.19   Hallie Flanagan] Hallie Flanagan Davis (1890–1969), founder of Vassar's Experimental Theatre and from 1935 to 1939 director of the Federal Theatre Project within the New Deal's Works Progress Administration.

4.27   "Lester"] Lester Lang, Flanagan's assistant at the Experimental Theatre, became its acting director while Flanagan ran the Federal Theatre.

5.7–8   Edna Ferber . . . George Kaufman . . . Gilbert Miller] Ferber (1887–1968), popular playwright and novelist whose works include *So Big* (1924), *Show Boat* (1926), and *Giant* (1952); she and American dramatist

George S. Kaufman (1889–1961) co-wrote several plays, including *Dinner at Eight* (1932). Gilbert Heron Miller (1884–1969) was a theatrical producer.

6.16–17 Sherry's or the Colony Club.] Beginning in the late nineteenth century, Louis Sherry (1855–1926) ran a series of luxurious New York restaurants. By the 1920s he was operating an expensive catering and confectionery business at Fifth Avenue and 58th Street. The Colony Club, a private women's club on Park Avenue and East 62nd Street in New York, was founded in 1903.

11.7–8 salmon wiggle] Salmon casserole with peas and white sauce.

11.11 Racquet Club] Men's athletic and social club founded in 1916 and located at 370 Park Avenue in New York City.

11.23–24 Katharine Cornell and Walter Hampden] Cornell, American stage actress (1893–1974); Hampden, Broadway actor (1879–1955).

11.25 John Mason Brown] Kentucky-born American theater critic (1900–1969).

11.27 Professor Baker] George Pierce Baker (1866–1935), teacher of playwriting at Harvard and later Yale, where he was a founder of the Yale School of Drama.

12.8 Russel Wright] Well-regarded industrial designer (1904–1976) of modern home furniture and colorful housewares.

12.9 Fly and A.D. and Porcellian] Private all-male "final clubs" at Harvard University. Students join a "final" club after having memberships in other clubs during their prior undergraduate years.

13.18 Daisy Chain] A Vassar commencement custom involving a chain of daisies and laurel, one hundred and fifty feet long, carried at the ceremony by distinguished sophomore students chosen by a committee of the senior class.

14.9–10 only the Cosmopolitan] Private women's social club on East 66th Street in New York; incorporated in 1911.

14.18–19 the old Hotel Brevoort] See Chronology for 1939. McCarthy's first husband, Harold Johnsrud, the model for Kay's groom, died in a fire at the Brevoort in 1939.

18.20–21 Women's International League for Peace] The Women's International League for Peace and Freedom, active on behalf of disarmament and mediation, was founded in Zurich in 1919. It had roots in the Woman's Peace Party, founded in Washington, D.C., in 1915, and in the international women's congresses held in Europe during World War I.

18.23 Vincent Club, Junior League] The Vincent Club, a Boston organization promoting women's health education. The Junior League was a chain of women's volunteer organizations that grew from the early twentieth-century

Junior League for the Promotion of the Settlement Movement in New York City.

19.21   a Patou model] Jean Patou (1880–1936) was a French couturier also known for his modern tennis outfits and eventually for perfume.

19.30   S.A.] Sex appeal.

20.36   Russeks] Fifth Avenue department store particularly known for its furs.

21.27–28   "as the laws of the Medes and the Persians"] A trope for implacability, derived from mention of these unrepealable laws in Daniel 6:8.

24.10   N.R.A.] The National Recovery Administration, the principal New Deal agency for the regulation of business and labor. Formed by President Roosevelt in 1933, the NRA was symbolized by a "Blue Eagle" displayed by businesses adhering to its regulations. The agency was dissolved two years later, when its founding legislation, the National Industrial Recovery Act, was ruled unconstitutional by the U.S. Supreme Court.

24.29   Lanvin] French fashion business founded in 1889 by Jeanne Lanvin (1867–1946). Its Paris emporium remained a favorite of McCarthy's during her long residence in France.

25.10   Riggs Clinic] The Austen Riggs Center in Stockbridge, Massachusetts, founded in 1913, offers treatment for psychiatric conditions.

26.14   Miss Lockwood's] Vassar alumna (Class of 1912) and English professor at the college from 1927 to 1956, Helen Drusilla Lockwood (1883–1971) was known for a course she instituted on "The Contemporary Press." She took a left-leaning and socially aware approach to literary study that was less appealing to McCarthy than the belletristic pedagogy of Helen Sandison and Anna Kitchel. In *How I Grew* (1987), McCarthy wrote: "Today the portentous Miss Lockwood seems like a grotesque caricature of the Vassar teacher as shaker-up."

29.16   Frazer] Sir James George Frazer (1854–1941), author of *The Golden Bough: A Study in Magic and Religion* (2 vols., 1890; 3 vols., 1900; 12 vols., 1906–15).

33.16   Krafft-Ebing] *Psychopathia Sexualis,* a series of case histories, was published in 1886 by the German psychiatrist Richard von Krafft-Ebing (1840–1902).

36.6   Empress Maria Theresa . . . court doctor] Maria Theresa's mother, Elisabeth Christine of Brunswick-Wolfenbüttel (1691–1750), was subjected to all sorts of supposed fertility treatments involving alcohol, diet, and erotic images, in order to help her produce a male heir for the Holy Roman Emperor Charles VI.

36.30–31   '*Post coitum* . . . poet said."] Latin: After sex every animal is sad; proverb ascribed to Galen (129–c. 199 C.E.), Greek physician-philosopher.

45.14–15   "an expense of spirit in a waste of shame."] Shakespeare's Sonnet 129, line 1.

49.19   Margaret Sanger] American birth control pioneer (1879–1966).

51.8   Clover Club cocktail] A gin cocktail that contains lemon juice, raspberry syrup, and an egg white.

56.18–19   Mrs. Pankhurst] Emmeline Pankhurst (1858–1928), aggressive campaigner for women's suffrage in Britain.

57.19   Threadneedle Street] London street running from Bishopsgate to Bank junction; home to the Bank of England and, until 2004, the London Stock Exchange.

57.30   Belasco] David Belasco (1853–1931), American theatrical producer and director known as "The Bishop of Broadway."

57.34–35   Jed Harris] Producer and director (1900–1979), whose Broadway hits include *The Royal Family* (1927) and *The Front Page* (1928).

58.31   Robert Moses] New York State's powerful "master builder" (1888–1981) from the time of Governor Al Smith in the 1920s to the gubernatorial days of Nelson Rockefeller in the 1960s and '70s. Celebrated for the building of bridges and the establishment of public parks, especially Jones Beach, Moses was also eventually reviled for putting the New York metropolitan area in thrall to the needs of the automobile.

59.15   Vincent Astor] Vincent Astor (1891–1959), philanthropic heir to the Astor fortune.

59.17   Sutton Place mansions] After World War I, the construction of commodious apartment buildings and private houses made Sutton Place, running along the East 50s close to the East River in New York City, increasingly upscale.

60.18   Slough of Despond] Allegorical bog of guilt awaiting the sinner in *The Pilgrim's Progress* (1678) by John Bunyan (1628–1688).

61.21   Fannie Farmer and that old Boston Cooking School] Fannie Merritt Farmer (1857–1915) edited the popular *Boston Cooking School Cook Book* in 1896.

62.39   Lucy Stoners] Supporters of the Lucy Stone League, founded in 1921, which urged married women to retain their maiden names.

64.29   Margaret Sanger] See note 49.19.

64.30–31   the long fight had been waged through the courts] Doctors in

New York State had been permitted to prescribe birth control assistance after a 1918 decision by the New York Court of Appeals.

69.31   *risus sardonicus*] Latin: an involuntary smile, one that appears to be sardonic, caused by muscle spasms.

70.21   Shubert] Three brothers from Syracuse, New York—Jacob, Lee, and Sam Shubert—formed the Shubert Organization at the end of the nineteenth century. It eventually owned many of the most prestigious theatres in New York City and other parts of the country.

72.25   a Hall Play] Vassar theatrical productions named for their venue, "Society Hall," the drama space inside the college's Avery Hall. In 1932 McCarthy appeared, along with Elizabeth Bishop, in a Hall Play called *Uncle's Been Dreaming.*

77.3   Sixth Avenue El] The elevated Sixth Avenue Line of New York's subway system, torn down in 1939.

78.3–4   the Maenads who destroyed Orpheus] In Greek myth, the Maenads, Dionysus's "raving" acolytes, rip Orpheus apart, perhaps because of his devotion to Apollo.

78.19–20   'outward and visible sign . . . grace,'] What, according to *The Book of Common Prayer*, the sacraments of the Church provide.

78.25   Senator Cutting] Bronson M. Cutting (1888–1935), Republican senator from New Mexico, 1927–35. A foe of government censorship and a proponent of self-determination for the Philippines, he supported Roosevelt for president in 1932, as well as early New Deal financial reforms.

78.32   Townley man] Arthur Charles Townley (1880–1959), radical agrarian politician, founded the National Non-Partisan League in 1915; he was an unsuccessful candidate for governor of Minnesota in 1934.

84.9   Hippolytus] In Greek myth, the son of Theseus, killed after spurning his amorous stepmother, Phaedra.

85.33–34   "Hell hath no fury like a woman scorned"] Common variant of a line from *The Mourning Bride* (1697), a play by William Congreve (1670–1729).

86.10   the Binet] The Stanford-Binet Intelligence Scales (1916), building on work by French psychologist Alfred Binet (1857–1911), were one of the most commonly used IQ tests in the United States.

88.12–13   Gump's in San Francisco] High-end home furnishings retailer established in 1861.

88.21   Alexander Meiklejohn] Leading educational reformer, dean of Brown University, and president of Amherst College (1872–1964).

89.28   *Morituri te salutamus*] Latin: Those who are about to die salute you.

What Roman historian Suetonius says the Emperor Claudius heard, in 52 C.E., from the mass of imprisoned criminals forced to fight a gladiatorial entertainment in front of him.

91.9–10   Fish House Punch . . . One Dagger Rum] A rum-based punch first concocted in Philadelphia in the eighteenth century, and a variety of Jamaican rum sold until the 1950s.

92.4   replaced Judith Anderson in *As You Desire Me*] Anderson, eminent Australian actress (1897–1992); she played the Unknown Woman in the New York production of Luigi Pirandello's *As You Desire Me* (1931), later filmed with Greta Garbo in that role.

92.8   Miss Sandison] Helen Estabrook Sandison (1884–1978); along with Anna Kitchel, "Darling Miss Sandison," as she is referred to in McCarthy's *How I Grew* (1987), was one of the author's favorite English professors at Vassar. Sandison chaired the department beginning in McCarthy's junior year. She used to write the college catalog; the document's lucidity was what convinced McCarthy to apply to Vassar.

92.10   the Scottsboro trial] An important civil rights trial of the 1930s in which African Americans charged with raping two white women were sentenced to death by an all-white jury in Alabama.

92.21   Walter Huston] Canadian-American theatre and film actor (1884–1950), noted for appearances in *Abraham Lincoln* (1930), *Rain* (1932), and *Dodsworth* (1936); father of director John Huston.

93.29–31   Gustavus Myers' . . . Mendel's Law] Myers (1872–1942) published *History of the Great American Fortunes* (1909–10) in three volumes; Poor's *Register of Corporations, Directors, and Executives* was published by what later became Standard & Poor's, the financial services company. Mendel's laws include those explaining dominant and recessive traits in matters of heredity.

93.37   the Lamont family] Corliss Lamont (1902–1995), longtime director of the American Civil Liberties Union, was a lifelong radical, the son of a wealthy New Jersey family. His father had been the chairman of J. P. Morgan & Co.

94.14–15   the Rich Young Man in the Bible] A favorite biblical story of McCarthy's; in Mark 10:17–31, Jesus tells a wealthy young man: "One thing thou lackest: go thy way, sell whatsoever thou hast, and give to the poor, and thou shalt have treasure in heaven: and come, take up the cross, and follow me." In the same episode he tells his disciples: "It is easier for a camel to go through the eye of a needle, than for a rich man to enter into the kingdom of God."

96.28   the Bennett School] A women's junior college that operated from 1890 to 1978 in Millbrook, New York, not far from Vassar in Poughkeepsie.

96.36   lays of the trouvères] Lyric songs of medieval poets of northern France.

97.6–7 "The Judgment of Paris,"] Greek mythological competition in which Paris, son of the King of Troy, decides which of three goddesses—Aphrodite, Athena, or Hera—should be awarded a golden apple.

98.18–19 Art Students League] Art school traditionally hospitable to amateurs and short-term students as well as more fully committed ones. Founded in 1875 and located since 1892 on New York's West 57th Street.

99.10 *toute proportion gardée*] French: All allowance being made.

100.35 *Dorothy* Wordsworth] Diarist and poet (1771–1855); sister of the Romantic poet William Wordsworth (1770–1850).

101.6 Dalcroze] Émile Jaques-Dalcroze (1865–1950), Swiss musician and composer who pioneered eurythmics, which seeks to induce an understanding of music through physical movement.

102.30 Hallie Flanagan] See note 4.19.

102.32 Philaletheis] Artistic, literary, and dramatic society (named for "lovers of truth") founded at Vassar in 1865, the year the college opened; it continues to this day.

102.36 Lester Lang] See note 4.27.

103.38 the Jalna series] Sixteen-volume fictional family chronicle by the Canadian novelist Mazo de la Roche (1879–1961). The first volume, published in 1927, won a $10,000 prize from the Atlantic Monthly Press.

105.27–28 the Furness *Variorum*] Scholarly edition of Shakespeare produced by Horace Howard Furness (1833–1912).

105.27–28 "Arthur Gorges,"] Poet, naval commander, and member of Parliament (1557–1625); a cousin of Sir Walter Raleigh, he fought against the Spanish Armada. Gorges was the main scholarly interest of Helen Sandison (see note 92.8).

105.29 "Dorothy Richardson"] English novelist (1873–1957), sometimes regarded as a forerunner of Virginia Woolf; pioneer of "stream of consciousness" in a series of thirteen novels, *Pilgrimage*.

106.3 Jane Cowl] Boston-born actress (1883–1950) on Broadway and in films. She performed with Katharine Hepburn in New York in 1930 in the play *Art and Mrs. Bottle*, by Benn W. Levy.

108.33 Tiger Flowers] Theodore "Tiger" Flowers (1895–1927) became the first African American middleweight boxing champion in 1926.

109.14 Lavoris] Brand of mouthwash made in the U.S. since the early twentieth century.

110.25–26 the Dead March from *Saul.*] Funeral march, once frequently played for important public figures, from Act III of Handel's 1738 oratorio.

113.26–27   'A Room of One's Own,'] Virginia Woolf's book-length essay, published in 1929, which recommended "a room of her own and five hundred [pounds] a year" as conditions necessary for a woman's creative success.

115.4–7   "Sister Ann . . . do you see anyone coming?"] Question repeatedly asked by Bluebeard's wife in the version of the tale by Charles Perrault (1628–1703).

115.31   Cary's] Cary's College View Inn operated at 10 College View Avenue in Poughkeepsie, near the Vassar campus.

115.37   3.2 beer] Beer with 3.2 percent alcohol content by weight, made legally available by the Cullen-Harrison Act in March 1933, prior to the overall repeal of Prohibition later that year.

116.5–6   *The Autobiography of Lincoln Steffens*] Memoirs of the muckraking journalist (1866–1936), published in 1931. Steffens made his reputation with exposés of political corruption in U.S. cities. An early supporter of the Soviet Union, he was famous for saying of it, "I have seen the future, and it works."

116.7   Georgia O'Keeffe] American modernist painter (1887–1986), known especially for landscape depictions of the American Southwest.

117.20–21   Marx's *Capital* . . . *Axel's Castle*] Karl Marx's *Das Kapital*, three-volume theoretical critique of capitalism, edited and completed by Friedrich Engels, published between 1867 and 1894. Vilfredo Pareto (1848–1928), Italian sociological economist, author of *A Manual of Political Economy* (1906). Oswald Spengler (1880–1936), German philosopher of history, author of *The Decline of the West* (1918–22). *Ten Days That Shook the World*, by American journalist John Reed (1887–1920), chronicled his witness of the October 1917 Bolshevik Revolution. *Axel's Castle* (1931), a study of symbolism in literature by Edmund Wilson, McCarthy's second husband.

117.29   Diego Rivera and Orozco and framed Stieglitz photographs] Mexican leftist-leaning muralists Diego Rivera (1886–1957) and José Clemente Orozco (1883–1949); Alfred Stieglitz (1864–1946) was a pioneering American expressionist photographer and the husband of Georgia O'Keeffe.

119.11–12   Sandison . . . Lockwood] See notes 92.8 and 26.14.

119.22–23   Flanagan . . . Newcomer . . . Rindge . . . M.A.P. Smith] For Flanagan, see note 4.19. Mabel Newcomer (1891–1983), professor of economics at Vassar from 1917 to 1957, held practical, progressive views and performed service for various New York State commissions. Agnes Rindge, later Claflin (1900–1977), professor of art at Vassar and director of the college's art gallery. Mrs. M.A.P. Smith was a member of the Vassar English department.

120.5   Old Miss Fiske] Christabel Fiske (1869–1956), a member of the Vassar English department from 1903 to 1940, edited the *Vassar Journal of Undergraduate Studies*.

120.32   Miss Kitchel] Along with Helen Sandison, Anna Theresa Kitchel (1881–1959) was one of McCarthy's favorite teachers at Vassar. A specialist in nineteenth-century English literature, particularly George Eliot, she was known for her warm personality. She shares, as does Sandison, in the dedication to McCarthy's memoir *How I Grew* (1987). Both women practiced an aesthetic and historical approach to literature that was at odds with Helen Lockwood's more political one.

120.32–33   Clive Bell and Croce & Tolstoy's *What is Art?*] Bell, Bloomsbury group art critic (1881–1964) and brother-in-law of Virginia Woolf. Benedetto Croce, Italian philosopher (1866–1952) interested in aesthetics. In *What Is Art?* (1897) Tolstoy saw art's purpose as the development of man's finer moral feelings.

120.35–36   "The spirit killeth, and the letter giveth life."] In "Baudelaire in Our Time" (1928), Eliot uses this inversion of 2 Corinthians 3:6.

121.11   Roger Fry] Art critic and painter (1866–1934) and member of the Bloomsbury group.

125.39   Miss Washburn's] See note 4.17–18.

127.17   Robinson Jeffers. "*Roan Stallion*,"] Narrative poem published in 1925 by Jeffers (1887–1962), a proponent of "inhumanism," which sought to persuade man against the idea of his own centrality in the universe.

128.1   Miss Beckwith's] Martha Warren Beckwith (1871–1959) held a chair in folklore in the Vassar English department from 1920 to 1938.

128.1–2   Ge, the Earth Mother] In Greek mythology, Ge, or Gaia, was the mother of all on earth and the ancestress of the gods; she was Zeus's grandmother.

128.2   chthonian cults] Performers of sacrifices for the underworld spirits of Greek mythology.

128.6   Miss Caroline Spurgeon] British literary scholar and Chaucer specialist (1869–1942) who in 1935 published *Shakespeare's Imagery and What It Tells Us*.

128.14–15   queen of hell . . . Corn Mother] The "Corn Mother" is an epithet for Demeter, Greek goddess of the harvest. Her daughter Persephone is the queen of the underworld.

128.18   Schrafft's] The Schrafft's restaurants, which operated for decades in Manhattan, were described in a 2008 article in *The New York Times*: "The chain sought associations with the well-to-do, or at least comfortable, and the typical restaurant was a relaxed white-tablecloth retreat from the midday hustle of the city."

131.18   Norman Thomas] Thomas (1884–1969) was Socialist Party candidate for president in six elections from 1928 to 1948.

131.24   Farmer-Laborites and Progressives] Supporters of the Minnesota Farmer-Labor Party (1918–44) and the Progressive Party, which continued in Wisconsin after the defeat of its presidential candidate, Robert A. LaFollette, in 1924. A version of the party also operated in California in the 1930s.

131.35   Veblen] Thorstein Veblen (1857–1929), American economic sociologist; author of *The Theory of the Leisure Class* (1899) and inventor of the concept of "conspicuous consumption."

134.35–36   Zeus . . . golden scales] In the *Iliad*, Zeus weighs the fates of Hector and Achilles on a pair of such scales.

134.38–39   *Si jeunesse savait . . . !*] French saying, "*Si jeunesse savait; si vieillesse pouvait!*": "If youth only knew; if age only could!"

136.27–28   Sir Walter Raleigh . . . diamond] The English poet and explorer Sir Walter Raleigh (1554–1618), a favorite of Elizabeth I, is legendarily believed to have scratched a verse ("Fain would I climb, yet I fear to fall") for the queen onto a pane of glass in her palace by using a diamond.

138.3–4   Dorothy Parker, Alexander Woollcott, Robert Benchley] Three members of the Algonquin Round Table of New York wits. Parker (1893–1967) wrote short stories and reviews; Woollcott (1887–1943) was a critic and radio personality; Benchley (1889–1945) was a *New Yorker* humorist who appeared in short comic films.

138.39   Heywood Broun] American drama critic, sportswriter, and radio personality (1888–1939), a left-leaning journalistic crusader and another member of the Algonquin Round Table.

140.18   '*Cherchez la femme*,'] French: "Look for the woman." A standard imperative in detective stories, beginning with *The Mohicans of Paris* (1854) by Alexandre Dumas père.

140.26   Inez Something Something] Inez Milholland (1886–1916), Vassar graduate and woman suffrage activist, who rode on a white horse while wearing a white cape in the Washington, D.C., Suffrage Parade of March 3, 1913, prior to Woodrow Wilson's inauguration.

142.20   Society Library] Subscription lending library on East 79th Street in New York City.

143.38   Piping Rock Club] Country club built in 1911 in Matinecock, New York, known for the prominence and wealth of its members.

144.11   Schuyler] Prominent family of Dutch origin, long active in civic affairs in New York.

144.15   Chapin] The Chapin School for girls was founded in New York City in 1901. Its alumnae include Jacqueline Bouvier Kennedy and Julie Nixon Eisenhower.

144.16–17   Miss Hewitt's] Caroline D. Hewitt offered private instruction to wealthy children in New York. In 1920 Miss Hewitt founded the Hewitt School for girls on the city's Upper East Side.

144.28 milk leg] Condition involving deep vein thrombosis afflicting pregnant women and those who have recently given birth.

145.15–16 the Brook or the Racquet or the Knickerbocker] Exclusive men's clubs on Manhattan's East Side.

146.7 Ben Turpin] American comic actor (1869–1940) successful in silent pictures and famous for his crossed eyes.

147.8 Benedictine] French herbal liqueur.

147.38–39 Holmes Protective man] Edwin Holmes began his electric burglar alarm business in Boston in the 1850s.

148.6 Apollo serving King Admetus] During a period of exile and punishment, the god Apollo worked as the herdsman for Admetus, King of Pherae in Thessaly.

149.18 "out of the mouths of babes."] Proverb derived from Psalms 8:2.

149.24–25 the catechism . . . "God is everywhere."] Question and answer number 15 in *The Baltimore Catechism*.

150.30 Percy Hammond] Drama critic of *The New York Herald Tribune* (1873–1936).

153.28 'Maud Muller, on a summer's day . . .'] "Maud Muller," 1856 poem by John Greenleaf Whittier (1807–1892).

154.13–14 'People who live in glass houses,'] Proverbial phrase: "People who live in glass houses shouldn't throw stones."

154.29 Chapin School] See note 144.15.

155.35 "pride goeth before a fall."] Proverbs 16:18: "Pride goeth before destruction, And a haughty spirit before stumbling."

156.28 Shreve Crump] The Boston firm of Shreve, Crum & Low, with origins in the late eighteenth century, sells luxury gifts and jewelry, and is known for the manufacture of prestigious trophies.

157.5 Chilton Club] Private club for women on Commonwealth Avenue in Boston.

157.10 Peck & Peck] Fifth Avenue women's store specializing in upscale, conservative women's fashions.

162.13 Banquo's ghost] In *Macbeth*, the guilt-inducing apparition of a onetime ally whom Macbeth had murdered in the furtherance of his own ambitions.

163.7–8 Judy O'Grady and the Colonel's lady] A reference to the last lines of

Rudyard Kipling's 1922 poem "The Ladies": "For the Colonel's Lady an' Judy O'Grady / Are sisters under their skins!"

163.23 *Peter Ibbetson*] Much dramatized 1891 novel by George Du Maurier (1834–1896); the tale's separated lovers manage to be together by insinuating themselves into each other's dreams.

167.11 'For want of a nail . . .'] An extended proverb of how, through a cascading chain of circumstances, the lack of a horseshoe nail eventually leads to the loss of a kingdom.

170.4–5 'Whither thou goest I will go. . . .'] Ruth's promise to Naomi in Ruth 1:16.

173.1 Miss Kitchel] See note 120.32.

173.7–8 "This hopeful beauty did create" (Carew)] From "Epitaph on the Lady Mary Villiers" by Thomas Carew (1595–1640): "This hopeful beauty did create / New life in Love's declining state."

173.15 *The Lady of Laws*] Novel published in 1929 by Susanne G. Trautwein.

173.17 Malatestas] Family from the Italian Romagna who controlled the city of Rimini in the fourteenth and fifteenth centuries.

173.35 "They flee from me that some time did me seek."] First line of Sir Thomas Wyatt's lyric poem of that name.

173.36–37 *Of Human Bondage*] Best-known novel of W. Somerset Maugham (1874–1965), published in 1915 and filmed in 1934 with Bette Davis and Leslie Howard in the leads.

173.37–38 Katherine Mansfield and Edna Millay and Elinor Wylie] Mansfield, short story writer (1888–1923); Edna St. Vincent Millay, prominent American poet (1892–1950) and Vassar graduate to whom Edmund Wilson, McCarthy's second husband, lost his virginity; and Wylie, American poet and novelist (1885–1928).

174.31–32 a Harkness] Philanthropic American family known for its patronage of education and the arts; Stephen V. Harkness (1818–1888) made the family fortune through investment in John D. Rockefeller Sr.'s Standard Oil Co.

174.34 Mark Cross] High-end leather goods retailer founded in 1854; its principal store was in Manhattan. From 1934 to 1955 the firm was run by Gerald Murphy, famous for being F. Scott Fitzgerald's friend.

174.37–38 Pelion on Ossa] To pile Pelion on Ossa is to add one impossible job to another. In Book XI of *The Odyssey*, the giants set one mountain atop another in order to reach the gods they are bent on overthrowing.

175.1–2 Katharine Gibbs Secretarial School] With her sister Mary, Katharine Gibbs (1863–1934) developed a chain of secretarial schools in U.S. cities;

"Katie Gibbs girls," white-gloved and well-skilled, were long prized by American employers.

175.12   Miss Amy Loveman] A founder and editor of the *Saturday Review of Literature* (1881–1955) and eventually head of the Book-of-the-Month Club's editorial department.

175.13   Mrs. Van Doren (Irita, the wife of Carl)] Longtime editor (1891–1966) of *The New York Herald Tribune*'s book review.

176.1   an "operative" in a Howells novel] In *Dr. Breen's Practice* (1881) by William Dean Howells (1837–1920), the mother of Grace Breen, a female physician, inspects a New England mill and discovers that "the operatives were deplorably destitute of culture and drainage."

176.12   *New Masses*] Socialist magazine published from 1926 to 1948.

176.13   *Anvil*] Short-lived left-wing literary magazine that was subsumed by *Partisan Review* in 1935.

176.14   *Partisan Review*] Intellectual magazine founded in the 1930s and edited for many years by Philip Rahv and William Phillips. Home for many years to McCarthy's "Theater Chronicle" as well as a number of her essays and stories. See also Chronology for 1937.

176.19   Lord Chesterfield] Philip Dormer Stanhope (1694–1773), fourth Earl of Chesterfield; Whig politician and orator; famously scorned by Dr. Johnson for his niggardly patronage of the *Dictionary*; author of the wearyingly strategic *Letters to His Son on the Art of Becoming a Man of the World and a Gentleman* (1774).

176.40   Odo-Ro-No] An early commercial antiperspirant; "Odor? Oh, no!"

178.38–39   a Dutch uncle] A blunt giver of sometimes unwelcome advice.

180.2   Mrs. M. A. P. Smith] See note 119.22–23.

180.32–33   the Cavalier Poets] English lyricists of the seventeenth century, including Richard Lovelace and Robert Herrick, who were supporters of Charles I during the English Civil War. Their poetry promoted worldly pleasures and "carpe diem," or the need to "Gather ye rosebuds while ye may" (Herrick).

180.33–34   Sidney and Drayton] Sir Philip Sidney (1554–1586), poet-soldier and model Renaissance man, author of *The Defence of Poesy* (c. 1582); Michael Drayton (1563–1631), English poet known for *Idea: The Shepherd's Garland* (1593) and *England's Heroical Epistles* (1597).

180.34–35   "Since there's no help . . . more of me . . ."] First two lines of Drayton's sonnet "Idea 61" (1619).

182.6–7   a Buchmanite boy] A follower of the Oxford Group, founded by the Protestant evangelical Rev. Frank Buchman (1878–1961); the Group held that "international problems are, at bottom, personal problems of selfishness and fear" and began a "Moral Re-Armament" campaign in 1938.

182.7 Sam Shoemaker] Samuel Moor Shoemaker (1893–1963), Episcopal priest, adherent of the Oxford Group, and rector of Calvary Episcopal Church in New York, 1925–52; his sermons reached a wide audience through recordings and radio.

182.26–27 Alice McCollister's] Alice McCollister's restaurant at 43 West 8th Street had been operating for decades. In the *Gothamist* website's report on "New York's Forgotten Restaurants," it is grouped with "rough places that were known for seafood right off the docks."

182.27 the Jumble Shop] Manhattan restaurant on Waverly Place.

184.12 Miss Peebles] Rose Jeffries Peebles (1870–1952) taught English at Vassar from 1909 to 1938; a proponent of "advanced, independent work" of the sort McCarthy published in the *Vassar Journal of Undergraduate Studies.*

185.40 Mr. Roselli] Bruno Roselli (1887–1970), Florentine immigrant to the United States, popular professor of Italian at Vassar from 1919 to 1933, and an enthusiast of Mussolini's early rule. Taught in Argentina and Peru in his later years; his students included Mario Vargas Llosa.

188.19 *Mezzogiorno*] Southern Italy, named for the bright sun in "the middle of the day."

189.18 Blanche Knopf] Cofounder (1894–1966) of what became Alfred A. Knopf, Inc., in 1915, a year before she and Knopf married. She acquired important Latin American and European authors for the house.

191.7 "The Birth of Venus."] Mid-1480s painting by Italian painter Sandro Botticelli.

192.25 Dr. Guthrie] During the 1920s, William Norman Guthrie (1868–1944) displeased his Episcopal bishop by incorporating pagan elements into worship at St. Mark's.

195.5 Ann Harding] The films of Ann Harding (1902–1981) include *Holiday* (1930), for which she received an Academy Award nomination as Best Actress.

197.37 Metternich] Prince Klemens Wenzel von Metternich (1773–1859), foreign minister of the Austrian Empire who chaired the Congress of Vienna in 1814–15. Its diplomatic settlement of the Napoleonic Wars remained largely in place for the next hundred years.

198.6 "*sortes Virgilianae*"] A method of fortune-telling, practiced since Roman times, that involves the random selection of passages from Virgil's *Aeneid.*

199.1 *E così via*] Italian: And so forth.

207.18 'The Milky Way'] Jacopo Comin, known as Tintoretto (1518–1594), painted *The Origin of the Milky Way* in the late 1570s. It depicts, from Greek myth, the painful nursing of Heracles by Hera, whose spraying breast milk forms the stars in our galaxy.

208.34 Skoal] Scandinavian toast (literally, "a bowl"); used in Britain from about 1600.

208.34 Rhine maiden] Mythological water nymph in Richard Wagner's *Ring* cycle of operas.

208.35–36 "Shakespeare," . . . pickled herring] In 1592, the playwright and man of letters Thomas Nashe wrote that "one of my fellows Will Monox," who is thought by some to be a reference to Shakespeare, consumed Rhenish wine and pickled herring at a banquet held in September 1592. That was a month before the death of playwright Robert Greene—but more than twenty years before Shakespeare himself died.

208.40 "The Passionate Shepherd to His Love"] Poem by Christopher Marlowe (1564–1593), famously rebutted by Sir Walter Raleigh in "The Nymph's Reply to the Shepherd."

210.18 Bendel's] High-end Fifth Avenue retailer of women's fashions and accessories.

211.15 the Wreck of the Hesperus] The title of Henry Wadsworth Longfellow's famous ballad of a shipwreck off New England, published in 1840. The phrase "looks like the wreck of the Hesperus" later entered the American vernacular.

214.23 Madam Perkins] Frances Perkins (1880–1965), the first woman to serve in a U.S. presidential Cabinet, was secretary of labor in all four administrations of Franklin D. Roosevelt.

215.27 new theory of history] Probably a reference to the work of the British scholar Arnold J. Toynbee (1899–1975), whose multivolume *A Study of History* began to be published, to much public discussion, in 1934. Toynbee argued that civilizations advanced by meeting challenges and accepting the leadership of "creative minorities" within their own populations.

222.4 *nolens volens*] Latin: willing or unwilling; whether one likes something or not.

235.24 Wanamaker's] Philadelphia's first department store, with later branches in New York, London, and Paris.

236.14 Ogilvie Sisters hairbrush] The Ogilvie Sisters, a company located in New York and Paris, sold women's hair products, including shampoo.

238.4 Hupmobile] Automobile manufactured by the Hupp Motor Car Company of Detroit from 1909 to 1940.

238.18 Brill's] Abraham Arden Brill (1874–1948), Austrian American psychoanalyst who translated Freud into English and founded the New York Psycho-analytic Society.

238.37 Shaw] George Bernard Shaw (1856–1950), Irish playwright and critic whose stage works and other writings presented a panoply of socialist and progressive views.

239.4–5 Intourist girl guide] An assigned guide and ideological minder from the official Soviet tourist agency who would make sure that travelers to the Soviet Union saw only what the government wished them to see.

239.5 Norman Thomas] See note 131.18.

239.7 Trotskyites] Leon Trotsky (1879–1940), early Soviet leader and head of the Red Army; advocate of "permanent revolution" and a measure of de-mocracy within the Communist Party; forced out of the Communist Party in 1927 and murdered by an agent of Stalin, in Mexico, in 1940.

239.8 Lovestoneites] Dissident faction within the American communist movement named for Jay Lovestone (1897–1990), who after his expulsion from the party in 1929 led his own communist group until 1941. He later had a long career with the AFL-CIO and cooperated with the CIA.

239.8 Musteites] In 1929, the Rev. A. J. Muste (1885–1967) founded the Conference for Progressive Labor Action as a more radical alternative to the American Federation of Labor (AFL).

239.23–24 Webster Hall] Constructed on East 11th Street in New York City in 1886; during the 1920s and 1930s the scene of dances, rallies, and meetings by radicals and artists. It hosts concerts and nightclub entertainments to this day.

240.6 El Campesino] Valentín González Gonzáles (1904–1983), anti-Franco military leader in the Spanish Republican Army during the Spanish Civil War (1936–39).

240.7 Vincent Sheean] American foreign correspondent (1899–1975).

240.9 Abraham Lincoln Battalion] American volunteer segment of the XV International Brigade that fought on behalf of the Spanish Republic and against Franco during the Spanish Civil War.

240.35 an Ayer] Edward Everett Ayer (1841–1927), a major collector of books and manuscripts that he donated to Chicago's Newberry Library and Field Museum, accumulated his fortune through the sale of timber to Ameri-can railroads.

240.35 Lord Acton] John Emerich Edward Dalberg-Acton (1834–1902), English political figure most famous for saying "Power tends to corrupt, and absolute power corrupts absolutely."

240.38 Döllinger's Old Catholics] Followers of Ignaz von Döllinger (1799–1890), German theologian.

240.39 Dukhobers] Russian pacifists (literally "Spirit wrestlers"), a portion of whom, even after getting to western Canada, would sometimes stage nude demonstrations to protest conscription.

252.18 "Poum"] The Partido Obrero de Unificación Marxista or Workers' Party of Marxist Unification, founded 1935, an anti-Stalinist Spanish communist party with Trotskyist elements. In *Homage to Catalonia* (1938), George Orwell recounts his service in the POUM militia during the Spanish Civil War.

257.23 Union Square] Public space near New York City's Fourteenth Street, long associated with protest demonstrations on behalf of radical causes.

260.4–5 'Each man kills the thing he loves,'] From Oscar Wilde's poem "The Ballad of Reading Gaol" (1897).

260.8–9 'Like the base Indian threw a pearl away, richer than all his tribe,'] *Othello*, V.ii.347–48.

260.25–26 "French leave."] Absence without permission and without having said goodbye.

261.3 her lamp trimmed like the wise virgins] In Matthew 25:1–13, the five wise virgins carry oil for their lamps when going to meet the bridegroom at a wedding; the five foolish ones miss his arrival when they have to go off in search of someone who will sell them more oil.

266.14–15 "*Il Penseroso*"] "The Serious Man," Milton's poetic expression of melancholy, published in 1645.

266.15 Dürer's engraving] Albrecht Dürer's *Melencolia I* (1514).

268.1–2 a pessimist in the tradition of Henry Adams] Adams's cultural gloom is displayed throughout his works, from his novel *Democracy* (1880) on through his third-person autobiography, *The Education of Henry Adams* (1918).

268.7 Politburo] The policy-making body of the Soviet Union's Communist Party.

268.33 Blum] Léon Blum (1872–1950), Socialist prime minister of France on three brief occasions, most lengthily from June 1936 to June 1937.

270.34 Borotra] Jean Borotra (1898–1994), nicknamed "the Bounding Basque," French tennis champion of the 1920s and 1930s.

277.9 Walter Duranty] Mendacious Moscow correspondent of *The New York Times* (1884–1957) from 1922 to 1936; a Stalinist sympathizer. In 2003 a posthumous attempt was made to strip him of his 1932 Pulitzer Prize.

285.15–16 Mr. Micawber . . . Prince Andrei] Mr. Micawber, amiable, debt-ridden character in Dickens's *David Copperfield* (1850). Mr. Collins, unctuous, self-regarding clergyman in Jane Austen's *Pride and Prejudice* (1813). Vronsky,

Anna's lover in Tolstoy's *Anna Karenina* (1878). Prince Andrei, complicated and introspective figure in Tolstoy's *War and Peace* (1869).

285.18–19   Dr. Lydgate . . . *Middlemarch*] Tertius Lydgate, the idealistic young physician in George Eliot's *Middlemarch* (1872).

285.19   *Silas Marner*] Novel by George Eliot, published in 1861, whose miserly hero is redeemed by his care of a motherless girl named Eppie.

285.21   Hector and Achilles] The dueling warriors—one steadfast, the other sulking and hot-headed—of Homer's *Iliad*.

285.30   Virgil's *Georgics*] Four-part agricultural poem (c. 29 B.C.E.) by Virgil (70–19 B.C.E.).

297.7–8   "I met Murder on the way. It had a face like my wife Kay."] Lines 5–6 of Shelley's "The Mask of Anarchy" read "I met Murder on the way—He had a mask like Castlereagh."

303.12   Lucius Beebe] Syndicated newspaper columnist (1902–1966) who covered "café society" in the *New York Herald-Tribune*.

304.21–22   *E io senti chiavar l'uscio di sotto/ all'orribile torre*] Italian: Below I heard them locking up the door / Of the horrible tower. Words spoken by Ugolino della Gherardesca in Dante's *Inferno*, Canto XXXIII, lines 46–47. T. S. Eliot also uses them in *The Waste Land*.

305.4   the Pathé rooster] A barnyard version of the MGM lion, heard crowing at the start of the company's newsreels, which were shown in theatres from 1908 on.

317.33–34   Behaviorist? Gestalt? Steiner? Klein? Anna Freud?] Contending schools of psychological thought and some of their proponents in the early and mid-twentieth century. Behaviorism emphasized the influence of an individual's experience, including the effects of punishment and rewards and reinforcement; Gestalt focused on the "global whole" formed by the mind as it organized itself amidst multiple stimuli. For Steiner, see note 327.22. Melanie Klein (1882–1960) and Anna Freud (1895–1982) were pioneering child psychologists.

317.38   Kuhn, Loeb] New York investment bank founded in 1867.

324.16–17   Margaret Mead] American cultural anthropologist (1901–1978) who achieved early fame with *Coming of Age in Samoa* (1928) and *Growing Up in New Guinea* (1930).

324.31   Pablum] Precooked cereal for infants, bland but rich in vitamins, introduced in 1931.

325.10–11   Gesell's studies at Yale] Arnold Gesell (1880–1961) did influential research in child psychology and development; known for the Gesell Developmental Schedules.

325.24–26   TVA, rural electrification . . . Wages and Hours] New Deal agencies and measures for economic relief and development. The Tennessee Valley Authority was set up by Congress in 1933 to promote flood control, electricity generation, and economic activity in the Tennessee Valley. The Farm Security Administration, established in 1937, replaced the Resettlement Administration as a bureau designed to alleviate poverty in rural areas of the U.S. The Wage and Hour Division of the Labor Department was created in 1938.

325.34   Danzig] "Free city" on the Baltic Sea from 1920 to 1939, created by the Treaty of Versailles, protected by the League of Nations, and conquered by Hitler during his invasion of Poland. In 1945 it became the Polish city of Gdańsk.

325.35   America First] The isolationist America First Committee (1940–41), determined to keep the United States out of the war in Europe; its supporters included aviator Charles Lindbergh.

325.40   Toynbee] See note 215.27.

327.19–20   the Monophysites or the Athansian Creed or Maimonides] Monophysites, believers that Christ had one divine nature rather than a mixture of the human and divine. The Athanasian Creed, an expression of the belief that all members of the Christian Trinity are equal. Maimonides, Sephardic Jewish philosopher (1135–1204).

327.22   Anthroposophist] Followers of Rudolf Steiner (1861–1925) who held that the spiritual world exists as an objective reality that can be reached through "inner development."

327.23   eurhythmics] See note 101.6.

327.31   *Pour les convenances*] French: For the sake of propriety.

337.8   *Luftwaffe*] Nazi Germany's air force, commanded by Hermann Goering.

337.13–14   "And all our flesh is as the grass" . . . Mass] *A German Requiem* by Johannes Brahms (1833–1897) was first performed in Bremen in 1868. "Behold, all flesh is as the grass" comes in the second movement, a funeral march.

337.21   Dr. Reiland] See note 3.6.

338.19   Sydney Carton] Sydney Carton is the self-redeeming "Jackal" of Dickens's *A Tale of Two Cities* (1859) who through some noble deception manages to substitute himself at the guillotine for the condemned Charles Darnay.

339.26   Fortuny's] The Spanish couturier Mariano Fortuny y Madrazo (1871–1949) founded his fashion house in 1906.

339.27   Duchess of Guermantes] Oriane, Duchesse de Guermantes, is the most beautiful aristocratic figure in Proust's *In Search of Lost Time* (1913–27). Throughout the novel special attention is paid to her elegant clothes.

341.36 Purcell] Henry Purcell (c. 1659–1695), English Baroque composer of both sacred and theatrical music.

342.35 the invasion of the Lowlands] Germany invaded the Netherlands, Belgium, and Luxembourg on May 10, 1940.

343.8 Mayor La Guardia] Fiorello H. LaGuardia (1882–1947), "the Little Flower," was New York City's colorful reformist mayor from 1934 to 1945. Franklin Roosevelt appointed him to direct the new Office of Civilian Defense in 1941.

344.4 America Firster] See note 325.35.

345.38 Mrs. Flanagan] See note 4.19.

346.2–5 "I am the Resurrection . . . shall never die."] John 1:25.

346.36–37 "Lord, let me know mine end, and the number of my days. . . ."] Psalm 39:4.

347.21–23 "In the morning . . . withered,"] Psalm 90:6.

347.32 *De Profundis*] Psalm 130: "De profundis clamavi ad te, Domine." ("From the depths, I have cried out to you, O Lord.")

348.4 *Si le grain ne meurt*] French: If it die. John 12:24–25: "Verily, verily, I say unto you. Except a corn of wheat fall into the ground and die, it abideth alone; but if it die, bringeth forth much fruit." The phrase is also the title of André Gide's autobiography, *Si le grain ne meurt* (1924).

348.17 Number 245: "He leadeth me."] Hymn number 45, by Joseph H. Gilmore (1834–1918), in the Protestant Episcopal Church's hymnal.

350.8 Bernard Berenson] Renaissance art historian (1865–1959), born in Lithuania, educated in America, and resident for many years at Villa I Tatti near Florence, where McCarthy visited him in 1956.

352.19 Schiaparelli suit] Elsa Schiaparelli, Italian fashion designer (1890–1973).

353.22 Castle Perilous] Where, in Malory's *Morte d'Arthur* and Tennyson's *Idylls of the King*, the Lady of Lyonesse, sister of Lynette, is imprisoned.

BIRDS OF AMERICA

366.3 SNCC, CORE, and SANE] Three activist organizations of the period. The Student Nonviolent Coordinating Committee (SNCC), organized in 1960, and the Congress of Racial Equality (CORE), founded in 1942, promoted civil rights; SANE originated in 1957 as the Committee for a Sane Nuclear Policy.

366.36–37 Eli Whitney and the inventor of the McCormick Reaper] Whitney (1765–1825) was the inventor of the cotton gin. The mechanical reaper, developed by Cyrus McCormick (1809–1884), had a similar industrializing effect on the production of grain.

367.28–29   like the Raven] The mournful, vocal title figure of Edgar Allan Poe's 1845 poem, who repeatedly says "Nevermore."

367.31   "Once more unto the breach, dear friends."] *Henry V*, III.iii.1.

371.37   Narcissus] Beautiful young figure of Greek mythology who fell in love with his own reflection.

375.35–36   Revenges . . . *Don Giovanni*] These three figures in Mozart's 1787 opera have suffered attempted sexual assault, jilting, and near-cuckoldry by the title character.

376.32   *Marie Celeste*] The mystery of this ghost ship (actually the *Mary Celeste*), found unmanned and drifting near the Azores in 1872, has never been satisfactorily solved.

378.20   Peterson guide] Roger Tory Peterson's *A Field Guide to the Birds of Eastern and Central North America* was first published in 1934.

380.16–17   Mannes School . . . Landowska] The David Mannes School, later the Mannes School of Music, founded in New York in 1916; Wanda Landowska (1879–1959), popular Polish harpsichordist who moved to the U.S. in 1941.

380.35–36   "*Mi piaceva il suo candore*,"] Italian: I liked her candor.

381.15–16   a Thomas Hardy poem . . . "Dear Lizbie Browne."] In "To Lizbie Browne," based on Hardy's youthful love for Elizabeth Sara Bishop, the name of the subject appears in the first and last lines of all nine stanzas.

383.29   *mains croisées*] A keyboard technique in which the right hand crosses over the left in order to play the bass part.

384.17–18   *Peter and the Wolf*] Sergei Prokofiev's 1936 composition, based on a story he wrote himself; often used to acquaint children with individual instruments of the orchestra.

385.16   "We Three Kings of Orient Are."] Christmas carol (1857) by John Henry Hopkins Jr.

387.27   Solon] Athenian lawmaker (c. 630–c. 560 B.C.E.) whose name is often used as a synonym for legislator.

388.23   the Lost Pleiad] Mythic star in the "Seven Sisters" cluster; perhaps in fact the variably bright star Pleione.

388.36–37   Fannie Farmer] See note 61.21.

389.8   Tafelspitz] Austrian boiled beef in broth, usually accompanied by horseradish, minced apples, and root vegetables.

395.18   "We GATHer toGETHer to ASK the Lord's BLESSing,"] Dutch hymn composed by Adrianus Valerius in 1597, after Spain's defeat in the Battle of Turnhout.

395.20   William the Silent] William I (1533–1584), Prince of Orange, led the Dutch rebellion against Spain. See also note 564.30–31.

395.29–30   'It is not good that man should be alone,'] Genesis 2:18; the Lord's spoken rationale for creating Eve as Adam's helper.

395.40   Aaron's Rod] Miracle-enabling stave of Moses's brother, mentioned in Exodus 7 and Numbers 17.

398.34   Queen Morgan le Fay] Sorceress of Arthurian legend, by some accounts the half sister of King Arthur.

400.32   *Carmen . . . The Seasons* by Haydn] Georges Bizet's once-scandalous opera premiered in Paris in 1875; Haydn's oratorio premiered in Vienna in 1801.

400.35   *E così via*] Italian: And so on.

402.27   "*cosa fatta capo ha*"] What is done is done.

408.14   a madman called Borromini] Francesco Borromini (1599–1667), angry, depressed, and eventually suicidal Baroque architect, whose significant religious work includes the structures of San Carlo alle Quattro Fontane in Rome.

408.16–17   the fox and the grapes] The fifteenth of Aesop's Fables, whose protagonist proudly decides that the grapes he desires and cannot reach are not worth having—i.e., "sour grapes."

408.22   *Stranieri*] Italian: foreigners.

408.28–29   Io after she had been turned into a cow.] Io, a mortal lover of Zeus, was turned into a heifer, either by him (for purposes of disguise) or by his wife, Hera (for purposes of revenge).

409.30   Franco] Fascist dictator of Spain from 1936 to 1975.

410.39–40   *Cultiver leur jardin.*] French: Cultivate their garden. A reference to the closing words of Voltaire's *Candide* (1759).

411.14   Goldwater] The 1964 Republican nominee for president, Arizona senator Barry Goldwater (1909–1998), a libertarian conservative and fierce anticommunist who said, in his convention acceptance speech, that "extremism in the defense of liberty is no vice." He suffered a landslide defeat at the hands of the incumbent president, Lyndon B. Johnson.

411.18–19   "Wood Alcohol—Your Poison."] During Prohibition, industrial methanol ("wood alcohol") was used in the making of illegal liquor, with sometimes lethal results.

411.29   "The John Birch Society."] Extreme right-wing American political organization founded in 1958 by businessman Robert W. Welch Jr.

420.24   Norman Thomas] See note 131.18.

420.25   Darlington Hoopes] The Socialist Party of America's candidate for president against Dwight D. Eisenhower and Adlai Stevenson in 1952 and 1956.

425.39   Simon Legree] The cruel slave owner in Harriet Beecher Stowe's novel *Uncle Tom's Cabin* (1852).

425.40   Adlai] Adlai E. Stevenson (1900–1965), Democratic candidate for president in 1952 and 1956.

430.1   *The Carpetbaggers*] Steamy, best-selling novel (1961) by Harold Robbins; the movie version premiered in 1964.

431.11   Lowestoft dishes] English porcelain china produced in the Suffolk town of Lowestoft during the second half of the eighteenth century.

432.27   Johnson] Lyndon B. Johnson (1908–1973), thirty-sixth president of the United States, 1963–69.

437.28–29   "*Se vuol ballare, signor contino*"] Italian: If you want to dance, my little count; aria from Mozart's *The Marriage of Figaro* (1786).

443.8   "*Oui, monsieur . . . Parfaitement,*"] French: Yes, sir. Absolutely.

443.12   "*On est en France, Pierre,*"] We are in France, Peter.

443.23–25   "*Essayez de comprendre . . . avec le train.*"] Try to understand, sir. . . . I am going to Paris by motorbike. I am not travelling by train.

443.30–32   "*Je n'ai pas de billet. . . . s'il vous plaît.*"] I do not have a ticket. I am going to Paris by motorbike. Give me back my luggage, please.

444.17   "*Mais je vous ai dit cinq fois, monsieur—*"] But I have told you five times, sir—

445.23   Sir Pellias the Gentle Knight] Lowborn member of the Round Table, a defender of Queen Guinevere, who in various versions of the legend is rejected by a woman of higher station.

445.26   Damsel Parcenet] Handmaiden of the lady who rejects Pellias.

445.27   Rosinante] Don Quixote's skinny, beleaguered horse.

445.36   Burke and neoconservatism or Plato's Philosopher King] The Anglo-Irish statesman and political philosopher Edmund Burke (1729–1797) strongly influenced the ideals of conservatism, most directly through his opposition to the French Revolution. "Neoconservatism" did not often appear in the American political lexicon until later in the 1970s, after McCarthy was writing, though the movement would attract some of her onetime colleagues from the anti-Stalinist left. She may be using the word—sometimes applied to conservative intellectuals of the Weimar Republic—in her own way, to indicate a brief ideological infatuation of some young people in Peter's generation, who temporarily affect Burke's ideas in the manner of "an Edwardian mustache." The

Philosopher King is the ideal ruler described in Book VI of Plato's *Republic* (c. 380 B.C.E.).

446.2 "weeping and commenting upon the sobbing deer."] "The melancholy Jaques," who gives the famous "seven ages of man" speech in *As You Like It*, II.vii, is the Forest of Arden's misanthropic philosopher; he is described as crying over a deer that has been wounded by perfidious man in II.i.64–65.

447.8 Harry's Bar in Venice] Famous spot for celebrities and tourists, opened in 1931 by Giuseppe Cipriani and named for Harry Pickering, an American to whom he once lent money, and who paid him back many times over with enough money to start the bar.

447.21 "*L'hai persa! L'hai persa!*"] "You lost it! You lost it!"

448.23 the Affluent Society] The title of John Kenneth Galbraith's socio-economic study of postwar America, published in 1958, quickly passed into the language.

448.29 LOT] Polish national airline.

449.14–15 *Arbres et arbustes de nos forêts et de nos jardins*] French: Trees and shrubs of our forests and gardens.

450.15–16 "*Via, bambini*," or "*Foutez le camp*."] Italian: Go away, children; French: Get lost!

452.32–33 five just men would have saved Sodom] Genesis 18:26–28: "And the Lord said, If I find in Sodom fifty righteous within the city, then I will spare all the place for their sakes. And Abraham answered and said, Behold now, I have taken upon me to speak unto the Lord, which *am but* dust and ashes: Peradventure there shall lack five of the fifty righteous: wilt thou destroy all the city for *lack of* five? And he said, If I find there forty and five, I will not destroy *it*."

452.36–453.1 'To thine own self . . . like Laertes] Polonius gives this famous advice to Laertes, his son, in *Hamlet*, I.iii.78–80.

453.34 *Ivanhoe*] Sir Walter Scott's novel of knighthood and medieval times, published in 1820; for generations a staple of English classes in American public schools.

457.32 Saint Jacques] St. James, apostle of Christ martyred in 44 C.E. and believed by some to have evangelized in Spain. His "trail" is the Camino de Santiago, which pilgrims take to his supposed burial place, Galicia's Cathedral of Santiago de Compostela.

457.33 Sir Percival of Gales] One of the principal knights of King Arthur's Round Table.

457.37 a giant Christopher] Because he is thought to have carried the young Christ across a river, Saint Christopher was long considered the patron saint of travelers, who in the twentieth century often carried medallions with his image in their automobiles.

462.23 Henry Adams] American historian (1838–1918), grandson and great-grandson of U.S. presidents. He published *Mont Saint Michel and Chartres* in 1904.

463.7–8 a whole book . . . by Prince Kropotkin] Prince Pyotr Alexeyevich Kropotkin (1842–1921), Russian anarchist philosopher, published *Mutual Aid: A Factor of Evolution* in 1902.

464.8–9 Samson Agonistes] The name of Milton's "closet drama" in blank verse (1671) on the subject of Samson, who in the Book of Judges loses his great strength when he is shorn of his hair.

464.20 Barry] See note 411.14. Goldwater was the son of a Jewish father and Episcopalian mother.

465.11 O brave new world!] Miranda in *The Tempest*, V.i.182–83.

466.40 the three Norns] Mythological Norse women who determine men's fates.

468.12–13 "*Descendez, monsieur. . . . Paris.*"] French: Get off, sir. Get off! You are in Paris.

468.21 "*Au voleur!*"] Thief!

468.27 "*On m'a volé mon vélomoteur!*"] They stole my motorbike!

468.29–34 "*A la douane, . . . vélomoteur!*"] At customs, sir! You will find it at customs. It must pass through customs. . . . There is your motorbike!

468.40–469.1 "*Monsieur! J'ai dédouané déjà—au Havre.*"] Sir! I have already cleared customs—at Le Havre.

471.7 the Lido] Cabaret on the Champs-Elysées that opened in 1946; noted for presenting Edith Piaf, Marlene Dietrich, and others.

472.26 "From each according to his abilities."] "From each according to his abilities, to each according to his needs." A coinage of the French socialist Louis Blanc in the 1850s; the formula was later made famous by Karl Marx.

473.27 Conscience doth make cowards of us all] *Hamlet*, III.i.82.

473.35 *chambres de bonne*] Literally "maid's room"; French term for a single-room apartment, often on the top floor of a building.

474.11–12 *une seule clef. . . . une seule porte*] One key . . . one door.

474.19–20 *per bene*] Italian: respectable.

475.1–2 "*Méfiez-vous, monsieur.*"] French: Beware, sir.

476.13 *praires*] Clams.

476.25–26 "*Ça ne me regarde pas,*"] It's none of my business.

478.22 Antonioni] Italian film director Michelangelo Antonioni (1912–2007); his films include *L'avventura* (1960) and *Blowup* (1966).

478.31 Monica Vitti] Italian actress (b. 1931) known for her work in Antonioni's films.

479.29 St.-Denis] The Basilica of St. Denis, north of Paris, was rebuilt in the Gothic manner early in the twelfth century under the administration of the Abbé Suger.

479.33 Abbé Suger] Abbot of St. Denis in the early twelfth century. An advisor to Kings Louis VI and VII.

481.3 *antipatico*] Italian: unpleasant.

481.9–10 FFV cookies] Famous Foods of Virginia, a brand name used by the Southern Biscuit Company in Richmond, whose products included cookies sold by the Girl Scouts.

483.35–36 "O what a rogue and peasant slave am I!"] From *Hamlet*, II.ii.550, part of Hamlet's self-loathing examination of his own cowardice—and his plan to overcome it.

484.26 Viollet-le-Duc] Eugène-Emmanuel Viollet-le-Duc, French Gothic architect (1814–1879); his restorations include Notre-Dame and the Basilica of St.-Denis.

484.40 Donatello] Italian sculptor Donato di Niccolò di Betto Bardi (1386?–1466).

485.10 a book by Salvemini] Gaetano Salvemini (1873–1957) was an Italian socialist and antifascist whose book *The French Revolution: 1788–1792* was first published in 1905.

485.12 *faible*] French: weakness or penchant.

485.13 Saint Denis] Third-century bishop of Paris and later patron saint of the city; he supposedly continued to preach, while carrying his own head, after his martyrdom by decapitation.

485.26 *ci-devant*] From a former time.

486.19–20 Out, damned spot] Lady Macbeth's guilt-ridden, sleepwalking utterance after the murder of Duncan in *Macbeth*, V.i.35.

486.23 OAS] Organisation de l'armée secrète (Organization of the Secret Army), violent rightist group opposed to independence for Algeria that carried out terrorist and paramilitary operations, including attempts to assassinate President Charles de Gaulle, during the early 1960s.

486.24   A BAS LES JUIFS.] French: Down with the Jews.

486.36–37   the Ciompi in Florence] Wool-carders at the heart of a four-teenth-century labor rebellion in the city.

487.1–2   that play about the man who came to dinner.] *The Man Who Came to Dinner* (1939), popular stage play by Moss Hart and George S. Kaufman; the obnoxious lead character, Sheridan Whiteside, was based on the critic Alexander Woollcott, a figure of the Algonquin Roundtable.

488.1   Castro] Fidel Castro (b. 1926), Cuban revolutionary and dictator from 1959 to 2008.

488.8   Good King Wenceslas] Tenth-century Duke of Bohemia, generous to the poor, immortalized in a Christmas carol by English hymn writer John Mason Neale in 1853.

489.20–21   the Urban League] The National Urban League, moderate civil rights organization formed in 1910.

489.21   the Brotherhood of Sleeping Car Porters] African American labor union, active in the civil rights movement, founded in 1925 by A. Philip Randolph.

495.28   Pierrot le Fou] French: Peter the Fool. Popular film that starred Jean-Paul Belmondo and was directed by Jean-Luc Godard. This is a slight anachronism—the film was not released until November 5, 1965—that would no doubt have bothered McCarthy if she'd caught it. While writing this novel she called the Paris weather bureau to make sure that there had actually been rain on the February morning when Peter learns about the U.S. bombing of North Vietnam (see p. 641 in this volume).

496.6–7   Brigitte Bardot . . . in *La Vérité*.] Thriller from 1960 directed by Henri-Georges Clouzot.

496.9   Javert] The police inspector who relentlessly pursues Jean Valjean in Victor Hugo's *Les Misérables* (1862).

496.11   Danton] Georges Jacques Danton (1759–1794), French revolutionary and briefly minister of justice. Guillotined by radicals during the Reign of Terror. The statue of Danton that Peter salutes stands in what is now the Place Henri-Mondor, near the Odéon metro.

496.17   Ecole de Médecine] Neoclassical building designed in the late eighteenth century by the architect Jacques Gondoin.

496.22   *le grand mal*] Severe epilepsy involving convulsions and the loss of consciousness.

499.18   *Guide des oiseaux d'Europe*] *Guide to the Birds of Europe*.

499.31   a Papagena] Lovely young birdcatcher who appears in Mozart's *The Magic Flute*.

502.6   Linnaeus'] Carl von Linné, known as Linnaeus (1707–1778), Swedish botanist who devised a classification system of plant and animal life.

503.12   *il pallone americano*] Italian: the American football.

503.25–26   "Mortal man was put . . . immortal plants."] Connected perhaps to a passage in the *Festal Menaion*, liturgical book of the Eastern Orthodox Church: "And I partake in faith of the life-giving tree in Eden, becoming once again a husbandman of immortal plants."

506.24   "*C'est beau, hein?*"] French: It's beautiful, eh?

508.12   *blouses de travail*] Smocks.

508.35   Magasins Réunis] French department store chain.

509.28   *témoins oculaires*] Eyewitnesses.

510.8   C'est leur métier.] It's their job.

510.18   *entendu*] Understood or agreed.

510.22   *panier à salade*] Black Maria, police van.

510.26   *bagarres*] Fights.

511.18   *carte de séjour*] Residence permit.

513.13–14   "*Oui, il a fait pipi dans mon escalier de service!*"] Yes, he has peed in my backstairs!

513.16–17   "*Le sixième, monsieur,*"] The sixth, sir.

513.18–19   "*Il n'était pas pressé,*"] He was not in a hurry.

514.3   Sydney Carton] See note 338.19.

514.12–16   "*Pardon, monsieur l'agent; . . . vous cherchiez.*"] Pardon, officer; I can testify for my countryman. He took no part in the demonstration. He did not hide in the lady's building. He was next to me, the whole time, on the pavement, a simple spectator. And he doesn't resemble in any detail the young man you are looking for.

514.22–26   "*C'est tout, . . . Je veux dire le trottoir.*"] That's all . . . Believe me. . . . I mean the sidewalk.

514.32   "*Sembrava un bosco di pioppi tremoli,*"] Italian: It looked like a forest of aspens.

514.37–39   "*Demandez aux autres . . . vérité!*"] French: Ask the others if you don't believe me! . . . Everyone here can confirm that I'm telling the truth!

515.4–5   "*Qu'il parle bien le français!*"] How well he speaks French!

515.7   "*Voici mon passeport et ma carte de séjour!*"] Here is my passport and my residence permit!

515.13 *"Quelle belle plante!"*] What a beautiful plant!

515.16–17 *"Qu'est-ce que c'est que ça?"*] What is that?

515.20–21 *"Bon. Merci, . . . Allons-y!"*] Good. Thank you, sir. Everything is in order. . . . Let's go!

515.27–29 *"Il a raison, . . . une honte."*] He is right, sirs. The American is telling you the truth. The other one was there for nothing. What are you doing? It's a shame.

515.32 *ô juste ciel*] Oh my goodness; literally, oh just heaven.

515.36–37 *"Soyez raisonnables! . . . des enfants!"*] Be reasonable! What are you doing? After all! A little calm! They are children!

515.39–516.5 *"Vos papiers! . . . Zut!"*] Your papers! . . . So what? . . . He doesn't have his papers. Heck!

516.28–34 *"Sais pas. . . . vous savez . . ."*] "Don't know." "Ah, no, sir, I could not tell you." "Perhaps at Beaujon?" "It's not my business. Ask the police." . . . "It's not worth it, man. They never say it. The police, you know . . ."

516.39–517.2 *"C'est pas un taxi, . . . la paix,"*] This isn't a taxi, sir, . . . OK, arrest me! . . . Give me a break.

518.1 "Perseverance, dear my lord, keeps honor bright."] *Troilus and Cressida*, III.iii.150–51; Ulysses speaking to Achilles.

518.15–16 *"Tenez, monsieur."*] Here, sir.

518.22 *hors de combat*] Out of combat.

521.25–30 *"Monsieur Dupuy . . . prochaine fois, Jacques."*] Mr. Dupuy, please . . . Good, I'll wait. . . . Hello, Jacques? It's us again. Not bad. And yourself? Yes, that's it. A little fight. As usual. You are aware? A certain Makowski, a student . . . Ah, good, good. Thank you. See you next time, Jacques.

522.25 *crise de foie*] Stomach upset.

523.23 Vouvray] Sparkling white wine from the Loire Valley.

526.35 *The Protestant Ethic*] Max Weber's seminal study, *The Protestant Ethic and the Spirit of Capitalism* (1905).

529.9 the Institut Pasteur] Parisian institute for medical research, especially concerning infectious diseases, founded by Louis Pasteur in 1887.

529.32 *"Vous êtes un trouble-fête, mademoiselle,"*] You are a troublemaker, miss.

532.6 *croulants*] Old people; literally, dodderers.

532.38–39 Kosygin] Alexei Kosygin (1904–1980), Soviet premier from 1964 to 1980 under Communist Party general secretary Leonid Brezhnev.

533.21–22   Belshazzar's Feast . . . out to eat grass.] In the Book of Daniel, the elaborate meal at which Belshazzar sees "the writing on the wall," which signals that, like his predecessor and possible father, Nebuchadnezzar, he will lose his realm.

536.27–29   "*Il s'est rallié . . . surtout, madame.*"] "He rallied behind the cause." "He signed up before the draft," . . . "Congratulations, young man. And you especially, madame."

537.8   food for powder, in the words of Falstaff] Cannon fodder; in *Henry IV*, Part I, IV.ii.65–67, Falstaff says, "Tut, tut; good enough to toss; food for powder, food for powder; they'll fill a pit as well as better: tush, man, mortal men, mortal men."

538.39   Foster Dulles] John Foster Dulles (1888–1959), U.S. secretary of state (1953–59).

538.39   "*lâcheté*"] Cowardice.

539.1–3   Dienbienphu. Suez. . . . The Left. Mendès-France. Geneva.] Under President Eisenhower, the U.S. refused to intervene to help French troops besieged by the Viet Minh in Dienbienphu (1954), or to help the British and French regain control of the Suez Canal from Egypt (1956). Pierre Mendès-France (1907–1982) was the left-wing prime minister who negotiated a cease-fire in Indochina and the withdrawal of French forces from North Vietnam at the Geneva Conference in 1954.

539.10–13   "*Mais la bombe, . . . N'exagérons pas.*"] But the bomb, of course. . . . One alone would suffice. . . . Atomic, naturally. Let's not exaggerate.

539.19   "*Ces Chinois s'en foutent,*"] These Chinese don't care.

539.29   "*Mais votre fils a raison, madame,*"] But your son is right, madame.

540.22–23   'His blood be upon us and upon our children,'] What the crowd says in Matthew 27:25, after Pilate washes his hands of responsibility for Jesus' death.

543.28   NATO shield] The Western defense alliance against the Soviet Union and its satellite states.

544.22   *gosses*] Kids.

548.17   Hautes Etudes] The esteemed École pratique des hautes études (EPHE) in Paris.

550.19–20   *Peaux-Rouges*] Redskins.

551.10–11   "*Papa, c'est un révolutionnaire; . . . maquis,*"] Dad, he is a revolutionary; he fought in the Maquis.

552.33   Chaliapin singing *Boris Godunov*] Feodor Chaliapin (1873–1938), renowned Russian opera singer; his signature role was the title character in *Boris*

Godunov (1874), Modest Mussorgsky's operatic adaption of Pushkin's play about Russia's "Time of Troubles" around the beginning of the seventeenth century.

553.1   *femme de ménage*] Cleaning woman.

553.2   *en panne*] Out of order.

554.4–7   "*Détergents? Qu'est-ce . . . savon!*"] "Detergents? What is that?" "This!" "But that is soap!"

554.16   "*Là, tu exagères un peu, mon ami. Quand même!*"] There, you're exaggerating, my friend. Really!

554.17–18   '*Après moi le déluge,*'] French proverb usually ascribed to Louis XV or his mistress, Madame de Pompadour. The sense of the words—After me, the flood—is that revolution and chaos are likely to follow the king's reign.

554.18   "*Qu'est-ce que j'y peux faire, moi?*"] What can *I* do?

554.31–33   "*J'en ai entendu . . . au courant.*"] I heard about it. . . . But I'm not exactly aware.

555.13–14   "*Ils se préparent pour la troisième guerre mondiale.*"] They are preparing for the third world war.

555.24   ("*Très bonne idée*")] Very good idea.

555.27   *mercerie*] Haberdashery, or dry goods store.

555.27   "*Tu plaisantes.*"] You're kidding.

555.30   "*A New York, . . . qu'on dit.*"] In New York, it works very well, is what they say.

555.33–34   "*Incroyable! . . . a trois.*"] Unbelievable! . . . Here there are three.

556.1   Krupp guns] German armaments manufacturer from the 1840s through World War II.

556.15–16   "*C'est très significatif, ce que tu dis là.*"] This is very significant, what you are saying.

556.26   *marchand de charbon*] Coal merchant.

556.28   "*Je viens chez vous ce soir,*"] I'm coming to your home tonight.

556.31–32   "*Les enfants adorent ce bougnat.*"] The kids love this *bougnat*. A *bougnat* was someone who had moved from the countryside to the capital.

556.35   *The Water Babies*] Satiric children's book by Charles Kingsley, published in Britain in 1863.

556.39–557.2   "*Les enfants-ramoneurs, . . . Un ivrogne.*"] The children-sweeps. . . . Yes, it was picturesque. . . . A drunkard.

557.9–10   *stoppeuse*] Seamstress.

557.14 *marchand de couleurs*] Art-supply store.

557.17 "*Oui! Il y a toujours une raison.*"] Yes! There is always a reason.

557.21–24 "*Saintes reliques . . . Ça pue.*"] Holy relics of people's illiteracy! . . . My dear, we must always be wary of the picturesque. It stinks.

557.29–30 *deux-chevaux*] The Citroën 2CV automobile, manufactured from 1948 to 1990.

559.3 Charles le Téméraire or Saint Louis] "Charles the Bold" (1433–1477), religious duke of Burgundy killed by the Duke of Lorraine's Swiss troops; Saint Louis IX (1217–1270), King of France from the age of twelve who participated in the Seventh and Eighth Crusades.

560.25 *dialogue de sourds*] Dialogue of the deaf.

561.11 Gislebertus] Twelfth-century French sculptor of ornaments for Autun's Cathedral of Saint Lazare.

562.1–2 "*On t'aime, Peter, tu sais,*"] We love you, Peter, you know.

562.20 "*Votre courrier.*"] Your mail.

562.31–32 *vacances scolaires*] School vacation.

563.32 Borromini] See note 408.14.

564.30–31 "*Il n'est pas nécessaire . . . persévérer.*"] "There is no need to hope to undertake, nor succeed to persevere," William, Prince of Orange (see also note 395.20). The remark is also quoted by McCarthy's ex-husband, Edmund Wilson, in *O Canada: An American's Notes on Canadian Culture* (1963).

565.4 *Multas per gentes et multa per aequora vectus.*] Latin: "Carried through many nations and over many seas," the first line of Catullus 101.

565.8 the Bambino's crib] Santa Maria Maggiore in Rome was originally called Saint Mary of the Crib (Sancta Maria ad Praesepe) for a relic believed to be a remnant of the manger or crib Christ was placed in at his birth.

565.13 Aracoeli] The Basilica di Santa Maria in Ara coeli.

565.15 Marcus Aurelius] Stoic philosopher (121–180 C.E.) and dutiful emperor of Rome, 161–80 C.E. His statue, erected in 175 C.E. in the Campidoglio in Rome, is now in the Capitoline Museums; it was replaced by a replica in 1981.

566.6 "*Se avessimo saputo!*"] Italian: If we had known!

567.13–14 "*Qui ne risque rien n'a rien*"] French: "Nothing ventured, nothing gained." Literally, who risks nothing, gains nothing.

567.32 "*Auprès de ma Blonde,*"] "Next to my girlfriend"; seventeenth-century French chanson, sung as both a military march and a nursery rhyme. See also the epigraph to *Cannibals and Missionaries*, page 653 in this volume.

569.2   *Gislebertus, Sculpteur d'Autun*] See note 561.11.

570.11   Tantalus] Figure of Greek myth who stands in a pool of water, always frustrated ("tantalized") by fruit that is just out of reach.

571.9   *béguin*] Infatuation.

571.13   Jumièges] Ruined Benedictine monastery along the Seine near Rouen.

571.14   St.-Wandrille] Benedictine monastery in Normandy, founded in the seventh century.

571.34   *emballés*] Thrilled or keen on.

572.5   Marais] Right Bank Parisian district (3rd and 4th arrondissements), home to many Jews and later gays. André Malraux, minister of culture at the time *Birds of America* is set, took a special interest in its architectural preservation.

573.8   *petit ami*] Boyfriend.

573.31–32   *comme il faut . . . chasse à courre*] Proper . . . hunting with hounds.

574.1   *dépucelée*] Deflowered.

574.18   Endymion] Figure of Greek mythology so handsome that he inspired the passion of Selene, goddess of the moon.

577.12–13   'Horridi dumeta Silvani . . .'] Horace, Book III, poem 29: The thickets of shaggy Silvanus.

578.13   *Timeo Danaos et dona ferentes*] Latin: I fear Greeks even when bearing gifts. *Aeneid*, book II, line 49.

580.35   the T.C.I. guidebook] Guide produced by the Touring Club Italiano, the national tourist organization of Italy since 1894.

581.4   Santa Maria in Cosmedin] Roman church in the Piazza della Bocca della Verità.

581.5   the Befana] Figure of Italian folklore; an old woman who brings children presents on the Eve of the Epiphany (January 5).

581.8   the Queen of Night] Figure in Mozart's opera *The Magic Flute* (1791).

581.27   "*Come parle bene!*"] Italian: How well you speak!

581.30   "*E bella l'Italia, signorino?*" "*Si, si!*"] "Italy is beautiful, isn't she, sir?" "Yes, yes!"

581.38   "*E chiuso! E chiuso!*"] Closed! Closed!

582.4   Bernini] Gian Lorenzo Bernini (1598–1680), Baroque sculptor and architect whose works include many fountains in Rome and the colonnade outside St. Peter's at the Vatican.

582.11   the sign of the figs] A contemptuous hand gesture, made by forming a fist with one's thumb between the index and middle fingers.

583.11   the Sapienza] Sant'Ivo alla Sapienza, mid-seventeenth-century Roman church designed by Borromini.

583.11   the Propaganda Fide] Roman headquarters of the Catholic Church's Sacred Congregation of Propagation of the Faith (now known as the Congregation for the Evangelization of Peoples). Bernini designed the north facade; Borromini designed the southern one.

583.27–28   the Re Magi] The three Wise Men. The Propaganda Fide contains the Re Magi Chapel designed by Borromini.

584.6   "*Come mai? Un ragazzo di dicianove anni!*"] Why? A nineteen-year-old boy!

584.9–10   "*In Francia ti piaceva il barocco?*"] You liked the Baroque in France?

584.13–15   "*Ma certo . . . E un capriccio,*"] Of course. Les Invalides! . . . It's a whim.

584.23   *principium individuationis*] The philosophical differentiation of one thing from another.

584.24   *flatus voci*] A name that has no corresponding objective reality.

585.4   *grappa*] Italian brandy distilled from the parts of grapes (skins, seeds, etc.) that remain after the grapes have been pressed to make wine.

585.14   *tartufo*] Truffle.

585.32–33   "*Che profumo!*"] What a fragrance!

586.2–3   *acqua corrente*] Running water.

586.6–8   *notevole facciata barocca . . . Bernini*] Remarkable Baroque façade. . . . Started in 1650 by Bernini.

586.9–10   *Ars longa vita brevis*] "Art is long, life is short." Greek aphorism of Hippocrates translated into Latin.

586.12–13   *apertura alla sinistra*] Opening to the left, term used for the decision by the center-right Christian Democrats to form a coalition government with the Socialists in 1963.

586.20   *cronaca*] News.

586.29–30   BRUCIATO VIVO, STRANGOLATA, IL MONSTRO DELL'AVENTINO] Burned Alive, Strangled, the Aventine Monster.

586.38   *le nouveau roman*] The "new novel," product of a postmodern French literary movement whose leading theoretician was Alain Robbe-Grillet (1922–2008). With its emphasis on surface description and its subordination of morals and character, it was hardly a genre to attract McCarthy's favor, though she admired the fiction of Nathalie Sarraute, who was often associated with it.

586.39　Althusser] Louis Pierre Althusser (1918–1990), Marxist philosopher.

587.2　Malraux's cultural offensive] As France's minister of cultural affairs from 1959 to 1969, André Malraux (1901–1976) carried out an ambitious series of programs for preserving and promoting the country's art and culture.

587.5–6　the Berkeley Free Speech movement, . . . did-the-CIA-kill-Kennedy?] Largely left-wing protest movement at the University of California, 1964–65; President Lyndon Johnson had a history of heart disease that went back to the 1950s; one of many conspiracy theories of the Kennedy assassination that flourished in the 1960s and beyond.

587.7　the Alliance for Progress] Kennedy-era program of economic cooperation with Latin America.

587.13　*Mario Savio*] Savio (1942–1996) was a leader of the Berkeley Free Speech movement.

587.30　"*Strano. . . . dei neri?*" "*Si!*"] "Strange. You are not interested in the problem of the blacks?" "Yes!"

587.33　the widow of Richard Wright] Following Richard Wright's death in 1960, Ellen Wright, the author's second wife, continued to live in Paris, where she worked as a literary agent for a number of prominent French authors. She died in 2004.

587.34　Professor André Chastel] French scholar (1912–1990) of Italian Renaissance art.

587.39–40　"*E cosa diceva . . . Stupidaggini.*"] "What did he say about Vietnam, this general?" "Rubbish."

588.12　"*nihil humanum mihi alienum puto*"] Latin: "Nothing human is alien to me," from *Heauton Timorumenos* (*The Self-Tormenter*) by Roman playwright Publius Terentius Afer, known as Terence (c. 186–c. 159 B.C.E.).

590.31–32　Cluny Museum . . . "Lady and the Unicorn."] Museum of medieval art on the Place Paul Painlevé; series of tapestries woven in Flanders (c. 1500).

591.21　*Itinerario Pittorico dei Musei Vaticani*] *Pictorial Guide to the Vatican Museums.*

593.14–15　'By the waters of Babylon.'] "By the rivers of Babylon, there we sat down, yea, we wept, when we remembered Zion." (Psalm 137:1).

594.28–29　"*Links, Gemälde Paradiso, recht, Inferno mit Teufels.*"] Left, a painting of paradise, right, Hell with Demons.

595.22   "*Per piacere, signori!*"] Please, gentlemen!

596.6   Steinberg cartoons] Romanian American artist Saul Steinberg (1914–1999), whose work appeared in *The New Yorker* for many years.

596.31   Deux Magots] Café on the Place Saint-Germain-des-Prés, known for its clientele of writers and intellectuals from the days of Hemingway through Jean-Paul Sartre and Simone de Beauvoir.

598.3   *gettone*] Token.

598.16   '*Questo è un luogo sacro*'] This is a sacred place.

598.37–39   *affreschi di scolari . . . cognato*] Much retouched frescoes by students of Pintoricchio; it was perhaps in this room that Cesare Borgia killed his brother.

601.39–40   Signorelli and Bartolommeo della Gatta] *The Testament and Death of Moses*, a fresco in the Sistine Chapel, is thought to have been painted by Luca Signorelli (c. 1445–1523) and Bartolomeo della Gatta (1448–1502).

603.16   that poem by Shelley] "Hymn to Intellectual Beauty" (1816) by Percy Bysshe Shelley (1792–1822). The poem's first lines tell us that "The awful shadow of some unseen Power / Floats though unseen among us."

603.34   Buonarroti] Surname of Michelangelo.

608.12–13   *al burro*] With butter.

612.11   'Barefoot in Athens.'] Play (1951) by Maxwell Anderson, later a television movie (1966), about the trial of Socrates.

613.24–27   '*Una sibilla, . . . Giocano.*'] A sybil, what? . . . No. They have children, like you. Playing.

617.23–24   *bistecca fiorentina, . . . cassata siciliana*] A Florentine steak and a Sicilian sponge cake made with fruit juice, ricotta, and a chocolate or vanilla filling.

618.32   "*Faccia due conti, per favore. Scusi.*"] Give us separate checks, please. Sorry.

619.14–15   "*Un sorriso, per piacere.*"] A smile, please.

620.19–20   "*Merde, alors! . . . Ta gueule.*"] French: Shit, then! . . . Shut up.

622.20   *carrefour*] Crossroads.

622.39   a *zinc* or a *pissoir*.] A modest café with a bar and simple menu; a public urinal.

622.40   DT's] Delirium tremens; an array of distressing and sometimes fatal symptoms, from delusions to shaking, that can result from the attempt to withdraw from prolonged and excessive alcohol consumption.

624.10   Queen Fabiola] Queen Consort of Belgium, married to King Baudouin from 1960 to his death in 1993.

624.28–29   "*Votre camarade a laissé la porte ouverte,*"] Your friend left the door open.

624.33   *bigoudis*] Curlers.

624.36–37   "*Ah, bon soir . . . Une femme.*"] Ah, good evening, Mr. Levi. I'm hunting already, you know. A woman.

625.5–8   "*Ah, monsieur, vous parlez. . . . l'employée?*"] Ah, sir, you say. This is not an asylum, our building. . . . You, Mr. American, or me, the employee?

625.12–13   *salauds . . . loge*] Bastards . . . lodge.

625.15   *voyou*] Thug.

625.29–30   "*Deux mégots, Monsieur Levi! Vous vous rendez compte?*"] Two butts, Mr. Levi! You realize?

625.35–36   "*C'était une femme, . . . Toujours la même.*"] It was a woman . . . Always the same one.

626.10–14   "*Mais vous, qui êtes jeune, . . . C'est tout.*"] But you, who are young, who have life ahead of you . . . And all the others, with their families, their distractions. Burning in a fire, is not gay. Well, here. I came to tell you. That's all.

626.24–28   "*Je suis bonne . . . pour ça.*"] I am a good Catholic, Mr. Levi. I know that these bastards are human beings of some sort. But I'm not the Christ. . . . I'm paid for that.

626.33–34   "*Chien méchant! Figurez-vous. Quelle honte.*"] Naughty dog! Imagine. What a shame.

626.37–38   "*Mon vieux compagnon.*"] My old friend.

627.1–2   "*Un chien de garde!*"] A watchdog!

627.4–10   "*Vous aussi, . . . un étranger!*"] "You also, Mr. Levi." "But no!" "I understand, it is a great responsibility." "Ah, you are good! Always so nice to me and courteous. You, a stranger!"

627.16   "*Comme les juifs,*"] Like the Jews.

627.33–34   "*Ils ne sentent rien, . . . vous et moi.*"] They feel nothing, Mr. Levi. They aren't like you and me.

628.32   *agrégés*] The highest grade of credentialed teachers.

629.12   '*Donnez-moi; j'ai faim*'] Give me; I'm hungry.

629.19 "*Basta,*"] Italian: Enough.

629.34 *strapontin*] Folding seat.

630.12 "*Jean! Qu'est-ce que tu fais là?*"] Jean! What are you doing?

635.3 *minuterie*] Automatic lighting.

635.10–11 A man's character was his fate—Heraclitus.] Greek pre-Socratic philosopher of mutability (c. 535–475 B.C.E.).

635.11 Atropos] Greek goddess, one of the Fates who cut the thread of life.

636.10 Eurydice] In Greek mythology, the daughter of Apollo and wife of Orpheus. After her premature death, her husband attempted to rescue her from the Underworld.

637.12 "*Voici votre lit, mademoiselle.*"] Here is your bed, miss.

637.20–22 "*Après. . . . Pain . . . Puis vin.*"] After. . . . Bread. . . . Then wine.

639.31–32 "*C'est pas un asile, notre immeuble.*"] This is not an asylum, our building.

641.24–27 49 AVIONS U.S. . . . LES ETATS-UNIS."] 49 U.S. PLANES (having launched from three aircraft carriers) BOMBARD INSTALLATIONS NORTH OF THE 17TH PARALLEL. JOHNSON TO AMERICAN FAMILIES: "RETURN TO THE UNITED STATES."

642.22 '*Ursus arctos Linné,*'] The brown bear, in Linnaeus's eighteenth-century classification; Aristotle remarks upon the maternal protectiveness of the she-bear in Chapter 30, Book VI, of *The History of Animals.*

643.15 Kosygin] See note 532.38–39. Kosygin was visiting Hanoi at the time of the American bombing.

644.6 a *renard famélique*] Scrawny fox.

644.30 '*Qu'ils mangent de la brioche,*'] Let them eat cake.

646.36 Aureomycin] Tetracycline antibiotic in use since the 1940s.

649.23 "*Theory of Winds,*"] Paper published by Kant in 1756; one of a number he wrote on natural and meteorological phenomena.

649.35 "'*Die schönen Dinge zeigen an . . .' Ach, ja!*"] From the "reflections" that were published after Kant's death. See page 30 of *Lectures on Kant's Political Philosophy* by Hannah Arendt, McCarthy's great friend, to whom *Birds of America* is dedicated. After Arendt's death in 1975, McCarthy devoted a great deal of energy to seeing Arendt's unpublished work into print. Peter Beiner, the editor of these lectures on Kant, acknowledges McCarthy's "constant help and unfailing kindness."

650.11 *mein kind*] German: my child.

CANNIBALS AND MISSIONARIES

653.1–4 *Dites donc . . . hollandais l'ont pris*] From the song "Auprès de ma blonde" (see note 567.32): "So say, my pretty one, where is your friend? He is in Holland, the Dutch took him."

662.12–13 'Let him who is without sin cast the first stone'] John 8:7; what Jesus said to the Pharisees and scribes who asked him what should be done with the woman taken in adultery.

665.9 a Biafra or a Pretoria] In 1967 the southeast region of Nigeria seceded and formed the Republic of Biafra. The secessionist movement was defeated in 1970 after a war in which more than a million Biafran civilians died from starvation as a result of a Nigerian blockade. Pretoria (Tshwane) has been the administrative capital of South Africa since 1910.

668.27 one of Paul's famous Laodiceans] In Revelation 3:14–22, the rich Laodiceans are described in a message from Jesus: "So because you are luke-warm—neither hot nor cold—I am about to spit you out of my mouth."

669.6 SAVAK] The fearsome Iranian secret police, active from 1957 to 1979, during the reign of Shah Mohammad Reza Pahlavi (1919–1980).

672.33–34 like Saul struck down . . . Damascus] The story of Saul's conversion, after hearing Jesus' voice on the road to Damascus, is told in Acts 9:1–9.

678.2–8 *Bon vol . . . Recteur d'université*] French: Good flight. . . . Friendly service. . . . Are you making this trip for Business □ Tourism □ Other reasons ____? . . . Educator . . . University Rector.

678.26 Lucy Skinner College] The college is fictional but probably owes something to McCarthy's time teaching at Sarah Lawrence, as well as her own days as a Vassar student.

685.3–4 signed the Stockholm Peace Appeal] Call for banning all nuclear weapons issued in 1950 by the World Peace Council, an international body that conformed entirely to the dictates of the Soviet Communist Party.

686.14–15 Naqsh-i-Rustan, . . . Isfahan] Four Iranian sites: necropolis in Fars province whose remains include those of Darius I; another name for Persepolis; the Tomb of Cyrus the Great, who built the Achaemanid Empire, was constructed in the sixth century B.C.E.; the capital city of Isfahan province, south of Teheran.

686.20 "Cube of Zoroaster," Darius's palace] Memorial structure at Naqsh-e Rustam built in the fifth century B.C.E., perhaps by Darius I, whose palace at Susa, discovered by nineteenth-century archaeologists, was still being excavated in the 1970s.

687.21 Sassanids] Inhabitants of the Persian Sasanian Empire, founded by Ardashir I in the third century C.E.

687.21 tombs of the Achaeminid kings] Four kings of the Archaemenid Empire (550–330 B.C.E.) have their tombs in the Naqsh-e Rustam necropolis.

688.33 *bouleversés*] Upset.

695.25 "hare's fur cup"] A Song dynasty cup with a dark streaked glaze thought to resemble the fur of a hare.

703.26–27 "*Aidez-nous à vous mieux connaître*"] Help us to know you better.

705.2–3 *Attachez vos ceintures*] Fasten your seatbelts.

705.8–9 *Asseyez-vous, madame! . . . à votre siège!*"] Sit down, madam! And you, sir, go back to your seat!

705.12–13 "*Regagnez votre siège, . . . Dèpêchez-vous.*"] Return to your seat. . . . Hurry up.

705.14 *Minou, minou*] Kitty, kitty.

711.39–40 *Tout le monde a son visa, j'espère.*] Everyone has his visa, I hope.

712.14–15 "*Monsieur Asad—oh . . . votre consulat?*"] Mr. Asad—oh, sorry! Mr. Mohammed, where is your consulate?

712.21 *périphérique*] Ring road.

716.34 Adlai Stevenson] See note 425.40. In addition to being the Democratic Party's presidential candidate in 1952 and 1956, Stevenson served as U.S. ambassador to the United Nations, 1961–65.

716.38 Harold Lloyd in *The Freshman*] Lloyd (1893–1971) was the winning, bespectacled comic star of many silent films, including *The Freshman* (1925).

717.30 Martha Mitchell's] Martha Mitchell (1918–1976) was the flamboyant, loquacious wife of Richard Nixon's first attorney general, John N. Mitchell. Her denunciations of Nixon during the Watergate scandal entranced the public.

718.10 Fanne Foxe] Stage name of Annabelle Battistella (b. 1936), the "Tidal Basin Bombshell," a stripper whose mid-1970s cavortings with Arkansas congressman Wilbur Mills, chairman of the House Ways and Means Committee, capsized his political career.

719.29 the Greek colonels] From 1967 to 1974 Greece was ruled by a military junta that came to power in a coup d'état.

720.9 SAVAK] See note 669.6.

720.21 *montagne russe*] French: roller coaster.

723.19 'Suffer the little children.'] In Matthew 19:14, Jesus says, "Suffer little children, and forbid them not, to come unto me: for of such is the kingdom of heaven."

725.2–5   "I beseech you . . . renewing of your mind."] Romans 12:1–2.

725.39–40   their Queen . . . Prince Bernhard and Klaus] Juliana (1909–2004) was Queen of the Netherlands from 1948 to 1980. She had been married to Prince Bernhard since 1937. She had four daughters, one of whom became Queen Beatrix (married to Prince Claus) in 1980, when Juliana abdicated.

726.15   Mr. Owl] Joop den Uyl (1919–1987), Labor prime minister of the Netherlands from 1973 to 1977.

726.29   genever] Dutch liquor flavored with juniper.

726.39   Queen Wilhelmina] Queen of the Netherlands from 1890 to 1948; inspirational head of the Dutch government in exile during World War II.

726.40   Spaak] Paul-Henri Spaak (1899–1972), Belgian statesman and a leading figure in the postwar integration of western Europe.

727.22   *Schwyzer-dütsch*] Swiss-German.

727.30   his Parker or his Waterman] High-quality American pens.

727.31   *landgenoot*] Dutch: countryman.

728.26–27   Frisian minority problem] The Frisians, a Germanic coastal people with their own language, have long sought increased autonomy within the Netherlands and Germany.

729.4   Clio] Greek mythological muse of history.

732.27   Khaddafi's] Colonel Muammar Gaddafi (1942–2011), a supporter of terrorism, was the military dictator of Libya from 1969 to 2011.

735.3   *On a le droit à savoir, je suppose*] French: We have the right to know, I suppose.

736.27   "And a star to steer her by!"] From the second line of "Sea Fever," by the English poet John Masefield (1878–1967), which opens with the words "I must go down to the sea again."

739.8   'Who steals my purse steals trash,'] Words spoken by Iago in *Othello*, III.iii.157, part of his speech about the greater importance of reputation than money.

742.27   Mystère and Mirage] The Mystère was a French fighter-bomber plane manufactured in the 1950s by Dassault Aviation; the company's Mirage planes were a later line of military jets, exported to Israel and other nations.

743.28–29   Bridget Rose Dugdale, the Price sisters] Dugdale (b. 1941), an English debutante who joined the Provisional Irish Republican Army, participated in 1974 in a violent theft of nineteen valuable paintings that the IRA then offered as ransom for Marian and Dolours Price, sisters imprisoned in England for their participation in IRA bombings.

744.34–35   the wise virgin always had her lamp trimmed] See note 261.3.

745.12   Stu Symington] Stuart Symington (1901–1988), Democratic senator from Missouri, 1953–76, and a foe of Senator Joseph McCarthy, who called him "Sanctimonious Stu."

745.26   Shirley Chisholm] The country's first female African American member of Congress (1924–2005), who represented her Brooklyn district from 1969 to 1983. She unsuccessfully sought the Democratic nomination for president in 1972.

745.35   St. Stephen's day] The Feast of St. Stephen, celebrating the first Christian martyr, is held on December 26.

746.15   Peter the Hermit] Priest from Amiens (c. 1050–1115) whose charismatic preaching attracted paupers and peasants to the First Crusade.

747.20–21   'Let me not to the marriage of true minds admit impediment.'] Shakespeare's Sonnet 116, line 1.

750.18   *détournement d'avion*] Hijacking.

750.33–34   Zutphen, . . . Sir Philip Sidney fell] While dying in the Battle of Zutphen (1586) after fighting on behalf of Dutch Protestant rebels against the Spanish, Sidney famously passed an offering of water on to another soldier, saying, "Thy necessity is yet greater than mine."

750.35   Hugo von Hofmannsthal] Precocious Austrian man of letters (1874–1929).

751.10   *Chapeau, Monsieur Charles*] Hats off to you, Mr. Charles.

751.14–15   shuffle off this mortal coil.] Hamlet speaks of "When we have shuffled off this mortal coil" during his "To be, or not to be" soliloquy in III.i.55–87.

752.27   Golda] Golda Meir (1898–1978), prime minister of Israel, 1969–74.

752.32   Nassiri] Nematollah Nassiri (1911–1979), director of SAVAK, 1965–78, (see note 669.6), who was executed by the Iranian revolutionary government.

753.11   St. Dominic's hounds] Domingo de Guzmán (c. 1170–1221), later Saint Dominic, founded the order of Dominican priests, whose members were sometimes called "Hounds of the Lord" ("Dominic canes").

753.21–22   'rape of Belgium.' . . . Kaiser Willy's troops] Lurid reports of atrocities committed early in World War I by the German army, including the bayoneting of babies, later came to be seen as propagandistic exaggerations.

754.23   Armstrong-Siddeley] Early twentieth-century automobile manufactured by a company that eventually became part of Rolls-Royce.

754.31   'I know not the man,'] Peter's words denying Jesus in Matthew 26:72.

755.3–4　'From each according to his capacities.'] "From each according to his capacities, to each according to his needs" was an idea put forward by the French socialist Louis Blanc (1811–1882) and made more widely famous by Karl Marx.

760.2　Schiphol] The Netherlands' principal international airport, near Amsterdam.

760.22–24　"*Les chats, vous savez, . . . des pouvoirs occultes.*"] Cats, you know, are a mysterious race. Very sensitive. Especially purebred cats. It lends them occult powers.

760.31–32　*anarchists de la bande Baader-Meinhof*] Anarchists of the Baader-Meinhof gang. See note 788.7–8.

760.32–33　*Des hollandais pur-sang, je vous assure*] Thoroughbred Dutch, I assure you.

760.39　*C'est le chef de la bande, paraît-il*] This is the leader of the gang, it seems.

761.9　"*La rage,*"] Rabies.

761.23　Antigone] In Sophocles's dramatic version of the myth, Antigone's brother, Polyneices, rebels against Creon, the King of Thebes. When Polyneices is killed, Creon insists that his body remain unburied as a warning to future opponents; Antigone defies his order.

761.31　"*Prenez vos affaires. Vous pouvez sortir,*"] Take your things. You can exit.

761.34　*Raus! Weg,*"] German: Out! Away.

761.38　*Maintenant vous sortez.*"] French: Now you exit.

761.39–40　"*Pas vous, madame,*"] Not you, madam.

763.13–14　*gereformeerde kerk*] Dutch: Reformed Church.

763.36–37　the French criminals at the Quai d'Orsay] How the hijackers would view the French government, whose Ministry of Foreign Affairs is headquartered on the Quai d'Orsay on the Left Bank. "Quai d'Orsay" refers to the apparatus of French foreign policy as "Foggy Bottom" does for the U.S. Department of State.

764.28　"*Is dat waar?*"] Is that true?

764.34–35　"*Bien sûr, . . . Mais soyons sérieux. Plutôt un DC-8.*"] French: Of course. . . . But let's be serious. Rather a DC-8.

765.8　an Identikit portrait] A composite picture assembled by police in which a suspect's different facial features are based on information from various eyewitnesses.

765.28   PFLP zealots] Popular Front for the Liberation of Palestine, Marxist-Leninist organization founded in 1967.

766.18   Tweede Kamer] The Netherlands' lower house of parliament.

767.18   *kievit* egg] Traditionally, the deliverer of the first egg from the kievit, or plover bird, would be rewarded by the queen.

767.21   "*Paete, non dolet,*"] After trying to overthrow the Emperor Claudius during the first century C.E., Paetus was sentenced to death. His wife, Arria, impaled herself and then told him, "Paetus, it doesn't hurt," while handing him the dagger she had used.

771.7   Mr. Schlesinger] James R. Schlesinger (1929–2014), U.S. secretary of defense under Richard Nixon and Gerald Ford, 1973–75, and later secretary of energy under Jimmy Carter, 1977–79.

771.25   Hell, as Sartre said, was others.] A line from his play *No Exit* (1944), which Sartre (1905–1980) believed had been mostly misinterpreted.

772.6   Giorgiones and Titians] Works of the Italian painter Giorgione da Castelfranco (c. 1477–1510) and the Venetian artist Tiziano Vecelli (c. 1488–1576).

774.1–2   Cupidity . . . root of all evil] See 1 Timothy 6:10.

775.23–24   the Patricia Hearst girl] American heiress (b. 1954) kidnapped by and then involved with the radical Symbionese Liberation Army during 1974–75. Her violent participation in her captors' activities and her subsequent trial—where the defense argued that her complicity had been forced—became one of the biggest American news stories of the 1970s. Convicted in 1976 for her part in an SLA bank robbery, Hearst later had her sentence commuted by President Jimmy Carter. She was pardoned by Bill Clinton in 2001.

776.16–17   Den Uyl] See note 726.15.

777.2   *Bitte, sagen Sie mir*] German: Please, tell me.

777.3   a Warsaw Pact force] The Soviet-bloc military alliance, the communist equivalent of NATO, in operation from 1955 to 1991.

777.5   *ja, sicher*] Yes, surely.

777.8   Schmidt] Helmut Schmidt (1918–2015), a Social Democrat, was chancellor of West Germany from 1974 to 1982.

777.11   Bundestag] The lower chamber of the legislature of the Federal Republic of Germany.

777.18   Joop] See note 726.15.

779.30   Zuyder Zee project] The enormous land-reclamation effort undertaken by the Netherlands from 1919 to 1986. Damming and drainage transformed the waterscape of the North Sea's Zuiderzee inlet and included the creation of the polders that became the province of Flevoland.

783.22   Full fathom five] *The Tempest*, I.ii.397.

784.25   the Japanese poet Bashō] Munefusa Matsuo, known as Matsuo Bashō (1644–1694), the premier artist of Japanese haiku.

784.29   Yoshitsune . . . the Taira] Minamoto Yoshitsune (1159–1189), Japanese general who defeated the rebellious Taira samurai clan.

785.23   *kabouter*] Dutch: gnome.

785.39–40   "*Vous êtes francophone, monsieur?*"] French: You speak French, sir?

788.7   the Price sisters] See note 743.28–29.

788.7–8   Andreas Baader, Ulrike Meinhof, Gudrun Ensslin] Baader (1943–1977), Meinhof (1934–1976), and Ensslin (1940–1977) founded the Red Army Faction, a left-wing West German terror group sometimes known as the Baader-Meinhof Gang. All three committed suicide in prison.

788.8–9   the adjutants of "Carlos" in Giscard's hands] Ilich Ramírez Sánchez, known as "Carlos the Jackal" (b. 1949), Venezuelan terrorist allied with the Popular Front for the Liberation of Palestine who was active in France in 1974–75. He was captured by the French in Sudan in 1994 and sentenced to life imprisonment. For Giscard, see note 839.27–28.

789.3   Reza Pahlavi's] For Pahlavi, the American-supported Shah of Iran from 1941 to 1979, see note 669.6.

790.33   Brueghel] Either Pieter Brueghel the Elder (c. 1525–1569) or Pieter Brueghel the Younger (1564–1638).

790.36   Che] Ernesto "Che" Guevara (1928–1967), Argentine Marxist who became the enforcer and sex symbol of Fidel Castro's Cuban revolution; killed by army special forces while attempting to instigate revolution in Bolivia.

791.12–13   Rilke and Hölderlin] Rainer Maria Rilke (1875–1926) and Friedrich Hölderlin (1770–1843), lyric poets.

796.14–15   Stubbses and Degas] The English painter George Stubbs (1724–1806), chiefly known for his equine canvases; Edgar Degas (1834–1917) is nearly as well-known for his paintings of horses and horse racing as he is for his studies of ballerinas.

796.15–16   Dufy . . . Ward] French artist Raoul Dufy (1877–1953) and English landscape painter James Ward (1769–1859).

796.18   Paul Mellon's] The art collector Paul Mellon (1907–1999), the son of Treasury secretary Andrew W. Mellon, was instrumental in the development of the National Gallery of Art in Washington, D.C.

797.8   Lord Acton] See note 240.35.

798.10   Augustus John] Post-Impressionist Welsh painter (1878–1961) best known for his portraits and his flamboyant romantic life.

798.12–13   Churchill's beautiful American mother] The Brooklyn-born Jennie Jerome (1854–1921) married Lord Randolph Churchill in 1874.

799.12   Jacqueline Bouvier] Jacqueline Bouvier Kennedy Onassis (1929–1994) was First Lady of the United States from 1961 to 1963.

799.31   Captain Molyneux] Captain Edward Henry Molyneux (1891–1974), British fashion designer operating in Paris. His dresses were prized for their elegant simplicity and exceptional tailoring.

801.2–3   "*C'est bien fait pour nous . . . N'est-ce pas, monsieur?*"] We've had it coming . . . Isn't it so, sir?

801.4–5   "*Sais pas, madame.*"] Don't know, madam.

807.13   Piper Cub] Nimble, bright yellow monoplane first produced in the 1930s.

807.14–15   *Jude the Obscure*] Thomas Hardy's novel (1895) about a rural stonemason's tragic aspirations toward a university education in Victorian England.

807.27–28   *Hans Brinker* . . . Mary Mapes Dodge] Dodge (1831–1905) was an American children's author and magazine editor. *Hans Brinker* acquainted U.S. readers with the story of the Dutch boy ("The Hero of Haarlem") who plugged a dike with his finger.

807.34   Rembrandt's glorious young wife] Saskia van Uylenburgh (1612–1642) married Rembrandt in 1634 and also modeled for him.

810.14   Lord Iveagh] Kenwood House, in the Hampstead district of London, was given to the British public in 1927, upon the death of Edward Cecil Guinness, 1st Earl of Iveagh (1847–1927), philanthropic heir to the brewery fortune.

810.15–16   that Getty boy's ear] John Paul Getty III (1956–2011), grandson of the enormously wealthy founder of Getty Oil, was kidnapped in Italy in July 1973. His grandfather agreed to negotiate a ransom payment only some months later, when the kidnappers sent young Getty's severed ear to the offices of an Italian newspaper.

810.36–37   Rijksmuseum "The Love Letter,"] Genre painting by Jan Vermeer (1632–1675) that depicts a young woman holding a musical instrument as her servant delivers a letter.

812.31–32   "Lighten our darkness, we beseech thee, O Lord,"] One of the evening prayers in the Episcopal *Book of Common Prayer*.

816.21–22   Beardsley first impressions, Klimt, Cocteau] Aubrey Beardsley

(1872–1898), English Art Nouveau illustrator. Gustav Klimt (1862–1918), Austrian Symbolist painter. Jean Cocteau (1889–1963), French writer and film director.

825.39–40 "*Ja!* . . . *Es stimmt nicht.*"] German: Yes! No. But, it's true. No. It's not true.

826.12 *Ja, ja! Hier!*] Yes, yes! Here!

826.22 *Merde!*] French: Shit!

838.30 *beste kamer*] Dutch: best room.

839.6 traditional Hindeloopen designs] Hindeloopen, a city in the northern Netherlands and a member of the Hanseatic League from 1368, became renowned in the seventeenth century for its colorful painting, decorative arts, and furniture.

839.8 *erfstuk* Reformed Bible] An heirloom copy of the bible of the Dutch Reformed Church.

839.27–28 the HLMs and bidonvilles of Giscard's police state] Valéry Giscard d'Estaing (b. 1926) was the democratically elected president of France from 1974 to 1981; HLMs ("Habitation à Loyer Modéré," "rent-controlled housing") are cheap housing units, home to many impoverished immigrants in France; *bidonvilles* are shantytowns.

840.32 *knabe*] German: boy.

840.33 *fedayin*] Catchall Arabic term for guerrillas and commandos.

842.34 *boenwas*] Dutch: wax.

844.38 General Pinochet's] Augusto Pinochet (1915–2006) ruled Chile from 1973 to 1990 after seizing power in a coup.

844.39 Franco's] Generalissimo Francisco Franco (1892–1975), fascist dictator of Spain for thirty-six years; Franco's rule of Spain moderated somewhat with the years but persisted until his death.

847.36 Japanese Red Army] Terrorist group bent on world revolution, founded in 1971 and involved in hostage-taking and airplane hijackings throughout the 1970s.

847.37 Wadi Haddad and his PFLP contingent] Wadie Haddad (1927–1978), a leader of the Popular Front for the Liberation of Palestine, was behind a number of hijackings from 1968, including the 1976 hijacking of an Air France plane that was landed at the Entebbe airport in Uganda.

849.12–13 "Hamburger Rundfunk"] "Hamburg Broadcast."

850.6 "*Dummköpfer!*"] German: Fool!

851.25–26 Omroepstichting] The Dutch Broadcast Foundation.

851.30–31 Hegel's "cunning of reason" or Adam Smith's "invisible hand."] Hegel wrote, in *Lectures on the History of Philosophy*: "This may be called the cunning of reason,—that it sets the passions to work for itself, while that which develops its existence through such impulsion pays the penalty and suffers loss." In *The Wealth of Nations* (1776), Adam Smith writes that "an invisible hand" may lead a person seeking "only his own gain" to unintentionally "promote the public interest."

852.5 *Schneeweiss und die sieben Zwerge*] Snow White and the Seven Dwarves.

852.38 Gereformeerd service] Service of the Reformed Churches of the Netherlands.

853.27 "*Genoeg!*"] Dutch: Enough!

856.39–857.1 Andreas and Ulrike . . . Irmgaard] For the founders of the Red Army Faction, see note 788.7–8. Jan-Carl Raspe (1944–1977) and Irmgard Möller (b. 1947) were additional members of the RAF.

857.4 the venerable prelate from Köln] Josef Richard Frings (1887–1978), German cardinal since 1946; known, when Archbishop of Cologne, for his protests against Nazi persecution of the Jews.

859.40 "*waarde*"] Dutch: value.

860.24 C.P.N.] Communist Party of the Netherlands.

861.15 Trotsky] See note 239.7.

861.17 repression of the sailors of Kronstadt] Brutal reprisals resulting from a failed rebellion by Russian sailors against the Bolsheviks in 1921.

864.1–2 "*Wunderbar, nicht? Unglaublich!*"] German: Wonderful, isn't it? Incredible!

864.10 *rommel*] Dutch: junk.

864.39 Ijsselmeer] Artificial lake formed in 1932 during the Zuider Zee project (see also note 779.30).

865.33–34 *sagt Anna, hat 8 grosser kinder*] German: says Anna, has eight large children.

866.10 "Widderhintere"] Ram's backside.

866.37 "*Wir haben das Wesentliche,*"] We have the essentials.

869.40–870.1 *Les très riches heures du duc de Berry*, Nixon's *Six Crises*] Fifteenth-century illuminated devotional manuscript created for John, Duke of Berry; Richard Nixon's memoirs of his early political career, published in 1962.

870.25 Silver Moon . . . Dorothy Perkins] Two varieties of climbing, flowering plants.

871.11 Vladimir Ilych Ramirez] See note 788.8–9.

873.33 Baucis and Philemon] In Ovid's *Metamorphoses*, the poor, elderly couple who, alone of their entire town, welcome the disguised Mercury and Jupiter into their home.

875.18 *The Possessed*] Novel by Fyodor Dostoevsky, first published in Russian in 1871–72; translated into English in 1916.

875.21 the Okhrana] The Russian secret police during the last decades of tsarist rule.

877.32 Baader-Meinhofs] See note 788.7–8.

878.25 the Hals in the Wallace Collection] *The Laughing Cavalier* (1624), one of the best-known paintings by Frans Hals (c. 1582–1666), is in the Wallace Collection in Hertford House in London.

879.39–880.1 'As of old . . . for His dear sake.'] From a Lutheran hymn, "Jesus Calls Us; o'er the Tumult" by Cecil F. Alexander (1818–1895).

880.34 'Malefactors of great wealth.'] Famous excoriation of the robber baron class by Theodore Roosevelt in 1907.

881.15 '*Alea jacta est*,'] Latin: "The die is cast." According to Suetonius, what Julius Caesar uttered as his army crossed the Rubicon.

888.37 There's many a slip] The full proverb is "There's many a slip 'twixt the cup and the lip"—similar to the warning not to count one's chickens before they hatch.

896.23 "Watchman, tell us of the night,"] Hymn by Sir John Bowring (1792–1872), Unitarian British editor, author, and governor of Hong Kong.

899.12 Kelley's cops] Agents of the Federal Bureau of Investigation, directed by Clarence M. Kelley from 1973 to 1978.

899.29 Laurencins] Marie Laurencin (1885–1956) was a French avant-garde painter associated with the Cubist movement; known for a delicate pastel style.

902.27 "*Voulez-vous que j'en cherche?*"] French: Do you want me to look?

909.17 *kermis*] Dutch: fair.

914.29 "*ontbijt*"] Dutch: breakfast.

918.16 in the watches of the night.] Psalm 63:6.

918.39–40 *Requiem aeternam dona ei Domine*] Latin: Eternal rest give unto him, O Lord. The first line of a requiem Mass.

927.10 *feste Burg*] The "mighty fortress" of Martin Luther's hymn, "A Mighty Fortress Is Our God" (1527–29).

927.15 *et in saecula saeculorum*] Latin: "a century of centuries." Rendered in the King James Version of the Bible (Ephesians 3:21) as "world without end."

927.28–29 Prester John] Mythical ruler, sometimes said to be descended from the Magi, whose Christian kingdom supposedly flourished in Asia or Africa.

928.17 *ite missa est*] Latin words announcing the conclusion of the Catholic Mass: "Go, you are sent forth."

932.9 Mandelstam's] Osip Mandelstam, Russian poet (1891–1938) and husband of writer Nadezhda Mandelstam, who died in a Soviet prison camp.

932.38 *grosso modo*] Italian: more or less.

933.16–17 like the sailors of Ulysses.] In the *Odyssey*, Ulysses' men stopper their ears against the song of the Sirens with beeswax provided by Circe.

935.37 Landseer and good old Rosa Bonheur.] English painter Sir Edwin Landseer (1802–1873) and French painter Rosa Bonheur (1822–1899), both known for their pictures of animals.

936.15 Maud Earl] London-born painter of dogs (1864–1943) who moved to New York during World War I.

936.29 a Stutz Bearcat] Expensive early twentieth-century American sports car.

936.29–30 Redon and Rouault] The French Symbolist painter Odilon Redon (1840–1916) and the French Expressionist Georges Rouault (1871–1958), whose work includes "The Old King" (1937). Redon is also mentioned in "The Friend of the Family," in *Cast a Cold Eye*.

940.27–28 the Hound of Heaven] See Francis Thompson's poem of God's relentlessness, "The Hound of Heaven" (1893).

940.31–32 "*qua se subducere colles incipiunt.*"] Latin: "that from where the hills begin to rise." Virgil, Eclogue (or Bucolic) IX.

941.20 Morgan and Frick] Banker J. P. Morgan Jr. (1867–1943); the American industrialist and art collector Henry Clay Frick (1849–1919) was infamous for his violent tactics against striking laborers.

941.21 Goering] Hermann Göring (1893–1946), the heavyset Nazi leader and war criminal, commanded the German air force, 1935–45, and was Hitler's designated successor from December 1934 until April 1945. Göring was notorious for stealing works of art from all over Europe.

944.13 the Pathé cock] See note 305.4.

947.5 Camay] Perfumed soap for women ("the Soap of Beautiful Women"), available since 1926.

955.3–4 the Empress Theodora in the Ravenna mosaic] Byzantine empress (c. 500–548), married to Justinian I. The Ravenna mosaic that depicts her is in the Basilica of San Vitale.

955.30 "*J'ai vu*,"] French: I saw.

955.33 Leidsekaas] Semihard Dutch cheese spiced with cumin seeds.

956.23 *Très malade*] Very sick.

957.18 Agatha] Saint Agatha of Sicily (231–251 C.E.), martyred under the Roman Emperor Decius after having her breasts cut off.

963.8 "*uit*" and "*weg*."] Dutch: out and gone.

966.24 'The Mystic Lamb.'] A panel of the Ghent Altarpiece painted by Jan van Eyck (c. 1390–1441); over centuries the object of thieves and foreign armies.

973.29–30 William the Silent or the boy with his finger in the dike.] See notes 395.20 and 807.27–28.

980.19 "*C'était un poète, madame*,"] French: "He was a poet, madam."

980.25–27 "*Il fallait tout détruire. . . . sa deuxième demande.*"] He had to destroy everything. . . . He was a Northern man, you know. I loved him very much. I understood him. Even his second demand.

980.30–31 "*Mais les tableaux . . . tout sacrifier.*"] But the pictures, Ahmed. Why? . . . He had to destroy everything, to sacrifice everything.

980.34–35 "*Le geste sublime d'un grand révolutionnaire.*"] The sublime gesture of a great revolutionary.

984.23 Isabella d'Este, François Iᵉʳ] Isabella d'Este, Marchesa of Mantua (1474–1539), formidable arts patron and fashion influence; Francis I of France (1494–1547), impresario of the French Renaissance, brought Leonardo da Vinci and other Italian artists to France.

984.38 Berenson, Duveen] For Berenson, see note 350.8; Sir Joseph Duveen (1869–1939), important British art dealer who helped build the holdings of significant American collectors, including William Randolph Hearst and Henry Clay Frick.

985.31–32 Cf. Kierkegaard on inferiority of aesthetic to ethical] Søren Kierkegaard (1813–1855), the Danish philosopher, broadly saw three "stages" in human development: first the aesthetic, then the ethical, and finally the religious.

986.5 Seagrams] The Seagram building in New York, designed by Mies van der Rohe and constructed in 1958 at 375 Park Avenue, is generally considered to be one of New York's most beautiful international-style skyscrapers. It was built as the headquarters of Seagram Company Ltd., a Canadian distillery.

986.9 Moissac] Southwestern French town renowned for the beauties of its medieval Saint-Pierre abbey. Now a UNESCO World Heritage site.

986.22 Union Carbide] Large chemicals-manufacturing corporation formed in 1917; a subsidiary of Dow Chemical since 2001.

987.38 Malraux] See note 587.2.

988.17 Arp & Brancusi] Jean Arp (1886–1966), French German sculptor and painter who moved from Surrealism to abstraction, and Constantin Brâncuși (1876–1957), Romanian sculptor who worked in France for over a half century, famous for his "Bird in Space" creations.

988.19 Henry Moore "King and Queen"] Large bronze sculpture of two seated figures, conceived in 1952 by the British sculptor Henry Moore (1898–1986); one cast of it is in the Sculpture Garden of the Hirshhorn Museum in Washington, D.C.

990.10–11 the claim of the ideal (Ibsen)] In Ibsen's *The Wild Duck* (1884), the character of Gregers Werle, the son of an industrialist, urges people to practice the "claim of the ideal," an uncompromising self-awareness and truth-telling.

991.23 David Niven] Debonair, pencil-mustached English film actor and bon vivant (1910–1983).

APPENDIX

995.7–12 Charlie Jackson . . . thirst for alcohol] Charles Reginald Jackson (1903–1968), author of *The Lost Weekend* (1944), a novel about alcoholism, had contributed fiction to *Partisan Review*.

998.3 Dumnorix and Diviciacus, the Haeduans] Diviciacus of the Aedui was Julius Caesar's Gallic ally in his conquest of Gaul. The Haeduans, or Aedui, were a Gallic tribe living throughout southeastern France.

998.6 Miss Mackay] Ethel Mackay appears as "Miss Gowrie" in "The Figures in the Clock" in McCarthy's *Memories of a Catholic Girlhood*.

999.16–18 boat from a Nazi submarine . . . Provincetown] A number of German U-boats were sunk by American forces off the eastern coast of the U.S. during World War II, including a U-550 submarine, approximately 70 miles off Nantucket, on April 16, 1944.

999.22–24 "The Meaning of Treason" . . . "The Heat of the Day"] *The Meaning of Treason* (1947) by the British journalist Rebecca West (1892–1983), a study of treason during World War II, contains an account of the trial of William Joyce (see note 1000.29). *The Heat of the Day* (1948), a novel by Elizabeth Bowen (1899–1973), concerns espionage and treason in London in the same period.

999.36–39 "The Bishops . . . loved his lass."] The last stanza of W. B. Yeats's "Come Gather Round Me, Parnellites," written in September 1936.

1000.18–19 ("Just for a handful . . . his coat.")] Browning's attack on Wordsworth, "The Lost Leader," published in *Dramatic Romances and Lyrics* in 1845.

1000.20 Annette, the French girl] Annette Vallon, the French woman with whom Wordsworth conceived a daughter, Caroline (b. 1792).

1000.29 Lord Haw-Haw or Tokyo Rose] Lord Haw-Haw, sarcastic nickname for Nazi propagandists, principally William Joyce (1906–1946), who broadcast in English during World War II; Tokyo Rose, nickname given to Ira Toguri (1916–2006) and other female broadcasters of Japanese propaganda to Allied soldiers in the Pacific Theatre.

1002.3 Dante's sick man] Cf. Dante's *Purgatorio*, Canto VI, lines 149–51.

*This book is set in 10 point ITC Galliard, a face
designed for digital composition by Matthew Carter and based
on the sixteenth-century face Granjon. The paper is acid-free
lightweight opaque that will not turn yellow or brittle with age.
The binding is sewn, which allows the book to open easily and lie flat.
The binding board is covered in Brillianta, a woven rayon cloth
made by Van Heek–Scholco Textielfabrieken, Holland.
Composition by Dedicated Book Services.
Printing and binding by Edwards Brothers Malloy, Ann Arbor.
Designed by Bruce Campbell.*

THE LIBRARY OF AMERICA SERIES

The Library of America fosters appreciation of America's literary heritage by publishing, and keeping permanently in print, authoritative editions of America's best and most significant writing. An independent nonprofit organization, it was founded in 1979 with seed funding from the National Endowment for the Humanities and the Ford Foundation.